BROKEN TRUST

Book One

R.A. SMYTH

PROLOGUE

He's back. I knew he was coming—he always does—same day every month. Not once in all the years I've been here has he missed a visit. When I was younger, I used to enjoy it. He'd bring me a toy and I'd get to play with it all day. We never got toys here.

Things have been changing over the last few years. Now, instead of toys, he brings jewelry and dresses. He likes me to get all dolled up for him, even though we don't go anywhere or do anything. The way he looks at me when I do as he says? It's not how you should look at someone over half your age. It's dark and possessive.

It's not just the gifts and the looks. It's the way he drags his seat right over beside me, the slow trail of his fingers down my arm, the casual graze on the side of my breast.

It's the way he talks about the future, like it's a given I'll be in it, with him. He says I'm going to go live with him someday. He'll buy me whatever I want, and we'll visit places all around the world. I've never gone anywhere before. I've never left this place. The thought of seeing *the world* sounds unbelievable. This place is not somewhere any kid should grow up or where any human should live. His promise could be my ticket out of here. I'd finally be free.

Yet, I don't miss the domineering way he fixes the necklace around my neck, ensuring it sits perfectly. I don't miss the low timbre of his voice as he whispers, "Mine," and rests his heavy hand possessively on my thigh.

He might be my escape out of this place, but he would only cage me in a different type of prison. I wouldn't be any freer than I am right now. If anything, the things he says he wants to do to me would only ruin me faster.

Hadley

CHAPTER ONE

I readjust my duffel bag on my shoulder while I take in the towering wrought iron gates in front of me. Who knew a set of gates could hold such significance? Most of the students here probably don't bat an eye as they pass through them, the cold iron representing nothing more than the start of a new school year. To someone like me, it symbolizes so much more. The opportunity for a private education. The chance at a new life, a future. Freedom.

Taking in the crest branded on the gates, my eyes hover over the three words the school has chosen to embody everything they stand for.

Felicitatem. Patientiam Operatur. Dignitate.

Prosperity. Perseverance. Prestige.

No, I sure as hell do not speak Latin, but I do know how to do a Google search. Only one of those words resonates with me. Perseverance. I've endured my fair share of shit so far in this reasonably short life. As for prosperity and prestige? Well, only the wealthy can afford that shit, and I'm sure as fuck not that.

Ignoring the judgmental eyes from the passing chauffeur-driven cars as they make their way through the gates and up the tree-lined drive, I trail after them, taking in the campus as I walk.

The campus is vast and fancy as hell, with its grandeur buildings, perfectly manicured lawns, and trimmed hedges. I can just about make out a football field and tennis courts, as well as some sort of sports center in the distance.

I walk past a large, even more prestigious building than the others. It's got more steps leading up to it than any average building needs, meaning it towers above me, with its large glass windows and dramatic floor-to-ceiling columns.

Above the large wooden doors, a plaque reads 'Davenport Hall'. Well, whomever the Davenports are, they have more money than they clearly know what to do with. What school needs a hall like that? I bet it's only used a few times a year. *What a waste!*

Strolling on, I watch as cars stop in front of another building up ahead of me. Students climb out, most of them with their parents, looking around warily before following their parents up the steps—freshmen kids, I bet. As they disappear through the front entrance, uniformed men rush over to the cars and start lifting luggage out of their trunks, placing them on carts, and, I'm assuming, taking them off to the student's accommodations.

Older students who have their own car—which appears to be everyone over the age of sixteen—climb out of their vehicles in the parking lot opposite the main building, greeting their friends, laughing and joking with one another as they slowly make their way toward the school. They all look perfectly poised in their school uniforms, not a crease to be seen or a hair out of place. With their white teeth, flawless makeup, and expensive haircuts, they look like models or celebrities, all oozing the confidence that only comes with having money.

I cast a quick glance down the front of my white shirt. The school had it delivered to me for today, but, despite it being exactly the same as everyone else's, it doesn't hug my slim frame or accentuate my boobs as it does on other girls.

I run my hand over the shirt, smoothing it out, pulling on the ends of my green, gray, and black tartan mini-skirt so it sits slightly lower. I'm not used to wearing short skirts, and it feels like a light breeze would give everyone a firsthand view of my basic white underwear.

Approaching the main school building, I follow behind a group of girls, only half listening to them as they catch up, ranting and raving about their summer vacations spent in far-off exotic countries, while my eyes roam over the building.

It goes without saying that this is yet another fancy as fuck ostentatious structure that resembles what I imagine a 17th-century manor house would look like. I have to crane my neck back to see all the way up to the roof, the three stories looming over me. It's built in the same fashion as the hall I just walked past, composed of dark stone and copious windows.

Walking between two large columns, I ascend the stairs, making my way through the huge entryway into the open foyer beyond. The atrium is the depth of the building, with prominent glass doors providing an unobstructed view of an enormous courtyard beyond, lined with shrubs. There's a massive marble fountain in the center, with picnic tables and benches placed around the open space.

Glancing around, I notice there are corridors branching to the left and right and a staircase leading up to the second floor, with a balcony overlooking the atrium. Students and their parents are dispersed around the room as they say their final good-byes, while others move out to the courtyard, where I can see others milling around.

"Finally," a tall girl with perfectly curled white-blonde hair, way too much makeup, and sky-high heels snaps as she strides toward me, her hips swaying seductively and her tartan skirt swishing against her thighs with every step she takes. "It's about time you showed up."

"Me?" I ask, looking behind me in case she's talking to someone else.

"Yes. You. Who else would I be talking to?"

She casts her eyes over my appearance, her lips pursing in disapproval as she takes in my curly blonde hair that's impossible to tame and my face clear of makeup. Self-consciously, I run my hand through the mass of curls in a vain attempt to flatten them a bit. I don't get a chance to say anything, not that I have any idea what to say to this weirdo who's snapping at me, when her eyes fall on my worn duffel bag.

"What is that?" Her nose scrunches up in disgust as she waves her hand toward my bag, her dislike of my non-designer, tattered duffel written all over her face.

"Uh, my bag?"

"Why do you have it here? You're supposed to leave all of your belongings with your driver for the bellboys to collect."

Drivers? Bellboys? What fresh hell have I subjected myself to?!

Seeing my utter confusion, she rolls her eyes, sighing in exasperation before looking around the hall.

"You," she calls out, waving over some guy in a uniform as he passes by us, heading out toward the parked cars. He looks like he should be working in a high-end hotel, not a high school.

Barely sparing him a glance, she gestures toward my duffle bag, "Take this...thing," she sneers, "to, uh"—she glances down at a page in her hand—"Hadley's room."

The guy goes to grab my bag and my hand instinctively tightens around the strap, preventing him from taking it from me. We remain in a standoff for a few seconds, him giving me a weird-ass look before I relax enough to let go, allowing him to walk away with every single thing I own in this world.

Turning back to the annoying girl in front of me, eyeing her up with a critical gaze, I ask, "Eh, who are you? How do you know my name?"

Her lips pinch together in disapproval as she looks down at me. At five-foot-six, I wouldn't call myself short, but between her height and the six inches her heels give her, she's a good head taller than me.

"I'm Bianca," she responds snootily, with all the arrogance of a rich brat, as she tosses her hair over her shoulder. She acts like I should already know who she is. Placing her hands on her hips, she sighs. "I'm supposed to show you around today."

Well, that statement was overflowing with enthusiasm. I'm guessing she wasn't given much of a choice in the matter, and I can't help wondering how she ended up stuck with the job. I have to bite my tongue to stop myself from letting her know I'm just as thrilled to have her as a guide as she is. "I take it you got a welcome pack? With a map?" she snarks, not really sounding like she cares one way or the other.

"Yeah, I did."

"Good, then I'm sure you can work it out for yourself." She raises an eyebrow at me. "You are here on an academic scholarship, after all."

Barely holding back my retort, I roll my eyes at her as soon as she turns her back to me, taking off across the foyer without bothering to check if I'm following her. I am, of course—I don't see that I have a choice. She forced me to hand over my bag, with my map and everything in it, to that guy. And I have no clue where the accommodation building is or what I'm even supposed to be doing this morning.

"This is the main building where most of your classes will be. There's an east and a west wing," Bianca explains, pointing to her right to indicate the East Wing before pointing out the West Wing on our left. I'm honestly surprised she's bothering to tell me anything, but I guess she feels like she needs to at least explain the basics. "The East Wing is where all the science, math, and computer classes take place. While the art classes, English, history, languages, all that sort of stuff, are in the West Wing. The music department has its own building, and anything drama related is held in the auditorium."

She pulls open the door into the courtyard, the buzz of other students chatting and calling out to one another reverberating around us, drowning out the noise of water trickling from the fountain. By now, the quad is filled with students from all years. A few of them hang back, lazing on picnic tables and laughing with friends, though most of them have joined the throng of students slowly making their way into what I'm guessing is the auditorium—a large stone building on the far side of the quad.

Bianca and I join the back of the crowd, slowly inching our way onward. I can feel the press of bodies around me, people jostling me as they join the crowd behind us. The more they push and shove, the more my heart rate starts to spike and my chest feels tight. *Why the fuck can't people respect personal boundaries. The quad is fucking huge, you don't need to be shoving against me.* I scowl at the girl behind me as her shoulder knocks into me for the third time, my dark glare succeeding in getting her to back up a step as Bianca scans the crowd. Oblivious to the students around us, it seems she's looking for someone in particular, most likely her friends. She doesn't spare me a glance when she says, "Stay in your lane, and you'll get through the year without any problems."

"My lane?" I question, confused about what she means.

She sighs, and I don't miss the snooty bitch rolling her eyes at me before penetrating me with a deadpan stare. "There's a you, an us, and a them," she explains, as though it's apparent and she shouldn't have to clarify any of this for me.

"A what?" I shake my head slightly, not understanding her at all.

"You," she sneers derisively, her voice making it clear she thinks she's so much fucking better than me. She roams her eyes over my less-than-perfect uniform, scowling, before dropping her gaze to my combat boots and wrinkling her nose in disgust. *Yeah, okay, the boots aren't exactly school attire, but they're sturdy, and I could do some damage to her with them if she doesn't stop staring at me like I'm shit on the bottom of her designer pumps.* "The scholarship students."

Ah, yes. Us common muck scholarship students who are unfortunate enough not to be born into a life of luxury and have to actually work for everything in life.

"Us refers to every other student. The ones who actually pay to attend this school," she says pointedly, once again emphasizing—in case it wasn't already obvious—that we're lesser because we don't have buckets of cash to spend on an education. I doubt she would be open to seeing my point of view if I tried to explain that hard work and dedication make me just as entitled to be here as her precious money does.

"And them?" I ask curiously, wondering who she could possibly be referring to. She's just lumped the entire school into the 'you' and 'us' categories...so who is left?

Her eyes flash up to something behind me. "Them," she repeats absently, her tone breathy, her eyes glazing over at whatever has caught her attention.

Spinning around, I see exactly what has her so distracted. Or, more specifically, *who*. Striding through the crowd, who all part for them like they are gods, are four of the most striking guys I've ever seen. I'm not sure if the whole courtyard quiets or if I just become so focused on them that everything around me fades into the background, but all I can hear is the blood pounding in my ears as I soak up the mouthwatering sight in front of me.

All four confidently strut through the crowd, looking like one of those sexy-as-hell TikTok videos. All they need to do is remove their tops and flex their muscles, except I'm pretty sure more than a few girls around me will faint. I can't even be sure I wouldn't be one of them.

I focus on the guy to the far left, who's tall and lean and perfectly put together in his gray slacks, white shirt, and forest green blazer as he strides across the courtyard. Every step is filled with arrogant confidence. My eyes roam over his face, noting his short, blond haircut, narrowed eyes, and pinched lips. Everything about him screams, 'stay the fuck out of my way'.

My gaze sweeps to the guy beside him. He's built like a fucking tank. At over six and a half feet tall and built like an MMA fighter, he's easily double the size of every other student around us. Similarly to the first guy, everything about him screams unapproachable. His features look like stone, with his sharp, angular jaw, high cheekbones, and icy glare. A few loose strands of his dark brown hair fall forward into his eye, somehow only adding to the fierce image he's working. I can feel my mouth dry as I drink him in before quickly glancing away.

The third guy is the complete opposite of the first two. His black tie hangs loosely around his neck, the top button of his shirt undone. His blazer is nowhere to be seen, and where the first two guys don't bother to pay attention to anyone around them, he constantly nods his head at guys as they call out 'hello's', sending flirty looks to the girls. He's got a tall, lean swimmer's body, built for speed and agility, and short yet stylish blond hair.

He catches me staring at him as he lifts his hand, running his fingers through his short strands. His eyes drop down my body, a salacious grin spreading across his face as he lifts his eyes back up to my face, giving me a dirty wink that I'd love to say doesn't affect me, but damn, I'm as much of a sucker for that wink as every other girl around here seems to be.

Embarrassed by the sudden racing of my heart and the heat in my cheeks, I quickly move on to the final guy in the group. Again, he's completely different from the first three. I can immediately tell he's the shy, quiet, studious one. He's got dark floppy hair that's hiding his face from my view, but as he flicks it out of the way, I can see that he's got a broad jaw and sharp features. He's wearing thick black-rimmed glasses, giving him, combined with his meticulous uniform, the overall appearance of a nerd. Although with his lean, slightly muscular frame, it looks super hot, like Superman before he puts on his cape.

His hand flattens over his shirt, ironing out invisible creases before his head snaps up, his intense gaze meeting mine, having apparently sensed me watching him. Unlike the flirty perusal the last guy gave me, his is filled with disinterest, his lips pinching together in what looks like disapproval. *What an ass. We can't all have perfectly ironed uniforms and look like gods.*

The noise filters back in around me as the four of them disappear into the auditorium. With them no longer occupying my every thought, I realize I've been standing in the middle of the courtyard gaping at them. *Talk about embarrassing.*

Glancing out of the corner of my eye to see if Bianca, or anyone else, noticed my moment of distraction, I find her still drooling after the guys. At least I wasn't the only one who lost some common sense in their presence.

"Who are they?"

Damn girl, get your inner slut under control, I mentally berate myself when my voice comes out all husky.

Bianca must pick up on it, too, as she spins toward me, her eyes narrowing. "Out of your league," she snaps before storming off, following them into the auditorium.

I cast a quick peek around me and see that most of the students have also disappeared. Not knowing what else to do, I quickly scramble after Bianca, trying not to lose her in the sea of students.

Passing through the large double doors into the hall, it takes a second for my eyes to adjust after the brightness of the California sun outside, but after a few quick blinks, the room comes into focus. There's a grand, empty stage at the front of the room, with a podium off to one side. The rest of the space is taken up with wooden pews that are slowly filling with students. *You'd think such a fancy school could afford something comfier than wooden seats.*

Spotting Bianca making her way toward a crowd of rich girls, I follow her. I don't particularly want to sit with her and her friends, but it's not like I know anyone else. I'm just about to slide inconspicuously into the last seat in the pew when Bianca glances up, noticing me.

"No. You don't sit with us," she snarks, her outburst garnering the attention of her friends, who all sneer at me. *They don't even fucking know me.* "Scholarship students sit at the front," she snootily states, pointing to the front of the hall.

Whatever. As I said, I didn't want to sit with them anyway. I guess our 'tour' is officially over.

"Oh, and Henry," she calls after me, deliberately butchering my name. I turn around to glare at her, my teeth gritted. She's wearing a sickly sweet smile, which morphs into a superior smirk when she sees she has my attention. "Welcome to Pac Prep."

Rolling my eyes at her cattiness, I ignore the other students whispering around me as I stomp down the aisle, slipping into an empty seat in the first pew as the headmaster steps up to the podium.

He casts his eyes over the room, taking his time to survey us, before leaning into the microphone. "Quiet down, students." His booming voice echoes out across the ample space, everyone quickly settling into a hush, focused on the front of the room. "For all of our new students, I am Mr. Phister, your headmaster."

Mr. Phister? For real? Glancing around me, I notice a few other students holding back a laugh.

"Welcome to the start of a new school year! I'm sure all of our returning students will make our new pupils feel welcome and help them adjust to life here at Pacific Preparatory."

Hmm, I somehow doubt that based on the less-than-stellar welcome I got this morning.

"You must be a new scholarship student," the girl beside me leans over and whispers, pulling my attention from the drivel coming out of the headmaster's mouth.

"That obvious?" I ask rhetorically, taking in the girl beside me. She's got short, black hair pulled back in a functional ponytail and an innocent-looking face—or maybe it just looks that way because she doesn't have layer upon layer of makeup caking her face like every other teenage girl around here.

It suddenly makes sense how Bianca knew I was a scholarship student. We just don't look like the other kids at Pacific Prep. Our hair doesn't have that same glow, and our skin doesn't look like it's been moisturized within an inch of its life.

I guess that's what happens when you don't have unlimited money to spend on haircare and beauty products.

The girl smiles back at me, showing me her slightly crooked teeth. It's a real, genuine smile, nothing like the fake, cosmetically enhanced ones Bianca's friends wore.

"Are you a senior?" she whispers.

"Yeah."

"I'm Emilia. Stick with me, girl. I'll show you the ropes."

Hadley

CHAPTER TWO

*A*fter what felt like a never-ending assembly, the headmaster reiterating the rules and reminding us of what he expects from us this year, he finally let us go.

"Ugh, thank god that's over!" Emilia groans as we get to our feet, the auditorium erupting into a cacophony of noise as conversations start up again and students make their way toward the exit. "Come on, I'll show you around."

"Thanks." I give her a grateful smile as we make our way back out of the auditorium, relieved I'm rid of Bianca and to have an actual guide to give me the lay of the land.

Once we step out into the blinding sun, Emilia turns to the other students who were in the pew. There are six of them in total—four boys and two other girls. "We'll catch up with you guys in a bit," she calls out.

Two of them mumble a goodbye while eyeing me warily as Emilia turns back to me with an excited grin on her face.

"Okay, so this is the main school building, obviously," she explains, waving toward the large building I met Bianca in. "The music department is over there, and the admin building is behind it," she points at a large rectangular building off to my left before tugging on my arm and taking off in the opposite direction. "Who was supposed to be your guide?"

"Bianca," I deadpan, giving her a look that says everything about how great an introduction to Pac Prep that was.

"Ha," the caustic bark erupts from her, "I bet that went well."

The main building is behind us as we head down one of the various paths. Off to my left is a dense-looking forest, with grass lawns to my right all the way down to an extensive-looking sports complex at the far end of the campus.

Emilia points to a large structure up ahead, saying, "That's the library. It's open pretty much twenty-four-seven. There's also a computer suite in the main building where you can go to do work or print stuff off, although no one ever really needs to print anything here. You'll have a tablet in your room where the teachers upload their worksheets for each lesson, and you just fill them in on that."

A tablet? Damn, that's fancy! Although I've never used one before, so I'm sure that's going to be a fun learning curve. What the hell is wrong with good old-fashioned pen and paper?

Strolling past the library, it's just as old and grandiose looking as everything else here, but there's something more inviting about it than the other buildings. Maybe it's because it's a place of solitude, of losing yourself in work or a good book, that makes it more endearing.

"So, what's your deal?"

"My deal?" I question, turning to look at Emilia. Her lips are puckered as she runs her eyes over me, trying to figure me out.

"What's your story?"

"What's yours?" I retort, not comfortable telling a complete stranger who I am or where I come from. I know she's more like me than the pretentious rich kids, however there's still a difference between coming from a poor family and having no family at all.

Instead of being put off by my prickly behavior, her smile grows wider, like my response has surprised her and she is more than prepared to rise to the challenge. Internally snorting, I can't help but think she's got a pretty massive hill to climb if she wants to be my friend. I don't exactly do friendships, or relationships, of any shape or form. I'm just not wired for that. As soon as that line is crossed, there's a requirement, a sense of responsibility. You're expected to be there, to show up, to give a damn.

From what I've seen, someone always lets the other person down, and it either blows up in your face or resentment slowly builds up, rotting everything good you once had from the inside out. Yeah, no thanks. I don't need anyone but myself.

Emilia shrugs her shoulders, not having the same reservations about divulging her life story to a virtual stranger. "It's just my mom and me. She's a nurse. We do okay—not anything like this." She chuckles, waving at our surroundings. "But we get by. Growing up, she always told me to strive for more, to want a better life. She works her ass off for everything we have." Her gaze turns distant as she falls into memories. "I'm here as much for her as for myself. I want both of us to have a better future."

"That's really admirable." I've never been close enough with anyone to take care of them like that. Everything I do is for me—to make *me* a better person, to improve *my* life. There's never been anyone else. Well...there *was* someone. But I don't let myself think about her now.

She once again turns that blinding smile my way.

"Okay, your turn."

Butterflies take flight in my stomach, and my palms sweat as I bite down on my lower lip. "I'm a foster kid." There, I said it. "I turned eighteen last month, so apparently, that makes me an adult now and responsible for myself."

"You can't be doing too bad if you're here," Emilia reasons, giving me a soft smile.

"Yeah, I guess," I acquiesce, not wanting to disagree with her and get into a whole conversation about it as we stroll through the grounds, the other students around us enjoying their last day of freedom before classes begin tomorrow. Some of them are crowded around benches on the various paths crisscrossing through the lawns, and a group of guys are tossing a ball back and forth.

"The dorms," Emilia points out, indicating two long, rectangular structures, "and that's the dining hall." Another large hall is situated between the two of them. All three buildings have the same gorgeous aesthetic as the rest of the campus. "Boys are on the right, girls on the left."

She directs me toward the girls' dorms, and we step into a bright foyer with a small seating area, a coffee bar off to one side, and a set of stairs leading to the upper floors. With the white painted walls and black fabric sofas, everything is sleek and modern looking, in complete contrast to the old style of the building.

"Scholarship students, regardless of what year they are, are all on the ground floor, then freshmen on the first floor, sophomores on the second floor, yadda-yadda. At least, that's how it is in the girls' dorms."

"What do you mean by that?"

"The boys' dorms are different. The Princes have had the whole top floor to themselves since their first year, and everyone else squishes into the lower floors." Emilia explains all this while she opens a door at the back of the foyer that leads down a wide, white-walled hallway with doors leading off it in both directions. Just like the foyer, everything looks freshly painted and sterile looking. Each door we pass has a girl's name on it, along with various stickers and posters personalizing it, distracting me for a second until her words register with me.

"The Princes?"

"Yup," she says, popping the 'p.' "They rule the school. If you think the teachers are in charge here, you're wrong. *They* are. Their great-great-whatever grandfathers founded the school or something. From what I've heard, everyone in their family has attended here and ruled the school when they did. It's a tradition thing." With a casual shrug of her shoulder, she waves it off.

"Right." I don't really understand what she means. How can teenage boys rule the school? All I've ever known is that adults are the leading figures and threatening their place of authority only ever ends badly.

"You probably saw them this morning. They're impossible to miss."

My mind immediately skips back to the four guys I saw earlier. With their superior presence and the way they caught everyone's attention, they must be who Emilia is talking about.

"Yeah, I think I did."

She nods knowingly, expecting that answer.

"This is me." She raps her knuckles on a door as we walk past, stopping outside the last room at the end of the hall. "And I'm guessing this one is yours since it's the only empty one."

She pushes the door open, and I step into a moderately sized room, my mouth hanging open as I'm met with more white walls and dark wood furniture. The room contains all the basic furniture needed—a bed, desk, wardrobe, bookcase, and a chest of drawers. Walking over to the window and peering out, all I can see is the surrounding forest. From this viewpoint, I'm unable to see the paths, meaning no one can peek into my room, providing me with some modicum of privacy.

"Most of us stick posters and stuff over the walls, or if you have your own bed covers or whatever. As long as we don't leave any permanent damage, they don't mind how we decorate." At Emilia's words, I turn back around to take in the room again. There isn't much space to move about, but it's more than I'm used to. Glancing at the bed, I let out a sigh of relief when I find my duffle already there, the stress lifting off my shoulders at seeing it again. It maybe sounds stupid, but when your entire life is in a bag, it's not easy to let it out of your sight.

"Your key will be in the door, and your tablet is on the desk. The showers are across the hall. Everyone on the floor shares them, but it's not too bad of a rush in the morning."

I don't know what to say. It might not look like much, but a whole room to myself? Not having to share with other people? And, looking at the door, I see there's a lock. I also noticed a lock on the window. This room could literally be my haven away from the world. I don't have posters or anything to decorate the place with, but regardless, I can picture myself living here doing my homework or reading a book. No one could come in and bother me or catch me unaware; I could be happy here.

Thankfully, Emilia doesn't pick up on my sudden muteness and after a few more minutes, asks, "Do you wanna check out the rest of the campus?"

I absently nod my head, my eyes still roaming over the room. "Sure, that sounds good."

We spend the rest of the afternoon wandering around. Emilia showed me the rec center, where they have several small cinema rooms for people to chill, a game room, a coffee shop, and even a small shop selling stationery, snacks, and anything else you could possibly need, before taking me over to the sports complex. I've never seen anything like it; you could more or less do any sporting activity you want. It even came complete with a sauna and spa. The entire campus is insane, resembling more of a self-contained village than a school. You literally don't have to leave the grounds for anything.

It's late in the day when we enter the dining hall for dinner. Apparently, breakfast is the only meal of the day with a set time for each year. For the rest of the day, the dining hall is open and you can come and go as you please.

A few of the tables are occupied when we enter, making our way toward the buffet tables. Instead of grabbing a tray, though, Emilia stops beside a kiosk with a computer screen, tapping away on it. I peer over her shoulder as she chooses what meal she wants from the online menu, selecting her table number before stepping to the side, so I can enter what I want.

"Hot meals are selected here, or you can use the app on your tablet. You can also order anything to go or grab something from the buffet," she explains as we make our way to an empty table at the far side of the room. She explains it all so casually, but this cannot be the norm at most high schools. It's definitely a far cry from what I'm used to.

She must see it written on my face as she releases a small chuckle. "I know, I know. It's crazy, right? It takes a bit of getting used to. I swear, I walked around here with my mouth hanging open for most of freshman year."

"Yeah, I bet. I'm struggling to wrap my head around it all. Everything just seems so…over the top."

"Ha, yeah. That's putting it mildly. Wait 'til you get to know the other students. Some of them…" She shakes her head like she's struggling to find the right word. "Let's just say they can be pompous, entitled assholes."

"From what Bianca said, I gather the scholarship students and the rest of the school don't get along?" I ask, keen to get more information on how everything around here works. I definitely don't need to go pissing off the wrong people right off the bat.

"Ahh, she gave you the whole 'you, us, and them' spiel?" Emilia shakes her head, rolling her eyes. "She's the worst, thinking she's so much better than everyone else. Just 'cause her daddy owns an oil emporium doesn't mean she doesn't eat, sleep, and shit like the rest of us. She's kind of right, however. We tend to stick to ourselves. It's not necessarily because the other students want nothing to do with us, but we just don't have anything in common. Bianca and her friends are the only ones that seem to openly dislike us."

Absorbing all the information she's sharing, I enquire, "What about the Princes?"

"They don't really have anything to do with us." She shrugs. "Or anyone, for that matter. They're a tight-knit group, mostly keeping to themselves and rarely interacting with anyone outside of the four of them, unless they're looking to get laid or someone pisses them off. Cam would be the most social out of all of them." My ears perk up at the name, remembering the guy who winked at me. He was definitely the outgoing one of the group.

The door into the hall opens before I can ask anything else, a reverent hush settling over the few students here as the guys themselves enter, not sparing a single glance around the room as they make their way toward the buffet table. My attention is immediately drawn to Cam, taking in his cocky swagger as he talks away to the guy beside him, seeming oblivious to everyone's eyes on him.

"Who are the other three?" I ask Emilia, unable to tear my gaze away from Cam.

"The guy Cam is talking to is West Warren."

West is the hot nerd from this morning. Unlike Cam, his eyes roam the room studiously before he turns back to respond to whatever Cam is saying. "The angry-faced one is Hawk Davenport, and beside him is Mason Hayes."

The four of them have such a beguiling presence, making it impossible not to watch their every move. They appear relaxed, talking to one another while they wait for their food. Except Mason's tense posture, and the way West flicks his gaze around the room, gives away the fact that they know everyone is watching them, and they aren't as comfortable with all the attention as they pretend to be.

"Earth to Hadley." Emilia laughs, my cheeks pinking at having been caught at practically drooling over them as I turn back to look at her. "I know, they're sex on legs," she continues to laugh, "but trust me, they aren't worth it."

My eyebrows jump up in surprise. "You've slept with one of them?"

"I fucking wish!" She chuckles. "Sadly, no, but every girl in this place wants in on that. The girls here are like sharks, especially when it comes to bagging themselves rich boyfriends. And *everyone* wants their very own Prince. If they smell blood in the water, they will tear you to shreds."

I'd like to see those rich bitches fucking try, but yeah, I don't need that drama. As tempting as they might look, I'm sure there's less problematic dick floating around this place that will do the job when my horny side surfaces.

"What's Cam's surname?" I ask before said horny side can make an unwanted appearance. Sadly, those gorgeous boys will only be featured on my nightly bean screen.

"Rutherford, why?"

I shrug my shoulders. "Just curious."

Only once the Princes leave the hall, everything returns to normal, with students returning to eating their meals and gossiping. It's crazy the effect four teenage boys can have on an entire room of people, but I can't deny that their magnetism doesn't affect me.

"We do a movie night on the first day of the term, if you wanna come and meet the other scholarship students?"

"Yeah," I nod my head, "that sounds like fun."

At eight o'clock, Emilia knocks on my door and we make our way across campus to the rec center, stopping at the shop on our way to meet the others. Using some of the allowances we're given as part of our scholarship, we buy snacks for the movie before heading to the cinema room that's been booked for the night.

The room comprises several rows of comfortable seats and a large screen taking up the whole wall, with speakers embedded on either side. Two boys are standing at the side of the screen, presumably getting everything set up, while the others are spread out across the front row, talking and laughing with one another, barely looking up when we enter.

"Hey, guys." Emilia smiles, walking down the aisle to the front row. "This is Hadley. She's a new scholarship student," she explains. "Hadley, this is Mary and Abigail." Emilia gestures toward the two girls, one of whom is stuffing her face with popcorn, giving me a quick wave when I glance in her direction, while the other is cuddling up to a dark, shaggy-haired boy. "That's Todd, Abigail's boyfriend. Michael and the two setting up the movie are Andrew and Samuel." The two tinkering with the screen glance over, waving hellos before focusing back on what they were doing.

Todd gives me a slight nod as Abigail smiles from his lap. "Hey, Hadley, nice to meet you." She giggles as Todd buries his face in her hair, distracting her.

"Nice to have a new face around." Michael smiles as Emilia directs me toward a spare seat beside him, sitting down on my other side. "I hope you like Blade. It's Samuel's turn to pick the movie tonight, and he seems to think we can watch all three in one night." He chuckles, leaning in closer to me so his arm brushes against mine on the armrest.

"I've never seen it," I admit.

His eyebrows rise with surprise. "Well, you're in for a treat then—as long as you like movies with blood, guts, and gore."

"I can definitely handle a little blood." I grin as the lights are dimmed, and Andrew and Samuel take their seats, the beginning credits of the movie rolling on the big screen TV.

We make it through two of the movies before midnight, and everyone agrees it's time to call it a night. I actually had more fun than I expected, listening to the others talk and bicker about the movie. I didn't have much to contribute, but watching them all laughing and getting along was interesting. It was all so *normal*.

We say goodbye to the boys outside their dormitory before walking to our own. "You have fun tonight?" Emilia asks once Mary and Abigail have gone into their rooms.

"Yeah, I did. Everyone seems really nice." I smile wearily. It's been a long, chaotic day, and the bed is definitely calling my name.

"They are. Anyway, I'll see you in the morning. You can get your first experience of the real Pac Prep." She laughs, opening her door.

Oh great, just when I was beginning to think maybe this place wouldn't be so bad.

"Night," she says, giving a final wave as she closes the door.

"Night."

Hadley

CHAPTER THREE

"What is your schedule like?" Emilia asks me at breakfast the next morning. I'm sitting at the same table as yesterday, pressed between her and Mary, listening to the others chat around me while I devour the delicious breakfast in front of me. I've always been a food lover, but I've *never* had food like this before. I swear I'd died and gone to heaven if it wasn't for the uncomfortable uniform I'm wearing and the sounds of other students echoing around us.

"Uh," I hesitate, trying to remember what classes I have today. It took over an hour after I got back to my room last night—of me trying to figure out how to use the damn tablet—before I finally managed to pull up my schedule. *What the hell is wrong with a printed timetable?*

"Gimme your tablet," she says, holding out her hand, quickly realizing she would be faster to look it up for herself. Grabbing it out of my bag and handing it over, I get back to my breakfast as she taps away on it, pulling up the schedule much quicker than I could have.

"Oh, we have English together this morning and a few other classes during the week. That's awesome, I can show you the way once we're finished eating."

Downing half my glass of orange juice, relishing the fresh, tangy taste, I nod at her, letting her know that sounds good. There was a paper version of the map in my welcome pack that I was able to look at last night, and I've shoved it in my bag for today when I inevitably get lost. The campus is just so widespread, it's impossible to remember where everything is, so I definitely won't be turning down her offer of assistance.

"What did you think of the movie last night?" Michael asks from across the table.

"I loved it." I barely get the words out between forkfuls of the fluffiest pancakes I've ever tasted. How do they make them so light? Doused in fruit and syrup, it's the best meal I've ever had.

A grin lights up his face. "We could—"

He doesn't get any further as the noise in the hall dies down to a deathly hush. The

Princes rise to their feet, and everyone forgets their food and conversations drop immediately to give the rulers their full attention. It was the same when they entered the hall half an hour ago too, everyone silently watching them as they headed to a table at the far end of the room.

The hall is designed so that the kiosks, buffet, and collection points are all on one side of the room, with large tables interspersed around the rest of the space. The best one in the room is by the large windows, overlooking the grassy lawn and boys' dormitory. Of course, that's the Princes' table, and no one is allowed to sit there unless invited, or so Emilia informed me.

"Today is the first day of senior year," Hawk shouts out. "So I'm sure you all know what that means." A round of excited whispers sound through the room before he speaks up again. "We each pick one girl who is ours for the month. That girl will be our date to parties, will sit with us at breakfast, and, basically, belong to us for the month."

"What is he talking about?" I whisper to Emilia.

She rolls her eyes. "It's a stupid-ass senior year tradition that was started by their forefathers, where they essentially pick a girl to fuck and flaunt for a month, then the next month they pick someone new and do it all over again."

"What the fuck?!" I whisper in shock, gaping at her. "Are you for real?"

"Yup," she confirms, nodding her head.

"What if the girls they choose don't want to be picked?"

Emilia snorts. "Girl, there isn't a person in this room that would turn down their offer."

I cast a glance around the room, taking in the excited looks in the girls' eyes as they whisper frantically to their friends, pulling their cameras up on their phones and tablets so they can check their makeup and peeking furtively toward the Princes. She's right. Every single one of them wants to be claimed by one of those idiots. *Talk about feeding their arrogance.*

"You mean you'd say yes if one of them asked you?"

"Hell yeah, I would! Have you *seen* them? They're real-life porn! My vagina would have to be a shriveled bean sack to turn down the fine-ass dick those boys have." I can't help snorting at her antics, despite the craziness of what she's saying. "Not that it matters, scholarship students don't get picked."

Why doesn't that surprise me?

My attention focuses back on the Princes as Hawk moves around from behind his table, his eyes scanning the room as he stalks across it like a lion on the prowl. He moves between a few tables before pointing at some girl I don't know. After a round of ear-piercing squeals from the nominated girl and her crowd of friends, they eventually settle down as Mason steps forward. The whole thing is ridiculous. I can literally hear the voiceover of some 'Animals in the Wild' documentary.

'Here we have the male Homo sapien prowling through the assembled females in search of his intended mate. Where the female primate gravitates toward males who ooze money and arrogance; the males are drawn to purely superficial matters like physical attraction, or whether or not she has a gag reflex.'

"So what, the girls are like their girlfriends for the month or something?" I ask as Mason chooses his girl, another round of squeals erupting in the otherwise quiet room. With his bulky size and bland expression, he's really not someone I'd want to spend much time alone with. Sure, he's hot and clearly popular, but he doesn't look like the type you'd have a titillating conversation with. He gives off that whole 'I could kill you and not even blink an eye' vibe. Not exactly alluring.

"I wouldn't necessarily say that, more like their fuck buddies. The girls get that elevation in status and the attention they crave, and the Princes get a sure thing booty call when they want it."

"Romance at its finest," I swoon, my voice thick with sarcasm.

"Ha." Emilia laughs. "Right?"

Cam steps forward next. Unlike the first two, he makes a complete show out of the thing, lifting his hand to run it through his short blond hair in a sexy 'I know I'm hot shit' kind of way, getting the crowd riled up and flirting with the girls before finally choosing some blonde chick. She jumps out of her chair in eagerness, flinging her arms around his neck, clinging to him like a spider monkey. As he gently, yet firmly, extracts himself from her embrace, I get a look at her face and actually recognize this girl.

Bianca.

Of course, it is. They're the perfect prom king and queen pair, with their same colored hair and incredible looks.

When he finally shakes her off, Cam heads back to his table. I expect West to move forward next, doing the same as the other guys, but he barely spares the room a glance, pointing absently at the closest girl to him before dropping into his seat and ignoring the final round of exciting murmurings as he stares pointedly at his tablet, working away at something.

"Pfft, what a farce." Samuel shakes his head, annoyed at the whole show. "They can get any girl they want, why do they need to make a spectacle of picking girls?"

"It's just another way for them to exert their dominance and control over the year," Todd responds dismissively. "Forget about it. It's not like it will make any difference to us."

The Princes settle back into their seats, indicating the end of this morning's events, as the rest of the hall buzzes with this morning's excitement. The tables with chosen girls are a hive of energy, the selected girls grinning and flaunting their new status while the others throw them jealous glares.

"I can't believe I just witnessed that," I mumble, mostly to myself.

Mary responds anyway, "I know, right? It's insane."

"Completely antiquated," I agree. "I just don't understand how every girl falls at their feet like that."

"They're the Princes." Emilia shrugs nonchalantly, as though that's justification for this whole insane thing.

"More like the Pricks," I grumble, rolling my eyes, and getting a laugh from the rest of the table.

"The Pricks of Pacific Prep." Emilia snorts. "Fitting."

The rest of breakfast goes by quietly, everyone chatting away and catching up after the summer. Michael tries to draw me into the conversation several times by asking about my summer and childhood, but I evade the topics with vague responses, and Emilia swiftly comes to my rescue.

"Come on, we better get to English if we want good seats," she says, grabbing her backpack and getting to her feet. I quickly follow her, giving Michael and the others a brief smile and waving goodbye as we head out.

Making our way over to the main building, Emilia navigates us through the west wing. Both wings have three floors to accommodate classes for each subject, with the top floor of the west wing comprising computer suites for classes and personal use.

We push our way through the throng of other students, finding their first class of the day, until I spot Mr. Greer's name on a plaque on the classroom door, recognizing it as the name of our English teacher. Stepping into the classroom, I notice a few other students are already there, chatting with one another while they wait for class to begin. Mr. Greer glances up as we enter, giving us a nod before returning his attention to the papers on his desk.

The tables are all set out in groups of two, and Emilia grabs my hand, dragging me over to an empty table on the far side of the room, where we can sit together. Dropping my bag, I pull out my tablet and a notebook, already knowing I don't have a hope in hell of taking notes on that thing. The screen is too tiny, and even if I could navigate to the virtual notebook, any time I attempt to use the stylus, it ends up zooming all over the place and making a mess.

It's not long until the room fills with people, only a few empty seats left when the bell rings. I'm bent over my desk, writing, so I don't see them arrive, but I do feel the room go still around me, signifying their presence. I don't even have to look up to hazard a guess as to who just entered since they draw my eyes to them like they are a hypnotic force pulling me in.

Cam and Mason stroll into the room like they own it. Well, if the names on some of the buildings are any indication, they do own it. I spotted all four of their surnames on various buildings around campus yesterday, making it more than obvious who owns this school.

Bianca has once again wrapped herself around Cam, fawning all over him while he's too busy making an entrance, putting on a show for the rest of the class, just like at breakfast this morning.

A pretty brunette is standing awkwardly beside Mason, casting unsure looks his way. I vaguely recognize her as the girl he chose this morning. Unlike Bianca, she's making a conscious effort to not touch him. I can't blame her. As if his size isn't intimidating enough, the whole stony expression he's got going on is a sufficient warning to stay the fuck out of his way.

He and Cam head toward the back of the room and claim a table together, as the girls follow and take the seats directly in front of them, whispering quietly to each other and casting coquettish looks back toward the guys.

The final few students stumble in, and when the class is full, the teacher gets to his feet, rounding the desk.

"Alright, class," Mr. Greer begins, casting his eyes over each of us before a huge shit-eating grin crosses his face. "Now that you've gotten comfortable in your new seats beside your buddies, you're all going to get up so I can put you in alphabetical order."

A resounding groan echoes around the room, and Emilia pouts, the expression making me chuckle as everyone clambers to their feet.

"Stand along the back wall," Mr. Greer calls out happily, deriving far too much pleasure from his students' grumblings, as we all do as he asks. "When I call your name, come and take your seat."

Starting at the beginning of the alphabet, he calls out, "Dustin Aberman," and a short, stocky kid quickly scurries toward the front of the class. This continues on for several more minutes until Bianca's name is called. With her hips swaying like she's striding down a runway and *not* simply walking across a classroom, she makes a whole parade of claiming her seat.

Emilia's name is called next and, with one final sulky look, her eyes silently begging me for help, she moves to sit next to Bianca. Neither girl looks happy to be sitting beside the other.

"Hadley Parker," Mr. Greer calls out several names later, pointing to a table against the wall at the back of the room. I hurry over to it, dropping into the chair as he calls out the next person's name. "Cameron Rutherford."

I have to physically restrain my eye roll as he strides toward me, his warm brown eyes alight with mischief and a confident smirk playing at the corner of his lips.

"New girl," he purrs, sliding into the seat beside me, leaning in as he drops his arm over the back of my chair. He flicks his tongue out, running it along his bottom lip in a deliberately seductive way. My eyes trail the movement like it's the most fascinating thing I've seen in a long time. *Hell, it's definitely the hottest.* How can he be such an arrogant ass and sexy as fuck all at the same time?

Unable to hold back that eye roll any longer, I let it loose, focusing on my workbook and deliberately trying to ignore the sex lollipop eyeing me up.

"Harley, right?"

What the hell is with these people and names?! How difficult is it to get someone's name right? Mr. Greer literally just mentioned it.

"No," I respond, still refusing to look at him. It's bad enough having him this close to me, where I can breathe in his stupidly expensive aftershave that smells like bad decisions. "Close, though."

I cave and glance subtly in his direction out of the corner of my eye. His eyes are narrowed in concentration as he tries to recall what the teacher said.

"Ahh," he exclaims, banging his hand on the table, having apparently figured it out. "Hadley." He appears triumphant, a proud grin spreading across his face.

Raising my eyebrows and pursing my lips in a sarcastic gesture, I bob my head, still not looking at him as I doodle in the corner of my notebook.

"Right, class," Mr. Greer calls out, having finished with the last few students. "We're going to start the term off with a project. Each pair is to pick a book from this year's reading list and write a ten-thousand-word report." Groans and murmurs erupt around the classroom that the teacher promptly ignores, raising his voice. "Everyone should contribute *equally*."

Great, now I'm stuck doing an assignment with Mr. Flirty pants. I highly doubt the Princes do their own homework either, so I'm probably going to be stuck doing the whole thing by myself. *Super fun.*

"You can spend the rest of the class discussing it in your pairs," Mr. Greer tacks on, solidifying the craptastic day this is turning out to be.

"Guess we're assignment buddies," Cam purrs, sounding way too pleased about it.

"Yeah, I guess so."

"You know what that means? A lot of late nights, alone in the library."

Why does his voice have me imagining all the dirty things we could get up to in the dark stacks? And the way he bites his lower lip has me wanting to replace his teeth with my own.

Snapping myself out of it, I focus on the project, instead asking, "What book do you want to do?" in an attempt to bring the topic back to safer territory.

"The first party of the year is this weekend," he states, completely ignoring my question. I may as well have said nothing. "You should come."

"I'll think about it." My reply is blunt as I once again attempt to shut down the conversation and get back to the assignment. Besides, I've never been invited to a party before, and I don't know if parties are something the other scholarship students go to. I'm also not sure I want to subject myself to the company of these kids any more than I have to.

"If you give me your room number, I can pick you up."

How sweet that would be, if he wasn't full of dirty intentions.

"I don't think your new girlfriend would be too happy about that," I respond, gesturing to Bianca who is glaring daggers at me from across the room. I don't know what she thinks is going on over here, but I have no doubt I'm the one she's going to have issues with.

Cam snorts, shaking his head. "That's just for show. It doesn't mean anything, it's just some stupid tradition."

"Then why do it?" I'm genuinely curious. If he and the others don't give a shit, why subject themselves to that? Wouldn't they rather be free to date and screw whoever they want instead of saddling themselves with a girl they couldn't care less about each month?

"Because it's expected of us."

There's something in the tone of his voice that makes me lift my head to look at him. *Really* look at him. I'm not sure what it was I heard, but his face gives nothing away. "It means *something* to the girls you chose."

He gives me an indulgent smile, leaning in even closer. "It would, to someone like you," he begins. I'm about to call him out on what exactly he means by 'someone like you' when he continues on, "But for them, it's got absolutely nothing to do with us. They want to be seen with us because of *who* we are and what we can offer them. If we fell to the bottom of the totem pole tomorrow, someone else would take our place, and none of those girls would give a shit about us. All they want is status, money, and power."

"And you get absolutely nothing out of it?" I argue, letting him know I'm not buying his whole 'woe is me' act. I wouldn't be surprised if what he's saying is true, but it's by no means a purely selfish gesture on the guys' part. He simply shrugs his shoulders. "Tit for tat. Everyone knows what they're signing on for."

I lean in so our lips are a hair's breadth apart. I'm playing with fire, I know it, but it doesn't stop me. "The look on Bianca's face says otherwise."

A cheeky grin lights up his face, excitement brimming in his eyes. "Don't tell me you're going to let something like that scare you off?"

"Please." I snort. "She's a kitty cat. I could destroy her in my sleep."

I mean it, but I'm not about to start drama just for Cam's amusement. There are enough idiots around here feeding his arrogance, he sure as hell doesn't need me adding to it.

"Mmm, I'd love to see that."

"Yeah, I'm sure you would. Too bad I don't go for rich dudes with fake girlfriends."

Hadley

CHAPTER FOUR

"Girl, you're sitting beside *Cam Rutherford*!" Emilia squeals as we leave English. "It's not as great as you're making it out to be. All he wants to do is flirt with me," I groan as she tucks her arm into my side, directing me to my next class. For real. We got nothing done the whole lesson. Whenever I brought up the project, he would divert the topic to something dirty. "And did you see the looks Bianca was sending me? I've barely been here a day, and I already have an enemy."

She cackles at my dramatics, but seriously, it's not the best start. I didn't want to make waves here. The goal was to fly under the radar and focus on my work before getting the hell out of here and moving on with my future.

"I think I'd happily flunk English if it meant Cam flirted with me." She sighs dreamily. "Any of them, really. Although Hawk and Mason are intimidating as fuck, imagine all that aggression being released in the bedroom." I fear I've lost her to her daydreams as she full-body shivers at whatever she's thinking about—I'm pretty sure I don't want to know...unless one of them is doing it to my body.

~

THANKFULLY, the rest of the day was uneventful. No other Princes were in my classes, and I didn't see them when I went to grab lunch with Emilia and the others. I don't know what it is about them. I can't deny their pull over me. Whenever they're around, I find myself watching their every move, wanting to learn more about them.

Unfortunately, my lucky streak ends on Tuesday afternoon when I sit in my business class and all four of them stroll in. The teacher literally takes one look at them and his eyes bug out of his head as he swallows around a lump in his throat, his voice becoming high-pitched. *Is he for real? He's a fucking teacher, and they're just students.* Maybe it's the fact that all four of them are in his class. They do have the air of an indomitable force.

The four of them move toward the back row, the couple of students already sitting there quickly scurrying out of their chairs to sit elsewhere. Cam winks as he walks past my table, deliberately brushing the back of his hand against my shoulder, sending an involuntary shiver through me. *Goddammit, how can he elicit that response from me so easily?*

"Alright," the teacher begins, starting the lesson. As he drones on about some cost-benefit analysis theory, my eyes roam over the class taking in the other students. Except for Mary sitting in the row beside me, there are literally no other females in the class. *Weird.*

Feeling eyes on me, I subtly glance out of the corner of my eye until I find Mason in the far back corner of the room, his intense gaze drilling into the side of my head. *What the hell?* His forehead is furrowed, and he's got a frown on his face as he leans over to Cam beside him, his hair falling forward to cover his eyes as the two of them whisper before Cam peers in my direction.

The teacher telling us to get started on a worksheet on our tablets pulls my attention back to the lesson, but I swear, for the next hour, I feel Mason's eyes on me. When the class finishes and the room empties, there's a crackle in the air as he walks past. Not knowing what to make of it, I shake it off and move on to the next class of the day.

As the week drags on, I'm constantly aware of their presence, subtly stalking them with my eyes when we're in the same room. There's just something about them and I can't put my finger on it, but it has me obsessing over them for no good reason.

As much as I've tried, I haven't been able to forget about the strange shock I got the other day with Mason, and it would be impossible to ignore the wetness in my panties every time Cam throws me a dirty wink—which is far too often. For the sake of my laundry, he needs to stop.

Every morning, my eyes inadvertently drift their way as they each sit with a girl draped all over them. Even the mousy girl, Vivian, who Mason chose, has come out of her shell. I can only imagine what went down between them to have her suddenly being more self-assured around him. The show we're all forced to witness every morning, though, is vomit-inducing. West is the only one who seems to have any sort of morning etiquette, blatantly ignoring the girl—Brittany—he chose. She certainly gives it her best try to garner his attention, in any case. It's almost painful to watch as she tries to get him to eat food from her fork and runs her hand suggestively down his arm until he shakes her off.

Hawk and Mason don't seem to have the same issue with their girls. Both of them spend the better part of breakfast attempting to see what base they can get to before someone in the hall stops them—newsflash, no one will ever stop them. I'm pretty sure one day, soon, we're going to walk in and find one of them full-on fucking a girl over the table. I'm going to have to start storing cereal bars in my room. Seriously, who wants to see that shit when they're trying to eat? Or, you know, *ever?* They have forever ruined pancakes for me, and I'm not fucking happy about it.

Cam is the most baffling. One day he seems to lap up Bianca's attention, flirting and getting on with her, and the next, he shoves her away, wanting nothing to do with her. Yet every day, he winks in my direction, always making a point of brushing up against me when we pass in the halls. Every time he does, my pussy fucking weeps for more. I like to think I'm a resilient woman, but damn, he's doing a good job of wearing me down. He doesn't even need to say anything to me. A dirty look and casual touch are all it takes, apparently. I'm not used to having to deny my sexual urges, and Cam is really testing my resolve.

When it comes to all four of them, I can't wrap my head around any of it. What confuses me the most is the way the guys get on. When they're around everyone else, it's like they wear these shields, hiding their true thoughts and feelings. However, I've caught glimpses of them alone, in the library, or sometimes late at night in the dining hall when they seem so much more relaxed, more open, joking, and laughing with one another. It makes no sense. This is supposed to be their domain, their territory to rule over, but most of the time, they look fucking miserable.

It's become a bit of an obsession, the way I watch them. I'd believe it was just my innate senses identifying a possible threat and reacting, yet the way my stomach takes flight and my every sense is attuned to Cam's closeness in English tells me it's so much more than that. I don't know what to make of it or what the hell to do about it. Ignoring it seems like the best option for now. I probably just have a stupid crush on him, although it will pass. If only we didn't have to do this project together, then I could actively avoid them all until whatever the fuck has gotten into me goes away.

"What do you think you're doing with Cam?" Bianca's annoying voice calls out, stopping me in my tracks. I should have known this was coming after my attempt to wind her up in English earlier in the week.

Slowly turning around, I narrow my eyes at her. "Excuse me?"

"He's mine. Don't think I haven't seen you panting all over him, hogging all of his attention."

I chuckle in disbelief. "Are you for real?"

"I saw you in English, flirting with him."

"You mean *talking* to him?"

Ignoring me, she continues her rant, going on about how it's her turn and he's hers. I don't know, I'm not actually listening to her.

"Look," I snap, cutting across whatever she was rambling on about, "I'm not interested in him." *Liar. Liar. Liar,* my inner slut insists, except I shut her down quickly. *We're living in denial, remember?*

"I'm serious," I assert when she looks dubious. "He asked if I could go to some party with him, but I told him no."

That's apparently the wrong thing to say, as her face turns red with steam practically pouring out of her. "He what?!" she screeches, her fists clenching in anger.

My eyes widen as I stand frozen, unable to do anything but gape at the volcano that's about to erupt in front of me. *What the actual fuck?*

"Stay away from him," she snarls. "I'll make your life here miserable if I catch you sniffing around him again."

She storms off down the hall, and I watch her go, utterly baffled as to what the fuck just happened. Choosing to forget about our little run-in, I saunter off in the opposite direction, continuing on my journey back to the dorms.

Rounding the corner, I crash into a solid chest. "Ouch," I cry as I bounce backward, rubbing at my nose. Who the fuck has a chest that hard? There's no way that can be normal.

"Watch where the fuck you're going," a deep voice snarls, his shitty tone immediately steeling my spine.

"Excuse me?" I bark back, glaring up into Hawk's dark, stormy gray eyes. There's something familiar about them, but I can't place it. Maybe it's the sea of anger I can see raging within them. Who knows!

"You heard me," he growls, shoving past me.

For fuck's sake, it was a bloody accident on both our parts. Is a simple 'sorry' too much to ask for? Evidently so.

"Fucking asshole," I grumble, shaking my head as I take a step forward. Getting back to my room before I run into any more rich shitheads is the best idea I've had all day.

"What the fuck did you just call me?" His voice is a low rumble, threaded with dark promises of violence, halting me mid-step as I slowly turn around to face him and take in his menacing expression. The hairs at the back of my neck stand at attention, a warning, if ever there was one, that this brute in front of me is a real and serious threat.

He's not the first man who thought he could intimidate me just because he was bigger and scarier looking, and he sure as fuck won't be the last. At this point, his shit slides right off me.

I raise my chin, unflinchingly staring him down. "You heard me."

A snarl rips out of his chest like he truly is part beast, but I continue to stand my ground, refusing to be cowered.

"Hawk, man, there you are," Cam calls out as Hawk takes a threatening step toward me. I have no idea what he was going to do, but it's probably for the best that Cam has shown up. "What's going on here?" he asks, his gaze bouncing between us, likely seeing the furious expressions on both of our faces and sensing the tension rippling in the air around us.

"Nothing," I spit out between gritted teeth. "Your buddy was about to make a horrible decision he'd later regret."

Another growl is the only response Hawk appears to be capable of right now. Cam instantly picks up on the pure rage seeping out of Hawk and angles his body between us...in some attempt to protect me? Either way, I've no intention of sticking around to find out.

I take a step back, then another, refusing to turn my back on either of them.

"Come on, man," Cam encourages, clapping his hand on Hawk's shoulder. "We've got shit to do."

It takes him another minute, but finally, Hawk seems to relent, giving a sharp nod and letting Cam steer him backward. His eyes never leave mine, though, until the two round the corner, disappearing out of sight.

Jesus, fuck. Can I not just get to my room in peace?

Later that night, I'm working in my room when there's a knock at the door. Expecting it to be Emilia, I answer in nothing more than an old pair of gym shorts and a ratty t-shirt.

"Michael," I gasp in surprise.

"Sorry." He looks embarrassed as he rubs awkwardly at the back of his neck. "I know it's late. I was craving some ice cream, and I thought I'd see if you wanted to grab some? I noticed your light was on, so I figured you'd still be up."

"Eh, yeah. Sure. Just give me a sec," I rush, caught off-guard and feeling flustered. Grabbing a baggy hoodie, I quickly throw it on over my top, grabbing my key and locking the door on my way out.

"How's your first week going?" he asks as we head outside into the cool night air. It's nearly midnight, and there aren't many students around as we walk to the dining hall.

"Yeah, it's going good. The workload is intense, but I'm slowly settling in."

"Good, I'm glad. It's been fun having you around this week."

His words take me by surprise, as I wrack my brain to think of even one moment that he could maybe classify as me being 'fun', but I come up empty. I've hardly spoken to any of the other scholarship students all week. Too busy with classes and four assholes whom have consumed my every thought.

Reaching the dining hall, he holds the door open, gesturing for me to go ahead. I step in, giving him an unsure smile, just as a hurricane of white-blonde hair barges past, knocking me against the wall.

"Out of my way, bitch," Bianca snaps as she storms past me, rushing out the door.

Turning to watch her, she power walks as fast as she can in her heels, racing back towards the girls' dorms.

"I wonder what that was about," Michael says, looking as bewildered as I do.

"No idea." I shrug, casting my eyes around the room. The hall is empty, except for the four assholes themselves at the back of the room. Cam is stomping across the room toward them, his brows furrowed and a scowl etched across his face as he runs his hand frustratingly through his blond hair. Hawk's stormy eyes zone in on me as soon as I step into the hall, like he has some sort of sixth sense that I'm here.

"Ice cream?" Michael prompts when I make no attempt to move from the doorway.

"Right, yeah." Shaking myself out of the distraction, I try to ignore their magnetizing presence pulsing from the back of the room, screaming at me to look their way. Instead, I follow Michael over to the freezer. I'm quickly pulled out of my thoughts by the vast range of flavors before me. In front of me are tubs containing every flavor of ice cream imaginable. I couldn't even tell you the last time I had ice cream. I remember eating it once as a child—some sort of fruity, berry flavor, I think. It was the sweetest thing I'd ever had.

Scanning the labels, I hum and ah for a good minute before deciding on a peanut butter one, grabbing the tub and then sitting down at what I've come to discover is the designated table for scholarship students.

My eyes once again flick up, seeing all four boys huddled at the back of the room at their usual table, deep in conversation. Forcing my attention back to Michael, I pop the lid off my ice cream, scoop out a spoonful, and bring it to my lips.

A soft moan escapes as my eyes drift shut, savoring the sweet, nutty flavor. *Oh my God, that is fucking delicious.*

"Good?" Michael chuckles quietly, digging into his own tub.

"So good," I agree, laughing too. "I, uh, don't get to eat much sweet stuff," I tell him, feeling like I need to explain myself.

"How come?"

"I, eh, grew up in foster care. You don't exactly get offered many niceties." Refusing to look at him, not knowing what sort of response I'll get, I focus on making designs in my ice cream with the spoon, the lighter tone from a moment ago now gone, along with my desire for anything sweet.

His voice tells me nothing about what he thinks of my childhood. "That must have sucked."

"Yeah." I give a sad sort of chuckle. "You could say that."

We lapse into silence. *Great, I've managed to make it awkward already.* How can I be so shitty in social situations?

"I'm sorry," I blurt when the silence becomes too much. "I didn't mean to put a downer on things. It was nice of you to invite me out."

"It's all good. I asked you out 'cause I wanted to get to know you..." His words drift into the background as movement at the back of the room pulls my attention, and I glance over his shoulder to see the Princes getting to their feet.

Cam still looks annoyed as he turns to face me, his eyes meeting mine, and he freezes in place, obviously not realizing I was here. Something passes between us. I don't know what it is. I don't even know how to describe it, but I can feel it throughout my entire body. This visceral reaction to him is kind of like an electric shock, lighting up my every nerve and snapping me to attention. It's more intense than anything I've ever experienced before. *What the hell is this?*

Someone knocks into him, breaking whatever weird spell between us, and I flick my eyes to find Mason glancing between the two of us, seeming confused. He says something to Cam, who shakes his head before they take off, moving to trail behind Hawk and West as they leave the hall.

"—would you want to go? Hadley?"

"Huh?" I focus back on Michael, realizing I haven't heard a word he's said. "Sorry, what were you saying?"

He glances quickly at the door before looking back at me. "I was saying there's a party tomorrow night, down by the beach."

"Oh, yeah, Emilia mentioned it to me."

"Yeah, all the scholarship students go, kinda like one final blowout before the workload piles up. I, uh, was wondering if you wanted to go."

"Sure," I agree, nodding my head. "Can't miss the first party of senior year, right?"

He's got a massive grin on his face. "Great. I can pick you up."

"I thought everyone went as a group?" I ask, confused.

"Well, I mean, yeah," he stumbles, his cheeks pinking. I don't know why he's suddenly looking so nervous, though.

"It probably makes more sense to walk down as a group," I reason, trying to ease whatever awkwardness he's feeling.

"Right, of course," he mumbles.

The conversation between us sort of dries up after that. I don't know what happened or what I missed, but neither of us seemed to know what to say to rectify things, and we soon call it a night and go our separate ways.

Firefly

CHAPTER FIVE

"What was that all about?" Hawk asks, tipping his head toward where a pissed-off Bianca just stormed out.

"Nothing." The scowl on Cam's face says otherwise as he stomps across the canteen toward us.

"Things have been weird between you two all week," I point out. He's been all over the place with her, like he can't decide whether he wants her or not. Something that is never usually an issue for Cam. If she's halfway good-looking with a decent set of tits, he'll stick his dick in her.

"It's nothing," he growls more vehemently, collapsing into the seat beside me, spreading his legs wide and slouching as he leans against the backrest.

Hawk gives him a once-over before glancing around at the rest of us, a serious expression on his face. "Who's the new girl?" he asks. "What's her deal?"

"Hadley?" Cam's head snaps up, his ire from a moment ago forgotten. Hasn't Hawk been listening to Cam all week? I swear she's the only thing he's been able to talk about. I'd bet my left nut she's the reason he's all over the place with Bianca. He's the only one of us who's been looking forward to the senior year tradition of picking a girl each month—although Hawk and Mason seem to be enjoying themselves alright—and now it's here, he couldn't care less. He thinks he likes the variability, the idea of always having a new girl, but really he loves the challenge of chasing after a girl. Now he's set his sights on someone unattainable. He knows scholarship girls are never chosen. Besides, it's not like our parents would ever be okay with us dating someone so far beneath us—their words, not mine. Personally, I have nothing against the scholarship students. If anything, I probably have more in common with them than the rest of the wealthy, vapid kids we go to school with. Certainly, they are my primary competition for the highest rank in the year.

"Yeah. Who is she? Why is she here?"

"Dunno." Cam shrugs. "She's a scholarship student, why?"

"Why are we even talking about her?" Mason interjects before Hawk can answer, his pinched, closed-off expression taking me by surprise. What's gotten up his ass? "We've more important things to discuss. West, have you found anything new?"

All eyes turn to me as I purse my lips, shaking my head in defeat. "Nothing," I growl, frustrated with myself. I've spent hours upon hours trying to dig deeper, but I've come up empty every time. "The two organizations are being treated like separate entities. The only thing I could find in common was the logo."

"That's it?" Cam gawks, staring at me in disbelief, but what did he expect me to find? "No employee logs or property reports, or second bank accounts or anything?"

"No, Cam. Nothing." He narrows his eyes, not appreciating my pissy attitude, but tough shit, I am pissed. I'm pissed at our parents for hiding all of this from us—hell, I'm fucking furious they're even involved in any of this. I'm angry with myself for not finding out sooner and for not being able to get all the information we need now. I don't even know how I feel about the fact that the futures we were expecting to have are all lies.

Rubbing his hands down his face, Hawk sighs, staring at me intently. "Keep trying. You might come across something. In the meantime, we need to devise another way of getting what we need."

We all nod in agreement, all of us on the same page. We can't do anything without more information, so for now, we just have to sit back and pretend life as a Prince is nothing but easy lays and keg parties.

The next day, I'm sitting at the computer desk waiting for the rest of the class to filter in. It's the last class of the week, and I can hear the excited hums of the students around me as they gossip about tonight's party. It's the first party of the year, and it's always a blowout.

I'm honestly too tired to give a shit. Between Cam's argument with Bianca last night and all the other shit we're already dealing with right now, we're barely keeping our heads above water. Not to mention I'm already regretting the decision to go along with this whole stupid girl of the month thing. Next month, I have to pay more attention instead of picking whatever random girl is closest to me. It hasn't even been a week yet, and Brittany is driving me mad, hanging all over me at meals and seeking me out between classes. It's completely insane. She's become a clingy, psycho, stalker girlfriend overnight.

What's even worse is that it's not because she's crazy in love with me or some shit like that. She sees me as a stepping stone to get to the others. All she ever does is ask me about them, and I've seen the way she ogles Mason. I get it. I'm not as buff or as in your face as they are. I don't have the angry, smoldering look that Hawk has, nor Cam's flirty charm. The girls even seem to like the whole silent, mysterious thing Mason has going on.

I'm the quiet, reserved one of the group, the nerd. I'm the guy the girls try to get close to, hoping to gain some insight into the others. At least, that's how it used to be. They quickly realized I was a vault.

Don't get me wrong, I still get girls willing to settle for me. After all, any Prince is better than *no* Prince. Apparently. But there's something about knowing someone is only with you because of what you are and who your friends are that makes it pretty damn difficult to find anything appealing about them. It sure as hell doesn't entice me to stick my dick in them.

So, while the others have been off getting their dicks wet on the regular, I've spent the last few years learning code and fine-tuning my programming skills. That's how I was able to dig up dirt on our parents' company. Dirt that changed our whole perspective on things. There's so much concerning our lives, our families, that we've been completely clueless about, until now. We've been running around being the entitled rich assholes everyone expects us to be, not giving a shit about our futures, while all this underhanded crap has been happening right under our noses. We've been too focused on getting girls and going to parties, but not anymore. This year is different. Shit has gotten fucking real.

The problem is, now that we're aware of exactly what our parents are up to, we have no idea what the fuck to do about it. It's been a point of contention between us, only made worse by all the petty shit we've had to put up with in school for appearance's sake and to keep our parents off our backs.

I'm barely paying attention to the room around me, too lost in the minefield that is our new reality, so I'm taken completely by surprise when someone sits down beside me. Everyone knows not to sit with us unless invited.

Turning my head, I guess I shouldn't be surprised to see the new girl sitting there. As I said, everyone else knows better. I watch her out of the corner of my eye as she checks out the whole setup; the computer screen, keyboard, and mouse before hesitantly moving the cursor around the screen, clicking on the username, and frowning at the desktop in confusion.

She glances around the room, her frown only deepening when she notices everyone else is already logged in and getting on with their work. There is a teacher—if you can call him that—who oversees the lesson, but since it's a computer science class, we're pretty much left to our own devices. Each lesson plan is already uploaded for us to work through, and Mr. Hughes usually pops his head in once or twice during the hour to ensure we're all behaving, but that's it. Mostly, the students fly through whatever we're supposed to be doing, then spend the rest of their time mucking around.

"Your login details will be on your tablet," I tell her absently, not removing my focus from my screen. I usually wouldn't get involved in other people's problems, except I tell myself I'm only helping her out because her mindless clicking of the mouse is already driving me bats.

"Oh," she replies, darting a quick glance my way. "Thanks."

She pulls out her tablet from her satchel and fumbles around on it. I try to tune her out, ignoring her sighs of frustration—*I did my part. I helped her, and I am under no obligation to do more*—as I struggle to focus on my own work, something that typically isn't an issue. Ordinarily, it's the other way around, and I forget the rest of the world exists until the bell goes or one of the guys pulls me out of my zone.

When it's apparent I won't be able to concentrate with her constant grumblings, I swivel around in my chair to face her and snatch the tablet off the table.

"Hey," she shouts, scowling at me as she tries to yank it back. Ignoring her, I tap away until I open up the document with all her login details, handing it back to her without another word. She looks at me quizzically, hesitating before reaching out and taking it from me. I don't know why she's giving me that look. Sure, people give us a wide berth, but it's not like I've done anything to her to make her so untrusting of me.

Glancing down at the screen, she gives me a final glance before turning back to her computer and typing in the details. Watching her is the most painstaking thing I've seen in a long time. She uses only her index fingers, taking forever to find the next letter on the keyboard. I swear it takes her five whole minutes to enter her username and password—it's like she's never used a computer before.

Once again, I try to ignore her presence, concentrating on my own work. I've already completed the advanced computer science course, but I had been planning on using this class to learn a new programming language, hoping it might help me find out the information I need.

"Um, do you know where I can find the lesson plan?" she asks, cutting through my thin veil of concentration. *Ah, who am I kidding? I have no idea what I had planned for today.*

This time, when I look her way, she's gnawing on her bottom lip, looking at me with an unsure gaze. The gesture captures my attention, drawing my eyes to her plump pink lips and the way the skin disappears between her teeth. I have this sudden urge to replace her teeth with mine. *I wonder what she tastes like.*

With her combat boots and how she keeps adjusting her uniform like it's a straitjacket, restricting her movements, she's a far cry from anyone else at Pac. Her mess of curly hair and sharp looks scream defiance and rebellion. I bet she tastes like trouble and every dirty thought I've ever had.

"Never mind," she blurts out, her cheeks blushing as she waves me away, mistaking my silence for a refusal. "I can work it out."

"It'll be on your personal drive," I rush out, shaking my head in an attempt to dislodge the dirty thoughts I was heading toward. *What the fuck is wrong with me?* It's been quite a while since a girl has gotten that reaction from me. And a scholarship student? She's probably only here to bag herself a rich husband. Definitely not the sort of drama I need to saddle myself with.

When she continues to look at me like I've spoken Klingon, I decide I may as well forget about my own lesson plan and help her out. It has absolutely nothing to do with the fact that she's uniquely attractive or intriguing, but because it's the polite thing to do.

Sliding my chair over beside hers, I'm enveloped by the vanilla and honey scent of her shower gel, losing myself for a moment in her eyes. I can't quite place the color—blue, but with a hint of something else. They're captivating, like looking at the sky just before it's about to rain.

She watches me with a mixture of wariness and curiosity as I adjust my glasses, grabbing ahold of her mouse. I show her how to access her drive, and it becomes clear pretty quickly that the girl hasn't spent much time around computers. She can barely use basic typing and spreadsheet programs. I want to ask her about it, but one look at the deep furrows in her forehead as she concentrates on what I'm telling her, combined with the nervous tapping of her nails against the table, and I can tell she wouldn't take it well.

She nods along with everything I explain, appearing to take it in and asking questions here and there when she needs something clarified. It takes the whole hour, but surprisingly, I don't mind. I'm not a dick. I'd help someone out if they asked for it, but it's usually begrudgingly, and I'm always ready to be done with them so I can get back to my own work. Not today, however. Maybe it was just her citrusy shampoo messing with my head, but I actually enjoyed showing her the ropes, watching her eyes light up when she learned something new, and how she bit the inside of her lip when she was processing what I was saying.

"Thanks," she says, her soft tone sounding genuinely grateful when the bell rings, which signals the end of class. Her teeth once again dig into her bottom lip in what I've learned is a nervous gesture. "For today. I really appreciate it."

"Anytime." The words blurt before I've had a chance to process what I'm saying.
Uh, what now? Anytime?

I'm not someone who invites people to hit them up when they need help. I like my own company and spending time with the guys, that's it. The last thing I want to do with my spare time is spend it with the students in Pac. I already have to show up at social events for appearance's sake. I definitely don't spend one-on-one time with any of them. Yet I've just told this girl, a virtual stranger, that she can ask me for help any time.

God damn, I knew her shampoo had scrambled my brain!

∾

THE SENIORS always host the first party of the year down by the lake. It's on the far side of campus and hidden from the view of the school by the forest, meaning no one is likely to bust us. Although I'm pretty sure the teachers are all aware of what we get up to, they just turn a blind eye. It's not like they could suspend or expel the entire senior class.

The lake is usually a tranquil spot, away from the usual furor of the rest of campus, but tonight it's alive with teenage energy, everyone buzzing for a good time. We've lit a fire on the pebbly shore—the flames sparking and fanning into the air, flaring like a beacon against the night sky—and dragged a few logs of driftwood to circle around it for makeshift seats. Music blasts over the speaker system and students sway to the beat while others sit up on the grassy embankment, chatting and drinking. There's a small dock stretching into the water, where a few kids are currently sitting—dangling their feet over the edge—and a boat shed at the other side of the lake.

The party is well underway when Hadley shows up. I notice her as soon as she arrives with the other scholarship students. They all stand out like sore thumbs, with their discounted clothing and cheap makeup, compared to the designer outfits and thousand-dollar shoes the rest of us are wearing.

Even with that distinction, she still sticks out from the others; with her wide eyes scanning warily over the party, drinking everything in. Not to mention she's the only girl here in a long sleeve top, baggy shorts, and combat boots, her mess of blonde curls blowing freely in the breeze. She looks like a vagrant, yet she appears much more at ease in what she's wearing than she did earlier in her uniform.

Their group makes a beeline for the drink table, and one of them—I think her name is Emily—shoves a drink into Hadley's hand. She sniffs it before wrinkling her nose, quickly setting it aside when her friend's back is turned. Everything about her is odd. Different. From her unusual behavior to her strange attire, I can't figure her out. I spent all afternoon trying to get a read on her. She came across as nervous sometimes, almost skittish, yet she was abrasive and acerbic. I'm a sucker for a good challenge, and Hadley may have just become my new puzzle to solve.

"Yo, West, man," Cam calls out, pulling my attention away from the girl who has been taking up way too much space in my brain.

"Huh?" I snap my head around to look at him before he can catch me staring at her. I can only imagine the ribbing if he caught me looking at the girl he's been talking nonstop about all week—although I don't think he's managed to make much headway with her.

"The girls are here." He sounds as enthusiastic as I feel. However, it's strange to hear him so uninterested in a party, but once again, this is a situation where the girl of the month crap isn't as much fun as he expected. Where's the excitement when you have a girl who's a sure thing? For a chaser like Cam, there's none of the adrenaline rush that comes from flirting with a girl, slowly building up to that moment when you find out if she's going to go home with you. Sure, I don't think anyone has ever turned him down, but there's still none of that anticipation he loves.

For me, I just don't want to be saddled with Brittany all night, or any other girl. I like doing the weird loner thing, watching everyone around me doing their thing. I don't need some chick hanging off me, trying to get my attention. *Ugh, why the fuck are we doing this stupid tradition again? Oh, yeah, because it's expected of us.*

Parties used to be when we could let loose, only inviting people to hang out with us if we wanted to, but otherwise sticking to ourselves. We could afford to drop the masks we wear in public. Not anymore. The rest of the day, I can get away with telling Brittany to leave me alone, but not here. Part of the deal is that they get to sit with us at parties. That exposure is half the reason they so quickly agree to be ours—the other reason being the bragging rights. And, of course, the faint hope that we might actually want something more with any of them.

"Great." I sigh, putting on a fake smile and heading over to where the guys are gathered round the fire pit. Bianca, Vivian, Melissa, and Brittany, each of our girls for the month, have joined them. Melissa is already in Hawk's lap, looking way too cozy as she runs her hand possessively over his large bicep, and Vivian is sucking face with Mason. I don't get how those two are so okay with all of this. They don't give a shit about those girls. They don't care that those girls don't give a shit about them. But then, it's nothing different from what they've been doing for the last four years. I just don't get it; it's not me. I'm not a meaningless hook-up person.

Brittany is sitting on the other side of the fire pit, glowering in Mason's direction. Or, more specifically, at the girl attached to his face. It should maybe annoy me that she's blatantly eyeing him up, but honestly, I just don't give a fuck. I didn't care at the beginning of the week, and with Hadley screwing with my brain today, I definitely don't give a shit now.

Cam seems to be back to wholly ignoring Bianca. An impressive feat, considering she's clawing at him like a cat in heat. He's been hot and cold with her all week, but I figured with a few beers in him tonight, he'd be all over that.

"West," Brittany purrs, jumping to her feet when she sees me in her line of vision. "I was wondering where you were."

Grabbing a beer out of the cooler, not bothering to offer her or any of the other girls a drink, I sit down beside Cam, all but ignoring her. It might come across as rude, but in all seriousness, if you give these girls an inch, they'll take everything you own and destroy you in the divorce.

"Why don't you two girls go dance?" Cam suggests, waving aimlessly toward the crowd of students in a bid to get rid of them.

"You want to watch me shake my ass for you, baby?" Bianca purrs, leaning in to lick Cam's ear. *Fucking gross.* I quickly glance away and take a large gulp from my beer can, ignoring whatever she's trying to do—what *is* she trying to do? Ear fuck him? *Jesus.*

"Sure." Cam's tone lacks all of its usual flirty undertones as he pulls away from her, though Bianca doesn't seem to notice any of it as she grabs Brittany's hand and sashays off.

"God, was she always that whiny and clingy?"

"Yes," I deadpan. "Why did you pick her anyway?"

He gives a casual shrug of his shoulder. "I heard she got a boob job over the summer. I was curious to see if her tits would be firm enough that I could stick my dick between them and get myself off."

I roll my eyes at that. *Of course, that was the reason.*

"And are they?"

"I dunno, haven't fucked her yet."

That takes me by surprise. Sure, he's got his sights set on another girl, but this is Cam. Even if he's lost interest, he'd still fuck her.

"Huh, I thought you'd be all about the monthly girls." We haven't actually talked about what's going on with him. Honestly, I thought he was just chasing after Hadley all while getting his dick wet in Bianca, but if he's not fucking her, then his head is more messed up than I realized.

"Yeah, me too," he agrees glumly. "And I was." He sighs, frustrated, downing a large gulp of his beer as his eyes scan the crowd until they catch on to what he's searching for. Turning to see, I spot Hadley dancing in a small circle with her friends. "Until I saw her."

"Just fuck her and get her out of your system." I have to push past the uneasy feeling in my gut at those words. I don't know what the hell that feeling is, but it can fuck right off. For Cam, it should be as simple as that. Yeah, okay, it sounds callous, but that doesn't make it any less true. It's what he does—lures a girl in with his charming ways, fucks her, and moves on.

He snorts. "I fucking wish, man, but she seems to be immune to my charms."

That gets my attention as I turn to look at him with wide eyes, my mouth slightly agape. "She's not interested?" Since when does a girl at Pac not want to fuck a Prince? The scholarship girls are much more reserved about it, but I bet if one of us asked them to suck our dick, they'd fall to their knees without a second thought. That's not me talking out of arrogance, I'm just stating a fact.

"I dunno, man." His brow is furrowed, his lips pinched in confusion as his eyes trail Hadley around the party. "I can't figure her out."

That makes two of us.

Hawk and Mason finally detach themselves from the girls and move over to join us as Vivian and Melissa go to dance with the other two.

"What are you two moping about?" Hawk asks, grabbing himself a beer, his eyes following Cam's gaze. "Are you fucking serious? You're still caught up on her?"

"What is your problem with her, man?" Cam snaps, finally stopping his stalkerish ways and turning to look at Hawk in confusion. "What happened the other day?"

"Nothing," he snarls. "She was just a bitch."

"Because she didn't fall to the ground, begging for mercy and offering you an apology blowjob like any other girl would do?" Cam chuckles, shaking his head, diffusing the tension from a moment ago.

Hawk just shrugs, refusing to answer. That's exactly what his problem is. He doesn't like to be challenged, and he's not used to any backtalk from girls. I bet he was shocked she dared say anything to him, and now he doesn't know what to do with it. It doesn't help that his head is already a mess with all this family shit we're drowning in. Mason's the only one who seems impervious to her distinctive brand of charm.

Hadley

CHAPTER SIX

The party is in full swing when we arrive. In fairness, we're over an hour late. Who knew it took girls so long to get ready? I sure as hell didn't. We spent ages in Emilia's room getting all dressed up. Well, she got dressed up—after finally giving up on forcing me into one of her dresses and heels, that shit ain't happening—while I flicked through the collection of girly magazines she had.

Looking out over the partygoers, I notice a crowd of people hovering around the drinks table, chatting, while others grind on one another on the beach, close to a set of large speakers that have been set up with some sort of dance music pumping out of them.

That same magnetism I feel around them has me looking toward the fire pit, finding all four perched around it. How are they able to lure me in and steal my focus in a crowd this size, with all the distractions that come with being at a party? I should be able to distance myself from them and forget they're even here.

"Cheers, girl." Emilia has a massive grin on her face as she pushes a plastic cup into my hand, bringing my attention back to her as she clinks her cup against mine, taking a large swallow from it.

Sniffing the straw-colored liquid, my nose scrunches as the sweet-vinegary-malt smell invades my senses. *Nope, no thanks.* Not that I'd drink anything with alcohol in it, but I definitely wouldn't touch anything here. I don't know these people. While their first impression hasn't been horrible, it certainly hasn't been warm and welcoming—only the scholarship students talk to me. Even if it was, life has taught me to keep my guard up and to always be on alert. Never be vulnerable. Never show weakness. Someone is always watching, ready to pounce at the first opportunity. I'm sure as fuck not about to give these rich assholes an opening.

The others quickly down their drinks, then Abigail, Mary, Todd, and Samuel all make their way toward the sea of dancing bodies, laughing, and getting into the partying mood. Emilia hesitates, and I can see she wants to go with them.

"Go," I encourage, ushering her away.

"Nah, I'm good here for now," she promises, pouring herself another drink and standing with me as we watch the party rage around us.

"So this is a Pac party?"

"Yup!" Emilia nods, her hips swaying slightly to the beat as we observe the party-goers around us.

"I thought it would be...bigger." Not that I have much to go on, but looking around at students slamming back shots, making out, or grinding on one another, I just don't get it. What's the appeal? Nearly every girl is parading around in sky-high heels and a barely-there dress, just asking for a broken ankle on the uneven pebbles, while the guys not-so-subtly eye up whatever girl they're hoping to get with for the night. From what I can gather, the whole night is about drinking, dancing, and sex. If two people want to fuck, why don't they just do it? Why do they need the liquid courage and the dancing warm-up? If I want a guy, I just go for him.

My gaze inadvertently flits back to the fire pit, watching Cam and West deep in conversation, ignoring everyone else around them. They're both casually dressed in jeans that hug their thighs, and Cam's t-shirt looks like it's been painted on him, every taut line of his muscles evident through the fabric. West has donned a pale gray shirt with rolled-up sleeves, showing off his lean yet sturdy forearms. Forearms shouldn't be attractive, right? I mean, they're just forearms, for fuck's sake. Yet, the flash of an image skitters across my brain of him pinning me against the wall with those forearms. *Yes, please.*

No. No. Off-limits.

Okay, so maybe I don't just go for it with *every* guy, but the Princes are the exception. They're a complication I can't afford right now. My body might want them, but my brain knows they're precisely what I don't need.

"Having fun?" Michael asks, interrupting my inappropriate thoughts. He'd been hovering nearby, talking to Andrew. However, turning to look at him, I see Andrew being pulled into the swelling crowd by some girl with a coy smile on her face, clearly knowing she's going to get lucky tonight.

"Eh, yeah." It's a less-than-enthusiastic response, but I think I've discovered parties aren't really my thing. Not that I know what my *thing* is. It's not like I've ever had the time or money to invest in extracurriculars, nor the friends to hang out with. When you spend your entire life simply surviving, you don't have time to discover who you are.

"You wanna dance?" Michael asks awkwardly, fidgeting with the tail of his shirt.

"Uh..."

Before I can work out how to tell him *no*, Emilia is already clapping her hands. "Yes," she shrieks. "That's an excellent idea." Grabbing my hand, I begrudgingly let her pull me into the crowd—it's not like I can refuse. The poor girl has been dying to dance all night but has been holding off so she can hang back with me. I can sense Michael at my back as we squeeze past bodies until we reach the others in the middle of the makeshift dance floor. Without letting go of my hand, Emilia gyrates her hips, tugging on my arm every now and again to encourage me to move.

Around me, everyone dances to the beat, closing their eyes and getting lost in the rhythm. I can feel Michael's body pressing into my side as Emilia keeps bumping up against me, the crowd pushing us all together.

I try. I honestly do, but I just can't get into it. Not only do I apparently have no rhythm, but I can't seem to lose myself in the music the way they do. Every time I close my eyes, I can feel the sweaty bodies shoving against me, the hairs prickling at the back of my neck as unknown hands sweep my body. My heart rate starts to climb, my breaths coming in short pants. Tearing my eyes open, I mutter an excuse to whoever hears me before pushing my way through the crowd, ignoring the others calling after me as I run off into the surrounding trees. I run until the noise of the party is nothing more than a soft drone in the distance, and there is nothing but fresh air and the hidden cover of the surrounding forest.

Pressing my back against the rough bark of a tree, I tilt my head back, taking a few deep, steadying breaths. What the fuck is wrong with me? Why can't I just be like everyone else? Be a typical fucking teenager for once, having fun and enjoying a party?

In the silence, I can feel myself regaining my composure, my heart rate slowing. Although, I can still feel a buzzing sensation beneath my skin, that nervous energy that only appears when I'm pissed off or stressed out. It's been building within me since I stepped foot on campus, except tonight has pushed it into overdrive, and it bothers me that I was so easily triggered. In hindsight, it was probably foolish of me to think I could simply escape my past and leave it all behind. I may be safe here, but I'm so used to being on the defensive, to expecting the worst. I can't just turn that off, unfortunately. Sighing heavily, I realize I may be more damaged than I even knew.

A twig snaps somewhere behind me, and I spin around, my head jerking toward the noise as I squint through the darkness. I'm searching to see which fuckface is out here with me, destroying my moment of peaceful solitude. *This* is why I can't be like all those other kids at that party. Shitty karma and dangerous situations follow me around like a bad fucking smell.

"Whoa," a deep voice calls out. "It's just me."

Squinting, I can just about make out the faint outline of someone cautiously approaching me. "West? What are you doing here?"

I don't relax my stance, eyeing him warily as he steps closer.

"I saw you run off and wanted to check on you."

"Oh." I don't know what to make of that. I've only spoken to the guy for the first time today. Everything I've heard and seen regarding the Princes indicates that I shouldn't so much as look in their direction unless I want to rain down hellfire on myself. Hell, some of the stories Emilia has told me are unbelievable...How, in their freshman year, they publicly humiliated a senior who wouldn't bow down to royalty younger than him; or the student they drove out of school because he made fun of West for being a nerd.

After my altercation with Hawk yesterday, I'd well believe he's capable of everything I've heard. Still, West was nothing but nice to me today, and the same with Cam, even though he definitely has ulterior motives.

It's difficult to make out his features in the dark as shadows dance across his face. However, everything about him says he's not a threat. His hands are tucked in his pockets, and his posture is relaxed as he strolls toward me.

"Are you?"

"Am I what?"

"Okay?"

"Oh. Yeah. I'm fine." Deciding he's not here to harm me, I lean back against the tree, closing my eyes and trying to find that sense of calm once again. It's no good, though. I'm hyperaware of his presence. It's the same awareness as earlier in class. The seat beside him was the only empty one in the back row, and I wanted as few people as possible to see how hopeless I was with computers. I didn't expect him to talk to me, let alone *help* me. None of the Princes are known for their hospitality. I hadn't counted on the strange nervousness his closeness elicited. And when he wheeled his chair over beside mine? My heart went into overdrive as his clean, musky scent enveloped me.

My eyes pop open as his arm brushes against mine, and I'm surprised to find him leaning against the tree beside me. Heat emanates from where his skin touches mine, that tiny bit of contact starting a chain reaction throughout my body, slowly settling me. And, for the first time since arriving here, that buzzing feeling dies down to a background hum.

I don't know what these guys are doing to me. I've felt physical attraction before—that sudden racing of your heart and twisting of your gut, the way you can't stop looking at them or picturing them naked. Those feelings are bland and superficial in contrast to the sheer visceral reaction I have to the Princes, the raw, intense awareness I get around them.

Licking my suddenly dry lips, I blurt out, "You, uh, don't have to stay with me. I'm sure your friends, or your, uh, girl of the month, or whatever, are looking for you."

A breathy laugh escapes him. "You looking to get rid of me?"

"What?" I splutter. "No. You, uh…I don't want you to feel you *have* to stay with me." I actually don't know if I want him to go or not, but he's been nice to me, and I don't need to piss off any of these guys by accident.

"Parties aren't my thing," he casually admits. He's not as social as the others, but I still figured he would be as much into this whole typical high school bullshit as everyone else.

"Apparently, they aren't mine, either." I don't know why I say that. I don't understand why I'm honest with him. Like earlier, asking for his help. It's like I lose my filter when he's around. Something about him comes across as genuine and truthful, making it challenging to be my usual stand-offish, bitchy self with him.

"Apparently?"

Eh, fuck. I've already given enough for him to deduce what I mean, so I may as well just blurt it all out. "This is my first high school party."

"Huh." I wait on tenterhooks, expecting him to say more. When it's clear he's not going to ask all the obvious questions, only then do I let out a relieved breath. Not that I was going to share any more of myself with him. Fuck, even that little tidbit of information has my heart hammering in my chest once more.

We lapse into silence, although it's not uncomfortable like the awkwardness with Michael last night. Honestly, I don't know what the fuck to make of it, but it's both settling and fraught with whatever this energy is between us.

"I should, uh, be getting back to my friends," I say tensely after several minutes, pushing off the tree.

"Sure." He shrugs, showing no signs of moving himself. Giving him a stiff, curt nod, I stride off and head back to the party, all the while ignoring the burning of his eyes into my back as he watches me go.

"Hadley!" Emilia calls out when she spots me, swaying in her heels as she stumbles my way. "Where'd you go?" Her words are slightly slurred as she essentially hangs off me, draping her arms around my neck.

"Wow, I think someone's had a bit too much to drink." I laugh, wrapping my arms around her.

"You have?" she gasps, staring at me with bright eyes and an unfocused gaze. "Naughty girl," she cackles, throwing her head back.

Jesus, was I gone long enough for her to drink that much?

"Come on," I urge, "let's get you a seat and some water."

Someone has dug out some old fold-up chairs and scattered them around the fire pit, so I ease her into an empty one, feeling eyes on me from the three Princes seated around us. Everyone else has avoided coming over here all night, but if she passes out on the ground, I'm worried I'll never be able to lift her.

She's half-unconscious as I glance around the fire pit, finding a cooler filled with drinks and bottles of water. Moving over to it, I reach out to lift one but snatch my hand back at the last second as the lid snaps shut.

"That's for us, not scholarship trash," Hawk snarls, his ice-cold glare penetrating through me as Melissa—perched in his lap—giggles, like Hawk's pissy attitude is fucking hilarious.

Ignoring her, I return Hawk's scowl with one of my own. "She just needs a bottle of water."

"There's an entire table of drinks over there," he snarks, waving his hand dismissively toward the drinks table. Yeah, but they all have fucking alcohol in them. Trust me, I checked when we arrived.

I sigh heavily, mentally telling myself not to start a fight with this asshole. "They don't have any water," I state, hoping to reason with him. I should have known there was a fat chance of that happening.

"So?" he snorts. "That's not my fucking problem."

My scowl darkens as I stare him down, but he's completely unfazed, unwilling to budge on his decision. I can feel Mason's eyes on me as he and his lap accessory silently watch the interaction. Seemingly, neither of them feels the need to speak up or intervene in this ridiculousness.

"She's practically unconscious," I hiss, grinding my teeth as I wave my hand toward Emilia as she's slumped over in the chair, her eyes shut. My words are falling on deaf ears, but I'm not about to back down from this shithead because that's exactly what he wants.

Flicking his gaze her way before returning his focus to me, Hawk nods his head slowly, only making me narrow my eyes at him in suspicion. "Okay." Nope. I'm not buying it. I don't respond, waiting for him to tell me what the catch is. "For a price," he adds with a smug smirk.

Pursing my lips, I stare him down, my mind racing through all the possibilities of what he could ask for. "I don't have any money on me."

"I don't want your money," he sneers. "Although I will take a blow job." A shit-eating grin spreads across his face, and it takes everything in me not to reach out and slap it off.

What the actual fuck? Is this arrogant dickweed for real? He can't seriously think I'd willingly do that. Melissa throws a pissy look my way, like *I* was the one that just offered *him* a fucking blow job for some measly water. If it wasn't happening to me, the whole thing would be laughable.

"Baby, I can give you a blow job if you want one," she purrs seductively, not happy at having Hawk's attention directed elsewhere. Her voice is low and breathy as her hand dips down between their bodies to places I don't even want to know about.

"No." Hawk grabs her wrist, halting her movements, his focus never leaving my face. Deciding he's fucking insane, I tear my eyes away from Hawk's hate-filled, stormy orbs to look at Cam, hoping he will back me up on this. He's been flirting with me all week, making it clear he's more than interested in getting in my pants. Surely, he will tell Hawk to stop being a douche. It's only water, for fuck's sake.

"Dude, it's just water." It's weak, lacking any sort of conviction, but whatever. If it gets Hawk to stop being a cumbucket, then I'll take it.

"She knows the price," he growls. "She either pays it, or she can get the fuck out of here."

Of course, Bianca and Brittany come stumbling off the dance floor at that moment, pushing their way through the crowd toward the firepit.

"What are you doing?" Bianca snaps, towering over me in a scrap of fabric that barely covers her...bits. "I've told you before," she hisses. "Stay in your lane and keep your pauper mitts off the Princes."

Seriously? Does she think I'm over here trying to get with one of these assholes? Puh-lease, like I'd ever sleep with any of these arrogant dickwads.

"What's going on here?" West's deep voice startles me, but before I can explain anything, Brittany practically launches herself at him. "Wes, baby!"

"Don't call me that," he bites out, glaring at her. "It's West. The name's already shortened, it doesn't need to be cut down any fucking further."

Her eyes widen in surprise, and her lip pops out in a pout. She doesn't unlatch her death grip from around his neck, and after a second, she shakes it off, giving him a sugary sweet smile again. "Where have you been? I've been looking everywhere for you."

"I'm sure you have," he grumbles in a low voice, mumbling something under his breath that I can't quite make out. Something about not being attached to Mason's face? I don't understand, and I don't give a shit.

"I just wanted a bottle of water," I explain wearily, baffled by how this is turning into such an issue, but he's the only one who's been halfway decent to me. Perhaps he can convince Hawk to part with a bottle of his precious water.

His eyes flick from me to Hawk before his lips pinch, an apologetic look flashing across his face before he carefully masks it, shrugging his shoulders.

Is he for fucking real?! Fucking jackass.

Fuck this shit.

"I wouldn't suck your disease-riddled pocket prick if it saved my life," I snarl, glaring darkly at Hawk before I turn my back on the whole fucking group of them, striding over to where a passed-out Emilia is sitting. I wrap my arm around her waist and haul her to her feet, ignoring her groan of protest.

Please don't puke all over me. I'll be seriously pissed if you do.

Feeling each of their eyes on me, I drag her away from the party and back to the dorms, silently cursing each and every Prick with every step. Yes, I may have said it in jest on Monday, but the whole fucking lot of them deserve the title.

With a serious amount of effort, I manage to haul Emilia's dead weight back to the dorms and into her bed, removing her shoes before tucking her in.

"Thought it was a date," she mumbles in her sleep, her words not making any sense.

"What?" I ask, confused. Was she supposed to be on a date tonight? Why didn't she tell me?

"Michael...You."

"What?" I repeat more urgently. What did she just say? She's drunk, and she's not making sense. She doesn't understand what she's saying...right? There's no way tonight was meant to be a date. I mean, I'd know if I was on a date, wouldn't I? Would I?

My brows furrow as I reflect on last night in the dining hall with him. Was *that* a date? He mentioned the party tonight, but he didn't actually ask me to go with him....However, he did ask me if I *wanted* to go. I thought he meant as, like, a group. Did he mean it as a date? If Emilia's drunken self is right, then yeah, that's exactly what he meant. How could I have missed that?

With a despairing groan, I close her bedroom door, slinking across the hallway and silently letting myself into my own room. What a fucking shitshow of an evening.

Hadley

CHAPTER SEVEN

It's barely eight a.m., and Emilia's drunken words have yet to stop playing on repeat in my head. I need to know for sure what she was talking about, because I have enough shit to deal with, with the Pricks, never mind throwing dates I'm apparently too clueless about into the mix.

"What?" Emilia whines when she finally answers the door. She's still in last night's clothes, her dark hair a bedraggled mess, and her makeup smeared across her face. "I'm dying today. Come back tomorrow." She goes to shut the door, but I wedge my boot in the opening, preventing her.

She doesn't even seem to notice me doing it, instead staring at the door in confusion before giving up and leaving it open, sluggishly stumbling back over to the bed and collapsing into it.

"Time to get up," I demand. "We have shit to discuss."

"Ugh, no," she mumbles, her voice barely audible through the pillow she's buried her face in.

"Yup," I enforce. "Go shower, and we'll grab breakfast. You'll feel worlds better."

She mutters something unintelligible. I'm pretty sure she's cursing me out, but when she still makes no effort to get up, I decide to add an incentive. "I'll tell you all about my run-in with the Pricks last night."

That gets her attention, and her head snaps off the pillow so fast I'm surprised she doesn't give herself whiplash. "What happened?" she exclaims, her eyes bright with intrigue, her hangover clearly forgotten.

"Go shower, and I'll tell you."

Half an hour later, we're sitting at our usual table with enough food between us to feed a third-world country.

"Spill," she demands, nursing her coffee like it's a lifeline.

I quickly rehash last night's events, observing as her eyes grow wider with every word.

"I'm sorry," she apologizes when I'm finished. "That's all my fault."

"What? No, it isn't," I insist, shaking my head fervently. "You didn't make them act like shitheads. That's all on them."

I sigh, pursing my lips. "I'm just annoyed that I misjudged Wes so badly. I thought he was a decent guy, but all of them are just as bad as each other."

She gives me a sympathetic look before her brows furrow. "Wes?"

"Ah, yeah," I chuckle. "Apparently, he hates it, so I've decided it's exactly what I'm going to call him."

"Even to his face?" she gasps, wide-eyed.

"Yup."

"Girl, you are going to get yourself in serious trouble if you antagonize them."

Giving her a flat look, I brazenly state, "Maybe they should have thought about that before pissing me off."

The look Emilia gives me says everything about how reckless she thinks I'm being, yet I'm not one to back down. I'm not going to go after them, but I also won't allow them to steamroll all over me, either. Enough people have tried to tear me down in life; I'm not about to let some control-obsessed teenage boys get the better of me.

We're finishing off the last scraps of breakfast, my stomach nearly bursting, when I broach the subject of Michael. "So," I begin hesitantly, flicking my gaze up to look at her, "you mentioned something last night."

"Girl, whatever I said, just ignore it. It was the ramblings of a drunken idiot." She laughs, waving me off.

"You said something about Michael thinking last night was a date?" I blurt out before I can talk myself out of it.

Emilia pauses with her mug halfway raised to her lips, her mouth falling open. She gapes at me before she cringes. "I did?"

"You did."

She sighs, setting the mug back down on the table. "Eh, yeah. He might have said something to me yesterday about how he asked you to the party, though you never brought it up, and it was clear last night that you weren't on the same page as him."

Burying my face in my hands, I release a frustrated groan.

"How did I not know it was supposed to be a date?" I grumble. "I've been playing our conversation from Thursday night over in my head and, I mean, I may have missed some cues. Although it's not like he outrightly said, 'Hadley, will you go on a date with me?' How was I supposed to know?"

She gives an empathetic chuckle. "I dunno, girl. Don't stress about it, in any case. I think he realized how clueless you were. He'll ask you again, and next time you'll *know* what he's getting at."

"Wait. What? He's going to ask me *again*?" I shriek in an embarrassingly shrill voice. I like to think I'm a cool, badass bitch most of the time. I've dealt with shit that would have most of the kids in this fancy-ass school shitting their pants, yet give me a high school boy that has a crush on me, and I don't have a fucking clue.

I lost my virginity last year to some biker dude in a back alley. I never even got his name, and all my *wham-bam-thank-you-ma'ams* since have been the same. I've spent a decent portion of my teenage years in seedy bars and dodgy warehouses, trying to make a buck to survive. They don't exactly come with the typical sweet, innocent boy most girls probably end up with for their first time, but, for the most part, they know how to use God's gift between their legs.

"Why would he do that? He doesn't even know me," I insist. Though even as I say it, the little demon voice in my head argues that I don't know any of the Pricks, and I have —had—some sort of strange reaction to them. Now that I've affirmed they're shit-heads; I'm sure whatever that was, has fizzled out. Even so, I don't know them, and they had that allure over me. I've definitely had several vibrator sessions thinking about Cam and how talented his fingers most likely are. You don't have to actually *know* someone to be attracted to them. Hell, if I've learned anything this past week, it's that you don't even have to like whoever you're attracted to. Hormones are a fickle thing.

Chuckling, Emilia shakes her head, rolling her eyes at me. "The whole point of dating someone is to get to know them. He evidently likes what he's seen so far, and he's clearly attracted to you."

"He is?" How did I not know that? I mean, I know Cam finds me attractive—he's blatantly obvious about it, but I had no idea Michael felt the same way. Maybe I'm just not used to subtle gestures or the way teenage boys flirt?

When I've picked up guys before, it's always been in dark, dingy bars, with guys willing to sink their dicks in just about anything, so it's not like I needed to have any game or make an impression. Literally, all you had to do was bat your eyes in a guy's direction and he'd drop his pants. When a man did approach me, it was unmistakable as to what he was after.

The problem is, Michael wants more than just sex. Even Cam, while all he wants is sex, is problematic. I've never had sex with someone I ever had to see again. Nameless, faceless sex, I can do. That's right up my street, but anything more than that, especially dating someone? Spending time with them? That's really not my thing. From what I've learned about Michael, he's quiet, shy, and innocent. He's not like me at all.

Emilia must be able to see my internal panic written all over my face as she bursts out laughing. "Girl, you're totally overthinking it. Ask yourself, are you attracted to him?"

I recall his whole image, picturing his short-cut dark hair and wiry frame. He's not unattractive, but there's no swirling in my lower abdomen, no fluttering as my heart rate increases. There's definitely not the same intense, indescribable reaction that I get in the Pricks' presence.

"No. I'm not."

"Then next time he asks, just let him down gently."

We spend the rest of the day spread out on the lawn catching up on homework while enjoying the last rays of sun before the seasons change, only making a move to head indoors when the sun starts to set.

That night we walked over to the rec center with the others for yet another movie night. Tonight is Mary's turn to pick the movie, and she chooses some rom-com I've never seen before. Turns out romantic comedies are not my thing—way too sappy and dull. Where's all the action? Not that I get the chance to focus much on the movie, with my stomach in knots, worried Michael will want to talk to me. I haven't worked out what to say to him yet. I don't want to hurt his feelings or say the wrong thing. The tension only drops out of my shoulders when we say goodnight to the guys, Michael giving me a soft smile when we part ways.

∼

"Hey, girl," Emilia greets, dropping into the chair beside me at our usual table in the dining hall. "Everything okay?"

"Yeah," I assure her. "I just couldn't sleep, so I thought I'd come for breakfast early." I tossed and turned all night, not that I usually sleep all that well, but last night was particularly bad.

Every year has a time slot for breakfast, with seniors getting the last one right before classes begin. Most students turn up not long before class, which, unsurprisingly, is also when the Pricks tend to arrive, so this morning I decided I was in no mood to watch their usual routine and made sure I was here just as the slot for seniors began.

I messaged Emilia before I left so she would know where I was if she came looking for me, which, it seems, she did.

"If you're worried about the Princes..." she begins, but I shake my head, cutting her off.

"I'm not. Not really. I'm neither afraid of them nor want any of their drama. I'm here to do the work, so I can have the future I want. I'm not about to let wayward hormones or devilishly handsome teenage boys interfere with my plans," I joke.

"Right." She laughs before growing serious. "But after Friday, Hawk's going to be pissed."

He's pissed? *I'm* fucking pissed!

I shrug my shoulders, not giving a shit about how he's feeling. "So? He can be pissy all he wants, so long as he leaves me alone."

She sighs, resigned. "Just don't do something that will only get you into more trouble with them."

The hall slowly fills up over the next half hour, and just before the time the Pricks usually arrive, I slide out of my seat, deciding I'd rather be ridiculously early to English than have to force myself not to spend all of breakfast watching them.

I saunter through the relatively empty corridors, slowly making my way to Mr. Greer's classroom. By the time everyone else filters in, I'm already sitting there, ready to begin.

Bianca throws a glare in my direction as she enters, although I pay her no mind. What the fuck is her problem, anyway? Is she seriously still annoyed about last week? Has Cam not fucked her good enough to forget about it?

"Morning, beautiful," Cam purrs as he slides into the seat beside me. Ignoring him, I stare pointedly at my black tablet screen until he sighs. "Okay, I get it, you're pissed." After a moment's hesitation, when he still gets no response from me, he continues, "It's complicated."

"Complicated?" I snort, turning to face him. "It was a bottle of water."

"It wasn't about the water. I mean, it was...but it wasn't."

He's not making any sense, and I roll my eyes at him, returning my attention to the desk again.

"Look," he begins, leaning in so no one around us can overhear our conversation, "it was about more than just the water. We have to present a united front in front of everyone else at this school. Yes, even over something as stupid as a bottle of water." He tacks on before I can interject. "With the girls watching, there was nothing I could do."

I give him a disbelieving look out of the corner of my eye. "So you're saying if the girls weren't there, you'd have given me the water?"

"I'm saying it wouldn't have been such a big deal," he responds immediately. He sounds sincere, yet he could simply be telling me what he thinks I want to hear.

"Unfortunately, words mean nothing when you can't back them up," I retort, not trusting what he says.

I'm still side-eyeing him, watching him closely, so I catch the pained expression that flashes across his face before he masks it. "For what it's worth, I'm sorry. Hawk was being a dickhead for no good reason. You managed to piss him off good with whatever happened between you in the hall last week."

My head snaps around so I can glare at him. "Nothing happened between us," I bark. "Just because I didn't back down from him like everyone else here does, doesn't give him the right to act the way he did."

Cam just nods his head, not saying anything, and thankfully the teacher brings the class to order, beginning the lesson before I can do something stupid like strangling him with my bare hands in front of all these witnesses.

For the next hour, I feel Cam constantly glancing my way, his leg bouncing annoyingly under the table. I can tell he wants to say more but has the foresight to realize I'm not in an understanding mood.

"Don't forget you need to be working on your projects outside of class hours," Mr. Greer calls out as the bell rings and everyone starts packing up. Fucking hell, how did I forget about the damn project?

"Meet me in the library after class tomorrow," I tell Cam as I shove my things back in my bag, walking off before he can argue with me.

"Damn, girl! That looked intense," Emilia says, catching up to me in the hall. I simply shake my head, not wanting to talk about it. I don't have any of them in the rest of my classes today, and I refuse to spend one more moment talking or even thinking about them.

"It was nothing, just sorting out our English assignment."

"Uh-huh." She lets the topic slide, and we soon part ways as she heads off to music and I go to my math class.

The next afternoon, I push open the library door and walk past the staffed front desk, spotting Cam alone at a table in the far corner of the room. I make my way through the large, circular tables, some of which have students working away at them, letting the hush of quiet conversations wash over me as I drop into the chair beside him.

"Hadley," he purrs, his voice thick and raspy in a way that makes my insides do stupid things. "Looking fine as always." He's back to his usual flirty ways, his remorse over Friday long forgotten.

"We need to sort this assignment out," I snap, getting straight to the point. "Did you read the book?" It's the only thing we've managed to sort out so far, although I don't for one second believe he's read it.

"Of course I did!" he gasps in mock outrage, his hand clasping his chest. I don't believe him, but whatever. As long as he does his half of the work and it's solid enough to pass, I don't give a fuck.

"Okay, I'll write the critical analysis of the book, and you can compare it to others from that period."

"I'll do whatever you want me to do," he replies, his tone suggestive.

For fuck's sake, Hadley, don't fall for it. Remember, he's a dickwad.

Glancing at him, I bite my lower lip as I cross my legs, 'accidentally' grazing them against his as I lean in. A sense of satisfaction courses through me as his pupils dilate, eating me up. Giving him my best seductive look, I lower my voice and breathe out, "I want...you to write your half of the book report." Pulling back abruptly, I lift out my notebook, flicking through the notes I made while reading the book.

I can feel Cam gaping at me before his wits finally return to him. Suddenly, he barks out a laugh, shaking his head like he can't believe he fell for my act before pulling out his tablet and finally getting into the assignment. We work in silence until someone drops into one of the spare chairs at the table.

"What are you doing here?" West asks suspiciously, like I'm doing something I shouldn't be. We haven't spoken since the party, not that I have anything to say to him. Glancing at Cam's work, he returns his gaze to me. "You're not doing his homework for him, are you?"

"What?" I can't do anything except gape at him. Why would he even think that? "Definitely not, *Wes*," I snark, not appreciating the inference that I'd willingly be someone's homework bitch.

His eyebrows raise in surprise, his lips pinching at my new name for him. He didn't like Brittany calling him that at the party, so I'm betting he won't be too pleased with me using it either, but I sure as hell won't let his pissy personality put me off.

"We're working on an English assignment together," Cam explains.

"Of course you are," West drawls. "Just don't forget about Bianca. Whatever you're doing, you should keep it on the down low."

"Excuse me?" I sneer, pissed off at his insinuation. Even worse than people thinking I'm Cam's homework bitch, are people thinking I'm his side piece. Regardless of how unofficial he thinks his monthly girls are, he is basically publicly dating Bianca, and I don't want to be anyone's dirty little secret. "We're not *doing* anything." When he just continues to look at me, like I'm bullshitting him, I spell it out for him. "I'm not fucking sleeping with him."

After another long, intense stare, West shrugs, offering a half-assed apology. "Sorry, that's just his MO."

"Dude," Cam hisses. "Shut the fuck up."

I'm undoubtedly missing something between them, but whatever.

"You think after your dickish behavior at the party last week, I'd be interested in any of you?"

"I apologized for that," Cam exclaims.

"That doesn't make it right."

West leans in closer, casting a surreptitious look at the other students around us before saying, "Look, we have to put up a united front when we're around others. We can't let anyone see any rifts or disagreements. It's nothing personal."

I just shake my head, not understanding him. It's essentially the same crap Cam spouted, but I don't get this whole social politicking. Who cares if they all agree or disagree on something? What does any of it really matter?

Ignoring the pair of them before I end up doing something I regret, I get back to work until two more assholes join us at the table.

Yay, the gang's all here now.

Mason stares at me with his sky-blue eyes for a long moment but doesn't say anything before glancing away. He's the hardest one to gauge. I never know what he's thinking. Sometimes I catch him staring at me, just like he was doing there now, only I don't know what to make of it. Hawk, on the other hand, glowers at me. "What is *she* doing here?" *Fucking asshole.*

"We're working on a project together," Cam reiterates, barely sparing Hawk a glance, utterly unfazed by his attitude.

I don't get what his problem is. He doesn't even know me. He can't seriously be that annoyed over our run-in last week. What mentally stable person holds such an intense grudge over a complete accident?

I've been observing him closely since the party, and he's the grumpiest dickhead I've ever met. He's surly and snaps at pretty much everyone around him. I don't know how Melissa puts up with him—although from what I've seen, they do nothing but make out and grope each other when they're together. I guess he can't say something shitty when her tongue is rammed down his throat.

The four of them settle down to get busy with their own work, occasionally sharing the odd comment before lapsing into silence again.

After about an hour, a rustling noise gets my attention, and I look up as Cam empties an entire bag of skittles into the middle of the table.

Seeing the confused look on my face, he gestures to the pile, "Help yourself."

Leaning forward, I stretch my arm across the table until I can grab a couple of green skittles, but a hand snags out and grabs my wrist before I can pull it back.

"The green ones are mine," Hawk snarls.

Fuck me, are we seriously doing this shit again?

Staring at him with wide eyes, aware of everyone around the table watching us, I give a hesitant nod. "Okay."

Releasing my hand, I make as though I'm going to set the candy back on the table and then at the last second, I pick up the last few green ones and shove all of them into my mouth before anyone can stop me, flashing Hawk a toothy grin across the table.

"Mmm, yummy. The green ones are my favorite."

The table is deathly quiet for a second before Cam bursts out laughing. "Fuck, I can't believe you did that. He's definitely going to kill you now."

I give a shrug of my shoulder, which only serves to annoy Hawk further as his hand clenches tightly around his stylus, threatening to snap it.

"There are plenty of other flavors," I appease, waving toward the candy.

"He only likes the green ones," West explains.

"Huh." Well, you snooze, you lose.

Hadley

CHAPTER EIGHT

The rest of the week passes in a blur of schoolwork. There are literally not enough hours in the day to do everything they ask of us. Plus, Hawk has taken to openly glaring at me when we pass in the halls, and students are starting to whisper.

"What's going on with you and the Princes?" Abigail asks on Saturday night at our weekly movie night.

"Nothing." I shrug, not wanting to get into it.

"There must be something," Samuel insists. "Bianca is going around telling everyone you're trying to steal Cam from her, and Hawk looks at you like he wants to rip your head off."

"Bianca is what?!" I gasp. How have I not heard of this? As for Hawk, well, that makes two of us.

"Sorry, girl," Emilia says sympathetically, cringing when I turn to look at her. "I heard it for the first time today. I was going to tell you later."

The audacity of that bitch!

"For the record, I am *not* trying to steal Cam from her. She's just annoyed that we're working on an assignment together." We've spent all week in the library, trying to hammer out this project, but unless it's work-related, we don't talk. He finally seems to have copped on to the fact I'm angry with him.

"Pfft." Samuel snorts. "Cam never does his own work. If he's spending time with you, it's because he wants in your pants."

"Samuel," Mary scolds. "You don't need to be so crass about it."

"What? It's not like it's not true." He shrugs unapologetically. "She's good-looking. Of course, he'd try it on the new girl."

"It's not like that," I assure them, but based on the dubious looks I'm getting, no one believes me.

"Well, what about Hawk?" Mary asks.

Rolling my eyes, I rehash my run-in with Hawk last week. By the end, everyone except Emilia, who has already heard the story, is gawking at me.

"It was just an accident," I reiterate, confused by their expressions. Why is everyone making such a big deal out of this? So what?

"You're so screwed," Mary gasps. "You better keep your head down and stay out of the Princes' way."

"Why?" I don't get it. Emilia has expressed concern several times and begged me not to antagonize them, but seeing everyone else looking worried has me on edge. "He's just one person. What can he possibly do?"

With wide eyes, Abigail shakes her head. "Nu-uh, if Hawk decides he doesn't like you, you're done for. Last year, Greg knocked into Cam while he and his friends were messing around on the lawn. He knocked him to the ground, but that was it. It's not like he hurt him or anything. Then, all four of them ganged up against him, claiming he had disrespected them. He was gone by the end of the month."

"What do you mean he was *gone?*" They can't have that power. What could they possibly do to him?

"He left. Dropped out of school."

As if that isn't disturbing, Samuel adds, "If you do anything to one of them or if one of them decides they don't like you, the others will back him up. They support each other in everything."

Remembering how the others sided with Hawk over the whole water incident and West's words about presenting a 'united front', their meaning is suddenly clear.

"I have no intention of pissing Hawk off any further," I assure them, making a mental note to try and stick to that promise. I plan on staying as far away from him as possible—we only have one class together, so it shouldn't be that difficult.

We all settle in to watch the movie after that, but there's a tension in the air that wasn't there before and when we're walking back to the dorms, Michael, who hadn't said a word all night, falls into step beside me.

"You need to be careful around the Princes," he warns. "I don't want them starting a witch hunt against you."

I give him a soft smile. He genuinely is a sweet boy, a good person, not at all like the complicated, convoluted Princes. If only I could be attracted to him like any ordinary girl. Although, I think the last of my sanity left me the day I entered Pac Prep.

"I can look after myself," I assure him.

"I'm sure you can," he agrees. "Just...don't trust them. They don't care about anyone but themselves."

"I don't," I promise just before we part ways.

～

It's late on Sunday night when the sound of my tablet vibrating from within my bag distracts me from the business homework I'm finishing. Fishing it out, the notifications show a new message from Cam.

Everyone has phones here, only they seem to prefer using the school's own messaging app on the tablet to communicate with one another.

Cam: Are you up?

I CONSIDER IGNORING HIM, since it's after midnight. For all he knows, I could easily be asleep by now. However the tablet goes off again, vibrating in my hand as another incoming message pops up.

> Cam: I'm stuck on our English assignment.

HE'S PROBABLY LYING to get me to show up. We basically had the whole thing wrapped up last week, but it's due tomorrow, and I've put a lot of effort into my half of it, so I don't want his annoying ass dragging my mark down.

> Me: Meet me in the dining hall in 5.

IT'S the only part of campus open at this time of night, and I'm sure as hell not going to bring him here. Stuffing my feet into my boots, I cast a quick glance in the mirror, my lycra leggings and hoodie more than sufficient, given the late hour. The tablet chimes again as I walk out of my room.

> Cam: Already here.

PULLING open the door of the dining hall, the place is empty, except for Cam sitting at the Pricks' usual table at the far side of the room. Going over to the coffee bar, I make myself a strong coffee and drop into a seat opposite him, taking a second to see what the view of the hall is like from here. I'm surprised to see that it looks exactly the same as it does from the scholarship table. I don't know what I thought it would be like, but it's rather disappointing.
"Not what you expected?" Cam asks, watching me closely.
"No," I admit. "I thought it would be...different." I guess I thought it would be more impressive? That I'd feel more important?
"Yeah." Cam sighs. "Everyone thinks that."
Turning to face him, he looks completely different than he does during the day. Sure, I've seen him and the others here late at night before, but I'm usually sneaking furtive glances their way, never really able to check him out this closely. His blond hair is rumpled like he's been running his hand through it all day, and his baby blue t-shirt strains against his defined muscles, giving me an up-close and personal view of how ripped he is underneath his uniform.
"But if they knew what it was truly like to be us, they'd quickly change their mind."
His words remind me he's not just a slab of meat for me to drool over, especially when he's being strangely open with me. Looking past his insanely good looks, I can see how

tired he is, like life has worn him down. How can that be possible? Don't guys like him have everything? I mean, look around us. He's basically the king of this campus. He can do whatever he wants, get any girl he wants. His family is loaded, so it's not like he ever has to worry about supporting himself or even finding a job. How much easier could his life get?

I really don't have any sympathy for him, yet that haunted look in his eyes resonates with me, suggesting there's something I'm not understanding, something about who he and the others are that I'm not seeing.

"What's it like to be you?"

The corner of his lip tips up in a smirk as his barrier slides back into place, cutting me off from whatever I saw. "Let's just say it's not all parties and pussy."

I don't know what to say to that. From what I can tell, that's exactly what it looks like.

Sensing he won't tell me anything more, I change the topic. "What do you need help with?"

Without a word, he taps on his tablet, turning it around so I can see. "Can you just read over these few paragraphs? I'm not sure I've got it quite right."

I'm taken aback, not expecting him to actually want to discuss homework, confident this whole thing was a ploy just to get me alone.

"Uh, yeah. Sure."

Pulling the tablet toward me, we sit in silence while I read over what he's written, becoming more impressed by the minute. Not only has he done the work, but he's done one hell of a job.

"Cam, this is good," I praise him. "I'd maybe swap these two paragraphs around, but other than that, it reads really well."

Nodding his head, he does as I suggest and re-reads it. "Yeah, thanks. That reads better."

Sipping on my coffee, I nod in acknowledgment, not knowing what to say. There's something about him tonight. He's different than normal. He's dropped the flirty air and seems almost vulnerable.

"Why did you come to Pac?" The question catches me by surprise, but of course, someone like him doesn't understand the desperate need to escape your current situation. To want to be better, do something *more* with your life.

"I couldn't live the life I saw unfolding before me," I respond honestly. "I needed to escape, to find who I am and lay out a future for myself that I want. One I can be proud of."

He nods, like he understands what I'm saying, yet I don't know if he truly gets it.

"I hope you find what you're looking for."

Scanning his face, I see nothing but sincerity there.

"You and the others, how long have you been friends?"

"Our whole lives. Our parents are all friends, and our families co-own a business. We all grew up in the same community."

"Huh. That must have been nice."

"It was," he agrees absently. "You might not believe it, but Hawk was a surly asshole as a kid."

"No way!" I gasp in fake shock. "I can't imagine that! He's such a cheery guy."

"Ha, right?" Cam laughs, his face lighting up with whatever memory he's thinking about. "When we were about nine or ten, I poured blue dye in his swimming pool." He barely gets the words out between fits of laughter. "The asshole was blue from head to toe for nearly a month. He looked like a smurf."

"Oh my God." I laugh along with him, not requiring much imagination to picture Hawk raging up a storm.

"It didn't matter what his parents did, they couldn't get it to wash off. We were always pulling pranks like that on each other." There's a fond smile on his face as he falls into the past, recalling old memories.

"And your parents were okay with stuff like that?"

He shrugs his shoulders. "None of them are really around all that much. So long as we don't publicly humiliate them and agree to work at the firm when we graduate, they generally don't care."

"Do you want to go into the family business?"

"Not particularly. None of us do, but it's not something we can simply turn down."

"How come? There are people out there that would sell their souls to be given such an opportunity."

He releases a defeated chuckle. "God, I probably sound like an entitled jerk right now."

"You don't," I assure him. When he just gives me a dubious look, I release a chuckle. "Yeah, okay, maybe a little."

Barking out a laugh, he gives me a small, genuine smile that's so much more enticing than any flirty grin he could throw my way. It's real, and it feels like some sort of achievement, like, in a rare moment of openness, he's showing me his true self.

"It's just…" He trails off, struggling to find the right wording.

"Complicated?" I supply, remembering his words when he tried to explain why he behaved the way he did the night of the party.

"Yeah." He sighs. "I know you don't get it, and I can't explain it to you. There's a lot of pressure on us from our parents, and we…" He once again trails off, sighing as he runs his hand through his hair in frustration, unsure of his next words.

Seeing how much he's struggling, wanting to remain loyal to his friends, I shake my head. "You don't have to explain yourself to me."

Giving a sharp nod of his head, understanding passes between us.

"I guess I should let you get some sleep." He gives me a soft smile, picking up his tablet and getting to his feet. Following him, we walk to the door together, but he pauses before pushing it open.

"You know, you're different from anyone else here." That same raw honesty is clear to see in his eyes as they roam over my face, like he's trying to memorize my features.

"How so?"

"I can guarantee you, if asked why they were here, none of them would say they wanted to become someone they could be proud of. They might not say it out loud, but everyone is here for selfish reasons. Whether it's money, familial obligation, or to find a rich husband, not one of them would give me the answer you did."

I don't know what to say to that and I'm not sure I agree with him. I've gotten to know Emilia, and she's the least selfish person I know. She's only here so she can provide for her mother. Isn't that the same with all the scholarship students? Sure, I've heard some of them discussing how, thanks to Pac, they have acceptances to top-line colleges and talking about high-flying careers, but isn't that all part of bettering themselves? They just seem to have more of an idea of what they want to do with their futures. I know I don't need a kickass career and money in the bank. I just want to be free to be me, to earn enough to be comfortable and be happy doing it, but beyond that, I haven't really figured my shit out yet.

∼

ON MONDAY NIGHT, I once again find myself walking toward the dining hall. I'm telling myself it's because I want some ice cream, but there's this pathetic little part of me that's hoping I'll run into Cam. Despite how much I try to tamp it down, part of me can't stop obsessing over him. That moment we shared last night seemed to change things; today, he was different. Don't get me wrong, he was flirting away in his usual fashion, only it felt more genuine than it did before. Like he wasn't just doing it because he's 'the flirty guy', but because he had a genuine interest in me. I'm most likely reading way too much into it, but the riot of butterflies in my stomach and this incessant need to watch him won't let me get over him.

Pulling open the dining hall door, I pause in the entrance. Cameron Rutherford is sitting at the *scholarship* students' table. Skipping the coffee this time, I head toward him.

"Well? Is it what you expected?" I ask, reiterating his words from last night.

"No," he admits, giving a small shake of his head. "It's better."

His words take me by surprise, something he must be able to read on my face, as he explains, "You're more hidden back here. It doesn't feel like you're on display the same way our table does. Back here, you're just a faceless person in the crowd. There's something to be said for not having people observing you all the time, judging your every move."

I have nothing to say to that, but Cam doesn't let us sit in silence for long.

"I wasn't sure if you'd show up."

Licking my lips, nerves flit through me. I don't know what we're doing here, flirting with danger. Neither of us should be doing this—whatever *this* is. It's asking for trouble.

"Tell me more about you and the guys growing up."

"Why?"

Shrugging my shoulders, I give him the honest truth. "I never had siblings or anyone to muck around with. I guess I wanna hear what it was like to have that."

Nodding his head in understanding, he thinks for a moment before his lip lifts in a small smile.

"Our parents own summer houses up in the mountains, right by a lake. Every year the guys and I head up there for a few weeks just to get away for a bit.

"A few years ago, we were out swimming in the lake, fucking around as usual. West was always more hesitant than the rest of us. It would take forever for us to coax him into the water. He was terrified of getting caught up in the reeds."

A sly grin crosses his face and I can immediately guess what he did. "You didn't?" I chuckle.

Cam lets out the most genuine, carefree laugh I've heard from him yet. "Oh, I did." He chuckles, bobbing his eyebrows. Everything about him screams mischief. I can only imagine he's kept the others on their toes all these years.

"Anyway, we finally got him out to the middle of the lake, and while Mason and Hawk distracted him, I ducked under, grabbing a hold of his feet. Man, he screamed bloody murder, kicked me right in the face too. I had a shiner for weeks after that."

"Sounds like you deserved it." I laugh along with him.

"I love that lake. It's where I learned to swim. I've had some of the best memories of my life up there."

"Do you still swim?"

"Yup," he says proudly. "I'm captain of the swim team. If all goes well, I'll be heading to the State Championships this year."

"Wow, that's incredible." I don't really know what that means, but it's obviously something he's excited for and cares a lot about.

"Your parents must be so proud of you."

"Yeah." He snorts. "I'm sure they're super proud." The words drip with sarcasm, my eyes narrowing in confusion. How could parents not be proud of a son like Cam? He's clearly liked, more so than the other Pricks. He does well in school, and he's good at sports? What's not to be proud of?

"My parents couldn't care less about me," he admits after a moment. "My father is never around unless it's to come to my competitions, but it's so that he can remind me that *Rutherfords are winners.*"

The lightness in his eyes from earlier is gone, his laugh lines faded, his face withdrawn as he stares glumly at the tabletop.

"I'm sorry." My voice is soft as I reach across the table, giving his hand a quick squeeze, ignoring how his skin feels against mine and how even that simple touch causes my breath to hitch, my heart hammering in my chest.

∼

FOR THE REST of the week, every night at midnight, I would pull open the dining hall door to find Cam waiting for me, even though every alarm bell was going off in my head, telling me I shouldn't be encouraging this.

On Friday night, I step into the hall, once again expecting to find him there...only the room is empty. *Huh.* Grabbing a tub of ice cream—this time deciding to try a cookies and cream flavored one—I take a seat at the scholarship table, where I usually find Cam sitting, ignoring the sinking pit in my stomach at the thought of him not coming.

It's nearly an hour later—I know, I shouldn't still be sitting here, it's pathetic—when the door creaks open, but it's not who I was expecting.

Mason storms into the room, stomping toward the freezer and lifting out a bag of ice. Turning around to head back out, he freezes in place, spotting me. Yeah, I must look like a weirdo sitting here alone in the middle of the night.

"What are you doing here?" he demands, his voice coming out as a growl as I climb to my feet.

"Just enjoying some late-night ice cream." Holding up the empty tub for him to see before I deposit it in the trash, I glance down, noticing his knuckles are all scraped and covered in blood. "What are *you* doing here?"

"That's none of your goddamn business," he snarks, his temper not much better than Hawk's.

"Whatever." I shrug. "But you're going to have a hard job holding that ice to both sets of knuckles at once."

He makes no effort to move or respond, simply continuing to stare at me with a mixture of hate and confusion. I can practically hear the static intensity of the energy around us, like an invisible force pushing us together.

After a moment, I sigh, rolling my eyes. "Come here." Before he can refuse, I snatch the bag of ice out of his hand and grab some napkins, walking over to the closest table. Opening it, I wrap a few cubes of ice in the napkin, giving him a look that says, 'what are you waiting for?' when he remains frozen in place. It takes a moment before he unglues his feet from the floor and comes to sit on the opposite side of the table, facing me.

This close, I can see the flecks of blood dusting his knuckles, both hands looking worse for wear than they did from further away. With both his hands lying flat on the table, I press one of the ice-filled napkins against his knuckles, a startled gasp escaping me when our skin touches. A static charge jumps between us before he pulls his hand back slightly, breaking the contact. With wide eyes, I stare up into his bright blue ones, swirling with confusion that's matched by the intense way he's looking at me. Like I'm an enigma to him, his brows pull down as he tries to suss me out.

Coughing to clear the lump in my throat, I murmur, "Sorry," making sure I don't touch him as I once again place the napkin on his knuckles before doing the same to his other hand.

It's only once I no longer have something to keep me occupied I realize how fucking awkward this is. I don't even know this guy, and I'm beginning to feel like a bug under a microscope with the way he keeps staring at me. *I can't be that bloody interesting to look at.*

After an awkward fifteen minutes where neither of us says anything, I remove the ice from his knuckles, using the now wet napkin to wipe away the blood until they almost look good as new.

Licking my dry lips, I focus on gathering the napkins and grabbing the bag of ice. "There you go. All done."

He *still* says nothing and after another awkward moment, I give a stiff nod and get up to dump everything in the trash and head out, leaving the mindboggling Prick behind.

The next morning, I wake up to a new message from Cam.

> Cam: Sorry about last night. Something came up.

WHY DO I get the impression that 'something' is the same reason Mason's knuckles were busted?

Hadley

CHAPTER NINE

My least favorite class of the week is gym. From the grumblings of the other girls in the changing room, it seems I'm not the only one. The problem is, it's not the actual physical exercise I dislike. I enjoy the class, although apparently, parents kicked up a fuss about their little princesses having to appear a sweaty mess in front of the boys in our year, so now the girls do yoga and pilates while the guys get to do whatever they want, basically. Even so, it's still enjoyable.

No, my problem is with the pre-and-post-gym changing routine. I always make sure I arrive early, ducking into a stall to change into a baggy top and yoga pants before anyone else shows up. Thankfully gym is the last class of the day, so as soon as it's done, I grab my stuff and get out of there, showering back in the dorms instead of in sight of the rest of the girls.

As I grab my clothes from my locker, I can hear the other girls whispering, wondering why I'm so weird. Just because I don't have the same desire to strip in front of them and have them all judge me. Emilia, Mary, and Abigail quickly copped on to my strange routine, though fortunately they haven't mentioned anything about it. They seem to be the only ones however, as each week the whispers become more and more prominent.

"What is she hiding?"

"Why does she refuse to shower?"

"I bet she's got, like, a horrible skin condition or something."

For the most part, I tune them out. Who cares what they say? They're vapid girls with nothing better to discuss. Unfortunately, Bianca has decided to make it my problem, as she and the other three girls of the month block my escape from the locker room after class.

"Where are you always running off to after gym?" she snarks, her arms folded across her chest, pushing up her tits that are already barely restrained by the thin, stretchy fabric of her sports bra.

"Why do you care?" I sigh, not in the mood to deal with this today. At this point, the entire school thinks I'm fucking Cam and, based on the dark looks being thrown my way, no one is too happy about it. I'm seriously starting to think I should just fuck him. If I'm going to be accused of doing just that, I may as well get something out of it, right? "Making sure I'm not running off to see Cam?"

Her face darkens at that thought, her eyes drilling into me. I don't know if she actually thinks I am sleeping with him or if it's just a rumor she started to gain some sympathy.

"Stay away from Cam," she snarls. "He's mine."

"Yeah." I snort. "For like another week, but then some other girl is gonna be warming his bed at night."

Her lip curls up in disgust, yet she doesn't argue with me, knowing I'm right. Instead, she takes a step forward so we're toe-to-toe. "Maybe so, but it will never be you."

What she doesn't get, though, is that I have no genuine interest in Cam. Yeah, he's smoking hot, and one look in my direction has my body fired up and willing to do whatever he wants to me, but I don't want to *be* with him. I'm not made for the rich, pampered life that would come with being with someone like him. I don't want the spotlight on me, all that attention. While it seems to be what most of the girls here are after, it's not me. I live in the dark, moving silently in the shadows. It's where I'm comfortable, where I belong.

My casual shrug seems to do nothing but confuse her, as she most likely was expecting another snarky retort, except I don't have space in my life for such petty drama.

I go to step around her, but she snatches my wrist, her nails digging into the skin. "You're reaching above your station. Stick to the scholarship boys. Trash should only date trash, after all."

Throwing a final glare her way, I yank my hand out of her grip—she should be fucking thankful that's all I do—and storm out of the locker room, leaving the lot of them whispering behind me.

I'm still in a rotten mood the next day when I arrive at computer science, not helped by the fact I *hate* this class. I have no fucking clue what I'm doing, and the online lesson plans may as well be written in French for all I can comprehend of them. So it's safe to say this class is kicking my butt.

I've actively avoided sitting anywhere near West since the party, but today I have to suck it up and ask for his help because I'm seriously at risk of failing if I continue on the way I am. Why it's compulsory to have at least a basic level of understanding of this crap is beyond me. What the hell am I ever going to do with spreadsheets? And I can't see myself doing a job where I have to give presentations. As far as I can tell, this whole course is just a headache. Nevertheless, it's one the school has mandated as necessary to pass before graduation.

Throwing my shoulders back, I make a beeline for West, claiming the seat beside him, the same one I sat in on the first day. I can tell by his tense posture he knows I'm here, yet he doesn't look away from his screen, his fingers flying over the keys as he types what looks like gobbledygook into some sort of program. He's definitely not following the same beginner's lesson plan I am.

"Hey," I begin hesitantly.

"Oh, so you're talking to me again?" he snarks, his eyes never leaving the screen.

"I was never *not* talking to you. I was just angry with you, which I had every right to be, by the way."

"Your temper is as bad as Hawk's," he grumbles, clearly not realizing how fucking insulting that is.

Gritting my teeth, I attempt to overlook it. *Remember, you need his help.*

"I was wondering if you could maybe help me?" I ask in my sweetest possible voice. Adding my best attempt at an innocent smile, too, when he glances my way. It must come off as more of a grimace if his suspicious look indicates anything.

"With what?" he asks dubiously.

"All of this," I gesture to the computer. "I'm gonna fail if I don't start improving."

After a long, tense moment of silence, where he attempts to ascertain whether I'm lying, he finally lets out a breath. "Fine, what lesson have you made it to?"

"Eh, lesson two."

"Two?!" His eyes widen in surprise, his lips pursing. "So you haven't managed to do anything since our first class?"

"Hey!" I defend myself. "It's hard when you're trying to teach yourself."

Rolling his eyes, he waves toward the screen. "Alright, sign in and I'll help you."

With a pep in my step, I jump to action, swiveling toward my computer and logging in. I can feel his eyes on me, and I once again feel that sense of calm he evokes in me as he rolls his chair over beside mine. My body has never settled the way it does when he's around. I'm always on alert, ready to jump into action. Life has taught me to be that way. Although with him, all of me relaxes, my body like a purring housecat around its master.

For the next hour, he takes me through the lesson plan, and I pick up on things so much quicker when he explains them than I do just reading the document. His passion for computers comes across with every word he says, every carefully thought out explanation, and instead of the class dragging like it usually does, the hour flies by. I'm still convinced I won't need to know half this crap, but at least I understand what I'm doing now.

I'm so focused on my task I barely notice the bell ringing. Grabbing my bag, I get to my feet. "Thanks, *Wes*," I throw over my shoulder as I leave the classroom, smirking at his glower before rounding the corner and disappearing out of sight.

∽

THE BRIGHT LIGHT of the alarm clock taunts me, silently mocking my inability to sleep. I've always been a bit of an insomniac; I'm lucky if I manage to get four hours of sleep. It's the only reason I've been able to stay on top of the workload since I got here, but thanks to Hawk's continued glares and Bianca spreading gossip, sleep has been nonexistent.

Seeing that it's already four a.m., I give up on trying to get some rest. It doesn't matter that I keep closing my eyes, focusing on my breathing, and blocking out the errant thoughts that keep probing at the corners of my consciousness. My body won't lie still; it won't switch off.

I've been so busy adjusting to my new routine here I haven't kept up with my regular exercise. Working out every day is something that was ingrained into me from a young age. I'd start my day with some simple stretches, followed by a five-mile run and a second cardio or weights session later in the day. I used to hate it, but being without that routine recently has thrown me off-kilter. My body feels sluggish and out of sorts.

Deciding to get back to it, I toss back the covers, quickly donning a sports bra, lycra shorts, and my ratty sneakers. Throwing a loose t-shirt over the ensemble, I pull my hair up into a messy ponytail, grab a bottle of water and my gym bag and head out the door. It's still dark out as I cross the campus, soaking up the pre-dawn silence. This is my favorite part of the day, before the rest of the world wakes up. It's so at odds with the usual noise and chaos of the campus.

Entering the sports complex, I follow the signs for the gym, stepping into the dimly lit, empty room. I don't bother to turn on any more lights, preferring the half-light atmosphere as I cast my eyes over the various machines, weight benches, and yoga mats before striding over to the heavy punching bag hanging from the roof in the far corner of the room. Dropping my stuff on the floor, I pull off my t-shirt and tug on a pair of fingerless boxing gloves, flexing my fingers to stretch the leather over my knuckles before swinging my arms to loosen the muscles, doing a few jumping jacks to warm myself up and getting into position in front of the bag.

With my weight centered and my arms raised, my thumbs un-tucked, and my fists clenched tight, I pivot on my back foot, pushing my body forward and driving my fist into the bag. It swings slightly, absorbing the impact from my knuckles. Even that one hit has the strange buzzing sensation I've been feeling recently, beginning to ease and quickly replacing it with adrenaline as I settle into a punishing rhythm.

Jab. Cross. Hook.

Repeat.

I lose all track of time as my whole world narrows down to that small sequence of movements. Nothing except the sound of my labored breaths and the satisfying blow as my punches land perfectly on the leather material.

I hit the bag over and over, giving it everything I've got. Pouring every ounce of frustration, anger, and determination I have into each and every punch until I'm an exhausted, sweaty mess. Even then, I keep going.

You don't stop until I say you can stop!

The angry bark echoes in my mind, taunting me as I continue to pummel the bag, fighting past the weariness settling into my arms.

I'm reaching my limit when I first sense I'm no longer alone, that ingrained feeling of being watched crawling over me. Not letting him know I'm aware of him, I continue on with my routine. Jab, cross, hook. Jab, cross, hook. However my attention is no longer on the movements, it's entirely focused on him. I'm expecting him to do something, but I don't sense him getting any closer to me. Nor do I hear him moving over to any of the gym equipment. *What the fuck is he doing?*

"Are you just going to stand there and watch me like a creep, or are you going to work out?" I pant, not bothering to turn around.

I knew it was him the second he entered the room. The crackle of electricity zinging through the air was a dead giveaway. Over the years, I've trained myself to pick up on the subtle changes that occur in the air when someone is nearby. I've learned to listen to my basic instincts, to pay attention when the hairs at the back of my neck stand up, or the feeling of eyes digging into the back of my head. Those instincts have saved my life more than once.

It's deeper than just being aware of his presence, though. It's like my body is primed to respond to him, to all of them. I don't just sense that *someone* is in the room, I instinctively know it's one of *them*. What's more, I can tell *who* it is. I don't even need to look over my shoulder to know Mason's been silently watching me for the last few minutes.

It's the same with all of them. Cam always has my body instantly going into overdrive when he's nearby. Just the feel of his eyes roaming over me makes my pulse thud and my breath stutter. He's pure sex appeal, and damn, when he's around me, I just want to tear his clothes off and fuck his bloody brains out.

With West, it's how his presence settles me in a way nothing else ever has. Even exercising only dulls the buzzing to a faint background noise, but when he's around, everything within me hushes. It all quietens, as though I'm responding to his steadiness. He dons an impassive expression, like he doesn't give a shit about anything around him, but I'm beginning to suspect he's just quietly confident that nothing will surprise him, that he can solve any problem thrown his way. That certainty resonates with me.

Hell, even Hawk's presence affects me. Not in the same way as the others. No, his is much more volatile. He just has to enter a room and he has unadulterated hatred pounding through my veins, and I instantly want to claw his eyes out. Nevertheless, that's before he opens his mouth and says something that makes me want to rip his nut sack off and shove it down his throat. Just thinking about that asswipe has me punching the bag harder, pretending it's his face I'm smashing my fists into.

For Mason, I can feel his penetrating gaze on me as soon as he walks into a room. He's always silently watching me, making me feel like he can see right through me. With just one look, he tears through every barrier I've ever erected around myself, leaving me exposed and entirely at his mercy. Everything between us is more subtle, though no less intense. When our skin touches, it's a jolt of energy, like I've just stuck my finger in a live socket. He makes adrenaline rush through my system, heightening my senses. I can practically taste the tension in the air around us. I'm just not sure if it's sexual on his part or something else. Hell, it could be pure fucking hatred for all I know. He's impossible to get a read on. It could honestly swing either way. I know *I* can't deny he's hot as fuck. With his broad, muscular frame and those thick biceps, how can I not picture his large palms squeezing my ass as he easily pushes me against the wall, punishing me with every savage thrust of what I am sure is a humongous dick. The type that eviscerates women and ruins them for all other men.

Now I'm hot and bothered, and it's got nothing to do with my morning exercise. Thank God Mason, who is still watching me from the doorway, can't tell what I'm thinking. There's no way he can know my red face is due to my dirty thoughts. That's the only reason I'm comfortable dropping my fists and spinning around to glare at him. *Why the fuck is he just standing there watching me like a creeper?*

I try my damnedest to ignore the way his heated eyes trail over my exposed thighs and naked torso, pausing on my heaving chest before meeting my face, thanking the lucky stars above I never turned on the lights. In the half-darkness, he won't be able to see my imperfections.

Realizing he never answered my question, I scowl at him. "Can I help you with something?" I bite out. My sharp words, combined with the death glare I'm giving him, must knock him out of whatever trance he's under because he quickly dons his usual look of indifference and stomps over to the weight bench, effectively dismissing me. Of course, this asshole gets an early morning gym session in before class, ruining the little bubble of peace I'd created for myself. I should have expected him to be here; he looks like he fucking lives in the gym.

I watch as he silently sets himself up, loading more weight plates onto the bar than any average human should be able to lift before getting comfy on the bench, planting his feet firmly on the ground and starting into a round of bench presses. He appears confident enough in his strength that he doesn't need anyone to spot him. *Talk about arrogance.* I'm sure as fuck not going to save his sorry ass if he drops all that weight on his chest. Not that I could possibly lift what looks like the equivalent of a small car in weights off of him if I tried. I'd need to be fucking superwoman to do that shit.

Once I'm satisfied that he's done paying me any attention, fully focused on his workout, I get back to mine. Now that I'm no longer in the zone, I can feel the ache in my fingers and the stiffness in my hands from taking out all of my pent-up anger on the punching bag.

Despite how hard I've been going at it, I can still feel that restless energy inside me, itching for more. Checking the time on my phone, I see it's still early. Class isn't for another few hours, and I'm still too worked-up to go back to my room. Besides, I can't let this fucker think his presence here is enough to send me running.

Downing half my bottle of water and wiping the sweat off my forehead, I move over to the treadmills, carefully selecting one that doesn't give me a direct line of sight to Mason—I don't want him to think I'm fucking watching him—but also enables me to keep an eye on him out of the corner of my eye. Most likely, he's only here to work out. He seemed pretty surprised to find me here, but the four of them are a conundrum I don't understand, and I can't afford to risk turning my back on any of them.

Setting a fast pace for myself, I sprint along on the machine. It doesn't take long for a new layer of sweat to coat my skin, my breaths becoming labored as I push myself harder than I probably should, considering I've neglected my regular running routine for the last few weeks. I'm a panting, sweaty mess when I climb off the machine an hour later, my legs like jelly as I slowly make my way over to where I left my towel and water. I've been slyly watching Mason out of the corner of my eye, however he still hasn't done anything other than cycle through various weight-based exercises, occasionally pausing between reps to stare at me with that same strange expression on his face that he had when he walked in. I don't know him well enough to understand what he's thinking. Hell, I don't know the guy at all. He could be picturing me naked or imagining a thousand different ways he could kill me and dispose of my body before anyone would even know I was missing. Choosing to put him out of my mind and in desperate need of a shower, I grab my stuff and head out of the gym, not looking back at him as I leave.

Little Warrior

CHAPTER TEN

She's fucking everywhere I go. Everywhere, even the fucking gym! The one place that gives me some peace, and she's fucking there, ruining it. What the hell is she even doing here so early?!

I'm stuck, frozen in the doorway, watching her pummel the shit out of the heavy bag. I can feel the rage coursing through her from here. Every move is carried out with perfect precision as she throws her entire weight into each punch. Taking in her form, straight back and wide stance, the accuracy of her hits and the sound the bag makes when you hit it just right, it's obvious she's had training. I had no idea she was a fighter, not in the physical sense. She's shown she can fight back with words, but she never resorts to physical violence.

As my eyes roam over her lithe body, taking in her sweat-soaked skin and heaving chest, I can feel my traitorous dick hardening in my shorts, not giving a single shit that this girl is off-limits.

The black marks of a tattoo curl around her hip, dipping beneath her shorts. Black lines swirl up her side until they form an abstract image, some sort of a bird, over her ribs.

Her tits look fucking incredible in that little bra thing she's wearing, rapidly rising and falling from the exertion of her workout. I've never really paid much attention to her tits before. Don't get me wrong, I noticed she had them. They're large and perky and would look fucking perfect with my dick shoved between them as I come all over her face. Sadly, she usually has them hidden under her uniform or the unflattering tops she wears that have apparently been hiding her hot-as-fuck body from the world. Such a fucking travesty. Someone with a body like hers should walk around naked all the time. It's a work of fucking art. She's skinny, but not the same kind of skinny as the other girls at Pac. It's got nothing to do with not eating and everything to do with how she's honed her body into a weapon. She's pure strength and muscle with her taut abdomen and powerful thighs. She's an athletic missile ready to rain down shit on whoever crosses her.

Her sharp words snap me out of my trance, pulling my gaze from her limber body up to her glowering eyes. The icy glare she's throwing my way reminds me that, although she may look like every one of my dirty fantasies, she's untouchable. Hawk has got a fucking bug up his ass about her. Besides, I'm pretty sure she can't stand any of us too. She certainly doesn't have the same level of respect and fear for us as everyone else. Although the way she looks at Cam sometimes, it's clear she's attracted to him, and I definitely caught her checking me out this morning. She might not like us, but she fucking wants us.

Regardless, she might be a hot piece of ass, although she's a distraction none of us can afford right now. Between school and our fucked-up families, we have enough shit going on. Hawk's right; we can't have a girl coming in and disrupting the balance, messing with our heads when we need our focus now more than ever. Guess I'm just going to have to continue getting my jollies from whatever mediocre girl of the month. It's bad enough that Cam has his sights on her. If she would just give in and fuck him, like I know she wants to, he'd get over her, as he has with every other girl. This back-and-forth she's got going with him is only creating more problems. He's fucking infatuated, and that's something we sure as hell don't need right now.

With that reminder, I wipe all traces of emotion from my face, not bothering to answer her as I quickly turn away before she can see the hard-on I'm sporting. I make my way over to my usual spot, pushing myself harder than normal, not leaving the gym until my arms and legs feel like wet noodles.

"Damn, man, isn't the gym supposed to make you all Zen or some shit?" Cam chuckles as I stomp back into our apartment, somehow more worked up than before I left this morning. All four of us have the top floor of the boys' dorms. We had the whole place renovated the summer before freshman year, so it has an open-plan kitchen and living space, four large bedrooms, and we updated the shower room.

It might sound crazy for four fifteen-year-olds to be able to do all that, but we were Princes the second we arrived on campus. A stupid-ass title, but whatever. We trumped every senior student. Of course, not everyone just rolled over and accepted that. It wasn't easy for the previous reigning seniors to give up their crowns, so to speak. Nevertheless, they were rulers because of their popularity. We rule by blood, by title. Our families are the founding families of Pac Prep. Every Hayes, Davenport, Rutherford, and Warren before us has ruled this school.

We had to stand up for ourselves and fight for our place, but one thing our families taught us is how to be ruthless, to take what's ours. People quickly learned not to mess with us, and since then we've been both revered and feared, a healthy combination.

Things have been pretty smooth sailing for the last four years. We can do what we want, fuck who we want, have whatever we want. But now that senior year is here, we're all starting to feel the tension. Where every other student is filling out college applications and preparing for the time of their lives, we are preparing to be inducted into the family business. There's no college education for us, no fraternities or keg parties. Only a boring pre-planned future at our parents' company.

Where our futures should be a vast expanse of the unknown spread out before us, we each feel like all the doors are slamming shut in our faces, and our world is closing in around us. The fear that, someday soon, we will be just like our parents is riding us hard.

It wasn't always this way. Sure, we've never wanted to be like our parents, but until last summer we were content with our lot in life. We accepted the future our parents had laid out for us.

But, fuck, everything changed this summer. Everything we thought we ever knew went up in smoke. The carefree life we've lived so blindly in came crashing down around us. Learning your parents aren't who you thought they were, is always a bitter pill to swallow. Hawk took the news the hardest and has been burying his anger in fights and pussy. Out of all of us, he thought he had relatively decent parents. The rest of us learned early on what assholes our parents were, so while still a shock, it wasn't a complete surprise.

Ignoring Cam, I storm into my bedroom, slamming the door behind me. Despite putting myself through a vigorous workout this morning, I can still feel all this pent-up energy thrumming through me. I couldn't fucking concentrate with her so close. Even after she left, I could still fucking smell her in the room.

I don't fucking understand it. Ever since that day in class, when I first saw her, I haven't been able to get her out of my head. I don't even know what it is about her that has caught my attention. She has this prickly attitude that's designed to keep people at arm's length—anyone paying attention can see that—yet, underneath it all, I can sense there's something more. There's something that resonates with me on a primitive level, not that that makes any fucking sense. It's kind of like my soul recognizes hers? I don't fucking know. It's confusing as hell.

I don't usually like other people. I have my boys, sure. We grew up together. We know everything there is to know about one another. But other people? Not my thing, and they don't understand me either. Neither do girls. They assume I'm not interested because I don't talk much, and my size tends to send most of them running for the hills. But something about *her* is different. I haven't been able to take my eyes off her. Not that I mean to, but my eyes seem to gravitate toward her whenever she's around. I don't have any fucking say in it. I'll be working away, minding my own business, and the next thing I know, I've been staring at her for god knows how long, my work long forgotten.

Sometimes, when I'm watching, it's like her mind is off somewhere else. There's a vacancy in her eyes. It's in those moments that my connection with her is the strongest. It's almost like I can sense her pain or some shit, like it's similar to my own.

A harsh bang on the door snaps me out of my funk. "What?" I growl.

"We've gotta go," Cam calls out, pausing a moment on the other side before I hear his footsteps as he walks away.

Fuck, I'm still far too worked up to make it through the day like this. I'll kill the first asshole who so much as looks at me wrong. Grabbing my bag, I head out the door, the four of us making our way toward the dining hall.

"I'll meet you inside," I call out, walking past the entrance toward the girls' dorm.

"What the hell, man?!" Hawk shouts after me. "It's changeover day!"

"I'll be there. I just need to sort something out first."

I hear him grumbling behind me, but I don't slow down or turn around. I need to release this feeling inside of me. Now. If I go into that hall with all those insipid fucking assholes watching my every move, I'm going to do something I regret.

Throwing open the door to the girls' dormitory, it bangs off the wall. The few girls in the foyer jump, looking at me with wide eyes, but I ignore them all as I take the stairs two at a time, making my way to the fourth floor.

Girls flatten themselves against the wall as I stride past, stopping outside a now familiar door and banging on the wood.

"What the...What are you doing here?" Vivian gasps. I don't know why she bothers, though. She knows the routine by now. I've never shown up looking as enraged as I feel right now, but even so, if I'm here, she knows why.

Pushing past her, I barge into her room as she closes the door. "Desk," I bark out, unbuckling my belt and popping the top button of my slacks. Moving past me, she perches on the edge of the desk, her ridiculously short skirt giving me a flash of her bright pink thong. "Turn around."

"Can't we do it my way this once?" She might think her pout is cute, but it makes her look like a child—a creepy as fuck one with all that makeup gunk on her face.

"No," I snarl, getting impatient.

Huffing, she finally does as she's told, bending over the desk as I dig a condom out of my pocket, rolling it over my hard dick. Pushing into her, I feel absolutely nothing. She used to at least feel good, but now she does nothing for me, and her fake pornstar moans only aggravate me further as I pound into her hard enough to hurt.

"Oh yeah, baby, give it to me," she moans in a breathy voice, her grating tone doing nothing but making it harder for me to pretend it's someone else I'm fucking.

"Shut. Up," I hiss through gritted teeth. Instead of the anorexic-looking brunette bent over the table, I picture an athletic blonde, authentic wanton moans escaping her plump lips as I hammer into her tight cunt. I only have to imagine myself fucking Hadley for a few seconds before that tingling feeling at the bottom of my spine ratchets up and I finally explode into the condom.

For the first time since seeing her this morning, I finally feel at ease, my whole body relaxing as I pull out, throwing the condom in the trash can and tucking myself away.

"Mmm, that was so good, baby." I don't even know if she came, nor do I give a shit.

I've just reached the door when she calls out, "Wait, are you at least going to pick me again?" The hopeful tone in her voice is fucking pathetic. Does she seriously think this means anything more than exactly what it is—a month-long fuck buddy?

With my hand resting on the doorknob, I snap out, "No," not bothering to turn around before opening the door and leaving her behind, finally feeling like myself again.

Breakfast is well underway when I arrive in the dining hall, ignoring Hawk's scowl. He's always been a grumpy bastard, but it's gotten so much worse since the summer. He's always loved the control he has over the school, the way the other students cower to him, but it's become something he craves. The slightest hint of defiance, and he'll ensure he squashes it, likely leaving whoever pissed him off fearing for their life. Not that he's ever had much control over his anger. Even as a kid, he would throw a motherfucker of a tantrum over the slightest thing.

Of course, Hadley is the one person in this place who doesn't flinch in the face of his rage. Instead of taking his anger as a warning, she seems to view it as a challenge, something to fight back against. Needless to say, her unwillingness to submit has only infuriated him more, and it's only made worse by whatever is going on between her and Cam. He thinks we don't know he's been sneaking out at night to meet her, except we all know. Fuck, I had to talk Hawk down from storming in there and tearing her fucking head off. Seriously, if she doesn't sleep with him soon so he can get over her, I don't know what the hell is going to happen.

Just like last time, Hawk gives us *the look* and we get to our feet, the room dropping silent in an instant. The buzz of excitement is suffocating as the girls all touch up their makeup and make sure their hair is sitting perfectly. The only girls who aren't preening are the scholarship ones. In fact, I'm pretty sure I catch Hadley rolling her eyes, sharing a comical look with the girl beside her. Sure, she's a scholarship student and knows she can't be chosen, but it's interesting to see how unimpressed she is by this whole farce. While the other girls at her table might not show the same level of excitement as the rest of the senior girls, I'd have to be blind to miss the wanting glint in their eyes. Even knowing they can't be chosen, they still *want* to be. Not Hadley, in any case. She looks like she couldn't imagine anything worse.

When it's my turn to step forward and select a girl, my eyes run over the sea of batting eyelashes and coy smiles until I find someone suitable. Cora Farber. She's got medium-length, blonde, curly hair and a bit more meat on her bones than Vivian had. She's not quite right, but she'll do. I make sure to keep a table between us when I point to her so she can't get any ideas about jumping all over me, and thankfully she stays seated as she squeals in excitement. I struggle not to roll my eyes at the whole scene as I stomp back to my seat and sit down, glad to be done with my bit as Cam steps forward to put on his usual performance. He does the same song and dance as last time, only I notice he doesn't have the same enthusiasm as before, and I don't miss his less-than-subtle glance toward the scholarship table before finally pointing to Missy Barton. It doesn't take West long to pick someone, and the four of us make our exit, leaving the hall in an uproar of excited squeals and murmurs.

The week drags by the same as every other week, except Friday is Cam's first swim meet of the year. He's determined to go all the way to the State Championships this year, and anyone who's seen him in the water knows without a doubt he will. Not only does he love the sport, but he's fucking incredible at it. He would have an impressive future on the Olympic team if it wasn't for our shithead parents and the legacy we have to maintain by following in their footsteps.

He's completely focused as he stands at the edge of the pool alongside the other swimmers—waiting for the whistle to blow—and when the race begins, he's the first one to hit the water, quickly getting out ahead of everyone else, a distance he easily maintains as he reaches the far side and swims back to the start. He wins the race by a landslide, a huge goofy grin on his face as he seeks us out in the crowd, lifting his arms in the air.

Swimming is one of the few times he lets his true self shine through. He loves the sport; the competitive nature, the energy that comes with winning. The smile only drops from his face as his father moves toward him. Of course, he's here. He never misses a race, but we'd hoped that since it was only a district meet, he wouldn't bother showing his face. The two of them exchange words—well, from the looks of it, Mr. Rutherford does most of the talking. Cam is occasionally nodding his head, his face pinched in annoyance. After a few moments, his father gives a final nod, storming out the door and leaving Cam glowering behind him. I'd be surprised if he can't feel the heat from Cam's hatred burning holes in his back as he leaves.

We quickly scramble from our seats, making our way down to the pool, all three of us with grins on our faces, offering our congratulations in an effort to put that smile back on his face.

"Come on, man." I slap him on the back, jerking my head toward the exit. "Let's get the hell out of here. We've got some celebrating to do."

Hadley

CHAPTER ELEVEN

Over the next week, things fall into a regular rhythm. I make an effort to stick to my regular gym routine—it eats significantly into my studying time, but it prevents at least one kid from ending up with a broken nose when they call me a slut. I thought that shit would die off when the Pricks all chose new girls, but it's only gotten worse. The only problem is that Mason shows up at five a.m. every morning to get his workout in too. Neither of us says anything, not even acknowledging the other's presence, but I'm aware of his every move.

On Tuesday, Bianca and Cam's new girl, I think her name is Missy, corner me between classes.

"Bianca." I sigh, as the two of them step in front of me. I'd stayed late to discuss my history assignment with Mrs. Beaufort, so now there was hardly anyone in the halls apart from the three of us. "Aren't we done with this? You're no longer Cam's girl. Shouldn't you be taking issue with Missy, who's *actually* fucking Cam, instead of with me?"

The two girls scowl at me, and seriously, I can't understand their problem. "I won't let you do to Missy what you did to me."

"And what exactly was that?"

"You took him! He was supposed to be *mine* for the month, and you stole his attention. He didn't want anything to do with me!" Her last sentence comes out in a broken sob, the tears gleaming in her eyes. I almost feel bad for her, except if Cam didn't want to spend his time with her, then that's between them. It has nothing to do with me. It's not my fault if he started chasing after me while he was with her. The guy is clearly a player, and I picked up on that on day one, so surely she knew what he was like. Besides, from what I've heard, it's not like there is any exclusivity clause in this whole antiquated tradition. Not that I've actually done anything fucking wrong here. "The other Princesses and I won't let you do it to anyone else."

"I'm sorry?" I struggle to hold back the snort threatening to spurt out of me. "You and the what?"

"The Princesses," she states with so much seriousness that I'm biting my lip hard enough to break the skin in an attempt to keep my composure. "The other girls that the Princes have chosen." She says it like that isn't the most ridiculous thing I've ever heard.

"The Princess Club?" The snort I was holding back bursts free. "What, like the mile-high club? You fuck a Prince, and you get a badge or something?"

Neither girl seems to find the whole thing as funny as I do, glowering at me with unimpressed looks until I roll my eyes.

"You have to be *chosen*," Missy emphasizes. "Trash like you could never be a Princess."

Aw damn, but I always wanted to be a Princess.

Does this idiot honestly think I want to be part of their stupid club?

"Missy." I sigh wearily. "I'll say the same thing to you that I said to Bianca. I'm not interested in stealing Cam from you. I suggest you learn from her mistakes and focus on your relationship with Cam instead of worrying about me."

Neither girl seems to know how to respond to that, so while they both gape at me, I step around them, having had enough of this pointless conversation, and head on to history before I miss the whole damn lesson.

What I said to Bianca and Missy is true, I don't have any interest in being a part of their stupid club, even though I continue to meet with Cam every night in the dining hall, where he regales me with stories of his childhood. He doesn't talk much about his parents or the company he and the others are supposed to take over, so we mostly stick to lighter conversation topics. Every now and again, he probes into my past, wanting to know more about me, but I manage to distract him, avoiding having to share much of myself with him.

It's late on Sunday by the time I leave the library and the sun has long since set, the glare from the pathway lamps my only source of light as I step into the cool, quiet night air. I was the last one left by the time I packed up my things, and I'm supposed to meet Cam any minute now. I'm pulling the door to the front entrance shut behind me when a brutal force crashes into me, throwing me against the solid wood; a large body presses up against me before I can bring my fists up.

Glancing up, I stare into the fuming eyes of Hawk. *Great, just what I need today.* His arms are outstretched, hands pressed firmly against the wooden door beside my head as he glares down at me. His stony expression and icy eyes are menacing, causing me to push back some dark memories and forcing myself to stay in the present.

The corner of his lip curls up in disdain as he snarls at me, "I don't know what the fuck you think you're doing with Cam, but leave him the fuck alone."

I don't react as all the different ways I could get him to back the fuck off flick through my mind. A well-placed punch to the kidney always does the trick. Or a knee to the balls, although he's a little too close to guarantee a direct hit.

"I don't like you, and I sure as fuck don't trust you. I don't know what you're playing at, but I won't stand by and let you screw with his head."

"I don't—"

"Bullshit," he snarls. "You taunt and tease him. You have him chasing after you, going to secret little midnight meetings with you—yeah, don't think I don't know about that. If you wanted him, you'd just fuck him. I don't know what it is, but you're up to something, and I won't let you mess with him anymore."

He pins me in place with his penetrating stare, the faint light enough to discern the glow of hatred in his eyes. Having seemingly said his piece, he stands up straight, giving me one last glowering look before stalking off into the night.

What a fucking douche.

His blitz attack has the adrenaline thumping through my veins, my hands shaking as I try to steady my nerves. Taking several deep breaths, I slowly exhale until my heart no longer feels like it's trying to break free from my chest. Once I feel calm again, I scurry down the steps and head toward the dining hall, pushing open the door. Hawk might have caught me off guard tonight and given me a scare, but he's going to have to do a lot better than that to get me to fall in line.

∼

"You have to come! You haven't been to one since the first party of the year," Emilia whines on Friday night.

"I'm just not feeling it tonight," I repeat for what must be the fifth time. When she continues to look at me like I'm deliberately being difficult, I tack on, "I just don't think parties are my thing."

I've managed to worm my way out of the last couple with one excuse or another, but Emilia isn't hearing any of it tonight. Pushing out her bottom lip and searing me with those goddamn puppy dog eyes, I can't help but roll my eyes at her antics. She's pulling out the big guns—how the fuck can I say no to that?

Gritting my teeth, knowing I'm going to regret it, I grind out, "Fine."

"Ahh," she squeals, throwing herself into my arms. "We're going to have a great time. Wait 'til you see."

"Uh-huh." I can't entirely agree with her view of tonight, but I guess if I'm going, I may as well make the best of it and try to enjoy myself.

"Here, wear this. You'll look fucking fine in it." Emilia throws a tiny piece of black fabric at me that I manage to catch before it hits me in the face.

"Uh, no. No way am I wearing that!" I insist, holding it out in front of me. Without even trying it on, I know it will barely cover my ass. Thankfully, the neckline is high so my tits wouldn't be on display for everyone to gawk at, but even so.

"Come on," she whines, and I can already see her lip starting to pop out in a pout.

"Fine," I cave, knowing it's easier to give in. "But you have to turn around."

Rolling her eyes and sighing, she turns around, giving me a modicum of privacy to change. "I've never known a girl to have such issues changing in front of other girls. Especially one that has as hot a body as you have."

Not responding, I quickly strip off my clothes, pulling the dress on over my head, ensuring it covers my ass as I glance in the mirror, adjusting the neckline slightly before pulling my hair over my shoulders and attempting to flatten the curls. I like the little, short sleeves that cover my shoulders and the fact it isn't backless like a lot of dresses the other girls wear. When I'm happy, I call out, "Okay, you can turn around now."

"Damn, girl, you are smokin'...but those boots? Hell no. Here, try these on with it." Emilia holds up a pair of stiletto heels, but I'm already shaking my head, adamant that I won't be wearing those death traps. Not tonight, not ever.

"Not a chance," I assert. "You'd have to pin me down and strap them to my feet, and there's no way I'm letting you do that."

Emilia roars with laughter as she drops the heels with a shrug, thankfully not pushing the matter. Pulling another dress out of the small closet, she strips down, not having the same issues with walking around in only her underwear that I do. She slips into a dark red dress similar to my own, except more revealing, with a plunging neckline and a pair of heels that finish off the outfit. I can't deny she looks amazing, her black hair and tanned skin contrasting perfectly with the dress and shoes.

"Don't we look pretty fucking hot?" She laughs, dragging me over to stand beside her in front of the mirror. I have to admit, I don't look half bad. The way the dress hugs my curves, highlighting my narrow waist, makes me look older somehow, sexier.

"Here, sit." Emilia pushes me into the chair at her desk where she has set up all her hair and makeup stuff for tonight. "I'll see what I can do with those curls."

An hour later, I'm probably more primped than I've ever been in my life. My hair has so much hairspray in it I could probably hang upside down from a tree and it wouldn't move an inch. Despite that, though, Emilia did a pretty fantastic job with it. I usually just let my hair drip dry, accepting that it's going to be a frizzy mess of curls. Somehow she's managed to get them all to behave and, with some product and a curling wand, they now sit in beautiful sleek ringlets down my back.

Regardless of how amazing I think I look, I'm already bored with this party. As I predicted, it is no better than the last one. Worse even, since this stupid dress keeps insisting on riding up my ass. I mentally curse Emilia out for guilting me into wearing the damn thing as I pull it down for the hundredth time, glancing around to check no one is watching me wrestle with it.

Everything looks just the same as the last party. The Pricks are once again congregated around the fire with their new girl of the month while the rest of the student's are spread out along the beach, most of them already looking worse for wear. I just don't understand the fascination with getting rip-roaring drunk and stumbling all over one another. Maybe it's because I've never been able to let my guard down enough to just live in the moment, but the thought of not being in complete control, of not being aware of everything going on around me, sounds terrifying.

"You don't exactly look like you're having fun," Michael jokes, coming up beside me. Emilia was whisked off to the dance floor with Andrew as soon as we arrived. I'm pretty sure he's got a bit of a crush on her. Recently he's been sitting beside her at our weekly movie nights and walking her to classes. It's adorable to watch, and based on how her cheeks flush and she gets all flustered when he's around, I'd guess she likes him too.

"Ha, yeah. I'm not really a party person."

"We could—"

A commotion over by the fire pit cuts off Michael's words as yelling, loud enough to be heard over the heavy bass of the music, reaches our ears. The whole party seems to come to a standstill, everyone turning to watch the unfolding drama. Emilia comes stumbling over from the dance floor, excitement dancing in her eyes as she drags me forward toward the scene. "What's going on?" I whisper-yell as we move closer, shoving our way through the crowd until we can get a good look at what's happening. All four of the Pricks have gotten to their feet, standing with the fire at their backs, looking like the kings of hell as they face off against a bunch of jocks. Running my eyes over them, I count eleven guys wearing jerseys, who I'm guessing make up the school's football team.

"What the fuck is your problem, Deke?" Cam growls, glowering at the guy standing front and center. He's tall and muscular with styled brown hair and a cold look in his eyes. He's nearly as tall as the Pricks and as broad as Hawk. Based on how the rest of the team swarms around him, I'm guessing he's their captain.

"You're our problem," he snarls. "None of the girls are interested in us 'cause they're all holding out for one of you assholes to pick them."

"Watch your mouth," West barks, the hostility in his tone and the dark look on his face taking me by surprise. I've never seen him confrontational before. Unlike the others, he goes out of his way to fade into the background, never seeming to have an issue with anyone around him. The West standing up there right now is very different from the everyday West I've watched far too intently for the last few weeks.

"You can't blame us if your usual groupies want an upgrade," Hawk drawls, a confident smirk lifting his lips. "Not our fault if the steroids have shriveled your dicks so much you can't satisfy them."

"You piece of shit," Deke growls and takes a step toward the guys, his boy band also stepping forward too, backing up their leader.

Hawk and the guys quickly adjust their stances as Mason stalks forward so he's chest-to-chest with the captain. Both boys are as tall as each other, but seeing them standing facing one another, it's noticeable Deke is nowhere near as broad or as muscular as Mason. Don't get me wrong, as a football player, he's stacked. It just doesn't compare to Mason or the rest of the guys. Even West, despite being scrawnier, looks more formidable. It must be some sort of air that comes with knowing you're invincible. In any other high school, Deke would probably be the typical reigning king, but here he's just another rich asshole in a sea of wealthy kids.

The two of them face off, the entire audience holding their breath, waiting anxiously to see what's going to happen next. West steps beside Mason, his gaze focused intently on the captain, sizing him up. I find myself, along with everyone else, leaning in to listen as his lips part. "Think very carefully about your next move, Deke. We'll tear you to shreds—and I'm not just talking about a social beat down in front of the entire senior class." West tips his head to the side, and Deke turns to look at us all. His eyes widen as he finds us watching them closely, wondering what his next move will be. "You and I both know Mason here could beat the crap out of you. You think you're having difficulties getting girls now? Wait until that ugly mug of yours is all purple and swollen." I've never heard West talk like this to anyone. Never even knew he was capable of it, yet the vicious smirk as he tears Deke down in front of the whole class says everything—he's fucking enjoying himself.

Where the other three—particularly Mason and Hawk—get their kicks out of beating the shit out of disrespectful students, West gets his from eviscerating them with his sharp words.

With a shit-eating grin on his face, Hawk steps forward, joining the other two. "Not to mention, one word to the coach and, just like that, you'd be off the team. You'd probably lose your football scholarship to Arizona State, too."

Deke is looking less and less confident about his stance with every word, his eyes flitting nervously around the crowd. Hesitant to back down and look weak in front of his team and the rest of the school, but equally realizing he hasn't a hope in hell of defeating these guys.

"Back down, Deke. Don't throw away your entire future over some pussy. There's a time and a place for this; here is not it." West's final cryptic words get through to him, and with an incomprehensible snarl, Deke stomps away toward the far side of the lake, the rest of the team following after him like good little lap dogs.

As soon as the tension dissipates, the rest of the class breaks out into murmurs, and it's only then that I realize someone must have stopped the music at some point. With the action over now, the music starts up again and people are quickly sucked back into the party, all drama forgotten for now.

"Wow, that was tense." Emilia chuckles. "But damn, what a showdown that would have been if Deke and Mason had gotten it on, right?"

"Sure," I say distractedly, my focus still on the four guys as they huddle together, whispering quietly to one another. Almost as though he senses me watching, Mason's head whips up as his gaze instantly zones in on me.

"Shit," I murmur, ducking my head and breaking eye contact with him, pulling Emilia through the crowd away from the Pricks.

Once we're safely on the far side of the beach, we drop down onto the pebbly shore. We're a bit of a distance from the main party, the thud of the music not as deafening over here, making it easier to talk to one another without having to shout.

"So...Andrew?" I glance at Emilia, a sly grin lifting the corner of my lip as her eyes widen in surprise. Yup, I might not be tuned into my own love life, but I've been paying attention to hers.

"You've noticed it too?" She groans into her hands.

"Yup. What's going on there?"

"Nothing...Something, maybe. I don't know." She lets out a heavy sigh. "He's been so sweet this week, but I don't know what it means."

"Oh, he definitely likes you." I laugh as she turns to face me, her lower lip caught between her teeth.

"You think so?"

"Oh, yeah. He's been following you around like a lost puppy, and he's constantly glancing at you at breakfast."

Her cheeks glow pink and I can see excitement brimming in her eyes.

"You like him." It's not a question; it's clear to see on her face that she does, but she nods anyway.

"Yeah. I mean, I always thought he was cute, but we've only ever been friends. I didn't know he was interested in me like that."

"Girl, he'd have to be deaf, dumb, and blind not to be interested in you," I say, bumping my shoulder against hers. "You're awesome."

Hadley

CHAPTER TWELVE

Dumping my bag on a spare table in the library, I pull out my tablet and workbook, ready to get stuck into yet another night of studying. If I didn't know any better, I'd swear they were trying to kill us through sleep deprivation. How does everyone else manage this workload?

Wrapping up my history homework, I move on to the next English assignment Cam and I have that is due next week. We need to compare and contrast two books from our reading list. Knowing what book I want to use, I get up and search for it, walking amongst the stacks until I find the aisle I'm looking for. I pause when I see West blocking my way as he scans the shelves in front of him.

I'm honestly not sure what to make of him. He's been a lifesaver, helping me with computer science, but we never talk about anything personal so, despite us spending an hour a week together, I don't feel like I know him at all. He's quiet and nerdy and more interested in his studies than girls and social etiquette, yet I've seen that same flash of violence that Hawk, Mason, and even Cam have.

Pretending he's not there, I saunter down the aisle in search of the book I'm looking for, ignoring when he notices my presence, his head turning slightly as he watches me approach. Finding it on the top shelf, I stretch up onto my toes, even though I don't have a hope of reaching it. Glancing around for a stool or ladder or something, I see absolutely nothing. *How the hell do other students get books on the top shelf?*

Eyeing the bookcase, I figure I can easily climb up and grab the book. Wedging the tip of my boot in a gap on a low shelf, I haul myself up until I'm several shelves off the ground and can grab a hold of the top shelf. With my free hand, I reach out to pluck the book, but just as my fingers touch the spine, my boot slips and I lose my footing.

"Aah." A small gasp escapes at the sudden movement, my hand instinctively clasping tighter around the shelf as I slide down the bookcase. Before I can regain my footing, an arm winds around my waist, catching me before I hit the ground and pulling me in against a hard, warm body.

"What are you doing?" a gravelly, breathy voice whispers in my ear. Holy shit, does he usually sound so irresistible? His voice belongs in an audiobook. It would have women everywhere panting. The timber alone has me close to orgasm.

"I needed a book," I respond, my own voice coming out husky.

West stretches above my head, keeping one arm wrapped around me as his tall frame and long arm enable him to reach the top shelf with his free hand effortlessly. The move has him towering over me even more, caging me in, and enveloping me in his clean, musky scent. His nearness is scrambling my brain, though, doing all sorts of stupid things to it.

"This one?" he asks, the rumble in his chest making my panties dampen as it vibrates through me. I'm incapable of doing anything other than nodding as he grabs the book I was after, lifting it down.

"Thanks," I murmur, taking the book from him. He holds on to it for another moment, neither of us moving. I can feel his breath on my cheek as he dips his head, inhaling the smell of my shampoo.

"You're welcome," he eventually whispers, slowly sliding his palm across my abdomen, like he's putting off letting go of me. *That would be crazy though, right?* Giving my hip a final squeeze, he steps away, the cold air replacing his heat at my back. I hear his footsteps as he walks off, but I don't look around, trying to calm my racing heart rate and understand what the hell just happened.

By the time I make it back to the study area, Cam has arrived, his stuff spread out over the table I was sitting at. As I head toward him, I scan my eyes around the room, searching for West or the other Pricks, only I don't see any of them. *Strange.*

"Hey," I greet, settling back into my chair, finding Cam reading through the few notes I've taken in my notebook.

"Why do you write it down in your notebook first instead of using the tablet? It'll take you twice as long to do the assignment that way." Cam laughs. Things have come a long way since we were handed our first assignment. Don't get me wrong, he still spends most of our time together flirting and driving me to distraction, but it's different than before, and I've let go of my anger over the first party of the school year. I'd say we're almost...friends? Maybe? I'm not sure you could put a name on what we are.   *People-who-are-friendly-but-also-have-an-insane-sexual-attraction-to-one-another? Hmm, that's a bit wordy.*

"Because it takes too long to write it on the tablet," I tell him. "By the time I've written a sentence, I've forgotten where I was going with it. At least this way, I get it all down while it's in my head, then I can just copy it across."

He shakes his head, rolling his eyes like I'm deliberately being difficult. "If you actually tried, you'd get better at it."

"Why?" I argue. "No one in the real world uses that crap. It's all pen and paper beyond these hallowed halls of yours."

Holding up his hands in defeat, he concedes. "Do it your way."

We settle down to work after that, getting an outline and draft written for our assignment. It's late by the time we finish up, and as I glance around, it appears we're the last ones left in the library. I lean over the desk to grab my things and put them in my bag when a presence behind me has me straightening and spinning around. Cam is standing right in front of me, his tall frame towering over me. I have to tilt my head back so I can see his face, the move bringing our lips within inches of each other.

"You're killing me, you know," Cam murmurs, his eyes roaming over my face, the brown flecks of his irises holding me captive. "I can't tell if you like me or if you seriously think we're just friends. There's no way you don't feel this tension between us, right?" He lifts my hand, placing it on his chest so I can feel his heart hammering against his rib cage. "Do you feel what you do to me?" As though the racing of his heart beneath my palm isn't enough, he rests his hand on my hip, the pads of his fingers pressing into my skin as he grinds his hard cock against my thigh. The action has my chest heaving, heat coiling in my lower abdomen. "Do I do the same to you?"

My mouth is too dry, my head too fuzzy, my senses intoxicated with his apple and lotus scent. I can't think past the feel of his hard body pressed against mine, his dick grinding so close to where I need him most. He places his palm over my chest, as though needing to feel for himself just how badly he affects me, before slowly sliding it up until his thumb rests over the pulse in my neck, likely feeling it thumping beneath his fingertip.

His eyes dart between my eyes and my lips as I watch him intently, waiting on tenterhooks to see what his next move is. I can no longer deny that I *need* to know what his lips feel like pressed against mine. That voice in my head, telling me this is a bad idea, that it's a line I shouldn't cross, is barely more than a whisper at this point.

I see it when he makes his decision, his hand sliding around the back of my neck, his thumb pressed against the underside of my chin, tilting my head as his lips brush over mine in a barely there kiss, testing the waters.

I gasp at the contact, that small touch affecting me more than any kiss has before. Our lips meet again, more firmly this time, his tongue flicking out to run along my lower lip. Opening beneath him, his tongue dips into my mouth, gliding slowly over mine. Everything about him is unhurried, deliberate, like he's thought about this a thousand times, and now that it's happening, he's going to savor every moment.

He pushes his hips against mine, leaning over me, pressing me into the table until I'm perched on the edge. My fingers thread through his short, soft strands as I pull him harder against me, every lustful feeling I've been trying to ignore rising to the surface.

He wedges himself between my legs, his hands slipping up my bare thighs until they dip under my skirt, his fingers trailing along the lining of my panties. My hips tilt up, telling him exactly where I need him. I feel him smile lasciviously into the kiss, his hand dipping between my legs. His fingers graze along the front of my panties before his thumb presses on my bundle of nerves, making me gasp into his mouth.

"Mmm, baby, you're so damn wet for me."

Pushing my panties aside, he slides his fingers through my pussy lips, moving them inside me. I pull my lips from his, my head falling back as I moan, my fingers digging into his shoulders. He runs his lips down my neck as his fingers expertly slide in and out of me, curling so he hits that perfect spot every time.

It doesn't take long until I'm a panting mess beneath him. Just when I think I'm about to combust under his touch, he pulls out of me. I growl at the sudden emptiness, but he simply gives me a coy smirk as he spreads my legs further apart, getting to his knees in front of me. Fuck, staring down at him kneeling in front of me, it's breathtaking. I feel powerful, like a fucking goddess he's about to worship with his hot mouth.

He stares up at me, his tongue flicking out, circling my clit. "Holy hell," I breathe, bucking against him. I press my hands flat against the table behind me, leaning back as he flattens his tongue, pressing it firmly against my already sensitive bundle. I can feel the familiar coiling in my stomach as he pushes two fingers inside of me once again, this time setting a faster rhythm that his tongue easily meets.

"Cam," I moan, just as that coiling in my stomach explodes, fire coursing through my veins until my fingers and toes tingle with a tantalizing orgasm.

He laps up every drop before fixing my panties and pulling down my skirt, then leans over me to press his lips to mine. I can taste myself on him as he slides his tongue between my lips, entangling it with mine, our combined taste flooding my mouth.

"I knew you'd taste fucking delicious."

We don't hang around for long after that, quickly grabbing our things and heading out. As we reach the door, I glance back, checking that I didn't leave anything on the table, when a movement out of the corner of my eye grabs my attention. My heart skips a beat at the thought that Cam just went down on me and someone was around to hear it. However, when I glance toward the movement, my breath catches in my throat, my eyes widening as they meet West's. It would be impossible to miss his heated stare or the hard-on in his pants as his gaze holds me frozen in place. Something passes between us. It's nothing like the usual calmness I feel in his presence. It's hot and energetic, palpable in the air between us. Before I can think too much about it, Cam calls my name, breaking the moment between us. Pulling my gaze from him, my mind is a jumbled mess of questions as I distractedly follow Cam outside.

~

THE NEXT NIGHT, I'm in Emilia's room as she gets ready to go on a date with Andrew. He asked her out last weekend and she's been talking non-stop about it since.

"What's going on with you and Cam?" she blurts out, her gaze focused on the mirror as she does her makeup.

"What do you mean?"

Turning to look at me, she lifts an eyebrow, silently saying, *are you serious?*

"Nothing." I shrug, ignoring the tingling between my legs from our library session yesterday. That was so fucking hot, and I'm more than ready for round two.

"Look," she sighs, turning around to give me a serious look, "I'm only bringing it up because the others have noticed, and, well, they're worried."

With furrowed brows, I ask, "Why?"

"Because we make a point of staying out of their way, of keeping our heads down and getting on with the workload. It's an unwritten rule that if we don't get in their way, then they won't make life difficult for us. But you're breaking all the rules."

"I..." I begin, not even sure how I was going to argue with that. She cuts me off anyway by raising an eyebrow.

"He's been hitting on you since the first day, and now you're telling us that you're friends? Except the Princes don't do friends, and Cam definitely doesn't do friends with girls."

My silence says everything to her. I never told her about my late-night chats with Cam, but I should have said something based on the hurt in her eyes. I tried to bring it up a time or two, but I couldn't get the words past my lips every time. I'm not used to having a girlfriend or talking about this stuff. It's not natural for me to simply tell other people about my private life.

"I'm sorry," I murmur, guilt hitting me hard.

She waves me away, finishing up with her makeup and coming to sit beside me on the bed. "It's fine. Forget about it. I know you're a private person. I copped on pretty quickly that you don't like to talk about yourself. Do I wish you felt like you could have told me? Hell yes! Although I can't be pissed at you just because it's not in your nature to share things. Now, how do I look?"

She jumps up, twirling in front of me, her purple skirt spinning out. In cute ankle boots and a leather jacket, she looks gorgeous.

"Andrew's brain is going to short-circuit as soon as he sees you." I laugh, making her grin wider.

Shortly after that, she leaves for her date, and I head out to the gym to work out my frustrations, running myself ragged before calling it a night. Flicking off the light switch, I exit the gym, finally feeling relaxed for the first time all day. How come it takes me being so physically exhausted, I can barely walk or think straight to feel at ease?

I'm slowly wandering up the path toward the dormitories when movement out of the corner of my eye catches my attention. It's well after midnight, so no one else should be out here. Hell, I shouldn't even be out here right now.

The lights along the path turn off at midnight—some sort of stupid notion that students are unlikely to stay out until all hours of the night if there are no lights on the path—so it's pitch-black out, but I can see the faint shadow of people moving amongst the trees.

Pausing, I stop and watch, seeing silhouettes flitter amongst the tree line as students, in pairs or individually, slip into the forest. Confused about where they could be going, I stand stock still in the middle of the darkened path until I don't see any more movement. I abandon my plan of heading back to my room and instead make a beeline to where the other students disappeared amongst the trees, curiosity getting the better of me.

Reaching them, I slip into the forest, moving carefully over the uneven terrain. What the hell are people doing out here in the middle of the night? Most parties are thrown in the dorms or down by the lake, and I hadn't heard anything about a party going on tonight.

I traipse through the dark, silent forest for several minutes before a noise up ahead draws my attention. Moving closer, light starts to filter through the trees, and I can hear people cheering. *Huh, maybe it is a party.*

A clearing opens up in front of me and I can see a crowd of boys forming a large circle in the middle of it. Someone has strategically placed flashlights amongst the crowd, providing an eerie glow and casting shadows that make the whole scene appear macabre.

Another roar goes up from the crowd, and, peering through the bodies, I can just about make out two boys in the middle of the circle. Both of them are topless and covered in sweat as one helps the other to his feet. One kid has a cut above his eyebrow, and if I squint, I think I can make out bloody knuckles. *Is this some sort of amateur fight club? How rich kid of them.*

The cheers from the crowd die down as Hawk raises his hand in the air. For the first time, I notice the four of them standing at the far end of the circle. I don't know how I missed them initially. They somehow tower over the other students, their demanding presence and steely aura drawing everyone's attention.

Mason strides forward into the makeshift ring in only a pair of boxing shorts. His head is held high, confidence oozing from every step. And why shouldn't he be confident? He's by far the largest guy in our year. He could snap some of the scrawnier ones in half without breaking a sweat. No one immediately steps forward to challenge him, and as he surveys the crowd, some of them even take a step back.

"Don't make me pick one of you pussies," he bellows.

After another tense moment of silence, someone steps forward. I can't make out who it is, but as the lights glance off his face, I am able to get a clearer look.

Deke. Of course, it is. After the verbal beatdown West gave him at the party, I bet he's been waiting for this opportunity to get some payback.

A cruel smirk cuts across Mason's face as he cracks his knuckles, making it clear he's going to enjoy destroying him.

Tearing his shirt over his head and piercing Mason with his own dark look, Deke flexes his muscles, widening his stance and preparing to face off against the muscle machine that is Mason. With both of them crouched low, ready to pounce, they stand and glower at one another, waiting for some sort of signal. After a tense moment, Cam barks out, "Go," and the two launch themselves at each other.

Deke is all pent-up anger and aggression, his hits sloppy as he attempts to pummel Mason, who, in stark contrast, delivers punishing blows to Deke's midsection as he ensures every hit counts. It's painfully obvious that Mason is the fighter of the two. His punches are well-aimed and intended to inflict pain, whereas Deke is just punching whatever part of Mason is closest to him. There's no skill or tact in his movements, no forethought to his hits. It's an unexciting match that quickly ends with Deke lying on the floor, barely moving. I scan my eyes over the other kids in the throng and quickly deduce that none of them would make for an enthralling fight, except maybe Mason and Hawk. I'd quite happily watch Mason beat the crap out of Hawk. Give me a seat and a cold can of coke, and I'll watch that shit all day.

A couple of other football players step forward to help a groaning, half-unconscious Deke to his feet while Cam claps Mason on the back, a dark grin on his face. Glancing at the other Pricks, I notice all of them are wearing matching sinister expressions, only made more terrifying by the half-light of the flashlights. Not wanting to hang around and risk getting caught, I slip into the darkness of the surrounding forest. Silently making my way back to the dorms, I replay what I just saw in my head, unable to forget the sadistic looks on all of their faces.

Baby Davenport

CHAPTER THIRTEEN

Storming back into the apartment, I slam the door behind me. Senior year is supposed to be *the* year, but mine is going to shit faster than I can blink. It's bad enough that I found out my parents aren't who I thought they were, but now I have some new girl who's shown up, defying me at every turn and messing with Cam's head. Why the fuck won't she just bow down to us? Every other girl here either worships the ground we walk on or is too afraid to come near us. Why the fuck can't she just fall into one of those categories?

Striding over to the fridge, I lift out a beer, twisting off the lid and bringing the cool bottle to my lips, my eyes drifting shut as I gulp down half of it. *If only alcohol was the answer to all of my problems.*

Finishing off the beer, I dump the bottle in the trash, striding across the living space to the bedrooms. I seriously need to wash this day off me or fuck it out of me. Maybe I'll stop by Tina's tonight. God knows, she and the last girl of the month have been taking the brunt of my anger.

Walking past Cam's door, the creak of a floorboard from within his room halts my steps, and I eye the closed door with confusion. I didn't think any of the guys were back yet, and Cam is usually the first one out of his room when anyone comes home.

Cautiously, I wrap my hand around the handle, slowly turning it. My muscles are tense, my body on alert and ready to confront whatever I'll find on the other side of the door. As it silently swings open, my eyes widen in surprise as an annoyed-looking Hadley is revealed, standing boldly in the middle of Cam's room.

"What the fuck are you doing?" I bark out, quickly scanning my eyes around the space and trying to determine if anything is out of order before returning my glare to her. Cam's room is such a mess, it's impossible to tell what she was doing in here. Her spine straightens as she grinds her jaw, returning my glare, like I'm the one in the fucking wrong here. Where the hell does this girl get off thinking she can do whatever the fuck she wants?

"Cam accidentally lifted my notebook the other day. He said I could stop by." The words come out confidently. No hesitation or stumbling, and she maintains direct eye contact. She's certainly not acting like someone caught in a lie.

"And you just thought you'd show up when none of us were here?" I question. "How did you even get in?" Despite her nonchalance, nothing is adding up here.

"You must have left your door unlocked." She shrugs. "I called out, but no one answered. I figured it would be on his desk or something and it would be no big deal, although I can't seem to find it."

I narrow my eyes on her, flicking them toward his desk, but I don't see anything that either corroborates or contradicts her story. Regardless, I don't fucking believe a word she's saying. I honestly can't put my finger on it, but something about her rubs me the wrong way. I just don't like her snarky personality or her shitty temper. She's constantly glowering at one of us, never giving us the fucking respect we deserve. The only person she seems to halfway like is Cam, which really just makes her seem more suspect. Not because she likes Cam; he is the most likable one out of us all, even though he's still as much of a dick as the rest of us. Yet she overlooks that quality in him while berating the rest of us. It makes no sense.

"What's your angle?" I ask, unable to figure her out.

"Huh? What do you mean?" Her eyebrows are scrunched together in confusion, but I don't miss the spark of...something in her eyes. Knowledge, maybe? I'm not sure.

"I don't know what you're after, but Cam's not stupid, and you sure as hell don't want to cross any of us." I pin her with a fearsome glare. One I learned from my father, which I *know* have made grown men shit their pants and run off to do whatever is needed. "Some scholarship kid like you?" I sneer, dropping my gaze to take in her unimpressive appearance. "We'll fucking destroy you." I expect to see fear and shock in her eyes. It's the typical response. Instead, I'm met with a steely resolve, a sly smirk lifting the corner of her lips.

What the fuck? What is wrong with this girl?

She takes several slow, deliberate steps toward me until we're only inches apart. Pressing up onto her toes, closing the height difference between us—not that it does much good, I'm still nearly a foot taller than her—she glares right back at me. "I'd love to see you try," she retorts confidently, my steely gaze and dark tone not affecting her. She fearlessly pats me on the shoulder, her arm brushing mine as she steps around me and strides out of the room. By the time I've worked out what the fuck just happened, she's long gone from the apartment.

I'm pacing back and forth across the open living space when the others come in. After she left, I had a good look around Cam's room, but nothing was out of place and I couldn't find anything obvious that was missing.

"Dude, what is eating you?" Cam chuckles as he collapses onto the leather sofa. West eyes me warily as he lowers himself into an armchair, bringing his leg up, crossing his ankle over his knee. Unlike Cam, he's much more refined. His movements are carefully thought out instead of slumping into his chair in a boneless heap.

I stop my pacing as Mason joins us, facing all three of them as I tell them about Hadley.

"I'm telling you, I don't trust her," I growl, getting annoyed that none of them seem to think her intruding on our space is a big deal. Cam just shrugged me off when I told him I found her in his room.

"She was just getting her notebook," he says easily. "She told me she'd be stopping by."

"She wasn't looking for any notebook," I snap. He wasn't there. He didn't see the look in her eye, hear the defiance in her tone. I might not know for sure that she was up to something but call it gut instinct. She was too calm, too confident, considering I'd just caught her red fucking handed. An innocent person would have shown a healthy dose of fear at being seen—not that any other Pac student is stupid enough to even think about coming into our personal space. "She was searching for something."

"Searching for what, man?" Cam sighs. "Unless she wanted condoms or something from my porn stash, there's nothing to find in my room."

I throw an exasperated look toward the other two, needing some sort of backup here. One of them has to be on the same page as me. They at least appear to be thinking over what I've told them, even if they aren't as angry about the whole thing as they should be.

"She said we left the door unlocked?" Mason questions, his brows furrowed, deep in thought.

"Yeah," I nod, "except there's no way any of us would do that."

West nods in agreement, remaining silent as he processes everything.

"I wouldn't," Mason agrees.

"Same," West concurs.

All three of us look in Cam's direction.

"I don't know," he moans. "I mean, maybe. I might have been distracted when I left this morning. It's possible I forgot to lock up."

"Dude, what the hell?" Mason grouches, throwing his hands up in frustration, pinning Cam with an angry stare.

"Say she *was* searching for something," West pipes up, playing devil's advocate. "What would she expect to find in Cam's room?"

Fuck. "I don't know," I grumble. This is the problem. She's up to something, and I fucking know it, only I don't know what she's up to or why.

"See," Cam states, waving his hand in my direction.

"She's a scholarship student. She could be after money or anything," I spit back, scrambling to think of some reason she could have been in his room.

Cam raises his eyebrows at me, giving me a *'are you fucking serious'* look. "She wouldn't risk her scholarship for some petty cash, and there are definitely easier students she could target than one of us," he reasons.

"I'm just saying, it couldn't do any harm to at least keep an eye on her," I say, pointedly looking at Mason and West to back me up in this since Cam's clearly thinking with the wrong head right now.

"Dude, you haven't liked her since she crossed you in the hallway." Cam sighs wearily, visibly done with the conversation. "Just let it go."

"I mean, it couldn't hurt," West points out, backing me and earning a glare from Cam. "If nothing comes of it, we'll leave her alone, and you can do whatever you want with her."

Cam sighs, rubbing his hand over his face. "Look, man," he says wearily, leaning forward in his seat, fixing me with a serious expression, "you're under a lot of stress right now. We've got a lot going on. It makes sense that you're looking for someone to offload all your issues onto, but, man, it can't be her. I actually like this chick."

With a heavy sigh, I run a hand through my hair, tugging on the ends in frustration. "If she's got nothing to hide, then it won't matter," I reason, piercing him with a deadpan stare until he concedes.

"Fine," he growls. "Honestly, though, I think you just need to get over it."

"I don't trust her," I grumble, repeating myself for the umpteenth time. "And she's got anger issues."

"So?" Cam snorts, looking at me like I'm crazy. "So do you."

"Man, she's basically the vagina version of you." Mason chuckles.

"Pfft, no, she's not. She's got no respect, and she shits a fucking brick over the slightest thing."

Mason raises an eyebrow in a *'are you for real?'* gesture, only annoying me further.

"And she's always got a smart remark."

"Again, so do you." Cam rolls his eyes, but the corner of his lip lifts in a small smile, his annoyance over our conversation fading.

Sighing heavily, I drop into an empty chair. "I just don't like her," I grouse. I might be able to talk Mason and West into being wary around her, but I will need something more to make Cam see her for who she truly is.

Letting out a bark of laughter, Cam retorts, "You don't like anyone."

～

THE SCHOOL THROWS a Halloween party every year. It's usually a complete bore, only the freshmen enjoying themselves while the rest of us make a quick appearance before heading to the lake to get started on the after-party.

The campus has been abuzz with excited chatter all week. All anyone can talk about is their costumes for tonight.

"I don't understand why we can't do a couple's costume," Tina whines that morning at breakfast. It's the gazillionth time she's brought it up this week. You'd think my adamant refusal the first few times would have made it clear to her, but apparently not.

"Tough," I growl. How do these girls not understand that just because we're fucking them, it doesn't make us a fucking couple? It's sex and a tradition we're forced by legacy to obey. I'm all for the anytime hook-up. It's great not having to put any effort into flirting with a girl or spending all night laying on the charm so she'll let you into her pants. Knowing I can just turn up at Tina's door any hour of the day or night and fuck her until I've exhausted my frustrations is perfect, especially with the amount of rage constantly coursing through me these days. It's saved more than a few asshole kids from having the shit beat out of them for pissing me off.

Nevertheless, dealing with the girls' whining is fucking exhausting. Thank fuck we get to switch them out every month. By the time they settle into their role and build up the confidence to get even more annoying, it's nearly time to move on to the next girl.

Tonight we'll have to spend time with the girls as part of the tradition, but that doesn't mean we have to wear whatever costumes they want or arrive with them. They get to be seen hanging out with us, and usually, they get to leave with us. But that's it. Besides, I've something else planned for tonight, something much more important than some stupid costume.

The day passes in a blur, everyone too distracted to focus on classes. That night, when the party is in full swing, we throw open the doors to the dining hall, all eyes falling on us. Cam is standing on my right, wearing nothing more than a pair of tight swimming trunks and flip-flops, with a plastic Olympic medal swinging from his neck. He's some famous Olympic swimmer.

Wearing all black and a trench coat and boots, I'm dressed as Neo from The Matrix, deciding to go old-school with my costume this year. When I was a kid, one of my nannies was obsessed with Keanu Reeves. I don't remember how many times I sat and watched The Matrix with her when I should have been in bed, asleep.

Beside me, West is dressed in a fancy suit with a weird ass hat on his head. I honestly have no idea who he's supposed to be. He tried explaining it to us, but it still made no sense.

On the other side of him, Mason is dressed in his usual casual attire of a muscle top, gray sweats, and a blank expression, dressed up as himself seemingly.

Scanning my eyes around the room, I take in the tacky orange and black balloons and the fake cobwebs strung up around the lights and windows. All the tables have been removed, opening up the space for students to dance, the buffet table overflowing with trays of Halloween-themed food and bowls of blood-red punch. There are students dressed in all sorts of weird and slutty costumes, dancing to the music on a makeshift dance floor, or congregating in groups around the outskirts of the room.

Each of our girls of the month pushes their way through the gaping crowd. Tina comes to latch onto my arm, a seductive smile curling her lip as her eyes roam over my outfit. She's dressed as a slutty nurse or something. Honestly, all I really notice are her pushed-up tits that are practically falling out of the white tube top she's wearing. Hell yeah, I'm so ready to watch them bouncing up and down while I fuck her brains out.

"Mmm, baby, you look so good," she purrs, running her hand down the front of my shirt. "Why don't we start this party off right?" She bites down on her lower lip, a coy look in her eye as her hand grazes across the front of my pants, giving my balls a squeeze. *Fuck yes!* Checking my watch, I've got some time before they announce 'best costume' and the real fun can begin.

Giving her a dirty grin, I let her drag me back out the door and around to the back of the building.

An hour later, the music cuts off as Mr. Phister calls the room to attention, a microphone and envelope in his hand.

"Alright," he calls out. "I hope you've all had fun tonight, but now it's time to find out which lucky student has won this year's 'best costume'. The winner will get to choose the theme for the Valentine's Day dance and head up the party planning committee."

I roll my eyes. Who gives a fuck about picking the theme or standing over a bunch of other students, making sure they pick streamers instead of balloons, or that the color they choose for the tablecloths is right?

Before Mr. Phister can announce the winner, I shove Tina off my arm, striding through the crowd, ignoring the confused looks on the other guys' faces.

Strolling up beside the headmaster, I say, "If you don't mind, Thomas, I'll take it from here," loud enough for the surrounding students to hear us as I take the microphone and envelope from him.

He gapes at me with wide eyes for a second before giving a hesitant, sharp nod, scurrying off to the side as I face the crowd, a cruel smirk on my face.

"Let's find out this year's winner then," I announce into the microphone, opening the envelope and glancing at the name printed on the page. "And the winner is...Abigail Cole."

I keep that same grin on my face as the crowd breaks into hushed whispers, everyone looking around them in confusion. A quick glance around the room is enough to know how much some of these kids spent on their costumes, and let me tell you, the scholarship students never win. They don't stand a chance, so the fact one of them has just won is unheard of.

The students near the scholarship kids all seem to take several steps back, a gap opening up around them as they all look at each other with confused and wary gazes.

"Don't be shy now, Abigail. Up you come." I wave her up onto the stage and, with one final wide-eyed look at her friends, she takes a hesitant step forward. Then another, clearly seeing that she has no other option but to come up here. *Good girl. It would have been worse for you if I had to come and get you.*

When she's finally standing beside me, an anxious look in her wide eyes that speaks right to me, feeding the inner part of me that lives off her fear, I wrap my arm around her shoulder, preventing her from running off. The poor thing looks like she's about to faint; she'll definitely bolt at the first opportunity if I don't stop her.

"Well, what do we think of Abigail's costume?" I ask the crowd. "Is it worthy of a win?" More whispered murmurs, and a few people shaking their heads, but no one speaks out to confirm or deny.

"I don't think so," I answer my own question, glancing over her thrown-together outfit. I don't even know what the fuck she's supposed to be, although at least she made an effort, unlike Hadley. I spotted her earlier, dressed in her usual attire of worn jeans, a baggy top, and boots, having made no effort for tonight.

"I don't think scholarship students should be allowed to enter at all," I continue, speaking into the microphone. "Don't we give them enough? They are already getting an education that *our* families are paying for, with *our* hard-earned money." My fingers dig into Abigail's skin, holding her in place as she subtly tries to shake off my grip and escape. "They shouldn't be given the opportunity to steal what is rightfully ours by birthright. They should cower in our presence, thank us for simply letting them walk these halls with us."

The murmurings are louder now, more than a few students nodding their heads in agreement. Whether they actually agree or they're just too afraid to disagree with me, I don't really give a fuck.

Pushing the girl away from me, she stumbles, scurrying through the crowd as tears run down her face, not stopping until she crashes into some guy's arms.

"Take this as a warning," I say, my steely gaze intent on the group of scholarship students. "If you mess with us, you *will* get burned." I stare at Hadley, making it clear to her that this is all her fault. This show is for her benefit, so she better heed my warning.

Hadley

CHAPTER FOURTEEN

"That was all because of you," Abigail cries, whirling on me. Her makeup is smeared, black tracks from her mascara running down her face as Todd hugs her against him. The others are standing in a semi-circle around them, all wearing tight expressions as they look at me.

"Me? That wasn't...I didn't..." I trail off, not knowing what to say.

She shakes her head, not wanting to hear my excuses.

"No. Everything was fine before you showed up. They left us alone." She sobs against Todd's chest. There's an unfamiliar tightness in my chest, guilt eating at me as I watch her fall apart. "As long as you continue to piss them off, just stay away from me."

She buries her face in Todd's chest and he wraps his arm more tightly around her, throwing a glower my way before whispering in her ear, the two of them walking off toward the dorm.

"She's right," Samuel speaks up, drawing my attention his way. "I think I speak for all of us when I say, stay away from us. All of us." Everyone but Emilia nods in agreement. Even Michael gives a hesitant jerk of his head, his lips pursed.

My eyes fall on Emilia as the others give me a final, stern look before turning their backs and walking off. Emilia's the only one who looks at me with sympathy and pain, but she doesn't say anything, looking torn between staying with me and following the others.

"Emilia, are you coming with us?" Samuel calls out.

"I told you they weren't worth messing with." Her voice is choked, tears gleaming in her eyes as she gives me a final empathetic look, her face pinched before turning on her heel and walking over to the others.

A sea of emotions flows through me as I silently watch them leave; rage, pain, and sadness swirl around like a tornado inside my gut. I'm torn between going after them and apologizing, and storming back into that hall and eviscerating Hawk. Did the others know what he was going to do? I didn't see their faces, too enraptured by the show of devastation Hawk was putting on for everyone.

Closing my eyes, I release a deep breath, weariness creeping into my bones.

"Are you okay?" Cam's soft tone only heightens the exhaustion. How did everything get so complicated? Coming here was supposed to make my life better. It should have been easy.

Turning around, I slowly take him in, trying to read from his face if he was involved in tonight's fiasco.

"What the fuck was that in there?" I sigh, waving toward the dining hall.

His lips are pressed tightly together as he gives a quick shake of his head, a gesture that doesn't tell me anything.

"He was pissed about finding you in the apartment."

For real? What right does that give him to do what he did?

I stare at him incredulously for a moment, not understanding him at all.

"So he took it out on Abigail? She never did anything to him!" My voice rises as anger sparks within me. "She didn't deserve what he did to her tonight. None of them did."

"I know." Everything about him is too calm, too at odds with the raging storm within me.

"But you never stopped him."

He shakes his head again, his shoulders dropping. "We didn't know he was going to do that."

My eyes narrow as I scrutinize him, carefully trying to suss out whether he's telling the truth. His open expression, uncrossed arms, and steady eye contact say he's not, although just because he didn't know about it doesn't mean he won't have Hawk's back if he goes after the others to settle his score with me.

He's got my head all twisted, trying to work out where he stands. It's too much. I can't handle any more tonight.

I shake my head. "I've gotta go."

The words are barely out of my mouth before he moves forward as though to stop me, but I quickly raise my hand. "Don't. Please. It's been a long night, I just wanna go to bed."

With a pained expression on his face, he gives a sharp nod and I turn on my heel, my gut swirling with upheaval as I walk back to my room, regretting ever leaving it tonight.

I toss and turn all night, sleep evading me. Any time I make it over into a semi-sleep, it's filled with nightmares. Hawk's face combined with *their* voices. I wake up in a cold sweat every time, my heart racing. In the early pre-dawn hours, I give up on sleep entirely and decide today I'll have to function off coffee alone. At least no one will be in the dining hall this early so I can avoid the judgmental looks and whispers from the other students and the awkward glares from the friends I had there for a little while.

Pushing the door open and stepping into the hall, I cast a quick scan around the room, expecting it to be empty, only I pull up short when I see West sitting at his usual table, alone. Why is one of those assholes always in here? They have that fancy-ass apartment with a kitchen and everything; they don't even need to fucking be here. Can't a girl catch a break for once?

Ignoring him, I make myself a coffee and order some breakfast. I hesitate as I glance over the tables, however. I'm probably not welcome at the scholarship table anymore, but I'm pretty sure I wouldn't be accepted at any of the others, either. Deciding it's not an issue for today—I'll be long gone before anyone wakes up and takes offense to my seating arrangements—I stroll over to my regular table and sit down.

My ass has barely hit the seat when West gets up from his chair. Instead of heading for the door like I was hoping, he comes toward me, sitting in the chair opposite mine.

"What do you want, Wes?" I sigh, not mentally fortified yet to get into an argument with him. Could he not have let me get caffeine in my system first?!

"Hawk said he found you in Cam's room the other day."

My eyes immediately snap up to him, narrowing in suspicion. Cam indicated as much last night—not that I'm surprised Hawk told the others.

"What were you doing?"

His tone is more curious than accusatory, which is the only reason I engage him.

"As I explained to Hawk, I was looking for my notebook. Cam must have accidentally lifted it. The door was unlocked, so I figured it wouldn't be a problem, but clearly, I was wrong. Next time I'll just leave it."

"Next time?" His brows pull together in confusion. "What exactly is going on between you and Cam?"

"Nothing," I insist, trying really hard not to think about what he did to me on that library table. But then I remember...West was watching us. My cheeks heat at the memory.

"You know, Cam is only interested in girls until he gets what he wants, then he drops them like yesterday's trash."

"Careful, *Wes*, you're sounding awfully jealous."

"Please." He snorts, his gaze not quite meeting my eye. "I'm not. I'm just letting you know how it is with him."

"Well, consider me warned."

He eyes me up for a moment before nodding.

"About last night..." He trails off, silence filling the space between us as he finds his words. "Hawk shouldn't have done what he did."

"Nonetheless, you're going to have his back anyway." I sigh. I can see it in his eyes. I don't even need him to confirm it.

"We're a team," he justifies. Something that I just don't understand. I'm more of a lone wolf myself. I play the game by my own rules, never answering or relying on anyone else.

After breakfast, I pull up my big girl panties and knock on Emilia's door, not happy with how we left things last night. She was the first person here to be kind to me, and she's been an amazing friend. I don't want to see that end the way it did last night.

I can hear her shuffling around in her room before the door creaks open a crack, revealing a still half-asleep Emilia in her bunny rabbit pajamas and fluffy slippers.

Her eyes widen as she looks at me. "Oh, hey," she says awkwardly, none of her usual morning loveable grumpiness to be seen.

Licking my lips, unable to stop myself from fidgeting with the hem of my top, I say, "I was, uh, hoping we could talk...about last night?"

She cringes, breaking eye contact with me. "I don't think there's anything to talk about," she mumbles, staring pointedly at her feet.

"Seriously? You don't think we need to discuss what happened?" I know she and the others are pissed at me, and I get that, but it's not like I *knew* Hawk would do that. If I'd known...

"Hadley." Her voice is strained, emotion heavy in that one word. "None of us can risk having the Princes, or anyone else in the school, ganging up on us. We just want to get through the year without any issues. I...I'm sorry, but we can't afford to gamble with our futures."

Before I can argue further, she closes the door in my face, the click of the lock engaging like a death knell on our short-lived friendship.

With a heavy heart, I let myself back into my room, anger and agitation making it impossible to sit still or focus on schoolwork. Glancing at the clock, I see it's still early morning, so I grab my gym bag and head back out. I wasn't feeling it when I first got up, but maybe a physically exhausting workout is exactly what I need to stop my obsessing over everything.

Over the next hour, I pummel the shit out of the heavy bag, my arms exhausted and my hands aching by the time I switch over to the treadmill, setting a fast pace so all I can focus on is putting one foot in front of the other. Mason entered the gym not long after I did, but he at least had the decency to stick to our silent agreement of not talking. He went straight over to the weights corner and has barely spared me a glance since.

The sweat runs into my eyes, and I wipe it away with the towel, faintly aware of the sound of Mason putting the bar back on the rack. Instead of starting his next round of pull-ups like he's supposed to, he crosses the floor toward me. It's clear he's got questions on his mind, and he looks determined as hell to get answers. His whole appearance gets my back straight and I'm immediately on alert as he stops in front of me.

"What's your deal?"

Not slowing my pace, I glare at him. "What's yours?"

The wankstain ignores me, his eyes narrowing as he tries to figure me out. I'm pretty sure it's something he's been trying to do since that day in business class. He hasn't managed it so far, so I doubt he's suddenly going to piece me together now.

Ignoring me, he runs his eyes over me, taking in the loose t-shirt sticking to my sweaty skin and my tight shorts. His gaze lingers on the flexing muscles of my thighs as I maintain my fast pace.

Returning his gaze to my eyes, he cocks his head.

"Poor parents?"

I don't give him anything, my face a blank slate.

"Absent parents, then?"

Still, I give him nothing, but my silence seems to be enough of an answer itself.

His eyes narrow and I can see the cogs turning in his head.

"Foster parents?"

I make sure my face remains a rigid mask, no part of me giving away any indication of who I am or where I come from to this probing asshole.

Yet, with his lips pinched, he nods his head.

"So that's why you're here? You're escaping a shitty foster home?"

How the fuck does he know any of that? I *know* my features are unreadable.

Slamming my hand down on the stop button, I hiss out, "What the fuck do you want?"

"I want to know what you're doing with Cam." His voice is steady, but there's a slight rumbling in his chest, giving away the fact he's not as indifferent as he's making himself out to be.

"What is everyone's obsession with Cam?" I snarl, jumping off the treadmill. "He's a big boy, he can look after himself." I run the towel over my face and the back of my neck, pushing past Mason to get to my bag. "I highly doubt you all take such a keen interest in every other girl he chases after, so why me?"

"Because," he growls, his hand snatching out, his fingers wrapping firmly around my arm as he pulls me back toward him, "there's something different about you."

I stare up at him in confusion, taking in his beautiful baby blues that are swirling with just as much chaos as I feel. What the hell does he mean by that?

∼

THAT AFTERNOON, Cam has a swim meet, and like the lovesick idiot I am, I show up. I am hiding at the back so he, and anyone else, can't see me. I'm not ready yet to face the backlash from the rest of the school. I just want to be left in peace to see that light Cam had in his eyes when he talked about swimming. I've never felt the kind of passion for anything that he has for this sport. I guess I'm curious what it's all about.

I can feel the vigor in the air as soon as I enter the room, the stench of chlorine combined with the buzz of excitement and nervous energy. Watching him in the water, he's like an art form come to life. He's captivating; mesmerizing to watch. I can't tear my eyes away from him. I'm not even aware that he's won—hell, I don't even register the others in the water—until someone claps him on the back.

The second his race is over, I slip away, wandering around the empty hallways until I find the entrance to the changing rooms. I'm not sure what I'm doing here or what I'm hoping to achieve. It's like I'm a puppet being pulled on by a string, some greater force leading me to this moment. Only I'm not sure what I'm supposed to do next.

Baby

CHAPTER FIFTEEN

"*R*utherfords are winners. You better not let me down out there today," my asshole of a father reminds me once again before stalking off, leaving me to warm up beside the pool. Like I don't fucking know already that Rutherfords don't lose. He's always been a belligerent asshole, except he's gotten worse in the last few months. I have no idea what's going on with him, but he's fucking unbearable, and that's saying something since I could barely tolerate his presence before.

Thank fuck, I hardly have to put up with him, except at these stupid competitions. It's almost enough of a reason to quit, but swimming is the only release I have, other than sex. Not that I'm getting much of that lately.

Since Hadley showed up, my dick has been on the fritz. I mean, I get it. She's hot as sin, and that mouth...Fuck, I can picture her doing so many things with that mouth. Not only is she hot, but her feisty attitude and how she talks back are apparently my thing. Who knew? I hadn't realized how fucking bored I was with girls willing to do anything we wanted. None of the rest has any backbone. They are too terrified to stand up to us, or too eager to suck their way to the top that they just don't care. Either way, I was bored out of my fucking mind, and I didn't even know it. Not until Hadley showed up and made me realize what I've been missing out on. The feisty blonde with combat boots and a snarky mouth is a hot little challenge I didn't know I needed in my life. Things have been so much more interesting around here since she arrived.

Just my luck though, that Hawk has gotten himself in a fucking tizzy over her. I don't think it's because he's attracted to her, although sometimes it's seriously hard to tell with him. I swear I've caught him fucking girls before and, honestly, it's impossible to tell if he's actually enjoying himself or hate fucking them.

When it's time for my race, I step up to the side of the pool, curling my toes around the edge of the concrete. I cast my eyes out over the crowd, quickly skimming over my father's sinister presence, spotting the guys cheering me on, like they always do on competition days. My eyes continue to search the stands, looking for a particular blonde. It's stupid. I know she won't be here, especially not after last night. Why would she be? I'm not even sure why I want her to be here. That's like girlfriend territory. Not something I do. Ever.

Yet, I can't ignore the disappointment I feel when I don't see her. Shaking off the feeling, I focus back on the water. Arching my body into the perfect dive pose, I steady my heart rate, focusing every one of my senses on the race in front of me, preparing myself for the loud blast of the whistle.

When it finally sounds, I push off with my feet, smoothly plunging into the pool. I've spent years honing my body, turning it into a machine that can move effortlessly through the water, barely causing a ripple. Kicking with my feet, I travel half the pool underwater before finally emerging. Gulping down a lungful of air, I skillfully glide through the water, propelling myself forward with my arms.

As I approach the far end of the pool, I duck under the water, tucking my head and flipping myself around to face the direction I just came from. Kicking off from the side of the pool, I speed back to the far end. Quickly traversing the distance, my hand slams down on the concrete as cheers ring out from the crowd in the stands.

Glancing back at the other competitors, I see I won by a decent bit, and, looking up at the timer, a large grin crosses my face as I fist-bump the air. I'm going to the State Championships baby, and that race was my best time yet. Hell yeah!

That should keep my father off my back.

Pulling myself out of the water, I shake hands with the surrounding coaches and other competitors, politely accepting their words of congratulations.

"Well done, son," my father praises, his hand squeezing my shoulder, his shitty attitude from earlier now gone, replaced with a proud smile, like my achievements somehow reflect positively on him. I know he's not actually proud of me. He couldn't give two shits about me or my accomplishments. He's barely present in my life except to dictate what I should and shouldn't be doing with it. Even growing up, he was barely around, and when he was, his mind was elsewhere. Who the fuck knows where, but it sure as hell wasn't at home with his family.

"Thanks, Dad," I respond, giving him a tight smile. Seeing the guys emerging through the crowd, I shake off my dad's hand. "I better go. The guys are waiting."

"Of course," he agrees, nodding his head, but he doesn't step aside to let me pass. Instead, he stares at me intently, his penetrating gaze seemingly seeing right through me. "Enjoy these last few months of freedom, son. You'll be graduating soon, and we need you to step up into the role we have set aside for each of you at the company." On that ominous note, he strides off, taking with him all of my joy from a moment ago.

As the guys approach, I plaster on a fake smile, accepting their congratulations before making my excuses to go shower.

∼

Turning off the hot water, I step into the locker room. I always wait until everyone else has left before showering off the chlorine. Sure, the post-race locker talk is invigorating, but I love this moment of quiet reflection after a competition, where I can replay every moment and analyze every second.

I'm running a towel through my hair when I hear the door open. Assuming one of the other guys has forgotten something, I don't bother to turn around, but when no one says anything, I glance over my shoulder, freezing when I see Hadley standing just inside the door.

Her eyes drop to take in my naked chest, the towel wrapped loosely around my waist, and she runs her tongue along her lower lip, her eyes becoming heated as she drinks me in. Fuck, seeing her turned-on like that is crazy hot. I don't know what it is about her, but she has my dick all tied up in knots. I barely even know her, yet something about her constantly draws me in.

Maybe the guys are right when they say I'm all about the chase. There's something thrilling about going after a girl, but the ones here give in too quickly. One wink in their direction, and they are practically ready to spread their legs for me. It's too easy. Hadley isn't anything like that. She's the perfect challenge. I know she wants me; nevertheless, the push-pull dynamic we've got going on is infectious. I can't get enough of it. Although it's more than just chasing after her. I can feel it. There's a hell of a lot of sexual chemistry between us, but there's also something more profound.

"What are you doing in here?" I ask, my voice husky. Her short skirt shows off her toned, milky thighs and her white shirt is clinging to her tits, sending all my blood due south. I couldn't talk my dick down even if I wanted to.

"You were great out there today," she murmurs, ignoring my question as she stares transfixed at my chest.

Her words catch me by surprise. I hadn't realized she was in the crowd. I didn't see her; honestly, I never expected her to be there. After Hawk's one-man show last night, I'm shocked she's even speaking to me.

"You were watching?"

She shrugs like it's no big deal; her gaze darting nervously around the room like she's embarrassed, but a seed of warmth sparks within me at the thought of her cheering me on from the stands. Sure, the guys always show up, and of course girls do too, but I've never actually wanted a girl there before. "Had to see what all the fuss was about."

I move quicker than I've ever moved before—which is saying something, considering how lean and agile I am from years of swim training. My lips crash down on hers, my hands wrapping around her waist, neither of us giving a shit that I'm getting her wet.

I've never felt so drawn to another person. It's like the shit in the movies where they have this undeniable chemistry. I never thought that crap was real, but there's no denying the pull she has over me, drawing me in like some sort of succubus.

Her tiny hands roam over my pecs, squeezing my shoulders and running down my back. Every part of me she touches lights up like a fucking Christmas tree, demanding more.

I shove her blazer over her shoulders and down her arms until it pools at her feet, reaching around to grab two handfuls of her ass cheeks and pulling her in against me as I grind my dick against her core. Groaning, she breaks our kiss, her head falling back as she arches into me, the movement exposing her neck. Her hands grip my shoulders and I dip my head, kissing and sucking as I use my grasp on her ass to lift her up, pressing her more firmly against the locker room door as she wraps her legs around me. I know I should take the time to strip her naked, lay her out and feast on her, but I'm too fucking desperate for her. I just need to be inside her. Next time, I'll make sure I lick every part of her before I have her screaming my name.

Using the heel of her weird-ass combat boots, she dislodges my towel, my dick springing free and immediately nestling itself between her spread thighs. Reaching between us, I run my finger up the front of her panties, groaning at how wet she is, loving her soft moans as she tilts her hips, increasing the friction of my finger and silently demanding more.

Giving her what she wants, I press down on her clit, rubbing tight circles until she's panting heavily. "Oh, Cam," she cries out, her grip on my shoulders almost painful as her fingernails dig into my skin. Slipping my fingers underneath her panties, I slide them through her pussy lips, sinking two fingers into her.

"Fuck," she moans, her hands sliding up into my hair, grabbing the strands and slamming her lips down on mine, using her grip on my hair to angle my head just how she wants it, her tongue sweeping deep into my mouth. My lips slide over hers, sucking her in further as my fingers pump in and out of her, the pace matching the clashing of our tongues. Her cunt clenches around me as her hand trails down the front of my chest, reaching between us until she's holding my cock in her hand.

She gently squeezes it, causing me to groan into her mouth as our kiss turns fierce, both of us getting lost in the passion. Her hand slides up and down my dick, providing the perfect amount of pressure. Fuck, most hand jobs are just meh, nothing to get excited about unless you're a pre-teen virgin, but holy hell, just the feel of her hand wrapped around me has my balls drawing up, that tingling feeling reverberating through me.

She tears her lips away from mine, her head falling back against the door. "Fuck, Cam, I'm going to come." Her eyes drift closed, her hand still pumping my dick as I circle my thumb over her clit and curl my fingers over that magical spot.

"Fuck. Fuck. FUCK," she cries, her pussy clamping down on my fingers, her juices dripping down my hand as she comes.

Pulling them out of her, I bring my fingers to my lips, sucking them into my mouth and groaning at her taste on my tongue. Her pupils are blown, and she watches transfixed as I lick her off me.

"Mmm, baby, you taste so good."

She licks her lips, her teeth digging into her bottom lip, her chest rapidly rising and falling with her heavy breaths.

"Cam," she breathes. "Condom." It's a husky demand, overflowing with hunger and carnal need.

"Yeah, baby," I agree, my lips meeting hers as I wrap my arms around her thighs, carrying her over to where I left my stuff. Dropping her to her feet beside my locker, I dig in my bag until I find a condom. She snatches it from between my fingers, tearing it open and rolling it down my dick before I've even comprehended what's happened. Damn, I love a girl who isn't afraid to go after what she wants.

Towering over her, my forearm leaning against the metal locker above her, I tuck my fingers under her chin, lifting it so she's looking up at me. I don't think I've ever wanted a girl more than I do in this moment. With raw lust in her eyes and heat on her cheeks, she looks fucking incredible. Dick-blowing. Literally.

My hand slides round the back of her neck, my lips descending on hers, loving that she can taste herself on me. She moans into my mouth, her tongue sparring with mine as we swiftly fall into that all-consuming heady sensation of being wrapped up with someone physically.

She lifts her leg, hitching it over my hip, the heel of her boot digging into my ass. Lifting my arm off the locker, I run it up her thigh, tucking her panties to the side before holding her leg securely in place as my cock stands at attention, aimed perfectly at her center.

Nudging at her opening, I slowly sink into her, our kiss breaking as we are both overcome by pleasure. My eyes drift shut, and I groan at the feel of her wrapped around me, her sweet heat like fucking ecstasy as I bottom out.

"I knew you'd feel fucking incredible," I breathe, my forehead pressed against hers.

Tilting her head, her lips brush over mine as I pull back. My hand clamps tighter around her thigh as I push into her again, savoring the feel of her clenching around me. Maintaining a slow pace, I thrust in and out. The tingling at the base of my dick spreads to my spine and I know I'm close to blowing my load, but I'm so not ready for this to be over yet. She feels far too fucking good.

Linking my fingers with hers, I pin her hand to the locker above her head. Holding her thigh in my large palm, I pick up my speed, ramming in and out of her, her soft moans of pleasure pushing me on as I bury my face in her neck, sucking and biting at the smooth skin.

I can feel her clenching around me, her soft cries letting me know she's close to coming. Inching my fingers up her thigh until I can feel her puckered hole, I dip lower, feeling my slick dick sliding in and out of her. Collecting some of her juices, I circle my finger around the rim of her hole, feeling her soft gasp against my cheek as she realizes what I'm doing.

I've barely pushed the tip of my finger inside her when she cries out, her walls slamming down around my dick in the best way, breaking through the last bit of resistance I had as I let go, grunting out her name as I go over the cliff with her, into orgasmic bliss.

We stay like that for a long moment after, both of us breathing heavily as we come back to reality. With my head still buried in her neck, I kiss her skin again, not wanting to leave this moment of contentment.

Eventually, though, she shuffles, and I have no choice but to lower her leg, pulling out of her. I keep the rest of my body flush with hers though, my hand wrapping itself in her hair.

"That was definitely not a one-time thing," I promise. "I'm nowhere near done with you."

∽

IT'S CHANGEOVER DAY AGAIN. I can't say I paid any attention to Missy last time, and why the fuck would I when I can be chasing someone like Hadley? And holy fuck, was she worth it! I knew it the second I slammed myself balls deep inside her—she's so much more than a simple fling. I don't know what the fuck she is or what it means, but I want to do it again and again.

That's why I've made my decision. Hawk's going to shit a brick, and West and Mason might be pissy about it, but I don't give a damn. It's the right thing to do.

The four of us stride into the dining hall, and all eyes turn our way, everyone following our every move as we make our way to our usual table. I hate that we have to eat here every morning. We have our own damn kitchen, yet we must come down here to appease the masses. It's a control thing, to remind the school who owns it, but I'd much rather have breakfast in our apartment every day, away from prying eyes.

After breakfast, all of us get to our feet. That buzz of excitement I felt the first month is back, and I can barely stand still as I wait for Hawk and Mason to take their turns. Mason again picks out a curly-haired blonde, and I cannot help but notice the similarities to Hadley. Is that just a coincidence? He barely knows Hadley. In fact, I don't think I've ever even seen him talk to her. Yeah, they've sat at the same table in the library once or twice, when the two of us have been working on our English assignment, and we all have business class together, but other than that, I don't think they ever cross paths, and he's never mentioned her before.

Realizing it's my turn, I shake myself out of that weird train of thought and circle around to the front of the table. Unlike the last two times, I don't make a whole song and dance out of the thing. I know what I want this month, and I'm not about to let another second pass without her.

Stepping into the middle of the room, I turn to face her, looking directly at her as I call out her name. "Hadley."

Hadley

CHAPTER SIXTEEN

"Hadley." That one word, my own goddamn name, obliterates the last shred of peace I had constructed for myself here at Pac Prep.

I slowly turn in my seat until I find Cam standing in the middle of the dining hall with a stupid-ass grin on his face, looking proud as shit. God damn, I just want to strangle the sexy idiot. He's got no idea the damage he's just caused.

Meeting his eyes, I try to communicate how sorry I am. I don't mean to hurt him, but that's precisely what I have to do because there is just no fucking way I can be a girl of the month. I don't even agree with the fucking concept, and I thought the idiot knew that.

Rising to my feet, I steel my spine, running my tongue along my suddenly dry lips. I cast a glance around the rest of the hall, ignoring Hawk's murderous glare and Mason's tight expression.

"No." The word comes out like a whip, swiping the excited look from Cam's face as it falls, shock and hurt evident for only a second before he composes himself, donning an impassive expression.

"You can't say no," Hawk barks out, surprising me. I thought he, of all people, would be more than happy for me to turn Cam down. He's been telling me to keep my distance for weeks now, and when I finally do as he asks, he's not happy? *Fucking infuriating shithead.*

"He's right," West agrees. Of course, he does, because when one of them decides something, the rest immediately jump on board and back them up.

"*He* can't choose a scholarship student," I retort.

"Also true," West nods, his brows furrowing as he tries to work out which is the bigger issue—Cam asking out a scholarship student or a girl turning him down.

"Who says I can't say no?" I question, adamant that regardless of whatever they say, I am *not* becoming a girl of the month. "Just because a girl has never said no before, doesn't mean it's not allowed."

West nods his head, that small movement allowing me to release the tense breath I'd been holding. He leans in to whisper in Hawk's ear, the two of them having a private conversation. I can't make out any of it, but I keep my eyes locked on them, refusing to look in Cam's direction and see the pain and confusion written all over his face. Why the fuck didn't he just talk to me first? I could have explained myself to him in private and saved both of us from this embarrassment.

"We need to discuss it," Hawk finally says, addressing the room. "We will have an answer for you by tomorrow."

What the fuck does that mean?!

Before I can argue, West quickly picks a girl and drags a still-frozen Cam back toward the table. Cam shakes him off halfway, though, storming out of the room.

With shaky legs, I sit back down at my table. I've been sitting alone since Halloween, but I can't help glancing toward where the scholarship students sit, finding all seven of them are gaping at me with mixed looks of awe, shock, and displeasure.

Fuck my life.

∽

"What the hell was that?!" I demand, sitting down beside Cam. I deliberately left the dining hall as soon as I finished eating, hoping to track him down before class. I looked everywhere for him before giving up and coming to English early; apparently, he's been here the whole time.

He doesn't even look at me or acknowledge I've spoken.

"Cam! Why didn't you tell me you were going to do that?"

"What does it matter?" he snarls, his head snapping my way so he can glare at me. "Would you have given a different answer if I'd consulted you first?"

"No," I respond truthfully. He gives a tight nod of his head, his gaze dropping back to his table.

"At least tell me why." His voice is quiet now, sad, and it only breaks my heart for him. I never wanted this to happen, but there was no way I could say yes; submit to someone like that, give them that power and control over me, not when I'm here to gain my freedom, to live my own life.

"I...It's complicated." I sigh weakly, rubbing my hands over my face in frustration, unable to explain any of it to him. "It has nothing to do with you, in any case. I just...couldn't say yes."

We lapse into silence, neither of us speaking again as the class fills up and Mr. Greer begins today's lesson. The air between us is fraught with tension, and the second the bell goes, Cam darts out of his chair like it's on fire, storming out of the room.

The rest of the day goes by in a blur, but I don't miss the glares thrown at me by the girls, everyone whispering, trying to work out why Cam would choose me. They aren't the only ones asking themselves that question. I can't understand why he would do that or openly acknowledge there's anything between us. Of course, the guys seem to have decided it's because I'm good in bed, and catcalls have been following me around the halls all day. It takes everything in me not to lash out at one of those motherfuckers, but I can't afford to lose my spot here, and *that* is the only reason several of them aren't sent to the hospital today with fractured arms or broken noses.

That night I've just flicked the desk lamp off—having crammed enough schoolwork nonsense into my brain for the day—and I'm getting ready for bed when my tablet goes off. Ugh, who could be messaging me so late? The only person who ever did was Cam, and somehow I doubt he's sitting in the dining hall wondering if I'm going to show up for our usual midnight date.

> Hawk: Dining Hall. Now.

Seriously? Does he think I'm some sort of lapdog who will come when ordered? The device vibrates with another incoming message.

> Hawk: Don't make us come get you.

WELL, I sure as hell don't need them turning up at my door and disturbing the whole dorm at this time of night. God knows there's enough drama involving me at the minute, I don't need to add to the rumors.

Not giving a flying fuck that I'm wearing a pair of boxer shorts, I throw on a hoodie and stuff my feet back into my boots, cursing out every single Prick as I storm out of the dorms and over to the canteen, throwing the doors open and glowering at the lot of them as they sit at their usual table. It's well after midnight, yet each of them looks better than the last. How is that fair?

Hawk's scowl only deepens as he takes in what I'm wearing, while Cam's face pinches when he sees me. I have to admit, that hurts a little, and I quickly glance away, finding Mason staring at my legs, and West with a slight blush in his cheeks which he hides by ducking his head.

"What is this about?" I bark, sitting down on the opposite side of the table, feeling all their eyes on me. It's unsettling, and I struggle not to squirm under the weight of their gaze, but I'm not about to let them know how on edge I am about all of this.

"It's about what happened today." Hawk's growl makes it clear he's still fucking pissed about this morning. *Yeah, you and me both, buddy.* "You can't say no."

"Excuse me?" My eyes snap to his. He's got to be fucking joking, right? "In case you missed it, I already did."

Cam mumbles something under his breath that sounds suspiciously like *nobody could have missed that*, but Mason jams his elbow in his ribs, shutting him up.

"We'll announce it to the school tomorrow. You'll be expected to sit with us at breakfast, come to parties with us, and essentially do whatever we say. You belong to Cam, so he's the only one who can fuck you, but it's in your best interest to just do as you're told."

Slamming my hand hard against the table, I jump to my feet. "I belong to no one," I snarl back, barely hearing the end of his sentence over the rage building inside me and the panic swirling in my head. I'm pretty sure most of it is shit he's just tacked on for me. Outside of breakfast and parties, I rarely see the girls with the guys unless they're willingly draping themselves all over them. But then I guess I'm the exception to all the other girls. The only one who doesn't want to be here.

A slow, cruel grin spreads across Hawk's face, and I swear to fuck, if it's the last thing I do, I'm going to wipe it off him. Make it so he can never fucking smile again.

"You do now, trash. Now run along, and don't be late tomorrow. You wouldn't want to miss your first breakfast with the Princes now, would you?"

My hands clench into tight fists as I grit my teeth, fighting back the urge to dive across the table and strangle him with my bare hands. Violence isn't the answer, and it will only get me kicked out of here. No, I have to play this smart. If he thinks he can forcefully keep me around, then fine, I'll make every second a living hell for each of them.

With my lip curled up in disgust, I flick my gaze between them, silently communicating the promise of pain, death, and destruction. Hawk only smirks back, rising to the challenge, while Cam still looks pissed. I'm beyond giving a shit that I hurt his feelings, though. Boo-fucking-hoo. Grow the fuck up and get over it. Mason is as impassive as ever, his penetrating gaze analyzing my every movement. I swear he can read every murderous thought flitting through my mind right now. West is the only one who looks uncomfortable, unwilling to meet my gaze.

"Fine," I snarl through gritted teeth. "But if you think you're going to get to me, you should know I give as good as I get." With that, I turn on my heel and storm out of the hall without a backward glance.

～

I TOSS and turn all night, and the following day I'm a ball of nerves, my hands shaking frantically as I struggle to button my shirt. Closing my eyes, I take several deep breaths, trying to steady myself. I'm being fucking pathetic. This is nothing I can't handle. Hell, this doesn't even make the top ten of fucked-up shit I've survived. I can do this. I'm going into battle, and I need to fucking prepare myself.

Snapping open my eyes, I'm pleased to find my old mask in place, the one I tucked away when I walked through those gates. This old thing has gotten me through everything I've had to face so far in life; I know it won't let me down now.

There's only fifteen minutes left of breakfast when I storm through the dining hall doors, a look of thunder on my face. If I'm going to do this, I'm going to make it very damn clear I'm not fucking happy about it, and hopefully, the dark scowl on my face will be enough to deter some of the weaker kids from thinking they can gossip about me.

"Ah, there she is," Hawk calls out, a shit-eating grin on his face that I can't fucking wait to rip off. "Come sit with us, Hadley."

As if I have a fucking choice.

Casting a glance toward the scholarship table, I find all eyes on me, Emilia's mouth agape as she watches me cross the room to the Princes' table to sit down beside Cam.

"I ordered you breakfast since you're late," Hawk says in a sickly sweet tone. Looking down at the plate, there's a slice of grapefruit in front of me. That's it. One measly slice of fucking grapefruit. Thankfully, I didn't undergo my usual exercise routine this morning, otherwise, I'd be fucking starving. Even so, who the fuck can live off that all morning?

Gritting my teeth, I don't bother to acknowledge Hawk, pretending I'm not insulted by the lack of food, and instead pick up my fork and dig in while ignoring everyone's eyes on me. No one says anything else to me for the rest of breakfast. The others are too caught up in talking to their new girls, and Cam is doing his best to pretend I don't exist. He doesn't even glance in my direction, and it's the longest fifte minutes of my life; but fucking finally, people start to filter out to class and the Pricks get to their feet. The second I am able to get away from them, I do, and other than having to endure their presence in business class, I spend the rest of the day ignoring their existence.

Of course, it's much harder to ignore the rest of the school, and Bianca and the other Princesses corner me that afternoon. Scanning my eyes over their scowling faces, I notice the group size has grown, the club having welcomed each new set of girls into their ranks. Somehow, I don't think they are here to give me my induction talk and welcome pack.

"How the fuck did you make Cam do that?" Bianca demands. She stands front and center, clearly the ringleader of this little band of fake royalty.

"I didn't make Cam do anything," I retort, crossing my arms over my chest.

"Then why would he choose you?" Missy's eyes run over me with confusion, like she can't understand what Cam could find so appealing about me.

"Why would you say no?" another girl demands. I think her name was Cora or something.

I scan my eyes over all of them, seeing the same question in each of their stares. "Because, unlike you, I didn't dream of growing up finding a Prick and living unhappily ever after," I snap, pushing through the crowd of desperate girls who are never going to understand why I'm not exactly like them.

"You're *never* going to be one of us," Bianca calls out behind me, causing me to pause, turning around to face her with an incredulous look.

"Bianca, understand this," I say evenly, "I don't *ever* want to be you."

As I turn away, I catch Mason standing in a doorway, watching the whole thing like some creeper in the shadows. I only stare at him for a second before forcing myself to look away and storm down the corridor.

The rest of the week goes by in much the same way. Cam doesn't say a word to me, Hawk takes far too much pleasure from the cheap shots he fires my way, and he's somehow managed to get the kitchen staff to only bring out fucking grapefruit for me every morning, even if I order something different. I've had to stock up on snacks from the shop in the rec center so I can eat something halfway decent in the mornings before I have to go to the dining hall, but, man, I fucking miss the pancakes.

The worst part of it, though, is that the scholarship students barely look at me. Any time I smile their way or dare to wave at them, they duck their heads and glance away, ignoring me. What hurts the most is Emilia's absence. I miss our easy friendship and her daily chatter.

On Friday, I show up early for computer class so I can sit as far away from West as possible, fully intent on going back to my original plan of teaching myself how to use the stupid software on these machines. Eating breakfast with them is enough torture, and while I know Hawk is the one behind most of this shit, the fact the others just go along with it pisses me the hell off.

Picking a seat on the far side of the room, I log in and open up today's lesson plan, only to be disturbed when someone sits beside me. His familiar scent washes over me and I snap my head around to glare at him. "What are you doing over here?"

Both of his eyebrows jump up, his surprise at my anger only infuriating me more. How can he not expect me to be pissy with him? Thanks to him and his stupid friends, I've had the week from hell.

"I thought you needed my help."

"I'm sure I can work it out by myself," I seethe, ignoring the little voice in my head that reminds me I tried to do that before and failed epically.

"Sure you can." He snorts. I don't respond as I mentally count backward from ten so I don't smash him over the head with my mouse. "Look." He sighs. "How about we leave all that crap outside the classroom?"

"You mean the crap where you're forcing me to be one of your stupid girls? That crap?"

Ignoring my attitude, West asks, "Why did you say no to Cam anyway? I thought you two were a thing."

Huh, why did he think that? Did Cam say something? Shame he couldn't have talked to me about us too, before making such a public and antiquated declaration.

"You can't just go around claiming girls and demanding they be yours, *Wes*. People are not possessions. You can't treat others like livestock to be traded at will."

A tense moment of silence fills the air between us as I wait for the verbal lashing that I've overstepped my mark, but instead, he surprises me. "You're right," he readily agrees. "I can only imagine how it looks to someone who hasn't grown up in our world, but it's tradition. Despite how it might look, it's bigger than us. We actually have very little say over any of this. Did you know most of the senior girls were enrolled here because of us? Because *we* were here. Everyone who's anyone in our circle knows the tradition. They enroll their daughters in the hopes they'll snag themselves a Prince for a husband. It's all part and parcel of being in the upper class. Hell, each of us will probably marry one of those girls someday. You're the first person I've heard of to fight back, to *ever* say no."

I take a moment to ponder his words, navigating through the various bomb drops. Parents pimping their daughters out, the Pricks marrying girls they don't have any respect for. I thought the life I left behind was pretty fucked-up, but this one is quickly coming in at second place.

"I just don't understand how you can be happy with any of that. How can you be okay with knowing girls are being pushed to be with you? How can you be happy spending your life with someone you don't even seem to like?"

"Happy?" West laughs, although it lacks any humor. "Who said anything about being happy? Despite what people think, happiness and money do not go hand in hand. You do what's expected of you, because that's what every generation before us has done. As for the girls...well, you've seen them. Do they look like they're being forced to you?" He has a point there. The girls are all chomping at the bit to be with the guys of their own free will. "They want us as much as their families want them to be with us, because we're rich and powerful."

"Doesn't hurt that you're all built like gods," I joke, but it falls flat when West simply stares at me, with surprise and confusion flitting across his face. I'm not sure what has him stumped, though. Surely he knows how hot he is?

After a moment he shakes himself out of whatever he was thinking, clearing his throat. "I'm sorry you got caught up in the middle of all of this. I don't know what's going on with you and Cam, but I know he's hurt, and he's going to take it out on you. Hawk's also going to do everything he can to make your life hell for the next month. There's nothing I can really do to stop either of them. All I can do is promise that, in here, we can continue on like normal. Leave all that shit at the door."

I stare deep into his forest-green eyes, wanting to believe him. In my head, there are two very different versions of West, the one he shows the world—the one he is when he's with the others—and this soft, gentle version that he is around me. I want to believe the version he shows me is genuine and not a ruse, except if I've learned anything these last few months, it's that I can't trust any of them. However, despite what I *know*, I *want* to believe in him. It's for that reason that I slowly nod my head in agreement. "Okay. We'll leave the rest of the world outside."

Hadley

CHAPTER SEVENTEEN

> Hawk: Get your ass to the lake! Now!

> West: It will be easier if you don't fight it.

Hawk and Cam are both assholes, and West clearly doesn't know me at all. I've been hiding out in my room for the last hour, trying to ignore the incessant buzzing of the tablet. There's a party tonight, and according to Hawk, attendance is mandatory.

With a groan, I get to my feet, rifling through my meager belongings. Finding the oldest, rattiest pair of shorts and a t-shirt with a middle finger on it, an evil grin lights up my face. Well, if they insist on my presence, I'm at least going to dress how I want.

Twenty minutes later, I'm strolling down the embankment toward the fire pit where, as usual, the four of them are chilling. Mason and Hawk have this month's girls on their laps. West's girl clings to his arm, trying to get his attention, even as her jealous gaze bores into Mason, Hawk, and Cam. What the hell is her problem? West is a fucking catch, you know, if you're into stupidly rich, pampered boys. The bitch should appreciate what she has.

Glancing Cam's way, I expect to find him with the same sullen look he's worn all week, but instead he's hitting on some chick I don't recognize. *Is he for fucking real?* I guess this is what West meant when he said Cam would take his hurt out on me, and, damn, the spike of jealousy that zings through me only annoys me further.

"What the fuck are you wearing?" Hawk snarls, tearing his lips away from what's-her-name. "You look like a fucking homeless person."

I mock gasp, bringing my hand up to my chest. "What? But these are my best clothes. Only the finest for a Pac party, right?"

Rolling my eyes, I snatch a water bottle out of the cooler and drop into a seat on the other side of the fire, as far from Hawk and Cam as I can get. Stretching my legs out in front of me, I cross my boot-covered feet at the ankle, looking chill as fuck as I unscrew the water and take a long gulp.

"You're an extension of us now. You have to dress the part."

The look I give him says everything about how few fucks I give about what he wants, but of course, his snarking has drawn the attention of the other girls around the fire.

"Eww." The girl Cam was flirting with scrunches up her nose in disgust. "Where did you even find those?"

I turn to look at her in confusion. "They were a gift, Stew gave me this hoodie."

"Who the fuck is Stew?" Hawk growls.

"The homeless man who let me share his cardboard box house with him for a few nights." Okay, so not quite the truth, however the gasps of shock and looks of revulsion are so totally worth it.

"If you wear that shit around us again, I'll strip it off you and burn it. See if you like walking around naked." Hawk's snarl is deadly serious. If he so much as laid a hand on me, I'd make him regret it. The thought of ending up in only my underwear in front of all these assholes has a skitter of fear running up my spine. *No fucking thanks.*

It's not long before Cam takes off to dance with the brown-haired bimbo he's been flirting with all night. Not that I notice. Hawk is practically fucking his girl in front of us all, while Mason and West talk quietly, both of them ignoring their girls. It's strange. While West frequently pays little to no attention to his girl of the month, it's the first time I've seen Mason ignoring his. He's usually all over that, although since I've sat down, he's barely looked her way.

Spotting Emilia and the others over by the drinks table, unease swirls in my stomach. Heeding their words, I haven't talked to any of them since Halloween, and I miss hanging out with them.

"Where the fuck are you going?" Hawk's growl has me realizing I'm on my feet, as though I was going to go over to them. Which is stupid—they wouldn't want me anywhere near them.

"For a walk," I lie, needing some sort of excuse to cover whatever I thought I was doing.

"No, you're not. Sit your ass down and shut up."

I grind my teeth together, my hand clenching around my water bottle until it crinkles under the pressure as my sadness quickly burns away in the heat of my anger.

"I'm not about to sit here and watch you attempt to fuck what's-her-name with your stunted dick. Trust me, you don't want anyone to see her fake as fuck orgasm."

With a venomous snarl, he gets to his feet, dragging blondie with him as he takes off into the forest. Only when he's gone, do I let out a laugh, shaking my head.

"Why do you have to wind him up like that?" West asks, reminding me there was an audience for that little showdown.

Shrugging, I take another sip of water. "He makes it way too damn easy."

He shakes his head, returning to his conversation with Mason while I sit and watch the scholarship students partying at the far end of the beach. After a while, my gaze comes back to Mason and West. The girl Mason chose, I think her name is Tiffany, has gone off to dance nearby, but every now and again she glances in this direction and scowls when she discovers Mason isn't watching her. On the other hand, West's girl stares star-struck at Mason.

"Why the fuck are you staring at Mason?" I bark at her, drawing not only her attention but also Mason and West's.

"What? I wasn't—" she splutters.

"Yes, you were. You have been all night. If you don't want to be with West, then you should have said no."

"Like you did?" she snarks, spitting fire at me.

"At least I'm not pretending to like one guy while eye-fucking his best friend."

With a glower, she storms to her feet, taking off toward Tiffany and dragging her deeper into the crowd and out of view. Two for two. I wonder who I can piss off next.

"You're on fire tonight, aren't you?" West deadpans, the pair of them still looking at me.

I shrug my shoulders in a *what can you do* gesture. "Hey, you guys are the ones that wanted me to come. Maybe next time you'll think better of it."

~

ON SUNDAY, I get a notification on my phone that a parcel is waiting for me in the post room. When I arrive, I find a stack of garment bags, each one containing a dress. *What the hell?* There are enough dresses to fill my entire wardrobe.

After getting help to carry them all back to my room, I flick through each bag, lifting out the dress and giving it a critical look before hanging it up. Each one falls to my mid-thigh and all of them are relatively conservative. No plunging necklines and none of them are backless—nothing like the strips of fabric the other girls wear. The most daring they get is a split up the side that I'm certain will show my panties. That I can totally live with.

I'm about halfway through the bags when I find a note stuck to one.

This should keep Hawk off your back for a while. W.

West. Why would he help me out, though? Not having any answers to that, I ignore it, instead focusing on my pretty new dresses. I've never had anything like them before—nothing designer, nothing that was just mine. I can't stop running my hand down the soft fabric, a goofy smile on my face as I continue sifting through the pile. I now have enough dresses that I could probably wear a different one to each party for the rest of the year and still have some I've never worn. That's crazy, right?

On Friday night, after yet another un-fun week of grapefruit slices, girls calling me a slut, and trying to avoid spending any more time than necessary with the Pricks, I'm dressed in one of my new dresses, strutting across the sand toward the fire pit. I have to admit; I feel like hot stuff right now.

All four boys are in their usual seats around the fire, but what's surprising is that they're alone. No girl of the month, or any other girl, in sight. Maybe that means they will let me off the hook for the night.

They all glance my way as I approach, various looks flitting across their features. While I see heat and surprise in Mason's, West appears almost smug, a rather unusual look on him. Cam takes one heated look at me and storms off. It's been yet another week of silence and avoidance from him, so I can't say I'm surprised. Hawk, as per usual, has his characteristic scowl firmly in place.

"Better," is all he says, barely glancing at the dress. "But you forgot the shoes."

"Nope, I didn't." I stick out my leg, shaking it in front of him so he can see my usual, impossible-to-miss, scuffed, chunky boots, enjoying the disgusted sneer that curls his lips.

"Heels go with dresses, not those monstrosities."

"Trust me, Hawk," I say sweetly, giving him a blindingly innocent smile as I drop into Cam's empty chair beside him. "You don't want me to wear heels."

His eyes narrow at me in suspicion. "Why is that?"

I make sure to keep my sugary sweet smile in place. "Because I won't be able to stop myself from stabbing you through the eye with it."

Unimpressed, he glares at me, and I swear I see West covering a laugh behind his hand.

"Beer?" Mason offers, stretching across to lift himself one.

"No thanks, I don't drink."

"You don't? Ever?" His eyebrows lift in surprise as he cracks the tab on the beer.

"Nope. Never."

"Huh. How come?"

I shrug my shoulders, not wanting to get into any of it. "I just don't. It's not my thing."

"What *is* your thing?" Hawk sneers. "You don't like parties, you don't drink. What the fuck do you like doing?"

"I like pissing you off," I retort sweetly. This time, both West and Mason snort, and Hawk turns his icy stare on them.

∼

THE SAME SORT of truce I have with West in the computer suite seems to apply to my time in the gym with Mason, where we both pretend to not notice the other as we go about our morning routine. Only, for the last two weeks, he's managed to secretly sneak a high-carb, high-protein snack bar—one of the fancy, expensive ones—into my gym bag without me noticing. I feel like I watch his every move, so I've no idea how he's managing it. They are so much more tastier than the cheap, unfulfilling shit in the shop, and Hawk still has the kitchen staff giving me only grapefruit for breakfast so I'm not about to argue.

I seriously don't understand it. He's not around when I eat the rest of my meals and the kitchen staff bring me whatever I order, yet he's intent on pissing me off every morning by dictating what I eat. What he doesn't realize is that every morning, as I tuck into my measly slice of fruit, I'm imagining all the horrific ways in which I'm going to get him back.

I'm putting my gym gear back in my bag after my workout when my tablet goes off. Pulling it out, I find a new message from Cam.

Cam: Library.

GOD, I'm getting seriously fucking sick of these demands. First Hawk, now Cam. I almost preferred it when he was ignoring me.

Grabbing my backpack, I take off for the library. Part of me fucking hates the fact I'm going to them as though summoned. Even though I might be playing along, I've been using the time I spend with them to learn about what I can from each. They think they hide themselves behind their public personas but don't realize how much they let slip; the small things about themselves that most people probably wouldn't pick up on. But I do. I note every detail they unwillingly offer me.

Entering the library, I don't see Cam, or any of the others, at their usual table at the back of the room. Glancing around, I don't see them anywhere. *If this is some sort of fucking joke...*

Someone waving catches my attention and I turn my head to find some dark-haired girl I don't know waving me over. Cautiously, I approach the table, unable to figure out what is happening.

When I just stand at the table, looking down at her, she must cop on that I'm not going to sit down.

"Oh, uh," she stumbles, flustered. "Cam wanted me to give you this." Peering at the pages she's holding toward me, I see it's Cam's half of our English project. *Seriously? He's getting minions to deliver his assignments to me? He could just have emailed the damn thing.*

"Why isn't he delivering it himself?"

She must not have expected me to question her as her eyes widen in surprise. "I don't know. He just told me to tell him when I was done and he'd get you to come pick it up."

Hold up. What did she say?

"When you're done with it?"

"Yeah." She's looking at me like she can't understand my confusion. With her hand still outstretched in a desperate bid to get me to take the pages, I skim over the work. It's painfully obvious this is not Cam's writing. What Cam wrote for our first assignment got us an A+, but this drivel is barely passable.

"You wrote this?" Obviously she did, but I want her to confirm it.

"Yeah." She smiles brightly, clearly proud of the job she did. She really shouldn't be, though. If this is who Cam has been using to do his work for him, it's no wonder Mr. Greer looked at us with suspicious eyes when he handed back our last two assignments.

"I'm not taking that," I state bluntly, gesturing to the pages. She finally drops her arm, gaping at me.

"Wh...what? But you have to."

"I don't *have* to do anything," I growl. Why the fuck is everyone making decisions for me and telling me what I can and can't do? I'm getting seriously fucking sick of it. This is not what I signed up for when I came to Pac. "Why would you do his work for him?"

She shrugs her shoulders. "He said he would pick me next month." The hopeful gleam in her eyes makes me bite back my words before I can snark out something insulting. I should have realized that was the reason.

Shaking my head. "It's really not worth...all of this." I wave my hand at the table where her textbooks are open. I want to tell her it's not worth the hit to her dignity, the selling of her pride, but I don't know her and I'm pretty sure anything I say will only come across as judgmental and bitchy. If she's going to be another Princess, I should probably at least try not to piss her off.

Turning on my heel, I head back toward the exit, ignoring her spluttered protests. Just as I reach the door, a hand wraps around my wrist, yanking me away from it as I stumble.

Spinning around, Cam is dragging me into the stacks. When I pull my arm back, trying to break his hold on me, he tightens his grip, and my teeth grit as my bones grind against one another.

When we're safely hidden from prying eyes, he lets go, using his larger body to push me up against the shelves. Cam glares down at me with fire in his eyes. It's also the first time he has looked at me in the last two weeks. Despite how angry he is with me and how frustrated I am with him, my body reacts instinctively to his nearness, remembering what it felt like to have him pressed up against me last time.

Staring unblinkingly at him, I can see he feels it too. Buried underneath all that anger, he still feels what I feel—the intense physical response we have to one another.

"Go back and take the assignment from her," he growls, his voice a deep rumble that sounds barely human.

"No."

His eyes narrow at my defiance, his jaw clenching.

"I'm not handing in something that isn't your work," I boldly tell him, not letting his icy glare scare me. "Do the damn assignment yourself. And don't use some lackey to give it to me. I know you have a set of balls, so fucking use them."

His nostrils flare, the brown around his eyes a thin ring as his pupils enlarge, his face darkening with rage.

His hand wraps around my throat, a move that takes me by surprise as his fingers press into the skin on either side of my neck. I can feel the strength in his grip as his fingers flex, the intermittent loosening and tightening of his hold as he struggles to decide what to do.

With a savage growl and a final squeeze, he drops his arm, storming away without a backward glance and leaving me sagged against the bookcase as I work to control my breathing.

Baby Davenport

CHAPTER EIGHTEEN

Still half asleep, I rub at my eyes, running my hand through my hair as I look at myself in the mirror. Reaching out for my toothbrush, I glance down as my fingers touch nothing except air. *What the hell?* I swear it was here last night when I went to bed.

As I peer around, I don't see it anywhere. Grumbling under my breath, I turn on the shower and step in, letting the hot water flow over me. I can look for the damn thing when I'm done. Tilting my head back and letting the water splash into my face and over my hair, I blindly go to grab the shower gel and feel bristles brushing against my fingers. Opening my eyes, my toothbrush is perched against the shower gel bottle. *What. The. Fuck?* I never brush my teeth in the shower.

Rolling my eyes at Cam's new idea of a hilarious joke, I make a mental note to tell him to grow up. This is the third time my shit has turned up in weird places. At first, I shook it off, thinking I had misplaced my backpack, but now it's clear Cam has been messing with me. I guess this is his way of handling his rejection from Hadley. I knew that girl was fucking trouble; I knew she would mess him up like this.

"Ugh," West groans, lifting up the couch cushions in search of something, when I enter the living room half an hour later.

"What's up?"

"I can't find my glasses," he growls, still digging around down the back of the sofa. I have a sneaking suspicion I know who might have taken them, though I decide to give Cam another day or two of being an idiot, then I'll tell him to wise up.

Once West finally finds them, hidden in the coffee canister, and Mason has managed to drag Cam out of bed—you'd think the idiot would want to be around to witness the havoc he's causing—we head down for breakfast, striding into the hall with our heads held high as we look down at our peers.

My lips pinch as I find Hadley's seat empty at our table. Why can't that girl be on fucking time? I shake it off as I sit down, Cindy immediately attaching her mouth to mine. Mmm, if she directs her lips further south, I definitely won't say no to a breakfast blowie. God knows, I need an outlet for all the tension I've been carrying around.

Hadley eventually storms in with her typical angry scowl, not looking at any of us as she takes her usual seat, stabbing her fork into her grapefruit. I've gotten way too much joy out of watching her grumble and glower at the little piece of fruit, slyly eyeing up Cam's loaded plate of food every morning. Any other girl here would probably think I was being sweet by setting that in front of them, but I knew Hadley would fucking hate it. Not just the shortage of food but the lack of control as well. She's just like me in that respect; she needs that control over her life. I saw it when I told her she belonged to Cam for the month. The hate in her eyes at my words, the spark of fear at her loss of control.

It's the same with the dresses and forcing her to come to our parties every Friday night. It's all about tearing her down. Although I have to admit, I thought she would put up more resistance. She's taken it all like a champ, despite the pissy look on her face. The problem is I don't know her well enough to know how to get to her.

That's why I take the master key from the admin office and let myself into her room while she's in class. I need to know more about this girl in order to understand how to get rid of her.

With the exception of a few stacks of books on her desk, a bunch of suspiciously new and expensive-looking dresses, and a few uniforms in her wardrobe, you'd hardly know anyone even lives here. Her bed is perfectly made with the standard white sheets provided by the school. She hasn't brought her own covers or put posters on the walls. There are no photos or anything personal in the room, either.

Rifling through her drawers, there are a few measly articles of clothing, but otherwise, it's empty. There's nothing under her bed or hidden in books on her bookshelf. Nothing here gives me any indication as to who she is or what makes her tick.

Frustrated, I slam my fist into the backboard of her bookcase, but rather than the solid knock, there's an echo.

I stare at the spot in confusion before scanning over the bookcase. It's a freestanding bookcase with a few books on one of the shelves, but otherwise, it's empty.

Yanking on one side, it easily pulls away from the wall and as I peer behind it, my eyes widen in surprise. *Sneaky bitch.* There's a hole in the drywall. Wedging myself between the bookcase and the wall, I slip in behind it until I can look in, finding a black duffel bag.

Lifting it out, I set it on the floor, bending down as I unzip it. The thing is basically empty, nothing except a few old clothes. In an inner pocket, I find a cheap, plastic ring, like the one you'd get out of a gumball machine. Chucking it back inside, I push aside her clothing, pausing when I find a notebook buried amongst them.

She's always writing in her stupid notebooks instead of using the tablet, only why would she hide her schoolwork in the wall? I dig it out of her bag, opening it up. Flicking through the pages, my eyes narrow, and I only become more confused the more I read. *What the fuck is this?*

Snapping it shut, I set it aside, zipping the bag up and shoving it back where I found it. I push the bookcase back in place and, with a final glance around the room to make sure nothing is out of place, grab the notebook and get out of there.

∽

SOME FACELESS BLONDE is giving me the best blowjob of my life as I fuck her face. Nutting in her mouth, she swallows every last drop of my cum before leaning back on her heels, smiling up at me.

Her mouth opens as she goes to say something.

"AHHHHH," she screams, the loud, high-pitched shriek making me jump.

What the ever-loving fuck?

"AHHHHH!" she screams again. I turn to look behind me, but I'm frozen, unable to move. I bring my hand up to cut off her screams, but again, my arm won't move.

What the fucking hell is going on?

I jolt awake, flying upright in bed, the screaming noise still pounding in my ears.

No, wait. That's not in my head. Someone is, honest to God, screaming.

My door bangs open, and Mason storms in.

"What the actual fuck are you doing in here?" I can barely hear him over the continued screams of some girl. My brain is too fogged with sleep to wrap my head around what is happening. Who the fuck is screaming?

Glancing around my room, Mason's eyes narrow on my desk as he stomps over to it and whips open the drawer. The action has the screaming getting even louder. *Holy fuck, my ears.*

He throws my phone on my bed—aggressively. I snatch it up, glancing at the screen. It's my alarm. My alarm is going off? I silence it, my head still fuzzy and swirling with confusion.

"What the fuck, man?" Mason grumbles. "Why is your alarm set for the crack ass of dawn? Turn the damn thing off when it rings. Some of us are trying to sleep."

He fires a final glare my way, not waiting for a response, grumbling about how even he shouldn't be awake yet.

Utterly confused, I look back down at my phone. It's barely four a.m. Opening up the alarm app, I notice it's set to go off every day at the same time, and the tone has changed from the usual soft wake-up one I use.

What the fuck? Seriously, Cam? I'm going to fucking murder you—in the morning, when I've had more sleep.

I've forgotten all about it by the time I wake up again, trudging into the kitchen in nothing but gray sweats. Pouring myself a bowl of cereal, I open the cutlery drawer, staring into it for far too long before it registers with me, and I slam it shut.

"Cam," I snarl, glaring daggers at him as he stumbles into the room, still half asleep with his hair sticking up in all directions as he lazily throws himself onto the sofa.

His head snaps up to look at me, eyes pulled together in bewilderment. "What?"

"Where the fuck are the spoons?"

The expression on his face would be comical if I wasn't so fucking furious right now.

"Dude, what the fuck are you talking about? They're in the drawer."

"No, they're not," I hiss through gritted teeth. "You've gotta stop this. It was funny the first few times, now it's getting annoying."

"Man, I seriously have no idea what you're talking about."

I stomp across the floor toward him, and he gets to his feet, facing off against me with that same stupid look of confusion on his face.

"No? So you didn't set my alarm to go off in the middle of the night? Or hide my backpack behind the sofa? What about putting West's glasses in the coffee tin? And all the rest of it. The amount of crap you've pulled the last couple of weeks is ridiculous."

His eyes widen, his mouth dropping open. "That's been happening to you too?" He runs his hand through his hair, turning away from me as he barks out a relieved chuckle. "Fuck, man, I was beginning to think I was losing it."

I scrutinize him, taking in the relief written clearly on his face, my mind running a mile a minute.

"It's not you?" I clarify, but I'm pretty sure it isn't.

"No, man." Realization dawns on him, the smile slipping off his face and I can see the wheels turning behind his eyes. "Who is it then?"

I shake my head, trying to figure that out.

"There's no way it would be West or Mason."

I agree. Cam is the only one who would do something so childish. Outside of the four of us, I know only one person who would dare to sneak into our private space and mess with us.

"Hadley," I growl, watching as Cam's eyes grow even bigger.

"No way," he gasps in disbelief, yet I can see he believes it too.

"That bitch," I snarl, unable to stand still, ambling back toward the kitchen.

"Hey, man. Now that's a bit extreme," he argues. His defense of her has me spinning around, storming back toward him.

"That's not all she's done."

He once again looks confused, but I push past him, not answering the questions in his eyes. He needs to see it for himself. Grabbing the notebook from my bag in the bedroom, I stomp back into the living room and slam it down on the table.

"Read that," I sneer, pointing at the book.

His gaze darts between me and the book before he hesitantly reaches out, lifting the book and opening it up to the first page.

I observe him closely as his brows draw together, his eyes skimming down the page before he flips over to the next one, doing the same. Page after page, his expression darkens, his eyes turning hard and his nostrils flaring.

"I don't...what the fuck is this? Where did you find it?"

"I don't know. She was hiding it in her room."

He focuses back on the notebook, and we stand in silence for several long moments as he flips back and forth through the pages. I've already read it several times over, trying to understand why.

When he's finally sick of looking at it, he lifts his head, his icy stare meeting mine.

"What are we going to do about it?"

It's about time we were on the same page. I just had to prove it to him, make him see for himself that she was no good.

A cruel smirk lifts my lip. "I have an idea."

Hadley

CHAPTER NINETEEN

You know that feeling when everyone is talking about you, but you have no idea why or what they're saying?

Yeah, that's exactly how I'm feeling right now.

I cast my eyes around the room, taking in the students gawking at me. Others are flicking their eyes back and forth between me and their tablets while some girls lean across the aisle, whispering to the student beside them. I don't know what the fuck is going on, but I can only guess it's not good. It never is.

My tablet is in my bag, yet something tells me I shouldn't look at it here, with people's eyes on me. By now, the whole room is watching me intently. Some students are even blatantly staring, waiting for me to react, to do something. I'm sure as fuck not about to give them anything. Whatever fresh torment Hawk has unleashed, I'm not about to make it fodder for these pathetic saps. Today is the last day of the month. On Monday morning, a new girl is chosen, and I'm supposed to be done with this shit. I should have guessed Hawk wouldn't let the occasion go without a memorable send-off.

Blocking them out, I pretend to focus on my schoolwork for the rest of class, impatiently counting down the minutes until the bell rings so I can escape and find out what's going on.

The last ten minutes of class feel like they last a lifetime. Every minute filled with hushed whispers and quiet chuckles under breaths. Not one person bothers to fill me in on what the fuck everyone is finding so funny, not even one of my old scholarship friends. I didn't really expect them to get involved, nor can I blame them—they're just trying to get through this school and start the future they've been working for the last four years.

When the bell finally rings, I remain seated in my chair, glaring down at every single student who looks my way as they pack up their stuff and leave the room. Only when the last person leaves, closing the door behind them, do I drop the tough girl act.

Bending down to dig my tablet out of my bag, I type in my pin and see a notification informing me that I have received a new email.

With clumsy fingers and sweaty palms, I eventually manage to open up the email. It appears to be a mass email that has, by the looks of things, been sent to every student in the school. *Excellent.*

There doesn't appear to be any text, however there's a video file attached.

My breath comes out in short, shallow pants, nausea churning in my stomach as my finger hesitates over the file.

Whatever this is, I can handle it. I have dealt with worse. I have fucking survived *worse.*

I slam my finger down on the screen harder than necessary, holding my breath as the video begins to play. The screen is black for the first few seconds until a light is turned on, illuminating a bedroom. *My* bedroom.

What the fuck?

I watch as I walk into my room, dropping my bag on the floor and closing the door behind me. From the looks of it, the camera's hidden in the bookcase by the desk, angled so that it pretty much captures the entire room.

I grab some clothes out of my dresser, dumping them on the bed before stripping off my uniform, in full fucking view of the camera. A tingling sensation travels under my skin as I watch myself strip off my clothes, unknowingly revealing the tattoo snaking up my side, along with every scar I've carefully hidden for the last couple of months. I feel every second of it as this new world I've precariously built around me comes crashing down. There's a reason I've kept those scars covered, and it's not because I'm embarrassed by them.

Now every superficial jackass in this fucking shithole that's masquerading as a prep school knows part of my deepest, darkest secret. They've seen the marks of my lowest moments. The times when I wanted to give up, when death felt like the only way out.

The video finishes then, with me dressed in a bra and fucking granny pants, a static image for every single student to roam their eyes over and do whatever the fuck they want with.

That tingling beneath my skin becomes a roar as shock is quickly replaced with insurmountable fury; that craving to punch something, to smash a particular someone's fucking face in.

Jumping to my feet, I grab my bag and storm across the room throwing open the door, ready to do just that.

My steps falter, though, as I find what must be every student in the senior class gathered in the hall, lining the banks of lockers like they're expecting some sort of show. Behind them, I can see pictures pasted all over the walls. Someone has strung the same static image I just saw on the tablet over every available surface.

With every poster I glance over, my fury heightens until it's an untamable storm. Eyes brimming with fire, I glower at every student, satisfaction coursing through me when some of them take a step back from me, their laughs faltering. The only faces I don't see are those of the other scholarship students. Well, at least they aren't here to witness whatever fresh hell this is.

Lifting my chin, I glare at every single fucker as I walk past them. Students talk to one another, no longer bothering to keep their voices low, so as I walk past, I pick up on some of their words.

Abuse. Self-harm. A traumatic accident.

All of them speculating about what the fuck happened to me. Like it's any of their goddamn business.

"Yo, Hadley! Nice panties," Deke, the fucker, yells while his buddies whistle and chortle, slapping him on the back. *Yeah, fucking hilarious, douchebag. You're clearly winning in life.*

I've only made it halfway down the corridor when the crowd at the end of the hall parts, revealing none other than the Pricks themselves. I wondered where they were. There was no way they would miss this little showdown of their own creation.

My eyes don't stray from Hawk as I storm toward them, ignoring every other asshole around us as I take in his stupid fucking smirk and the glimmer of satisfaction in his eyes. Gritting my teeth, I throw him my coldest, most brutal glare, dropping my bag as I close in on him.

"What the fuck is wrong with you?!" I snarl, shoving him in the chest with every ounce of strength I have. He has to take a step back to steady himself, but it's nowhere near enough. I want to see him flat on his ass, staring up at me, wondering how the fuck I bested him.

The smirk drops off his face, his eyes narrowing as he scowls at me, mirroring my own dark look.

It takes everything in me not to go apeshit on his ass as just enough common sense gets through to me, reminding me *he's* the Prince and I'm a nobody. I'll be out of here so quickly I won't have time to process what the fuck happened before I'm dumped on the sidewalk with no education, nowhere to live, and no prospects for the future.

"You fucking proud of yourself?" I seethe, finally turning away from Hawk to glare at the other three fucktards, making sure they know I'm talking to them too. They are each as responsible as he is.

Mason wears his usual look of indifference. He could be watching paint dry right now, that's how unbothered he looks by this whole thing. Flicking my gaze to West, he at least has the decency to seem uncomfortable. His lips are pinched and I can see what might be a semblance of regret in his eyes. Too fucking late, buddy. Regret does me fuck all good now. Where was your conscience when you were recording me? When you were clicking send on that email?

Shaking my head in disappointment, I finally look at Cam, my lips parting with a quick intake of breath at the molten hatred in his eyes. His posture is tense, back ramrod straight, as his hands clenched in tight fists. Everything about him says he's a raging inferno ready to explode, the intensity of his fury suffocating. The extent of his animosity seems out of place, only I can't work out what I could have done to warrant such loathing.

Did he know? Did he tell them? My shirt was on when we had sex, but he might have seen something. His fingers could have possibly grazed over a scar.

Confused, I move my hardened gaze back to Hawk.

"You didn't think I'd let you get away with walking around these halls defying me," he simply states, like somehow this is all my fault because I didn't listen to them before now. "Making fools out of us."

Stepping in so I'm inches from him, I snarl, "I didn't do anything to you, but you can bet I'm going to do something now." Glancing at the other three again, I add, "I'm going to burn your pathetic little lives to the ground."

Snatching up my bag, I keep my head held high as I storm out of the school, making a beeline to the only place that brings me peace in this hellhole.

I pummel the heavy bag over and over, not giving a shit that I'm in my uniform and my bare knuckles are turning red. Throwing everything I have into each hit, I pretend it's Hawk. West. Mason. Cam. Every single one of them deserves my wrath. What the fuck is their problem? Hawk has had it out for me since that first day, when I ran into him in the corridor, and he's only gotten madder since then as I got closer to Cam.

Maybe he's got a hard-on for Cam? I snort at that thought. Damn, that would be pretty fucking funny. Cam is most definitely a vagina lover, though. What other reason could he have? No normal person gives that much of a shit about who their friend is in to. Maybe it's because of who I am? My past. The whole 'you, us, and them' crap Bianca spouted on the first day. Cam has definitely deviated out of his lane by pursuing me.

Based on the look on his face today, Cam fucking hates me. I set that friendship on fire and destroyed everything we might have been. I didn't mean to, but since when did that matter? Regardless, you'd think Cam's newfound hatred would have appeased Hawk. Fuck, I don't know. Who the hell understands the inner workings of teenage boys' minds?

I have no idea how long I pound on the bag, but based on the ache in my hands and the sweat making the back of my shirt stick to me, it's quite a while. The rage is still pouring off of me when that crackle of electricity alerts me to his presence. *Great, what the fuck is he doing here?*

"Go away," I growl, only getting more frustrated when I hear him move further into the room.

"You need to do something more than beat on a bag," Mason says, somehow knowing exactly what I need.

I continue to ignore him, instead pounding even harder on the bag. He's fucking right, however. Sure, this is working to drain some of my energy, but it's doing absolutely nothing for my rage.

"Come on," he taunts, "show me what you've got."

I bark out a caustic laugh. "So you can tattle on me and get me kicked out? Yeah, I don't think so."

"I won't."

I don't move, though. I can't trust him, and as much as I want to beat his face into a bloody pulp, I want to remain enrolled in this school more.

"Everyone in the school just saw you at your most vulnerable." His words only fuel my anger. "Guys are going to jerk-off to your image for the rest of the year." I try to zone him out, knowing he's baiting me, except every single one of his words worms its way into my brain. "I was surprised to see the scars. After all, I've seen you in just your sports bra, but then I realized you always keep most of the lights off when you're in here."

Another beat of silence as I fight against my desperate need to throat-punch him.

"You know, they're all out there right now, speculating about what happened to you," he continues. "Some people have invented an entire sob story for you. A tragic car accident that killed your parents and left you with all those scars." I can't help the snort of laughter that leaves me at that notion. *If only.*

"Others think you're a self-harmer. That your life is just so damn pathetic, you need to cut yourself open in order to feel normal."

I roll my eyes at that emotionally dense and equally wrong theory; the ongoing strike sound as I hit the bag is my only response.

"I think they're wrong." I can't deny I'm curious as to what his theory is. None of the pretentious twats in this place could even wrap their judgmental little minds around the truth of how I got these scars. They have no fucking clue of the life I've endured. They all sit up there in their ivory towers, perched on their thrones of money, judging the fucking world around them, yet the truth is they wouldn't have survived in the world I grew up in. So they can whisper and speculate and judge, but at the end of the day, it all means nothing, for I've already been to hell and back, and I'm still fucking standing.

"I think someone did that to you. I think you *let* someone do that to you," he clarifies. "Or maybe you were a weak, pathetic, helpless little girl, and someone saw that you weren't made to survive this world, so they did what they had to do to toughen you up."

His words penetrate deep through my tough exterior, embedding themselves under my skin, sucking me into their dark depths. I'm not in the gym anymore. I'm not eighteen. I'm not a fighter. I'm exactly as he just said. I'm a weak, helpless little girl, crying and begging for *them* to stop. Promising I'll do better as blood drips onto the floor.

I don't know when I stopped punching the bag, nor do I remember closing the distance to Mason, but the next thing I do know, is my fist flying into his face, finally shutting him the fuck up.

It's too late, in any case. I'm too far gone. I can take the shit that's been thrown my way since I stepped into Pacific Prep. I can deal with the whispers and taunts. I can even handle the speculation about my scars. What I can't fucking cope with is being thrown back to that little girl who couldn't fight for herself. I might not be her anymore, but she's still very much a part of me.

I watch as I rain down punch after punch on him, barely grasping what I'm doing. I feel like a spectator in my own body. Rage, fear, hurt, and hopelessness, the feelings of both my past and present, melding together and creating one hell of a firestorm inside of me and using my body as a vessel to let it all out.

Mason doesn't even try to fight back as my fist collides with his jaw, snapping his head to the side. Another blow to his kidney has him grimacing, while a well-placed right hook has a cut opening up at the edge of his brow.

The whole time, he just stands there, taking every blow like the fighter he is. I have no idea how long I attack him like he's my own personal punching bag, but I don't stop until I've exorcised myself of every painful emotion, and I'm so exhausted I can no longer stand upright.

He catches me in his arms as I sag forward, barely able to keep my eyes open from the exhaustion slamming into me as my adrenaline finally burns off. He wraps his arms around me, slowly lowering me until we're on our knees, his body propping me up.

He feels so warm, the regular rhythm of his heart steadying as I come close to giving in to this bone-deep weariness. I don't have the brainpower or emotional bandwidth to understand what we are doing right now. I should not be letting him hold me like this, but I just can't bring myself to give a shit.

It's like my body was a bath. The plug was in and the tap was on, and I was overflowing with emotions, unable to contain them. At some point, when I was beating the crap out of Mason, the tap was turned off and the plug pulled out, allowing everything I was feeling to drain away. What's left is a vast, empty tub; a void within me.

The next thing I know, we're lying on the floor, my body draped over his. I feel him stroking his hand over my hair, but my eyes refuse to open, a small groan escaping me.

"Shhh, you're okay. Sleep. I'll look out for you."

As though he's just said the magic words, my body gives up the fight, and I succumb to sleep, letting it suck me into its dark depths.

When I next wake up, I'm back in my room, tucked into bed with wet bandages wrapped around my knuckles. I don't remember how I got back here, but there's only one person who could have done it.

Mason.

But why?

Little Warrior

CHAPTER TWENTY

*I*t starts out slow, with one or two kids whispering. I barely even notice, but when a low hum of activity settles over the library, I can no longer ignore it. Glancing over at the other tables, students are staring wide-eyed at their tablets, some of them laughing.

"Eww, no wonder she's been trying to hide *that* all year," I hear a girl at a nearby table say to her friend.

A couple of jocks are sitting at the table beside me, leering eagerly at whatever is on the tablet.

"Damn, even with all those marks, she's fucking hot."

"Right? I'd totally fuck her."

"Hell yeah, I'd have tried with her sooner if I knew she looked like that under those crappy clothes she wears."

What the hell are they talking about?

Setting the tablet in front of me, I open up my email, finding a video file attached to a recent unopened email. That must be what everyone is whispering about.

Pressing play, I stare transfixed at the video, unable to believe what I'm seeing. There's only one person who would do this, but to go this far? My hand clenches tightly around the device, a notification popping up, showing a new message in our group chat.

> Hawk: Meet outside the east wing at the end of class.

Not willing to wait that long, I stuff my things in my backpack and storm out, arriving at the east wing just as the bell goes off. West is already there, his face pinched as he glares at the passing students. The entire way here, I heard them all whispering about her, about the video. Are their lives so goddamn empty that they have to talk about a girl they don't even know, speculating about the damage that's been done to her? What the fuck is wrong with them?

"Did you know?" I snap at him as I arrive.

He grits his teeth, frowning at me. "No. Of course not."

"He's gone too far this time," I growl, my body practically vibrating with rage.

His eyes run over me, taking in my clenched fists and wide stance. "You can't do anything here. Let's just get through whatever he has planned, and then we can talk to him."

I fucking hate that idea. What the hell else does he plan on doing to her? He's right, though. I can't say a goddamn word until we can get back to the dorms, and I can ream him out in private.

So instead, I grit my teeth, donning my usual mask of apathy and watch as Hadley fights fire with fire, showing us just how resilient she is as she tears us a new one before stomping off.

"Show's over, get the fuck out of here," I roar at the lingering students after Hadley's departure. Everyone quickly jumps into action, scurrying away from us, until we're the only ones left in the hall.

"I don't know what the hell you were thinking," I snarl, rounding on Hawk. "But we're going to fucking discuss this later."

Before I can give in to the urge to punch him, I storm out, ignoring him as he calls after me.

I know where she would have gone to, and while I'm probably one of the last people she wants to see, I also know exactly what she needs right now.

～

FOR THE LAST FEW MONTHS, I've watched Hadley beat on the heavy bag harder than some trained professionals, ridding herself of whatever she was feeling. However, watching her today, she was completely different.

Sure, the rage coming off her was a palpable thing sitting heavy in the air, but it was more than that. She seemed almost haunted, as though her demons were pressing in around her. I know that feeling. I understand it.

When I wrapped my arms around her, I was only trying to catch her before she collapsed, but holy fuck, holding her against me—she fit perfectly in my arms. I've never held anyone like that, never mind someone so vulnerable. Whether it was due to some part of herself trusting me, or she was just so lost to her pain—pain that we caused—whatever the reason, holding her like that hit me in a way I never expected.

Tucking her in, I brush a stray strand of hair from her face. Even in sleep, it's scrunched up. *What the hell happened to you?* Brushing my thumb lightly across her cheek, the lines on her face flatten out and she leans into my touch. Grudgingly, I turn away from her, ignoring the pit in my stomach, the part of me that wants to go back and stay with her, as I silently close her door behind me. With anger coursing through me, I storm back to our dorm. Hawk and I need to have some fucking words after that shit he pulled today. What he did was fucked-up. And not to tell us? Dick move.

Throwing open the door to the apartment, I find Hawk sitting in the living room.

West is standing over him with his arms crossed and a similar scowl to my own on his face.

"What the hell was that about?" I bark out, slamming the door shut behind me and glaring at him as I close the distance between us, coming to stand beside West.

Hawk's eyes widen as he takes in my appearance. Yeah, I imagine I look like shit. I can't say I thought I'd ever be beaten up by a girl. Not only do I deserve it, but I'm so fucking turned-on by her ability to beat the shit out of me; I don't even care that everything hurts.

"What the fuck—" West starts, but Hawk cuts across him.

"I did what was necessary," he says with a nonchalant shrug.

"Necessary? What the fuck does that mean? You completely violated her privacy."

"What the fuck do you care?"

Unable to answer that, I purse my lips.

"You saw her scars. You *know* what leaves marks like that," I spit the words out between gritted teeth, the ink-black tone of my voice giving away the roiling emotions within me as I fight to block out the traumatic memories of my past.

Maybe that's the difference between me and Hawk. Where he saw scars and pain and an opportunity to strike; I see a five-year-old boy struggling to hold himself together as blood flows down the shower drain, crying out in pain as the water hits the open lashes on his back.

The guys all know what I've been through, but there's a difference between hearing about that shit, and actually living it. I've let him go around, putting her in her place all semester, all in the name of presenting a united front to the rest of the idiots at this school. Today crossed a fat fucking line, though. What he did is *not* okay. The second he saw that video, he fucking *knew*, yet he *still* sent it out to everyone.

"How has Cam not already torn you a new one?" I snarl.

Looking utterly unfazed by my aggression, he snorts, shaking his head, a cocky grin lifting his lips.

"He knew what I had planned."

I gape at him, his words playing on repeat in my head.

"He what?" West barks at the same time I blurt, "Cam knew?"

The man himself comes strutting into the room, looking far too fucking nonplussed, given all the shit that's gone down today.

"I knew what?"

"You fucking knew what he was going to do?" I growl, turning my glare on him.

What the actual fuck is going on here? I know he's butt-hurt over her rejection, however he needs to get the fuck over it. After what I saw today, her insistence that she belongs to no one makes even more sense. How can he not fucking see that?

His features shutter as he locks down whatever emotions he's feeling, making it impossible for me to read him.

"I found this in her room," Hawk informs us, dropping a notebook on the coffee table. It looks just like every other one Hadley owns. She's one of the only students who insist on writing everything instead of using her tablet.

"Her workbook?" I ask, frowning at it in confusion. Picking it up, I flick through the pages, hesitating when, instead of school notes, I find clip outs. The first few pages are all of Cam's dad, followed by a handful of news articles on the rest of our parents and their company, each one with handwritten scrawls beside it.

"What the fuck? What is this?" I can't tear my eyes away from the damning pages in front of me. Insights into our parents, into our lives. Information she could only have gained from us.

"I don't understand."

What the fuck is this? Why does she have it?

West tears the notebook out of my hands, his eyes narrowing as he slowly scans each page, his computer brain analyzing every word.

"She was clearly using us," Cam seethes, venom thick in his tone. His hands are clenched, his lip curled in hatred. *Fuck, he's pissed.* It takes a hell of a lot to enrage him, but he is fucking furious right now.

"For what?" I can't make sense of it all. What does she want with our parents?

"How the fuck do I know. She's street trash. She probably wants what every other girl wants—money, security, and a better social status."

"I told you she couldn't be trusted." I round on Hawk so quickly that the room spins, glowering at him. That shit isn't fucking helpful right now. Ignoring him, I turn to look at West, who is still flipping through the notebook.

"What do you think?" I ask him, needing someone with a sensible head to have some sort of input into this asinine conversation.

"It doesn't fucking matter," Cam yells, waving his hand toward the notebook. "Why she has all this...information, or what she's doing, doesn't matter. Hawk's right. She's been using us this whole time. Everything she said, every move she made, was some preconceived plan designed to bring us closer to her."

My eyes narrow on him, trying to read between the lines. He's never said anything, but he's way too annoyed about all of this for Hadley to have simply been another girl he was chasing after. Something more must have happened between them for him to be this pissed-off. "She's been using us, manipulating us all year. What she got today was the least she deserved."

After listening to him wax fucking poetic about her all year, it's a shock to hear the bitterness in his tone as he spits out each word. Sure, he was hurt after her rejection, but he's hardly said anything about her since then. Not a bad word against her, except the rage coming off him is a flagrant thing reverberating in the air around us. Underneath it all, though, he's concealing a hell of a lot of pain over her betrayal. It snuffs out some of the fire I came storming in here with, taking the edge off my anger at Hawk.

I still don't agree with what they did, but this notebook certainly complicates things. What the hell is she up to? What interest does she have in our parents?

"By forcing her to be Cam's girl, we gave her exactly what she wanted," Hawk snarls.

"But she turned him down," I argue, still not totally in agreement with his assessment of her. He hasn't been thinking straight when it comes to her. She was the first person of the year to cross him, and he's decided to make her life miserable for it, only there's no real reason for his dislike of her.

"What do we do now?" Cam asks, still looking furious over the whole thing.

"Let the rest of the school deal with her. After today, they'll hopefully tear her to shreds," Hawk states. "*We* have nothing more to do with her. We can't give her any more information than she already has."

"Don't you want to know what she's up to?" I ask, surprised.

"No. I don't give a shit. You all just need to stay the fuck away from her, okay?"

"Do you always sneak into other people's rooms in the middle of the night?"

Flicking on the lamp, she spins toward me, her eyes wide when she finds me watching her from a chair in the living room.

I've been waiting for her all night. I knew she would show up at some point. She's spent all semester putting together this notebook on us all, and there's no way she would just let it go. Besides, she's shown how capable she is at getting in and out of our rooms undetected. Even after we changed the locks, she still managed to get in and mess with us. Last week she took all the cables for the TV and game consoles and hid them amongst towels in the airing cupboard. It took us a whole day to find them.

"Holy shit, you nearly gave me a heart attack," she whisper-yells. "And I don't think you can say anything about sneaking into others' rooms."

I ignore her dig, refusing to be sidetracked from my task of getting some answers out of her.

"What are you doing here, Hadley?"

The lines around her eyes tighten as she frowns at me. "I need my notebook back."

"Why?"

Come on, just tell me something. Give me some reason as to what this is all about.

"I just do."

"You've gotta give me something." I sigh. "Hawk and Cam are convinced you're using us—well, Cam—to get to our parents...Is that the case?"

She pauses, her eyes simmering with defiance. Before she even opens her mouth, I know she won't give me the necessary answers.

"Is that why you sent everyone that video? Because you found my notebook? Or are you just so bored with your life of privilege that you need to destroy someone else's just for shits and giggles?"

Her head tilts slightly as she scrutinizes me, trying to get a read on me and understand the motives behind today.

"No," I seethe, annoyed that she thinks any of this is just fun and games to us. "We—"

"Did you think that would break me?" she snaps, cutting me off before I can say anything further. Not that I had any clue what I was going to say. "A video? I guess someone like you couldn't possibly understand what I've had to endure."

Unable to bare the distance between us, I cut across the space until I'm standing right in front of her, her chest brushing against mine. I'm angry at Hawk and Cam, at her. I'm confused and need answers, but despite all that, I still can't ignore this connection I feel with her. And after this afternoon, it's only gotten more intense. I need to feel her small body pressed up against mine, wrapped around me once more.

Towering over her, I drop my head so our faces are inches apart. "You assume you're the only one with a fucked-up past, Little Warrior?" I murmur, staring deep into her volatile eyes, swirling with so many emotions that I can't identify them. "Do you truly think that just because we have big houses and fancy cars, we don't have our own traumas we're working through?"

She returns my intense gaze, trying to gauge my carefully concealed thoughts. "Yes," she murmurs honestly, the word barely more than a whisper against my lips.

"I wish that were true." I give her a small, sad smile. "Although you should know better than anyone, everyone wants to keep the scars of their past a secret, and just because they might not be visible doesn't mean they're any less real."

A tense moment of silence stretches between us until she speaks again.

"So, Mason, if we're sharing war stories, what are your scars?"

"What are yours?" I rebut, not willing to share any more of myself with her. She already sees too much, knows too much.

Her eyes bore into mine, showing me all of her, every painful crack and open wound she always keeps so carefully hidden. At the same time, I can feel her probing inside me, peering in hidden boxes, delving into my dark secrets, each of us letting down our walls, however briefly.

"Why do I feel like our pain is the same?" Her words are a barely heard breath, but with our lips basically touching and my every sense honed in on her, it would be impossible to miss her slightest movement.

"Because, baby, it is."

She doesn't say anything for a long time, and I expect she's not going to respond. Our lips hover dangerously close, and all I can think about is kissing her, but my loyalty to my brothers holds me back.

Eventually, her lips part and her tongue flicks out to wet her lower lip. I trace the movement with a keen eye until her words distract me from wondering what she tastes like. "It was, at first…about finding information on your parents." She pointedly directs the conversation back to somewhat safer territory and something about the way she says it comes across as vulnerable, honest. God help me, but I'm inclined to believe her.

"Why?"

She shakes her head. "I can't tell you that."

I grind my teeth together. I need fucking answers. "What *can* you tell me?"

Again, she pauses. "Your parents aren't who you think they are."

My hands come up, squeezing her shoulders firmly. "What do you know about our parents?" There's no way she can know. Hell, we only just found out. How the fuck could *she* know?

"I can't tell you," she reiterates, her refusal to tell me what I need to know pissing me off as a growl of frustration rumbles through my chest. How can I go from wanting to kiss her to wanting to throttle her in mere seconds?

Taking a deep breath, I ask a different question, "What about now?"

"What?"

"You said you were using us at first…what about now?"

"Things have changed."

"With Cam?"

She gives a small, sharp nod of her head. "And with West…and you."

Me? Does she feel whatever the fuck this is between us? What does she mean by 'things changed with West'? I didn't know they were close. Every word out of her mouth is only raising more fucking questions.

"And Hawk?"

"Hawk can choke on a bag of dicks for all I care."

I have to hold back a laugh at that, silence falling between us once again as I think through everything she's said. She hasn't really given me anything to go on. No reason why she's got that stupid notebook, no understanding of what she's up to. Yet something in my gut wants to trust her.

Staring into her eyes, her gaze roams over my face and she grimaces as she takes in the myriad of bruises starting to appear. She doesn't apologize, nor do I expect her to.

I don't understand this connection between us, but I do feel like she gets me better than anyone ever has.

"I'll get you your book. Give me a few days."

Her eyes widen in surprise before her brows pull down. "Why are you helping me?"

That's an excellent fucking question.

"I have no fucking clue."

Hadley

CHAPTER TWENTY-ONE

The days after the video are a dark blur. The headmaster calls me into a meeting, demanding answers I can't give him, wanting to know who did this to me and why. Not once does he actually mention the video or the posters. He doesn't ask who I think is responsible nor does the word 'bullying' even pass his lips. It's a complete farce. Everyone knows who did it, but because they're the fucking Princes, they get away with it.

Nonetheless, that's okay. I don't need the school to dole out punishment. I'm more than capable of taking revenge into my own hands. In fact, I prefer it that way. I want to see their faces as I ruin them and rip their perfect fucking world apart.

Except Mason's words come back to me.

Do you really think that just because we have big houses and fancy cars, we don't have our own traumas we're working through?

There was no faking the pain I saw in his eyes. I got a good look at his inner torment, and he made it sound like the others have experienced their own suffering too.

It doesn't make any sense. What could have happened to him that was so bad? But I *felt* it. I felt how similar our pain was, like he'd survived the same fucked-up shit I had.

A knock on the door pulls me out of my ruminating thoughts. Ever since the video, I've spent every spare moment I'm not in class hiding out in my room. It's pathetic, I know, yet I can't fucking take the looks and whispers from the other students. Also, if I have to see the stupid, smug smirk on Hawk's face one more time, I'm going to do something I regret.

I haven't even gone to the gym. Too afraid of running into Mason. I don't know what the fuck to make of him after our chat the other night. Things got heavy and far too...real. All this time, I've firmly believed they are just like their parents. I've thought of them as these rich, controlling, pampered dicks with nothing better to do with themselves, only now Mason has me thinking I have them pegged all wrong.

When I mentioned their parents, he was angry and surprised, but there was also a hint of fear in his voice, a spark of worry in his eyes. Why? Was that concern for me? Or because I might've found out something I shouldn't have, and he's worried about the repercussions to his family and business?

Nevertheless, he took care of me that day, going so far as to tuck me into bed, and he was true to his word. I found an envelope with my notebook inside shoved under my door two days later. Not to mention the strange connection between us, and the steady strength I feel around him.

No, I can't afford to think like that. I can't allow a couple of nice gestures and some stupid feelings to soften my hatred. I need to hold on to this anger and use it to fight back against them, to show them they haven't beaten me down.

Opening the door, I stare speechlessly at my visitor. I don't know who I thought it would be, it's not like many people want to hang out with me these days, but I definitely wasn't expecting Emilia. She was already not talking to me after Halloween, so I expected this latest incident to be the final nail in the coffin of our friendship.

She's fidgeting nervously with her hands, glancing everywhere but at me. "Uh, hey." She gives me a weak smile, still not meeting my eyes.

"Hey." My voice lacks any of its usual warmth when talking to her as I peer past her, checking to see if she's alone. There's no one else around, making my posture relax a bit.

"I, uh...I wanted to see how you were doing after, you know...everything."

Huh, I wasn't expecting that.

"I'm fine."

What else can I say? We haven't spoken in over a month.

She nods her head, probably having expected that answer. She knows me well enough to know I'm not a 'pour my heart out' kind of person.

"Right. Well, I just wanted to check that you were okay."

She turns around to walk away, but I call out her name, halting her mid-step.

"Why?"

I'm not even sure what I'm asking. Why did she come here? Why now?

When she turns around, regret flashes across her eyes as she chews her bottom lip, taking a step back toward me.

"I thought about knocking on your door every day. I wanted to, but I was scared. It probably sounds stupid to you, but I like the quiet life I have here. I don't think I could handle the Princes messing it up for me or having the whole school...well, you know."

Yeah, I do. The last week, since the video, the students have been relentless. If it's not some meathead jock asking if he can see my fucking panties, it's the girls scowling at me like I'm disgusting, ensuring they don't accidentally bump into me, like I'm fucking diseased or some shit.

And, of course, there's also Bianca and the other Princesses. They didn't waste any time cornering me to make fun of my humiliation and remind me just how much I'll never be one of them. It doesn't help that Cam chose Bianca *again* for a second month, a fact she likes to rub in my face every time I see her. As if the twisting in my gut at seeing Cam superglued to her side all the fucking time isn't bad enough.

"Nevertheless, I couldn't go another day without at least checking on you." She licks her lips nervously. "You maybe want nothing to do with me, and I wouldn't blame you...but if you ever wanna talk, I won't push you away again."

I don't know what to say to her. Instead, I end up staring at her like a wide-eyed idiot while she glances awkwardly around the hall before giving a sharp nod of her head and slipping into her room.

That afternoon, I wander over to the admin building. It's a two-story structure on the far side of campus, as old as every other building, where the school reception is, along with offices for the headmaster and teachers. It's also where the school nurse is based and the school counselor, who I've been mandated to see—even if I think it's a complete waste of both our times.

I rap my knuckles sharply on the door before I can talk myself out of it. It's not like I have any fucking say in the matter, so I may as well get this shitshow over with as quickly as possible.

"Come in," a gravelly voice calls out from inside the room. With one final deep breath, I wrap my hand around the handle and push the door open, stepping into the small office.

"Hadley?" the counselor questions when I walk in. I have to say, he is not at all what I pictured when I was told I'd have to see a fucking shrink. He must be newly qualified. There's no way he's older than twenty-two or twenty-three.

He's got neatly styled dark brown hair, moss green eyes, and just a hint of dark stubble dotted along his sharp jaw, all of which gives him a classically handsome look.

Paired with his black shirt and cute black waistcoat, he has that whole 'hot for teacher' thing going on. Although, I guess it's more 'hot for therapist'?

"It's nice to meet you," he greets, getting up from behind his desk and moving around it to stand in front of me. "I'm Mr. Jacobs." He holds out his hand, giving me a friendly smile and showing off his perfectly straight, white teeth.

"Yeah, hi." My greeting is much less enthusiastic than his as I ignore his outstretched hand.

His smile doesn't falter, and I could swear his eyes flare at my attitude, but it's gone before I can be sure.

Lowering his hand, he gestures for me to have a seat on the couch. *Talk about cliché.* Ignoring the sofa in the corner, I stride over and plonk my ass in one of the chairs in front of his desk.

Thinking I hear him huff out a chuckle, I turn around to look at him, only to find him watching me closely. Too closely; his expression unreadable. After a moment's hesitation, he saunters to the desk himself, sitting in the spare chair beside me, not seeming phased by my unwillingness to bend to his will.

Neither of us says anything for a moment, each of us scrutinizing the other. He's definitely not what I expected, but that doesn't mean I'm about to just spill all my dark secrets to him.

"I understand you just started at Pacific Prep this year," he begins. It's not a question, so I don't bother to answer him. Something he must realize after a beat of silence as he continues on, "How have you been settling in?"

I take in his overpriced haircut and expensive outfit, ignoring how his fancy aftershave has annoyingly permeated the air in the room, suffocating me with his cedarwood and eucalyptus scent. It's strangely comforting, yet I remind myself it's a false sense of security designed to lure in fucked-up people like me and get us to bare our souls.

Not. Fucking. Happening.

Pinching my lips, I sigh. "Why don't we just get down to why I'm here," I say, ready to get this stupid session over with.

"Alright," he agrees readily, giving me a nod. "Why are you here?"

I narrow my eyes at him. He knows damn well why I'm here.

I don't say anything to his stupid-ass question, and he eventually tries a different tactic.

"Why don't you tell me what happened the other day?"

"There's nothing to tell," I grind out between gritted teeth. I, sure as fuck, am not about to rehash that fiasco.

When I don't elaborate, he leans forward in his chair to rest his elbows on his knees and looks me straight in the eye. "Listen," he begins, a serious expression on his face, "I know you don't want to be here, telling your problems to some stranger."

"Does anyone want to be here?" I snark, gaining a small smile from him, and damn, it's cute as all fucking hell.

"You'd be surprised." He leans in even closer as though we're sharing a secret. "These rich kids don't give a damn. They just want an engaging audience while they listen to themselves speak."

Cocking my head, I roam my eyes once again over his outfit. Yup, definitely designer. "Aren't you one of those rich kids?"

He doesn't answer my question, quirking his lips up in a sly smile.

"The school has raised some concerns. Given your less-than-ideal upbringing, they felt it would be in your best interests to come and talk to me."

Less-than-ideal upbringing? That's putting it mildly. I don't think he could have found a more diplomatic way to say 'the fucked up shit you've been through'.

"Of course they have." I snort, shaking my head at their audacity. "They're worried about how I got some old scars, but they don't seem to give a flying fuck about the threats, the dirty looks, or anything else that's happened since I rocked up to this hellhole."

"You're being bullied?" He phrases it as a question, even though he doesn't sound surprised. And why would he? I'm sure, just like everyone else, he's already heard about the video and the posters.

"Well, I didn't post that video or put those pictures up all over the school myself now, did I?" I reply sarcastically, feeling my body heat with anger once again over the whole goddamn situation.

Overlooking my attitude, he continues to stare intently at me. It's as though he's worried if he blinks or looks away for a second he will miss some vital tell. I'm better than that, however. I'm not that easy to read, and he's soon going to realize that. "How bad has it been?"

I glance away, not wanting him to see how affected I am by everything.

I sigh, so done with this whole stupid meeting. I knew it was going to be a waste of time. "I'm not here because of that. It's nothing I can't handle. The school referred me to you because they were obligated to do so, but there's nothing for them to be concerned about."

He stares at me intently for a long moment, and I can feel him trying to dig under my skin and work me out. *Fat fucking chance of that.*

"Hadley, I'm going to be honest with you," he says, his lips pinching as though he doesn't want to say the next words but knows he has to. Then again words like that are never followed by anything good. Before he even says it, I know what he will say.

"I saw the pictures of you."

Before I can cuss him out—I mean, that's gotta be all sorts of inappropriate, right?—he holds up his hand, silencing my unspoken words.

"It was purely so I would know what the school was talking about. They were worried you were self-harming."

"And you don't think that?" I ask curiously, guessing from his tone that he hasn't drawn the same conclusion.

He observes me for a long moment, the silence building between us until he shakes his head slightly. "I don't."

I swallow around a lump in my throat, not entirely sure why I'm suddenly feeling emotional.

Coughing to clear my throat, I lick my unexpectedly dry lips. "Then what am I doing here? You know I'm not self-harming, and I'm sure you're aware that any 'issues' with my home life before I came here are redundant now that I'm eighteen and no longer legally a child of the state."

"Because, regardless of whether or not you're still in a dangerous environment, someone did that to you. That kind of abuse leaves more than just physical scars."

I have no words. I literally have no idea what to say to that. He's more right than he could possibly know, but I'm still not telling him shit.

He seems to realize he isn't going to get anything out of me, not today at least. So rather than the probing questions I am expecting, he lets me go.

As I reach for the door handle, his words stop me.

"I think we should meet for the rest of the semester. Same time next week?"

It's not really a question, not one I can refuse anyway. So with gritted teeth, I give him a tight nod, not saying anything else as I pull open the door and stalk out.

I have no idea what the hell he thinks he's going to achieve by having me come to his office every week. Does he think he'll wear me down? That if he forces me to sit and talk to him, I'll eventually spill all my dark, dirty secrets? *Ha. If that's the case, he's got another thing coming.*

∼

It's late on Sunday when I pull open the dining hall door, not really paying attention to the few other students milling around as I make a beeline for the freezer, my head already debating which flavor of ice cream I should go for today.

Deciding on strawberry shortcake, I turn to head back to my room when I spot Emilia sitting at the scholarship table. I haven't spoken to her since she knocked on my door. I have no idea what to say to her, but I miss her. I miss our friendship.

Hesitantly, I take a step toward her, gnawing on my bottom lip as I approach.

"Hi." I stand awkwardly on the opposite side of the table, smiling—although it feels more like a grimace—as Emilia looks up from the book she's engrossed in, her eyes widening when she sees me standing there.

"Hey." A small, hopeful smile touches her lips. "How have you been?"

"Fine. I'm fine. You?"

"I'm good." She nods, the two of us staring awkwardly at one another.

"How are things with, uh, Andrew?"

A light brightens in her eyes, a genuine, happy smile taking over her face.

"Things are going really well."

I can't help but smile at the happiness radiating from her as I sit down, digging into my ice cream as she catches me up on everything that's been going on with her recently, the two of us falling easily back into our old chatter.

Sweetheart

CHAPTER TWENTY-TWO

This job is boring as hell, but when you're fresh out of college, neck deep in debt, and you get offered a ridiculously overpaid job to listen to the pathetic problems of over-privileged rich kids all day? Yeah, you'd have to be brain-damaged not to take it. Still, it's a total fucking bore. Who cares if Daddy won't buy you a new car or Mommy spent most of her summer vacation fucking the pool boy?

Well, I guess I'm supposed to give a shit. Although growing up in a tiny apartment in a rough neighborhood, learning to fend for myself at a young age because my mom was too busy working three jobs to make ends meet, makes it seriously fucking difficult to have any sympathy for these spoiled brats.

I'd just been going through the motions, barely paying attention to the kids who walked through my door, until *she* walked in. I know there are a handful of scholarship students here, but ironically, none of them ever need to see me. I reckon, like myself, life has taught them how to suck it up and get on with it, even when shit is hitting the fan. So when my first scholarship student walks through the door, I'm intrigued, especially given the reason she's here. The bullying doesn't surprise me. What does surprise me, though, are the images.

I've gone over case studies of children of abuse. I've read files and studied psychological theories, and learned about therapeutic treatments, except I've never had to actually deal with one. It was the last thing I expected to have thrown at me in this pretentious school of pampered princes and princesses.

I was taken with her the second I saw her picture. It had nothing to do with her scars, and it sure as fuck wasn't because she was mostly naked. I could barely tear my eyes away from her face to look at anything else. It was the same when she stepped into my office. She was the embodiment of everything I've read, yet she completely contradicts what I expected.

With her hostile demeanor, prickly attitude, and wary manner, everything about her screamed distrust. Her dry wit and evasive answers are defensive measures designed to keep people at arm's length. All of it is a protective defense, so no one can hurt you if you don't let them in. No one can catch you unaware if you're constantly on alert.

Despite the ugly reason she ended up in my office, I couldn't help but be excited that she was here. She's exactly the distraction I need right now. A challenge I didn't know I was looking for.

Unlike the other kids who come storming in here, immediately blurting out their problems and expecting me to fix them, I'm going to have to actually work to get Hadley to talk to me. It will take patience, careful prodding, well-placed questions, and tactful information sharing.

I get the impression that if I can get her to trust me, to open up to me, to allow me to see the real Hadley she hides underneath all that sass and snark, she's going to make me question everything I've ever known.

The knock on the door alerts me to her arrival, and I immediately sit up straighter in my chair, running my hand through my hair and smoothing it out. *Jesus, I feel like a tween about to go on his first date.* I'm a riot of nervous energy. Clearing my throat, I call out, "Come in."

The door swings open, and Hadley storms in, her face shuttered and back straight. Does she walk around the school with that attitude, or is it just for me?

"Have a seat." I gesture to the chair in front of the desk, assuming that's where she'll sit since it's where she chose last time. Then, with a raised eyebrow in my direction, she strides over to the couch, dropping her bag on the floor and making herself comfortable as she sinks into the couch cushions.

I have to force my lips not to hitch up as I swallow my laugh at her defiance. She never does or says what I expect.

In all the literature I've read, it explains how children of abuse grow up to be closed-off, independent individuals. Hadley is undoubtedly all of those things. Only where the textbooks say they are also broken, nervous, anxious people; Hadley is all strength and defiance.

"I have some work to finish up. I figured you probably have homework you could start on, or there are books on the shelf so feel free to look through them."

Her eyes narrow slightly, the only indicator of what she's thinking. If I am to guess, I've taken her by surprise. She was expecting prying questions into her childhood and whatever is going on at school, but I've already ascertained that that won't work for her.

I need her to trust me. I *want* her to trust me, and that starts with getting her comfortable in my presence. Saying nothing, she bends down, pulling out a tablet and notebook before getting to work.

Neither of us says anything for the next hour, both of us working away in silence. Only once the hour is up, do I stop focusing on the pages on my desk and peer up at her. She's lost in her work, scribbling away in her workbook, transcribing notes from the tablet. Her face is softer than I've seen before, making her look more her own age. Just seeing her relaxed and focused like that feels like a victory in itself.

As though sensing my eyes on her, she snaps her head up, her face hardening as she glares at me. "Sorry," I state, looking at her for a second longer before breaking eye contact. "That took longer than I expected. Our time is up."

"No worries." She shrugs, shoving her belongings back into her bag and throwing it over her shoulder.

Just before she heads out the door, I call out, "Same time next week." Her steps falter, and she hesitates, not once looking my way before giving a sharp nod and pulling open the door to leave.

Once she's gone, I sit back in my chair, replaying our very limited interaction. She didn't give me much, yet she said more than she realized. The fact she turned up is telling in itself. It's not like anyone would track her down and force her to come here if she didn't show.

Equally, when I told her I was busy, she didn't try to worm her way out of the session by suggesting we reschedule. So without even saying a word, she's told me a lot. She showed me she's used to following orders, doing as she's told, even if she doesn't agree or internally rebels against it. My guess is the scars have something to do with that—pain and torture are excellent methods of compliance. The fact that she was comfortable enough to focus on her schoolwork tells me that, while she may not want to be here, she feels safe enough in this room, in my presence, that she doesn't need to be constantly on alert. I have no doubt she's still finely tuned into her surroundings, but she doesn't perceive me as an immediate threat—something I'll take as a win.

Our subsequent few appointments go the same way. Me finding excuses not to conduct our session so I can silently observe her and give her time to get comfortable in my space. Each week I see her getting more and more relaxed, growing used to the routine. However, today I can tell I will only be able to continue with this tactic for a bit longer. She's fidgety, unable to focus on her work, constantly casting glances my way. She knows it's only a matter of time before this silent truce between us comes to an end and the hard questions begin.

Before she can ask whatever questions are rattling around in her head, I speak up. As I said, this only works if we trust one another. To do that, I will have to share a part of myself with her.

"I grew up in a run-down one-bedroom apartment in Black Creek. You've probably never heard of it—"

"I've heard of it." Her eyes are narrowed, skepticism written all over her face as she takes in my fancy-as-fuck suit and styled hair. Yeah, I'm a far cry from the Black Creek kid I used to be. I may not be that scrawny street rat any longer, but this suit isn't me, either. It's the persona I donned when I agreed to this job—the person I had to become to fit in with the uppity staff and pretentious kids.

If I'd shown up in my worn jeans and faded t-shirts, they all would have taken one look at me and sent me packing. It's been made very clear to me that appearances matter here. Everything ultimately boils down to how you look and come across to others. It's got absolutely nothing to do with who you are or how good of a person you are. It's all superficial bullshit. But the other students I see would be straight on the phone to their parents, demanding a 'real therapist' if they knew I wasn't one of them. So every morning, I put on my unfamiliar, pretentious clothes, don my fake smile and pretend I actually enjoy this platitudinous job.

The only problem is that every step I've taken to fit in with the people here has created a wall between Hadley and me. One I now have to carefully deconstruct, forcing me to put my trust in her that she will keep anything I share to herself.

"You don't look like anyone I've ever met from Black Creek."

The fact that she knows *anyone* there surprises me. The only people in Black Creek are mobsters and gangbangers. Not exactly your everyday folk, and according to her file, she's been bounced about from home to home all over California, though she's never lived in Oregon.

Rolling up the arm of my shirt, I show her the crude tattoo on my forearm. It's jagged and uneven, appearing like a botched job. In fairness, it was. That's what happens when a bunch of thirteen-year-olds with nothing better to do attempt to tattoo themselves. I've added other professional ink around it over the years until the entire length of my arm is covered in various tribal designs, yet this one still stands out.

Looking at the ink, I have to swallow around the emotion in my throat, shrugging away the painful tug in my chest. Each harrowing memory hits me like a punch to the gut. Despite its prominent position, making it impossible for me to overlook every day, I never allow myself to reminisce on the past and all the things the tattoo once represented.

Setting aside her workbook, she stands up from what has become her usual position on the sofa and cautiously approaches me, as though I might be trying to lure her into a trap.

When she's in front of the desk, she leans down, getting a better look at the symbol on my arm. It's a crude shape of the number four, with the words 'Reaper Rejects' encircled around it in barely legible writing.

"Reaper Rejects? I've never heard of them."

"They aren't anyone." I sigh. "A bunch of kids who thought they were all that, wanting to grow up way too fast, except when their world crashed down around them, they didn't know how to handle it."

Her eyes flick up to mine for a moment as if wanting to test the truth of my words, before she looks back down at the ink. "What happened to them?" Her voice is a low whisper, like she's afraid if she talks any louder it will break this moment of truthfulness between us.

"We all went our separate ways. I don't know what happened to the others."

For the first time since I laid eyes on Hadley, her walls are lowered. It's still impossible to get a read on her, but there's now an understanding sitting heavy in the air between us. The sense of shared trauma and unresolved pain, memories we would both rather leave buried in the past.

Clearing my throat, I glance down at my watch. "Our time is up." I had planned all along to tell her who I am, who I was, but I never intended to bring *that* up. That part of my past is not something I talk about. It's not something I *think* about. I spend a considerable amount of my day pretending it never happened, so to bring it up so readily and to share it with her, has left me raw and unsure of my next move. I can't think straight when my head's a mess like this, and her close proximity is playing havoc with my brain. I can't afford to do or say something that might undo the little bit of progress we've made today.

She stares at me for a moment longer. Her eyes are softer than before, like she's finally seeing past the privileged, rich, white guy facade I'm wearing and glimpsing the real me.

Giving a slight nod, she murmurs, "Okay," before moving back to the sofa and hastily shoving her things into her bag, pausing as she passes the desk on her way to the door.

"Same time next week?"

Unable to look at her, I give a quick jerk of my head. "I'll see you then."

It's only when the door clicks shut behind her that I let out a shaky breath, loosening the tie around my neck and bending down to lift out a bottle of bourbon and a coffee mug I keep hidden in my bottom drawer.

Pouring a small measure, I knock it back in one-go, leaning my head against the headrest and closing my eyes, letting the memories flash behind my eyelids.,

Despite our impoverished upbringing, we were always laughing and smiling. We never complained about being hungry or not having the latest technology. Black Creek was our playground, where we made games out of dumpster diving and constructed toys from the trash littering the streets. Together, we were happy. We had each other, and we were naive enough to believe that was enough.

I'll never forget that day; the gunshots, the screams. Everything changed and before I could come to terms with it, my mom pulled us out of there, carted me off to a brand new town and made me promise I'd never step foot in Black Creek again or reach out to my old friends.

It's been nearly ten years since that fateful day. Nearly as long since I last thought about them all, shrugging off any notions with false pretenses that they are probably okay out in the world living their lives. In actual fact, they're most likely dead or in prison at best.

Fuck it, I decide, pouring myself another glass of bourbon. It's not like I have any more students today, and I'm already in a piss-poor mood. May as well drink my pain away until I'm too far gone to think about them, until I can numb the gnawing guilt inside me for never going back for them, for never getting them out of there.

Hadley

CHAPTER TWENTY-THREE

I hesitate with my fist in front of the door. Goddammit. Why did he have to go and mess with our usual routine of silence? Does he expect me to open up to him now after our little powwow last week?

Whatever happened in his past must have sucked, and he's clearly not the typical rich asshole I first thought he was. I was too quick to judge him, although just because he decided to share some deep dark part of himself doesn't mean I'm obligated to do the same. Trust me, despite how fucked-up his history might be, mine is worse.

Straightening my back, I take a final deep breath and rap on the door, opening it when he calls out.

"I'm swamped with work today. Do you mind just working on your own stuff?"

I let out a silent breath of relief at his words. I know he's bullshitting me. Why would he insist on me coming here every week if he's just going to do paperwork? It's a tactic. Yet, each week I show up, and not once have I said I could skip the week's session if he's busy.

If I'm being honest with myself, I've come to enjoy the undisturbed hour in this room, away from the prying eyes and hushed whispers of the other students. I enjoy the companionable silence, often finding myself letting down my guard and getting comfortable. That's not something I ever thought I'd do around other people. Life has taught me not to trust anyone, yet I trust him enough to be relaxed in his presence.

I have no idea what that means. Every time I think about it, it freaks me out and I tell myself I'm not going to show up to our next session. Yet every week, here I am, standing in his office like I just can't help myself.

"Yeah, that's fine," I respond, heading over to my usual spot on the sofa and pulling out my tablet and books, and getting to work.

I'm too distracted this week, however. Just like last time, I constantly find my attention drifting, my eyes repeatedly flicking up to drink him in. Maybe it's because I know this quiet peacefulness we have going has to come to an end soon, but I also can't deny I'm just insanely curious about him, especially after what he revealed last week. He's more like me than I thought, than anyone else here at Pac could ever be. If there was one person who might ever understand what I've been through, it would most likely be him.

Despite the fact that this is all a ruse, he appears to be actually working. His brow is furrowed in concentration as he taps away on his laptop, and he doesn't seem to be aware of me watching him. It allows me to look him over with fresh eyes. He's wearing yet another one of his ridiculously expensive-looking waistcoats and shirts. Today's waistcoat is light gray, paired with a pale blue shirt; the combination makes him look professional and straight-laced in an *'I just stepped out of a hot male model photoshoot'* kind of way.

Unlike in our first appointment, where I saw the extravagant suit and ritzy hairstyle, I look beneath all of that while taking in the haggard lines on his face and the knowing look in his eyes that only comes from being forced to grow up too quickly. When you realize at a far too young age that the world fucking sucks. It's filled with horrible people willing to do whatever they want for their own gain, and there isn't a fucking thing you can do to stop it.

Taking in his hands as they fly across the keyboard, typing at a speed I could never hope to replicate unless I wanted to write gibberish, I notice the toughened skin and calluses that come from manual labor. Those are not the hands of an upper-class kid raised with servants at their beck and call and taught to delegate work instead of doing it themselves.

"What made you want to be a school counselor?" I ask, surprising myself. I had no intention of engaging him in conversation, but I'm genuinely curious now that I've asked it.

His hands pause on the keyboard as he looks over at me, a mixture of surprise and something else I can't place before it disappears. "I wanted to help kids like me. Help them realize there is more to life than violence and gang wars. Give them more options than I had growing up."

All of that makes sense, and yet...

"I wouldn't think too many kids at Pac end up involved with gangs and drug lords."

A surprising burst of laughter erupts from him, like he wasn't expecting my sarcastic response, a slow smile growing across his face. Holy shit, does he look fucking magnificent when he smiles. His whole face lights up, his eyes sparkling. It's almost like smiling is a rarity for him, only when he does, he puts everything he has into it.

It leaves me a little breathless, and I have to subtly swipe my finger along my lip, ensuring no drool slips out. All the while, I ignore the weird fluttering sensation in my lower abdomen. I've felt something similar on the odd occasion, when Cam gives me a heated look or when West was pressed against me in the library, however it's never felt this tumultuous before.

"No, I'm sure they don't." He chuckles. "But college isn't exactly cheap, and I'm working toward my master's, so I couldn't afford to turn down such a well-paid job."

I simply nod my head, not sure what to say to that.

"Do you know what you want to do with your life?"

The question takes me by surprise and I let out an inelegant snort. "Not a clue. It's not like I had any prospects before Pac, and I keep expecting this all to blow up in my face and I'll end up back where I was."

He nods in understanding. "Life has taught you that when things are going well, it's too good to be true. It's ingrained in you not to trust the happy periods of your life because they won't last."

"I don't know if having the Pricks hate me and the school whispering about me is necessarily my life 'going well'," I retort with a snark.

His brows pull together at something I've said. "The Pricks?"

"Oh." *Crap.* I hadn't meant to refer to them out loud like that. It's one thing to call them that in my head or to Emilia, but the fewer people who know about my less-than-pleasant pet name for the assholes, the better for me. "The Princes," I clarify, figuring he's probably already deduced who I'm talking about, and even if he hasn't, what we discuss here is confidential. I don't believe he would run off and tell them. He doesn't strike me as someone who would let themselves get stuck under the Princes' thumbs. He's probably one of the few adults in this place who might actually stand up to them or would at least resist them.

Once again, his face brightens with that brain-melting, panty-soaking smile of his, another deep, rumbling laugh escaping him as he shakes his head. "Very fitting."

A small smile lifts the corner of my lip, and I have to mentally tap that shit down. This isn't a friendly bonding session. In fairness, I don't know what this is, but it's definitely not that.

He must be able to recognize when I erect my walls again as, without even looking at his watch, he says, "Our time is up."

I begin shoving my workbooks back into my bag. "Same time next week, Mr. Jacobs?"

"Yeah," he agrees. "And Hadley, you can call me Beck when we're in this room."

I peer over at him, finding him watching me closely. "Okay...Beck." The word tastes like dark chocolate and cherry, and I can suddenly picture myself crying out his name as he does very unprofessional things to my body.

With my cheeks stained crimson, I duck my head and scurry out of his office, desperately trying to forget the way my name rolled off his tongue in his rich, husky voice.

∽

IT'S pitch black out as I slowly make my way through the forest. I noticed the others sneaking out earlier, so I know tonight is fight night. Tonight is *my* night. I don't know how often they run these things, but I've been patiently waiting for this opportunity.

After the first time, I promised myself I wouldn't come here again, that I wouldn't insert myself into the fights, but Hawk has driven me to this point. Punching a bag isn't enough. I need blood. I need pain. I need to watch these idiots beat the shit out of each other for no other reason than because they want to.

Each step I take is silent as I traverse the forest floor, approaching the clearing. The howls and cheers of bored, over-privileged teenage boys guiding my way.

Reaching the same clearing as last time, I hide in the shadow of the trees, ensuring I stay out of the beam of the flashlights while scanning the crowd in the makeshift ring. Just like last time, the boys form a wide circle around the fighters—two juniors who can't punch for shit. The Pricks stand out like a sore thumb at the far end of the ring, the other students keeping a respectful distance, unwilling to get too close and accidentally jostle them.

I focus back on the piss-poor fighters right as one of them lands a lucky shot, knocking the other guy to the ground. Lying in a heap, he slaps his hand against the compact dirt, tapping out.

A couple of his friends rush into the ring, lifting him up and dragging him out of there while the other fighter does a victory lap, people in the crowd clapping him on the back as he passes by.

The sounds of victory quickly die down as Hawk steps forward into the ring, the previous winner rushing to the sidelines before he can get pulled into another fight. Everyone here knows he wouldn't stand a chance against Hawk.

With his usual arrogant look and a slight curl to his lip that promises pain, Hawk surveys the crowd, shrewdly selecting his victim.

This is my moment.

I stride out from between the trees, cutting silently across the clearing toward them until I'm standing unseeingly at the back of the crowd. Thanks to my smaller stature, the boys in front of me prevent any risk of me being seen by Hawk or the other Pricks.

"Who will it be tonight?" Hawk calls out, slowly turning in a circle, eyeing each and every boy, all of whom quickly glance away. The resonating silence is deafening as everyone looks at the person beside them, not one of them having the balls to take him on.

"Me," I shout out from the back of the crowd. The guys in front of me turn round, their eyes widening when they see me standing there. As I step forward, they jump to the side, everyone parting to let me through.

I focus on Hawk as I step into the ring, watching his eyes widen and brows lift in surprise before he covers it with a sneer.

"You?" He snorts derisively. "Please, I'd wipe the floor with you."

With an impassive expression, giving nothing away as per usual, Mason steps forward into the ring to come to stand beside him as he whispers something in his ear. He's probably trying to convince Hawk to back down. He's the only one who has seen me in the gym. Annoyingly, he's also probably telling Hawk he can't fight a girl—just because I have ovaries doesn't mean I should be underestimated.

I didn't come to Pac to get caught up in fistfights and brawls, but apparently, that's precisely what I'm going to have to do. I'm sick of taking Hawk's shit. I'm not someone who can sit back and let people walk all over them. I was raised to be a fighter, and taught how to give as good as I get. I've been letting him go around acting like the big man on campus because I didn't want to disrupt the hierarchy here. I've had more important things to focus on, but enough is enough. I'm fucking done. If this asshole won't leave me the fuck alone, then I'm more than happy to show him exactly who he's provoking.

Hawk swats Mason away, not heeding his warning.

"Then what are you so afraid of?" I taunt, smirking back at him.

"I'm not about to have everyone going around telling people I beat the shit out of a girl," he snarls in response.

I nod my head like I agree with what he just said.

"How about," I begin, tilting my head to one side, as though I'm thinking through what I'm about to say. The truth is I know exactly how to play this to ensure I get what I want tonight—my fists crashing into his stupid, pompous face. "You pick one of these...boys." I gesture to the gathered crowd, watching our exchange with a mixture of excitement and apprehension. "And I'll fight them. If I win, then it's your turn. No excuses, no bullshitting."

He looks completely relaxed, his arms crossed over his chest as he snorts. "Sure," he agrees readily, not for one second believing I could beat any of these wimps. "Why not? It'll be your funeral."

I catch Mason shaking his head. I wish I knew what he was thinking right now. He's seen my moves, felt the power behind my hits, so he probably knows I can hold my own, but he's never seen me against an actual opponent.

West looks conflicted, as though he's torn between intervening and letting Hawk do whatever he wants. We all know he won't dare contradict Hawk in front of everyone, though. God forbid their subjects see them arguing. *Fucking pathetic.*

I deliberately avoid looking at Cam, a skill I've become quite adept at. Things between us have gotten so fucking complicated. Between his betrayal and my own deception, neither of us can trust the other, leaving us in this weird stalemate where we awkwardly pretend the other doesn't exist. It's fucking exhausting, and I miss his easy, flirty banter.

"Marcus," Hawk barks, pulling my attention his way as he points to a lean-looking junior behind me. Turning around, I run my eyes over him as he steps forward without hesitating. Shrugging off his top, I can tell he's packing some muscle—not much, but a bit. Flexing so he can show off for the crowd, I immediately know he's all about the performance, not the actual talent and skill. He already thinks he's won—a fighter's worst mistake.

Mason seems to agree as I hear him snort behind me, likely knowing as well as I do I'll have this idiot tapping out in no time.

I pull my hoodie off over my head, leaving me in only my sports bra and lycra leggings as I flex my fingers, stretching the leather of my fingerless gloves over my knuckles.

"Fuck me," I hear one of the Pricks behind me murmur, but I can't tell who, and I'm not about to take my eyes off my opponent. Throwing my hoodie to the edge of the circle, I ignore the hushed whispers as, for the first time, every male in the school gets an up-close and personal view of the phoenix tattoo covering my ribs and the various scars I'm sure they've all seen from the video or pictures.

Widening my stance, I raise my fists, Marcus mimicking me, except he's got a cocky ass grin on his face that I can't wait to demolish.

The second someone shouts 'go', I pivot forward, sidestepping his undeniable right hook and grabbing a hold of his wrist as I swiftly move behind him, yanking his arm up behind his back. He cries out in pain as the shift forces him to lean forward.

Honestly, this is probably enough of a demonstration, but I've been taught not to stop until someone isn't just down but out. Besides, I saw that glint in his eyes. He was looking forward to having the upper hand and taking me to the ground, so why the fuck shouldn't I give him a taste of his own medicine.

Without hesitating, I step around him while maintaining my firm grip on his wrist, holding it in place as I bring my leg up, and relishing in the satisfying snap of broken cartilage as his nose collides with my knee.

Letting go of my grip on his arm, he drops like a sack of shit, blood running down his face. "You broke my nose, you bitch!" His words come out slurred as he spits blood everywhere.

I should probably feel at least a little bad about that, but something inside of me is inherently broken. I *can't* feel the same remorse other people would. I get little sparks of it here and there. Moments of humanity, usually when my emotions are running high, or I'm under a lot of stress. I also find myself feeling more...human, more alive, when I'm around Mason, Cam and West...*and Beck*. Hell, even Hawk ignites more fire in me than I've felt in years. It's pure, unadulterated hatred, yet still, it's something.

Ignoring the sniveling idiot on the ground, I lift my gaze to Hawk, finding him staring at Marcus with wide eyes. Glancing behind him to the other three, West and Cam are wearing similar expressions of shock and surprise, whereas Mason looks smug...almost proud?

Returning to Hawk, he catches me smiling smugly at him and scowls back.

"You owe me a fight, Davenport."

With a sharp nod of his head, he agrees, "A deal's a deal," stepping confidently into the ring as Marcus stumbles to his feet and into the gathered crowd, giving Hawk and me room to circle one another.

"You better not hold back just because I'm a girl, Davenport."

"I wouldn't dream of it, Parker."

Unlike the first fight, when someone shouts, "Go," Hawk and I continue to circle one another, each of us analyzing the other, getting a feel for the other's style, movements, strengths, and weaknesses.

In the first few seconds, I have learned that he's well-trained. His footwork is impeccable, and he never once lowers his fists, giving me a solid opening. However he is cocky, extremely sure of himself, and *that's* his weakness.

We dance back and forth, both of us testing the other with a few practice strikes, although it doesn't take long before Hawk gets bored and makes his first real move. His first real mistake.

With swift, confident advances, he lands a punch to my ribs and another to the side of my head, causing my ears to ring. I'm faintly aware of the crowd cheering around me, but I zone them out as I retaliate, landing a few punches of my own—nothing with lasting impact, yet enough to get him to back off.

His wide conceited grin pisses me the fuck off, and he doesn't hesitate before coming at me again, this time trying to sweep my legs out from underneath me and take me to the ground.

Self-defense 101–never let them get you to the ground. As soon as they do, they have the advantage, especially if the asshole is easily double your size, like Hawk.

My smaller stature makes me lighter on my feet, faster, meaning it's easier for me to avoid his swipes as I dance out of his way whenever he comes near me.

He quickly becomes frustrated, not expecting it to be this difficult or to take this long, and that's when he makes mistake number two. Rather than using his knowledge and insight, he comes at me with annoyance and indignation.

The combination of his arrogance and anger makes him sloppy and big-headed. We each share another few blows, neither of us doing much damage. He's got a split lip and I can feel the smarting of a bruise on my cheek and another one over my ribs, but nothing serious.

As we continue back and forth, my punches grow weaker and sloppier, and it soon becomes evident to everyone around us that Hawk is the better fighter displaying more strength and stamina.

On my next hit, he grabs a hold of my wrist and yanks me toward him, giving me no other option than to let him pull me in. He spins me around using his grip on my arm, and wraps his thick arms around me.

"Tap out," he growls in my ear. I ignore him, wriggling helplessly in his arms. "You can't win this," he snarls. "It will only get worse for you."

His grip on me tightens to the point of pain, however he's already given me the in I need.

Slamming the heel of my boot down on the top of his foot, I throw my head back, feeling it connect with his nose. There's no satisfying crunch this time, even though it's enough that he loosens his grip, and I can bring my arms out, breaking free.

While he's still stunned, I spin around to land a quick jab to his kidney, then his spleen, followed by several sharp blows to his head.

Kicking out with my foot, it connects with the side of his knee, making it buckle. Between the instability and the disorientation, he drops to his knees.

"Tap out," I demand, not bothering to keep my voice low like he did. "You can't win this. It will only get worse for you."

While my words are defiant as he looks up at me, I am secretly pleading him with my eyes to just tap the fuck out. *Don't make me do something more severe just to get you to stay down.*

Of course, the shithead knows how to push my buttons and his glare turns rebellious. He's got no intention of giving up, of losing to a girl.

Before he can move an inch, my fist flies forward, connecting with the soft tissue surrounding his windpipe. As the impact from my hit forces his airway to close over, preventing oxygen from getting in and out of his lungs, his eyes bug out of his head as his hand comes up instinctively to grasp at his neck as he gasps for air.

"What the fuck? You throat-punched him!" West panics, running over and bending down beside Hawk, frantically looking him over as Hawk gasps and wheezes. The crowd whispers around us, everyone shoving against one another to get a better look, but I ignore them all.

"He'll be fine," I assure him, waving off his concern. "He wasn't going to stay down. It was that or knock him out. I figured this was the better choice."

"You...what?" he stutters, frantically checking Hawk over. He's already starting to recover though, his pharynx opening back up as he gulps down lungful's of air.

"See?" I wave toward a very alive and well Hawk. "He's fine."

Lifting my gaze, my eyes catch on Mason and Cam who haven't moved from their position just outside the circle. Cam is staring at me in shock, frozen in place with his mouth agape as he tries to compute what he just witnessed.

On the other hand, Mason appears like he's trying really hard not to laugh. His reaction takes me by surprise, honestly. I expected him to be as angry as West. I certainly didn't expect him to be holding back laughter. I don't think I've ever seen him laugh...or smile, for that matter. He doesn't exactly show his emotions much. Even when we're alone in the gym, he wears his usual stony expression.

The sound of Hawk coughing up a lung pulls all of our attention his way as he climbs unsteadily to his feet. I expect his typical glare to land on me, but when he glances over my shoulder instead, I remember that we aren't alone and that I've just shown-up the reigning asshole of the school in front of everyone.

As though realizing the same thing, West matches Hawk's glare, adjusting his glasses as his steely gaze roams over the crowd. "Get the fuck out of here," he barks. "Tonight didn't happen. You didn't see anything, and if we hear so much as a whisper, you'll regret it."

His threatening tone and icy expression once again remind me he has a darker side

I know very little about, one he reserves for times like these—when there is a threat to their reign.

The crowd jumps into motion, everyone scattering back through the trees like the hounds of hell are on their ass. It takes no more than a minute before the clearing is empty, and the sounds of people running through the forest grow distant before tapering out; the stillness of the night air again returning.

"You tricked me," Hawk wheezes, his voice coming out harsh against his bruised throat.

"You let your arrogance rule you," I retort. "You assumed you'd already won, so you got sloppy. You're only a winner when your opponent is on the floor. Remember that next time, and you might not lose."

The glower he throws my way would have anyone else pissing themselves; only I simply roll my eyes as he storms off into the trees to head back toward the dorms.

Cam doesn't spare me a glance before taking off after him, an action that has my chest tightening painfully. With a heavy sigh, West steps away to pick up the flashlights strategically placed around the clearing. He turns them off as he lifts each one until only one is left on, providing just enough light as he walks back toward me.

"You coming?" he asks Mason.

"Yeah, I'm right behind you."

As he passes by me, he pauses and stares at me for a long moment. We haven't spoken since before the video. I've made a point of sitting as far away from him in computer class, and he hasn't tried to talk to me—whether that's out of respect for my need to be alone or because he's pissed over the notebook, I'm not sure. I can't say I'd blame him if he were angry with me, not that I can explain anything to him. I shouldn't have even told Mason what I did, but when he was looking at me with those eyes full of questions and doubt, it fucking bothered me.

It's impossible to read anything in his expression in the dim light of the flashlight. Still, after a second, he glances away, shoving a spare flashlight into my hand before following after Hawk and Cam. The yellow beam lights a path through the forest as he leaves behind Mason and I in the darkness.

Neither of us moves or makes a sound, listening to the noise of twigs breaking and leaves rustling as the three of them head back toward the dorms.

Silence once again surrounds us when Mason speaks. He had been standing several feet away from me when West walked away, and I didn't hear him move. Nevertheless, his voice comes from right in front of me, inches from my face. I can feel his warm breath on my lips. "I never thought a woman would bring any of us to our knees, but you're constantly surprising me, Little Warrior." His voice is like gravel, dark and sinful, thickly coated with lust. Every word oozes sex, not to mention his nickname sends shivers up my spine.

There's something about the inky black of darkness, of being unable to see your surroundings or make out faces or read emotions. It bolsters confidence and makes people act in ways they otherwise wouldn't. The dark is where depraved things happen, and secrets come to hide. It can push people to carry out disturbing acts, commit crimes, and inflict pain. Yet, it's also in the dark where we find the courage to take our first steps, to do something reckless, like, for example, kissing Mason Hayes.

It's only since shadows conceal us, and I'm still riding the high of the fight, that I reach out, wrapping my hand around the soft fabric of Mason's shirt to pull him in against me.

It's because no one is around to see us, that tomorrow we can both pretend this never happened, that he lets me.

Our lips collide in an explosion of fireworks, the magnetism an undeniable force spreading outward from where they touch, running through my nerves and setting fire to my skin.

My lips part, his tongue sweeping in to stake his claim as I lose myself in something for the first time in my life. In someone. He tastes exactly how I'd expect—all quiet contemplation and steady reliance. I get lost in him, in the feel of his strong arm wrapped around me. His hand tangles in the strands of my hair, pressing firmly against the back of my head and holding me captive.

We take our time, savoring the taste of one another, like we have all night. I have no idea how long we kiss for, neither of us taking it any further and simply enjoying this moment. Knowing as soon as it's over, we will go our separate ways and pretend it never happened.

Using his tight grip on the back of my head, he deepens the kiss, our tongues sweeping hungrily over one another. He kisses me like I'm a lifeline, like he's barely been surviving, but now he only wants to live on the taste of me.

When we break apart, I feel like my whole world has been realigned. I'm not the same girl from a few minutes ago. My world feels brighter, and I don't feel so alone. Like, somehow, Mason has taken some of my burdens off my shoulders, lightening my load. It's almost as if I'm no longer fighting this battle alone.

Mason knows nothing of the secrets I carry or the darkness I bear, yet I get the impression he *knows* at least some of my burden; he understands my pain.

I'm still lost in the taste of him, my lips still tingling as his arm slides from my waist. As his hand untangles from my hair, he slips into the shadows, disappearing as if he was never here. Like this was nothing more than my imagination.

I stand in the darkness for who knows how long, wrapping my mind around what just happened. Deciding there's no point in overthinking it and flicking on the flashlight, I grab my hoodie and follow after the four confusing as fuck men who have my head all screwed-up.

Sweetheart

CHAPTER TWENTY-FOUR

I always sneak out to watch the fights. It would be impossible not to know when they're happening. It's the worst-kept secret. You can see it on the boys' faces—the antsy anticipation, the way they stare down others who have crossed them or done their circle wrong, ready to call them out in the ring.

Watching the fights is the only thing in this damn place that gets my blood pumping —well, until Hadley showed up at my door. I can't participate in them, nor would I be welcome, but I can hide in the trees and watch. Even from a distance, the violence and bloodshed satiate that restless inner part of me. I should probably be reporting them, except who the fuck would I tell? Not a single teacher here, Mr. Phister included, would stand up to the *Princes*. It's a complete fucking joke.

I spotted Hadley before anyone else as she strode up to the back of the crowd, her back ramrod straight, with focused determination written all over her face. Once again, she takes me wholly by surprise, for I never expected to see her here. Then again, of course, she is. Where every other girl would scrunch their nose up in disgust and turn their back on the whole thing, pretending it doesn't exist, she wants to dive right into the middle of it and bathe in the chaos.

Hiding among the shadows of the trees, I watch as she rises to Hawks' challenge, unlike every other wimp pretending to be tough. Not one of them knows what it's like to actually fight for your life, to fight for survival and not just for sport. Although it's apparent Hadley knows—not that I expected anything less.

Standing prepared for battle in a fighter's stance, with her glove-covered fists raised, the swirls of black ink dipping beneath the lining of her leggings and up over her ribs, she looks like a fierce warrior. Combined with the impassive mask on her face, she's all business, not someone to mess with or take lightly.

I'm captivated as she takes down the first kid without breaking a sweat, not that he was much opposition. But Hawk...she gave as good as she got, neither one of them holding back. I admit, at one point, I nearly blew my cover and stormed over there to break them up, worried he was going to injure her. The contempt in his eyes was enough for me to know he would have no issues doing whatever it took to win, regardless of how much it could hurt her.

I should have known she had it all worked out. Every move she made had already been planned out before she even stepped into that ring. She likely already knew what sort of a fighter he was; if she didn't, one look told her all she needed to know to use his weaknesses against him.

The whole fight had me rock-fucking-hard in my jeans. Who knew watching a girl beat the crap out of someone bigger than she could be such a turn-on? Although, I'm pretty sure it had more to do with the girl being Hadley.

I was already taken by her. Her quiet, strong composure intrigues me, but seeing her mete out justice tonight has pushed me over the edge into obsession.

I have to have her.

I have to make her mine.

I never thought I could find a girl who would understand my past and accept the part of me that is still very much a Black Creek kid at heart.

Regardless of the overpriced suits and expensive haircuts, violence still thrums in my veins. Anger still swirls in my core, only expanding every day that I have to remain in this insipid school, pretending to give a shit about vapid, self-obsessed students. This is not what I went to college for; this is not the future I wanted for myself. Unfortunately, I'm not here for just myself. As much as I might hate it, this opportunity can help me do a lot of good in the future. I just need to get through the here and now.

I feel my phone vibrate in my pocket as West barks out for everyone to get lost, and I slip into the inky darkness of the forest, heading back toward the staff accommodation on the far side of campus before anyone can catch me lurking.

When I'm far enough away from the clearing, I pull out my phone. Two missed calls from a private number. The phone goes off again in my hand, the same unknown number calling.

With a low groan, I answer the call, knowing that ignoring it any longer will only infuriate him more.

"What?"

"Watch your tone with me!" he shouts, already infuriated, and we haven't even gotten to the reason he's calling. "Why didn't you answer the first time?"

"I was busy. I don't just sit around and wait for you to call. I have a job, you know."

"I'm hardly going to forget the job *I* got you now, am I?" he sneers, making me grit my teeth. I should have known such an opportunity would come with strings, but I was too blinded by the prospect of it all. I was too naive to this world to realize how fucking corrupt the people in it are.

"What do you want?" I spit the words out, wanting this conversation over with as soon as possible.

"Lunch at my house on Christmas day. Two o'clock. Don't be late."

"I can't, I'm going home." It's a lie. Mom is working all of Christmas—it's always easy to pick up extra shifts around the holidays. Plus, people are always more generous with tips at this time of year, so it just makes sense—not that he needs to know that.

"Cancel. You're coming here. I won't hear otherwise. We have things to discuss. I had to use favors to get you that cushy job of yours, and it's about time you paid me back."

Before I can get a word out—not that I know what to say to any of that—he hangs up, the silence from the disconnected call reverberating in my ear.

I squeeze the phone tightly in my hand, fighting the urge to throw it against a tree. *The fucking infuriating bastard.* It's moments like these that I seriously contemplate just leaving. What the fuck am I even doing here? Then I think about the number of other graduates who are in retail or working minimum wage, dead-end jobs because no one is hiring school counselors in a recession. Despite having him hold shit over my head, I'm lucky to have the job I have. Not only that, but I'm getting my degree to become a professional. Something that will open doors for me and create better opportunities, as well as being able to send money home to Mom to help her out a bit. It's the least she deserves after all she's done for me. I can suck it up for one meal and deal with him. How bad can it be? At least I'll get to eat the best turkey dinner I've probably ever had.

Baby

CHAPTER TWENTY-FIVE

*I*t's three a.m.

It's three a.m., and I've got the biggest swimming competition of my life tomorrow, not that it really matters. I may be quickly working my way up to qualifying for the Olympic team, even though my family will never let me actually compete at that level, not when there's a business to run and responsibilities to uphold. My father just wants to brag that I made it. He'll push me all the way there just to dangle the golden ticket in front of me, then tear it away, and he'll get off on it too. *Sadistic bastard.*

Despite how painful it's going to be to turn down my dream, I want to win. I want to go all the way, even if I have to say no. I want to live that dream for even a moment. God knows I will need something to hold on to when I'm stuck behind a desk, bored out of my fucking mind.

Yet, regardless of how much I want it, it's three fucking a.m. and I'm wide awake, thinking about *her*. I've done everything I can think of these past two months to get her out of my system. Despite Hawk insisting she be forced to hang around us like a fucking gnat, I ignored her, blocked her out. I even went as far as to flirt and mess around with other girls right in front of her, ignoring the fact that my dick was like a wet noodle the whole time, only coming to life when she was nearby. Breakfast was fucking torture, having her sit beside me...smelling her. It only infuriates me more that she can get to me like that, and I don't seem to affect her in the slightest.

Her turning me down in front of the whole class, no less, was a hit to my ego. There's no denying that. No one has ever said *no* to me before, but, of course, I should have fucking expected that to be her answer. She's always saying no to me. She's only ever given herself over to me twice, and I stupidly mistook that for her wanting more, for her feeling what I feel.

Finding that notebook has just pushed me over the edge. How could I have been so fucking stupid? Of course, she didn't want me. She wants my father, or one of our fathers. We're just stepping-stones she's happy to crush beneath her boots on her way to getting exactly what she wants—money. Hawk has been saying it since the beginning, and I should have fucking listened to him. Well, I'm listening to him now. I've been avoiding her ever since, just like he told us to do.

Bianca's been a somewhat decent distraction. With some imagination and her face shoved in a pillow, I can get myself off...eventually. But seeing her last night, the way she took down Hawk like a trained professional, holy fuck, my dick's been stuck in erect mode ever since, and Bianca's C-grade pussy just isn't cutting it.

Anger pulses through me. How fucking dare she have this effect on me. She continues to walk around this school—*our* school—like nothing fucking happened, like she didn't try to pull one over on us, on me. But you know what? I'm fucking done with that. I'm fucking done with ignoring her. It isn't enough. That video wasn't enough. She needs to be taught a fucking lesson, to know she can't just mess with people like that. She can't mess with *us* like that.

Throwing back the covers, I jump out of bed, fired up and ready to aim my anger at the one person who deserves it most. Not bothering to throw on any clothes, I amble out of the apartment in just my boxers, making it over to the girl's dorm in record time.

The scholarship girls all have the ground floor, and it doesn't take me long to find out which room is hers. It's the only one without any personalized crap on the door. Of course, she never shows anyone anything about her true self. She keeps everything about herself locked down tight. I should have fucking realized.

All those nights in the dining hall, chatting, I thought we were getting to know each other. However, looking back on it now, I can see the probing questions from her, asking about my parents, my father, my childhood, yet she expertly dodged every question *I* asked *her*. Not once did she give me a scrap of info on her childhood, any idea of her inner thoughts. Her wants. Her desires. *How the fuck did I not notice that?* I was too busy thinking with the wrong head, that's what was wrong. Well, not anymore.

I bang on the door far too loudly for this time of night, but who gives a shit. Hopefully it will only make her life here harder if people get wind of me coming to her room in the middle of the night. I raise my fist to bang again, except the turning of the key in the lock halts my movements as it swings open with a sleepy, disheveled Hadley standing in front of me in a pair of barely there sleep shorts and a tank top. The scars across her chest and the tops of her arms are fully on display now. I've noticed that recently, too. Since the video, she's stopped wearing her baggy, oversized t-shirts. She now wears these tight, revealing tank tops that make her tits look unbelievable as she walks around, not giving a shit that everyone is gaping at her damage.

I thought for sure that video would break her. She's been hiding those scars all semester, and there's got to be a reason. If it's not because she's embarrassed, then why?

"Cam?" Sleep is thick in her voice, but one look into the fiery pits of rage in my eyes and her eyes widen, her back snapping straight. Barging into her room, I don't give her any choice but to merely move aside, inspecting her inner space as she closes the door behind me. Again, there's nothing personal here. No knickknacks, no photos, nothing that tells you anything about the girl who's lived here the last few months. Whatever, I no longer care who she is.

"Cam, what are you doing here?" The sleep is gone from her voice, leaving her sounding both weary and on edge. What the fuck does she have to be weary about? I'm the weary one. I'm fucking exhausted, tired of all the lies and deception.

"Is that why you came here?" I ask, still refusing to look at her. "To get close to one of us? Did you honestly think you'd get to our parents through us? What would you have done then? West's dad is the only one who openly cheats on his wife, or were you happy enough to settle for the role of mistress so long as you were paid enough?"

I finally turn around to face her, seeing my own fury reflected in her face as she glowers at me, her teeth grinding as her eyes spit fire in my direction. *Yeah, give me that fire, baby. Burn me with it, because if I'm going to hell, I'll be bringing you down with me.*

Taking a step toward her, she doesn't falter. I've seen her in the ring, I know how tough she really is. Tougher than I ever realized, yet her hostility and refusal to answer just piss me the fuck off.

"You never back down, never give up," I snarl, taking another step toward her. "You didn't even flinch when I wrapped my hand around your pretty little neck."

She tilts her chin, staring me down. The angle accentuates her neck, drawing my attention. Her eyes scream defiance, but something about the move almost feels like she's daring me to try.

How can I hate her and want her all at the same time? My head and my dick have never been at odds like this before, and I'm getting pretty fucking sick of not knowing what to do.

I came here to hurt her. To quiet that rage that's been simmering inside me for the last two months, but now that I'm here, my dick already hardening in my boxers, I don't know what to do. Do I hurt her or fuck her? The answer comes out of nowhere, hitting me like a strike of lightning. For the first time in too long, every part of me is in agreement—do both!

My hand snaps out, wrapping around her throat, feeling her steady pulse thrumming beneath my fingers. Is she truly not afraid of me? Of the power I have right now? My dick, that's constantly sporting a semi around her, stands to full attention. Like a soldier reporting for duty and more than ready to dive into battle so long as the fight ends in it being buried deep inside her.

Squeezing ever so slightly, she doesn't move an inch, doesn't speak up or fight back. Why? If anything, she's shown us how much of a warrior she is, so why isn't she fighting me now? Does she know something I don't? Does she think I won't hurt her? *I'm* not even sure of that right now, so how could she be?

With my free hand, I push down her shorts, tearing at the thin straps of her top until I can push that down too, leaving her naked in front of me so I can see every perfectly flawed part of her. If anything, her scars only enhance her beauty.

My fingers flex around her neck as I take my time looking her over, drinking my fill. I can feel every struggling breath she takes, yet that power, that control, only makes my dick harder. For too long, I've been feeling weak. I think it's time I claimed back some of that power.

Using my tight grip on her neck, I push her backward until her back slams into the door. Still, she says nothing, only glaring at me with defiance—*and is that a flare of lust?* —as I push my boxers down then wrap my hand around my painfully hard dick. Unable to look her in the eye, I kick her legs apart and slam into her in one quick motion, surprised at how wet she is as I feel her spasm around me, adjusting to the intrusion.

Fuck me, is she enjoying this?

A slight moan escapes her lips even as I tighten my grip on her neck, cutting it off while I pound into her at a ferocious pace, every thrust meant to rid myself of this helplessness I feel. Of this rage I have toward her that's intended to punish her for her betrayal, for her lies.

My anger still isn't sated, but it has somewhat abated by the time the familiar tingling starts and my balls draw up, my eyelids drifting closed as I explode inside of her, not even giving a shit that I didn't wear a condom.

Her pussy spasms around me as though she's about to come. My eyes snap open, taking in her lidded eyes, blue-tinged lips, and the crimson flush rising on her cheeks and cascading down over her heaving chest. The blush *could* be due to the lack of oxygen, but there's no denying she's about to cum all over my dick.

Before she can do just that, I pull out, not letting her see my surprise as I fix an impassive look on my face. Her eyes snap to mine, the lust from a moment ago quickly replaced with irritation as she glares at me. Smirking at her, I use my still tight grip on her throat to fling her body toward the bed, where she lands in a heap, my cum smeared over her inner thighs as it leaks out of her. Ignoring the twisting in my stomach, I tuck myself away, not turning back as I open the door and leave her behind.

∽

Feeling like my old self, I strut out of the changing rooms to cheer from the stands. I once again dominate in my race, beating the other kids by a mile, a huge, shit-eating grin on my face as I throw my arms in the air, facing the crowd.

As students line up for the next race, I spot my dad standing at the far side of the pool. Grabbing a towel and running it through my hair, I drape it over my shoulders as I head toward him, knowing he won't leave until he's once again reminded me Rutherfords are winners. Doesn't he know by now that every time he spouts that crap, it only encourages me to do the opposite? I'd deliberately lose at swimming to piss him off if I didn't actually give a damn about winning. I don't have the same reservations about my grades, though, so he's just going to have to accept I'm barely scraping by.

As I get closer, I notice he's avidly watching someone up in the stands. I'm standing right behind him, when I hear him murmur under his breath, "Elizabeth?" Glancing up, I scan my eyes over the crowd, yet I don't see anyone I recognize with that name. The only person who stands out to me is Hadley. Her head is ducked as she scurries away, attempting to hide in the crowd, likely trying to get out of here before one of the guys or I spot her. I don't even know what she's doing here. She's made it clear she doesn't give a shit about me, so why even bother showing up? If she was hoping her presence would throw me off my game, then the joke's on her. Nothing could interrupt my focus when it comes to swimming.

"Who?" I ask, pulling my gaze from Hadley and searching again for whoever my dad saw. He startles at the sound of my voice, not having heard me approach.

"Who was the student I just saw? The new girl."

I shrug my shoulders, not wanting to talk about her with him. "Just some scholarship student who started this year."

"Huh," he puzzles, frowning. "I didn't realize the school was taking on any new scholarship students."

I shrug my shoulders again. *What the fuck does it matter?*

"What's her name?"

I give him a weird look out of the corner of my eye. Something about his tone is off. It's sharper than usual, his eyes beadier looking. Maybe he's on something?

Whatever, not my fucking problem.

Knowing if I don't just hand over the name, he'll make me, I say, "Hadley Parker."

He probably just wants to dig into her file. He's a control freak, always needing to know everything about everyone around him, so he probably thinks he's doing his due diligence by checking her out, making sure the school hasn't accidentally accepted an application from some delinquent. I'm sure the school does its own thorough background checks on new students, but whatever.

"Why?" Despite the fact I tell myself I don't care, I ask the question anyway.

Waving me off, he simply says, "Just curious. You know I like to stay informed of who attends Pacific Prep with you. Good job today, son. You did the Rutherford name proud. I can only hope you'll bring the same drive and determination to the company with you."

Right. Unable to think of anything constructive to say, I give him a tight smile.

"You'll be home for Christmas break in a few days. We'll talk more then. We have a lot we need to discuss with you boys."

Yeah, I bet you do. Like maybe the fact that the company we've always been told we'll inherit one day is actually a front for a mercenaries-for-hire organization in the black market. Well, too late. We discovered that little nugget of information on our own, thanks to West and his next-level genius skill with computers.

It blew our minds. Fucking obliterated them. Our parents have always been cold, detached...ruthless, almost. But then, aren't all prominent businessmen? I remember West telling us once that some of the most successful business leaders are psychopaths, or have similar traits to them. Something like that, anyway. Sure, our parents are successful, and they share some of the tendencies West mentioned. They're definitely egotistical and apathetic, and they certainly never gave a shit about us beyond how our successes or failures reflect on them. Even so, I never would have thought them capable of this.

We've discussed every scenario, but regardless of what we come up with, there is no denying they are involved. We haven't been able to find out anything regarding the inner workings of it all, only that all four families co-own and oversee the overall running of the organization. Maybe we'll get more answers when we're home over Christmas.

My father takes off to speak to the coach as I spot the guys leaving the stands. After a quick shower, I meet them outside the changing rooms, all three sporting huge grins as I pull the door open.

"Well done, man," Hawk congratulates, bumping my fist as West slaps me on the back.

"You were on fire out there," Mason enthuses.

Their praises light me up. Why can't my father show such genuine happiness at my successes? These guys make it seem so easy. We always have each other's backs and support one another. I can trust them to stand behind me in anything. That kind of loyalty is hard to come by, but what we have is forever. No girl will ever come between us, and absolutely not someone like Hadley.

"Come on." Hawk jerks his head toward the exit. "We've got some celebrating to do."

CHAPTER TWENTY-SIX

I don't know why I went to that stupid swim meet, especially after what Cam did last night. I'm not only repulsed with myself but also shocked at *his* actions and, most disturbingly, turned-on by the whole thing. I'm clearly sick in the head. I've spent my entire life around abusive, dominant men, and I know that exposure has seeped into my sex life. I like my sex rough—although I never hand over control like that—but last night was on a whole other level. I was lightheaded and on the verge of passing out when he released his grip on my neck.

I've no idea why I let him treat me like that. I could feel the pain pouring off him, and I guess I felt...guilty?

Yet, despite his hatred of me and the anger emanating from him, I went to that meet. I had to know he would win. I had to see him in action, because I do care about him regardless of what he might think. He made me fucking care. I was never supposed to fall, never supposed to give a damn. Except all those late nights I spent with him, trying to find out more about their parents and listening to him talk about his childhood, it made me see him as more than just the flirty guy I needed to get close to. Combine that with the way he used to look at me like no one else in the room mattered, not to mention the unbelievable sex...how could I not fall for Cam Rutherford?

Shaking him out of my thoughts, I walk through the campus gates. This is the first time I've been outside these walls since the day I arrived. I meant to do this ages ago, but, well, life kind of got in the way. Crossing the road, I head down the wooden steps to the beach. It's insane that the school is this close to the ocean with this view, yet they stuck the dormitories at the back of the campus.

Stepping onto the beach, the smell hits me first. The brine of seawater is so strong I can practically taste it. Peering around the uneven shoreline, strewn with rocks, shells and chunks of seaweed, I find myself alone, except for some man at the far end of the beach. My boots sink into the sand, and I hastily kick them off, feeling the hot grains between my toes with every step I take toward the ocean. The crashing waves and seagulls crying are the only sounds I can hear.

Just before I reach the water's edge, I drop my boots and sit on the sand, my legs outstretched in front of me as I slide my hands through the rough grains, enjoying the feel of it beneath my fingers. My eyes soak in the sight in front of me, the steady push and pull of the tide, the waves rolling inland before they dissolve into foam on the beach. It's bliss. Here I can forget about Pac Prep, the Pricks, the Princesses... The reason I'm here.

Tilting my head back, I close my eyes, letting the sun hit my face as it warming it; the cool breeze just enough to offset the heat of the day. For a long while, I pretend I'm just some woman on a beach, enjoying her day of relaxation, until I feel someone watching me. Snapping my eyes open, the guy I saw earlier has walked down the beach and is headed toward me. He's dressed casually in jeans and a t-shirt, with a tattoo covering one arm.

With the glare of the light, it's impossible to make out his face, but as he gets closer, recognition dawns.

Beck.

"Fancy seeing you here," he calls out, approaching me. "I thought you'd be busy packing for the end of term."

"Foster kid, remember? I'll be spending all my holidays here for the rest of the year."

"Ah, I wasn't sure. Do you mind if I sit?"

Shaking my head, he lowers his athletically-built body onto the sand beside me, keeping a respectful distance between us. God, I thought he looked good in his preppy waistcoats, but holy shit, he's fucking lickable right now. I hadn't realized his tattoo went all the way up his arm, and his t-shirt does nothing to hide the fact he clearly works out.

His eyes roam over my face, lips thinning as he takes in the purple bruising on my cheek. Emilia lent me some of her makeup to cover up the worst of it from prying eyes and whispering students, unfortunately though, the swelling and discoloration are still noticeable up close.

The two of us sit in silence for a bit, comfortable enough in each other's presence now that neither of us feels the need to say anything. Only a few short weeks ago, I wouldn't have been able to sit beside him like this. Not without my every sense in overdrive, waiting to see what he would do, ready to react if he made one move I didn't like. Instead, my nerves are ablaze for an entirely different reason.

"It's beautiful out here." His voice is filled with awe as he takes in the view, seeing the same beauty as I do.

"It is," I agree. "I've never had time to just sit and take it in before. I've caught glimpses of the ocean and watched other kids playing in the sand, however I've never just sat and enjoyed it."

He doesn't pry further, something I appreciate. I think that's what has endeared me to him most. If anything, he's shared more with me than I've shared with him. He's entrusted me to keep his secret about who he really is, without asking anything of me.

Licking my lips, I pull my legs up in front of me, wrapping my hands around my knees before blurting out, "When I was thirteen, my only friend was murdered in front of me." He doesn't respond, even though I can feel his eyes on me. I don't look away from the rolling ocean, knowing I have his full attention. "She was killed because she wouldn't do what some scumbag lowlifes wanted her to do."

I rarely let myself think about Meena, but it's thanks to her I'm finally free. If only she hadn't had to die for me to realize there must be more to life than what we'd been subjected to.

"She always talked about coming to the beach," I say in a flat, monotone voice. "We'd tell each other all the things we were going to do when we got here. I promised her we'd see it one day, together."

My chin trembles as tears prickle behind my eyes, my chest aching with the grief of her loss as I press my forehead against my knees and take a few deep breaths to collect myself.

Beck remains quiet, not saying anything, as he gives me the time I need to gather myself. Eventually, I sit up, leaning back on my arms and press my hands flat against the sand. "She would have loved it here," I murmur as I look out over the frothy sea-green water, taking in the sun's glow on the horizon. It's so picturesque. Better than anything we could have dreamed up.

The feeling of a warm hand on mine pulls my attention back to Beck. His features are soft as he looks at me with empathetic eyes, a sad smile lifting his lips.

"I think she'd be proud of who you've become," he murmurs gently. "The depth of your strength is incredible."

We both sit in silence for the rest of the day, only making a move back toward campus when the sun starts to set, its yellow-red rays painting the sea a bright amber.

Despite not having done much with my day, I'm exhausted by the time I make it back to my room, and I'm really not in the mood when I find West leaning against the wall beside my door.

"What are you doing here, Wes?" I sigh, unlocking the door and pushing it open.

"I need to talk to you." His tone is pressing, brows furrowed, and his lips pinched, making him look more serious than usual as he watches me closely. Unable to handle his overbearing gaze, I push through into my bedroom, not giving a crap if he follows me or not.

Dropping my bag on the desk, I turn around to face him, crossing my arms over my chest.

"Okay…" I raise an eyebrow impatiently, wishing he would hurry up and get to the point and tell me whatever he has to say so he can leave me alone.

He steps hesitantly into the room, closing the door behind him and standing awkwardly in front of it, glancing around like he's never seen the inside of a girl's bedroom before, even though I know he's been in this exact bedroom. Hence, I've no idea who he's trying to fool.

"I like what you've done with the place."

The room looks pretty much the same as it did the day I moved in. *Sarcastic asshole.*

"We don't all have money or time to waste on decorating," I snipe at him. If he's just come here to insult me, I'm going to be fucking pissed.

I notice his eyes lingering on the bookcase.

"I've found a new hiding spot, in case you were wondering."

"I wasn't."

His words have my eyes narrowing on him. Is this some sort of recon mission? Are they trying to get the notebook back?

Taking another step toward me, he holds out a file I hadn't even noticed he was carrying. Staring at it warily, like it's a bomb and not a collection of papers, I make no effort to take it from him.

"What the hell is that?"

"You said you were raised in foster care, right?"

I hesitate before confirming, my thoughts racing as I try to figure out what he's getting at, my eyes flicking up from the envelope to his watchful gaze. "Yeah."

Fuck, if he's been doing some digging, he'll have discovered my backstory is a complete lie. There's no way he can know the truth, in any case. Even if he did somehow stumble across it, there's no fucking way he would believe it. No one in their right mind would.

My heart races, every muscle tense. Everything inside of me is screaming that this is not good.

"Do you know who your real parents are?"

"What are you getting at, Wes?" I demand, snapping at him, disliking where this line of questioning is going.

The fucker just raises his eyebrows, waiting for me to answer him.

"No," I snap, "I don't."

Realizing I'm not going to touch whatever the hell is in that folder, he inches toward the bed, dropping it on the covers. My stomach churns this gut-wrenching feeling that I know exactly what is in that folder, making me feel physically sick.

"What did you do, Wes?" I glare at him. Who the fuck is he to stick his nose in my business. Why the fuck would he even go looking for my parents. Does he think he's doing me a favor? Just because he's got the perfect rich family, he thinks we all want to know where we come from?

Wrong!

We can't all have picture-perfect families like his. Why the fuck would I want to know what teen mom or druggie parents decided they didn't want me?

"I don't want to know who they are," I blurt out before he can tell me anything I *know* I don't want to hear, looking pointedly at the floor, not wanting to see the judgment on his face. This is my decision to make. If I don't want to know, then I *don't want to know*. That's my prerogative. I won't let him make me feel bad for that.

He nods his head. "I get that." There's something in his voice that makes me peer back at him. I can't place it, but when our eyes connect, it's like he gets me. Understands my need to not know.

His lips press together, a pained expression flashing across his face. "However, in this case, I think you need to know."

What the fuck does that even mean?

"Ever since you showed up, I've been noticing things. Small—"

"Nope," I seethe, my sharp tone cutting him off as I shake my head vigorously. "No. Get out! I don't want to hear any of this." Striding toward him, I'm not even able to enjoy that usual calming energy between us as I slam my hands against his chest, failing miserably at shoving him toward the door. The fucker doesn't budge an inch, standing his ground as I continue to push against him.

His hands come up, his long fingers wrapping around my upper arms in a tight grip, holding me in place as he gives me a quick shake.

"Hadley." His voice is a firm bark, and I slowly lift my eyes to meet his. My head shakes from side to side as I silently beg him not to say anything more. I know. I just fucking *know* his next words are going to eviscerate me. I can already feel the cracks as my world shatters around me. Hasn't he done enough damage? Does he need to inflict more pain on me?

I can see he doesn't relish being the bearer of this news, but, despite the regret in his eyes, he hardens his resolve, sticking to his guns. He doesn't give a shit how much this is going to fuck me up; he's going to tell me, anyway.

"I honestly thought I was imagining things. I didn't think anything would come of it," he murmurs, more to himself than to me. "It was a long shot, ruling out an impossibility more than anything else."

I don't say anything. I'm incapable of saying anything, the lump in my throat blocking any words I might have. I feel utterly numb, his words coming at me through a dense, incomprehensible fog.

"Hawk is your brother."

Silence reigns in the room, his words bouncing around in my head as I stare at him stupidly, my mouth agape as I struggle to comprehend his words.

"What?" I croak, frowning at him. There's no way I heard him right. "What did you say?"

That numb, earth-shattering feeling is quickly receding, the familiar fire of anger replacing it.

"Do you think I'm fucking stupid?" I snap, shoving him again in the chest, shaking off his grip on my arms. "Do you *seriously* think I'd fall for that shit after everything you guys have done to me?"

I bark out a sharp, caustic laugh as I take a step back from him, shaking my head as I increase the distance between us. My heart reshapes and hardens with every inch of space I create.

"Playing the family card?" I growl, every muscle in my body quivering with uncontrollable rage. "That's so fucking low of you! I expect this shit from Hawk, even Cam, but you?" Sneering at him, I shake my head in disappointment.

"What? No!" he exclaims, but I'm not hearing any of it. I can't bear to listen to another fucking word that comes out of his mouth.

"I get that you all sit up there in your ivory tower, laughing at the rest of us plebs down here trying to survive one day to the next, but you have no idea how fucking difficult it is to go through life without knowing who your family is. Not knowing who *you* are or where you come from, and the fact you'd do all this as some sick joke is just fucking disgusting." I'm yelling by the time I'm done, my chest heaving as I glare at him. I'm practically vibrating with anger, so fucking done with their shit and pissed off with myself for expecting anything more from any of them. They aren't capable of being decent human beings. Tonight just proves that.

"I thought you were better than that," I sneer, staring at him with hate-filled eyes. "I guess I was wrong."

"Hadley, no—"

"Get out!" I demand, cutting him off once again. When he still doesn't seem to be getting the message, I make it super fucking obvious for him.

"GET THE FUCK OUT!" I yell, my fingers wrapping around the first object they find, throwing it across the room. The fact that my aim misses only infuriates me further.

Seeing how close I am to going full psycho on his ass, he finally concedes, dropping his gaze from mine. With a final sigh and shake of his head, he turns on his heel, not looking back as he lets himself out of my room.

I stomp after him, slamming the door shut and flicking the lock behind him. My legs give out beneath me as I slide down the door, my hands shaking as I curl into a ball on the floor as an uncontrollable wave of emotion crashes over me. I've been holding myself at bay for so long. I think I finally found my breaking point.

I don't know how long I lie there, curled up in the fetal position by the door, wholly numb to everything around me. When the tears finally stop, and I feel like I can get back to my feet, I make my way over to the bed, intent on crawling under the covers and blocking out the rest of the world, hoping the sweet oblivion of sleep will claim me quickly.

The crinkling of something underneath me as I drop onto the covers, has me rummaging around in the sheets, trying to find what I'm lying on. Pulling out the envelope, I stare at it for a long moment, torn between seeing what's inside and chucking the whole thing in the trash.

I told West I didn't want to know. But is that the truth? I spent my whole life wondering who my parents were, and the answers are right here in front of me, in some stupid nondescript envelope. It's not like knowing is going to change anything. They're probably long dead by now. Even if they aren't, it's not like I have to go track them down.

I stare unseeingly at the envelope for a while, going back and forth before curiosity finally wins out, and I tear open the sealed tab to pull out the small pile of papers. Looking at the first page, it's headed with the name of some sort of lab. *Okay, not quite what I was expecting to find.* Scanning through it, most of it is a bunch of medical jargon I don't understand. However, one paragraph sticks out.

FIND ENCLOSED *a detailed analysis of the provided DNA samples. We can confirm that the DNA provided by one Hadley Parker and one Hawk Davenport share common markers, indicating the tested individuals are biologically related.*

SHUFFLING THROUGH THE OTHER PAGES, they all say something along the same lines: all reports from different labs. Spreading the papers out on the bed, I sit and stare at them. What does this mean? Is this all an elaborate prank? What if it's not?

Noticing an address and phone number at the bottom of each report, I do a quick Google search. When nothing suspicious stands out, I grab my phone off the bedside table and dial the number for the first lab. When a receptionist answers, confirming it is, in fact, Synex Labs, I do the same with the second and third reports, getting the same corroborating response.

With my head spinning and thoughts jumping all over the place, I gather the papers in my hand and storm toward the door with the intent of getting some answers from the assholes themselves. There's no way I'll be able to focus on anything else until I get to the bottom of this.

Flinging open my bedroom door, I freeze when West falls backward into my room.

"What the—" I gape down at him in confusion. He must have been sitting on the floor, leaning against my door. How long has he been sitting there for? Has he been here since I kicked him out?

"What is this?" I demand, shoving the papers against his chest as he climbs to his feet.

"I tried to tell you," he snarks, glaring at me as he throws his hands up in the air. "I believe you didn't want to listen to me."

"Well, I'm all ears now," I throw back, crossing my arms and planting my feet, waiting impatiently for him to explain himself.

"I told you." He sighs, jerking his head toward the papers. "Hawk's your brother."

"You tested his DNA?"

"Yeah, against yours."

"How did you even get mine?" I demand before quickly changing my mind. "Actually, don't answer that. I'd rather not know. I don't understand what made you even *think* to do that."

"I'm perceptive." He shrugs, like that explains anything. "I pay attention."

"What the fuck does that mean?"

"I noticed things. You have Hawk's eyes. You both have fucking awful tempers."

"Are you serious? That's *all* you had?"

He sighs heavily, gritting his teeth. "It was more than that, though it's hard to explain. As I said, I thought it was all in my head, but Mason and Cam also picked up on it. They mentioned something off-hand about how similar you both were, which got me thinking. I started paying more attention, and that's when I sent the samples off. It was an off chance that I *may* be on to something. I honestly didn't expect to be right."

I don't know how long we stand there; me lost in thought, openly staring at West with an unfocused gaze as his words echo in my head, nothing really resonating with me.

I have a brother? And not just any brother, but fucking *Hawk*, a fucking asshole who I hate. *Of course, my luck is that shitty.*

"What does this mean?" I eventually murmur.

He gives me a small, sympathetic half-smile, his hand reaching out as though he's going to, I don't know, comfort me? Whatever he was going to do, he decides against it, dropping his arm back to his side.

"I don't know," he answers softly, giving a slight shake of his head as he shrugs his shoulder.

Licking my lips, I nervously ask, "Have you told Hawk?"

"No." His reply is instant. "I haven't talked to anyone about this. I figured you'd want to know first."

I'm surprised he put me above his friend like that. I don't understand why he would, but I appreciate his thoughtfulness. It gives me time to come to terms with this bomb drop and prepare for Hawk's backlash.

"I need to tell him, though. He has a right to know. I, uh...I wasn't sure if you would wanna be there when I talk to him?"

"No, definitely not." I adamantly shake my head. "It will be better for everyone if I'm not there." Hawk hated me when he had no good reason to. I can only imagine how well he will take this development.

"It's not like that," West tries to explain, clearly knowing where my thoughts have strayed. "It's not you. He hasn't had an easy life."

"An easy life?" I interject, barking out a sarcastic laugh, unable to believe his audacity. "Yeah, I'm sure the poor prince has had it rough," I snarl. "Spare me the pathetic *woe-is-me* bullshit. I don't wanna hear it."

With his lips pressed together, he gives me a tight nod, saying nothing else as he takes the DNA reports from my hand, leaving me alone with my tumultuous thoughts, the soft click of the door closing behind him resonating around the room.

Firefly

CHAPTER TWENTY-SEVEN

Fuck.

I lift my glasses off, rubbing my eyes and pinching the bridge of my nose in frustration. Putting them back on, I run my hand through my hair, not caring that I'm messing it up. Well, that went about as horrendously as I expected—worse even. Seeing her shocked expression as I blew apart her world and, Jesus, listening to her faint cries through the door. I nearly kicked the damn thing in, the urge to comfort her riding me hard.

I've been humming and hawing for nearly a week now over what to do with the results. They both needed to know. Only I couldn't work out how to tell them. There's been a strange sort of stalemate between us for the last month. All four of us have actively been pretending we don't notice her when she's around. Cam only pays attention to Bianca the second Hadley enters the room. Mason has wholly ignored his girl all month, and I've caught him watching Hadley when we're in the same room. Of course, I've only noticed it because I've also been watching her.

Seeing her and Hawk fighting the other night just made it all the more clear that they needed to know. Now. They need to get past this shit. They're fucking family. Whether or not Hawk likes it or Hadley wants to be, she's one of us. I don't know what the fuck happened for her to end up with the life she's had, but all these years...she should have been with us. Should have grown up with us, been at the cabin with us in the summers, and attended Pac with us the last four years.

A lot is going on with her that we don't know or understand; nevertheless, all the issues between us and her need to be resolved. Hawk's too caught up in his need to control her, and Cam's too lost in his hurt. Both of them are too proud to be the bigger person. I honestly don't know where Mason stands with her, so I guess that leaves me to try and create some peace between us all.

Pulling open the door to the boys' dorms, I release a heavy breath. As badly as that went with Hadley, I know it will be ten times worse with Hawk.

Letting myself into our apartment, I glance around the open living space, checking if he's around. He's slouched on the sofa, playing a video game as I make my way over to him.

"Hey, man." My steady voice doesn't give away any of the jittery nervousness I'm feeling.

"What's up?" His eyes never leave the TV as he races around a corner on a motorbike.

Taking a deep breath, I know I need to just rip off the Band-Aid. Sitting down on a chair opposite him, leaning forward, with my elbows resting on my knees, I pierce him with the same serious expression I used on Hadley. "I need to talk to you."

He must sense the gravity in my tone as he pauses his game, setting the controller down before shifting to look at me. "Sure, what is it?"

"I found something out about Hadley," I start, unsure of how to say the words to him. This is so much harder than it was when I broke the news to Hadley, and that was fucking difficult. Seeing that pain on her face. I've never seen her look so broken. She puts on this impenetrable front, always acting like everything bounces off her. It makes me sometimes forget that she's fucking human underneath it all. She's still got the same insecurities as the rest of us. Hell, I have a feeling she's got more issues than most.

Growing up the way she did, not knowing who her family was, I can only imagine what a bombshell it must be to suddenly find out you not only have a family but that they're right under your nose, and they're stinking rich. And on top of that, to know your own brother has been your tormentor for the last few months? Yeah, that must sting.

"You did? What did you find?" His voice is threaded with excitement, a wide grin on his face. Fucking hell, he needs to get over his infatuation with her. Now more than ever. I know he's had a lot going on, we all have, and I know he was worried she was using Cam. I'm honestly not sure what the hell was going on there, and I can't explain the notebook we found in her room, although I get the feeling there's more going on here than he and Cam seem to realize. I don't know how I know that; I just do.

"Man, I don't get it," I admit, needing answers before sharing what I've found with him. "What is your problem with her? And don't tell me it's about the notebook. You and I both know this started long before that."

I have to tell Hawk this news—he has a right to know. However, after seeing Hadley, after hearing her sobbing her fucking heart out through the door, I can't let him do any more damage to her. I need him to explain this vendetta to me.

"I just don't like her." He scowls. "I don't trust her. She's up to something."

I sigh wearily, not understanding his cryptic answer. It's the same bullshit he's been saying all year, only there's never an actual fucking reason. "Are you sure you're not just worried 'cause Cam has feelings for her? It's the first time any of us has actually given a shit about a girl before."

His eyes narrow on me. "Don't bullshit me. I know you've taken an interest in her too."

I simply shrug my shoulders, unable to deny it. What can I say? The girl intrigues me. There's something about her. She's tough as nails and fiercely independent. She's got walls so thick I don't think she's ever allowed anyone in. Then there are moments like today when I see a rare vulnerability in her. All of it speaks to one complicated woman.

As if that wasn't enough to have me curious, there are odd things about her I just can't explain. I want to know about her inability to use technology, why she doesn't drink, and the wariness in her eyes when she's around others. I can't understand any of it, which of course, only fascinates me more. I can't help it, I'm a sucker for a puzzle, and Hadley is precisely that—a complex enigma that's just screaming at me to be solved. She draws me in. It's like she's begging me to figure her out, to understand her. I want to know everything about her, which is fucking weird because I've never given a damn about a girl. Never even been all that interested in them until Hadley showed up.

"Look." I sigh, preparing myself for the Hawk shit-storm that's about to rain down on me. "You're not going to like what I've gotta say, but you know me. I've done my research, and I've checked everything out. I have the proof right here," I say, waving the same file I showed Hadley. "What I'm about to tell you is the truth, and I need you to not lose your shit over it."

"Jesus, man." Hawk chuckles nervously, confusion apparent across his face. "Just spit it out already."

Fuck. Here we go.

"Hadley's your sister."

He looks at me for a moment before bursting out laughing.

"Fuck, man. You totally had me! That's hilarious." He continues to laugh, shaking his head as he grabs his controller from the table and relaxes back onto the sofa again, getting back to his game.

He's still laughing when I drop the file of lab reports on the sofa beside him. "I'm being serious," I state, gesturing to the file when he glances my way.

He casts his eyes down to the brown envelope before flicking them back up to look at me. His brows pull together in confusion as he takes in the tight press of my lips and the critical look in my eye.

His game forgotten, he slowly sets down the controller to pick up the file and rifles through the pages.

"What the fuck is this?" he finally asks in disbelief, his words an echo of Hadley's as he continues to scan his eyes over the pages.

He's not really asking me, so I don't answer, waiting patiently for him to take in what I've just said, what's written in black and white on the pages in front of him.

"I don't understand," he finally murmurs, glancing up at me. "You tested our DNA? Why the fuck would you do that?"

I again try to explain to him what I struggled to explain to Hadley, but it isn't easy to find the words. It was a gut feeling, a hunch as much as anything else. Simply saying they have the same unique shade of stormy blue-gray eyes and fiery tempers isn't enough justification.

It was every time one of the guys laughed off how similar they were. It was in the small mannerisms they share, the green skittles. It was the way her jaw clenches and her nostrils flare when she's pissed off, the slight tilt of her head when she's concentrating. How she absently plays with the hem of her skirt or a pen or the corner of a page when she's distracted. All things Hawk does, too. All things no one who doesn't know Hawk as well as I do, or pay as much attention to Hadley as I do, would ever piece together.

I'd sound insane if I said all that, or like a creepy fucking stalker.

"There must be a mistake," he insists after another long moment of him trying to internally process the news. "There's just no way this is true. For starters, I'd fucking know if I had a sister. My parents would have said something, or there would be some sort of proof somewhere, a photo or something at our house. Even if she was my sister, how the fuck did she end up in foster care?"

These are all excellent questions that I've been trying to figure out the last few days too.

"I dunno, man," I admit. "I don't have the answer to that. I just know the tests don't lie."

"Well, I don't fucking believe them," he seethes, his anger finally making an appearance like I knew it would. "They've made a mistake. There's an error."

"By five different labs?" I reason.

"I don't fucking know," he yells, jumping to his feet. His hand grips the pages tightly, crumpling them. "But there is no fucking way this is true!"

He paces furiously back and forth across the apartment, grumbling to himself as he tries to come up with an alternative to what is right in front of him. Knowing there's no point in arguing with him when he's like this, I get comfortable in my chair to watch him as he wears a hole in the hardwood, stomping the length of the open space and back. His thoughts running a mile a minute.

I don't know how long we stay like that for, but eventually, the front door opens and Cam and Mason walk in. They stop inside the door, immediately catching on to Hawk's angry state.

"What the hell's going on here?" Cam asks, eyeing Hawk warily as he moves over to claim the spot on the sofa Hawk vacated.

Mason doesn't move from the doorway, his eyes following Hawk as he continues pacing, ignoring their arrival.

"Hadley and Hawk are related," I say, not beating around the bush.

Cam's head snaps toward me, his mouth dropping open. "They're what?" He gapes. "Like distant relatives? Second cousins twice removed or some shit like that, that doesn't even count?"

"More like siblings," I clarify.

Even Mason's eyebrows raise at that piece of information. "Wow," he exclaims.

Cam, clearly incapable of forming words, continues to gawk at me.

"What? When? How?" he finally splutters.

"In the same way as any other siblings," I retort sarcastically. "If no one's had the birds and the bees talk with you yet, I'm sure as fuck not explaining it."

He scowls at me, unimpressed with my scathing tone. "Don't be such a dick. You know what I mean."

Finally ungluing his feet from the floor, Mason pulls his eyes away from a still-pacing Hawk, coming to join Cam and me.

"How did we not know Hawk had a sister?"

I shake my head, not having an answer for him.

"Hawk, man, stop whatever the fuck you're doing. We need to sort this shit out," he barks. His words must get through to Hawk in some way as he stops pacing to spin and glare at all of us.

"Sort what out?" he demands, storming over. "There's nothing to sort out. So what if she's my sister or whatever? That doesn't mean anything. No one even has to fucking know. We can just tear this shit up," he rants, waving the pages in the air, "and pretend none of this ever happened."

"Dude, what the fuck? You can't do that!" Cam snaps, reaching out to tear the pages from his grasp, glancing quickly at them before handing them to Mason.

"Why the fuck not? Clearly, my parents have decided she doesn't exist. Why can't I?"

"Because you're not them," I seethe at him, unable to believe he's even thinking of burying this shit. "You may be acting like an ass right now, but you're not the same dicks your parents are."

Hawk grinds his teeth, glaring at each of us. But he doesn't argue the issue any further, knowing damn well we're right.

"You haven't told her, have you?" he demands, his pissed-off expression drilling into me.

Cringing, I respond, "Yeah, actually. I have."

"She knows?" Cam exclaims before Hawk can tear me a new one. "Not that I care," he tacks on, mumbling under his breath.

Sharing a look with Mason, I roll my eyes at him. Between him and Hawk, I'm not sure who's being the greater asshole right now. Cam needs to get the fuck over his hurt pride and see the bigger picture.

"She must be a mess right now," Mason says softly, his forehead furrowed in concern. Huh, the fact his thoughts immediately went to Hadley is proof enough. I knew he was interested in her by how he observes her, but now he also seems to actually care about her.

How did that happen?

When did it happen?

I mean, I get it. There's something about her that draws you in, that makes you want to give a damn about her, even when alarm bells are going off in your head. Walking out of her room and leaving her there after I had just dropped that life-altering bomb on her was so much harder than I thought it would be. Even now, my thoughts continually stray back to her, wondering what she's doing or how she's coping with it. Is she on a rampage like Hawk is? Unable to sit still, stomping around her room? Or has she withdrawn into herself, blocking out everything around her while she tries to process what all of this means?

"You told her?" Hawk barks, reminding me I have my own Davenport problem to deal with. He grinds his teeth as he glares at me, his hands repeatedly clenching into tight fists, like he's imagining ripping my head off. "Why the fuck would you do something stupid like that?!"

"She had a right to know," I respond calmly. "Just the same as you do."

"I'm supposed to be your best friend," he shouts. "You should have told me first. I should have been the one to decide if she should know or not."

"And that's exactly why I didn't tell you first," I snap, getting annoyed. "Because for some stupid reason, you're on a mission to destroy her and it's blinding you. You can't fucking see that this affects her just as much, if not more so than it affects you."

Hawk doesn't say anything, but I'm pretty sure he's picturing his hands wrapped around my throat. I'm not stupid enough to think his silence means I've gotten through to him or that he agrees with me. He's just so fucking furious right now he can't even talk.

Sighing, Mason interjects before tensions can escalate any further. "Regardless of whether or not she knows, this raises a lot of questions. Questions we need answers to."

"Yeah," Cam agrees, nodding his head in agreement. "Like, why the fuck your parents never told you about her."

"Or how she ended up in foster care," Mason adds.

"Do you think she knew?" Cam questions. "Is that why she had the notebook?"

All three of them turn to look at me. "No way," I insist, giving a vigorous shake of my head. "She didn't have a clue. She threw the same hissy fit you're having right now." I wave my hand toward Hawk, who still looks like an angry bear with his arms crossed over his broad chest as he stands, towering over the rest of us.

Hawk finally unclenches his jaw enough to suggest, "She could have been lying to you. Look how she manipulated Cam all year; she's clearly gotten inside your head, too."

My fingernails dig into my palm, my fists clenched tight as I try to reign in my anger. "She wasn't," I spit through gritted teeth, scowling at him before turning my frustration on Cam. "And I don't believe everything between you and her was a lie, either. Do you not see the way she looks at you? The two of you need to talk and sort out your shit. You can't keep going around blaming her for everything. I know there are a lot of unanswered questions," I say, holding my hands up to get him to keep quiet, "I know she hurt your pride, but, man, you've gotta get over it."

He doesn't say anything, pressing his lips together, not pleased with the reality-check I just hit him with.

"How the fuck are we supposed to get answers to any of these questions?" Hawk challenges. "Hadley's a closed fucking book, and it's not like I can just say to my parents, 'hey, remember that other kid you had that you never told me about and apparently forgot ever existed? Well, she's enrolled at Pac now and knows all about the rich family that abandoned her.'"

"Well, you probably shouldn't say it quite like that," Mason retorts unhelpfully, making me scowl at him.

"You shouldn't say anything to them at all," I snap.

Hawk's eyebrows rise in shock at my words.

"Your parents kept it a secret for a reason," I explain. "Just do some snooping while you're home over Christmas break. We need more information before we confront them or anyone else finds out about this."

Before he can argue with me any further, a sharp knock on the door draws all of our attention, and I get up to go shoo away whatever idiot thought it was okay to just turn up at our apartment unannounced.

Hadley

CHAPTER TWENTY-EIGHT

I pace back and forth for god knows how long before giving up and storming out the door. West can't seriously drop that bomb and just expect me to sit here and stew in it.

I have a family. A fucking family.

Except that family is Hawk.

I'm not sure how I feel about that.

Why couldn't I have had a nice little cookie-cutter family with a white picket fence and a dog?

Oh yeah, because this is me we're talking about, and even when I get something I never thought I would have, life still has to go and fucking shit all over it.

I climb the steps to the fourth floor of the boys' dormitories, pulling open the stairwell door and walking into a small hall. Unlike the other floors, there's no hallway with numerous doors along it. Instead, there's just the one door right in front of me.

Pursing my lips, I bang my fist against the door and wait impatiently for someone to open it.

West doesn't seem surprised to see me, although he sure as hell doesn't seem pleased about it as I stomp past him into their dorm to find the other three assholes spread out around the open living space. They all look my way, only I can't tear my gaze away from Hawk as I run my eyes over his face, trying to see whatever West saw. I'm not surprised when all I see is the arrogant dickwad I've seen every day since the first day of school. Sure, his eyes are maybe similar to mine, and his nose is straight like mine, but that's it.

His eyes narrow as he turns to face me, and Cam jumps to his feet beside him as the two of them stride toward me. At a slower pace, Mason stands up but stays back by the couches, assessing the situation from a distance. "What are you doing here?" Hawk demands.

"I'm guessing West told you the good news, *brother*." His icy glare promises all sorts of heinous acts as he practically snarls at me. I shrug away his shitty attitude. West said we had similar tempers? There's no way I'm as infuriating as this asswipe.

"He shouldn't have fucking told you," Hawk growls, briefly flicking his glower from me to West.

"Are you for fucking real?" I yell, directing his ire back at him. "Of course, he should have fucking told me. You think I wanted this to be my fucking reality? Wanted *you* to be my brother? I'd take pretty much anyone else."

"Please," he snorts. "You just landed yourself the answer to all your fucking problems."

When I look at him like he's got three heads, not understanding what he's going on about, he continues, "That's assuming you didn't already know about any of this." Hawk's penetrating gaze stays firmly pinpointed on me, scrutinizing my every move. "Is that what that whole notebook was about? You were learning everything you could about us before coming clean about who you really were?"

"What?" I gape in shock, but of course, that's what he assumes the stupid fucking notebook is about. "No."

"She's telling the truth, man," West insists. "I saw the look on her face. She was as shocked as you."

"So you claim, but as I said, she's a good liar."

I glance at Cam, taking in his thinned lips and the distrustful look in his eyes, trying to forget the uncharacteristic softness I saw in them after our rendezvous in the locker room.

I look right at him when I speak the god's honest truth. There is a lot they don't know about me—not that they've earned the fucking right to know any of it—nonetheless there is one thing I am certain of. "The feelings I had for you were real. The...time we spent together? All of it meant something to me."

I swear his eyes soften just a little. But it's also highly possible I'm only seeing what I want to see because the rest of his face is still shut down, pinched tight in anger.

Mason coughs uncomfortably, drawing my attention as he rubs the back of his neck in awkward embarrassment. Noticing my attention on him, his gaze latches onto mine, a private moment passing between the two of us. I have no idea what it means, though. I don't know what that kiss meant in the clearing or what any of this means, really. I'm beyond confused at this point. None of this is what I expected to find at Pac.

"I don't give a shit who you are or what you are to me," Hawk snarls, his nose wrinkling in disgust as his gaze drops to take me in. No part of me meets his standard, obviously. The sheer hatred in his eyes stalls the breath in my throat as I stand frozen, gaping at him. "As far as I'm concerned, you're unwanted trash. I don't care if we are related, I don't want anything to do with you. These idiots are letting their dicks make all the decisions for them right now, but pretty soon, they'll see you for who you really are—a pathetic nobody trying to fuck her way to a pampered future as some old guy's mistress."

Despite how fucking infuriating he is, his words cut deep. He might not be what I want in a family, but he *is* my family. Something I've wished for and dreamed about my entire life, and he's just shit all over it with his nasty, untrue words and revulsion. I'm not sure what I expected when I came up here. I knew it wouldn't be all hugs and celebrations. It's Hawk. Of course he's going to fight it tooth and nail, but the unrelenting hostility in his voice is painful to hear. I can feel my chest cracking open with every foul word he spits my way.

I try so goddamn fucking hard to hold it all together, except I feel it when the mask slips. It's only for a second, but it's enough. It's more vulnerability than I've shown anyone, ever. Before I can do something downright embarrassing, like cry, I duck my head, spinning on my heel and nearly running over West in my hurry to get out of there and away from Hawk's toxic malice.

Fleeing from their apartment, I don't stop until I'm slamming through the doors of the gym. I'm not sure why I came here, of all places. I'm not dressed for the gym, and I don't have my gear with me. I guess I knew it would be empty so late at night.

Skirting my way around the darkened room, I wander through into the swimming pool. Other than when I came to watch Cam's swim meets, I've never set foot in here. Since I'm a shitty swimmer, it seems wise to avoid coming anywhere near a deep body of water, especially with all the enemies surrounding me these days. All it would take is one little push. I can guarantee you none of those bitches would dive in to rescue me, and Hawk would happily stand idly by and watch me drown.

There's something oddly peaceful about this place, however. The gentle lap of water, the way the lights shine from the bottom of the pool. Even the stench of chlorine is strangely comforting.

Keeping a safe distance from the edge, I carefully walk around until I'm at the shallow end, on the far side of the room. Before I can think better of it, I strip out of my jeans and top, take off my bra and panties, and set them on a bench before dipping into the warm water. I'm probably insane for doing this, but the water calls to me. I can feel the tension draining from my body as it laps against me, soaking my skin. With my feet firmly planted on the bottom of the pool, I bend my knees, slowly lowering myself until the water hits my shoulders.

Spreading my arms out, I trail my fingers through the surface of the water, watching the ripple effects of my movements. Life's a lot like that; someone does or says something that causes a chain reaction. Their behavior influences everyone else around them, for better or worse. Most of the time, we don't even consider how our actions might affect those around us. Or people like Hawk just don't give a shit. But it's folks like me who have to live with the consequences of others' crappy choices.

A sudden noise from the gym next door has me snapping my head up. I quickly duck to the corner of the pool, hoping I won't be noticed in the dim lighting. I barely breathe as I listen for any signs of someone coming this way.

The door to the pool bangs open, and Beck storms into the room, seeming just as furious with the world as I imagine I did when I first arrived.

Reaching behind his back, his large bicep flexes as he grabs his shirt, pulling it over his head in a sexy-as-fuck move that has me drooling. My mouth is suddenly parched as his sculpted torso is revealed to me. I've spent weeks wondering what he's hiding underneath his fancy waistcoats. I thought he looked pretty damn fine earlier in his t-shirt, but *hot damn*. Naked, he's a mouth-watering masterpiece of perfection. He's got a panty-melting swimmer's body—all lean with sharp edges. A firm chest, with a sprinkling of dark-colored chest hair, giving way to a prominent six-pack just begging for a girl to run her tongue over. My eyes follow the faint outline of a treasure trail down to the lining of his swimming trunks, which sit snugly on narrow hips and wrap around his muscular thighs.

Throwing his shirt carelessly behind him, he plunges into the water in what I imagine is a perfect dive. There's barely a splash as his body is submerged, gliding smoothly through the water.

He doesn't come up for air until he's halfway across the Olympic-sized swimming pool, his arms moving in synchronization as they rise out of the water, one at a time in a perfect arch, propelling him forward.

I watch in awe as he reaches the shallow end of the pool, doing some fancy flip under the water before kicking off the side with his feet and gliding effortlessly back to where he started. Back and forth he goes, never faltering or slowing as he swims from one end to the other. I can't do anything except hide and gawk at him, mesmerized as he moves like an unstoppable machine.

After several lengths, he must feel my stare on him, for he stops mid-stride, his gaze jumping about the room until he finds me lurking in the corner of the pool like a typical stalker.

"What the—" he breathes, squinting to see who would be creeping about in the pool this late at night.

Taking a small step forward so I'm not hidden in the shadows, I try to swallow around my suddenly dry throat.

"Hadley?"

"Sorry, " I begin, "I, uh, needed to clear my head. I didn't think anyone would be here."

He doesn't say anything as he swims toward me, stopping when we're a few feet apart.

"Is everything okay?"

"Yeah," I breathe out, my automatic response to fob him off coming out before I've even thought about the question. "No…I don't know." I give a small chuckle. "It's been a crappy day. I…" I trail off, the words getting stuck at the back of my throat. I want to tell him about today, about Hawk, but I'm fucking shit at telling anybody anything. It doesn't come naturally to me, and apparently, it's harder than I thought to blurt out stuff about yourself.

"I'm a mess," I eventually admit. Not what I want to say but fuck if it's not the truth.

His eyes roam over my face, taking me in, likely seeing for himself how true those words are. My eyes still feel puffy from earlier, and despite trying to fix my mask back in place after running away from Hawk, it no longer fits quite right.

"You are far from a mess." His words take me by surprise. He listens to the whining and superficial problems of teenagers all day. I'm pretty sure I'm the most complex case he has, though. "You're the embodiment of strength…I don't know what you've been through," he murmurs, trailing a finger along an old scar on my collarbone, making me aware of how close we've drifted as he towers over me in the water. "But I can tell you're a survivor. Your scars? Your pain? They only make you more beautiful."

I swallow around the lump in my throat, my heaving chest only inches from his, my stomach a riot of butterflies as I watch rivulets of water trail over his pecs and down his abs. I've thought about this moment for months now, wondered what would happen if we were alone like this.

"I've wanted you from the moment you stepped into my office," he murmurs. His voice barely more than a whisper, the gravel tone scraping under my skin as it ignites my nerves.

Tilting my head back, I look into his eyes and see his usual bright moss-green irises darkened with lust. "I don't do this. I don't seduce students, but I just can't seem to stop myself with you."

"So don't," I whisper the words so quietly I'm not sure he even hears me. He gazes into my eyes for a moment longer before his hands slide around my neck, his fingers tangling in my hair as he angles me just perfectly. His lips hover over mine, both of us savoring this before everything changes.

Unable to hold back any longer, his lips descend as they move slowly, teasingly, against my own. My eyes drift shut as my body lights up. His kiss is like a thousand volts of electricity, making me feel alive.

I open beneath him, moaning as he sweeps his tongue into my mouth, our tongues sliding over one another in the most delicious kiss. He unhurriedly explores my mouth, driving me wild as he takes his time getting to know every part of me, memorizing my reactions to his every touch.

We drift closer until our chests are pressed up against each other, my arms winding around his shoulders, my fingers running through the tiny hairs at the back of his neck.

Using the buoyancy of the water, I wrap my legs around his hips, seating myself in his lap, relishing the feel of his hard length pressing against my core.

His hands stroke their way down my body, roaming over my back and sides until he grabs a handful of my ass cheeks in each palm, groaning as he realizes I'm completely naked. Tugging me in closer to him, he grinds against me.

"Beck," I murmur, tearing my lips from his as my head falls back, granting him access to my neck. His lips feather across my skin as he licks and nibbles his way down my throat and across my collarbone. Every light touch has me panting harder, grinding against him.

I want nothing more than to pull down his trunks, wrap my fingers around his cock and slide myself down his length, but he needs to be the one to take control here. He has to make that move. After all, he's the one risking everything right now.

His hand slips down between our bodies, his fingers deftly sweeping over my clit before they sink inside me. He meets no resistance with me being so wet. I don't need any working up at all—more than fucking ready for him.

"Fuck," he groans. "You feel so good, and you taste so sweet. I need to be inside you." He hesitates before sheepishly adding, "I don't have, uh, a condom."

"I'm covered."

I've barely gotten the words out before he's pulling down his trunks, his pink, veiny erect dick springing free. I reach down between us to wrap my hand around him, angling him at my entrance as I sink down on top of him, gasping while I adjust to him. He's got a slight bend that rubs perfectly against my G-spot, eliciting a dirty moan from the back of my throat as he seats himself deep within me.

"Fuck," he hisses between gritted teeth, his hands tightening around my hips, leaving half-moon fingernail marks in my skin.

I can't do anything but wrap myself around him tighter as he begins to move. With every thrust, he hits that perfect spot, and I cry out, quickly rushing toward oblivion as I meet him thrust for thrust.

My fingernails dig into his back, leaving scratch marks as I lose myself in the feel of him pounding into me.

"Beck," I cry out, feeling that familiar, intense uncoiling in my lower abdomen. I can feel him swelling within me, close to coming himself as his pace turns erratic.

I fall over the edge as his cum hits my inner walls, both of us collapsing into one another, our chests rising in symphony together. He loosens his grip on my hip, wrapping his arms around me as he lazily kisses me. His tongue tangles with mine in slow, lavish strokes, both of us catching our breaths and coming back to reality, yet still refusing to leave this perfect little bubble we've created for ourselves.

"You're incredible," he murmurs between kisses. "I want to see you again. I want to get to know you, to spend time with you."

"You mean an hour a week isn't enough?" I joke.

His voice is serious when he responds, "Not even close."

Eventually, we pull ourselves apart, climbing out of the pool and getting dressed. He even offers me his towel to dry off with so I don't have to attempt to pull my jeans on over wet skin. With one final passionate kiss, he watches as I take off back toward the girls' dorms, replaying the unexpected end to this bizarre day in my mind.

Hadley

CHAPTER TWENTY-NINE

The next day, excitement is in the air as parents and drivers arrive, and everyone gets ready to leave for two weeks. Everyone except me, apparently.

I thought even some of the scholarship students would stay behind—not that any of them talk to me—but nope. It's just going to be me and an empty campus. *That's not creepy at all.*

On the plus side, with no one around, I should have plenty of opportunity to sneak out to see Beck. My cheeks turn red just thinking about him and what we did in the pool last night. I swear, I'm not going to be able to keep a straight face at Cam's next swim meet.

The thought of him swimming through our juices nearly has me bursting out in laughter. I hope he accidentally swallows some pool water. It would be exactly what he deserves.

Most of the students seem to be gone, the halls eerily quiet as I make my way through the school. Rounding a corner, I come to an abrupt halt when I find Beck and West at the far end of the corridor. That in itself isn't necessarily strange, but the dark scowl on West's face is surprising. He only ever looks like that when he's with the other Pricks and they're making a stand in front of the entire school. Even then, I've never seen him look at anyone the way he's looking at Beck. It's similar to how Hawk looked at me yesterday, disgust and vehement hate written all over his face. What issue could he possibly have with Beck to instill such violent emotions?

"Don't fucking bother. I don't want anything to do with you," West snarls before storming off. Beck watches him leave, running a hand through his usually perfectly in-place hair. Sighing heavily, he shakes his head before following West, the two of them disappearing out of sight.

What the hell was that all about?

For the next three days, I focus on completing the mountain of homework they gave us to do over the break. It's strangely peaceful having the whole place to myself, eating alone in the dining hall, and being the only one in the library. However, after several days of solitude, I'm officially bored. I tell myself the desire to talk to another human being is the reason I'm standing outside his door. Although, if I'm being honest with myself, I just want to see him again.

Despite how opposed I was to this whole counseling thing—and still am—I've found solitude in this room over the last few weeks. Found comfort and safety in Beck's presence. Growing up always on alert, never knowing where the next danger will come from or when the next hit will strike, that's saying something.

Unsure if he will even be here—it is Christmas break, after all, I'm sure he has better things to do—I rap my knuckles on the door. Turning the handle, I'm actually shocked to find the door opens when I push on it.

"Hadley," Beck says, pleasantly surprised, an easy smile on his face as his eyes drink me in. I'm wearing jeans and a tank top, but he obviously didn't get the memo that no one else is here, since he's dressed in his usual attire of a preppy waistcoat and chinos—not that it matters. He honestly looks hot in anything.

"Hey." My reply is much more awkward and uncertain as I step into the room, closing the door quietly behind me. "I, uh, wasn't sure how to get in touch with you, so I figured I'd see if you were here."

"You hunted me down?" There are laugh lines around his eyes as his smile stretches wider.

Rolling my eyes, I retort, "I was bored," as I sit in the chair in front of his desk, bringing my knees up in front of me.

"Well, we can't have that now." He leans forward in his seat, his arms resting on the desk as he watches me. "I'll give you my number, and you can text or call me anytime."

Biting my lip, I nod my head. My heart is racing, smashing against my chest, and my palms are sweaty. I don't even understand why I'm so nervous. I've never been like this around him before.

"I can see your thoughts running a mile a minute. What are you thinking about?"

"I...What are we doing?"

His lazy smile returns as he gets up and circles around the table, perching on the edge of the desk.

"I believe they call it dating." He still looks like he's enjoying himself way too much at my expense as I shake my head.

"I don't know how to do that. I've never..." I trail off, my unsaid words hanging between us. How pathetic is it that I've never gone out with anyone before, never been on a date with a guy?

"Hey," he soothes, crouching down in front of me. "We don't need to put a label on it. We'll just do us—go at whatever speed you want, do whatever you're comfortable with."

I stare into his deep green eyes that easily ensnare me, holding me captive, allowing him to truly *see* me. See all the insecure, fucked-up parts of me I keep carefully locked away.

"What if I'm bad at it?" The words are barely more than a whisper, and I don't think I've ever felt so exposed, so vulnerable. Not even when that stupid video was going around.

He reaches out, tucking a stray bit of hair behind my ear, running his fingers through the messy strands.

"I don't, for one second, believe you will be. I was captivated from the minute you strolled in here, full of fire and quick wit. It had nothing to do with what you've been through. It was just *you*, your inner strength, your tenacious ability to thrive when anyone else would crumble. The hour I spend with you is the highlight of my week."

"You must have a very boring life if that's the case," I grumble, deflecting him away from the heat in my cheeks and the fluttering feeling in my chest that I can't place.

A slow smile makes its way across his face. "I'm pretty sure I could spend my free time skydiving and base jumping, and I'd still say you were the best part of my week."

Fucking hell, he's trying to kill me with sweet sentiments.

Leaning forward, I lower my legs, planting my feet on either side of him as I bend down and kiss him. Not wasting a second, his hand slides around to the back of my head, holding me to him as our tongues dance together, affirming every sweet word he just said to me.

He untangles his hand from my hair, slipping his hands beneath my thighs and lifting me up, making me wrap my legs around his waist. I feel him growing hard as I am pressed against him, neither one of us breaking the kiss as he carries me over to the sofa, dropping down onto it so I'm straddling him.

Before we can get too carried away, he pulls back. "We've gone about this all backward," he breathes. "I want us to do it right."

"Are you saying no to sex?" I tease, nipping on his earlobe before kissing down his neck, loving the feel of his fingers digging into the flesh on my hips.

"I'm definitely not saying that," he growls. "God, all the dirty things I want to do to you right now." I can hear the strain in his voice as he holds himself back, and as much as I want him to do precisely that, I want him to be comfortable in this thing between us, too. He's already assured me we can go at my pace, but I want him to enjoy this, and if he wants to do it 'the right way', then who am I to stop him?

Pulling back, creating a bit of distance between us so I can work through my hormone-addled thoughts, I look him in the eye. "How do we go about doing that?"

"We start by getting to know each other." He must feel me tense in his lap because his hands start rubbing soothing circles up and down my back. "Nothing big, nothing you don't want to share. We'll start with the small, simple stuff." He's got no idea that nothing about me is *simple*, and what he's asking is much more complicated than he thinks. Yet, I find myself giving him a hesitant nod.

The pride in his eyes at that one small concession almost makes it worthwhile, although it doesn't calm the thudding in my chest or the nervous flutter in my stomach.

Pulling me in closer, he lies back on the sofa and takes me with him so I'm lying on top of him, my head resting on his chest. When he doesn't immediately start firing off questions, I slowly relax, kicking off my boots and entangling my legs with his as I get comfy. His fingers dip beneath my top, drawing lazy circles on my hip, while his other arm is bent at the elbow, with his hand resting underneath his head.

Holy hell, why have I never done this before? There's something to be said for just lying with a guy, feeling the steady thrumming of his heart beneath your palm and his body pressed against yours. It's calming, stabilizing, reassuring. I never knew I could feel this way with another person. Whenever I tried to picture doing crap like this with a guy, it always looked awkward and uncomfortable. I could easily fall asleep on him, and I'm pretty sure it would be the best damn nap I've ever had.

I'm lying half-asleep on top of him when I feel him move, his lips kissing the top of my head in a strangely sweet gesture that has every girly part of me squealing in delight. I have to bury my head in his shirt to hide the stupid grin on my face.

"What's your favorite color?" he murmurs, the question taking me by surprise. *Okay, that I can easily answer.*

"Umm, blue, I guess, but like a deep, rich blue-green color. Like teal."

I can feel the rumble in his chest as he chuckles. "I should have known you wouldn't just come out with a standard, generic color. That you'd actually have given it some thought...I like that."

I glance up at him through my eyelashes. His eyes are closed, and he's got a small, peaceful smile on his face.

"What about you?"

"I've always been a fan of bluish-gray shades, kind of like the color of your eyes." I lift my head to catch him already watching me, enraptured, as I look down at him. "There's something so...energetic but calming about it. The outward appearance of composure and determination, yet you get the impression there's so much more going on beneath the surface."

I simply gape at him, unsure of how to respond. Probably sensing my internal panic, he leans up to give me a quick, reassuring kiss.

"What about your favorite ice cream?" he asks, moving the conversation along.

With a grin, I settle back into my position on his chest. "Well, I'm slowly making my way through every flavor in the dining hall. So far, my favorite is lemon and lime."

"What?!" he gasps. "Tell me it isn't so! Lemon and lime? That has got to be one of the worst flavors. You could only top that by saying vanilla."

I chuckle at his dramatics, enjoying the easy banter.

"Alright, Oh Wise Knower of Ice cream Flavors. What is your favorite?"

"Chocolate fudge brownie, obviously," he states, like there could be no other option.

"I haven't tried that one yet."

"You haven't—?!" he sputters, shaking his head. "Well, we'll have to rectify that as soon as possible."

The fact that he doesn't ask me why I'm working my way through the flavors in the dining hall or how I've never had such a typical flavor as chocolate fudge brownie, means more to me than he can ever realize. We spend the rest of the day just lying there, talking. There's no awkwardness like I thought there would be, and any time he hits a sore spot, he quickly waves away the question and asks something different, never prying or asking for more than I'm willing to give.

I've never felt so at ease around another person, so accepting of sharing a part of myself with them—even if what I'm sharing is light and superficial. It's still more than I've shared with any one person before.

Before I leave, we swap numbers and he pulls me into him, planting a heated, passionate kiss on my lips.

"Just because I didn't fuck you, doesn't mean I didn't spend all day thinking about bending you over that desk," he murmurs against my lips, the deep gravel in his voice only making me wish he'd done exactly that.

"Next time," I whisper, sealing the promise with a kiss.

I can't fight the smile on my lips as I make my way back to my room. Maybe being the only ones left on campus isn't so bad after all.

The rest of the Christmas break goes by uneventfully. Beck and I text back and forth, and I even get a few messages from Mason and West. I don't hear anything from Cam or Hawk, not that I'm surprised. Anything Hawk would have to say to me would only be more hateful words I don't need right now. Nevertheless, it does bother me more than I'd like, when I don't hear anything from Cam. I even went so far as to pull up his details on the tablet and stare at the screen, re-reading the last few messages we sent to each other, not knowing what to say and eventually closing out of the app altogether.

We've done too much damage to one another. We've both destroyed any trust there could have been between us—me with my deceit and him with his betrayal, assuming he was the one that told Hawk about my scars. If he didn't, well, I guess it's all my fault. I broke us. But how was I to know he would come to mean something more to me? That I'd actually give a damn about him.

Hell, I came here to kill him, not develop a fucking crush on him. But standing over him that night, I couldn't fucking do it. He might have been nothing more than a flirtatious idiot back then, then again he wasn't at all what I expected. He didn't deserve what I had planned for him, so I devised an alternative plan to exact my revenge. Of course, that kind of blew up in my face, too. God, I was never this sloppy or off my game before I got here. All these guys are messing with my head, preventing me from thinking straight and distracting me from my goals.

On Christmas day, the kitchen staff put out a feast, even though it's just me here, and I spend most of the day sampling a bit of everything. It's all delicious, and I'm annoyed every time my stomach threatens to blow the button on my jeans and I have to begrudgingly stop eating.

All too quickly, the end of the holidays approaches, and the day before classes commence again as students start to return to campus.

A sharp rap on my door pulls me out of the book I was reading, and I swear I'm going to fucking murder whoever is disturbing me. Not only was I at a particularly juicy scene, but the book was doing wonders at making me forget about tomorrow.

Unfolding myself from the bed, I don't even care that I look like a hot mess in a baggy t-shirt and tight boxing shorts, with my hair scraped back in a messy bun, as I answer the door. I've barely gotten it open when someone shoves their way through it, storming past me.

"What the hell?" I shriek, spinning around to glare at my intruder.

Hawk.

Of course, it's fucking Hawk.

My fucking brother, a fact I still can't wrap my head around. I've gone back and forth all throughout the break, between fixating on the matter and pretending West never stormed in here and turned my world upside-down.

I wasn't sure if he would be hell-bent on making my life even more miserable now that he knew exactly who I was or if he was intent on forgetting the whole thing ever happened. Based on the sneer he's sporting and the burning pits of hatred in his eyes, I guess he's decided he's still pissed. Evidently, two weeks wasn't enough time for him to simmer down.

Glaring back at him, he's impossible to ignore in the confines of my room. He's got such a demanding presence, his larger frame seemingly taking up all the space in my small room.

"I don't see it." His head is tilted to one side as he scrutinizes me in much the same way I imagine I'm looking at him.

"Yeah, well, neither do I," I agree, standing taller and keeping my head up to glare at him.

He trails his eyes over me, taking his sweet fucking time, while I stand there awkwardly. Curiosity swirls with the ever-present hatred in his eyes, his brows drawn together in confusion.

"What do you want?" I snap out when I can't stand his eyes on me anymore.

He holds out a shoebox-sized box he was gripping, not bothering to answer my question with actual words.

"What is that?" I ask hesitantly, once again sensing I don't want to know what's in that box. While it might give me answers, I get the impression it will only further solidify this whole 'brother' thing. I've been living quite a nice life of denial the last two weeks, and I'm not sure I'm ready to burst that bubble just yet.

"Stuff I found at the house," he grunts out, stretching his arm out further to get me to take the box. I still don't move though, frozen in place as I stare at the unassuming item. How can something so small and innocent-looking hold all the answers to the questions I've given up on asking?

When it becomes clear I'm not going to take it, he closes the space between us, shoving the box against my chest until I have no other choice but to grasp it or risk the contents spilling out all over the floor.

Once it's in my hands, I can't resist the curiosity brimming within me. Moving over to set the box on the desk, I hesitantly reach out, lifting off the lid and absently setting it on the table as my eyes settle on the first thing I see. A picture of a girl, a toddler. She's got white, blonde hair, chubby cheeks, and a mischievous grin. Her clothes are covered in dirt, with soil smudged on her face. Standing beside her, clean as a whistle, is another white-haired toddler. This one's a boy. His eyes are narrowed as he scowls at her, but there's a slight curl at the corner of his lip, like he's trying hard not to laugh.

"This is...us?" I whisper, the words barely audible. It's a redundant question, however. Of course that's us. I'd recognize Hawk's glower anywhere. I can't tear my eyes away from the photo. We're so young. I look so happy. *I don't ever remember being that happy before.*

Despite not needing to, he answers me anyway, "Yeah." The word is barely a grunt, but the closeness of his voice catches me off guard, and I pull my gaze from the picture, looking up to find him standing right behind me, staring into the box. *When did he move so close?*

Pulling out the photo, I carefully place it to one side. There are a couple of other pictures of a baby that I'm guessing are of me as well. Not lingering on them, I move on to the page underneath them. Tugging it out, I'm still processing what I'm looking at when Hawk states the obvious, "That's your birth certificate. It's got your real name on it and the day you were born."

My eyes hover over the name on the page, the words feeling both foreign and familiar at the same time.

Elizabeth Jane Davenport.

Elizabeth? I don't feel like an Elizabeth. Hadley is a much more suitable name for me. Elizabeth sounds like it belongs to a pampered princess, someone who's lived a life of luxury, who's never had to fight every day of her life, who hasn't had to endure the pain and torture I've had to live through.

Maybe I was an Elizabeth once, but I'm not that girl anymore.

Not feeling comfortable with this new identity I'm trying to reconcile myself with, I swiftly move on, glancing further down the page until I find a date of birth.

"I was born on January eighth?"

"*We* were," Hawk says over my shoulder.

We? We're twins? I guess that makes sense. I probably should have thought of that before.

"That's only a few days away," I murmur absently, staring obliviously at the birth certificate until Hawk pulls out a brown envelope from his pocket, setting it down in front of me.

"What is this?" I ask, wariness creeping through me.

"Why don't you open it and see." His haughty tone immediately has my back straightening, and with shaky hands, I reach out and break the seal, lifting out the folded pages inside.

The first page is a photocopy of yet another birth certificate, only the name and date of birth are different.

"I don't..." My words trail off as I move on to the next page. This one is a photocopy of a passport with the same name and date of birth as the certificate.

Hadley Parker. Born August twenty-third.

Except, the image on the passport isn't of me. It's a girl with long dark hair. She's got a wide smile on her face, which shows braces on her teeth. This Hadley looks nothing like me. She's carefree and full of life.

Looking at the next page, my heart thumps rapidly in my chest as I scan my eyes over the photocopy of a newspaper article.

'Teenage girl dies in a tragic car accident'.

Quickly skipping over the article to the next page, I can taste bile at the back of my throat as I again see my name on another page. This one is a death certificate.

Apparently, I died three years ago last month.

"What is this?" I choke out. But it's a futile question. I *know* what this is. I didn't know this girl; I've never seen her picture. I didn't know how she died, but I knew she was dead.

"This was the *real* Hadley Parker," Hawk growls from behind me, his voice regaining its harsh quality that he seems to reserve only for me.

He reaches up, spinning me around and grabbing on tightly to my shoulders, his fingers digging painfully into the bones. He towers over me, standing so close there's nowhere else for me to look but into his menacing eyes overflowing with distrust and malice.

"So the question is," he sneers, "who the fuck are you?"

EPILOGUE

"*I* found her."
    I finally fucking found her.
"What do you want to do?"
"I want her back," I snarl down the phone. "She's mine."
She thinks she can escape me? I've waited *years* to have her, and right when she was about to become mine, she disappears. Well, I won't let that happen again. I searched fucking everywhere for her. I never thought I'd find her at a fucking prep school, of all places.
Not that it matters, she'll soon be back where she belongs, and I'll do what I should have done years ago. I'll make her *mine*—in every possible way. She won't *ever* get away from me again. I'll chain her to my fucking bed if that's what it takes.
"I'll put in a call."
His blunt, professional tone settles some of the anger that's been coursing through me recently, and I disconnect the call knowing he'll get the job done. He doesn't have a fucking choice.
I won't throw away years of hard work, years of plans in the making. I've been patiently playing the long game, but I'm fucking done. She might not realize it yet, but we belong together.
I hope you've enjoyed your freedom, Dove, because I'm coming for you.

Little Warrior

THE TIME WHEN HADLEY BEAT UP HAWK

"Who will it be tonight?" Hawk bellows. I scan the crowd, sizing up and quickly dismissing each student. Not a single one of the pathetic wimps in front of us meets Hawk's punishing gaze. Not that I can blame them exactly. Other than me, Hawk is the best fighter at Pacific Prep. Unless called out, no one here has the balls to stand against him—or any of us.

So when I hear a voice rise above the crowd, I'm stunned. Even more so when the crowd parts and Hadley strides confidently to the front. Of course this enigma of a woman has more balls than the rest of the guys here. The woman has a spine of steel, and for some reason, she loves pissing off Hawk.

Maybe she's got a thing for him. Then again, the vitriol she's spitting at him right now indicates it's more than a simple *hate to love him* kinda thing.

"You?" Hawk snorts, unimpressed. "Please, I'd wipe the floor with you."

Despite Hadley's brass balls and the skills she's displayed in the gym, I'm worried that wiping the floor is exactly what Hawk's going to do with her. He wouldn't go easy on her either. That's not Hawk's style, even if she is a woman. And irrespective of Hadley's skill level, Hawk is taller, bigger, broader. One well-aimed punch and he could easily knock her out.

Before I've fully thought through what I'm doing, I step up beside Hawk, leaning in to whisper in his ear. "You can't do this, man. Not here. Not with her."

Instead of listening, the asshole ignores me as he stares down Hadley.

Of course, the stupid woman has to piss him off further by taunting him. "Then what are you so afraid of."

I bite back my groan, not that anyone would have heard me over Hawk. "I'm not about to have everyone going around telling people I beat the shit out of a girl."

At first, when Hadley nods her head, I naively hope that that will be the end of it, but of course Hadley wouldn't back down so easily.

"How about you pick one of these boys"—she gestures to the watching crowd—"and I'll fight them. If I win, then it's your turn. No excuses, no bullshitting."

THE TIME WHEN HADLEY BEAT UP HAWK

This time I don't bother stifling my low groan, because I know exactly what's about to happen. Hawk will take her bait, Hadley will kick whatever idiot's ass Hawk picks, the two of them will end up in an all-out brawl to the death, and I'll be left to bury one of them before the sun comes up. *Great. Exactly my idea of a good time.*

"Sure," Hawk unsurprisingly agrees. "Why not? It'll be your funeral."

For a second, Hadley's gaze clashes with mine, and I subtly shake my head, telling her to back down. Not that it does any good as she shifts her attention to West, lingering for a moment. She spares Cam a split-second's glance before averting her gaze.

"Marcus," Hawk barks, indicating a wide-eyed junior. It takes all of a forced breath for me to confirm Hadley will make mincemeat with this lanky kid, and snorting out a laugh, I decide to sit back and watch the ass-kicking he's about to receive.

Getting into position, Hadley pulls off her hoodie, and I roll my eyes when Cam curses, "Fuck me," under his breath. I totally agree, though. I'm used to seeing Hadley in her sports bra and leggings at the gym, the shine of skin along her scars reflecting in the overhead lights, and the stark contrast of the dark ink over her ribs, but her beauty still takes my breath away every time.

It's not just that she's attractive—which she most definitely is—but it's the way she carries herself, with a confidence that can't be faked, yet she's not arrogant like a lot of the self-righteous girls at Pac. No, Hadley's confidence is sexy, alluring, drawing you in like a moth to a flame.

When Hawk yells, "Go," Hadley moves with a fluidity that can only be obtained with years of practice and honing one's skills. She turns fighting into a work of art as she ducks, weaves, and jabs, and just as I'm getting into it, the fight ends with the loud snap of broken cartilage as Hadley breaks the twig's nose.

The entire fight couldn't have lasted more than two minutes, and a shocked silence settles over the crowd, before Marcus spits blood onto the ground, barking, "You broke my nose, you bitch!"

No one pays him any attention. I sure as hell don't. My entire focus is on Hadley as she lifts her gaze to Hawk's and fucking smirks at him. Fuck, why is that so sexy?

"You owe me a fight, Davenport."

Hawk grinds his molars, but he's been called out and he sure as hell isn't about to back down. "A deal's a deal," he states confidently, stepping into the ring as Marcus stumbles his way out of it, his pathetic attempt at fighting already forgotten by the crowd.

The two of them begin to circle each other, like lions pacing, each waiting for the prime moment to pounce on their prey.

"You better not hold back just because I'm a girl, Davenport."

God, why does she insist on riling him up?

I had no worries when it came to her going up against Marcus, but Hawk? Hawk's a different ball game, and my muscles tense as I wait for the fight to begin, almost as though I'm ready to dive in and protect her should Hawk go too far.

Hawk smirks. "I wouldn't dream of it, Parker."

I believe him. It wouldn't matter who his opponent was—he wouldn't go easy on them—but being that it's Hadley, he's *definitely* not going to hold back. If anything, this is the outlet he's needed for weeks now. Since she first crossed paths with him.

Reluctantly, I shout, "Go," but instead of jumping into action, the two of them continue to pace, measuring each other up. I'm very familiar with Hawk's fighting style. I know every one of his moves before he even makes them, so it's Hadley that I focus on, trying to read her, wanting to know what she will do.

I quickly learn that she has far more patience than Hawk does. She'll taunt and tease him all night, never laying a finger on him, but Hawk prefers to dive right in, and after a moment of the two of them dancing around one another, he makes the first move.

Things escalate from there, and with every hit he lands on Hadley, my heart slams against my ribs, and it's a struggle to maintain an impassive facade. The rest of the crowd shouts and cheers with each one of Hawk's strikes, but West, Cam, and I are silent as we observe Hawk annihilate Hadley.

It's almost painful to watch. She gets a few punches of her own in, but it's not enough to have any significant impact, instead only forcing Hawk to back off for a second before he's coming at her again.

However, she manages to hold her own, dragging the fight out longer than I'd expected, something that appears to piss Hawk off based on the aggressive way he strikes. Despite that, Hadley soon runs out of energy, her hits becoming weak and sloppy, giving Hawk the upper hand he needs to win.

My heart sinks, knowing she's lost the fight as Hawk grabs hold of her wrist and succeeds in pinning her against him. He murmurs something in her ear, too low for any of us to hear, but whatever the hell he said sparks something primal in Hadley.

Her eyes flare with an intense anger before she slams her heel down on top of his foot while throwing her head back, connecting with his nose. Stunned, Hawk loosens his grip and she easily breaks free, turning the tables as she lashes out, hitting his kidney, spleen, and head, effectively disabling him.

As if that wasn't enough, she swipes his legs out from beneath him, taking him to his knees. All I can do is gape at the scene in front of me, shocked and impressed as hell.

"Tap out," she demands. "You can't win this. It will only get worse if you do."

Listen to her, you idiot, I silently yell at Hawk.

Of course, Hawk has to be the stubborn asshole that he is instead of conceding. I can see it in the angry snarl as he glares up at her. There's no way in hell he's going to yield to Hadley.

A choked laugh slips past my lips when, before he can move a muscle to retaliate, Hadley's fist flies out, landing a solid punch to his windpipe.

"What the fuck?!" West yells, rushing toward a coughing and spluttering Hawk. "You throat-punched him!"

The way Hadley waves off his concern has me rock-fucking-hard in my sweats. *Sexiest fucking thing I've ever seen!*

"He'll be fine," she assures West, displaying the same level of concern as a psychopath would. "He wasn't going to stay down. It was that or knock him out. I figured this was the better choice."

"You... what?" West splutters.

"See?" Hadley waves toward a barely breathing Hawk, slumped on the ground as he fights to get his lungs to cooperate. "He's fine."

Yes, clearly.

It's probably inappropriate that watching a girl beat the crap out of my best friend has me so turned on, but *holy crap*, I wish I'd recorded that so I could rewatch it later when I'm alone. I'll definitely be jerking off to the memory. My Little Warrior.

"Get the fuck out of here!" West barks, drawing me back to the conversation and the entire male population of Pac who just saw Hawk get his ass kicked by a girl.

Great, a new problem we didn't need.

"Tonight didn't happen. You didn't see anything, and if we hear so much as a whisper, you'll regret it," West continues before the crowd hastily disperses, everyone moving back through the forest to the dorms.

"You tricked me," Hawk wheezes when we're alone.

"You let your arrogance rule you," Hadley retorts. "You assumed you'd already won, so you got sloppy. You're only a winner when your opponent is on the floor. Remember that next time and you might not lose."

Wise words, ones Hawk would do well to heed. I wonder who taught her to fight. Who instilled that mentality in her. The way she moved and counter-moved, not giving up until she was confident both opponents were incapacitated, it's almost as though she's used to fighting for survival, rather than as self-defence or for exercise purposes.

The others begin to gather everything up, Cam leading the way as he storms off toward the dorms.

"You coming?" West asks.

My gaze flicks to Hadley before I respond. "Yeah, I'm right behind you."

I wait until the guys have disappeared into the trees, listening to the sounds of their feet as they move across the forest floor and watching as the beams of light from their flashlights are swallowed up by the darkness.

Cloaked in shadows, I approach Hadley, this urgent need to touch her, to hold her, to do a hell of a lot more than that, driving me forward. "I never thought a woman would bring any of us to our knees, but you're constantly surprising me, Little Warrior."

I know Hawk says she's off-limits. I know that there is something going on between her and Cam. But this compulsion cannot be denied. I crave her like I never have before. Hell, I didn't even fight tonight, and yet blood pounds through my veins as though I did. But it's all her. She makes me feel this way. Makes me feel alive.

I'm not sure who moves first, whether she pulls me to her or I pull her to me, but each of us latches on to the other, her hand fisting my shirt as mine snakes around her waist. We're drawn to one another like opposing magnets, my lips finding hers in the dark and devouring everything she gives me.

That energy thrumming through my veins begins to boil over, consuming me until all I can feel is her; taste, is her. She's in my blood, and goddamn, I don't ever want her to leave. I've never felt so corporeal. Like a live wire, I'm raw and exposed, overtly stimulated by the slightest touch. Except the only touch I'll respond to is hers.

Firefly

THE DNA REPORT

I stare at the stack of envelopes on my bed, knowing I need to suck it up and open one. I deliberately waited until I received responses from a number of different labs—at least, that's the excuse I've been telling myself. In reality, I'm just putting off the inevitable, because what's inside these envelopes could change absolutely everything.

Fuck, just do it, I say subconsciously, trying to psych myself up. *You've come this far. You may as well read the measly letters. You were probably wrong anyway, and in a minute you'll be laughing over how crazy you were to think there was even a possibility that...*

"Fuck," I hiss, ripping open the first envelope and pulling out the letter before I can change my mind. I scan the contents, certain words popping out, but I stop dead over the words *probability of relatedness: 99.7%.*

Fucking hell, I was right?

I skip to the end of the letter, reading the summary just to be sure.

Based on testing results obtained from analyses of the DNA loci listed, the probability of siblingship is 99.7%. From this analysis, we can conclude that Mr. Hawk Davenport and Miss. Hadley Parker are biologically related.

"Fuuuuuck."

I hadn't really expected to be right. I mean, I suspected. There were similarities. Similarities that I could never really explain, but once I noticed them, I couldn't stop seeing them. Their eyes, the Skittles, Hawk's temper, Hadley's defensiveness. Just a general gnawing feeling when I saw them together, like there was something there that I couldn't quite put my finger on...

But suspecting and being proven right are two very different things.

And now that I know it wasn't all in my head, I can't just sit on this knowledge.

Hadley deserves to know.

Fuck, I need to tell Hawk and hope he doesn't decide to kill the messenger.

Just to be sure, I rip open another envelope, then another, both confirming the same thing. Hawk and Hadley are fucking siblings.

But how? None of it makes any sense, and this information only raises questions none of us have answers to. Like where the hell Hadley has been all these years, and why. Why Hawk's parents never told him. What it means if they find out she's alive and at Pac of all places.

It's too much of a coincidence that she's here, right? Out of all the scholarships at all the prep schools, is it really just sheer luck that Hadley ended up here?

What if she knew all along who her parents were? Is that why she had that book with information on each of us?

God, I'm getting a headache, each question only serving to send me deeper into an unanswerable spiral.

I have to tell Hadley, right? Not only does she have a right to know, but telling her would answer some of these questions. Based on her reaction, I'll be able to determine if she already knows, although my gut tells me she doesn't. And if she doesn't, I'm going to be completely blindsiding her with this.

However, it's not like I can keep it to myself.

Sure, she and Hawk are constantly at each other's throats, but perhaps knowing they are related will help channel some of that hatred into sibling rivalry.

I stew over what to do for the rest of the week. Anytime Hawk and Hadley interact, I watch them closely. Now that I know the truth, it seems so obvious, but each interaction has me growing more concerned about how devastating the truth will be, for both of them. I wish I could say for certain that Hawk would ease up on his hatred of her if he knew the truth, but I fear it will only drive a bigger wedge between them. Which is the main reason I've put off the inevitable. However, with each passing day, the secret that I'm keeping from both of them gnaws at my insides, until I can't take it anymore.

Grabbing each of the letters, I place them all in one giant envelope and head for Hadley's dorm room, thankful that I don't run into Hawk or any of the guys on my way there.

Reaching her door, I rap my knuckles against it, my foot tapping on the floor as I wait. When she doesn't answer, I try again. After my third attempt, I have to admit that she isn't in, pacing back and forth in front of her door as I decide what to do.

I can't risk going back up to my room in case I run into Hawk or one of the others. No, my best bet is to stay here and wait for Hadley to return. Which is exactly what I do.

Thankfully, I don't have to wait too long before I see her striding toward me, her lips pulling into a frown when she spots me standing outside her door.

"What are you doing here, Wes?"

"I need to talk to you."

I watch her stomp into her bedroom, making it very clear that I'm an unwanted visitor and she wants me to fuck off, before following her over the threshold and closing the door behind me.

Buying time as I try to organize my thoughts, I glance around her room, mumbling to myself while noticing the lack of personal touches. If you stripped the bed, cleared the desk, and removed her few necessities, you'd never know she lived here.

"I like what you've done with the place," I mutter.

Her face instantly clouds over. "We don't all have money or time to waste on decorating," she snipes, following my gaze to her bookcase. "I've found a new hiding spot, in case you were wondering."

"I wasn't," I confess. The truth. It was that damn notebook I was thinking about. The information she had in it, and why she had it. Does it all relate back to the information clutched in my hand?

Shaking my head to dispel the theories, I take a step toward her, holding out the envelope of letters.

She eyes it like I'm trying to hand her a tarantula. "What the hell is that?"

"You said you were raised in foster care, right?" I question, my thoughts all over the place, as my quest for answers and need to know she's not a part of whatever this is wars with my desire to explain everything to her.

"Yeah." Her eyes narrow on me, her gaze sharp.

"Do you know who your real parents are?"

She's immediately on the defensive, "What are you getting at, Wes?"

I don't cave beneath her hostile glower. This is a question I need her to answer before I can decide my next move.

"No," she eventually barks, and damn it, I have no substantial evidence, but I'm inclined to believe her.

Her eyes dart between me and the envelope in my hands, her initial defensiveness giving way to fear.

"What did you do, Wes?" she hisses as I drop the letters on the bed. "I don't want to know who they are." Her voice has lost its angry edge, tinged with the same panic that's shining in her pupils.

Any suspicions I had about her fall by the wayside, and instead I hate myself for what I'm about to do. "I get that," I say, nodding. "But, in this case, I think you need to know." I pause, waiting to see if she's going to start screaming at me to leave. When she doesn't, I continue. "Ever since you showed up, I've been noticing things. Small—"

She's already shaking her head, as though that can dispel the truth of my words. "Nope. No. Get out! I don't want to hear any of this."

Closing the distance between us, she slams her hands against my chest as the tears she refuses to let spill over shine in her eyes. Sensing she's on the verge of falling apart, I grab her upper arms and give her a little shake. What I really want to do is pull her against me and tell her it will be okay, but I hold myself back.

"Hadley." Her name snaps off the end of my tongue, gaining her attention. Her eyes lift to mine and she silently pleads with me to stop.

I don't. I can't.

"I honestly thought I was imagining things. I didn't think anything would come of it. It was a long shot, ruling out an impossibility more than anything else." I'm rambling. I know that. But, *fuck*, this is even harder than I thought it would be.

Gathering my emotions, I take a deep, steadying inhale before ripping off the Band-aid. "Hawk is your brother."

There, I did it. It's done. It's out there in the world now and there's no taking it back.

"What?" The word is a quiet croak, her brows pulling down in confusion. "What did you just say?" In the span of a blink, her entire demeanor changes, and instead of the fracturing, pleading woman clinging to me like I'm the only thing keeping her upright, fire spits from her eyes. "Do you think I'm fucking stupid! Do you seriously think I'd fall for that shit after everything you guys have done to me?" Shaking her head, she shoves me off her as she barks out a sharp, slightly unhinged sounding laugh. "Playing the family card?" Her lip curls in disgust as she sneers at me. "That's so fucking low of you! I'd expect this shit from Hawk, even Cam, but you?"

Finally getting over the shock of her sudden and intense anger, I manage to find my words. "What? No!" God, that's what she thinks? That this is some prank? Does she really think that lowly of us?

Of course she does. You've terrorized her all year. What is she supposed to think when you come barging in her room spewing this shit?

I'm an idiot. I should have expected this reaction. Instead, I was completely caught off guard, and all I can do is watch as she continues her tirade.

"I get that you all sit up there in your ivory tower, having a laugh at the rest of us plebs down here trying to survive from one day to the next, but you have no idea how fucking difficult it is to go through life without knowing who your family is. Not knowing who *you* are, or where you come from. And the fact that you'd do all this as some sick joke is just fucking disgusting."

If a look could kill, I'd be six feet under by now.

"I thought you were better than that, but I guess I was wrong." She looks at me with such disgust and loathing that I almost wish I *was* six feet under. I've never felt so unworthy, so undeserving. I know I didn't do what she thinks I've done, but the realization that she thinks I'm even capable of playing such a cruel joke on her sickens me. The last thing I ever want to do is hurt her. Hell, if it were possible, I'd do whatever it took to *stop* her from experiencing any more hurt.

"Hadley, no—"

"Get out! Get the fuck out!" She's screaming now, and when she begins throwing objects at my head, I know it's time to go. Nothing constructive can happen while she's so worked up. I'm better off letting her calm down and trying again later.

Making a hasty retreat from her room, I flinch as she slams the door shut behind me. Releasing a defeated sigh, I make myself comfortable at the foot of her door and wait. She just needs time. She has the letters. Once she's calmed down, she'll read them and have questions. And when she does, I'll be waiting. Not because I have any answers for her, but because I want her to know she isn't in this alone. That I'm here for her, whatever she needs.

BRUTAL LIES
Book Two

R.A. SMYTH

Baby Davenport

PROLOGUE

I don't waste a second once I'm home, dumping my stuff in my room before starting a search of the house. If Hadley really is my sister, there's got to be something hidden here to prove it. Not that I doubt West or those stupid lab reports, but why the fuck did he have to go digging and stirring shit up.

Heading straight for my dad's office, where he keeps his safe, I type in the code, lifting out various files and folders and flicking through each of them for signs of anything related to Hadley.

Coming up empty, I groan in frustration. He's got some vague-looking work papers, insurance documents, the deed to the house. Even our birth certificates and passports are in here, but nothing that hints at anything about a long-lost daughter.

Is it possible West is wrong?

I run my hand through my hair as I look around the room before pulling open drawers. I even flick through books in the bookcase in case he's got a secret photograph hidden amongst the pages. Nothing. There isn't a single trace of her here.

Racking my brain for anywhere else they could hide something, I stride up the stairs. Instead of turning right toward my room, I head left, opening the door to their suite.

I haven't been in here since I was a little kid, and even then, I was rarely allowed to come in. Usually, only if I had a nightmare, which wasn't often, and more frequently than not, the nanny was left to deal with me when I did have one. Glancing around the neat bedroom with the made bed and perfectly positioned decorative cushions, I search through their nightstands first, once again finding nothing useful.

Heading into the attached dressing room, I push sweaters and shoes aside, searching the shelves before dropping down to the ground and rifling through a bunch of shoe boxes.

I'm about to give up when I spot a small safe tucked in the back left corner of the closet. Moving closer, I stare at it, my mind racing with the possibilities of the secrets it could be hiding. I know it's not jewelry or important documents—all that shit is kept in the main safe I just searched through. So, what could they possibly be hiding in this one?

Pressing the buttons, I enter the standard pin my dad uses for everything, not even questioning that it could be anything else. But when the safe bleeps, the screen flashing with a red *error* sign, I'm taken by surprise. *What the hell else could the pin be?*

I stare, baffled at the keypad, thinking over the possibilities before trying my birth date—0108. Nope, another error message flashes across the screen. Confused, I try a few random combinations to see if I have any luck.

After several more annoying bleeps, I sigh in frustration, rattling my brain for another combination. Something personal that could be related to Hadley...or to me. Or to both of us?

On a whim, I type in 8946—the numbers spelling out T-W-I-N.

The screen flashes green, the satisfying sound of the lock disengaging as the door clicks open. After gaping slack-jawed at it for a moment—*seriously? Fucking twin?*—I pull open the door. Inside, there's a small stack of documents and nothing else.

With nerves fluttering in my gut, I lift the pile out, my eyes landing on the top page —a photograph. It's of two toddlers—a boy and a girl, each with white-blonde hair and mischievous looks—sitting in highchairs, their faces smeared with food as they laugh at one another. There's a brightness in her eyes and a goofy grin on his, neither of which belong to the adults these kids became.

With a strange twisting in my stomach, I set the photo aside, flicking through the others in the stack before coming across a birth certificate. Something tugs at the corner of my brain, a memory I can't quite grasp. A strange familiarity comes over me as I read her name, Elizabeth Jane Davenport.

Hawk and Elizabeth.

There's something so familiar about that. Like I've heard it a hundred times, but I don't ever *remember* hearing it.

Somehow, I can't picture Hadley as an Elizabeth. It sounds too uppity or something. Not her at all. It's the kind of name you expect the other rich superficial girls at Pac to have, but not Hadley. She's never been one of them, never fitted into the same world as the rest of us, so why would her name be any different?

What stands out to me is the date of birth on the certificate. It's the exact same as mine, confirming my suspicion. We're not just siblings, we're fucking twins—assuming of course, this *is* Hadley, although I can't deny it's getting more and more difficult to refute that assumption.

Not sure what to make of any of this, I grab a shoe box, emptying out the pair of overpriced Manolo Blahnik heels and shoving the contents of the safe into it. Lifting the first photo I came across, I pause, once again looking at the cheerful smiles on the toddlers' faces before stuffing it in my back pocket, choosing not to think about the fact I'm holding on to it.

Quickly leaving my parents' room before they can come home and find me snooping, I text the guys.

> Hawk: Found something.

> Mason: What did you find?

> Hawk: I'll show you tonight.

THAT NIGHT, the guys come over and I turn some football game on the TV, letting it play in the background. Ensuring the door to the den is closed in case my parents come home—not that they often do—I hand out beers to the guys.

My ass has barely hit the seat when West opens fire with the questions.

"Well, what did you find?"

Sighing, I lift the box from beside my chair. As I stretch forward to set it on the coffee table, West leans in, snatches it from me and flips off the lid. Silently, he takes his time as he goes through every photo before looking at the birth certificate.

Mason leans in close beside him, looking over his shoulder so he can see the documents too. Cam, on the other hand, glowers at the box like it's at fault for the fucked up state of his *whatevership* with Hadley.

Both Mason and West's eyes widen as they move through the few photos.

"Damn, I didn't know you knew how to smile." Mason laughs as I throw my bottle cap at him.

"You were both pretty cute as kids. I don't think I've ever seen a photo of you this young before."

"Yeah," I agree, ignoring West's statement about me looking cute. I was never fucking cute looking. "I guess we know why."

"So it's true then?" Cam questions, eyeing the photos in West's hands like they're a bomb that's about to go off and not some innocent pictures. "She really is your sister?"

I shrug, not fully having an answer. "It seems like it. I guess it's possible the kid in the photos isn't her."

It's probably fucked up that some part of me hopes that's true, but even as I say the words, I know it's only wishful thinking. Something that's confirmed by West's deadpan expression.

"It's her," he assures us.

Mason's brows are furrowed as he ponders something. "How the hell did she end up in foster care? And after all these years, she just so happened to turn up at Pac? What are the chances?"

"Too fucking unlikely." There's no way it's just a fucking coincidence. A lot more is going on here than we know, and I don't fucking like being left in the dark.

Setting aside the last photograph, the two of them finally read over the birth certificate.

"Her name is Elizabeth?" His voice hitches at the end, and he tilts his head slightly, like he can't make the name fit with the girl he's come to know.

Cam's head snaps up, his eyes narrowed on Mason. "What did you just say?"

His harsh tone has all three of us turning to look at him, confused at his hostile reaction. I get it, he hates the girl, and so he should, but it's just a fucking name.

"Elizabeth?" Mason repeats slowly, looking at Cam in bewilderment.

Cam's up and out of his chair in the blink of an eye, snatching the certificate from West's hands, nearly tearing the damn thing in his urge to see it.

"Watch it!" I bark, yet the asshole ignores me. His face pales as he looks at the words on the page, confirming with his own eyes that her name is, in fact, Elizabeth—how many bloody times does it need to be mentioned?

"Cam." West uses a gentler tone, his hand resting on Cam's forearm, jolting him out of whatever fucking trance he was caught in. "What's going on?"

I can see the wheels spinning in his head as he looks at each of us, confusion and something much darker marking his features.

"My dad knows her."

"What?" all three of us demand at once.

"That's not possible," I insist.

"What makes you think that?" West questions, staring intently at Cam, just like I am.

"At my last swim meet, I heard him say her name," he explains vaguely, his thoughts straying back to that day as he tries to recall what happened. "He didn't hear me approach, but I heard him say *Elizabeth*. I followed where he had been looking up into the stands, except I didn't see anyone with that name."

Scoffing, I wave him off. "He could have been talking about anyone."

"He was looking right fucking at her," Cam seethes, turning to glare at me. "He was looking right at her, and afterward, he asked me who she was. He claimed he didn't know there was a new scholarship student and wanted to ensure the school had done their due diligence."

I take a moment to think through what he's saying, but none of it adds up. "So...what does that mean?" I finally ask. "That he knows her?"

"What else could it mean?" Cam demands.

"I mean, all of our parents must know about her," West suggests. "Is it possible he recognized her?"

"From when she was a toddler?" I snort, waving my hand at the stack of photos. "She looks nothing like she did at that age."

"No," Cam spits the word out between gritted teeth, his lip curling back in a sneer as he shakes his head. His eyes are still narrowed as he attempts to put the puzzle pieces together. "She knows my dad. She has to. Nothing else makes sense."

"How, though?" Mason questions. "How the fuck would a foster kid like her know your dad?"

"I don't know," Cam grits out in exasperation, throwing his hands up in the air. "Maybe he tracked her down and brought her to Pac?"

"That wouldn't explain why he was surprised to see her at your swim meet," Mason reasons.

"Then maybe she's sleeping with him," Cam argues.

The rest of us remain silent, no one having a reasonable rebuttal to that statement.

"What about the notebook?" West eventually asks. "She had all of our parents in it. What was that about?"

"Blackmail?" Cam suggests, clearly full of theories. "Maybe she decided to blackmail my dad and was using us and whatever information she could find on our parents to do it?"

I slowly nod my head as I try to work my way through it. It's not an impossible assumption. Hell, it's the best one we've got, the only theory that fits the few puzzle pieces we have.

"If your dad knows who she is," West begins, looking up at Cam with the same questions the rest of us are asking ourselves. "How come he never told her? There's no way she knew anything about being a Davenport," he insists for like the fiftieth fucking time.

He's so sure she wasn't pulling the wool over his eyes. I'm not so fucking sure, however. She's made it more than evident that she can manipulate us and pull our strings on a whim. I don't believe one fucking word out of her mouth.

No one seems to have any answers, all of us just looking at each other.

"We need more information. We need to learn more about her, where she came from, how she could have met Cam's dad." I glance pointedly at West. "You need to do some digging."

His lips thin, not exactly happy with that idea, but he doesn't argue, simply nodding his head in agreement. "I'll see what I can find."

∼

ON CHRISTMAS DAY, the house is abuzz with energy as staff run back and forth between the kitchen and dining room, preparing for our guests. Everything is tastefully decorated with a tree and other Christmas decorations in some vain attempt to get us all in the Christmas spirit.

All our families eat together on holidays, our parents usually finding time in their busy schedules to come home and check in with all of us, however briefly or unwanted it may be.

The guys' families will be over later this afternoon so all of us can sit down to dine together. My father pulled me aside this morning to tell me that they need to talk to us after dinner, so we're not to disappear after we've eaten.

A quick text to the guys confirms they've been told the same thing.

We've been debating what it could be, and we're sure they're finally going to spill the beans on what their company—Nocturnal Enterprises—actually does to earn most of its money. After all, they want us to come and work for them in a few short months. They'd have to tell us sooner or later.

Of course, they're several months too late.

Over the summer, we were searching for something—anything—we could use against them, to blackmail them into letting us live our own lives for a few more years. So we could go to college and simply enjoy our youth. West was digging into their company to see what he could find, and fucking hell, did he find something alright.

It was a single breadcrumb at first, yet the deeper he dug, he discovered Nocturnal Enterprises is nothing more than a front for the fucked-up shit they're really involved in.

It turns out there's a whole other covert side to their business—Nocturnal Mercenaries. Our parents have been using their connections from their legitimate business contracts with the military to recruit people who have been discharged and are looking for lucrative, private work. From the employee bios we found most of the men they hire are highly trained, having done time on special-ops teams. However, they have a history of issues with authority and aggression problems and ultimately ended up being dishonorably discharged. That's when our parents swoop in and offer them employment...as fucking mercenaries, accepting contracts from all sorts of low-life scum, wanting to dick over or piss off someone who has wronged them.

To say we were shocked is an understatement. Our minds were fucking blown, each of us trying to compute this new information with what we knew about our parents and trying to rifle through our memories to work out what tells we missed that could have had us clued in years ago.

Then, as if that wasn't enough, Hadley had to blow into our lives right after that, fucking shit up even more.

It's a toss-up, which has come as a bigger shock—finding out my parents aren't who I thought they were or finding out I have a sister who has been conveniently missing for the last sixteen years, and she just so happens to pop up out of nowhere when shit starts to go south.

My parents have always been distant, never really seeming to give a shit about me. Now, looking back on it, I wonder if any of that had to do with Hadley. Maybe things would have been different if whatever the fuck happened to her hadn't happened. I guess it's just one more thing I can blame her for.

My phone buzzes in my pocket and, pulling it out, I see a new text from West.

> West: We're in the pool house.

WEST MESSAGED INTO the group chat last night saying he'd found some information about Hadley, and we agreed to meet today before the festivities begin. With extra staff in the house, not to mention my parents floating about, there are too many eyes and ears to risk not being overheard.

As I make my way out to the pool house, my mind runs through all the possibilities of what West could have uncovered. The best option is that he's found out she's not my sister, and this has all been one hellish mistake, though I doubt I'm about to be so lucky.

If she really is fucking and blackmailing Cam's dad, maybe we can pay her off to just leave us the fuck alone. Although, I'm not entirely sure money is what she's after. The look she gave me when I told her she'd just won the life lottery was the opposite of what I had expected. Every other kid at Pac would have a heart attack if they discovered they were a Davenport—or any one of us. All you'd be able to see is dollar signs in their eyes, but not Hadley. No, she seemed pretty affronted at the accusation that she was in it for the money.

What the fuck is her deal? Money is the primary motivator of everyone I know. Why is she so different?

Slipping into the darkened pool house, I find the other three waiting for me. "Well?" I ask, getting straight to the point. It won't be long until their families all start to show up and we get called in to spend the day with fake, polite smiles on our faces, pretending we give a shit about whatever our parents are talking about.

West lifts a rolled-up envelope out of his back pocket, flipping the tab and pulling out a few pages. With an unreadable expression, he hands them over to me and I quickly take them, scanning the pages.

"What the fuck? What is this?" I bark, unable to tear my eyes away from the pages. Instead of providing any answers, all of this only raises more fucking questions. There's a photocopy of a passport, the name matching Hadley's, but that picture sure as fuck isn't her.

Another page has a photocopy of a news article stating that a 'Hadley Parker' died in a car accident three years ago and as I flick to the final page, it's a death certificate with the same name on it.

When I don't get a response, I tear my eyes away from the papers in my hand to look at West, seeing the same questions swirling in his eyes that are rushing through my mind right now.

Hadley isn't even fucking Hadley?

But if she isn't Hadley Parker, who the fuck is she?

"Is this all you were able to find?" I demand, flapping the pages at West.

"So far. I need more time, but I'll keep digging."

"We need to find out who she is and why she's here," I growl. West nods his head, confirming he will get the job done.

It's not long before we're all being summoned inside to begin this whole farce of a day. I spend the next hour downing glasses of bourbon and nodding my head at appropriate intervals, pretending to listen to whatever Mr. Warren is saying, sending up a silent prayer of thanks when the server calls out that dinner is ready. We all make our way into the dining room to sit down and eat.

Everyone, even West's fucking half-brother who showed up out of the blue—yet another fucking surprise—is here, looking as pleased about it as I am.

The meal is relatively uneventful, our parents yattering away to one another about work and whatever else that I don't give a shit about. Honestly, my mind is still out in the pool house, mulling over the newfound information, trying to make sense of all of this.

If Hadley isn't her real name, then it's an alias. Only why would she need one? All so she could come to some fucking prep school? Somehow, I doubt that. If she doesn't know any of us like she claims, then why would she feel the need to hide who she really is? Unless she's hiding from someone else, maybe some drug lord or pimp from her old life? Who the fuck knows. West wasn't able to find anything else. The real Hadley died three years ago, and there was nothing associated with her until nearly a year ago, which is when our Hadley must have taken on her identity. As for who my sister is, West couldn't find a thing. The girl is a damn ghost.

A swift kick to my shin has me scowling at Mason from across the table, clenching my knife tightly as I debate throwing it at him.

Giving me a look to tell me I missed something important, he subtly jerks his head toward the far end of the table where my father is sitting, and I realize he must have been talking to me.

"Sorry, what were you saying?" I ask politely, turning to look at my father and ignoring his disapproving frown.

"I was explaining what was going to happen tonight," he repeats, his words not making any sense. What the fuck is happening tonight? I thought it was just a conversation.

"Tonight?" I question, sounding like a total fucking idiot as I slyly glance at Mason from the corner of my eye, gauging his response. He seems as bothered by this news as I do. Right, so I wasn't the only one left out of the loop about tonight.

"Yes," my father emphasizes. "All five of you will need to prove your loyalty to the company before you can take your rightful places."

"All five of us?" I sound like a fucking parrot at this point, and it must be getting on my father's nerves as his eyes narrow on me in a stern warning.

"All four of you"—he gestures to me, Mason, Cam, and West—"as our rightful heirs, will stand up and claim your place tonight as the future of our company."

Nobody misses the emphasis he puts on rightful heirs, making it clear to West's older half-brother that his blood is tainted. As the eldest-born child, he should be sitting in West's place and should have led his life, but instead, he was the stupid mistake of a fling; a bastard child. From what I can gather, West's dad wanted nothing to do with him growing up, pretending he didn't exist. Something has evidently changed though if he's sitting here today.

"What about him?" West sneers, glowering at the guy—hell, I don't even know his name, never mind what it is about him that hits all of West's buttons. West is the most unlikely to resort to violence out of the four of us, but his tense stance and hostile glare are enough to show me how close he is to losing his shit. Fuck, if this guy is going to be hanging around, I'm going to have to talk to West about what his problem is.

"We have other plans for him," West's dad interjects, not explaining anything at all as he pins West's half-brother in place with his intense stare.

The way the guy grinds his teeth and glares at his old man is telling enough. He hates the guy. Interesting.

"You make it sound like some sacrificial blood thing." Cam laughs in a vain attempt to lighten the mood. It doesn't work, however, as each of our parents eyes us up as if determining which of us will have the gall to cut it.

What the actual fuck is going down tonight?

Hadley

CHAPTER ONE

"*Who the fuck are you?*"

Hawk's words ring in my ears.

Who the fuck am I? What a great fucking question.

I'm Elizabeth Jane Davenport.

I'm Hadley Parker.

I'm D.

I've been avoiding all of them since Hawk stormed out of my room, a look of thunder on his face at my refusal to answer him. Did he honestly expect me to spill all my dark, dirty secrets just because he demanded it?

He hasn't earned my truth. None of them have.

I locked myself in my room the rest of the day, worried they would be waiting for me, firing questions and demanding answers I couldn't give them.

When there's a knock on my door that evening, I hesitantly move toward it. "Who is it?" I call out, refusing to open it. Every time I blindly open the damn thing, an asshole strolls in like he fucking owns the place—yeah, yeah, alright, technically they all fucking do, but this is my fucking safe space. *My* sanctuary.

"Girl, what the hell, are you rubbing the nub or something in there? Open up!"

I roll my eyes at Emilia's ridiculousness, the tension draining out of me as I unlock the door and open it to let her in. She pounces on me like a madwoman, her short black ponytail whacking me in the face as she throws her arms around my neck.

"Ah, girl, I missed you!" she exclaims, almost deafening me as her lips are right beside my ear.

"It's only been two weeks." I chuckle, hugging her back. Damn, I missed her too. Given everything that happened last semester, I never thought we would be this close again, but after I approached her in the dining hall, things just fell back into a normal rhythm for us. Except I made her promise to sit with the other scholarship students at meals. I don't want her being targeted just for hanging out with me, and none of the other scholarship students seem interested in having anything to do with me now—not that I blame them. Still, I don't want Emilia's friendship with them to suffer because of me. "How was your break?"

"It was good," she says, beaming as she detaches herself from me and walks over to my bed, dropping down onto it and getting comfortable. "Quiet. Mom had to work most of it, but we got to spend some time together and catch up, which was nice."

Emilia's mom is a nurse and works crazy hours, meaning it's difficult for her to visit often, so I'm glad they got to spend some downtime together.

"What about yours? Was it creepy here all by yourself?"

"No, it was good." I have to bite my lip to stop the smile from spreading across my face as the dirty thoughts of everything I got up to with Beck over the break flit through my mind. Nights spent at his, wrapped around him as we talked about absolutely nothing, and afternoons spent in his office, both of us working away on our own things. "I mean, it was weird being here alone, although it was nice and peaceful."

A part of me wants to tell her about Beck, which is surprising in itself—I never feel a need to tell anyone *anything*. I'm pretty sure she wouldn't judge me, but it's not just myself I need to think of. I trust Emilia. I do—again, something that doesn't come naturally to me. *What the fuck is happening to me that I'm starting to open up and trust people?*

Nevertheless, Beck could get in serious trouble if anyone found out about us, so the fewer people that know, the better. At least for now. It will be a totally different story when I graduate in a few months. I just hope she will understand why I had to keep it a secret.

"Sounds boring," she grumbles, making me smile as she lifts the book I was reading from earlier before Hawk stormed in, and skims through the pages.

I might not be able to tell her about Beck, but there is something I can share with her. Something that has been itching under my skin, driving me insane. Something that, if I don't share with someone else, is going to drive me crazy.

"Hawk is my brother," I blurt out.

Smooth, Hadley. Super smooth.

Emilia freezes for a moment, her eyes slowly peering up to meet mine. Her head tilts slightly to one side as she tries to read me, assessing whether or not I'm bullshitting her.

"Is this your idea of a joke?" she asks, her nose scrunching up. "If it is, you really need to work on it. Maybe start with a knock-knock joke and build up from there. Or maybe jokes just aren't your thing. Not everyone can have a good sense of humor."

"Nope, not joking," I say seriously, shaking my head.

Her eyebrows climb up her forehead until I'm sure they're going to disappear into her hairline as she gapes open-mouthed at me, looking like a fish out of water.

"How? When did you find out? Did you know before you started at Pac? Oh my god, does Hawk know? I bet he's *so* pissed. Does this mean he and the others will back off?" she rapid-fires questions at me until she runs out of breath, finally taking a gulp of air and giving me a chance to actually get a word in.

Sitting down on the bed beside her, I tell her everything. How West had some weird gut instinct—that I still don't understand—about Hawk and me, and that he tested our DNA. How the report came back confirming the samples were a match and what a complete shock it was to me, and to Hawk, judging from the look of utter outrage and animosity on his face—an image forever burned into my brain. And how I have no idea what the fuck this means or where I go from here.

My stomach churns with unease, something that's become recurrent over the last two weeks, every time I think about Hawk and the fact I have a family—a very wealthy, corrupt family, but a family nonetheless. It's something I had given up thinking about. As a child, I used to lie awake at night, wondering who they were and why they didn't love me enough to keep me. How they could hate a baby so much that they left me in the hands of complete psychopaths.

I don't know what the fuck happened or how I ended up in the life I did. Deep down in my gut, I just know that this revelation isn't going to culminate in a happy family reunion. The little I know of the Davenports—of all four families—is enough to ensure that. Throw in all the questions I have, and then the tension that's been brewing between Hawk and me all semester.

Not to mention the unadulterated hatred he feels toward me, and, yeah, any idiot can see this whole thing is a fucking shitshow that's about to detonate. Like a fucking car crash you can see coming—when the whole world slows down, and no matter what, there's never enough time to stop the impending collision. You can't do anything but stand there and watch it happen. Well, I can see the pile up from here, see everyone slowing down to watch the train wreck that will be my relationship with Hawk, and probably every other Davenport.

"That's insane," Emilia breathes out when I'm done telling her everything. "Like legit crazy."

"Ha, yeah."

"How did West get your DNA?"

"The asshole must have snuck into my room."

"No way," she gasps. "Dickhead."

I shrug. "In fairness, I may have been sneaking in and out of their dorm, messing with their shit," I admit, a smile lifting my lips as I picture their confused faces as they try to work out what the fuck is going on.

"You didn't." Emilia giggles, slapping me playfully on the arm.

"I did." I wiggle my eyebrows, making her laugh harder.

"Oh my god, girl, I can't believe you're still walking around with all your limbs attached."

I shrug nonchalantly, unable to tell her about my fight in the ring with Hawk or the fact they could damn well try to tear my limbs from my body, but I'd fight them tooth and nail. I don't need her asking questions about how I know how to fight like that or have her thinking I'm even crazier than she likely already thinks I am.

We spend the rest of the evening chatting and catching up before Emilia grabs her laptop and some snacks from her room and we watch a movie until we're both on the verge of falling asleep.

"Breakfast tomorrow?" she asks hopefully as she leaves my room.

I grimace. "Better not," I say, feeling guilty. It's not that I don't want to, it's that I don't want to come between her and the scholarship students. "I think I'll skip breakfast tomorrow, what with avoiding Hawk and all."

She nods in understanding, sadness tugging at her features as she says goodnight and slips out of my room. Changing into a pair of sleep shorts and a loose t-shirt, I climb under the covers, exhaustion quickly claiming me and tugging me down into a dreamless sleep.

I spend the next day avoiding Hawk and the guys, like I told Emilia. I skip breakfast, slipping into English just as the bell goes off. Cam gives me his usual cold shoulder, not looking my way when I arrive, something that I'm becoming annoyingly familiar with.

I'd hoped the knowledge that I was Hawk's sister might have calmed some of his hate toward me or at least opened the lines of communication, but I guess not. If anything, he seems more on edge than normal as he shuffles his chair away from me. His leg bounces irritatingly, his eyes laser-focused on his tablet as he pretends I'm not sitting beside him.

Rolling my eyes, I decide two can play that game and ignore him right back. I have just as much right to be angry as he does.

When the bell rings to signal the end of class, his arm accidentally brushes against mine as he pushes his chair back. That small amount of contact sends sparks up my arm as he freezes, glaring at his forearm like it behaved of its own accord by moving against his will.

Just that slight touch has flashbacks zipping through my head of our few intimate moments together. How fucking hot it was when he went down on me in the library, driving me insane with his talented tongue and deft fingers. The out-of-this-world sex in the locker room. I'd never felt so connected to another person before. The look in his eyes…well, whatever was in that look is long dead now, replaced with ire and vitriol. Even when he was fucking me into the door, using me to purge himself of the unwanted emotions I could see swirling in his shadowed eyes, I could still feel that connection between us. I intuitively knew he wouldn't hurt me, despite how he snarled at me or the promise of pain in his rough touch. I have no fucking clue how I knew that; I just did.

Glowering at me, like I am the one responsible for whatever that spark is between us, I gasp at the darkness seeping out of his eyes. The way he looked at me before the break was cold, but this is on a whole new level.

What the fuck could I have possibly done now?

Gritting his teeth, he snatches his bag off the floor, pushing past the other students as he storms out of the room without a backward glance, leaving me to gape at his retreating back.

"That looked intense. Are you okay?" Emilia asks, coming to stand beside me as I shove my things in my bag, the rest of the class filtering out of the room.

"Yeah, it's nothing." I wave away the moment, ignoring the churning guilt that has my stomach in upheaval.

Fuck, I could hardly bear his pain-filled hateful gazes, but there was no trace of the Cam I knew and had come to like in that look. It was overflowing with a malevolence so powerful it actually scared me. It reminds me too much of someone I'd rather not think about.

Pushing it to the back of my mind, Emilia and I leave the room, heading to our next class. With the exception of the smug looks thrown my way by the Princesses, the usual taunts about my scars, and the lewd smirks from shithead guys—because why be an adult about it and leave all that shit in our last semester—the day goes by in a peaceful blur. At the end of the day, the halls are quiet as I walk through them, making my way back toward the dorms. I had to stay behind after math class to talk to Mrs. Fenway, so most of the students had already fled the building for the day.

I round the corner coming to a stop, when I see two of the assholes I've been actively avoiding all day standing guard at the other end of the hall. Thinking on my feet, I spin around to head back in the direction I just came, my blonde mass of curls swooshing out behind me at my quick one-eighty turn, but a hand reaches out and grabs me before I can run off.

Raising my fist as I attempt to pull my arm out of the fucker's tight grip, I turn around, coming face to face—well, more like face to chest—with Mason.

"Mason? What the fuck? Let me go!"

"Sorry, Little Warrior," he murmurs, keeping his voice low. "No can do."

I snarl at him, but movement on my other side draws my attention as I snap my head around to find Cam staring down at me with a spiteful grin on his face.

The look in his eyes stalls the air in my lungs for a second. It's the same one he speared me with earlier. What the fuck happened to the happy-go-lucky, flirty guy I met on the first day of school? He looks completely different. Did I do that to him? Did I cause all that hate he's carrying around?

I fall silent in Mason's arms, unable to look away from Cam's furious gaze as I hear the others approaching.

"What do you want?" I bite out, finally tearing my eyes from Cam to stare down all four of them as they form a semi-circle around me, enclosing me against the wall.

"We need answers," West demands with an impassive expression. His tone has an authoritative edge to it that I've never heard directed at me before, although the look in his eyes is pleading with me to cooperate.

"No," I argue. Didn't Hawk get it into his thick skull yesterday? Does he not fucking understand the meaning of *no*? Why would I open up and leave myself so vulnerable to people who fucking despise me?

"Yes," Hawk retorts flatly. "Whatever the fuck you are up to, involves us. We have a right to know."

Jutting my chin out in defiance, I stare them down, refusing to talk.

"Who are you?" Hawk barks, his voice losing that calm, collected tone as his anger gets the better of him.

I can tell I'm quickly burning through the last threads of his patience, with my repeated refusal and constant denial pissing him off. Good, because his incessant fucking questions and lack of respect for personal boundaries have pissed me off all the way to hell and back.

"I'm Hadley Parker," I state, holding my head high, daring him to say otherwise.

He sighs, shaking his head in disappointment. "We know that's a lie. Stop playing games with us."

"I'm not. My name is Hadley Parker," I repeat more forcefully, carefully enunciating every syllable. He better goddamn believe it, because, as far as I'm concerned it's the motherfucking truth.

I don't miss the flash of rage as his nostrils flare, his hands forming fists at his side as he holds himself back. He's seconds away from snapping and closing the small amount of distance between us, but as he takes a step forward, Cam beats him to it, storming toward me.

"Stop it," he snarls. His palms press into the cold stone on either side of my head as he looms over me, forcing my back against the wall. With his face inches from mine, flecks of spittle hit my cheek when he bares his teeth, seething out, "Hadley Parker is dead. *You* stole her identity."

"Maybe." I shrug, pretending like reading that news article about her accident and seeing her death certificate didn't bother me. Jesus, I'm not a fucking psychopath. I can feel bad at the loss of a young, innocent life, even if it was an accident. "But who I was doesn't matter. Hadley is who I am. Who I am always going to be." I emphasize the last words, cementing to both them and myself that this is who I am. She may not be who I was born to be, or who I was raised to be, but she's who I fucking *want* to be.

Elizabeth is long gone. Her life snuffed out before she had a chance to really live. D is my past. The darkest part of me, trapped in a cage born of the environment she was brought up in and forced to become someone she wasn't. But Hadley...Hadley is free. Hadley can be anyone she wants to be, do what she motherfucking pleases.

Hadley. Is. Me.

The real Hadley may be dead, however I can live on in her name, live the future she should have had. Not only for me, but for her. Tragic as her death was, it's allowed me to live a life I could never have dreamed of. A life that I plan to live to its fullest.

"Fine," Cam hisses, his nostrils flaring. "Who you are or were doesn't matter. I want to know what you're doing with my dad."

His eyes watch me intently, scanning for every micro-movement I make.

Keeping my voice even, my face an impenetrable mask, I respond, "I don't know what you're talking about."

I've barely got the sentence out before his hand wraps around my throat and he pushes me further into the wall, his body pressed against mine with every sharp line digging into me. This is nothing like the last two times he's exerted his supposed dominance over me. There's no sexual tension thrumming in the air. Today, it's all pent-up rage and aggression. Still, I don't fight back, sensing he needs this to feel some semblance of control.

His fingers flex against my throat, except he doesn't tighten his grip. He's not restricting my airway or preventing me from talking. Every twitch of his fingers against my neck, every press of his hips against mine, is for show.

With his face inches from mine, I can make out the faint circles of fatigue under his eyes and the ticking of his jaw as his stern gaze bores into me.

"What the fuck are you up to with my dad?" His voice is a low rumble, the words coming out slow and controlled, sounding more ominous than his displays of rage ever have.

I tilt my head back to look him straight in the eye. "What are you talking about?" I snap. I can't deny my heart rate has picked up, and he can most likely feel my pulse hammering against his thumb. *Why does he think I'm up to anything with his father? What would even make him think we know one another?*

"Bullshit," he snarls, using his firm grip on my throat to pull me forward before slamming me back against the wall. I notice Mason take a small step toward me, but I don't—for even one second—look away from Cam's thunderous expression, not once letting my focus shift from the threat hovering in front of me. "You see, we *know* you know each other. He even pointed you out to me."

What the fuck does that mean?

I somehow manage to maintain the impassive look on my face. "What are you talking about?" I'm relieved when the words come out as more than just a panicked croak.

My heart rate is skyrocketing to dangerous levels, my breaths coming in short pants that have nothing to do with Cam's hand around my throat and everything to do with the fact that my lungs no longer feel like they can function properly.

"Oh, you thought he would keep you his dirty little secret?" he goads, fake pouting with a cruel glint in his eye. "Nope. Sorry." He doesn't sound the slightest bit apologetic as he looms over me. "See, my father's not really the reliable type. He only ever looks out for himself, so whatever you think you have going on with him, you're the one who will lose in the end."

Black spots appear in my vision, Cam's words reaching me as though through a tunnel, echoing around in my head while I struggle to make sense of them. All the while I'm doing my best to act as if I'm not in the middle of a serious freak-out.

"What do you mean he pointed me out?" The words come out firm, reflecting none of my inner turmoil, except the next words I hear unravel the thin hold I have on my emotions, confirming my worst nightmare.

"At Cam's meet before Christmas," someone says—I don't even know who—"Cam's dad saw you there. He knew your real name."

I can feel vomit rising up the back of my throat, further interfering with my ability to breathe as I'm sucked into the past. Dark, frantic thoughts batter my mind as I battle to keep my wits while I'm in the middle of what I'm pretty sure is a panic attack.

He found me. He knows I'm here.

Fuck.

Fuck.

I'm so fucking screwed.

"But...that was weeks ago," I murmur, no longer seeing the school hallway or the four assholes standing in front of me. I can't feel Cam's hand on my throat any longer as my body begins to tremble, memories destroying my mental walls and threatening to pull me under.

We belong together, little Dove. You and me. Nothing can come between us.

No. I can't go back there.

I can't let him cage me.

I'd rather die.

Firefly

CHAPTER TWO

I watch as Cam pins her to the wall, his hand wrapped possessively around her neck. I should probably interfere, but I can see that he needs this, and I won't let him go too far. I wouldn't let him actually hurt her—not that I think he could, even if he wanted to.

"What the fuck are you up to with my dad?" he snarls, his face inches from hers.

I see the defiant glare in her eyes, the confused look on her face, although there's also something else she's hiding beneath it, something I can't quite put my finger on. Regardless, she knows more than she's letting on.

What secrets are you hiding, you sly seductress?

"What are you talking about?" she growls, unfazed by the snarling blond in front of her, or the rest of us crowded around them, blocking the view of anyone who might stumble upon us. Not that anyone would dare interfere or tattle on us. "I don't even know your father."

Cam tips his head to the side, observing her closely. "Bullshit," he bites out. "You see, we *know* you know each other. He even pointed you out to me."

Her eyes widen, and I swear I see genuine fear flash across her face, but she masks it a second later which only causes me to wonder if I imagined it.

"What are you talking about?" The words are strained as her tongue flicks out to lick her lower lip in a nervous gesture.

Cam's grin is maniacal. There's no other way to describe it as he towers over her, his face so close it encompasses all of her vision.

"Oh, you thought he would keep you his dirty little secret?" he goads, fake pouting. "Nope. Sorry. See, my father's not really the reliable type. He only ever looks out for himself, so whatever you think you have going on with him, you're the one who will lose in the end."

That defiant glare is back in her stare as she scowls at him. "What do you mean he pointed me out?" she growls, seeming unfazed by Cam's words. However, I can see her chest rising and falling in rapid succession, giving away that she's not as calm and collected as she's letting on.

"At Cam's meet before Christmas," I interject before Cam can toy with her more. "Cam's dad saw you there. He knew your real name."

The blood drains from her face, making her appear washed out, almost ghost-like. I can see the wheels spinning, her brain working overtime to sort something out.

"But...that was weeks ago." The words are barely more than a terrified whisper, her breaths coming in short pants as she hyperventilates, her gaze unfocused as she slips away from the present.

"Who gives a crap when it was?" Cam snarls, clearly not picking up on the same cues I am.

"Cam," I call out in warning, right before Hadley's body gives out, her head falling forward as vomit spews out of her mouth.

"What the fuck?" Cam shouts, jumping back to avoid being hit. He's too late, though. It's all over the arm he was using to pin her to the wall.

Without his support, Hadley drops to the ground like a ragdoll, her whole body shaking as she dry heaves onto the floor.

I rush toward her at the same time Mason does. Moving in behind her, he pulls back her hair, as I crouch down in front of her, careful to avoid the puddle of puke. I've never seen her look so weak, so vulnerable. She can barely hold herself up as her arms tremble, her whole body trembling, but why?

"What the fuck is wrong with her?" There's a hint of hysteria in Cam's voice, despite the angry tone of his words. His eyes widen with panic and confusion as he strips off his blazer, using the sleeve to wipe some stray vomit from his shoes.

She struggles to catch her breath, and Mason loosely wraps an arm around her from behind, gently pulling her back against him. I lift out a tissue from my pocket to wipe at the corner of her mouth. She doesn't even register my presence, and her skin is flushed and clammy under my touch.

"What the fuck is going on with her?" Hawk barks from right behind me, sounding more confused than angry for once.

"Fuck, is she pregnant? Did my dad knock her up?" Cam demands, pacing back and forth as he throws furtive glances her way.

"Shut up, asshole. She's not fucking pregnant," I snap, rolling my eyes at his idiocy. "I think she's having a panic attack."

I reach out and grasp her chin securely between my thumb and index finger. "Hadley," I say her name firmly, but she gives no indication of hearing me, too lost in whatever the fuck is going through her head right now.

"What the fuck do we do, man?" Cam asks, his voice frantic as he continues to pace. It's a far cry from the cold tone he was using on her a moment ago.

Sharing a look over her head with Mason, he gives a small shrug, feeling as unsure as I am.

"We need to get her to the nurse." I have no idea what else we can do. None of us are equipped to deal with this. Fuck, none of us can handle a woman crying, never mind something like this.

Nodding in agreement, Mason tightens his hold around her, but that seems to set her off again, and she launches a frenzied attack on his arms by scraping and clawing at them.

"NO! NO!" she screams. The sound is ear-piercing and I wince as the high-pitched noise assaults my eardrums, bouncing off the stone walls of the otherwise empty hall. The panic in her voice unsettles me. Where the fuck is she in her head that she's behaving like this? "I won't go back there!" she shouts.

Mason keeps a firm grip on her as she twists and contorts her body in an attempt to get free, his teeth gritting as she digs her nails deep enough into his skin to draw blood, leaving shallow half-moon-shaped cuts along his forearm.

He manages to get to his feet, pulling her up against his body as she writhes in his arms.

I step in front of her. "Shhh," I soothe, rubbing my thumb along her cheek, not knowing what else to do to try and calm her. It takes a moment, but she eventually begins to settle at my gentle touch, falling limp in Mason's arms and sagging against him. Now that she's no longer fighting him, he's able to get his arm under her knees and lift her up to carry her.

"I can't go back there," she whispers in a broken voice that fucking eviscerates me. Her words are so soft that only Mason and I hear them. I share a concerned look with him before staring into her eyes again. They're unfocused and glazed over. She's still lost in whatever nightmare she's trapped in.

I can't take my eyes off her as she buries her face against Mason's chest, her arms wrapping loosely around his neck.

Go back where?

Seeing her like this only makes me even more determined to find out what the fuck happened to her. Not so my brothers can have answers or so Hawk can use it to get rid of her. It's only so I can keep the promise I'm making here and now to never let any fucking harm come to her again.

I don't know what the fuck she's been through, but today has made it painfully apparent that more is going on here than we know. More than just her possibly fucking Cam's dad—not that I believed that for a second—or her trying to blackmail our parents or whatever the fuck she might be doing.

Something is seriously fucking wrong. This fierce, defiant girl has demons nipping at her heels, tormenting her and making her live in fear. Well, I won't fucking have it. I knew I gave more of a damn about her than I had let on to the guys or that I was willing to believe myself. Now, I'm accepting it. She's gotten under my skin and infiltrated my mind, and I'm going to make damn sure she's safe. I will get to the bottom of what's happening, then destroy whoever thinks they can fuck with her like that—even if it's Lawrence Rutherford himself.

Rushing through the school, we dash into the administration building, practically running down the corridor toward the nurse's office. Hadley doesn't speak or move the entire way there, and I'm not sure if that's a good thing or not.

A faculty member steps out of an office just up ahead of us, but we don't slow our pace as we race toward him. Hearing our footsteps slapping against the tile, he turns toward us. My lips pinch in irritation as I recognize him, his eyes widening at our approach.

"What's going on here?" Beck barks in an authoritative voice, stepping further out into the middle of the hall to block our path. I've half a mind to bowl him over, except the look on his face says he'd trail us to the damn office demanding answers if we don't stop.

All four of us stutter to a halt.

"Out of the way," I seethe. Now is not the fucking time for him to be sticking his nose where it doesn't belong.

His eyes fall on Hadley lying limp in Mason's arms, her face still pressed against his chest.

Stepping in front of Mason, he demands, "What's wrong with her?" His eyes roam over her as though checking for any injuries.

"We need to get her to the nurse," I bark urgently, pushing past him. He suddenly grabs my arm, refusing to step out of Mason's way. Scowling where his hand is wrapped around my bicep, I meet his gaze, glaring at him.

In the few interactions I've had with him, he's always been cordial, polite, but the look on his face now is pure thunder as his grip tightens to the point of pain. "What did you do to her?" he snarls. His aggression and accusation take me by surprise. Why the fuck would he think we've done anything to her?

Yanking my arm out of his grip, my lip peels back. "*We* didn't do anything to her. She's having a panic attack. She needs to see the nurse."

He tears his eyes away from me, looking back at her as though I hadn't spoken. Reaching out, he brushes her hair away from her face. Her chest is still heaving with rapid breaths, even though it's impossible to see her face, which is still buried against Mason's shirt. So I've no idea if she's still in the throes of a panic attack or if she's come around a bit.

"Get her into my office," he barks. "Now!" He practically shouts the word when none of us move. Everything about him is no-nonsense and I share a quick look with the others, but Mason is already moving toward the door to his office, Beck beside him as he pushes it open. "Set her on the couch."

He strides in behind Mason, the two of them setting her down on the couch and getting her comfy as the rest of us filter in behind, closing the door and standing awkwardly in the small space. She curls up on her side in the fetal position with her head burrowed into her chest. Her eyes are squeezed shut as she tries to block out the world around her. I can't take my eyes off her, and my palms are sweaty with worry.

Mason sits on the arm of the sofa ensuring he doesn't touch her, although close enough that if she needed him, he'd be beside her in a hot second. His fingers run anxiously through his dark hair, pushing it out of his eyes as he watches Hadley intently. I've never seen him behave the way he is right now. He's usually cold and emotionless, especially with girls. It's almost like he cares for her, too. I had caught hints here and there that he was interested in her, but this is next level. The way he's looking at her is more than just sexual attraction or physical chemistry.

Beck crouches down in front of her, his fingers tucking her wayward hair behind her ear before clasping her small hands in his larger ones as his gaze roams over her face. She's no longer panting heavily, but her face is still leached of all color and small tremors intermittently shake her body.

"Hadley," he murmurs, getting no response.

"She needs a nurse," I reiterate, throwing my hands up in exasperation when he ignores me. *Fucking asshole. Does he think just because he "counsels" students on their problems, that he's a fucking doctor?*

Mason pulls a blanket off the back of the sofa, draping it over her trembling legs.

Reaching out, Beck trails his thumb over her cheek in a strangely intimate gesture miming how I touched her earlier. Tucking his finger underneath her chin, he slowly tilts her head upward until their faces are inches apart and, if she opened her eyes, she would see nothing but him.

"Hadley, sweetheart. I know you're in there. I know you can hear me. It's just us, baby. I've got you."

What the ever-loving fuck am I hearing right now? Sweetheart? Baby?

I glance at Mason. His body has tensed up, but his face is as impassive as ever. Side-eyeing Cam and Hawk beside me, I see similar looks of confusion on their faces too.

When I look back at Hadley, her hand is fisted in Beck's shirt and he's stroking her hair. She's finally opened her eyes and they're transfixed on his as he does some weird-ass breathing thing.

"That's it. You're doing great," he encourages. Whatever he's doing seems to be working as her breathing appears to return to normal. With every passing moment she seems to relax, her muscles untensing and her breathing stabilizing, I can feel my heart rate steadying.

"Beck?" she murmurs.

What the fuck? How does she even know him?

"I'm right here, sweetheart," he promises, the sentiment making my lip curl up in contempt as I swallow the growl threatening to escape.

We all stand silently for fuck knows how long as he settles her. She doesn't look at any of us, ignoring our very existence as he calms her and convinces her to get some rest, tucking a pillow under her head and pulling the blanket around her tighter.

Once she seems to have drifted off to sleep, he gives her one last soft look before turning toward the rest of us, a hardness in his stare I've never seen before.

"Out," he mouths, pointing toward the door. We all dutifully traipse out of his office and back into the hall. However, as he closes the door, I turn on him.

"What the fuck? You're sleeping with a student?" I snarl, my fists clenched tight in anger as I struggle not to fucking punch him. How dare he take advantage of her, the sick fuck. Can't he see how fucking vulnerable she is? Does he get off on that, pulling the strings and toying with susceptible students who come to him for help? Fucking disgusting is what it is.

His eyes dart around the hallway, confirming no one else is listening in before he pins me with a serious look as his jaw ticks with anger.

"Shut the fuck up," he hisses.

"You know this is grounds for dismissal," I threaten, stepping into him so we're standing toe-to-toe. I can feel the others close in behind me. They know of the animosity between Beck and I, and they'll have my back regardless of how this plays out.

He snorts. "You and I both know it wouldn't matter if you went tattling to the headmaster."

My teeth grind, knowing he's right. Our father would never let something as mundane as fucking a student jeopardize his plans. I don't know what the fuck his agenda is with Beck, but for some reason he got him a job here, so I guess I'm stuck on campus with my fucking half-brother until he's done with him.

Knowing he's won that argument, he steps back, his hard gaze sweeping over the others. "What happened today?"

"Nothing," I snap before anyone else can give him an answer.

"Don't fucking lie to me," he hisses. "You did something to her. Now, what was it?"

"We didn't do anything," I insist. I still don't even know what happened. It seems pretty fucking obvious what triggered that, but why? How? There're still so many unanswered questions, all the numerous possibilities giving me a fucking headache. Regardless of what happened, I'm sure as fuck not about to divulge any of it to him. Thankfully, the rest of the guys seem to agree as they all keep their lips shut.

His hand snaps out, gripping the front of my shirt as he slams me against the wall beside the door.

"I *know* it was you. *You* sent that fucking video around school, and she didn't even blink an eye, so whatever fucking bullshit stunt you pulled today, you better stop it. You saw how easily she beat the shit out of your buddy last time. If you do *anything* to her again, it won't just be her wrath you'll be facing."

My eyes go wide at the knowledge that he saw that fight and at the fierceness of his promise. He's not just fucking her. Whatever might be going on between them, it's not just sex, and for some reason that knowledge doesn't sit well with me.

Mason comes over, resting a hand on Beck's shoulder. "We were just talking to her, man. We didn't mean to…" He trails off and I can see regret in his eyes, the same regret that's eating away at me. I wouldn't have let Cam do what he did if I thought it would cause that reaction. She's always seemed so fierce, so strong. I had no idea we would set her off so easily. "We didn't mean to." Mason sighs, shaking his head.

"Just get out of here," Beck growls, done with our vague responses, as he releases me and takes a step back. Adjusting my glasses, I fix my uniform, running my hand over the creases to iron them out before I step away from him; Hawk and Cam standing beside me as a unit.

Mason hovers behind us for a second, glancing at the door where Hadley is sleeping on the other side, his face tight, as though he's torn between leaving and staying.

"I'll make sure she's okay," Beck promises him quietly, seeing the same indecision on his face as I do. After another moment's hesitation, he gives a tight nod, striding toward us and the four of us leave the admin building and the shitshow that just happened behind us.

None of us say anything until we're safely in the privacy of our dorm. The second the door closes behind us, Cam looks at us with wide eyes. "What the fuck was that all about?"

Dropping down onto the sofa, I remove my glasses, rubbing at the bridge of my nose and trying to relieve the tension building behind my eyes. Mason brings over a six-pack of beer from the fridge, holding a bottle out to me before sitting at the other end of the sofa.

"Dude, your brother is fucking her," Hawk snickers, leaning back in the chair opposite mine. His easy banter only serves to irritate me further.

"Yeah, I picked up on that," I deadpan, not bothering to look at him as I take a swig of the beer, the cool liquid doing nothing to quiet the raging inferno within me.

"I wonder how long that's been going on," he continues, oblivious to Cam's tightening expression and grinding teeth. Despite how much he might be pissed at Hadley right now, it's noticeable to anyone who's watching that he's still fucking obsessed with her. "Do you think she was fucking him when she was supposed to be your girl?" he directs at Cam.

"Shut up, man." Mason sighs, sounding exhausted as he gives Hawk a piercing glare.

"Whatever, like I give a shit." The asshole shrugs, taking a large gulp from his own bottle.

I tune out the conversation around me as I analyze what went down today. Hadley had been fine, or so it seemed until we brought up Lawrence. Specifically, until she found out he knew she was here....but why? Why would it matter if he knew she was here? *Fuck.* I can feel the headache throbbing in my temples as I try to work it out, none of it making any sense.

Not to mention the fact she's sleeping with my fucking half-brother. What the hell is that all about? I swear, if I didn't know any better, I'd think she was deliberately screwing him to mess with me. Her way of getting back at me for the video and posters, but there's no way she knows who he is. Beck is as reluctant as I am to tell anyone the truth about who he is, although fuck knows why *he* doesn't want anyone to know. He's already pretending to be a preppy rich guy. Why not add a fancy fucking family name to it too?

I'd never fucking met the guy, had no fucking idea he even existed until right before the school year started. The night before school started, Dad insisted on a family dinner and brought him home, introducing him like it wasn't the weirdest fucking thing ever. The next day, the asshole was waltzing into Pac like he fucking belonged here in his stupid fucking waistcoats.

What the fuck does my father even want with him? He and the others made him partake in that fucking ambush with us at Christmas before they spilled the dark secrets of Nocturnal Enterprises, but why? Why do they need him if they have us?

It seems he was the only one who didn't know about Nocturnal Mercenaries, if the shocked look on his face was anything to go by. His face turned pale when our families threatened him, threats they'd happily deliver on if he didn't fall in line. So here the five of us fucking are, falling in line like good little soldiers and waiting for our marching orders.

In the meantime, the four of us are doing everything we can to get out from under our parents' thumbs. And work out who the fuck Hadley is, where she's been all these years, and why she's suddenly shown up here now. Yeah, our plate is pretty fucking full right now, never mind tossing the bullshit from today onto the pile.

"Did you find out anything else about her?" Hawk asks, looking at me.

"No." I push my dark hair out of my face, fisting the strands in frustration. I've spent every spare moment trying to find a lead on her. It seems like she became 'Hadley' a year ago, but before that? I haven't a fucking clue who she was or where she had been living. I've gone through her school records, but they're all fake, along with the history of her foster care placements. Not only is she using an alias, but she's given herself an entirely fake background.

How did she even manage to achieve all of that? She's definitely not tech-savvy, and hiring out a job like that would be costly.

"I can't find anything on who she is."

Strangely, I also can't find anything on Elizabeth Davenport, either. No record of her birth, and any of the articles I could find on Mrs. Davenport were about her simply being pregnant. Electronically, Elizabeth never existed. If I hadn't seen her birth certificate and the photos of her and Hawk, not to mention the irrefutable DNA reports, I'd almost believe she really wasn't his sister.

Hawk's lips pinch, not happy with our lack of progress.

"You saw her today," Hawk says, his words drawing me back to their conversation. "We could break her. If we kept pushing her, she'd crumble."

"What the fuck, man?" I snarl, glaring at him. Is he seriously considering what I think he is?

"What?" He shrugs, not the slightest bit bothered by the fact he's suggesting breaking his own sister. "It would get us some answers."

"At what cost?"

"West is right," Mason insists. "The way she looked today." He grits his teeth as his hand runs through his dark hair, once again pushing the strands away from his face, tugging on the ends until they're sticking out all over the place. "Fuck. I don't want to see her like that again. It was fucking brutal."

Hawk rolls his eyes. "Jesus, she's got you two fucking pussy-whipped."

"We're not doing that to her," I assert, pinning Hawk with an intense stare until he rolls his eyes again and grumbles a half-assed agreement. I then glare at Cam, who has been disturbingly quiet during the argument, giving him the same no-nonsense demeanor until he agrees as well.

"Yeah, yeah, okay, man. I won't push her on it, but she's fucking hiding something about my dad, and I wanna know what."

I get that, but there was something off about the whole thing. "I agree she knows stuff about your dad, but, man, it's not what you think it is. Her face...she was fucking terrified when you told her he knew she was here."

"I agree," Mason says. "She went into the ring against Hawk and didn't bat an eyelash. She's taken everything we've thrown at her and fought back without showing an ounce of fear or hesitation, but today she came across...broken. I don't know what could cause such fear in someone so fearless, but it must be something horrific."

Hadley

CHAPTER THREE

My body feels like lead, my eyelids weighing a ton as I roll onto my back. Fuck, I can absolutely skip the gym today. What difference is one day going to make?

Except, something isn't right. My bedsheets feel different than normal against my skin, not as light or smooth.

Cracking an eye open, I take in the darkened room. Beck is sitting in his chair as he reads a book with only a reading lamp turned on at his desk.

How the hell did I end up asleep in his office?

It takes a second, but flashes of earlier dance behind my eyes. The fuckheads cornering me in the hallway. Cam towering over me as he tells me his dad knows I'm here.

He knows I'm here.

My breath picks up speed, air coming in and out in quick pants. Beck must pick up on my distress as he's at my side in an instant, his hand running over my cheek, pushing my hair back.

"Shhh," he soothes. "You're okay. You're in my office. You're safe."

Despite how untrue his words are, his soft touches and comforting voice soothe me somewhat as my breathing evens out. Rolling onto my side, I stare into his beautiful green eyes, not that I can really make them out in the dark, but it grounds me nonetheless.

"What happened?" My voice comes out as a croak, husky from lack of use, and I suddenly realize how dry my mouth is as I lick my parched lips. "How did I get here?"

Getting to his feet, Beck moves over to his desk to grab a bottle of water and returns to the sofa. I prop myself upright, accepting the drink from his outstretched hand and downing half the bottle in one go before relaxing back against the cushions.

He watches me intently with concern etched into his features as he crouches in front of me, reaching out to intertwine his fingers with mine. "Let's get out of here. We can discuss it at my place."

"At yours?" I practically squeak. "I can't go back to yours. What if somebody sees us? You could lose your job."

A soft smile curls the corner of his lip. "It's well after midnight, sweetheart. No one will be around. Besides, if you think I'm letting you out of my sight after today, you're wrong." He practically hisses out the last few words, his ire getting the better of him as his face tightens.

Biting on my lower lip, I nod my head. I don't want to go back to my dorm and sleep alone anyway. The thought of being curled up with him for a few hours sounds like exactly what I need. Pulling me up from the sofa, he grabs my backpack and flicks off the desk lamp before wrapping his hand around mine and escorting me out of his office.

We make the journey across campus to the staff accommodations in silence. The fresh air feels amazing against my skin. The evening chill makes me feel more alert as I inhale a few deep breaths. I can finally breathe for the first time since this afternoon. I wrack my brain to remember how I ended up in Beck's office, but it's all disjointed flashes that I can't piece together. The last thing I remember is the sheer terror that consumed me at finding out Lawrence knew I was here. Just thinking about it has my palm sweating in Beck's, and he looks down at me, worry and confusion engraved on his face.

God, he's going to have so many questions. He's going to want to know what happened today, why I freaked the fuck out. I'm going to have to give him something. I want to tell him everything—an utterly terrifying thought. I've never been able to trust anyone, never been close enough to anyone to *want* to tell them anything. But Beck gives the illusion of safety.

During our sessions and over the last few weeks of our relationship, he's been nothing but patient and understanding. He's made me laugh more than I remember ever laughing before and provided me with a sense of comfort that I didn't know I was craving. He's become my safe haven, my port in the otherwise raging storm of shit going on around me, but that's what scares me. What if I open up to him and he decides he's done, that I'm too much effort and he can't do it? I wouldn't blame him, even though the thought of him leaving me, of not having him in my life anymore, is honestly more terrifying than facing Lawrence.

Despite my reservations however, he deserves some answers and to better understand what he's gotten himself into by going out with me. Especially if Lawrence knows I'm here. He could have eyes on me right now. I could be putting him in danger just by being seen with him.

That thought has my stomach flipping with uneasiness and I subtly cast my eyes around us, trying to pick up any moving shadows in the darkness. I don't see anyone, although that doesn't mean they aren't out there lurking, watching my every move.

Most of the staff live in a large apartment block at the far end of campus. Unlike the main buildings or the student dorms, theirs is new and modern. Much like the sports and rec centers, the structures stand out in complete contrast to the old buildings on campus.

I've been to Beck's apartment a couple of times before, over the Christmas break, when no one else was around, except this is different. Everyone is back on campus now. Anyone could peek out their window and see us.

Beck doesn't seem to have the same concerns as me, in any case. He confidently strides up to the front door, pulling it open and gesturing for me to go ahead. I hesitate for only a second, glancing through the glass window to check that no one is in the foyer. Seeing it's empty, I dash inside, hurrying toward the stairs and rushing up to the second floor where his apartment is.

Peeking through a slit in the door to check the coast is clear, I powerwalk to his apartment, fidgeting and darting my eyes up and down the corridor until he unlocks the door and I can slip in. I hear him chuckle under his breath at my paranoia, and I have no idea why he's so chilled. Why isn't he more concerned? He's explained how much he needs this job, so surely he should be more worried about the possibility of losing it.

I don't relax until he closes the door behind him, flicking the lock and moving to turn on a few lamps as I fall onto his sofa. His apartment is nothing special. It's a decent size, with an open-plan living, kitchen, and dining area, along with a bedroom and bathroom. Everything is new and modern looking—all white with fancy appliances, a flat-screen TV and a large sectional sofa separating the kitchen and dining area from the living room.

I notice that, just like my room, there's nothing personal. No photos or any indicators of who Beck is underneath his fancy waistcoats. In fact, the space barely seems lived in.

Beck pulls the blind across the large window, which offers a view of the lawns toward the sports center, before moving into the kitchen.

"Are you hungry? I can make us something to eat."

I really don't feel like eating, still out of sorts from today's events and nervous about the conversation that I know is coming. Yet my stomach grumbles, letting me know it's not happy it hasn't been fed since lunchtime.

"I'll take that as a yes." Beck chuckles, turning to the fridge and pulling stuff out to make us a midnight snack.

As he gets to work, I pop into the bathroom, grabbing the spare toothbrush Beck dug out for me the first night I stayed over. It tastes like something died in my mouth, and I desperately need to brush my teeth. Once I'm done, I take a hard look at myself in the mirror and note how my hair is even more out of control than usual, sticking out at odd angles. There are bags under my eyes and my pale complexion makes me look like a zombie. This day has done a number on me.

Pressing my lips together, I look away, heading back to the living room and getting comfy in the same spot I was in before, just as Beck brings a large plate piled high with sandwiches, a bowl of chips, and two glasses of water over, setting it down on the coffee table in front of us as he situates himself beside me on the sofa.

I stretch forward and grab a couple of sandwiches off the plate. Beck does the same before he wraps an arm around my shoulders, pulling me in against him. It's the best feeling in the world, being tucked up against his large, taut body. When we're like this, everything else fades into the background. It's exactly what I needed, especially after today.

We eat in silence, and when I'm full I snuggle in against him, breathing in his comforting cedarwood and eucalyptus scent. When I first smelled it, I thought it was his cologne—I imagine expensive cologne has the capacity to smell so divine—but regardless of the time of day, he always smells the same. I swear I've had some of the best nights' sleep in the last few weeks, cuddled up against him, sniffing him like a fucking weirdo as slumber overtakes me.

I watch as he finishes off the stack of sandwiches like a starved bear, barely chewing as he swallows them down before reaching for the next one. He was clearly hungry. I guess, thanks to me, he ended up skipping dinner. The thought makes me feel guilty as he relaxes back into the couch cushions, pulling me even tighter against him as his fingers stroke random patterns up and down my arm.

"Do you want to talk about today?" he asks softly, his cheek resting against the top of my head, his warm breath tickling my ear.

No. Not really. But he deserves answers.

"Okay," I say hesitantly, wringing my hands as nerves flutter in my stomach. I don't dare look at him, not wanting to read any pity or judgment on his face. Knowing that so much as a glance in his direction will have me changing my mind and shutting down.

"Did they hurt you?" The words come out as an angry rasp, and I can feel his body tense against mine.

"No, they didn't." They might have been assholes, but what happened today wasn't their fault. They couldn't have known how badly I would react to their words. "There's so much you don't know. So much I haven't told you," I confess, my eyes drilling a hole in my lap as I refuse to look at him.

"You don't need to tell me anything you don't want to." The soft, reassuring cadence of his voice soothes me, softening my hard edges and putting a dent in the barrier I built around myself at a young age. The fact he's not pushing me, that I *know* he would drop the subject if I said I didn't want to talk about it, means more than he can ever know. Nevertheless, the time for secrets between Beck and I is over, and I need to be honest with him. I don't need to tell him everything about my past, but I do need to tell him about Lawrence and Hawk. I need to explain to him why I'm really here.

I slowly begin to tell him about Lawrence, the monster who haunts my dreams, threatening to ruin me. I can't look at him, and honestly I don't need to in order to feel the anger building up within him with every word that passes my lips.

When I'm done, he holds me tightly, like he's afraid if he lets go, I'll disappear. We end up sitting like that for a while as he processes everything.

Eventually, he breaks the silence. "So you came here to seek out Cam? Then what? What were you going to do?"

I shake my head, unable to tell him the fucked-up plan I had in place for Cam. I can only say that I was in a dark place when I came up with it, and I clung to it like a lifeline until I was free.

"It doesn't matter. I couldn't go through with it. Cam might be an asshole, but he's nothing like his father."

"So now what?"

I shake my head, defeated. "I don't know," I admit. My first thought when I found out about Lawrence was to run, to get as far away from here as quickly as possible, but then I thought about Hawk, *the insufferable dickhead*. Regardless of how angry he makes me, or how much he despises me, he's family. I've spent my whole life dreaming and wondering who they could be. Now that I can get some answers about them and find out what happened to me, I can't just walk away from that. And, despite how futile it seems to hope, I can't help but wonder, if I stayed, could Hawk and I one day maybe even be friends, or at least tolerate one another? Not to mention, the thought of leaving Beck behind and never seeing the others again doesn't sit well with me.

"There's more," I say on a heavy sigh, knowing I'm probably about to push him over the line with the amount of information I'm throwing at him out of left field.

"More?" he repeats, his voice hitched in disbelief.

"Hawk is my brother."

The words still sound foreign on my tongue, yet they roll off it easily like they're familiar. Something I should have been saying to people my whole life. "I only found out a few weeks ago, just before Christmas."

Silence sits heavy in the air between us, practically suffocating me as my thoughts spin out of control, wondering what he's thinking. I know he knows of the Princes, but I don't think he knows them that well. Beyond his name and the fact he's friends with Cam, he probably doesn't really know who Hawk is.

"That's...a lot to take in," he eventually says, drawing a small, humorless chuckle from me.

"I'm sorry I didn't tell you sooner."

Until now, he hasn't tried to get me to look at him. He listened patiently as I told him everything at my own pace and in my own way. Now that I've run out of things to say, his fingers press firmly against the side of my chin and he turns my face to look at him.

"You have nothing to apologize for." His voice is earnest, his eyes never breaking contact with mine. "Thank you for telling me." Leaning in, he presses a quick kiss against my lips, the brief touch saying more than words ever could.

Placing his hand in mine, he gets to his feet. "Come on," he says, tugging me to my feet. "We should get some sleep."

"That's it?" I ask, shocked at how laid back he seems. "You don't have any questions?"

"I have loads of questions, sweetheart." He chuckles. "But it's nearly dawn, and you need some sleep. The rest of it can wait."

Too gobsmacked by his easy acceptance of everything, I let him lead me to the bedroom. He grabs me an oversized t-shirt out of his drawer, and I quickly peel off my uniform and tug it over my head, slipping between the cool sheets as he slides in the other side. He wraps his arms around me as I lean my head on his chest and tangle my legs with his, the steady thumping of his heart the last thing I remember as I fall asleep.

∼

THE WEAK MORNING sunlight peeks around the corner of the blinds on the bedroom window as I open my eyes, letting me know it's still early morning. I can feel Beck's body pressing along my back and the weight of his arm draped over my hip. I must have only slept for a couple of hours, but I feel refreshed.

I don't want to leave my warm cocoon, except I've already been here too long. People will be waking up soon, and with the sun out, it won't be so easy for me to slip away without anyone seeing me. Sliding out from between the sheets, careful not to wake him, I silently put on my uniform from yesterday and sneak out of his bedroom. I scribble a quick note on a scrap of paper I find in his kitchen before ducking out of his apartment and stealthily using the fire exit to walk out of the building unseen.

I stick close to the shadows of the forest as I make my way toward the sports center. As the last remnants of sleep are blown away by the morning breeze, I feel the telltale sign of being watched. The hairs on the back of my neck stand upright as I subtly scan around me. Listening intently, I try to discern the shuffling of leaves and snapping of twigs that could signify someone is nearby, but I don't hear anything untoward.

Keeping my senses on alert, I pick up my pace until I'm far enough away from the staff accommodations that my presence on the path wouldn't seem suspicious.

Still feeling that tingly sense, I duck out of the cover of the forest onto the path, peering over my shoulder. I don't see anything suspicious, even though it definitely felt like someone was watching me.

Once on the path, I slow my pace, taking my time as I walk, breathing in a deep breath as I soak up the pre-dawn silence. There's something about this time of day. The dew is still wet on the grass, and the mist clings to the air as if refusing to be removed by the heat of the sun. The sounds of birds chirping in the trees as they start their day, making their nests and finding food for their young. It's a blissful solitude that only heightens the rawness of my wounds. As the cover of darkness is pulled back, the truths I laid bare to Beck come to light.

While I don't regret any of what I told him, there's no denying that I'm not on edge, panicking that this could change everything between us. I've never trusted anyone with my secret before. I don't know what I would do if I didn't have his understanding and acceptance.

A shadow crosses my path, jolting me from my thoughts. Even lost in my own head, I knew he was nearby. It would be impossible to miss the static charge of electricity in the air.

"I can't today, Mason." I sigh wearily before he can bombard me with more questions. Of course, the asshole ignores me, stepping right into my personal space and blocking my path. His hand slides into my hair, gently tugging on the strands until I tilt my head back, gazing up at him.

His lips are pressed together as he roams his eyes over my face. I don't have the energy to affix my usual mask in place, instead allowing him to see every broken, damaged part of me. Maybe when he realizes how incredibly scarred I am, he and his dickhead buddies will leave me alone.

"I needed to make sure you were okay," he murmurs, his thumb stroking down my cheek as if he's confirming that I'm real, that I am indeed standing in front of him and not just some figment of his imagination.

He glances behind me toward the staff accommodations, likely putting two and two together as his teeth grind and my body stiffens, preparing for the onslaught of his hate.

Beck relayed everything to me last night about how I ended up in his office after I fell into the throes of my panic attack, so I know he and the others are aware of our relationship, or they at least know that something is going on between us. I'm not sure if that knowledge will make them resent me more. So long as they don't target Beck, I can take whatever they throw at me—just not today. Today I need to let myself burn in my damage, and tomorrow I'll rise from the ashes with my armor back in place, ready to take on the world.

"Did he hurt you?" His words puzzle me, and I assume he's talking about Beck, although I don't understand why. Before I can tell him he's got it all wrong, that Beck isn't like that, he clarifies, "Cam's dad. Did he do that to you?" He runs his finger along a scar on my collarbone, that simple touch igniting my body, sending a newfound energy coursing under my skin. It pushes back the final remnants of exhaustion that clung to me from yesterday.

"No." The word comes out husky and croaked, a combination of the intense feelings he evokes in me and the broken parts of myself that I can't cover up today. "He didn't do that, but he's capable of so much worse. If he had his way, he would turn me into a walking, talking mannequin trained to do as he demands. He would scoop out my insides, carving me into a hollow version of myself that no one, not even me, would recognize." Looking into his eyes, I give him the truest words I can. "I've been to hell and back and survived, but there would be no coming back from that."

Hadley

CHAPTER FOUR

I don't go to class that day, or the next. Nor do I answer the door when someone bangs on it—I'm guessing it's Emilia. Instead, I stay hidden in my nest of blankets, pretending the outside world and its problems don't exist. Beck is the only person I talk to, just to check in with him and let him know I'm okay.

By Thursday, Emilia has had enough of me avoiding her.

"If you don't open this door right now, Hadley Parker, I'm going to...I'm going to...well, I'm going to do something, and you won't like it!" she shouts, her fist banging on the door.

Checking the time, she should be at breakfast with all the others, not here making a racket that I'm sure people on the fourth floor can hear.

A dull thud comes from the door, followed by an "Ow, fuck, that hurt," as, I'm assuming, Emilia kicks the door with her foot. Rolling my eyes, I get out of bed, listening to her grumble and curse through the wood.

"What the hell?" she exclaims when I open the door, throwing her arms up in the air as she stomps into my room, her sore foot suddenly forgotten. "What happened? Why are you hiding out and avoiding me?"

Spinning around, she scrutinizes me. "What did they do now?"

"Hi to you too," I greet, ignoring the sharp daggers of her eyes as I dismiss her probing questions.

Crossing her arms over her chest, she pops out her hip, making it clear she isn't going anywhere until I give her some details.

Sighing, I roll my eyes yet again.

"It was nothing," I assure her. "I just wasn't feeling great and felt like hiding from the world for a couple of days, that's all." I ignore the tightness in my chest as the lies flow effortlessly from my tongue.

It's for her own good. The less she knows, the better.

She studies me for a moment longer with narrowed eyes before her face smooths out.

"Oh, I'm sorry. Are you feeling okay?"

The guilt on her face for barging in here when she thinks I'm not well, has the tight band around my chest constricting further, and I have to look away from her. Pretending to get myself ready, I bustle about the room.

"Yeah, I am."

"Good. Are you coming to class today?"

"Ehh." I cringe, not ready to go back and face all of the assholes, but I guess I have no choice. At least I don't have any classes with them today, so I can probably avoid them. "Yeah, I guess," I finally respond unenthusiastically.

Seeming satisfied, she bounces over to my bed and makes herself comfortable while I throw on my uniform. Now that the beans have been spilled about my scars, I don't mind changing in front of her. It wasn't like I covered myself up out of embarrassment. I just didn't want to deal with any awkward questions or pitying looks.

Emilia barely glances my way, her finger scrolling along the screen of her tablet. Thankfully, she's never asked me about the scars. I don't want to lie to her any more than I need to.

"Ohhh," she exclaims in a high-pitched voice that has me looking over at her. "There's a party tomorrow night. You *have* to come."

"I don't know," I respond hesitantly, already flicking through my mental list of excuses.

"You *have* to," she repeats. "It's going to be a total blowout."

Raising my eyebrows at her from across the room, I deadpan, "It's going to be like every other party by the lake."

"Nope." She shakes her head. "It's Hawk's birthday. The Princes always go big for their birthdays."

My eyes widen—*fuck, of course! How could I forget?* —and Emilia's jaw drops as she realizes the significance of what she just said.

"Holy fuck," she squeals. "It's your birthday, too! Well, you can't miss out on it now."

"It's not my party," I retort, my head still stuck on the fact I'm turning eighteen —again.

"So?" she argues, like I'm being unreasonable. "It's still your birthday. You deserve to celebrate it. Don't let Hawk have all the fun. Besides you know it will piss him off if you show up."

Ah, damn. She's got me there.

She smirks, knowing she's said the magic words.

"Fine. But I'm only going to piss that asshole off."

"Sure, whatever you wanna tell yourself."

∼

THE NEXT NIGHT, I have my hair thrown up in a ponytail and I'm dressed in a pair of Beck's black boxers, with a matching sports bra and my trusty combat boots—because apparently tonight is some sort of boxers and boots party. I have no idea what the fuck that is, but Emilia insisted this was the dress code. If she's playing a trick on me and I'm the only one that shows up in this ridiculous get-up, I'm going to be fucking furious with her.

Pulling open the door, I look at Emilia with confusion.

"What are you doing here?"

"Going to the party with you, silly." She rolls her eyes like I forgot some sort of conversation where we discussed this, but I'm fairly certain we didn't.

"You're supposed to be going with the other scholarship kids. I don't want you to lose their friendship over me, or for Hawk or the guys to use you, if they find out we're friends again."

"It's fine," she assures me. "It's your birthday. Of course, I'm going with you." Something about the tone of her voice is off. As I observe her closer, I can see her eyes are rimmed red as though she has been crying recently.

"What happened?" I demand, the words snapping out harsher than I intended.

She cringes, unable to look me in the eye as she wrings her hands. "I told them that you and I were talking again…"

"And?" I prompt when she falls silent. That's clearly not all she has to say, and based on the way her nostrils flare and her lips purse, whatever happened isn't good.

"And they told me I had to choose—you or them."

My jaw drops open. *Shit.* I thought they would tell her not to talk to me, insist on it even, but giving her an ultimatum? That's cold. My own anger flares on her behalf. How fucking dare they try to dictate who she can and can't hang out with. I get that they don't want anything to do with me, and I've accepted that, but what's their problem if Emilia and I are friends? I highly doubt any blowback from Hawk or the guys will circle back on them.

"Emilia." I sigh sympathetically, not sure what to say. I can tell she's upset, and the fact she's standing here right now instead of at the party with them tells me everything about who she chose. Don't get me wrong, my heart is doing all sorts of happy dances at the fact she picked me.

She fucking picked me. No one has ever chosen me.

She shakes her head, gritting her teeth, even though I can see the hurt in her eyes. These kids were her friends for the last four years, and they just threw her friendship away like it meant nothing. Fucking shitstains.

"What about Andrew?" I ask slowly, getting my answer as tears well up in her eyes and she swallows around a lump in her throat.

Her tongue flicks out to lick her lips. "He said he couldn't afford to risk his scholarship by going out with me if I insisted on jeopardizing everything for you."

Yup. Now I'm royally pissed-off. She must be able to see the steam coming out of my ears or the bloodlust pounding through my veins, demanding vengeance, because she quickly shakes her head, reaching out to grab onto my arm.

"He's not worth it. If he can throw away what we had so readily—if all of them can—then they aren't worth it. I want friends who will always be there for each other, who have each other's backs. You've been looking out for me, pushing me away because you're worried about what will happen if I'm seen with you, but I'm a big girl, and I can look after myself. I just need to know you'll always be there if I need you."

I stare at her for a long moment, a mixture of awe and shock at her heartfelt words.

Damn, she's going to make me cry.

"Always," I promise her, my words garnering a tearful smile from her.

Taking a deep breath, she swipes under her eyes, pulling herself together and casting a look down at my outfit.

"Damn, girl," she says in true Emilia fashion, a proper grin on her face now. "Who knew boxers would look so hot on you?"

"You're one to talk." I laugh, taking in the bright pink neon boxers she's wearing.

"Where did you even find those?" Combined with an equally blinding pink crop top and black high-heeled boots that go all the way up to her thighs, she looks like a hooker Barbie. A hot hooker Barbie.

"I spent all week dying these babies from their plain old boring white color to this." She laughs.

I glance down at the plain old boring black underwear I'm wearing, along with the black boots. *God, we couldn't be more opposite if we tried.*

"Come on," she whines, tugging on my arm and dragging me out the door as I stuff my room key between my tits and my phone into the waistband of my boxers—yeah, the outfit doesn't exactly come with many places to store stuff.

Stepping into the night air, I can hear the boom of music in the distance as I turn to head toward the lake, but she slides her arm into mine, pulling me in the opposite direction.

"Where are we going? Isn't the party at the lake?"

"Nope, not tonight. I told you, it's a special party."

"I don't know what that means," I grumble.

"You'll see," she sings eagerly, practically bouncing in her heels.

The throng of students gets more prominent as we head toward the back of the campus, everyone chattering excitedly. By the sounds of it, the Princes' birthdays are a big deal. I swear I even heard someone say that last year one of them had a superhero-themed party, and the entire cast from the movie came. It meant nothing to me—I didn't recognize the name of the film, but the student was talking about it as though it was a big deal, and the fact they can make something like that happen is just insane. What normal teenager has a birthday party like that? Although, I guess these guys aren't normal teenagers.

There's ample open space between the rec and sports centers, where students usually sit and study or play games when the weather is good, which is where everyone seems to be heading, and the music gets louder as we approach. The crisp quality of it makes me think it's not coming from a sound system.

As we step out from the side of the rec center, the area opens up in front of us, and I can see it's been completely converted into what looks like an outdoor concert with a stage where a band is rocking out. A guy wearing only a pair of jeans, showing off his tattooed skin and toned, sweat-glistening abs, screams lyrics into the microphone while the rest of the band slams on guitars or beats on drums.

I don't recognize them or the music, but the sound of his husky voice is impossible not to love. I'm noticeably not the only one who thinks so, as all the girls in the crowd are screaming at him as they stare up at the stage with hearts in their eyes.

"Wow," I gasp, taking in the scene. It doesn't feel like I'm on a school campus, and apparently we're done with the pre-tense of sneaking out to the lake to drink and have fun. There's no way every teacher here doesn't know what is going on right now.

"Told you," Emilia breathes out, unable to tear her eyes from the sight in front of us. Students are everywhere—do this many kids go to our school?—and off to the side. Along the treeline, tents have been set up where I'm assuming the drinks are.

Tugging on my arm, Emilia directs us over to the tents and I see that, yup, there is a bar setup with a bartender and everything. How is that even possible when we're clearly on school grounds and everyone is a minor?

Emilia orders some fancy cocktail thing while I ask for a coke, both of which come in large fancy-ass glasses with mini umbrellas and a straw. Giggling, Emilia sucks down a large gulp of her drink before we saunter through the crowd. The tent next door is set up as a seating area with big puffy chairs and tall bar tables interspersed around the area. Mood lighting has been placed strategically, making it appear dark and mysterious. I can only imagine what couples are getting up to in the dark corners of that tent.

Moving on, we walk past another bar, a tent with a dessert bar offering frozen yogurt in dozens of different flavors and a topping station with various containers of all sorts of sugary treats. *Damn*, I've never seen anything like it.

The final tent, closest to the stage, has its sides rolled down so we can't see inside, and a rope across the front of it that runs all the way to the stage, preventing people from getting too close. Standing at the entrance is a massive guy dressed all in black and wearing a serious as fuck expression. His size alone could rival Mason's.

"What do you think is in there?" I ask Emilia, pointing toward where a couple of girls wearing next to nothing and positively do not look like they are teenagers slip through the gap in the tent, disappearing inside.

"VIP area, probably," Emilia responds, shrugging. "The guys are most likely in there along with whoever they invited."

"Huh." Well, if they're in there, then they aren't out here, and I don't run the risk of running into any of them. Good. I don't need their drama tonight. It is my birthday, after all, even if it doesn't feel like it.

Finishing off our drinks, we circle around the perimeter, getting as close to the stage as we can before the crowd becomes too thick, everyone pressing together in an effort to get as close as possible.

The soft, crooning voice of the male singer blasts out of the speakers, soaring over the screaming crowd.

Throw the pieces over you
Turn my back and count to ten
Feel it crashing on my skin
I just need to breathe again
Why did it have to be this way?

"Who are these guys?" I shout, turning my head so my lips are close to Emilia's head so she can hear me over the thumping base.

"*Death on a Matchstick*. Haven't you heard of them?"

I shake my head, and she laughs. "Have you been living under a rock?" She chuckles, not realizing how close to the truth her words are.

Song bleeds into song as we stand there, letting the music flow over and around us, the two of us dancing. Well, Emilia dances and I give the occasional sway of my hips, but that's it. Despite the fact this shit isn't really me, I'm enjoying myself more than I have at any other party—it helps that the music is out of this world, and there isn't a single Prick in sight.

My phone vibrates in my boxers and, pulling it out, I find a new message from Beck.

> Beck: You look downright fuckable in my boxers, sweetheart.

My head snaps up as I search around me, trying to see where he's hiding. I haven't laid eyes on him since I left his place on Tuesday morning. He messaged me yesterday to say he had to cancel our session this week—not that we're really continuing with the sessions, but they're an excellent cover for some alone time. No one would ever question if they saw us talking to one another on campus.

Before I can find him, my phone buzzes with another incoming text.

> Beck: If we weren't in public, I'd peel them down your toned thighs and run my tongue along your wet pussy. I'd suck your clit and fuck you with my mouth until you came all over my face and screamed my name into the night.

Holy Jesus fuckballs. Fucking asshole has me soaked without even touching me. Once again, I glance around me, but with so many people, it's impossible to see him.

"I've gotta go to the bathroom," I say distractedly to Emilia. "Will you be okay here?"

"Yeah, yeah, you go, girl. I'm going to grab another one of these," she responds, shaking her empty glass. "Meet you back here in a bit?"

I nod my head in agreement. "Sounds good."

I keep my eyes peeled, peering left and right as I walk past the tents, slowly moving away from the thick of the crowd. I don't even know where the closest bathrooms are. The rec center, maybe? Probably. Unless they got Porta Potties for this whole event. Do rich people even piss in Porta Potties? Perhaps you can get fancy golden-plated ones for privileged shitheads.

Not that I need to pee anyway, I only wanted to get away from where everyone else is so I can find where Beck is lurking like a creeper, watching me.

My phone buzzes in my hand and I glimpse down.

> Beck: Getting hotter, baby.

I fire off a quick response as I continue moving away from the stage, back toward the rec center.

> Hadley: Wetter too.

I swear I hear a groan travel on the breeze toward me, but gazing into the darkness, I can't see anyone. Shifting toward the sound, my senses are on high alert as the noises of the other students start to fade into the distance.

> Beck: Hotter.

> Hadley: Wetter.

ANOTHER FEW STEPS into the darkness and I'm now out of sight from the party. Ducking around the side of the rec center and keeping close to the wall, making it harder for me to be spotted by anyone who might wander out this way, I continue squinting into the dark while typing on my phone.

> Hadley: Maybe I should just finish myself off?

I HEAR him just as he steps up behind me. One arm encases my waist, and his other hand slides up my throat as he presses his hard length against my ass with his lips hovering over my ear.

"There will be none of that," he growls in my ear in response to my text, his dominant tone only making me soak the boxers more.

Damn, I really should have brought a backup pair, not that I've any idea where I'd have kept them.

His fingers grip my jaw firmly and he uses his hold to tilt my head, giving him better access as he brushes his lips over the column of my neck. His arm tightens around me, pressing me firmly against the hard planes of his torso as he grinds his erect dick into my ass.

He sucks and licks his way up my neck, his hand pushing under the waistband of my boxers—*his* boxers—until he slides his fingers through my wetness, groaning as he discovers how turned-on I am. I'm completely fucking soaked for him.

He bites my earlobe at the same time he pushes two fingers inside me, the combination eliciting a low moan as I grind down on his hand, my head falling back against his chest.

"You're so tight, baby," he groans. "So fucking wet for me."

"All for you," I breathe as he presses his thumb against my clit, and I buck wildly against him, chasing that high I can feel catapulting toward me.

"Beck," I pant, feeling the telltale hot, tingly feeling sweeping over me.

"Come for me, baby. Show me how fucking good I can make you feel."

Just as I go to scream out my release, he uses his grip on my chin to tug my lips to his, swallowing my cries as ecstasy radiates out from my pussy, washing over me, and I collapse against him.

My lips move passionately over his, our tongues sliding along one another as he pulls his hand out of my boxers, turning me, so we're chest to chest. His hand slides around from my neck to fist my ponytail, holding me still as he devours my mouth.

His body pushes against mine, forcing me to take a step back, then another, until I'm pressed against the cold cement of the rec center.

Breaking our kiss, he licks along my jaw, sucking on that sensitive spot behind my ear before trailing a hot path down my neck to my shoulder, then he runs his tongue over the scar along my collarbone before kissing his way down my chest.

His hands brush over the curve of my breasts, thumbs grazing my peaked nipples which are screaming for attention. Attention that he gratefully gives them, twisting them through the fabric of my bra.

His mouth moves to lick my nipple over my bra before he sucks it into his mouth, my eyes drifting shut as I moan my delight. Moving to the other, he gives it the same attention before bending down in front of me, licking and sucking his way down my abdomen to the waistband of my boxers.

Oh fuck, he's going to deliver on his promise, and I am so here for it.

I should probably give a shit about the fact we're getting hot and heavy out in the open for anyone to see, but that rational thought is a quiet voice, barely more than a whisper, at the back of my head. One that's quickly snuffed out as Beck hooks his fingers under my waistband and slowly pulls the boxers down over my hips and thighs until they're curved around my ankles, and I can step out of them.

With wide eyes, he stares at my pussy as he licks his lips, seeming like a man starved. *Well, who am I to deny him such a meal?*

"Spread your legs, baby." His words come out in a low husk flooded with lust, and I quickly do as he says, his lip quirking at my obedience.

His eyes never leave the promised land as he leans in, flicking his tongue between my pussy lips as he licks me from cunt to clit.

"Fuck, Beck," I moan, my hands tangling in his hair.

He laps at me before circling his tongue around my clit, his hands gripping my ass cheeks as he pulls me closer against him, holding me still while he sucks my sensitive nub into his mouth.

Oh, mother of mercy, that is next-level shit.

His tongue slides down, and he drives it into me, tongue-fucking me exactly as he promised while his ministrations cause my breaths to come out in quick pants. Lifting a hand, I squeeze my heavy tit, kneading the skin and twerking the nipple until I feel myself constricting around his tongue. Just as I'm about to detonate, he pinches my clit between his fingers, the sharp sting catapulting me into oblivion as I cry out, unable to hold it back.

My body sags against the wall as he laps up my juices, moaning like it's the best damn thing he's ever tasted. Helping me step back into my boxers, he pulls them up my legs and gets to his feet. The second he's standing in front of me, I wrap my arms around his neck and dig my fingers into the back of his scalp as I press up onto my toes, slamming my mouth against his.

It's a clash of teeth as I struggle to satisfy the need to get closer to him, sucking and biting at his lips in a frenzy. His pelvis grinds against mine, his jeans doing nothing to hide the python in his pants.

Grabbing his shoulders, I spin him around, pushing him back against the wall like he did with me. Running my hands down over his top, I slip them underneath, feeling his heated flesh under my palms and groaning as his muscles flex under my touch.

I stroke my way down to his jeans and hastily pop the button, shimmying them and his boxers over his ass just enough to pull out his hard length. Running my hand along it, I swipe my thumb through the bead of precum, smearing it over his sensitive flesh.

He jerks into my hand, groaning at the pressure as I give him several hard, firm pumps before falling to my knees in front of him.

He grunts, his pupils blown with need. "Oh, baby, you don't need to do that," he groans, but despite his words, every other part of him is telling me he wants this just as much as I do.

"I want to," I reassure him. "I need to taste you. I need to feel you deep in my mouth, with your cum spilling down my throat."

He gets a feral look in his eyes as his hands thread through my hair, practically pushing my lips over his dick.

Parting them, I slide my tongue over his tip, his moan of encouragement driving me on as I suck him further into my mouth, my tongue working him over.

"Oh fuck, Hadley. You feel fucking incredible. You look amazing with my dick buried in your mouth."

Blushing at his praise, I pull back, bobbing up and down on him until he loses the last of his restraint. His hands fist in my hair, holding me still as his hips piston forward, driving him deeper into my mouth. I struggle not to gag, but I focus on relaxing my jaw, and when he thrusts in again and manages to go even deeper, he hits the back of my throat.

Tears well up in my eyes, but I blink them away, not wanting them to obscure my vision as I gaze up at him through my eyelashes. His face is relaxed, his eyes boring into mine, silently saying sweet nothings that are in complete contrast to the way he's using me right now as he moves faster and faster, chasing his impending orgasm.

Raising a hand up to cup his balls, he groans, his cock swelling in my mouth just before his hot seed hits the back of my throat and I swallow it down.

He slowly pulls out, tucking himself away before helping me to my feet. His eyes are glued to my swollen lips as he leans in, kissing me gently, almost reverently, like I'm the most fragile thing he's ever held.

Hadley

CHAPTER FIVE

With a final searing kiss just out of sight from the partygoers, I leave Beck behind and head off in search of Emilia. It's definitely been way longer than the fifteen-twenty minutes it should have taken me to find the toilet and get back again.

Pushing my way through the students, the music from the band practically deafens me. I freeze when I spot Emilia talking to none other than Mason Hayes. *What the fuck is he doing here? And why is he talking to Emilia?* Picking up my pace, I sprint toward them, flexing my fists in preparation to get him to back off. Those assholes came between us once, and I won't fucking let them do it again.

As I approach, Emilia throws her head back and laughs at something Mason says. Motherfucking laughs. At Mason. Mason doesn't make jokes. Mason doesn't even smile. The only time I've seen him even halfway smile was when I throat-punched Hawk in the ring.

Warily, I approach them, and Emilia turns to smile at me. "Hey girl, I was beginning to wonder where you disappeared off to."

"Sorry, long line," I mumble, my gaze darting between her and Mason.

"I just came over to ask if you both wanted to join us in the VIP section." Using his thumb, he points over his shoulder at the tent I saw earlier with the Mason-like bodyguard.

"Ahh, no, I do—"

"Yes," Emilia squeals over the top of me, clapping her hands together. "We'd love to. Wouldn't we, Hadley?" She turns to face me, the smile still lighting up her face as she pins me with a pointed look.

"Uh, yeah. Absolutely," I say, with zero enthusiasm, giving her a quizzical look.

Mason gives me an easy smile which I return with a frown and a look that says if he's fucking with either of us, I'm going to castrate him with a fucking melon baller. Ignoring my glare, like the insufferable shithead he is, he turns on his heel, heading toward the VIP section.

Emilia makes a move to follow him, but I snap out my hand, grabbing a hold of her arm.

"What's going on?" I demand, leaning in so I can hear her.

"Nothing." She shrugs like this isn't the weirdest fucking thing ever. "He came over a few minutes ago, wondering where you were and asked if we wanted to join them in the VIP section."

"And you want to?" I stare at her, completely baffled.

She gives me another infuriating shrug. "I'm not about to say no to the VIP section. He said the band would be there once they finished their set. Besides, it's your birthday, so you're a VIP as much as they are."

I really don't agree with her on that last point or understand why she would willingly suffer their presence to get close to a band, but whatever. If she wants to go trotting into the lion's den, then that's what we'll do.

Following Mason, the bodyguard doesn't blink an eye as we step past him. Mason pulls aside the slit in the tent and gestures for us to go in ahead of him. Walking inside, the tent is dimly lit with fairy lights strung across the roof and fire-like heaters placed around the ample, enclosed space. One side has been rolled up, leaving an unobstructed view of the stage. It's a much better view than we had from outside, and we're far enough away that we don't have to yell at one another to be heard.

Which is why I hear him the second he sees Emilia and me in his space.

"What the hell is *she* doing here?" Hawk snarks in his usual hostile tone, directing my attention toward him and the other two Pricks. All three of them are sprawled across large, comfortable-looking seats while a couple of women wearing next-to-nothing dance around a stripper pole situated at the far side of the tent in front of a small bar. Another scantily clad woman approaches the guys with a tray full of drinks which she sets down on a table between them. As she saunters away, swaying her hips seductively, she trails her fingers up Cam's arm, and he gives her a flirty smirk that has me rolling my eyes and ignoring the she-beast inside me that wants to tear the bitch's hair off.

Feeling eyes on me, I turn to look at West, just in time to watch his tongue run along his lower lip in a hot-as-hell move. His eyes roam over my long legs and toned abdomen, eating me up. Holy fuck, the carnal need in his eyes has my body humming.

"Drop it, man." Mason sighs. "She has as much right to be here as you do."

Whether he's referring to the fact it's my birthday, or that I'm a Davenport, I'm not sure. Regardless, his comment about me belonging only has Hawk's lip curling back as he sneers at me. I must admit that the thought of me belonging here with them leaves me with mixed feelings. A voice in my head screams *no fucking way*. I'm not one of them. I don't belong in this uppity class where everyone seems to think they can demand whatever they want. Yet, a part of me has to admit that it feels right, like this is where I always should have been. Clearly, that part of me has lost her fucking marbles, so I shove her back into the dark recesses of my mind and ignore her.

"Can I get either of you drinks?" Mason asks cordially as he steps toward the bar.

"I'll take a vodka and cranberry, please," Emilia responds, sounding more subdued and nervous than before we came in here. *Yup, I bet she's regretting that decision right about now.*

"Water for me," I respond.

Nodding, he goes off to get our drinks, and I grab Emilia's hand and tug her toward the seats, ignoring the three assholes following our every move. We're here now, and I'm not about to let them run us out.

The seats are laid out in a large semi-circle, all facing the stage, so I lead us to the ones furthest from where the guys are, sitting down and getting comfy as I ignore them muttering beside us.

"Oh my god," Emilia breathes, her eyes glued to the lead singer. "This is amazing. Isn't he just lickable?"

I laugh, letting my eyes roam over him. He's definitely hot, with his ripped jeans and dark hair, not to mention the myriad of tattoos on display, giving him that bad-boy image.

"Totally," I agree, just as Mason approaches with our drinks. He hands Emilia her glass and me a bottle before sitting in the chair beside mine so he can still interact with the guys beside us, but can also talk to Emilia and me.

Unscrewing the lid, I take a large gulp, the cold liquid only mildly easing the heat I can still feel from West's passionate look, as I try to ignore the crackle in the air zinging between myself and Mason.

No, libido. He's an asshole—a hot, sexy-as-sin, domineering asshole that I bet could have a woman screaming all night.

I squeeze my thighs together, my thoughts unwillingly drifting back to that tingling kiss I shared with Mason and wondering how much more explosive things between us could be.

No!

Jesus, what is wrong with me? I was just screaming Beck's name not even twenty minutes ago, and now I'm hot and bothered all over again. I swear, my vagina turns into such a slut around these guys.

"Are you a fan?" Mason asks, gesturing with his head toward the stage as he leans into me so no one around us can eavesdrop on our conversation.

"Yeah." I shrug, trying to focus on his words and not the scent of his aftershave—an unusual combination of citrus and spice. I swear I can practically taste the grapefruit and bergamot, swirling with hints of cinnamon and chilli. The mixture suits him perfectly and has my thoughts falling back into the gutter once again. It encompasses his strength and resilience but also the uncharacteristic moments of softness he's shown that seem so at odds with the uncaring, cold exterior he portrays. "They seem good."

"Good?" He chuckles. "They're number one in the charts right now."

My eyes widen at his words. *Damn, that's impressive.*

He tilts his head, reading something on my face. "You don't know who they are, do you?"

"No, I've never heard of them." I may as well be honest about it; he's evidently already deduced as much.

Looking at me, I can see the questions in his eyes. Before he can ask any of them though, I blurt out, "If they're that famous, how were you able to get them to agree to perform at a teenager's birthday party?"

For a second, he doesn't respond, continuing to watch me closely. "We can get pretty much anything we want," he eventually answers.

Something about the way he says it has me asking, "What can't you get?"

"The one thing we all really need—freedom."

I can see the truth in his eyes, how trapped he feels, how suffocating the weight of it is. What I don't understand is how he can feel so imprisoned. They have all the money in the world. If that doesn't buy freedom, what does?

Whether or not I understand the reason behind it, I recognize the suffering in his eyes. I know that feeling, that clawing need to escape. While the thought of freedom can empower you, knowing you'll never experience it is stifling. It can blow out the last flicker of hope, leaving you alone in the darkness.

Looking into Mason's sky-blue eyes, they're darkened with grief over the loss of a future he believes he will never obtain. That flame of hope is weak and dies a little every day. It's only a matter of time before a light breeze blows it out completely. What will happen to him then? When there's no hope left to fight for?

"Mason." Hawk's warning tone pulls Mason's attention from me as he glances over at him.

"What?" Mason snaps, his tone surprising me, and apparently Hawk, if the raising of his eyebrows is anything to go by.

"I hear you have a pet baby chick," I say sweetly to Hawk, cutting off whatever biting remark he was about to fire.

Everyone turns to look at me, confusion etched across their features.

"What?" Mason asks, turning his head to look at me.

"Dude, what is she talking about?" Cam looks at Hawk.

Hawk's eyes darken, and his jaw ticks as he attempts to shoot me dead with his glare.

"You didn't tell your friends about her?" I pout. "That's not very nice."

"What are you going on about?" West asks, his gaze darting between Hawk and me.

"His pet baby chick," I reiterate with a tone that says *duh*. "I hear she's been keeping you up at night with all her chirping."

A sly grin crosses my face as Hawk jumps to his feet, striding toward me. "Shut. Up," he snarls venomously.

Mason is immediately on his feet, his arm outstretched as his palm connects with Hawk's chest, pushing him back. All the while I sit there, relaxed as a cucumber, smiling sweetly up at Hawk, unfazed by his aggressive stance and threatening eyes.

"Dude, chill out," Mason warns. "What's going on?"

"That *bitch*," Hawk sneers, "put some sort of recording device in my room, and every fucking night it plays a chirping noise, but I can't fucking find it anywhere."

I suck my lips between my teeth, forcing myself not to burst out laughing. I've been sneaking in every other day to move the device to a new hiding spot, and I only play it a few times during the night to piss him off, but not enough to have him tearing his room apart...yet.

Cam has no issue holding back his laughter as it bursts out. "That's fucking hilarious," he gasps, clutching his stomach as he wipes away a stray tear. Seeing him laughing like that has me captivated, unable to look away. It's been so long since I've seen him laugh. I fucking miss it.

Emilia cracks up beside me, laughing just as hard as Cam, nudging me with her elbow. "That's genius, girl."

West joins in too, and even Mason releases a small chuckle at Hawk's expense. All of us laughing does nothing to calm Hawk nonetheless, his anger only escalating until he explodes.

I give him an innocent shrug. "Just making up for lost time, *brother*."

I have no idea what shit normal siblings get up to, but this is the dynamic Hawk has created for us, and I can't deny I love knowing I'm the reason for the throbbing vein in his forehead right now.

"It's not fucking funny," he roars, glaring at his friends before storming out of the tent.

Meh, whatever. If he wants to have a hissy fit over it, that's his problem.

With the threat gone, Mason lowers his large frame back into the seat beside me, Cam and Emilia still chuckling away. As their laughing eases off, the tension grows in the air, and none of us know how to react around one another.

The last time I was around any of them, I was in the midst of a panic attack. The whole reason I've been avoiding them all week is so they wouldn't ask me any questions. Nerves take flight in my stomach, worried they might bring up the conversation now, though I don't think they would in front of Emilia.

Leaning in, Emilia murmurs, "I've, uh, gotta go to the bathroom. Will you be okay?" *Well, there goes that idea that they won't say anything in front of her.* I nod, letting her know I'll be fine, even though the thudding of my heart ratchets up, and my stomach churns at the thought of being left alone with all three of them as she gets to her feet and leaves the tent.

And then there were four.

Silence reigns supreme between us. Even the music from the band seems more distant, swallowed up by the thick layer of everything that's happened straining between us.

I lick my lips nervously, and I swear all three of them track the movement with searing, heated stares. *Whoa!* Even Cam, although he does it with a scowl on his face, one that deepens, as though he's annoyed with himself for his reaction.

"Hadley," West begins, and I just know what he's about to say.

"No," I fire out before he can say anything further. "We're not talking about the other day, and I'm not telling you anything about me or my life."

Cam's brows furrow in annoyance, and I can see he's about to say something dickish.

"How would any of you like it if I pried into your lives, asking questions you weren't comfortable answering? Why don't we talk about you guys; your childhoods, your families, your deep, dark secrets."

All three of them grimace at the thought of that. Maybe they finally fucking realize how intrusive they've been. If they aren't comfortable telling me things about themselves, why should they expect anything different from me?

"Exactly. You want to know things about me? Wanna know who I am? Try getting to fucking know me."

I jump to my feet, having said my piece, and storm over to the edge of the tent, keeping my back to the infuriating assholes behind me as I cross my arms over my chest and watch the band perform on stage.

Standing there, I listen to them playing several songs, and as the latest one comes to a close, I feel a presence behind me, just before West murmurs in my ear.

"Can I talk to you? Alone."

"Wes," I sigh wearily.

"It's not about that, I promise. I just want to talk."

Looking at him over my shoulder, he gives me a small, shy smile—reminding me of the boy who would sit and talk me through my computer lessons—which has me caving too easily.

"Yeah, okay."

His smile grows more prominent, reaching his eyes as he steps past me, brushing his arm against mine and causing goosebumps to erupt over my skin.

He tilts his head for me to follow him and, after a second's hesitation, I comply in following him as he walks away from the party toward the forest.

Stepping past the treeline, we walk in silence for a beat until the noise of the band is nothing but low background music, and you can barely see the lights from the party through the thick density of the trees.

I can hardly make him out in the darkness, just discerning his outline, until he flicks on his phone light, casting a yellow glow around us.

"I, uh, wanted to give you this," he says sheepishly, holding out a small box with a bow wrapped around it.

Looking between him and the offered box, I've no idea what to make of it.

"What is it?" I ask in a quiet voice, my eyes on the inconspicuous box as I hesitantly reach out to take it.

"A birthday present."

My eyes raise to meet his, my suddenly dry mouth preventing any words from getting out.

Slowly looking back down at the box, I pull the ribbon to unravel it and lift off the lid. Inside, there's a beautiful silver necklace. A delicate link chain with a heart hanging from the end. It's refined and gorgeous, and I can't help running my fingers over it.

"It's beautiful," I whisper, unable to take my eyes off it.

"Here." West moves closer to me. "Let me put it on you."

Carefully, he lifts the necklace out of the box, handing me his phone before I turn around. Draping it over my neck, he fastens the clasp at the back, gently turning me back to face him.

"I wasn't sure what to get you," he murmurs, his fingers fixing the heart so it sits perfectly. "But I saw this, and I couldn't stop picturing you wearing it."

"It's beautiful," I whisper once again.

He lifts his eyes from the necklace to meet mine, his fingers tucking a stray strand of hair behind my ears. "You're beautiful."

God, what is this boy doing to me?

West and I don't know each other well. I probably know him the least out of all the guys, but he's always been the sweetest.

His thumb glides softly down my cheek, his hand cupping my jaw, and *god*, do I want him to kiss me right now. Instead, he drops his hand. I sigh and take a small step away. What are these guys doing to me? I have Beck...shouldn't that be enough?

"There's a party at the Davenport's tomorrow night, for Hawk," he begins, his words killing the moment. "I was wondering if you'd like to go with me?"

"Why?" Suspicion coats my tone. Why would he even suggest that? Does he not remember what he and the others did to me last semester? Why would I want to go anywhere with them, never mind the Davenport house, of all places?

He shrugs his shoulders. "I just thought you might want to see where you should have grown up and meet your parents...They don't know who you are," he quickly tacks on, probably seeing the look of terror on my face. "I understand if you don't want to go, but I thought I'd offer in case you were interested."

I can't deny I'm not intrigued. Curious about the house where I spent the first few years of my life, the house I *should* know like the back of my hand, where I should have spent my childhood. Not to mention the parents that spawned me. Did they give me away? I have so many questions about them. I told Beck I'd stay here, despite the threat of Lawrence, because I had to know more about my family. This would be my shot.

"Okay," I agree, before I can change my mind. "I'll go."

An easy smile graces West's lips. "Okay. I'll pick you up at seven."

I nod, and, after a moment's hesitation when he doesn't say anything else as he looks at me intently. I assume we're done and turn to head back toward the party, except he grabs onto my arm, spinning me back around as his hand cups the back of my head. His other one grips firmly to my hip as his lips descend on mine, moving confidently as he licks along the seam, demanding entry.

My hands come up of their own accord to rest on his shoulders, my fingers digging into his skin as my lips part beneath him, and his tongue dips in to taste me. The whole thing is so out of character for the shy, reserved West I know, but *ohmygod*, his dominance shouldn't be this much of a huge fucking turn-on. And his lips...Mmmm, I need to feel them all over my heated skin.

I moan, and he quickly swallows it, his lips moving over mine as his tongue takes its time exploring. My body is flush against his, loving the feel of him pressing up against me as he pillages my mouth.

When he breaks off the kiss, he stays holding me in place with his face inches from mine as we both catch our breaths.

"Wear the dark green dress I got you," he whispers in a dogmatic tone that has me instinctively nodding in compliance before I even realize what I've agreed to.

Pressing one last punishing kiss to my lips, he grabs my hand and drags me out of the forest. I'm honestly too stunned to do anything other than follow him blindly back to the party, my mind replaying that kiss on repeat the whole way.

Hadley

CHAPTER SIX

By the time we return to the party, the guys' current girls of the month have joined them.

Oh, yay, now it's a celebration.

Since I skipped breakfast on Monday and classes for most of the week, I haven't had to watch them with any of the girls. My jealous she-bitch is raising her ugly head when we step back into the VIP section, and I see some floozy pressing her obviously fake tits up against Mason. For a few months last year, he seemed to have a type—blonde and athletic—but this month, he's gone for the total opposite. Mercedes is tall and stick thin, with long black hair that hangs down to her ass. Mason doesn't appear to be paying her any attention, though, as he sips his drink and taps away on his phone.

Unable to stand watching them any longer without storming over there—a reaction that concerns me, for I definitely should not be feeling territorial over that asshole. I glance away, my eyes landing on Hawk at the bar. Two girls are vying for his attention. Attention he appears to be more than happy to give them.

Seeing us, one of the girls—I'm pretty sure her name is Kendra—jumps away from him, adjusting her boobs in her skin-tight dress—no boots and boxers for her apparently—before sauntering over to us, swinging her hips, and licking her lips like she thinks she's hot shit.

"West, baby," she purrs when she approaches us, dragging her nails down the front of his shirt. "I wondered where you disappeared off to."

Finally noticing me standing beside him, she glances my way, her gaze dropping down my body as a sneer curls at the corner of her lips. "You didn't have to go off with her." She sulks, her lower lip pushing out. "I'll give you anything you want."

"No need," I assure her with a sweet ass smile on my face. "I sorted him out."

I swear I hear West chuckle as Kendra snickers at me, but when I glance at him out of the corner of my eye, he's piercing me with a stern look, clearly telling me not to stir shit up.

Me? I would never.

"He's not yours," she snarls, stepping threateningly toward me. West's arm whips out, halting her progress.

"I'm not yours either," he growls at her, fixing her with a vicious look. "I believe I'm free to do whatever I want."

"Oh…of course," Kendra quickly agrees, her eyes wide as she nods her head.

"Apologize to Hadley," West demands.

"But I didn't do anything," she whines.

"Apologize." The word is barely more than a growl, West's face hardening with every passing second that she doesn't do what he ordered.

Looking my way, she doesn't look or sound the slightest bit apologetic, not that I give a shit, as she mumbles a sorry.

"Good, now get the fuck out of here," West barks. She stumbles away from us, practically tripping over her heels in her haste to escape West's ire.

"Wow." I slowly release a breath, unable to tear my eyes away from him. It's fucked up that his aggression turns me all the way on, right? Oh hell, who gives a shit? It's crazy hot. "I don't know why, but I always forget your demons are as dark and depraved as the others."

His hand comes to rest low on my hip, his thumb dipping below the waistband of my boxers, the sensual touch making me gasp. His other hand comes up to grab my jaw, tilting my head up so he can stare deep into my eyes, getting a read on me before he smirks.

"Does my demon turn you on?" He chuckles, leaning in closer so our mouths are a hair's breadth apart. The heat of his breath hits my lips with his next words. "You want me to be rough with you, baby? Throw you around the bedroom and pin you beneath me?" His voice is a husky rasp that goes straight to my clit and sets it on fire.

Oh fuck, yes, please. Sign me up.

Releasing his hold on my jaw, he trails his lips over my cheek until he reaches my ear, whispering, "All you have to do is beg."

Too afraid to say anything in case nothing but a dirty moan escapes, I stand and stare at him like a horny idiot as he gives my hip a final squeeze, slipping his thumb out and striding away.

"Girl, you okay? I got worried when I came back and you were gone," Emilia says, walking over to me. I didn't even realize she was here. "Did something happen with West?"

"Huh? No, nothing. Sorry. You having fun?"

Before she can reply, I hear our names being called. Looking around, Mason is striding toward us.

"Come meet Axel and the boys," he says, jerking his head behind us. Turning, I see the band coming this way. Huh, I hadn't even realized they'd stopped playing.

All three of them look like sin. The guy on the far left has long brown hair tied up in a top knot. His shirt is tucked in the back pocket of his dark jeans, showing off his toned chest, dotted with colorful splashes of ink, and he's absently twirling a drumstick between his fingers.

I recognize the guy beside him as the lead singer. Holy hell, I thought he looked hot on stage, but as he strides toward us, he looks even better. Arrogant confidence oozes off of him with every swagger of his hips. This guy knows he's hot shit. His dirty blond hair is sticking up all over the place. I'm not sure whether that's his style or sweat causing it to sit that way, but the mussed look only adds to his overall sex appeal.

The final guy has dirty red hair and stubble on his face. He's got what looks like a fresh t-shirt on, not a drop of sweat on it, and a dark scowl on his face as he approaches, seeming like he'd rather be anywhere but here.

"Oh my god," Emilia squeaks beside me, practically bouncing in her heels as she wraps her hand around mine in a death grip to tug me toward them, with Mason on my other side.

"Hey, guys," Mason calls out. "Great show."

"Thanks, man." The lead singer smiles warmly at Mason, the two of them sharing a slap-on-the-back bro hug thing before separating.

"Guys, this is my friend Hadley and Emilia. This is Axel." Mason gestures to the lead singer. "And this is Jared and Foster." He indicates the guy on the left, then the right.

"Hey," I greet, giving them a wave.

"Hi," Emilia chirps, her cheeks flaming red as their eyes fall on her. Various expressions range from humor to lust to indifference as they take her in. Interesting.

"You guys sound amazing," I tell them, taking the attention away from her. I can feel her palm sweating in mine and I have to hold back my laughter.

"Thanks." Axel gives me an easy smile. "You a fan?"

"Umm…"

"Hadley here is a newbie." Mason laughs, throwing his arm around my shoulders. Now it's my cheeks that flame red.

"Oh, cool." Although Jared sounds surprised, he doesn't act as though it's weird that I've never heard of them. "It's not often we get to meet someone who isn't a die-hard fan. It's refreshing."

I give him a grateful smile.

"I'm sure you guys are thirsty," Mason says, playing host. "There's a bar in the tent. Go help yourselves."

"Thanks, man." Axel gives Mason a slap on his shoulder. "It's great seeing you. Let's catch up before we have to leave later."

"Sure thing," Mason agrees.

"Wanna show us the way to the bar, sweet thing?" Jared asks Emilia, his eyes eating her up as she gapes, utterly starstruck, at him.

When she doesn't respond, I subtly nudge her with my elbow, causing her to jump.

"Huh? Oh yeah…yes. I'd love to."

Jared has a shit-eating grin on his face, and Axel looks at her with an expression I can't place as they step to either side of her. Jared throws his arm casually over her shoulder in a similar gesture to Mason's as they walk back toward the tent.

I turn to watch them go, dislodging Mason's arm from my shoulders. Emilia glances back at me over her shoulder, her eyes wide with excitement and nerves, and a huge grin plastered to her face. I chuckle at her.

Damn, girl might just get lucky tonight with a rockstar.

"She looks like she just woke up in her favorite fantasy." Mason chuckles beside me.

"Thanks for doing that for her," I say. "How do you know them anyway?"

"Axel's family and mine are friends. He spent a lot of time with the guys and me when we were kids."

My eyebrows lift in surprise. "How did he end up in a rock band, then? It doesn't exactly fit in with the whole wealthy, 'grew up with a gold-plated spoon in my mouth' vibe I get from the rich assholes here."

Mason lets out a deep rumble, his shoulders shaking with unrestrained laughter.

"Yeah, no, he kinda broke the mold," he says in a wistful tone, growing serious once again. "He's been crowned the black sheep of his family." He doesn't expand, and I don't push. It's not any of my business, even though I can't understand how parents could turn their back on their son just because he chose a career that wasn't what they wanted for him. "You know, technically, you're one of those rich assholes now," Mason informs me, changing the subject.

"Ha, yeah, I don't think so," I retort, shaking my head.

"How are you doing with all of that anyway?" His voice is soft and understanding as I sense his eyes on me.

"Okay, I guess." I shrug, unsure of how to respond to that. I mean, what is someone in my shoes supposed to say?

"I'm sure you have questions."

I snort. "Yeah, you could say that." Looking up at him, I blurt out, "West invited me to Hawk's party tomorrow night."

His eyes widen, and I suddenly need to know what his opinion is on the matter. Am I making a mistake by going?

"What did you say?"

"I said yes. I guess I'm…curious."

He nods his head. "That's understandable. I don't know if you'll get the answers you want, but you deserve to see the life you should have had."

The life I should have had…fuck, I can't even imagine what that looks like. I don't get the chance to ask him anything more, although I'm not sure I want to know anything about my parents or their life.

"Mason," Hawk shouts, "What are you doing, man? Come on."

"Yeah, I'll be right there," Mason calls back. The fact he isn't immediately jumping into action has Hawk scowling at me, but I flip him the bird and he stomps off.

"You two certainly know how to get under each other's skin." Mason chuckles, taking a step toward the tent. "You coming?" he asks, watching me when I don't make a move to follow him.

"I think I'm done," I reply, suddenly feeling exhausted. "I'm gonna call it a night."

His eyes search my face before he nods. "Do you want me to walk you back to your dorm?"

"No." I snort. "I can get there on my own."

He shakes his head, a small smile curling at the corner of his lips. "I don't doubt it. Just being a gentleman."

I raise an eyebrow. "Since when have you been a gentleman?"

Huffing out a laugh, he shakes his head and says, "See ya later, Little Warrior," before walking away.

I stand and watch him as he heads back to the tent, trying to make sense of everything. Mason has a closed-off exterior, never giving anything away, but he's let his guard down somewhat tonight. Most of the time we're around one another, we pretend the other isn't there. However, over the last few months, there have been moments—when he caught me sneaking into their apartment after I beat Hawk, and the other day—when I've felt like he and I are one and the same.

I still have no idea what he's thinking or where he stands, in any case. Same with West. At least I know Hawk and Cam hate me, but West and Mason only leave me confused. They don't seem to hate me. If anything, the way they look at me, how it felt when I kissed them, I'd say they might actually like me. But the fact they mindlessly go along with Hawk and back up whatever stupid shit he says and does pisses me off.

I'm not going to figure any of it out tonight. I'll just have to wait and see how things play out this semester. While I've really only targeted Hawk for the video so far—I'm pretty sure he's the primary culprit of that fiasco—I've no issues going after all of them if they pull any of the shit they did last semester.

I lift my phone out of my boxers, firing off a quick text to Emilia to let her know I'm leaving so she doesn't worry.

Choosing to walk back to the dorms along the back of the tents instead of trying to push my way through the crowd, still partying hard to what sounds like a DJ, I walk carefully along the treeline of the forest, enjoying having a moment alone for the first time all night.

I've just reached the rec center when I feel it. Eyes on me. It's a feeling that has been gnawing at me all week. Glancing subtly around, I don't see anyone, yet I can feel them nearby. The hairs at the back of my neck stand on end, and that, combined with that intuitive feeling of being watched, is enough for me to know something isn't right. Whoever this fucker is, they've been watching me all week and tonight might be the night they finally make their move.

It's possible it's just Hawk being a dick and trying to scare me, but I didn't see or hear anyone leave the VIP area behind me. I bend down pretending to tie my shoelace as I slip a switchblade I keep in my boot into my hand, flick it open, and listen intently for any sounds around me. Remaining vigilant, I continue walking back toward the dorm, ensuring I act normal, not wanting to warn this asshole that I'm on to him.

I decide to keep walking along the treeline, hoping that will draw him out rather than heading to the main path where I know I'd be safer—what good will that do me if some fucker is hiding in the woods watching and waiting for the right opportunity to strike?

Honestly, I've been expecting this since Monday. It was only a matter of time. If anything, I'm surprised someone hasn't shown up sooner. I've been on high alert all week, waiting for this moment. Paranoia has become my constant friend, and it seems I'm about to be proven right, as I hear a faint rustle in the woods beside me.

Another stretch of silence as I take my time. I've just reached the boys' dorms when a snap infiltrates the air, a twig breaking beneath someone's heavy boot. Dear, dear, someone forgot all of their training. He must be a newb. I'm going to be seriously fucking offended if Lawrence thought I'd be that easy to wrangle.

Knowing his cover's been blown, a black shadow rushes out of the woods. A large, muscular body slams into me, sending the two of us rolling across the grass as we grapple for the upper hand. I hold tightly to the switchblade and, as we come to a stop, him hovering over me with a confident grin on his face, I slam the blade into his side.

I vaguely remember his face. I've seen him around over the years, although I don't know anything about him. Not who he is or how he ended up stuck in the same hellhole as me.

I smirk up at him as the fucker grunts in pain. Bringing my head up, I smash my forehead into his face, ignoring the pain as I shove him off me and yank the knife out of his side, not even giving a fuck that I'm getting blood all over myself. His job is to bring me in, but I bet he's been told to do it by any means necessary. Well, I'm sure as fuck not going to make it easy on him.

"Fuck, D," he rasps. "I heard you were good."

I rattle my head, trying to remember his name, except there were so many of us and he was several years behind me. When I left, his age group was only just being allowed out on jobs this challenging.

"This is your only warning," I growl. "Get the fuck out of here."

He gets to his feet, shaking his head. "You know I can't do that."

Fuck. Yeah, I do know.

He rushes me, attempting to use his size and weight to tackle me to the ground, all while trying to grab a hold of my wrist and wrestle the knife out of my hand.

Ducking low at the last second, my shoulder connects with his gut, sending him flying over the top of me and he lands on his back on the grass, a whoosh of breath escaping him. He's quick to scramble to his feet, but I don't give him the chance to come at me again. I deliver a roundhouse kick, my foot connecting with the side of his head, knocking him sideways as I move in closer. Kicking out again, this time at his knee, I hear the satisfying snap as the cartilage tears, his leg buckling beneath his weight as he drops to the ground.

"Fuck," he hisses, although he's not down yet.

A dark laugh leaves him as he fights through the pain, once again getting to his feet.

"Damn, I knew you'd be an excellent match. I think I'll reward myself when I beat your ass." His eyes drop down over my half-naked body, the gleam in his eye making nausea churn in my stomach.

So much for trying to convince him to run. They've undoubtedly stripped away any humanity he had.

Adjusting my stance and pushing my shoulders back, I prepare to go again. This time, when he comes at me, he manages to deliver a solid blow to my midsection, winding me as I fight to get free of his tight grip on my arm. Spinning around in his hold, a move that has me pressed up against him instead of pulling away like he's expecting, I stab the knife into his side and back repeatedly. His grunts echo in my ears as he tries to push me off him. By the time he succeeds, he's bleeding profusely and my body is slick with his blood.

"You bitch," he snarls, stepping toward me. However the blood loss, combined with his damaged knee, has him stumbling and once again crashing to the ground.

Keeping a safe distance, I slowly circle him. Coming up behind him, I yank on his short, dark hair, pulling his head back to look at me and exposing his neck.

"I may be a bitch, but I'm the last thing you're going to see." I slash the knife along his throat, blood streaming like a river down over the base of his neck and soaking into his black top as his face turns ashen.

I watch apathetically as the life dims in his eyes, flickering before it finally extinguishes, his body sagging. Letting go of my hold on his hair, he sinks to the ground.

Fuck, now I have to get rid of him before anyone notices a dead fucking body.

Wiping the knife on his trousers, I tuck it back in my boot. Grabbing him by the legs, I wrap my arms around them and slowly drag him into the forest, all the while trying to decide what to do with him. I'll have to move quickly. It's getting late, and it's only a matter of time before students start filtering back to the dorms.

Once I've hauled him deep enough into the forest that I don't think anyone will accidentally come across him, I leave him there, running through the trees as quickly as I can in the dark back toward the rec center. There is a small gardening shed down there and I can only hope it has what I need.

The sounds of the party get louder the closer I get. Once I reach the shed, I glance around, checking that the coast is clear, then jimmy the lock and slip inside. Locating a wheelbarrow, some plastic sheeting that looks like it's used for landscaping, and a bunch of rope, I check my surroundings again before sneaking outside and rushing away, all while pushing the how-to-hide-a-dead-body supplies over the grass back toward the now dead asshole.

Dumping his body in the wheelbarrow, not giving a shit that I'm not showing the dead any respect—if he wanted respect, he shouldn't have jumped me—I stick as close to the treeline as I can in the hopes the dark shadows will be enough to hide me if anyone just so happens to peer out their dorm window.

I only relax slightly once I've made it past the dorms, navigating slowly over the uneven floor of the forest to get to the lake. Sweat is dripping down my back, and I'm exhausted by the time I make it to the boathouse on the far side.

The door to the boathouse is unlocked and it creaks open when I tug at it. I push the wheelbarrow inside and close the door behind me, sighing in relief that I made it this far.

I fish out my phone from my boxers—which miraculously survived the fight—and turn on the flashlight app, searching around the boathouse. There's a small gas-engine boat and a similar-sized rowboat. The engine boat would be so much easier, but I risk being heard if I use it, so I wheel the dead body over beside the rowing boat.

Unrolling the sheet of plastic and dropping the rope on the floor beside me, I tip the body onto the sheet, positioning him so I'll be able to completely wrap him in the plastic. Glancing around, I'm reluctant to leave him, but fear that he won't sink out on the water has me rushing from the boathouse, scanning along the shore for any large rocks I can use to weigh him down. I grab as many as I can carry before heading back, placing them along his body so I can then wrap the plastic tight around him. Tying the rope around the plastic, sweat drips down my back as I roll him into the rowboat, where he lands with a solid thump.

I untie the boat from the dock and climb in. God, please don't let this rickety thing have a hole in it. I do not want to fucking drown in this goddamn lake. Grabbing hold of the oars, I row us out to the middle of the lake. When we are far enough from the shore, I lift one of the oars and stick it into the water to check how deep it is. When the bottom of the oar doesn't connect with the ground, I'm satisfied it's deep enough. Lifting it back into the boat, I cautiously shift around in the small space until I can lift the asshole up over the side without the risk of capsizing the damn thing.

His body splashes into the water, the boat rocking dangerously at the weight displacement. Clinging to the side, I'm unable to tear my eyes away as the body floats on the surface for what feels like forever.

Why isn't he sinking?!

Eventually, the body dips beneath the surface. It's quickly dragged down into the dark depths of the lake, and I collapse back onto the bottom of the boat, suddenly feeling so exhausted it's suffocating. I'm not sure how long I lie there, staring at the stars. Fuck, I can't believe I did that. I've never had to dispose of a body on the fly like that. Usually, I leave them behind as a calling card. If someone wants the body to disappear, then it's a carefully thought-out plan, not a spur-of-the-moment thing.

I finally find the strength to haul myself up and row back to the boathouse. Grabbing the wheelbarrow, I push it back to the treeline, where the forest separates the lake from the dorms. My skin is sticky with dried blood, and I can't risk being seen like this.

It will look weird enough that I'm walking around with a wheelbarrow in the middle of the night.

I walk back toward the lake, kicking off my boots and leaving my phone beside them, as I step over the sharp stones into the freezing cold water. Fuck, that's unpleasant. I walk in until the water comes up to my waist, bending down and using my hands to wash away the blood. Once I'm satisfied that my body is clean, I splash water on my face and neck, the cold water waking me up and rejuvenating me some. My clothes are soaked, but hey, better to look like a drowned rat than the victim of a massacre.

Not wanting to waste any more time, I shove my feet back in my boots, grab my phone and haul ass back to the wheelbarrow. Without the dead weight in it, it's much easier to traverse the rough forest with it—thank fuck—and I'm soon running along the smooth grass. I can hear students near the dorms now, making me think the party must be winding down. I'll have to be extra careful not to be seen.

Moving as quickly as I can, I rush past the dorms, then the rec center. The music has stopped, the noise replaced with drunken hoots and hollers. Once I reach the shed, I put the wheelbarrow back where I got it and slip out into the night again.

Just before I reach the dorms, I step out onto the path, looking like any other student heading back to the dorms. The ones around me seem too drunk to notice that I'm wet.

"Oh, someone went swimming." Some girl giggles, pointing at me. "We should go swimming! Let's go to the lake, guys," she yells, a round of cheers and shouts of agreement going up into the air. That's probably a terrible idea, given their drunken state right now, but whatever.

Finally making it back to my room without incident, I grab my stuff, needing a quick, warm shower, before I collapse into bed. Less than thirty minutes later, exhaustion claims me, and I pass out underneath the covers.

Hadley

CHAPTER SEVEN

I'm dead to the world the next morning when a loud thud rings out from my door.

"Girl, I know you're not hungover! Answer the damn door," Emilia shouts through the wood, following it up with another bang of her fist.

Groaning, I stumble out of bed and over to the door. Who knew the cure to insomnia was killing a guy and dragging his dead ass halfway across campus?

"You're just getting up?" Emilia gasps, when I let her in. "But you left so early."

"I was tired," I say vaguely, moving back to the bed and dropping down onto it. Muscles I didn't even know I had ache every time I move, and my side fucking hurts from that shitstain's punch. Noticing Emilia scrutinizing me, I ask, "How was the rest of your night?" in an attempt to distract her.

It clearly works as she collapses onto the bed with a dreamy look in her eye. "I think I'm in love." She sighs, making me laugh.

Oh, fuck, no. Don't laugh. That hurts. Painkillers. I need painkillers.

"With Axel?" I precariously lean back against my pillow, careful not to jostle my side.

"Yes…and Jared. And maybe Foster, but he's a grumpy ass."

"So, I take it things went well last night?" My eyebrows jump up and down in a saucy gesture, Emilia's cheeks turning pink at the innuendo.

"No way," I gasp. "I was joking, but oh my god, you totally slept with one of them, right?"

"What? No!" She hits me playfully on the arm, biting her lower lip. "I may have done other stuff…with two of them."

"Oh, you dirty girl." I laugh. "Good. You deserved it."

She gives me a shy smile, which I return with a genuine one of my own.

"So?" I ask, when she doesn't tell me anymore. "How was it? I bet it was hot…two guys at once? Yes, please!"

"Shut up." She laughs. She's silent for a moment before she loses the battle to keep her secrets to herself. "It was amazing. Best I've ever had. Axel's tongue, oh, and Jared's fingers. Holy hell, I was pretty sure I was going to die from orgasm overload at one point."

We both burst out laughing, and she spends the next half hour regaling me with every tiny detail of last night. I have to admit, it sounds fucking hot. I sure as hell wouldn't say no to having two guys loving on me at the same time.

"I'm so happy for you," I tell her sincerely.

"Thanks. I mean, it was only a one-night thing. They're heading away on a European tour next week for several months, and it's not like they said anything about seeing me again." I can't tell if she's okay with that, or if she wants more.

"Still, it's an excellent way to get over Andrew."

"Oh, it definitely is," she agrees, laughing. "I highly recommend it as a method to get over an ex."

We crack up laughing again.

"So, what are your plans for today?" she asks once we come back down.

"Uh, well, I might have agreed to go to Hawk's party at the Davenport's tonight," I blurt out the final few words, watching as Emilia's jaw drops open and she gapes at me for a long moment.

"You're what?" she screeches. "For real? You're going to meet your parents?"

"Yup," I say, popping the *p* while nodding.

"Wow. That's huge. Like really huge. Like *epically* huge."

"It is."

"How do you feel?"

"I'm freaking the fuck out." Four months ago, I wouldn't have felt comfortable telling her or anyone about that. Of letting them see how uncomfortable this whole situation makes me. Only, Emilia and Beck have done a hell of a job at getting under my skin and coaxing me out of my self-imprisoning shell.

"Do you know how you ended up in foster care?" she asks quietly.

"Not a clue. From what I can tell, they never filed any missing reports or anything. So unless they gave me up for adoption…"

"But why would they give you up and not Hawk?"

"I don't know." I sigh, frustrated. I've been all over the place, trying to figure out what could have happened. How I ended up living a life of torture and fear, while Hawk was handed everything he could ever want, but I keep coming up empty. I'm hoping I'll get a read on them tonight. Maybe I could even do some snooping, find out something, *anything* that could point me toward the answer to that question.

"Do you know what you're going to wear? Oh, I have to do your hair and makeup. You'll look amazing. Drop dead gorgeous." She jumps off the bed with an excited glint in her eye, flinging open my wardrobe and commencing to throw dress after dress onto my bed.

I guess that answers the question about what I'm doing today.

∼

AT SEVEN ON THE DOT, West knocks on my door. I'm a riot of nerves as I swipe my sweaty palms across the front of my dress. Emilia made me try on every damn dress in my wardrobe, and I ended up choosing the dark green one West wanted. Not because he wanted me to, but once I tried it on, I knew it was the one.

It's the most formal dress out of the ones he bought me. I don't know where he thought I'd wear it when he bought it, as it falls all the way to the ground, with a slit running up to the top of my thigh on one side. It's got a boatneck neckline that's high enough to cover the scars on my chest but still looks fashionable, with thick straps that cover the tops of my shoulders. It clings to my boobs, cinching in at my waistline and emphasizing the small curves of my hips before flowing down to the ground.

Emilia has done my hair, pinning the top half of it back and using her curling iron to tame it into soft beach waves. Along with a little foundation, mascara, and lipstick, I look like a completely different person when I look in the mirror. It's shocking. I even let her talk me into wearing a pair of heels with the damn thing. She must have argued with me for half an hour about how I couldn't show up in combat boots. I have to admit—but not to her—that when she finally convinced me to try the heels on instead, I couldn't get over the difference they made. Instead of looking like a grungy teenager playing dress up, I look like a fully-fledged woman. I almost look like I belong in the Davenport world. I'm just not sure if that's a good thing or not.

My mouth is dry as I pull open the door, revealing West in a black suit and white shirt. I swear, my ovaries just combusted. My eyes roam over him, from his dark hair which is styled back to keep it out of his face, to his black Clark Kent glasses and sharp suit. The whole combination is just...yum.

"Wow," he breathes, eyes examining me in much the same way, his pupils blown with lust. "You look beautiful."

I blush at his compliment, tugging my lower lip between my teeth.

"Thanks," I murmur, clearing my throat. "So do you."

The hunger burning in his eyes is doing totally inappropriate things to my insides as he continues to roam his gaze over my outfit, his desire only escalating when he spots the necklace he gave me last night still hanging on my neck.

He steps in closer, lifting his hand so his fingers wrap around a loose curl of my hair, running it through his fingers before he touches the heart on my necklace. His finger trails along the chain, inadvertently brushing my skin, the light touch making me shiver.

My eyes are glued to his, and when he raises his gaze to meet mine, I close the distance between us. My hands slide up the front of his suit jacket, gripping onto his shoulders as our lips connect and our tongues tangle together. It's soft and sweet, and everything West is on the surface.

Neither of us lets the kiss get too out of hand, pulling back after an intense moment, our eyes still fixated on one another.

Breaking the moment, West clears his throat. "We should go." His voice is a sexual husk that only dampens my panties further as I slip my hand under his cocked elbow, and he escorts me down the hall on shaky legs.

We walk through the campus, keeping the conversation light as we make our way toward the student parking lot. Nearing a fancy white Aston Martin, West pulls the keys out of his pocket, pressing a button that makes the halogen headlights turn on, lighting up the ground in front of the car as he walks me around to the passenger side. Like a gentleman, he holds the door open while I slide into the plush leather seats. The interior is clean and shiny, with more screens and buttons than any car should really need.

West slides in behind the wheel, and his fresh scent envelopes me in the small confines. I love that he doesn't wear aftershave or cologne. That everything about him is real, genuine.

He starts the engine, the soft purr vibrating through my seat as we move down the driveway and onto the main road. We drive in silence for a while, slowly winding our way up the side of a cliff until the sea is miles beneath us. Looking out my window, all I can see in the darkness is the white foam splashing into the air as waves crash against the rocks far below me.

Nerves get the better of me, the higher we climb. I must swipe my hands over my dress a thousand times, ironing out non-existent creases as my leg bounces with anxious energy.

After what feels like forever, yet no time at all, we pull up at a large wrought iron gate. West lowers his window and types in a code, the gate slowly sliding open. I lean forward to watch, just about able to pick out the tops of houses amongst large hedges and trees lining the property.

"We live in a gated community," West explains, answering my unasked question.

"Just the four of you?"

"Yeah. Our parents built it back when they formed the company before we were born. I guess they wanted their privacy."

"Fancy."

What else am I supposed to say?

Pulling through the gates, the four properties are spread in front of us, spaced in a wide semi-circle, lights on in the garden, and windows of each one. All four houses are the same—large, white, plantation-style structures.

"Don't go wandering too far from the house," West warns, pulling my attention from the opulent wealth surrounding me as I turn to look at him in confusion. "We're on a precipice. It's impossible to see in the dark, but if you stray too far from the houses in any direction, you'll reach the cliff's edge and tumble down to the rocks below."

I gape at him. *Is he for fucking real? What genius builds their house on a precipice? What if the entire thing breaks off and goes crashing into the ocean?*

"Eh, what?" I squeak.

"It's fine." He chuckles. "We're safe. Just don't go near the edge."

Well, I'm sure as hell not going to do that.

A bunch of cars are parked along the driveway and over the grass at the mansion on my far left, and we pull onto the driveway, crawling up it and stopping at the bottom of a large set of steps.

I reach out to pull on the door handle, but West's hand on my knee stops me and I turn to look at him.

"Nothing's going to happen tonight. I'll be with you the whole time."

He's probably noticed how stressed I am, and his words ease some of my tension. I offer him a soft smile, which he reciprocates before getting out.

"Stay there," he calls, as I reach for the handle again.

Doing as I'm told, I wait for him as he walks around the front of the car, fixing his suit jacket as he goes. He opens my door for me, holding out his hand and helping me out of the low seat.

A guy in uniform approaches as we near the bottom of the steps, and West drops his keys in his hand, nodding his head at the guy as we ascend the stairs.

Looking back over my shoulder, I watch as the guy climbs into the driver's side and starts the engine, driving off in the car.

"What the…"

West laughs. "He's a valet. He's just parking the car."

"He's parking your car for you?" I ask, looking up at him in surprise. "Talk about laziness."

Laughing again, West explains, "The rich believe they're too important to do such mundane things themselves, so they pay people to do it all for them—cook, clean, look after their kids, park their cars."

"So basically, they pay someone to live their lives for them?"

"Yeah, more or less."

"Sounds kinda sad if you ask me."

He doesn't respond as we step through the front door into a large, luxurious foyer. Men and women in elegant dresses and smart suits loiter around the large space, talking and laughing while sipping on drinks. A crystal chandelier hangs from the roof far above us, the lights twinkling against the glass and illuminating the numerous expensive-looking pieces of art meticulously placed around the room.

Placing his hand on my lower back, West navigates me through the crowd, stopping at a bar on the far side of the room.

"What can I get you to drink?" a bartender in a black uniform asks.

"I'll take a coke." I smile at him in thanks as he nods his head, then looks at West, taking his order before going off to get our drinks.

Looking out over the other guests, it seems like every kid from school that isn't a scholarship student is here, but the number of adults far outnumbers the kids our age.

"I thought this was a party for Hawk?" I question.

West follows my gaze. "It is. Technically. Our parents use any excuse to show off to their friends and colleagues. The whole purpose of events like these is to network and socialize. Talk your sons up to potential employers or rivals and pimp your daughters out to the next Elon Musk."

I grimace at that notion. Silence settles between us as the bartender places our drinks in front of us.

"Shouldn't you have brought your girl of the month then?" I ask, when he saunters back down the bar to take another order.

"Ha, no." West laughs, shaking his head. "That shit is just a control tactic for school. Our parents view those girls as nothing more than floozies to pass the time. They would consider it a serious insult if we arrived with one of them."

"But Cam mentioned once that all of you would probably end up marrying one of them one day," I say, remembering Cam's words from one of our earlier late-night talks —back when things between us were so much easier.

"Yeah, he's probably right," West agrees, his lips pressed in a tight line as he gives a reluctant nod. "Anyone we marry will be because it makes good business sense, not because we chose them once, or they made any impression on us.

"While their daughters are at school, sucking up to us, their fathers are negotiating business deals with our parents. Hoping that having their daughters attend the same school and possibly gain our attention will sway our parents in their favor instead of choosing a rival company to do business with instead.

"Our parents view us running the school as like a training exercise to make sure we're ready to step up and do what is required of us when we graduate."

"Cam made it sound as though running the company wasn't something any of you wanted, though?"

"It's not. But despite what you may think, we don't have a choice in any of this. I don't know what they'd do if we failed them, and after what I've seen and learned these last few months, I don't want to know."

I can't do anything except look at him as I wonder what he's seen, what he knows.

A slight blush creeps up his cheeks like he's embarrassed by the tiny bit of insight he's given me into his life.

"So, uh, yeah, to answer your question, the girl of the month stuff doesn't mean anything. They're nothing more than sure things for the guys to fuck."

I scrunch my nose up in disgust.

"Eww, gross. You do remember I was one of those girls, right?"

He steps closer to me, his fingers tucking a wayward strand of hair behind my ear. "You were never one of those girls. Everything about you is the opposite of them."

My throat feels dry as I remember the feel of his lips pressed against mine, the taste of him as his tongue slid into my mouth. His eyes gaze into mine, the swirling greens hypnotizing me as the sounds of the party fade into the background, the world around us falling away until it's just the two of us.

My hand reaches out, my fingers hooking into his belt, pulling him closer to me as his hand slides around the back of my neck, our faces so close I can't see anything but him.

"You taste so much better than I imagined," he murmurs, his words surprising me as his gaze darts down to my lips. I wonder if he's replaying the kiss in his head the same way I am.

"You thought about kissing me?"

"Only every day since you sat beside me in class."

My lips part, my chest heaving, as my breasts brush against his shirt with every rapid breath I inhale.

"Next time, it'll be somewhere private, where I can do so much more than kiss you."

I press my thighs together, desire very likely plain to see on my face as I stare wordlessly at him, unable to string together a coherent sentence as my thoughts drift to everything I want to do to him behind closed doors.

Breaking eye contact, he takes a step back, ending the moment between us as he lifts his glass of bourbon from the bar to take a sip. I do the same, the fizzy taste of the coke refreshing my parched mouth.

"Let me give you a tour," he says, wrapping his hand around mine as we move away from the bar. He walks me through the various rooms of the house, stopping every now and again so I can take in family photos of Hawk and his—our—parents. He looks like a surly ass kid in every single one, glaring at the camera.

Most of the students we pass give us a wide berth, stepping away when they see West coming, although I don't miss the Princesses gathered together in a huddle in the far corner of the living room, glaring daggers in my direction when they see me entering on his arm. I can practically see the steam coming out of Kendra's ears from here.

With his hand firmly pressed against my lower back, West ignores the daggers we are receiving from the girls, directing me through the crowd away from them. I spot Mason across the room, standing beside an older, gray-haired version of himself. I'm guessing that's his dad. He's got the same sharp jaw and piercing gaze, but there's a disconnect in his eyes that makes him appear less human somehow.

Looking back to Mason, his whole face is shut down. I've never seen him looking so impassive or cold, which is saying something, considering his usual resting bitch face.

His father lifts his hand as he laughs at something the guy he's talking to says, the innocent movement making Mason flinch. It's an involuntary response that he manages to get under control as his father claps him on the shoulder. His whole body is taut, his muscles tense and rigid. He looks like he's trying to resist the urge to shake off his father's hand and flee.

As I take a step toward him, feeling an overpowering sense to rescue him from the situation, a group of people move into my field of vision, blocking my view of Mason, as West, his palm placed flat on my lower back, steers me into another lavish room.

Having finished our drinks, West takes mine from my grip, setting both on the tray of a passing server. We've only taken a few steps into the room when I pause, gasping as I see Hawk talking to two people I recognize from the photos I've seen placed around the house.

Looking to see what has me frozen in place, West steps in closer beside me, his body pressing against my arm and side as if he can sense my need for comfort and strength, when he spots my parents and brother. The three of them make a picture-perfect family, with their matching blond hair and expensive clothing.

Hawk is the spitting image of our father. His hair is cut short, like Hawk's, his clean-shaven face stern and serious looking. He's about the same height as Hawk, with a lean body. His suit fits him perfectly, with no pot belly in sight, like it was designed just for him.

My mother is wearing a long black dress that hugs her curves, emphasizing her flat stomach and toned arms. Her blonde hair is perfectly straight, cut in a long bob that finishes just above her shoulders.

The three of them are talking to someone, however, his back is to me and I'm too captivated by the sight of my parents that I barely even register his presence.

My mother laughs at something someone says, but the sound is fake. Her smile doesn't reach her eyes as her red-painted lips lift and, with her long, manicured nails, she trails her hand down my father's suit jacket.

I'm not sure how long I stand there, simply staring at them. I can't tear my eyes away, and I feel strangely numb as I watch them. I don't know what I expected, but I guess too much is up in the air for me to feel anything positive at the sight of them.

Seeing the bored look on Hawk's face as he throws glares at his parents when he thinks no one is looking, settles me a bit. Maybe I haven't missed out on much if that's what he thinks of them. Despite the opulent house and sheer wealth exuding from them, perhaps they've been shitty parents. But then, regardless of how absent they might be, it's still better than not knowing who your parents are. Still better than the childhood of abuse and violence I was exposed to, right?

The person they are talking to excuses himself and steps away from them, turning to face me.

The air stills in my lungs as my eyes connect with his, my hand clenching around the fabric of West's suit trousers. His eyes widen with surprise before they narrow, his jaw ticking in anger as he glares at me.

"Oh shit," West murmurs beside me, tugging on my arm as he attempts to drag me out of the room. Even as he tows me behind him, my eyes never leave Lawrence's. He was surprised to see me here, and I'm guessing that's because he expected the guy from last night to have done his job and captured me—I bet he assumed I was on my way back to where he thinks I belong—or maybe he just never expected me to stumble back into this life.

Even though seeing him again has me breathing unevenly, my head fuzzy with swirling thoughts, I don't let him see how easily he affects me. Instead, I smirk at him, watching as his features darken and his stare becomes more menacing, just before West tugs me out of the room.

He pulls me along with him down several hallways, leaving the crowd behind us. I'm barely paying attention. Now that I don't have to put up a front for Lawrence, cracks begin to appear in my façade, as I recall the last time I saw him.

"It won't be long now, Dove," *he promises, fixing my hair over my shoulders just how he likes it.*

The way his eyes dilate with an intense hunger as he looks down at the dress he bought for me today has me suppressing a shiver.

He bites his lower lip, shamelessly adjusting himself in his pants as his eyes devour me.

"Not long now at all," he purrs. "I've waited so long to have you. Too long." He growls the last two words, anger flaring as his fists clench.

"Do you know how long I've waited?" he snarls, his lip peeling back as his hand wraps around my hair, messing it up. His mood swings give me whiplash with how quickly he jumps from one emotion to the next. "You were supposed to be mine. I saw you first, but he stole you from me." He laughs. It's a dark, ominous sound that has fear skittering up my spine. Leaning in, he tightens his grip on my hair to the point of pain, and I bite my lip to hold in the whimper. "But I won in the end, Dove. Now you're all mine."

I have no idea what he's blabbering about. I don't know who 'he' is or how he stole me. As far as I'm aware, I've never belonged to anyone other than him. No one else comes to visit me here or gives me the attention he does—not that I'd want it.

"Isn't that right?" he snarls when I don't respond how he wants me to.

"Y-yes," I stutter.

"SAY IT," he yells, yanking on my hair. This time I can't hold back the gasp of pain, his pulling on my hair enough to have my neck bent back at an awkward angle, forcing me to stare up into his gruesome face.

It's not really gruesome. To anyone else, it's probably handsome, attractive even. But to me, it's the face of the devil. The person who thinks he owns me, who thinks I'm his. When I look at him, all I see is pure evil.

"I'm yours," I cry out, knowing if I don't say it, it will only get worse. He hates when anyone else lays their hands on me. He gets enraged when he comes for his visits and finds new cuts and wounds on me, insisting the others only hurt me in places he can't see, but he doesn't seem to have the same issues with causing the damage himself. A black eye here, a split lip there. It doesn't matter to him.

Hadley

CHAPTER EIGHT

I'm yanked back into the present as West tugs me into a darkened room, the lights dimmed low. He closes the door behind us and pushes me back against the door.

"What's going on?" I hear Mason demand from somewhere deeper in the room, though I can't see past West's frame as he stands in front of me, so close he's blocking my view of the room.

He gently places his thumb and forefinger over my chin, slowly lifting my head until I'm peering into his eyes.

"You're okay," he soothes. "Everything is okay."

Everything is definitely *not* okay, but now that Lawrence is out of sight and I'm hidden behind a closed door with West, I don't feel as panicked as I did a moment ago. I knew he was going to be here. Of course, he would be here. Although, knowing that and actually seeing him are two very different things.

I should have known seeing him would be too much. I convinced myself I was stronger than that, but despite how tough I may *think* I am, facing one of my greatest fears will always break me down into that weak girl I used to be, worn down by dominant men and a hopeless situation.

"What the hell is going on?" Mason demands again, his voice coming from right behind West. Planting my hands on West's chest, ignoring as his flesh shivers under my touch and a small gasp escapes him, I give him a nod to let him know I'm fine, pushing off the door and forcing him to step to the side.

"Nothing," I assure Mason as West moves, no longer blocking his view of me. Mason's eyes widen, obviously not realizing I was here.

His eyes drop to take in my outfit, his lips parting. He seems stuck for something to say, his gaze lingering on the curves of my hips and swell of my breasts before he finally gazes at my face.

I feel West step up behind me, his heat seeping into my back as I melt against him. His hand splays across my hip in a possessive gesture without giving me the creeps like

Lawrence's covetous touch does. No, this is the exact opposite. I feel heat pooling between my legs, noticing Mason's eyes are drawn to the way West is touching me. Desire and...jealousy, maybe, flaring in his eyes.

West's other hand comes up to pull my hair over my shoulder, exposing my neck. I can't take my eyes from Mason. The way he salivates over every move has my skin warming and my heart beating faster against my chest.

West runs his nose up the column of my neck. "Our girl could do with some destressing," West explains to Mason. His breath tickles the sensitive skin behind my ear before he presses a chaste kiss to my heated flesh. *Our girl?* My head is too clouded with hormones to analyze what that means. Instead, I tilt my head in invitation, one he quickly accepts, as he slowly trails hot kisses along the side of my neck. Pulling me back against him, he presses his hard, lean chest more firmly against my back, causing his erection to dig into my ass.

My eyes never leave Mason's, waiting to see what he's going to do. Indecision is written across his face, his posture tense as he wars with himself. Yet, regardless of how unsure he seems, his pants tent where his dick hardens, watching West work his way down my neck, taking in my heated gaze as I ogle him.

It feels like we are staring at each other for a lifetime, but eventually, he makes a decision and takes a confident step forward, quickly closing the short distance between us until he's towering over me. Lowering his head, his lips brush mine before his hand slides along the back of my head and he deepens the kiss, his tongue pushing its way past my teeth in a move that's all hunger and long-denied passion.

I moan into his mouth, kissing him back just as fiercely. I feel West's fingers as he trails them along my exposed thigh, climbing higher and slipping beneath the slit in my dress until he's running his finger along the lining of my panties.

Breaking the kiss with Mason, my head falls back against West's chest as I pant. Mason moves effortlessly to kiss along my jaw and down my neck, sucking and biting as he goes.

My hands roam over his chest, pushing his suit jacket over his shoulders until it falls in a heap on the floor. Pulling on the bottom of his shirt, I untuck it from his pants and run my hands over his warm skin, trailing my fingers teasingly along the valleys of his abs.

He grinds against me as West slips his fingers under my panties, sliding them through my wetness.

"Mmm," I moan, tilting my hips, seeking his fingers where I need them most. He pushes two fingers inside me, pumping them a couple of times before pulling out and circling my clit, the motion causing me to cry out as my pelvis jerks and he sinks his fingers into me again.

"You're a wet, greedy little thing, aren't you?" West purrs in my ear, his dirty words only making more wetness coat his fingers.

What the hell? This is so not the West I know. I expected him to be shy and nervous in the bedroom, reserved, just like he is in public. Damn, I bet if girls knew how talented his fingers were and how filthy his mouth was, they wouldn't always be wishing one of the other guys chose them.

Not that I'm about to give them a chance to find out. West has me perplexed, trying to figure out who he is. Whenever I think I have him worked out, he shows me another side of himself. I want to get to know the real him, and I have a feeling this is the first step—not that I'm about to complain. I love this wicked side of him.

My nails scrape over Mason's chest as the signs of an impending orgasm take over my body, and I cry out as fireworks explode, my eyes squeezing shut in ecstasy.

My chest is heaving as Mason moves back to kiss me, my hands on either side of his face as I express my thanks with a passionate kiss. He pulls away as West slides his fingers out of me, fixing my panties back in place.

I turn to look at him as he raises his fingers to his lips, sucking one into his mouth.

"Mmm, brother, she tastes so sweet." His pupils are blown with lust as he observes me, lifting his hand to offer Mason his other finger.

Holy shit, they're going to have me coming again at this rate.

Mason parts his lips, granting West access, groaning as he tastes me on his best friend's skin.

"Mmm, so good," he rasps.

I can't do anything but glance between them, speechless.

West's lips capture mine in a brief, heated kiss.

"I told you I'd do more than kiss you when I got you somewhere private," he murmurs against my lips, making me laugh.

Turning back to Mason, I watch as he stuffs his shirt back in his pants.

"Not that I'm complaining, but what exactly happened out there?" he asks as West leads me further into the room, and I sit down on a vast, comfortable armchair.

Glancing around, it looks like we're in some sort of game room. There are several similar-looking armchairs spaced around the room, all angled to face a large TV that spans one wall with various gaming consoles set up in a low cabinet.

"What were you doing? Hiding out in here?" West asks, deflecting for me.

With a lingering look, Mason drops the subject and collapses into an armchair facing me as he runs his hand through his dark hair, pulling the strands back from his face.

"I just needed a minute," he responds vaguely.

We sit in silence briefly until the door opens again, and Hawk storms in in his usual aggressive fashion.

"Why the fuck does it sm—" He stops mid-sentence, freezing when he finds the three of us sitting there—well, when he finds *me* sitting there.

"What are *you* doing here?" he snarls, his eyes drilling into me.

"Dude, chill," West interjects before I can snap at him. "I invited her."

"What would you do an idiotic thing like that for?" he demands, whirling on West.

"Because she had a right to see where she should have grown up and to meet her parents."

Hawk stares at him for a long moment before glancing at Mason. "Did you know about this?"

Mason shrugs his shoulders, the gesture and obvious affirmation only further infuriating Hawk.

Grinding his teeth, he spins to face me. "Well," he snarks, "have you been adding up the price of every piece of art you came across, trying to work out how much you might get if you tell the world you're a Davenport?"

I gape at him. Is that seriously what he thinks?

"What?" I exclaim. "No. Of course not."

Getting to my feet, satisfaction courses through me when my heels have me looking him square in the eye instead of staring up at him for once. "I don't want any of this," I tell him, waving my hand to indicate the extravagant mansion he calls home. "I didn't ask to be a Davenport, and I don't want to be one."

"Then why are you here?" he argues. "If you don't want anything to do with us, then why, every time I turn around, are you there?"

I purse my lips, thinking over the answer before I tell him anything.

"Because I'm still curious about who I am. I might not give a shit about your money, but I do have questions about my parents and how I ended up with the life I have." I hesitate before I add, "I've been alone my whole life. You can't blame me for wondering who my family is."

He continues to glare at me, trying to ascertain whether I'm bullshitting him. Eventually, he must decide I'm telling the truth. I think I also almost see understanding or at least acceptance in his eyes, but he blinks, and it's gone before I can be sure.

Taking a step back, he crosses his arms over his chest in a defensive move. "What do you want to know?"

His easy agreeability and open question take me by surprise, and I gape at him for a second before gathering my wits. This might be the only opportunity I get to ask any questions I have. I need to make the most of it.

"Did you know about me?" Based on his shitty reaction to the news, I'm sure he didn't, but I need to be sure.

"No, I didn't." He grinds his teeth, clearly annoyed at being blindsided by such big news. Or maybe he's just annoyed that it's me he's stuck with as a sister. Probably both.

Silence falls between us again as I wrack my brain, trying to think of something useful he might be able to tell me. I swear I'm constantly asking myself questions, but now that the opportunity has presented itself, I'm struck mute.

"What was it like to grow up here?" That's really not an important question, but now that I've asked it, I can't help but wonder what my life would have been like if I'd grown up here. How different would it have been?

He shrugs his shoulders. "It was fine. Quiet. Mom and Dad were rarely around, so I was left in the care of nannies as a kid. By the time we were twelve, all of our parents figured we were old enough to look after ourselves. We spent basically all our time together anyway."

I can't imagine what that was like, spending your childhood hanging out with friends and just having fun. There's a tightness in my chest as I wonder if I would have fitted in with the four of them. Would I have spent all my time hanging out with them too?

"Oh." The word comes out a little choked, giving away the riot of emotions swirling within me.

I'm saved by the door opening again, the stench of perfume hitting me before I register my mother entering the room.

"Hawk, there you are," she chastises. "Your father has been looking all over for you. He wants you to meet the Clearwaters."

Her eyes quickly run over me before she dismisses me, smiling politely at West and Mason. "Boys, so nice to see you both again."

West moves to stand at my side. "Mrs. Davenport, this is Hadley. She goes to school with us."

Her lips pinch as her gaze settles on me again, taking in my unprofessionally styled hair and makeup and home nail job with disdain.

"Hadley?" she questions. "What's your surname?"

"Uh, Parker," I respond, confused, my mind too caught up on the fact my mother is standing in the same room as me—and she's inspecting me like I'm a stain on her expensive shoes.

"I don't know any Parkers," she responds dismissively. "Who are your parents?"

"Uhh…" How the fuck am I supposed to answer that? My brain is short-circuiting as I internally freak out.

"She's a scholarship student, Mom," Hawk interjects, saving my ass. Or perhaps not, based on how one side of her lip lifts in disgust.

"I didn't know you boys hung out with…*them*." Disdain drips from her voice, destroying the last bit of hope I had that maybe we could have some sort of relationship one day.

"We don't," Hawk cuts across before anyone else can answer. However, I don't know if either of the guys were going to speak up. I sure as hell had no response for her. "You said Dad was looking for me?" he asks, tucking his mom's arm under his and escorting her out, neither of them looking back.

I gape at the door for who knows how long after they're gone.

"Are you okay?" West murmurs eventually, breaking me out of my reverie.

"Yeah," I croak, coughing to clear my voice. "I'm fine. We should probably get back, right?" I plaster a fake smile on my face, trying to take some of the attention off me. "Can't hide out here all night."

"You can leave if you want," Mason offers, seeing right through my facade. "One of us can drive you home."

"No." I shake my head. "I'm honestly fine."

I can't let something stupid like feelings prevent me from using this opportunity to learn more about the Davenports or the rest of them. I'm in the one place that might hold some answers, so I need to make the most of it while I can.

Seeing the resolve written on my face, West escorts me out of the room, Mason behind us as we mingle with the crowd. It's not long before Mason is called away by his dad. He sighs heavily, mumbling a goodbye before taking off. The noise and the way he closes in on himself, hunching his shoulders and dragging his feet as he crosses the room, has me watching him with concern until a large, robust man blocks my view.

"Son," the man—clearly West's father—says. "Where have you been hiding all night?"

He's short, shorter than me in these heels. He's also got a large, round belly with hair that's clearly been dyed to hide the gray, as the tint doesn't quite match his eyebrows.

He doesn't give West a chance to respond.

"Have you seen your brother? He's supposed to be here, but I haven't seen him all night."

"No, I haven't," West responds, his voice tight. "I'm not his keeper."

My eyebrows lift. Brother? I didn't know he had a brother. He's obviously a lot younger, or older than us. I'd know about it if he attended our school.

His dad's eyes narrow on West in irritation before he moves his gaze to me, his eyes dropping to run down my dress. There's something sleazy about him that I don't like, and I immediately stand taller, staring right back at him.

He chuckles, shaking his head.

"Brave of you, son, to bring someone like her here."

What the fuck does that mean? My eyes narrow on him, not that he seems to notice as he claps his son on the shoulder.

"Better than one of your monthly flings from school, though. Bringing a girl like that would only give her ideas, but a girl like her"—his gaze lingers inappropriately on my cleavage, a disgusting smirk lifting the corner of his lips— "she knows her place. Isn't that right, girlie?"

Blood fills my mouth from biting my cheek so hard to stop the hateful words from spewing out of my mouth.

"What the hell, Dad?" West exclaims, glancing apologetically at me. "Not all of us sleep around with hookers." He snarls the final sentence in a low hush, an angry flush staining his father's cheeks.

"Watch your tongue, boy," his father growls before composing himself, straightening his shoulders and adjusting his suit jacket. "Now, park your date at the bar and come with me. I want you to meet the Clearwaters."

He strides away, West sighing as he leaves.

"Sorry about him," he apologizes, turning toward me with a grimace.

I wave off his apology. It's not his fault his dad is a whore loving sleazeball.

"You should go," I encourage him, gesturing in the direction his father disappeared. "I'll be at the bar when you're done."

He gives me a lingering look before nodding and striding off after his father. I watch him go, admiring how his ass looks in those pants, before walking toward the bar and ordering another drink.

With an ice-cold glass of coke in my hand, I lean back against the bar, scanning the room. Watching the fake greetings guests give to one another, the heated glances men share with other women across the room behind their wives' backs.

Most of the students from school are being dragged around the party by their parents, introduced to countless people who I'm sure they won't remember once they say goodbye. It all seems futile. What teenager would willingly attend an event like this?

I watch as a guy in his fifties escorts a girl I vaguely recognize from school, who I'm assuming is his daughter, toward another older gentleman. The guy practically drools all over the girl as she bats her eyelashes at him, blatantly flirting with a man who looks like he's the same age as her father. Meanwhile, her dad stands beside her, appearing proud as punch, as the two of them flirt back and forth.

What a weird fucking world this is.

I feel a presence step up beside me at the bar as Lawrence's slimy voice rings in my ear.

"Fancy seeing you here, Dove," he purrs, toying with me.

My body is rigid as I stare straight ahead, doing my best to ignore him.

"You know, I looked high and low for you after you left. I had everyone out searching for you, but here you've been, hiding right under my nose, at a prep school with my son." He sneers out the last word, angry at my close proximity to Cam, or maybe he just doesn't like his kid. It wouldn't surprise me if he was jealous of Cam and the attention he gets from girls. He's the type to get annoyed when all eyes aren't on him. "Play your games, little Dove, but don't forget who you belong to. I *will* be coming to collect, and if I find out you've let any of the boys at that school touch what's mine, there will be hell to pay."

I have to suppress a shiver, forcing my face to remain neutral as I refuse to look at him.

He just laughs at my little act of defiance, leaning in so his lips are at my ear. It takes everything in me not to pull away, but I know he will only get a rise out of that. He loves having that control over me.

He growls, annoyed he's not getting the reaction he wanted.

"I'll be seeing you real soon, Dove." He flicks his tongue out to run along the shell of my ear as I grit my teeth, forcing myself not to flinch away from his touch.

Feeling eyes on me, I spot Cam standing not far from us. I'm surprised I don't drop dead on the spot from the hateful glare he's throwing my way as his father finally steps back, enabling me to breathe again as he walks away, oblivious to his son's eyes glaring daggers at me.

I can only imagine how that looked to Cam—like two lovers flirting. He's probably not close enough to see the fear shining in my eyes, and I know no other part of my facial expression gave away how uncomfortable I was in Lawrence's presence.

Snarling, Cam turns on his heel, storming through the crowd and out of the room, leaving me exhausted as I prop myself up against the bar. Jeez, who haven't I had a run-in with tonight? No doubt the Princesses will be all over my ass before I leave.

I'm not left by myself for long, sucking down a third glass of coke in an attempt to rid myself of the horrible taste in my mouth and the churning anxiety in my stomach.

"Sorry about that," West says when he reappears. "You okay?"

"Yup, all good," I respond, forcing a smile. I must overdo it as his eyes narrow on me in suspicion before he glances at my now-empty glass.

"How many of those have you had?"

"Umm, three?"

He rolls his eyes. "You're going to be on a sugar high all night."

I shrug my shoulders, not too worried about a sugar high. It's not like I'll be able to sleep after everything tonight anyway.

West is saying something to me when I catch a flicker of movement out of the corner of my eye. There's something about it that I recognize, and I turn my head to get a better look, my mouth dropping open as I take in the scene before me.

"Beck?" I breathe, my eyebrows scrunching in confusion. I watch him from across the room as he shakes hands with some old dude. He's dressed impeccably in a dark navy suit, his hair slicked back, looking like he belongs among these pretentious assholes. "What is he doing here?"

"About time that dickhead showed up," West grumbles beside me, his words not making any sense to me. "Dad was all over me to find him."

I don't understand. Why would his dad want him to find Beck? How does Beck even know these people? He's a Black Creek kid. Our kind doesn't know people like this. We don't just shake hands with wealthy business tycoons.

"I don't...why is he here?" I can't tear my eyes away as Beck nods along to something the man he's talking to says.

"Dad invited him." West sounds less than pleased about that. "Basically ignored him his whole life, but now he's decided to take an interest, inviting him to these events and introducing him to everyone."

I'm just getting more confused by the second.

"But, why?"

I can feel West's eyes on me, but I still don't look away from Beck.

"Didn't he tell you?"

"Tell me what?" I finally tear my eyes away to look at West, taking in the wrinkles on his forehead and the furrow between his green eyes as he looks at me in confusion before his eyes widen, surprise passing through them.

He grimaces. "Beck is my half-brother."

He's what?

The room seems to tilt. How many more bomb drops can I handle?

"What?" I croak, turning to look at Beck again, my eyes scanning his face and analyzing his posture, trying to find some clue that I missed.

As though sensing my eyes on him, he turns my way, his bright green eyes widening as he finds me standing beside West, the two of us staring at him. I have no idea what I look like, but based on the way he quickly makes an excuse to whoever he's talking to and starts pushing past people, heading in my direction, his eyes narrowed and his lips pinched as he comes this way, he can tell I know the truth about him.

Why didn't he tell me? Why would he keep this from me? After I opened up to him. After I told him my truth.

Not giving it much thought, just knowing that I can't do this with him here and now, I jump down from the bar stool and take off, pushing past West as I run in the opposite direction from Beck, ignoring West calling my name as I flee from the hall.

Tears stream down my face, blurring my vision as I run aimlessly down a hallway. I don't even know where I'm going, not that I make it far before I crash into a rigid body, someone's arms wrapping around me, steadying me before I fall to the ground.

I'm unable to make out his face through my tears, but I don't need to, to know who it is. I've only had the luxury of being in his embrace a handful of times, but I'd recognize the heat of his skin against mine anywhere.

"Are you okay?" Cam asks, not removing his tight grip on my waist. I blink away the tears, his face coming into focus. For the first time in months, there's genuine concern in his eyes.

Swiping under my eyes, I sniffle. "I'm fine," I reply automatically, not giving the response much thought. My brain is still too numb from what I just witnessed to construct anything more coherent.

His body tenses against mine as he quickly withdraws his hands from me, my dismissal of his concern getting his guard up.

"Oh, I get it. I'm the wrong Rutherford, right?" His harsh tone is back in place as he snarls at me. "You're after Daddy Dearest. Although I bet you don't call him that...or maybe you do," he sneers, tilting his head slightly. "Do you get off on calling him Daddy when he's balls deep inside of you and fucking you like a whore? 'Cause, that's all you are to him."

I slap him before realizing I've even done it, the noise reverberating across the otherwise empty hall as we stand frozen, staring at one another with hate-filled eyes. The stinging of my palm and reddening of his cheek confirm I didn't hallucinate that action.

Fresh tears leak out of my eyes, trailing down my face, and I know I look a mess. But Cam's words have anger coursing through me, heating me from the inside out as I power toward him, shoving him hard in the chest so he stumbles back against the wall.

"Listen here, asshole," I snarl. "I've had enough of your shit. I've let you talk down to me, terrorize me, *use* me because I thought it would help you through this anger and, yeah, I felt guilty. But I'm fucking done with it now. I'm not just going to stand here and take your shit. If you come at me again, I won't just stand there and take it. I know I hurt your feelings, and I'm sorry, however there is so much worse shit going on than me refusing to belong to you like a fucking mail-order bride."

Glaring back at me defiantly, he says, "What about lying to me?"

"I haven't lied to you about the things that matter." I hold his gaze, dropping my barriers briefly so he can see the swirling storm of emotions that crash through me every time I look at him. "I never lied or faked what I felt for you. I felt what you felt. Every beautiful moment of it."

"Felt?"

Pain flashes across his beautiful brown eyes, but I'm too emotionally drained to feel guilty about it.

"Yeah, Cam." I sigh wearily. "Past tense."

Pushing off him, I continue up the hall, away from him. I rush through way too many fucking corridors before I finally find a door leading outside and yank it open stumbling out into the night.

I take several steps into the garden, bending over and placing my hands on my knees as I drag in a deep lungful of air. I repeat the action over and over until my head stops swimming and my pounding pulse slows down to a more normal rate.

Standing upright, I tilt my head back, staring up at the starlit sky for a long moment, my body feeling completely wrung out from tonight's events.

"What happened to you?" a voice asks, breaking through my quiet moment and letting me know my freak out wasn't private. *Just great.*

Turning toward Hawk, I eye him leaning back against the wall beside the door I just exited, having clearly missed him standing there as I stumbled out into the night, desperate for a breath of fresh air.

"None of your business." My voice lacks its usual snark, weariness draining me of any energy to fight with him.

"You look like a mess," he unhelpfully comments, taking in my tear-stained face. *No fucking shit, Sherlock. Someone give this guy a medal. His observation skills are top-notch.*

I scowl at him as he pushes off the wall, a smirk on his face as he walks along the side of the house, fishing his car keys out of his pocket.

Just before he can disappear around the corner, I call out, "Wait."

He stops, throwing a look over his shoulder at me.

"Are you, uh, going back to campus?" I ask hesitantly, my voice sounding way too vulnerable for my liking.

He doesn't say anything, only staring me down.

"I, umm, need a lift. Can I…" I trail off, unable to finish that sentence, and lower myself to actually ask him for help.

He leaves me hanging for what feels like forever, his eyes squinting as they roam over my face.

"Sure," he finally acquiesces, his easy agreeability taking me by surprise. "It's not like you can show your face at the party again looking like that."

Ah, there we go. That's the brother I know and hate.

I scowl at him harder, reluctantly trailing after him as he disappears around the corner, not looking back to check that I'm behind him.

He walks toward a large garage off to one side, away from where the guests' cars are parked, opening a side door that slams shut behind him. *Fucking douche has no manners.*

Mentally berating him, I yank open the door and stomp into the dark garage, my eyes widening as I find a lineup of expensive cars.

"Wow," I breathe, trailing my fingers along a beautiful red Jaguar convertible. I learned to drive when I was fourteen, but I've never been behind the wheel of something so beautiful.

A car's engine further up the row starts, a dark-colored SUV pulling out of the space and stopping beside me, the halogen glow of the headlights illuminating the dim space. There must be at least twenty cars in here, each one more expensive than the last.

"Come on, Princess, I don't have all night," the asshole calls out through the lowered passenger side window.

I scowl at him. "Don't call me that," I snap, pulling open the door and climbing into the front passenger seat. As we approach it, the garage door opens automatically, and Hawk is gunning the engine, flying through the gap before I'm even confident the door is open wide enough to let us through.

I gasp, scrambling to buckle my seatbelt, suddenly regretting the decision to get into the car with this maniac. Hawk laughs beside me as he takes off down the driveway and out through the main gate.

We drive in silence for a while, the low sound of the radio playing in the background.

"So, are you going to tell me what happened tonight?" he asks.

"No. Why would I tell you anything?"

He's silent for a moment. "I can guess if you prefer. Let me see." He taps his finger against his lips as though he's thinking. "You're upset Mommy didn't recognize you at first sight."

"No," I respond, but I can't deny her inability to recognize her own daughter, never mind her complete dismissal of me, did sting.

"Hmm," he ponders. "Did the guys finally fuck you out of their system and now they want nothing to do with you?"

"You wish," I snap, anger sparking within me.

"Maybe you're upset because Cam's dad couldn't get it up for you. You worried you've lost your touch, and he's not going to keep you as his side piece?"

I grit my teeth, my hand wrapping around the fabric of my seat beside my legs. *You can't punch him when he's driving, Hadley*, I remind myself, trying to take a couple of slow, deep breaths.

"Ha." He laughs, smacking his hand against the steering wheel. "That's it, right? I fucking knew it."

"No, asshole," I sneer, turning to glare at him. "That is...so far from the fucking truth."

"Then tell me what the truth is," he growls, his hands tightening around the wheel. "'Cause from where I'm standing, you're stringing my friends along, making them fall for you and question everything."

My stomach twists at that knowledge. "I'm not stringing them along," I insist.

"Oh, so you've no ulterior motive then?" Hawk laughs humorlessly.

"Not anymore," I say honestly.

"But you did." It's not a question, so I don't bother to answer him, keeping my gaze on the front window as we drive back down the cliff. "And it has something to do with Lawrence."

"Yes," I finally admit, hoping I'm not making a mistake by saying that much. "And before you ask, no, it's got nothing to do with money, social status, or any of that crap. I couldn't care less about any of that."

"Then why?"

I turn my head to look at the side of his face. He must feel me looking at him as he glances briefly my way before focusing back on the road.

"He's the devil." I move to look out the window again as Hawk turns to stare at me. I can feel his gaze burning into the side of my head, trying to figure me out.

He focuses back on the road, his jaw tight as he says in a low, defeated tone, "All our parents are bad people."

I don't respond, but yeah, he's right. I'm beginning to realize as much for myself.

Sweetheart

CHAPTER NINE

"What the hell have you done?" I snarl, storming toward West as Hadley flees in the opposite direction. Every step she takes away from me has my heart slamming against my chest, desperate to go after her.

How is she here? I never expected to see her here. I would have told her the truth if I'd known, but it's clear from the look on her face that West spilled the beans.

I never wanted her to find out like this. I knew I should have told her everything after she poured her heart out and told me about Lawrence, but I didn't want to add any more to her burden. She's already carrying so much, and I was worried my familial ties to the Warrens and how close all four families are, would cause issues with us. Maybe it was stupid. I just wanted to be there for her, and I was scared that her knowing that asshole spawned me would make her second guess whether or not I was on her side.

"You're the one keeping secrets, big bro." West shrugs, his nonchalance pissing me off.

"Why the hell did you bring her here? Do you have any idea what could have happened to her?"

He gives another infuriating shrug, and if it wasn't for the concern I could see that he's doing his best to hide, I'd have fucking decked him. I don't give a shit about these pompous assholes or what they think of me. I'd have happily laid him out flat on his back with one solid punch.

Wrapping my hand around his tie, I yank him toward me. "You have no idea what you've just done," I snarl, using my grip to push him backward. He stumbles, but I'm already shoving my way past nosey onlookers, trying to chase down my girl.

My shoulder bangs against Cam's when he enters the room as I exit, both of us glaring at one another. I don't slow down though, quickly moving past him into the corridor beyond, throwing open doors and calling out Hadley's name.

I must search half of the damn house before I give up. She's not here. With Lawrence lurking about, I don't think she would storm off somewhere alone, not for this long. Lifting my phone out of my pocket, I dial her number, but it just keeps ringing out as she ignores my calls. I open the app to message her, staring at the screen for a long moment. *Dammit, I don't want to have this conversation over goddamn texts.* I want her to see my face and hear my voice when I apologize to her. Frustrated, I stuff the phone back in my pocket, running my hands through my hair as I sigh. It's going to be fine. She's pissed and has every right to be, but I can fix this.

Defeated, I return to the party, seeking out West and his asshole buddies in case they found her anywhere. The three of them are standing against the wall in the living room when I arrive, their heads close together as they whisper to one another.

Not giving a shit if I'm interrupting, I head toward them, all three looking in my direction as I approach.

"Where is she? Have you heard from her?"

"She's fine, dude." Cam waves off my concern like I'm being an overprotective momma bear, but he doesn't know the risks she took just by coming here tonight. I can understand why she came, that same curiosity is how I got sucked into all of this shit as well. But I don't want that for her. Like I said before, Hadley has enough to worry about. She doesn't need to get caught up in the shit these families have going on.

Fuck, even I can barely wrap my head around what they've been doing all these years. I knew my father was a scumbag—any guy who cheats on his wife, and is a deadbeat to his son, is—but a group of rich assholes presenting one face to the world, pretending to be upstanding citizens while secretly fronting an organization of hired assassins? Yeah, there's a special place in hell for people like that.

I knew my father had his own motivations for why he got me the job at Pacific Prep. He inferred as much himself, but I was utterly fucking floored at Christmas when, standing in a windowless room with those other four assholes, he and the rest of our parents proceeded to explain to us how their company really keeps them in the life they've become accustomed to.

Not only did they blow my mind, but they ensured we would remain silent.

"Hawk took her back to campus," Cam says casually, his easy tone making my eyes narrow in concern. After everything that happened last semester, and Hadley told me about his response to finding out she's his sister, it's safe to say I don't trust him alone with her. He might not do anything to hurt her physically, but as someone who grew up not knowing one whole side of his family, I can understand the draw to find out and get to know said family, even if they don't deserve your time or attention. Every time he rejects her, it cuts through her, deeper even than she may know. The fact she's still here, enrolled at that school despite the threat of Lawrence, says everything about how much getting to know her family means to her. Hawk is her first connection, and if that asshole keeps denying her, he and I are going to have issues.

"He better not hurt her," I snarl.

"He won't do anything to her," West says confidently, rolling his eyes like I'm being dramatic. "He is her brother, after all." He watches me closely, looking for a response, but I just scowl back at him.

"That's exactly what puts him in the prime position to do the most damage," I sneer.

"You knew?" Cam gapes at me.

"So she spilled her secrets, but you didn't tell her yours?" West snarks, driving the knife in deeper. As if I don't feel guilty enough for keeping it from her.

Mason stands silently, eyeing me intently as though he's trying to size me up.

"What else did she tell you?" Cam's question has me turning my glare on him. The way he's looking at me, like he's trying to read what I know about Hadley from my face—fat fucking chance of that.

"Anything Hadley tells me is none of your fucking business," I snap.

"Because you're her boyfriend, right?" West tilts his head, staring at me in much the same way Cam is. What the fuck is with these guys? Are they just looking for dirt to hold over my head? They all know they can't get me removed from the school by threatening me with Hadley.

"Yes." The word comes out sharp as I straighten my spine and glare at all three. They can say whatever they want. Judge me, I don't care. I sensed it as soon as she walked into my office—that feeling of being lost. It resonated with me. I've never quite felt like I belonged anywhere since leaving Black Creek. You can't see the shit I've seen, survive the childhood I had, then expect to just integrate into normal society like it hasn't left you emotionally scarred.

When I started at my new school at the age of thirteen, everyone around me was so fucking ordinary. They didn't jump when someone slammed their textbook down on the desk, thinking it was a gun going off; they hadn't had to learn to scope out the exits in a room to ensure you always had a getaway if shit went down. They didn't fucking know what it was like to live constantly on edge, always prepared to fight. But Hadley, she got it. The way she carries herself, how her eyes roam around a room—it spoke to my inner damage. No one ever really understood me before, but with one look, I knew she would fucking get it. And even if there were parts of me she couldn't understand, she'd accept me anyway, because she's just as fucked up as I am.

"It didn't seem like she had a boyfriend earlier." West smirks, his insinuation making my eyes twitch as I glare at him.

Okay, so "boyfriend" might have been a stretch. We're dating, but we're taking it slow. I know this is all new to her but is what West's implying true? I'm not sure how I feel about that. Honestly, I'm more pissed that the asshole would do something with her and then try to use it against me.

"What the fuck are you trying to say?" I snarl, stepping closer to him. Cam and Mason stand taller on either side of him, acting like bodyguards. "If you're messing with her just to piss me off, it won't matter how rich you are or how many friends you have."

"Man, chill out," Mason says, eyeing me closely as I clench my fists, fighting the urge to make a scene. "It's not like that. We're not messing with her."

We? What the fuck does he mean by "*we*"?

I scrutinize him, but Mason is like a blank fucking slate. I've never been able to get a read on him. Glancing at Cam, he just looks pissed off and frustrated. I don't know what the hell his problem is.

Looking back at West, there's a steely resolve in his eyes that I'm pretty sure matches the one I'm giving him. I don't exactly know what's going on between them and Hadley, but there's definitely something. Despite his callous words intended to rile me up, he's not backing down or disputing what Mason is saying.

"I guess we'll see." Casting my eyes over them a final time, I walk away, completely done with this night. I don't give a shit if my father wants to show me off to more people. I'm fucking sick of him introducing me to associates as his *long-lost son that he never knew about*, trying to gain some fucking sympathy. It's pathetic.

Loosening my tie while I wait for the valet to bring my piece of shit car around, I pull my phone out of my pocket. No messages, no missed calls. I guess what was I expecting?

Getting into my car, I redial her number. It rings out, the same as it did earlier, and I toss my phone in the passenger seat, driving back to campus. Parking the car in the lot, I sit for a moment, tapping my fingers against the wheel as I look over toward the student dorms.

Glancing at the time, it's late. Too late. The last thing I want to do is add to her stress by getting caught sneaking in or out of her room at this time of night. Decision made, I huff out a breath as I grab my phone and get out of the car. Walking toward the apartment building, I fire off a text to her.

> Beck: I get that you're pissed. I'll give you your space tonight, but hear me out tomorrow.

Not expecting a response from her, I stuff my phone in my pocket as I climb the stairs to my floor, letting myself into the apartment. I'm fucking wrecked after tonight. Who knew faking an interest in the shit that comes out of rich people's mouths was so exhausting? But with the blackmail my father now has over me, he can force me to do whatever he wants, including turning up at completely pointless events. I'm nothing more than his walking, talking monkey right now. Something I fucking hate.

Collapsing onto the sofa, I lean back, my legs spread wide as I undo my top button and pull my tie off over my head. Sighing, I burrow my head in my hands, groaning. I can't tell her any of the shit I know about our parents, but I need to apologize for keeping the fact that I'm West's brother a secret. I also have questions of my own, like why she risked going there tonight and what's going on between her and the others.

We've never really talked about the guys. Before I found out she was Hawk's sister, I just assumed the only time they ever interacted was when one of them was pissing her off. But being related to Hawk makes things more complicated. Any relationship she has with him will inevitably include the others, too—the four of them are thick as thieves. The tight-knit relationship pissed me off when I was first offered the job at Pacific Prep and my father informed me I actually had a brother. At first, I blamed them for West not feeling the same need as me to get to know one another. In hindsight, I guess I was jealous. I figured if I was in his shoes, I wouldn't care much about him or his rejection if I had a solid group of friends.

Shaking off the trip down memory lane, I focus back on the present. I don't believe Hadley would have gone with West, or any of the others tonight, if she didn't feel safe in their presence, especially considering she had to know she would come face to face with Lawrence. Based on their prying questions, they don't know anything about her, so she clearly doesn't trust them enough with her past, but she does trust them enough to go there with one of them tonight.

Unanswerable questions circle round and around in my head, and it's nearly dawn by the time I set all of it aside and drag my ass off the sofa and into the bedroom, stripping down and climbing into bed. Exhaustion cloaks over me, knocking me out like a light, and I'm asleep as soon as my head hits the pillow.

It feels like I've just closed my eyes, which are dry and scratchy as I pry them open. Something woke me from my deep sleep, but my sleep-fogged brain doesn't remember what.

The sound of someone clearing their throat has me turning over and sitting up in bed, instantly on alert. Squinting, I can't make out anything more than a silhouette. Not taking my eyes off them, I stretch out and turn on the bedside light, illuminating the room.

Hadley stands in my doorway, her arms crossed over her chest, with an eyebrow raised and an unimpressed look on her face.

"You said you wanted to talk."

"Uh." I rub at my eyes. "Yeah...yes, I did."

"Right, well, get up. I'll take a coffee." With that, she leaves me alone.

Glancing at my alarm clock, *yup, I've barely gotten an hour's sleep.* Groaning, I get out of bed, grab a pair of sweats and stagger into the living room. Hadley is sitting on the sofa, her eyes trailing me as I walk into the kitchen and start the coffee machine, grabbing two cups for us. There's none of the hurt or pain that I caught a glimpse of yesterday. Today she's all deadly eyes and hostile aggression.

Once the coffee is ready, I carry our cups into the living room, handing one to her and taking a seat beside her on the couch.

Turning, so her back is against the arm of the sofa, she brings her legs up in front of her, watching me intently over the rim of her cup. She doesn't seem angry or upset. I'm not actually sure what she's feeling right now. She's just watching me, waiting patiently for what I have to say. It's a little unnerving. Aren't girls supposed to be pissed when you keep secrets from them? I expected her to shout and yell at me, so I'm not entirely sure what to make of this silence. I should have known she wouldn't react the way other girls would, though; she wouldn't get all emotional about it. She's a practical thinker, someone who thinks things through.

I take a large sip of my coffee in an attempt to wake up the cogs in my head.

"I should have told you," I begin, my voice sincere as I return her serious expression. "I don't have an excuse. After you told me about Lawrence, I didn't want you to regret trusting me. I don't want anything to do with my father, or the others, and I guess I was worried you'd think I did. Or that you'd think I was in cahoots with West and the guys, when I'll only ever be on your side."

"You could have just explained it to me," she reasons, still watching me with those gray-blue eyes that tear right through me, prying me open for her to analyze. Hopefully, that means she can see the truth in what I'm saying.

I nod my head in agreement. "I should have." What else can I say? She's right.

"So explain it to me now."

Swallowing another mouthful of coffee, I tell her about how my parents met. "My father met my mom when he was up near Black Creek on business. My mom was only eighteen, working as a stripper in the rundown shithole he entered. Somehow, they got to talking, and let's just say nine months later, I was born.

"I don't think she told him about me. Not until she decided to take us out of Black Creek. She never said anything, but I think she reached out to him for help. I remember him coming to visit us one day shortly after we moved, and I overheard him demanding that she give him regular updates on me, but I never saw him again until a year ago.

"I was neck deep in student loans, just about to graduate, and he showed up at my dorm one day, offering me a job here and telling me all about a brother I knew nothing about."

"And he wanted nothing in return?" she asks dubiously, an eyebrow raised, letting me know she doesn't believe he gave me this opportunity out of the goodness of his heart.

I laugh humorlessly. "He wouldn't tell me, but honestly, an offer of a well-paid job in an economy that wasn't hiring, and the opportunity to meet a brother I never got the chance to know, was enough of a temptation, regardless of what he might want in return."

"I can understand that."

Of course, she can. She's in the same position with Hawk.

Setting my mug on the coffee table, I scoot toward her, running my hands over her knees and down her thighs.

"I'm sorry. I should have known you'd understand. I didn't want to give you anything else to stress over, but that was stupid of me. You're more than capable of looking after yourself."

"I am." She hands me her mug, and I place it on the table beside mine. When I turn back to look at her, her eyes have softened, and she has a slight smile on her lips. "But it's kinda nice to have someone else looking out for me. I know you're not like West or the others. Not that they are bad people, but...I don't know how to explain it. I can just tell that you're like me. Does that make sense?"

"It does. I feel it too."

Her legs part, and I don't miss the opportunity to wedge my upper body between them, lining my torso up with hers, our faces inches apart.

"Are you keeping anything else from me?"

She asks the question I hoped she wouldn't. I can't lie to her, but I can't tell her the truth.

"There are things you don't know that I can't tell you."

She nods, not arguing with me. "There are things I can't tell you either."

I can't deny I'm not curious about that, but it's only fair. Everything between us is still new and it takes time to share things about yourself with others, especially when you're like us and aren't used to opening up to people.

"I think I need to tell the others about Lawrence," she blurts, nibbling on her bottom lip.

"What's going on between you and them?" I ask. "I was surprised to see you with them last night."

"I don't know. West and Mason have always been nice enough to me, but things have felt different this semester." Her brows furrow. "I'm beginning to think they might not have been involved in the video last semester. They've been sticking up for me against Cam and Hawk. West even told me about the whole brother thing before he told the guys. And he invited me last night, so I could see where they all grew up and meet my parents."

That surprises me. From what little I've seen and heard, it's the four of them against the world, so West breaking rank like that is unexpected.

"Can you trust them?" She clearly knows them better than I do, but I can't imagine Cam taking such news about his dad well. And if he decides he doesn't believe her, the others will most likely support him.

"I don't know." She sighs. "But the secrets are only making things worse. Cam hates me. He thinks I'm fucking around with his dad." She visibly shudders at the thought. "And Hawk thinks I'm only here for the money. They couldn't think any worse of me than they do right now."

"Alright then." I'm worried about how it could all backfire on her, but it's her decision to make. "Do you want me to go with you when you tell them?"

She smiles. It's soft, but it reaches her eyes as she leans forward, closing the distance between us as her lips caress mine.

"It's probably better if I do it alone, but thank you."

"Anytime. I'm always here for you."

"Beck." She hesitates over my name, worry haunting her eyes as she nervously licks her lips. "Last night…" She swallows. "I kissed West and Mason. We—"

Before she can explain further, I cut her off, running my hand over her hair.

"It's okay," I assure her. "You don't owe me an explanation."

Her eyes widen in shock, but I've had all night to think this through. I'm not a big fan of the so-called Princes. They're entitled assholes. But I'm worried about Lawrence. I don't know if Hadley can see it, but he's basically been grooming her her whole life. He's not going to just let her slip through his fingers. I'll do everything I can to protect her, but having four more sets of eyes on her would help.

As long as they aren't just messing with her. If I hear one fucking word about what goes on between them behind closed doors, I won't hesitate to make their parents heirless.

"We never said we were exclusive, and if they can help bring Hawk around to the idea of having you as a sister, then who am I to argue?"

"I don't think Hawk will ever accept that I'm his sister." She laughs, but it's disingenuous, and I can see the pain those words cause in her eyes. He might annoy the hell out of her and piss her off, but she wants him to like her or at least accept her.

"I don't think West will ever accept me either," I tell her somberly.

She runs her fingers through my hair. "It's a good thing we have each other, then."

I feel her smile against my lips as she kisses me again, her legs wrapping around me as she pulls me into her.

Hadley

CHAPTER TEN

It's late afternoon by the time I tear myself away from Beck's apartment, sneaking out the emergency exit at the back of the building by the forest and slinking through the trees until I come out near the sports center.

After our serious talk we got a little caught up in, well, other things, but I left his place with a mission—to tell the others about Lawrence. Except somehow, it seems even more daunting than it did when I was talking to Beck about it.

My palms sweat as I walk across the campus toward the boys' dorms. Am I seriously going to tell these assholes who have been harassing me since I stepped on campus the most shameful part of myself? The part that will make them see me as a victim? I initially walked onto this campus with my head held high, back ramrod straight, refusing to take shit from anyone, including them. But the second I tell them, they're going to know all that bravado is just that—a defense mechanism to stop people from looking too closely at all my jagged edges.

The closer I get to the boys' dormitories, new fears take flight. What if they don't believe me? What if they think I'm making it all up? I'm about to accuse a wealthy, well-respected businessman of essentially grooming a minor. We all know how well shit like that usually goes over.

Sighing heavily, I nervously fiddle with the necklace West got me that is hanging around my neck, twisting the chain around my fingers. *Jesus, who the fuck have I become, giving a shit what others think of me?* This school has changed me, and I'm not entirely sure it's for the better.

I can't fucking stand Hawk, yet some stupid, naive part of me wants him to like me, to respect me. I want to close this gap between us, mend the bridges *he* burned with his stupid shitty attitude. My hand clenches around the heart on my necklace, anger drowning out my nerves from a moment ago.

Okay, I probably shouldn't go rocking up at his door looking pissed at him.

He made an effort last night—a very fucking small one, but an effort all the same. While I can blame his crappy behavior on why we don't get along, his piss-poor personality isn't the only reason we are where we are. Maybe if I'd been honest with Cam when I realized he wasn't like his father, to begin with. Or maybe if I could have told Hawk when I found out he was my brother.

So many what-ifs. Regardless, I know I wouldn't have done anything any different. I didn't trust them. Fuck, I still don't, but I guess Emilia's friendship, and spending time with Beck, have made me realize you have to take a leap of faith sometimes. Besides, if they snap this olive branch I'm offering, I can just beat the shit out of them and bury their sorry asses in a deep, dark hole in the middle of the forest.

Pushing through the entrance into the boys' dorms, I climb the stairs to the top floor, wiping my palms on my jeans before I knock on the door. My heart slams against my chest as I wait anxiously for someone to answer.

After what feels like forever, I hear the latch and the door opens, with Hawk's scowling face in the doorway.

"What do you want?"

Charming as ever, I see.

Rolling my eyes, I swallow the snarky retort on the tip of my tongue.

"I wanted to talk."

He raises an eyebrow in expectation. "So talk."

What was I saying earlier about his pissy personality not being the reason we don't get along?

"Let me in, asshole." *Oops, there goes the hold I had on my snarkiness.* "I have something I need to tell you all. Now, do you wanna hear it or not?"

He stares me down for another moment until his curiosity wins out and he opens the door.

"Fine." He huffs as I move past him, glancing around the empty apartment.

"Where's everyone else?"

Being the chivalrous host that he is, he ignores me as he walks toward the seating area, plonking himself down on the sofa that separates the kitchen from the living room. Seated in front of the wide-screen TV, he picks up a controller and restarts whatever video game he was playing, all while I stand there watching him.

"Mason and Cam are at the gym, and West is at the library," he responds, not pulling his attention away from the screen where he seems to be killing zombies or something.

Moving over and sitting down on the opposite end of the sofa, I watch him for a few minutes as he stealthily moves through some sort of desert terrain, shooting at anyone who comes near him.

He doesn't bother to ask me why I'm there. In fact, I'm pretty sure he's pretending I'm not here at all. I'd planned to tell all of them at once, but now that I'm here, I just want it over with. I can feel the words lodged in the back of my throat, and I don't think I'm going to be able to breathe properly until I spill them all out. My leg bounces up and down, and I feel physically sick.

Spotting a second controller on the coffee table, I reach forward and snatch it up, needing some sort of distraction. "Does this game have two players?"

I know, I know, I'm totally stalling. I just need a moment to relax so I can think straight to get the words out.

The asshole snorts. "Do you even know how to play?"

"If you can do it, I'm sure I can figure it out," I snark back.

Shaking his head, he comes out of the game, setting it up so the screen is split in half, each of us looking through the eyes of the character we're playing.

"You have to kill all the zombies before they eat your brains."

Sure, that makes total sense.

It takes a few minutes for me to work out what each button does—because the asshole beside me doesn't bother to tell me—and how to smoothly maneuver my character across the screen. Still, after a few near misses from the zombies, I figure it out, and it's not long before I'm throwing axes at their heads like a pro and shooting them with a gun I managed to pick up somewhere.

We silently play the game for a while, the two of us working together to destroy the zombies. Once he's realized I'm not going to get myself killed and that I might actually be an asset in whatever the fuck the goal of the game is, he starts directing me so the two of us can take out larger groups.

"You're going about it all wrong," I argue. "You need to attack them from this side, and I'll take the other."

"No, two of us attacking one side will be better than splitting up."

"I'm telling you, you're wrong."

He sighs. "Fine, we'll try it your way, but when we die, we're doing it my way next time."

"Whatever," I grumble. We aren't going to die, so it's a moot point.

Taking opposite sides, we manage to fight and kill our way through the biggest hoard of zombies yet, revealing a glowing golden chest in the center that they were apparently protecting. When Hawk's character approaches it, it is full of food to restore our energy—'cause, yeah, a group of the undead protecting a chest of food, that makes total sense.

What the fuck is this shit?

Having seemingly completed the level, the game returns to the main menu and I turn to smirk smugly at Hawk as I set the controller on the table.

"Told ya."

He just scowls at me, but he does appear mildly impressed at my ability to shoot and kill undead things in a video game. If only he knew what I could do in real life.

"I didn't realize foster kids got much of a chance to play video games."

His words wipe the smug look off my face as I glower at him. "They don't. It's not exactly difficult to work out how to press a few buttons and aim and shoot."

He turns in his seat to lean his shoulder against the back of the sofa as he brings a leg up and crosses his arms, running his gaze over me. Every time he looks at me like that, scrutinizing me, it's like he's trying to make sense in his head of how I'm his sister. It's like he still hasn't come to terms with it. Or maybe he just can't figure me out.

"What did you want to talk about?" he asks after a long moment of awkward silence, the two of us analyzing one another. When we aren't arguing or pissing each other off, we really have no idea how to act in one another's presence.

"Ehh." I look away from him, suddenly becoming very interested in the patterns the grains of wood make in the floorboards underneath my feet as I try to gather my courage. What I'm about to tell him will change everything; for better or worse. "You wanted to know about Lawrence."

I glance up at him out of the corner of my eye, taking in his raised eyebrows and look of surprise before he masks it.

"And you're going to tell me?" He scoffs.

Looking away again, I pull on a loose thread on the sofa, tugging and wrapping it around my finger.

"He would visit me once a month," I begin, ignoring his shitty tone and keeping my eyes focused on my fingers as they fiddle with the loose thread. My voice suddenly sounds unnaturally high-pitched, my throat dry and scratchy, and I cough in an attempt to clear it. Instantly feeling somewhat better when my next words come out stronger. The only way I'm going to get the words out is if I emotionally detach myself from the subject; pretend none of it happened to me but to some other girl. "Has done ever since I was a kid. I didn't understand back then why he was giving me all this attention, although as I got older, his...intentions became clear." I can feel Hawk, stiff as a board on the other end of the sofa, watching me intently as he hangs on my every word. "I started to resent the days he would come. The things he would say...the way he would touch me." My voice breaks over the final words as my composure crumbles and memories crash over me.

"You're mine, little Dove," *he whispers against the shell of my ear, his hand clamping possessively around my shoulder. "We belong together. Soon I'll be able to take you away from here. You'll finally be where you should always have been—at my side, day and night."*

His hand trails down my side, his fingers deliberately brushing over my breast, his sigh of pleasure twisting my stomach as I struggle to maintain my composure.

"Wouldn't you like that, Dove? Being mine."

"Yes, sir."

The words come out robotically, not that he notices, his fingers digging painfully into the flesh of my hip as my response excites him and he fixes his gaze on my red-painted lips, a wild and hungry look in his eye that scares me more than anything else I've experienced in this cruel world.

As though his possessive promises that sent shivers of fear skittering up my spine weren't enough, the raging monster he had lurking beneath the surface that would raise its ugly head when I did anything wrong—when I didn't move fast enough, didn't respond quick enough, didn't say or do what he wanted—was even more terrifying. It's like he became a entirely different person. His whole face would rearrange itself into something unrecognizable and looking into his eyes was like looking into the flaming pits of hell. There was no redemption there, no mercy to be seen.

I quickly learned to be and do precisely what he wanted, tucking the real me into a box in my mind on the days he would come to see me, pulling out a version of myself I had to pretend to be in order to make it through his visits.

"I knew it was only a matter of time until he would make true on his promises. As I got closer to turning eighteen, he pushed the boundaries more and more with every visit." Even now, I can feel his skeevy hands and hungry looks on me, the way they dug under my skin, rotting me from the inside out as I slowly withered.

"I was going to make a run for it, disappear into the unknown and never look back, except one day I heard him on the phone. He mentioned Cam and Pacific Prep. He'd never told me anything about himself. I didn't even know his name, yet as soon as I could, I got on a computer and found the school's website and a picture of Cam with the rest of the swim team. I did more research on him and the Rutherfords and, well, I wanted Lawrence to pay."

I wanted him to experience the same kind of torture he had inflicted on me with every visit, with every dark-laced promise and controlling touch.

I can't tell Hawk what my initial plan was—that I came here to get my revenge on Lawrence by killing his son. I had assumed Cam would be every bit as demonic as his disgusting father, and honestly, I couldn't see past my own need for vengeance. Of course, Cam—sweet, funny, loveable Cam—was nothing like his father. He has some of the same anger burning underneath the surface, but it's not born out of greed and malicious intent like his father's. Cam's anger is forged from pain, a pain he's been carrying for a long time. Pain that I added to, pushing him over the edge until it consumed him.

"And that's why you got close to Cam." It's impossible for me to tell from his tone whether Hawk believes me. His voice is cold, detached, carefully concealing his thoughts about what I've said. "To learn something you could use against his father."

He didn't phrase it as a question, however I answer him anyway. "Yeah. That's why I spent time with him at first, but things changed as I got to know him."

He doesn't say anything, and I don't know if he believes me.

"But the notebook had information on all of our parents. Why, if he was your target?"

I shrug my shoulders, not willing to give him an answer to that yet. "Know your enemy and all that."

He lapses into silence, thinking through everything I've just told him as I continue to stare at my lap, repeatedly swallowing as my fingers pull and pry absently at the thread, slowly unraveling the stitching on the lining of the couch cushion.

He abruptly gets to his feet, the sudden movement startling me as I stare up at him, watching warily as he walks around the sofa into the kitchen area. Opening the fridge, he lifts out a beer for himself, twisting off the cap and tilting his head back so he can down over half the bottle in one gulp.

Standing on unsteady legs, I move around to the back of the sofa, meticulously watching Hawk's every move on the other side of the kitchen. Not being able to gauge what he's thinking means I don't know what to expect. Is he going to yell and lash out at me?

His hand tightens around the bottle as he glowers at the counter. Just when I think he's going to blow a fuse and throw the bottle, he tosses his head back, downing the beer.

"You need to tell the others," he says, slamming the empty bottle down on the island counter between us. He doesn't look at me, and I don't know what to make of that. Does he believe me? Is he holding back his judgment until he can get the guys' opinions?

Fuck, not knowing is going to give me an ulcer.

"Yes, well, that's why I'm here."

He nods, but I don't think he's really listening to me at this point. I've no idea where his head is at.

I open my mouth to ask him if he believes me, only the words stick in the back of my throat and I end up gaping at him like a fucking fish before snapping my jaw shut. *Jesus Christ, Hadley, you aren't this fucking fragile.*

The sound of a key in the door has both of us jerking our heads toward the noise as the door opens and Mason and Cam walk in. Whatever they were discussing dies on their lips as they take in Hawk and me standing in the kitchen, their gazes flicking between us as they no doubt pick up on the tension lying thick in the air. I don't know what we look like. Hawk's expression is unreadable, yet I feel too emotionally exposed, like every inch of what I'm feeling is displayed on my face for them to see.

"What's going on here?" Mason asks warily, stepping up to the island separating Hawk and I, acting like a physical manifestation of all the secrets hanging in the air between us.

Cam hangs back by the door, and even though I don't look directly at him, I can feel his eyes on me. After last night, he's probably even more pissed at me, yet I am holding on to the small hope that he actually heard what I said to him. Who knows how he will act around me after today, though. Will he be surprised? Or has he always suspected, or perhaps even known, that his dad is a deranged lunatic?

"Hadley's finally decided to tell us the truth," Hawk grits out, somehow sounding both furious and distant at the same time.

Both Mason and Cam look at me, confusion and surprise readable on their faces. Hawk still doesn't meet my gaze. He hasn't looked at me since I told him everything, and it's beginning to freak me out.

He goes back to the fridge, grabbing three more beers and hands one each to the guys. Mason goes to refuse, but Hawk laughs dryly. "Trust me, you're going to need it."

Reaching out to take the bottle from him, Mason glances in my direction asking a silent question, but I shake my head.

Cam crosses his arms over his chest, quirking a brow when I look his way, letting me know he's all ears.

"We should wait for West," I state bluntly, my cold tone matching Hawk's. I can feel the vulnerability I showed him earlier, slowly diminishing as my usual walls rebuild themselves. Having their eyes on me stresses me out, and the thought that Hawk doesn't believe me, or worse, he does believe me but doesn't care, is too much for me to handle.

"I've already texted him," Hawk says, taking a swig of his second beer.

As the seconds slowly tick by, all four of us stand in awkward silence, no one knowing what to say or do. I'm suddenly regretting ever opening my goddamn mouth. Why the fuck did I think trusting these assholes was a good idea? *Fuck me*, I'm going back to being a socially inept hermit after this.

A fucking eternity passes before the sound of the key in the lock breaks through the tension. I breathe a sigh of relief even though butterflies take flight in my stomach, and I feel sick at the thought of having to repeat myself. At least we can finally get on with it.

"Hadley?" West asks as he enters the apartment, his gaze landing on me before darting to the others. "What's going on?"

Before Hawk can open his big mouth, I blurt out, "I need to tell you guys why I'm here at Pacific Prep."

Three sets of eyes narrow on me in a mixture of confusion, suspicion, and surprise. I can feel my legs going weak beneath me, and I move to sit on a barstool at the island.

My stare falls on Cam, regret coursing through me at the thought I might be about to tear apart his whole world. He's already implied his parents aren't good people, but there's bad and then there's *bad, bad*. And Lawrence Rutherford is the fucking worst.

He must see something in my eyes as his hard stare falters, his brows drawing together in confusion. I wasn't able to look at Hawk at all when I poured my heart out to him. Although this time I can't seem to take my eyes off Cam as I once again tear myself open, showing all of them the darkest, most damaged parts of myself.

His eyes widen to the size of saucers the more I talk, and he occasionally shakes his head as though his refusal to believe the words will make them just that—untrue.

When I'm finished, the weight of the silence that falls in the apartment is suffocating. It's like there's no oxygen left in the room. My body sags, collapsing in on itself. Shedding the weight of that secret has drained me, somehow leaving me feeling heavier than I did before.

I just want to curl up in my bed, left alone to drown myself in my dark thoughts and even darker memories. Cracking open the tightly sealed door I had on my past has taken a greater toll on me emotionally than I expected. Knowing what a shitty existence you have is one thing, but sharing that history with others is something else. It's so much easier to pretend you don't have it that bad when no one knows just how fucked up your life is.

Not saying anything, Cam turns on his heel and storms toward the door, throwing it open and leaving.

Fuck, that can't be good.

My gaze darts to Mason, who seems torn between staying here and going after Cam, but he eventually sighs and throws me a sympathetic look before following after him.

Good, he shouldn't be alone right now. God only knows what thoughts are running through his head.

Without saying anything, Hawk walks past me, his beer in hand, as he disappears down the hallway toward the bedrooms. His response, or lack thereof, finally breaks me, a single tear slipping out and trailing down my cheek.

I quickly wipe it away before West can see, although he's watching me like a hawk, so there's no way he missed it.

Taking a deep breath, I lock down all the pain and heartache I'm feeling right now, rearranging my tough exterior.

"You don't need to do that," he says softly.

He's wrong, though. I need to lock all those feelings up tight and throw away the key. I have to get back to my roots, where I don't give a fuck and don't let people in. What fucking good does it do when they'll turn their backs on you anyway?

As though he can read my thoughts, he closes the distance between us, a stern look on his face.

"Don't do that," he growls, his hand wrapping around my jaw, his thumb and forefinger pressing firmly into my cheeks. "Don't shut yourself off. Hawk and Cam just need time. They'll come around."

"What about you?" My voice is void of emotion. I'm not sure whether that's because I'm just so emotionally drained or because I've locked it all back up. I'm honestly too wrung out to think straight.

He loosens his grip on my jaw, his hand gliding lightly down my neck, making goosebumps pebble under his touch. His fingers caress the skin until they trail along the delicate chain of the necklace. I haven't taken it off since he gave it to me. I'm not even sure why. I'm not exactly a jewelry person, yet something about having it on me brings me comfort.

A pained expression crosses his face, mixed with anger and hate. "You should never have had to go through that." The menacing tone of his voice catches me by surprise.

It's nothing like the demanding husk he occasionally uses with me that has my panties melting, or even the alpha tone he used on Deke and the jocks at the party, or when he told everyone to get lost after the fight night. His voice is pitch black, filled with shadows, and plagued by monsters.

"You're not in this alone now," he promises, wrapping his arms around me and pulling me in for a hug. The caring gesture threatens to have tears streaming down my face, and it takes me a second to respond. Still, I slowly relax into his embrace, my hands grasping the back of his t-shirt as I press my face against his chest, willing the pressure behind my eyes to subside as I breathe him in.

I've gotten used to cuddling with Beck over the last few weeks—I'd deny it if anyone asked, but I actually quite like it—but being hugged by West feels completely different. Maybe it's because I'm feeling so exposed right now, but the steady calmness his embrace brings me is soothing. It's like listening to one of those nature audio tracks to help you fall asleep. Instantly, my erratic heart rate starts to settle, and all the stress seems to fade away. Nothing matters but this moment right here.

I don't even know if his words are true. Not that I think he's lying to me but based on the way Cam and Hawk stomped off, I think he's going to have a hard time convincing either of them to even be in the same room as me after today.

Pulling back so he can look down at my face, his arms still loosely wrapped around me, he says, "I'll talk to the guys. It'll be okay."

I want to believe him so badly it hurts, but if life has taught me anything, it's to not have high hopes in the face of such overwhelming odds. Cam already hated me. If anything, this is even more reason for him to want nothing to do with me. And Hawk...I don't even know what to think when it comes to him.

With emotion clogging my throat, I simply nod my head. I go to step back, breaking out of his hold, but he tenses his arms, preventing me from getting away.

I glance up at him through my eyelashes just as his lips press against mine in a lingering, chaste kiss. There's nothing heated or passionate about it, but it's so much more meaningful than any kiss has a right to be. With that brief touch, he tells me he's here for me. That he believes me, and he's going to do everything he can to sort it out with the other guys.

That one kiss obliterates my heart and permanently marks it with his name.

Hadley

CHAPTER ELEVEN

I can't settle after leaving the guys' dorm, and I toss and turn most of the night, finally giving up in the early hours of the morning and deciding to work out my frustrations in the gym instead.

When I'm dressed in my gym gear, I throw my hair up into a messy ponytail and open the door, coming to a halt when I find Cam sitting on the floor opposite my room. His long legs are stretched out in front of him, his head leaning back against the wall. He's sound asleep, a soft snoring noise coming from him. His face is relaxed, void of the usual tight lines and angry frowns he's been donning these days. He almost looks peaceful. The way he's sitting does not look comfortable, though, and he's going to have a crick in his neck if he stays like that for too long.

Bending down in front of him, I gently shake his shoulder.

"Cam?"

His head snaps forward, nearly colliding with mine and I quickly lean back out of the way just in time. He blinks the sleep out of his eyes as he wakes himself up.

"What are you doing out here?"

There are bags under his eyes, and he looks more haggard than yesterday. I guess that's the toll of finding out your father is a sleazy scumbag.

"I came to see you." His voice is thick with sleep, giving it a husky quality that makes my vagina clench like a greedy whore. I haven't forgotten how fucking good he felt with his body pressed against mine as he drove me to insatiable heights. Any time I'm around him, my body seems to come alive, craving more of him. Even when he looks at me like he'd rather strangle me, I still want him.

"You have to actually knock on my door for me to know you're out here," I jest awkwardly, not sure what to say. The fact that he's even here has my heart dancing an irregular rhythm, my thoughts racing a mile a minute, wondering why.

"It was late." He runs a hand through his blond hair, mussing it up before climbing to his feet. I stand along with him. "I didn't want to wake you." An awkward silence passes between us, both of us staring transfixed at one another before he blurts out, "What you said yesterday was true? My father really did that to you?"

He watches me closely with his warm brown eyes that simultaneously heat me up and put me on edge. They've been full of so much hostility lately, all aimed at me, and I can't blame him. But today, they're brimming with questions, his gaze curious and unsure.

I maintain eye contact when I answer him so I don't miss the pain in his eyes when I confirm what I'm pretty sure he already knows. He just needed to hear it from me.

I notice his jaw ticking a split second before he loses his cool. "Fucking hell," he roars, raging down the hall away from me. His body is coiled tight, fury practically radiating off him as his arm snaps out and he punches the wall.

I gape at him, surprised at his outburst as he runs his hands through his hair, pulling on the ends and groaning. It's an agonizing sound composed of pent-up fury and pain. I can't see his face, but his back is tense and his muscles are rigid as he attempts to restrain himself.

He lashes out again, punching the wall in the same spot. I know I should tell him to stop, except I'm completely frozen, watching him inflict pain on himself.

His third punch cracks the plaster and leaves red speckles of blood on the white wall, his knuckles busted from the force.

He drops his fists, his shoulders rising and falling sharply as he tries to regain control of himself. When he turns around again, he looks utterly distraught, his face pale and sunken. I thought he appeared haggard when he woke up, but he now looks like a completely different person.

The pain and loathing in his eyes tear me apart. Not because it's aimed at me but because he's going through all that. I knew telling the truth would be difficult for him, only I never wanted to put him through any of this.

His gaze falls to the scars running across the top of my shoulder. "Did he do that to you, too?" he growls through gritted teeth.

"No." I shake my head. "That was someone else."

I didn't think it was possible, but somehow those words seem to shatter him even more, his face crumbling with the last of his composure dissipating.

"That's why you refused to be my girl of the month. You didn't want anyone else to pull the same possessive bullshit as my dad." The words are a harsh croak mostly spoken to himself, but I nod anyway, confirming it.

"Oh my god." Any remaining color leaches from his face, and he looks like he's about to puke. "I...fucking hell, I practically raped you."

"What?" I gasp. How the hell did he reach that conclusion? "No, you didn't." I finally manage to unstick my feet from the floor, rushing toward him, but as I reach out to touch his arm, he pulls back, stepping out of my reach and shaking his head.

"Cam," I snap in a sharp voice. "You didn't."

He's not listening though, mumbling under his breath as he shakes his head.

I don't know what to do or how I can help him, so I stand there helplessly.

"I'm so sorry, Hadley." His voice is broken. Beyond broken. He sounds wholly destroyed, and when he looks me in the eye, it's like a core part of himself is missing. He's a mere shell of the man he was only moments ago.

He takes off down the hall without a backward look, ignoring me as I call after him. Pushing open the door at the end of the hall that leads into the foyer, he strides through it, disappearing out of sight and leaving me gaping after him.

Fuck. I've no idea how to fix him. Hell, I don't even know how to fix myself.

A couple of doors crack open as other students peer out, probably having heard our early morning commotion. Ignoring them all, I grab my gym bag off the floor where I dropped it when I found Cam and glare at each of the nosey assholes as I stomp past them out into the morning air.

∼

My head's not in the game at the gym. My punches are sloppy. None of my hits are landing quite right, and they're making my knuckles hurt and my arms feel heavier quicker than they should. I've just given up on the bag, pulling off my fingerless gloves when Mason arrives, halting my movement toward the treadmill.

He freezes just inside the doorway, both of us watching one another. He took off after Cam yesterday, so I never got a chance to determine his reaction to everything.

I try to read something, anything, from his expression. However, he's as unreadable as ever, his features blank. He's the hardest one out of the four to figure out. Does he feel the same static charge in the air I do when he's nearby? Sometimes, the way he looks at me, I think he does. Then on days like today, I can't work him out at all. Perhaps those moments are all in my head.

Sometimes I think about that kiss after I fought Hawk, and the other night at the Davenports'. Jesus, was that only two nights ago? So much has happened since then. My lips tingle just remembering the feel of his mouth against mine, my tongue flicking out at the memory. His eyes zero in on the movement, my heart skipping a beat at the heat that rises in his eyes.

"Have you seen Cam?" he asks, tearing his gaze from my lips to look into my eyes.

"Yeah. I think he spent the night sitting outside my room."

He nods his head like he expected that. "Is he okay?"

"I don't think so. He stormed off before I could really talk to him."

Mason sighs, his shoulders slumping as he nods his head again, a strand of hair falling into his eyes. He brushes it out of his face, searing me with an intense look.

"Are you okay?"

It's the first time someone has asked me that, and I actually don't know the answer. *Am I okay?* I didn't just have my whole world torn apart like Cam or have a heavy bomb dropped on me like the rest of them. But everything feels different now, and I'm not entirely sure if it's a good different or a bad one.

"I don't know," I reply honestly, exhaustion hitting me like a freight train.

"I understand why you didn't tell us earlier. I'm not even sure why you would tell us now. What changed?"

"I'm sick of all the secrets." I sigh. "What good are they doing any of us?"

He nods his head knowingly. "I'm guessing Beck knows all of this too?"

"He does." He must pick up on the hint of steel in my tone as he quirks an eyebrow. He needs to know I won't take any shit from any of them about Beck.

"You sort stuff out with him?"

"Not that it's any of your business, but yes."

He takes a step toward me, his head tilting to one side.

"So, you're dating now? 'Cause according to him, you are." Another giant stride in my direction. "Yet you were in that room with West and me." He steps forward again, his gaze warming with every step he takes as the electric charge in the air intensifies and my pulse skyrockets. "You let us put our hands on you, kiss you." He focuses on my mouth as, with another large step, he places himself in front of me. "You liked it."

"Beck knows he doesn't control me." I intend the words to come out defiant, yet the breathiness of my voice betrays how fucking turned-on I am right now.

"Does he know what we did?" His gaze dips, taking in my sports bra that gives him an eyeful of my tits and lean stomach. The way he's looking at me has my chest heaving and my nipples peeking below the thin fabric.

"He does."

His head lifts, my words surprising him as his wide eyes meet mine. A split second later, his irises darken with hunger, like the idea of Beck knowing that, of him thinking about what Mason and West did to me, is turning him on.

"Does he know you're going to do it again?"

His voice is a seductive growl, deepened with lust, the combination of it and his words making me clench my thighs. A small step has him closing the last little bit of space between us, his body brushing against mine, the fabric of my bra rubbing against his polyester muscle shirt.

"Yes." The word is nothing more than a low whisper, but the second it leaves my mouth, his lips descend on mine, his tongue sweeping into my mouth in what can only be described as a claiming. With every sweep of his tongue, Mason marks me as his.

My fingers dig into his shoulders, clinging to him as I moan into his mouth. Tugging on his shirt, I pull it up over his head. Our kiss breaks just long enough for me to remove it before he wraps his arms around me, yanking me into his hard chest.

My hands roam over his large biceps and the corded muscles of his chest as my tongue delves into his mouth.

His hands slide down over my workout pants, squeezing my ass before he effortlessly lifts me, my legs wrapping around him as he walks us over to some exercise mats. He lowers us to the ground, hovering over me. His pale blue eyes devour me, drinking in every inch of my flushed cheeks and heaving chest.

He dips his head, kissing along the side of my neck until he reaches my collarbone, running his tongue along one of the scars there. He takes his time, slowly kissing his way down over my chest, undoing the front zip of my bra so my tits spill out into his hands.

Kneading one in his large palm, I can see his knuckles are split, something I hadn't noticed before, the angry red lines reminding me of the sheer force that is Mason Hayes.

He runs his tongue along my peaked nipple, eliciting a moan as I arch my back. His pelvis presses against mine, providing some much-needed friction as he sucks my nipple into his mouth, biting gently on the sensitive skin. The sting of pain only intensifies the pleasure though, and I begin grinding against him hungry for more.

Moving on to the other one, he lavishes it with the same attention before trailing his tongue over the phoenix tattoo over my ribs.

The combination of his hands and tongue drives me wild as I writhe beneath him, mentally cursing him for not rushing and getting to where I need him most.

My hands run down his back, and I notice the telltale lines of scars crisscrossing over his back. *Huh, I never noticed that before.* Looking down, I can see white lines similar to my own cutting sharp lines across his skin.

Our conversation from before comes back to me.

Why do I feel like our pain is the same?

Because, baby, it is.

Is that what he meant? That he knew the physical pain I'd experienced to leave those scars?

His tongue travels over the swirls of black ink as he follows the line down my side to my hip, distracting me from my wayward thoughts as his fingers dip beneath the waistband of my leggings. He deftly tugs down my leggings and panties in one move, pulling off my trainers and dropping them on the floor beside us as he leans back over me, his tongue picking up where it left off on my lower hip.

His lowering lips move agonizingly slow while his hand trails a heated path up my inner thigh. His fingers brush teasingly over my core, and I practically jump at the light contact, making him chuckle against my skin. He's got me so worked-up and on edge I'm fucking weeping for him.

I release an impatient growl, telling him without words to hurry the fuck up, but instead of doing as I want, he stops, lifting his head as he looks down quizzically at my tattoo.

"Is that a design mixed in with the tail of your phoenix?"

"Seriously?" I growl. "You want to stop what we're doing right now to talk about my tattoo?"

Leaning forward, I capture his lips with mine, distracting him. My fingers run over his muscular chest, trailing the hills and valleys of his abs until I reach the waistband of his shorts. Slipping underneath, I wrap a hand around his hard dick. He groans into my mouth, questions over my tattoo long forgotten as I slide my hand along his hard length.

With my free hand, I push his shorts and boxers down. He fishes out his wallet, pulling out a condom before kicking off his clothes and settling between my thighs again.

He swipes his fingers through my pussy lips, easily sinking two fingers inside me as he rubs his thumb over my clit. My head falls back, my eyes closing as I moan.

He lowers his head, once again sucking my nipple into his mouth as he adds a third finger, stretching me.

"Mmm," he hums against my skin. "So tight."

"Mason," I moan, anxious for him to get on with it. His fingers just aren't enough.

Chuckling, he uses his teeth to tear open the condom wrapper and roll it down his long length. Positioning himself above me, he slides inside of me, one glorious inch at a time, until he's fully seated. My walls spasm as they adjust to his girth.

"Fucking hell," he groans as I whimper, lifting onto my elbows so I can kiss him. It's a languid, sloppy kiss, both of us overwhelmed with pheromones and the need to get closer to one another.

He pulls back until he's nearly all the way out before slamming back into me, as we both chase our release with a quick, desperate rhythm.

Wrapping my legs around him, I lean up, pushing on his shoulder until I'm on top and he's lying on his back, watching me.

At this angle, he can get so much deeper, and I moan as his length slides against the perfect spot. His hands cup my breasts, kneading them as I ride him.

"Fuck, I could get used to this," he groans. His eyes are half-lidded with lust as I dig my nails into his chest, using the leverage to pick up a faster rhythm, which he readily meets thrust for thrust.

As we get lost in the throes of pleasure, our movements become erratic. He grips my hips, his fingers pressing firmly into the skin as he takes control, slamming up into me and hitting the spot with every thrust until I'm crying out his name.

With another few thrusts, I feel his dick swell within me as he comes. "Jesus, fuck, Hadley," he grunts, his arms wrapping around me as I collapse onto his sweaty chest, both of us breathing heavily.

"That was not the workout I had planned when I came down here today." He chuckles, making me laugh.

"Shit," I panic. "What time is it? Class must be starting soon." I push myself up, his dick sliding out of me as I climb off him and pull my clothes back on.

"Yeah, we've got about an hour," he says casually, moving to dump the used condom in a trash can at the edge of the room and retrieve his own clothes, getting dressed.

"Crap, I've gotta go."

Getting to my feet, I retrieve my gym bag from the far side of the room.

"Well, can't say I've ever been pumped and dumped before," Mason quips before I run out of the gym.

The guy's all jokes today. It is amazing the effect great sex can have on a personality.

Throwing him a smirk over my shoulder, I rush out of the gym, leaving him behind me, staring at my ass as I go.

Hadley

CHAPTER TWELVE

There are only five minutes left of breakfast when I rush into the dining hall. I almost trip over my feet when I find three of the four Pricks sitting alone at their table. The only time they are alone at the table is on the first day of the month when they choose a new girl, except they just started a new month last week. Cam is missing—something that concerns me after the way he was this morning.

Quirking an eyebrow at Emilia as I move to grab a banana and granola bar for a quick breakfast, she shrugs her shoulders, telling me she doesn't know what's going on.

Looking around the rest of the room, students are huddled together in groups at various tables, whispering and shooting glances at the guys, everyone speculating about why they're eating alone and wondering where Cam is. There hasn't been a single day where one of them has skipped breakfast. It's like their morning ritual, reminding us all who's in charge.

I must admit, I really didn't want to walk in here and have to watch the girls drooling all over them. I've always hated seeing that. It does stupid things to my stomach, yet after the few intimate moments with West over the weekend and this morning with Mason, I was not looking forward to having to watch the usual attention-seeking-bitch-in-heat show while trying to eat.

"What's going on?" I ask Emilia as I sit down opposite her at what has become our new table. I've been avoiding the dining hall at breakfast as much as possible since I stopped hanging out with the other scholarship students, and even more so since the stupid video. The first time I came in here after being exiled from the scholarship table, I hadn't a clue where to sit. There were only a couple of students at this table, so I'd chosen it, but as soon as I sat down, they quickly vacated their seats, leaving me alone. Not that I gave a fuck. The few times I ventured in here after that, this table was always free, so I claimed it as mine.

It's nice having Emilia sitting with me—even if the reason for it pisses me off. The thought has me seething at the scholarship table, not that any of them notice.

"I have no idea," Emilia answers, sounding way too excited about the drama. "But the girls are *pissed*."

Looking around the room again, I notice what I may have missed before. All of the Princesses, past and current, are gathered at a table near the Princes. Some of them are comforting a couple of this month's girls, while the rest of them glare daggers at the guys. One of them, I think her name is Deirdre, is actually fucking crying. Huge sobbing tears. You'd think her fucking pet had died with the way she's getting on.

"Jesus," I mumble, rolling my eyes.

"Right?" Emilia laughs. "It's fucking hilarious. Why aren't they sitting with the Princes, though?"

She looks at me like she thinks I should have the fucking answers.

"How should I know?" I respond evadingly.

"Oh, you know, 'cause I'm pretty sure three of them are crushing on you."

I choke on my granola, coughing like an idiot to dislodge it from the back of my throat.

"What?" I wheeze. "Why would you think that?"

"Please, girl. They practically eye fuck you when you enter a room. There's absolutely something going on with you and them." She leans forward across the table, lowering her voice to a conspiratorial tone. "Right?"

She must read something in my expression as her face brightens, a grin stretching across it as she squeals. "I fucking knew it. Spill the beans, girl. I need all the deets. Man-meat like that must be talented between the sheets."

I can't help but laugh at her antics. Damn, I fucking missed her and the crazy shit that comes out of her mouth.

"I'm not telling you anything," I grumble, faking annoyance which makes her pout. "And they don't eye-fuck me."

"Girl, you're blind if you can't see it."

"Well, Cam doesn't eye-fuck me," I argue.

"Ehh, yes, he does. He's the most obvious."

"I think you're confusing lust for hate. When he's looking at me like that, he's thinking I'd make a pretty corpse."

She just laughs, shaking her head.

"But *something* has happened, right? With the other two? They were nice to us at Hawk's party."

Rolling my eyes again, I sigh. "Yes," I admit, only making her grin broaden.

"Eeekkk," she squeals. "With which one? Oh my god, with both of them?"

I don't say anything, which is telling enough, her eyes widening to the size of saucers as she gapes at me. "Oh, you dirty minx!"

"You're the one who got it on with *two* hot rock stars!" I snort.

She waves me away. "We're not talking about me right now. We're talking about you. So? Which one? Oh, no, wait, let me guess." She turns around in her seat, not even trying to be subtle, as she looks at West and Mason. They have their heads bent together, talking, while ignoring the stares and whispers around them.

"West. No, Mason. Oooh, a West and Mason sandwich—now that would be hot!"

My cheeks flame, thinking about Saturday night and the feeling of being pressed between the both of them. I would be perfectly okay with doing that again, the three of us going even further.

Jesus, it's not even midday, and my brain has fallen into the gutter. Emilia is such a bad influence.

"Holy shitballs," Emilia gasps. I hadn't even realized she had turned back in her seat to look at me. She can plainly see where my thoughts had drifted off to as she gapes at me, excitement dancing in her eyes. "It's totally both of them."

The bell goes off before I can think of a response, not that I really need to confirm it, and there's obviously no point in denying it. She would know I was talking crap.

Walking into English, Cam's seat beside mine is empty and he doesn't show up for the rest of the lesson. I barely pay attention to Mr. Greer at the front of the room, instead spending most of the class looking at our chat on the tablet, ruminating over messaging him. I need to know he's okay, but I'm pretty sure he doesn't want to hear from me.

When the bell rings indicating the end of class, I stuff the tablet in my bag and head to my next class. I decide to find one of the guys before the end of the day and ask them how he's doing.

~

I HAVE a free period before lunch, so I go to the library to try and get some work done.

"What do you think you are doing?" Bianca's whiney voice breaks through my concentration, shattering the thought I had as she shouts across the library and causes heads to turn in our direction as she stomps toward me.

Dammit, I need to get this history report done today.

Carefully setting my pen down on the table, I scan my eyes over the other students working silently in the library before scowling at Bianca. Her face is blotchy, and her eyes are glaring daggers at me.

"What do you want, Bianca?" I sigh, speaking at a much more appropriate volume, considering we're in the middle of the library.

Standing right in my personal space so she's towering over me in her ridiculously high heels, she places her hand on her hip.

"Do you think I'm stupid?" she spits.

I hope that's not a serious question. She's not going to like the answer if it is.

"We all saw you at that party with West, then suddenly the Princes are eating alone at breakfast and having nothing to do with us. You can't just come in here and mess with the rules," she snarls.

"I'm not messing with anything. I have nothing to do with the guys not wanting any of you money-grabbing idiots hanging all over them."

Bianca's hand slams down on the table, the slap of her flesh hitting wood pulsating across the quiet room, and again drawing students' attention our way.

"You have no idea what I or the others will do to ensure we get a Prince," she threatens, leaning down, so her face is uncomfortably close to mine. I can see the layers of makeup caked on her face, clogging up her pores and making her look years older than eighteen.

"You realize there are only four of them and like twenty of you, right? That math doesn't exactly add up."

"*You're* the one getting in my way," she growls. "I *will* get myself a Prince, and if you don't keep your hands off of what doesn't belong to you, we *will* be forced to get rid of you."

I have to hold back my laughter.

Bring it on, bitch. I'd love to see you fucking try.

Having said her piece, she storms off, and I roll my eyes before quickly forgetting the interruption and getting back to my history report.

Emilia sends me a message as I walk into the hall for lunch, telling me she has choir practice and can't make it for food. That girl is in so many extracurriculars it's insane. I don't know how she does everything and keeps on top of her schoolwork.

Ordering food for myself at the kiosk, I sit at my new regular table, ignoring the other students around me. It's much more pleasant coming here at lunch than it is for breakfast. The hall isn't as busy, with most students choosing to eat elsewhere on campus, or too busy with extracurriculars, and it's a mixture of all-year groups. I'm pretty sure the whole school knows about the Pricks' vendetta against me and the stupid fucking video, but the younger year groups don't seem to give a shit, something I find refreshing. They probably have enough drama going on in their own year group to worry about ours, but still, it's nice not to be bombarded with hateful looks and cheesy pickup lines.

I thought that shit would have died down this semester. I mean, get over it. It was one fucking video of me in my underwear. So what? I'm pretty sure the Princesses—god, even in my head, that sounds pretentious as fuck—are keeping it going by encouraging the other students to be shitheads. Deke and the jocks have been the worst, catcalling and asking when the next photo shoot is every time I walk past them.

They all seem to have forgotten I beat Hawk in the ring, and I'm beginning to think it's past time for another demonstration. Let's see what the assholes have to say when I hand them their asses at the next fight night.

Sitting down at the table, I reply to Emilia's message. Too engrossed in responding to her and not expecting any company, I'm taken by surprise when someone sits down opposite me.

Looking up from my tablet, I quirk an eyebrow before glancing at the other tables. "Ehh, what are you doing here?" I ask Hawk, watching him warily as he casually leans back in his chair.

Looking around for the other guys, I notice West slipping out of the hall. Did that dipshit seriously just abandon me to deal with Hawk? Doesn't he realize how dangerous that is? We'll have leveled the whole damn building by the end of lunch if the infuriating ass starts anything with me.

I also don't miss how the other students openly gape at us, waiting to see what Hawk will do to me. I scowl at each and every one of them until Hawk's voice has me focusing back on the asshole himself sitting at *my* table.

"Are you always so aggressive?" he bites back, his eyes narrowed as he watches me closely.

Why the fuck is he always looking at me like that? Ever since the whole sibling bomb dropped, anytime we're around each other, it's like he's trying to dig under my skin and figure me out.

"Nope." I smile sweetly. "I guess you just bring it out in me."

A waiter arrives with my food, setting down a plate of spaghetti and a side of mashed potatoes. It's a total carb fest, but I'm fucking starving after barely eating anything for breakfast.

Picking up my fork to dive in, I pause when the waiter sets the exact same dish down in front of Hawk.

What the fuck?

Looking from his side of mashed potatoes to his face, his eyes are wide with surprise and bewilderment.

The first time I ordered this combo in front of Emilia, she looked at me like I had three heads. I'm pretty sure it's just me that thinks potatoes with pasta isn't the weirdest combination ever.

Although, as I watch Hawk shovel spaghetti into his mouth, following it up with a forkful of potatoes, I'm beginning to wonder if it's a fucking Davenport thing.

"When did you learn to fight?" Hawk asks me after we've been eating in silence for a while. By now, I'm seriously fucking confused. What the hell is he doing sitting with me? And why hasn't he said something to piss me off yet? This is *not* how interactions between us typically go.

"I'm confused. What are you doing right now? Why are you sitting with me?" I ask, ignoring his question.

Finishing off his meal, he leans back in his chair, once again studying me.

"It's called making an effort."

I tilt my head to the side, my eyebrows pulling together as I try to understand what he's saying.

"An effort to do what? Creep me out?"

He frowns. "I'm trying to get to know you."

Oh.

"Why?" I ask, scrunching my nose up. It's not that I don't want him to, I'm just confused about the sudden change in his attitude. "Is this because of what I told you? 'Cause I don't need a pity friend."

"No," he growls, grinding his teeth.

I quirk an eyebrow, squinting at him. "I also don't need you to sit here and pretend to care just because West told you to."

"I'm not," he snaps, getting irritated. "Would you just shut up for a second?"

Is it weird that I feel a bit more at ease when he's being all snappy with me?

He sighs, still surly at me. He purses his lips like his next words taste bad in his mouth, but he manages to force them out anyway. "We're...family." It looks like it physically pains him to say that. "And the guys think we should try to get along."

My eyebrows climb toward my hairline. I guess West's chat with him yesterday got through to him.

"And there's obviously shit going on that we need to all talk about and sort out."

I glance nervously around the room, except no one is sitting near us.

"Okay," I agree. "How do we do that?"

He shrugs. "No idea."

His words are said with much reluctance; however, it is the beginning of a tentative, albeit hostile...friendship?

For the rest of the week, Hawk joins me for lunch. One of the guys must have spoken to Emilia as they are all strangely absent every lunchtime. The two of us simply sit in awkward silence, occasionally making stifled conversation.

I don't get much of a chance to speak to West or Mason all week, although they have started sending me messages every day, checking in and asking how my day is going. It's all superficial, yet it makes me feel all giddy inside when I see their names on the screen—*I know, I'm turning into a sappy love-struck idiot.*

At my session with Beck on Thursday, I rehash everything—about telling the guys about Lawrence and my concerns about Cam. I even confide in him about the feelings I've been denying that I have for West, Mason, and Cam. It's the first time I've openly said as much. Until now, I've been telling myself it's only sexual chemistry, but I don't know. Things have been different since they returned after the break—at least they have with West and Mason. There's always been something there, although it feels more serious now. Like none of us can ignore the pull toward one another any longer. Nevertheless, I still have no idea what is going on between us, and with all the other shit we need to discuss, it's low on the priority list.

Beck reiterated what he had said the other day, that he was okay with me exploring whatever this is between the other guys, but the dark promise in his words when he threatened to make them regret ever being born if they hurt me, had lust burning through my veins. What's not to love about a guy who's willing to destroy your enemies for you?

Cam returns to class on Friday. I don't know where he's been all week, but when I asked the guys, they assured me he was okay. He doesn't look alright, however. He's got rings under his eyes, and he's not sporting any of his usual light-hearted, flirty banter. He's withdrawn, ignoring everyone around him and snapping at the slightest thing. It concerns me how much he's changed since the beginning of the year. Can he ever get back to being that person? I hope so. I miss who he used to be. I could do with some of the light he used to emit in my life so easily right about now.

All week, none of the guys have a girl at their table. Not even Hawk. While I'm secretly pleased to see West, Mason, and Cam without anyone hanging all over them, with each passing day, the girls get more and more worked up. They've been taking their anger out on me, upping the petty bitchiness. It used to be Bianca who led the bitch train when she walked past me in the hallways, but now all of them call me catty names and sneer when they see me.

In the face of everything else going on, I couldn't give a single fuck about them, but I know the longer the guys ice them out, the angrier they are going to get. Since they can't take out their resentment on the Princes, it appears I've become their target. Shame they don't know who they're messing with.

There is a party on Friday night, but I've convinced Emilia to stay in and watch movies instead. While she sets up the tablet with a film, rearranging her cushions into a makeshift sofa, I go to the dining hall to grab us some ice cream.

I can hear the noise as soon as I open the door.

"You're not upholding your end," Bianca argues in her usual annoying high-pitched tone. "You've been ignoring the girls all week. We won't stand for it any longer."

Someone snorts.

"What are you going to do about it?" Mason's detached, callous tone rings out, and I peek through the door gap. All four guys are facing off against the Princesses. There must be about twenty of them by now. "If we want to not deal with any of you for a week, that's up to us."

"And what about next week?" Bianca demands. She and the other princesses have their backs to me, so I can't see their expressions, but I can only imagine the pissed-off look on their faces.

"I guess you'll find out next week."

"Well, what about the party tonight?" some girl pipes up.

"We won't be there." Hawk's face is impassive as he scowls at the girls, showing how little of a fuck he gives about the conversation.

"This is ridiculous," Bianca whines, the other girls murmuring their agreement.

Cam cackles, a sound that verges on hysteria, showing just how close he is to losing his shit.

"Tough shit, B, it's not like you missed out on your turn or anything."

Bianca cocks her hip, straightening her shoulders.

"Sort your shit out, boys. Things better be back to normal next week."

She turns on her heel, striding across the dining hall in her sky-high heels, her entourage following behind her as they head my way.

Before she reaches the door, I pull it open, striding into the room. Bianca's scowl deepens when she sees me, the other girls wearing matching expressions.

"Oh, look," she drawls, "it's the scholarship trash."

I smile sweetly. "At least I'm not a fake bitch. Is any part of you not filled with silicon?"

As she approaches me, I notice each of them is wearing matching pink pins on their shirts, in the shape of crowns that say *Princess* across them. *Dear lord, just when I thought their little group couldn't get any more pathetic.*

"Aww, my pin must have gotten lost in the mail." I fake pout.

"Even if all four Princes chose you, you'll still never be a Princess," Bianca snarls.

Okay, well, that's just gross considering one of them is my brother.

I shrug. "Queens don't need crowns."

Anger blossoms on her cheeks, her eyes narrowing to slits as she glowers at me.

"See, that's the thing about true power." I lean in toward her as though I'm sharing a secret, not bothering to lower my voice. "You don't need to constantly remind people you're all that. They just fucking know it."

Her lip quirks up as she sneers at me, a high-pitched growl coming from her as she stomps her foot and storms past me. The rest of the princesses scowl and whisper words like 'bitch' and 'slut' as they pass, yet I just continue to smile sweetly at them. Kill them with kindness and all that bullshit.

When the door closes behind them, I let the fake-ass smile fall off my face as I roll my eyes.

"Such lovely girls," I retort sarcastically.

"I didn't know they gave you any hassle," West says, a tight expression on his face.

"It's nothing I can't handle," I assure him, waving off his concern. Please, a few high-heeled bitches who couldn't land a punch if their lives depended on it? The thought of them getting the better of me is laughable.

"All of us need to sit down and talk," Hawk states, looking at me like he's expecting me to argue. For once, I'm in agreement. I don't really know their thoughts after last weekend, and they've had plenty of time now to process everything.

I nod my head. "Yeah, we should."

"We can take food back to our dorm."

"Tonight?" I lift an eyebrow.

"Yeah, why not? You got something better to do?" Fucking asshole always has to phrase things in such a way to deliberately piss me off.

"Yes, actually. I do," I bite.

"Well, drop it. This is more important."

I stand taller, his demanding tone straightening my spine. "I'm not about to just drop my plans because you demanded it," I snap. "I'm not your fucking monkey. When you say jump, I'm not going to ask you how high.

"Now, I have plans tonight, but I can do tomorrow if that suits you, your royal highness." My voice is heavy with sarcasm.

Before he can reply with some snarky response that will only escalate things, West steps forward, sighing wearily as he pins Hawk with a look, silently telling him to shut up.

"That's fine," he agrees. "Come over to ours tomorrow night."

"Will do."

I cast a glance at Cam, but he's looking pointedly at the floor, ignoring my existence. Not knowing what to do or say to him, I sigh, shaking my head before moving over to the freezer, grabbing as much ice cream as I can carry and ignoring all four of them as they watch me walk back across the hall and out the door.

Baby

CHAPTER THIRTEEN

*H*er words play on repeat in my mind like a fucked-up song I can't get out of my head. Every replay only sickens me further as fury, self-hatred, and shame all fight for dominance within me.

I couldn't stand being in that school any longer. Couldn't bear the thought of being anywhere near her. Just standing in the same corridor as her, seeing the concern and worry in her eyes, was driving me fucking insane. How can she look at me like that? How can she be okay being anywhere near me after what my father has done to her, after what *I* have done to her?

When I stormed away from her in the dorm, I headed straight for my car, not even thinking about where I was going. I just drove and drove. I could feel my phone vibrating like crazy in my pocket, the guys wondering where I'd disappeared off to, but I just didn't have it in me to respond to them.

I don't know how long I drove for before I wound my way up the private road to where our parents live—not that they're ever fucking here. They spend a lot of time away on business and own apartments closer to work that they tend to use during the week. Usually, I like knowing they won't be here, but as I idle at the gate, I wish just this once that my fucking scumbag of a father was home. With the amount of rage coursing through me, I'd probably kill him, and I wouldn't even fucking feel bad about it. Hell, it would be fucking cathartic.

Driving through the gates, I pull into my driveway. Parking in the garage, I skirt around the side of the main house and walk through the garden to the pool house. As I said, I highly doubt my father is home, but I can't risk running into him. With the way I'm feeling, I wouldn't be able to hold back, and as much as I might want to hurt him, I don't fancy doing twenty-five to life for killing the fucker. Nor do I want to give away the fact that I know what a sick piece of shit he is.

Letting myself into the pool house, I close the blinds, blocking out the whole fucking world as I help myself to the liquor cabinet going straight for the top-shelf vodka and downing it directly from the bottle.

The pool house is just one large room with a seating area comprised of a couple of sofas and a large-screen TV. Off to one side is a small kitchenette and a door leading into a bathroom.

I'm halfway through the bottle of vodka before Hadley's voice starts to become fuzzy, her words finally dying down, enabling me to think straight. Well, as straight as one can think when they're half-cut.

How the hell can my father do that? He's been fucking grooming her, for years. Like a fucking online predator, only worse, 'cause he fucking visited her wherever the hell she was.

Where was she? Where were the adults who were supposed to be looking out for her, protecting her from sickos like him?

My blood boils and I throw the now empty bottle of vodka across the room, the sound of it smashing against the wall and shattering into pieces doing nothing to quiet the raging storm within me.

Grabbing another bottle—I don't even know what the fuck I'm drinking now—I gulp down the burning liquid.

What were my father's intentions? What the fuck was he going to do to her when she turned eighteen? Marry her? How the fuck did he think that was going to go over with the other families and me when he brought home a bride the same age as his fucking son? Not to mention the fact it would clearly have been a forced marriage. What would he have done to Hadley to keep her here?

Vomit rises up the back of my throat, and I make it to the sink just in time to throw up, washing the acrid taste away with more alcohol.

I can be disgusted at my father all I want, for I'm just as bad. Fucking hell, I'm worse. I did what my father never got the chance to—I fucking raped her. All because my fucking pride was hurt. Because I thought she didn't want me, when she just didn't want to be 'owned.' Jesus, fuck, she even told us as much, and I just refused to listen.

Stumbling back to the couch and downing a quarter of the bottle I'm gripping, my head falls back against the sofa as my eyes drift shut. Images of all the shit I did to her flash across my closed lids. The hurtful words, the rough way I would grab her, the video. The stupid fucking video. Fucking hell, how could I have been so dumb as to encourage Hawk with that. How the fuck did I see those scars and not think that she's been through enough shit.

It only raises new questions, questions I should have asked myself ages ago. Did my father inflict those wounds on her? Did he cause that pain? Even if he didn't, he didn't put a fucking stop to whatever was happening to her.

The night I shoved my way into her bedroom flashes across the back of my eyes next, like a fucking movie reel. The way I taunted her, how I wrapped my hand around her throat. Jesus, I squeezed her neck so fucking hard. Her lips were practically blue. Yet, she didn't cry out or fight against me.

A fresh wave of nausea washes over me as I remember pushing my way inside her, taking what I wanted and not giving a shit about her. I don't make it to the sink this time; I don't even try as I lean over the side of the sofa, throwing up on the tiles. My stomach clenches painfully, nothing left inside it to bring up.

Swiping at my eyes, I can feel wetness on my cheeks, tears marking tracks as they run down my face.

How can I ever make right what I did to her?

I can't. I'm pretty sure they don't sell gift baskets with cards saying: '*Sorry, I fucking violated you*'.

I must pass out somewhere near the end of the second bottle of alcohol, and over the course of the next few days, every time I wake up, I drink. I drink enough to dull the pain, to forget what a shitstain I am. To forget what a fucking disgusting family-line I come from.

I don't know how fucking long I've been hiding out, but it doesn't feel like long enough when voices break through the fuzzy haze in my head. My mouth tastes fucking disgusting and I'm pretty sure I'm still drunk. I can't get any part of my body to cooperate enough to move or form words as I lie on the sofa, zoning in and out of the guys' conversation.

"Jesus Christ, it stinks in here," someone grumbles.

"Smells like he hasn't showered in days."

"Yeah, and he's vomited too."

"Come on, let's just get him cleaned up so we can get out of here. I already feel like I need a shower."

Someone jostles me, and I groan.

"Cam, come on, man, you've been hiding out for four days now. That's more than long enough. Shit needs to be dealt with."

Four days is nowhere near long enough. A fucking lifetime wouldn't be long enough.

"No," I growl, although it comes out more as a slurred, unintelligible grunt.

Ignoring me, someone—my eyes are glued shut; I literally can't pry them open—grabs onto me and hauls me into an upright position. My stomach revolts, but there's nothing left to bring up. I don't even remember the last time I ate. It was before I got here, anyway.

"Cam, dude, come on, you weigh a fucking ton," Mason grumbles.

Fucking liar, asshole could lift three of me without breaking a sweat.

"Leave me alone," I groan, trying to push him off me, except I've no strength in my arms.

"Fucks sake," he murmurs. In the next second, his hands leave me and I sink back against the couch cushions. Their voices fade away as I fall back into sleep.

The next thing I know, something ice cold breaks me out of my snooze. My eyes fly open as cold water drips down my face, soaking through my shirt and effectively blocking out the pounding headache behind my eyes as I glare at a smirking Hawk.

"What the fuck?" I snap. I don't have the energy to put any heat behind my words, though.

"Morning, sunshine." He's got a shit-eating grin on his face. "Although, technically, it's nearly midnight."

"Get in the fucking shower," West demands, handing me a clean pair of sweats and a t-shirt that they must have brought with them. "You fucking stink."

Scowling, I carefully get off the sofa, my balance unsteady as I take the clothes from his outstretched hand and stumble toward the bathroom.

After a shower, I still feel like death, but at least I don't smell like it anymore. By the time I leave the bathroom, the guys have the place mostly straightened up. They've lined up five or six empty bottles of alcohol, brushed up the broken glass, and even cleaned up the puke from several days ago.

Man, sometimes I really love these guys.

"How you feeling?" West asks, handing me a bottle of water which I gratefully take and down in several large gulps.

"Like shit."

"Yeah, a drunken binge will do that to you."

"Right, well, now that you've got the pity party out of the way, we have a lot of shit to discuss and deal with," Hawk says unsympathetically. Asshole can't even let me get some solid food in my stomach before starting into it.

"Here, eat this." Mason hands me a cream cheese bagel. *Mmm, that'll do.*

Careful to avoid the wet patch from my ice-cold wake-up call, I collapse onto the sofa and practically inhale the food, washing it down with a second bottle of water. West sits beside me, and Hawk and Mason take the couch opposite us.

I eye Hawk while I finish my food, wondering how he's taking Hadley's news. His face is set in its usual angry scowl, so it's impossible for me to tell how he's feeling.

"How's Hadley?" I ask, looking at West. Not that I should be asking about her. I told myself I wouldn't. I need to stay as far away from her as I can. I'm not any good for her. Fuck, I don't even know how she can look me in the face and not see my father staring back at her.

"She's doing okay. She's been asking about you."

Why? After the way I've treated her, she should be happy I haven't been around all week. My face scrunches, wishing she would just forget about me.

"What are we going to do about all of this?" Hawk asks.

"What do you mean?" I ask, rubbing at my temples, my head still too muddled with the remnants of alcohol to think straight.

"We all know your dad," Hawk explains. "If he wants something, he gets it. Do you honestly think, just because Hadley is at Pac, that he's going to let her go?"

Fuck. I should have thought of that, but I'm also surprised to hear Hawk talking about protecting Hadley. That's a one-eighty from how he's been behaving toward her all year.

Running my hand through my still, damp hair, I sigh and let my head fall against the back of the sofa.

Staring up at the ceiling, I ask, "What are we supposed to do?"

"Dude, what the hell?" West snaps. "You spent most of last semester chasing after her, and now you sound like you don't give a shit. Does what she told us not mean anything to you?"

West rarely gets angry, especially at us. Not that he's not capable of being as ruthless as Mason and Hawk, and he has a similar darkness to my own; he's just usually above it all. I think he secretly gets off on people underestimating him. Everyone thinks that he's a nerd or weak because he wears glasses, studies hard, and doesn't work out as much as us. But he can be just as cutthroat as the rest of us. If anything, it just makes him more terrifying when he does give people a glimpse at the monster lurking within him.

I glare at him. If I had it in me, I'd fucking hit him. Of course, what she said meant something. "It changed fucking everything," I snarl. "Why the fuck do you think I'm here, drinking myself stupid?"

"You aren't responsible for your dad," Mason tells me, throwing in his two cents.

"Maybe not, but I'm responsible for my own actions," I mumble, only half telling the truth. I feel like I bear some weight from what my father did. I know it's stupid, it's not like I knew or could have done anything to stop it, but I feel like I *should* have known. I've always hated him; he's a possessive, controlling asshole. It's why I act out so much, trying to regain as much control over my own life as I can. I never thought he would have the same influence over someone else's life. And Hadley had to go through it all alone—at least I had the guys for support.

"You've been shitty to her since she turned you down, so what? Now you know why. Just apologize and move on."

Of course, the guys don't know the extent of how fucking horrible I've been to her.

I shake my head. "I don't want anything to do with her," I say adamantly. "It's best for everyone if I stay away from her. I'll help with whatever you need to protect her from my father, but as for her and I, we're done."

Hawk must see the determination on my face. That, or he's happy he's finally gotten his wish, since he doesn't argue or say anything. He just simply nods his head like he agrees with that decision.

"What about you two?" he asks, looking at West and Mason.

We've never really talked about the fact that all three of us have become fucking obsessed with Hadley. I flick my gaze between them, curious about their responses—not that I give a shit. As I said, I'm done with her now. She can do whatever she wants.

Mason shrugs, but West's response surprises me.

"I'm not letting her go."

He's never shown any genuine interest in girls. There were a few when we first discovered how good it felt to stick our dicks in pussy, but after some bullshit rumors in the first year, he's been like a fucking nun. He must be a born-again virgin, by this point.

Hawk's eyes narrow on West before shifting his gaze to Mason. "And you?"

"I'll see where it goes," he responds vaguely. He's always kept his cards close to his chest, but if it was just sexual attraction to him, he would have said as much.

Hawk doesn't look happy by their responses, but the fact he doesn't throw a hissy fit at either of them blows my mind. What the fuck happened to the Hawk from a week ago? He's suddenly 'Team Hadley' now?

"Alright," he agrees reluctantly. "Just don't let your dicks get in the way of keeping her safe."

I gape at him. "For real? You're okay with the fact they want to fuck your sister, but when I wanted to, you bitched me out over it?"

His face scrunches, looking repulsed. "Don't say it like that. That's fucking gross. And I think we have more important things to worry about right now, don't you?"

"So, what, you trust her now? You're over the bullshit from last semester and embracing the whole twin thing?"

"I'm not saying that," he growls, getting frustrated. "However, I'm not a complete fucking asshole. She's…" He sighs, gritting his teeth like he's admitting something he really doesn't want to acknowledge. "Family." He says it like those are words he's been repeating to himself all week in some sort of attempt to help him bite his tongue.

Well, at least he hasn't completely changed. It would just be creepy if he was suddenly all buddy-buddy with her. Not that I don't want her to get to know her brother. After the shit she's been through, it's the least she deserves.

Hawk is an asshole but fiercely protective of the people he cares about. Although a selfish part of me doesn't know how I'd cope if all three of them suddenly insisted on including her in everything. I can't afford to lose my brothers, but I can't be around her, not all the fucking time. It's going to be difficult enough seeing her around campus and occasionally having to be in the same room as her when we all get together to sort out this shit with my dad.

"I have an idea about what we can do," West states, getting us back on track. He glances at Mason and me before fixing Hawk with a look, thinning his lips. "But neither of you will like it," he says, meaning Hawk and Hadley.

"What is it?" Hawk demands.

"If your parents knew about Hadley—"

"Absolutely not," Hawk cuts across him, shaking his head. "No fucking way. I've been doing as you asked all week, making an effort with her, but I'm not ready for the whole fucking world to know."

My eyebrows lift at that bit of knowledge. Damn, I'd love to be a fly on the wall for those little chit-chats. I imagine it's mainly silent glares and sharp retorts thrown at each other.

"This isn't about you, man," Mason argues.

"It would offer her more protection," West continues, like neither of them spoke. "It would make it harder for Lawrence to get to her. He might even back off altogether. There's no way he would jeopardize his position in the business by risking your parents finding out what he's been up to all these years."

Hawk scowls, still shaking his head in denial.

"After the shit that went down with our parents, you honestly think bringing another heir out of the woodwork is a smart idea right now? Look how well that worked for you."

Ooh, low blow.

West seems to agree as he glowers at Hawk.

"I think it's a risk we need to take to keep her safe," he retorts icily.

There's no love lost between West and Beck, yet things have been even worse since Christmas, with West blaming the guy for the position we're in now with our parents. Although, the way I see it, we were always going to end up here, whether or not he existed. West isn't hearing any of it, though.

"She's not cut out to be a Davenport," Hawk argues, trying a different tactic. "The other rich fuckers our parents are friends with, not to mention the kids at school, would tear her to shreds."

"She might surprise us," West retorts, not letting Hawk dissuade him. "And we can watch her back at school. If we accept her, everyone else will have no other choice but to do the same."

"But I don't accept her," Hawk growls, too agitated to sit still any longer. Getting to his feet, he paces back and forth across the small space. "I don't fucking accept her. What she's been through sucks, and it answers some questions, but there's still too much we don't know about her."

"Well, being an asshole to her didn't get you anywhere," West snaps, getting irritated as he stands too, glowering at Hawk. "You want to know all her secrets? Get to fucking know her, idiot. If we hadn't been such shitheads to her, maybe she would have felt comfortable talking to us months ago."

Can't deny he has a point there.

Marching back toward him, Hawk scowls, but he doesn't argue further knowing West is right.

"Fine," he growls. "Only don't blame me when she fails to live up to the standard expected of us."

With that settled, the four of us lock up and head back to campus. West might have gotten Hawk on board with his plan, but now he has to convince Hadley, and she's a whole other kind of storm to navigate.

CHAPTER FOURTEEN

"What the fuck is he doing here?" West barks, jumping out of his seat as soon as Beck and I step into their dorm.

My eyes flick to Cam who is lounging in an armchair, deliberately not looking in our direction as Mason silently closes the door behind us. Hawk, appearing angry as always, watches us closely from his seat.

"You said we needed to talk," I state, crossing my arms over my chest. West might be sweet with me, but he can be a right asshole when he wants to be. From what Beck has told me, West has no reason to be so hostile toward him. "Beck knows everything, so he should be here for this conversation."

"Not that I was going to let you guys continue to be dicks to her." Beck narrows his eyes on all four of them, placing his hand on my lower back as we move over to the empty sofa. He sits down, pulling me into his lap in a blatantly obvious gesture of possession.

Mason watches us closely, and even Cam lifts his head. West's scowl deepens as he glares daggers at where Beck's arm wraps around my waist. The jealousy and annoyance in their eyes have me clenching my thighs. *It's totally wrong that seeing how easily I can get under their skin turns me on, right?* Beck's possessive behavior should be setting off alarm bells, the way my inner thoughts would scream at me to get the fuck away from Lawrence when he acted like a possessive psycho. But I know Beck isn't like Lawrence; his actions might be intended to tell the guys I'm his, but he's already told me he's okay with me pursuing whatever is between the guys and me. I'm not sure how accepting of it he actually is, but the fact he's not trying to put restrictions on me only has me falling harder for him.

Beck doesn't miss the slight movement as my thighs press together, and he glances down at me. His brows raise in surprise, a knowing smirk lifting the corner of his lips as dirty thoughts dance in his eyes.

Someone clears their throat, and we both shift our heads to look at the other guys as they watch us closely.

"So, what did you want to talk about?" I ask, leaning back against Beck, taking strength from having him here with me.

Mason sits down on the other end of our sofa, giving West a pointed stare until he sits back in his seat beside Hawk.

Throwing a glare at Beck over my head, he looks at me, his eyes softening.

"Do you have a plan for dealing with Lawrence?" he asks.

My gaze flicks to Cam, who is watching me closely, but there's a shield around him preventing me from getting a read on his thinking. He almost looks detached. Like he's here in the room, paying attention, only he's not letting himself feel any of it. He still looks tired and worn out, but he's not as pale as yesterday.

Glancing back at West, I shake my head. "No. Not yet. Nothing that doesn't involve me leaving Pac."

He raises an eyebrow, but it's Hawk who speaks up.

"You thought about running?"

I can't tell by his flat tone if he wants me to do exactly that, and fuck off right out of his life.

"It crossed my mind."

"It wouldn't do any good even if she did run." Beck's arm wraps tighter around me, not liking the thought of me disappearing, so I run my hand soothingly over his arm to help calm him. It's a gesture he does to me when I'm anxious and helps me, so hopefully it does the same to him.

Thankfully, his words steer the attention off me before Hawk can pry any further. I'm not about to tell him my reasons for staying here. He would have a fucking field day if he knew the lunches we had this week had given me some hope that we can learn to get along and further solidified that I can't just up and leave this place.

Pacific Prep was only ever meant to be a pit stop on my journey to get as far away from here as humanly possible, but everything has changed now. Not only do I have answers to questions I've spent my whole life wondering about, but I have Beck and Emilia, and I don't want to give them up. They make me feel more human, more alive. Everything in my life has been about survival, endurance, and pain. But since I met them, I'm beginning to realize there's so much more to life. I want to laugh and let loose. I want to have those quiet moments with Beck and talk shit with Emilia. Lawrence has been a black cloud hanging over me for far too long and I refuse to let him control my life any longer.

"A guy like that, he'd only chase her until he got his hands on her again."

My body tenses. What he's saying isn't news to me, yet the thought of it doesn't sit well. It's the life I had planned for myself—constantly on the run, evading Lawrence—but now that I'm settling in here, it's no longer a life I want.

His hand slips under my top, the warmth of his palm relaxing me as he lightly strokes his fingers across my side.

The guys all nod in agreement with his assessment of Lawrence.

"We need a plan then, if you're going to stay here," West says.

"We?" I question, looking at him in confusion before flicking my gaze around the other three. "I didn't tell you so you'd sort out my problems for me."

"We know that, but we want to help."

Now I know that's a crock of shit.

I go to call him on it, but Beck squeezes my hip. "What were you thinking?" he asks.

Both West and Mason grimace, and I know I'm not going to like whatever West says next.

"We need to tell Mom and Dad about you," Hawk blurts out through gritted teeth, the words barely more than a snarl that makes West's head whip toward him as he frowns.

"What?" I gape open-mouthed at Hawk. "You want to tell your parents about me?"

"Technically, they're *our* parents." He doesn't look happy about that fact, but the shithead is completely overlooking the point.

"If your parents know, everyone will know. It will make it next to impossible for Lawrence to do anything. Did he, uh, ever say what his plan was when you turned eighteen?" West rubs his hand along the back of his neck, awkward as fuck. I can't blame him, it's not exactly a pleasant conversation to bring up.

"Nothing specific." I shake my head. "He'd say that we would get married and live together, but I don't know where or anything."

All four of their faces darken, and I can feel Beck's chest vibrate with anger against my back. Cam jumps up from his seat, mumbling something under his breath as he storms into the kitchen behind me. No one says anything as he bangs around, and I hear a drink being poured. He must down it because there are more sounds of liquid hitting a glass before he stomps back to his seat with a tumbler filled with dark brown liquid.

West pins him with a disapproving look, but Cam ignores him, drinking from his glass.

"I don't want everyone to know," I tell them, getting back to the topic.

"Don't you want to meet your parents?" Hawk asks, tilting his head to the side and pursing his lips.

"I..." I don't know. After the brief introduction to Mrs. Davenport and the snooty way she looked at me, I'm not exactly chomping at the bit to be in her presence again. "Not like this, under these circumstances. And I definitely don't want the whole school to know who I am."

"Why? You'd automatically be above all those girls talking shit to you yesterday."

I quirk an eyebrow at him. "I'm not in competition with them. I don't give a shit what they think of me, and I have no interest in being above them in any sort of social hierarchy."

Hawk just doesn't get it. Maybe in his world everything is about besting the people around you, but as far as I'm concerned, that's just another reason for me to stay the fuck out of it.

"Look." I sigh, shifting my gaze back to West. "I appreciate you wanting to help and all, but I've got this."

"Clearly." Hawk snorts, rolling his eyes. He thinks I'm some helpless girl who can't look out for herself, but he has no fucking idea what I'm capable of.

"Oh, so you want the whole world to know we're related?" I fire back, making him scowl at me. "You want us to be forced to attend social events together and sit opposite one another at family dinners?"

His grimace tells me all I need to know about what he thinks of that idea.

"Exactly." I look at West and Mason before fixing my stare on Cam. He's too busy observing his nearly empty glass, but he must sense my eyes on him as he looks up. "I told you about Lawrence to clear the air between us and because I felt you should know."

Tearing my gaze from Cam, I spear the other three with a severe look. "*Not* because I need your help. Thanks for your input, but that plan's just not going to work."

I climb out of Beck's lap and get to my feet, heading toward the door. I can sense Beck behind me, and I'm pretty sure I hear Hawk grumbling about how he knew I wouldn't agree to the plan as I open the door and walk out.

"Hey." Beck reaches out to stop me as we descend the stairs, turning me round to face him. "What are you thinking?"

"Nothing." I shrug, making him arch an eyebrow at me.

"Their plan has merit."

"Seriously? You want me to come out as a Davenport."

"No. Maybe." He shrugs. "I want you to do whatever you're comfortable with. I'm just saying it's not a terrible idea."

"Why didn't you say any of this in there?"

"And agree with West?" He snorts. "He would ditch the plan just to spite me."

"In that case, you should definitely have said something." One side of my lips lifts to let him know I'm joking—partially—and he smirks back, tugging me into him.

His hands slide around my hips as I wrap my arms around his neck. "I'm on your side, I'll support whatever you want to do, but I think you should give some thought to their idea."

"You know, if I agreed, you'd be dating a rich, pampered princess."

He grins. "And you'd be going out with a guy from the wrong side of the tracks."

I laugh. "Sounds like my kind of guy."

Stretching up on my toes, I press my lips to his.

"I'll think about it," I tell him, and he rewards me with a dirty kiss that's all tongue and makes me not give a single fuck that we're making out in a public stairwell where anyone might see us.

A cough has us instantly jumping apart. We both glance up and find West standing at the top of the stairwell, looking uncomfortable. He's got a slight blush on his cheeks, and his lips are pressed tightly together, the only sign that he's annoyed by what he just witnessed.

"I wanted to talk to Hadley," he states, looking pointedly at Beck. "Alone."

"I don't wanna talk about that anymore today, Wes." I sigh.

"It's not about that."

Roaming my eyes over his face, I relent. "Okay." I sigh, turning to Beck. "I'll see you later?"

"Definitely," he murmurs, leaning down to kiss me again before looking over his shoulder at West and taking off down the stairs.

West doesn't say anything until the door at the bottom of the stairwell slams shut behind Beck.

"What's up?" I ask when it becomes clear he isn't going to speak first.

"Do you, uh, wanna go for a walk?"

He seems strangely nervous, much more like the shy, reserved guy I know, and not the asshole he becomes around Beck or when anyone at school threatens the guys' reign.

"Sure."

We head down the stairs in silence, making our way out into the dark, crisp night. It's a Saturday, so there are several other students around, making their way to the dining hall and rec center to hang out with friends.

He directs us past the dorms toward the lake. Since there isn't a party tonight, there's no one here but us. The lake is surprisingly peaceful when no one else is around, and we sit down on the short pier, our legs dangling over the edge.

The dark water is calm, the light breeze occasionally causing a ripple to run across the surface. There's no noise except the sound of the wind blowing amongst the trees. Tilting my head back, there's a bright crescent moon and the sky is full of thousands of tiny stars, the cloudless night making them stand out.

"It's beautiful out here," I breathe, unable to tear my gaze away from the stars above me.

"It is." West tilts his head back too. "I never come out here when there isn't a party."

We sit in peaceful silence for a moment before I glance away from the sky above us to look at him. "What's your deal with Beck?"

His head falls forward, and he sighs. "I dunno. Nothing really. It's more what he represents."

I don't say anything, waiting him out to see if he will continue.

"Since my mom found out about Beck, and my father's affair, she's been living in Europe. I was six when it happened. I've only seen her a handful of times since then. I basically have no relationship with her, and my dad's a self-serving asshole who constantly compares me to the other guys, so I don't exactly get along with him."

"I'm sorry, that sounds rough." I press my shoulder against his, unsure how I'm supposed to react or comfort him. "I, uh, don't understand what Beck has to do with that, however. You know none of that is his fault, right?"

He nods his head, leaning forward to see into the water. "I know. Logically, I know that, but when I'm around him, I just get so angry. It was easier to pretend he didn't exist and everything was okay when I didn't have to see him every day."

"I get that." I do. When Hawk isn't glaring daggers or scowling at me like I shit in his cereal, it's much easier for me to pretend he doesn't exist; that he isn't fucking related to me.

But at the end of the day, he is, and I have to accept that, just like Hawk has to accept I'm his sister, and West needs to accept Beck is his brother.

Leaning forward, I nudge West's shoulder. "He's a good person. I think you'd like him if you gave him a chance."

Adjusting his glasses, he pushes his dark hair back out of his face. Turning to look at me, he must see something in my expression. "You like him."

I can feel my cheeks flush as I nod. "I do. He..." I trail off, trying to find the right words. "He gets me." I don't know how to explain it to him, not without giving away any part of Beck's past or my own.

He nods his head though, like he understands, getting to his feet and holding out his hand to help me up. My hand lingers in his, enjoying the feeling of his soft palm against mine, before I reluctantly pull away. He looks at his hand when I let go. *Did he feel the same tingling sensation I felt when we touched?*

Shaking off whatever he was thinking, he turns to walk back down the pier.

"Didn't you have something you wanted to talk about?" I call out, causing him to face me.

When he looks at me, the moonlight reflects off his glasses. There's a sadness in his face that wasn't there a second ago.

"It was nothing important." With a final lingering look, he says, "I'll see you around."

He doesn't wait for me to respond, tucking his hands in his jeans' pockets and strolling across the beach and into the trees.

~

THE FOLLOWING WEEK, the weird lunches with Hawk continue, except there's more hostility and tension in the air between us after Saturday.

"Look," I say on Wednesday, sick of the friction hovering in the air and ruining my lunch every damn day. "You don't have to sit with me. I don't need to feel all of your anger directed at me while I'm trying to enjoy my goddamn food."

"I'm not angry," the idiot responds, barely sparing me a glance as he dives into his lunch.

"Right." I roll my eyes. "And I'm worth a million bucks."

He opens his mouth, likely to deliver some snarky response, except a high-pitched whine cuts him off.

"I can't fucking believe this." Bianca's grating voice slices through the air as she heads toward us, her Princess minions trailing behind her like good little puppy dogs. "I heard you were sitting with the trash last week, and I thought maybe you were toying with her, but here I find you *still* entertaining this degenerate." She sneers at me before fixing Hawk with an infuriating look. "What are you and the others playing at?"

"We aren't playing at anything, Belinda." Hawk sighs, deliberately getting her name wrong as he leans back casually in his chair, throwing his arm over the seat beside him.

"Then why are you sitting with her?" she whines.

Hawk shrugs. "Wanted a change of pace. She's much more interesting than any other girls we've had to put up with this year."

Despite knowing he's only saying that to get under Bianca's skin, my brows climb up my forehead in surprise before I carefully mask my expression.

"Then I'm sure you won't mind if I join you." She gives a falsely innocent smile as she moves to slide into the chair beside Hawk, but he pulls the chair away.

"Actually. We do," he states.

"No fake bitches allowed," I say, smiling sweetly at her, making her hateful glare fall on me.

She slams her hands on the table, leaning in toward me.

"I warned you," she threatens.

My brows scrunch together as I tap my lips with my finger.

"You did? I don't remember that."

Releasing a pathetic girly growl, she stomps her feet and throws Hawk a pissed-off glare before she takes off across the hall.

"Has she been threatening you?" Hawk demands as soon as her posse disappears.

"Did you just compliment me?" I retort.

"What? No. I was only trying to get under her skin," he snaps.

I smirk. "Sure you were."

Hadley

CHAPTER FIFTEEN

Over the next week, the semester settles into the usual mundane routine of classes, homework, and the gym. Cam seems to be going out of his way to avoid me. He never comes to English, and I've only caught brief glimpses of him around campus. Even West seems to be avoiding me, and I don't understand why.

The only person who doesn't seem to be pretending I don't exist, is Mason. He's driving me crazy in a completely different way, teasing me with his hot as fuck sweaty body every morning in the gym as he works out.

Every time I'm here, all I can think about is that glorious O he brought me to on the mats. It's fucking distracting. He hasn't been holding back since then, throwing me heated glances and snatching private moments to make out. It's hot as hell.

On Thursday, I'm walking through the main school building when a door swings open in front of me. Mason leans out, grabs onto me, and tugs me into the dark supply closet, pulling the door closed behind me.

"What the—" I gasp.

He cuts my words off, his lips slamming down on mine. Our kiss is heated. Both of us too worked up from the flirting back and forth over the last few days to need any warming up.

His hands slide around the back of my thighs, lifting me up and perching my ass on the edge of a shelf as he grinds his rock-hard erection against me.

I break off our kiss, my head falling back as I moan. I'm fucking drenched. I haven't been able to think about anything except the feeling of him inside me all week.

His hands slip under my skirt, and I groan.

"I can't," I pant, kicking myself for saying those words. "I have a counseling session with Beck now."

"He won't mind if you're five minutes late," he murmurs against my neck, sucking and biting his way along it.

He strokes his fingers along the front of my panties, humming at how wet he finds them. As he pushes them to one side, his tablet goes off in his bag. Ignoring it, he sinks two fingers into me, making me buck against him.

His stupid fucking tablet vibrates again, and he pauses before once again choosing to ignore it, pumping his fingers at a rhythm that has me panting.

When his phone starts ringing from inside his blazer, he growls and pulls it out of his pocket.

"What?" he snaps. He resumes finger-fucking me while listening to whoever is on the other end of the phone. His pupils are blown as he hungrily watches me come apart on his fingers.

"I'm busy right now."

Whoever is on the other end mustn't accept his response because they keep talking. He adds a third finger, pressing this thumb against my clit, and I have to bite my lip to hold back a whimper. He smirks as I squirm, a challenge entering his eyes as he rubs my clit in rough, fast circles, quickly bringing me to the brink of an orgasm.

"Uh-huh." He's barely paying any attention to his phone call, focusing solely on me.

He grins as I begin to spasm around his fingers and then he curls them up, hitting that perfect spot that causes me to detonate, and I cry out, unable to hold it in.

"Nothing, I'm just watching porn."

He smirks, and I release a breathy laugh as he slips his fingers out of me, sucking them into his mouth all the while keeping his eyes on mine.

He releases them with a pop.

"Look, I've gotta go. Yeah, yeah, I'll be there."

Not waiting for a response, he hangs up and pockets his phone before fisting the front of my shirt and pulling me toward him, kissing me fiercely, the taste of me dancing on his tongue.

"To be continued," he murmurs against my lips. "Have fun in therapy."

"It's not fucking therapy." I laugh, shoving him back.

"What do you two do in there anyway?" he asks, helping me down from the shelf. "A weekly fuck session?"

"You're such an ass." I laugh, fixing my uniform. This is a side of Mason I've truly enjoyed getting to know. He's got such a dry sense of humor. "It's the only time we can be together without worrying about anyone catching us or suspecting anything."

"Well, I hope he enjoys my hard work." He chuckles, slapping my ass and pulling open the door before I can call him out.

Going our separate ways, I head toward Beck's office. Of course, my little session with Mason has barely scratched the surface of what I needed, and his joking has dirty ideas flitting through my mind.

As I step into Beck's office, I flick the lock behind me, biting my lower lip as I lean back against the door. He glimpses up at me from behind his desk, raising an eyebrow when he sees the intentions visibly written on my face.

My eyes eat him up, taking in his preppy waistcoat and shirt combo. Along with his short stubble and styled hair, he looks thoroughly fuckable.

"Well, well," he purrs, leaning back in his chair and watching me with lust in his eyes. "Look at you, eye-fucking me like a starved person."

I smirk, crossing the distance and scooting my ass onto his desk. He rolls his chair back a bit, giving me just enough room to slide in front of him. Kicking my boots off, I press my feet on his chair on either side of his thighs. My skirt hikes up, giving him an unobstructed view of my panties as I spread my legs, leaning my palms back against the desk.

His eyes drop to the gap between my thighs as he licks his lips, his eyes practically turning black with desire. His palms run up my calves and over my thighs, pushing my skirt up to my hips as he runs his fingers along the seam of my panties.

"Do you know how many times I've sat here, watching you as my dick strained to get to you?" he asks in a rough growl.

Hooking his fingers under the lining of my panties, I lift my ass enough for him to pull them down my legs and over my feet, and he discards them on the floor pushing my thighs open wide.

"I don't think I'll ever get enough of tasting this pussy," he murmurs, his eyes glued to the gap between my thighs as though he's talking directly to it.

The way he looks at me, knowing I affect him as much as he affects me, has me gushing. My juices drip down my inner thighs, running onto the table, making him groan and bite his fist to muffle the noise. "Beck," I whimper, squirming a bit. Finally, he lowers his head, flicking his tongue out to run along my slit. I'm so sensitive from Mason that the light touch is enough to have me bucking into his mouth as I moan.

My hands thread through his hair, mussing it up as I grip the strands, holding him in place as his tongue circles my clit before he sucks on it.

"Fuck, Beck," I cry, my head falling back as I grind on his face.

He groans against my pussy, the vibrations making me gush more and whimper. He laps up my juices, inserting three fingers into me and I gasp at the intrusion, loving how I stretch to accommodate him.

"That's it, baby. Show me how fucking good I make you feel."

"Fuck, fuck, YES," I cry out, the combination of his dirty words and talented fingers and tongue lighting the match. Sending me up in flames. I'm barely aware of the fact that I'm in his office, and those sorts of noises should definitely not be coming from behind his door. Not that he seems to give a shit as he smirks up at me, sliding his hand through my hair and pulling me down to kiss him, tasting myself on his tongue.

I can't get close enough to him. Running my hands over his shirt, I tug on the buttons until I can get his waistcoat off and do the same with his shirt until I can roam my hands over his hard chest.

Shrugging my blazer over my shoulders, he quickly removes my shirt so I'm sitting in front of him in just my bra and skirt.

He pulls back, breaking the kiss as his eyes take in my heaving chest and the peaked nipples evident through the thin fabric of my bra.

"Turn around," he growls in a low husk that has my pussy clenching. Doing as he says, I lean over his desk with my ass in the air. Peering back at him over my shoulder, his eyes are glued to the globes of my ass as he folds my skirt back, grabbing an ass cheek in his hand.

His fingers circle my clit, before he slides them back to my pussy, appearing mesmerized.

"I've thought about fucking you over this desk since the first time you walked through that door."

"What are you waiting for then?" I taunt. His eyes meet mine as a dark grin curls at his lips.

Pushing his chair back, he gets to his feet, deftly unbuckling his belt and pushing down his pants and boxers. Holding his thick dick in his hand, he pumps it as he inserts two fingers inside me. I'm more than fucking ready for him and I push back against his hand.

"Beck," I growl loudly, my impatience making him chuckle.

"Quiet, baby, or I'll have to gag you." *Holy shit, yes, please.* My eyes roll back just at the thought, and I moan a little louder while wiggling my ass against him. A palm hits my ass cheek, and his hand grips my throat, pulling my back against his chest.

"Such a naughty girl." His voice is a deep rumble as he shoves his tie into my mouth and slams my chest back onto the wood.

He positions himself at my entrance, thrusting into me in one swift move that knocks the air out of me. His hands grip tightly to my hips, and he groans as he begins to move.

At this angle, he's so deep inside of me I know I'm going to feel the ache of him between my thighs for days to come.

"Hadley," he moans. "You're so fucking tight."

His thrusts pick up speed and I push back against him, causing him to slide even deeper inside me as his balls smack against my clit.

My pussy spasms around his dick, and he grunts, "Not yet."

Ah, fuck, that demand is so fucking hot.

Sweat coats my forehead as I struggle to hold back, the denial only pushing the pleasure higher. Fuck, when I do explode, it's going to be cataclysmic.

"Beck," I whimper, the sound muffled around the tie. He has me downright delirious. I just need to come.

His hands slide through my hair, and he pulls on the strands, causing my back to arch. The angle enables him to sink impossibly deeper inside me as my head tilts back at an awkward angle. He holds my hair in such a way that I can see him out of the corner of my eye as he rams into me.

His eyes meet mine. "I said, not yet." His voice is strained, and I know he's pushing off his own release.

I focus on the feral look in his eyes, using every bit of my resolve not to combust as every thrust threatens to send me careening over the edge into oblivion.

He smacks my ass, which is my undoing, and I spasm as he roars, "Now."

I feel him swell inside me as my pussy clamps down on him, both of us groaning our release as he collapses against my back and kisses along my spine.

Pushing the hair away from my neck, he caresses the sensitive spot behind my ear while removing the gag, and when I've finally caught my breath, I turn my head so our lips meet in a brief yet passionate kiss.

He pulls out, cleaning both of us up before I put my shirt back on. Once he's tucked himself away, he doesn't bother getting dressed again as he tugs me over to the sofa, pulling me in against him as we cuddle.

"How's your day going?" he asks, kissing my forehead.

This is what I love about Beck. He can fuck me like an angry caveman, then kiss me like I'm some sort of precious gem. He knows I'm not fragile or weak, but he also pushes me out of my comfort zone.

"Good." I sigh, pressing my face against his chest and breathing him in. This has become the norm for our sessions this semester. Well, there isn't usually amazing desk sex—although I'm totally adding that to our sessions from now on. We usually sit together on the sofa and talk about anything and everything. I'm like a completely different person from the girl who walked in here several months ago. Don't get me wrong, there are still topics I refuse to discuss, but he doesn't pry and is always accepting of my boundaries.

"Have the guys been bothering you much?"

"The opposite, really. I've hardly seen them all week. I think they're avoiding me."

"It's a lot for them to process, especially Hawk and Cam. They will come around."

"What if they don't?" I ask nervously, putting words to the thought ruminating around in my head all week. I lean up on my elbow so I can look down at him, needing to see his face when he answers me.

He reaches up, tucking a strand of hair behind my ears. "Then it's their loss, but I don't think you need to worry about that."

Lying back down on top of him, he asks, "Have you given any thought to telling people who you are?"

I cringe. "Ehh, not really."

A chuckle vibrates through his chest.

"You said you would think about it," he reminds me.

"I know. I will. I just...I don't think I'm ready for all of that. My blood might make me a Davenport, but everything else about me screams street trash. I'm not going to fit into their world."

"Do you want to?"

"No. Beyond maybe getting to know my parents, I have no interest in any of it."

"Then why worry about fitting in? Just be you. If your parents don't like you for who you are, then it's no loss, right?"

He makes a good point.

I tilt my head so I'm looking up at him. "Sometimes you say wise things."

"Only *sometimes*?" He chuckles as I kiss him, both of us quickly losing track of the conversation as we get caught up in the feel of one another.

My "session" is long since over when I emerge from Beck's office, a pleasant pain between my thighs as I cut across campus back toward the dorms.

I'm nearly at the girls' dorms when someone calls my name and I turn around to see Michael coming toward me.

"I thought that was you," he says, smiling at me.

"Uh, yeah. Hi." I glance warily around, looking to see if any of the other scholarship students are with him. We haven't spoken since the whole debacle at the Halloween party—when Hawk made a total ass of himself and hurt some of the only friends I ever had—but he's acting like we're still friends, so I'm just a little confused.

"Do you wanna grab a coffee?"

"Uh, Michael, what's going on? We aren't friends anymore."

His face falls, *and now I feel like a bitch.*

"I'm sorry. You're right." He rubs awkwardly at the back of his neck, his eyes darting around us. I've undoubtedly made him uncomfortable. "I feel awful about all of that. After what happened with Abigail on Halloween, we kind of freaked out. I want to be your friend still."

Not buying into his pretty words and offer of friendship, I stare at him with distrust. "Why now? What's changed?"

"Eh, well, the Princes don't seem to be hassling you anymore, right? It seemed safe to reach out."

I sigh, rubbing at my eyes. He had every right to stop talking to me after Halloween.

Emilia did the same and I forgave her, so I guess I should give Michael the benefit of the doubt too.

"So... do you want to get that coffee?"

"Sure," I say wearily, giving him a weak smile. "Coffee sounds good."

He rambles on about schoolwork as we enter the dining hall and fix ourselves coffees, before he follows me to my usual table. It's early evening, and a few other students are milling around, grabbing a late dinner and catching up with friends.

He updates me on everything going on with him and the other scholarship students, not that I really care about them, and he asks me about my Christmas break and how I'm getting on with the workload this term.

At least he's making an effort, and I try my best to engage with him. My attempt to give him my attention is thwarted when West walks into the hall. His eyes search the room, landing on my table, and his face pinches as he goes to make himself a coffee.

"Do you think you'll go to the Valentine's Day dance?" Michael asks.

"Ehh, maybe. When is it?"

His brows pull together. "Umm, February fourteenth. Valentine's Day."

"Oh yeah, of course." I shake my head, laughing off my faux pas.

"If you don't have anyone to go with—"

"What's going on over here?" West asks, cutting across Michael's words.

When I look up at him, he's scowling at Michael.

"Michael and I were just talking about the Valentine's Day dance," I tell him, giving him my own death glare. The asshole can't ignore me all week and then come over here because he's what, jealous?

His eyes narrow on Michael as his jaw ticks. "Were you now?" he asks warningly.

"What?" Michael splutters. "No. I mean. We were. But I was only asking if she was going. I wasn't—" His eyes dart around the room, searching for some sort of escape while simultaneously appearing like he's on the verge of hyperventilating.

"Didn't you say you have to get going, Michael?" I ask, offering him an out that he gladly accepts, his shoulder sagging with relief as he nods his head.

"Y-yes. I do. I, uh, I'll see you around, Hadley."

"Don't count on it," West growls as Michael practically scurries out of the hall.

"What the hell is your problem?" I hiss at the asshole, getting to my feet and striding across the hall to go outside.

"My problem?" West barks, having followed me out. "What is *yours*? You're supposed to be dating Beck, and I find you in there on a fucking date."

I snort, spinning around to glare at him. "It was fucking coffee. We were only talking."

"He wanted to do a lot more than just talk, Hadley," he snarls.

I throw my hands up in the air in exasperation. "What the hell do you even care? I thought you hated Beck?"

"It's got nothing to do with Beck," he seethes, stepping closer to me.

"Then what is it about?" I demand, not letting him intimidate me as I straighten my spine and tilt my head back to glare up at him.

"It's about the fact I've left you alone all week. I've been trying to purge you from my system so that you can go be happy with *Beck*," he sneers his name, "and I can finally get over you."

My eyes are wide as I gape at him.

We're chest to chest as he frowns down at me. "And here I find you with some other guy. If you're going to cheat on Beck, it's not going to be with some scholarship wimp."

His lips crash against mine, his hand pressing firmly against the back of my head as he pushes his tongue past my lips.

For a split second, I kiss him back before his words penetrate through the lusty fog. Placing my hands on his shoulders, I shove him back. The crack of my hand slapping his cheek reverberates in the air, and he stares at me in shock.

"You asshole," I snarl. "I would never cheat on Beck."

"Then what do you call what happened between you, me, and Mason at the party?"

God, give me some motherfucking patience with these idiots.

"Beck knows all about what happened between us," I inform him. "He's okay with it." West's eyes widen in surprise. "Because he's not a fucking man-child. If you want a relationship with me, West, fucking ask me. Don't stomp around here ignoring me all week, then get pissed because you find me talking to another guy."

Not giving him a chance to dig himself any further into a hole, I shove past him and stalk off toward the girls' dorms.

Hadley

CHAPTER SIXTEEN

"Ugh, I'm so tired," Emilia groans at breakfast on Monday morning. "I'm so not ready for this math test today."

We were up half the night studying for the damn test. Between that and my not getting much rest since the term started, my eyes feel scratchy from lack of sleep.

"Eh, hey," Michael says awkwardly. I'm so tired I hadn't even noticed him approaching our table. "Can I sit with you guys?"

Emilia and I stare wide-eyed at him before regarding one another. She shrugs her shoulders, letting me know the decision is mine.

"Sure," I agree, smiling at him.

It's the least I can do after West had ran him off on Thursday night.

He returns my smile, his awkwardness receding as he sits beside me.

"Did I hear you talking about the math test?" he asks.

"Yeah, we were up all night studying. Cramming everything we've learned into one test is just cruel," Emilia whines while I dig into my syrup-soaked pancakes.

"Same," he agrees. "We should all study together next time."

Emilia and I exchange a look.

"What about the others?" Emilia asks him, referring to the other scholarship students. Glancing their way, the four of them are huddled together, leaning over the table as they have a hushed conversation, occasionally looking our way.

Michael shakes his head. "I didn't agree with what they said to you. They shouldn't have made you choose between them and Hadley. I've been wanting to, uh, apologize to you. As I told Hadley on Thursday, I'd like it if we could all go back to being friends."

Emilia glances my way, and I shrug. It's up to her. I understand why he distanced himself from me, but what they did to Emilia isn't okay. Michael is a follower, though. He doesn't like to upset the balance. Nevertheless, if he's finally found his balls and picked a side, then sure, we can try to be friends, but only if Emilia is on board.

She scrutinizes him for a moment before nodding slowly. "Okay," she agrees. "Apology accepted."

A huge grin lights up his face.

"But," I interject, his smile deflating, "if you're going to be our friend, then you're all in. No running away or changing sides if shit hits the fan."

"Is, uh, shit going to hit the fan?" he asks nervously, peering around anxiously like said shit is going to jump out of nowhere and attack him.

With the Princes lurking around every corner, pissing me off? Most definitely.

"Maybe." I shrug. "You never know what can happen."

"Okay, yeah. I'm one hundred percent in. No backing out."

His brows are drawn, lips set in a straight line. As I stare him down, he manages not to break eye contact with me.

"Alright then."

Deke and the jocks have impeccable timing as they choose that moment to walk past our table.

"Alright, babe," Deke says with an infuriatingly cocky smirk. "When's the next show? My dick's getting bored of watching the same one every night." He bites his lower lip in a way that's intended to be sexy, even though it's anything but. His eyes roam over my body as if he can see right through my uniform.

I clench my fists, reminding myself I can't go apeshit on his ass in the dining hall. I'm seriously going to have to find a way into the fights if he keeps this shit up. A public beatdown would do wonders for putting him in his place.

"Fuck off, douchebag," I snap at him. "If you can't get your dick up, it sounds like a *you* problem. Might wanna get it checked out before rumors start spreading."

The lascivious look drops off his face as he scowls at me.

"Frigid bitch," he snarks back as his friend shoves him in the shoulder, silently telling him to keep walking.

Flipping him the finger, I turn back to the table and arch a brow at Michael. "See? You never know when assholes like him will crawl out of the woodwork and start something."

After that, the three of us fall into easy chit-chat about the weekend and our plans for the week until the bell goes off.

I stumble over my feet as I walk into English beside Emilia, unable to tear my eyes away from what I'm seeing. Cam is sitting in Emilia's usual seat beside Bianca, listening to her as she rambles on about something, all the while running her grubby little mitts all over his arm.

"Ah, girls," Mr. Greer says when he spots us. "There's been a change in the seating plan. Emilia, you're now sitting next to Hadley."

Unable to move, I gape dumbfounded at the two of them before peeking at Mason. His face is tight, and he shrugs his shoulders when he catches me looking, not knowing what new game Cam is playing.

Emilia drags me to my chair and as we walk past Cam, I stare so hard at his head I'm surprised the force of my gaze doesn't dent it. Regardless, he still doesn't look at me. I know he can sense me nonetheless, as his whole body stiffens when I pass.

When I don't get any response from him, I glance at Bianca, but she just throws me a haughty look. *Fucking bitch.*

"What the hell is going on?" Emilia whispers as we take our seats and Mr. Greer starts the lesson.

"I don't know."

I'm unable to focus for the next hour, my gaze constantly straying to Cam and

Bianca on the other side of the room. The bitch keeps pawing at him and laughing obnoxiously loud at whatever he says. The sound is driving me fucking crazy. She sounds like a fucking hyena.

Why is he sitting with her? I get it if he doesn't want to sit with me. I've been trying to give him his space, and I know he just needs more time to process everything—but *her*? Seriously? He could have picked literally anyone else, and I would have accepted it. I wouldn't have liked it, but I would have fucking accepted it.

As soon as the bell goes off, I'm up out of my seat, calling out his name, but he ignores me, speeding toward the exit with Mason hot on his tail, looking just as pissed as I feel.

"Desperate much?" Bianca sneers, and I pull my gaze away from Cam's back to glare at her.

"Shut up."

She smirks. "Look who's jealous. I'm going for round three with Cam, and it seems like he's all but forgotten about you. Guess you can fight it out with the rest of the girls for one of the other Princes."

Fuck me. If he picks this bitch for a third time, I'm going to be seriously pissed. What the hell does he even see in her? I scowl at her as she turns on her heels, swaying her hips as she strides toward the door and out into the hall.

I can't stop thinking about either of them all day, and by lunch, I'm in a horrible fucking mood.

"Jesus, who pissed in your cereal?" Hawk asks, sitting down opposite me.

"No one," I snap, biting into my burger and tearing off a huge chunk.

Hawk looks at me with a raised eyebrow, like I'm some kind of wild animal he's never seen up close before.

I simply scowl at him around a mouthful of food, the two of us collapsing into our usual silence.

"Why is Cam letting that bitch dangle all over him?" I snap, unable to keep my thoughts to myself any longer, making Hawk look at me with raised eyebrows.

"You'll have to be more specific than that."

"Bianca," I spit out the word like it's poison on my tongue, and Hawk rolls his eyes, not the least bit surprised.

"It's nothing," Hawk says, waving it off as though I'm acting like an overzealous girlfriend.

"It's not nothing," I argue. "She had her hands all over him today."

Hawk's eyes narrow on me as he studies me. "Why do you care?"

"What?" I splutter. "I...don't."

He quirks an eyebrow disbelievingly.

"I don't," I insist. "But she's a bitch who's only after him—any of you—for your money."

Hawk snorts, shaking his head. "Everyone here is. Look around you." I slowly move my head, taking in the tables around us where students whisper and avoid our stares. "Every guy is here to make friends with us so they can use us for whatever future business bullshit they are involved in, and every girl is here to offer up her pussy in the hopes of getting a ring at the end of it all."

I scrunch my nose up in disgust, yet my chest tightens in pity for what Hawk and the guys have had to endure for the last four years. No wonder they stick to each other, never making friends with anyone else. It would be impossible to trust anyone.

Never knowing if they are true friends or just associating with you for their own gain.

"Cam's having...issues right now. Making stupid decisions that will bite him in the ass, but none of these girls mean anything to him."

I'm surprised he's offering me any reassurance, and while his words don't exactly calm the green bitch within me, I guess I can sit back and make sure Bianca doesn't dig her claws into him any further. God knows, Cam has enough shit to deal with, never mind that conniving slut.

We lapse into silence, eating our meals until the door to the dining hall opens and Michael steps in, his eyes furrowing when he sees Hawk and me sitting at the same table. I half expect him to turn around and leave—honestly, that would probably be for the best. Only, he steels his spine, walking past the kiosk without ordering anything and making a beeline for our table.

I groan, fixing Hawk with a stern look.

"Be nice," I demand in a low tone just before Michael approaches the table.

"Is, uh, everything okay here, Hadley?" he asks, his voice quivering as he observes Hawk and me. He's shaking like a leaf, but I'm a little impressed he had the backbone to come over here.

"All good," I assure him, smiling sweetly.

Hawk scowls at him. "What do you want?" he demands, making me roll my eyes at him.

"I was, um, going to ask Hadley if she wanted to grab some lunch." Michael turns his gaze from Hawk to me, but before I can respond, Hawk answers for me.

"Well, as you can see, she's already got a lunch date."

Pinning Hawk with a glare, I smile sweetly at Michael. "Thanks, Michael. I'm a bit busy today, but how about tomorrow?"

"Oh, yeah. If you're sure." He glances between Hawk and me, his meaning clear.

"What the fuck am I going to do to her in the middle of the dining hall?" Hawk barks, picking up on what Michael means.

"I'm sure," I assure him, ignoring Hawk's outburst. "Hawk's nothing but a grumpy teddy bear, nothing to worry about."

I hear the asshole himself scoff as I press my lips together, holding back my laughter.

Michael's eyes widen at my words, likely thinking I'm digging my own grave, but he nods his head, stuttering out a goodbye before racing away from the table.

"What the hell was that?" Hawk barks, waving his hand in the direction Michael ran off.

"What was what?" I ask, picking up a now cold fry and chewing on it.

"You're having lunch dates with that beanpole?"

"I don't remember it being any of your business who I eat lunch with," I snark back.

"Jesus," he snarls. "You're just accumulating a whole assortment of dicks, aren't you? Is one not enough?"

"Excuse me?" I drop my fry back on my plate, losing my appetite as anger ignites at Hawk's words.

"You've got the boys' brains all scrambled, chasing after you, all while you're fucking West's brother. And now you're also leading that kid around by the balls?"

Slamming my hand down on the table, I stand up, not giving a shit if I'm making a scene.

"Fuck you, Hawk. You know nothing about me or my relationships, and last time I checked, I didn't owe you any fucking explanations."

I stalk off and ignore the asshole for the rest of the week, not setting foot in the dining hall at lunchtime, so he can't track me down and piss me off.

At my session with Beck on Thursday, I mention my friendship with Michael. West and Hawk's reaction has me thinking that maybe I have been doing something wrong, even if I can't work out what.

"I just don't understand what their problem is. Should I not have guy friends?" I ask Beck.

"You should be friends with whoever you want to be friends with," Beck reassures me. "West is just jealous."

"And Hawk?"

"Hawk's feelings are more complicated. He's trying to look out for his friends, and things between you two are still new. He's probably just unsure how to navigate everything."

"So, I'm not doing anything wrong?" I clarify.

"Do you have feelings for Michael?" he asks. He doesn't sound jealous like West did, or angry like Hawk. He's genuinely curious.

"No, definitely not," I assure him. "Everything between us is strictly platonic."

"Does Michael know that?"

"Ermm..." I trail off, unsure how to answer that. "Emilia did say he had a crush on me when I first arrived here, but that was ages ago."

Beck gives me a soft smile.

"That's probably what the guys are picking up on, then. He likely still has feelings for you, and the guys are getting territorial."

"You're not getting territorial."

"That's because I know I have nothing to worry about," he says, wrapping his arms around me on the sofa. "You and I have a solid foundation. We're learning to talk to one another and trust each other. You're not there yet with the others, and they're letting their fears get in the way."

I don't really understand what he means by that, but it's not his job to psychoanalyze them for me.

"So, it's okay if I'm friends with Michael?"

"Of course it is. It's good that you have friends. You need some balance in your life. The guys are all after something more with you, even if they don't realize it yet. And your relationship with Hawk is complicated. You need other people outside of them and me who you can go to if you need to. You should have as many friends as you want," he reassures me, tucking a strand of hair behind my ears.

"I think two is enough for now."

Feeling better, I leave his office, determined to fight for my friendship with Michael and not let any of the Pricks drive him off. I'm perfectly entitled to have friends. It's a normal part of the high school experience, and one I want to enjoy without four alpha assholes breathing down my neck.

Choosing to focus on my friendships and ignoring all the fucked-up shit going on in my life right now, I spend the entire weekend with Emilia and Michael.

We skip the standard party on Friday night, booking a cinema room in the rec center and binge-watching old movies all night while stuffing our faces with popcorn.

"Why has Hawk been eating lunch with you all week?" Michael asks as the movie credits roll down the screen. I should have known the question was coming since rumors have been circulating all week, with everyone speculating about what's going on.

Honestly, some of the stuff I've heard is just sick. If students aren't assuming what Bianca did, that Hawk is messing with me, they are assuming we're in some sort of relationship, or that I'm his side piece—talk about fucking gross!!

"He's just being an ass, trying to piss me off," I respond vaguely. "Nothing I can't handle."

Michael eyes me with suspicion, not believing what I'm saying.

"Who wants to watch another movie?" Emilia jumps in, saving my ass. "I vote *Bridesmaids*."

"God no, not some romcom shit," Michael groans, thankfully getting distracted as the two of them argue back and forth over what to watch next, and I mull over what the hell I'm going to do about Hawk. The entire school is gossiping, and as much as I don't want them to know who I am, I sure as fuck don't want people thinking I'm his fuck buddy. Just thinking that in reference to him has my gag reflex working overtime.

On Saturday, we take the bus into the nearby beach town, spending the day window shopping and walking along the beach. We grab lunch at a cute little restaurant along the waterfront and eat ice cream from a vendor on the pier. It's a great day out, and I can't believe I haven't ventured into the town before now. It's so quaint and picturesque—a sleepy fishing village filled with hard-working, pleasant people. It's the kind of place where I can see myself living a quiet life. No rich bitches or drama, no Lawrence or memories of my past. Just sunshine and the ocean.

By the time Monday rolls around, I'm feeling pretty fucking relaxed. It's amazing what a weekend without schoolwork and asshole boys can do for a girl's zen.

Little Warrior

CHAPTER SEVENTEEN

On Monday morning, we walk into the dining hall, all eyes falling on us. It's changeover day again, although this month's girls are throwing scornful expressions our way. All of them are pissed about being ignored for the last two weeks. Not that I give a fuck. I don't even remember the name of the girl I picked. I wanted nothing to do with her even before things with Hadley heated up. That was an unexpected turn I'm certainly enjoying. I'd been struggling for months to find my release in any other girl, but since we started fucking, I haven't even looked at anyone else. All I can think about is her. Watching her in those tight lycra shorts that cling to her ass and thighs and how her tits bounce in her flimsy bra when she's working out, is the best form of torture. The flirty banter between us is also scorching hot.

All of that is why I've made the decision I have. It's going to piss a lot of people off, but I don't fucking care. I'm done with this fucking farce. Why should I have to let some slut who's only after my surname and money hang all over me at parties when it's Hadley I wanna spend the night with?

A hush falls over the hall as Hawk stands, drawing everyone's attention. I don't give a single fuck about any of them, only having eyes for Hadley.

She's stabbing her fork into her pancakes like they've personally offended her, pointedly not looking in this direction. She's the only one in the hall not staring in our direction. I can practically see the anger and jealousy radiating off her. Strangely, it doesn't make me feel good. Usually, I don't give a fuck about a girl's jealousy. Actually, it can be such a thrill watching a catfight break out when two girls want you—such a confidence boost. But as I watch Hadley tear her pancakes to shreds, I just feel guilty.

The scholarship dweeb leans in to whisper in her ear, and a smile curls at the corner of her lip as she chuckles. What the fuck did that asshole just say to her?

My hand curls around my knife as I watch her respond to him. Why the fuck does she let him sit beside her every day? The dude's practically coming in his pants from how she looks at him. Can she not fucking see that?

I'm not even paying attention as Hawk picks his girl. Too busy wishing I could shoot the scholarship dickhead dead with just a look.

He finally fucking feels my eyes drilling into him, his head snapping up to look at me as the blood drains out of his face and his eyes widen to saucers.

He nearly falls off his chair in his haste to scoot away from Hadley as quickly as possible, and I smirk when he appears like he's about to piss his pants. *Yeah, buddy, get your hands off my girl before I tear your arms from their fucking sockets.*

Hawk's elbow jams into my ribs, breaking my stare-off with the wankstain and I focus on the rest of the room, realizing everyone is looking at me and waiting for me to take my turn.

Getting to my feet, I scan the room before focusing on Hadley. She's still not looking our way. Regardless, I keep my gaze on her as I say, "I choose...no one."

The room is silent for a second. So quiet you could hear a pin drop. Hadley's head snaps to mine, her lips parting in a gasp as she stares at me. In the next second, the hall erupts into shouts of outrage, girls jumping to their feet as they yell.

I can feel Hawk's eyes on me, yet I don't remove mine from Hadley. From the corner of my eye, I see him raise his hand, telling the crowd to calm down. It takes a few minutes, but eventually the hall hushes to murmured whispers, which Hawk talks over.

"We'll come back to Mason in a few minutes," he says pointedly. "Cam, you go next."

Cam doesn't even bother to stand. The fun guy who was soaking up the attention at the beginning of the year is long gone. This year has taken its toll on him.

Waving his hand dismissively, he says, "I'm done too. I'm not picking anyone."

More murmurs and yells of fury ensue, but Hawk barks over the top of them. "West," he growls, furious with us. If I'd known Cam was going to do the same, I'd have talked to him and discussed it with Hawk ahead of time. *Oh well, bit late now.*

"No one," West says as well. I half expected him to do the same as me after his declaration in the pool house last week. Although he's been avoiding Hadley since then for some reason, so I wasn't sure if he had changed his mind about her.

Most of the senior-year girls are on their feet now as they shout and yell at us, their faces scrunched in anger and stained red with rage.

"You can't do this!" Bianca screams, somehow managing to make her voice heard above the chaos erupting around the hall. "This is not how it's supposed to be."

"Shut up," Hawk roars over the noise, everyone instantly falling quiet. He glares around the room, daring anyone to speak. Hawk has one of those faces that can haunt your nightmares. A steely glare or a curl of his lip and his face darkens to something hellish. They say the devil has an angelic face that can trick you into following him into the pits of hell; well, Hawk could send you running for the gates, begging to be let in to escape him.

Satisfied that he's thoroughly scared everyone within an inch of their lives, he nods. "We are well within our rights to not choose a girl if we don't want to," he shouts loud enough to be heard around the room. He's speaking out of his ass. All four of us know that's not the case, but the great thing about our brotherhood is that we all have each other's backs. I can tell by the subtle ticking of his jaw that Hawk is fucking furious with us right now, but despite that, he will stand beside us.

"Bullshit," Bianca argues, not having the same feeling of fear or common sense the rest of the student body appears to have.

Hawk's icy glare could kill a lesser woman, but Bianca gives as good as she gets when she lifts her chin and stares him down. "Most of us are only at Pac because of this stupid tradition," she argues, several girls around the room nodding their heads in agreement.

"Yeah, 'cause your parents are hoping we'll want to marry one of you." Hawk's voice is cruel as he chuckles at her. "I hate to break it to you, but that shit ain't happening." He doesn't sound the slightest bit apologetic about what he's saying.

Several gasps ring out, whispers rising from some of the girls. Apparently, that news was a shock to some of them, or maybe they just don't like being talked down to like that in front of the rest of the year.

"You have an obligation," Bianca argues, not giving up.

"Why?" West disagrees. "So you can be seen with us? What the fuck do we get out of that?"

"You get us," Bianca growls, clearly thinking her vagina is fucking gold.

Cam laughs a dark, malicious sound. "Why would we want your saggy, worn-out pussies?" His lip curls in disgust as he sneers at her. "We just need to look in your direction, and you're fucking gagging for it. Where's the fun in that?"

Bianca gasps, her hand slapping against her chest in a dramatic as fuck gesture that has me rolling my eyes.

The warning bell goes off, telling everyone to get their asses to class. No one moves at first, until Hawk yells at them. "What the fuck are you waiting for? Get to class!"

The senior guys all start grabbing their stuff, probably not really giving a fuck about this morning's events. If anything, they're probably relieved—Deke certainly looks smug, like he's somehow going to get more pussy now. Spoiler alert, he won't. Just because we aren't choosing girls anymore doesn't mean they aren't going to continue ignoring every other guy in Pac and keep on throwing themselves at us in some vain attempt to gain our attention.

The girls reluctantly follow behind them. Bianca is one of the last to leave, standing with her hands on her narrow hips as she stares us down, looking like a pissed-off housewife.

As she storms out the door on her high heels, I see Hadley being tugged across the room by her friend. Her eyes flick between each of us, confusion swirling in her icy blues.

When it's just the four of us left in the hall, Hawk turns toward us. "What the fuck was that?" he demands, throwing his hands up in the air. "You assholes couldn't have given me a fucking heads-up?"

"In fairness, I didn't know these two shitheads were going to jump on my bandwagon," I defend.

"This is about Hadley," he states, realization dawning. "Seriously? Do you know the shit you're starting?!"

"I'm done with all this shit," Cam grumbles, still slumped in his chair as he kicks his legs up on the table, pulling out a fucking hip flask from his blazer pocket and knocking back a measure of whatever the fuck he's got in it. *For real? He's got to get his shit together and stop with the day drinking.*

Hawk rolls his eyes, scowling at Cam before pinning West and me with a glare.

I shrug, not seeing any point in denying it. "Yeah, it's about Hadley. I'm fucking her, and it feels weird to be doing all this bullshit while I'm doing that."

His eyebrows climb to his hairline before his face scrunches in disgust. "Fucking gross," he grumbles.

"You're what?" West exclaims. "How long has that been going on?"

I shrug. "Since the party."

He shakes his head, running his hand through his unruly dark locks. "Doesn't it bother you that she's dating someone else?"

"Not really." I don't give a shit about that. It should probably bother me, but for all I know, it could be a passing fling. There's no way he has the same connection with her that I feel.

"Whatever," he grumbles irritably, checking his watch. "We need to get to class."

"What the hell are we supposed to do about the senior girls?" Hawk asks, not giving a shit about class.

"Fuck 'em." Cam shrugs.

"The fact you *don't* want to fuck them is the problem here," Hawk snarks. "There's no way our parents aren't going to find out about this eventually."

"I don't really give a damn. After the shit they pulled at Christmas, they can fuck off," I growl. "What are they going to do? Threaten us? Oh wait, they're already doing that."

"Now is hardly the time to go pissing them off," Hawk argues.

"I'm fucking done playing by their rules," I spit. "What has it ever gotten us? We're neck-deep in their shit, and they'll only suck us in more after graduation."

Hawk's lips flatten and he doesn't argue with me, knowing I'm right.

"Look," West interjects, always the peacekeeper. "What's done is done. The girls will just have to get over it. As for our parents, we'll deal with them when it becomes an issue."

With none of us having a better plan, we agree—albeit Hawk is still reluctant—and head off to class. I don't have any interest in whatever they are trying to teach us this morning, however. Now that I've made my stand, I only want to find Hadley.

I skip out early from my last class before lunch, walking toward the dining hall and waiting there so I can catch Hadley before she goes in. Seeing her strolling down the path toward me gets my blood pumping like nothing else. She's so fucking sexy in a wholly unique way. It's refreshing, watching her with her combat boots, short unpainted nails, and face free from makeup. She isn't fake or pretending to be somebody she isn't. She shows the world every barbed part of her, and it's up to everyone else if they want to take her or leave her. I sure as fuck want to take her—in every position she'll let me.

I stride toward her when she sees me.

"What are you—" she begins, but I grab her arm and pull her toward the girls' dorms.

She lets me tug her along as I push open the door into the foyer, making a beeline for the corridor where the scholarship students stay.

"Which room is yours?" I ask, peering over my shoulder at her.

"You mean you don't know?"

"Why would I know that?"

"The video..." She trails off, her words making me stop and turn around.

"You think I was involved in that?"

She shrugs. "I wasn't sure."

I can't blame her for suspecting me, but I wouldn't say I like the thought of her thinking I was involved in that. I will always stand beside my brothers in whatever hair-brained shit they do, but this is Hadley. I want her to know the truth, and we don't need to always present a united front to her. She's not going to see any cracks in our friendship and pry them open.

"I didn't know about any of it until it was going down," I tell her. "And neither did West." Yeah, I'm throwing Hawk and Cam under the bus, but they deserve it.

Her eyes widen at my admission, her eyebrows lifting in surprise. When she just stares at me, I ask again, "Which room is yours?"

"That one." She points to the last door at the end of the hallway, and I link my fingers with hers before walking toward her room. I press my chest against her back as she inserts the key in the lock, feeling her breath hitch at the contact as the air between us seems to crackle with sexual tension and something more meaningful.

I slide my hand onto her hip and she presses back against me. The feeling of her ass rubbing against my crotch snaps the last of my restraint as I use my grip on her hip to spin her around and push her against the door. Shoving my thigh between her legs, I use my weight to press her into the door as I kiss her savagely, plunging my tongue into her mouth and refamiliarizing myself with how she tastes and melts against me, her body fitting against mine perfectly.

I've been substituting her all year with girls that look like her, but none of them can compare to the real thing. It's like I've had nothing but oatmeal my whole life—bland, cardboard-tasting oatmeal—and now, I've discovered something much more appetizing. Now that I've had a bite, I'm never going back.

She rubs herself against my thigh, moaning into my mouth as her fingers dig into my back, pulling me in closer to her. While I still have some awareness of where we are, I blindly reach out, unlock the door and hold her against me as I swing the door open. Stepping forward, I force her to step back until we're in her room and I can kick the door closed behind us.

My hands are on her waist as I direct us to the bed, pushing her down onto the mattress as my eyes remain glued to her bouncing tits. Shrugging off my blazer, I undo the buttons of my shirt, watching as her pupils dilate and her tongue runs along her lips. Her eyes are transfixed on my every move with avid interest.

She follows my lead, quickly taking off her shirt so she's in her bra and skirt, looking like the dirtiest schoolgirl I've ever seen. Pushing my slacks down my legs, I step between her thighs, widening them as I lean down, hovering over her.

Her hands fist the duvet behind her as she tilts her head back, her long hair falling away from her face as she meets my stare. We remain frozen for a moment, watching one another with lust-clouded eyes.

Both of us move at the same time, closing the distance as our lips collide. Her tongue delves into my mouth as I slide mine over hers, my hands gliding into her hair.

She scoots up the bed, and I follow, keeping my weight off her as I settle between her legs. Moaning, she grinds against me, and I reach my hand between her thighs, more than happy to give her what she needs.

Grabbing the flimsy fabric of her panties, I easily tear it off her and she breaks our kiss, surprised at the torn material. "Fuck, that's hot," she murmurs, desire dripping from every word.

I smirk. "You haven't seen anything yet," I tell her, pushing two fingers inside her. She's so fucking wet, I easily slide right in to the knuckle, the sensations making her eyes drift shut as her head falls back and her hips rock, pushing my fingers in deeper.

Leaning down, I use my teeth to pull down her bra, sucking her nipple into my mouth while I finger-fuck her. The way she arches her back and her soft moans encourage me as I pick up speed.

"Mason," she moans when I bite down lightly on her nipple, the sting sending her racing headfirst into an orgasm as her walls spasm around my fingers, and she cries out.

I go to climb off her to find a condom, my balls fucking aching with the need to be inside her, but she grabs my arm.

"Don't. I'm covered. I just need you inside me."

I hesitate for a second, but my desire to feel her clenching around me is too strong so I hastily kick off my boxers, lining up, and slam into her in one swift thrust, making both of us groaning.

She feels fucking incredible. Not too tight as her wet warmth hugs me perfectly, like the best fucking dick warmer. The way she responds to me, her cheeks staining red and her tits rising with each heavy breath, is mesmerizing. There are no fake moans or warm-ups required, unlike every other girl who only lets us do what we want to them so they can have our inheritance when the time comes.

The whole bed creaks as I pick up speed, hammering into her hard and fast. I press her hands into the mattress above her head, hovering over her and loving the way her tits bounce every time I slam into her.

She meets me thrust for thrust, small whimpers leaving her parted lips that make my balls draw up. I press my lips against hers in a hard kiss as she falls apart, her back arching and her pussy spasming. The way her cunt squeezes mine steals the last of my restraint, and I explode inside her, grunting against her lips.

Collapsing onto the bed beside her, I pull her in against me as we breathe heavily, and my lids close as a wave of exhaustion hits. The feel of her sweaty, naked body pressed against mine feels amazing.

She snuggles in against me—something I've never let any girl do before—and before I know it, I'm sound asleep as my soft breaths blow against the top of her head.

I fall into a deep, dreamless sleep which is eventually broken by the best wet dream. I feel my dick growing hard as something warm and wet slides along its length before it's sucked into a warm incubator, the suction making me groan in my sleep as my dick grows to its full length.

Fuck, whatever that is feels incredible. There's a humming vibration against the sensitive skin, and I jerk forward. My hands move to jerk myself off, fucking desperate for a release, but instead, my fingers touch a head of hair. My eyes pop open as I watch Hadley as she's perched between my thighs, her plump pink lips wrapped around my dick and her heated gaze watching me.

Jesus, it's the best fucking sight I've ever woken up to.

"Fuck, baby," I groan, sliding my fingers through her hair and pushing her down on me, lightly thrusting into her mouth.

She doesn't push back or resist, slowly taking all of me in. Her tongue swirls around my head as she lets me take control, holding her in place as I thrust into her mouth. Her hand cups my balls, squeezing gently, and I completely lose my shit.

"Fuckkkkk," I grunt as I come in her mouth. She swallows all of me, slowly pulling her lips back and wiping me clean with her mouth.

"Get up here," I growl, reaching out to pull her up my body as she giggles, smirking down at me. "Sit on my face."

She doesn't hesitate, placing her thighs on either side of my head and lowering her pussy onto my mouth. Wrapping my arms around her thighs, my hands squeeze her ass and I run my tongue along her slit, lapping at her juices as she moans.

Her hands press against the wall behind my head as she rocks back and forth. I slide my tongue around her clit, sucking it into my mouth, satisfaction coursing through me as she gasps. "Shit," she murmurs as I feel her clenching.

Releasing her, I glide my tongue down to her pussy, flicking it in and out of her tight hole.

"God, yes," she cries, throwing her head back as she seats herself more firmly against my face.

Dipping my fingers between her ass cheeks, I coat one in her juices before sliding it around her puckered hole, testing her response. She drives back against me, and I take that as all the consent I need to push the tip of my finger into her ass.

"Oh," she gasps as I slowly push in further, my tongue still fucking her pussy. "Fucking hell, Mason." She shifts back more. My finger is fully seated inside her, hips jerking with the onslaught of sensations.

Slowly pulling my finger out, I pump it in and out of her, her rising cries of pleasure compelling me until I feel her clenching around my tongue and finger.

"Shit. Jesus. Fuck," she groans as her pussy floods with the release of her orgasm. I lap it up, holding her in place with my tight grip on her thighs until I'm done feasting on her and she's squirming on top of me.

When I let her go, she collapses onto the bed beside me, panting.

"What a wake-up call." I smirk, rolling onto my side and leaning up on my elbow as she laughs breathily.

Reaching out, I place my palm on her stomach, getting momentarily distracted by the contrast of her pale skin beneath my tanned hand and the way she responds to even that simple touch.

When she's recovered, she looks up at me with so many thoughts running rampant in her mind.

"What happened this morning? Won't you get in trouble for what you did?" she asks, creases forming across her forehead as she frowns.

I lift my hand, running a finger between her eyes, flattening them out.

"You don't need to worry about that," I assure her. "It won't be anything I can't handle."

My words fail to settle her, and her lips flatten as she presses them together before sighing.

"Did you…" she trails off, appearing unusually vulnerable. It's not a side of herself she displays often, yet I've gotten to see tiny flashes of it recently. I love her tough-as-shit attitude, but there's something about seeing her unguarded that makes me feel proud as shit. Like I did something to earn that glimpse into her inner psyche. "I don't understand why you did that."

"I wasn't going to pretend to be fucking some girl of the month when I'm with you," I tell her, observing her face closely for her reaction.

Her lips part slightly as she looks up at me.

"Is that what we're doing?" she asks softly. "Dating?"

My heart hammers against my chest as I nestle myself between her thighs. I've never asked a girl out before, not that that's what I'm doing now. I'm not giving her a choice; I'm *telling* her I'm all in.

"Yeah, Little Warrior. It's you and me." I press my lips to hers in a chaste kiss, which she returns.

"And you're okay with me dating Beck?" she clarifies, her eyes jumping back and forth between mine.

"Sure," I agree, leaning down to kiss her again. My dick has woken up, and he's more than ready to solidify this new relationship.

She pushes against my shoulders though, moving me back until I'm looking down on her again.

"I'm serious," she says sternly to me. "I'm not giving him up. I..." Another flash of vulnerability crosses her face before she tucks it away, shaking her head.

"Okay," I tell her seriously, seeing how much he means to her—way fucking more than I thought he did. I don't know what to make of that, but I'm all in, even if I have to share her with him. "Keep dating the old man, but when you see the stamina I have, you'll quickly change your tune." I smirk down at her as she laughs, hitting me playfully on the shoulder as she wraps her legs around my waist to pull me against her.

"Promises, promises," she murmurs against my lips, kissing me before I can reply. No problem however, I'll just have to show her.

Hadley

CHAPTER EIGHTEEN

Mason and I spent the rest of the day in bed, skipping our afternoon classes to stay wrapped around each other, until the guys started blowing his phone up non-stop.

There's a skip in my step the next morning as I get dressed and head to breakfast. The other girls on campus might be blowing a gasket over the guys, but I feel on top of the world today, and it must be written all over my face.

"Girl, what has you in such a good mood?" Emilia laughs as I sit down opposite her at breakfast.

She leans in closer before gasping. "You had sex!" she admonishes loud enough for people at nearby tables to overhear her.

"Who would want to have sex with scholarship trash?" Bianca sneers as she walks past, having obviously heard Emilia's comment.

"Well, Cam didn't seem to have an issue," I say sweetly, batting my eyelashes innocently at her. She scowls at my comment before storming off.

"Sorry," Emilia grimaces, but I wave off her apology.

"Don't worry about it."

Quickly moving on, her face lights up. "So, who was it? Ooh, it was Mason, right? Apparently, nobody could find him all afternoon," she explains, seeing the *what the fuck* look on my face.

Jesus, seriously? Are people stalking his every move?

She looks toward the Princes' table, where all four are eating, ignoring everyone around them. Unlike the usual jealous looks and revered glances, girls are whispering and scowling in their direction today.

"He looks so intimidating," she whispers, as though he might hear her from all the way back here. "His face almost seems permanently stuck in that position. Does he have any other facial expressions? Is that his jizz face too?"

She turns to look at me with a serious expression, but I just throw my napkin at her. "I'm not telling you that." I laugh.

"Not telling her what?" Michael asks, coming to sit beside me.

"Nothing," Emilia and I blurt at the same time, making Michael glance between us.

"She was asking inappropriate questions," I explain vaguely.

He nods his head in understanding, clearly used to her quirky ways.

"We need to sort out dresses for the Valentine's Day dance," Emilia informs me, changing the topic. "I want something that says *'I want to get laid'* but isn't slutty."

I snort. "Does such a dress exist?"

"Dunno." She shrugs. "But I'm going to find it if it does."

"Are you going with anyone, Em?" Michael asks.

"Nope," she says, popping the *p*. "I'm keeping my options open." She glances around the room, eyeing up the guys before scrunching her nose. Yeah, I can imagine high school boys don't compare after being with rock stars. Not that she really has many—or any—guys to choose from. The non-scholarship kids wouldn't date any of us, and the only scholarship guy we talk to is Michael.

"The three of us should go together," I suggest. Emilia and I were going to go together anyway, and since Michael doesn't have anyone else anymore, it seems rather mean to exclude him.

"Oh," he responds, his gaze flicking between Emilia and me. "Eh, yeah, sure."

I smile at him. "Yeah, it will be fun…unless you were already planning on going with someone?"

"What? N-No."

"Cool," Emilia adds. "Let's go into town this weekend. We can use some of our stipends to find something to wear."

Michael and I both agree, and the rest of the week trails by. Mason and I get a few quiet moments together, and I have my Thursday session with Beck. He seems a bit off when I see him, but when I ask him about it, he just tells me he's having a crappy day and not to worry. I wish I could spend more time with him, but it isn't easy with everyone on campus. I worry about him, in any case. I get the impression a lot is going on that he doesn't talk to me about, and it concerns me to think about what his father might expect from him in return for offering him this job.

On Friday, I've got computer science with West. Things have been a bit stifling between us recently, and I'm not sure why. Ever since I told him about Beck and me, he's been keeping his distance, even though he got all upset when he saw me with Michael, and then he refused to pick a girl this week. So I don't understand any of it.

"Hey," he greets, sitting beside me, and giving me a brief smile.

"Hey." My eyes roam over him. He's always impeccably dressed. I swear he must iron his clothes when he lifts them out of the closet every morning. There's not a single crease, even now at the end of the day, as if he's just put it on.

He types in his password, logging into the computer and pulling up whatever he's working on today. It's just a black screen with a bunch of random words, numbers, and symbols strung together. It makes absolutely no sense to me, yet he seems to understand it as he nods his head, making a few changes before closing out of the program.

"How's your week going?" I ask.

Seriously? How's your week going? Geez, I sound like his damn mother.

He turns in his swivel chair to face me, head tilting to the side as he drops his eyes over my uniform, slowing when he reaches my bare legs before raising again to meet mine.

Scooting toward me, he reaches out, turning my chair so I'm facing him. My legs are pressed between his spread thighs. Leaning forward in his chair, his hands are planted on either side of my hips, holding the chair in place as his face hovers in front of mine.

This close, I can see the swirling green of his eyes. Usually, they are a bright moss color, but today they are clouded with so much emotion that I can't identify anything he's feeling.

"You're dating Beck," he says quietly so no one can overhear us.

My brows pull together. "I am."

"And Mason?"

"Yes."

He doesn't say anything for a second as his gaze darts between mine.

"You said if I wanted to ask you out, I should just do it."

"I did." The words are a breathy whisper as my heart rate picks up and my pulse races.

"Well, I'm not about to do it here, but will you go to the dance with me?"

My eyes widen. That's…a big deal. That wouldn't just be going to the dance, it would be coming out to the whole school. After his refusal to pick a girl this week, there's no way everyone wouldn't see us together and not put two and two together.

"I…can't." I sigh. "I'm going with Emilia and Michael."

His face tightens when I mention Michael, but he wisely doesn't say anything. "But I can save you a dance or whatever."

"I want a lot more than one dance with you," he murmurs, his husky tone and heated gaze doing crazy things to my insides. "But it's a start."

Fuck me, he must be able to smell my arousal. I love when he goes all alpha. Because he doesn't exude that alpha-ness the way the other guys do, it's so fucking hot when he does.

My tongue runs along my lower lip, his eyes trailing the movement.

"Girls have no idea what they're missing out on when they skip over you to get to the others," I tell him sincerely, the admission making his eyebrows lift.

He shrugs. "I prefer it this way. Girls don't usually get me."

My head tilts to the side. "What's not to get?"

Giving me a dirty smirk, he trails his fingers along my thigh, sliding lower when I part my legs slightly. His eyes fall to follow the movement of his fingers as he gets closer to the hem of my skirt.

"I like certain *things* when it comes to sex. Things most people don't. Girls think they want the rough, kinky shit, but when it's truly offered to them, they freak out. I don't need the school whispering about what a freak I am."

As much as his words annoy me—he shouldn't be ashamed or need to hide who he is—I'm dying to know what he's into. I got a glimpse of it at Hawk's party, except I get the feeling he's going to open me up to a host of new experiences—and I'm here for all of it.

I spread my legs wider, giving him better access as his hand glides over my upper thigh, and he touches my panties, pressing his thumb into the fabric and running it up my center. Thank fuck we're sitting alone in the back row, and someone would have to turn around to see us. Even then, they can't see under the desk to know what he's doing.

"But you don't have the same reservations with me?" I ask breathily, pushing against his thumb as he rubs it over my clit.

He shakes his head, his eyes heating as he seductively bites his lower lip.

"I'm pretty sure you can handle it," he purrs.

He goes to lean back, his thumb lifting off my clit. Only my hand snaps out, grabbing onto his tie and yanking him back toward me, his chest pressing against mine.

"You better not be about to leave me hanging," I growl.

My neediness makes him smirk.

"I'll let you come when I get that dance," he murmurs against my lips, pulling out of my slackened grip as I gape at him.

~

On Saturday, Emilia, Michael, and I catch the bus into town.

"I'm so excited to get away from school for a bit," Emilia enthuses. She is practically bouncing up and down as we jump off the bus in the center of town.

"Where to first?" I ask, glancing around. Liberty Point is a sleepy little beach town, and being a Saturday, there are people milling around window shopping. Tourists who have ventured down to the beach for the day and a few other kids from school are also wandering about, enjoying their day off.

"Should we try the thrift store on Fifth?" she suggests.

"Sure." I don't know any of the shops here, and we have a minimal budget. The scholarship came with a small stipend primarily intended to use in the shop or at one of the cafes on campus. Still, since you can eat anything you want from the dining hall for free, most of the scholarship students save their stipend for precisely this occasion.

I do have a little money squirreled away from jobs I worked before I started at Pac, but I'm saving it for a rainy day—a dress emergency does not count as that, despite what Emilia might say.

We walk the short distance to the store and spend the next hour rifling through the racks and trying stuff on.

"Oh, girl, no. Just no." Emilia laughs when I emerge in a lime green dress that has excess material gathering around my boobs and is way too tight over my ass. Emilia and I have tried on several dresses, yet each one has been worse than the last.

I laugh, turning to check myself out. I look ridiculous, something Michael clearly agrees with. His nose scrunches up as he steps out of his changing room.

"Wow, Michael," I exclaim, looking at him in the mirror. "That suit is sharp."

"You think so," he asks, running his hand over the jacket before doing a little twirl.

"Definitely," Emilia agrees, nodding her head.

He's wearing a smart-looking pale gray suit with maroon and dark green threads woven through it. He even found a maroon tie to pair with it.

I step aside so he can look in the mirror.

"You should get it," I tell him, stepping back into the changing room so I can get out of his hideous dress.

"Yeah, I think I will," he responds as I pull my jeans and top back on, hanging the dress on the hanger.

Once he's paid for the suit, the three of us make our way out into the street.

"I'm starving," Emilia whines. "Food next?"

"Yes, that sounds great." My stomach chooses that moment to grumble, letting me know it's gone too long without attention.

We go to the same cute cafe on the waterfront we visited last time. It's painted in white and pale blues with beach paraphernalia over the walls. Large family-style booths are interspersed along the window front and back wall, with tables spread across the rest of the open space. It's a proper tourist trap for sure, but it's bright and airy.

Choosing a table by the window with an unobstructed view across the road and out over the beach, I slide into the booth, Emilia sitting beside me as Michael slides in opposite us.

We sit in silence, each of us reading over the laminated menus on the table.

"Welcome to The Shack," a girl—not much older than us—says. She's wearing a tight white top with a small black apron wrapped around her waist over the top of her jeans. She has a bright smile on her face, her dark hair pulled back into a high ponytail as she makes a point of looking at each of us. "What can I get for you?" she asks, pulling out a pad of paper and a pen from a pocket in her apron.

I order a burger with fries and a shake, and Emilia and Michael recite what they want before the girl collects our menus and puts in our orders.

Michael and Emilia start talking about a music project they are both working on, and I zone out of the conversation, staring out the window and watching families enjoying a day out at the beach. Kids are building sandcastles and running in and out of the water as it rushes up the coast. A group of older kids have a game of volleyball going, and a few surfers are out riding the waves. The place is teaming with life, everyone enjoying themselves. It's not even that warm outside, but it doesn't seem to faze anyone.

My phone goes off in my pocket and I pull it out, finding a message from West. Beck is the only person who usually messages me. Everyone else uses the school tablets, but of course, I didn't bring mine when I left the school campus this morning.

> West: Heard you are out shopping in town today?

Surprised, my fingers fly across the screen as I respond.

> Hadley: Who told you that?

The message comes up saying it's been read as soon as I send it, and a second later, the bubbles at the bottom of the screen that tell me he's responding pop up.

> West: Can you stop by Belles for me? Give them my name. Everything is already paid for.

Of course the asshole just ignores my question. Rolling my eyes, I've half a mind to tell him to do it himself, but he'll probably just ignore me *again*. I'll need to remind him I'm not his goddamn errand girl to his face when I give him his crap later.

"Who's that?" Emilia asks, leaning in to read my message over my shoulders.

She gasps. "Belles? Oh, hell yeah, I've always wanted to know what it's like inside."

I give her a quizzical look, and she rolls her eyes.

"Belles is a high-end fashion store. All the Pac students go there to get their outfits for dances, but it's crazy expensive."

"He probably wants me to pick up his suit for him," I grumble.

"Who cares what you're picking up, so long as we can get a peek inside," Emilia exclaims, practically jumping up and down in her chair.

After lunch, we head to Belles, which turns out to be a gorgeous shop right on the beach. The window displays are filled with elegant formal dresses and James Bond-type suits. As beautiful as they are, I feel completely out of place as the three of us stroll into the shop in our bargain clothes.

The bell chimes above the door as we enter, the few other shoppers turning to glance our way as we walk in.

Of course, Bianca and a few of her friends are at the checkout, paying for dresses hidden in garment bags.

Bianca's lip curls as she sees us.

"You've got the wrong shop, trash," she sneers. "The thrift stores are on the other side of town. You couldn't afford to so much as breathe on the clothes in here."

Narrowing my eyes on her, I quickly dismiss her, turning instead to look at the woman behind the counter who is watching our exchange with curiosity.

"I'm picking something up for West Warren?"

I hear Bianca snort beside me, and, with a sigh, I reluctantly focus my gaze back on her to hear what witty remark she will make next.

"West's got you running around for him?" She laughs. "At least you've finally learned your place in life."

The woman behind the counter glances between Bianca and me with a raised eyebrow before her eyes rest on mine. "Yes, Mr. Warren said you'd be stopping by. Hadley, right?" Her knowing my name catches me by surprise, although I guess West had to give it to her so she knew who to hand the items over to. Whatever he's bought probably cost a small fortune. She wouldn't want to give them to the wrong person.

"That's me," I confirm, smiling tightly.

"He said there would be three of you." She glances at Emilia and Michael standing behind me. "Are these your two friends?"

Well, now I'm just confused. How much fucking shit did he buy if he needs three of us to carry it for him?

"Uh, yes?"

"Fantastic." She smiles brightly and waves for us to follow her. "Right this way, we have a private room at the back all set up for you."

"The private room?" Bianca interrupts with a gasp, her voice a touch higher than its normal annoying whine. "There must be some sort of mistake, she can't afford to buy anything here." Bianca is seething as she glowers at me.

"Mr. Warren has taken care of all of the costs," the woman reassures me, all but ignoring Bianca.

I still have no fucking idea what is going on, though. What happens in the private room?

The woman steps out from behind the counter, and Emilia moves to follow her, not having the same reservations I have.

"But—" Bianca whines again as Michael and I share a look. Shrugging my shoulders, I smile sweetly at Bianca, giving her a sassy finger wave before following the woman and Emilia toward the back of the shop.

I can still hear Bianca complaining to whoever will listen as we walk into a room at the back of the store. I instantly forget all about her as I peruse over the numerous railings filled with more dresses than I've ever seen. Emilia's eyes look like they are about to pop out of her head, and she rushes over to the closest rack and starts rifling through it.

Tearing my gaze away from the dresses, I notice the far wall is comprised of one large mirror running along the entire width of the room. There's also a small seating section and a curtained-off changing area in the corner of the room. All of it is designed to provide the ultimate private experience while you find the perfect dress.

"I don't know what West said to you—" I begin, shifting to address the shop assistant in a mixture of confusion and shock.

"He made it clear we were to help you and your friend find the perfect dress for a dance."

He did?

Emilia turns to gape at me, excitement brimming on her face. She seems like she's died and gone to heaven.

"Have a look through the racks and pick out anything you like. Let me know if you need a different size, and I'll have someone bring in a bottle of champagne for you all. You have the room for the remainder of the day, so no rush."

After an awkward silence, none of us capable of forming a coherent response, she nods and leaves the room.

"Oh. My. God," Emilia squeals. "Pinch me. There's no way this is real." She holds her arm out. "I'm serious, pinch me."

Shoving her arm away, I laugh. "I'm not going to pinch you, you idiot."

"Why would West do all of this for you?" Michael asks suspiciously, glimpsing around the room.

I share a look with Emilia. She knows all my dirty secrets with the Princes, but I'm not ready to tell anyone else yet.

"Ehh," I start, scrambling to come up with a reasonable explanation.

"He's trying to apologize for the video fiasco last semester," Emilia blurts out, looking at me with wide eyes and shrugging.

"Right," I agree, nodding. Sounds like as good an excuse as any.

He glances questioningly between us, but the door opens before he can question us further, a shop assistant carrying an ice bucket with a bottle of champagne in it and another bringing glasses for us.

"Let us know if you need anything," the one carrying the bottle says as the other pours each of us a glass.

"Will do," I respond, giving her an awkward smile. I'm not used to any of this, and I'm not entirely sure what to make of it.

As soon we are alone, Emilia starts going through the dresses, lifting out the ones she likes.

"Oh, here, this one would look gorgeous on you," she says, shoving a dress into my arms.

The red satin material glides through my hands; it's so soft. Holding the dress in front of me, it's got thin straps going over the shoulders, the thin material looking like it will cling to my small curves before falling to the floor. There is a high slit up the leg and as I turn it around, it's backless, with a slim neat row of white buttons running down over the curve of the ass. It's beautiful, but it's also more revealing than anything I've ever worn. I definitely don't think it's something I can pull off. Every single one of my scars would be on show for everyone to gawk at. I wouldn't say I'm a self-conscious person, but equally, I've never voluntarily put myself on display like that.

"Come on, girl," Emilia encourages. "At least try it on."

Michael makes himself comfortable on one of the sofas while I go into the dressing room to slip on the red dress.

When I step out from behind the curtain, Emilia gasps.

"Holy fuck, I've never been so annoyed that I'm not into girls."

A nervous laugh barks out of me as I awkwardly slide my hands over my stomach, feeling naked.

"Girl, you look amazing," she says in all seriousness, grabbing me by the shoulders and turning me to face the mirror. "Doesn't she, Michael?"

Michael coughs, clearing his throat. "Yeah...yes, she does. Gorgeous."

My cheeks flame, but I can't tear my eyes away from the mirror. The fabric stretches over my breasts, molding to them, emphasizing my flat stomach and narrow waist before curving round my hips. I've never looked or felt so sexy.

"Here, these would look amazing with that dress." Emilia shoves a pair of black strappy heels into my hands.

I attempt to argue, but she cuts me off with a shake of her head.

"You are not ruining that dress by wearing boots, woman. You'll take the heels, and you'll wear them like a goddamn goddess."

Michael smothers a laugh behind his hand as I silently take the heels, knowing when I've been put in my place.

Emilia and I spend the rest of the afternoon trying on dresses, the three of us laughing and joking while the two of them steadily make their way through the bottle of bubbly. I snap a few pictures of Emilia and me in different dresses and of the three of us goofing around and then send some of them to West, thanking him for arranging all of this.

No dress looks as good on me as the first one I tried on, and I decide to get it while Emilia chooses a gorgeous blue-green dress that subtly changes color as it falls down her frame. She looks incredible in it.

"You've gotta try some of this," Emilia says several hours later, holding her glass of champagne out for me. Based on the way she's giggling, the bubbles have gone to her head. "I googled it. It's like a two-thousand-dollar bottle. When will you ever get the chance to taste something so expensive again?"

She does have a point there. Taking the glass from her, I sniff the fizzy liquid, my face scrunching when the bubbles go up my nose. Sipping on it, a slightly acidic, fruity taste coats my tongue. *Huh, not bad.* I take another couple of sips before handing the glass back.

The shop is closing by the time we take our dresses to the cashier. I'm still expecting the shop assistant to ask for money, only breathing out a full breath of relief when she once again confirms that the dresses have already been paid for. West must have spent a fortune to cover all of this. For all he knew, we could have picked the two most expensive dresses in the shop, not to mention the cost of having the private room all day.

With our garment bags in hand, all three of us traipse back to the bus, heading back to campus. I have to say, suddenly, I'm feeling pretty damn excited about this dance.

Hadley

CHAPTER NINETEEN

When we step into the hall on Monday, it has been completely redone. There are white, red, and pink decorations plastered everywhere, announcing the fact that it's Valentine's Day soon. Is it really that big of a deal? From what I gathered from a quick Google search, it seems to be a fake holiday made up by card companies to increase their sales. Why the fuck would anyone want to celebrate that?

The rest of the school has been decorated in the same colors, and the other girls spend the entire week in a frenzy, too busy bragging about their dresses and sharing ideas of how they want their hair styled to do any actual work.

Cam continues to actively avoid me. Whenever I see him, he's a disheveled mess, smelling more and more like a brewery every day. I haven't missed the hip flask he not-so-discreetly pours into his coffee every morning and drinks from during the day. He still sits beside that bitch in English, letting her rub herself up against him, while he sits slumped in his seat, with his head on the table every time we're in Business.

The guys cast worried looks his way, and one of them is always trying to take the flask from him when they see it, except the next time I see him, the flask is back in his hand. He's going to drink himself into an early grave at this rate.

Hawk and I go on with our awkward, silent lunches. I'm not sure what good they do, but at least he's making some sort of an effort, right? Michael is absolutely getting suspicious, though. He's been asking questions about the Princes and me all week that I've managed to avoid with vague, bullshit non-answers. However, it's only a matter of time before he figures it out, or I end up telling him just to stop his nagging questions.

On Friday, Mason and I are finishing up our separate workouts in the gym. It's become our routine every morning, except the now angry glares have been replaced with heated glances and enough sexual tension to set off fireworks.

He has a towel draped over his shoulders, having just run it through his hair to gather the excess sweat while I gulp down a mouthful of water.

"I have something for you," he says, bending over to rummage through his gym bag.

When he stands back up, he's got a small flat gift box in his hand, which he holds out to me.

"What's this for?" I ask, accepting it.

It's adorably wrapped in crinkled, pink wrapping paper with a red ribbon tied around it in what I think was meant to be a bow but looks more like a twisted knot. It's certainly not a professional gift wrap job, but the fact that he even tried is sweet.

When he doesn't answer me, I catch him looking uncertain as he rubs his hand nervously through his hair.

"It's, uh, a Valentine's Day gift."

My eyes widen.

"Oh. I didn't realize we were supposed to exchange presents."

"We don't," he rushes out, looking flustered. It's a weird look on him and one I'm undoubtedly enjoying.

His hand reaches out to take the present back, but I tighten my grip.

"What are you doing?" I ask, refusing to give up the present. It's the first one he's ever given me, and I'm not about to let him take it back.

"Forget it," he grumbles. "It's a stupid thing anyway."

"No way," I argue, pulling it out of his grasp and stepping back so he can't try to take it from me again.

"Hadley," he growls in warning.

A warning I ignore.

"Nu-uh." I shake my head. "You can't take a gift back once you've given it to someone."

"It's stupid," he repeats, his lips pressed tightly together.

"So?" I look back down at the present, digging my fingers into the wrapping paper and tearing it off, lifting out a pair of black fingerless gloves. Turning them over, the stitching is all pink, and the words 'Badass' and 'Bitch' are etched across the knuckles of each one.

Dropping the wrapping paper, I slide the gloves on, flexing my fingers and loving how whoever I punch with them is going to see the writing as I slam my fist into their face.

I have a huge goofy grin on my face when I look up at Mason, finding him watching me intently, still awkward.

"I love them," I tell him earnestly, jumping up and wrapping my arms and legs around him as I kiss him. His arms slide around my waist, hands grabbing my ass cheeks and taking some of my weight.

"You do?" he questions when we break apart, still looking uncertain, as if he thinks I'm lying to him.

"Why wouldn't I?" I laugh. "They're perfect."

He shrugs. "I dunno. I've never given a girl a present before, and you seemed surprised."

Now it's my turn to feel awkward. "I just didn't realize gifts were exchanged on Valentine's Day." I grimace. "It's not something I've ever done before, and I feel bad that I don't have anything for you."

"I can think of a few things you can give me," he murmurs, kissing me again as I laugh against his lips.

"I'm sure you can," I tease, "However, right now, we have to get ready for class."

Groaning, he squeezes my ass harder, effortlessly grinding me against his growing erection before dropping me to the ground.

"You're going to the dance tomorrow, right? West said you got a dress."

"I am," I confirm, taking off my new gloves and tucking them in with my other stuff back into my gym bag. "I'm actually looking forward to it. I've never been to a school dance before."

"You're not missing much." He shrugs, grabbing his bag and slinging an arm around my shoulders to tuck me in against him. "But I'm sure I can come up with a few things to make it special for you," he jokes, giving me a dirty wink as we walk out of the gym.

∽

EMILIA and I spend most of Saturday getting ready. She curls my hair, getting it to sit in neat ringlets down my back while pinning the sides away from my face. Then, she does my makeup—something subtle but with a slash of red across my lips to match my dress.

"Did Bianca ever corner you about Belles?" Emilia asks as she puts the finishing touches on my hair.

"No, she didn't." I'd completely forgotten about her threats. She seems to have backed off since the guys proclaimed they wouldn't be taking a girl of the month. I'm sure she's deep in her planning cave, working out how to get one of them wrapped around her pussy.

"There you go, all done," she says excitedly, stepping back so I can look in the mirror at the finished product. I appear so much older and sophisticated, but she's done a fantastic job of dolling me up while making me still look like me.

She steps in beside me at the mirror. "We are smokin'." She laughs, making me grin. She's got her hair styled in cute little beach waves that stop just above her shoulders, and she's gone with smokey eyes and a pale pink lipstick that somehow makes her appear both innocent and naughty.

When we're both ready, I snap a photo on my phone, sending it to Beck.

> Beck: You look amazing, baby. Have fun tonight.

Michael knocks on the door as I tuck my phone away in my purse.

"Wow, ladies," he exclaims. "You both clean up well." I notice his eyes don't leave me, though. I'm pretty sure he's still got a crush on me, yet I've no idea what to do about it. I don't want to bring it up and embarrass him or risk destroying our friendship. "Shall we go?"

Both of us link arms with Michael, laughing as we walk down the corridor and out the door toward the dining hall. The school has had people in and out of it all day, decorating and setting up for tonight.

"Wow," I gasp when we step out of the girls' dorm.

Students mill around on the path and lawn outside, taking photos and lining up to walk down the red carpet into the dining hall—yes, there is an actual red-carpet entrance. Lights have been set up, so heart-shaped lights dance over the front of the building, lighting the area up.

"This is insane." I can't tear my eyes away from it all as we join the back of the queue.

As we shuffle closer to the front, I can see a photographer set up to take photos as students strut down the carpet, posing as though they are heading into the Oscars.

When it's finally our turn, the three of us walk rather self-consciously along the carpet, not doing the same song and dance as everyone else.

Stepping into the hall, I'm once again left speechless. The usual large tables and food counters have been replaced with a large dance floor and DJ area. There's a table set up with drinks and snacks, and more circular tables are placed around the outer edge of the hall for sitting.

Heart-shaped balloons have been strung up all along the ceiling, and some sort of snow-blowing machine is blasting out little pieces of heart confetti, the paper blowing everywhere and sticking to everything. There is already a crowd on the dancefloor, and Emilia tugs us in that direction.

I'm still an awkward as fuck dancer, although I've gotten used to having people around me in a crowd. So as long as no one is too close, my brain doesn't go into freak-out mode.

Several songs later and my feet are killing me. Why the fuck do girls wear heels to dance in? Sure, my legs look like they're a mile long, but what good is that when I can hardly walk?

"I'm going to go get a drink," I yell over the top of some loud pop song, pointing toward the drinks table.

Emilia nods, shouting that she's going to stay and dance.

"I'll go with you," Michael shouts, leaning in toward my ear so I can hear him.

Nodding, the two of us push our way through the crowd. The air immediately feels less suffocating once we leave the packed dance floor, heading over to grab some drinks before sitting at a nearby empty table.

"This is all so over the top," I say absently, staring at the glowing heart-shaped lamps on all the tables, providing a dim, atmospheric ambiance.

"Everything at Pac is," Michael responds. "You get used to it."

I honestly don't think I ever will.

"That dress really does look incredible on you," he says after a moment, his words making me blush as I sip on my punch.

"Thanks." I smile at him, unsure of how to respond. He looks good, too, all dressed up in his suit, only he just doesn't evoke that overwhelming sense of attraction and chemistry I get around the guys.

"Oh, look, it's the trash, and she brought a date," Bianca sneers, coming up to us, with a couple of the other Princesses trailing behind her.

She's wearing a sheer black cocktail dress that barely covers her vagina, her huge fake tits practically bouncing out of the top of the material. If anyone looks like trash, it's her. *Talk about fucking desperate.*

"Your dress seems to be missing some bits," I retort, making her scoff.

"Because you know so much about high-end clothing." Her eyes take in my dress with disgust. "Everyone knows red is the color of sluts."

Says the girl wearing fucking lingerie.

I roll my eyes, not giving a shit what she says.

"Why don't you just leave us alone, Bianca." I sigh, trying to get rid of her.

A commotion by the door draws all of our attention as the Princes enter. They are immediately surrounded by people, guys trying to buddy up to them and girls attempting to garner their attention.

"Ah, my boys are here," Bianca says slyly. "Cam already promised me the first dance."

My teeth grind together. I'm pretty sure she's bullshitting me, but with the way Cam has been avoiding me for the last few weeks, I can't be sure.

Narrowing my gaze on the man himself, he doesn't look the slightest bit interested in being here. He's got a scowl on his face, like a grumpy bastard, as he shoves his way through the crowd to sit at a table on the far end of the room and pull out his ever-present, trusty hip flask.

"Well, have fun with your date," I say sweetly. "He looks like he's in a partying mood."

The other guys break through the gathered crowd and follow Cam over to the table. Each one of them looks better than the last. Hawk is dressed all in black—black suit, black shirt, black tie—looking as sharp and unapproachable as ever. Mason is in a navy-blue suit with a white shirt and has forgone the tie and undone his top button. While he's still wearing his usual cold, *fuck-off* expression, his body is screaming for me to touch it. West is wearing a pale gray suit with a pale pink shirt and a cute as fuck bowtie that is perfectly him.

Cam, on the other hand, looks like he's barely made an effort. Wearing a pair of cream chinos and a light blue shirt that's rolled up at the sleeves, he's the most casually dressed person here. Not that he's any less handsome for it. If anything, it suits him better than an all-out suit would.

"He'll be all over me after a few drinks," Bianca jibes before fixing her dress around her tits and striding toward their table, her hips swaying, giving everyone a clear view right up her hoo-ha.

"She's such a bitch," I grumble, rolling my eyes.

My hand clenches around my drink, the plastic cup crinkling underneath the pressure as I watch the bitch slide onto Cam's lap, running her fingers through his hair. He doesn't even seem to notice she's there, too busy guzzling down whatever is in his flask. He must already be three sheets to the wind to not even acknowledge her presence.

West snatches the flask from Cam's grip, the two of them exchanging heated words before West turns to glower at Bianca. It looks like he's telling her to fuck off, but she only winds her arms tighter around Cam, refusing to leave.

I'm on the verge of going over there and dragging her off him myself, when Cam seems to realize she's there. His unfocused eyes land on her, seeming utterly bewildered that she's sitting on his lap before he reaches up and shoves her off.

She crashes to the floor with a squeal, drawing people's attention at nearby tables. The whole scene totally makes my night as I burst out laughing.

Climbing to her feet, she glowers at all four of them, saying something I can't hear from this far away before storming off. *Fucking priceless.*

Michael and I sit for a while longer, watching the party unfold around us.

"Do you wanna dance?" he asks eventually.

"Eh, sure," I agree. We should probably get back out there and check if Emilia is doing okay. I've seen glimpses of her dancing with a few guys, so she seems to be having fun, at least.

As we head back toward the dance floor, West walks over and blocks our path.

His gaze goes straight to Michael, narrowing on him like he's the enemy. *Stupid, dumb boys.*

"West," I greet, steering his attention to me.

His gaze immediately drops when he looks my way, falling down my body as he takes in my dress. His pupils dilate, his tongue running along his lower lip as he drinks me in.

"Wow." The word comes out in a low, breathy tone as his eyes slowly travel back up my body and come to rest on my face. "You look incredible."

I can feel my cheeks turning red at his compliment, the way he's looking at me turning me into a puddle of goo.

"I believe you owe me a dance."

"Oh, we were ju—"

West's sharp gaze snaps to Michael as though he had forgotten he was even there.

"N-nevermind," Michael murmurs as West takes my arm, threading it through his and leading me toward the dance floor.

Turning to look over my shoulder, I mouth an apology to Michael feeling bad about ditching him.

"That was mean," I chastise, although there's no heat in my voice as West pulls me onto the dance floor, wrapping his arms around me. His palms land on my bare skin, and he groans at the realization that the dress is backless.

I lean my arms against him as we sway back and forth, getting caught up in his hypnotizing eyes.

"If you didn't look so damn irresistible, I wouldn't have to stake my claim," he murmurs huskily. "Every guy here is checking you out."

I roll my eyes at his macho bullshit, but then he spins me around while holding onto my hips as he presses his front to my back.

He leans down to whisper in my ear, "See?"

I glance around the room. When my gaze lands on the Princes' table, I catch all three of them watching us.

I meet Mason's heated gaze first, and he sends me a dirty wink that has me clenching my thighs, and West growls behind me as his hand squeezes my hip.

Next, I look at Cam. The same desire is in his eyes, but it's clouded by alcohol and self-hatred, making me sigh.

"He'll come around," West whispers, as though he knows where my thoughts have gone. "He's just struggling right now."

My heart clenches for him as I look at Hawk. His jaw is ticking from how hard he's gritting his teeth, confusion and anger warring for dominance on his face.

Is he angry that I'm dancing with West? Something tells me that's not quite right.

"He's worried I'm putting a target on your back by dancing with you in front of everyone."

I snort. I highly doubt that is why he looks like his head is about to explode.

Turning back around, I wrap my arms around West's neck.

"I'm sorry I was an ass," he apologizes, making me raise my eyebrows in surprise. "I hope the dress made up for it."

"It did, but you didn't have to do any of that for me. I don't need expensive things. Your apology is enough."

A genuine smile crosses his face as he looks down at me with adoration.

"You're something special, you know that?" he murmurs.

I don't know how to respond to that, staring at him wide-eyed as his gaze drops to my lips, both of our thoughts heading in a direction that we can't act upon in public.

"You've had my attention since that first day in class," he says softly, his words barely more than a whisper, but we're standing so close it would be impossible to miss them. "Every time I'm around you, it feels like I'm where I'm meant to be, like it was always supposed to be you and me. Even if I have to share you, I just want to be able to stand next to you and call you mine."

Stepping back, I wrap my hand around his and tug him across the room. His words have my heart racing and my pussy dripping. I'm so over this dance and ready to see what mischief we can get up to for the rest of the night.

Little Warrior

CHAPTER TWENTY

I watch, enraptured, as Hadley pulls West across the dance floor, the pair sneaking into the kitchens at the back of the hall.

"They're being stupid," Hawk grumbles, frowning at where the two disappeared. "The girls will skin her alive if they find out she's fucking all of you."

"She's not fucking me," Cam unhelpfully mentions.

Ignoring him, I call Hawk out on his bullshit. "I didn't know you cared so much."

"I don't," he growls. "We just don't need to be dealing with more shit."

Right. I'm pretty sure the idiot is starting to care about her more than he wants to admit.

"Where are you going?" he demands when I get to my feet.

"I need a drink," I grumble, walking away, but instead of heading toward the drinks table, my feet carry me in the direction Hadley and West disappeared.

Pushing open the swinging door, I slide into the darkened room. The only lights on are the ones above the cookers, barely providing enough light to see where I'm walking. Not that I need to see. I can hear Hadley's breathy moans and, following them, I walk toward the back of the kitchen.

"Arms above your head," I hear West growl. "Grab the edge of the counter."

As I reach the back of the kitchen, I find Hadley lying on her back on a steel countertop, her arms raised above her head, hands wrapped around the edge of the counter. The position has her back arching and her tits pushed up into the air as her chest rises and falls with each rapid breath. I can see her nipples erect through her dress, begging to be sucked as she looks up at West with lust-filled eyes.

West stands between her parted legs, looking down on her, his pupils dilated as he watches her spread out before him like a feast.

The slit in her dress gives him easy access as he pushes it aside, sliding his hands up her thighs.

"Do you have any idea how fucking tempting you look?" he growls, bending down to kiss her inner thigh.

I'm so fucking riveted, my dick pressing painfully against the zipper as I watch him slowly making his way up her leg, her sweet, breathy moans ringing out in the otherwise silent room.

Hadley's head snaps in my direction, noticing me standing there, watching them. I freeze, suddenly realizing how fucking creepy this looks. I've walked in on one of the guys fucking another girl, but I've never actively watched any of them. However, something about seeing Hadley lying on the table willingly at West's mercy is captivating.

West works his hands higher up to her thighs, and Hadley groans, her eyes rolling back in her head as he touches her.

"Mmm, so wet," West murmurs, his lips trailing over her inner thigh. "You like Mason watching you, don't you, dirty girl?"

Her eyes widen, as do mine, neither of us aware West knew I was here.

"Answer me," he demands when he doesn't get a response from her.

I've heard the rumors from girls years ago about what West was like in the bedroom, but we never asked him about it. None of us are soft or sweet, so he wants to boss girls around or tie them up? Who gives a fuck? There's absolutely nothing wrong with that, and from the way Hadley's breath hitches, she's totally into what West is doing.

"Yes," she whimpers, her hips lifting at West's touch.

He pushes her dress higher up her hips, exposing her to me. I move closer, getting an unobstructed view of her pretty pink pussy as West pushes his fingers inside her, her cry echoing around the room as he sinks into her to the knuckle.

"So tight," he purrs, pulling out before sliding in again. "Keep your eyes on Mason," he demands. "What do you want him to do?"

His fingers work her over as her eyes stay fixed on me, her gaze roaming over my body, pausing when she sees the noticeable bulge in my pants.

"I want him to touch himself," she moans, biting on her lip as I deftly unbuckle my pants, pushing them and my boxers down enough to palm my dick. I'd do pretty much anything she asked of me right now.

I swipe my palm over a bead of precum, using it to lubricate myself as I pump my dick, pretending it's her hand wrapped around me.

"Pull her dress down," I demand in a husky tone.

West does as I command, sliding the strap over her shoulder and pulling down her dress to expose her breast. He cups her tit, her back arching higher. Leaning over her, he sucks her nipple into his mouth, and she tilts her head back, moaning loudly.

I pump harder on my dick, unable to tear my eyes away from my best friend pleasuring my girl. *Our girl.* I never thought I'd be into this shit, but it's the hottest fucking thing I've ever seen.

"West," she groans, her hands white-knuckling the counter as she writhes beneath him.

"You like what West is doing to you, baby?" The words come out in a deep rasp as I work myself over, watching Hadley getting closer to the edge.

"Mmm," she whimpers, unable to form words. Her eyes are transfixed on me, glued to where my hand is wrapped around my dick.

Her nipple pops out of West's mouth, and he squeezes it tightly in his palm, kissing his way over the fabric of her dress, down her stomach, until he's buried between her thighs.

"Oh shit," she moans as his tongue laps at her clit.

I feel the telltale tingling at the bottom of my spine as my balls draw up, keeping my gaze on Hadley as she falls apart under West's touch, her thighs squeezing his head as she cries out her orgasm. My own release hits me, and I grunt, catching it in my hands.

"Doesn't she taste amazing?" I pant, grabbing a paper towel from a dispenser at a nearby sink and cleaning myself. West licks her clean, groaning as I tuck myself away.

"She does," he agrees, lifting his head, and climbing back up her body until he's kissing her.

When they break apart, he fixes her dress back in place. I close the distance as West helps Hadley to her feet. The second she's standing, I wrap an arm around her waist, tugging her off her feet as I yank her into me. My other hand slides into her hair, crashing my lips against hers in a passionate kiss, as my tongue tangles with hers as she clutches onto my shoulders, kissing me back. The taste of her lingers from West's kiss, and I groan into her mouth, the flavor fast becoming one of my favorite things.

"Hi," I murmur, feeling her smile against my lips.

"Hi."

"You look amazing." I kiss her again.

"We better get back before your friends come looking for you," West says from behind Hadley before either of us can get lost in one another.

She nods, and the three of us rejoin the party, slipping out of the quiet kitchen into the busy hall. With a final smirk, Hadley slips away, going to join her friends, while West and I head back to the table Hawk and Cam are still sitting at.

They make quite a pair, the two of them scowling at everyone and everything around them. They've even managed to send the students at nearby tables scurrying away.

I reclaim my seat, the four of us watching the party rage around us. Guys come over, trying to start up conversations with us, and girls grind on one another in front of our table, giving us "fuck me" eyes in the hopes we'll go over and join them. We don't. I barely spare them a second glance, too focused on the vixen dancing with her friends. I'm captivated as she throws her head back and laughs at something one of them says.

She's always wound so tight, always on alert, and never allowing herself to just let go and have some fun. I can't exactly complain; I'm made the same way, but carefree looks good on her. Really fucking good.

The night passes in a slow, monotonous blur. My eyes rarely leave Hadley, and all I can think about is getting her into my bed. I wonder if West would be game to join us. That shit was hot earlier.

At some point, she stumbles off the dance floor. Her arms are hooked through her friends as they move to a table at the back of the room. I lose sight of her, unless I want to turn around in my chair and make it very fucking obvious I've been watching her all night.

I honestly wouldn't give a shit, but I don't want to draw any more unwanted attention her way. I let my dick lead the way earlier, except what Hawk said is right. Until she agrees to come out as a Davenport, we must be careful. If people—specifically the girls—notice where our attention has gone, they won't leave her alone until she's a bedraggled mess on the ground. She might know how to handle herself in a fight, but the girls at Pac don't use their fists. The boys have rules—all issues are resolved in the ring—but the girls fight dirty. They wouldn't hesitate to do whatever's necessary to eliminate a threat, and that's precisely what Hadley will become if any of them discovers she's the reason we've strayed from the standard Pac tradition.

I'm downing a beer that West procured from who knows where, when a cry rings out and everyone in the hall seems to fall deathly silent, everyone looking toward the back of the room.

Hawk, West, and I are immediately on our feet, turning toward the back of the hall, where a crowd has already formed. Cam stumbles to his feet behind us, very unsteady as he wobbles. *Fucking hell, he's going to trip over his own feet.*

As a unit, we move toward the commotion, the crowd parting to let us through. As the last students move out of our way and the scene unfolds, a red mist coats my vision.

"What the fuck is going on here?" I bark, making Bianca jump as she gets to her feet. She turns to look at me with fake, innocent wide eyes and a shy smile on her face. *She won't be fucking smiling if I strangle her.*

"She tripped. I was just trying to help her up."

Shoving her aside, I look down at Hadley. The straps of her dress are torn, and she needs to hold the thin bits of fabric over her breasts to prevent the whole fucking hall from getting a view of them. A dark patch down the back of her dress makes it clear she didn't just trip.

"Oh shit," Cam unhelpfully comments, and I hear someone whack him upside the head.

I reach out to help her up, but her fiery eyes meet mine as she slaps my hand away.

"Get away from me," she snarls, getting to her feet as her friends finally push their way through the crowd, looping an arm through each of hers and helping her up.

"Hadley?" West questions, sounding confused, but she cuts him off, shaking her head.

Once she's standing on her feet, she shakes off her friends, straightening her back. With punch dripping from the ends of her hair, the back of her dress stained, and her arm holding the fabric over her breasts, she should look a mess, but the flames in her eyes have me captivated, even if she does seem pissed as all hell.

Her pissed-off, stormy eyes meet mine before she flicks her gaze to my brothers, pain and betrayal slashing across her features.

She lingers on Hawk, shaking her head.

Shrugging off my jacket, I hold it out to her so she can cover herself up, but she doesn't take it.

"Don't bother." She sighs, not looking me in the eye. "I should have known I couldn't trust you. Any of you."

She pushes her way past us, none of us stopping her as she takes off across the hall and out the door, her friends hot on her tail.

The second the door clicks shut behind them, I wheel around to glower at the crowd until I find Bianca.

Everyone must see the murderous rage on my face as they all step back when I take several large strides toward the bitch, wrapping my hand around her throat and slamming her head against the table.

"What the fuck did you do?" I roar, forcing myself to hold back from actually killing the bitch.

"N-nothing," she stutters, her denial only making me tighten my hold around her neck.

"Don't fucking lie to me," I snarl.

I can feel the guys creating a circle around me, preventing unwanted eyes from seeing what I'm doing, and I faintly register one of them telling everyone to fuck off.

Tears are streaming down her face now, not that they make me feel sorry for her. If anything, they just make her look more pathetic. Hadley would never fucking cry so easily.

"I on-only di-di-did what he wa-wanted," she cries.

"Who?"

I have to restrain my hand from tightening any further. She's already struggling to get the words out between rapid pants.

"Cam," she wails.

My eyes snap to Cam. Even though he's still drunk, he's managed to straighten himself out somewhat and simply shrugs his shoulders, not understanding what she's talking about.

"What are you talking about?" I demand, leaning down to snarl in her ear. The loud boom of my voice makes her jump, and she cries harder. *Fucking pathetic.*

"C-Cam kept saying h-he wan-wanted her t-to leave him a-alone."

Now I'm going to fucking murder Cam.

Using my tight hold on her neck, I throw her on the floor, stepping over her pitiful, sobbing frame as I grab Cam and shove him toward the kitchen doors where I was watching my girl come apart only an hour ago under my best friend's fingers and tongue.

The second the door swings shut behind us, I throw him up against a steel cabinet.

"What the fuck have you been saying in front of her?" I snarl.

The asshole glowers at me. "Nothing," he argues.

"Well, clearly, you've been saying something. Whatever that bitch said to Hadley has her not trusting us anymore."

He shrugs his shoulders, his nonchalance tipping me over the edge as my fist swings out, colliding with his cheek.

"You need to sober the fuck up," I yell at him as West steps between us, fixing me with a pointed look which I promptly ignore.

The blood is rushing through my veins, scratching just under the surface and begging me to expel some pent-up aggression.

"Stop it," West barks, sounding much calmer than I do. I don't miss the hint of steel in his voice, though, letting me know he's just as angry. He just does a better job of hiding it. "It doesn't matter what Cam said to her. Bianca's been gunning for Hadley for a while now."

Glowering at him, I spin away, pacing across the room.

"Fuck this shit. I need a fight." I scowl at West until he nods in agreement.

"Alright. We'll get the boys together in the clearing."

~

I LOSE myself in a blood-soaked haze, quickly working through pathetic wimp after pathetic wimp in the ring, unable to stop seeing Hadley's pained expression every time my fist lands against flesh.

Sweat coats my skin, and my knuckles scream in pain as blood splatters my hand

and chest, but I keep going, fueled by rage and the fact that I might have lost the only girl I've ever connected with before I even got a chance to really know her.

I don't know how many students I work my way through before Hawk claps a hand on my shoulder, telling everyone to get lost.

I snarl at him, not nearly done with any of them. He comes to stand in front of me, a hand on each shoulder as he observes me.

"You're done," he states in a tone that tells me there's no arguing with him. "Sending half of the school to the hospital isn't going to solve the problem."

Shrugging out of his hold, I reluctantly nod, and we trudge back toward the dorms. I still can't look at Cam. Too fucking furious with him right now. What the fuck has he been thinking, hanging around with that bitch the last few weeks. We all know it's been some fucked up tactic to get Hadley to lose interest, but what he doesn't seem to realize is she isn't going anywhere. His actions only make her watch him with increasing concern.

"She's not answering any of my messages." West sighs as we walk through the forest.

"Just leave her alone." Hawk's monotonous tone makes it sound like he couldn't give a shit, and his blasé attitude has me wanting to lash out at him next, but I know he's more concerned than he's letting on. He's spent weeks having lunch with her, and I know he's starting to develop some sort of connection with her. "You can talk to her tomorrow."

Sighing, West silently agrees, tucking his tablet away.

When we reach the dorms, I walk away from the boys without saying a word, and they don't call after me, likely knowing where I'm going.

Ignoring the few students still loitering around from the dance, I push into the girls' dorms, striding down the hall until I reach Hadley's door.

I stand and stare at it for a long moment before knocking. When she doesn't answer, I knock again, harder this time.

"She's not there," a voice says from behind me, making me turn around.

Her friend, Emilia, I think, is leaning against the doorframe. She's wearing weird as fuck looking rabbit pajamas, complete with ears and fluffy feet with her arms crossed as she looks me over, taking in the blood stains and the rage still looming in my eyes.

"Where is she?" I sound more defeated than angry now, just wanting to fix everything.

She shrugs. "I don't know, but even if I did, I wouldn't be a very good friend if I told you."

Fair point. As annoyed with not getting an answer makes me, I have to respect the fact she's being a friend to Hadley. I get the feeling she needs one of those in her life.

"Do you know what happened tonight?" I ask instead.

She doesn't immediately respond, taking her time to look me over. Her eyes don't hold any lust or jealousy. It's more like she's trying to figure me out, figure out if I'm worthy. She must decide I am as she uncrosses her arms.

"Bianca had it all planned out," she begins, gritting her teeth in anger. "As soon as Michael and I stepped away to get drinks, a crowd formed around Hadley. She poured punch down her back and tore the straps of her dress."

My fists clench as the urge to lash out again rises within me, but I squash it down, for now.

"She must have done more," I insist. "Hadley's stronger than that. Why would she say she couldn't trust us?"

Emilia doesn't sugarcoat her words, giving them to me straight. "Bianca said Cam told her to do it. She said you all knew about it."

Well, now I wish I'd fucking killed Cam when I had the chance.

I crack my knuckles. Just thinking about punching him again sates some of the raging flames flickering inside me.

"Why would Hadley believe her?" I growl. Haven't we shown her that we can be trusted?

Emilia laughs. The girl evidently has a death wish as I narrow my eyes on her.

"Do you even know her at all?" she snarks, not fazed by my deadly stink eye. "Hadley doesn't trust. Like at all. She's starting to open up to me, but she still keeps a large part of herself closed off. And I've never done anything to make her not trust me, so why the hell would she trust you guys?"

She sighs. "Look, I know Hawk is her brother." My eyebrows lift at that information, but she continues before I can question her. "For that reason, she's been trying to let down her guard with all of you, but for someone like Hadley, that's not an easy task, and the slightest thing will have her walls slamming back into place. If you don't give her a reason to trust you, she'll close herself off, and you'll never get the chance to see how incredible she truly is."

Hadley

CHAPTER TWENTY-ONE

After fleeing from the dance, I assured Emilia and Michael that I was fine and just wanted to be alone. Once I'd changed out of my ruined dress, I snuck out into the forest and hid in the treeline as I circled the campus to the staff accommodation.

From the second Bianca's hateful words registered, all I wanted was to find Beck and curl up in his arms. I honestly don't know if what she said, about her only doing what Cam had told her, was true or not. With the pain I've inflicted on him, plus the way he's been ignoring me and flaunting Bianca in front of me for weeks now, even though he refused to pick a girl for the month, it makes it very difficult not to believe her words. I'm not sure if that means I can't trust the others—they are an unbreakable unit, after all. Regardless, I wasn't about to hang around and let them make bigger fools out of me.

The second Beck opens his front door, I fall into his arms, the tears I've been holding back trailing down my face. I never fucking cry, and the fact that those fuckfaces have me showing any weakness only pisses me off further.

Because he's a fucking godsend, he just holds me until I'm calm enough to tell him the whole horrendous story of this evening.

How could everything go so wrong so quickly? It was only a few short hours ago that I was spread out on the counter in the industrial kitchen, being eaten out by West while Mason eye-fucked me, yet it feels like a fucking lifetime ago now.

By the time I've told him everything, I'm exhausted, and the last thing I remember is falling asleep in Beck's arms as he strokes my hair and tells me everything will be okay.

I hide out in his apartment for the rest of the weekend, ignoring my phone and tablet, which keeps buzzing.

"You're going to have to respond to them sometime," Beck says on Sunday afternoon.

"Maybe so, but not today."

He sighs. "You can't trust whatever Bianca says. She's a vindictive bitch that wants them for herself. The only way you'll resolve anything is if you talk to them yourself."

I know he's right, but I just want to ignore it all for a little while longer.

Climbing onto his lap so I'm straddling him, I run my fingers through his hair. I love seeing it like this. When he's not at work, he doesn't have it styled back to within an inch of its life. Instead, his hair runs wild, all mussed up and sexy looking.

"I don't want to talk about them," I tell him, seating myself over the growing erection in his sweatpants and grinding against him.

He groans, placing his hands on my waist as he directs my movements.

"In fact, I don't want to talk about anything," I purr, leaning in to drag my lips over the sensitive skin on his neck.

∼

Sadly, on Monday, I have to confront the masses. I skip breakfast and show up early to English so Emilia can sit beside me, in case Cam gets any funny ideas about switching seats again—not that he even bothers to show up.

I haven't spoken to any of the guys—I haven't even read their plethora of messages from the weekend—and I don't know if the jig is up and they're done with me or if they're all in apology mode. Either way, I don't think I'm ready to see them yet.

Unfortunately, it's not so easy to avoid the whispers and pointed looks in my direction. I swear I will slash a bitch if one more person looks at me the wrong way.

"Hadley, the headmaster would like to speak with you," Mrs. Dean, my biology teacher, says. Her words cut off my glare to the bitch on the other side of the classroom, who keeps turning around in her chair to look at me, like I'm a fucking zoo animal to be gawked at.

"What?" I ask, confused, tearing my gaze away from the student to look at the teacher, certain I heard her wrong.

Fixing me with a stern look, she repeats more sharply, "The headmaster wants to see you. Now."

I quickly gather my belongings while trying to figure out what the headmaster could want. My hands shake with nerves. Am I failing out? What if he's discovered my identity is fake? I'm just starting to make a life here for myself, I can't get kicked out now.

My stomach somersaults the entire way to the headmaster's office, my legs feeling like lead as every step takes me closer to a fate I have no control over.

I feel my phone vibrate in my pocket as I enter the administration building, although I don't bother to look at it. Whatever it is can wait until later. I barely register the bell ringing, signifying lunch, as I reach the headmaster's door, wiping my sweaty palm down my blazer before lifting my fist and knocking.

"Come in," a deep voice calls out.

Opening the door, I step into his spacious office. There are bookcases along the walls, with a large wooden desk taking up most of the space. I don't take in any more than that as sitting in a chair opposite the headmaster's desk is none other than Lawrence Rutherford.

His eyes eat me up as he slowly lifts his gaze up my bare legs, taking in my short skirt and form-fitting shirt before his dark eyes meet mine, a challenge written in them.

"Hadley, come in." Mr. Phister waves me into the room and, with a dry mouth, I try to swallow down the bile rising at the back of my throat as I close the door behind me.

"What's this about?" I croak.

"Don't worry, dear," Mr. Phister says, chuckling. "You aren't in trouble. Mr. Rutherford here just wanted to meet our new scholarship student."

Bull-fucking-crap.

I stand awkwardly near the door, refusing to move any further into the room, and I'm sure as shit not about to sit beside that asshole.

"It's nice to meet you," I say politely, gritting my teeth and hating that I have to pretend to be nice to this fucker. "But I should probably be getting back to class. I wouldn't want to fall behind."

Lawrence just smirks at my attempt to get away.

"Miss Parker," Mr. Phister barks authoritatively, looking both embarrassed by and furious at my response. "Mr. Rutherford is from one of the founding members of this school, and if he wants to get to know a student of mine, then you can damn well miss one class to accommodate him."

My back straightens. Clearly, the headmaster is going to be zero fucking help; he's just offered me up on a silver platter.

"You can have my office for your conversation," the headmaster says, looking at Lawrence. "I have a few things to take care of."

Is he shitting me right now? He's just going to fuck off and leave me here alone with him?

I open my mouth to protest, but the headmaster throws me a stern look that has me snapping it closed. Why even bother? It will only please Lawrence, hearing how uncomfortable I am in his presence.

Getting to his feet, Mr. Phister shakes hands with Lawrence, pinning me with a look, telling me to behave, as he walks past me, striding out of the room without a backward glance.

As soon as the door clicks shut behind him, Lawrence is on his feet, prowling toward me.

"You don't look happy to see me, Dove." One side of his lip lifts in a victorious fucking smirk that simultaneously makes my blood boil and has fear skittering up my spine.

Planting my feet, I refuse to let him intimidate me, clenching my hands so tight to stop them from trembling that my short nails dig into the skin. I need to work out how to get out of here. Now.

"I always did love seeing you in short skirts," he purrs when standing right in front of me. "I have a whole closet of them for you at my house."

No fucking thanks.

I force my features to remain neutral. He'll only get off at seeing my distress, and any disgust at the idea will anger him.

"I hope you haven't been letting any of the boys here touch you," he sneers, glancing down at me as if he can tell by simply looking at me if I've been faithful to him. "Have you?" he barks, the loud roar of his voice making me jump. His hand wraps around my upper arm, squeezing it painfully as tremors take over my whole body.

"No," I choke out, panic building within me as I struggle and fail to devise a plan of how to get away from him.

His hold relaxes, his facial features evening out as he strokes his hand down my hair. "That's my little Dove," he coos. "I knew you wouldn't do that to me."

"You have been a naughty girl, though," he tuts. "You should have been mine by now."

I feel his fingers grazing against my bare thigh, the slight touch making my entire body freeze.

Leaning in, he runs his nose along my hairline. "You owe me," he growls against my ear. My body is rigid, my heart slamming against my chest at his insinuation. He's never forced me to do anything. He's never done anything to me either, but it seems he's done with all the lines between us.

His hands press firmly against my shoulders, applying force as he tries to push me onto my knees at his feet.

Fighting against him, I shake my head helplessly. "No," I plead in a quiet voice, hating myself for uttering that one word.

He laughs maliciously. "You brought this upon yourself. You know how much I hate to be kept waiting."

I continue to shake my head, deciding I no longer give a shit about getting out of this without pissing him off or causing a scene. I just want to get the fuck away from him.

"Don't think I didn't see you at that party with West," he sneers. "Do you know how it felt, watching him put his hands all over what's mine?" He hisses out the word *mine*, his body practically vibrating with anger, and he bares his teeth as he glowers at me. "I wanted to kill him." His fingers dig painfully into the skin on my shoulders, making me flinch, but he doesn't seem to notice or care.

"I saw the way you looked at him," he snarls, his hands releasing my shoulders as he grabs my face, his fingers squeezing the soft flesh enough to push my cheeks between my teeth. I don't need to look in a mirror to know he's leaving crescent moon indents from his nails. I can feel them driving into my skin.

His head tilts to one side, fury spitting from his eyes. "Did you develop a crush on the nerdy Prince?" He laughs like that's hilarious, before his features darken over again.

His hand comes out of nowhere, my face whipping to the side. The sting of his hit is the first realization that he's slapped me before heat emanates from the tender spot.

"You. Are. MINE!" he roars. "That boy is easily replaceable. It wouldn't be difficult to get rid of him. So unless you want that to happen, I suggest you get down on your knees and show me who you belong to."

He watches me patiently as hopelessness crashes through me. He no longer needs to physically force me to my knees. His words have cemented my fate. He's psychotic enough to follow through on his promise, and I know he has the means to execute it. I can't let any harm come to West just because I couldn't bring myself to give the old fuck a blowjob. Despite how messed up things might be with the guys at the minute, I'm not going to sign West's death warrant just because I can't trust them.

With a heavy heart and feeling physically ill, I slowly lower myself to my knees, deliberately not looking into his eyes, unable to bear the sick gleam of satisfaction I know I'll see in them.

He unbuckles his belt, lifting out his small, erect cock and pressing it against my lips.

"Open," he growls.

I part my lips as I recede into myself, pretending I'm anywhere but here, until it feels like this is happening to someone else. This is some other girl's life.

"Fuck," he groans as he pushes deeper inside my mouth, his hand roughly gripping the hair at the back of my scalp, pushing me further down on him.

His grip is painful as he holds me still, tears spilling over and running down my cheeks as he thrusts in and out of me. The room is silent, except for his labored breathing and the sound of his balls slapping against my chin.

Blocking it all out, I retreat into the corner of my mind where I used to visit when I was being punished. When I was a kid, I used to come in here and pretend I led a different life—one where I had parents who loved me. We lived in a lovely home, and we had a dog. Sometimes I even had siblings that annoyed me, but I loved them anyway.

As I got older, I stopped pretending that could ever be my life. Instead, I looked to the future. I made a list of all the places I wanted to visit and pictured myself there—the first time I walked on the beach, swimming in a hot spring, getting soaked at Niagara Falls.

I'm safely tucked up in that little corner of my mind when the sound of the door slamming against the wall snaps me out of it and back to reality. Lawrence's dick falls out of my mouth as I blink away the tears, humiliation and shame suffocating me as I look up at Hawk standing in the doorway.

Fury burns in his eyes as they run over me. However, in the next second, he blinks and all traces of emotion are wiped from his face as he flicks his gaze to Lawrence, dismissing me as though I'm nothing more than the cock-sucking slut I feel like right now.

"Hawk, my boy, haven't you ever heard of knocking," Lawrence admonishes, tucking himself away, not sounding the slightest bit ashamed at having been caught with his dick shoved down a student's throat.

"I did," Hawk responds in a monotonous voice. "You mustn't have heard me."

Lawrence chuckles like it's a fucking joke, taking a step back from me as he turns toward Hawk. "I was a little preoccupied," he jokes. "What are you doing here, son?"

"I heard you were here; I was hoping we could talk."

"Sure, sure," Lawrence agrees, sitting down in the headmaster's chair behind the desk.

Hawk glances my way, where I'm still sitting in a heap on the floor, not having the strength to get to my feet. There's nothing in his eyes. No emotion that could give me any insight into what he's thinking.

"We probably shouldn't discuss this in front of *her*," he says, his lip curling back as he sneers.

Lawrence glances my way, pursing his lips. "Fine," he reluctantly agrees on a sigh before focusing his gaze on me. "Go," he demands. "We can finish this next time."

My legs shake, threatening to give out beneath me as I scramble to my feet. Grabbing my bag that I dropped at some point, I rush out of the room without a backward glance.

I race blindly down the hall to the first bathroom I see. I don't even notice if it's for females or not. I just push my way inside, rush into a cubicle and collapse on the floor in front of the toilet bowl.

Tears trail silently down my face as I stick my fingers down my throat, forcing myself to be sick—anything to get the taste of him out of my mouth.

Crouching over the toilet bowl, I empty my stomach before falling back onto the floor and leaning back against the toilet door, resting my head against the wood as I close my eyes.

My hands shake as I swipe at my damp cheeks, fury and shame fighting for dominance. It's not even that I'm ashamed of what I did. I did it to keep West safe, and I don't regret that. It's the fact that Hawk saw me like that. What the hell is he going to think of me now? I've probably just destroyed the tiny bit of progress we'd made over the last few weeks.

I don't know how long I sit there before I hear the bathroom door open and someone walk in. The person stops outside my stall. All I can make out are their black loafers and gray slacks.

"It's only me," Hawk says. "Lawrence is gone. You can come out."

I want to tell him to leave me alone, too ashamed to look him in the eye. Nevertheless, he moves to stand by the sinks, and through the gap at the bottom of the door, I can tell he's leaning back against the counter with his legs crossed at the ankle, prepared to wait me out.

Sighing, I wipe the back of my hand across my mouth and get to my feet, fixing a mask in place over my features before I unlock the cubicle door and step out. Not looking at him, I cross the space to the sink. I deliberately don't look in the mirror, not ready to look at myself yet, as I turn on the tap and cup my hand under the faucet to gather water, bringing it to my lips and swishing it around my mouth before spitting it out.

"Here." Hawk holds out a packet of mints for me to take. I gratefully accept it from him, removing one and popping it into my mouth, the minty freshness hitting the spot.

"Did you, uh, know I was in there?" I ask hesitantly, keeping my gaze firmly on the white-tiled floor as I lean against the counter beside him.

"I thought you might be." His voice isn't the same monotonous voice he used in the headmaster's office. There's a heaviness to it that I've never heard before. A weariness, likely he's suddenly exhausted. "Beck saw Lawrence heading into the headmaster's office earlier and messaged us to give us a heads-up that he was on campus. When you didn't turn up at lunch, I got worried."

He was worried about me? That's...new.

"What he..." He trails off, gritting his teeth as he pushes off the counter, storming across the small space. His hands form fists as he tries to control his anger, losing the battle as his arm snaps out to punch the tile and it cracks. The sudden aggression shocks me. Since he walked into that office, he's been calm and collected, not giving me any insight into the rage he was harboring.

He runs his hand through his hair, his back to me as he takes several deep breaths before spinning around to look at me. I can't not look into his dark eyes as he strides back toward me. His face is like thunder, jaw tight, and his eyes swirling with so much rage. I'm pretty sure he's about to tear me a new one, probably thinking the story I told them about Lawrence was all bullshit since I so easily got on my knees for him.

I'm entirely taken by surprise when instead of yelling, he steps into me. His arms wrap around me and he pulls me into his chest. He's....hugging me? My body is tense for a moment, and I've no idea what to do with my hands as I just stand there.

"I'm so sorry," he murmurs in a cracked voice that shatters my resolve as a tear runs down my face, and I wrap my arms around him, burying my face in his chest. "I'm so fucking sorry," he says over and over again, holding me tightly as I fall apart in his arms.

When he finally steps back, I wipe away the tears, trying to get myself under control again. I can't say I ever thought I'd cry in front of Hawk. And crying twice in the span of a week, what sort of pathetic cry-baby am I turning into?

He doesn't move far, standing right in front of me. His gaze roams over my face and his jaw ticks as he fixates on my cheek. I can still feel the sting from Lawrence's slap, and I'm sure if I looked in the mirror, I'd find the skin red and swollen.

"What happened?" he growls, looking furious.

"I...he threatened to kill West if I didn't..." I trail off, not needing to explain what I had to do. He saw it for himself. Something I'm pretty sure he's not going to forget any time soon.

"I'm going to fucking kill him," he snarls, anger building within him again. "I've half a mind to track him down and shove my fist in his face right now." He stares at the bathroom door as if he's seriously thinking about chasing after Lawrence and doing just that.

"Don't do that," I plead, tugging on his sleeve to get him to look at me. "His death is already fated, but if you go after him now, he will know everything. He'll know we're siblings, that *we* know who I really am. We can't give him any more ammunition."

"But—"

"No," I snap, latching onto my own anger. "It was nothing I couldn't handle."

"Hadley, he had his dick in your mouth," he snarls, stomping across the bathroom.

"I fucking know that," I bite back. "And I'd let him do it again if it kept West safe."

When he turns around to look at me, he looks anguished. Torn between wanting to kill Lawrence on my behalf and keeping his friend safe.

He looks at me for a long moment before sighing.

"Fine," he relents, walking back toward me. "But he's never getting his hands on you again."

The promise in his words makes my heart clench. It's always been me against the world. I've somehow managed to collect an army of guys who would protect me, but having Hawk firmly on my side has emotion clogging my throat. It's something I've secretly hoped for, and I know we were making some progress. But having him tolerate my presence at lunch and hearing him say he'll fight for me are two very different things.

"I won't argue with that."

"About the other night," he begins, talking about the dance. "None of us knew what Bianca was going to do." He grits his teeth. "She'll pay for her actions, but you shouldn't blame the guys."

I stare at him, stunned for a moment. No doubt, accepting that I'm his sister *and* that I'm dating two of his best friends, has been challenging for him, so the fact that he's trying to save my relationship with West and Mason when he could so easily just leave them to sort it out themselves, is surprising, to say the least.

I swallow around the emotion in my throat. Unable to speak, I give him a jerky nod as he moves toward the door.

Just before he pulls it open, he turns back toward me.

"The guys don't need to know about what happened, if you don't want them to."

He looks at me for a moment before pulling the door open and walking out.

"Oh," he says as if he just remembered something he forgot to tell me, turning back to face me and glancing around the room. "You should probably get out of the boys' bathroom before anyone finds you here—what would people say?" A small smile graces his lips and I give a weak chuckle as the door closes, blocking my view of him.

CHAPTER TWENTY-TWO

I'm pacing back and forth across our dorm when the sound of our tablets going off stops me mid-stride and I spin to look at Cam sitting in the chair with his already empty glass of scotch.

"She's fine." He sighs, lifting his glass to his lips. He pauses when he realizes it's empty, scowling at it before getting up to make himself another drink.

Idiot needs to stop fucking drinking his problems away and talk to Hadley. You'd think after the other night he would have realized his drinking is getting all of us in trouble. Still, nope, if anything, he's been drinking more the last few days. I haven't missed the fact he's also wearing sweatpants instead of his school uniform and his hair is all mussed up like he just got out of bed before I arrived back.

Ever since Hadley told him about his dad, he's constantly drunk or hungover, looking like shit with bags under his eyes and sallow skin. It's only a matter of time before his lack of attendance raises flags, and Lawrence comes asking questions. That's the last thing we all need.

I breathe a sigh of relief, my shoulders slumping. When we heard Lawrence was on campus, we all freaked out. Even more so when Hawk said she hadn't turned up for lunch, and Beck confirmed she hadn't responded to his message either.

All of us wanted to go chasing after her, but Hawk shut us down, saying it would be too suspicious if we all showed up. He's right, I knew he was, but it doesn't make it any easier to deal with. Where the fuck was she? Was she with Lawrence? What the hell did he do to her if she was?

My stomach churns as the number of possibilities, each one worse than the last, runs through my head.

"Hawk's demanded a meeting," Mason informs me, reading the rest of the message that Cam failed to look at.

"What do you think happened?" I ask him.

He shakes his head, running his hand through his hair. His body is tense, adrenaline still coursing through it. "I dunno, man." He sighs. "He'll be here in a few minutes, so we can ask him then."

Parking my ass on the sofa, my leg bounces impatiently while we wait for him to arrive. As soon as we hear the key in the lock, Mason and I jump to our feet, spinning to look at the door in sync.

"What happened?" I demand as soon as Hawk walks in, my eyes narrowing on the asshole behind him. "Why is *he* here?"

Hawk rolls his eyes at me, but I don't miss the darkness shadowing him. Something fucking happened that has him furious, even if he is trying his best to hide it.

"It's going to take all five of us to keep Hadley safe," Hawk states in a no-nonsense tone that only raises more red flags. "So get over whatever the hell your problem is with him."

My eyes widen at Hawk's pissy attitude. He has always been on my side when it comes to Beck. He's definitely never told me to just 'get over it' like I don't have legitimate reasons to be pissed at him.

"Is she okay?" Mason interjects. "What did he do to her?"

I can hear the promise of death and destruction in his voice as he growls.

"Yeah, she's okay," Hawk assures us. "I got there in time."

He doesn't meet our eyes, however. What the fuck is that about? Got there in time to stop what?

My vision turns red at the thought of what could have happened to her. I usually leave the violence to Mason and Hawk, but right now, I'd happily drown that sick fuck.

He and Beck move to join us, sitting down in the remaining seats. Hawk runs his hand through his short blond hair, rubbing at his eyes. He seems exhausted.

"We need to get Hadley to agree to come out as a Davenport," he says, bringing up the original plan that Hadley had shut down several weeks ago.

"Are you sure that's a wise idea?" Beck asks, leaning forward in his seat to stare intently at Hawk. "You know your parents better than I do, yet I can't say they're my favorite people. They're just as involved as the rest of our parents." His eyes flit over to me briefly. "They're already holding West over our heads. Do we want to give them any more ammunition?" His words make me grind my teeth as flashbacks of Christmas day assault me.

"Where the fuck are we going?" *Cam grumbles from beside me. The five of us were ushered into the back of a car after dinner. A blacked-out partition separates us from the driver, blocking our view out the windshield, not that we can see much. It's pitch black out, the country road not even having streetlights to indicate where we are.*

We've been in the car for nearly an hour now, and I've long since given up on trying to follow the turns and work out where we are being taken. Somewhere inland, but that's about all I can figure out.

"Did they say anything to you?" I demand, glaring at Beck sitting opposite me in the back of the car.

"Why would they tell me anything?" he retorts. "They're your parents."

The five of us go silent as the car turns off the main road, the crunch of gravel heard under the wheels before we stop. We can hear the driver mumbling something to someone and, squinting out the window, I can make out a guard and a gate behind him.

Where the fuck are we?

The guard signals for the gates to be opened and we slowly pass through, the car trudging along the dirt road before stopping at a small, one-story building.

The partition between the driver and us is lowered, and I catch a glimpse of him for the first time. Some dude I don't recognize.

"You're to go into that building," he states indifferently. "Your parents are waiting for you."

Why the fuck this conversation couldn't have been had back in the house is beyond me.

The five of us climb out of the car. Glancing around me, I squint through the darkness, unable to make out much of anything. We're in the middle of fucking nowhere, with nothing but a lone building surrounded by fields and open space.

Running his hand through his short blond hair and sighing, Hawk shakes his head and moves toward the building, flanked by Mason. With a final wary look around us, I follow after them, Cam beside Beck and me bringing up the rear.

All five of us are on alert, our postures stiff as we approach the door, Hawk yanking it open. Inside is dark, making the hairs rise on the back of my neck. Something isn't adding up here. There's no way our parents are waiting for us in a dim room.

Looking over his shoulder, Hawk spears each of us with a silent look to be on guard as he steps through the doorway. The rest of us follow behind him, moving as a unit. Even Beck moves with us, his body stiff and arms raised, ready to strike, as his eyes dart around our surroundings.

As soon as we're all inside, the door bangs shut behind us, and the overhead lights flicker on, momentarily blinding me.

I hear it before my eyes can adjust to the light, the sound of scuffling, the oomph as the air is knocked out of someone's lungs.

What the fuck is going on?

Blinking rapidly, I finally take in the sight before me. Mason and Hawk are fighting some guy dressed in all black and built like a machine, appearing more menacing than anyone I've ever seen.

Hawk's arm snaps out, delivering what I know is a solid right hook that could have even a trained fighter knocked backward. The guy barely even moves as Hawk's fist connects with his abdomen, scowling before he takes a step in Hawk's direction.

I don't get to see what happens next as another guy drops from the fucking ceiling behind Cam, his arm going around his neck in a headlock, cutting off his air supply.

I react on instinct, not comprehending I've even moved until I'm standing right behind the guy, lashing out at his kidneys with all my strength. I'm the weakest of the guys, and if Hawk's punches barely fazed the guy he's fighting, then I might as well be tickling the guy holding Cam for all the good it does me.

He looks over his shoulder, his lips peeling back as he snarls at me like a rabid animal.

Who the fuck is this dude?

With one swipe of his hand that connects with my face, my head snaps to the side, sending my glasses flying across the room.

Fuck.

The images around me go blurry, but despite being unable to see, I focus on the blur in front of me, punching him repeatedly.

Another blurry image appears in my field of vision as my breathing comes in rapid pants, the mixture of adrenaline and fear from not being able to see taking control of my body.

"It's me," Beck grunts, as I hear a pained groan come from in front of me.

Another flurry of movement, and someone grabs my arm. Pulling back against the grip, I swing my arm out. Shit, I hate being fucking blind. If I'd known I was going to be getting into a fistfight, I'd have put my fucking contacts in.

"Wow, man, it's alright," Cam's voice calms me as he tightens his grip once again, leading me somewhere. "Just stay here, okay? Don't move. I'll find you your glasses."

I frown, but I know it's not his fault I'm fucking useless to any of them.

Instead, I do what I do best. As the sound of skin hitting skin and grunts echo around the room, I try to figure out what the fuck is going on and how to get us out of here.

Before I can work any of it out, something smashes into me, knocking the wind out of me as I crash to the ground, a weight landing on top of me.

Whoever it is releases a groan as they sag against me, and I reach out blindly, squinting to try and make out who it is.

My hand lands on a warm chest that rises in rapid pants, feeling the buttons of the person's shirt as I make out a blur of blond-looking hair. Hawk or Cam, then. Neither of the guys who attacked us was wearing a shirt.

"Dude, stop feeling me up," Cam groans again.

"Are you okay?" I ask in a panic. "What the hell is going on?"

"Not sure, but I found your glasses."

He pushes my glasses into my hands, and with shaking fingers I put them on. One of the lenses is cracked, obscuring my vision, but it's still a step up from not being able to see anything more than moving blobs.

Running my eyes over Cam as he lies sprawled half on top of me, I notice he's got blood trickling down the side of his head, and his face is scrunched up in pain.

"Are you okay?" I repeat, looking him over for further injuries.

"Just dandy," he retorts sarcastically.

Asshole. He can't be too bad if he's fucking joke.

I focus back to the fights, noticing Mason is sporting his own war wounds as he rushes the guy he's fighting. His shirt is half torn, showing what looks like a fucking knife wound to his side, blood flowing freely down over his white skin. As I watch, his punches become sloppy, his energy waning the more blood he loses.

Hawk and Beck appear to be faring a bit better as they tag team the other guy who attacked us, managing to give as good as they get. It's clear that although we outnumber these assholes, they outmatch us, and it's only a matter of time before we all fall like dominos.

Tearing my eyes away from the fight as the guy delivers a punch to Hawk's face that is guaranteed to leave a black eye, I run my gaze over the walls, not seeing any other way out of here other than the door we came through.

"We need to get to the door," I tell Cam, urgency making the words come out rushed as I stand and pull him to his feet, ignoring his grimace. The way he's holding himself makes me think he has bruised, if not broken, ribs. He meets my eye, nodding at my silent question before we start to make our way around the outer edge of the room, keeping close to the walls and moving slowly so as not to distract the others from their fights.

As we're about to reach the door, a blaring alarm goes off and the lights start flashing.

What the fuck is happening now?

As soon as the noise starts, the guys who attacked us stop fighting, stepping away from the others as they move into an empty corner of the room, their faces impassive.

All of us stare at them with confusion and wariness, yet the sound of the door unlocking and being opened snags our attention as our parents move into the room. All of them are forming a line across the only escape.

The five of us drift into the center of the room, remaining vigilant as we form a circle, simultaneously keeping an eye on our parents and the two guys now standing silently at attention in the corner of the room.

"What the hell is going on here?" Hawk seethes, the words coming out in short pants as he recovers his breath, swiping away a trickle of blood from his brow before it can run into his eye.

His father's eyes narrow on him. "This is a demonstration," he begins, his eyes roaming disinterestedly over us as though we aren't standing sweaty and bleeding in front of him.

"It's time for all of you to step up and claim your places in this company," my father tacks on cryptically.

"What the hell does that mean?" Beck bites out, looking frazzled. He's the only one of us who doesn't have some idea at this point what this is all about.

My father's eyes flick to him, his jaw ticking. "Boy, we are the owners of the most successful mercenary conglomerate in the Northern hemisphere." The words are spoken so matter of fact, that it's clear it takes a moment for them to register with Beck. I almost feel sorry for him for a second, finding out like this. It was a struggle for us to wrap our heads around it before, and we didn't even have the shit nearly beat out of us either. Then again, it's not my problem. He's the one who inserted himself in this mess. If he'd stayed gone in whatever hick town he came from, he wouldn't be neck-deep in this shit now.

A weak, unhinged-sounding laugh escapes him and his gaze darts over each of our parents as his brows pull together. "You're fucking kidding, right?"

When he doesn't get the appropriate response, he glances to each of us, and I can almost see the pleading in his eyes, wanting someone to tell him it's all one big, massive joke.

No such luck, bro.

When he catches Hawk's eye, Hawk gives a quick jerk of his head, cautioning him to shut up.

"Boys, you will be stepping into your roles at graduation," Mason's dad pipes up, ignoring Beck's outburst. "Between now and then, we will be familiarizing you with everything and preparing you for your future positions."

Each of our parent's eyes fall on Beck, our father speaking up again, "Beck, we have a specific job we need you to do. I'll discuss it with you in private later."

"Fuck no," Beck snarls, glowering at each of them, disgust and shock plainly written on his face for everyone to see. "I'm having no part of this."

Our father barks out a cold, uncaring laugh. "I think you'll find you have no choice." There's a hint of warning in his tone. "You agreed to my conditions when I gave you that cushy job at the school."

Beck's lip curls back as he practically snarls in outrage.

"And in case that isn't enough," our father continues, ignoring the death glare Beck is throwing his way. "This little meeting tonight"—he gestures toward the two men, that I've now ascertained are mercenaries, in the far corner—"has been a demonstration of sorts, to show you what our men are capable of."

The threat is crystal clear in the stern tone of his voice.

"Are you threatening us?" Hawk growls, fixing each of our parents with his own menacing glare. "You can't get rid of us. You need us."

The second my father's eyes connect with mine, realization sets in, fury bursting into flames in my chest—at him, at Beck, at this whole fucked-up situation.

"Is that so?" my father drawls, an evil smirk playing along his lips. "I have two sons now. I don't believe I have a need for both of them."

"You'd...You wouldn't..." Cam's voice trails off, his already pale face draining of the last of its color as understanding dawns.

Mason's dad steps forward, his cold eyes boring into Mason, who lifts his chin defiantly. "None of us have a need for heirs who don't fall in line and do as they are told. Disappoint us, and West will find out what it's like to come face to face with one of our men when they aren't holding back."

Holding back? Fuck, we struggled two on five as it was. I don't want to know how capable these scumbags are when they go all out.

"Fail to follow our instructions, and we will pick you off one by one."

It's not my fault my dad decided to get his dick wet and spawn a bastard child, but here we are, and I'm the first to go if any of us step out of line. *Fucking great.*

"Do you have a better idea?" Hawk seethes, pulling me back into the conversation. "Our parents are pieces of shit, but none of them are as bad as Lawrence. Yeah, they'll probably dangle her over our heads to make us do their bidding, except I'd rather have that than whatever she might suffer at that fucker's hands."

Hawk has utterly lost the thin hold he had over his emotions. He's practically foaming at the mouth, he's so goddamn angry.

"What the hell happened today?" I demand. Hawk has always had issues with his anger. He's never been able to control it, but this is on a whole other level.

"Nothing." The word is said on a frustrated growl, lines furrowing across his forehead as he scowls.

"You're lying," I shout, getting to my feet and glowering at him. He can't keep fucking secrets about her from us. She might be his sister, but she's dating us—well, kind of. After last night, I don't know where we stand, but I'm not about to just let her go. I got a taste of her, and now I need more. The way she obediently obeyed me, grew fucking wet at my demands…it was so fucking hot. Not to mention the trust she placed in me to make her feel good. Nope, there's no fucking way I'm letting Bianca's little bitch-fit fuck this up for me.

"He thinks he can come in here and just demand to see her," he snarls, lost in his thoughts as his hands clench into tight fists, nostrils flaring. "The headmaster had left her alone in his office with him. He fucking left her alone with that…predator." He yells the last sentence, losing his thin hold over his anger again as he storms to his feet, throwing the first thing he can get his hands on—the TV remote—at the wall.

My heart slams against my chest, needing desperately to know what happened while simultaneously hoping Hawk continues to rant and rave, taking his sweet time getting there.

"She's not safe here," he hisses, looking at Beck.

"And you think if everyone knows she's a Davenport, she will be? That he won't be able to get his hands on her?" Beck questions, desperate hope shining in his eyes.

"I think it will make it harder for him." He sighs. "He won't want word to get back to our parents if he's caught alone with her or seeming too interested."

"So, nothing happened today?" I interject, watching him closely.

"No." He sighs. "I told you, I got there before anything could happen."

"You know your parents will only use her for their own gain." There's a defeated tone in Mason's voice, mixed with anger and frustration, and I immediately cop on to what he's getting at.

"No way," I bark out. "Fuck that. She's ours."

Even Cam, who has contributed the sum total of fuck all to this conversation, grimaces, while Beck's eyes dart between us, seeming confused.

"We won't let anything happen to her," Hawk insists, getting annoyed once again. "We can protect her from anything my parents might try to do. Besides, it's better than letting Lawrence get his hands on her."

"I don't understand what's going on right now," Beck says, still looking at each of us. "But if you think this is the best plan, then you need to try and convince Hadley of that. I've already told her to give it some thought, but ultimately, I'll support whatever decision she makes."

"Seriously?" I sneer, my lip curling up. "You're that pussy-whipped that you'll let her do whatever the fuck she wants. Even if it ultimately results in her ending up locked in some basement that only Lawrence knows the location of?"

Beck's hand is around my throat before I've even finished speaking. His green eyes, so similar to my own, clouded over with anger.

"Don't you fucking dare talk like that," he snarls, spittle hitting my face. "Unlike you entitled fucking shitheads who have always had each other, she's had no one her entire life. So yeah, I'll try and get her to make the best decision. But regardless of what she decides, I'm going to be on *her* side and have *her* back, because she's never had someone be there for her like that before, and I'm sure as fuck not about to let her down."

Using his grip on my neck, he pushes me backward, away from him, and I stumble into the sofa behind me.

Straightening out his stupid little waistcoat, he turns to Hawk. "I take it we're done here for today."

"Yeah, we're done," Hawk responds on a sigh.

Beck gives him a tight nod before stalking out of the dorm without a backward glance.

"Well, that went well," Cam unhelpfully pipes up, finishing off the remainder of his scotch as we all turn to scowl at him.

Huffing out a breath of annoyance, I state, "I'm heading out," not bothering to look at any of them as I head for the door. They already know where I'm going. I don't give a fuck about class. If Hadley's not going to be there, then neither am I.

"Hold up," Mason calls out, "I'm coming too."

Hadley

CHAPTER TWENTY-THREE

I look relatively okay when I check myself in the mirror before I leave the bathroom, other than looking paler than usual with red-rimmed eyes and the faint outline of a handprint on my cheek. It's not like I'm going back to class anyway. Not after that fucking shitshow. As far as I'm concerned, today's canceled. I'll give life a go again tomorrow.

Once I'm back in my room, I shower and change out of my uniform into a pair of shorts and a tank top, flopping down on my bed. The second I close my eyes though, images flash across my eyelids until I jump out of bed, pacing back and forth across the small room.

I'm fuming. Absolutely fucking furious. All the rage I should have been feeling at the time, drowned out by fear and weakness, is crashing through me like a tsunami. It feels like it's going to break through my skin and tear me to shreds if I don't find an outlet for it.

There's a knock at the door, and I pull it open with more force than necessary, probably appearing like someone possessed.

Mason and West are both standing there, their jaws set and their eyes telling me they have no intention of leaving until we sort stuff out.

Cocking my head, *I guess I've just found my outlet.*

Snatching my hand out, I grab onto the front of Mason's shirt and all but yank him into the room, slamming my lips against his in a kiss that's all-feisty aggression. He remains rigid for a moment, not responding to my attack, but after a few seconds, he jumps into action as his arms come up to drag me further into his embrace and kisses me back with just as much fervor.

I'm faintly aware of West closing the door as he crosses the threshold, and I feel his body heat against my back as he brushes my still-damp hair out of the way, biting and sucking his way along my shoulder.

"Not quite the welcome we were expecting," West murmurs against my neck, the soft vibrations as his lips move over my skin making me shiver. Tearing my lips from Mason's, I tilt my head back, giving West better access as I moan to the ceiling.

"Not that we're complaining." Mason chuckles in a dark tone, filled with sexual promises.

"Shut up and fuck me," I snap impatiently.

The two of them share a look over my head, one that says they're about to do nasty things to me. *Hell. Fucking. Yes.* This is exactly what I need after today.

West trails his fingers down my bare arms before circling my wrists and tugging my arms behind me. The move has me arching my back, my breasts grazing against Mason's shirt as my nipples stiffen. He slides his hands up my sides, flicking his thumbs over my nipples and rolling them between his fingers.

My panties grow damp as I rub my thighs together.

"No, no, sweetheart," West purrs in my ear as Mason wedges his thigh between my legs. "The only relief you'll be getting is at our hands." He slips his hand under the waistband of my shorts, slowly gliding his finger over the sensitive skin along the line of my panties, teasing me mercilessly. "By our tongues." Using his teeth, he pulls down the thin strap of my top before licking a trail over the scar on my shoulder. "From our cocks." He grinds his dick between my ass cheeks, letting me feel how turned on he is.

His dirty words and light touches are making me delirious as my system floods with rampant hormones.

All the while, Mason is slowly stripping off his uniform, starting first with his tie, which he slowly unloops from around his neck. Dropping it on the floor, he begins to undo his shirt buttons one at a time. Never taking his eyes from where West touches me, drinking in my reactions—my heaving chest, my panting moans, the flushed rosiness of my cheeks.

Shrugging off his shirt, he smirks as he catches me licking my lips. Mason is like a Greek god—all hard muscle and warm skin. He's got muscles on muscles on muscles. I bet he could probably bench-press me with one arm. Every flex of his arms and tensing of his pecs draws my attention.

My gaze drops to the firm ridges of his abdomen and the glorious V that's begging me to run my tongue over it. I spot the thin layer of hair that trails down to his belt as he deftly unbuckles it, shucking his gray slacks as he kicks off his black loafers until he's standing in front of me in nothing more than skin-tight boxers.

I was so caught up in Mason's strip tease that I hadn't noticed West doing the same behind me until I felt his bare arm pressing against my back.

His fingers hook under the hem of my top, pulling it over my head as Mason shrugs down my shorts and takes my panties with it until I'm standing between them naked.

They both stare at me, making me feel self-conscious despite the obvious hard-ons they're sporting and the heat in their eyes.

"So sexy," West murmurs against my skin, his hand trailing across a scar that cuts across my hip. From where he's standing behind me, he's got a clear view of the worst of my scars, yet the way he's tracing them…there's none of the disgust or hesitation I'm used to. Instead, his eyes flare as they roam over my skin. "I love how fucking strong you are," he murmurs, more to himself.

Mason steps up in front of me. "A Phoenix is fitting," he says. "You had to go through hell in order to rise from the ashes and emerge as the warrior you are."

I don't know what to say in response to either of them, my heart swelling at their words as I stare wide-eyed at them.

Except this is meant to be a down-and-dirty fuck session to escape this day, and I'm too strung out after what went down this afternoon to wrangle my way through any more emotions, so I do what I do best and deflect.

"Why am I the only one that's naked?" I pout, staring pointedly at their boxers.

Not needing any more encouragement, both of them strip out of their boxers, and I feel West's long length rubbing between my ass cheeks as Mason fists his cock, his eyes heating with molten lust, practically turning black; he's so turned on.

"You want us both, Little Warrior?"

How could I not want them when they look at me like that?

"Yes," I respond in a husky voice. Looking over my shoulder so I can see West, I say, "But I'm in charge."

He tenses, then gives me a curt nod.

Spinning around until I'm fully facing him, I kiss him deeply and it swiftly turns frenzied as he pushes me back toward the bed. I turn at the last second, shoving him down on the bed and straddling him. I hover above him as he rubs his dick through my slick wetness, lubricating it before positioning it at my entrance.

Done with waiting and knowing I need it quick and rough and dirty, I slam myself down onto his long length, letting out a silent gasp as he keeps sliding into me until I can feel him hitting my cervix.

He groans in pleasure as I rock against him, quickly picking up the pace as I bob up and down on him.

"More," I moan, peering over my shoulder to find Mason jerking himself off as he watches me fuck his friend.

When he catches me looking at him, he comes toward us.

West shuffles us further back on the bed so Mason can climb in behind me. Reaching down between us, until he can feel West's cock sliding in and out of me, he gathers my wetness on his fingers and uses it to lubricate my ass before pushing a finger inside.

I shift back against him, relishing the slight burn and needing more.

"More," I repeat in a pleasure-induced groan.

"So demanding." Mason chuckles, but he does as I say.

Placing his cock at my puckered hole, he slowly pushes his way inside. The burning sensation increases, but the pleasure-pain combo only makes me wetter as I push back against him, feeling more full than I ever have before.

When he's seated inside me, neither of them moves, glancing at one another as though waiting for a signal.

"Move," I snap, growing impatient.

The two of them jump into action, quickly finding a rhythm that works for the three of us until I feel my pussy clenching. Both guys groan, and Mason slides his hands from my hips to my aching nipples, giving them a pinch as West claims my lips, kissing me with so much passion my pussy spasms. Both of them tremble as I explode, a gush of wetness coating my thighs.

"Fuck," West growls, his face scrunched up as his cock swells within me, his hot seed coating my inner walls as I cry out. Feeling Mason pull out behind me a second before his cum hits my back, I collapse forward onto West, exhausted.

I rest against West, panting heavily as I hear Mason moving behind us. A few seconds later, he returns with a cloth to wipe my back before pulling me off of West.

He drags me into his large arms, not caring that West's cum is dripping down my inner thighs. West drops a kiss on my shoulder as his hand rests on my hip.

"Not what I was expecting to happen when we came over here," Mason smirks, a cocky grin on his face.

"So fucking hot, though," West responds, leaning in to whisper in my ear, "but next time, I'm in charge."

My pussy clenches like the wanton hussy she is. *Hell yes, I'm dying to see how alpha-dominant West is in the bedroom.*

A moment of silence falls between us, each of us enjoying our post-orgasmic bliss, yet it's not long before tension bleeds into the air.

"About the other night," West begins hesitantly, "none of us had anything to do with what Bianca did. She's a dead girl walking for pulling that shit."

"I know," I respond wearily, suddenly feeling exhausted and far too comfy nestled between them. "Hawk explained it."

"So, you're not angry with us?" Mason asks. I can feel him watching me, but I don't lift my head to look at him.

"No."

"But you don't trust us," he states, picking up on what I'm not saying.

"No," I confirm. "Not yet."

"That's okay, Firefly," West murmurs against my skin, his warm body pressing along my back and his nickname for me making my stupid girly heart melt. "Your head might not trust us yet, but your body does, and that's good enough for now."

∼

Today is Cam's first race of the semester. Since I told him about everything, he's been off, drinking every day and skipping class. I'm worried about him, and even though the guys have assured me he will kick ass today, I'm nervous. A future in swimming is something he wants. He may not think that's possible, but I don't want him to throw away all hope of that today just because he's in a dark place.

Unable to stay in my room and wonder how the race is going for him, I head to the sports center. I can hear the announcer before I step into the room, just as a whistle goes and the race begins.

I'm high up in the stands and take a seat in the back row, not wanting Cam or Lawrence to see me. Scanning my eyes over the other students and parents around me, I spot all three of the guys sitting in the front row, watching the events with keen eyes.

As I'm watching them, something off to the side catches their attention, various looks of hatred and contempt crossing their features. I lean forward in my seat, looking down toward the pool, wanting to see what's annoyed them, and find Lawrence and Cam huddled in a corner near the changing rooms. A shiver runs down my spine at seeing him again, and my stomach revolts as mental images of being back in the headmaster's office with him batter my vision.

Closing my eyes, I take several deep, calming breaths in through my nose and out through my mouth, letting the smell of chlorine ground me and remind me of the time Beck caught me hiding in the pool. I remember the shocked look on his face before he moved closer to me.

. . .

Tilting my head back, I look up into his eyes, seeing his usual bright moss-green irises darkened with lust. "I don't do this. I don't seduce students, but I just can't seem to stop myself with you."

"So don't," I whisper the words so quietly I'm not sure he even hears me. He gazes into my eyes for a moment longer before his hands slide around my neck, his fingers tangling in my hair as he angles me perfectly. His lips hover over mine, both of us savoring this moment before everything changes.

I think back to one of the best nights I've ever had, feeling some of my anxiety and tension slip away before opening my eyes again and focusing back on Cam.

I'm guessing Lawrence is doing his usual pre-race routine that I've seen him do with Cam before his other races. Whatever it is he says to Cam only ever seems to piss him off, and today is no exception as Cam scowls, storming away from his dad as his race is called.

Standing at the edge of the pool, he glowers at the water as he waits for the whistle to blow. Nerves beat a steady tune in my stomach as the seconds seem to last forever until finally, the whistle goes and Cam dives into the water.

All of them are strong swimmers, their arms arching through the water as their legs kick out like their lives depend on it. Cam's neck and neck with another swimmer, both of them fighting for the number one spot, but as he reaches the far end and starts back toward the starting point, Cam increases the distance, pushing into first place as his hand slams against the side of the pool and he is announced as the winner.

There's not a trace of the usual celebratory smile on his face or any fist pumping the air. The moment he's done, he effortlessly hauls himself out of the water, still scowling at everyone and everything around him as he drapes a towel over his shoulder and storms off toward the changing rooms.

Glancing around, I don't see Lawrence anywhere. I guess now that his son has once again proven he's a winner, he's returned to his own life. *Good riddance.* Slipping out of the back row, I keep an eye out in case Lawrence is still lurking around here somewhere as I head down to the changing rooms. Cam did well today, but the outcome could have been completely different. He's going down a dangerous path, and I can't help but feel at least partially responsible for it.

He's been avoiding me for weeks, but I'm fucking done with it now. We need to talk this shit out. He needs to know I don't hold anything against him. His father's sins are not his to bear, and the shit he's done to me in the past, is just that...in the past.

I wait outside the changing room until the door opens and a group of guys emerge. None of them pay me any more than a cursory glance, all of them too hyped up on their wins and ready to celebrate to linger outside the changing rooms.

A few more stragglers filter out before the door stops opening. Pressing my ear against it, I don't hear any noise inside, so I'm hoping that means Cam is alone. Silently pushing open the door, I slip in, glancing around to ensure no one else is here. I can hear the shower running, but there's only one locker with clothes in it—the same one Cam's stuff was in last time.

Locking the door behind me, I sit and stare at the locker as I wait for him to finish up in the shower. Things were different the last time I was here. How I wish we could go back to that, but then, none of it was real. I was keeping secrets and lying. Yet, despite that, my feelings for Cam were always real.

I hear the shower turn off, and a moment later, Cam walks into the changing room only wearing his swimming trunks as he runs a towel over his hair.

Lifting his head, his eyes widen as he stops midway across the room, glancing around before focusing his gaze back on me. His eyes darken as his lips flatten, not happy with my intrusion.

"What are you doing here?"

He starts walking toward me again, stopping at his locker to lift out some clothes before dropping them on the bench, ensuring he leaves a decent gap between us.

"We need to talk."

"No, we don't," he growls, not looking my way as he swipes the towel over his chest, catching a few trails of water as they drip off his hair.

"You've been avoiding me."

He doesn't respond, continuing to dry himself off before turning away from me, giving me a perfect view of his tight, muscular ass as he pulls his shorts down, quickly donning a pair of boxers instead.

Sensing I'm running out of time, I get to the point.

"Cam," I say in a softer voice. "None of what happened is your fault."

He spins toward me, his face firm with anger.

"How can you say that?" he snaps furiously.

"You are not responsible for what your father did—"

"No, but I'm responsible for what I did. I let my anger get the better of me, and I took advantage of you."

"Cam." I sigh, my heart breaking for what he's putting himself through. "No, you didn't."

He's already shaking his head, not believing me.

Getting to my feet, I step toward him. "I've wanted you since the first day I saw you on campus."

He goes to speak, but I hold up a hand to silence him. "Even when you were angry with me and hated me, I still wanted you." I'm looking him right in the eye, hoping he can see the truth in my eyes when I say, "You never did anything to me that I didn't want."

Pain and heartache are written across his face as he stares at me, and I think I might have gotten through to him, might have finally gotten him to stop with all the self-hatred. But then, after a moment, he breaks eye contact and shakes his head.

"Still, you're better off staying away from me."

"Jesus, Cam," I growl, my own anger getting the better of me as I storm across the small changing room so I don't reach out and strangle him for being a stubborn idiot.

"I came here to kill you," I blurt out, throwing my hands in the air, no longer giving a fuck. If he thinks he's so much worse than me, then I'll show him just how fucked up I am.

"You what?" He quirks an eyebrow, gazing at me in disbelief.

I guess I can't blame him for not believing me.

"After everything with Lawrence," I begin, watching him closely. "When I found out about you, I couldn't think straight. I just wanted to get back at him. I found out you were at Pac, and instead of running away as I'd planned, I decided to come here. I was in a dark place and assumed you'd be just like your father. However, as I got to know you, I realized you were nothing like him. I…" I trail off, licking my lips nervously.

"After we started talking, you told me about your childhood…" I shake my head. "I couldn't do it."

He gapes at me with wide eyes for several moments.

"If you were just here to kill me, why even bother enrolling? Why not just sneak onto the grounds and be done with it?"

"I didn't know anything else about Lawrence then. I didn't even know his name. All I knew about him was you. I guess it wasn't just about getting vengeance, but about trying to understand what happened to me. Why he chose me."

"Besides, it kind of worked out in your favor that I didn't just sneak onto campus." I give him a rueful smile.

"Right." He nods his head, even as I can see his thoughts running a mile a minute. "Because you were going to kill me."

I can tell he doesn't know what to believe as he drops down onto the bench, staring absently at the wall of lockers opposite him. I sit down on the far end of it, deliberately keeping my distance from him so I can give him time and space to process everything.

I'm not sure how long we sit there, but it's a good while. When he doesn't speak up, I slowly shift down the bench toward him.

"We all make bad decisions and do stupid things when we're angry or upset," I say softly. "I've spent a lot of time analyzing your father, but I knew by the end of our first class together that you were nothing like him. Your heart is good, Cam."

The way he looks at me, like he wants to believe what I'm saying, has me wanting to wrap my arms around him and hug him. Although I don't think he would be too accepting of that after everything I've just told him.

"So much has happened between us," I continue. "I don't know if we can ever go back to the way things were, but I'd like to be friends…if that's possible."

He's still looking at me, watching me closely, his thoughts all over the place.

"Friends?" he questions, his brows drawing together like he can't comprehend how that would ever work. It makes my stomach clench. I miss talking with him and hanging out with him. He was always such a bright light that I never knew I needed in my life.

"Yeah. We can just put all of this behind us, leave the past in the past, and start fresh."

Deciding to take the initiative when he just keeps sitting in silence, staring into space, I close the final bit of distance between us and hold out my hand for him to shake.

"What do you say? Friends?"

His eyes meet mine, and I smile. It's hesitant, but I let him see how much I want us to get past this.

"Yeah, okay," he responds, still appearing unsure. "I've never been friends with a girl before, but sure. Friends."

His palm presses against mine as he shakes my hand, and I ignore the searing heat radiating from his touch or the way my lower belly clenches, smiling brightly at him.

"Good, now finish getting dressed. I'm sure the guys want to celebrate your win with you."

∼

There's a fight night tonight. Despite the itch that's been clawing under my skin, screaming at me to beat the living shit out of someone, I've been avoiding them ever since I beat Hawk in the ring—not wanting to draw any more unwanted attention my way.

It's truly a testament to their power over the school that no one has ever breathed a word of that night. None of the guys in school have so much as given me a second glance after that fight. Honestly, it's a tad disappointing. Is it bad that I want them to be afraid of me, to whisper to one another about what a badass I am? Instead, they have all moved swiftly on as though it never happened.

Just because I can't participate, doesn't mean I can't watch. Beck confided in me that he sometimes sneaks out to watch the fights, so tonight I decided to join him. It's the closest I can get for now, and I'm hoping it will sate some of the bloodlust.

It's about half an hour before the fights begin, and I'm walking through the forest toward the clearing with my phone in my hand, the torch lighting my path when it vibrates, a message from Beck coming through.

> Beck: Leaving now, meet you in five.

Not bothering to respond, I keep walking through the forest. I'm not far from the clearing when I hear rustling behind me. Thinking it's Beck, I turn around, smiling as I shine the torch back in the direction I came from.

Before I can call out or say anything, a body crashes into me, sending my phone flying as I lose my balance.

"Ooof." The air is forced out of my lungs as I hit the ground, a firm body landing on top of me. *What the fuck?*

Someone begins pulling on my arms, yanking them behind my back. I start to buck furiously, fighting with everything I have. Arching my back, I throw my head back, colliding with something hard and causing stars to dance across my eyes as I scrunch my face up in pain.

"Fuck," the asshole snarls, yet the move is enough to distract him. Knocking him off balance the next time I buck, I dislodge him enough to wriggle out from beneath him.

Jumping to my feet, I raise my fists as I spin around, clocking him around the head before kicking out. My foot connects with his side and causes him to double over.

He's dressed all in black, and I don't need to see his face to know who sent him and why he's here. I just know I need to get rid of him before Beck or anyone else finds us.

The guy recovers quickly, lashing out with a jab that hits me right in the ribs, making me groan in pain as I struggle to breathe through it and land a punch of my own. Snarling in anger, I launch myself at him, grabbing a hold of his shoulder and swinging myself onto his back. I wrap my arm around him in a chokehold, squeezing him with everything I've got.

He stumbles backward, slamming me against a tree as his hands scrape at my arm. I can feel the rough bark tearing through the skin at the base of my back, yet still, I hold on while tightening my grip around his neck.

He keeps staggering backward through the forest, except I'm barely aware of any of it as I focus on maintaining my hold around his neck, feeling his Adam's apple bob against my arm as he struggles to breathe.

As he starts to run out of air, his movements grow frantic, smacking my arm and digging his fingers into the skin. When that doesn't work, he starts hitting me around the head, and I duck, burying my face in his neck as I hold onto him. *He must be about to pass out, just a few more seconds.*

He trips and falls, knocking the air out of me once again as I hit the ground beneath him, using the last of my energy to squeeze the fucking life out of this asshole.

"What the fuck?" I hear someone roar from somewhere nearby as the fucker gurgles his last breath, finally going slack in my grip.

My head falls back against the dirt, and I sag in relief.

"Hadley?" the voice yells again, just before someone pushes the dead guy off me.

"Hadley!" Beck's voice finally registers with me. "What the hell? Are you okay? What happened?"

He carefully pulls me up into a sitting position, his hands on either side of my face as he runs his worried gaze over me.

"I'm okay," I reassure him, wincing as I breathe a lungful of air. *Yup, fucker bruised some ribs.*

Beck slowly helps me to my feet, and I stretch my back out, aches and pains flaring as I move.

"What the hell happened? Who is that guy?"

I scowl down at the dead fucker, not recognizing him. "I don't know," I tell him. "He attacked me out of nowhere."

Beck crouches down beside him, getting a better look at him as he reaches out to press two fingers against the pulse point in his neck.

"He's dead," he states bluntly, looking up at me. "You killed him."

There's no judgement in his tone, he's only stating a fact.

"He was going to kill me."

He nods absently, getting to his feet and looking around.

I glance around us, realizing that at some point in the scuffle we stumbled into the clearing where the fights are held.

"We have to get him out of here," Beck rushes out, speaking my thoughts aloud. "People will be heading this way soon."

"I lost my phone when he crashed into me," I tell him, pointing in the direction we came from.

"Go get it. We can't leave anything behind. I'll stay with the body and work out what to do."

I dart into the trees, rushing back to where I was when the asshole attacked me. I can't fucking believe Lawrence would try that move again. Didn't he learn from the first time? I'm not that fucking easy to take out.

Despite how pissed-off I am, nerves spark to life within me. He's only going to keep trying, isn't he? The longer I stay here, the higher my chances of being caught. *I can't go back to him. I'll kill myself if that's what it takes to escape him.*

Spotting the glow from my phone light up ahead, I rush through the undergrowth, picking it up and blowing out a breath of relief when I find it isn't damaged, before heading back to the clearing. Beck is standing where I left him, glancing nervously around him.

"Got it," I whisper as I approach.

Before either of us can say anything else, a masculine voice rings out across the clearing, making both of us jump.

"What. The. Fuck?"

Baby

CHAPTER TWENTY-FOUR

"**W**hat. The. Fuck?" I bark.

Literally, what the actual fuck am I looking at right now? Is that guy dead?

Hadley and Beck's heads snap up, staring wide-eyed at us, both raising a hand to block the light as our flashlights run over them.

"What happened?" Mason demands, striding across the clearing, the rest of us hot on his heels.

When he reaches Hadley, he pulls her in against him, hugging her, as West kneels next to the dead guy on the ground.

Hawk's eyes run over Hadley, but he doesn't say anything.

She looks okay. Her cheeks are flushed, her hair is a mess, and there are scratches over her arms, but otherwise she seems okay. She doesn't even look all that freaked out.

"He's dead," Beck confirms.

"What happened?" Hawk demands when neither of them seems like they're about to answer.

"I was coming to watch the fights," Hadley begins. "And he attacked me. He came out of nowhere. I...I don't know what happened, but the next thing I knew, he was lying dead on top of me."

I don't understand how the fuck that happened, but I guess she's in shock.

West reaches out, tilting the dude's head to one side, his expression growing more severe at what he finds.

"Look," he says, pointing at the back of the guy's neck.

The rest of us huddle around him, and Hawk shines his torch at where West is pointing. There's a tattoo painted on the back of his neck, and as the light hits it, I gasp. It's a tattoo of an owl, with a knife driven down through its head. It's not just any tattoo though, it's the symbol of our parents' mercenaries.

"What's that?" Hadley asks, looking up at us, her brows furrowed in confusion.

"That's the symbol for a group of mercenaries," Hawk states bluntly, glancing away from the dead body to stare at her.

She focuses her attention on him. "How do you know that?" Her words come out sharp as her gaze narrows on him, suspicion brewing there.

Hawk looks around at each of us before focusing back on Hadley, resolve in his eyes. None of us say anything or try to stop him. It's time she knew. She's clearly in danger, and keeping this from her isn't going to do her any good.

"Because they work for our parents."

Silently, we all wait on tenterhooks for Hadley's response. She gapes at Hawk for several moments before turning to each of us, seeing the same truth on our faces.

"And you all knew this?"

Her eyes have a wild look, most likely from shock and everything she's already experienced tonight.

"We found out over the summer," West explains, his words causing Hadley to look at him as he gets to his feet. "Although our parents officially told us at Christmas."

Thoughts race through her mind for a moment before she turns on Beck. "You knew too," she says in a quiet voice.

Beck moves to stand in front of her, his hand cupping her face in an intimate gesture that makes me feel like I'm intruding, not that I bother to look away or give them any privacy. "We couldn't say anything to you, sweetheart. We were trying to protect you."

"Right." Her voice is blank, giving nothing away as she swallows and flits her gaze away from him. "Of course."

Looking at each of the guys, they're all wearing guilty expressions that probably match my own. She shouldn't have had to find out like this, but Beck is right. Not only were we sworn to secrecy—and West's life depends on that secrecy—but if our parents found out that she knew, it could put her in even more danger.

"So, Lawrence ordered one of his own men to come and get me," Hadley surmises, correctly connecting the dots as she looks down at the fucker.

"Yeah, looks that way," Beck agrees.

"We can discuss this all later," Hawk interjects, going into leader mode. "We need to get rid of him before anyone else shows up. Cam, text everyone and tell them tonight's fight is canceled," he orders, taking control of the situation.

Nodding, I lift out my phone and do just that.

He frowns at the dead body, before looking expectantly at each of us. "Anyone have any ideas what to do with him?"

I share a look with West, shrugging my shoulders. It's not like we've ever been in this situation before. How does one get rid of a dead body without getting caught?

Surprisingly, it's Hadley who speaks up.

"What about the lake?" she asks, glancing at each of us. "We could tie rocks to him, so he sinks."

Everyone shares another round of looks, nobody disputing the idea or coming up with anything better.

"Lake it is then," Hawk agrees with a nod. "Mason, take his feet. I'll get his head."

The two of them easily lift the guy off the ground, carrying him between them as we move through the forest. No one says anything as we walk, not wanting to alert anyone who might happen to be in the woods. It's slow going, but we finally make it out of the trees by the lake, walking over to the boathouse and dropping the dead sack of shit on the ground.

"We need rocks and rope," Hawk barks, each of us quickly jumping into action.

I head to collect a bunch of rocks from the beach while the others spread out around me as they do the same. Once my arms are full, I head back to the dead body, dropping the rocks beside him. Hawk has found an extended length of rope, and the two of us begin tying the rocks to him.

A few minutes later, Hadley comes over, closely followed by Mason. As she steps into the beam of our torch, I notice her movements are stiff as she bends awkwardly, biting her bottom lip as she drops the rocks beside me.

"What's wrong?" I demand, noticing how sweat is beading on her forehead.

"Nothing," she pants, pain lacing her voice. "The asshole got me in the side, but it's fine."

Mason is beside her in a second, dropping his pile of rocks and pulling up her top so he can inspect her. Grabbing the torch, I shine it in her direction as Hawk and I move to examine the damage.

"It's nothing," she grunts, swatting us away. There is a large purple bruise over her ribs, though, and she winces, pulling away when Mason touches it.

Growling, he drops her top, moving over to the dead guy and slamming his foot into his stomach. Mason kicks him over and over again, swearing at him.

"Dude." I clap a hand on his shoulders. "He's dead. You're only exhausting yourself."

"He fucking hurt her," he snarls.

I nod. "I know." But Hadley is tough as nails. Evident by the fact that she's already bent over the dead guy, stuffing rocks down his pants.

"Just go sit over there and let us sort this out," I demand, gently pushing her aside and taking the rock from her hand. "We've got this. Just…go and relax."

She grumbles something under her breath but shuffles away, sitting to one side as West and Beck saunter back, and Hawk and I resume tying rocks to every part of him we can.

Once we're done, Mason and Hawk dump his sorry ass in a rowing boat. Mason climbs in, the boat creaking dangerously. Before Hawk can climb in and overload the rickety thing, I step forward.

"I'll go," I tell him. "You stay here with Hadley."

He purses his lips but nods as I get into the boat, grabbing an oar, and we head out onto the lake.

It's a gloomy night, the clouds blocking any light from the moon, casting everything in shadows as we row into the middle of the lake.

"This should do," Mason says eventually. The boathouse is nothing more than a faint black outline in the distance, and there's no noise except the rustling of the wind as I pull the oars out of the water.

Between us, we manage to lift the guy up. With all the rocks, he weighs a fucking ton, and as strong as I may be, I don't have the same strength as Mason or Hawk.

Sweat is trickling down my forehead by the time he rolls over the edge of the boat, splashing as he hits the water. He only bobs for a second before the weight pulls him under, and he quickly disappears.

"So long, fucker," I murmur as the murky depths swallow him up.

As we are rowing back toward the boathouse, I ask the question that's been rattling around in my head for the last hour.

"How the fuck did she manage to kill him? When we had to go up against those guys, we lost badly, even though we outnumbered them."

"I dunno." Mason shrugs. "The guy looked younger than the ones we fought. Maybe he's not as well trained."

Maybe. Still, it's impressive shit.

"What are we supposed to do now? Hadley's not safe here if my dad is sending fucking mercenaries after her."

Hatred wars within me as I grit my teeth and squeeze the oar tighter. How can my father be such a piece of shit? To send mercenaries after a teenage girl? That's fucking sick. It was bad enough that he turned up here, demanding time alone with her and scaring her. I can't even think about what would have happened if Hawk hadn't gotten there in time.

Now he's trying to kidnap her in the middle of the fucking night? Not fucking happening. I don't know how we are going to manage it yet, but I won't let my father torment Hadley any longer. There's got to be a way to keep her safe until we can get rid of him for good.

"I think we're going to have to convince Hadley to go along with West's idea of telling her parents." Mason sighs. "I wasn't sure about it at first—it's not like we can trust them either—but it might offer her some protection while we work shit out."

"Man, none of our parents can be trusted," I argue. "They're all threatening to kill West if we step out of line."

He nods his head in agreement. "I know, but Hawk's parents have always been the nicest. You and I both know our parents never gave a fuck about us, but Hawk's seems to care about him to some extent. Surely, they will feel the same way about Hadley?"

There's a hopefulness in his tone, and I can tell he wants to believe they'll give a shit about her, protect her even, once they know about her existence. I'm not sure I share that same faith in any case. "We don't even know what happened there. What if they gave her up? I doubt they would be too pleased to see us return her if they got rid of her."

Mason shrugs his shoulders, not having any answers to my questions. "It might be a risk we have to take."

∽

ALL SIX OF us traipse back to our dorm once Mason and I get back to shore.

"I need a shower," Hadley grumbles as we enter the dorm.

"Let me get you some clothes," Mason insists, pressing his hand against her lower back and steering her toward the bedrooms. The guy has turned into a fucking sap over her. He's usually so cold and detached, so to see him jumping to Hadley's every whim is weird as fuck.

"I need to change my clothes," Hawk grumbles, taking off as well, which leaves West, Beck, and I alone in the living room. Talk about awkwardness. I don't fully understand West's problem with Beck, but he needs to get over it. They're both dating the same girl, for shit's sake.

"Beer, anyone?" I offer in an over-the-top cheery voice. Anything to break the awkward tension.

"Sure," Beck agrees. Opening the fridge, I lift out a six-pack, offering Beck a bottle before carrying the rest over to the coffee table and setting them down. I imagine the other guys will need a drink after tonight too.

Beck follows behind me, sitting down on one end of the unoccupied sofa. At the same time, West is watching him closely. Hesitantly, he snatches up a beer and sits as far from Beck as physically possible.

"What's the deal with you two?" I ask, looking between them.

"Keep your nose out of it, Cam," West snaps, and I roll my eyes.

"Dude, you're going to have to sort your shit out. You're both with Hadley, unless one of you plans on giving her up at some point?"

"No," they both respond at the same time.

Well, that answers that question.

Studying Beck, I ask him, "Did you do something to piss him off?"

"You mean other than existing?" he quips back.

West snorts, shaking his head. "Is that not reason enough?"

"Dude," I interject, before the two of them start an argument. "You can't be angry at him just because he was born."

"Well, what about for being the older, better son? For barging into *my* life and essentially making me redundant? For not having to grow up in this life but being handed all the benefits of it anyway—the fancy job, the money, the connections?"

Oh, wow. I opened the floodgates, and now West is off on a verbal rampage.

"I didn't ask for any of this," Beck argues back.

"You didn't say no either," West retorts.

"Neither would you if you had nothing," Beck barks, his anger flaring as his hand clenches around his beer bottle and he glares at West. "And for the record, I only accepted when I was told about you. I only agreed to come here so I could meet *you*."

"Right." West snorts. "The money and being entitled to your half of the inheritance means nothing."

"I couldn't give two shits about the money." Beck jumps to his feet, furious now. "Do you think I wanted to be caught up in this shit? Getting involved in fucking mercenary companies and having to keep secrets because if I tell anyone, you'll die? I've seen and had to do a lot of fucked up shit in my life, but I can guarantee you, this tops any of it."

"What's going on here?" Hawk yells, entering the room, his gaze bouncing between West and Beck.

"Nothing," West grumbles as Beck sits back down, still looking livid.

"It better be fucking nothing," Hawk states. "We have enough shit going on, and Hadley needs us all to get along if we're going to keep her safe."

I don't know what the fuck happened the other day between the two of them, but it's like he's finally come to accept he gives a shit about her. It's good to see. It's been obvious to the rest of us for weeks that he was warming up to her, but he was still in denial. So, whatever happened the other day, I'm glad.

Mason enters the room with a satisfied smirk on his face and his dark hair still damp from his shower with Hadley. *Lucky bastard.* Not that I'm jealous. Nope. Hadley and I agreed to be friends, and that's what we are—even if my dick does jerk awake when she's nearby, and jealousy raises its ugly head when one of them touches her.

Grabbing a beer, he sits on the other end of the sofa West is occupying, twisting off the lid and bringing the bottle to his lips.

Hawk claims the seat beside Beck as Hadley walks in wearing an oversized white shirt she's tied at the waist and gray joggers rolled up so they don't drag along the floor.

How does she look even hotter, just out of the shower, with her wet hair thrown up in a messy bun, wearing another guy's sweats?

Glancing around, she strides over to West and Mason, sliding between them and smiling softly at Beck before focusing her gaze on Hawk, her features hardening. Not in the same way they used to, though. None of the anger or dislike is there. It's more like she knows she's not going to like whatever Hawk is going to say, and she's preparing herself for it.

Before Hawk can start on her, she holds up her hands, searing him with a grave look.

"I already know what you're going to say, and before you do, I have some questions."

She waits for Hawk to nod his head in agreement, giving her the floor. Once he does, she looks at each of us before focusing back on Hawk.

"Are all of your parents involved?"

"Yes." Hawk's response is instant.

"What do they all do? Do you know?"

West answers this one. "They haven't told us much yet, but from what we can gather, your parents are responsible for the security and marketing aspect. My dad is involved with the clients, meeting with them and securing deals. Cam's dad runs the day-to-day stuff, and Mason's is in charge of the financial aspect and recruitment."

Hadley nods, chewing on her bottom lip as she takes it all in. All of that is a bit of a guess on our part, based on the paper trails we have been able to find and what little we know about our parents' schedules, but we're pretty sure it's accurate.

"And you've all known about this since the summer."

"I only found out at Christmas," Beck says, at the same time, Hawk says, "Yes."

Hadley's eyes are on Beck when she asks, "What happened at Christmas?"

West answers her, his voice coming out strained.

"Our parents didn't know we already knew," he begins. "Before this year, we thought they ran a legal, legitimate enterprise." He shakes his head like he can't believe they fooled him all this time. He's not the only one. How the fuck none of us realized before now, but then, why would we? They never gave anything away. They clearly went to great lengths to ensure we never suspected anything.

"They..." He trails off, lifting his glasses and rubbing at his eyes as he sighs heavily.

Hadley's eyes bounce all over his face, worry crossing her delicate features.

No one takes over for him. West started the explanation, so it must be vital for him to tell her.

"They bought our silence by threatening to...kill me, and then the rest of us if any of us told anyone."

"What?" Hadley exclaims, looking at us for confirmation.

Looking around the room, we all are wearing similar expressions of fury.

"They can't do that."

"They can." I sigh. "Supposedly, they have the means, and, as they've pointed out to us, Beck can take over as an heir if anything were to happen to West."

"But..." She looks at Beck with wide eyes, her words trailing off.

Beck grits his teeth, looking absolutely furious. I actually feel kinda bad for the guy, especially if he only came here because he wanted to get to know West. Not only has West made that impossible for him, but he's now been forced into protecting a brother who wants nothing to do with him. And buying our silence is only the beginning. None of us would jeopardize West's life, and our parents know that. They could ask literally anything of us. That's what is so concerning."

Her eyes harden, and she glares at Hawk. I can practically see the steam coming out of her ears.

"And you want me to tell these people who I am?" she seethes. "Are you serious?"

"It would protect you from Lawrence," Hawk argues, not the slightest bit bothered by the death glare she's giving him.

"You don't know that," she retorts. "I'd only be one more thing for them to hold over your heads."

I shift in my chair as Hawk grinds his teeth. Based on the tight expressions on the other's faces, none of us like the sound of that.

"It's a risk I'm willing to take," Hawk growls, looking at each of us.

We all murmur agreements, gaining our own glares from Hadley.

"Well, I'm not," she snaps, crossing her arms over her chest. "I'm not about to be a pawn on a chessboard that can be pushed about to make you guys do whatever they want."

"It won't be like that," Mason says softly from beside her. "Your parents have never been as cold as the others. I'm sure they will just be glad to have their daughter back."

"You don't know that."

Sighing, Hawk leans forward on his elbows. "Regardless of what might happen, I don't see how we have any other choice. Lawrence has tried to get to you twice now." A look passes between them that I don't understand. "Tonight just proves how far he's willing to go to get you back."

"We can't be sure that me telling everyone who I am will make him back off," Hadley continues to argue, but her voice is softer than it was before, losing some of its defiance.

"No, but it will buy us more time to figure out what to do."

She purses her lips, peering at the rest of us before her gaze lands on Beck.

"What do you think?" she asks him.

His features are tight as he looks at her, before getting up and moving to crouch where she's sitting.

He tucks a damp strand of hair behind her ear.

"I'll do whatever you want, but I can't find you the way I did tonight. I thought..." His voice cracks, and he coughs to clear his throat. "For a second, I thought you were dead. I can't go through that again. I don't care what it takes, I'll do anything to keep you safe."

The two of them share an intense look, a private conversation happening between them. After what feels like a lifetime, Hadley releases a long, defeated sigh. "Okay," she agrees hesitantly, tearing her gaze away from Beck to look at each of us. "I'll tell them."

Hadley

CHAPTER TWENTY-FIVE

How the fuck did the guys talk me into this? It's been nearly a week since the mercenary and my talk with the guys. I've put off going to meet my parents for as long as I can, but Hawk finally snapped yesterday and put his foot down, telling me we were going today, even if he had to drag me there kicking and screaming—infuriating bastard!

I still can't get over the fact the guys all knew about the whole mercenary shit and kept it a secret. I completely understand why they did. I wanted to kill every one of those fucking shitheads for threatening West's life, and I know none of the guys would jeopardize his life for anything.

As much as I appreciate them opening up and telling me the truth—not that I left them with much choice after what they found out in the woods—it only makes me feel more guilty for the secrets I'm still hiding.

Of course, they asked how I managed to kill a trained mercenary, and I fobbed it off as an accident; pure fucking luck, but that's far from the truth. I didn't tell them about the last mercenary I took care of. Killing one by accident might be luck but killing two of them would definitely have them asking questions I'm not ready to answer. They all seemed shaken enough when they discussed finding out what their parents were up to and the expectations for them to take over in due time. How the hell would they handle knowing it's even worse than they think? That I'm more involved in it than they could ever know?

I've been staring into my wardrobe for who knows how long, trying to figure out what one wears when they go to meet their parents for the first time, when suddenly there's a knock on my door.

Abandoning choosing an outfit, I go to answer it.

"Hey," I greet, smiling at West. "What are you doing here?"

"Thought you might like some company." He shrugs, his thoughtfulness making my smile broaden.

"Sure." Opening the door wider, he steps into my room.

"I was just trying to decide what to wear," I explain to him as I walk back toward the wardrobe. "I don't exactly have a 'long lost daughter' outfit, and the last time I met my mother, I was wearing a fancy gown and heels, and she still looked right through me."

He comes over to stand behind me, his arms wrapping around my waist as he draws me in against him, his eyes scanning over my closet.

"So just be yourself this time. Trust me, if you turn up in your usual get-up, you'll have your mom's attention."

"That doesn't sound like a good thing." I chuckle.

He shrugs. "I know you want them to like you, but just be yourself. You're pretty amazing, and if they can't see that, it's their loss."

Feeling stupidly happy at that statement, I give him a kiss on the cheek.

"So, jeans and combat boots?" I laugh.

"Your mom might have a heart attack if you wear those ugly boots into her house. What about those ballet flats, instead?" he suggests, pointing out a pair of flats belonging to Emilia that I borrowed once. The damn things kept slipping off my feet, but I guess it's a compromise. At least I'm not wearing heels, right?

Lifting a few items out of the closet, I strip down as West makes himself comfortable on my bed.

"How are you feeling about tonight?" he asks.

"Nervous. What if they don't like me? Or I don't like them?" I look up at him as butterflies take flight in my stomach for the gazillionth time today. "I know you all say they're nice enough, but we don't really know anything about them. What if they were involved in what happened to me?"

"Hawk will keep you safe tonight," he promises, trying to reassure me.

I don't need Hawk to take care of me, though. I can do that all on my own. I just want answers—which is the main reason I agreed to this in the first place. Yes, getting Lawrence to back off for a while will be great, assuming he does, in fact, do that. But mostly, I want to know how I ended up so far removed from the life I should have had. How did I end up in a life where I was beaten regularly, and forced to witness and do things no child should ever have to experience? I thought I could live without knowing those answers, but it's been nagging at me ever since I set eyes on my parents at Hawk's party.

I was initially reluctant to agree to this plan—I still am, if I'm being honest—but I can deal with everyone knowing my last name if it gets me the answers I've always wanted.

I can look after myself if they try anything, but what worries me is how this could impact the guys. I am not okay with being another tool their families can hold over their heads to keep them in line. We've all agreed to act like we barely know one another when we are around the parents. We don't want them to know how close we have all gotten or have them think we mean something to each other. If their parents believe they don't care much about me, then I'm less likely to be used as a bargaining chip. Even so, we are still taking a considerable risk, and I don't know how I feel about that.

"Has Hawk told them anything?" I ask, pulling on my jeans.

"Just that he needed to speak to them tonight."

"How are we even going to explain all of this to them?"

"Hawk says he's got it all figured out," West replies confidently, not even questioning Hawk's ability to take care of it.

I wish I had the same faith.

"Come here." Likely picking up on my frazzled state, West waves me over to where he's lounging on my bed. Climbing up beside him, he wraps his arms around me, the two of us falling back against the duvet as he pulls my body against him. I rest my head on his chest, the steady thumping of his heart soothing me. I don't know what it is about him, but I feel so much more at ease when he's near me or holding me like this. The stress that has been gnawing away at me all day dissipates, and I feel like I can finally think straight.

"We will take it one step at a time, okay?" he says softly against the top of my head, running his hand over my arm as it rests on his chest.

I nod, not saying anything, just enjoying this quiet moment of peacefulness with him. I've no idea what's going to happen next. I just want to enjoy this moment.

∽

SEVERAL HOURS LATER, West and I are still wrapped up in our cocoon when Hawk knocks on the door.

Sighing heavily, I remove myself from my comfortable position of being curled up beside him to answer the door.

"You ready?" Hawk asks, looking me over.

He's wearing a dark red shirt with dark blue jeans and brown loafers, looking smart yet casual, whereas I just look casual. He doesn't pull his usual face at my poor dress code, only nodding his head before glancing over my shoulder at West. A look passes between the two of them.

"Yeah," I answer, grabbing my keys as we step into the hall and I lock the door.

West pulls me into him for a final hug. "Everything's going to be fine," he promises in a whisper against my ear.

I wish I could believe him. Regardless, I wrap my arms around him, squeezing him tight as I breathe him in a final time before we part. He presses his lips to mine in a quick kiss that I wish I could get lost in, but the grumpy asshole behind me coughs obnoxiously and I scowl at him as the three of us move down the hall.

Once we're outside, West, with a final goodbye, heads off toward the boys' dorms while Hawk and I walk toward the car park.

"Have you told them anything about me?" I ask, twisting my hands nervously as we walk.

"No, I figured it would be better to do it in person."

I nod. *Makes sense, I guess.*

"How do you think...What do you think..."

Ugh, my thoughts are too scattered, my heart beating an unnatural rhythm as it threatens to crash right out of my chest.

"I don't know," Hawk answers, somehow knowing what I was going to say. "I've gone over the conversation in my head, and I've no idea how they'll react or what to expect. Either way, their reaction should give us an idea of whether or not they were involved in whatever happened to you."

That's true.

"Do you think they were?"

He sighs, running a hand through his perfectly styled hair.

"I hope not," he responds tersely. "The thought of them giving you up, or getting rid of you, or being involved in whatever the fuck happened, makes me feel sick."

His honesty surprises me. We have been getting on a lot better since that day he found me in the headmaster's office with Lawrence—don't get me wrong, he's still an asshole, but he's been almost nice at times. It's weird, and certainly will take some getting used to.

"Our parents were always nice to me growing up," he continues. "Mason's dad…" He trails off, shaking his head. I remember the scars I saw along Mason's back, not needing Hawk to tell me what sort of a childhood Mason had to endure. "Mason had it the worst, and West's dad wasn't much better. Cam's dad was never here. In comparison, my parents seemed like good parents. They always took more of an interest in what I was doing than the guys' parents did.

"Now though, with all this shit coming to light and the lengths they are willing to go to to get us to cooperate, it has me second-guessing everything I thought I knew about them."

"I'm sorry," I murmur, linking my arm with his. I have no idea how to comfort him, and based on how he tenses up, he wasn't expecting me to offer any sort of solace. Except, he was there for me the other day, so I can at least try to be here for him now.

After a moment, he relaxes, and we walk arm-in-arm in silence the rest of the way to the car.

Climbing in, we take off out of the school gates and along the coastal road. The closer we get, the more anxious I feel, wiping my sweaty hands down my jeans. Hawk must get annoyed with my fidgeting as he sighs, reaching out to turn on the radio and cranking the music.

We drive in silence, and I swear, by the time we pull up at the gate to their private residence, I'm on the verge of barfing all over Hawk's expensive leather seat.

Pulling into the driveway, he stops the car, turning off the engine before looking at me.

"You don't need to say anything," he reassures me. "Leave it to me. I'll explain it all to them."

I'm pretty sure I'm going to be sick so I just nod my head, more than happy for him to take the lead and do all the talking tonight.

He looks me over for another moment, probably seeing just how much I'm panicking.

"Hadley." His sharp tone pulls me out of my freak out, as I finally tear my gaze away from the huge white house in front of us to look at him. "Just breathe," he encourages. "I'll be with you the whole time."

Doing as he says, I suck in a deep breath, holding it for three counts, before exhaling. I repeat the motion until I feel calmer. When I'm ready, I nod, and Hawk climbs out of the car.

Tossing up a wish to whatever god exists that this isn't a complete shit show of an evening, I open my door and get out of the car to meet Hawk at the hood before we walk up the steps to the front door.

With a final glance over his shoulder, silently asking if I'm ready, I jerk my head not feeling the slightest bit ready for this.

Nodding, he turns back to face the house, pushing down the handle. The door swings open, officially starting the evening on the night that will change everything.

Sweetheart

EPILOGUE

Getting into my heap of junk car, I leave the campus behind, driving down the coast until I reach a small parking lot for the beach. During the day, the lot is packed with people coming to walk along the beach or go surfing, but it's the middle of the night and there isn't another person in sight.

Getting out, I lean against the hood as I look out toward the ocean. The moonlight reflects off the water, the sound of the waves crashing against the shore, the only noise as I breathe in the sea-salt air.

My thoughts drift to Hadley, as they often do when I'm alone. I'm riddled with guilt at hiding all this shit from her, but it's for her own safety. Not even the guys know about this aspect of their parents' business—and I want to keep it that way. No one should get caught up in this shit, least of all a bunch of high school kids. They should be free to just be kids while they still can. I was forced to grow up way too fucking fast, and so was Hadley. I want her to have some time to be a teenager for once.

A black Rolls Royce pulls into the lot, and a driver gets out, opening the back passenger door. I restrain my eye roll at the pretentiousness of it all as my father steps out of the back of the car.

"I don't understand why you don't use some of the money I give you to buy yourself a decent car," he grumbles, sneering at the rusted piece of junk. I'd love a new car, but I'm not about to use his dirty money to buy it. Instead, every blood-soaked penny is sitting in a bank account, and I've no idea what to do with any of it.

When I don't answer him, he sighs and hands me the folder, getting down to business. Begrudgingly, I take it from his outstretched hand, feeling dirty just holding it.

"Same as last time," he states bluntly. "I'll get a list of names from you next week."

I give a sharp nod of my head. It's the same every time; I know the deal by now.

"Remember, West's life is on the line if you don't deliver."

I grit my teeth, not needing to be fucking reminded of that.

"I'll get it done," I grind out.

Nodding his head, he gets back in his car and drives off, leaving me alone once again, except the sound of the ocean isn't as calming as it was before.

Staring out at it, for a single moment, I seriously consider walking out into the water until the current carries me out to sea. Only then does Hadley's soft smile and flyaway hair flash across my mind, and I know I couldn't do that to her. This is the unwitting price I agreed to pay when I decided to come to Pac and get to know West. Hadley has been an unexpected plot twist, but she's been the light in this whole dark tunnel.

With a heavy sigh and one final glance out over the crashing waves, I get in my car and drive back to campus, shoving the folder in a drawer. I know I'll have to go through it, but not tonight. Tonight, I pour myself a glass of cheap whiskey and pretend this isn't my fucked-up life.

~

"Have you gone through the folder?" my father asks a week later.

Of course I've gone through it, and he damn well knows it. He's made it perfectly clear what will happen if I don't.

"I have."

"And?" he snaps impatiently.

Closing my eyes, not knowing for sure but having a fair idea of the impact of my next words, I sigh. "The seven-year-old girl and five-year-old boy," I tell him, swallowing down the bile.

"Good, good," he responds absently, probably taking note of the two profiles I picked. "From now on, we'll need you to do a face-to-face evaluation. None of this on paper nonsense. You'll get a better idea of these kids and their capabilities if you meet them in person."

"What?" I exclaim, horrified by his suggestion. It's one thing to look at pages in a file and make a decision. At least that way I can fool myself into pretending I'm not destroying children's lives, but if I have to see them, look them in the face, and make a decision…There's no way I could do that. "No." I bite the word out with force, my teeth clenched in fury at what he's asking from me.

He laughs, and it's a cold, depraved sound that washes over me like ice. "Boy, this isn't up for discussion. A car will pick you up next time and take you to the compound. You can meet the new initiates and do a full assessment, decide who could cut it and who can't."

Swallowing around the lump in my throat, I force back the bile and ask a question to which I'm pretty sure I don't want to hear the answer. "What happens to those that can't?"

He snorts, acting like we aren't discussing the lives of young children. "We have no need for them."

Baby Davenport

THE BATHROOM SCENE

I storm down the hallway toward the headmaster's office, my fists clenched. A secretary steps out from a room in front of me, and the second she sees me, her eyes widen and her jaw drops on a gasp before she scurries back inside, slamming the door shut behind her. Yeah, I bet the look on my face is fucking murderous.

I'm so pissed right now, beyond fucking pissed. I'm furious at Lawrence for thinking he can just come in here and do whatever the fuck he pleases. This is *our* territory. *Our* kingdom. I'm angry at the guys for pushing me to eat lunch with Hadley and get to know her. They made me fucking care about her. I'm even fucking annoyed with Hadley. *She* made me care about her.

All those stupid lunches where she wolfed down platefuls of food, not giving a fuck about carbs or being thin or whatever other bullshit nonsense the girls here harp on about, and scowling at every student who dared look in her direction, all while watching and assessing me closely.

This sister I never wanted has fucking wormed her way under my skin with her tough-as-nails attitude and inherent stubbornness. Her ability to fight and stand up for herself is beyond impressive. And, *Jesus, fuck, I can't believe I'm saying it.* But the way she's always stood up to me, never once cowered to my hatred or my status within these walls, has fucking earned her my respect—my *reluctant* respect.

I don't know what shit she's been through in her past, but I'm guessing she's had to deal with more than just Lawrence. Cam and Mason both said she told them the scars didn't come from him, which means not only has she spent her life being groomed by a sexual predator, but she's also had to endure physical pain as well. There are plenty of people who wouldn't have survived an upbringing like that. Most would have crumbled, given up and closed in on themselves, said 'fuck it' and shot their brains out. But not Hadley. She fucking fought. And endured. She fucking escaped. And now he wants to come after her, *again,* on *my* turf? Not fucking happening.

I pause outside the headmaster's door, taking a deep breath and trying to calm myself the fuck down. It won't do any of us any good if I go storming in there with all my fucking emotions on display.

Closing my eyes, I inhale deeply, feeling my heart rate settle and the cold facade ripple over my skin as my mask attaches itself to my face. When I'm certain it's well and truly glued to my exterior, my barriers impenetrable as always, I push open the door.

The sound of heavy panting and grunts has the hairs standing up along the back of my neck, and for the first time ever, I feel that impenetrable mask threatening to slip. The door opens wider, and there isn't enough bleach in the world to remove the sight I'm greeted with.

My facade drops. Unadulterated anger courses through me so intensely that it's all I can think about. For a second, it consumes me. It burns its way through my veins, sinking its venomous teeth into my cold, dead heart, making it jolt to life with a cry of vengeance. *Hurt. Kill. Destroy.* These three words play on repeat in my head as the door handle slides out of my grip, the metal knob crashing against the wall.

Hadley's eyes flash to mine, and the look in them fucking floors me. The shame and embarrassment is hard to take in, but it's the fear that gets to me the most. It's not fear of Lawrence, although I'm sure she feels a healthy dose of that too. No, it's fear of what I'll think of her. Fear of what I'll do to her. That fucking look will stay with me for the rest of my days. I've never felt guilty before. Never felt bad for the way I've treated some of the kids here—it's just the way things had to be. I always did what was necessary. But right now, guilt over the way I've treated Hadley makes me fucking nauseous.

Lawrence, the colossal shithead that he is, takes his sweet fucking time removing his dick from my fucking sister's mouth, and I'm careful to ensure I've corrected my mask before he turns to look at me.

"Hawk, boy, haven't you ever heard of knocking," he admonishes, tucking himself away. His movements are unhurried and sure, like me catching him getting a blow job —a nonconsensual blow job—from a student is no big fucking deal.

Even though I know my guise is firmly in place, giving nothing away, I'm relieved when my voice comes out impassive. "I did. You mustn't have heard me."

He smirks, effectively dismissing Hadley as he turns toward me. "I was a little preoccupied," he jokes. "What are you doing here, son?"

"I heard you were here; I was hoping we could talk."

He moves to sit in the headmaster's chair—of course the arrogant fuck has to claim the most influential seat in the room.

"Sure, sure." He waves for me to get on with it, but honestly, I have no idea what the fuck to talk to him about. I don't want to talk to him at all. I just want to get Hadley out of here.

I glance her way, without really seeing her. If I take in the dejected slump of her shoulders, or the way her hands are trembling, I'll never fucking get through this without Lawrence realizing how much we know—how much *I* care.

"We probably shouldn't discuss this in front of *her*." I force my lip into a sneer.

Lawrence glances her way before reluctantly agreeing. "Fine." Pinning his gaze on Hadley in such a way that I want to rip out his fucking eyeballs, he barks out, "Go. We can finish this next time."

Hadley stumbles to her feet and scurries from the room. I don't once look at her, only watching her from the corner of my eye and sighing internally when I hear her heavy boots smacking against the tiles in the hall as she runs as fast as her legs will carry her.

"What is it you want to discuss?" he asks impatiently, his intense gaze focused on me. Now that we're alone, his tone is sharper than it was before, giving away how angry he is with me for interrupting him.

I spout out the first thing that comes to mind. "Cam has the state championship race next week."

Lawrence lifts an eyebrow, silently telling me to get to the point.

"He's done amazingly this year. He should have the chance to pursue swimming competitively before he starts working for the company."

"Is that so?" His deadpan expression lets me know how futile this conversation is. I hadn't planned to bring up Cam's dream. Any previous conversations we've had with our parents, about giving us a few years to pursue whatever the fuck we wanted before coming to work for the company, have all been quickly shut down with the excuse of familial responsibilities—like our parents know anything about being a family. "So you want him to go to college for four years, then you'll probably want him to try out for the Olympics, and what? When he's got a high-flying swimming career, he's going to just give it all up? I don't think so." The glee in his voice at knowing he's squashing his son's dreams is sickening, and I have to work not to let any of my anger show.

"It would only be for a few years," I argue weakly, knowing there's no point in pushing harder.

He pushes to his feet and steps out from behind the desk, standing opposite me. "Freedom is a fickle thing," he says, making my eyebrows pull together. "Give someone the slightest bit of it, and they'll keep wanting more." I get the impression he's talking about more than just Cam, but before I can mull over his words any further, he pierces me with a stern look. "Trust me, son, we're doing you boys a favor." Straightening his suit jacket, he casts a glance around the room. "I'd better be going." His lips thin, before he tacks on, "Since I won't be getting what I came here for."

My thoughts white out, and it's a fucking miracle that I don't lash out here and now and kill the sick fuck. Instead, I nod curtly and watch as he makes his way down the hallway and out the door. I wait another moment before I go in search of Hadley. She won't have gone far. I know she won't want anyone on campus to see her looking so weak and fragile—not that she looked like either of those things, but I'm guessing that's how she views herself right now.

When I reach the first bathroom in the hall—a men's bathroom—I push open the door, peeking my head in to check if she's there. One of the stalls is closed, and I can see Hadley's bag dropped on the floor just inside.

Walking over, I pause outside the door with my hand raised, unsure of my next move. I don't know how to react around her. I can tell she's wary of me—and I can't blame her—and right now, all of her damage is going to be on display. She probably doesn't want me to see any of it. Maybe I should get one of the guys? Beck's just down the hall. I could go and grab him. Yet my feet don't move. And, after a moment, I say, "It's only me. Lawrence is gone. You can come out."

I don't get a response, and she doesn't move, but that's okay. It's not like I'm going back to class, and even though I can feel my phone buzzing incessantly in my pocket, the guys can all fucking wait. I can feel the importance of this moment for Hadley and I. The way I react to today will either make or break us, and God fucking help me, I don't want to break us. Despite my insistence all year that the guys keep their distance

THE BATHROOM SCENE

and don't fucking fall for her, that's exactly what they're doing. More so, I can see the positive impact she is having on them. Mason has dropped his guard and opened up. Even around us, he's laid-back and chattier than he's ever been before. West is slowly getting over his insecurities and the rumors from first year, and Cam... well, Cam's a fucking mess, but that's not Hadley's fault. The idiot needs to pull his head out of his ass and face his problems, instead of running from them, but again, that's all on him. Regardless of how fucked up in the head he is at the moment, all three of them are fucking obsessed with her, and I don't want to be left on the outside, having burned all my bridges, if whatever the fuck is going on between them turns out to be the real deal.

It's more than that though. It's not just about being left out. I want my own relationship with Hadley. She's earned my begrudging respect, and fuck, I've even had to force back a smile or two at her snarky behavior. She always comes across as being so strong, completely unbreakable. But, *fuck*, seeing her on her knees in that office, with that shitstain's dick in her mouth, the hopeless acceptance and vulnerability in her eyes, it fucking broke something in me. She might be fierce and headstrong, but she's also fucking human. She bows and bends just like the rest of us, and it's about fucking time she had someone in her corner helping her stand tall and fight her demons. She's my family—words I've been saying on repeat all semester but am only now fully comprehending. She's my fucking sister. My twin.

I lean against the sink counter, patiently waiting her out, until she finally flicks the lock. I have to say I'm fucking nervous when she first steps out, especially when she doesn't look at me.

My tongue flicks forward to lick my dry lips and, not knowing what else to do or say, I reach into my blazer pocket and withdraw a pack of mints. "Here," I offer, presenting it for her to take.

She hesitates before accepting it from my outstretched hand, popping one into her mouth and turning to lean against the counter beside me. Her gaze stays fixed to the floor, and I can practically hear her thoughts racing a mile a minute. Eventually, she speaks up, her voice sounding quiet and drained, and nothing like her usual self. "Did you, uh, know I was in there?"

"I thought you might be. Beck saw Lawrence going into the headmaster's office earlier and messaged us to give us a heads up that he was on campus. When you didn't turn up at lunch, I, uh, got worried." Fuck, I'm no good at talking about fucking feelings, and I can tell she doesn't believe that I was worried about her. But that's exactly what I was—worried. "What he..." I trail off, gritting my teeth as I push from the counter and storm across the small space toward the stalls.

Fuck. FUCK. I've been keeping a tight rein on my emotions, but seeing her looking so small and unsure of herself is undoing that leash, and the burning anger I felt before once again makes itself known. Red mist coats my vision and I lose all control, barely registering the pain in my hand as I punch the tile wall. I want to do so much more than punch a goddamn wall. I want to tear the whole fucking bathroom apart, the entire school. The roaring fire of my anger is so vast it would take a tsunami to put it out.

Somehow—don't ask me how because I have no fucking clue—I manage to cage it, turning the fire down to a low simmer. It takes all of my self-control. One slow, deep breath at a time. But eventually I manage it. Only then do I turn back around, storming toward her, knowing if I don't hug her right now, I'm going to lose any semblance of control I have left.

Reaching her, I wrap my arms around her shoulders, pulling her into my embrace. I feel Hadley stiffen, but I ignore it, resting my chin on her head and closing my eyes. "I'm so sorry," I murmur, the crashing waves of my emotions threatening to pull me under. "I'm so fucking sorry."

I feel her relax into my embrace, her small hands coming to fist the back of my blazer as she buries her head in my chest. I just hold her as she falls apart in my arms, her tears soaking my shirt. I don't know how long we stand there, me whispering apologies in her ear as she sobs into my chest, but eventually she quietens, and I pull back, looking down at her as she quickly brushes away the tears, like she's embarrassed to have shown so much weakness in front of me. She shouldn't be. Crying isn't a weakness. Even if it were, I want her to show me her weaknesses. Not so I can exploit them or use them for my own gain, but because it means she trusts me. That she's comfortable enough to be herself around me.

My eyes pause on the red palm print on her cheek, and the guilt eating away at me is quickly burned off by the flames of rage.

"What happened?" The words come out in a furious growl and she tenses for a second before she relaxes, her face grimacing.

"I... he threatened to kill West if I didn't..." She trails off, but I don't need her to finish the sentence. Like I said, that disgusting image is branded into my brain.

"I'm going to fucking kill him," I snarl, the flames of anger growing taller. "I've half a mind to track him down and shove my fist in his face right now."

"Don't do that," she pleads, tugging on my sleeve to get my attention. I tear my gaze from the bathroom door as well as the internal debate I was having about seriously tracking him down and fucking castrating him. "His death is already fated, but if you go after him now, he's going to know everything. He'll know *we know* we're siblings, that we know who I really am. We can't give him any more ammunition."

"But—"

"No," she snaps before I can say anything further. "It was nothing I can't handle."

"Hadley," I growl, "he had his dick in your mouth."

"I fucking know that," she bites back, and damn does that flare of anger settle something in me. She isn't Hadley if she isn't breathing fire and making guys piss themselves with a single look. "And I'd let him do it again if it kept West safe."

Fuck. Those words floor me. My best friend or my sister. That's the impossible choice I'm being asked to make here. I look at her for a long moment, taking in her determined stance and hard resolve before I sigh. "Fine, but he's never getting his hands on you again." The words are an angry growl but she doesn't cower at the fierce promise underscoring them or the anger radiating off me.

Instead, her steady gaze meets mine. "I won't argue with that."

I watch her for a long moment. Something I can't place passes between us. A truce, maybe? Or acceptance, maybe?

"About the other night," I hesitantly start, my brows pulling together as I continue to watch her closely. "None of us had any idea what Bianca was going to do." Yet another spark of anger rises to the surface as I think about that bitch. "She'll pay for her actions, but you shouldn't blame the guys."

Her eyes widen in surprise before she nods her head. This time, I can tell she believes me. Unsure what else to say, and having had my fill of fucking emotions for

THE BATHROOM SCENE

the day, I make my way toward the door, knowing I'll have to get back to the guys soon, or they'll all come looking for us. I'm sure that's the last thing Hadley wants or needs.

On that note, I turn back to look at her. "The guys don't need to know about what happened, if you don't want them to."

I guess the dynamics are changing. My boys will always come first, but I need to think about Hadley too. I have no idea how I'm going to navigate these new waters, but I want to do right by her.

I pull open the door and step out. It's only when I see the stick man symbol that I remember we were in the male toilets. Not that I think Hadley really gives a shit, but it does make me chuckle under my breath.

I pop my head through just before the hinge closes. "Oh, you should probably get out of the boys' bathroom before anyone finds you here—what would people say?" My lip curls up in a small smile, and her weak chuckle is like music to my ears as the door closes behind me.

BEYOND VENGEANCE

Book Three

R.A. SMYTH

Dove

PROLOGUE

Very sneaky, Dove. Very sneaky, indeed.

You've proven to be much more of a challenge than I expected. I wouldn't say I like having to chase after you, but I've worked too hard to let you slip through my fingers now. It was fate, the way things worked out. I was only keeping you nearby for insurance; instead, I became infatuated with you. Watching you grow older, with your blonde hair and petite features so strikingly similar to your mother's, I knew I had to have you. With you, I could finally have everything I always coveted, and this time no one would take you away from me.

The compound was the perfect place to hide you. *I'm* the one who runs all the day-to-day operations. None of them spend any time there. They prefer to hide in their offices and fancy houses—pretending the torture and pain required to make cold, unquestioning soldiers isn't happening—but I live off watching those children become what I want them to be.

When you were younger, your eyes used to shine with such fierceness. You took every punishment I inflicted on you like a champ, and it only seemed to make you stronger, more defiant.

Well, I couldn't have that. I needed you broken and pliable, so I could build you into who you were always supposed to be. I gave your mother too much freedom, and she left me. For *him*. I wasn't about to let that happen again. I had everything planned. I was going to do things right with you. Make sure you could never leave me.

Having your little friend killed was your breaking point. I should have had it done years ago, but better late than never. Watching the light go out in your eyes was the greatest thing I have ever witnessed. You have no idea how fucking hard I was when I showed up for my monthly visit, and you were barely a shell of your former self. I'd have fucked you then and there, but it wasn't the right time. You needed more training, and I could wait.

I was patient. I was *nice*. I brought you gifts and complimented you. I was willing to wait until you were old enough to ultimately mine. While I waited, I dedicated years to training you, to mold you into my perfect wife.

And you thank me by running away mere months before all of my plans were due to come to fruition.

I thought I had you all worked out. That I'd broken you down, but you've been deceiving me all this time. Pretending to be what I wanted you to be, all the while planning your escape. What you don't realize, however, is that I'm not letting you go.

You might have done an excellent job of masking the defiance in your eyes, but I now know you've been planning too. I wonder what kind of friends you've made at that school, how they've been able to protect you against not one but two of my men. Whoever they are, they won't be enough to save you from me. They'll pay for their transgressions…and you'll pay for yours.

Hadley

CHAPTER ONE

"Hawk, dear, is that you?" a female voice calls out from deeper in the house as I follow Hawk into the mansion and close the door behind me, ignoring my racing heart and sweaty palms.

Hawk's already walking into the posh-looking seating area, not bothering to check if I'm behind him.

"What is this all about? You know we're b—"

Hawk's mother—*my* mother—stops when she sees me loitering awkwardly in the foyer. She's dressed in a black flared pantsuit, dolled up to the nines as her high heels echo on the tiled floor.

"Oh. You brought a...girl home," she states blandly, her face pinched which tells me exactly what she thinks of me. There's no recognition in her eyes, and I'm not sure if she remembers me from the party last month.

Her gaze drops to take in my thrift store jeans and worn top, her face scrunching up in disgust. She doesn't even have the common decency to hide her dislike of me.

"Yeah, Mom, this is Hadley. Is Dad around? We need to talk," Hawk says, diverting his mom's attention.

"Yes, yes, you said as much on the phone." His mother waves her hand, dismissing his words. "I don't understand what this is all about."

"Well, when Dad gets here, I'll tell you," Hawk responds, getting irritated.

"I'm here, I'm here," an older gentleman calls out as he comes down the stairs, buttoning a suit jacket, seeming like he's about to head out for the evening.

Reaching the foyer, he all but ignores me as he strides over to his wife, kissing her on the cheek. Seeing them standing side by side, I realize they *are* on their way out for the evening. There's no way they would be so dressed up for their son's visit.

Staring at them standing together, I recall the few details I know about them that I have written in my notebook—*the* notebook. Maria and Barton Davenport. Married for thirty-one years. The two of them, along with Wilbert Warren, Lawrence Rutherford, and Frank Hayes, attended Pacific Prep together. However, I couldn't find any information on whether or not she was one of his girls of the month, or whatever they called it back then. The first mention of them being a couple that I could find was whenever they were at college together.

"What's this all about?" Hawk's father asks him.

Noticing me *still* standing awkwardly by the door, his father gives me a once-over, his blank expression giving no indication of his initial thoughts about me.

"Who's this?" he asks, turning to look at his son.

"This is Hadley," Hawk repeats. "Let's just sit down, and I'll explain everything."

With his lips pinched in displeasure, Barton escorts his wife to a couch. When I hesitate to follow, Hawk pins me with a stare, jerking his head for me to move. Reluctantly ungluing my feet from the floor, I follow Hawk, and the two of us sit opposite...our parents? *God, that sounds weird.*

Hawk sits back on the uncomfortable couch, his legs spread wide, looking far too at ease considering the awkward as fuck conversation we're about to have. Meanwhile, my back is as straight as an arrow while I perch on the edge of the seat, ready to flee at any moment.

His father's eyes dart between us, lines marring his forehead as he frowns at us. "I think I know what this is about." There's a serious ring to his voice, and he shakes his head, frowning at Hawk in disappointment.

My eyebrows climb up my forehead as my gaze jumps from him to Hawk, confused. *How can he possibly know what's going on?*

Barton sighs disappointedly. "I thought I taught you better, son. We want to *avoid* scandals like this." With pursed lips, he side-eyes his wife. "Maria, you have Dr. Mitchell's number, don't you?"

His mother gasps, her hand coming up to cover her lips. I am beyond confused at this point. I honestly have no idea what they're talking about.

"Oh my." She stares pointedly at my stomach before answering her husband, "Yes. Yes, I do. I'll phone him right away. He can take care of the, eh, problem."

What the fuck is going on right now? What has a doctor got to do with any of this?

"How far along are you?" Her tone has a sharp edge as she sears me with an unimpressed look.

"I don't—"

"Jesus, Mom," Hawk exclaims, outraged, having caught on to what his parents are talking about. "She's not fucking pregnant."

My eyes must be the size of saucers as I gape at the three of them, unable to string a sentence together. Hawk's face is scrunched up, and he looks like the idea makes him physically ill.

That makes two of us.

"Well, if you haven't knocked her up, what is this all about?" his father demands.

"Fucking hell," Hawk growls, leaning forward in his seat as he runs his hand through his short blond hair. "She's my fucking sister."

Well, that's not exactly how I saw them finding out about their long-lost daughter.

Silence reigns supreme as his parents first gape at Hawk before their attentions focus on me, making my skin itch as I tug on the hem of my shirt, looking everywhere but at them.

"What are you talking about?" his mother snaps, eyeing me critically.

Hawk rubs at his eyes before he answers her. "Hadley enrolled at Pac this year.

Since the first day, there was something about her I couldn't put my finger on. With her blonde hair and eyes the same unusual color as mine, I felt like I knew her."

I guess we're skipping over the whole part where we hated each other.

"I couldn't put my finger on it," Hawk continues, "so I did a DNA test."

He pulls pages out of the back pocket of his jeans—the same reports West received from the DNA labs. I hadn't even realized he'd brought them with him tonight. "They came back positive."

His parents stare dumbfounded at the pages when Hawk sets them on the coffee table, neither reaching out to lift them. Instead, they glance at the reports from a safe distance as though they are a bomb about to go off. *I guess that's not far from the truth.*

"What...I don't—" His mother's voice trails off as she continues to gape at the ominous pieces of paper. "There must be some sort of mistake."

Ouch.

Hawk sighs, pinning his parents with a 'cut the crap' look.

"I found the stuff in the safe in your bedroom," he states bluntly, letting them know he's not buying their splutters of denial. I can only assume he's talking about the birth certificate and photos he showed me.

His father's gaze turns to steel as he scowls at Hawk. "You know you're not supposed to be in our room," he barks out.

Seriously? That's the main concern right now? Talk about fucking priorities.

Hawk silently meets his father's gaze, although I'm too focused on Maria, who hasn't stopped staring at me. I can't decipher the look on her face. A mixture of confusion and doubt, possibly.

She casts her eyes over me with a critical look. I look exactly the same as when I walked through the door, and I didn't meet her high standards then, so I doubt she will find anything about me that she likes now.

"I really don't think that's the issue," Hawk grinds out between gritted teeth, his thoughts on a similar wavelength to my own. "How come you never told me I had a sister, let alone a twin?"

His father—fuck, *our* father—hasn't looked at me once since Hawk spilled the beans. It's as though he's concentrating on pretending I'm not there.

"What's to tell?" Maria shrugs, sounding a tad defensive. "One day, she was here and the next, she was gone. We looked for her everywhere, but when no one could find her, we had to accept that she was gone for good. After all these years, we assumed she was dead."

She says it with such indifference. If I were more emotional, her detachment would have left me feeling like she had just ripped my heart out and stomped all over it. The child who used to cry for her long-lost family would have been sobbing on the floor by now, but thankfully, I learned to harden my heart. I've carefully wrapped it in barbed wire, placing it behind a sharp fence where no one can get to it.

Hawk's thigh presses against mine in a silent act of comfort, yet he needn't bother. Other than a twinge of tightness in my chest at her cruel, heartless words, I feel nothing. The white-picket-fence childhood, with smiling parents who hugged and adored me, was only a fantasy. Something I dreamt about in the dark of night to keep the demons away. I've known for a long time that it would never be my reality.

I haven't sussed out my father yet, but my mother is clearly a conniving bitch, only giving a damn about her own self-preservation. I call fucking bullshit at her words, though. The child of a wealthy family just disappears, and no one asks any questions?

There's no investigation? I've already done my research. I *know* the police were never contacted. No report was ever filed, and no official search was ever conducted.

Whatever is going on here—and there sure as fuck is something strange going on—she and her husband are up to their necks in it. They fucking know a lot more about what happened to me than they are willing to share.

Barton looks at his watch, the lines around his eyes and mouth tightening. "Look, we have to go," he says, glancing up at Hawk. "I'll make an appointment for the, uh, girl" —he can't even say my name—"to meet with our doctor this week. I want him to do another DNA test. We can talk again when we get the results back."

Without waiting for a response, he stands, holding a hand out to help his wife get to her feet. With a final nod at Hawk—still fucking ignoring me—he escorts his wife from the room.

"Come on," Hawk practically growls once we're alone. Not waiting for a response from me, he gets to his feet and strides toward the door. I scurry after him, because I sure as fuck don't want to be left alone in this house with either of them.

"Well, I'm so glad you talked me into doing that," I gripe once I've closed the front door behind me, earning an unimpressed glare from Hawk as he strides over to the car. Following him, I climb into the passenger seat. We sit silently, staring out the front windshield at the extravagant house. Lights shine out from the foyer and front room, lighting up the circular gravel drive and manicured shrubs lining the garden.

"They know more than they're letting on," Hawk grits out. Starting the ignition, he puts the car in drive and we head away from the house.

Hawk's hands repeatedly flex around the steering wheel, and I can feel the tension radiating off him on my side of the car as the gates out of the private residence slide open. He guns the car down the dark lane that winds its way along the cliff toward the school.

I wait him out, staring unseeingly at the night sky out the passenger side window as he stews for a long while.

"I can't fucking believe them," he eventually spits out, jolting me out of my inner thoughts as I turn to look at him. "He couldn't even look at you, and my mom was a complete bitch." He shakes his head, scowling out the front windscreen at the dark road ahead. "I don't even recognize them anymore. I can't work out if they've always been this cold and selfish and I just never saw it, or if I've been deluding myself this whole time."

"I'm sorry."

Hawk whips his head around to look at me, his brows furrowed.

"What are *you* apologizing for?"

I shrug. "It must suck realizing your parents aren't who you thought they were." I mean, they're supposed to be your role models, right? The people you turn to for help and advice. I can't imagine asking either of the people I met tonight for anything.

"Well, yeah, but you're the one who had to grow up without parents." He doesn't say it in a nasty way, more like he can't understand why I would feel sorry for him when, in his opinion, I got dealt a worse hand.

"Maybe so, but you can't miss what you never had," I tell him easily, being honest. Sure, I've always wondered who they were and what happened. Except after having met them tonight, I'm honestly glad they weren't in my life. They can't disappoint me or let me down, because they've never been there or shown me a different side of themselves.

I message Beck on our way back to campus, telling him to meet us at the guys' apartment. Once we are all together, Hawk relays the whole—relatively uneventful—evening. All of them are angry at our parents' blasé attitude, but none seem surprised. The one thing we're all in agreement on is that they know more than they're letting on.

∽

ON TUESDAY, Hawk drives me to some fancy private clinic where a doctor swabs the inside of my cheek and takes some blood. We're in and out in less than half an hour, and it all feels so anticlimactic, considering the outcome will change everything.

I still have so many reservations, and having now met my parents, I'm even more hesitant to dive further into this world. Do the answers to my questions about my past truly matter this much? What will it change? Nothing. Ultimately, it doesn't matter how I ended up in the life I have. I'm here, surviving and doing the best I can.

Nevertheless, the second Hawk told them the truth about it, the choice to back out of this hair-brained plan was eradicated. Sure, I could still run. There's no denying the thought crosses my mind several times a day. However, every time I picture myself somewhere else, living a life without Emilia or the guys, or even Hawk—*I know, I can't believe I'm even thinking it*—I get this strange tightness in my chest, and I realize it's not as simple as running away. There's some sort of connection between the guys and me. I don't know how to explain it, but it's pulling us all together. It's a force that would be impossible to fight, and frankly, I don't want to. I'm sick of fighting. Fighting for my life, fighting for freedom, fighting to be happy. I just want to live. To enjoy the easy moments with Beck, soak up the strength I get from Mason, and bathe in West's calmness. I don't know what will happen with Cam, but I need to help him find his light again. I need to see his easy, carefree smile and assure myself I haven't completely broken him.

So no, while running might seem like the easy solution, it's not the answer.

After we leave the clinic, I spend the next few days on tenterhooks, waiting for the phone call that will upend my life. I already know what the test results are going to be. Even so, it's the final confirmation the Davenports need before anything more happens —although I have no idea what comes next. Somehow, I doubt we will dive straight into family dinners and vacationing together on the holidays.

"Do you want to talk about what happened with your parents?" Beck asks during our Thursday session. We're lying on the sofa, which has become our usual position during this hour every week.

"Not particularly," I grumble.

He wraps his tattooed arm around me and I lean against his chest.

"What was it like when you met your dad for the first time?" I ask.

"Well, I was just a kid when I first met him—after my mom and I moved out of Black Creek—but I knew as soon as I laid eyes on him that he would never be any sort of father figure. Not that he hung around long enough to even try and get to know me.

"Most of the kids I grew up with didn't have fathers. If they weren't in prison or dead, they were neck-deep in gang life. That was always their priority over their own kids, so I never felt like I was missing out on much.

"When he showed up last year, it became painfully obvious he saw me as a pawn. Someone he could manipulate into doing his bidding. Which is precisely what happened. After growing up in Black Creek and all the lowlifes I met there, I thought

I'd be able to handle whatever he wanted in return. I stupidly figured whatever he would ask of me would be worth it." He sighs dejectedly. "But things have gotten so fucked up."

Yeah, he can say that again.

"What does he want from you?"

There's a moment of heavy silence.

"I'm not sure yet." His voice sounds tense, tighter than it did a moment ago.

I glance up at him through my eyelashes, noticing the deep frown on his face, and the moss-green of his eyes seems duller than they did when I first walked in. It's possible that not knowing what's going to be asked of him has him on edge. Why wouldn't it when he knows what he does—but if that's the case, why do I feel like he's lying?

"Maybe he's just using you so he can threaten West's life," I suggest. I've been trying to think about it, to determine what use Beck could be to the company. Honestly, being used as a tool to threaten the rest of them is the best-case scenario, but I'm concerned they will want to use the skills he's learned through his degree, analyzing people and figuring out what makes them tick. If that's the case, our parents might want to involve him with the new recruits, somehow. I know Beck is tough, and he's seen and done some fucked-up things in his youth, but I don't know how well he—or the others— would handle knowing their parents don't just offer mercenaries for hire. In actuality, they train them, more or less from birth, ensuring that each child grows into a formidable machine. Some of these kids become so removed from their humanity that they barely even see their targets as human beings.

"Yeah, maybe." The hopeless tone of his voice has unease churning in my stomach, only intensifying the feeling that there's something he's not telling me. Worry for him courses through me. If Beck was forced to devise new and creative ways to dehumanize those kids, or differentiate the weak from the strong, I don't think he could live with himself.

He coughs, clearing his throat before changing the topic. "How have things been going with you and Hawk?"

As much as I want to know what he's hiding, I welcome the change in conversation. I trust Beck enough to know he'll tell me when he's ready.

"Okay, I think." I shrug. "He doesn't seem to hate me, which I guess is a win. Things are still awkward, though. Neither of us knows how to be around one another without biting each other's heads off."

He chuckles softly. "It'll get easier with time. At least he seems to be trying."

"Yeah, he's still a dick most of the time, in any case. Especially when he doesn't get his way. I really don't understand how West put together that we were related. I'm nowhere near as infuriating as him."

Another rumble of laughter vibrates through his chest.

"Did you get things sorted with all of them after Valentine's Day?"

"Yeah, I think so. Well, West and Mason explained that none of them had anything to do with Bianca's stunt. And now that I've had time to think about it, Cam has been so busy beating himself up, I don't see that he would do something to hurt or upset me. It was stupid of me to believe Bianca at all. I was just…"

"After everything you've been through with them, it's understandable that you weren't sure what to believe. The main thing is that you worked everything out."

"We did, yet I still don't like how much trust to put in them. We're blindly going along with this plan of theirs. What if it blows up in our faces, or they turn on me?"

"Unfortunately, they know more about their parents than we do, so I don't see that we have any other choice but to listen to their advice for now," Beck says, voicing my own thoughts. "I don't believe you have anything to worry about, anyway. Hawk's been different with you recently. As for the other guys, well, the way they look at you...I don't know how the whole school hasn't caught on to it."

"On to what?" I question, confused. All four Princes have always watched me closely, but they're perpetually attuned to their surroundings, constantly observing everything happening around them.

"Their feelings for you."

He says it like it's obvious. Something I should already know. I mean, I know Mason and West like me, but I wouldn't say there is anything obvious about the way they look at me. As for Cam...well, I can't deny the way my body flushes when I feel his eyes on me or how my heart rate picks up when he's nearby. Regardless of my body's physical reaction, we're just friends. After everything the two of us have been through, I don't see how we could ever be anything more.

"Don't talk crap," I grumble, pushing up onto my elbow so I can scowl down at him.

"I'm not," he insists with a small laugh, as though he can't understand how I don't see what he sees. "I realized it the first day I saw them with you, when you had your panic attack. Sure, they were freaking out, but they were genuinely concerned for you. Mason wouldn't even leave until I reassured him you'd be okay."

Well, if my sappy little heart doesn't go all gooey at hearing that.

"And Cam is determined to do whatever it takes to make it up to you. The steadfastness in his eyes that night they found us in the clearing was more than obvious."

"That doesn't mean he has feelings for me," I argue.

"Maybe not," he reasons. "Although the fact he said he was done with the tradition and was using Bianca to taunt you is."

I'm not sure what to make of his words as I mull them over. "None of that means they're trustworthy, however."

"It doesn't," he agrees readily. "But they did help us get rid of a dead body, so maybe they deserve the benefit of the doubt."

Hmmm, maybe.

Baby

CHAPTER TWO

"You need to stay here while we're gone," Hawk orders in his usual no-nonsense tone. You'd think he would have worked out by now that that's not the way to handle Hadley. The second the words are out of his mouth, her back straightens and she frowns at him.

"Now I know you didn't just *order* me to do something," she snaps, defiance glowing in her eyes.

She's so fucking sexy when she's spitting fire and ready for a fight. I'm used to people cowering and bending to our every whim, but Hadley doesn't take any of our shit. She's never given a damn about our power or influence.

I agreed to be friends with her—so my dick definitely shouldn't be getting hard as I watch her stand up to Hawk—but *fuck me*. Friends? I haven't got the first fucking clue how to be friends with a girl, and there's no way Hadley and I can just be friends. Not with how my dick strains to get to her every time we're in the same room.

I've never been so attuned to someone's presence before. My whole body comes alive when she's nearby. My skin heats and my cock swells, not understanding that this girl is off-limits. Despite my body's reaction to her, my brain isn't on the same page. I don't know how to behave around her. The easy banter we used to have is no longer there; instead, we're left making awkward conversation, neither of us sure how to respond. It's fucking exhausting.

"I'm not a fucking idiot," Hadley seethes, drawing me back to her argument with Hawk. "I'm not about to go wandering around in the forest after what happened, but I'm perfectly safe in *my* room."

Hawk got a phone call earlier today from his dad. Apparently, all of our parents are demanding a meeting with us. Our guess is Hadley's DNA results are in, and they want to discuss what that means for them and our ruling over the school.

The five of us were chilling in the apartment; Hadley was playing a video game with Mason while I watched them—well, *her*—and West was fiddling around on his laptop, before Hawk had to open his big mouth and start this argument. He looks ready to strangle her as he gives her a look that has most other students pissing themselves, ready to do just about anything to get him to stop staring at them like that.

Jesus, are siblings supposed to be so aggressive toward one another? The only difference between them since finding out they're twins is that Hawk's dickishness no longer comes from a place of hate, yet they still snipe at one another like they want to tear each other's heads off.

"Your room is on the ground floor," Hawk argues. "Anyone could break in."

Hadley throws her hands up in exasperation. "I'm pretty sure killers can climb stairs," she snarks. Her comeback has Mason not-so-subtly swiping his hand over his mouth, hiding his chuckle behind his large palm. The girl has an answer for everything.

"You could invite Beck over. Then you'll both be here for when we get back," I suggest, earning a glare from West.

Both siblings turn to look at me. Hadley has a thoughtful look on her face before a cunning smile graces it.

"That works," she agrees far too easily, and Hawk gives her a suspicious look, most likely trying to work out her angle.

She's probably thinking about fucking Beck on Hawk's bed just to piss him off. *Damn, why does that thought have my dick twitching?*

∼

THAT EVENING, we are picked up in a chauffeur-driven car and taken into the city to the modern office building which houses our parents' company. Our families own various properties throughout California, but the base of their operation is here. This building is the powerhouse of Nocturnal Enterprises.

An hour later, we exit the vehicle and make our way into the building, pushing open the glass door into the vast, mostly empty foyer. At forty stories, the high-rise is tall and sleek, comprised entirely of glass that reflects the setting sun, causing a glare that burns my eyes.

Besides the security guard manning the door—who doesn't even bat an eyelash as we walk past him—and a couple of women seated at a reception desk, the ground floor is otherwise empty as we stride toward the bank of elevators. No one stops us or says anything. Everyone here knows who we are, even though we rarely visit.

None of us say anything—you never know who could be listening—and all too soon, the doors are opening onto the thirty-seventh floor. Our parents own the entire building, renting out all but the top three floors. Everything from the thirty-seventh floor up is all Nocturnal Enterprises. How much of that is actually Nocturnal Mercenaries? I'm not sure.

"Welcome, boys," the receptionist greets, a seductive purr to her words. She's got curvy hips and is lasciviously licking her lips as her eyes bounce between the four of us, her pupils dilated with desire. Any other visit and I'd be all over that, but my dick doesn't even stir. Frustratingly, only one fiery blonde gets any sort of response out of me anymore, even though I'm not supposed to think about her like that.

It's not for lack of trying. No matter how many times I tell myself I can't go near Hadley and that I've fucked things up so badly I should be grateful she's even talking to me, my dick still doesn't get the message. Neither does my heart, based on the way it picks up speed whenever she's around. It's making it impossible to be near her, yet, I can't stop gravitating her way. I guess I'm a glutton for punishment.

The receptionist escorts us toward a large boardroom. "Can I get any of you a drink? Your parents should be here momentarily."

"No, we're fine," Hawk responds succinctly, barely sparing her a glance as we filter into the room.

Nodding, she turns to leave, but not before casting one last longing look over each of us.

"Well, let me know if you need anything." Her voice drops to a husk as she says 'anything,' and she trails her finger down my arm before she steps out of the room, leaving us alone.

Scowling, I uselessly wipe down my arm as though her touch might have left cooties or some shit. Mason snorts, shaking his head at my antics as he follows Hawk toward the table.

The four of us take our seats along one side of the long glass table, looking out the floor-to-ceiling windows that offer a spectacular view of the city skyline. We're only left waiting a minute before our parents filter in—Maria and Barton Davenport, Theresa and Frank Hayes, Wilbert Warren, and last but not least, Daddy Dearest. West's mom is off god only knows where, pretending she doesn't have a son or a cheating sleazeball of a husband, and, well, I never really knew my mom. She was nothing more than an egg donor.

I can barely look my dad in the eye as he struts into the room, not a care in the fucking world, and it takes everything in me not to throw myself across the table and murder the fucker right here. I've already been given a stern warning by Hawk not to do something stupid. We need the element of surprise if we stand any chance of taking him down. He doesn't know it, but he's a dead man walking, even if I have to kill him myself. He's never been a father to me. There's no love lost between us, and even if there was, nothing could negate his actions. What he's done to Hadley is beyond fucked up, and he clearly knows where she's been all these years.

From what Hawk said, their parents know something too, but we can't be sure if they were in on whatever the hell went down, or if they're just covering up the reason for her disappearance. Regardless, all six of our parents are suspicious as fuck.

I can't tear my eyes away from my father as all of them sit down on the opposite side of the large boardroom table. He looks so normal. Yeah, he's got a suffocating air of arrogance around him, but he doesn't look like someone who would be involved in the kidnapping and grooming of a little girl. Shouldn't he give off some sort of sicko signal?

"We need to discuss this new development with Elizabeth," Hawk's dad states, his words slicing through my thoughts. It sounds so weird to hear her being called Elizabeth, and I turn the name over in my head. *Yeah, I can't imagine calling her that.* It was Hadley I called out when I was dick-deep inside of her. Hadley is what she will always be to me.

"I take it you got the DNA results back?" Hawk asks.

"We did. She is who you thought she was."

Obviously. Who the fuck else was she going to be? We had our own DNA results, but of course, that wasn't good enough for any of them.

"What happened to her? Where has she been all this time?" Hawk demands, staring pointedly at his father.

"We're looking into that."

That doesn't help in bringing me any sort of comfort.

"What does that mean? How did she even go missing in the first place?" Anger, as per usual, gets the better of Hawk as he practically snarls out the words, and his father's eyes narrow, not appreciating his son's tone.

"Watch it," Barton growls in a warning.

Everyone else is observing us closely, their faces void of any emotion. I can't keep myself from repeatedly glancing toward my father, trying to pick up on any little tell that he was involved in any of this. I mean, he *has* to be, right?

"As your mother told you the other day, she just disappeared."

"How?" Hawk is walking a dangerous line with his tone, not that I can blame him. We're all anxious for answers, him and Hadley most of all.

"We were having a party, and the two of you were up in your room. The nanny had put you to bed and claimed she didn't hear anything all night. The next morning when she went to get you, Elizabeth was gone." He casually shrugs his shoulders like that discovery wasn't life-altering for him or his family. "We questioned everyone who attended the party, but no one had seen or heard anything suspicious. When we couldn't find any leads, we had to accept that she was gone."

That was it? They asked a few fucking questions, and then they just gave up on her? What the fuck is wrong with these people?

It takes everything in me to hold my tongue. Out of the corner of my eye, I can see Mason's body coiled tight, just as furious as I am about the bullshit coming out of Barton's mouth.

"And you didn't think to go to the police?" Hawk argues.

"You know we couldn't have done that. Not with the line of work we're in," West's dad pipes up dismissively.

Right. Can't have the authorities finding out about your little mercenary business. Much more important than finding your missing daughter. *The whole fucking lot of them are nut jobs.*

"We hired a PI at the time," Barton states, as if that's some compromise for not going to the cops. "However he never uncovered any leads."

It's clear Hadley meant nothing to them. She wasn't worth investing the time or resources into tracking down, and they noticeably don't give a shit where she's been living or what she's been through the last fifteen-odd years.

"The more pressing concern is what we do now that she's shown up," Maria Davenport speaks up, not sounding the slightest bit relieved to have her daughter back. If anything, she makes it sound like this new development—the return of her fucking daughter—is an inconvenience.

"What do you mean?" I question, struggling to keep the sharpness out of my tone.

"We need you to keep an eye on her and find out what you can about her."

"We've already looked into her past," Hawk informs them. "She's just a foster kid who got a scholarship here. Pac is one of the most prestigious schools in the country, so it's not much of a stretch that she would end up there."

"It's good to see you taking some initiative, son," Barton says, a proud gleam in his eyes. "Lawrence has already confirmed the same, but nonetheless, we can't be too careful. Especially now."

Well, that's not suspicious as fuck that my dad confirmed her background. And what the hell does he mean by 'especially now'?

"Alright, we'll stay close to her," Hawk agrees, sounding reluctant. It's all for show. If anything, this works in our favor.

"We've also been hearing from disgruntled parents that you boys refused to pick a girl last month," Mason's dad takes over, looking furious as he brings up the topic. "What the hell is going on there?" he demands, his sharp tone enough to have Mason sitting straighter in his chair.

That man has fucked his son up good. Mason does his best to hide it, but there's no denying his dad has done one hell of a number on him.

"When we found out about Ha...Elizabeth, we decided it was time for a change in traditions," Hawk explains easily, as though it's no big deal.

"Did you now?" There's a warning growl in Frank's voice. "Don't you think you should have discussed this with us?"

Hawk's jaw tightens. "I thought you wanted us to prove to you we could control the school."

"What Frank is trying to say," Barton interrupts, "is that we don't understand your decision to do away with a tradition that's been effective for generations."

"The senior girls were getting too big-headed about it. They've formed a club and everything, and it's only serving to make them harder to control. I figured changing things up and having Elizabeth take over control of the girls would be a good way to test if she's cut out to be a Davenport."

Our parents are silent as they think over Hawk's proposal.

"It's an interesting idea," Barton speaks up. "Nevertheless, let's stick with the tradition for now. We'll see how Elizabeth handles coming out as a Davenport, and then go from there."

"Elizabeth should also be included in the tradition," Maria chimes in. "It will be good to see how she handles the vultures. She's pretty enough. We could get some useful contracts out of her."

What the fuck? Does this woman only see her daughter as a bargaining chip?

Tension seeps into the air, none of us keen on the idea of Hadley being involved in the tradition. Casting a subtle glance toward my father, his eyes are narrowed and jaw clenched. Nope, he's not a fan of that idea, either. I wonder what he'd think if he knew three of us have fucked her—four, if you count Beck, which I'm assuming we can. Not that I'd tell him any of that. He's controlling enough to do something reckless if he ever finds out. Something that would only put Hadley in greater danger.

"Yes, a good idea," Barton agrees, neither of them giving two shits about the fact they're essentially pimping out their daughter to the senior boys. To what end? The whole point of the tradition is so the next generation of male heirs can prove to their parents they are capable of running a multimillion-dollar conglomerate one day. Sure, families from all over the country enroll their children in Pac Prep in the hopes that they can make friends—or more—with us and gain their families a foot in the door when it comes to doing business with our parents. But what do our parents truly gain from it all? They have their pick of companies to do business with. Is it all a control thing? A way for them to seem more important than they are?

None of us can protest or say anything about involving Hadley in the tradition without raising any red flags that might have our parents realizing we care more about her than we're letting on. Instead, we're all forced to nod and agree with their asinine idea.

How the fuck this is going to work is beyond me. I might not be dating Hadley or anything, but she still consumes my every thought. The idea of sticking my dick in any other chick is seriously unappealing. Despite the fact it's been fucking ages since I had sex, my cock doesn't even stir at the thought of having a sure-thing lay. All it wants—all *I* want—is Hadley, and the idea of watching some douche from school with his arm draped over her, acting like she's his, pisses me the fuck off.

"Right, now that we've sorted that out, let's move on to Easter break. The four of you will be spending the break at the company, shadowing each of us and learning the ropes. You'll also be expected to attend our "Annual Open Day" later in the year so you can all get an understanding of the quality of recruits we have. Then, when you graduate, you'll start taking on some of the more minor responsibilities."

"What about Beck?" West asks in a tight voice. "What's his job?"

"Don't worry about him." Wilbert waves off his question. "He's already doing his job."

Huh. We didn't know that. What the hell is he doing for them? Maybe it's time we had a little chat with him, especially if he's keeping secrets. We've let him in because he's West's brother, not to mention he's dating Hadley. And he *appeared* genuinely shocked and horrified at Christmas when he found out what our parents did, but what the fuck do we actually know about him? Typically, West would have researched the fuck out of someone new in our lives. However, he's completely buried his head in the sand when it comes to his brother, choosing to pretend he doesn't exist. Well, he's done with that shit now. If his brother is involved in stuff with our parents, we need to know whose side he's on. And if it's not ours, he needs to go.

Having seemingly discussed everything they needed to, our parents get to their feet.

"Oh, one more thing," Barton begins. "We will be announcing Elizabeth's return home tonight. We expect you all to be there. Let her know."

Without waiting for a response, the six of them filter out, and once we're alone, the four of us share a knowing glance.

"Not here," Hawk states in a quiet order, when I open my mouth to speak. Nodding, we exit the boardroom silently, none of us saying a word as we leave the building and get into the car to head back to campus.

"Not it!" I rush out, throwing my arms in the air the second we're all standing back on campus, watching the car drive away. "I'm not telling her." No fucking way do I want to be the one to tell her that not only do West and Mason have to continue picking a girl each month, but she has to pick a guy too.

"Not it," West and Mason echo quickly, making Hawk scowl at all of us.

"I'm not fucking telling her," he insists. "She'll tear my balls off. At least she has a vested interest in you keeping yours."

"Sorry, dude." I shrug. "You lost."

He presses his lips together, mumbling something about 'not it' being a stupid fucking way to decide anything as he stomps toward the dorms. I'd laugh, but I'm reasonably certain he's walking into his own funeral.

Hadley

CHAPTER THREE

"What the hell, Hadley?!" Hawk barks out. *Oh great, he found me. Now he can yell at me in person instead of via text.*

He and the others got back several hours ago, and I got a string of pissed-off messages when he discovered I wasn't in his apartment where he *ordered* me to stay. *Yeah, that shit was never going to fly.*

"Calm your tits, big guy." His eyes narrow to deathly slits, and I have to swallow my laughter. "I've been here the whole time. See"—I wave my hand over myself—"totally fine."

Such a fucking temperamental bastard. All I did was come to the library, where I've been surrounded by students. It's not like I decided to go for a walk alone in the forest. Even if I decided to do that, I can handle myself. Although, I guess he doesn't know that, so fair enough. I have every right to be pissed off, though. I didn't fucking escape Lawrence and everything else just so he, or anyone, could boss me around. Hell no. There's no fucking way.

When he continues to frown at me, I change the topic. "What happened at the meeting?"

Sighing, he lets go of some of his anger, sitting beside me so we can whisper quietly without worrying about nosy students nearby overhearing us.

"Not much. We have to spend Easter break with them, learning the ropes." He scrunches his nose up, not fond of that idea.

"That sucks," I empathize. "But it could be a good opportunity to get some dirt on them or find something we can use to help bring them down."

Hawk's eyes roam over my face for a second before he responds, "Is that what we're going to do? Destroy them?"

The way I see it, there are only two options. "Well, do you want to work for them, knowing the truth of what they do?"

"Hell no." He stares at me with wide eyes like I'm insane.

I shrug my shoulders. "Then we have to take them down."

After a second, he chuckles, shaking his head like he can't believe what he's hearing. "You make it sound so simple when it's going to be anything but. Not only do they have the financial means and know-how to evade discovery all these years, but they have a fucking army at their beck and call."

He's right. It's a Herculean task if ever there was one. Nevertheless, escaping the compound seemed impossible too, and I achieved that all by myself. So why can't the six of us accomplish this?

Dropping the topic, for now, he leans back in his chair, running his hand through his hair as he watches me closely.

"Our parents are throwing a party tonight," he blurts out.

"Okay." I shrug, not caring about some meaningless party filled with rich assholes who all think they're god's gift to humanity, focusing my attention back on my homework. "Have fun with that."

The guys may have had a face-to-face meeting today with the parents, but no one has reached out to *me* since I took the DNA test. Although Hawk hasn't mentioned it yet—it looks like he's getting the mundane news out of the way first. I'm assuming the results were discussed today, but jeez, is it asking too much to pick up the phone and let me know too? Apparently so. I guess they've been too busy planning a party to bother with little old me.

Despite my complaining, I'm more than happy for them to leave me alone. I just don't like decisions being made about me behind my back, and I'm sure that's what happened this afternoon.

"We're all invited. You too." The bottom of my stomach drops as I tear my eyes away from the homework I was working on, giving Hawk my full attention.

"I'm what? Why?"

"The DNA results are back."

What the fuck...That doesn't explain anything.

Seeing my utter confusion, he continues, "This is how things are done in our world."

Nope, he's still not making any sense.

He taps a finger against the wooden table, leaning in toward me. "You best put on your finest jewelry, 'cause tonight you're coming out as a Davenport." Hawk's words send an ominous chill down my spine. "Welcome to the family, Elizabeth."

∼

WEST HAD YET another dress delivered for me to wear tonight. The fact that my wardrobe mainly consists of fancy, overpriced dresses does not sit well with me. I'm a jeans and t-shirt girl. All this expensive shit is just not me. I want to open my wardrobe and see clothes that I *want* to wear, something that is me.

Regardless, the dress he bought is beautiful. It's a deep, midnight blue, with a high jewel neckline—West once again ensuring my scars aren't on display for every asshole to gawk at. It falls to the floor at the back, with the front lifting so it finishes mid-thigh. Diamonds are sewn into the fabric on either side of my waist, looking like twinkling stars against the dark material when the light hits them.

Emilia again does my hair and makeup, her constant chatter helping to ease the nausea that keeps rolling through my stomach, as sweat coats my forehead and makes my palms slick.

"You need to calm down, girl," she admonishes, seeing how fucking stressed out I am. She moves to stand in front of me, pinning me in place with her serious expression. "You've stood tall against Bianca and her bitches, and the Princes all year. You've got this."

It's a decent pep talk, and I give her a weak smile in thanks, but dealing with Bianca and the guys was nothing compared to what I'm going to face tonight.

I'm not ready. I don't want this.

Why the fuck did I let those shitheads talk me into this?

I lift my hand, fiddling with the necklace West got me for my birthday, closing my eyes as I try to draw some semblance of calm from it.

My heart rate starts to settle, the churning in my stomach slowing, but a knock on the door breaks me out of my reverie, and I scowl as I stomp toward it in my heels.

Yanking the door open, I glower at Hawk, pissed off that he interrupted the zen I had going, not to mention the fact he talked me into this stupid, half-cocked idea. Really, I'm just happy to cling to my anger rather than sit in the sickening anxiety I've been struggling through since he informed me about tonight.

Ignoring the dark glare I'm giving him, he roams his eyes over my dress and matching heels.

"It'll do, I guess," he laments, looking unimpressed with my ensemble. I bark out a half-hysterical laugh, finding some reassurance in his dickish behavior. I just hope Emilia didn't hear him. She'll have a bitch fit that her hours of primping weren't acknowledged.

A small smile lifts one side of his lip, and I think it's the first time I've ever seen him do it. Not that you could really call it that. It's so small, barely more than a twitch, and he quickly wipes it off his face.

"Where are the others?" I ask, peering past him, half expecting to find the rest of the guys standing in the hall behind him. One is rarely far from the others.

"They're already on the way there. It's better if they arrive separately."

Right. Can't let any of our parents know how close we've all gotten in the last few months. *God, things are getting so complicated.*

Emilia chooses that moment to come bouncing over. "Doesn't she look amazing? She'll have no issues fitting in with you pompous pricks."

Hawk's eyebrows climb up his forehead, and he stares slack-jawed at Emilia as another—more genuine—laugh bursts out of me. I don't think he's ever heard her talk so condescendingly about the Princes, or the upper class in general. I love that she's no longer afraid to be herself around them. I don't know if she thinks she has immunity against their tyrannical ways because of who I am now, or because I'm basically dating two of them. Whatever the reason, I wouldn't hesitate to cut a bitch—even if that bitch is Hawk—if they tried to put her in her place.

"Have fun tonight, kids," she chuckles, turning toward me with a giant smile on her face that's totally out of place, considering the tension in the air and the nerves still somersaulting in my stomach. "Remember, you're a badass bitch, and the Davenports can go fuck themselves if they don't see how great you are." Still, with that blinding smile in place, she glances at Hawk before tacking on in a sickly-sweet voice, "No offense, Hawk."

Hawk continues to stare at her quizzically, likely trying to work out what the fuck is happening right now, as I bite my lip to stifle my laugh. Kissing me on the cheek, Emilia skips past him and down the hall to her room.

"Is there something wrong with her?" he asks, eventually finding his words.

"No, you asshole." I shove him in the shoulder as I close the door behind me, the two of us making our way down the hall.

"Then she must have a death wish."

I yank on the sleeve of his jacket, bringing him to a stop.

"If you do anything to her, I will become your worst living nightmare," I threaten in a deadly tone. "You think getting throat-punched was bad? Touch her, and I'll slice open your stomach and use your intestines as a noose to hang you with."

"Fucking hell, Hadley." He rolls his eyes like I'm being melodramatic, unfazed by my grave threat. "I'm not going to do anything to her. I'm just not used to anyone being so uncaring if they piss me off."

"I don't care if I piss you off."

"Yeah, and you're the first person to be so cavalier with their life."

Eh. What's life, if not odd moments of peace between staring death in the face and giving it a big, old fuck you.

Stepping outside the dorms, the light breeze blows my hair back out of my face as we walk along the path. "You realize they all just bitch about you behind your backs, right?"

Hawk's eyes narrow, and he gives a lethal glare to some random student walking in the opposite direction, making them whimper as they pick up their pace, practically running to get away from him.

"They better not be," he snarls, making me roll my eyes. We reach the car, both of us hopping in and leaving the school behind as we drive toward the Davenports' mansion.

By the time we arrive, the party is in full swing. People are milling about everywhere, drinking expensive champagne and pretending to give a shit as they listen to each other droll on about their pathetic little lives.

I recognize many of the kids from school as they gather in groups and traipse around with their parents. It looks like just about everyone the Davenports know or have ever spoken to has been invited, and nerves do a jig in my stomach as Hawk and I make our way across the foyer.

We're barely across the hall when I feel eyes boring into me, and I turn my head to find Lawrence's menacing gaze watching me intently. He looks more haggard than the last time I saw him, in the headmaster's office. *Good. It serves him fucking right.*

The last time I was in the same room as him, I was on my knees, having reverted back into the scared child I used to be as he shoved his dick in my mouth. Straightening my spine as my eyes meet his, I stare defiantly back at him and refuse to let him make me cower this time.

It's easy when there are other people around and I know he can't do anything to me, but when he had me cornered alone in that office, it was just like every other time I've been around him. I felt scared and helpless, frozen in terror. It doesn't matter that I'm a big, badass assassin bitch. When he's around, I'm nothing more than a frightened kid, willing to do anything to avoid his punishments.

Nonetheless, I've made a stand against him now. I've moved my chess piece, and while I may not have him in checkmate yet, based on the daggers he's throwing my way, I've certainly made the game more difficult for him to win. I smirk before dismissing him, something that I know will piss him off. *The arrogant asswad always did love it when all my attention was focused on him.*

Walking beside Hawk through the crowd, I spot the guys interspersed throughout the room, stuck in various conversations. West catches sight of me from across the room as I walk by, throwing me a dirty smirk before responding to whoever he's talking to.

Beck is standing nearby, and his eyes trail me across the crowded room as he absently nods his head at whatever the person he's engaged in conversation with says, his intense gaze heating my skin. The lighting in the room emphasizes just how tired he looks, the bags under his eyes worryingly dark. I'm becoming increasingly concerned about him. The light in his eyes isn't as bright as when I first met him, and it doesn't look like he's sleeping much, if at all.

"We should find our parents," Hawk murmurs in my ear, steering my focus back to the room. His eyes dart around the crowd as he searches for them, so he misses the way my face scrunches at his words. *Our parents.* I'm never going to get used to that.

Giving Beck a soft smile, I tear my eyes away from him as Hawk and I continue pushing our way through the partygoers. Hawk is stopped several times by men who shake his hand and look keen to engage him in conversation before he politely blows them off, and all the women do is eye him up like a piece of meat, quickly dismissing me. Currently, I'm a nobody to them. I can't do anything that would benefit them, so in their eyes, I'm not worthy of their precious time.

Spotting our parents—*cringe*—we make our way toward them. Maria Davenport notices us first, her shoulders sagging in relief as she waves us over, scowling at Hawk.

"There you are," she chastises. "It's about time you showed up." Barely sparing us a glance, she gains her husband's attention. "Barton, they're here. Let's get this started."

Get what started?

Before I can ask, Barton excuses himself from his conversation with some random old dude and nods his head at his wife, taking off toward the front of the room as Maria follows dutifully behind him.

Hawk tugs on my arm, indicating that we're to follow, and my legs become heavier with every step I take, until it feels like I'm trudging through marshland.

My hand squeezes Hawk's upper arm, my fingernails digging into his suit jacket. My grip is so tight I'm sure it must be painful, but he doesn't shrug me off, his face impassive as we reach the front of the room.

Barton coughs loudly, tapping the side of his glass with a butterknife—*where the hell did he get that from?*—until the rest of the room quiets down, conversations coming to a halt as everyone turns to look at him. At us.

"Thank you all for coming tonight," he begins when he's gotten everyone's attention. "We've gathered you all here to share some special news."

It would be impossible to tell from his blank expression—creepily similar to Hawk's—whether or not the 'special news' of the return of his long-lost daughter is good or bad. *Does he even give a shit that I'm alive and well?* He hasn't spared me a glance, never mind a kind word, so I've no idea.

"Fifteen years ago, our family was struck by a terrible tragedy," he says, pausing dramatically as a few people whisper and gasp in surprise. "Not many people know that when Hawk was born, Maria also gave birth to a baby girl. She was stolen from us, and although we have dedicated extensive resources in the hopes of finding her, we feared the worst."

What the fuck is this shit he's spouting?

I glance at Hawk out of the corner of my eye, giving him a 'what the fuck' look, which he returns with a roll of his eyes, clearly used to his parents spinning stories to suit their own agenda.

"Now, however, we are over the moon to have finally found her. Tonight, I'd like to introduce you to our daughter, Elizabeth Davenport."

They make it sound like *they* were the ones to find *me*, not the other way around. I don't, for one second, believe they've put any time or money into searching for me. I've been right under their fucking noses all these years, trapped inside the confines of their own goddamn organization.

Lawrence made sure to hide me away on the rare occasion the other benefactors—which I now know are our parents—came to the compound, but even so. Surely, I should have been easy enough to find?

My father holds out his arm, pointing me out to the gathered crowd, and suddenly all eyes are on me as whispers break out around the room. My cheeks stain red under their scrutiny, and I self-consciously press my shoulder against Hawk's, as if he can somehow hide me from these money-hungry gawkers eyeing me up as if I'm a weak link in the Davenport stronghold that they could manipulate their way through.

Men step forward to shake hands with Barton, congratulating him like he fucking achieved something.

"Come." Maria's sharp tone snaps my attention in her direction, where she's got a forced smile on her face. It's painfully fake, only further emphasizing this is all a sham and that there's no real happy family reunion in my future. "There are people we need to introduce you to."

As she strides forward, her eyes focused on whatever rich dickhead she feels the need to force on me, Hawk moves to follow after her, obviously more used to blindly obeying her orders at these things.

"Hawk, dear, you're not needed. Why don't you go mingle with the other guests."

Hawk's lips flatten, the only tell that he's not happy with that order, although he reluctantly nods his head before pinning me with a look. Basically, telling me with his eyes to behave.

What does he think I'm going to do? Cause a scene? I would never! It's just not in my nature to do such a thing.

I watch him disappear into the crowd before reluctantly chasing after Maria, nerves fluttering in my chest. She drags me around the party, introducing me to people whose names I immediately forget, but I've noticed a trend by the fifth introduction. All of the couples I've met have entitled-looking fuckers as sons, all of whom seem to be in and around my age.

As we walk away from yet another couple whose names I don't care to remember, I blurt out, "I have to go to the bathroom." I've had enough of being paraded around like I'm a new piece of art they've acquired. I can feel a headache forming behind my eyes, and I'm so beyond done with all the fake happy family bullshit for one night. If I have to hear this bitch tell one more person how fucking happy she is to have her daughter back home, even though she hasn't talked directly to me all night, except to order me around, I'm going to lose my ever-loving shit.

Her face tightens in disapproval, like I'm being rude, but what does she expect me to do? If I have to pee, I have to pee.

"Fine," she relents. "But hurry back. There's a lot of other people you have to meet tonight."

Yeah, that shit ain't happening.

Turning my back on her, I shove through the crowd, feeling everyone gawking at me as I go. I don't even know where the fuck I'm going; I just know I need to get out of here.

Hadley

CHAPTER FOUR

Mason must catch sight of the murderous look on my face as I push through the gawking crowd, desperate to get away from them all before I snap and do something I'll regret. Like a fucking white knight, he comes striding toward me. "Follow me," he murmurs quietly before taking off again, leaving me confused as I trail after him.

He walks purposefully through several rooms filled with guests, his stony expression enough to deter anyone who appears as though they're about to approach him, until we reach a door that leads outside. Once we're alone, he slows down, waiting for me to catch up.

"You looked like you needed a break."

"Yeah, you could say that. I don't know what I expected, but this was not it. I'm pretty sure my mother was just trying to pimp me out."

"Oh yeah." He chuckles, like it's no big deal. "I guarantee you she was."

My face scrunches. Having him confirm my suspicions only makes me feel worse. Nothing about tonight was designed to reunite us as a family or get to know me. It was all a publicity stunt, so they could turn my arrival into something they could use to elevate themselves.

"Where are we going?" I ask, changing the subject before I can get myself even more worked up about the whole thing. I'm not even sure if I'm hurt, disappointed, or just pissed-off. A mixture of all three, probably.

"The pool house. It's where we go when we need a break from everything in there," he explains, gesturing toward the party we left behind.

Circling the side of the house, we skirt around a large pool before coming upon the pool house. The door is unlocked, and we let ourselves in. Mason flicks on a lamp that provides a dim glow, showing a large room with a wide-screen TV, several sofas and chairs, and a small kitchenette.

The place is empty, and Mason pulls me toward the nearest sofa, dropping onto it and dragging me onto his lap.

"Don't let them get to you. It's the same with all of our families. Everything is about presentation. It's all a show for other people. None of them give a fuck about us beyond what they can use us for."

"What is it they want?"

"Dutiful children who will continue their legacy and marry into the right families, thereby boosting their status and financial earnings," he cites off, as though someone has repeatedly explained to him his purpose in life.

His eyes meet mine, the trapped look in them flooring me. "They'll do anything to ensure they get what they want. Remember that."

I watch him closely, noticing the shadows clinging to him in much the same way they did when I saw him with his father at Hawk's birthday party. Something about being in that man's presence brings Mason's darkness to the surface, and seeing him so depressed doesn't sit well with me. He's always quiet and subdued, his features carefully kept blank when he's around others, but the world is missing out on a whole other side to Mason Hayes. Despite whatever abuse he's experienced in the past, he's got a big heart and a wickedly dry sense of humor.

Wanting to help quiet his demons, I run my fingers through his dark hair, brushing the strands back from his face. "It was your parents, right?" I don't need to elaborate any more than that. His eyes are shrouded in misery as his hold tightens around me.

"Yeah, Little Warrior." His words are a soft sigh filled with sadness.

I lean against his chest, breathing him in and hoping my presence can lift some of his emotional baggage. "Parents aren't supposed to treat their kids that way." It baffles me how people can do that to their own flesh and blood. How can anyone be so callous? I would make sure my kids knew they were loved and cherished every moment of every day. I'd go to the ends of the earth to protect them and personally castrate anyone who so much as thought about causing them harm.

"No, they aren't, but who's going to stop them?"

His dejected tone has anger burning in my gut. How dare his parents try to destroy this giant marshmallow of a man.

Vengeance has flowed through my veins for so long now. It's an integral part of who I am. For years, my goal has been to get back at the people who have wronged me, the people that killed the only friend I had growing up. Mason's parents, as are all of ours, have since been added to that list, but seeing how much they tried to beat down their son and turn him into what *they* wanted, has me fighting the urge to track them down and eviscerate them.

We sit in silence for a moment, each of us lost in our own thoughts.

"I used to pretend I had a family out there," I tell him, my words barely audible. "Parents who wanted me, who missed me, whose lives had been completely upturned in their search to find me. I used to picture how it would all unfold if we were reunited. It definitely wasn't anything like the reality is turning out to be."

Mason's eyes roam over my face, and I wish I knew what he was thinking when he looks at me so intently, as if he's trying to read everything there is to know about me.

"Where were you all these years? We know you weren't in foster care. West checked into the fake background you gave the school, and he couldn't find anything about you. It's like you didn't exist until you showed up at Pac."

"I didn't." At least, that's how it feels. My life didn't begin until I got my fake ID and escaped the compound. "I was trapped in my own personal hell, and I didn't know how to escape it. I didn't think I could. Only when I learned about Cam did I feel like I had the power to fight back against Lawrence. Against all of them."

Finding out about Cam changed everything. I was falling down a dark hole of accepting my bleak fate, unable to see any way out of my cemented future. Before that day, I knew nothing about Lawrence. Not his name, who he was, or what he had to do with the mercenary organization I had somehow become a part of. Knowing that little thing about him gave me the strength to stop accepting the shitty hand I'd been dealt in life. All of a sudden, I didn't feel so helpless. It wasn't much to work with, but it was more than I'd known before, and I was desperate to find out everything I could about Cam and his family.

HIS EYES EAT *me up as they slowly climb up my slim frame. He always gets a carnal look in his eyes when he sees me dressed up in whatever outfit he brought—usually some sort of form-fitting dress that highlights my newly developed curves and pushes up my perky breasts.*

"Perfect," he breathes. "You can always wear clothes like this when you come to live with me. Won't that be nice?"

"Yes, Sir."

I've learned by now that there's no point in arguing with him. It's best if I grin and bear his visits, nodding and agreeing with whatever he says.

As he tucks my hair behind my shoulder, his cell phone goes off in his pocket, making him frown. The call rings out before starting up again, and he tugs harshly on a strand of my hair as agitation gets the better of him.

Huffing out a breath, he digs his hand into his pocket, retrieving his phone and moving to the corner of the room, getting as far away from me as possible so he can gain some modicum of privacy before answering the call.

"Yes," he hisses, the blatant rage more than obvious.

Great, I'm going to be the one that pays for this intrusion with brand-new bruises on my body.

I slowly edge toward him, intent on overhearing his conversation.

"Now isn't a good time...Yes, I understand my son has been acting out."

My eyebrows lift in surprise. He has a son? He's been coming to see me my whole life, and I know absolutely nothing about him. I don't even know his fucking name. He's always insisted on me calling him 'Sir,' and he's never divulged anything about who he is. I stupidly assumed he didn't have any family. But a son? That could be useful to know. A possible weakness I could use against him.

I've been trained to identify people's weak spots and to poke and prod at them until they become gaping holes. The problem is, Sir has never given me anything to work with...until now.

"Fine," he snarls, after whoever is on the other end of the line has droned on for several moments regarding whatever new issue there is with his son. "I'll speak to Cam. No, I don't think a meeting with the headmaster is necessary."

Now I have a name. It's not much, but it's a hell of a lot more than I had this morning.

Another moment passes where he fumes at whatever the person on the other end is saying. He repeatedly glances my way, as though expecting me to disappear or jump him—I fucking wish I could, but fear freezes me in place every time I so much as think about taking him on.

"Listen here," he growls, furious at whatever is being said to him. Based on his tone alone, I know I'm in for a rough afternoon of slaps and degrading comments as he takes his anger out on me, but right now, I don't care. I'll take anything he throws at me if it means I can finally learn

something I could use against him. "You seem to have forgotten who you're talking to. My family is one of the founding families of Pacific Prep. My son can do whatever the hell he wants. He answers to me, and me alone. If you have a problem with that, I'm sure Mr. Phister will happily help you find an alternative place of employment."

He hangs up the phone before whoever is on the other end can respond, spinning in his overpriced loafers to face me. His nostrils flare as he grits his teeth, anger consuming him. I hate when he's like this. He's truly terrifying. Completely demonic looking.

"What are you doing just standing there?" he snarls, startling me into action.

"S...Sorry." I lick my lips nervously as I fumble with my hands, frantically trying to stop them from trembling. "C...Can I get you anything?" I ask. "Perhaps a drink?"

Normally, if I'm not training, I'm in my room. Except, on visitation days, I'm brought here to this room with a bed in the corner, a small living area, and a kitchenette. I have no idea how to cook—not that Sir seems to mind. He loves it when I offer to make him a drink. I don't understand why, but right now I'd do pretty much anything to tamper down the rage inside of him and ease the onslaught of abuse I know is coming my way.

I've barely gotten the words out before he's striding toward me, quickly closing the distance between us until his chest is pushing up against mine. His hand wraps around my hair and he yanks it back, so my neck is bent at an awkward angle.

"Do you think a drink is going to solve my problems?" He's so close, spittle hits my cheek as he yells at me.

His eyes drop down my body, hovering over my heaving chest. With how he's stretched my neck, my back is arched, pushing my boobs out in an inviting gesture.

He growls as he grits his teeth, the grip on my hair tightening to the point of pain, and I bite the inside of my cheek to hold in my whimper.

"There's only one thing that would make this better, and your worthless ass can't give it to me until everything's in place."

Tugging on my hair, he throws me across the room, and I go crashing to the ground, not understanding what he's talking about. Honestly, the intent behind his words is crystal clear, and whatever the reason he may be holding back, I don't give a fuck, so long as it keeps him away from me.

THAT CONVERSATION CHANGED EVERYTHING. Cam has no idea, but he saved my life that day. I don't know what he did to instigate that phone call, but regardless of what happens between us, I'll be forever grateful to him.

"Hey, where did you go just now?" Mason asks. I hadn't realized how closely he was watching me. His eyes are filled with concern, and I quickly shake away the thoughts of the past. Lawrence is still an ever-present threat, but I have so much more to fight for now. I'm no longer trapped and, more importantly, I'm no longer alone.

I press my lips to his in what I intend to be a chaste kiss, a thank you for being here. I don't know how temporary what I have with him and West is, but for the time being, I'm glad to have the two of them in my corner.

He responds immediately, his hand resting on the back of my neck and holding me to him as he deepens the kiss, both of us getting lost in the taste of one another.

As heat spirals in my lower belly, I shift in his lap, hiking up my dress as I straddle him.

Now, this is a much better way to spend the night.

His hands slide up my thighs, and he groans as I grind against his growing erection.

Trailing my hands over his shirt until I reach his belt buckle, I deftly undo it and lower his zipper, reaching into his boxers. I wrap my hand around his thick girth, testing the weight of him in my palm. I need to feel him inside me...now. I sit up on my knees, hovering above him as he pushes my panties to the side, and I don't waste any time lowering myself onto him, my head falling back as he easily slides inside, filling me to the brim.

We're both breathing heavily as he fully seats himself, and I look deep into his eyes, the connection between us stronger than ever as the air crackles around us. My pussy clenches with desperate need and he grunts in pleasure as I rock shallowly against him.

The squeaking of the pool house door has me freezing as I tear my gaze away from Mason's blissed-out expression to find West standing in the doorway, his pupils dilated at finding us fucking.

"Don't mind me," he purrs huskily, moving to lean against the wall, obviously intending to watch us. *Fuck, why does the thought of that make my pussy spasm?* Mason groans again as I practically strangle his dick, and his hands move to grip my hips, holding me still as he thrusts into me, setting a faster pace. I moan, my eyes drifting shut as he hits that perfect spot deep inside me.

I don't even hear *him* approaching, but in the next second, I feel a tug on my hair as my head is pulled backward and my eyes snap open, staring up into West's lust-hazed green ones.

"Don't close your eyes," he growls, his rough voice coated with sinful promises, only making me wetter.

He releases his hold on my hair, moving to undo the zip at the back of my dress until he can push it down my arms, exposing my breasts. The fabric of the dress made it impossible to wear a bra with it, and my nipples peak as the cool air hits them.

Mason leans forward to suck one into his mouth as West's hand once again entangles itself in my hair, pulling until my head is bent back and I'm looking up at him. The angle has me pushing my tit further into Mason's mouth, my back arching. Mason's dick slides impossibly deeper as my lips part, and a wanton moan escapes me.

I keep my eyes glued to West as Mason picks up his pace, rapidly sending me toward the edge as he palms a tit in one hand while sucking and biting on the other.

My face is flushed as Mason thrusts frantically, every pant a breathy moan. I'm so lost in my pleasure that I don't hear the door opening and someone new arriving to the party.

West obviously hears it, though, as his eyes snap up to see who entered. Mason doesn't stop his relentless pounding, and I try to turn my head to look at the newcomer, but West's grip tightens, keeping me in place for a second before he uses his firm hold to turn my head. I see Cam standing slack-jawed in the doorway, seeming both unsure and turned-on.

My eyes drop to his crotch, taking in the noticeable bulge, and *fuck me*. Even though we agreed to just be friends, the way he's looking at me, and the dirty thoughts I'm having about him joining in, are anything but friendly.

My pussy spasms as I picture him closing the distance and slamming his lips against mine—oh, how I've missed the taste of him—and Mason groans.

"Fuck, baby, I'm gonna blow if you keep doing that."

Cam stares transfixed at the three of us, frozen in the doorway.

"Well, are you in or out?" West barks impatiently.

Cam's eyes widen in surprise, not having expected the invitation, his gaze bouncing between all three of us—not that Mason is paying him any attention as he licks along the column of my neck, rolling my nipple between his fingers as I buck against him. Between his magical dick, hot mouth, and talented fingers; plus West's controlling nature, and feeling Cam's eyes on me, I'm about to combust.

"I..."

Even though I know what his answer will be, I'm still wracked with disappointment as he shakes his head.

He doesn't get a chance to turn me down with words since Hawk chooses that moment to storm into the pool house next—*great, now it's really a fucking party*—his eyes widening to the size of saucers at what he sees.

"What the fuck?" he roars, slamming his hand over his eyes and quickly turning around. "Someone tell me I didn't see what I think I saw," he growls furiously.

I try to climb off Mason's lap, but West is still holding tight to my hair, and as I attempt to move, Mason's hands grip my hips, cementing me in place so he can continue slamming into me, unfazed by Hawk's presence.

"Get out if you don't want to see it." His words come out in an angry tone. However the breathless quality as he maintains his relentless pace, not sparing Hawk a second glance, shows where all of his focus is right now.

Mason circles his hips, causing him to grind against my clit, and my eyes fall closed as I bite my lip to hold back a moan. Fairly certain Hawk won't appreciate that.

Hawk's voice is nothing but background noise as he rants before stomping out, and when I crack open an eyelid, both he and Cam are gone.

West directs my head so I'm looking up at him standing behind me.

"Forget about him," he says softly, referring to Cam, before he seals his lips to mine in an all-consuming kiss.

Mason's fingers move to rub my clit, and that light touch is the final straw as I come apart on his dick, crying out my release while staring into West's lustful gaze. I feel Mason swell within me after another couple of thrusts, his seed hitting my inner walls.

"So beautiful," West murmurs, his lips brushing over mine.

Knowing it won't be long before someone other than one of the guys comes searching for us, we quickly clean up and redress, reluctantly heading back to the party.

West and Mason disappear into the crowd, leaving me alone as I do a loop around the room, smiling politely at people before hurrying off through the crowd in a vain attempt to avoid getting dragged into any unwanted conversations.

I can't find my mother, which suits me perfectly fine, though I do catch sight of Lawrence at the far end of the room. His eyes are trailing my every move like laser beams, making my skin itch with the intensity of his gaze.

Shivering, I move as far away from him as possible, ensuring enough people are between us that he can't see me as I head to the bar, ordering a coke with ice. I sit and watch the party going on around me, picking out each of the guys, all of whom are stuck in various conversations appearing as bored as I feel. As I sip on my drink, I can feel everyone's lingering stares on me, hear the whispers behind their hands as they speculate about where I've been all these years.

I'm only halfway through my drink when I cannot take it any longer. Staying in one place is the worst thing I can do. It's better if I'm constantly circulating through the crowd. At least that way, I won't feel the eyes on me as much.

Getting to my feet, I push through the gawking herd, already needing another break from all this bullshit. Just when I think things couldn't get any worse, Bianca steps up to me, an ugly scowl on her face. "Don't think just because your surname happens to be Davenport that you're no longer trash," she sneers. "Someone like you isn't worthy of such a name."

"And you are?" I laugh coldly.

She frowns. "You don't deserve it," she whines, like the entitled bitch she is. "I've been doing everything the Princes want for *years*, and you just waltz in here and get handed everything I've worked for? It's not fair!"

I'm surprised she doesn't stamp her feet like a two-year-old having a fucking tantrum.

"*Life* isn't fair," I snap, getting irritated. She thinks just because she bent over and swallowed their dicks when demanded that she *deserves* to be given one of their surnames?

I tilt my head slightly, thinking. "You're a self-centered bitch, and I think it's past time someone reminded you of your place." An evil smile plays at the corner of my lips as I step in close to her, my heels putting us at eye-to-eye level. "I've wanted to slap that pretentious fucking look off your face since the first day we met," I tell her quietly enough so that no one nearby can overhear us. Her eyes widen. *Is she seriously surprised at my admission?* "And now I have the immunity to do it." She gulps, and I'm sure her face has paled, not that you can see it under her layers of makeup. "I may be trash, but I'm trash that can do whatever the fuck she wants," I say sweetly, a broad grin on my face that I'm sure looks maniacal.

Oh yeah. I think I might have found a silver lining to this whole Davenport name bullshit.

~

IT'S LATER THAT NIGHT, and I'm contemplating the appeal of alcohol—God knows you need something to drown out the boring as fuck conversations—when I recognize West's father as he comes hobbling toward me, his pudgy belly straining the buttons of his shirt. His cheeks are ruddy from too much alcohol and sweat clings to his temples.

"Elizabeth, it's so great to meet you. I'm Wilbert, Westley's father." His words make me think he doesn't remember meeting me before. Of course, I was only his son's whore that night, so why would he?

"You're quite a beautiful young lady, aren't you?" I don't miss the way his gaze heats as it lingers on my tits. *What is with all these rich assholes being sleazy perverts?*

He licks his lips with no zero shame, and subtly adjusts himself in his pants. *Fucking gross.* It takes everything in me not to wrinkle my nose in disgust, not that his gaze ever ventures further north than my chest, as he continues with his conversation.

"The day you disappeared was a somber day indeed," he goes on, nodding his head in agreement with himself. "We were all distraught."

Yes, it sure seems that way.

"What happened?" I ask, deciding I may as well try and get some information out of him. I'm hoping the alcohol I can smell on his breath might loosen his lips enough to let slip something that could be of use.

"Oh, I couldn't say." Wrinkles form across his forehead as his eyebrows draw together and he frowns. "It was a long time ago."

"Of course," I agree readily. "But it must have come as a shock that someone could get onto your well-secured property here and steal one of your own children."

His eyes bulge. "Oh yes, we were all very shocked." He looks like a bobblehead as he nods vigorously. "Took us all quite by surprise." He lifts a handkerchief out of his pocket, dabbing at the sweat along his hairline.

"And you never found out who did it?"

"Oh, well, you know how it is. The trail ran cold and all that."

Yes, I'm sure the trail did run cold when you didn't put any resources into following it.

"You truly are quite stunning," he repeats, his gaze once again falling back to my tits. It's not like they're even pushed up or falling out of my dress. There isn't an inch of skin on display, yet he can't stop fucking gaping at them like he's never seen boobs before in his life.

I notice Beck in the crowd and silently beg him with my eyes to come save me from his father. Because he's a fucking godsend, he switches directions, coming toward me.

"Ah, this is my other son," West's father explains, spotting him. "He's actually a counselor at your school."

"Nice to meet you." Acting as though we're complete strangers, Beck's tone is nothing but polite as he holds his hand out for me to shake.

"Likewise." I smile innocently up at him as I slip my palm into his, and his hand squeezes mine, holding it for a second longer than is socially appropriate before letting it go.

Mr. Warren flicks his gaze between us. "Maybe you two know each other?"

"I don't think so," I respond, giving Beck a once-over as though I'm trying to work out if I recognize him from around campus, when in reality, I'm picturing stripping him out of that suit.

"I think I'd remember someone like you." The seductive undertones in Beck's baritone voice have goosebumps pebbling on my skin. Heat flares in his eyes, and he runs his hand slowly down the length of his tie, drawing my attention to it. My panties grow damp as I remember how, the last time he wore it, he stuffed it in my mouth to silence my cries while he hammered into my dripping wet pussy.

His pupils seem to dilate, a dirty smirk flitting along his lips as similar dirty thoughts likely dance through his head.

His father chuckles, clapping his son on the shoulder, not noticing the dark scowl Beck fires his way.

"She's a pretty piece, isn't she?" he expresses to Beck, like I'm some sort of fucking possession and not a human being standing right here listening to him. Utterly unaware of the ticking of my jaw or the clenching of Beck's fists, the arrogant dickwad keeps talking. "Beck here only recently came into the fold himself. I didn't even know I had another son until last year." The idiot chuckles, lying through his teeth. "But he's been a great addition to our family and has been instrumental in increasing the efficiency of our business."

My eyebrows rise in a silent question as I sear Beck with my probing gaze. *What the fuck does his father mean by that?*

"Is that so?" Beck's lips pinch and his father rattles on, oblivious to the silent conversation going on between us.

"Oh, yes. He's been very helpful, but my apologies. It's rude to talk business at a party." He laughs.

I give him a tight smile.

"If you'll excuse me, I should be finding my parents," I tell him politely—look at me acting like a fucking Davenport—not waiting for an answer before taking off, storming out of the hall as questions swirl around my head.

I fucking knew Beck was keeping secrets!

Knowing what I do about our parents' company, whatever they have Beck doing is bad. Seriously. Fucking. Bad. The fact that his dad singled him out instead of saying he *and West* have been helping only confirms my suspicions that Beck has been more involved than the other guys.

Storming outside, I can hear Beck's heavy footsteps smacking against the ground as he chases after me. When he catches up to me, his large palm wraps around my forearm, and he uses his grip on my arm to drag me toward his parked car, his free hand yanking open the passenger door with more force than necessary.

"Get in," he snarls between gritted teeth, pushing me forward and giving me no choice. Doesn't he know I want fucking answers from him? He doesn't need to drag me. *Stupid fucking testosterone-fueled male.*

My ass has barely hit the nylon seat before he slams my door shut, stomping around to the driver's side and climbing in. His car is nothing like Hawk's. It's old and rusted, with the dash scored, the seats worn, and the odd tear here and there. The engine sputters for a second before starting, and Beck takes off, the two of us sitting in silence as we drive to god knows where. All I know is that it's not back toward the school.

"What do they have you doing?" I demand when I can no longer keep my questions to myself, regarding him out of the corner of my eye.

His hand on the steering wheel tightens while he irritably runs his other one over the coarse hairs of his short stubble. His jaw is clenched and the stubborn asshole shakes his head, refusing to answer me.

"Fine," I seethe, throwing my hands in the air in exasperation. "How about I guess, and you just let me know when I get it right."

There's only one reason I can think of why his dad sought him out and dragged him into all this bullshit, and the thought makes my blood boil. My vision blurs red as the urge to demand Beck turn this car around so I can go back and slice his father open from sternum to groin rides me hard.

I sigh, yet again knowing I will have to give up more of myself by talking about this. Talking about Lawrence was one thing. What he did…that was something that was done *to* me. Other than making me look like a victim—something I seriously hate thinking of myself as—it was unlikely to negatively affect how Beck, or anyone else, would look at me. But this…*this* is who I am. Once Beck knows this, it will change everything. He'll never look at me the same, and who could blame him?

I keep my gaze fixed firmly on the inky blackness out the window. It seems fitting that we're shrouded in darkness as I spill my secrets for the first time. Akin to splitting open my skin and showing him how black my blood runs, he's about to get a glimpse of how demoralized I really am.

"They have you psychoanalyzing the kids, right? Helping to pick recruits and turn them into mindless soldiers." My voice is hollow, my heart cracking as I accept how deeply Beck has been dragged into all of this. My chest constricts as I think about what fresh hell the new kids these sickos find have to go through. Isn't what they're doing bad enough? Why do they need to find new and inventive ways to strip the soul from these innocent children too?

Another moment of silence, this one fraught with tension, the weight of our topic of conversation suffocating.

Beck pulls over to the side of the road, slowing the car to a stop, and the two of us stare out the windshield, seeing nothing in the darkness. We're in the middle of nowhere, surrounded by woodland and fields.

Eventually, he turns to look at me, letting his eyes roam over what he can see of my face before he asks, "How do you know about that?" His deflated, pained tone makes me suspect he already has an idea of the answer. As I turn to meet his gaze, I can see the pleading in his eyes, begging me to refute it.

Dropping the last of my barriers so he can see into every dark crevice I keep carefully hidden, I stare back at him, revealing to him every little bit of my suffering. I show him every strip of humanity they took from me every time they tore my skin open and tried to break me. I allow him to see how much every death affected me, even if I was murdering people just as corrupt and devious as our parents. I let him see how much it killed me to stand back and watch while they punished and tortured other children, some of whom were no older than five or six.

When he's seen all he can bear to see, he tears his gaze from mine, staring unseeingly out the windshield as he shakes his head in denial.

"Don't," he pleads.

But I've come this far.

I *have* to say it.

"Because I was one of those kids." It's barely more than a whisper, but in the silent car, the words are akin to a gunshot, confirming his worst fears.

Sweetheart

CHAPTER FIVE

Because I was one of those kids.
Those words echo around in my brain, giving me a headache that beats a steady drum against my skull.

I have so many questions.

How did she end up there? Why? How did I not notice or put it together?

Everything suddenly made so much sense as soon as she uttered the words. The scars, her closed-off behavior, her insane fighting skills, and how she so easily killed that mercenary. After the blitz attack at Christmas, I *know* how well-trained they are. They're fucking machines. The five of us were struggling to fight off two of them, so I didn't much like my odds in a one-on-one battle.

Yet I thought she got fucking lucky getting the better of one of them? I snort just thinking about it. There was nothing lucky about it.

The truth of her words sits heavy in the air between us, strangling any sort of conversation. I don't even know what the fuck to say to that. I'm professionally fucking trained to deal with people who have been through fucked-up shit, but this is next level. It's not like there was a class that taught me the appropriate way to respond when the girl I'm falling in love with tells me she's a trained mercenary.

Thankfully, I'm saved from having to think of a reply when Hadley keeps talking. Focusing on her, her eyes are cloudy and her face is withdrawn as the memories hold her hostage.

"Lawrence didn't want me to learn to fight like the other kids, but the guys in charge of us didn't share his opinions. When he wasn't around, I was thrown in the ring and treated to the same grueling training as everyone else. They would work us until our legs couldn't hold us up and we were puking our guts out. Anyone who couldn't hack it was made an example of."

Her expression darkens, and there's so much sorrow in her eyes that I don't know how she doesn't drown in it.

"They were never short of cruel and inventive ways to torture us. Beatings, food and sleep deprivation, preying on our fears."

She shudders, withdrawing further into herself. I want to reach across the short distance between us and drag her into my lap, but I sense she wouldn't respond well to that. It's clear she was seriously deprived of gentle touch growing up, and wherever she is in her memories right now, I fear any physical contact would only trigger her further.

"The normal fears any kid would have. They would lock me in the dark, alone, for what felt like days. I hated it." Her voice breaks and tears start to leak out of her eyes. "It was their punishment of choice, especially when we were getting close to another visit from Lawrence. He didn't like when they touched me, although he was always in agreement with their methods to keep me in line in his absence, so long as the scars didn't show." She snarls out the last sentence, anger burning away the despair in her features as her hands form tight fists.

"After Meena died, I stopped fighting. I was never getting out of there, so what was the point? I became what all of them wanted. A soldier. A fighter. A doll." A caustic, unhinged laugh breaks free, and she shakes her head. "The funny thing is I became an asset to them. One of the best fighters they had. Rather than putting all my energy into fighting them, I became one of them. But I couldn't switch off my humanity the same way the others did.

"Every death stuck with me—even if it was deserved. We were hired by bad people to torture and kill other bad people." Sighing, she shakes her head again. "I didn't want to. Every time I did, I could feel a part of myself revolting, screaming at me to stop. But I was too far gone. Too lost inside myself to do anything except blindly follow their commands."

She lapses into silence, and when it doesn't look like she's going to tell me any more, I ask softly, "What happened?"

Lifting her gaze, she looks at me through watery eyes. "Cam did. Lawrence had been talking more and more about me coming to live with him. I'd shut down years ago. I was a mere shell of myself, yet I knew whatever he had planned for my future would destroy the last thread of who I am. I...I would have done anything to avoid that."

I don't like the way she's talking, and it only makes me more furious at Lawrence for the pain he's inflicted. As though stealing her from her home—because there's no way he wasn't involved—and hiding her in his own company, away from the rest of society, guaranteeing she was isolated and alone wasn't enough. He had also to destroy any hope she could have for a future by ensuring she would forever remain chained to him.

I can feel my blood boiling as it pounds through my veins, demanding vengeance. Every single one of those sick fucks is going to pay for what Hadley has had to endure. I'll rip their fucking heads off myself.

As the adrenaline pumps through my body, anger swelling like a tsunami within me, I throw open the car door, barely getting my seatbelt unclipped before I launch myself from the vehicle. The cool night air does nothing to calm the raging inferno as I walk away from the car, wishing the darkness would just suck me up and expunge my brain of the last fifteen minutes. Knowing what Lawrence had put her through was bad enough, but this...*I* don't even know how to handle this.

I faintly register the car door opening somewhere behind me and before I've given more than a passing thought to the action, I'm striding back toward the car. Hadley is perched on the hood appearing like an angel of darkness in her long dark gown that stands out in such contrast against her alabaster skin as she watches me approach, her face unreadable.

I open my mouth to say something—what I was going to say, I haven't the faintest clue—but Hadley beats me to it.

She peers up at me with vulnerability shimmering in her eyes. Nonetheless, she juts out her chin, righting her armor, and preparing for battle. Although I have no idea what war she thinks she has with me.

"If this changes things between us, I understand."

Her words grind me to a halt as I stare at her in confusion. When I don't say anything, she swallows—the only tell showing she's nervous—and continues speaking.

"I'd get it if, you know, you didn't want to be together now. Knowing what you know. It's a lot to take in, and well, you didn't know what you were signing on for when we agreed to try this dating thing. So, yeah, I, uh, would understand...I guess."

She's rambling, and it would be cute—laughable, really—if it wasn't for the heaviness of her honesty sitting like a lead balloon in the air between us. Unable to go another second without feeling her in my arms, I reach out and wrap my hand around her wrist to tug her toward me.

I sink my other hand into her soft, luscious curls, crushing my lips against hers and swallowing her gasp of surprise as I drown in the taste of her.

She thinks this could change things between us? She's so fucking wrong. It only makes me want her more. Not only is her strength awe-inspiring, but I want to be the one to show her what love is. I want to be the one to hold her when she has a nightmare, to bring a smile to her face on rainy days, to bask in the light that is Hadley Parker when she laughs. Most importantly, I want to be at her side when she gets the justice she deserves. I'll ride into battle with her, bleed every fucker out, and when we're done, we'll burn that motherfucking compound to the ground.

Her small hands fist my shirt, pulling me impossibly closer as our tongues clash like weapons, our kiss ferocious and hungry. I could never get enough of this. Of her.

Pulling back just enough to break the kiss but also so I can still feel her breathless pants against my lips, I stare into her turbulent gray-blue eyes. They're chaotic, churning with so much emotion, and her pupils are dilated as she stares back at me. I'm seeing all of her for the first time—every little part. She's got nothing left to hide. For me, she has peeled back all the layers she usually keeps carefully hidden, revealing all the grim parts of herself that she never allows anyone to see.

I stare deep into her eyes, feeling as though I'm seeing into her very soul. "I love you. There's nothing you could say or do to make me change my mind."

Her eyes widen in surprise, her features softening even though she looks unsure, like she doesn't believe what I'm saying. I get the impression she's never heard those three words before, and why would she? She didn't have anyone to tell her, to *show* her what love was.

After a moment's hesitation, she tightens her hold on my shirt, yanking me toward her, her lips closing over mine. Her kiss is scorching and my body comes alive, acknowledging her touch. It's heated and desperate, but it's also a promise. As my tongue slides over hers, I can taste everything she feels but doesn't know how to put into words.

"I'm not sure I know what love is," she whispers softly, making my heart ache for her. "I've never experienced it before. I don't know what it feels like…but if there were ever someone I thought I could fall in love with, it would be you."

Cupping her cheeks in my hands, I kiss her harshly, taking as much from this moment as possible and burning it into my memory. Our time is running out. We'll have to head back to campus soon, and the second I tell her so, she'll re-erect her walls. I want to remember every second of this moment, when I had all of her.

Eventually ending the kiss, I rest my forehead against hers, committing to memory how fiercely beautiful she looks at this moment, before I murmur, "We should probably get back to campus."

Agreeing, the two of us head back to the car. As I open the door, I can hear my phone vibrating in its holder in the center console, and it goes off again as I start the engine. Sighing, I already suspect who is blowing up my phone as I lift it out. Yup, as expected, it's Hawk, wondering where we are. I fire off a quick reply, letting him know I'm taking Hadley back to campus. As soon as it's sent, a notification pops up saying it's been read, and dots appear at the bottom of the screen. *Great. He has more to say already.*

> Hawk: Drop her off at her door and meet us at our apartment.

Such a demanding asshole. I can understand why he grates on Hadley's nerves. She would deny it if asked, but as much as his bossy attitude annoys her, I think she secretly likes the fact that he cares enough to boss her around.

"Everything okay?"

"Yeah, fine. The guys are just checking in, wondering where you disappeared off to."

Ignoring Hawk's demand, I throw my phone back in its holder as Hadley rolls her eyes. Starting the engine, I laugh, and the two of us head back to campus.

We're halfway down the road when she says, "You never answered my question." Her detached tone tells me she's carefully tucked her heart away again and re-erected her walls, just like I knew she would.

I let out a long exhale. I'd been hoping to avoid discussing it, but I should have known she wouldn't let it slide.

"They have me going through profiles and telling them which kids I think could be molded into what they want and which ones won't hack it."

I glance briefly at Hadley, finding her jaw clenched tightly. Her leg bounces in irritation.

"How do you even know that?" she asks, a curious ring to her voice.

"I don't, really. For some of the older kids, I can look at their history. If the police have brought them in for fighting or assault or anything like that, but for the most part, it's just looking at how shitty their upbringing has been and trying to work out if that's enough to help them survive what our parents are going to do to them."

The way I say it, with no emotion in my voice, makes it sound so clinical. Over the last few months, I've managed to remove myself from the reality of what I'm doing. I've learned to set aside the wrongness of what's being asked of me when my father hands me those profiles every week and tells me to pick the best ones. The first few times, the guilt nearly ate me alive. I barely ate or slept for weeks. I *had* to learn to live with the fucked-up decisions I was being forced to make. It wasn't only my life that relied on it but West's too. He might not trust me—hell, he doesn't even know me—but where I come from, family matters. Whether it's the family you're born into or the one you make for yourself, it *means* something. A fuckton more than whatever 'family' means to the rich assholes here; they don't give a shit about anyone but themselves.

"They want me to go to the compound and start assessing them face to face," I say bleakly, noticing how Hadley tenses beside me. "I have to go. They'll hurt West if I don't."

I spare her a quick glance, and she nods her head sharply, understanding why I have to go, but I don't miss her tight expression as I return my gaze to the dark road in front of us. In fairness, we don't know for sure that they would hurt West. Maybe it's all a bluff, and they wouldn't really hurt one of their own kids. But is it a risk worth taking, testing them to see what they do? Hell no.

Driving onto campus, I park my car in the staff parking lot and walk Hadley to her dorm. Very few people are around. Most of them are probably still at that pointless party, and anyone left on campus has better things to do than lurking outside the dorms on a Saturday night.

"Lock your door when you get in."

She gives me a placating smile that's full of attitude. *Yeah, yeah, I know she can take care of herself. Doesn't mean I'm not going to worry, though.* Rolling my eyes, I gently push her back, nudging her toward the building.

"Get in there, you pest."

She chuckles, waving at me over her shoulder before disappearing behind the door.

When she's out of sight, I take off toward the guys' dorms, climb the stairs to the fourth floor, and knock on the door.

With a perpetual scowl gracing his face, Hawk answers. "You should have told one of us you were leaving," he snarks before I even enter their apartment. Seriously, what is so permanently lodged up his ass that he can't even give me a fucking hello before ripping into me?

"It wasn't exactly planned," I drawl dismissively as I walk past him into their open-plan living and kitchen area and spot the other three musketeers sprawled out across the sofas.

"What happened?" Hawk demands, gaining the attention of the others as their eyes pin me in place.

"Nothing. Our father was killing her with boredom," I respond calmly, looking at West. His features tighten, but I ignore him, turning back to glare at Hawk. "What the hell were your parents thinking, throwing her into that party tonight?"

"I think the better question is, what are *you* doing *for* our parents?" West snaps from behind me, making me spin to face him.

"What are you talking about?"

"We had a meeting with our parents today, and they so kindly informed us that you were already working for them. So what the hell have you been doing that you didn't think to tell us about?"

I grit my teeth. "I can't tell you."

West scoffs. "Of course not. That's not suspicious as fuck. How do we even know you're on our side? You could be a mole, reporting back everything we say and do."

"Seriously?" After all the shit I've had to do the last few months—shit that has slowly eaten away at my soul—all in order to keep his ungrateful ass alive, and he accuses me of this?

Before I know it, I've closed the distance between us. Wrapping my hand around the front of his shirt, he glowers back defiantly as I hiss at him, "Everything I've done has been to protect you. You have no fucking idea what I've had to do to keep you safe. To keep *you* alive."

Hesitation and confusion flicker across his face, but they're gone in an instant.

"I never asked you to do that," he bites back, infuriating me further.

"Why would you do that?" Mason asks, interrupting the stare-off between my brother and I.

"Because where I come from, family means something." I take a step back from West but keep my gaze on his. "You can be pissed at me all you want, but we *are* family, and that means something to me."

"What do you even know about family?" West sneers, even though there's a curious lilt to his voice, which is the only reason I don't fucking punch him.

"I lost the closest thing I've ever had to a sister and, not long after, my brothers. I've been mourning their loss every day for years, so don't tell me I don't know anything about family." The words are nothing more than a furious snarl, and I'm practically shouting by the time I'm done.

It shouldn't be this fucking difficult. After feeling alone for so long, I just wanted the opportunity to get to know West, to maybe find somewhere I belong. Since we have the same blood running through our veins, I wondered if he felt as lost and confused in this world as I do, but it's obvious he doesn't. Unlike me, he's managed to hold on to the family he built around him, and he's made it painfully clear he's not looking to add to it —not in the form of a brother, anyway.

Yet, the thought to cut and run, and leave him to stew in this fucked-up shit, never once crossed my mind. Maybe it's because I know I'd be leaving Hadley too, or perhaps it's the urge to protect West, no matter how big of an asshole he might be to me. He might not want me as a brother, but in my heart, he's always been mine. So regardless of whether or not he wants me here, I'm fucking staying.

The sound of the front door banging open has all of us turning to face the intruder, everyone on alert and ready to jump into action.

My eyes widen as I take in all nearly six feet of Hadley standing in the doorway, glowering at Hawk and the guys. She's changed out of her dress into a pair of short shorts and a loose t-shirt. Her hair is piled up on top of her head, with loose strands already falling out of it. She shouldn't look intimidating, but with the dark look on her face and the glint in her eye that is intended to deter anyone who so much as thinks of crossing her, she's pretty fucking scary looking. *Why do I find that such a fucking turn-on?*

Her abrupt and unexpected appearance breaks the tension in the air and, thankfully, stops any of these dickheads from asking me any more personal questions.

"What the—" Cam murmurs, gaping at her with hearts in his eyes. *Pathetic sap.* I give him a week before he realizes he can never just be friends with her and makes his move.

"What are you doing here?" Hawk barks.

"I saw Beck coming this way, and I know what you four idiots are like, always sticking together and ganging up on everyone. I figured if you were at least going to give him a hard time for not telling you we left, the least I could do is be here so he has someone on his side."

"We weren't—" Mason begins, earning a raised eyebrow from Hadley.

"How did you even get in here?" Hawk demands, ignoring her little speech. I have to say though, it feels kinda good that she came to back me up. Not that I give a shit what these assholes have to say, but still, it's been a long time since I had anyone in my corner.

She shrugs, giving him a quizzical look. "Who doesn't know how to pick a lock these days?"

Hawk grumbles under his breath, something about normal people not knowing how to do half the shit she can, except he's got no idea just how far from *normal* Hadley truly is. She's exceptional.

Rolling her eyes, she slams the door shut behind her, stalking across the space toward us with all the attitude in the world.

"Well, I guess since we're all here, we, uh, have some news," Hawk declares, looking reluctant to broach whatever he needs to discuss as he moves the conversation on to a new topic—*thank fuck*. He's rubbing the back of his neck and looking anywhere else but at Hadley. His behavior is making me nervous. *What the fuck could he have to tell us?*

Glancing at the other three, they look equally uncomfortable.

I feel Hadley's arm lightly brush against mine in a silent act of reassurance, likely having also picked up on the sudden tension in the room.

"Our parents want us to continue with the girl of the month tradition," Hawk blurts out quickly, similar to ripping off a Band-aid.

Hadley opens her mouth to protest, only Hawk speaks again before she can say anything.

"And they've insisted you take part as well."

Eh, what now? There's no way Hadley's about to publicly date some rich pompous fucker with a permanent hard-on. Hell no. Based on the various looks of disgust and anger on the other guys' faces, they agree.

There's a moment of silence while everyone waits with bated breaths—like the calm before the storm. You know shit's about to hit the fan, but you can't do anything but wait for it to come.

"What?" The word is a sharp bark, but her voice sounds slightly higher than usual. "You'll have to repeat that. I'm certain I heard you wrong 'cause there is *no fucking way* I'm going to stand up and pick one of those sorry sacks of shit to fake date."

She looks wholly revolted by the idea as she uses her fingers to make air quotes.

"We don't like the idea either," Mason assuages. "However they've already threatened West's life if we don't do as they say."

"Yeah, but that's for the business, right?" Hadley's eyes jump between the four of them. "They wouldn't kill him just because you refuse to date some girl at school."

The guys all look at one another, a silent communication occurring between them that Hadley nor I are privy to.

"Honestly, we don't know." Hawk sighs, running his hand through his short blond hair in irritation, mussing it up.

"I've been thinking about it," West musses, his brows furrowed in thought. "And I don't think they would. I'm their only bargaining chip. If they offed me, there wouldn't be anyone else to threaten all of you with."

"Maybe so, but that sounds like too big a risk to take." As much as I don't want Hadley having to act like a piece of arm candy to some rich prick or see her upset at having to watch the guys do the same, I equally don't want West to end up hurt or dead just because they decide to push the boundaries of what they can and cannot get away with.

"It's your decision, man," Mason says to West. "It's your life that's at stake. We'll all do whatever you want."

Hawk and Hadley both nod their heads in agreement, the movement strangely synced and oddly similar in a freaky twin way.

West's gaze focuses on Hadley, the two of them sharing some sort of moment before he reaches his hand out for her to take. Slipping her hand into his, he tugs her toward him so she's standing right in front of him.

"Fuck them," he states confidently, his eyes never leaving Hadley's face. "Let's run the school our way."

It takes a second, her eyes jumping back and forth between his, as though she's checking if he's sure about his decision. She must see the resolve in his eyes as a bright grin splits her face. His decision to go against our parents worries me. I have no idea what they might do in retaliation, but I can understand that none of them can continue doing our parents' bidding with this stupid tradition. Especially if Hadley is now going to be involved.

Wrapping her arms around his neck, she gives him a quick kiss before he spins her around in his arms, her back flush to his chest and his hands resting possessively on her hip and abdomen.

"Alright then," Hawk agrees. "Fuck them."

Hadley

CHAPTER SIX

"No." I shake my head, adamant I'm not letting Hawk browbeat me into doing what he wants. "I am not sitting at your table."

Hawk glowers at me, like I'm deliberately being difficult. "You have to."

"I don't *have* to do anything," I bite back.

"We have to present a united front. If everyone sees that we have accepted you into the fold, they will treat you with the same fear and respect they treat us."

"I don't care what any of those rich assholes have to say about me."

Hawk throws his hands up in exasperation. "You have no idea what it's going to be like. You're basically living every girl's fantasy right now, and the guys will be all over you, hoping you might be their meal ticket."

I scrunch my nose, but Hawk's words don't scare me.

"I can handle myself. I did kill a mercenary, after all," I snark with a devilish grin, making him roll his eyes.

"Yeah, by accident."

The smirk drops off my face, quickly replaced with a fierce glower as my hands clench into fists, and I hold back the urge to show him exactly what I'm capable of. It was no fucking accident—just like the other mercenary I killed.

"Have you forgotten I beat your ass without much effort?" My voice is sickly sweet, and I top it off with a deadly grin, making him scowl. Well, tough shit. It's something I'll happily hold over his head and taunt him with when he's being an asshole, which is pretty much all the time.

"It's the *Princes'* table," I argue. "Meaning it's only for boys. Obviously, no previous daughters of the founding families have been forced to sit there."

"That's because no daughters have ever come to Pac," he retorts.

"What?" I gape, surprised. "Why? Where do they go?"

"Some finishing school for girls." He shrugs. "Mason could tell you. His sister is at one."

"His what?" My head is spinning with all this new information. "Mason has a sister?"

"Yeah. She's a couple of years younger than us. I haven't seen her since we were kids. I'm pretty sure Mason's only seen her a handful of times."

"Doesn't she come home for the holidays?"

"Maybe for a bit over the summer."

What the hell? I have so many questions, yet it's clear from Hawk's vague responses that he's not going to be able to give me any actual answers.

"Are you going to be picking a girl this month?" I ask, moving on to a different topic. I know we discussed this last night, but there's really no reason for him—or Cam technically, but my stomach churns violently when I think about that—to not pick someone, and at least keep their parents happy. However, if he thinks I'm about to sit at that table and watch him make out with some tramp while I try to eat my breakfast, he's got another thing coming. It was nauseating enough having to witness it from across the hall.

"What do you mean?"

"I know Mason and West agreed not to pick girls anymore, but that doesn't mean you can't pick someone."

"None of us will be picking girls." He must see the surprise on my face as he explains, "We stand together. If one of us decides something, we all go along with it."

"I thought that just applied to bullying," I snide.

Yeah, I'm still a little pissy over that.

I don't understand that level of loyalty. Of just blindly following someone else's orders because you have such a tight bond with them. It makes no sense to me. I think it's beyond stupid how easily the others fell in line with Hawk just because he didn't like me. What the fuck was all of that about anyway?

He rolls his eyes. "It applies to everything. That's what loyalty is."

"Loyalty is all of you being total dicks because *you* decided for no reason you didn't like me?"

I can feel my blood heating at the reminders of what assholes they all were—Hawk refusing to give me a bottle of water, the others not standing up to him or telling him what an asshat he was being, the stupid fucking video he and Cam emailed to everyone, the *grapefruit*.

"It's having one another's backs," he retorts. "It's understanding that, no matter what, someone will always be on your side—even if you're wrong. It's knowing that you're not alone. When you grow up not being able to trust anyone, knowing you have three people who will support you in anything you decide…it makes life bearable."

A heavy silence falls between us, threaded with tension, although underneath it, there's a slither of similarity. We both grew up not being able to trust the people around us. Not knowing who we could rely on and who would only use us for their own gain. The difference is that Hawk never had to survive on his own.

"I wouldn't know." There's a heaviness in my voice as I wonder how different things might have been. "I didn't have anyone I could trust."

The anger bleeds out of his face, the tight lines smoothing until he's looking at me softly. What appears like regret flashes across his eyes, but it disappears so quickly I'm left wondering if I imagined it. It's most likely that I only saw what I wanted to see.

He sighs as he steps toward me, closing the distance between us. "I know I was an ass to you." *Understatement of the year.* "But things are different now."

"Because I'm your sister," I say, spelling it out. The thing is, I don't want things to be different just because I'm related to him. Maybe it's stupid, but I want him to actually *like* me. To *want* to be friends with me. I don't want him to just put up with me because we share the same DNA and the guys have forced him into it.

"I guess you're kinda growing on me," he grumbles with a small, barely there smile lifting one side of his lips. "Like unwanted mold."

I snort, breaking the tension between the two of us before his expression sobers once again.

"I'm serious, though. I'm sorry you've had to go through life alone, but that's not the case anymore. Whatever happens between you and the guys, I'll still be here for you."

Well, fuck me, this grumpy brother of mine might just have a heart, after all.

～

"So," I begin hesitantly, gnawing on my bottom lip. It's early evening, and I'm curled up on Emilia's bed with her. She's been nagging me all day to catch her up on the events at the party last night. Having just spilled all the very unexciting details, I'm now trying to broach the subject of me sitting at the Princes' table.

Yup, the fucking asshole suckered me into eating with them. The other three shitheads agreed with Hawk—of course—and I was totally outnumbered, with no actual argument for why I didn't want to sit at their table. Other than that, I just didn't want to.

Emilia looks at me impatiently with a quirked eyebrow.

"Ihavetostarteatingattheprincestable," I blurt out, the words all running into one another in my haste.

Her eyes widen as she tries to comprehend what I just said. "You, what?"

Grimacing, I repeat myself, "I have to start eating at the Princes' table for breakfast."

"Yeah, I figured you would," she remarks sadly before plastering on a smile.

"I'm sorry." I reach for her hand, giving it a squeeze. "I'd much rather sit with you than up there being gawked at."

Her smile turns genuine. "I know you would, except no girl in their right mind would turn down eating breakfast with all that hotness."

I can't help but laugh. She does have a point.

"Besides, we can eat lunch together on the days I'm not busy, right?"

"Definitely," I promise.

"And I'll still have Michael in the mornings."

"Crap. Michael. I should probably explain all of this to him before he finds out tomorrow, right?" My eyes widen as realization dawns. "He probably already knows. Most of the school was there last night."

Emilia shrugs. "He might not. The scholarship kids rarely listen to the school's gossip. It's up to you, in any case. You could tell him when we see him later."

We're meeting Michael tonight for our standard weekly movie night. Usually, we do it on Friday or Saturday, only things have been a little hectic the last few days, and I had to push it back. I guess tonight is as good a night as any to tell him.

Several hours later, the three of us are sprawled out in the movie theater with our popcorn while Emilia hums and haws over which movie she wants to watch. I don't know why it's such a big decision. She can always pick the other movie next time it's her night to decide—or, more likely, she'll sucker me into picking it on my night.

On the plus side, it gives me the perfect opportunity to broach the whole Davenport subject with Michael. Emilia is the only other person I've told, and I'm a nervous wreck as I try to find the words to tell him. It's strange because I didn't feel this way when I told Emilia. Sure, I was nervous, mainly because I didn't want to lose her again. However, with Michael, it feels different. I'm not sure why, though.

"Uh, Michael. Can we talk for a sec?"

He looks up from where he was typing on his phone beside me, and I notice Emilia giving me an encouraging smile from his other side before focusing back on her movie choices, trying to give us some semblance of privacy. We discussed it earlier, and she offered to sit out tonight if I wanted time to talk to Michael alone, but I feel more confident with her here. I worry I would have chickened out otherwise.

"Sure, what's up?"

Biting on my lower lip, I swallow around the lump in my throat before continuing, "So, some stuff is going to come out tomorrow about me, and I wanted you to hear it from me first."

"Okay," he says hesitantly, drawing out the word as he looks at me with wary confusion.

"Uh..." I fiddle with a strand of my hair, glancing away from him. "This is kind of difficult to say, and I only found out a few weeks ago, so I get it. I struggled to wrap my head around it too. Honestly, I'm still coming to terms with it all—"

"Hadley." His tone is sharp but soft, halting my rambling as he places a hand on mine. "Just spit it out."

"I'm a Davenport."

His eyes widen before his brows furrow, confusion evident in his brown irises.

"What?"

"I'm a Davenport," I repeat. "Hawk's my brother."

"I don't...How?"

I explain the craziness of the last few weeks to him, skipping over a lot of the details and leaving out anything that would raise red flags to the fact I'm dating two of the Princes—he definitely doesn't need to know that yet.

"Wow, that's insane," he mutters when I'm finished, still trying to wrap his head around everything I've told him.

"Yeah, you can say that again." I chuckle awkwardly.

"Is that why they've been nicer lately?" His brows furrow. "But they've been acting differently toward you all semester. How long have you all known?"

"Oh, well, the guys knew before they told me," I blurt. I don't know why I lie. I guess I don't want him to know I've known for two months and I'm only telling him now. We are supposed to be friends, after all, but there's no other explanation for the guys' behavior.

"And they had some making up to do after the shit they pulled last semester," Emilia tacks on helpfully.

Michael nods like that all makes sense, lapsing into silence as he mulls it all over.

"Okay, *The Princess Diaries*, it is," Emilia proclaims excitedly, having finally made her decision. I groan internally. *Great, another rom-com.*

∼

THE DINING HALL falls into a deathly hush as we walk in the next morning. Eyes follow us as we stride toward the Princes' table—can it still be called that now? Pretty much every asshole in here was at the party, and whispers have been running rampant all weekend, so even the other scholarship kids probably know who I am by now.

Reaching the table, I stand beside Hawk, with Mason on my left, Cam on the other side of him, and West at the far end of the table.

"I'm sure you've all heard by now," Hawk begins, his voice booming across the otherwise silent room as everyone clings to his every word. "Hadley is my long-lost sister, Elizabeth."

Just one more fucking thing I can't get used to. Apparently, the change of name is non-negotiable. The school has already updated its system, and everything now says 'Elizabeth Davenport'. I was even offered the top floor of the girls' dorm to do with as I please—an offer I quickly refused, to the shock of the admin woman who couldn't seem to understand why I would want to keep my room on the same floor as the scholarship girls.

"That means she's one of us. No one is to mess with her." He looks pointedly at Bianca, who is glaring daggers in my direction, steam practically pouring out of her ears as she vibrates with silent fury. I guess she's feeling more confident today, surrounded by her friends and peers. "Or they will deal with us."

Jeez, he makes it seem like I couldn't handle any of these pampered pricks myself, and I have to hold back an eye roll at his words. I swear, I roll my eyes so much at the shit that comes out of his mouth, they are going to stick to the back of my head one day soon.

I'm so not done with Bianca, though. After the abuse she has hurled my way all year, not to mention the shit she pulled at the Valentine's Day dance, making me doubt Hawk and the guys, she is in for some serious hurt this semester. The fact I'm practically invincible now has a smirk curling at the corners of my lips as I smile darkly at her, causing her eyes to widen a fraction. *That's right, bitch. You better sleep with one eye open 'cause I'm coming for you.*

"What about the girl of the month tradition?" someone calls out.

"Yeah, is she going to get to choose a guy?"

Whispers break out at that suggestion, and I have to force my facial expression to remain neutral, not giving away how unappealing that idea sounds. There isn't one sniveling idiot in this hellhole I'd willingly put up with for a whole month.

"No," Mason growls, glowering in the direction of whoever spoke up. Based on the guys' pissed-off expressions the other night, they didn't like the thought of me being included in their stupid tradition any more than I did. Still, we haven't had a chance to actually discuss it—it kind of seemed redundant since we've decided to fuck the whole tradition. However, Mason's sexy growling tone makes it obvious how much he hates the idea, and I press my lips together to restrain my smirk at his possessive nature. *What can I say, his jealousy makes me feel all sorts of sappy, girly feelings.*

"There will be no more girl of the month tradition," Hawk continues, speaking over the top of them and sparking an uproar of disagreement amongst the girls in the hall.

"Why?" someone shouts.

"This is ridiculous. You can't just ignore tradition," an angry voice calls out, and several others nod their heads in agreement before Hawk raises his hands.

"The decision is final," he barks, glowering at the crowd with steely eyes, daring anyone to question him. "Things are going to change around here." Whispers break out around the room as students share unsure looks with one another. "Everyone seems to have forgotten *we* are in charge. *We* are the Princes, and what we say is law."

As the warning bell goes off to tell everyone to hurry their asses up and get to class, his penetrating gaze roams around the hall, his cold expression enough to silence any other complaints.

"Get to class," Mason barks in a threatening tone that has everyone jumping into action.

The hall is a chaos of noise, students gossiping and complaining to one another, speculating about the turn of events as they get up from their tables and head to class.

"Well, that was fun. So glad you talked me into all of this," I grumble sarcastically, my attitude earning me an eye roll from Hawk, which I promptly ignore, focusing on Cam and Mason. "English?"

"You two go on. I'll catch up." Mason winks at me, and I can't tell if he's trying to give Cam and me some time alone or if he genuinely has something he needs to do before class. There's no denying that things have been tense between Cam and me lately. There's still none of his old flirty banter and easy conversation—which I miss terribly. Instead, everything feels stifled and awkward, but at least he's no longer avoiding me, so I guess there's that.

"Alright, we'll catch you later." Cam grabs his bag, and with a final wave at the others, we head out of the dining hall.

As we make our way to class, everything is a complete one-eighty to how it was last week. Girls I don't even recognize greet me by name—the wrong name, of course—and guys blatantly check me out, giving me flirtatious smirks as I walk past.

"What the hell?" I whisper to Cam. "What is happening right now?"

He snorts, shaking his head. "Welcome to the top of the food chain. Now everyone wants to be your best friend, or date you."

I scrunch my nose up. "No thanks."

"Hey, Elizabeth," some guy calls out as I reach the classroom door, giving me a typical dude chin-lift greeting as he walks past.

"Who the fuck is that?" I ask Cam, confused.

"One of the many leeches that will crawl out of the woodwork and attempt to stick themselves to you."

"Gross. Make them stop," I groan, taking my usual seat and lifting out my notebook and tablet. I'm already not liking all of this extra attention.

Cam laughs at me, but I'm being serious.

"No can do," he unhelpfully sing-songs as he sits beside me, taking far too much pleasure from my pain. "It's all part and parcel of being a Davenport. May as well get used to it, *Elizabeth.*"

"Don't call me that," I snarl, my sharp tone making him raise his eyebrows.

"It's only a name."

"My name is Hadley." I seethe out the words so it's perfectly fucking clear for him. "Regardless of what other name these idiots call me, *that* is my name. It's the name *I* chose. Hadley is who I am. Not Elizabeth, or anything else. Had-ley." I spell it out for him loud and clear while he looks at me in bewilderment.

He doesn't get it, and why would he. He's never had to live his life as someone he never wanted to be. I grew up being D. A fucking letter. The same as everyone at the compound. I don't know if the D was for Davenport, or D for Dove, or if it was just the next letter in the alphabet when I walked through the door. It doesn't even matter what it stands for because D is my past.

D is the scared kid who cried herself to sleep every night. D is the assassin who had to kill people to ensure her own survival. D is *not* who I am anymore. And I'm sure as fuck not Elizabeth, either. After having so many rights withheld from me, the least I fucking deserve is to pick my own goddamn name. I picked Hadley. I *am* Hadley. The rest of these assholes can call me whatever the fuck they want, but Cam and the others, *will* call me by my goddamn name.

He raises both of his hands in surrender. "Okay. Sorry. I was only teasing. Hadley suits you much better, anyway."

When he looks at me like I'm crazy, I realize I probably went a little overboard. He was only joking, after all. Blame it on the stress of the last few days and the complexity I'm developing from carrying around so many different identities. After everything this morning at breakfast, and all the unwanted attention I've been getting, his little joke just sent me over the edge.

The rest of the day is the same. I swear more people have tried to engage me in conversation today than have spoken to me since I arrived at Pac Prep. By the time lunch rolls around, I'm fucking exhausted.

I'm not paying any attention as I order food at the kiosk and take a seat at my usual table. The Princes' table is always free, but I'm more than happy to only sit there when I have to. I've had enough people staring at me today; I don't need them all gawking at me while I shovel food in my mouth.

I drop my bag on the chair beside me, sagging back in my seat and closing my eyes, needing a moment to myself. They've only been closed for a few seconds when the sound of someone sitting down opposite me has me huffing out a breath. Assuming it's Hawk, I open my eyes to scowl at him, yet I'm taken by surprise to find another weirdo I don't know slouching in a chair at *my* table with a cocky smirk on his face, acting like he fucking belongs here.

"Who the fuck are you?" I snap.

Yup, I've totally lost any control I had over my composure. Can't I just eat a fucking sandwich in peace?!

His eyes widen at my sharp tone, but my closed-off expression and unmistakable fuck-off vibes aren't enough to get him to take a hike.

"You should come to the party with me this weekend, baby." The guy leers at me in such a way that he's obviously thinking about all the dirty things he'd do to me at the party—evidently, he has a death wish.

I pretend like I'm giving his offer some consideration, letting my eyes roam over his face before dropping down to take in his broad chest and muscular biceps. He's attractive, but the stench of arrogance coming off of him is suffocating. I know Mason, West, and Cam all have that same air about them, but somehow it comes across as sexy and domineering. On this guy, it just makes him seem like a pretentious dickwad.

I scrunch my face, letting him know I'm unimpressed by what I see and internally preening when his features tighten and his jaw ticks.

"No, I don't think so. Finishing the night unsatisfied is not my idea of a fun Friday night."

His body tenses and he leans forward in his seat, losing his calm, cool façade as his hand clenches into a fist. Rising out of his chair until he looms over the table in an attempt to cower me, he growls out in a menacing tone, "What did you just say?"

Unfazed, I lean back in my chair. *The poor guy must have a hearing problem. Maybe I need to speak louder.*

"I said," I begin in a much louder tone, attracting the interest of students from nearby tables, "even in your dreams, your teeny-weeny peen couldn't get a girl off."

Students at the tables around us snicker behind their hands as they watch us. The guy's face reddens with anger, and he looks like he's about to launch himself across the table when a large hand slams down on his shoulder, anchoring him in place.

"What's going on here?" Mason demands, his usual impassive expression in place as his eyes dart between the two of us. The only hint that he's angry is the dangerous gravelly tone of his voice as he spears the nameless dude with a cold enough stare to have his heart stuttering to a stop.

"This guy was trying to get me to go to the party with him this weekend and didn't seem to like my answer." I shrug innocently.

"You were being a bitch," the guy protests.

He winces as Mason's grip on his shoulder tightens to the point of pain, the move a muted demand for the asshole to watch his tone.

"You were being an arrogant asshat," I argue back. "Next time, try getting to know a girl for five seconds first. And for god's sake, fucking ask her instead of acting like a cocky shithead."

"Fuck off, Joshua, and don't talk to her again," Mason snaps, shoving the guy away from the table.

Stumbling over his feet, he glowers at us before stalking off, not daring to face off against a Prince.

"Why are you always pissing people off?" Mason huffs, sitting down in the now vacant chair opposite me.

"Me? He's the one that came over here and was bothering me. Besides, if you'd had the day I've had, you'd snap at some fucker too."

He grins. "I might have something that will cheer you up." I perk up at his words, curious as to what it could be. It would have to be something pretty fucking spectacular to get me out of my crappy mood.

"What is it?"

He leans forward in his seat so no one around us can overhear him. "There's a fight night tomorrow. I thought you might like to come."

Excitement thrums through me. *Hell yes! Beating the shit out of some assholes is exactly what I need.*

"You can't fight, though," he tacks on, pouring cold water over the happy light beginning to spark inside me at the thought of slamming my fist into some idiot's face.

"That's not any fun." I pout.

"Babe." He chuckles. "There's no way any of the guys here would fight you after last time. And we can't let you fight us in front of them."

I tap my finger against my chin as an idea comes to mind.

"What if we had our own fight night afterward?"

I see the second he misinterprets my words, lust flaring in his eyes as they dilate. "You want me to pin you beneath me and fuck your brains out, Little Warrior?" he growls in a sexy as fuck husk that has my panties growing damp.

"I'm not going to say no to that." A coy smile plays on my lips as I lean in toward him, crossing my legs in such a way that my foot deliberately runs up his calf under the table. "But that's not quite what I was thinking. The six of us could have our own exclusive fight club after everyone else has fucked off. That way, no one can witness you get your asses kicked by a girl." I smirk, shrugging a shoulder innocently like it's no skin off my teeth if he says no. He's not going to say no, however.

His eyes sparkle in exhilaration, more than ready to rise to the challenge I've just laid down. "The six of us?"

"Beck too. He usually comes to watch the fights. I'm pretty sure he could even give you a run for your money," I jibe.

"Ha, I'd like to see the old man try." He laughs, making me shake my head at him. Beck's only like three years older than us. Certainly not *old* by any definition.

"So you're game?" I ask, delight threading my voice at the promise of violence.

"Little Warrior, I'd agree just to watch you throat-punch Hawk again. That was fucking priceless."

A grin lights up my face as I laugh. *Yeah, that was pretty fucking epic.*

"Speaking of the asshole, where is he?"

"Ah, we usually have lunch at our place, away from prying eyes, so I figured I'd come to get you."

When my food arrives, I get a to-go box for it, and the two of us leave the inquisitive eyes of the dining hall behind us as we head for a quiet lunch with the others.

Hadley

CHAPTER SEVEN

There's a buzzing under my skin, and I'm on edge, bouncing on the balls of my feet as we make our way toward the clearing in the forest. Blood and violence are exactly what I need after the last few days of being gawked at like a fucking zoo animal. I miss being a fucking nobody. I've been feeling stifled, suffocated under everyone's attention and this newfound fame. But it's nothing a sweaty brawl can't rectify.

"You have the same excited look on your face that other girls get when they find the perfect pair of shoes." Cam laughs.

"It's been far too long since I've been in a fight, and beating on a bag hasn't done anything to shake off the annoyance from the last few days."

"You just killed a mercenary the other week," Hawk argues.

"Yeah, but I've had to put up with your shitty attitude," I quip. "It would make any sane person crave an outlet for all their pent-up aggression." He snorts like I'm being melodramatic, but it's not like he's had a personality transplant. He might not hate me anymore, but he's as cranky and dickish as ever. "Just be thankful I haven't taken it out on you yet," I say sweetly, fully intending to change all of that tonight.

He grumbles something under his breath that I'm sure would only piss me off, but I get distracted as we enter the clearing. West gets to work setting up flashlights, spacing them out so they form a large circle while Hawk and Mason stretch.

"How did all of this start?" I ask, looking around the ring. The glow from the flashlights makes it look eerie and ominous, and a shiver of anticipation rolls down my spine. "Is it another tradition?"

"When we started at Pac, our parents made it clear we had to prove we could control the other students. Some sort of bullshit about proving ourselves capable of taking over for them when we graduate," Cam begins. "Technically, *that* is the tradition. Our forefathers started the girl of the month tradition to control the girls and keep them in line, and there have been various methods used on the guys."

West takes over as he walks back toward us, having placed all of the flashlights around the clearing. "We decided scheduling regular fight nights where the guys worked out their issues with one another would fit best for us."

"What if someone breaks the rules?"

There's a malicious grin on Hawk's face. "They fight us." The dark thrill of excitement in his voice tells me he gets off on inflicting pain just as much as I do. I wonder if that's a Davenport thing or a 'kids with fucked up lives' thing.

"Like with Deke? When he called you out at that party, then Mason fought him in the ring."

"How did you know about that?" Hawk questions, looking up at me from where he's bent over at the waist, stretching out his hamstrings and lower back.

"It was the first fight I snuck out to watch. It was hot as hell."

Mason grins darkly, throwing me a dirty wink that immediately drenches my panties.

"Exactly," West nods, getting us back on topic. "It only took a few fights back in freshman year before the rest of the guys realized they didn't want to be on the other end of Hawk or Mason's fists."

"Smart," I praise. "And the girls would do whatever you wanted, because they thought they might get a chance of being a girl of the month when senior year rolled around," I say thoughtfully, voicing my thoughts aloud.

"Yup." Popping the p, Cam confirms my line of thought.

"What are you going to do about them now, then? The girls weren't too happy after your little speech yesterday. It won't be long before you have an uprising on your hands. And I'm guessing any grievances amongst the students will get back to your parents."

"Us?" Hawk laughs darkly. "Oh no. *We*"—using his finger, he points at himself and the others—"are in charge of the guys. *You* are now in charge of corralling the girls."

"Me?" I gape. "You must be fucking crazy. I have no idea how to keep those pretentious bitches under control."

Hawk—the infuriating fucking dickhead—shrugs, evidently not giving a shit.

"Seems only fair," he says. "Everyone's gotta prove themselves. And if our parents think you can be useful, they're less likely to retaliate to our little rebellion."

Fuck, he has a point there.

"Fine, the girls can have a fight night too. I'm more than happy to beat the shit out of Bianca and her princess posse."

"Fuck yeah," Cam hoots. "Everyone has to wear bikinis and we'll get a mud pool."

"Unless you're also wearing a bikini and rolling around in the mud, then that's a hard no," I snark, rolling my eyes.

"I mean, if that's what you're into." He gives me a playful wink. It's the most banter I've gotten out of him in a long time, and it's great to see him acting like his old self. He's still awkward when it's just the two of us, but around the others, I can almost pretend that there isn't so much tension between us.

"There's no way that will work with the girls," Hawk argues, tearing apart my fantasy of pummeling the ever-loving shit out of Bianca. *Spoilsport.*

A less exciting yet just as satisfying idea comes to mind. "Do you guys keep dirt on the other students?" I ask.

"Of course we do." Hawk's 'duh' tone grates on my nerves, making me scowl at him. "Why?"

"I have an idea. I need to see what you have, though."

"Yeah, okay. I'll get them for you later," West promises as the noise of students approaching permeates the otherwise quiet evening.

It's not long before a crowd has formed around the makeshift ring. It looks like every boy in the school is here, and I don't miss the confused glances my way. I don't think they're used to seeing a girl present at these things. The clearing is silent as everyone looks at the five of us—well, the four guys—waiting expectantly for…something. Do they ring a bell or beat on a drum or something as some sort of commencement signal?

"This is supposed to be guys only," Deke calls out, glutton for punishment.

"She's one of us," Hawk states in a non-negotiable tone. "She has as much right to be here as we do."

"If we're done with the stupid questions," West drawls, "we're here to fight. So someone get in the ring."

Everyone hesitates for a moment before a freshman steps forward. He calls out another freshman and explains his issue with him—apparently, the other guy slept with his girlfriend. Personally, I'd be taking issue with the girlfriend, but whatever. Then the fight begins. It's all rather…civilized.

They're stick-thin freshmen with no meat on their bones or muscles to pack a punch, so the fight is pathetic. I know ten-year-olds who could have them unconscious in seconds. Still, as the other guys egg them on, the atmosphere is enough to ease some of the buzzing under my skin.

The fight doesn't last long before another one begins, and on and on it goes. I lose myself in the thrill of it. In watching blood spill as lips are split, the redness that rises to the skin's surface as any accessible body part is bruised. It's nothing like the fast-paced, athletic, deadly fights I'm used to watching, but it's sufficient to quell some of the bloodlust I've been craving.

I'm so lost in watching some guy grab another in a headlock that could easily be broken that I nearly miss a flash of movement in the trees opposite me. My body stiffens, immediately suspecting that it could be another mercenary lurking in the dark, but I relax when I catch sight of Beck, hidden just behind the tree line. He's engrossed in the scene of violence playing out in front of us, watching it with hawk-like eyes.

He needs tonight as much as I do—possibly more. Everything he's had to manage by himself for the last few months has taken its toll on him, but tonight, he can let all of it go. He can exorcise his demons and expel all of his rage on Mason and Hawk. Tonight should help him clear his head and stabilize him a bit, so we can work out our next move. Because there is no fucking way I am letting any of our parents continue to use and abuse us like this.

I've fallen so deep into my own thoughts, sucked in by the idea of bloodshed and retribution, that I don't even realize the fights have ended and the boys are all breaking apart, some of them starting to make their way toward the tree line.

The five of us stand and watch as the other students disappear into the trees one by one or in small groups. As the sound of their voices fades into the distance, everyone else making their way back to the dorms, Beck steps out of the trees.

Out of the corner of my eye, I notice West tense, and I make a point of walking past him on my way to greet Beck. The two of them—well, West in particular—need to sort out their shit.

"Behave," I growl in his ear, not giving him a chance to respond as I close the gap between Beck and us. I meet him on the far side of the ring with a smile on my face as I wrap my arms around his neck and kiss him.

"Right, let's get this show on the road," Hawk calls out, making me smile against Beck's lips.

"Yeah, let's see what you've got, old man," Mason taunts.

Beck gasps in outrage. "What did he just call me?" he murmurs, in a low voice that only I can hear.

I chuckle, turning back toward the guys. Mason is now standing in the center of the ring, staring brazenly at Beck, while the other three are still lined up along one edge.

"No, me first," I call out across the open space, walking back toward them, sensing Beck following behind me. "Then you can let Beck kick your ass."

I smile sweetly as I meet Mason in the middle of the ring, and he scoffs, looking affronted at my suggestion. *I guess we'll soon find out.*

"Alright, Little Warrior, whose balls are you planning on busting tonight?"

I smile wickedly at Hawk. *Obviously, it was going to be him.* I definitely want to try my skills out against Mason someday, but I need him good and fresh for his fight with Beck.

Hawk smirks confidently as he steps forward. "No problem, baby Davenport. Let me prove to you that last time was just a fluke."

Beck snorts behind me before he and Mason both move to stand with West and Cam at the edge of the makeshift ring. "Five bucks she beats him," I hear Beck say.

"Pfft, there's no way I'm taking that action," Mason retorts, shaking his head. "We all saw her last time. There's no way he's beating her."

My smile only grows more prominent at their friendly ribbing, although Hawk doesn't look impressed as he throws them a dirty look over his shoulder before pulling off his top and throwing it toward the outskirts of the ring.

I do the same with my hoodie, leaving me in my sports bra and lycra leggings. In this outfit, I've got plenty of flexibility to move, and with my hair pulled back, nothing can get in my way. Tonight, Hawk's all mine.

"No dick blows," Hawk announces, making me roll my eyes.

"Fine, but no titty shots then. That shit hurts."

"No hitting each other's faces either," West calls out. "We don't need the whole school speculating about what you two have been up to."

Dammit. He's got a point, but still, he's totally killing my fun. Nothing is more satisfying than seeing your opponent walking around with a shiner you delivered.

When Cam calls the fight, we circle each other, both of us testing the waters with glancing blows. We spar back and forth. Occasionally, one of us lands a solid hit to the other's chest or abdomen, but it's not enough to have any lasting impact.

I can tell Hawk is much more focused this time. Although he walked into the ring with a confident attitude, there's not the same cockiness in his movements, making it much harder for me to find an opening to take him down.

It takes a while, but as he goes in to deliver a punch to my kidneys, I get the shot I've been waiting for. Hawk drops his arm just a little, but it's enough for me to knock him round the head, quickly following it with a kick to his leg. He moves to try and grab ahold of my calf, in an attempt to take me to the ground, leaving his head and chest completely exposed. Side-stepping him, I knock him around the head twice more, disorientating him.

On reflex, his arms come up to cover his face, giving me an opening. I rush in, delivering two lightning-quick jabs to his kidney and stomach that have the wind knocked out of him as he doubles over.

"Fucking hell," he wheezes.

Swiping his legs out from underneath him, he crashes to the ground, and I'm left victorious, standing over him with a satisfied grin on my face.

As easy as that.

"I win," I sing-song as Hawk coughs and splutters in the dirt.

"Fuck me, next time you can beat on Mason," he rasps, making me laugh. Stretching out my arm, he slaps his hand into mine, and I help him up off the ground.

"You did well. Much more focused and less cocky than last time."

"Remind me again where you learned to fight like that?" he questions, still sounding pained.

"Just something I picked up along the way." I shrug casually before shouting, "Mason and Beck next," in a feeble attempt to change the subject and distract him as the two of us make our way toward the others.

Beck is dressed more informally than the guys have probably ever seen him. He's wearing a pair of dark-colored basketball shorts and a matching muscle shirt that shows off his large, well-defined biceps and toned arms, giving me a nice view of his tattoo sleeve. His usually styled hair is messier, giving him a more rugged appearance, especially with the short stubble he's rocking. All in all, it's a pretty irresistible picture.

Oops, was that a bit of drool? Subtly swiping at the corner of my mouth, I watch as the show gets even better when both Mason and Beck take off their shirts. *Oh, yes, please.* Both men are built to perfection. While Mason is broader than Beck, and packing more muscle, Beck is leaner and defined but no less powerful looking as he stalks into the middle of the ring with Mason following closely behind.

"Same rules as last time," West calls out.

"Yeah, man, don't hit my titties," Mason jokes, making the corner of Beck's lip tilt up as I belt out a laugh.

The two of them face-off against each other in what is my favorite wet dream come to life, and when Cam calls the start of the match, there is no slow build-up like there was with Hawk and me.

The two men launch themselves at one another, going straight in for brutal attacks as they pummel any part of their opponent they can reach. It's violent and ferocious—and so fucking hot. My panties are a wet mess. Other girls might get off on their guys being sweet and caring, but this right here—this battle of power and brutality—*this* is what gets me revved up.

It's a fast-paced fight, and for the most part, it's impossible to tell who has the upper hand. The two are evenly matched as they block each other's hits and deliver merciless punches of their own, neither of them holding anything back.

Just when I'm beginning to think there won't be a winner—unless we spend all night standing out here, which doesn't sound all that appealing now that the cold air is blowing against my sweat-coated skin, and my stomach is starting to grumble—Beck delivers some fancy maneuver so quickly that I hardly see it. The next thing I know, he's got Mason in a headlock, his arm squeezing his neck.

Mason fights him like a rabid animal, twisting and turning his torso and punching at any part of Beck he can get at. However, Beck holds firm around his neck until I'm concerned that Mason is going to pass out—he's too much of a heavy fucker to carry all the way back to the dorms.

I don't even realize I've taken a step forward into the ring, until I notice Mason smacking his hand against Beck's arm, the signal that he's tapping out.

"Woohoo!" I cry out, racing toward the two as Beck lets go of his hold around Mason's neck. Mason bends over, placing his hands on his knees as he coughs and splutters. After giving Mason a slap on the back, Beck shifts to face me with a grin. "Underdogs for the win," I shout out, laughing as I launch myself into his open arms, and he spins me around.

It's a rare carefree moment, and I soak up every second of it because you never know when things can take a turn for the worst. One second you can be loving life; the next, everything around you has crashed and burned. So yeah, I take in every aspect of this moment—Beck's white teeth as he laughs and how his arms tighten around my waist. How Mason has a small, rare smile playing at the corner of his lips and the feel of the other guys' eyes as they watch us. In this peaceful moment, Lawrence doesn't exist. I didn't grow up isolated in a compound where I was beaten and tortured into becoming a killing machine. I wasn't robbed of getting to know my brother.

Nope. Instead, I'm a normal teenage girl, feeling content in the arms of the boy she's falling for, while she senses the heated stares of her three other crushes warming her up from the inside out. Like I said—normal.

Setting me back on the ground, Beck keeps an arm around my waist as he turns to Mason, holding out his hand. "Good fight, man," he praises in an act of sportsmanship.

Mason shakes his head with a defeated chuckle, slapping his hand into Beck's. "Yeah, you too, old man. Didn't know you had it in you."

Cam comes strolling over. "Well, well, I never thought I'd see the day Mason got his ass kicked," he exclaims. "Man, you'll be getting beat by baby Davenport next if you aren't careful."

He laughs, and Mason clocks him around the head. "Shut up, asshole."

"You are not calling me that!" I argue.

"Why not?" Cam pouts. "Hawk did."

"He's not calling me that, either. I'm several seconds younger than that dickhead, and I'm not a baby anything. I'm a strong, fierce warrior."

"Yeah, you are, baby." Mason swoops in, draping his arm over my shoulder and tugging me in against him, planting a kiss on my temple. Of course, Beck refuses to move his arm, so I end up wedged between their sweaty chests. Their sweaty, naked chests that look so hot and lickable.

"I think this calls for a celebration," Cam hollers. "Drinks at ours!"

"Sounds good," Hawk shouts back before saying something to West that's too quiet for us to hear. West doesn't look pleased, though he doesn't argue either, so I guess that's progress.

"Dude, I lost," Mason says, looking at Cam in bafflement.

"Exactly." Cam gives him a shit-eating grin. "We're celebrating your first-ever loss. It's the end of an era, man."

I laugh at their antics as Hawk and West start collecting the flashlights and meet us in the middle of the ring. Handing a flashlight each to Cam and Mason, the six of us make our way back through the dark, quiet forest toward the dorms so we can start the celebrations.

Firefly

CHAPTER EIGHT

All six of us pile into the apartment, spreading out on the couches and chairs. I get comfortable on the sofa, leaning back and resting my arm on the armrest while Mason unglues himself from Hadley's side to grab beers from the fridge and hand them out to everyone.

Grabbing Beck's hand, Hadley walks my way, giving me a soft smile before sitting beside me. Her thigh presses against mine, and I have to resist the urge to wrap my arms around her and drag her into my lap. That urge only increases when Beck sits on her other side, and I have to push it down, taking a gulp of beer to distract me from her tantalizing scent. The usual subtle vanilla and honey tones of her shampoo are wrapped up in the muskiness from her fight, and the heady aroma has gone straight to my dick as it presses uncomfortably against the zipper of my jeans. I have to shift awkwardly in my seat, trying not to draw attention to myself.

After our parents insinuated that Beck was working for them, and his outburst the other night about how he'd lost the closest thing he'd ever had to a sister, I did some digging. Not that I found much beyond the usual college and school records.

No evidence of an actual sister, or any other siblings, but I wasn't expecting there to be. When I investigated more into the possible deaths in the Black Creek area to see if I could find this 'sister' he was talking about, it was like looking for a needle in a haystack. The number of people every year who are run down, outright shot, or killed assassination-style, is shocking. Even when I searched for teenage girls—guessing that that's probably the age Beck and his friends were when whatever happened, happened —I still came up with too many potential cases.

Honestly, it sickened me to see so many kids pointlessly killed, all in the name of gang wars. Kids hit by stray bullets while they were out playing or gunned down on their way home from school. Even if they were lucky enough to make it past their childhood, from what I could tell, they wound up dying for whatever gang they'd pledged their allegiance to. All of it seems like such a senseless waste of life. Yet it looks like the police have all but given up on the town, pulling their men and resources from it and leaving its citizens to fend for themselves.

Is that how Beck grew up? With death and danger on every corner? There was no faking the raw emotion pouring off him the other night when I accused him of not knowing the significance of family. I've never experienced actual loss, but I only had to look into his eyes to see that he had. Whoever his self-made family was, they were everything to him. Is that why he kept seeking me out when he first showed up? Did he see me as some sort of emotional Band-aid that could curtail his grief? I just don't understand why he would come here, if not for money. He claims it was to get to know me, but I don't understand how that could be the case. I'm nobody special or important. So why would he sucker himself into becoming a pawn for our father just to be near me? It makes no sense.

Yet, watching him now as he tilts his head back and laughs at something Mason says before glancing down at Hadley with what looks a lot like love in his eyes, he seems relaxed. More himself than I've ever seen him. Out of his stuffy suits and away from the fake persona he wears on campus, he seems so much more like one of us.

He must sense me staring at him as he glimpses over. Our gazes catch for a second before I break away, taking another swig of my beer, but I could have sworn I saw something in that split second—a rare moment of vulnerability or openness. I'm not sure whether he meant to show me so much; even so it was the most open with me he's ever been. Usually, he keeps himself guarded and closed off, rarely allowing anyone to see behind the mask he carefully dons. Hadley seems to be the only one who has seen the real him.

"West." Cam calling my name breaks me out of my thoughts, steering my focus back to the room and whatever they're talking about. "Tell them how much you love to go swimming in the lake at the cabin."

I groan, giving a fake shiver of horror as everyone else laughs. "You couldn't pay me to get back in that lake."

I always hated the lake. I hated the fact that you had no idea what was swimming around in the murky water beneath you. There could be dead bodies or anything just sitting decaying down there. Why would anyone be okay with swimming in that?

The last straw was Cam sneaking up on me and pulling me under the surface. I swear to god I thought an eel or something had gotten ahold of me, and I was going to drown and be forever lost to the muddy lakebed. I've never been more terrified in my life. Strangely, I never set foot in the lake again after that day, and now I get ribbed mercilessly for it.

"What about the time in freshman year when you thought you had herpes." I smirk, causing Cam's face to redden with embarrassment as he glowers at me.

"I thought we agreed to never talk about that again," he hisses.

I shrug, all the while laughing. It was fucking hilarious. He was convinced his dick was going to drop off at any second. Considering the fact it was freshmen year and girls had only just started showing an interest in all of us—well, mostly them—he was freaking the fuck out.

Hadley gasps, her face scrunching in disgust. "You got an STD? Eww, Cam, that's gross!"

"No, he didn't," I admit, coming to his rescue. "Turns out he had poison ivy all over his junk from fucking some girl in the bushes by the admin building."

Everyone bursts out laughing. It doesn't matter how many times we bring this story up, it's still fucking hilarious.

"Oh, dude, that must have been painful." Beck laughs. "You sure everything still works alright?"

"Don't you worry, old man, it's all good as new," Cam volleys, adopting Mason's nickname for him. He gets to his feet and strides toward us. Lifting his hands, he pops the top button on his jeans. "Wanna see for yourself?"

Beck throws his hands out to try and stop him from coming any closer. "God, no, I'll take your word for it."

Cam's gaze falls on Hadley, the cocky swagger falling out of his shoulders as heat blooms in his eyes. I can feel Hadley's entire body tense beside me, reacting to whatever moment they are sharing. It doesn't last longer than a few seconds before Cam coughs and drops his gaze, breaking whatever connection between them. There's no way we all didn't feel the sexual tension heating the room, though. It's only a matter of time until they fuck and make up. And surprisingly, I'm okay with that.

"You got any funny childhood memories, Beck?" Hawk asks as Cam saunters back to his chair and collapses into it, suddenly appearing more withdrawn than he did a minute ago.

"Umm." Beck picks at the label on his beer as he ponders over Hawk's question. After a few seconds, a fond smile grows on his face, and he chuckles.

"There was this one night my friends and I managed to get our hands on one of our parents' liquor stash. We were only eleven or twelve, so we were fucked up from like half a can of beer."

The guys all laugh—we've all been there.

"Cain, he was always doing reckless shit. I'm pretty sure he thought he'd be dead before he was twenty-five." There's a sadness in his tone, but he quickly shakes it off. "Anyway, we were just walking around the neighborhood, thinking we were cool as shit, when Cain spotted an old merc parked at the curb. His dad had just taught him that week how to disable the alarm on one and hot-wire the engine so he could steal it, so he wanted to try it out for himself. Of course, none of us had a fucking clue how to drive. A problem we didn't consider until we'd already broken in and messed with the wires.

"All four of us were sitting in the car, arguing over what to do, when a light switched on inside the house beside us. Well, I'm pretty sure I shit my pants." Everyone laughs again, and I have to admit, I'm pretty caught up in the story. It's a million miles away from the life we had growing up. Sure, the guys and I all had each other and got into some shit, but never anything illegal. It was the one thing drilled into us from a young age—not getting the police involved in our lives. We thought our parents just didn't want the bad publicity, but obviously it was more than just their social standing they were concerned about.

"So I dove into the front seat, practically sitting on Cain's damn lap, as I tried to work out which pedals did what and quickly tore off down the street. Thank fuck it was an automatic, or I wouldn't have had a clue. Not that it was much help when I could hardly see over the dash. I hadn't had much of a growth spurt yet, and once Cain wriggled out from underneath me, I was doing well to see over the wheel. We were veering all over the place, all of us freaking out that whoever was in the house was coming after us.

"We made it a few streets before I accidentally side-swiped a bike. Then we were really fucked. Less than five minutes later, there was this deafening roar behind us as a dozen bikes chased us down the road, shooting at us. Fuck, we were shitting our pants by then. I didn't know what the fuck to do. Stop? Keep driving? I'm pretty sure I was crying like a baby." He chuckles. "They eventually hit one of our tires, and the car spun out, losing control. We were still dazed when they tore the car door off and shoved their guns in our faces, but, fuck, the look of surprise when they realized it was a bunch of kids in the car. I think they thought it was a rival gang trying to piss them off."

Hadley gasps as the rest of us laugh. "What happened?"

Beck shrugs. "They made us promise that if we were ever looking to get into the life, we'd go with them. I think they were impressed with our recklessness."

"Holy shit, that's insane." Cam laughs, watching Beck with what looks like respect, or at the very least, a modicum of admiration. It doesn't sit well with me how easily the guys seem to be letting him into our circle. What happened to not trusting him? Are we seriously done with that because he *claims* whatever he's doing is to protect me?

The six of us chat for a while longer, before tiredness starts to kick in. Leaning in, my shoulder brushes against Hadley's as I whisper in her ear, "Stay with me tonight?"

I've never asked a girl to spend the night with me. Except things have been chaotic lately, and now that she's so close, sitting right beside me, I can't stand the thought of her leaving to go sleep alone in her own bed.

Her eyes roam over my face, and a small, shy smile crosses her features as she nods. "Course I will."

Damn, well, now that I've gone and asked her, I'm done with the rest of this night. I don't think I've ever been more ready to call it a day and go to bed, although the thought of having her soft curves pressed against me all night has my thoughts heading down a filthy track. Thankfully, it's not much later when Beck gets up to leave.

"I'm gonna stay here tonight," Hadley explains when he looks at her.

I expect to see some jealousy or anger at that. Most people wouldn't be okay with their girlfriend sleeping at another guy's house. Especially when he knows damn well she will be sleeping in either mine or Mason's bed. Instead, he almost looks relieved to hear that.

"Okay. I'll see you on Thursday."

He leans down to give her a quick kiss before waving goodnight to the rest of us and heading out.

The other guys begin to tidy up, placing the empty bottles over by the sink.

"Right, well, I'm going to bed," Hawk says. "I don't wear headphones or listen to music while I sleep, and I'm not about to start." He gives each of us the stink eye before sauntering down the hallway toward the bedrooms. Cam lingers in the space between the living room, where Hadley and I are still sitting, and the hallway. He's glancing back and forth, looking unsure about what to do as Mason joins us on the sofa, sitting in Beck's vacated spot. After a tense moment of awkward silence as Cam debates what to do, he makes up his mind and mumbles out a hasty goodnight before he saunters down the hall after Hawk.

Hadley worries her bottom lip as she watches him disappear into his room. "Is he doing okay?" she asks softly after we've heard the click of his bedroom door shutting behind him.

"He's actually been doing a lot better," I reassure her. "He's stopped drinking, and has been going to class more."

Some of the tension drops out of her shoulders. "He doesn't know how to act around me anymore."

"He seemed to be doing pretty well tonight," Mason supplies.

"When we're all together, he isn't so bad. When it's just the two of us, it's… awkward." She sighs heavily. "Talking to Cam used to be so easy. I miss it."

I lace my fingers through hers as Mason drapes his arm over her shoulder, tugging her in against him.

"You'll get back to that," I promise her.

The way she looks into my eyes, I can tell she wants to believe me.

"You will," Mason agrees. "It's in the way he looks at you. He's fighting with himself because he doesn't know how to handle his feelings, but it's a losing battle. Just give him some time."

Hadley leans her head on his shoulder, and the three of us sit in comfortable silence for a bit, with each of us lost in our own thoughts until Mason yawns. That starts us all off as Hadley and I yawn in reflex.

"Well, I'm heading to bed," Mason announces, gazing at Hadley. "Which one of us do you want to sleep with?"

"I was going to sleep with West, if that's okay?" She suddenly looks nervous and I don't like seeing that expression on her. She's got no reason to be nervous. Not that Mason or I have really talked about it, but our dynamic with Hadley feels right. Like this is how it was always meant to be.

Mason tucks his finger under her chin, lifting it so she's looking into his eyes. "Of course that's alright, Little Warrior. You never have to be embarrassed about spending time with one of us or Beck." He presses a kiss to her lips and her hands come up to slide through his hair, holding him to her as she deepens it.

It's probably creepy as hell that I'm just sitting here watching my best friend and my girlfriend suck each other's faces, but it's too fucking hot to look away from. Watching them get lost in one another is captivating.

They're both breathless when they break apart, their lips swollen.

"Night, Little Warrior," Mason murmurs before getting to his feet and smirking at me before leaving the room.

"Ready for bed?" I ask, unable to tear my eyes away as Hadley's tongue sweeps out to lick her lower lip, likely tasting the last remnants of Mason on her skin.

Fucking hell, that should not be hot. I'm curious to know what he tastes like, mixed with her, and before I can second guess myself, I lean forward and capture her lower lip with my teeth, sucking it into my mouth. "Mmm." I release her lip with a pop, watching her pupils dilate and her eyes widen as her cheeks and chest flush with need.

"Come on, Firefly, bedtime." Taking her hand in mine, I lead her to the bedroom. I hesitate outside the door, the thought of bringing her into my personal space weighing on me more than I thought it would. It's stupid. I know she's been in here before when she snuck into our apartment, yet somehow, this feels different.

I've never brought another girl back to my room. Never invited anyone other than the guys in here. Not that it's anything unique or particularly personal, but it's *my* space. Where I come to get away from the world. Once upon a time, my bedroom was the one place I could come and be comfortable in my own skin. Where my father wasn't judging me for not being strong enough, man enough, buff enough. Despite knowing I can be whoever I want to be at this school, and no one would dare say anything, my room is still that safe space for me. So, letting someone new into that is unnerving.

She gently squeezes my hand in hers in a comforting gesture, and I take some strength from that as I turn the handle, pushing open the door to my sanctuary.

Flicking on the light, it illuminates a forest-green room. I have a large desk lining one wall, with several computer screens covering it, along with various pieces of hardware and other technical items. A large king-size bed is in the middle of the room, taking up most of the space, and I have a bookcase, a reading chair, and another desk with all my school stuff scattered across it on the other side of the room.

A large window opposite the bed overlooks the woods that run along the back of the dormitories and dining hall. Moving over to it, I pull the blinds, tidying up the desk and whatever other clutter I can shove in the drawers—I probably should have tidied up before asking her to stay the night—until I feel a warm palm on my back.

Clutching the book in my hand, I turn to face Hadley. She looks so beautiful, standing there in only her sports bra and tight leggings.

"Can I have a top or something to sleep in?" she asks.

"Right. Yeah, of course." I drop the book in my hand and cross the room to my chest of drawers, lifting out a t-shirt and handing it to her. I don't know why I feel so awkward. It's not like we haven't been alone before. I've seen her naked and coming all over mine and Mason's dicks, for Christ's sake. Yet I can't handle her being in my bedroom? What the hell is wrong with me?

She smiles softly as she takes the t-shirt from my outstretched hand before moving to the bed. With her back to me, she peels off her skin-tight bra while I stand there starstruck like a total fucking idiot until she slips the t-shirt over her head, cutting off my view.

Hitching her thumbs under the top, she wiggles her ass in an inviting manner that has my dick hardening until her leggings peel down her legs. Kicking off her battered trainers, she steps out of them and looks back at me over her shoulder. "Are we getting into bed or what?"

When I don't respond, unable to do anything more than stare at her standing there in only my t-shirt that just about hits the top of her thighs and gives me a front-row view of her long, toned legs, a small smile graces her lips.

"West," she coaxes gently, "which side of the bed do you sleep on?"

"Oh." I tear my eyes away from her legs, slowly lifting my gaze to her face. "The right side."

She peels back the covers on the left side and slips between the sheets, appearing like every wet dream I've had about her in my bed.

"Well, are you going to join me or just stand and stare at me all night?" Her words and inviting smile jolt me into action as I quickly strip off my top and jeans and climb in beside her, wearing only my boxers.

"Why are you so nervous?" she asks, scooching closer to me until the bare skin of her arms and legs are pressed up against mine. Heat radiates out from where our bodies touch, making goosebumps pebble along my skin. How does she have such an effect on me? I've never been this nervous or awkward around a girl before. I like to be the one in charge. If I sleep with a girl, I'm the one making the rules and telling her what to do. Only I don't feel any of my usual confidence right now.

"I don't know," I admit. "I've never had a girl in here before."

Shifting onto her knees, she lifts her leg over mine until she's seated in my lap and, *holy fuck*, does she feel fantastic with her warm, wet pussy pressing against my straining cock. Nothing but the thin fabric of her panties and my boxers separating us.

"I like that," she murmurs, trailing her fingers over my pec. I don't have any of the muscles that Mason or Beck, or even Cam, have. I'm much leaner—skinnier looking—and I can only imagine what she thinks when she looks at me.

Lifting her gaze, she looks into my eyes. "I like you, just the way you are."

"You don't wish I was more of a fighter like Mason?" I half-joke, suddenly feeling self-conscious. Not only am I built entirely differently to Mason, but I also think and behave differently from him too. We probably couldn't be more opposite.

"You're more like Mason than you think." Her words catch me by surprise, and she must see it on my face as she explains. "Where Mason uses his fists, you use your words to eviscerate your opponent. I see the same darkness in you as Mason; it just manifests differently. That's good, though. It means people underestimate you. They think you're incapable of destroying them, but they don't realize that your sharp tongue can do more damage than a roundhouse kick ever could."

My hand slides into her hair as I lean forward, pressing my lips to hers. I can feel her fingernails digging into the soft flesh of my chest as I tug on her hair tie until her hair falls down around her shoulders in long, wavy strands.

My other hand slides under her t-shirt, gliding across the smooth, warm skin of her back and pressing her more firmly against me. She grinds against my cock, our tongues sliding over one another while I groan into her mouth and she sighs. She tastes like everything I never knew I needed, and I can't get enough of her.

Eventually, I push her back, breaking our kiss even though my dick starts up a protest, and Hadley regards me in confusion.

"I didn't ask you to stay over so we could have sex. I just wanted to spend the night with you."

She smiles seductively. "I kicked Hawk's ass tonight, for the second time," she says, confusing me as to why she's bringing up her brother right now.

"Do you know what I like to do after a fight?" She bites her lip seductively, trailing her fingers down my chest. "I like to fuck."

Hadley

CHAPTER NINE

The second the words are out of my mouth, my vision tilts. The next thing I know, I'm on my back with West's lean body wedged between my thighs and his hard-on pressed perfectly against my wet panties as he hovers over me.

"You asked for it, Firefly," he growls in a dark, seductive tone that has me grinding shamelessly against him. "You're going to have to be quiet, though, unless you want your brother to come in here before I can make you see stars. Can you do that?"

He pins me in place with a serious look. *This* is the West who likes to be in control. The one who is in charge behind closed doors. Seeing him go all alpha and taking control only makes me wetter as I nod my head, biting down on my lower lip. I'm already suppressing a whimper and he's barely even touched me.

He gets a feral look in his eye at my obedience before slowly roaming his gaze over my body as though trying to decide where he should start. Tugging on my top, I sit up slightly so he can remove it, and he does the same with my panties until I'm lying naked on the bed for him to feast his eyes on.

His tongue runs along his lower lip as his pupils dilate, and his hands trail over my hips and up my stomach before he grabs my tits, pushing them together and squeezing them.

My head falls back and a small moan escapes me, having already forgotten about my promise to keep quiet.

A sharp slap across my nipple has me gasping, and I snap my gaze to West's. He gives me an admonishing look as he massages the spot he just slapped, and even though it was supposed to be a punishment, I can't help the way my eyes roll back in my head as the bite of pain goes straight to my clit.

"I'll have to stop if you can't keep quiet," he growls in warning.

Fuck no. He can't stop.

I bite into my lower lip, more than willing to make myself bleed if it means he'll continue to make my body come alive under his touch. His hands glide down my torso and over my thighs before he pushes them further apart.

"Fuck, you're already dripping all over my sheets, Firefly."

As soon as his fingers touch my clit, I jump off the bed, already so sensitive and eager for him.

He chuckles darkly, pleased with my reaction. With a hand pressed against my lower abdomen to pin me in place, his other hand trails through my wetness before he inserts two fingers into me, making my back arch as I fist the bed sheets and bite my lip harder.

I'm practically vibrating with the need to come as he slowly slides his fingers in and out of me, driving me wild as I buck against him. It takes everything in me to stay quiet, which is only heightening my desire.

When he presses his thumb against my clit, I go off like a bomb. Blood floods my mouth as I pierce the skin with my teeth, barely feeling the sting as pleasure flashes through my body, my legs trembling.

West doesn't give me a chance to recover, and I'm still experiencing the aftershocks of my orgasm when he pushes his boxers down his legs and, in one swift move, slams all the way into me.

I can feel myself spasming around him and my mouth drops open as he bottoms out, the tip of his cock hitting my cervix. "Ohh," I moan, losing any control I had over my ability to stay quiet. My brain is hazy with the surge of hormones from my climax, and all rational thought has left the building.

Unfortunately, West hasn't forgotten the rules, and just as quickly as his fucking amazing dick sunk into me, he pulls out, leaving me feeling empty. I whimper at the sudden loss, searing him with a pleading look.

"If you can't keep quiet, Firefly, I'll have to stop," he threatens, all the while running the head of his cock up and down my pussy lips, smearing my juices and teasing me. "Do you want me to stop?" He presses the tip of his dick against my already highly sensitive clit, and I can't do anything but shake my head. "Are you going to keep quiet?"

I nod my head this time, silently begging him with my eyes to shove his dick back inside me and make me fall apart.

"Good girl," he purrs, slightly rocking his hips to tease me before pushing his way back in. He never breaks eye contact with me, his intense gaze holding me hostage as he picks up the pace, chasing his release. I wrap my legs around his narrow waist, my heel digging into his ass, urging him on as I race toward the light.

My pussy constricts and my back arches as I fist the bedsheets. I can feel it, that intense tightening in my lower belly, and I know, regardless of my promise to keep quiet, I'm not going to be able to.

West must sense it too, as his hand clamps down over my mouth, silencing my scream as a blast wave explodes outward from my core, racing through my nerves all the way to my toes.

Panting heavily, I can hardly move when I'm suddenly tossed onto my stomach, his nails digging into the soft skin of my hips as he hauls them up off the bed, lining me up before slamming into me. I bury my face in the pillow, silencing my whimpers as he hammers into me relentlessly, quickly sending me crashing toward my third fucking orgasm of the night.

This time, he dives off the cliff with me, grunting out his release as his cum hits my inner walls, before pulling me down onto the bed beside him.

"Fuck," he pants breathlessly as he tugs me into his arms. He plants a fierce kiss on my lips, his tongue pushing its way past my teeth, and I suck him greedily into my mouth as our tongues clash together.

Despite how wrung out I am, I can feel my body gearing up for round two when he breaks away, climbing off the bed to get some tissues and wet wipes so we can clean ourselves up. Throwing the used tissues in the trash, he climbs back into bed, placing his glasses on the bedside table before once again wrapping his arms around me so I can rest my head on his shoulder, our legs intertwined. A tired, sex-hazed bliss surrounds us as sleep pulls me under, dragging me into oblivion.

∽

I'M AWAKE EARLY the next morning in exactly the same position I fell asleep—both of us must have slept like the dead.

Peeking up at West through my eyelashes, I see he's still out for the count. His face is relaxed, with none of the usual hardness scoring his features. He looks so peaceful, like he doesn't have a worry in the world. I wish that were the case.

Carefully, I untangle myself from him and slip out from between the sheets, pulling on the discarded t-shirt he gave me last night and slipping out of the room.

The fantastic thing about sleeping over here—and the same at Beck's—is that I don't have to make myself look semi-human before caffeinating my system. So it doesn't matter that my hair resembles medusa's or that I have a terrifying resting-bitch face first thing in the morning.

If anything, Mason seems to find it amusing, as he chuckles when I enter the kitchen, not at all deterred by the dark scowl I throw his way.

"Aren't you a sight for sore eyes in the morning." He laughs.

He's sitting at the barstools, drinking his own freshly made cup of coffee, but before I can throw something at his head, he gets up and grabs me a mug, filling it as I take a seat next to him.

"Mmm," I groan as I wrap my hands around the hot mug and take a sip of the hot life force within it.

"You have fun last night?" he asks with a knowing smirk, throwing me a dirty wink as I roll my eyes at him.

"I don't kiss and tell."

He scoffs. "I'm pretty sure you were doing much more than just kissing last night."

Tossing him a dirty look, I snark back, "What were you doing, standing at the door listening to us?"

He throws his head back and laughs. "I wish, babe. If I'd heard those sweet moans coming from your lips, I wouldn't have been able to stop myself from turning your two-way into a three-way."

Well, damn. I totally would have been okay with that.

"Instead, I settled for jerking myself off to the thought of your hot mouth bobbing up and down on my dick."

Fucking hell, he's going to have me wet and needy before I've even had breakfast.

His gaze zones in on my lips as my tongue inadvertently flicks out, making him groan.

"Head out of the gutter, Little Warrior," he murmurs, like I'm the only one whose thoughts have strayed to a dirty place. "Your brother will be in here any minute. We're going to the gym. Do you wanna come?"

I take another sip of my coffee as I think over his offer. Last night satisfied my urges for now, and honestly, I'm still a little sore from the fight. Not to mention the delicious ache between my thighs from West last night. "Nah, I'm good. I think I'll just stay here, if that's okay?"

"Of course it is. You can come here any time. I'd give you a key, but it would seem you can just let yourself in."

Hawk saunters into the kitchen, still looking bleary-eyed in his gym gear. "Morning," he grumbles as he pours himself a coffee and sits down on the opposite side of the island.

"Good to see you look as shitty in the morning as I do." I smile sweetly, feeling more alive now that I've finished my first cup of the day.

Mason laughs. "Ha, you think Hawk is a grouchy shithead during the day? You should get on his bad side first thing in the morning."

"Shut up, asshole," Hawk snarls, taking a large gulp of his coffee. "It's a fucking ungodly hour of the day to be awake. Why do you go to the gym this early?"

"Why did you agree to come then?" Mason retorts, unfazed by what I'm guessing is Hawk's typical early-morning cantankerous nature. "You could have said no."

"I must have been drunk. It's still fucking dark out. No human should be up before the sun."

Someone's clearly not a morning person. I might look like death warmed over first thing in the morning, but I'm definitely an early bird like Mason. I love being up before everyone else and watching the world come to life around me. Maybe it's because I spent so many years locked away in the compound, barely allowed to experience much of the outside world, but now that I'm free to do whatever the fuck I please, I want to soak up every second of it.

I share a look with Mason as he rolls his eyes at Hawk's pissy attitude.

"Make sure you get whatever information you need from West today," Hawk reminds me. "Now that we've announced the second month of not picking girls, they're going to be out for blood."

"Great," I snark sarcastically.

I guess I'll just have to show the pampered girls of Pacific Prep exactly how things will roll under my reign.

There's bound to be dirt on every girl here. It's just a matter of finding it. I'm hoping whoever the guys are getting their intel from has enough for me to pull this off. Otherwise, I'm out of ideas. I haven't the first idea how to befriend these girls or get them to do as I say, so there's no chance I can endear them into accepting that the girl-of-the-month tradition is finished.

I huff out a frustrated breath when Hawk stares pointedly at me. "I'll get it done," I assure him.

It might be a job I couldn't give less of a shit about, but I'll do whatever I have to to make myself seem useful to our parents and avoid any backlash on any of the guys.

Seemingly satisfied, he nods, downing the last of his coffee before getting to his feet.

"Right, we going?" he asks Mason.

"Sure thing."

As Hawk walks toward the door, Mason swoops in to plant a quick, searing kiss on my lips, leaving them tingling as the two of them leave the apartment.

Once I'm alone, I swivel slowly on my stool, taking in my view of the kitchen and living space from here while I ponder what to do with myself. We still have several hours before we have to head down for breakfast. I don't know what time West or Cam get up, but I'd guess Cam is a last-minute kind of guy. I'd imagine West likes to take his time, so he'll probably be awake in another hour or so.

Getting up, I refresh my coffee from the pot and saunter over to the living room to curl up on one end of the sofa and face the TV. Grabbing the remote, I surf through a few channels before finding something that looks half-decent to watch.

I couldn't even tell you the last time I just sat and scrolled through various television channels. Watching TV wasn't something we ever had the opportunity to do at the compound. Occasionally they would put on a movie as a reward, but it was once a year at best. After I managed to escape, I mostly lived on the streets for the few weeks before starting here. There were a couple of nights when I sprung for a motel that sometimes came with a TV, yet for the most part, I had to conserve every penny I had. It took me over a year to save that money and get everything in place for my big escape. I couldn't just throw it away for the sake of a hard, lumpy bed for a night.

Leaning back against the cushions, my whole body relaxes as I get engrossed in a crime show where some woman has been murdered, and the detectives are running around in circles as they try to uncover her murderer. It's painfully apparent the guy killed his wife; how the police can't see that is beyond me.

Although, whoever the show's producer is, clearly didn't know anything about what happens when you slit someone's throat. The best way is to stand behind the person so that way, you have the necessary force to pull your knife through their throat. It's no easy job cutting through all that skin, muscle, and cartilage, especially if you want to be sure they'll bleed out quickly and not gain a second lease on life for long enough to call the police after you've gone. Plus, it stops you from getting completely saturated in the blood, which is always a win.

Only by the looks of things, the guy on this TV show had barely more than grazed the dead woman, and the angle of the wound was all wrong for someone of his height. It's laughable how inaccurate it all is.

My stomach grumbles as the show ends a half hour later—they caught the guy eventually, but what took me two minutes to piece together took them the whole forty-five-minute episode to figure out.

When my stomach grumbles again, I realize I won't be able to wait until breakfast, and decide a raid of the guys' pantry is in order. It's already bad enough that I have to sit and be gawked at every morning while I eat. If I go in there hungry and someone pisses me off, it will only cause more problems that none of us need.

Baby

CHAPTER TEN

Maybe it's knowing that Hadley is currently asleep mere feet away from me, that only a thin wall separates me from her. Whatever it is, I'm awake at the ass-crack of fucking dawn. I toss and turn for a while before eventually giving up and deciding I may as well get up, throwing on a pair of sweats and a t-shirt before leaving my room.

As I walk into the kitchen, I come to a stop, watching Hadley as she bends down to reach into a cupboard. Her firm ass in the air acts like a red flag to a bull as my dick hardens in my sweats.

I stand and watch her—something that has become my norm—unable to keep my eyes off her. It doesn't matter if she's just sitting and studying, interacting with the guys, or full-on fucking them. Apparently, I've turned into a complete fucking pervert and will watch her do just about anything.

I've lost count of the number of times I've jerked myself off to the image of her fucking Mason while West stood behind her, pulling on her hair. It's the hottest thing I've seen since I watched her come all over my dick—the second most commonly played video in my spank bank.

She doesn't notice me as she lifts a bowl from the cupboard, standing upright. The only thing she's wearing is an oversized t-shirt that barely covers her ass—most likely West's if the banging of his headboard against our adjoining wall is any indication of who she spent the night with.

I'm happy for him. I know West has had issues in the past when it comes to girls and sex, so if he can find someone he can be himself with in the bedroom, then that's great, but that doesn't mean I'm not jealous as fuck.

The way the top clings to the curves of her ass makes her look absolutely fuckable, and despite me mentally berating my dick to calm the fuck down, it's as hard as a fucking rock in my pants. Not an uncommon occurrence when Hadley's around. Though it's sure as fuck not comfortable, and jerking off to the image of her is a shitty substitute for the real thing.

I don't even remember moving, but the next thing I know, I'm standing beside the island in the kitchen, close enough that the overwhelming scent of her washes over me, flooding my senses. The combination of vanilla, honey, and sex is intoxicating. My mouth waters at the thought of tasting her again, my dick twitching to remind me of his presence and ensure I haven't forgotten about him and his needs.

As if I could forget how fucking much I want to be buried balls-deep in that tight pussy, having her scream my name as her juices drip down my dick.

Sensing someone behind her, she spins to face me. Her fists are clenched tightly as though she's about to hit me. *Why does that only make my dick strain harder to get to her?* I'm on the verge of coming in my pants like a fucking virgin.

Her eyes widen in surprise, and she drops her fists.

"What are you doing creeping up on me?" she snaps, although there's no real heat behind her words.

"Sorry," I mumble distractedly, my attention caught on where her nipples are peaking through her shirt. *Is she as turned-on as I am right now?*

I don't know if she can read something in my expression or see the obvious fucking hard-on in my pants, but her pupils dilate.

"Cam?" Her voice is breathy. That one word has so much confusion, hesitation, and heat. I can't blame her for being confused and unsure. Ever since I opened my fat mouth and said her name in the dining hall, everything's been so fucked-up. I can't believe I was so stupid as to think that wouldn't change things. How did I not see that that's the last thing she would have wanted? I was so busy thinking about claiming her publicly and showing her off so every other asshole in this place would know to keep their hands off her, that I didn't think about what *she* wanted.

Her tongue flicks out to run along her lower lip. There's no way she doesn't feel whatever the fuck this is between us, right? Even when I was furious with her, wanting to bury her ten-feet under, thinking she was fucking my father, I still couldn't ignore how much I fucking wanted her.

Despite how intense this chemistry is between us, she still shouldn't want anything to do with me. After what I did to her...What my father has done to her. The same blood runs through my veins as is in his. It's no longer bright red and flowing but black and sluggish, like tar. It's sick and tainted, poisoned by generations of malicious hate and greed. The Rutherford blood is infected. *I'm* infected. Diseased to the fucking core. I should come with a fucking hazard sign.

"Stop it," she seethes, somehow able to tell my thoughts are spiraling out of control. "I'm sick of watching you drown yourself in self-hatred."

"You would too, if your family was as heinous as mine."

She steps toward me, closing the distance between us.

"You can't be held responsible for anyone's actions but your own." Her tone is soft yet insistent, and I can see the truth of her words in her eyes. "As for your own actions...you have to learn to live with them. I've already forgiven you, but you have to forgive yourself."

"I don't..." I trail off, sighing while I shake my head. "How?" I don't know how to move on from what I did. I don't understand how *she* can forgive me. As far as I can tell, there's nothing within me worthy of forgiveness.

"I have done far worse shit than you can ever imagine," she murmurs. "The reasons behind your actions are what matter. Yours came from a place of pain; mine were for survival. We do what we must, to scratch out some sort of existence for ourselves and hope we can live with the consequences of our decisions. You need to learn to accept everything that's happened and move forward with your life. It doesn't do you, or anyone else, any good to drown in it all."

While there's sorrow in her eyes, it's clear, whatever she's done, she doesn't regret her actions. I find it impossible to believe her, in any case. Sure, she's probably had to do some fucked-up shit to get by, and who can blame her? But there's no way it can be as bad as what our parents are involved in. Or what my father has done to her. Just like I don't fully believe she came here to kill me. They're just words she's said to try and make me feel better, to try and ease my guilt, and while I appreciate her effort, it's not necessary.

She reaches out, linking our fingers together, her palm resting on the back of mine. "I can think of much better things we could be doing with our time instead of hating on one another," she whispers in a low, seductive purr, peering up at me through her eyelashes, a coy smile dancing along her luscious lips.

She slowly directs our hands toward the hem of her shirt, using her hold to place my hand over her pussy so I'm cupping it.

I groan at finding her naked and my fingertips instinctively curl, sliding through her wetness, eliciting a moan from the back of my throat. She's fucking soaked already, and I can't remember ever needing someone the way I ache for her. My balls are blue and ready to fall off, not the slightest bit impressed at having been denied her sweetness for so long.

She pushes against my hand as her fingers and mine slide into her tight channel. Her lips part on a breathy gasp, and I stare transfixed at the glisten of moisture on her lower lip as I slide deeper into her, feeling her walls spasm around us.

I want this—her—so badly, but disbelief that she could want me after everything stills my fingers inside of her, even as my dick practically screams my ear off for putting a stop to this when he was so close to getting where he's been dying to be for months.

"You already have the others. Why would you need me?"

Her eyes dart back and forth between mine, a rare vulnerability taking over her features. She walks around with walls so high and thick that nothing can break through them. Except, right now, she's letting me see a part of herself she doesn't show many people. In fact, when I think back to her wary, barbed-wire attitude when she first arrived at Pac, I'm not sure she let anyone get close to her before she showed up here.

"None of them are you," she says in a quiet whisper, looking deep into my eyes and letting me see just how much she means what she says. "You constantly remind me of what I've been fighting for. When I found the strength to escape Lawrence, my entire focus was on survival, but you've shown me what it's like to live. The nights we spent in the dining hall, when you told me about everything you and the guys used to get up to when you were kids, made me realize what I'd been missing my whole life. I craved that sense of belonging, of having friendships, and feeling that deep-seated loyalty the four of you share.

"You were the first one to *see* me. To make me laugh and forget about the dark past I was running from and the uncertain future I was heading toward. With you, I was able to live in the moment and enjoy it.

"I miss that. I miss *you*. I miss how your touch burns my skin and ignites a fire in my soul. I want to feel that again. I don't want to go another day without you."

Well, fuck me raw and piss on my grave. What the hell am I supposed to say to that?

There's nothing I can say. Nothing I can do except give her exactly what she wants. With my fingers still deep in her pussy, I flex them, pressing against her sensitive bundle of nerves. Removing the last bit of distance between us, my chest pushes against hers as I wrap my hand around the back of her neck, drawing her toward me.

I slant my lips over hers, swallowing her moan of pleasure when I press my thumb against her clit. Her small hands fist the front of my t-shirt as I pump my fingers in and out of her, repeatedly gliding over her G-spot until I feel her clenching around me, her soft cries driving me on.

"Cam," she pants in a half plea-half moan just before she finds her release, her juices running down my hand while I continue to finger-fuck her through her orgasm.

As her scent permeates the air around her, I lose myself to my basic needs. Carnal hunger takes control as I wrap my hands around her thighs, lifting her up onto the island.

She gasps as her bare ass hits the cold marble, and I fist the bottom of her t-shirt, tearing it over her head and exposing her to me. Her nipples harden in the room's cool air, and I dip my head, licking her areola before sucking her nipple into my mouth, biting teasingly on the sensitive skin.

I push against her chest until she's lying flat on the island, staring up at me with half-lidded eyes, her pupils blown with desire. Her breaths come in rapid pants that make her tits bounce up and down in the most inviting way.

Fuck, I want to stick my dick between them and come all over her chest.

But I want to taste her more. I've been fucking dreaming about eating her out again. I swear, some mornings, I've woken up with the lingering taste of her on my tongue.

Pushing her thighs apart, I lick my lips as I devour her glistening pink pussy with my eyes. She's so fucking wet, the evidence from her last orgasm still coating her folds.

Lifting her legs so they rest on my shoulders, I lower my head between her milky thighs, nibbling on the soft skin until she's a writhing mess beneath me.

Only when she's practically begging for it, do I push my tongue between her drenched pussy lips, moaning against her skin as I lap up her juices. When I place my lips over her clit to suck it into my mouth, her hands thread through my hair, smooshing my face against her pussy, and I inhale her scent. She smells like the best wet dream: all dirty sex and carnal desire.

"Fuck, Cam," she moans, grinding against me as I slide my tongue down her slit until I push it inside her.

With one hand wrapped around her thigh, I use my other one to undo the drawstring of my sweats, shoving them and my boxers down my thighs until I can free my cock. Gripping my length, I give it a few quick pumps, groaning in pleasure and causing her to moan at the vibration.

Her hands tighten in my hair, and she tugs on the strands, pulling my head back.

"You're fucking amazing at that," she pants, "but I need your dick in me. Now."

Yes, ma'am.

I don't waste a second shucking out of my sweats and boxers as I pull my top over my head.

The height of the island has her swollen pussy lined up perfectly with my throbbing dick, and I don't give a single fuck about how unhygienic all of this is as I push inside of her.

The feel of her wrapped around me has my balls tingling, and I'm close to spilling my load already, but there's no fucking way I'm coming so soon. I focus on reciting the months of the year backward until the feeling subsides and only then do I dare pull back until only the tip of my dick is left inside her.

I can feel her clenching, as if trying to stop me from pulling out, and I smirk down at her as she gazes up at me in a blissed-out haze before I slam all the way in.

Her mouth drops open on a silent gasp as I repeatedly hit that magical spot inside her until I feel her spasm around me, and her head tilts back, eliciting a scream from her.

I hope Hawk isn't around to hear that, or I'll be getting an earful later—totally worth it, though!

I continue to pound into her as she gushes all over my dick until my balls draw up and I find my own release, grunting as I come.

"Fuck, that was way better than I remember," I groan, leaning down and kissing her as she chuckles breathily against my lips.

"Let's not wait so long to do it again." Her voice is raspy, her cheeks flushed, and she looks royally fucked. Just looking at her has my dick twitching within her, and we both groan before I reluctantly pull out. I doubt we'd get a second round uninterrupted. I'm surprised no one has disturbed us already, and I don't really want Hawk to tear my balls off for fucking his sister on the kitchen counter.

I'm handing Hadley her top and pulling up my sweats when West's voice takes us by surprise.

"About time," he quips, leaning against the kitchen doorway in his perfectly pressed uniform. *How long was that asshole watching us?* I can't get a read on his expression as he pushes off the doorframe, clapping me on the shoulder as he walks past. Moving in front of Hadley, he plants a heated kiss on her lips. He doesn't appear to be the slightest bit bothered by the fact I just fucked his girlfriend.

Hadley smiles into their kiss.

"Morning," he murmurs against her lips, sounding like a sappy idiot. What the fuck has this girl done to all of us?

"Morning." She smiles at him before jumping down from the counter. "I'm going to go shower." With a final, lingering look my way, she walks out of the room, leaving me feeling awkward as fuck as I blatantly ignore West's gaze drilling into the side of my head.

"So, that happened."

"Yup," I respond dismissively, grabbing food out of the fridge to make omelets for breakfast and putting on a fresh pot of coffee for everyone. I'm the only one who knows how to cook. Growing up, there wasn't much to do, and when I wasn't with the guys, I'd be bored out of my mind. One day, I accidentally flicked onto the cooking channel and thought it would be a laugh to give it a go. After setting off the smoke alarm and somehow managing to start a small fire in the pan, our housekeeper agreed to help me, so long as I promised to never attempt anything when she wasn't around.

After that rocky start, I quickly discovered an enjoyment in the process. It was a great distraction when my dad was even more of a prick than usual or when none of the guys were free.

I don't cook often—there's not much of a need when the dining hall is right beside us and you can order food to go from it—but every now and again, I like to immerse myself in it and forget about whatever problems we're facing—or distract myself from awkward questions and unwanted opinions from West.

"I'm glad, man. It's about time you stopped moping around."

My eyebrows pull together. "I haven't been *moping*," I argue.

"Well, whatever you wanna call it, it will be good to have the old Cam back."

He squeezes my shoulder before lifting down two mugs and filling them with coffee while I chop the vegetables and make us breakfast with a bit more pep in my step than I've had recently. *Nothing like morning sex with the girl you can't stop thinking about to put you in a great mood.*

"Mmm, something smells good," Hadley states as she walks into the room, wearing her hoodie and leggings from last night, her damp hair framing her face.

Grabbing a mug she must have been drinking out of earlier, she refills it before sitting at the island.

"Where's Hawk? He not up yet?" I ask, lifting out plates and cutlery for us.

"He went to the gym with Mason," Hadley informs us.

"More for us then," I grin at her before dishing up the food and setting all three plates down on the island and putting out plates for Mason and Hawk in the oven for when they get back.

"Mmm, this is delicious," Hadley blurts out around a mouthful of food. She eats like a half-starved savage, shoveling her food into her mouth as quickly as possible. It's as if she's afraid that someone will take it away from her if she doesn't eat it quickly enough. What sort of childhood do you have to endure to grow up with such a mentality?

"I wouldn't have pegged you as knowing how to cook," she says as she finishes off the last remnants and pushes her plate away. West and I are barely halfway through our meals, and I notice him watching her closely out of the corner of his eye, likely picking up on the same behavior I am.

"I'm just full of surprises." I give her a dirty wink across the island, making her laugh.

"Oh, can I get whatever information you have on the other students?" she asks, turning to West.

"Sure, I'll get it all together and give it to you tonight."

"Thanks." She smiles at him like he hung the moon for her instead of just grabbing a bunch of folders from his room. "Well, that was delish, but I'd better get back to my dorm before anyone thinks I'm doing the walk of shame." She laughs at her own joke as she slips off her stool. "See you at breakfast," she calls over her shoulder before heading out the door.

Hadley

CHAPTER ELEVEN

I've spent the last few evenings going through the files West gave me, completely sucked in by all the drama going on here over the past four years. Girls cheating on guys; guys cheating on girls. Friends sabotaging friends. It's downright vicious. And that's before you even start in on the blackmailing of teachers to improve grades and the threatening of other students to do people's bidding.

Then there's the out-and-out illegal shit. This is where things get seriously fucked up. Apparently, our fifty-five-year-old chemistry teacher moonlights as the school's drug dealer. The great thing is that he offers flexible payment plans to his clients. Can't front the cash for your coke or Ritalin? No worries, he's happy to accept payment in the form of underage sex. The best part is, he's not fussy as to whether it's dick or pussy. You won't get any sexism from this guy.

The downside is that most of these kids don't realize they're being recorded as they perform these sexual acts, and based on the videos on the teacher's OnlyPorn account, he's uploading them and selling them as soft porn. *Fucking gross.*

It actually pisses me off that none of the guys have put a stop to this. Are they seriously okay with this dude getting away with that? I fucking hope not; I had higher expectations of them. All of us have been flat out with schoolwork and ensuring the Princes still have control of the school, so I haven't had a chance to call them out on any of it yet, but you can be sure that talk will be coming real soon.

For now, my focus is on the material I can use against the girls. Whispers and rumors have been spreading all week as girls speculate about the reason behind the Princes' change in behavior. I've heard everything from the plausible to the hilarious, to the downright absurd. I swear I overheard some guy telling his buddies he was certain the guys were all in one big gay relationship together—I laughed my head off at that.

Of course, the rumors mainly revolve around me. It's far too coincidental that I show up this year, and the guys suddenly change things up. Thankfully, no one seems to have worked out the truth. I don't know if it's because Hawk's my brother and the guys very much give off the impression that they do everything together, that has people not immediately jumping to the fact I'm sleeping with two—well, now three—of them, but whatever the reason, I'm glad. The last thing I need is the girls breathing down my neck or our parents finding out about us. The most popular theory seems to be that our parents have demanded the change due to my sudden reappearance—a theory we are all happy to go along with.

Regardless of the reason, though, the girls aren't happy. None of them have acted on it yet, but it's only a matter of time. The discontent is heavy in the air. It's in every conspiratorial look they share. It's in the hurt, angry, confused glares they throw at the guys and the sneers and dismissive looks at me. None of them are pleased, and it won't be long before they make their objection known.

Bianca has kept her distance since the party, but I've noticed her watching me, as though she's measuring me up and trying to decide if I'm a threat. If she hasn't figured out by now that I am, there's no hope for her. She should know by now I'm the big bad wolf. I may look innocent, but my claws are sharp, and I like to bite. If she pisses me off any further, I'm going to tear her to pieces, and I'll fucking enjoy it.

But then, because I'm a sick bitch, I actually *want* her to come at me. We've been butting heads since day one, and the tension is only rising. I'm just waiting for her to present me with the perfect opportunity to bring her down and then show the whole school what happens if they mess with me.

I've spent the last few nights familiarizing myself with all the possible blackmail information I have, trying to work out who people are and remember their names in case I need to recall any of this shit on the fly. It's been the perfect distraction from the nauseating butterflies doing somersaults in my stomach. Cam asked if I wanted to meet him in the dining hall tonight, just like old times. Ever since I agreed, my stomach's been in knots. I don't know what the hell has come over me. This is *Cam*. There's nothing for me to be anxious about. We've done this a dozen times before.

A giddiness takes over me as I gather up the folders and pull the bookcase away from the wall so I can drop the folders into the hole I made. It feels like it's been forever since Cam and I had one of our late-night chats, and I'm pleased to see him reaching out. I was worried he'd be awkward after what happened the other day. It was unexpected, but honestly, I think it's what we needed to move forward.

Throwing a hoodie over my head, I shove my feet into my boots and grab my key as I head out the door, trying to ignore the fact I feel like someone who's going on their first-ever date—at least, that's how I imagine it feels like.

With sweaty hands, I pull open the door to the dining hall, but the high-pitched whine of fucking Bianca has me hesitating in the doorway. Shifting my body so I'm hidden behind the door, I hold it ajar to eavesdrop on them. I know, I shouldn't be listening, but I'm curious as to what they're talking about and, well, I guess I wanna hear what Cam has to say. After his back and forth with her all year, who can blame me?

"I don't understand what's going on," I hear Bianca grate. "Why have things suddenly changed?"

"Bianca." Cam sounds tired, making me wonder how long she's been bothering him for. "Things change. Just accept it."

"But why?"

God, she sounds like a stropping two-year-old.

"Because of *her*?" she sneers, the venom clear to hear in her tone.

"It's got nothing to do with *her*," Cam seethes, making me wince. I know he's only trying to get rid of her, and he can't let her think there's anything between us, but damn, that hurts.

"But we used to be so good together." I can picture the pout on her face as she changes tactics, trying to suck up to him instead. Peeking my head around the door, I see she has stepped closer to him. So close her breast grazes against his arm, momentarily making me see red. A little voice in my head snarls, *Mine*, and even though that's not technically true, it *feels* fucking right.

"I even got these for you," she goes on to say, lifting her tits. It would be fucking impossible to miss her double D's that are so out of proportion to the rest of her slim body. "Because I know how much you liked to fuck them."

Eww! Yup, that lasagna I had for dinner does not taste so nice on its way back up.

Cam grimaces. "You shouldn't have done that, B. It was just sex. Nothing more."

"So what, you're fucking celibate now?" she gripes, instantly dropping the 'woe is me' act as her temper flares. "Don't bullshit me, Cam. If you're not getting it from me, you're getting it from someone else. What makes *her* so fucking special, huh? You know when the school finds out—and they will find out—they'll crucify her."

Cam's hands dart out and grab onto her upper arms, shaking her roughly. The expression on his face is like nothing I've seen on him before. Even when he wanted to murder me, there was always this spark in his eyes that told me he would never take things too far. Only today, that spark is gone. His gaze is ice-fucking-cold, his eyes nothing but a blank void as he towers over her.

"You better be careful, Bianca," he snarls menacingly. "Threats like that will get you in real trouble one day."

In the next second, he shoves her away from him, shrugging his shoulders indifferently and tucking his fingers into the front pockets of his jeans. A complete one-eighty from the gargoyle he resembled a second ago.

"Anyway, you're wrong. There's no girl. We're graduating soon—moving on to bigger, better things. The four of us are just over the whole skanky, desperate thing. We want someone with more…substance. With a bit of a backbone. Not a whiny bitch."

Having heard enough—and admittedly feeling a tad smug after Cam's little speech—I push open the door, announcing my entrance before Bianca can start on another unwanted tirade.

Bianca's back is mostly turned toward me, so Cam notices me first. A wicked glint enters his eye.

"I wondered what that smell was." My voice echoes around the otherwise empty hall as I wrinkle my nose in disgust and grimace.

Bianca turns in her obscenely tall high heels, giving me the stink eye. "What smell?" she says irritably.

"The stench of desperation that's coming off of you. I could smell it all the way from the dorms."

Cam barks out an arctic laugh as Bianca's eyes narrow and her lips purse.

"Get out of here, trash. Cam and I are busy."

I scoff. "Yeah, I don't think so."

"Fuck off, Bianca. And stop sending me twat shots. I don't wanna see that shit," Cam sneers, going into full-asshole Prince mode.

Her cheeks tint in embarrassment, or rage—probably both—and she throws each of us a scathing look, but I don't miss the hurt in her eyes.

"Word of advice, girl. If you don't want to be treated like a walking, talking cumbucket, don't act like one." It might sound harsh, but it's a life lesson she evidently needs to learn. Although if the murderous look she tosses my way is anything to go by, she doesn't appreciate the advice.

Oh well, you can't help people who refuse to help themselves.

With a venomous snarl, unable to form any real comeback, she stamps her feet and storms out in typical Bianca fashion.

"Twat shot?" I chuckle after she's gone.

Cam shrugs. "Like a female dick pic. I'm going to need therapy if I have to look at them anymore."

"Just stop looking at them," I retort, rolling my eyes.

"You think I look at that shit?!" He fake gags. "Hell no. The image automatically appears at the top of my screen when I get a notification. That's enough to have me wanting to pluck out my eyeballs, never mind looking at it on the full screen." He shudders, looking thoroughly sickened.

I can't help but laugh at his dramatics, although, yeah, I'd probably feel the need to scrub the image out of my eyes, too, if I had to see that shit.

"Anyway, enough about her. I, uh, wasn't sure if you'd want coffee or ice cream, so I grabbed us a coffee-flavored ice cream to share, if that's okay?"

His demeanor has wholly changed from the asshole he acted like in front of Bianca. Now he seems nervous as he rubs awkwardly at the back of his neck, seeming unsure.

I smile reassuringly at him. "Coffee ice cream sounds awesome." The tension drains out of his posture immediately, and he smiles back as I close the distance between us to sit down in a chair facing him. Neither of us talks as he pops the lid off the tub and hands me a spoon, the two of us digging in.

The tub is nearly empty by the time my stomach screams in protest, and I lean back in my chair, watching as Cam finishes it off.

"I missed this," I say quietly, as though the truth of the words would be too much to handle if I spoke them any louder.

Cam glances up at me, setting the empty tub on the table along with his spoon. A softness enters his eyes, and a sad smile dances along his lips.

"Yeah, me too."

Awkward tension burns up the air between us until Cam laughs sheepishly. "I don't know how to act around you now. I have no idea what we're doing. Do we go back to the way things used to be? Is that even possible?"

"I don't know," I admit, chewing anxiously on my bottom lip. "What do you want to happen?"

He takes a second to think over his answer, but a heated resolve enters his eyes.

"I want all the things with you." His voice has taken on a deeper tone. A hungry rasp that has my vagina waking up and suddenly paying attention. "I want what we had before, and so much more."

My eyes bulge at his admission. *Well, damn.* I'd kind of hoped that's what he'd want. I can't explain it, but this pull between us is irresistible. Fighting it is exhausting. I was fully expecting him to go back to trying to put distance between us, and while I'd respect that if it's what he wanted, I'm honestly tired of all the hate and anger. If he's willing, I want to see how amazing things could be between us.

Slipping out of my chair, I round the table and slide onto his lap. His hands instantly come to rest on my hips, as though he couldn't bear to go another second without touching me.

"I want all that too," I murmur, looking into his eyes, right before he crushes his lips to mine and the two of us lose ourselves in one another. My fingers tangle with the still-damp strands of hair at the nape of his neck, Cam having most likely come straight from a training session at the pool. We shouldn't be doing this here, where anyone could walk in and see us, but the heat between us is an unstoppable force. We're like two magnets being pulled toward one another, and there's no stopping the inevitable collision.

All too soon, we pull apart.

"Come with me." He hurriedly gets to his feet, pulling me up with him.

"What...Why? Where are we going?"

He steps into me, his nearness ratcheting up that magnetic pull between us. "If we stay here, I'm not going to be able to hold you. I won't be able to kiss you or do any of the things I want to do to you."

Well, when he puts it like that. "Lead the way."

A bright grin lights up his face, reminiscent of the old Cam that I've missed so much. I love seeing that smile on his face, and I'd do pretty much anything to ensure he never loses that happiness.

Leaving the dining hall, we step into the gloomy night. It's nearly midnight, so not many people are about, but we still need to be careful.

"Are we not going to your dorm?" I ask when he starts to walk in the opposite direction. I'd just assumed that's where we were going.

"If I take you there, I'll have to share you with West and Mason." Leaning down, he whispers in my ear, "I want you all to myself for a little while." The tickle of his breath against my ear and the sexual husk in his voice have me suppressing a shiver as my pussy clenches, already hungry for him.

He's all but sprinting as he pulls me after him, and I giggle as we quickly make our way through the forest toward the lake. We continue at a hurried pace, skipping past the boat house until we reach the tree line on the opposite side of the lake. I've never been to this part of campus before. It's so far away from everything that I just assumed there was nothing out here. Hidden amongst the trees is a small hut and a short boardwalk that goes out into the water.

We walk to the end of the boardwalk, and Cam shrugs out of his jacket, setting it down on the wooden boards. He sits down, patting the space beside him. Doing as he commands, my thigh presses against his, our legs dangling above the dark water.

Neither of us speaks. Instead, we sit and listen to the slight breeze whistle through the trees overhead as we look out over the cavernous lake.

"So," Cam begins, back to his initial awkwardness, "my dad's trying to trap you into being his bitch bride."

I snort. Of course, Cam has to turn the whole fucked-up situation into a joke.

"I guess that makes me almost your bitch mommy."

His face scrunches in disgust before he bursts out laughing. "Fuck, that would have been super weird."

"You're telling me," I agree.

The two of us chuckle before Cam's features grow serious. "So, how did you get away from him?"

I glance away and peer out over the lake as I contemplate the answer to his question. "I ran away." It's difficult. I can't give him many more details without coming right out and telling him about the rest of my fucked-up past. I'm not entirely sure why I'm still keeping it from the guys. I told Beck, after all. But out of all of them, he was the easiest one to open up to. And not because the others have made me feel like I can't be honest with them. I guess it's since they're closer to their parents, and they're the direct heirs of the company. It makes it that much harder to be entirely open with them.

"Why now? Why didn't you run away years ago?"

I sigh. It's a good question. "Have you ever been so consumed by your fears that they've immobilized you?"

"Like night terrors?"

"Yeah, but when you're awake. That's how I felt every time your dad was around me. I wanted to fight back, yet I was frozen with fear. He was the scariest thing in my universe—and that's saying something. Over the years, he convinced me I could never get away from him. He swore he'd never let me go. Hearing that over and over messes with you. The words get into your head and make you believe they're real. It took me a long time to realize his words were just that—words.

"One day, when he was with me, he received a call from the school...about you. You'd done something that had obviously warranted a call to him. Before then, I knew nothing about this man who visited me once a month and brought me unwanted gifts. I felt powerless, which further reinforced his influence over me.

"However, that day, he said your name and the name of your school. I know it wasn't much, but it was enough for me to work with. Enough for me to feel like I had some control. Something I could use to fight back with."

"So you made a plan to escape?"

I nod my head. "More or less."

"And came to Pac?"

I nod again.

"To kill me."

It's not a question, and I can tell by the tone of his voice that he doesn't believe me or believe I'm capable of doing something like that. He's seen me fight twice now, so he knows I have the skills to do it, but there's a massive difference between physically being able to overpower someone and being mentally strong enough to take someone's life. If only he knew I could do both. Despite the darkness that lives inside him and likes to rear its ugly head now and again, Cam is all light and happiness. Honestly, he's the one I worry about the most when it comes to telling them my truth. I don't think Mason will be all that shocked, and I believe West will be able to rationalize it. Hawk, I'm not sure about yet, but Cam...I worry it will be too much for him.

"Yeah. I know it sounds far-fetched—"

"Not really," he admits, shaking his head. He's deep in thought, lines furrowed across his forehead. "You're physically capable, and you've proven you can get in and out of our apartment without us noticing. If you'd wanted to, you probably could have done it ten times over by now."

More like fifty, but who's keeping count?

"So why didn't you?"

He looks genuinely confused, and it breaks my heart a little. I've seen true evil. I've stared it in the face every day for years, so I *know* Cam is anything but evil. Yeah, he's got demons within him, but who doesn't? This world tries to beat you down every damn day. It's only a matter of time until all that locked-up anger and resentment takes on its own form. We all like to think we're not capable of horrible things, but in the right circumstances, with the right incentive, we're capable of anything. We all have demons inside of us; some people's are just more vile and barbaric than others.

I shift onto my knees and move to straddle him, needing him to see the honest truth in my eyes. I've told him this before, but I get the impression that he wasn't really listening, or he didn't believe what I had to say, so I want him to genuinely hear me now.

With my face taking up his whole field of vision, I press my palms flush against his cheeks, so he has no option but to look at me. "Because you are nothing like your father." I see the protest forming on his lips, and I quickly lean in, pressing a chaste kiss to shut him up.

"You are the sunlight on a dark day, the rainbow when it pours, the lighthouse in a storm. You're *my* sunlight. *My* rainbow. *My* lighthouse. I was barely alive when I turned up here, but *you* helped me learn to breathe. You made me see there's more to life than just surviving. I *need* you in my life, making me laugh and reminding me of the good times when things go wrong. So please, *please* don't let all this self-hatred and guilt you're carrying around swallow you up, because I don't know what any of us would do without you."

A tear leaks out of the corner of his eye and runs down his cheek, catching on the edge of my thumb before I swipe it away. The way he looks at me…I don't know how to describe it. It's almost like reverence. No one has ever looked at me like that, like I'm some sort of angel sent to guide them.

His hand wraps around the back of my head, his fingers tangling in my hair as he draws me in. His lips collide with mine, hungry and eager. It's more than just carnal need, however. The way he kisses me, it's like I'm his lifeline. The only thing keeping him alive right now.

I kiss him back with as much fervor, needing him just as badly as he needs me. Our hands are everywhere as our bodies burn up. Tearing our clothes off, Cam wastes no time sinking into me in the most delicious way possible. It doesn't take long before we're both cresting that peak, and I cry out my release into the night sky.

"I hope you know I'm never letting you go," he pants in my ear.

That suits me perfectly fine. I have no intention of going anywhere.

Hadley

CHAPTER TWELVE

I storm into the computer suite, sending the door banging off the wall as I sear anyone who so much as dares glance in my direction with a heart-stopping death glare.

We knew the girls would do something, but this has Bianca's dirty fingerprints written all over it. I'm going to tear out her fucking ovaries and force-feed them to her.

"Wow, why do you look like you want to murder someone?" West asks, cocking a brow as I dump myself in the seat beside him.

"Have you seen this?" I snarl, opening my tablet for him to see. Navigating to the page, I thrust it under his nose and watch as his eyes widen and his features tighten, a scowl forming across his face.

That dead fucking bitch set up a website where any Tom, Dick, and Harry can watch that stupid fucking video Cam and Hawk released last semester. I make a mental note to tear them new assholes when this class is over.

"Look at the number of views." I'm practically vibrating with anger in my chair. "And do you see what it says about me? That *bitch* even got her hands on fake medical records that say I've been in a fucking psychiatric unit all this time. She's got the whole school thinking I'm fucking unstable. No one will even look at me today. One kid nearly peed himself when he accidentally walked in front of me."

He quirks an eyebrow. "Thought you hated everyone trying to get your attention."

"Doesn't mean I want them thinking I'm about to go apeshit on their asses."

I know he's about to come back with another stupid retort, but he sees my deadpan stare and thinks better of it—smart boy. He focuses back on the tablet for another few seconds before setting it down, pulling the same screen up on his computer, and split-screening it along with one of his gibberish code programs.

"What are you doing?" I ask curiously. "Can you take it down?"

"Better," he assures me with a smug smirk, his fingers flying furiously over the keyboard.

I want to know what he means by that, but I don't want to distract him when he's busy, so instead I sit and watch, not having the faintest idea what he's doing.

After about fifteen minutes, he hands the tablet back to me. "Okay, refresh the page and play the video."

"What? West, I really don't need to see that thing again. I know what my body looks like, thanks."

He rolls his eyes at me like I'm being deliberately obtuse. "Just play the damn video, Firefly."

"Fine," I sigh dramatically, doing as he asks.

I'm only half-watching as the video begins to play, but the second I realize I'm not looking at myself but at Bianca's head on a blob of a body, jiggling as it does some sort of weird naked dance, I throw my head back and burst out laughing. *Holy shit, that's fucking amazing.*

"How did you do that?" I exclaim, a massive grin on my face. Damn, I want to kiss him so badly right now. "And what about the other stuff?"

He's got a wicked glint in his eye as he smirks back before concentrating on the screen, hopefully getting rid of the fucking article that claims my scars are all self-inflicted and the reason why I was locked away in a psych unit all these years. It's the fake medical records that infuriate me. They look fucking real, and they bluntly state that I'm a danger to myself and others and that I was removed from the facility against medical advice. Fucking bitch is going to pay for this.

"I've erased everything else on the website," West confirms. The tension immediately drops out of my shoulders as I collapse back in my chair. "As for the video, it's pretty easy, really. I've done it before, so it took no time at all to recreate it."

"You've done this before? To who?"

"You read through all the files I gave you, right?"

"Of course." I made sure to read through them all the night he handed them over to me, and I've been keeping them safe since then, scouring through them at every available opportunity.

He nods his head, having expected that answer. "So, you know about our chemistry teacher."

"Yeah, I've been meaning to talk to you guys about that."

Again, he nods his head, pulling up the chemistry teacher's OnlyPorn account on the computer. I'm guessing he was able to bypass whatever website restrictions the school has in place. Somehow, I doubt they would be okay with their students having easy access to such sites during class.

"Did you play the videos he's uploaded?"

"What?! No. Why would I do that? Why the hell haven't *you* taken them down yet if you're so damn talented?" I argue.

The smug look he throws me lets me know I've underestimated him. He passes me an earphone so I can hear the sound as he clicks on the video. Instead of the underage porn I was expecting to find, I have the horrific pleasure of watching Mr. Dillman, our chemistry teacher, trussed up like a thanksgiving turkey as some dominatrix woman spanks his ass, and he screams like a little girl. West pauses it just as the woman produces a monster dildo—there's no other word to describe the ten-inch black dick that's lined up with his asshole, sans lube.

"What," I stutter, flapping my hand at the screen in protest. "It was just getting good."

West laughs as he exits the site.

"How did you manage to do that?"

"It took a lot of work, and required Cam to scare the crap out of him so I could record that girly scream you heard."

I laugh. "Damn, that's amazing. I need a copy of that."

"You seriously thought we just left those videos up there for anyone to see?" he asks, looking hurt. His expression makes me wince.

"Why haven't you gotten rid of him, though? That's all well and good," I say, pointing toward the monitor, "but he's still preying on vulnerable students."

West grits his teeth. "I know," he spits out. "We haven't been able to get rid of him. He's in our parents' pockets, along with several other staff members. We have a mountain of evidence against him, but if we take it to the police now, our parents will just get him off and the school will sweep it under the rug. We're waiting until graduation to release it. We figure by then our parents won't care as much about who in the school is on their payroll."

Well, that makes sense, and now I feel bad for thinking the worst of the guys.

"I'm sorry," I grimace.

West sighs, moving his chair so our knees are pressed together. His fingers come up to press firmly on either side of my chin in a dominating hold that ensures I can't look anywhere but at him.

"It's okay. I know you have difficulties trusting people, and I know you don't fully trust us yet. We might be assholes, but we don't condone what he or our parents are doing." He releases his hold on my chin, clasping my hand between his large palms. "Hawk told us what you said to him, about taking down our parents and the company."

I nod my head.

"We're all in. We're sick of them controlling us. I'm sick of them holding me as leverage over everyone's heads."

I stare at him slack-jawed. "You want to help take them down?"

"Yeah, Firefly. We're going to destroy them, once and for all."

~

WEST'S little computer trick with Bianca was pretty awesome, and it's certainly become the gossip of the school. The video spread like wildfire until Bianca locked herself away in her room, refusing to come out. That was over a week ago, and no one has seen hide nor hair of her since. But, it's not enough. People are still whispering about me. Don't get me wrong, I kinda love the way the color drains out of their faces when I enter a room, but *I* want to instill that fear in them, because they know what I'm capable of, not because some fake document states that I'm mentally unstable. It's crucial that I exert my control over the girls, and the only way to do that is to make it perfectly clear that *I'm* the one with all the power around here.

So that's why I've gathered all the girls in the dining hall this afternoon. Okay, so I had to get the guys to spread the word that *they* were the ones that wanted to speak to the girls, to clear the air with the whole girl of the month thing—I'm pretty sure no one would have shown up if they thought it was me asking for the meeting—but either way, the method worked. Casting my eyes over the crowd as I step into the hall, I see it looks like every senior girl is here. *Excellent.*

With my head held high, my school skirt swishes around my thighs as my combat boots smack against the wooden floor, effectively silencing the crowd as I stride to the front of the room. The guys wanted to join me, but it would make a much more powerful statement if I did this on my own.

When I reach the Princes' table, I pull out a chair, lifting my foot onto it before I step up onto the table so I'm standing above the crowd.

"Where are the Princes?" someone shouts out.

"Are they reinstating the tradition?"

Jesus, is sex with the Princes all these girls think about?!

"No, the tradition is *not* being reinstated," I bark out more harshly than is necessary.

"Then why are we here?"

Oh, look who climbed out of their hidey-hole to join us today.

"Ah, Bianca. It's so great you could be here," I say in a sugary sweet voice, topping it off with a cherry smile.

Breaking eye contact with her, I look out over the assembled girls.

"As you are all aware, a website was set up this week containing slanderous allegations and a compromising video. A video that I did not consent to. Now, if the person who did it will step forward and own up to what they did, this can be sorted out quietly." Whispers erupt in the crowd. I know Bianca did it, and Bianca knows she did it, but I'm guessing most others don't know who the primary suspect could be.

"*If* the offending party does *not* own up to their actions, then everyone will suffer," I declare threateningly. Honestly, I don't expect Bianca to ever own up, but putting the fear of God in the rest of the girls will ensure they think twice before stepping out of line.

"What does that mean?" a nervous voice near the back of the room asks.

"Excellent question. What does that mean? Well, I guess it means that the secrets all of you have that you don't want everyone to know about will start coming to light."

Another round of whispers as girls gasp and frantically consort with the person beside them.

I don't miss Bianca's scoff, though, or how she rolls her eyes. "Do you have something to say, Bianca?" I smile politely at her, like I've all the time in the world.

Huffing, she crosses her arms across her ample chest, cocking her hip. "Please, you've only just started here, and you've been a pariah all year. You don't know anything about any of us."

A few head nods and murmured agreements are scattered throughout the crowd, and my polite smile turns positively vicious as I drop the act and let them see every part of the predator I am.

"Is that so? Let's see." I tap my finger against my lip in time to the tapping of my boot against the tabletop. "I know Tiffany has chlamydia that's gone untreated for over a year." A gasp comes from somewhere on the left side of the room.

"How dare you," Tiffany yells, sounding offended.

"Am I wrong?" I question her with a raised eyebrow. "Would you like me to show you the proof?"

Lifting my phone out of my blazer pocket, I shrug my shoulders like it's no big deal, because *it is no big deal*. With a press of a few buttons the swoosh of an email being sent echoes around the room—okay, so West spent over an hour teaching me how to attach a document to an email and mass send it, but that's so not the point right now—and a few seconds later, everyone's tablets and phones go off.

There is another round of gasps and whispers as everyone reads my email. Attached is the latest letter sent by Tiffany's gynecologist, urging her to contact him immediately regarding her positive chlamydia result from over a year ago. It also lists the long-term consequences of the disease, and trust me, that shit is nasty. Why the fuck she doesn't just get it treated is beyond me.

Tiffany starts screaming a litany of abuse my way, but I just give her a megawatt smile in return, feeling fully in my element right now as I bring all these bitches to heel.

I notice a movement in the far back corner of the room, and my attention flicks to the doorway leading into the kitchen, noticing it's slightly ajar. I have to restrain my eye roll when I spot Mason and Cam squinting through the crack. *Idiots.* They just had to check out what I was doing, didn't they! Noticing me looking at them, Cam gives me a thumbs-up in encouragement, and Mason winks. Ignoring them, I focus back on the girls before me. They are much more subdued than when I first entered the hall.

"Alright," I yell over Tiffany, who's still screaming like a banshee. "Who's next?"

"We don't know who leaked that video," one girl near the front cries out.

"No?" I swivel my gaze around the room before landing on Bianca. She looks paler than before, but she holds her ground—gotta give her credit for that. "None of you have a clue?"

Everyone shakes their heads adamantly.

"Bianca?" I question. "You have no idea who did it?"

"No," she bites out, but I don't miss the quiver in her voice.

I sigh in disappointment, shaking my head as I press another button on my phone. Once again, the flurry of notifications goes off across the room a few seconds later.

After my initial excitement, I was particularly shocked at this revelation, and I didn't even get it from West's blackmail pile. Nope, I found this little beauty all by myself, when I had to pee in the middle of history class. It's amazing…The gossip you overhear while sitting in a bathroom stall.

My eyes stay pinned on Bianca as whispers crescendo around us. For a long moment, she stares back at me, refusing to lower her gaze. Eventually, though, the need to know exactly what bomb I've dropped that will destroy her life gets the better of her, and she glances down at her phone. The color leeches out of her face as her hands start to tremble. She peeks nervously at the girls around her, all gaping with open mouths in her direction.

"Is it true?" I hear someone ask her.

With tears shining in her eyes, she spins on her heels and rushes out of the room, the door closing echoing behind her.

"Take this as a warning," I shout out, making sure everyone can hear me loud and clear. Now that I've dropped the giant bomb, I'm keen to get this shit show over with. "Do not cross me. Do not cross the Princes. Do. Not. Step. Out. Of. Line. I am watching you and will gladly reveal your deepest, darkest secrets to the rest of the school. There's a queen on the throne now, and she won't be taking any prisoners." I pin every single girl with a fierce look that shows them how fucking serious I am. "Now get the fuck out of here," I bark in my best impression of Hawk and Mason.

Everyone jumps into motion, eager to get away from me as quickly as possible. As the girls push and shove their way out the door, I hop down off the table, landing solidly on my feet.

"Holy shit, babe, that was amazing," Mason praises, once we're alone in the hall, pushing his way through the kitchen door with Cam hot on his heels. Gathering me in his arms, he swings me around, making me laugh.

"Seeing you go all demonic on their asses was hot as fuck." Cam is bouncing on the balls of his feet as he waits impatiently for Mason to let go of me, pulling me in for a heated kiss as soon as he does.

"Yeah? You think I made my point?"

"I think you made them piss their pants, Little Warrior." Mason laughs, looking weirdly proud. His praise makes me grin, even if it's a little sick and twisted. "But you have to tell us, what dirt did you have on Bianca?"

I smirk. "She has a secret baby."

Cam gapes at me with wide eyes, and I can see the wheels churning in his head.

"She, what?" Mason exclaims. "How did you find that out?"

"I overheard her arguing with her mom about it one day in the bathroom. I got West to do a little digging, and we uncovered the birth certificate."

"It's not mine, is it?" Cam asks in a strangled voice, sweat forming along his brow.

"No," I assure him, reaching out to squeeze his hand. "It's not."

"Thank fuck," he breathes out, relieved.

Fuck, that would have been a catastrophe. There's no way Bianca would have kept that a secret, however. She's been trying to hook Cam all year—and now I think I know why—but if he was the baby's father, she would have made sure to use it to lock him down tight. Thank fuck for condoms, right?

Word spreads through the campus like wildfire, and by the end of the day, everyone knows about Bianca's not-so-secret baby and Tiffany's untreated chlamydia. The latter quickly packed her bags and escaped campus amidst a bunch of enraged boys.

"Holy shit, girl. Do you have any idea of the mayhem you have unleashed?" Emilia giggles that evening. "Everyone is terrified of you now."

"They should be." I laugh.

"I don't get why you had to do it," Michael chimes in, bewildered. "Or why the guys are no longer picking girls?"

"I had to exert my dominance," I explain casually. "When the guys arrived freshman year, they had to prove they were the top dogs or no one would take them seriously, so now I have to do the same. Stopping the tradition they had with the girls, means I'm the only one in control of them. It makes me look more powerful if I'm doing it on my own instead of riding their coattails."

I didn't really understand why I had to do it, either. Still, now that I've done it, and seen for myself how effective it was at getting everyone to fall in line and see me as the new queen of Pac, I can admit that rush of adrenaline you get from knowing you're the biggest, baddest bitch around is intoxicating. I think I'm a little high off of the power.

"What now?" Emilia asks.

"I'm not sure. I guess I don't need to do anything unless someone steps out of line."

"So." Emilia gets an excited glint in her eye. "Bianca's baby…"

We spend the rest of the day speculating about who the baby daddy is. There was no name on the birth certificate, and apparently Bianca disappeared all of last summer. She told everyone it was because she was getting her boobs done—which it seems she also did—but the main reason she wasn't at any of the summer parties was that she was having a friggin' baby.

Of course, when I first overheard Bianca in that bathroom, my initial concern had been that Cam was the dad—what a fucking disaster that would have been—but West and I were able to work back from the date on the birth certificate. We calculated that she must have gotten pregnant in October or November, and West assured me Cam only started sleeping with her last spring after she was already pregnant. The lucky bitch must have had one teeny-tiny baby bump to pull that one off.

I don't really give a damn who her baby daddy is. Although I'm guessing he's not rich or of the 'right breeding' since she's not shoving a diamond engagement ring in everyone's faces and is instead chasing after *my* filthy rich boyfriend.

Hadley

CHAPTER THIRTEEN

Everything falls into place after my little show in the dining hall. The girls rightfully look at me with fear as I walk past, always either saying nothing or stuttering out a polite hello before scurrying off.

The boys are still annoying as hell, trying to flirt with me at every opportunity. The fact none of them knew my name before all this Davenport crap came to light shows they're just after me because of my supposed money and status. It's repulsive, and I don't have the time of day for them. Yet, they have the audacity to think *I'm* the rude one when I tell them to fuck off. The arrogance of some people!

Over the next week, I try to stay on top of my homework—and fail miserably—and I get to spend time with my friends and the guys, both as a group and some one-on-one time. Life actually feels good right now, except for the dark cloud that is our parents constantly hanging over our heads.

I'm sitting in my room, trying to blast through some of the backlogs of schoolwork I have, when my phone ringing interrupts my concentration.

No one ever calls, so I'm surprised when I see Hawk's name flash on the screen.

"Hey, is West with you?" he blurts out before I can say anything. The unusual strain in his tone has me instantly on alert as I drop my pen and focus on the call.

"Uh, no. Why?"

"Fuck," he curses. "None of us have been able to find him."

"What do you mean?" I rush out, frantically trying to remember when I last saw him. He was at breakfast this morning, but we didn't have any classes together, and I grabbed lunch with Emilia and Michael today, so I haven't seen him since then. "You checked the library and computer lab?"

"Yeah." I can hear the worry in his voice, and it only makes me panic more.

"Have you talked to Beck? Maybe he's with him?" It's a long shot, but it's the only idea I have right now.

"No, I haven't."

"I'll phone him now."

Not waiting for his response, I hang up and dial Beck. He picks up on the second ring.

"Hey, sweetheart, what's up?"

"Have you seen West?" I rush out, sounding panicked as I get straight to the point, a sick feeling settling in my stomach.

"Uh, no, why, what's going on?"

"No one has seen him all day. We were hoping he might have been with you."

I can hear rustling in the background and the flurry of movement before the sound of a door slams shut.

"He's not. I'm coming over now."

"Okay, meet you at the guys' room."

Hanging up, I jam my feet into my boots and rush out the door while my brain frantically tries to think of where he could be. I'm desperately making excuses to myself that he's gotten caught up in his computer stuff or something and lost track of time—anything to stop me from thinking of the alternative—that something has happened to him.

I take the stairs to the guys' floor two at a time, banging my fist on the door.

"Anything?" I ask hopefully, when Hawk answers.

"In the last two minutes? No."

Ignoring his pissy attitude, I stride past him, saying, "He's not with Beck. He's coming over now to help."

Cam and Mason are sitting at the island. Cam's typing on his tablet, and Mason sighs as he hangs up his phone. "His cell just goes straight to voicemail."

"He's not answering any of my messages either," Cam tacks on.

"Has he ever done this before? Is it possible he's just working on a project and lost track of time?" My voice is tinged with optimism, even though I know it's futile.

"Nah. He wouldn't not answer his phone," Cam insists. "He must have about twenty missed calls from us by now."

I absently nod my head as I contemplate where else he could be. "Is there anywhere he likes to go on campus that you haven't checked yet?"

"No. We've already looked everywhere he usually hangs out."

I've only been in the apartment for a few minutes when there's another knock at the door.

"What's going on?" Beck demands, sounding slightly breathless from his rush to get over here as he strides into the apartment in his workout gear, a serious expression on his face and a tightness around his eyes.

"We don't know yet," Hawk responds. "The last we saw West was at lunch. He had physics and biology this afternoon, but none of us are in those classes with him."

"It's seven o'clock. How are you only realizing now that he's missing?" Beck growls angrily, causing Hawk to glare in his direction.

"Not that you would know, because you don't know anything about him," Hawk snarls, digging the knife into Beck's chest, "but he usually goes to the library or computer lab after class. It was only when he didn't show up at dinner and none of us had heard back from him that we suspected something wasn't right."

"Guys," I bark. "This isn't helping. We need to work together."

"We should split up and scour the campus," Beck insists.

Hawk scowls at him but nods his head. "I agree. Between us, we should be able to cover most of it pretty quickly. Mason, check the rec and sports center. Cam and Beck, both of you check the main school buildings, then when you're done, meet Mason and spread out to search the forest at that end of the campus. Hadley and I will search the forest behind the dorms and work our way toward the lake."

Everyone nods and quickly gets to their feet.

"Here, take these." Mason hands each of us flashlights. "In case it gets dark before we find him."

His voice is tight, and his words leave an ominous chill in the atmosphere that none of us want to acknowledge.

"Everyone keep their phones handy, check in every half hour and let the rest of us know if you find anything," Hawk directs before we all set off out the door.

⁓

"I'm really beginning to worry," I reluctantly admit an hour later. We've searched most of the forest, and there has been no sign of him. Although, honestly, I'm not sure if that's a good thing or not. I mean, what the fuck would he be doing all the way out here? *This is where you'd take a dead body to dump it.* That's the thought that keeps playing on repeat in my head. As the sun starts to set, making the shadows grow longer, every fallen log and pile of leaves that looks like it could be a dead body makes me shiver in fear as nausea churns my stomach, freezing me in place for a second before I can gather my wits and convince myself it's nothing more than foliage.

"He's stronger than he looks," Hawk assures, sounding like he's trying to convince himself as much as me. The two of us are about six feet apart, scouring the ground and surrounding forest to our left and right with every step we take.

"I know, but I keep thinking about what if our parents got to him. If they sent someone after him, he wouldn't stand a chance against them."

"He's fine," Hawk growls, refusing to believe anything else.

We walk on in silence for another beat until the crack of something hidden in the leaves underneath my boot has both of us freezing and staring down at the ground.

Hawk rushes over to me as I lift my boot, revealing a now cracked phone. He bends down to lift it, but all I can do is stare at it. This has got to be a bad omen, right?

"Is it his?" I croak out.

He looks it over before attempting to turn it on, but the thing is nothing more than a black brick.

"I don't know." He blows out a breath in frustration.

I mean, it *has* to be his. Only a few people come this deep into the forest, and anyone who dropped their phone would search for it. They wouldn't just walk off and leave it.

He tucks the phone away in his pocket. "Come on, let's keep searching." His eyes roam over the area, looking for any other clues before he fixes his stern gaze on me. "This doesn't tell us anything, and it might mean nothing. We have to keep looking."

The sharpness of his words is what gets through to me and locks down the out-of-control swarm of emotions I'm feeling right now, forcing myself into the headspace I've had to engage so many times when I was out on a job. Emotions have no place when you need to keep your head and think rationally, so all this fear and worry won't do me—and it certainly won't do West—any good. Shoving all those useless feelings into a box, I nod my head, ready to keep going.

After another fifteen minutes of searching, we reach the edge of the forest by the lake. By now, the sun has set, and the dark sky makes the deep water look more sinister than I ever remember it being. A deep-seated sickness flows through me as I look out over the water, and I feel Hawk tense beside me as he does the same. Both of us know the best place on campus to get rid of a dead body is in that lake.

We shine our torches over the pebbled shore as we walk along it toward the boathouse.

"Over there!" I point toward where something glints in the glow of my flashlight slightly further down the beach. "What is that?"

The two of us rush toward it, hoping it's a clue and fearing it's something bad.

I gasp as I skid to a stop on the stones. "They're his." My voice is strained, emotion choking me as I bend down to lift the broken pair of glasses. The lens in one eye is missing, and I can see small fragments of glass on the ground. "He must have gotten into a fight."

Frantically, I shine the light around us, desperately wanting it to show us another clue. Something. Anything. He must be nearby. He wouldn't have been able to get far without these.

Not seeing anything, I squint into the darkness, barely making out the outline at the far end of the beach.

"Hawk," I gasp. "The boathouse."

We share a glance before we take off, running full-force toward the small shack, no longer taking our time to search as we go. He *has* to be there.

I beat Hawk there by mere seconds and take a steadying breath, mentally trying to prepare myself for whatever we might find on the other side. Alert for any sound that could indicate an ambush, I push the door open, and we peer into the dark interior. There's nothing but silence which only makes me feel more on edge as we step inside, our flashlights sweeping over the weathered floorboards.

"Oh my god," I breathe, when Hawk's flashlight washes over a pair of legs—a pair of very still, unmoving legs. I scramble forward, Hawk right behind me as he moves his light to show us West's body and battered face.

His uniform is torn and bloodied, and his face looks like it was used as a punching bag.

"West," I cry out, dropping to my knees beside him. My hands hover over him, unsure of what to do or how I can help without causing him further pain.

When he doesn't respond, I shout again, "West!"

Hawk crouches down on his other side. "West, man," he calls out, shaking his shoulder. "It's me. Come on, we gotta get you out of here."

West groans, and I release a sigh of relief. *Thank fuck he's alive!* The stress from the last few hours vanishes, quickly being replaced with concern as I try to assess how bad his injuries are.

"West," Hawk yells, shaking him roughly again.

Another groan and a feeble swipe of his hand as he tries to dislodge Hawk's hand from his shoulder.

"That's it, man. You're gonna be fine," Hawk assures him before looking at me. "Stay with him, and I'll phone the others. Then we've gotta try and lift him out of here."

I absently nod my head, not once removing my gaze from West's face while Hawk gets to his feet and heads outside. He leaves the door open though, so we can still see each other.

I lean down so our faces are inches apart. "West?" I murmur softly, running my fingers through his hair, ignoring how the strands feel wet and sticky.

"Firefly," he whispers so quietly I barely hear him. "Not safe."

"It's okay," I reassure him. "Hawk and I are here. Whoever did this to you is gone."

He tries to nod his head, groaning at the pain that little movement causes him. I press my forehead to his, not giving a shit that he's sweaty and bloody.

"I'm so sorry," I murmur. "This is all my fault." My voice breaks and tears fall onto his closed lids, making them flutter.

"Shhh," he soothes, wincing as he lifts his arm, cupping the back of my neck. He manages to peel his eyes open, and it takes a second for him to focus his gaze on me. The pain I see in them only heightens my guilt. "This was *not* your fault," he insists in a tight voice, sounding hoarse from lack of use.

"It was. I was the one that said we should go against them. Look what they did to you," I croak. "They beat the shit out of you. They broke your glasses." A broken sob escapes me, and he lets out a pained chuckle, which quickly morphs into a groan as he winces. "I have a spare pair, don't worry about them. Just kiss me."

I press my lips to his, needing to be as close to him as possible to reassure myself he's actually alive. Intending to keep it quick, knowing he's not exactly in the right condition for a prolonged, dirty kiss, I go to pull back, but his hand on the back of my neck holds me in place as he deepens the kiss.

A snort behind me has us breaking apart, and I peer back over my shoulder.

"He can't be that bad if he's able to kiss you like that." Hawk scoffs, looking disgusted as he comes toward us. "Right, man, let's get you up. The others are on their way."

West gives a slight nod of agreement, and between Hawk and I, we manage to get him on his feet.

"Fuck, everything hurts," West groans. "Why the hell you and Mason do this to yourselves for fun is beyond me."

Hawk gives a small laugh. "Well, we don't usually go so hard."

West grunts, and we start moving. All conversation ceases as we focus on taking one step at a time. The sweat is dripping off West's forehead by the time we've reached the far end of the boathouse. Before we've even reached the edge of the forest, Hawk and I are pretty much supporting all of his weight, and it's making my thighs burn.

Rustling and the sound of footsteps has my body tensing while Hawk awkwardly tries to shield a more or less passed-out West with his broad frame. The two of us share a quick glance as we wait to see who's out here with us.

When Mason, Cam, and Beck come bursting out of the trees, I let out a breath of relief. I don't know what we would have done if the mercenaries who beat up West were still around. I'm not sure how many I could take at once, and with West's condition, we need to get him back and check him over for any internal injuries.

Spotting us, all three of their eyes widen as they see the state of West.

"Fuck, are you okay?" Cam asks, looking him over.

"He'll live," Hawk answers brusquely. "But we need to get him back to the dorm."

Mason steps up in front of me, obviously intending to relieve me of West's weight that I'm supporting, but I hesitate and glance at Beck. The same concern is in his eyes as is in the others. I can see he wants to help, but he's holding himself back, unsure of what West would want.

Stepping out from under West's arm, Mason takes up my position, and he and

Hawk manage to carry West through the forest with the three of us silently trailing along behind them. Sensing what a nervous mess I am as I worry about the extent of West's injuries, Cam reaches out and wraps his hand around mine, giving it a reassuring squeeze. Holding on to him, I link our fingers together and hang on to his small act of comfort as we slowly walk back to the guys' apartment.

It takes forever for Hawk and Mason to navigate up the stairs while carrying a nearly passed-out West between them. Although, we all eventually make it and the two of them get West settled on the sofa.

Cam rushes off to get his spare pair of glasses while I sit down beside him. Sliding my palm into his, I take comfort from the warmth of our touch—a solid reminder that the blood is still flowing through his veins, telling me he's alive.

"Should we call a doctor?" Hawk asks Mason, the two of them eyeing West critically. He's sitting with his head resting on the back of the sofa, his eyes shut, only cracking open a lid when Cam returns and hands over his glasses. Putting them on, his eyes drift shut again, his face scrunching at a flare-up of pain.

"I dunno." Mason purses his lips.

"Of course, we should," I argue. How could they think otherwise?!

"It would be our parents' doctor," Hawk explains, making me realize their indecision.

"No doctor," West groans, peeling his eyes half open. "I'll be fine."

"You're clearly not fine," Beck snaps. His expression is dark and angry, yet I can feel the concern coming off him in waves as he hovers uncertainly behind Hawk and Mason, watching West like…well, like a hawk.

He thinks on something for a second before stepping up beside Mason. "I'm by no means medically trained, but I've seen and patched up my fair share of battle wounds. I can take a look…if you want." He tacks on the last few words, indicating his hesitation.

Usually, he acts all tough and confident around the guys, but right now, he wants to be here for his brother, to help in some way, but he's got no idea how or if West would even want his help. The rocky state of their relationship breaks my heart. The two of them need each other more than they realize. West needs to wise up soon before Beck gives up trying altogether, and he misses out on what could be a pretty incredible relationship.

West dawdles, and I give his hand a squeeze, silently asking him to try. For his sake and Beck's.

"Yeah, okay," he relents with a sigh, sounding too tired to argue.

Giving Beck a small, reassuring smile, I help West remove the tattered remains of his shirt while Beck asks one of the guys if they have a first-aid kit and to get it for him.

I gasp as West's body is revealed. Bruises are beginning to form over his ribs and abdomen, and there are a few shallow cuts scored along his chest, the straight lines giving away the fact that a blade carved them. *I'm going to murder whichever fucker thought they could get away with that.*

The wounds are superficial. Intended to make a statement rather than do any actual harm and, honestly, I've seen far worse damage on some of the kids after they came out of the ring at the compound. The difference is that I didn't give a shit about any of those kids. Sure, I empathized with them. I felt awful for them, but I didn't have a smidgeon of the feelings I have for West.

Other than Meena, I've never had to see someone I care about get hurt. As I watch

West wince, his breathing shallow, as he tries not to inhale too deeply and spark a flare-up of pain, the bloodthirsty assassin within me screams out for retribution. It's a debased part of myself I usually keep locked-up tight, only letting her out to play when I'm on a job or my life is on the line. Since leaving the compound, I haven't had to become that person—other than when I finished off those two mercenaries. However, right now, I welcome the coldness that seeps into my veins as my baser instincts rise to the surface, dulling and heightening my emotions as I burn the fuckers' unknown names into the muscle around my heart. Promising myself their death will be at my hands.

I move out of the way, giving Beck space to assess his brother as he approaches with the first-aid kit. His gaze roams over West, assessing the damage, his face pinching when he spots a particularly nasty-looking discolored patch over his left kidney.

We all watch as Beck pokes and prods West, inspecting his cuts to make sure they're as superficial as they look.

"Are you sure you know what you're doing?" West growls when he flinches for the fifth time under Beck's touch, grunting as the move causes him pain.

"Yes, I'm sure." Beck groans frustratedly, getting irritated at West's lack of trust in him, and fixing him with a look that says, 'stop being a baby'. "My friends and I were constantly patching each other up when we were kids. It's not like we could go to a hospital with every possible broken bone or deep cut. No one in Black Creek could afford healthcare, and gang life isn't a career path that comes with health insurance, so you quickly learned the basics of examining, disinfecting, and stitching up any sort of injury."

Despite his obvious pain, West watches Beck closely, scrutinizing his every move. "What if it was life-threatening?"

Beck shrugs indifferently. "Then you'd probably die before anyone could do anything. *Maybe* a buddy or someone would have driven you to the hospital, but if you were lucky enough to live after that, you'd be saddled with a hefty bill that would only push you into taking greater risks for whatever gang you were working for. Risks that would ultimately get you killed later on down the line anyway." Beck paints such a hardened, bleak picture of Black Creek, it has me feeling sorry for any kids who have to grow up in such an environment.

I was sent quite a few times myself when I was out on the job, and I have made a couple of contacts there, but it's not a place I'd rush to visit any time soon. The people there are all hardened by the things they've had to see and do. Their souls are black, or various shades of gray at best. I've always gotten the heebie-jeebies when I was there. That ick feeling when far too many unwanted eyes are watching your every move. Even with my blatant 'leave me the fuck alone' face on, it never stopped cocky shitheads who thought they were all that because they carried a weapon and wore special gang tats from approaching me. Assholes who thought I'd happily fall all over their dick just because they thought it was cool to be in a gang. Honestly, for the most part, everyone there are a bunch of children, playing at being tough and fighting over territory like it's their favorite toy. The whole lot of them need to grow the fuck up.

"Some of the bigger crews, like The Feral Beasts or the Antonellis, would have had a doctor or medical person under their thumb who could sort out any gnarly wounds. On the other hand, anyone who wasn't a part of their crew, or any gang at all, just had to pray no injury was too serious."

It's the way Beck says all of this so nonchalantly, like that's just how things were.

Like it's normal, that is the most devastating. It's all incredibly fucked up, is what it is. I don't know what happened that resulted in his mom finally dragging them out of there, but I'm glad she did. Based on the worry lines on his forehead and the way he glances down at his Reaper Rejects tattoo on his forearm with a dejected look, I know whatever happened was something terrible. Something that he's carried with him, alone, for far too long.

As Beck says all of this, he continues his careful prodding of West, all the while ignoring him as West scans over his face. The way West is looking at him, with a sad and thoughtful look in his eyes that I noticed last time Beck opened up and shared some of his childhood with us, has a spark of hope igniting within me. Hope that one day these two can get past their differences.

"Well, what's the verdict?" Hawk asks as Beck gets to his feet, finished with his assessment.

"The cuts are all superficial. They just need to be cleaned and bandaged to ensure they don't get infected. His ribs and kidney are bruised, but I don't think anything is broken. He'll be stiff and sore for a few weeks, but he'll be fine."

"Good." Hawk's voice is gruff, and if I wasn't getting to know him better or seeing for myself how much he cares about these guys, I'd think he didn't give a shit. Even as his gruffness is chock-full of emotion that he doesn't know any other way to express.

Taking the kit from Beck, I slip back into my seat beside West and begin cleaning him up as the guys talk around me.

"So, are we all thinking this was our parents?" Mason begins, taking the chair opposite me as Cam brings over beers for everyone before sitting on my other side.

A resounding "yes" comes from everyone except West, who hisses when the antiseptic I'm using touches his cut.

"It definitely was," he assures us, looking a bit more alert than earlier. "There were three guys. They wore masks so I couldn't see their faces, but the way they moved was similar to the guys who attacked us at Christmas. They were so coordinated, and the level of precision..." He trails off, shaking his head, sounding both impressed by their skills and aggravated that he got jumped. "It was obvious they were highly trained and used to working as a team."

I grit my teeth and focus on stopping my hand from shaking with anger as I move on to clean another cut just beneath his pec. I'm going to gut every single fucker who touched him, and then I'm coming for the conniving sickos who call themselves our parents.

The roaring in my ears as I try to control the rage consuming me drowns out the continuing conversation around me, and I'm only pulled out of it when the loud ringtone of a phone going off penetrates through the red haze coating my mind.

Everyone looks at Hawk, whose lips are pressed tightly together as he stares at the phone before answering. Immediately putting it on speaker for the rest of us to hear, he tosses each of us a look to be quiet.

"I'm disappointed, son." Barton's voice comes out clearly across the speakerphone as he sighs. "I thought we told you to resume the tradition with the girls, yet we had to find out through another source that our own sons were defying us?" He snarls out the last few words. It's the first time I've heard him sound anything other than indifferent, and it's the first hint at the darkness within him—the same controlling darkness in all of our parents.

"We wanted—" Hawk begins.

"I don't care what you wanted," Barton yells down the phone. "You will do as we say. You will *all* go back to the old tradition with the girls."

He waits silently for Hawk to agree, but Hawk hesitates, staring at each of the guys for confirmation.

"Tonight was only a warning," Barton threatens when Hawk takes too long to respond. "We can do far worse. And not just to Westley."

Sighing silently, Hawk agrees—it's not like he has a choice.

"Okay. We'll start up the tradition again."

"Good. And Elizabeth is to join in as well, for now. We'll let you know when that changes."

What the fuck is that supposed to mean? The five of us share confused, worried, and angry glances. No one is entirely sure what exactly Barton means by those cryptic words.

Hawk looks at me, as if waiting for my confirmation that I'm okay with that, but, just like him, I have no other choice, so I reluctantly nod my head in agreement.

"Okay," Hawk responds to his dad.

"Good. Pick someone for her. You know who's suitable. Take this as the warning it was intended, son. Next time, do better."

With that, Barton hangs up, leaving us all staring dejectedly at one another and working out what the fuck we're supposed to do now.

Hadley

CHAPTER FOURTEEN

I spend the night with West, the two of us sleeping fitfully. He tosses and turns all night, struggling to get comfy with his injuries, and his restlessness keeps me awake.

At five a.m., I give up and slip out of bed, grabbing a pair of sweats to pull on underneath the oversized t-shirt I borrowed last night before sneaking out the door. I creep down the hall, not wanting to disturb the others so early. It was after two before we all went to bed, exhaustion getting the better of us after the day's events. It felt like we got nothing sorted last night, the conversation going round in circles as we discussed what we were going to do about this stupid tradition and, ultimately, what our plan was to get rid of our parents, because it's become abundantly clear we can't continue to live under their rules and restrictions. I refuse to let anyone else dictate my life for me ever again, and I won't let them drag the guys deeper into their shit or tarnish Beck's soul further with the horrendous job they've asked him to do.

I pause in the threshold of the open plan kitchen and living space, studying Beck as he sleeps on the couch wearing only his boxers. His blanket is on the floor, having kicked it off at some point during the night. He refused to leave last night, and thankfully, no one argued with him, the others understanding his need to be close to his brother after everything that had gone down. Even if they had taken issue with it, I wouldn't have let him walk out of here. I needed to know all of us were safe last night, and the only way to be sure of that was if we were all together.

Instead of heading toward the kitchen for coffee, I veer off course, moving on silent feet toward a softly snoring Beck. Careful not to disturb him, I ease my knees onto the cushions on either side of his hips and hover over him. My eyes drift to his Reaper Rejects tattoo as I again wonder what happened in his childhood. He's alluded to the loss of someone close to him, but he's never volunteered more information, and I've never asked. He doesn't push me to tell him anything I'm uncomfortable with, so I won't do that to him. I trust that when he's ready to share, he'll let me in—and, hopefully, the others too.

Twirling around the tattoo are various black tribal designs, extending down to his wrist and shoulder. There's also a smattering of color intertwined with the other, smaller designs, making them stand out. From this angle, I can make out a compass with the words 'stay true' scrawled underneath, an image of a tree bare of leaves, and another one of an hourglass with the sand mostly run through.

Following the designs until my gaze lands on his face again, I can't help but stare at him. He's stunning when he's awake—all rugged handsomeness and wicked intent—but he's beautiful when he's asleep. The tight lines that far too frequently mar his face have faded away, letting his true age show through. He's so much younger than you'd think when you initially look at him. His past and life experiences have hardened him, both on the outside and inside, but he's not much older than the rest of us. Yet, he's trying to take the weight of all of this on his shoulders so the guys and I don't have to. I know that's why he's never mentioned what our parents are making him do. He's willing to risk the guys not trusting him if it means he can let all of us be kids a bit longer. It's selfless, really, but how much is bearing that burden alone going to cost him? I'm thankful that he opened up to me the other week. Hopefully, now, he knows he's not as alone as he thought he was.

"Morning, creeper." His deep voice is thick with sleep and he still doesn't open his eyes, but his hands slide up my thighs, resting on my hips and pulling me down so I'm sprawled across him.

"I didn't mean to wake you," I murmur against the soft skin of his neck.

"Then you probably shouldn't have been climbing all over me."

Okay, fair point, but he just looked so peaceful I had to get a closer look.

"How's West?"

"He's doing okay. He didn't sleep well, so I'm letting him rest a bit longer."

He nods his head, his eyes still closed as his fingers trace lazy circles on my back.

"How are you?" I know last night got to him, regardless of how well he tried to hide it.

He sighs, finally peeling his eyes open to look at me with a soft smile. He kisses the crown of my head before resting his head back on the pillow and staring at the ceiling above us.

"I was so worried about him," he admits. "I only just found him, and he still fucking hates me. The thought of something bad happening to him before we have a chance to get to know one another..." He trails off, but he doesn't need to finish that sentence. I know what he means. Hawk drives me fucking insane, but we're only beginning to get to know each other, and the thought of losing him now, just when things are starting to go well for us? Well, I can't bear to think about it.

"I don't know how to make things better between us." The tightening of his fingers on my hip tells me how much the friction between him and West is getting to him. "I've tried opening up about my childhood, so he could get to know me, however he doesn't even want to spend time with me. I don't know what else I can do."

I run my fingers through his hair, hoping it will take away some of the tension that has his body wound so tight. He snorts at whatever he's thinking, shaking his head at his inner thoughts. "I stupidly thought admitting why I was doing what I was for our parents, and why I couldn't tell anyone about it, would help him warm up to me. I thought if he knew I was doing it all for him, to keep him alive, it would make a difference. Not because I want him to owe me or because I feel obligated to, but because I want to be in his life. I want us to have a future where we have the opportunity to get to know each other."

"So, you really are only doing it for me?"

Beck and I both jump. My eyes dart up to look at West standing in the doorway in his pajama bottoms, staring bleary-eyed at Beck. I carefully climb off Beck so that he can sit up.

His gaze never leaves West as he responds, "Yeah."

"What about the money? And the fancy job and better career prospects?"

"I don't care about any of that. Every cent our father has given me is sitting in a bank account. I've never touched it, and I don't plan on it. As for the job, I can't deny it's not an amazing opportunity that I'm hoping will benefit me someday, but I wouldn't have accepted his shady offer for that reason alone."

West's eyes dart between Beck's, trying to ascertain the truth in his words. "So why did you take it, then? You had to know it would come with strings you wouldn't want to pull on."

Beck nods his head slowly. "I did, but after losing touch with my brothers all those years ago, the opportunity to connect with you, my *real* brother, was more than I could pass up. It's not like I ever expected us to be friends or anything, but I wanted the chance to get to know you. To see that you were doing okay, and, yeah, I hoped we could maybe have some sort of relationship one day." He shrugs casually like it's no big deal, except this is a huge fucking deal, and I can practically feel the stress radiating off him as he waits to hear what his brother says next.

West's eyes bounce to me, and I silently implore him to give Beck a chance. He's got no idea how fucking worth it it will be.

Looking back at Beck, he takes another few seconds to mull it over before nodding his head.

"Okay," he agrees slowly. "I'll stop icing you out."

No longer able to hold back my grin, I squeeze Beck's arm in excitement.

"But if it turns out anything you're telling me, or any of us, is bullshit, you'll be out of here so fucking fast it will all feel like a distant memory. You won't see me, or Hadley again."

Okay, I don't appreciate him making decisions like that for me, and I make it clear with the scowl I aim his way. My glare is sharp enough it could pierce a hole in the front of his forehead, right between his eyes. But I let it slide because I know that won't happen. I understand he still doesn't trust him fully, and I—of all people—can appreciate that.

"Alright, now that we have all agreed we're on the same team, sit your ass down," I tell West in a no-nonsense tone, getting to my feet. "I'll get you some painkillers. You should still be in bed, resting."

"I'm fine," he assures me, ambling slowly over to one of the armchairs and carefully lowering himself into it so as not to jostle any of his many bruises. In the light of day, and now that the blood has had time to rise to the surface of his skin, he looks fucking awful. Still hot as sin, of course, but it's painfully obvious he was put through the wringer last night.

Despite his insistence that he's fine, he doesn't argue with me when I give him the meds and a glass of water, quickly downing them and relaxing back in his chair as I go to make us all some coffee. I have a feeling we're going to need it.

NONE of us go to class for the rest of the week. Since West isn't a fighter like Mason or Hawk, his sudden bruised appearance will only raise unwanted questions, and with the gauntlet hanging over our heads, the rest of us need to strategize about our next moves. So the five of us hole up in their apartment, relying on gossip from Emilia and Beck to keep us up to date on what's going on in the rest of the school.

The only time we leave is to go to Cam's swimming competition on Saturday. He's in the regional championships, which means nothing to me, but it's something he's proud of, and we all want to be there to support him. He's been in the pool every spare minute he's had—which admittedly is not as much as he probably would have liked considering all we've had going on. With a hoodie pulled up over his head, hiding the last of the bruising on his face, West is able to join us as we watch Cam once again kick ass—looking fucking panty-melting doing it.

Of course, Lawrence can't let the occasion go by without a visit. This time, he's standing poolside with his gaze fixated on me as I sit in the stands beside Hawk. I do my best to ignore it, but his eyes burn into me like a laser. I have to curtail my enthusiasm for Cam's win, not wanting to alert Lawrence to my intense feelings for his son. However, as Cam stalks into the locker room afterward and the guys get to their feet around me, I can't help glancing his way. I instantly regret it as the corner of his lip curls up in a confident sneer, momentarily immobilizing me.

"Ignore him," Hawk whispers in my ear, a scowl etched across his face as he gently nudges my shoulder, pushing me forward. Ripping my eyes away from Lawrence, I follow the guys out of the stands, but I swear, even after we're back in our dorm and Lawrence is long gone, I can still feel his eyes on me.

On Monday morning, our masks are firmly in place as we throw open the doors to the dining hall and make our way to the Princes' table amidst murmurs from the rest of the crowd. Taking our seats, I do my best to ignore the gawking and obvious whispers as breakfast is delivered. The five of us eat in silence—not that I manage to eat much with the lead lining my stomach—and once we're finished, Hawk gives us the signal and we all get to our feet.

"We understand there have been issues regarding recent changes to the girl of the month tradition." Hawk's voice echoes around the room, loud and clear for everyone to hear.

My hands clench tightly around the edge of the wooden table, hating that we have to do this, but we've discussed it in depth over the last few days, and none of us can see any way around it. Not yet, at least. Not without putting West, and all of us, at risk.

"When we first discovered Elizabeth was a Davenport, we stopped the tradition as she needed the opportunity to come into her own here in the school. Now that that has been achieved, she has agreed to join us with the monthly tradition."

I grit my teeth as excited whispers break out around the room from both guys and girls. It takes everything in me to hold back the truth I desperately want to let slip. It's all a bunch of bullshit, yet we can't afford for the school to think we're being forced into this. They need to believe *we* are in charge, and this was the best excuse we could come up with after a week of mulling it over.

"So," Hawk bellows, bringing everyone's attention back to us. "Starting today, all five of us will choose a girl, or guy, for the month. The same rules as before apply."

Without further ado, Hawk points out some girl, and the same song and dance as every other time ensues. The other guys do the same, and despite the fact they barely spare whatever random girl they choose a second glance, every time they pick someone, it makes my blood boil. Mental images of me stabbing our parents flitter across my mind as I make a silent promise that those thoughts will one day be a reality.

All too soon, it's my turn. When Hawk first mentioned me participating in this archaic tradition, I'd just assumed I'd pick Michael. Except after Barton's little 'you know who's suitable speech,' we all agreed it couldn't be a scholarship student.

The guys gave me a few names of families our parents would deem 'suitable' who weren't total assholes, yet looking out over the eager crowd, I don't know who any of them are.

As I roam my eyes over the rest of the hall, I play 'eenie meenie miney mo' in my head with each of the names I was given—it seems like as good a way as any to pick one.

Hawk coughs, a wordless gesture telling me to hurry the fuck up and get this over with, and after mentally cursing him out in my head, I call out the last name I was thinking.

"Daniel Fairweather."

Roars erupt from a table in the middle of the room, and guys clap some nerdy-looking kid on the shoulder as his ears pinken. At least he looks more likely to keep his hands to himself. Meh, even if he doesn't, I can just break them. That will teach him not to touch without permission.

After breakfast, the chosen girls all crowd around the guys, and rather than have to watch that shit, I wander off to find Daniel. He approaches me through the crowd, looking both cocky and unsure at the same time.

"Alright, Daniel," I begin before he can say something that will only make me dislike him more, "this is how things are going to go. In public, we have to make it look like we're dating, but do *not* touch me. Do *not* kiss me. There will absolutely be no sex. Got it?" His face falls with every order I bark, and he nods his head dejectedly. "Oh, and you can't have sex with anyone else either for the month."

I know. I bet he's real happy about being the chosen one now, but I can't have word spreading that my fake date is fucking other girls while he's supposed to be with me. It would undermine everything I've spent the last few weeks achieving here.

"What—"

"Those are the rules," I state, cutting him off. "It's too late. You can't back out or change your mind. And if you break any of them, you'll have the distinct pleasure of meeting my bad side. Fair warning, she can be a downright bitch. Just ask Tiffany and Bianca."

He pinches his lips, looking annoyed—not that I can blame him—but he nonetheless agrees to my crappy terms.

"Great." I plaster a falsely bright smile on my face. "You can walk me to class then."

The rest of the day isn't too bad. I think I put the fear of God into Daniel as he does nothing more than graze my shoulder as he walks me to my first class, and I'm pretty sure it's by accident because every time he does, he jumps a mile and mumbles an apology. I don't see him for the rest of the day after that, and the guys manage to shake off their girls as well, so the six of us hide away in their dorm for lunch. Beck has started joining us for lunch most days, and it's been great having everyone together. I've even noticed him and West talking a bit. It's not much, but it's an awesome start.

On Tuesday, the good mood leftover from yesterday drops right out of me as we enter the hall and the girls practically throw themselves at *my* guys. None of them look happy about the physical assault and are quick to extricate themselves. Still, seeing it fucking pisses me off. It only gets worse when we all sit down, and I overhear Hawk's girl telling him the fucked up shit she can do with her mouth. Hawk's eyes fill with lust as he adjusts himself under the table, utterly oblivious to the dangerous churning in my stomach. On my other side, Mason's girl is pushing her tits against his arm, trying to gain his attention as he all but ignores her as he shovels his breakfast into his mouth like it's a race. It's a little funny but still annoying as hell.

"So," I snap, turning my attention to Daniel in a bid to distract myself from going apeshit in front of the whole room. "Tell me about yourself."

Daniel spends the rest of breakfast blathering on about his hopes and dreams. In fairness, he doesn't seem like a total asshole, and the tension drops out of his shoulders with every passing minute that I don't tear him a new one.

When the bell goes off for class, we all get to our feet, and I give the guys a wistful smile as I let Daniel lead me out of the hall. He's back to his nervous self as we walk toward the main building, and I can see his thoughts running rampant as he mulls something over. Not caring what's going on in his head, I let him stew as we walk on.

"Look," he eventually blurts out. "I don't know what your deal is." I'm about to tear into him when he rushes out, "And I don't care. You're hot, and if you were interested, that would be awesome, except you're not...right?"

"No," I state bluntly.

"Right." He nods like he expected that answer. "So if this is all for show, it needs to look legit." I ponder over what he's implying and, realizing I'm open to listening to what he has to say, he continues, "You saw the way the girls are with the guys."

I give him an unimpressed look, shooting him a snarky response. "I don't need you pawing all over me, thanks."

He laughs nervously. "That's not quite what I was thinking. Although people will expect me to have my arm around your shoulders or carry your stuff. Things like that."

I scrunch my nose. "I don't need you to carry my shit. I've two perfectly good arms to carry it myself."

He shrugs. "It's just what guys do for girls they're dating. I'm not talking making out in the hallway or anything like that, but there are a few small things we could do that would prevent people from asking questions that I'm guessing you don't want them to ask."

Huh, maybe he's not an asshole at all.

"And what do you get out of it?" I ask.

He shrugs. "I'm not looking for anything. Sure, if one day in the future you wanted to take pity on me and give me a job in your parents' company or something, I wouldn't say no, but just call it a gesture of goodwill."

"Don't you come from money? I'm sure you can find your own job or have your own company you'll run someday?"

"My parents have money, but it's my uncle who has made our family name popular. He's the one that paid for me to come here, but he runs a vineyard, and I'm really more of an indoor person. I prefer working with computers and gadgets rather than with people."

Huh. "Alright, Daniel. You have yourself a deal."

A huge grin lights up his face, and he cautiously throws his arm over my shoulder. I tense at the contact, not used to anyone other than my guys or Emilia touching me, but I slowly relax as he talks my ear off about his college and future plans, and we make our way to class.

Sweetheart

CHAPTER FIFTEEN

A week after West's run-in with our parents' mercenaries, I'm climbing into the backseat of a blacked-out SUV on my way to my first-ever visit to the compound. My first visit should have been weeks ago. But, for whatever reason my father neglected to share with me, it kept getting pushed back—not that I'm complaining. I'd secretly hoped he'd changed his mind. It's the last place on earth I want to be, especially knowing what I do about Hadley.

To say I'm nervous would be an understatement. I don't know what the fuck I am. I'm a whirling vortex of emotions. I'm apprehensive about what I'm going to see and find here, sick at the thought of what will be expected of me, and fueled by molten rage at knowing whatever I see today was Hadley's entire life until recently.

The car journey takes two hours, but finally, we pull up to a staffed gate. I've been looking out the window most of the way, mentally cataloging any useful signposts that could help guide us back here, should we need it. The last town we passed was nearly an hour ago, and really, calling it a town is a stretch. It was a rundown, one-street backwater place that looked like it barely had more than a gas-and-go.

Since then, it's been all open fields interspersed with little pockets of forestry, with barely a house in sight.

Turning off the main road, we veer onto a narrow dirt track that looks like it leads to nothing but more fields. I guess that's the point. After bumping along it for another five minutes, a long fence line appears out of nowhere, littered with warning signs indicating this is private property and trespassing is prohibited.

A wide gate with barbed-wire coiled around the top and yet more warning signs attached to it blocks the road forward in front of us, and two guards wearing black combat uniforms stand guard on either side of the road.

As the driver talks to the one closest to us, the other guard inspects the car, checks the trunk, and waves some device underneath the vehicle. Both guards are armed with guns strapped in their holsters, and their thorough professionalism and the way they carry themselves make it obvious they're no amateurs. These aren't the lazy wannabe cops who sit in guard houses outside rich people's properties, watching TV instead of doing their jobs. They come across as highly-trained, dedicated soldiers.

The driver says something that I can't make out through the divider, and a minute later, the gates roll back and we drive into the compound.

No turning back now, I guess.

We bump along the track for another few minutes until we come up over the hill, at the bottom of which is a large, low-lying building shaped like a hexagon. Several other large facilities are dotted around the place and, beyond that, fields as far as the eye can see. We really are in the backass of nowhere.

Making our way down to the main hexagonal building, the car comes to a stop outside the entrance where a broad-shouldered, muscular man, who looks more like he belongs in Black Creek with the thugs and gangbangers, is waiting. He taps his foot impatiently as I get out of the back of the car and head toward him. He's dressed in similar tactical gear as the guy at the gate, the guns on his belt immediately drawing my gaze.

"Beck?" he asks—well, it sounds more like a demand.

"That's right."

He gives a curt nod as he holds out his hand for me to shake, and I reluctantly slap my palm against his. "Welcome to Nocturnal Mercenaries. I'm Major Bowen. I'm in charge of this place when Mr. Rutherford isn't around."

In return, I give him a tight smile and a professional nod of my head.

"Follow me." He turns on his heel and heads into the building, leaving me no choice other than to follow him even as my stomach fills with lead, and I swallow roughly around my dry throat.

"I have to apologize. You should have been here weeks ago, but we had a security breach that needed to be resolved first."

"Of course, I understand," I pacify, keeping my questions about what happened to myself.

"I've set aside an interrogation room for you to use. I, uh, wasn't sure what all you would need, but you can just let one of my men know and we will do our best to accommodate you," he explains in a bland tone, not realizing his use of the words 'interrogation room' in reference to young children has bile crawling up the back of my throat.

Unable to speak, I give a sharp jerk of my head as he leads me down a brightly lit corridor.

"This building houses the gym, boxing rings, dining hall, and interrogation rooms. The recruits are split into teams based on their competence and age, and housed in the surrounding buildings you probably saw on your drive in."

"Teams?" I query, knowing I need to say something. I can't just continue to nod my head like a moron every time he opens his mouth and spews more words that make my skin itch to get out of here.

"Yes. We throw them all in together when they first arrive, but as they progress in their training, the weak are weeded out. We put them in teams, for which they remain in for when they go out on jobs, etcetera. They eat together, work together, sleep together. That way, they can learn to work cohesively as a team and get along with each other in confined spaces, should that be necessary for the job." He chuckles, even though I don't see what he finds so funny. "It's not always fancy kills and exciting getaways like in the movies. There are a lot of boring stakeouts and long hours spent following a target. It's important that each team can work through whatever challenges they may face in order to get the job done."

"Do the teams interact much during their training?"

"Not really. We hold a monthly challenge night where the teams face off against one another. We find it to be a healthy form of competition between them, enabling us to compare their skill sets and identify any issues. Other than that, they're kept pretty separate."

"Where, uh, are all the recruits?" I ask. We haven't passed a single person, child or otherwise.

He laughs before explaining, "This corridor loops round the whole building and is for staff only. There's a separate recruit entrance at the back, with a secure hallway leading into the middle of the building, where the main workout area is."

Coming to a thick, steel door, the guy swipes a card against a reader, the light turning green before he opens the door.

"Each section of the building is subdivided for security reasons," he explains.

Security reasons, my ass. More like safety measures to ensure no one escapes. How Hadley managed to break out of this place is a miracle in itself.

Entering another similar hallway, we continue walking. "So, from what Mr. Rutherford explained, you're going to assess which kids are the best candidates for training and which are duds." The guy says it with such casual indifference, like we're talking about the fucking weather, further intensifying my disgust for him.

"That's right." That's the only response I can spit out, knowing if I say anything else, I won't be able to keep the edge of anger out of my voice.

"Cool. That would be helpful. We invest a lot of time and effort into finding suitable kids, but we don't always get it right. Currently, one in five of the kids we think could hack it, end up washing out."

Why do I get the impression that when he says 'washing out,' it's not like in college when kids drop out and decide to do something different with their lives? No, the way he says it makes it sound much more permanent, and I have to suppress my shiver of revulsion.

"How do you find these kids and determine which ones are worth your time?" Even though I am curious, I'm not convinced I want an answer to that question, although it's probably expected of me to have some questions, especially about the recruitment phase, since that's why I'm here.

"We have lookouts on the streets and contacts in the foster system and in children's homes that report back to us if they find someone they think would be fitting. Someone with no family, anger issues, prone to getting in fights, acts like a bully, that sort of stuff. Then we put surveillance on them and set up incidents where we can test them to see how they react. If they don't meet our expectations, we move on; if they do, we either approach them or take them.

"The younger we can get them, the easier it is. We can't test them the same way as the older kids, but they quickly learn here that it's a survive-or-die environment. We've discovered most kids, if they're younger, will adapt quicker and question us less."

What he means is that the younger kids are easier to condition. Probably because they don't remember life outside these bloodstained walls. The older kids, even if they did come willingly at first, most likely come to regret that decision or at least go through a phase where they want their freedom back.

"Honestly, I think your help would be better suited during the surveillance stage before we bring them in, but Mr. Rutherford wants you to look at the last set of recruits we picked up a few weeks ago."

"How many kids do you have here?" I ask, changing the topic before he can dive too deep into what I'm going to do. Honestly, I have no idea what the fuck I'm going to do when I'm placed face to face with some tear-stained kid and asked to decide their future.

"Thirty." There's a proud lilt to his voice, like coaxing and kidnapping young children and forcing them into a life most people wouldn't willingly choose, is some sort of achievement. It takes everything in me not to lash out and throw him against the wall. "We have a lot of adults that we train too," he continues, unaware of the boiling rage inside me. "Guys that have been discharged from the army or from private security, who are looking for a new, lucrative gig. The board only started recruiting kids about twenty years ago. We now have three active teams, and the rest are still in training, but so far, they've proven to be much more effective than those that come to us as adults."

We stop at another door, and after yet another swipe of the keycard, we step into a different sector.

"Alright, these are the interrogation rooms," he says, taking me to a door on the right. Scanning his keycard, the door beeps and unlocks to allow us entry into yet another hallway. This one is a complete juxtaposition to the one we left behind. It's dark, lit by dim, intermittent overhead lighting, and I'm not sure if it's my imagination or not, but I swear I can smell piss and fear all around me. It's potent, activating my gag reflex, and I struggle to lock that shit down.

Thick steel doors are placed at intervals down both sides of the wall, and I don't miss the hatches in each of them—one at eye level and a larger one closer to the floor. The whole area resembles what I imagine the confinement section of a prison looks like.

Bowen stops outside one of the doors, where a guard stands to attention. "We've set you up in here," he states as I follow him into the windowless room. A single bulb hangs from the ceiling, providing an eerie glow that only adds to the foreboding pit in my stomach. Maybe it's for the best that I can't make out any more of the room. The smell of piss is more pungent in here, combined with a tangy rust smell that I know all too well. Blood. I knew, based on the little Hadley has shared with me, that I'd see some shit here. And I thought I'd prepared myself, but every instinct in me is screaming for me to run, to get the fuck out of here and never come back.

There's a small table in the middle with two chairs on either side. Other than that, the space is empty.

"I wasn't sure what all you would need to do for your assessment, but Officer Gordo will be in the hall. If you need anything, ask him."

I nod my head. I'm not physically capable of doing anything more than that right now.

"We have five kids for you today. We've already vetted them from a physical aspect, so I guess you're here to see if they can withstand the psychological aspects of training. Honestly, I don't really understand what it is you'll be doing, but if you can stop us from wasting our time surveilling and training washouts, then I don't care." He laughs at his own joke. "Alright, I'll get someone to bring in the first kid. Hang tight."

He walks out, pulling the door closed behind him. A loud clatter rings out around the dark, depressing space as the door slams shut and a bolt is slid into place, locking it. The sound is so final, like the lid closing on a coffin, sending a shiver of fear skittering down my spine. If I'm afraid, I can only imagine the utter terror those poor kids feel when they're dragged in here unwillingly.

Just when I'm beginning to reach my limit of uncomfortableness, and I'm debating banging on the door and demanding they open it, I hear the grate of the bolt unlocking and the door is yanked open.

The guy guarding the door, Gordo, marches a young boy into the room. He gives me a brief nod and says, "Let me know when you're ready for the next one." The kid holds his head high, refusing to be cowered. There's a stern resolve in his eyes. He jumps, however, when the guard slams the door shut, leaving the two of us alone in the room. I also notice how his eyes are darting nervously around the darkened space.

Fuck, this is going to be a long day.

A headache is beating a drum against the inside of my skull, and I'm both physically and mentally drained by the time I finish up and Major Bowen comes to escort me out.

Instead of leading me back the way we came, though, he directs me deeper into the compound. We walk through room after room where kids are being put through grueling exercises as trainers yell and threaten them, even when the kids shudder in terror and cry out with exhaustion.

I hate to admit it, but it gets to the point where I try not to look, instead attempting to block it all out until I'm finally directed back to the initial corridor and can let out a silent breath of relief. There's a tightness in my chest, and the adrenaline in my body is pushing me to go back and help them. Witnessing that and not being able to do anything about it, not even *trying* to stop it, goes against my very nature. Only there's nothing I can do right now to help any of them. Every time I saw a guard hitting or screaming at a young kid, all I could picture was Hadley. How the hell she endured this place and didn't turn into something cold and detached is beyond me. It's a true testament to her strength. Most people would break eventually. You can only hold on to hope for so long; once that flame goes out, all that surrounds you is darkness.

When we're finally back outside the building, I bid a hasty farewell to the sick fuck masquerading as a Major, greedily gulping down the fresh air. I already know I'll be burning these clothes and jumping in the shower as soon as I get home. I can feel the fear and hopelessness that cloaks this place clinging to me like an unwanted second skin. One that's not going to be so easily washed away.

∽

STEAM BILLOWS out of the bathroom behind me as I step back into my room, wearing nothing but a towel wrapped around my waist after a long, hot shower that did nothing to remove the grime adhering to my skin from today. I pause, finding Hadley lounging on my bed, a sight for sore eyes in her shorts and t-shirt. I smile softly when she catches my gaze.

"What are you doing here?"

"I wanted to check on you after today." Her eyes probe against my skin, and I know she's trying to read me, to gauge the lasting impact of the horror I had to witness. She slides across the bed as I sit down on the end and leans her head on my shoulder.

"I don't know how you survived it all those years. I could hardly stand being there for an afternoon."

I feel her shrug, feigning nonchalance. "I think you become indifferent to it all. It's the only life I know."

I let out a long breath, closing my eyes as I soak in the feel of her pressed against me. "I couldn't stop picturing you there, imagining what it must have been like for you—"

"You can't think like that," she chastises, reaching out and wrapping her hand around mine. "I'm here now, with you, and that's all that matters."

∽

ON FRIDAY, I knock on the guys' apartment door at lunch. Ever since West got attacked, and they all had to resume the stupid tradition, it's become the norm for all of us to hang out here at lunch. I have to admit, it beats eating alone in my office or making stifled conversation with the other faculty members in the staff room, plus it's given me more of an opportunity to hang out with West.

I'm pleased to say he looks a bit better every day, and the bruises have faded considerably. True to his word, he's stopped icing me out, yet things are still awkward as fuck between us.

The door swings open, and the man himself stands in the doorway.

"Hey," I greet, striding past him into the apartment. Glancing around, I don't see anyone else.

"Hey, everyone else should be here in a few minutes. The guys are just grabbing food."

"Sounds good." Sitting down on one of the bar stools, I scan my eyes over him. "How are you doing?"

"Much better. Still sore over my ribs, but nothing like what it was." He takes a seat on the opposite side of the island, and we stare awkwardly at one another, neither of us sure what to say.

"This thing you have with Hadley," he begins. "It's serious?"

"As serious as it is between you and her." I know, just from the way he looks at her, how much she means to him—to all of us.

"And you don't care that she's dating three other guys?"

"It's not quite what I'd pictured for myself," I admit. I don't think many people plan to end up in a poly relationship. Certainly, any pre-Hadley fantasies I would have had about the idea included more women than men in the relationship, but Hadley is more than enough woman for all of us. "But she deserves to be happy. If you guys make her happy, then I'm not about to stand in the way of that." I hesitate before continuing, "I've spent most of my teen and adult life feeling like I don't fit in anywhere, yet with Hadley, I feel like I'm exactly where I'm supposed to be."

He stares at me for a long moment. "You love her."

It's not a question, but I answer anyway. "I do."

We don't break eye contact, and I tap my finger thoughtfully against the countertop as I mull over my question before finally just blurting it out, "How do you feel about sharing?"

"It feels natural with Mason and Cam. We've never shared a girl before, but with Hadley, it just feels right."

A lump forms in the back of my throat. I'm painfully aware he didn't comment on sharing Hadley with me and, good or bad, I need to know his thoughts about it. I'm not going anywhere, regardless of what he says, but I still need to know. "And with me?"

He doesn't say anything for a moment, nerves making my palms sweat. It's ridiculous that, as a fucking adult, I want to be accepted—by him, by the others, but dammit, I feel like I'm so close to finding somewhere I might actually belong.

"I thought it would be weird…seeing you with her. But I see the way she is with you. Because of you, she dropped her barriers and let us in after everything we did to her." He hesitates. "I should probably be thanking you, old man." One side of his lips quirks up in an easy smirk, the tension dropping out of his shoulders when I bark out a laugh. *Damn, I'm never getting rid of that stupid nickname, am I?*

The jingle of the keys in the lock alerts us of the others' arrival and cuts off whatever else West might have said. Hadley strides in, a large grin on her face when she finds us both sitting here, with all of our limbs still attached, and not—for once—yelling at one another.

"Hey," she purrs, wrapping her arms around my neck as I draw her into me.

"Hey, sweetheart." I plant a quick kiss on her lips before she extricates herself to go say hi to West. I watch as he winds his arms around her waist, recognizing the look in his eye as he smiles at her. He loves her too.

∾

"LOOK AT THAT SMUG FUCK," Mason snarls, glaring daggers at Daniel. I'm surprised he can't feel our angry stares drilling into the side of his head as he laughs at something Hadley says.

I was heading to my office when I came across Mason leaning casually against a bank of lockers in the corridor, staring at a classroom door further down the hall. It all made sense when he said he was waiting on Hadley's class to finish.

"Thinks he can just walk around with his arm around our girl."

Of course, when the door opened and Hadley walked out, Daniel was right by her side, his arm draped over her shoulder. She's grown more comfortable with his nearness as the week's drawn on, and even though I trust her, it doesn't stop me from wanting to rip the asshole's head off any time I see him touching her. I rarely come into the main school building, choosing to stay away from the majority of the student body so I just have to deal with whatever students are sent my way. Then again, all week, I haven't been able to stop myself from wandering through the halls just so I can check up on her and make sure the little fuck, Daniel, isn't overstepping his mark. Hadley is like a breath of fresh air in this place, so I don't trust that he won't get as infatuated with her as we are.

I can feel the rage coming off Mason, his jealousy fueling my own.

"Miss Davenport," I bark out in a menacing growl that makes several students stop and stare in my direction. Freezing, Hadley turns to face me, Daniel's arm dropping from her shoulder. "A word."

She glances wide-eyed at the other students, an impassive expression on her face. She gives a tight nod of her head, whispering something to Daniel before coming toward us.

"Yes?" Although that one word sounds polite and patient, the fire burning in her eyes tells me she's not happy about being called out in front of everyone. But I don't care. I'm sick of seeing that shithead glued to her side every time I walk through here.

"In private. My office. Now."

Her lips flatten as she presses them together.

"You coming?" I ask, turning to Mason. He's staring at Hadley with a mixture of carnal need and jealous rage, but he grits his teeth and shakes his head at my question.

"Can't. I have class."

With one final, longing glance at Hadley, he takes off. I turn on my heel and stride through the emptying hallways with Hadley trailing behind me, until we reach my office.

"What the hell—" she begins as soon as the office door closes behind her, but I cut off her words, slamming my lips against hers and sucking her tongue into my mouth.

"Do you have any idea how difficult it is to watch him with you all day, every day?" I growl, my body pressed flush against hers, pinning her to the door.

Some of the anger melts out of her expression.

"That still doesn't mean you can act like a caveman and boss me around."

I tilt my head a fraction, staring into her mesmerizing gray-blue eyes that suck me in like a vortex. "You like when West does it." My voice is a low husk as I grind my erection against her core, loving the way she sighs, her hands squeezing my shoulders as lust overtakes her body.

"That's different." The breathy quality of her tone gives away how much I'm affecting her. *Good.* I hope I affect her even half as much as she consumes me. She's infiltrated my every thought, my every action. Thoughts of her dominate every spare minute in my day, and it's still not enough. I just can't get enough of her.

My lips hungrily meet hers, our tongues clashing as we give into our need for one another, neither of us coming up for air until we've sated our urges.

"I'm sorry you have to see me with him," she says twenty minutes later, when we're re-dressed and in our usual position on the couch. "I feel the same way when I see the girls all over the guys."

Well, now I feel like an asshole. Of course, this is as difficult for her as it is for me. We're all struggling.

Leaning up on her elbows, she stares into my eyes. "It's not fair to you, though. You're not even part of the stupid tradition, and you still have to see all that." A soft smile graces her lips. "One day, it's going to be your arm around me in public while we walk down the street, or go to the theater, or out for a meal. Everyone will know you're mine."

"Is that so, sweetheart?" I grab her ass cheeks firmly with both hands, dragging her on top of me. "And are you mine?"

She leans down, her wavy hair falling around us, hiding us from the world. With her lips a hair's breadth from mine, she whispers, "Always." After a second of hesitation, she adds, "I love you."

I didn't need to hear the words to know she felt that way about me. I can see it every time she looks at me. It's in her every action, but the fact she now knows how she feels, and has the courage to say the words aloud, shows how far she's come since she first arrived here. My heart swells with pride as I close the distance between us, both of us getting lost in one another for the rest of the period.

Hadley

CHAPTER SIXTEEN

*I*t's Friday, which means there's a party. One that we all have to attend with our stupid tradition dates. I hate parties as it is, so I'm already not looking forward to this one as I bang on the guys' door.

Mason's eyes instantly fill with heat when he answers. His gaze roams over my skin-tight black vest top and black skinny jeans with rips along the thighs. Paired with my black combat boots, and my blonde hair flying loose around my shoulders, I look like one sexy badass bitch.

"Damn, Little Warrior, you sure know how to dress up for your fake boyfriend," he teases, a hint of jealousy underlying his humorous tone.

"Shut up, asshole." I roll my eyes as I try to push him aside to let me in, but the immovable bastard just stands there.

"Don't you know you've gotta pay the doorman before you can get in," he jokes, a dirty glint in his eye.

"Is that so?" I purr, playing along as I run my finger down his navy shirt until I reach the belt buckle on his dark jeans. He looks hot as fuck, all dressed up for tonight. "And what's the price of entry?"

"Hmm, I'm not sure yet. It might be more than you can afford. I think you'll have to tempt me into letting you in."

With a playful smirk, I step in toward him, my body pressing up to his and ensuring my breasts graze against his chest. Wrapping one arm around his neck, I trail my other down his pec and over each ridge of his six-pack.

With my lips inches from his, I breathe out, "Is that so?" before rubbing my hand over his growing erection.

He groans when I squeeze his shaft. Diving in to close the distance, his lips crash against mine in a wet, heated, sloppy kiss that instantly has me skyrocketing to dizzying heights. His hands grab large fistfuls of my ass, holding me in place as he grinds his now hard cock against my jean-clad pussy.

"You may be going to the party with that asshole," he grunts, "but you'll be coming all over one of our dicks before the end of the night."

Fuck, the way he says that is so hot, and I'm so here for coming over *all* of their dicks tonight. I mean, why choose, right?

With another dirty kiss and enough grinding to have my panties soaked and my pussy clenching around air, he lets me go, and with my cheeks flushed, I step into their apartment.

Daniel is meeting me here, and the six of us are heading over to the party together. The guys never arrive with their dates, but apparently, it's expected of me to arrive with mine. It's fucking sexist, is what it is. This whole thing is ridiculous. The guys get away with treating their girls like crap, and it's presumed that the entire tradition is nothing more than fucking for the month. Although, as a girl, I'm held to a higher standard. I can't just pretend to use Daniel as a fuck toy like they can. No, I have to act like I'm fucking dating him. As I said, it's ludicrous, sexist bullshit.

Before I get too caught up in my anger over the whole thing, Mason drags me over to the sofa, pulling me down so I straddle his waist. His lips descend on mine and his hands go back to squeezing my ass, as the two of us kiss like the horny teenagers we are. I soon forget where I am and my anger is snuffed out as I grind shamelessly against him.

I'm completely lost in the feel of him, more than ready to strip him naked and climb aboard his dick, when there's a tug on my hair. Breaking our kiss as my head is pulled backward, I find myself staring up at West upside down.

Smirking, he leans in to kiss me, his pillowy lips soft against mine. His kiss is no less possessive than Mason's as he pillages my mouth with his tongue. I'm faintly aware of Mason's hands skirting up underneath my top, hitching it up.

I gasp into West's mouth when Mason pulls down the cup of my bra, exposing my nipple to the cool air in the room. While I grind harder against him, he brushes his thumb over the peak before running his tongue around it. Flashbacks of the last time we were in this position drive me wild, and my eyes drift shut until West pulls on my hair again, forcing my head to tilt so I'm looking at Cam. He's standing in the doorway, watching us with a prominent bulge pressing against his pants. I lick my lips invitingly, and he moves closer, quickly closing the distance as he comes to join us.

West steps to the side, maintaining his firm grip on my hair as Cam's lips replace the ache West left behind. Cam's kiss is more hesitant at first. Nevertheless, the moment I bite down on his lower lip, causing him to groan, he stops holding back and gives me everything he's got as he fucks my mouth with wild abandon. Mason stops with the ministrations on my tits and instead moves to undo the button on my jeans, shoving his hand inside until his fingers are pressing against the sopping wet fabric of my panties.

"Jesus," he groans. "She's fucking drenched. You love having all of us worshipping you, don't you, baby."

I can't do anything but moan into Cam's mouth as West pulls down the thin strap of my top, exposing my shoulder so he can lick, suck, and nip his way along it. Fuck, having all three of them touching me is like nothing I've ever experienced before. It's too much and not enough all at once.

"Better hurry up and make her come, man, before Hawk shows his face," West growls to Mason.

"She's fucking ready to explode," he assures him, pushing his fingers inside me.

He's not wrong. I can already feel the telltale tingling in my fingers and toes. Mason sets a fast, rough rhythm, his other hand pushing its way beneath my jeans to play with my clit. It takes mere seconds before I'm rushing toward the cliff, crying out into Cam's mouth when West bites my shoulder.

Cam doesn't stop kissing me right away. Rather, he slowly eases the pace before breaking away.

"That was the hottest thing I've ever seen," he says, staring at me with blown pupils and lust-filled eyes.

Mason fixes my panties back in place and rebuttons my jeans, and I climb off him so he can go wash his hands while I fix my bra and shirt. By the time Hawk makes an appearance, we're all sitting casually on the sofas like nothing ever happened.

A knock on the door signifies Daniel's arrival, and I get up to answer it. Only Mason, with his stupidly long legs, manages to get there before me, blocking the doorway with his large frame as he glowers at the poor guy. He's a good head taller than Daniel, painting an intimidating picture as he looms over him.

To say it's been difficult, balancing the stupid tradition with our relationship, would be an understatement. There's been jealousy on both sides, and I've lost count of the number of times one of the guys has pulled me into a dark corner of the school and kissed me stupid, reminding me that no matter what it might seem to everyone else, I'm theirs. As if I could forget, especially when they drop to their knees and make me see stars. But we all agreed the only way to get through this was if we trusted one another and talked it out if any of us were unhappy at any point. Not that there's much we can do, but open and honest communication can resolve many problems.

"Let him in, asshole," I huff, shoving Mason in a futile attempt to get him to step aside.

With one last threatening glower, he steps aside, letting a slightly terrified-looking Daniel into the apartment.

"Ignore him," I placate, trying to put him at ease with a smile. It doesn't work though, because as soon as Mason closes the door, Hawk appears along with West and Cam. All four assholes form a brick wall of muscle behind me.

"You keep an eye on her all night," Hawk begins threateningly, making me roll my eyes as I throw my hands up in exasperation. I just can't with these boys sometimes. "Do not give her alcohol or let her out of your sight. If she comes back here with so much as a scratch on her, you're a dead man, got it?"

"Y-Yes."

"No touching and sure as fuck no kissing," Cam growls out.

"No p-problem." By this point, Daniel's head is bobbing up and down like a bobble-head. I'm pretty sure he'd agree to a blood sacrifice if it meant they would leave him alone.

"Guys, stop being assholes," I seethe. "I plan to sit by the fire all night with you guys, so I don't know what you think is going to happen."

Tonight will be the first true test of whether or not we can all survive this. It's one thing watching each other with another person at breakfast. However, at a party where there's alcohol and dancing, as well as the girls having certain expectations, it's going to be exponentially more challenging.

Not long after, when the apartment is so thick with tension you can hardly move, we all pile out into the fresh air of the evening.

"Fuck," Daniel breathes out from beside me. "I thought they were scary from a distance, but they're so much worse up close."

I can't help but laugh.

"I'm sorry. They're not usually that bad. This is all a bit of a fucked-up situation," I explain vaguely, unable to tell him anything more.

He snorts. "I'll say. I'm surprised my balls are still attached to my body. You're dating all three of them, right?"

I give myself whiplash with how quickly my head snaps to look in his direction, my eyes wide as I gape at him. He laughs at my shocked expression. "It was obvious as soon as I arrived tonight."

He must see the fear in my eyes as he quickly tacks on. "Don't worry. I don't think anyone else will realize. I didn't even suspect it until tonight. I figured you were maybe dating someone, but I had no idea who. Nonetheless, the whole alpha dominant thing they were doing, yeah, that was a dead giveaway."

"You can't tell anyone," I implore him, still fretting over the fact someone else now knows about us.

"Hey," he soothes. "I won't. Promise. It's none of my business. And after what I saw tonight, there's no way in hell I'd willingly cross those guys." When I scowl at him, he rightfully adds, "Or you. You're pretty scary too."

"I'll have you know I can make whatever they do to you look like child's play." There's a pressing note in my tone and a menacing smile on my face, and I can tell he doesn't know whether or not to take me seriously.

"So, Daniel." Cam throws his arm over his shoulder in some weird bro thing that I'm pretty sure he isn't doing out of friendliness, pulling him slightly to the side as he whispers something in his ear that I'm not able to hear. West slips in between us, the back of his hand occasionally grazing the back of mine as we follow the rest of the crowd toward the increasing noises of the party at the lake.

For the most part, the party isn't too bad. Michael and Emilia arrive shortly after we do and join us around the fire. If I ignore the half-naked girls rubbing themselves against *my* guys and constantly trying to gain their attention, it's a pretty decent night. We all sit in a circle around the pit, talking, and the rest of the school avoids us as usual.

Halfway through the night, Daniel goes off to join his friends. Unfortunately, the girls refuse to leave the guys' sides, and as the alcohol starts to course through their systems, they become bolder about their intentions.

When one of the sluts tells Cam how she can't wait for him to feed her his giant cock, and places her hand over his crotch, I've reached my limit of what I can handle. I jump to my feet as Cam brushes her hand off, failing at masking his disgust.

"I'm going for a walk," I snap out, not waiting to hear their protests as I stalk off through the crowd. I don't even know where I'm going, but I need to get the fuck away from here before I break that bitch's arm.

As I reach the tree line, I hear footsteps chasing after me, and Cam catches up just as I slip into the forest. Out of view of the partygoers, he pulls on my arm, spinning me to face him and wrapping his arms around me. "I'm sorry," he murmurs against my ear, even though he didn't do anything wrong. He's just playing his part—a hell of a lot better than I am.

"This is so difficult," I mumble into his t-shirt, resting my head on his shoulder as I breathe in his apple and water lotus aftershave, trying to draw some comfort from it.

"I know, but none of it's real. I wanted to cut her hand off every time she touched me, and I know the others feel the same."

I sigh wearily. "I know, but it doesn't stop it from hurting." I lick my lips nervously, drawing back to look into his eyes. "I've never felt this way before."

A tender smile graces his lips as he peers down at me. "Neither have I," he admits. With his palm on my cheek, he leans down to kiss my lips softly. It's slow and steady but no less passionate than his other kisses as he conveys just how little that slut by the fire means to him.

"Come on." He tugs on my arm, pulling me deeper into the forest.

"Where are we going?"

"My girl's not happy, so I've gotta find a way to put a smile on her face." He tosses me a dirty wink that has my panties melting.

Hmm, I can think of a few ways he can improve my night.

Half an hour later, we're both fixing our clothes back in place before we reluctantly return to the party, when I hear a rustle in the trees.

"Did you hear that?" I whisper, snapping my head in the direction where I swear I just heard a twig snap.

"Probably just an animal." He shrugs, unperturbed.

I squint into the darkness between the trees for another minute, but I don't see or hear anything else. *Yeah, he's probably right. I'm just being paranoid.*

Shaking it off, the two of us return to the party, and I ignore the scowl on Hawk's face as I reclaim my seat.

"Where are Emilia and Michael?" I ask no one in particular.

"Emilia's over there." West points toward where she's grinding on some dude, both of them looking drunk enough that they'll likely regret their decisions in the morning. "Michael went to get a drink. Are you okay?"

"All good." I plaster on an over-the-top cheery smile. The girls are so drunk by now I could probably fuck West in front of them and they wouldn't even remember it.

Thankfully, everyone calls it a night not much later, and the guys drop off their mostly passed-out dates back in their dorms while Daniel walks me to the guys' apartment. I can see the questions in his eyes, except he wisely keeps them to himself, dropping me off and saying goodnight before disappearing back down the stairwell.

West is the first to return, and I can sense how close he is to losing it the second he enters the apartment. Tonight was hard on all of us, and I get the impression he's feeling particularly out of control at the minute—a feeling I know he hates.

His alpha persona is in full control right now as he storms toward me, grabbing me firmly by the wrist and tugging me behind him as he strides toward his bedroom. I have to jog to keep up with his long legs—damn tall man.

The second the door slams shut behind him, I know I'm in for a fun night of blissful orgasms and watching West in his element.

He makes me see stars three times before pressing a final searing kiss to my lips. "I love you," he murmurs. The second the words spill out, his body stiffens. I keep running my fingers through his hair as I kiss him, pulling him back into that noxious cloud of passion until he's once again relaxed.

"I love you too."

Collapsing onto the bed beside me, he sets his glasses on the bedside table and wraps his arms around me, and the two of us fall into a peaceful sleep.

The first time I said those words aloud to Beck, my heart was slamming against my ribs. Before then, I'd never spoken the words aloud to another living soul, but since he said them to me several weeks ago, I've been thinking about it a lot, trying to put a name to this feeling I have for each of the guys. Now I've come to the conclusion it has to be love. There's nothing else it can be. No other word feels big enough to encompass all of these complicated feelings I have for each of them.

∼

"Ahhh, look! Look!" Emilia screams, waving a page in my face as she bounces into my room. She didn't even knock before barging in, making me jump out of bed, thinking some madman was chasing her.

"What is it?"

I snatch the page from her outstretched hand as my heart rate settles back to normal.

"Oh my god, Emilia, this is amazing!" I exclaim. "Congratulations!"

She beams at me with an authentic, brilliant smile showing how thrilled she is at this moment. And so she should be. She just got a full-ride scholarship to one of the most competitive colleges in the state.

She bounces into my arms, and I happily return her hug, letting her squeeze me half to death in her excitement.

"I can't believe it. I mean, I know that's what the last four years have been for. Why I've been working my ass off, but I can't believe it's real. That it's really happening."

"Believe it, girl. You're amazing. Of course you deserve this."

Taking the letter back, she falls onto my bed with a dreamy sigh, staring at the page like it's a love letter. I guess to her, it is.

"What are your plans after school?" she asks, looking up at me.

I move to sit opposite her on the bed. "Eh, I'm not sure. I haven't given it much thought."

"What? How? It's your future!" She gapes. Neither of us has really talked about the future in much depth—well, *I've* never talked about the future. I know all about Emilia's prospective plans. They mean everything to her, but as much as having a feasible plan in place is vital to her, not having any idea what's in store and just seeing what happens along the way is important to me. At least it means I have a future that's all mine. Other people have mapped out my whole life, but now *I* get to decide what I want to do with it. I haven't quite worked out the 'what' yet, but the fact that I have options is everything.

"I know. I just haven't decided what to do with it yet." I shrug as she keeps staring wide-eyed at me.

"I'd just assumed you'd applied somewhere and were keeping it on the DL until you heard from them."

"Nope." I shake my head, but all this talk has me wondering, do I want to go to college? I'm not exactly academic. If it weren't for my fake transcripts, I wouldn't be here at all. I'm barely scraping by this year. Even so, isn't college like one of those things you have to experience? It's not like I have any ideas of what I want to do with my life, so college could be the perfect place to figure out who I am and what I like.

Equally, I've probably missed all the application deadlines. I don't know if I can even afford to go, and I can't see my parents being accepting of me just going off and deciding my own life. I feel like I'm forgetting another reason...Oh yeah, the fact Lawrence is trying to drag my ass back to the compound and we're in the middle of trying to figure out how to take down all of our parents and their fucked-up company.

Yeah, college plans might have to wait.

Hadley

CHAPTER SEVENTEEN

Emilia, Michael, and I are ordering lunch at the kiosk when Daniel and his friends walk in. He smiles when he sees us. "Hey."

"Hey," I greet awkwardly. Other than breakfast and parties, we don't interact much and are rarely around other people where we have to pretend to be something we aren't.

"Dude," his buddy hisses, jamming his elbow in his ribs. "Ask her to sit with us."

"Oh, right, do you, uh, wanna sit with us?" He rubs the back of his neck in obvious embarrassment.

"Sounds great," Emilia answers for me, earning herself a 'what the fuck' look. She knows this is all for show.

When her eyebrows waggle up and down a couple of times, I catch on to what she's silently trying to say. Basically, the guys are hot, and I'd be a horrible friend to rob her of this opportunity.

"Sure." I sigh, giving Daniel a tight smile.

He quickly puts in his order, and we follow him over to his table as his friends put in their lunch requests.

"Sorry," he whispers in my ear as we take our seats.

"It's fine." I smile so he knows I'm serious. It's actually hasn't been too bad spending time with him. It would be fun if we weren't busy pretending we're in a fake relationship. He's a genuinely nice guy and easy to get along with.

His friends all join us, and Daniel introduces them. Their eyes all bounce inquisitively between Emilia, Michael, and me.

"Oh, this is Emilia and Michael."

"Aren't you guys scholarship students?" one asshole asks.

"So?" I snap, glowering menacingly at him, daring him to say one bad word.

He holds up his hands in surrender. "Didn't mean anything by it. It's just that the Princes don't hang around with the scholarship kids."

"Do I look like I have a dick swinging between my thighs? I'm not a Prince, and I'll be friends with whomever I want to be friends with."

"That's cool. Like I said, I meant nothing by it," the guy persists, nodding his head frantically.

The rest of lunch goes by without any issues, but I catch Michael looking quizzically at me several times over the hour. Especially when Daniel nudges my shoulder and whispers in my ear, making me laugh.

"Are you actually dating him, or is it just for show?" Michael asks later that afternoon as we head to the library.

"Why?"

He shrugs. "You just looked comfortable today at lunch. You're rarely like that."

I guess I had fun. I am learning to let down my walls a bit, and all the frequent touches from the guys have helped me feel more at ease around others.

"It was fun, but no. I barely know the guy."

"Are you dating anybody?"

I hesitate, wondering how much to tell him and why he's even asking. I know he had a crush on me when I first arrived, but I thought that was long over. I mean, we're friends, right?

"Eh, no. Things have been a little hectic, what with the whole Davenport bomb drop and adjusting to that, never mind throwing a boyfriend in the mix." I laugh tensely.

Whatever weird tension was in his shoulders drops out. "Cool." Before I can ask him why he's suddenly interested in my love life, he continues, "We should hang out and do something fun sometime soon. It's been ages since we caught up."

"Yeah, we should," I agree, feeling bad. Sure, the three of us hang out together a lot, but I haven't spent much one-on-one time with Michael, and like Emilia, he gave up the only other friends he had when he agreed to be friends with me. So I do really need to make more of an effort.

"We could book a theater room for tonight. I'll grab us some ice cream and coffee."

I hesitate for only a second, thinking of the guys, but I'm not that needy girlfriend who has to be with them every spare minute of the day, so I quickly chastise myself and agree to tonight.

We spend the rest of the afternoon in the library getting some work done, and that night I stop by Emilia's room, wanting to get her two cents on the conversation I had with Michael earlier, before I head out to meet with him. I still struggle with navigating these newfound friendships, and I can't figure out if Michael was off earlier or if I'm reading too much into it.

"Hmm, sounds like he still has a thing for you," Emilia unhelpfully tells me, making me groan.

"What am I supposed to do about that?" Now I feel super awkward and don't even know if I should meet up with him tonight.

"Nothing. You're not leading him on. He's a teenage boy, he'll get over it."

"So you think I should still hang out with him tonight?"

"Absolutely." She nods her head. "You're still his friend, and he's probably confused about everything going on with you lately. What with you spending a lot of time with the guys, and now with Daniel. He could be feeling insecure that you don't have time for him anymore. Tonight will hopefully put him at ease."

Feeling reassured, I head to the rec center to meet him. The night turns out to be good fun, and I remind myself to make more of an effort to spend time with him. As the movie credits roll across the screen, Michael turns to face me.

"How are you coping with everything that's happened recently?" he asks.

Sighing, I rest my head back against the seat. "It's been a lot to take in, but I'm doing okay."

"And you're getting along with Hawk and the guys alright? You've been spending a lot of time with them."

"Yeah, they've been great, actually." I have to suppress my smile as I think about them. "There's been a lot to work through with Hawk, but we're turning a corner now, and the others have been accepting me into their fold."

A look I can't place crosses Michael's features, but I blink, and it's gone. Studying him for a second longer, he looks like his old self, so I brush it off. Probably just the way the dim lights in here glance across his face.

"So you're like friends with them all now? Even though they bullied you throughout the first semester."

There's a harshness in his voice, and I don't appreciate the accusatory tone he's using as I turn to look directly at him.

"Things are different now," I snap. Yeah, it sounds weak to my ears, and I can't blame him for thinking I'm insane, but he doesn't know everything that's going on or what we've had to deal with.

I sigh, trying my best to let go of my anger. "It's complicated. Nevertheless, they've apologized, and we're working through it," I tell him.

Gathering our stuff, we start to head back toward the dorms.

"We should do this again," he says. "Sunday night?"

"Ehh, let me get back to you. Things have been hectic recently, and I just want to make sure there's no Davenport nonsense I need to deal with." I know I'm being a bitch by blowing him off, but I do have a lot on my plate right now, and Sunday is only a few days away. Plus, we still have our standard Saturday night movie night with Emilia, so I don't really see a need to do two.

"Oh, yeah, sure."

∽

I'M SITTING in the library, with Daniel beside me and his friends taking up the rest of the seats at the table. When Mason comes in, his slut of the month is draped all over him. It's been three weeks since we started up this stupid tradition again, and I still can't get used to seeing any of the guys with one of them. Uncontrollable rage overtakes me every time I have to watch them with one of their sluts. It's a miracle no one has gotten a knife in the eye or a fork to the hand yet.

He's clearly not having a good day—if the furious look on his face is any indicator—but if he looked pissed off when he entered, it's nothing compared to the look on his face when he notices me sitting with Daniel and his friends. His head looks like it's about to pop off his shoulders, and I can't do anything except silently apologize with my eyes as he stomps over to a nearby table and bangs his bag onto the surface, not giving a shit that he's disturbing everyone around him.

It's not my fault. I was just sitting here minding my own business when Daniel and his friends walked in. I saw him try to convince them to go to another table, but they weren't having any of it and practically dragged him over here to sit with me. So now we're stuck playing pretend while we do our best to focus on our schoolwork.

Of course, now that Mason is here, zero work will get done. I watch as his little slut follows him to the table, oblivious to his rage as she tries to sit in his lap, laughing like it's some game when he shoves her off him.

I try to ignore him, focusing back on my workbook and tablet, but I can feel his furious stare like laser beams burning into the side of my head. Giving up on trying to ignore him, I decide the best thing to do is give him an outlet for all that rage. Biting on my lower lip in thought, I decide to play a dangerous game with the fuming beast glaring at me.

Leaning in, I whisper in Daniel's ear, "Play a game with me?" I flick a glance in Mason's direction, and he hesitantly agrees. "Put your arm around me," I whisper, squashing my smirk.

Doing as I tell him, he leans in and drapes his arm across the back of my chair, his fingers dangling over my shoulder. Pretending to focus on my work, I peer up at him through my eyelashes, watching Mason's features narrow, his jaw clenching as he strangles his stylus, oblivious to the girl who may as well be doing naked star jumps beside him.

Daniel bends down to whisper in my ear, and to anyone else, it would look like two lovers sharing a secret. "You're going to get me killed," he says, half joking. I let out a girly giggle, batting my eyelashes at him like he just said the sweetest thing.

"He's going to bury my body out in the forest. Tell my family that I love them. Make sure my brother gets my baseball card collection." He sighs dramatically. "I never got the chance to tell Wendi how amazing I thought her tits were." My laugh is real this time as he continues with the theatrics.

"Jeez, will you two get a room already," one of his friends hollers, his words loud enough to carry across to Mason's nearby table.

It's the last straw for Mason as he jumps to his feet, sending his chair crashing to the floor as the bimbo gasps in shock, and he stomps toward us to haul me out of my seat.

Glancing back over my shoulder, I ignore the shocked looks from the other guys at the table as I give Daniel a conspiratorial wink, and he shakes his head while rolling his eyes at me.

Mason yanks me behind him until we reach the back of the library, where the private study rooms are. Barging into one with people in it, he barks, "Out," glowering at everyone as they hastily gather their stuff and run out of the room like their asses are on fire.

He slams the door shut behind them, pushing me against the door with his large body.

Fire glows in his bright blue eyes, mixed with carnal need and desire. Shoving his hand between my thighs, he cups my pussy and curls his fingers beneath the fabric of my panties before tearing them clean off in a move that leaves me panting.

Clamping my dripping wet pussy in his hand, he growls, "This cunt is mine." He slides his fingers through my slick wetness, coating them before sliding further back, pressing the tip of his finger against the tight ring of muscle. "This ass is mine." His eyes flick down to my lips, the thumb of his other hand pushing its way past my teeth. I suck him into my mouth, licking his thumb with my tongue. "That dirty mouth of yours is mine."

He watches, enraptured, as I suck on his thumb before slowly removing it with a pop. His hand moves to take mine, placing it over his rock-hard erection. "Just like this dick is yours." I squeeze his shaft, and he groans, his hips involuntarily thrusting into my grip.

Using his grip on my hand, he pulls it away and slowly slides my palm up his shirt until it's resting over his heart, as the look in his eyes softens. I can feel the steady beat of it beneath my hand, and I can't look away from the unusual vulnerability I see in his eyes. "This heart is yours. *I* am yours."

I swallow around the lump of emotion in my throat.

"You're perfect for me, Little Warrior. We were always meant to be together. You're mine—not because you belong to me, but because you own every part of me."

Well, fuck me. Give this man a standing ovation, because that was one hell of a declaration.

My voice is hoarse as I lick my dry lips. "You own all of me, too," I admit, clenching my hand into his shirt and using it to yank him toward me.

Our kiss is brutal. All teeth and violent possession as we assault one another. My hands roam frantically over his chest, pulling and tugging on his clothes until they come apart. In no time, he's throwing me back against the door and driving into me, making my eyes roll back in my head.

His hand clamps down over my mouth, silencing my cries. The sex is rough and intense, but with our faces inches apart, our eyes never straying from one another, it's intimate and overflowing with raw emotion. All too soon, I feel him swelling within me, and as his cum hits my inner walls, I fall apart, my ecstasy muffled behind his hand.

When we're done, he removes his hand from my mouth, resting his forehead against mine.

"I love you," I pant, loving how his eyes soften and a boyish grin graces his lips.

"I love you, baby. You're mine, and I'm yours. That's the way it's always going to be." He kisses my forehead, and the two of us share a moment of blissful contentedness before he speaks again. "I actually came here to get you. West found something."

"He did? What?"

"I dunno yet. He wanted to wait until all of us were together."

Satisfied and with a renewed purpose, we quickly redress and leave the study room. I quickly gather my belongings, blurting out an excuse to Daniel and his friends before rushing out of the library with Mason.

By the time we make it to the guys' dorm, everyone else is there, waiting impatiently.

"About time," Cam grouses. "What took you so long? This asshole won't tell us anything."

"Sorry. We're here now. What's going on?" I ask, skipping over the reason for our tardiness and wedging myself into the space on the sofa between him and Hawk.

When we all are seated, we stare impatiently at West, waiting for him to share his findings. He's sitting opposite us, with a laptop open in front of him on the coffee table.

"So, I've been monitoring the security cameras at both our parents' offices and their homes. It's all been pretty boring stuff, but today I was reviewing the footage from last week when I came across this from a few days ago." He turns the laptop around, and we all huddle together to see the screen as he presses play.

The footage is of the kitchen in one of our parents' houses. At first, it's just an empty room, but after a second, a woman in a revealing dress and sky-high heels enters the frame. We can't hear what's being said, but based on her frantic hand gestures, she's upset. I don't recognize her, but I do recognize the man who enters the room next—Frank Hayes. His face is thunderous, and it looks like he's yelling at the woman. An argument ensues, and I gasp when he slaps her across the face hard enough to have her stumbling sideways into the kitchen counter.

She stares at him in shock, cradling her stinging cheek in her hand, but Frank is on a roll now. He stalks toward her, his cheeks reddening as he yells in her face. I can see the terror in her eyes as she tries to backtrack, cowering and most likely apologizing to him. The asshole isn't hearing any of it though, too lost in his rage as his hand grips tightly around her upper arm, easily throwing her across the room.

The woman goes flying, crashing onto the tiled floor. She curls in on herself, but Frank still manages to get his foot in as he kicks her relentlessly. Not caring what body part he connects with.

It feels like it goes on for ages, and based on how the woman's muscles slacken, she must pass out at some point. Nonetheless, it's not enough to stop the sick bastard from beating on her. I have to look away, unable to watch anymore. My hands begin to tremble as I struggle to force back long-buried memories. My gaze lands on Mason's hard one. His body is wound tight, his fists clenched as he watches his father beat the ever-loving shit out of an innocent woman. I can only imagine the extent of the beating he took as a kid. For that reason alone, the fucker in the video needs to pay.

When the woman is bloody and lifeless on the ground, Frank finally stops his assault. Panting heavily, he stands and stares at her with a vacant stare. There's no remorse over the fact he's just killed someone. No guilt. Nothing.

As he storms out of the frame, leaving the woman lying on the cold floor, West pauses the recording. "This was three days ago."

"He killed her?" It certainly looks like she's dead, but I need to know for sure.

"Yeah, he did. He got some guys from their organization to come clean up his mess."

"Who was she?"

"Lacee Hamilton," Mason supplies, staring off into space. "Her family owns a chain of high-end jewelry stores." He grits his teeth, looking ready to explode as he pushes himself out of his seat, pacing back and forth across the living room.

"How do you have this?" Hawk asks. "Surely he would have wiped the tapes?"

"I've been downloading all of the security footage onto my own secure drives, so we'll still have a copy of it even if they delete anything."

"So what do we do with this?" Cam questions, watching Mason out of the corner of his eye.

Mason turns on his heel to face us. His features are dark and terrifying as he struggles to deal with what he just witnessed. "We use this to put that sick fuck away for good."

Hadley

CHAPTER EIGHTEEN

> Hawk: We've been summoned for dinner tonight. 7 pm.

I groan, already predicting how bad tonight will be. If the last two times I've met my parents are any indicator, it's going to be pretty grim. I haven't seen either of them since the night of the party, nor have I spoken to them. Which is totally fine with me. I've decided it's much better to skirt by, lurking on the periphery of their awareness. I'm not sure they know what to do with me yet, but I have no doubt they're contemplating how they can get the best use out of my unexpected arrival.

The problem with maintaining as much distance as possible from them is that I'm no closer to finding out what happened to me or if they are involved. I mean, they have to be on some level, right? Even if they aren't, they're shitty parents for not funneling all of their resources into finding me and instead putting the priorities of their company first.

Sighing, I fire off a less-than-enthusiastic response to Hawk as I lean back against my headboard, trying to think of a way to get the information I need from my parents. They aren't just going to come out and tell me the truth about what happened.

I spend the rest of the day going back and forth between homework and thinking about all of our parents and what the hell we're going to do. West finding that footage of Frank enables us to finally fight back. It's a small step, but a step forward nonetheless. West sent a copy to the local police, the state police, and another one to the family. He's also kept a secure copy for us, which could come in handy. Now, all we have to do is wait and let the chips fall where they may.

As for the other parents, the six of us have thrown around a few ideas, but we need to sit down and come up with a real strategy for tackling them, and the company. The end of the school year is quickly approaching, and things will only get worse once the guys graduate and work full-time for them. I don't even know—or want to know—their plans for me after graduation. I can hazard a guess that the future they've mapped out for me is not the one of freedom I envisioned when I escaped the compound.

By the time Hawk knocks on my door that evening, I'm dressed in a pair of jeans and a t-shirt. I've done my best to flatten my hair, and I even borrowed another pair of flats from Emilia—look at me making an effort!

"Ready?" he asks when I open the door.

"No," I grumble. "What do they want this time?"

"No idea, guess we'll find out soon."

We make our way out of the dorm and along the path to the parking lot, before I speak up again. "West told me you all want out from under your parents' thumbs."

"Yeah," he agrees. "Obviously, we've never wanted to head up the company. Initially, we'd hoped we could at least talk them into letting us go to college first, so we could buy ourselves a few more years of freedom and enough time to come up with a better exit strategy, but now..." He shakes his head. "None of us want anything to do with what they're involved in. They want us to spend some time shadowing them over Easter break at the company, but honestly, I can't imagine anything worse."

"After the way the guys were treated growing up, and the threats our parents have been shoving down our throats this year, I can't stand to be in the same room as any of them."

"Even your own parents?" I ask cautiously, knowing his relationship with his parents was nothing like what the other guys had to endure.

"Them most of all," he growls out. "Yeah, the other guys had a harder time growing up, but at least they *knew* their parents were shitty. I thought mine were okay. Not overly affectionate or around much, but they never harmed me or made me feel like a failure. But this past year, they've been completely different. Nothing like the parents I had when I was a kid. It's making me doubt everything I thought I knew growing up, and I hate that. I hate how I can't trust any of my memories and that I'm second-guessing every second I have spent with them," he growls in frustration. "I probably sound like an asshole. Compared to Mason or West, or fuck, you, I have nothing to complain about. At least I had those years where things were good with my parents, right?"

I bump my shoulder against his. This is the most he's opened up to me, and while it's a complicated, convoluted subject, I'm silently squealing like a girl on the inside at the new level we've reached in our relationship.

"You're entitled to feel whatever you're feeling," I assure him. "It doesn't matter what anyone else's past is. That doesn't negate what you have experienced or how you feel with all these new developments."

"I can understand where you're coming from. You felt more blindsided than the others because you didn't think your parents were as bad as theirs. The others had time to prepare, so while the whole mercenary discovery might have been a shock, the fact their parents were caught up in that shit wasn't a complete surprise."

"Exactly." He sighs, lapsing into silence as we reach the car, and he starts the engine, driving us out the campus gates.

As we enter the house, Maria saunters toward us. "There you are," she scolds, like we're late, but I know for a fact we're exactly on time. The clock in the car read seven on the dot as we got out of it. "Hair and makeup are waiting for you, Elizabeth."

Uh, what now? Why the fuck do I need my hair and makeup done?

"What's going on, Mom?" Hawk asks.

"We're having a couple of guests this evening. It's important everyone looks their best," she answers vaguely, looping her arm through mine as she drags me away from Hawk.

I glance over my shoulder, begging him with my eyes to get me out of this, but he shrugs his shoulders, not showing any signs of coming to my rescue. *Fucking asshole.*

Sighing in defeat, I accept my fate as we climb the stairs. All the while, Maria rambles on about some shit or other. The woman honestly baffles me. Right now, she's almost acting as though we're friends, except she's barely said more than a handful of words to me before now. Most of them have been snapped out in irritation—guess I know where Hawk gets his shitty personality from.

Directing me to a bedroom where two women are waiting, Maria lifts a garment bag off the bed. "Put this on," she orders, shoving the bag against my chest and leaving me with no choice but to catch it before it drops to the floor.

She doesn't bother to turn around as I strip out of my clothes, opting to avert her eyes instead, like that's going to do any good. I don't give a fuck what this bitch thinks of me and my scars, so if she wants to watch, then fine. I shimmy into the skin-tight dress that I have to stretch over my breasts. It clings to my hips, the sheer black material barely covering my ass.

Maria gives up all pretense of pretending not to watch, staring openly at me with her lips pinched as she assesses me.

"Not bad." She taps her index finger against her lip in thought. "We might have to do something about that tattoo, though. It's unseemly. Thank goodness the dress covers it all for tonight." Before I can tell her she's not doing shit with my tattoo, she twirls her finger in the air. "Turn around."

Not seeing that I have a choice, I bite my tongue and do as she says, hearing her gasp when she notices the scars covering my shoulders and back. If you look at me from the front, you can hardly notice them. There are only a few faint, white lines along the tops of my shoulders and my collarbone, but when you look at my back, it would be impossible to miss the prominent white lines marring the skin.

"Oh my," she breathes.

You'd think this might be the moment she softens toward me, now that she realizes what hardships her daughter has had to face. However no such kindness or compassion exists in this hard shell of a woman.

"We can't have that. I'll make an appointment with my plastic surgeon."

"No," I bark out sharply as I spin around to glare at her. There is absolutely no fucking way I am letting anyone come near me with a scalpel. My scars are a part of who I am. Yeah, they might be an eyesore, but anyone who can't bear to see them can just look the fuck away.

Her lips purse and her eyes narrow in warning at my outburst, but she doesn't push the matter, for now.

"Stella, make sure her hair covers that…atrocity on her back."

I grit my teeth, biting my tongue against the nasty words that I want to pour out, knowing it will do nothing but rile her up more.

"Yes, ma'am," a demure woman responds, nodding her head.

Happy with that acknowledgment, Maria exits the room, leaving me alone with the women who usher me into a chair in front of a floor-to-ceiling mirror. I can't do anything but let them fuss over me like mother hens, too overwhelmed with everything to tell them to stop.

"You have such thick curls," the one sorting out my hair coos as she runs her fingers through my thick locks before attacking it with a brush, while another woman wipes my face and starts to apply gunk to it. Between them, they tug on my hair, and direct me to close my eyes and push out my lips until they're satisfied with my appearance.

"Much better," Maria praises when she enters the room nearly an hour later. Her gaze roams over my too-short dress, primped hair, and over-the-top makeup. I've never been so dolled up in all my life, and I don't mean that in a good way. I look like some sort of expensive, high-end prostitute.

"Put these on." Her words are a sharp order as she hands me a pair of black peep-toe high heels. I sway dangerously as I struggle to get my feet into them, not seeing the point in arguing with her. God knows, my inability to wear heels will only give her another reason to dislike me. Before I even stand upright in my new shoes, she's already ushering me out of the room, looking impatient. "Come on. Our guests are waiting."

Cement forms in my stomach at her words as I try to figure out what the hell is going on. I'd naively thought tonight we were all going to sit down and discuss what would happen now that I was a Davenport. I'd hoped I would finally get some answers to what happened to me, but with each passing second, that is looking less and less likely.

When we enter the dining room, Hawk, Barton, and two men I don't recognize are sitting around the dining table. All four stop mid-conversation when we enter, their attention turning to us.

Hawk's eyes widen, and his lips press together as he struggles to hold back a laugh. *Yeah, I bet I look fucking ridiculous—like a five-year-old who got into her mom's makeup.*

I 'accidentally' knock my elbow against the back of his head when I walk past his seat. He glowers at me as I sit in the empty chair beside him to take in the guy opposite me. He looks around our age, with wavy, tousled chestnut brown hair. He's got a broad chin and dimples in his cheeks as he smiles at me. It's a dirty smirk that, combined with his honey-brown eyes that twinkle with mischief, lets me know his thoughts are in the gutter.

There's something wild about the look in his eye. It's not quite normal, yet I can't put my finger on what it is. Shrugging it off, I flick my gaze to a similarly built older man with tints of gray in his hair and lines around his eyes and lips sitting beside him, watching me intently. The way he looks at me makes my skin crawl, as though he's trying to determine my measure.

I quickly look away from him, but I continue to feel his eyes on me as Maria takes her seat at the end of the table, sitting opposite her husband.

"Benjamin, meet our daughter, Elizabeth," Barton introduces, barely sparing me a glance—as has become his usual. I don't know what it is about me that he can't bear to look at. Maybe it's guilt eating him alive?

"She's certainly something, isn't she?" the guy—Benjamin—says, only increasing the creep factor.

I sneak a glance at Hawk out of the corner of my eye. His face is its usual impassive mask, and I can't get a read on what he's thinking or what the hell is going on here.

"I understand she's been missing for quite some time," the guy continues, his beady eyes still watching me far too closely for my liking.

"Yes, that's right. She was kidnapped as a toddler and somehow ended up in the foster system under a new name, which is why we weren't able to find her all these years. It was a fortunate coincidence that she ended up at school with Hawk this year, and the connection was made as to who she really was."

Since my so-called father has never asked me about my past, I'm guessing he's gotten his hands on my fake records and put together his own theories, which he's now passing off as fact.

Servers bring out food for each of us, cutting off their weird conversation. A plate of something tiny and fancy is placed in front of me, and it's only then that I notice three different sets of knives and forks on either side of the plate. *What the fuck? What's wrong with using the same utensils for every course?*

Once everyone has been served, and we're once again alone, I subtly cast my gaze around the table, watching to see which set of cutlery everyone else starts with. I feel so far out of my depth right now, and while I mostly don't give a shit, a small part of me wants to fit in with these people. I don't understand it. Why do I care so much about what these people think when they clearly don't care about me?

I inadvertently catch the gaze of Benjamin's son—whose name I still don't know. He must have been watching me and picked up on the fact that I have no idea what I'm doing. He points to the smallest set of cutlery furthest away from the plate, silently letting me know that's what I should be using for this course.

"Wilder will be joining you at Pac for the rest of the year," Barton informs us—well, he's looking at Hawk, so his words are meant for him.

"It's a bit late in the year to transfer, is it not?" Hawk responds, looking between his father and Wilder.

Wilder has a wide grin on his face that makes him look every bit his namesake—wild.

"Yes, well, I think getting to know him and his family better will be very fortuitous for all of us," my father responds cryptically. Hawk's eyebrows pull together as he darts his gaze back and forth between the two men, as if he can somehow telepathically read their thoughts and figure out what's going on if he just stares hard enough at their heads.

The rest of the meal drones on. Barton and Benjamin talk about mundane work things that I struggle to follow, all the while ignoring Wilder's gaze boring into my head and the tension radiating off Hawk beside me. It's safe to say it was not the most fun meal I've had, even if the food was pretty decent.

"Why don't we leave the kids to get to know each other while we go over the finer details of the contract," Maria suggests after we've all finished eating.

"Yes, what an excellent idea, darling. Hawk, you'll see that Wilder follows you back to campus when you're done?"

Barton spears Hawk with a look that makes it clear his request isn't optional.

"Sure," Hawk reluctantly agrees. Benjamin and Maria stand from the table and leave the room without a backward glance. Barton hesitates, however, as if he has something else to say. His mouth opens and closes wordlessly before he decides against saying anything at all, and he silently follows after the others.

The minute we're alone, Hawk glowers at Wilder. I must admit, it's nice not being on the other end of that menacing look for once.

"What are you really doing here?" he demands.

Wilder leans back in his chair, casually placing his napkin on the table. His other hand plays with a knife left behind after dinner, and he absently runs his thumb over the pointed tip and down the sharp blade. There's a gleam in his eye as he smirks knowingly at Hawk, enjoying lording over the fact he knows something we don't.

"You mean you haven't figured it out yet?"

Hawk's eyes narrow to slits. "I can hazard a guess," he growls.

My eyes flick between the two of them, not having any idea what they're talking about.

"Uh, would one of you like to enlighten me then?!" I snark, getting annoyed at being left in the dark.

Wilder focuses his intense gaze on me as a crazy-looking grin splits his face. This guy is definitely off his rocker. There's no way he's right in the head. He looks like a deranged psycho right now.

"Sunshine, you and I are getting hitched."

A strangled laugh escapes me.

I mean, he's obviously joking. He has to be…right? He's so deep in crazyville that he's talking out of his ass.

An animal-like growl sounds in Hawk's chest, and he slams his hand against the table, jumping to his feet. The chair squeaks against the wooden floor as it's pushed backward.

"No, you're not," he snarls.

"Well, no, not yet," Wilder says casually, not at all intimidated by the fact Hawk looks ready to gouge his eyes out. "I'm sure our parents will want to work out the fine print first."

I'm half expecting Hawk to launch himself across the table, so I'm surprised when he reaches out and all but yanks me to my feet.

I just about manage to pull my dress down, ensuring I don't give Wilder a free show as Hawk drags me out of the dining room. I have to run in my heels—which is fucking tricky—in order to keep up with his giant strides. He's grumbling under his breath, but I can't make out what he's saying.

"Hey," Wilder calls after us, and I hear his chair being pushed back before the sound of his shoes slapping against the floor chases us across the foyer. "You're supposed to show me the way back to campus."

Hawk ignores him, pulling open the front door with more force than necessary and, still with a tight grip on my arm, he tugs me out the door and down the steps. Doesn't he know I'm as keen as he is to escape the crazy madman following us?

Two cars are parked at the bottom of the steps. One is Hawk's black SUV, and another is a dark green classic Mustang convertible. It looks beautiful, and I can't help but admire it as we approach.

Hawk comes to a stop, fishing his keys out of his pocket, giving Wilder time to catch up to us.

"Get in the car, Hadley," Hawk growls.

"Wifey should probably come with me." Wilder throws his arm over my shoulder before I can move out of his way, acting as if we're best buds and he's not some weirdo I just met. "We need some 'getting to know you' time."

"I think I know all I need to know," I snark, jabbing him in the ribs with my elbow —hard.

The psycho just laughs as he doubles over in pain, and I shove him.

"Sunshine, you're going to give me an erection in front of my new bro-in-law. Not cool."

Hawk and I share similar 'what the fuck is this guy on' looks, ignoring him as I round the car, getting in, and Hawk climbs in behind the wheel to start the engine and take off down the drive.

Hadley

CHAPTER NINETEEN

"Who the hell was that guy?" I ask as Hawk hurtles down the road, driving recklessly in his attempt to get away from his parents' house and the deranged psycho stalking us.

"His dad is Benjamin Clearwater," Hawk states, as if that explains anything.

I get irritated when he doesn't elaborate, seething out, "Am I supposed to know who that is?"

"His company manufactures personal body armor, like Kevlar vests. He would provide the police and army with a ton of their gear." Hawk thinks for a moment before continuing, "It was recently announced that he was branching into weapons production. I'm guessing he and our parents are looking to get into business together." He turns his head to look at me. "And you're the bargaining chip."

My stomach churns violently. "What does that mean?" I ask, not truly wanting an answer. I can already guess for myself.

"If what Wilder said is right, they're marrying you off to him in exchange for whatever business Benjamin agreed to do with them."

"But, I don't understand." I'm ashamed to say my voice comes out more high-pitched than I'd like, although I think it's perfectly acceptable since I'm freaking the fuck out right now. "They wanted me to get involved in your whole stupid tradition, so why would they do that if they were just going to marry me off to some rando anyway?"

Hawk shrugs his shoulders, not having an answer for me. "No idea. Benjamin is a big fish, though. It would take the company to a whole new level if they got him on board. I know they had some business deal in the works with him years ago, but something happened and it fell through." He taps his finger rapidly against the steering wheel, still driving like a fucking maniac down the dark road. "They aren't going to let this deal fall through." His grim tone only exacerbates my unease as we drive on in silence, each of us lost in our own thoughts. What the fuck am I supposed to do now? I'm not about to marry that lunatic, or anyone else for that matter.

We're nearly back at campus when Hawk breaks the heavy silence in the car. "I don't know where the nearest strip club is, but I'm sure I can find one if you wanna earn a few dollars in that getup."

"Ha ha." I laugh sarcastically, slapping him playfully on the arm. "I look like a fucking hooker *and* I left all my clothes behind in our rush to get out of there."

Hawk laughs. "Oh yeah, they've probably been burned by now."

I groan. "Those weren't even my shoes."

"So just buy a new pair." Hawk shrugs, like it's no big deal.

"We're not all made of money, asshole. Some of us know the price of a dollar."

He glances away from the road, cocking an eyebrow at me. "You do realize being a Davenport comes with some benefits, right? Like a bank account with more money than you've probably ever seen."

"What? No."

He laughs, shaking his head. "I have one, so you should too. I'll talk to Dad this week and set it up for you."

"I don't need their dirty money," I grouse.

"No," he admits, "but you might as well get something out of this shitty situation."

Well, he has a point there.

Parking the car in the student lot, Hawk fires off a quick message to the group chat, telling everyone we need a meeting. *Great, this new, fucked-up development will be super fun to explain to the guys.*

Not hanging around for Wilder to find us, we quickly head back to the guys' apartment.

"What's going on?" West blurts out as soon as Hawk and I step into the apartment, finding all four of them already there. Beer bottles are sitting out on the table, someone having already figured it was going to be one of those kinds of talks. "And what the hell are you wearing?"

Oh, right, I forgot I look like a common prostitute.

I kick off my heels and walk over to the sink, splashing water on my face to wash off the gunk that feels like it's clogging my pores. I still look ridiculous in this dress, but at least my face doesn't scream 'street walker'.

Feeling slightly better, I sit in the free armchair. All eyes are on me as I sigh, suddenly exhausted after this evening's events. "Uh." I hesitate, unsure how to explain tonight's weirdness as I take in each of my guys. "I think I'm engaged?" If I sound confused, it's because I am.

"You're what?" Mason roars, jumping to his feet, his face like thunder.

"What the hell are you talking about?" Beck demands, anger lacing his words.

"You *think*?" West questions.

"It's pretty much a done deal." Hawk sighs, rubbing at his eyes before grabbing a beer, ignoring the murderous look Mason is giving him.

"Explain," Mason spits out between gritted teeth, slowly lowering himself back into his chair. I move to sit in his lap, sensing he needs some comfort, and he swiftly wraps his arms around me, pulling me in flush against him. I rest my head on his shoulder, my fingers tracing soothing circles along his forearm as Beck lifts my feet onto his lap and massages my arches.

Holy fuck does that feel good after having them crammed into heels for the last few hours.

"What the hell is she talking about?" Beck fires at Hawk.

Hawk explains what happened after we showed up at our parents' house tonight, and I can feel the tension rising in the room until it feels like lighting a match would be enough to set everything on fire.

"Absolutely not," Beck insists. "There is no fucking way she is marrying anyone other than one of us. Least of all him, he sounds fucking unstable."

My eyes widen. *What was that now? Marrying one of them?* Is that something he's given thought to? I have so many questions, but now isn't the time to ask any of them, and honestly, the thought of his answer makes me a little nervous.

The other guys nod their heads in agreement. None of them look like they're having the same internal freak-out over Beck's words that I'm currently experiencing.

Mason must sense the tension suddenly stiffening my muscles as he presses a kiss by my ear. "Don't overthink it," he whispers.

I glance up at him in confusion, seeing the laughter in his eyes. The asshole is enjoying watching me squirm and panic.

A loud knock at the door has all of us shifting our heads toward it before looking at each other and shrugging. Cam, being the closest, gets up to answer it.

"Bro, not cool," Wilder calls out, pushing past a stunned Cam. Hawk immediately jumps to his feet, and I'm unceremoniously dumped on the couch cushions as Mason and Beck jump up as well. "Insane driving, however. You'll have to teach me how to do that one day. I had no hope of keeping up with you."

"What the hell are you doing here?" Hawk growls as I scramble to my feet, pushing my way around Mason even as he tries to keep me out of sight behind his back. I don't know what he thinks Wilder will do; he's no immediate threat.

"I had to make sure Wifey got home safe and sound."

A chorus of growls erupts from each of my guys, making Wilder laugh. If I had any doubts about his sanity before, I know for sure now—he's certifiable. No sane person would laugh when they have five growling, beastly men glaring at them with murderous intent in their eyes.

"Oh, this just got more interesting." His wild gaze focuses on me, where I'm still partly sequestered behind Mason's brick of a body. "Good on you, Sunshine. I didn't know you had it in you." He winks. He fucking *winks*, like this is all some hilarious joke and he's not seconds away from being torn limb-from-limb and thrown into the lake.

Ignoring the death glares he's receiving, he saunters over to the armchair I vacated in favor of Mason's lap and sits down, grabbing a spare beer off the table.

He looks at each of the guys. "I'm guessing you four are the fearsome Princes I've heard all about," he says, pointing a finger each at Hawk, Cam, West, and Mason—what the fuck, he's been here for like five minutes—before his gaze lands on Beck. "And you are?"

"I think the better question is, who the hell are you?" Beck snarls.

Wilder gasps, clutching his heart with his hand. "Excuse my manners, so rude of me. My name's Wilder Clearwater, husband-to-be of Sunshine here." He gestures in my direction before holding his hand out to Beck as we all share 'what the fuck' glances. He doesn't seriously expect Beck to shake his hand, does he?

Beck sneers at his outstretched hand before smacking it away.

"Drop the act," Hawk snaps. "What do you want? 'Cause despite what our parents might think, you're not getting my sister."

Wilder shrugs, leaning back in his chair as he eyes me critically. I don't get the same itch under my skin that I did when his dad looked at me. Tilting my head, I stare at him curiously. He's impossible to get a read on, and his behavior too erratic to gain any sort of stable baseline. But despite the crazy glint in his eyes, I don't think he's any sort of a threat.

"Meh, blondes aren't my type, anyway. No offense, Wifey. I'm sure we could have had a blast."

Wriggling out from behind Mason, I stand in front of him, ignoring his huff of frustration.

"So why are you doing what your dad wants then? Why does your dad even want you to marry me?"

"He thinks a wife will help keep me in line." He snorts, but I don't miss the darkness that clouds his eyes. I'm not sure anyone else noticed it, and it's gone as quickly as it appeared, but it was definitely there. "As for why I'm going along with it...I have my reasons," he responds vaguely. "Just like I'm sure you have yours."

"What does your dad want out of this deal?" Hawk asks.

"No idea. He was on the fence until a week ago, then something changed." Before anyone can ask, he tacks on, "I don't know what. But all of a sudden, he was more than willing to sign the contract."

That has all of us exchanging uneasy glances.

∾

MONDAY MORNING IS the start of a new month, meaning we all have the joy of picking new people we're stuck with for the next four weeks. Hawk got a call from our father last night, informing him that I was to choose Wilder. It was obviously asking too much for him to phone and tell me himself—although I doubt he would have appreciated my colorful response.

Despite the guys making a fuss, I didn't argue about it too much. I had no idea who I was going to pick anyway, and at least Wilder has admitted he has no interest in being with me. Plus, he knows about me and the guys, so it's probably best that we keep a close eye on him until we can determine his motives.

After breakfast, the usual routine begins: each guy picks a girl. I notice Wilder slip into the hall as Cam takes his turn, propping himself up against the wall by the door and winking when he catches me staring. I have to admit, he looks good in his uniform —well, what he's wearing of his uniform. His tie is missing, his shirt is half unbuttoned and rolled up at the sleeves, and there's no blazer in sight. Looking down at his feet, I stifle my laugh. Instead of the standard black or brown loafers every other guy wears, he's got on multicolored Air Jordan's that look totally out of place with the school uniform.

When it's my turn, I quickly call out Wilder's name, ignoring the whispers and confused looks around the hall, everyone wondering who the hell Wilder is as the five of us get the fuck out of there.

"Wifey, I'm touched," Wilder says dramatically, swinging his arm over my shoulder. "You chose me out of all the reprobates in this place."

"Don't let it go to your head," Cam grumbles from Wilder's other side, looking decidedly pissed at the way his arm is slung around me. "She didn't have a choice."

"So what happens in this little tradition, then?" Wilder asks, ignoring Cam. "Do we get to make out in the hallway and grind on each other at school parties?" He waggles his eyebrows suggestively, making me laugh. I don't know what it is about him, but I can't take him seriously despite his constant flirtiness. The flirty banter doesn't meet his eyes, and I know it's all for show to wind up the guys, or maybe because he thinks that's what people expect from him. I'm not sure.

"Only if you want your teeth knocked out," Mason growls.

"Basically, you eat breakfast with me, escort me to class, and we go to parties together. That's pretty much it." I shrug. "People just need to think we're fake dating."

"Fake engaged," he corrects, earning another scowl from the guys.

"Not yet," I remind him.

"Sounds pretty boring. I thought it would be so much dirtier than that."

"I mean, it used to be." I shrug.

"Before you all started one big gangbang."

"Eww, gross." I jam him in the rib with my elbow. "Hawk's my brother."

"Right, that would be a bit awkward. Sorry, bro." He tosses Hawk a pronounced frown, and I can tell Hawk has no idea how to respond to that, choosing instead to ignore him.

"Well, I guess I should get the Wifey to class then." Wilder grins, well, wildly, earning more than one glare from the guys. "Don't want her to be late."

The rest of the week goes by in a blur. Between showing Wilder the ropes, catching up with Michael and Emilia, keeping on top of homework, and carving time out for each of my guys, it's hard to find a single moment of peace.

I have to admit, I actually quite like Wilder. He's definitely a weird one, and most of the school seems wary of him. Hard not to be when he spends most of breakfast with his feet kicked up on the table, twirling a knife in his hands like a certifiable lunatic. I dunno, he speaks to a deeper part of me that I've kept carefully buried since I escaped from the compound.

Of course, the guys all *hate* him with a passion. It doesn't help that Wilder makes a point of skipping so far over the line of what the guys will tolerate him doing with me, that it's nothing but a distant blur. Where Daniel only did the bare minimum of what was expected of him, Wilder has quickly weaved his way into my friendship group with Emilia and Michael, joining us for lunch most days and even inviting himself to our weekly movie night this weekend.

"Why does your father think a wife would keep you in line?" I ask Wilder. We're sitting in the theater room, waiting for Emilia and Michael to arrive. I've tried to broach the subject a couple of times this week, but whenever I mention his father or his past, he clams up. I can see him doing the same right now, closing himself off. It's a feeling I know all too well, when someone pries into shit you don't want them to see.

I expect him to shoot me down again, fobbing off my question with some fake-ass line, but he surprises me by actually opening up. "I got caught up in some shit last year; friends of mine died."

That's some heavy shit to deal with. The tight set of his jaw and the guilt in his eyes emphasize how much he's struggling to come to terms with whatever happened.

"My only friend died when we were kids," I share with him. "After she died, I gave up. I more or less wrote myself off as dead. It took a long time before I remembered I was still alive."

He stares at me thoughtfully. "Yeah, but I bet you didn't kill her."

As quick as it appeared, the vulnerability in his eyes disappears. Within a blink, he's pulled down his shutters and closed himself off. A maniacal grin splits his face. "So, tell me, Sunshine. Something I've always wondered… Are girls into period sex, or is that just a guy fetish?"

I'm looking at him with wide eyes, confused out of my ever-loving mind, when Emilia comes bouncing in with Michael following behind her.

"Hey, guys. What's going on?"

I break away from the intense stare-off with Wilder, ignoring his inappropriate question, as I smile at Emilia. "Hey. Nothing. What's up?"

Michael glances furtively back and forth between Wilder and me before slipping into the seat on my other side, narrowly missing being squashed by Emilia's ass as he sneaks in behind her to steal the seat.

She pouts before laughing it off, claiming the chair on his other side while Wilder starts up the movie he'd selected. It's technically my turn, but I never know what to choose, and if Emilia suckers me into picking one more romcom, I'm going to throw a bitch fit. Thankfully, Wilder had the good sense to go for an action movie.

"Hey," Michael whispers, smiling.

"Hey."

"We should grab a coffee this week, just the two of us."

"Sure, sounds good."

# Hadley

CHAPTER TWENTY

A week after we sent off the footage to the authorities, we get the news we've been waiting for.

"Dad's been arrested," Mason announces as he comes barging into the apartment. I'm kicking Hawk's ass in some shooting game, while Cam is showing Beck videos on his phone, and West is tinkering on his laptop.

We immediately stop what we're doing, sitting up and paying attention to Mason. "What? For real?" Cam exclaims.

"Yeah." Grabbing the remote, Mason switches over to the TV, flicking on a local news channel.

"—day's news, Frank Hayes, one of the founders of Nocturnal Enterprises, a high-profile private security company, was arrested today for the murder of Lacee Hamilton of Hamilton Jewelry. Police have not yet released any information regarding the case but they…"

"Fuck, this is really happening?" Cam gasps as we all stare wide-eyed at the TV. I mean, this is what we wanted, but I'm not sure any of us thought it would be that easy. Yeah, it's only one family of the four out of the equation, but it's a start.

Hawk's phone goes off, and I pull my attention from the image of Frank Hayes being escorted into the police station in handcuffs on the TV, to look at him as he fishes it out of his pocket, and Mason mutes the television.

"Son, I'm sure you've heard the news by now." Barton's voice comes out loud and clear over the speakerphone.

"Yeah, we just saw it on the TV."

He sighs wearily. "Yeah, it's a disaster. Not what we need right now. We have lawyers on it, though. Everything will be fine. We'll need all of you to step up in Frank's absence." There's no emotion in Barton's voice. Other than sounding stressed, he doesn't seem to be bothered by the fact that his friend and business partner is currently in jail for murder. "Especially Mason. He will have to start taking on some of his father's responsibilities. We will discuss it when you come to the office for Easter break."

He hangs up before Hawk can figure out how to respond to any of that.

"What does he mean, you'll all have to step up? What are you going to have to do?" I stare at Hawk before swiveling my gaze to the others, but none of them appear to have the answers to my questions.

"No idea. Guess we'll find out at Easter."

∽

WEST TUGS me down the hallway and into his bedroom, backing me up to his bed as his lips press against mine. His tongue sweeps in to claim my mouth as I moan. Stepping back, he pushes me down onto the mattress, and I bounce before he climbs on top of me, fusing his lips to mine again. His fingers trail over my clothes, slipping under my skirt until he's rubbing circles around my clit, making fireworks ignite behind my eyelids.

I honestly don't have time for this. I need to go and get ready for tonight, but I know the guys have been stressed out lately about this whole situation with Wilder, so if West needs this moment of comfort to remind him that I'm all his, then so be it. I'm sure as hell not about to say no when he's already got me soaring toward oblivion.

Pushing my panties to the side, he slides his fingers through my wetness, sinking deep inside me as he scissors his fingers, stretching me perfectly. "Always so fucking ready for me, aren't you, Firefly?"

I moan my agreement as I ride his fingers, cresting quickly toward the edge. Just when I feel my core tightening, he pulls out of me, and I whimper when he chuckles darkly, climbing off me to move to his bedside table.

His body blocks whatever he's doing, but a second later, I hear the drawer click shut and he comes back, pushing my thighs apart as he gets on his knees at the end of the bed, his mouth inches from where I need him.

Holding eye contact with me, he leans in and swipes his tongue from my slit to clit before pushing his fingers back inside me, once again starting the ascent toward heaven. I'm quickly losing myself in his touch when I feel him push something into my pussy.

"What the...Ho-oly fuck," I cry out when the thing starts vibrating. The extra stimulation has me hovering right on the precipice of an orgasm. Just when I expect West to send me soaring over the edge, he pulls back, tucks my panties back in place, and flips down my skirt, stopping the incredible vibrations.

I gape up at him with love-drunk eyes, trying to unscramble my thoughts so I can work out what's going on.

"What...why'd you stop?"

He smirks down at me, looking both deviant and wicked.

I press up onto my elbows, glowering at him as he leans down to hover over me, careful not to touch me.

"You didn't think you deserved a reward right before you're about to go off on a date with another man, did you?"

"So you're sending me out there turned on and needy?!"

"Exactly." His voice is a smug, seductive purr. He lifts a small black remote and presses a button. The vibrations start up again, making my body shiver as I moan. "And every time this goes off in your tight little pussy, you better think of me and remember exactly who owns you. Maybe I'll let you come when you get home if you're a good girl and don't touch yourself all night."

I whimper, so unbelievably turned on by his authoritative tone and the little vibrating device inside me that's doing crazy things to my pussy.

Pressing another button, the vibrations stop, and I can once again regulate my breathing as I clamber off the bed. "Now you better go get ready, wouldn't want to be late for your date." With a slap on the ass, he nudges me out the door with an evil chuckle, and I curse his name out in my head all the way back to my room.

An hour later, I'm showered, dressed, and sitting at a table in a fancy restaurant with Wilder and his father. The vibrator hasn't gone off since I left the guys' apartment, and I'm on tenterhooks with every passing second, waiting for it to start up. I have no idea how I'm going to keep from embarrassing myself when it does.

"So, you two have been getting to know one another?" his father inquires. I really don't like this man. The way he catalogs my every movement has the hairs standing to attention along the back of my neck, and every time I look at my steak knife, I imagine driving it into his neck.

"Yes. I'm her guy of the month," Wilder answers while I sip on my glass of water. *Ugh, I wish this evening would hurry up and be over already.* If I'd had any say, I wouldn't be here at all, but of course, I didn't, and, not wanting to piss off our parents any more than we already have, I have no option but to just grin and bear it.

"I didn't attend Pacific Prep," Benjamin explains, looking at me—his eyes have rarely left me all evening—"so I don't understand this tradition of theirs. Sounds emasculating to me." He grumbles the last bit under his breath, and somehow, I doubt he would say the same if I was Wilder's *girl* of the month.

Wilder just shrugs his shoulders, not giving a shit if it's emasculating or not. He's not one to follow the rules or give a shit about societal norms. He follows his own path in life, not caring if it pisses other people off.

I jump, gasping when the vibrator in my pussy comes to life, mumbling an apology as I take another sip of my water, ignoring both men's eyes as they observe me.

Thankfully our starters arrive then, and even though eating is the last thing on my mind, I'm grateful for the distraction as the two of them discuss something or other—I'm too busy clenching my thighs and wishing I could sneak off to the bathroom to rub one out to pay attention to what they're saying.

The meal goes on, and I slowly get more and more worked up every time the device starts up. Sweat coats my skin, and I've drunk about a gallon of water in an attempt to stave off the moans of pleasure that keep creeping up the back of my throat. My panties are soaked, and I've never been so grateful for a bra as my stiff nipples chafe against the fabric. I'm absolutely going to murder West once I get home—after he's made me come at least five times.

"Are you a virgin, Elizabeth?" Benjamin's question comes out of left field, making me choke on my drink.

"Excuse me? I don't think that's any of your business," I snap.

"Well, it is if I'm going to sign a contract that makes you a part of my family."

"Dad," Wilder hisses. "Everyone has sex before marriage these days."

His father's gross, beady eyes stay focused on me. "How many guys have you been with?"

I grit my teeth, refusing to answer as I glare daggers at him.

"Dad," Wilder hisses again, but his words fall on deaf ears.

"It's only a number. One, two, five? How many?"

"I dunno." I shrug casually. "I lost count."

A spark flashes through his eyes that makes goosebumps form along my skin, but it's gone so quickly I can't place what it was.

"I'll be asking for an STD screen and pregnancy test before the wedding then," his father responds blandly all business. I can't shake off whatever I saw in his eyes, though.

With the exception of that weird blip, the rest of dinner is uneventful. Benjamin hardly spares me anything more than a passing glance, talking with his son for most of the meal.

"Excuse me, I'm just going to freshen up," I say after dessert, smiling politely even as the vibrating demon in my pussy starts up again. Fuck, I've never been so desperate to come in all my life. I swear to God, I'm not going to let West come ever again without edging him for a good fucking hour beforehand.

Slipping into the bathroom stall, my hand snakes under the waistband of my jeans, hovering above my throbbing clit. I debate back and forth between touching myself or not, finally groaning when I decide West would probably be able to tell and make me go all night without a proper orgasm.

Frustrated, horny, and so fucking done with this stupid dinner, I throw open the stall door causing it to bounce off the wall, but I barely hear it as I stand frozen.

What the fuck? Am I seriously so turned on that I missed hearing this asshole follow me in here?

"What are you doing in here?" I snap, immediately on the defense, as Benjamin Clearwater leans casually against the wall in front of the bathroom door. His arms are crossed over his chest as he blocks my exit with his body.

"You and I both know why I'm here." He disgustingly leers at me. "You've been gagging for it all night."

I open my mouth to protest, but he cuts me off, "Ah ha, no need to lie. You've been squirming in your seat all night, thinking about my cock."

I barely contain my snort, knowing that a knock to his ego will only make this situation ten times worse. *It's sure as fuck not his cock I've been thinking about all night.*

"You're a little old for my tastes, but I'm not one to disappoint someone as gorgeous as you."

I'm a little old for his tastes? What the fuck does that mean? *I'm* barely legal, and he looks like he's in his forties.

"Besides, you were meant to be mine all those years ago, so it's only fair I take that pussy for a test run. It's the least I deserve for how long I've had to wait.'

"What?" I croak out, my head spinning off its axis at all the confusing information he's throwing my way.

"Well, technically, you were always meant to end up with Wilder, but you should have been mine first."

As bile burns its way up the back of my throat, my head spins with everything he's saying, and I decide I'm now officially done with this sick conversation. I force myself to hold still as he prowls toward me. I know that look in his eye; I've seen it more times than I care to remember. He'll only restrain me if I resist or fight back, and I need my arms and legs free to escape him.

The stupid fucking demon in my pussy chooses that moment to start up again, and I swear it's more intense than it was before, making me whimper as the sick fuck in front of me grasps two fistfuls of my ass cheeks in his hands, using his hold to grind me against his pathetic half-dick.

"Yeah, I knew when I looked at you that you were a dirty slut," he growls in my ear, squeezing my ass to the point of pain.

Pushing past the confusing sensations between his grimy presence and the fucking vibrator, I hitch my leg over his hip. Unfortunately, it opens up my pelvis more, giving him ample room to rub himself against me. I have to push past the vomit in my mouth as I lean in, brushing my tits against his shirt so I can reach into my boots and lift out my pocketknife—see, *this* is why you should never go anywhere unarmed, not even to the bathroom.

He's groaning in my ear, but the gullible asshole is so far gone in thinking I'm as into this as he is that he doesn't expect my sudden movement. Quick as lightning, I grab his wrist and slap it against the bathroom wall. Not giving him a second to yank out of my tight grip, I slam my knife into his palm, driving it in all the way to the hilt, embedding it in the wall.

He starts screaming bloody murder, and I know I have to get out of here ASAP.

"You fucking, bitch. What did you do? My hand!" he wails.

"Don't touch what isn't yours, you sick fuck," I snarl, quickly running my hands under the tap to wash off the blood and wiping down my knife before tucking it back in my boot and making a hasty exit out of the bathroom.

Trying not to draw suspicion, I move as quickly as possible through the tables toward Wilder.

"We've gotta go," I rush out, a hint of urgency in my tone.

"Dad's just paying—"

"No, he's not—"

A high-pitched scream followed by a deep bellow that rings through the restaurant, and my eyes widen to saucers. "Let's go."

Not needing any more of an explanation, Wilder jumps out of his seat. Pulling out his wallet, he drops a bunch of hundred-dollar notes on the table—*way* more than what the meal cost—and the two of us scurry out the door.

"What do you know about the old deal that fell through between your dad and my parents?" I ask him as we climb into his gorgeous dark green mustang.

He looks at me like I'm fucking insane, which is an interesting role reversal. Backing out of the parking space, he guns it toward campus. "You gonna tell me what happened in there?"

"Only if you answer my question."

He laughs, shaking his head before getting serious.

"I don't know much about it. I know something happened on your parents' end that caused it to fall through."

"When was the deal?" I ask, a sick pit opening in my stomach.

"I dunno." He shrugs. "Like fifteen, sixteen years ago?"

"Right around the time I went missing," I mumble to myself.

"I guess so. Why?"

"Just something your dad said," I respond vaguely, knowing I'll have to give him more details soon, just not tonight. My head is a mess with everything, and as the stupid vibrations start up in my pussy again, the only thing I can think about is putting West's tongue to good use when I get home.

Sighing, I lean back against the headrest, closing my eyes until Wilder snorts.

"Let me guess, West?" He waggles his eyebrows, making it pretty obvious what he's referring to.

"What…" I splutter. "How?"

He scoffs. "That guy loves control too much. Of course, he wouldn't send you out tonight without making sure you thought about him all evening."

"That obvious?" I can feel my cheeks burning, and it's not from how turned on I am.

"Ooh, yeah. You couldn't sit still every time it started, and you barely ate a thing. I sit beside you at breakfast. I *know* how much you fucking love to eat."

Can't argue that.

He pulls into the student car park, and we get out of the car.

"Are you going to tell me what happened tonight?"

I sigh. "Can we do it tomorrow? It's nothing that can't wait."

His gaze roams over my face in a rare moment of seriousness. "Yeah, sure. You probably can't think with all those hormones floating about in your head anyway."

By the time I let myself into the guys' apartment, the need for release is all-consuming. I can't think about anything else, and when I spot West and Beck sitting and talking in the living room, desire so potent you can taste it in the air, courses through me.

If I wasn't so turned-on, I'd be ecstatic to see the two of them sitting and chatting to one another, but as it is, all I can think about is West's hot mouth on my body as Beck's dick drills into me.

West must know where my thoughts are as he gives me a dirty smirk. "Have fun tonight?" he teases, heat flaring in his eyes.

"I swear, West, if you don't make me come right fucking now, I'm going to do it myself."

He growls as Beck's head bounces back and forth between us, confusion and desire crossing his features.

"Bedroom, now," West barks, his dominant tone that he saves for the bedroom surprising Beck as his eyebrows climb up his head.

I hesitate, looking at Beck, wondering if he's going to join us. West must pick up on my hesitation or sees my need for both of them, as he turns to Beck.

"Do you wanna come see just how wet our girl is from thinking about us all night?"

Beck's eyes darken, and he smirks. "Lead the way, brother."

Oh, holy shit, I'm about to be the filling in a super fucking hot brother sandwich.

We all pile into West's bedroom, and I swear, my skin feels like it's about to melt off my bones with how they both look at me.

"Out of those clothes, Firefly. Show us how much you need us."

Well, you don't have to tell me twice. My movements are desperate as I kick off my boots and throw off my clothes, until I'm standing naked before them.

"Lie back on the bed. Spread your legs."

Doing as he says, I lie back, spreading my legs as wide as they can go so they can get a crystal clear look at my glistening wet pussy as I drip onto West's sheets.

"Fuck, she's drenched," Beck grunts in a gruff voice, adjusting himself in his jeans.

I'm already panting heavily, but my head falls back and I moan to the ceiling as West starts up the demon device again, setting it at a more intense speed than it was in the restaurant.

"Did you think about us every time you wanted to come?" West's silky voice flows over me, making my nipples pebble.

"Yes," I moan.

"Did you touch yourself?"

"No."

"Firefly," he growls in a warning tone, promising me retribution if I lie to him right now.

"I didn't," I groan. "I thought about it, but I didn't."

"Good girl." His praise makes me pant harder. I'm going to self-combust if I don't come right now. I feel a wet tongue sliding through my folds, making me nearly jump off the bed at the titillating sensation, and I tear my half-lidded gaze away from the ceiling to watch Beck as he licks and sucks his way to my clit. His stubble rubs against my inner thighs, only pushing me closer to the edge.

"Don't come yet," West growls from beside me, as if sensing how close I am.

"West," I plead.

Beck laps at my clit, and my legs quiver with the need to come. Just when I think I'm not going to be able to hold out anymore, West barks out, "Come, baby," and bright lights flash across my vision as I cry out, the buildup resulting in one of the most intense orgasms I've ever had.

I sag against the mattress as Beck continues to lick and suck at my juices, and West slowly rolls the vibrator down through the settings, easing me down from my release, until finally, he turns it off, and Beck retrieves it from my overly sensitive pussy.

"Firefly." West's husky voice has me leaning up on my elbows, ready for round two, even though I'm not sure my legs can hold me up.

Lifting his finger, he beckons me toward him. "Come here."

I stand and move toward him on shaky legs, and he pushes me onto my knees in front of him. Slowly, he unbuckles his jeans and pushes them and his boxers down low on his hips so his dick springs out, bobbing in front of my face. I lick my lips, holding back the urge to lick him until he tells me to.

Grabbing a hold of his long length, he pumps himself. Pre-cum beads on his tip, and he rubs it along my lips before pushing his way into my mouth. His eyes become hooded as he watches me take all of him until he hits the back of my throat. He holds himself there for a second before pulling back, repeating the movement over and over as he slowly picks up speed.

With each movement, I swivel my tongue along his head and down his shaft, causing him to groan as heat gathers between my thighs. I move to touch myself, but fingers wrap firmly around my wrist, yanking my hand away.

"Mine," Beck growls, moving in behind me. I can feel his skin against mine. He must have removed his clothes at some point. His fingers rub my clit, and I moan around West's shaft.

Beck lifts me slightly, lining his dick up with my entrance before pushing into me, and he and West quickly find a rhythm that has all three of us rushing toward the edge of the cliff.

Cleaning up, the three of us collapse onto the bed. I can feel my eyes dropping as tiredness takes over.

"Go to sleep, Firefly," West murmurs.
"You owe me at least three more orgasms," I grumble, half asleep.
I feel Beck chuckle behind me.
"Plenty of time for that in the morning, sweetheart."
Well, okay then.

Hadley

CHAPTER TWENTY-ONE

A commotion the next morning pulls me out of my deep sleep, and I'm instantly annoyed that whoever is talking so loudly is disturbing my quiet time with West and Beck. I've definitely decided my new happy place is being snuggled between these two.

"Where is she? Is she here?" I hear someone snapping from elsewhere in the apartment. "HADLEY!"

Oh, damn. That's Wilder.

"What's going on?" West mumbles as Beck yawns.

I quickly scurry out from between the two of them, grabbing the first items of clothes I find—Beck's t-shirt and West's sweats—before yanking the door open and rushing down the hallway. Only to find Wilder facing off against Hawk and Mason, all three of them looking downright furious.

"It's the crack ass of dawn," Cam grumbles, stumbling out of his room, still looking half asleep. "What are you two doing?"

"You put a *knife* through my father's hand?" Wilder barks when he spots me, making everyone else stare in my direction as West and Beck come out of the room and join the party.

"In fairness, he put his hands on me first." I shrug.

"He what?" several voices bellow, furious tones flying all over the place.

"When were you going to tell us this?" Hawk snaps.

"This morning, after I'd had coffee."

"You should have said something last night," West argues, making me give him the stink eye. Maybe I would have, if I wasn't so crazed out of my mind with need—need that *he* caused.

"Let's all sit down, and we can talk about this," Beck rationalizes, stepping around me and moving between Wilder and Hawk, glaring at both Hawk and Mason until they take a step back. Cam stomps over to the coffee maker, filling it up as the others claim their seats. Mason makes a point of dragging me into his lap, scowling over my head at Wilder, who promptly ignores him.

"Did you finally get that release you needed last night, Sunshine?" Wilder winks, making Mason growl behind me.

"I'm still a few releases short," I admit. "Someone interrupted this morning." I scowl at him, and he gives me an oopsies face—it's literally the only way I can describe the look he's sporting.

Cam sets a tray of mugs on the coffee table for everyone to help themselves. Lifting two, he places a cup in my hands, kissing me on the forehead and mumbling a 'good morning' before sitting beside Mason and me.

"So, wanna explain what happened last night?" Hawk directs at me when we're all seated and adequately caffeinated.

I take them through the previous evening's events, only having to stop every few words when one of them curses up a storm. *Finally* we get through it, and everyone falls into silence, thinking through the various information drops.

"You keep a knife in your boot?" Cam asks, sounding shocked and having picked up on what I would have classified as one of the least significant things I said, but whatever.

"Yeah. Why, where do you keep yours?"

He just looks at me like he doesn't know whether to take me seriously or not, before mumbling something about not keeping a knife on his person.

Hmm, we'll have to sort that out. What idiot walks around unprotected?

"So I'm guessing you spoke to your dad today?" I ask, looking at Wilder.

"Yeah," he grumbles, looking unimpressed. "He phoned me when he was released from the hospital this morning—at four a.m." He glowers at me, likely not happy that the phone call disturbed his beauty sleep. *Oopsies.* "Going on about how he might need surgery."

I scoff. "Please, it was barely more than a flesh wound."

Wilder cocks an eyebrow. "You went right through his hand and out the other side." Despite the harsh tone in his words, he sounds hella impressed. At least, I think he does. I'm going to pretend he does, regardless.

"Is that why you always insist on wearing those boots?" Cam questions, clearly still stuck on the whole knife-in-the-boot thing.

"One of the reasons."

"What are the others?"

"They're comfy, and I know how to move silently in them."

"So it sounds like our parents agreed for you to be married off to Wilder when we were kids," Hawk theorizes, his brow furrowed in thought.

"Yeah, after he'd had his turn with me first." I shiver in disgust, burrowing deeper into Mason's chest as he tightens his hold around me. I take comfort from the soft vibrations in his chest as he growls deep in his throat.

"Did you know about that?" Hawk snaps, fixing Wilder with an intense, murderous look.

He holds his hands up in surrender. "All I knew was that a contract was drawn up, and then it fell through. I had no idea it included Hadley or I or anything else."

"So what, he's into little kids?" Cam scrunches his nose up, his face blanching at the thought.

All of us look at Wilder for confirmation.

"Honestly, it's news to me if he does."

"How do you not know?" Hawk snaps, making Wilder quirk an eyebrow at him.

"Do you know everything about *your* parents?"

Well, he's got a point there. Hawk seems to agree as he quickly shuts his mouth.

"So, what happened this morning?" I ask Wilder.

"Nothing, really. I don't think he'll be looking to spend much time with his new daughter-in-law."

Suits me just fine.

"He's not breaking off the agreement?" I ask.

"Nope. He didn't even mention it. Whatever he's getting out of it must be worth handing me over to a stabby psycho." He waggles his eyebrows. "By the way, I'm all for knife play in the bedroom, Wifey." He winks, even as the guys glower and curse him out, laughing like the crazy idiot he is before once again growing serious. "He's signing the contract today." His words settle in my stomach like lead as I glance nervously at the others. "Guess it's about to be official, Wifey. We're getting hitched."

∽

Three days later—*three fucking days*—and I'm wearing a stupid-ass gown—walking into the Davenport house for *my* engagement party. Okay, admittedly, it's another gorgeous piece selected by West.

My dress is a floor-length pale blue-gray that perfectly matches the color of my eyes and rises high on the back, once again ensuring my scars are covered from prying eyes.

My arm is linked with Wilder's, just as Hawk, Mason, Cam, and West form a protective circle around us, looking sharp as ever in their suits. Each one of them has something that matches my dress, be it their tie, handkerchief, cufflinks, or in Cam's case, his shoelaces. It's their silent way of letting me know they're here for me, and my heart just about stuttered to a stop when I saw all of them lined up. I know Beck is here somewhere, too, supporting me in his own inconspicuous way.

"Let's get this show on the road," Hawk huffs, straightening his suit jacket before moving away, weaving through the crowd as he makes his way to the bar.

The other guys break away, going to mingle while ensuring they keep me in their sights.

"Right," Wilder starts, his gaze sweeping around the room before focusing on me, "which set of shitty parents should we tick off the list first. Yours or mine?"

Ugh, what a crappy choice to choose between. "I'm sure my lovely mother will hunt us down fairly quickly."

"Bar it is then."

I laugh as he escorts me through the crowd. People constantly stop us, wishing us congratulations, starting up a conversation with Wilder, and complimenting me on my dress, which takes forever for us to reach our destination.

Eventually, we make it, and Wilder orders a scotch for himself and a water for me. I'm sipping on the drink, relishing the feeling of the cold liquid in my mouth, when I feel eyes on me. I knew it was only a matter of time until he sought me out. Making sure my mask of indifference is firmly in place when I turn my head, I search through the crowd for Lawrence, only it's not Lawrence that's watching me. It's Barton. *What the fuck?* He's barely spared me a glance or said a word to me since I returned, so what's with the creepy as fuck stalking now?

We've just finished our drinks when my mother spots us, piercing me with a stern glare like she knows I was deliberately avoiding her, as she marches toward us. "What are you doing? You should have found us as soon as you arrived," she seethes in my ear before standing to her full height and plastering on a sweet smile. "Wilder, dear, don't you look handsome as ever."

Wilder, the socialite suck-up that he is, laughs congenially. "Why thank you, Mrs. Davenport, but it's all your lovely daughter's doing. She makes me look good."

My mother's smile tightens, neither confirming nor denying his statement. "My husband would like to say a few words, if you'd both follow me," she says cordially, leading the way to the front of the room.

Seeing us approach, Barton gains the room's attention, beginning his speech.

"Ladies and gentlemen, I am honored to have you here this evening. We have some momentous news to share with you all. Not only are we lucky to have our blessed daughter back in our lives, but she has found true love in Wilder Clearwater."

I cough, hiding my snort as Wilder elbows me in the ribs, appearing equally amused. I'm sure the guys are somewhere nearby, grumbling under their breaths.

"The two met at a family gathering, and it was love at first sight." The audience coos and awes—are they seriously that fucking gullible?! "Tonight, I am so very pleased to introduce to you my soon-to-be son-in-law, my daughter's fiancé, Wilder Clearwater." The room erupts into claps and cheers as Wilder practically drags me up to stand beside my father.

"We haven't finalized a date for the wedding yet, but the two of them are excited for a short engagement"—*We're what now?!*—"so I'm sure we will have a date for you all very soon."

Somehow, amid all this mayhem, I forgot there would be an actual wedding. I'd kind of figured we'd be engaged for at least a year. I mean, that's what most people do, right? I definitely thought it would be enough time for us to wrangle our way out of it before it occurred, yet my father is making it sound like it's *weeks*, *months* at most, away.

I'm pretty sure I'm sporting a 'deer caught in the headlights' expression as Wilder maneuvers me back into the crowd, quickly fobbing everyone off as he ushers me out of the room.

"Wilder," I whisper-hiss, clinging onto his arm for dear life. "I am not marrying you."

"Oh, Sunshine, you wound me. There I thought we were in love." I try to scowl at him, but the whole panicked eye thing kind of ruins it, and he chuckles at my freak out. He directs me into a back kitchen, quickly kicking the few staff members out, and grabs me a glass of water while I collapse onto a stool.

I'm not someone who freaks out. Usually, I'm pretty calm in the face of challenging situations. Give me a surprise dead body any day, and I'll happily deal with it, but *this* is unchartered territory. I've never really given any thought to marriage. Growing up the way I did, it's not something I thought I'd have the luxury of experiencing—unless it was to Lawrence, in which case, fuck no—but now that it's a real-life possibility staring me right in the face, I'm kind of fucking panicking.

"What's wrong with her?" Mason snaps out, barging into the kitchen.

"She's fine. Chill your nuts." Wilder rolls his eyes. "She's just freaking out a little."

"What is she freaking out about? What did you do to her?"

"I don't think she was expecting an actual wedding," he says far too casually. How is he not freaking out as badly as I am?!

The next thing I know, Mason has bumped Wilder out of the way, taking the glass of water from my hands and setting it on the table. He cups my face in both hands and focuses my gaze on his eyes.

"Hey, Little Warrior." His soothing voice washes over me, and he smiles when he sees I'm looking at him.

"Mason, I can't marry him," I whisper.

"You're not going to, baby. It's all for show, remember?"

"But Barton made it sound like we'd be getting married in a few weeks or a few months." The pitch of my voice climbs with each word.

"These things take time to plan, and we're not going to let that happen, okay?"

I want to believe him, but I don't. He must see it in my eyes—as his own harden—and he moves his hand to pinch my chin.

"If you're marrying anyone, it will be one of us. You got that?"

The steely resolve in his tone breaks through my panic, and I nod my head. Seeing that I trust in what he's saying, he dives in, sealing his words with a searing kiss that I can feel all the way to my toes.

"Good, now get back out there and put on a show so I can tear that dress off you later and make you forget about this whole night."

He goes to move away, but I wrap my hand around his blue-gray tie, pulling him back into me. He searches my eyes as I repeat the words he said to me in the library. "You're mine, and I'm yours."

His eyes soften, and he plants another kiss on my lips. "I'm yours, and you're mine, baby. To the end."

"Truly heartwarming," Wilder drawls when we break apart. "Armor back in place, Wifey?"

I give him a firm nod.

"Excellent." A bright grin spreads across his face, a wicked glint entering his eyes. "Let's go freak the fuck out of some conservative assholes."

Heading back to the party, we do a lap of the room. Wilder is undoubtedly the most fun person to be with at one of these stuck-up events. He turns everything into a game. We spend the next hour trying to figure out who is cheating on whom, while working to see how quickly we can make the women clutch their pearls with our outlandish stories.

"This was me in Italy last year," Wilder explains, showing some middle-aged lady his photos from Europe. "And this is me beside the Eiffel Tower." Swiping across the screen of his phone to the next image, the woman tilts her head at the phone in confusion, and Wilder feigns shock. "Oh, oops. My bad. I thought I felt something weird on my ballsack. Such a difficult angle to get a photo."

The woman gasps, taking a step back from us, while Wilder continues muttering to himself. I can no longer contain my laughter as she rushes out with an excuse to leave. When a little bit of pee dribbles out from laughing so hard, I know I can't hold off my bathroom break any longer and excuse myself to search for one in this ridiculously massive house.

Refreshed and with a now empty bladder, I pull open the bathroom door, but before I can step out, I'm herded back in. Panic flares as I stare into Lawrence's cold, hard face as he slams the door shut behind him, flicking the lock. Somehow, in all the fun I was having with Wilder, I forgot this fuckface was lurking about. He never openly approaches me in front of any of our parents, showing nothing more than a passing interest in my arrival, but of course he would take the opportunity when out of sight of the other partygoers to corner me.

"You've been a hard woman to get a private moment with, Dove."

"Are you here to congratulate me?" I struggle to keep my voice from shaking, even as my hands tremble and my heart rate skyrockets.

His hand snaps out, wrapping tightly around my neck, and my mind goes blank as utter terror consumes me. If he were anyone else, I'd be cool and collected right now, strategizing and working out my best move to get out of this situation, but because it's *him*, I'm frozen in fear, unable to move as he towers over me.

It's fucking ridiculous. I was in a similar situation with Benjamin, and I was able to fight my way out of it without a second thought, but replace that person with Lawrence, and I'm reduced to that scared kid I used to be.

His face is the thing of nightmares, encompassing my entire field of vision. "You think I'm going to congratulate you," he sneers in disgust. "Have you forgotten who you belong to, Dove?"

His hand tightens around my throat, his other one pulling on my hair so I'm forced to stare up at him. I don't know how it's possible, but his features somehow darken. "Has he fucked you yet?"

His hand untangles itself from my hair as he roughly pulls up my skirt, not caring that he's tearing it in his haste.

"Has he?" he barks, roughly cupping my pussy and squeezing it. His loud voice echoes around the small bathroom, making me jump.

"N…No."

Curling his fingers under the fabric, he tears my panties clean off.

I should be fighting back, kicking out or hitting him—doing *something*, but my whole body feels numb as he shoves two fingers inside me.

"Who does this cunt belong to?" His words are a possessive snarl, leaving no questioning as to who he thinks it belongs to.

When I don't answer fast enough, he removes his grip on my throat, smacking me across the face.

"Answer me!" he bellows.

"Y…you."

"And has anyone else had a taste?"

"No," I respond immediately, making an evil smirk light up his face in the most menacing way. It's a look that will haunt my nightmares for years to come.

He curls his fingers roughly inside me, hurting me more, before finally pulling out and sniffing them.

"Good. It better stay that way. I'm getting impatient, Dove. You've made friends at that school, haven't you? The scholarship kids? If you don't fall in line soon, I might have to get one of my men to pay them a visit."

Tears are streaming down my face as I all but cower in front of him, my weak state only bolstering his confidence as he preens.

Wrapping his hand around my throat once more, he presses his lips roughly to mine, his fingers digging into my cheeks until I open for him, allowing him to shove his tongue into my mouth. He takes and takes until he's satisfied. Finally letting me go, he sneers down at me, "Clean yourself up. You're a state."

Turning, he lets himself out of the room, and I collapse to the floor, tears flowing freely as I beat myself up for being so weak around him.

I'm supposed to be a badass bitch. I can gut people without a second thought. Slit their throats, drive blades into their heads. You name it. Although I can't stand up to one measly cretin of a man? I'm pathetic. Completely fucking pathetic.

I don't know how long I sit there before finding the strength to get to my feet. Looking in the mirror at my tear-stained face and the pins that once held my hair in place, now hanging uselessly from the loose strands, I decide there's no fucking way I'm going back to that party.

With shaking hands, I lift my phone out from where I stored it between my boobs, texting Cam to meet me round the side of the house. I'm hoping he's the least likely to ask questions and just take me home.

Working my way outside, I notice Cam coming toward me.

"Hey," he says quietly, keeping his voice low. "What's going on? Is everything okay? Ooh, is this a booty call?" I can just about make out his eyebrows waggling in the darkness, and I release a teary chuckle that immediately has the coy smile falling off his face as he rushes to close the distance between us.

His hand cups my face gently, and his eyes darken as he takes in the red palm print smarting my cheek. "What happened?" he growls.

I extricate myself from his grip. "Can we just go to the car, please?" I plead.

He doesn't move. His body is practically vibrating with rage. "Did my father do that?"

I don't need to answer that question; he can see the truth in my eyes as he lets go of me, storming away before pacing back toward me, looking like a restrained beast as he fights to unleash all his pent-up anger.

"Cam," I plead. That one word is enough to snap him out of his murderous thoughts, and he freezes in front of me.

"Right, yeah, come on, baby." He drapes an arm over my shoulder, drawing me in against him as he leads me to the car.

He surprises me when he opens the back and slides in behind me instead of opening the front passenger door for me to climb in. Closing the door, he pulls me into his lap, and I burrow my head in the gap between his neck and shoulder, breathing him in. He rubs soothing circles along my back, neither of us saying anything for a long time.

"I need to know what happened, baby," he eventually murmurs.

"Can't we just go home?" I peer up at him through my eyelashes, imploring him with my eyes.

He grimaces. "We all came together, so we have to wait for the others."

"Oh." That's all I'm capable of saying. I don't even think I care. Other than wanting to get out of this ruined dress and into bed, I'm comfortable here with Cam, pretending the rest of the world outside our little car bubble doesn't exist.

"Tell me what happened," he repeats with more insistence.

Sighing, I rehash what happened with his dad in the bathroom, feeling the mounting rage within him with every word out of my mouth. By the time I'm finished, I'm sitting tensely on his lap, waiting for him to go absolutely apeshit, except he surprises me by burying his face in my hair.

"I'm so sorry," he murmurs in a broken voice. I can still feel all that rage pouring off him, but more than that, I can feel the devastation he feels for what I had to endure. For not being there for me, and most of all, for the part he feels he plays in all of this by being related to that monster. "I'm going to kill him someday. I won't let him get to you again."

I shush him, running my fingers through his golden hair. Not because I don't believe him, but because his father's death is mine. I don't know how since I'm not capable of even lifting a finger in his presence, but *somehow, someday*, he will die a slow, painful death at my hands.

Hadley

CHAPTER TWENTY-TWO

I don't know how long Cam and I sit in the car, mostly in silence, occasionally exchanging the odd word, before the back door is wrenched open.

"Why are you two hiding out in here?" West asks. When he opened the car door, it activated the overhead light. So as he slides into the seat beside us, my swollen eyes and torn dress render him motionless as he frantically checks me over, his features hardening.

His gaze flicks to Cam's before landing back on me, and he quickly climbs into the backseat, closing the door behind him and bathing us in darkness once again. "What happened?" His voice is a low, menacing growl. I don't have it in me to go over it all again, so I let Cam explain the gist of it—no doubt it will all need to be brought up *again* with everyone back in the dorm.

Leaning in, West presses his forehead against mine. "You did so good, Firefly."

I scoff. "I was pathetic. I'm so weak around him. He just has to look at me, and I turn into a little girl again. What's the point in knowing how to fight when I'm frozen in place whenever he's nearby?"

"You're not weak," he assures me. The fire in his voice almost makes me believe him. "You've got so much power in you, you don't even realize how strong you are. He's been your monster under the bed for so long that you don't know how to overcome him, but you're not alone anymore. You've got us. We're just one more weapon in your arsenal against him."

When I look at him in confusion, he explains.

"He thinks you're all alone. He believes you're too brainwashed by him to let anyone else in, that you're too broken to love anyone. However, you've proven how wrong he is. He thinks he owns every part of you, but *you* are the one who decides who you give yourself to. No part of you is his."

"All of me is yours," I whisper, catching on to what he's saying.

He shakes his head no. "It's all *yours*, Firefly. Your heart, your body, your mind, your soul…every part of you is yours to give away to whoever you choose, *when* you choose."

"I gave all of it to you," I murmur, realizing that I've given each of these guys—my guys—small parts of myself at various intervals over the last few months. So much that, collectively, they now own enough that they could destroy me—yet I don't, for one second, believe they would. Glancing at Cam, I add, "All four of you. I'm all yours."

"And we're yours," they both echo.

"Lawrence doesn't know you've got an army of guys ready to dive into battle for you. You're no longer alone in this, Firefly. Whatever you decide to do, we'll be right beside you."

Cam nods his head in agreement with West's sentiment. "Every step of the way."

I smile softly, relaxing back into Cam's touch. When push comes to shove, I don't know whether these guys will stay. Taking on our parents, the compound, and Lawrence is one hell of a battle. For now, though, I'll take comfort in their words and the fact that they're here with me.

West pulls out his phone and sends out a text, and then a few minutes later, he gets a reply.

"The guys are getting a lift home with Wilder." He turns to Cam. "Let's get our girl home to bed."

∽

THE NEXT MORNING, I wake up wedged between two deliciously hot bodies. I fell asleep between Cam and West last night. So when I peel my eyes open to find a very thick, muscular arm that definitely does not belong to either of my leaner guys, cupping my tit, I realize Mason must have climbed into bed with us when he got home—and mostly likely shoved Cam out of the way to steal his spot. A faint smile graces my lips at the thought. I didn't even hear any of them get back last night. After the adrenaline rush of the evening's events, I crashed as soon as my head hit the pillow.

Looking away from Mason's broad arm, my eyes roam over West's peaceful, sleeping face. He seems so different without his glasses on. He wears them all the time, even during sex, so I rarely get the opportunity to just look at him without them on.

Moving my gaze away from his face, I stifle a chuckle when I see a broad, tattooed arm draped over his hip.

Beck is snuggled up against West's back, his arm hanging over him, the back of his fingers brushing against my stomach.

"They make a cute couple, don't they?" Mason murmurs sleepily in my ear. His hand slowly massages my boob, making my back arch and pushing my ass against his morning wood.

"Mmm." It's the only response I can give, both in answer to his question and the way he's making my body slowly come alive.

He trails his fingers down my abdomen, slipping beneath my t-shirt, and he groans against the sensitive skin on my neck when he discovers I'm not wearing any panties. After Lawrence divested me of mine last night, I decided to go commando when I got home, not seeing a need to put on a fresh pair just to get into bed.

Hitching my thigh over his leg, he pushes down his boxers, sliding his thick length through my folds before slowly pushing his way inside me. He bites down on my earlobe, causing me to moan softly as I push back against him, the two of us thrusting in a slow, easy, early morning rhythm that is just as tantalizing as a good, hot fuck.

His hand is clamped over my thigh, holding it in place, and my eyes are shut as I get lost in the feel of him stretching me, so I'm startled when another hand starts rubbing my clit in time with Mason's lazy thrusts. Glancing down, Cam's hand slowly works me over, and as I pant and grind, chasing my release, I catch West watching me, a feral glint in his eyes.

He pushes my top up, exposing my tits. My already hardened nipples stiffen as he tweaks and pulls on them, driving me mad with all their teasing touches.

I'm approaching the edge, when I feel yet another hand slide down over my lower belly, and I know the last of my guys has joined in the fun, bringing a content smile to my face as Mason picks up his pace, finally giving me what I need.

Skimming over my clit, where Cam is rubbing me furiously now, Beck pushes two fingers inside me, along with Mason's dick, stretching me that extra little bit that sends me catapulting over the edge and into oblivion.

"Damn, we should wake up like this every morning," Cam states as Mason slows and pulls out. He's still rock-hard, letting me know he managed to hold off on reaching his own release. Keeping an iron-tight grip on my thigh, he returns to gliding his dick along my slit. Every time he thrusts forward, the head of his cock bumps against my sensitive clit, making me whimper.

West is watching me closely, and he must be able to see the need still burning through me, as he smirks wickedly.

"I believe I owe you a few more orgasms." There's a dark husk to his tone that has my pussy immediately weeping.

"I believe you do." My own voice is dripping in lust; the thought of having all my guys together makes me hot and needy.

In one swift move, Mason moves onto his back, taking me with him so I'm sprawled on top of him, my head resting on his shoulder. He drapes my thighs over him, spreading me wide for the others to see.

"So pretty and pink and swollen," Beck purrs as he moves between my thighs, flattening his tongue and giving me one long, languid lick that makes me moan and writhe against Mason's hard body.

Getting his hands beneath me, Mason spreads my ass cheeks, running his dick through my juices, ensuring it's slick before slowly pushing past the tight ring of muscle.

I gasp and tense at the slight burn, but then Beck goes back to creating magic with his tongue, and my whole body relaxes under his delicious touch.

Mason slides all the way in, filling me up, before giving a few shallow, testing thrusts.

"Fuck." I grind, pressing my head back against his shoulder.

"That feel good, Little Warrior?"

"So full," I groan.

"Just wait, sweetheart, you're about to feel so fucking stuffed," Beck growls possessively before slamming his dick all the way into me in one hard thrust.

I cry out, nearly coming there and then. "Oh, Jesus," I whimper. "I need to come so bad."

"Not yet, Firefly," West demands. "You still have two more dicks to take." His dirty words make me whimper again, my pussy clenching at the thought of having all of them at once. Both Mason and Beck curse when I strangle their dicks.

"Fuck, she's gushing all over me. She loves the idea of having all of us, don't you, baby?" Beck's voice gives away how much he's getting off on this too, as he struggles to hold himself back while thrusting impossibly deeper into me.

Glancing up at West, he jerks his head at Cam, who quickly comes to sit behind Mason and me. I adjust myself so my head is falling off Mason's shoulder, putting me at the perfect angle as I open my mouth and relax my jaw, enabling Cam to slide past my lips and down my throat.

Fuck, I've never been so full in all my life, and as all three of them start to move in a coordinated rhythm, I know I won't last long. Yet there's still one guy missing and, as Cam pulls back, I look at West out of the corner of my eye, holding my hand out for him in a silent gesture.

He smirks, coming toward me on his knees and lifting out his heavy dick, weighing it in his palm before letting me wrap my hand around him. I tug and pull on him as Cam repeatedly hits the back of my throat, spilling soft curses every time; all the while, Mason and Beck drill into me, the multitude of sensations driving me crazy with ecstasy. This is what being on drugs must be like. That heady, all-consuming feeling, like you can't take anymore but it's still not enough.

Cam comes first, spilling his cum down my throat before kissing my lips and moving to lie beside me. His fingers stroke my sweat-slicked skin, pinching and rolling my nipples as West takes his place. Unlike Cam, he doesn't wait for me to open. As soon as he's settled, he pushes the tip of his cock against my lips, smearing on the bead of pre-cum as he silently demands entry.

He shoves his way inside, groaning as my teeth graze along his skin until he hits the back of my throat, blocking my airway. He stops, holding himself there until my lungs feel like they're about to burst, before pulling back and letting me gulp down a large breath, only to do it again.

The lack of oxygen only heightens the sensations, and I quickly lose it. My moans vibrate over West's dick as he comes down my throat, and my pussy clenches, causing the other two to lose the last bit of control they had as they come inside me.

After getting dirty, passionate kisses from Beck and Mason, the five of us collapse into a sweaty pile on the bed. Mason removes himself from beneath me, and I flop onto Cam's chest, sated and content, not giving a shit that we're all lying in cum-filled bedsheets.

Just as I'm about to drift back to sleep, a loud knock on the door startles me awake.

"Get up, family meeting." Hawk barks.

"Ugh," I groan.

"Asshole seriously needs to get laid," Cam grumbles, unwrapping his arms from around me and climbing out of bed.

As the others grab clothes and towels to go shower, I lean into West. "Why do you normally wear your glasses during sex?"

His fingers trail tenderly over my face. "I want to see every bit of pleasure I make you feel."

He plants a quick kiss on my lips before getting up. *Damn, there's something so hot about his need for control.*

Half an hour later, we're all in the living room with cups of coffee. Hawk, Beck, and Mason are all staring at me expectantly, so I'm guessing this is where I have to once again go over what happened last night.

Sighing, I lean back in my seat and bring up my knees, wedging myself into the corner of the sofa before explaining what happened to them.

By the time I've finished, Hawk is stomping about the place like an angry bear, Mason looks like he's on the verge of hunting Lawrence down and killing him himself, and Beck is looking at me with a sad expression in his eyes, like this is somehow all his fault.

Grumbling under his breath, Hawk stalks over to where I'm sitting. Crouching down in front of me, he rests his hand on my knee. "Did he...?" He can't finish the sentence, his mouth clamping shut in refusal to even utter the words.

"Not as bad as last time," I whisper. However, West, astute as ever as he sits stoically beside me, overhears.

"What do you mean *last time?*" he growls, his pitch-black tone enough to draw the others' attention our way.

Hawk and I share a look, and he picks up on my silent plea for him to be the one to tell everyone else.

Sighing defeatedly, he nods, standing to his full height and looking at each of the guys.

"The day Lawrence came to campus, and I found Hadley alone with him in the headmaster's office—"

"You said she was fine," Mason barks, cutting across Hawk, already able to tell the end of this story isn't a good one. "That nothing happened."

"I know." Hawk sighs. "I lied." I can see it in his eyes. He's still beating himself up about not getting there sooner.

"I asked him to." I fix each of them with a look so they don't start shouting at Hawk for lying to them. He was only doing right by me. Glancing at me, I can tell he's surprised. We both know that's not what happened. He *offered* not to tell the guys. He put me first, above people he's been friends with his whole life. It's not something I'm going to forget any time soon.

Now that I've spoken up, all four of my guys look at me. "What did he do?" Mason's deep baritone and menacing growl send a shiver skittering up my spine. If I were Lawrence, I would run very far away, pretty fucking quickly, before Mason has a chance to gut him like a fish.

"He tried to get me to suck his dick," I blurt out, refusing to meet anyone's gaze. I don't want to see any the pity or disgust on their faces.

"How far?" Mason doesn't seem capable of saying anything more, but he doesn't need to. His meaning is clear enough.

Hawk sighs. "It was in her mouth when I walked in."

I close my eyes against the onslaught of tears threatening to leak out, burying my face in my hands. I jump when something goes crashing against the wall.

"Cam!" West calls before the front door slams shut. The sound of Cam leaving shatters the last of my restraint as tears drip from between my closed lids into my palms.

Broad arms wrap around me, and I breathe in Beck's cedarwood and eucalyptus scent. Usually it calms me, but today it just makes me feel more lost as I burrow deeper into his chest, internally freaking out about how this new development might change everything.

I just got Cam back. What if this breaks him? What if the others don't want to be with me anymore, knowing what I did? I mean, that's kind of cheating, right? Our already complicated relationship is still too new to survive this, and I'm too emotionally stunted to know how to save it.

I hear the others whispering nearby, but Beck holds me close, rocking back and forth while he strokes my hair. Not long later, I hear the front door open and close again. Someone probably went to check on Cam.

Silence envelops the apartment as I keep my head firmly pressed against Beck's chest.

"I'm sorry," I mumble into his t-shirt, when I finally find my voice again.

He stops rocking, and his fingers wipe away the tear tracks on my cheek, slipping under my chin and forcing me to look up at him.

The devastated look in his eyes nearly breaks me all over again.

"Don't be sorry." There's a husk in his voice, giving away the overwhelming emotions he's experiencing, yet the sternness in his tone is very real. "You didn't do anything. This is all on him. *I'm* sorry. *We're* sorry we didn't get to you on time." There are tears in his eyes, and I've never seen him look more emotional before. "We failed you."

"You're not angry I didn't tell you?"

He shakes his head. "Do I wish you'd felt like you could? Yeah, of course. But I understand why you didn't."

"I wanted to pretend it never happened."

He nods, understanding.

"He threatened West if…if I didn't."

He clenches his teeth, his nostrils flaring in anger, as he continues to stroke his thumbs over my cheeks reverently.

"We won't let him get away with this," he promises. There's so much hostility and determination in his words, I can't not believe him.

Glancing around the room, I realize we're alone.

"Did the others go after Cam?" I ask, worrying my bottom lip.

"Yeah, and to give us some time alone."

I nod my head absently, leaning in against him.

"Do you think he'll be okay?"

"He just needs some time. He'll be back."

I hope so. I can't do any of this without him.

We didn't stay on the sofa for long before Beck carried me back to West's room, lying down with me. After everything that happened in the last twenty-four hours, it didn't take long before I fell asleep.

When I come to, the sun is low in the sky, the bright red shining through the window. Beck is gone, and Cam is lying on his side, his head propped on his hand as he watches me with sad, broken eyes.

"Hi," I croak, my voice dry and thick with sleep and emotion. His fingers skim over mine and I interlink them. "Are you okay?"

His eyes lift to mine. "I should be asking you that."

Closing the distance between us, I wrap my arms around his waist and he falls onto his back, taking me with him.

"That was the first day Hawk stepped up and had my back," I tell him. "I hate that he had to see me like that"—Cam's fingertips dig into the skin on my hip—"but it strengthened our relationship tenfold. So rather than thinking about what happened that day in that room, I remember Hawk hugging me and how he looked at me—like he finally realized we were one and the same. Because of what happened, I now know what it's like to have a brother and, for the most part, it's been pretty awesome."

Cam pulls me up his body so my face is inches from his. "You're incredible," he murmurs, awestruck.

I shrug. "When you're used to awful things happening to you, you learn to focus on the positives."

Hadley

CHAPTER TWENTY-THREE

When Cam and I emerged from West's room, Mason and West scooped me into their arms with reassurances that they loved me. Even Hawk gave me one of his rare hugs, and we all finally sat down to discuss what Lawrence said at the engagement party. All of us agreed that the fact he threatened the scholarship students means he doesn't know how close I've gotten with the guys, which is good.

We also discussed the plan for Easter break. Mason, Hawk, Cam, and West will be at their parents' office building for the whole week. While we're all unsure of what new responsibilities they will have to take on, especially Mason, now that Frank is out of the picture, we've all decided it's the best opportunity we're going to get to dig up dirt on all of them. They'll have easy access to snoop around and, hopefully, find something we can use to not only take down our parents and destroy the company but free ourselves from the lives they have planned for each of us.

Beck relayed any details he could about his visits to the compound, without giving away the fact our parents are training kids. He and I have been talking a lot lately about what he's seen and had to do there. As we all get more entrenched in all of this, he's been encouraging me more and more to tell the guys the truth. I keep jumping back and forth on the matter. Part of me—okay, *most* of me—wants to be honest with them, but I'm scared. I don't think many relationships could survive when one finds out their significant other is a ruthless assassin who has killed, maimed, and tortured people. I think I'm getting there when it comes to telling them. The more time I spend with them and learn to trust them, the more I find myself wanting to. I'm just not quite there yet. The guys leave at the end of the week for Easter break, so I think I'll spill the beans when they get back—I know, I'm a total pussy. Beck mentioned that our parents might tell the guys what's really going on at the compound over Easter break—they have to eventually, right? But I think it might be better that they've had some time to stew in that little revelation before I add even more to their plates. *Yeah, basically, I'm making excuses.*

Unfortunately, none of us know what to do about Lawrence. He has been keeping his distance since it was announced to the world that I'm the long-lost Davenport daughter, but we're all a little worried the news of my sudden engagement will be enough to tip him over the edge. If last night is any indicator of what's to come, he will be gunning for me. Other than being on high alert and not going anywhere alone, I'm not sure what else I can do. If he sends any more mercenaries after me, it's not a problem, I can more than handle my own. Although if he comes for me himself, it's a totally different ballgame. I don't know how to get over my fear when it comes to him. It's utterly irrational, given that I could easily take him, but that doesn't make it any less real. It's like people being afraid of spiders. You know you're the predator in the room, that you can easily squash the spider beneath your boot, but it doesn't stop your body from locking up when the damn thing scurries across the floor.

I'm making my way down the corridor toward Beck's office when I hear the headmaster's door open further down the hall, and a girl in a school uniform steps out.

She's not looking my way as she flattens her hair and tugs down her skirt, but as my boot squeaks against the wooden floor, her head snaps up, looking in my direction, and I notice the girl is none other than Bianca.

She's got flushed cheeks and swollen lips, appearing freshly fucked.

My eyes dart back and forth between her and the headmaster's door, easily putting two and two together as my eyebrows rise up my forehead and a smirk crosses my lips.

"Well, well, what do we have here?" I sing cheerily, taking pleasure in her shocked, panicked expression.

I gasp, bringing my hand up to cover my mouth in fake dramatics. "Oh my, is he your baby daddy?"

Bianca has been staying out of my way since I announced her little secret to the whole school, but that doesn't mean I've stopped keeping an eye on her.

Instead of talking back to me like she usually does, she glances quickly at the door before rushing off. I quirk an eyebrow as I watch her disappear. *Weird.* I really thought it would have taken more than announcing one measly secret to put her in her place.

Shrugging it off, I quickly forget about her as I turn the handle and step into Beck's office.

"What has you looking so happy today?" Beck asks, getting out of his chair as I close the door behind myself and flick the lock. Striding around the table, he approaches me, planting a panty-melting kiss on my lips.

"Just caught someone doing something—well, someone—they shouldn't have been," I say cryptically.

As he pulls away, I reach out, placing my palm on his cheek and forcing him to stay as my eyes roam over his face, taking in the dark bags under his eyes. There's none of the usual light there, and his smile is tight.

Concerned creases furrow along my forehead as I run the pad of my thumb under his eye. "You got in late last night."

"Yeah, they had me going through all their surveillance tapes for their next targets. It took hours."

My lips pinch. He's going to end up in an early grave if he continues traveling to the compound and doing what he's doing.

"Come on, I just want to hold you."

He tugs me over to the sofa, and I curl up beside him, wrapping my arms around his waist.

"When do you have to go back?"

"Not for a few weeks."

Good. The guys will be back from Easter break by then. "Maybe we'll have something useful by then," I say hopefully.

"Yeah, maybe."

I hate the dejected tone in his voice. He's always really low after he comes back from visiting the compound. Not that I can blame him, but I hate seeing him like this. He always seems so strong, like nothing could get to him, but underneath his rough exterior, he's as vulnerable as the rest of us.

"You know what's weird?" he muses. "I thought I saw Wilder's dad there."

"At the compound?"

"Yeah. I remember him from the engagement party, and I'm sure it was him. But what would he be doing there?"

"How does he even know about the compound?"

We lapse into silence, and I can feel something tugging on my brain, a memory that I can't quite pull to the surface. Thinking back over my minimal contact with Benjamin Clearwater, I remember the night Wilder and I met him for dinner. Him blocking me in the bathroom. What he said.

I gasp as I lean up on Beck's chest. "What if the deal he made with my parents was so he could have access to the recruits?"

Beck looks at me, confused, not following. *Right, probably need to explain it better.*

"The night Wilder and I met him for dinner"—Beck's eyes darken and his jaw clenches, remembering exactly what happened that night—"he said how I was older than his usual preferences."

Beck's face scrunches up in disgust but understanding dawns. "You think he demanded access to the underage recruits as part of the business contract?"

"Why else would he be there? I don't imagine it's easy to get your hands on underaged girls, but our parents have a bunch of them just sitting at the compound. Nobody cares about them. No one is going to save them. Hell, most of the guards have probably already taken their turn, so why not pass them around to one more person."

My stomach revolts even as I say it, and the dejected look in Beck's eyes confirms I'm right about the guards. "I've heard a few things on my visits," he verifies in a hollow voice. I'm pretty sure the only reason I wasn't violated in such a way was because of Lawrence. Not that I can be grateful to him for that small mercy, considering I'm pretty sure he's the one that stuck me in that godforsaken prison in the first place.

"Well, at least we understand his motives now." He sighs.

True. He's just another name to add to the list of fuckers I want to watch burn.

∼

"So," Emilia asks, waggling her eyebrows. "What's it like to be an engaged woman?"

We're in the theater room, having our usual weekly movie night. Wilder decided to duck out of tonight. I think he realized I needed a bit of time with my friends, although I haven't told Michael the truth. Having discussed it with the guys, we agreed that the fewer people who know, the better. No one outside of Wilder, Emilia, and the six of us knows that the engagement is fake, and neither of us intends to go through with it. Unfortunately, that means I'm stuck pretending to be a happy bride-to-be tonight.

"Exactly the same as being *un-engaged*, except I have to cart this heavy rock around," I joke, flapping my hand in front of her face.

I nearly died when Wilder presented it to me this afternoon. It's legit worth more than anything I've ever owned, and it weighs a fucking ton. On the plus side, it would do a hell of a lot of damage if I decided to swing my left hand at some fucker's face. Small wins, I guess.

"You're seriously going to marry him?" Michael scoffs, looking disgusted. He and Wilder don't exactly see eye to eye, but I think Michael's just jealous. He's used to being the only guy in our group, and if he's still harboring a bit of a crush—which Emilia thinks he is—then he will be put out by Wilder's sudden appearance.

I shrug. "It's mostly a business arrangement, but I mean, I can think of worse people to marry."

"He's undeniably hot enough," Emilia agrees. "And rich. Other than being a little weird, he's the total package." She sighs. Clearly, she's given the idea of marrying him way too much thought.

"I thought you didn't care about money?"

I look at Michael in confusion. "I don't. I told you, it's mostly a business deal."

"Why do you care about agreeing to a business deal? You've hated the Princes and all the rich assholes in this place since day one. Now all of a sudden, you're fucking them and marrying someone just like them?"

You could hear a pin drop in the room as Emilia and I gape at Michael, shocked at his outburst.

"It's none of your business what I decide to do," I snap back.

He scoffs, looking repulsed. "Then don't have sex where anyone can see you."

I mentally wrack my brain, trying to figure out who he could have seen me with, but dammit, I've had sex in a public space with both Mason and Cam. It could be either or both of them.

Thinking back, I recall the night of the party when Cam and I snuck off into the forest. I was sure I heard someone in the trees that night, and when we came back, Michael was gone.

Gasping, I exclaim, "Was that you that night in the forest? Were you watching us?"

"What the hell, Michael?" Emilia gapes.

"You're just like everyone else here," Michael yells, "a two-faced bitch."

My jaw drops open in shock as I stare at him, flabbergasted, my fists clenched at my sides. "I'm not sure what I did to upset you," I start, trying very fucking hard to keep my temper under control. "And I'm sorry if I hurt you, but you have *no* right to talk to me that way."

Not waiting for him to dig himself any further into a hole, I stalk out of the room.

"I can't get over him," Emilia fumes when she catches up to me on the path back to the dorms. "And he saw you with one of them? Do you know who?"

"I think it was Cam." I sigh. "But that was *weeks* ago."

"And he never said anything?" she gasps.

"Nope." I pop the 'p', wholly baffled at what the fuck just happened in there.

"Damn."

Something in Emilia's tone has me looking over at her. "What?"

She grimaces. "Well, he must be hurt and confused. He's had a crush on you all year, then he catches you sleeping with someone you've spent half the year hating, and now you're 'happily engaged' to someone else."

Damn, the girl makes a lot of sense sometimes.

I sigh heavily, rubbing my eyes with my fingers.

"I fucked up, didn't I?"

"Maybe a little, but he also fucked up massively tonight. He should have just talked to you."

If the asshole wants to apologize and explain himself tomorrow, then fine, but otherwise, he can go fuck himself.

∽

THE NEXT DAY, the guys all leave for Easter break. They'll be staying at their parents' houses for the next week since it's closer to the offices. None of us are happy about being separated, yet I'm hopeful this will be the perfect opportunity for us to gain some leverage. It *has* to be, otherwise I've no idea what we're going to do.

"Don't go anywhere alone," Hawk reiterates for like the nineteenth time. "And don't go out in the dark." I roll my eyes behind his back as he lifts his bag off his bed. "In fact, just spend all of your time with Beck. He won't have any sessions so he can entertain you."

"You realize I'm not a puppy or a child, right?"

"I'm being serious," he snaps, with a deathly scowl.

"So was I." When he continues to glower at me, I sigh. "Okay, I promise. I won't so much as insert a tampon without telling Beck."

His face blanches. "Gross," he grumbles.

I grin brightly, bouncing over to him and throwing my arms around him. "I'm gonna miss you, big bro."

He hesitates for a fraction of a second before returning my hug. "I'll miss you too, little sis," he mutters, sounding reluctant, even though I know it's all an act. We've made heaps of progress in the last few weeks and I really am going to miss the ornery fucker.

It takes forever to say goodbye to the other guys—mainly because Cam refuses to let me go. However, with one final kiss, they all head out, and my shoulders slump as the door closes behind them.

"None of that," Beck chastises, pulling me back against him. "We have the whole apartment to ourselves. I bet you we can't have sex in every room before they come back."

Laughing, I turn around in his embrace. "Oh yeah? I'll take that bet."

I press up onto my toes, fusing my lips to his, wondering what room we should start this bet in. Hmm, the sofa's the closest, so the living room it is.

Despite my teasing of Hawk, I spend pretty much every moment of the next week with Beck. The guys check in frequently, and they send me plenty of sexts and dick pics which I use as fuel to win my bet with Beck. We don't talk much about whether or not they've managed to find anything useful, preferring to wait until we're all back together in person to discuss it.

Still, as the holidays draw to a close, my excitement at seeing them all again, and possibly taking some actual steps forward with the plan for our parents, has me bouncing around like a madwoman.

I'm in the guys' apartment—where I've basically sequestered myself for the last week, under the guys' orders—with Wilder. We're trying to watch a movie, but I just can't sit still.

"Sunshine," he gripes. "You're driving me crazy."

"Sorry. I'm just so sick of being in this apartment, and the guys are coming back tonight, and it just feels like it's been forever."

He chuckles, shaking his head at me. "Ah, to be in love."

"Shut up," I grouse, punching him hard enough to give him a dead arm.

Flicking off the TV, he turns to me. "Right, well, if you aren't going to let me watch my movie, you can at least teach me some of those knife-wielding skills of yours."

I cock a brow. "You wanna learn how to stab your daddy in the hand?"

"Or anyone else who crosses me." He gets that dark psychotic look in his eyes that should probably be a warning not to teach the guy to use sharp weapons, but I'm bored, and I haven't gotten to play with my knife in ages.

I spend the rest of the afternoon teaching him how to properly hold a knife and the best body parts to aim for if you want to do the most damage. The throat is a nice, bloody one, but it doesn't have to be messy. A well-aimed slice through the ribs is relatively blood free and will pierce a fucker's lungs. They'll be drowning in their blood in no time. Likewise, a nick to the spleen will have the blood pouring out into their abdomen so fast they won't even know what happened. The femoral artery is another good one, albeit the blood spray is just as impressive as the carotid.

It also doesn't have to be all about the deadly blows, however. A slice to your opponent's Achilles will have them crashing to the ground, unable to walk. Similarly, if you go through the back of their knee, you can tear through their ligaments and really fuck up their leg. If you're looking to do lasting damage to their upper arms, then going through their armpit and destroying their brachial plexus will have them losing all feeling and function in that arm. There are just so many ways to beat down and kill your opponent with a knife. That's why it's my favorite weapon.

We set up a target against one wall, and I get him to practice throwing. It's a lot harder than it looks, and the first few times—despite his cocky attitude—he throws it all wrong and the handle ends up tearing through the paper target.

I can see, with every new trick I teach him, questions linger in Wilder's eyes. He's most likely wondering how I know all of this. Yeah, some of it you can probably pick up, but as I get caught up in the comforting feel of palming my knife and twirling it in my hand, I think he picks up on the fact I'm more than just self-taught. Thankfully, he keeps his questions to himself. That's the great thing about Wilder. He never oversteps the mark. Even if he did ask a question, he'd just laugh and shrug it off if I told him to mind his own business.

I'm laughing my ass off as Wilder misses the target *again*, his inability to hit it getting to him as the color rises in his face, when my tablet pings.

Retrieving it from the kitchen, where I plugged it in to charge, I notice a message from Michael. I haven't heard from him since he blew a gasket in the movie theater. He's been keeping his distance from me and vice versa. I figured I'd let him cool off and he'd come to me when he was ready to talk.

> Michael: Can we meet? I think we should talk, and I need to apologize.

I guess he's ready to talk.

Little Warrior

CHAPTER TWENTY-FOUR

This week has been the week from Hell. When our parents said we would be working for them over Easter, I thought it would be boring business meetings at the office and horrifying visits to wherever they keep and train their mercenaries, but nope. Since my dad is no longer around to do his part, I have to step up. Apparently, as part of his job, he would take quarterly trips to Black Creek. Without him around, no one else has been able or is willing to go in his place, so I was the lucky sod that was tasked with going.

I've spent most of the week here, meeting with shady fuckers. I was told to collect the packages, and that's it. I'm not allowed to open them or ask questions. Literally, just pick up the packages. So I'm basically a glorified delivery man. Yet every time one of the crazy-eyed druggies hands me the parcel, I'm torn between needing to know what's inside and feeling like I'd be better off if I never found out.

"This place is disgusting," I grumble, sneering at the sticky bar table that I'm fairly certain is going to give me hepatitis. I've never missed home more than I have in the past few days. The G&T is a rundown shack of a strip club, and even though it's barely midday, the place is packed with what looks like homeless vagrants. I'm pretty sure it's just how the people here look—gaunt and skeletal, like they're barely surviving. I naively assumed G&T stood for gin and tonic, but after making a passing remark about how it didn't make sense that they didn't stock any gin, the bartender informed me it stood for guns and titties. It makes much more sense, especially when I glanced around the bar and realized how many guys had a gun stuffed down the back of their jeans.

Some even have them sitting out in the open on their table while they lean back in their chairs, warily observing their surroundings. Obviously, carrying a firearm is a requirement in Black Creek.

The bodyguard I've been assigned chuckles. His eyes never leave the crowd, though, roaming over everyone and constantly assessing for possible threats. He looks far more at ease here than I do. Although being one of our parents' trained mercenaries, he's as broad as I am, so the two of us stick out like sore thumbs.

According to Barton, my dad never came here alone. A bodyguard was always assigned to him for personal protection, but I'm not sure if that's the truth or if it's just our parents' way of keeping an eye on me while I'm up here. Either way, I've been careful to watch what I say around him. For the most part, we've gotten along fine. He doesn't talk much, so getting a read on him is hard.

"Aye, it's a shithole, but it spits out the best recruits."

I have to squash my look of disbelief as I peer around at the people sipping their drinks and hollering at the half-naked women on stage. No one stands out as being mercenary material here. They're all druggies or alcoholics, skin and bone with zero muscle mass. No way is anyone here like the men they had attack us at Christmas.

"If you say so."

"Not people like this." The guy looks unimpressed at the riff-raff in the room. "But, yeah, there's a lot of untapped potential in Black Creek."

Cryptic. I don't dare ask him anything further, despite the number of questions dancing on my tongue. I can't be sure he won't report anything back to our parents, and I also don't know how much he thinks *I* know. He's more likely to let something slip if he thinks I already know everything our families are up to.

We sit in silence for a while longer, the guard constantly scanning the room. We're in this dingy bar to meet some guy who apparently has information for me that I need to take back to our parents, but I don't know who the fuck he is or what information he has, so I guess we're stuck here waiting until he shows up.

The crowd gets riled up, shouting and hollering when the music switches and a new dancer comes on stage. I'm guessing she's their favorite.

Following their gazes, I look up to the stage where a skinny girl, a few years older than me, with perky tits and a nice ass, sways her hips seductively. Her long coppery-red hair, I'm sure, has most guys here probably imagining twisting it around their fists as they fuck her. She doesn't do it for me personally, but I can see the appeal for why she would be a favorite among the men.

A greasy-haired man in a ratty trench coat approaches our table, gesturing with his head for us to follow him. Without question, the guard gets to his feet, indicating I should go in front of him as we trail the guy into a back room. It must be soundproofed since the noise from the bar dies as soon as he closes the door. I can only imagine what this room is used for, and I make sure not to touch any of the furniture or walls.

"You're not the usual guy." He eyes me warily.

"No. He couldn't make it. I'm here in his place."

Finishing his assessment of me, he moves on to the guard, giving him a once-over. He still doesn't relax his tense stance, and I'm getting annoyed with every passing second I have to spend in this STD-infested room.

"Well?" I snap impatiently. "Have you got information for me or not?"

Focusing his gaze back on me, he hesitates before nodding his head.

"Everyone's been fightin' over Beast territory the last year," he begins. I've gleaned enough from the last few days to know the Beasts were a formidable gang that ran half the town until a few years ago when something happened. No one seems to know what exactly, just that they're dead and buried, and their territory is up for grabs. "But The Reaper Rejects have been makin' a name fer themselves recently. They've been claimin' the land fer themselves."

Reaper Rejects? The name sounds strangely familiar, though I can't place it. I can't think where the fuck I'd know a Black Creek gang name from. "Who are they?"

The guy shrugs. "No one knows. They're small, but they're gainin' territory fast enough to be noticed."

The guard lifts out a wad of bills and hands them over. "Keep an eye on them. We'll want to know more when we're back next time."

Snatching the money out of the guard's hands, the guy mumbles an agreement and scurries out of the room. I don't know what any of that meant, or why it matters to our parents.

∽

I'VE SPENT the past several hours lying on top of my bed in my motel room—yes, that's right, a fucking *motel*, and a run-down ramshackle one at that. I'm fucking around on my phone, texting the guys to see how they're all getting on, which doesn't seem like they're fairing much better than I am, while also chatting with Hadley. Thankfully, we're heading home in the morning, and I'll be back in bed with her by tomorrow night. I've missed her more than I thought I would. It's weird, I've never felt this way before. Obviously, I care about the guys, but I've never felt this overpowering need to spend all my time with another living soul. Still, if the distance between us this week has taught me anything, it's that I can no longer live without Hadley in my life, in my arms, every fucking day.

She's started sending these teasing videos every day into the group chat with me, West, and Cam that West set up before we left for Easter break. As I respond to the guys' latest string of messages in our own private chat, a notification comes up from her, showing there's a video attached.

Clicking into the chat, an image comes up showing her very naked chest, with the triangle 'play' button in the middle of the picture.

Faster than lightning, I jump up from the bed and cross the small space to flick the lock between mine and the bodyguard's adjoining rooms, and I do the same with the door leading outside before collapsing back on the bed and getting comfy.

There's already a reply from Cam, but I ignore it as I press play, watching as she lifts the video, giving me an up-close view of her soft, puffy lips and hooded eyes before she slowly trails her fingers down the valley between her breasts, moving the phone to follow the movement.

She stops to massage her tit, pulling on her nipple as she moans softly, and I push my hand beneath my boxers, tugging on my growing erection. Moving back to the center of her body, she paints a line with her finger all the way to her clit as I pump myself.

Just as she sinks her fingers inside herself, she moans, ending on an evil-sounding giggle before the video comes to an end.

What the fuck?

After staring, bewildered, at the screen for a second, I start frantically typing a reply, ignoring Cam's grievances about leaving him hanging.

> Mason: Touch yourself.

Her reply is instantaneous.

> Little Warrior: I am.

> Mason: Show us.

An image pops up of her fingers knuckles-deep inside her dripping wet pussy. Only it's not enough. I need to hear her come.

Pressing the button for a video call, it rings once before she accepts, and I get to see her beautifully flushed cheeks.

"You wet for me, baby?" I smirk, running my thumb over my tip and wetting the head of my dick.

"So wet," she pants.

"Show me." The words are barely more than a growl as she lowers the phone to give me the perfect view of her pussy. She lazily pumps her fingers as I watch, jerking harder on my dick as I pretend I'm sinking into her hot center.

"Rub your clit, baby."

She moans as she does what I tell her.

"That's it, baby. Tell me what you're picturing."

"You," she pants.

"What am I doing?"

Another few breathless pants before she responds, "You're using your mouth on me."

"Yeah, I'm working you up real good."

"Uh-huh." They're the only words she seems capable of forming.

"Are the others there too?"

"Yeah."

"What are they doing?"

"West's—"

I pump faster on my dick as I add the guys to the video call. Cam's topless, and by the looks of things, he's halfway to getting himself off already, while West looks as stoic as always.

Before either of them can say anything, Hadley moans, and I focus back on her image, clicking on it so it fills the whole screen—I definitely don't need to see either of those guys' jizz faces.

"Fuck, baby, yeah. I'm fucking your ass so hard right now," Cam growls, making Hadley moan.

"Pinch your nipples, Firefly. Pretend it's my teeth," West commands. After another moment of breathy moans, West fires out his next order. "Reach into my bottom drawer. There's a rabbit and some lube. Lift it out."

Doing as he says, she lifts out the vibrator and lubes it up.

"That's it. Pretend it's Mason's dick filling you up."

I watch, enraptured, as the pink device sinks into her sweet cunt. I'm staving off my own release, not ready for this to be over with, but her moans are making it so goddamn difficult as I twist and pull on my cock. I imagine I'm actually sinking into her wet heat.

"Mason," she moans.

Hadley cries out our names as she comes, and a second later, I hear a door open. "Well, well, what do we have here? Looks like I'm missing out on all the fun," I hear Beck say.

In the next second, the phone is tossed onto the floor, and all I can hear is Hadley giggling before she starts to moan again, the unmistakable sounds of fucking coming down the line. *Lucky bastard.*

I quickly disconnect and clean myself up, deciding to go check with the bodyguard about what we're doing for dinner tonight. Maybe I can ply him with greasy food and a few beers and whittle some useful information out of him.

I knock lightly on the door between our adjoining rooms. When he doesn't respond, I flick the lock, testing to see if his side is unlocked. It is, and the door swings open.

Before I can announce my presence, I hear him talking to someone. Peering my head through the doorway, I catch him looking at something on his laptop at the small two-person table.

"This kid, he's impressive," he says to whoever is on the other end of the line. Focusing on his laptop screen, there's a video playing and as I watch, a kid barely older than eight or nine tackles a kid who looks twice his age with all the ferocity of a grizzly bear. Taking him to the ground, the kid beats on his opponent until he's unmoving and bloody beneath him. "He'll make an excellent recruit. We should get someone out there to pick him up ASAP."

What the fuck? I stand frozen in the doorway, unable to comprehend what I'm seeing and hearing. The shitty tequila from earlier must have warped my brain. There's no way I fucking heard that right. Kids? They're recruiting kids? Surely not. I must have misunderstood.

"There's a couple of other potentials too." He laughs. "In the tape I watched yesterday, one kid lit another on fire over a loaf of bread. He's definitely worth bringing in."

Fucking hell. There goes the idea of misinterpreting him.

"Oh yeah?" Pausing the video, he exits the program while I stand there frozen. "Got it, one sec." Clicking on something, another recording pops up. This one is of a dark room and it's difficult to make out what's happening from this far away, but as a high-pitched scream blasts out from the speaker, I shudder. I've never heard anything like it. The loud cry is filled with unimaginable agony before it suddenly cuts off, making the room feel even quieter than before.

"Fuck, I love it when they scream." The bodyguard chuckles, staring riveted at the screen. Bile climbs up the back of my throat and I stumble back to my room in a daze, that scream playing on repeat in my head. I couldn't see what was happening on the screen, but I didn't need to. Whoever it was, was being fucking tortured.

My mind races as questions fly across it. What the hell was going on in that video? Why are our parents recruiting kids? I mean, *kids?!* I can't wrap my head around it. I always knew my dad was a sick man. The glee in his eye when he'd bring his belt down on me with all the force he could muster was enough of an indicator of the cruelty he hid inside him, but *this?* It's a whole other level of sick and twisted.

Ensuring the lock on the adjoining door is engaged, I collapse onto the bed. My hunger is long gone as I stare unseeingly at the damp ceiling. Kids. That's what all of this is about. And they're fucking torturing them. Why? As punishment? To keep them in line?

Sighing, I rub the heel of my hand against my eyelids as I try to erase the echo of that girl's pain-soaked screams from my brain. It's so much fucking worse than we ever imagined. Being involved in the black market assassins-for-hire services is one thing, but stealing kids off the street and forcing them to become monsters is just…fuck, I don't even know the word. Mind-blowing. Sick. Incomprehensible.

How did our parents ever expect us to be on board with this? Or is it their plan all along to get us so wrapped up in the illegal shit they're up to that when they do eventually tell us, we'll have no way out of it all.

I'm still in a daze the next day. Thankfully, my usual quiet demeanor and the hard, cold mask I wear around others come in handy, and the bodyguard doesn't pick up on the maelstrom inside my head. All the way home, I kept opening up the group chat with all six of us, desperately wanting to tell them what I found out, but we agreed to keep any information until we were all face to face, just to be safe.

After a final debrief in our parents' offices—one I don't pay any attention to—the four of us exit and quickly get in the car to head back to campus. The mood is subdued, and I have the feeling I'm not the only one with grim news to share. On the bright side, I get to spend all day tomorrow in bed with my girl. Nothing like a lazy Sunday with your best friends and your girl to reset your mood after a shitty week.

It's late by the time we arrive back on campus, and there's a cold chill in the air now the sun has set. Hawk's phone goes off as we're all grabbing our bags from the trunk. "Yeah?" he answers. I'm not paying him much attention as I reach for my own duffel, closing the trunk. "What the hell do you mean *you can't find her?*"

Those four words, combined with his snarling, venomous tone, have all of us focusing on him. *What the fuck has happened now?* His jaw is clenched so tight I'm surprised his teeth don't shatter as he listens to whatever is being said on the other end of the line.

"We're coming now. We'd better find her, or you're a dead man."

Hanging up the phone, he looks at each of us with unadulterated fury blooming in his eyes. The next words he bites out destroy any hope I had of curling up with my girl for the rest of the night.

"Hadley's missing."

Hadley

CHAPTER TWENTY-FIVE

My head feels like it's been stuffed with cotton wool. *Where the fuck am I? What the hell happened last night?* It's not like I drink or do drugs....drugs.

The flicker of an image skitters across my memory, but I lose it before I can catch a hold of it. I try to dig deeper into my forgotten memories, desperately trying to find something that could tell me what happened last night, but I only succeed in giving myself a headache.

Something doesn't feel right, though. The pounding in my skull as I try to turn my head only confirms that, and when I lift my arm, something cold presses painfully against the skin, a rattle echoing around the room as something pinches my wrist.

What the fuck?

I pry my eyes open and squint down at my hand. It takes me a second to focus, and I blink furiously. Even once my vision clears, I still can't process what I'm seeing. There's a metal cuff around my wrist, the other end attached to a ring on the wall, chaining me to it like I'm a fucking animal.

My heart rate picks up as sweat breaks out along my forehead and down my back, and I force myself to think through the fog in my head. My eyes dart around the dimly lit room, nausea churning in my stomach, and I have to swallow it down before I throw up all over the floor.

This is my worst nightmare come to life. I slam my eyes shut, breathing past the nausea as I plead to whatever God is above that this is a dream. There's no way this is real. It can't be. I already escaped from here. I won't live to escape a second time.

Another memory flashes across the back of my eyes, and I manage to latch on to it before it disappears. Flashes of meeting Michael at the dining hall—he wanted to apologize—followed by flickers of the two of us walking toward the lake. I vaguely remember it was a lovely evening and he suggested going for a walk.

Everything after that is hazy. God, do they have Michael too? Is he okay? Another round of bile works its way up the back of my throat, and it takes everything in me to swallow it down. No way am I going to puke up my guts and let whoever comes in next realize how deathly terrified I am.

Time passes in a meaningless blur, and I'm still trying to come to terms with my new reality when the door unlocks and swings open, the light from beyond blinding me and painting the large man blocking the doorway in darkness, preventing me from seeing who it is as I squint up at him from my less-than-ideal position on the narrow bed.

"Ah, good, you're awake." Lawrence's cold voice runs over me like water, instantly chilling me to the bone. Being back here is one thing; being back here with *him* is something else entirely.

As he strides into the room, the door slams shut behind him. I hurriedly try to sit up, wanting to be in a better position to defend myself should I need to, but my muscles feel like jelly and I fall back down when I put my weight on my free arm.

The asshole laughs at my attempt. "It will be a while longer before you gain full control of your muscles, but that works in my favor for now." His smug tone and the way his lip curls maliciously have me swallowing around the lump in my throat.

He moves to stand in front of me, so I'm forced to tilt my head back and look up at him. He reaches his hand out to stroke my hair and the second his fingers wrap around the wavy strands, I jerk my head away. His other hand whips up to slap me across the face faster than I can blink, my head snapping to the side. The sudden movement only adds to the pounding headache I've got going, and I can feel the sting and flush of my cheek as blood rushes to the surface.

He goes back to stroking my hair reverently as though nothing happened. "Tut tut..." He laments disappointedly, sounding as though he's reprimanding a disobedient child. "I told you, Dove. I told you, you were mine. I wanted to give you everything."

"Yeah, everything but my freedom," I seethe. I have no idea where the sudden courage has come to talk to him like that. Maybe it's the drugs or knowing I'm probably going to die in this cell—or even worse, wishing I had.

He shrugs uncaringly. "Your mother had freedom, and she made the wrong choice. I couldn't have you do the same."

My mother? What the fuck does she have to do with any of this?

"Yet you still found a way to defy me. At first I kind of liked the challenge of chasing you." His fingers move to stroke over my cheek before running down my neck, the light touch making me shiver with revulsion.

In the next second, his hand is wrapped securely around my throat, squeezing until I can't inhale more than the slightest wisp of air. "But you just had to take it too far, didn't you? You just had to fuck him, you dirty slut."

I'm barely paying attention to his words as I focus on trying to push him away with my hands, but there's no energy in my movements.

He moves to straddle me, pinning me beneath him as panic courses through me. It's been a long time since I've felt this helpless, and my fear only escalates as dark spots bloom in my vision as he uses his weight to push me further into the thin mattress.

He lowers his face in front of me so it's all I can see, even as blackness creeps in at the edges of my vision. "You're exactly like your mother," he growls furiously. "Whores." Spittle hits my lips and cheeks as he sneers down at me. "But that's fine. You want to act like a slut, I'll treat you like one. I was going to give you everything. Now, I'm going to lock you away here and leave you to the mercy of the men who have been dying for a taste of you since the day you arrived." He laughs spitefully. "You thought this place was a nightmare you needed to escape before? You'll be wishing for death by the end of the week.

"I was too soft with you. I thought killing your little friend would be enough to break you." My eyes flare at that revelation, even as my vision blurs his devil-like features. "Clearly, I was wrong. Well, I won't make that mistake again. You'll be well and truly broken this time. Who knows, maybe then, when you're nothing more than an empty shell, begging for death to claim you, I'll take you back and save you from this hell." His fingers trail down over my abdomen and he pushes his way beneath my panties while his other hand tightens around my throat painfully, cutting off the last of my air. My energy quickly wanes as the black spots become large blobs. The last thing I'm aware of as everything goes black is the feel of his fingers shoving their way inside me.

The next thing I know, I'm jolted awake to the sting of freezing cold water being hosed over me. I gasp as the horrific realization that this was not some fucked-up nightmare settles in my bones, weighing me down.

"Wakey, wakey, rise and shine, Princess," a cold voice sings from somewhere in front of me. It takes a second for my brain to come back online after the ice shower, and I almost regret it when it does, because the sight that faces me is bleak and hopeless. I'm completely fucking screwed. I'm shackled to the stone wall behind me, splayed out like a starfish, butt fucking naked as *Bowen* sprays me down with water so cold my body already feels frozen solid.

Another pass of the water has me crying out, and he laughs cruelly when my whole body wracks in shivers. Bowen is the worst guard here. I guess that's why he's in charge, but he's as coldhearted and morally rotten as our parents are. The glint in his eye as he comes closer tells me I'm about to experience first-hand just how sick he truly is.

Despite fear beating a quick rhythm through my cold veins, I glare at him as he approaches. He smirks, more than ready to rise to the challenge of breaking me as he unsheathes a knife from his waist, rolling it back and forth in his hand. All the while, his gaze is roaming over me.

"I always did like cutting you up." There's a sick reverence in his tone that has goosebumps rising to the surface of my skin. He lifts the blade and traces the scar along my collarbone. Every one of my scars occurred at his hands. The twisted fuck gets off on inflicting pain onto others and watching them bleed out in front of him. I know for a fact that begging and crying only spur him on, so I learned to hold my tongue a long time ago. He could literally stab me in the kidney, and I'd refuse to so much as whimper in front of him.

The thing is, I got so good at acting broken when I was here, at pretending they'd beaten me down and turned me into an obedient soldier ever-ready to do their bidding, that they've never seen my fire. All those years, they thought they crushed me, but they were only adding fuel to the building inferno of hatred inside me. I'm burning so fucking brightly, brimming with fire and hate and malice. So he can fucking bring it; I'm ready for him.

I let him see every ounce of contempt I feel for him, for this compound, for the fucking board that runs this hellhole. His eyes widen at the realization of just how alive and ready to fight I really am, before darkening. His lip curls up on one side, and his eyes sparkle with sick excitement.

"Oh D, I'm going to enjoy breaking you," he promises, dragging the blade down between my exposed breasts. He applies just enough pressure to bring blood to the surface, occasionally nicking the skin and causing tiny red droplets to form before they drip down over my white skin. His tongue flicks out to lick his bottom lip and he digs the blade in deeper. My body tenses, preparing for the slash of pain when he breaks the surface. Instead of pushing the knife all the way in, he loosens his hold to trail it further and further south until a red line runs from the base of my neck to my pubic bone.

"Nothing gets me harder than having my prey all trussed up and covered in blood." He smiles wickedly before pushing the blade through my folds, the cold steel making me gasp as my body freezes.

"I haven't been allowed to play with you the way I want," he pouts, pulling the blade away from my body. My muscles relax now that I don't need to worry about him nicking any of my sensitive bits right before a perverted grin crosses his face. "But my time is coming. Soon I'll have claimed every part of you."

~

FACING Bowen has become a daily part of my routine. For several hours every day, I'm splayed out for him to slice and dice like a slab of meat. Of course, just to drive the knife in deeper, he opens up the gallery for any and every fucker to come and watch the 'Humiliating Hadley' show. It becomes the only way for me to tell the passing of each day. Based on my count, today is day number four. I've been here for *four* days.

It already feels like a lifetime.

The frozen water blasts over my skin—again—and I grit my teeth against the shivers wracking my body, blocking out the hoots and hollers from the guards. All of them are getting off on seeing me strung up and at Bowen's mercy. The tangy smell of blood in the air as Bowen trails the tip of his blade along my skin, decorating my body with brand-new scars, drives the men wild. They're like rabid dogs, biting on the bit and itching for a taste.

"Just like old times, D. I remember how much you and your little friend *loved* being chained to my wall." He leans in, whispering in my ear, "Keep fighting, D. Every day you hold out is another day Lawrence gets closer to caving and letting me do what I want with you." A wicked glint enters his eye as he presses the flat side of his knife against my nipple, getting distracted as he trails a circle around it. "In the meantime..." He nicks my skin, a bead of blood swelling before it spills over onto my milky skin. "Why don't we give the guys a show." The smirk that lifts his lips is positively vicious. "Let's see if I can make you scream."

Sweat beads my skin over the next hour as I strain and grunt, refusing to give these fuckers what they're craving—my pain. When Bowen is finally done making me bleed for the day, and I'm panting from the exertion, he steps away. One by one, the guards approach me with lecherous looks as they unzip their trousers, jerking themselves off until their cum hits my thighs, my abdomen, my hip—whatever body part they can reach.

"They're all going to get a piece of you one day, D," Bowen calls out. "You're only delaying the inevitable."

I don't have the energy to digest what he's saying. Instead, I let his words wash over me like rain, tuning him out, along with everyone else in the room. Disconnecting myself from my reality, I let my mind slip away to a better place. It's something I've become adept at doing, and it's only when my knees collide painfully with the stone floor that I abruptly crash land in the present again.

I'm a sticky mess on the floor, blood and cum combining and crusting on my skin. Without my restraints holding me upright, my body no longer has the energy to stand unaided. Instead, I'm a boneless heap sprawled out on the ground. I've had nothing to eat or drink since I arrived, so my muscles are running on nothing but grit and sheer determination at this point, except my adrenaline is quickly wearing off. I'm exhausted; beyond exhausted. Fucking numb.

The assholes don't even wash me down before dumping me, naked, back in my cell. I'm not sure how long I sit on the floor, staring absently at the stone slabs before I gather enough energy to drag myself onto the thin, lumpy mattress on my cot.

Just as my eyes droop, sleep threatening to drag me down, the screaming and banging start.

No. Please no. Not again.

It's the same death metal they blast every time exhaustion is about to pull me under. The lights start flashing next—a painfully bright strobing that has my retinas burning, even though I squeeze them shut and bury my head in the mattress.

Everything they're doing is intended to break me and, *fuck*, I think it might be working. I can feel myself slowly giving up the fight. The only thing that keeps me alive is the thought of my guys. Images of them all, of Emilia and Hawk, and even Wilder, flitter across my mind, providing me with the only source of energy to keep me going. I can't help but wonder if they're out there looking for me. Do they know where I am? The music, if you can even call it that, blares through the speakers into the cell, threatening to drive me mad as I clamp my hands over my ears. I need sleep. I need food. I *need* to get out of here.

I don't know how much more of this I can take.

Even if my guys do find me, will there be anything left to save?

Hadley

CHAPTER TWENTY-SIX

Today's the day. The day I finally take control of my future. I can practically feel the sun on my face, heating my skin; the light breeze whispering 'freedom' as it whips around me. By the time the sun sets today, I'll be standing on the other side of these tall, concrete walls, free to do whatever the fuck I want with the rest of my life.

That, or I'll be dead.

Lights out was hours ago, and I've been sitting impatiently in my small room ever since. Waiting. By the time I hear the lock disengaging, I'm a ball of nervous energy, no longer able to sit still. I've been pacing back and forth across the space for a while now, and the sound of the door opening freezes me in my tracks.

"Hurry up," a deep voice hisses. The guard is nothing but a dark silhouette in the narrow slit of my open door. Not wasting any more time, I close the distance and slip out the door without a backward glance, and he closes it soundlessly behind me.

He doesn't say anything, but I can see the tick of annoyance in his jaw as he strides down the corridor. Glancing nervously around at the other closed doors in the block, each one containing a sleeping soldier behind them, I scurry silently after him and catch up as he reaches the door leading outside.

I suck down a deep breath of the cool night air, but I'm not free yet. Without a word, the guard takes off. He doesn't look over his shoulder even once to see if I'm following. He probably hopes I'll change my mind. That won't happen. Nothing will stand in my way tonight. The only way I'm going back into my room is if they drag me kicking and screaming.

I trail the guard in silence, the two of us stealthily making our way across the dark yard to a garage at the far side. I've never been to this part of the compound. Although I'd hazard a guess, there's a lot of this place I've never seen—not that I care to. The sleeping barracks and main building where we train, eat, and receive punishments are the only two buildings the recruits have any reason to be in. Whatever is in the other outbuildings I've seen is nothing more than an assumption to me—one I don't care to find an answer to.

"Get in and stay down," he orders in a low whisper, opening the back door of a compact sedan. There's junk strewn all over his backseat, and as I quickly wedge myself into the floorboard, squirming as far under the front seat as I can, he shoves some of it down on top of me to ensure I'm well hidden. I hate having to rely on him to get me out the gate, but what choice do I have? I've done all I can to guarantee he doesn't turn on me. I wiggle, arching my back so I can slip the knife I stole from a guard earlier out of my pocket. When he slips into the driver's seat, his weight further pinning me to the floor of the car, I poke my arm out from beneath the junk on top of me, sticking it through the small hole between his seat and the door of the car, and angle the blade at his kidney. I hear it—his gasp—when the sharp edge digs into his skin.

"Don't get any funny ideas," I bark out in a low, threatening growl.

I've been bribing Stevo, the guard so kindly helping me this evening, for the past year. Any time my team is sent on a job, he's ordered to come along to keep an eye on me. I'm precious cargo, after all—can't have Lawrence's plaything getting killed or disappearing. He's also up to his ears in gambling debts, so it wasn't difficult to coax him into taking a cut of the 'off book' jobs I accepted any time I was away from the compound.

It all started as sheer fucking luck. Right place, right time, sorta bullshit. We were on a job up in Black Creek, and I was running surveillance on our target. On my way to the rendezvous point, I came across some bikers harassing a curvy redhead. I wasn't about to let that fly, and I quickly pulled them off her. She offered to pay me if I taught her how to hold her own in a fight. It sounded like a bunch of bullshit to me, but she produced the cold hard cash there and then. I didn't ask why she wanted to know this stuff. That's her business. My guess would be, living in Black Creek, an attractive girl like her would stand out by a mile with her red hair, well-sized rack, and curvy ass. She probably just wanted some basic self-defense tactics to protect herself from sleazy scumbags. Whatever the reason, I accepted her offer.

With that first wad of cash, I bought myself a burner phone and rented out a locker at the rundown bus station in Black Creek. That way, I had somewhere to keep my money and a way to contact the redhead—Red—when I was next in town.

So, after that, any time we were sent up to Black Creek for a job, we'd meet up. I'd either make up some bullshit excuse for why I needed more time to do my job, or I'd bribe Stevo into letting me out for an hour. Red was a lifesaver. She was able to put me in touch with a guy who makes top-of-the-line fake IDs, and she even secured me a couple of quick and easy jobs, delivering cars to chop shops and running drugs, to help me get the money together.

Once I had papers sporting my brand new name, it was only a matter of waiting for Pacific Prep applications to open, and finally, last week, when I checked my PO Box, I had received my acceptance letter. With everything in place, there was no reason for me to stay here any longer. I lifted as much cash as I could from my locker and bribed a reluctant Stevo into helping me tonight. Of course, it's a big fucking difference between him letting me slip out for an hour and him actually helping me escape. It took a lot of haggling and threatening for him to finally cave, but that doesn't mean I'm about to trust him. Anyone who can be bought, can't be trusted.

I roll my eyes as he grunts and curses me out under his breath, the car slowly making its way through the compound. As we roll to a stop, I hiss out, "Remember, I can kill you faster than you can blink."

He ignores me, rolling down his window, and I pray the guards won't be able to make out the white skin of my arm wedged around the side of the seat or demand to rifle through the stuff in his backseat.

"Alright, Stevo," the guard greets. "Where are you off to tonight?"

"Off to drown my sorrows, man. The Cubs were supposed to be a sure thing." Stevo sighs, and his disappointment sounds too genuine to be fake. He probably had all of the bribe money I'm about to hand over to him riding on tonight's game.

"Ouch, man." I hear the guard chuckle sympathetically. "You won't be the only one drinking away the loss." There's a pause, and unable to see what's going on, I press the tip of the blade more firmly into Stevo's skin, only stopping when I hear him hiss. "You're all good, Stevo. Catch ya later, man."

There is another tense moment as Stevo waits for the gates to slide open before he rolls the car forward, and we drive through. Sweat coats my skin and my heart hammers against my chest. I keep expecting one of the guards to call out for him to stop, but no one does, and we drive down the dark road.

"Where am I going?" he growls, letting his anger show.

"Just keep going." I wiggle out from beneath the seat, shoving all of his shit off the backseat so I can sit on it. My eyes dart all around us, half expecting some sort of ambush, but there's only darkness.

We drive in silence for twenty minutes before I tell him to pull over. I've no idea where the fuck we are, but it doesn't matter.

The car idles at the side of the road, and I lean forward in my seat.

"Sorry about this," I apologize in a bland voice before jabbing the knife into his kidney.

He screams, "What the fuck?" as blood soaks through his shirt, and he scrambles for the door handle, getting out of the car. I follow quickly behind him, and the second he stumbles onto the road, clutching at his side, I launch myself at him. I slice the knife quickly through the soft skin of his neck, jumping off him as he collapses to the ground, gurgling and gasping.

I couldn't let him live. I couldn't run the risk that he would raise the alarm. It's why I chose to escape from the compound rather than when we were out on a job. It would have been so much easier to run then, but someone would have noticed me missing much sooner. I need every second I can get to grab the last of the cash and things from my locker at the bus station and disappear.

With Stevo dead, I know that no one will realize I'm missing until the morning. That gives me several hours to do everything I need to. Dragging his dead body into the undergrowth along the side of the road, I wipe off the few flecks of blood on my skin and climb in behind the wheel.

I flick through the radio channels until I find one I like, cranking it all the way up as I speed down the country lanes to freedom.

I'M in and out of consciousness, barely alive, when I hear the steel door of my cell being pulled open. *No. Not yet. I'm not strong enough to survive another round already.*

"Up," a deep voice snaps.

When I don't move—because I'm not physically capable of it—he grabs onto my upper arms and yanks me up roughly. Once I'm in a sitting position, he shoves a tray of food in front of me.

"Eat."

Clearly, he's only capable of monosyllabic words.

I don't even have the energy to lift my spoon, and the smell of the soup has my stomach threatening to revolt.

When I make no effort to follow his instructions, he pinches my cheeks painfully, forcing my mouth open and starts shoveling the food into me. It's not long before I'm gagging and puking up what little he managed to get down my throat.

Vomit splashes over the front of his shirt, and he's quick to react, slapping me across the face as he curses me out. I don't know what he expected to happen when I haven't eaten anything in god knows how long.

Wiping himself down, he returns to his task of force-feeding me. I'm fairly certain most of it ends up on the ground or over both of us, but eventually the tray is empty.

When we're done, he hauls me out of the cell, dragging me into a large room with a drain in the middle of the floor. Grabbing a hose, he douses me in freezing cold water. The thing about being blasted daily with ice-cold water is that you never get used to it. You know it's going to be a shock to your system, but no matter how prepared you are, you still flinch away when it hits your skin. I can't do anything but lie there, shivering and naked on the floor as the water washes over me. I no longer even give a shit that I'm naked. That requires energy—energy I don't have.

I must pass out, as the next thing I know, I'm back in my cot. The same routine continues the next few times someone comes to my cell, and slowly I start to regain my strength, managing to keep the food down and feed myself. The question is why. Why are they feeding me? Why now? I highly doubt it's because they've taken a sudden interest in my well-being.

The next time the door clangs open, Bowen is standing there, looking as menacing as ever. I haven't seen him in several days, and while it's been a small reprieve, the panic of wondering when he'll come back and what fresh hell he'll have in store for me, has slowly worn me down.

"Put this on," he orders, throwing a pile of black tactical gear at me.

"Why?" My voice is hoarse from lack of use. *When was the last time I spoke?* Looking at the clothes, I do my best to keep the longing for actual clothes off my features. I've been naked since he first shackled me to the wall seven days ago, or was it eight? They are all starting to run together.

The wicked smile that brightens his heinous features has me forgetting all about the clothes.

"Tonight's challenge night."

On challenge nights, we usually work as a team, every team competing against one another to achieve a common goal, but I get the impression I'm not going to be working as part of a team tonight.

Standing on unsteady legs, I quickly pull on the black trousers and matching top, noticing the asshole didn't bring me shoes.

"What's the challenge?" I ask, making sure to sound uninterested.

"Why, D, I'm so glad you asked." He grins menacingly, his next words making me blanch. "You are. You're going to face off against all twenty recruits in your age bracket and see if you make it out alive."

Fuck.

"As an added incentive, if you lose, you'll get to find out what it feels like to have my blade shoved up your ass."

Fighting hard against the shivers threatening to overtake my body, I focus on trying to remain positive. Sure, I'm beyond exhausted, half-starved, and I haven't trained—or so much as stretched my legs—in far too long, but I used to be the best recruit here. That's got to count for something, right?

"And if I win?"

The maniacal look in his eye doesn't give me any reassurance.

"Then you'll only get to see what the handle feels like."

The sick fuck escorts me to the fight hall, and I'm unceremoniously shoved through the door. Based on the roar of the crowd, everyone is here, including the adult mercenaries who are here of their own free will; who *chose* this life.

Passing a few younger kids, their eyes are wide with terror, but as I meet the gaze of others my age, that terror is replaced with steely resolve. By the time you're our age, you've accepted your fate, if not grown to revel in the bloodshed.

Not about to let anyone think I'm weak, I throw my shoulders back and lift my head. Shaking off the sentinels tasked with ensuring I don't try to escape—where the fuck would I even go?—I make my way unaided into the ring. The ring itself is enclosed with a large wire fence that goes all the way to the roof, preventing the crowd from pushing against the ropes and stopping anyone from trying to flee if things don't go their way. As I step through the gateway, it's closed and locked behind me, locking me in with my opponent—a heavy-set beefy man I vaguely recognize. He wasn't one of my team members, so I only know him in passing. *Good, that should make it easier.* I didn't spend any time with my team members outside of training, and while there was a professional acceptance of one another, there was nothing more between us. Still, it's going to be awkward if I come face-to-face with one of them tonight.

The second the bell rings to start the fight, he charges at me, and despite his size and the fact I've been locked in a cell the last few days, I'm still agile and light on my feet, and I easily maneuver out of his reach, quickly coming up behind him. With a few well-placed kicks and an elbow to the head, he goes down.

Fight number one over. Only nineteen more to go.

I steadily make my way through opponent after opponent, bringing them to the ground or knocking them out. The room becomes blurred as I zone out, ignoring the roars and chaos around me. The only thing I focus on is the guys. They're all that matter. I know over the last few months I've grown softer. I've learned to relax into a hug and enjoy small touches. I'd deny it until I was blue in the face, but nothing beats a snuggle sandwich on a cold morning. Some might think that learning to rely on the guys has made me weak, but as I pull on the well of strength I can feel glowing within me, I know those people are wrong.

The guys are what I'm fighting for. Every time I punch, kick, and maim my opponent, it's because I'm fighting to get back to them. When I first found out about Cam and devised my plan to get out of here, it was because I wanted to survive. It was a novel goal, but now I want so much more. Now I want to live—for the guys. *With* the guys. The will to do whatever is necessary to get back to them is why I'm going to win every one of my fights tonight. It's why I'm going to survive this hellhole yet again. Everyone here is fighting for survival, but I'm fighting for love, which is why I'll win every time.

Everything hurts. The cuts Bowen carved in my skin have torn open and are freely bleeding, and I have a fresh set of cuts and bruises to match. My legs are shaking uncontrollably, and I can tell I'm minutes from passing out as, with the last of my energy, I take my final opponent to the ground, pinning them to the mat until they tap out. When the whistle is blown, I roll off them onto my back, fighting to remain conscious. *I can't pass out yet. Not here, surrounded by enemies. I need to get back to my cell.*

All I can hear is the rushing of blood as it pounds through my ears, and I stare absently at the ceiling high above me until the face of a monster obstructs my vision.

"Looks like you've still got it, D." He pouts. "Guess my blade will just have to play with your asshole a different day."

On those lovely words, I promptly pass the fuck out.

CHAPTER TWENTY-SEVEN

MASON

Where the fuck is she?
 I throw my mug at the wall as yet another lead turns out to be a dead end. Beck and Wilder filled us in on what had happened when we returned to campus—not that they seemed to know much. Hawk went absolutely apeshit on them, giving Wilder one hell of a shiner when he confessed he was the one that let her leave on her own. She was only going to the dining hall to meet Michael, so he thought it would be fine. Fuck, I wanted to hit him too, but honestly, I'm more pissed at myself for not drilling it into him that she wasn't to go *anywhere* alone. As much as I want to blame him, it's not like he knows the fucked up shit that's happening with our families or what a threat Lawrence is to her. Surprisingly, he hasn't tried to pry or ask questions about any of it, although, no doubt, he suspects *something*.

 Once Hawk chewed the two of them out, we spent the rest of the night scouring the campus for her. We tracked down Michael, who confirmed he had coffee with her that evening but claimed that after they were done, he went to the library, and Hadley was making her way back toward the guys' dorms. So what the fuck happened to her? She didn't just fall off the face of the earth.

 Even weirder, we found her phone down by the lake, but after interrogating everyone in the school, no one was able to confirm if they remembered seeing her down there that night. It's fucking infuriating.

 I hear them before they enter, Emilia's loud voice carrying as she demands answers and updates. That girl will not stop, and it's made me realize just how perfect her friendship with Hadley is. She's been on our asses since the minute she stepped back on campus after the break. Hadley hadn't been answering her calls or texts all day Sunday after she disappeared, and Emilia showed up breathing fire, demanding to know where she was.

 It was a difficult one to explain. It's not like we could tell her anything about our parents or the compound. She also wasn't buying our bullshit about Hadley being in bed, sick, so that basically just left us telling her that something had happened, but we didn't know what, and that we were doing everything we could to bring Hadley home. I think it's fair to say she took that news about as well as Hawk did, and she's been demanding daily updates ever since.

Hawk sighs as the three of them come through the door. "I told you we'd let you know when we had something," he gripes.

Emilia spits fire at him with her eyes. "Right." She scoffs. "You wouldn't tell me anything if I didn't harass you daily."

Turning toward her, he pins her in place with a serious expression. "I promise we're doing everything we can to find her."

Emilia's brows are slightly furrowed as she studies him. I'm pretty sure she's trying to determine if she can trust him or not. Surprisingly, Hawk lets her look her fill. The two of them stare at one another for so long it grows uncomfortable to watch, but finally Emilia gives a tight nod of her head.

"Okay," she admits reluctantly. "I still want updates in any case."

Without waiting for a response, she turns on her heels and walks out. No one else would dare talk to Hawk—or any of us—like that and then turn their backs on us. They'd be asking to get their asses handed to them. But despite her meek appearance, there's a lot of defiance in that girl. She reminds me of Hadley. Thinking of my fierce Little Warrior has a now familiar ache forming in my chest, and I glance hopefully between Hawk and Cam, eager to see if they found anything. "Well?"

"Nothing," Hawk grits out.

"You?" There's a wistful look on Cam's face that only intensifies as I shake my head. He grimaces. "Maybe West has something."

Yeah, maybe. He's been glued to his computer screen, going through security footage on campus, verifying students' stories and trying to find glimpses of Hadley so we can see where she went after meeting with Michael.

It doesn't make any sense, though. She wouldn't just wander off on her own. She *knows* to stay with one of us when she's out. She spent all week with Beck and Wilder, so why, the night she knew we were due back, would she decide to go off alone?

The only thing we can think of is that Lawrence somehow got to her. Maybe he threatened her into meeting him or going with him somewhere. I don't know. I can't think of any other explanation. Of course, after we'd searched every inch of the school, we went home to make sure Lawrence didn't have her hog-tied to his bed or some sick shit like that, or her parents hadn't done something stupid, but there was no sign of her there.

West has been tracking Lawrence's phone and scouring the security footage for both our parents' homes and their office building, so we have eyes on him everywhere. The problem is, he hasn't gone anywhere suspicious—the office and home. That's literally all he does.

"We need to find out where she was before she came here. Maybe he's holding her there," Hawk growls in frustration.

I look between him and the others, clueless. She's never told me anything about her past. I know whatever happened was fucked up, but I don't know where she was.

Cam shrugs too, as unhelpful as I am.

"Seriously?" Hawk snaps. "She didn't tell you anything? You didn't think to ask?"

"Did *you* ask?" I argue, riling him up.

He snaps his arm out, shoving me. "*You're* supposed to be in love with her. *You're* supposed to get past her barriers and get her to open up to you."

"Yeah, and if you hadn't spent all of the first semester making her hate you, maybe she would have opened up to you!"

"Hey!" Cam yells, barging his way between us. "Stop it." The look he gives us is lethal, and it's enough to have us dropping our fists. "None of this is helpful. If we can't work together, then we don't deserve to get her back, so pull your heads out of your asses!"

Cam rarely raises his voice, and it's yet another reminder of how close we all are to losing it without her.

Cam flops down into one of the armchairs, scrubbing his hands over his face and groaning. "If he has her, I don't know where my dad would have taken her."

"He literally hasn't gone anywhere except home and the office all week," West updates us, strolling into the kitchen in a pair of sweats and a stained t-shirt. He goes straight to the coffee machine and fills his cup to the brim before joining us in the living room.

The door opens again, and Beck walks in, looking as bleary-eyed and exhausted as the rest of us. "Anything?"

The three of us shake our heads, and his shoulders slump in defeat.

"We're trying to work out where Lawrence could be hiding her," I explain as he collapses into a vacant chair.

Pursing his lips in thought, he asks, "What about the compound?"

West shakes his head. "Nope. Not since I hacked into his GPS, anyway."

"Still, he could be keeping her there," I argue.

"I just think it's too obvious, right under our parents' noses," Hawk dismisses.

"It might not be completely implausible…" There's an odd look on Beck's face as his eyes dart between each of us, making us sit up straighter in our seats.

"What the fuck does that mean?" Hawk snarls, sounding like a rabid dog.

Beck's lips flatten, and he looks reluctant to share whatever he knows. "She should really be the one to tell you this, but you need to know."

There's a sadness in his eyes when he looks back at Hawk, and I know whatever he has to tell us is something significant.

"Hadley grew up in the compound."

Hawk scoffs, waving away his words. "Yeah, right, like Lawrence could hide a kid in the compound all those years without any of our parents hearing about it."

I grimace. "Actually, that might be more plausible than you realize."

The attitude drops from Hawk's face as he stares at me, his gaze intense and slightly confused. I feel bad having kept this from them for so long, but with everything we've been dealing with since we got back from Easter break, there hasn't been the right moment to tell them all.

"When I was up in Black Creek, I, uh, uncovered something about Nocturnal Mercenaries."

I quickly rehash everything I overheard, and my words are met with stunned silence.

"Kids? What, like eighteen-year-olds?" Cam asks, confused, while the other three sit quietly, mulling over what I've just said. It's not every day you're told your parents are grabbing kids off the street to turn them into weapons. So I fully understand the shock they're experiencing right now—hell, it's been nearly a week since I found out and I'm still in shock.

I shake my head. "The kid I saw on the video looked more like eight or nine."

Beck leans forward in his seat, resting his elbows on his knees. "So they're taking kids from Black Creek?" he questions. I get why that would bother him, having grown up there himself.

"Amongst other places, but Black Creek seems to be their main feeding ground. They have some sort of deal with the leading gangs there."

Beck purses his lips, but unlike the other three, he doesn't seem surprised at what I've said.

"Fucking kids?" Hawk snarls in disgust. "What the fuck is wrong with them? Is it not enough that they're already performing a black market service for god knows what sort of underground criminals?!"

My gaze is still focused on Beck's contemplative ones as Hawk goes off on a rant, cursing out all of our parents.

"Why are you not surprised?" I demand, watching him closely.

Beck looks up at me, sighing before leaning back in his chair and looking at the others. "I knew."

"You knew?!" West repeats, sounding outraged.

"And you never told us?" Hawk snaps, turning on him. He's been ready to beat the shit out of Beck every day since Hadley went missing, so this is probably only adding fuel to the fire.

"I couldn't," Beck responds, unfazed by Hawk's glower.

"That's the secret job they were getting you to do by threatening me," West states, successfully putting all the pieces together with his computer brain.

"Yeah." Beck sighs, rubbing at his eyes. He looks ten years older than he did before the guys and I left for Easter break. Although, glancing at the others, we all have bags under our eyes. Without Hadley, we're struggling.

He spends the next ten minutes explaining precisely what they've had him doing, filling us in on all the details he'd previously left out when he discussed his visits to the compound.

Rage consumes me as he tells us all the fucked up shit he's been involved in. The haunted look in his eye is enough to see how much it's all been getting to him. Now that I see it, I don't know how I didn't pick up on it before. He's obviously expended a lot of energy trying to keep all of this from us. Simply keeping up the act of pretending he's not losing a part of himself every time he goes there must be exhausting. I get that he was protecting West, but we're a team. The guys and I always lean on each other when we need to. Beck needs to understand that he can do the same. He's one of us now.

"You could have told us, man."

He shakes his head. "Nah. This shit eats away at your soul. I didn't want that for you." He looks pointedly at West, before glancing at the rest of us. "For any of you."

Fuck, well, if that doesn't endear me to him, then nothing will. The fact he's been looking out for us all this time, even when West was pushing him away, makes me like the guy even more. I've never had any issue with him, other than doubting whether or not we could trust him in the beginning, but it's hard not to like the guy, especially when he looks at my girl the way he does. He solidified our friendship and his place in the group with me, when he kicked my ass in the ring. It's been a long time since anyone managed that, and I sure as shit didn't expect him, with his preppy waistcoats, to be able to best me, but he's clearly spent a fair bit of his youth at the gym, working out.

I know Hawk's pissed at him at the minute, but honestly, Hadley's disappearance could have happened under any of our watches. I'd be kicking myself if it happened to me, and I've seen the guilt in Beck's eyes every day since we got back. He's beating himself up enough for all of us. There's no need to lay it on any thicker.

Cam's laidback, so he's never been too bothered about having Beck join our group. After everything that happened between him and Hadley, I think he'd accept anything if it made her happy.

West has been the most stubborn, but it's been good to see him opening up to Beck over the last few weeks. A couple of times, I've come home and found them chatting in the kitchen over beers. I think it's been good for him to have another person in his life he can talk to. They're total opposites, apples and oranges, but they haven't let that get between them.

"So, it's actually possible that Lawrence could have taken her back there," Cam muses.

No one jumps to respond to him as we all contemplate the possibility. I mean, it's not *im*possible.

"I have to go back there in a couple of days," Beck eventually tells us. "I was planning on doing some snooping; try to find out if he was keeping her there."

"I still can't believe you've been doing all of this for me," West murmurs, still looking shell-shocked. "How have you coped, carrying that burden all by yourself?"

"Hadley figured it out—"

"Jesus Christ." Hawk throws his arms up in the air, stalking back and forth across the apartment as his anger consumes him. "It's like we don't even fucking know her. What other secrets is she keeping?"

Hawk grounds to a halt when he sees Beck's expression, and the look he pins him with is fucking lethal. "What?"

He hesitates before stating, "It wasn't luck that she was able to kill that mercenary. She had all of the skills to do much worse to him."

"There's no way." Cam scoffs, but I can tell he's not sure what to believe. "If that's the case, why didn't she kill my dad and run off years ago?"

"Lawrence is her Achilles heel. He's terrorized her since she was a little girl. All the attitude and combat skills in the world won't help her if she can't stand up to him psychologically."

∽

THE SOUND of the door crashing inward has all of us spinning around as Beck comes rushing in, a grim yet hopeful expression on his face.

"I know where she is."

"What?"

"How?"

"Where?"

All three of us fire off questions, not giving him a chance to respond. He ignores all of us anyway.

"West!" Beck yells, waiting until he comes to join us in the kitchen. West's clothes are disheveled, and he smells musty, like he hasn't showered in a few days. I'm pretty sure he hasn't, and as I subtly sniff my armpit, trying to remember the last time I showered and took a nap. I reckon I probably look and smell as bad as he does.

"What?"

Beck's gaze bounces between each of us. He looks as haggard as we do, with bags under his eyes and his hair sticking up.

"She's at the compound."

"You have proof?" Hawk demands.

Beck grimaces. "Sort of."

"What the fuck does that mean?" I bite out.

"Last night, I heard the guards talking about a recent challenge night they did. One fighter bested twenty of their older recruits."

"So? That doesn't tell us anything?" I can hear the frustration in Hawk's voice as he clenches his fists.

There's a glint in Beck's eye, and fuck do I not want to hold on to that look of hope he's sporting. "The fighter was a girl."

No one says anything for a moment, and I can tell the others want to believe him too. I mean, our girl is one hell of a fighter, but to beat twenty trained professionals? Even I have a hard time believing that.

"That doesn't mean it's her," Cam says, albeit reluctantly.

"It's her," Beck continues to insist, making Hawk throw his hands in the air.

"You can't fucking know that," he snarls.

Beck gets to his feet, coming to stand chest-to-chest with him. "It's. Her."

"We need proof," Hawk snaps, not letting the hope of Beck's words get through his tough exterior. "We can't go off hearsay. We need to see her for ourselves."

"The open day," West reminds us. "It's next week. We can look for her then, see if she's there."

"She's there," Beck growls in frustration.

I guess we'll find out next week.

If you are there, baby, hold on, we're coming for you.

Firefly

CHAPTER TWENTY-EIGHT

"Do you really think she's going to be here?" Cam whispers. We're in the back of the car our parents sent to take us to the open day.

"I have no idea," I tell him. "I don't even know if I want her to be or not."

My words are met with silence. We've heard enough from Beck to know the compound is not somewhere you want to be kept against your will, and if what he's saying is true, that she grew up here, then it's a miracle that she not only made it out alive but with her humanity intact.

I can't wrap my head around the reality of that. If Beck is right, then our girl is a motherfucking mercenary. Bearing that in mind, some of the things we've seen her do, and the way she behaves, makes sense—like her blasé attitude after stabbing Benjamin in the hand, her ability to pick locks, and the fact she was able to kill that mercenary. She was the one that came up with the idea to dump the body in the lake—is that because she knew it was the best place? Had she done something like that before? My mind is a chaotic mess of questions as, with every passing minute, the car takes us closer to possibly finding her.

When we're officially far from civilization, we pull up at a manned gate. After the driver says a few words to the guard, the gate rolls open and we drive in, and a few minutes later, we crest a hill and see the compound laid out before us.

There are a lot of other cars on the road, heading in the same direction, and when we pull up out front of the main building, the small car park is already full.

We've already been warned to be on our best behavior today. None of our parents are here, preferring to leave the demonstrations to whoever is in charge of this hellhole, and they'll wine and dine whichever rich assholes are interested in investing or making use of their services, but apparently, being present today is part of our induction into the business. Just like Easter break, when I was forced to attend client meetings with my father. Some of them were for the legit aspect of our parent's company, providing private security to government officials, celebrities, and whoever else needs it. Still, for the most part, the meetings involved discussing targets, negotiating prices for hits, and setting realistic time frames—it was absurd. Like something you'd see in a movie.

"Ah, you must be the up-and-coming heirs of Nocturnal Enterprises," a slimy man greets, holding out his hand for each of us to shake. "I'm Major Bowen. Follow me. I'll show you to the hall where we'll be conducting today's demonstration, then I'll get someone to give you a tour of the facilities."

The four of us silently follow him through the bright corridors toward an auditorium.

"What will today's demonstration involve?" Hawk asks, miraculously managing to keep the contempt out of his voice.

"The whole point is to show off to potential clients and future investors why *we* are the best. Our men and women are ruthless because we push them to be. Today, we'll show everyone our best fighters, as well as demonstrate our recruits' abilities to handle various weapons. We'll also have several recruits competing in an obstacle course to show their agility, speed, and flexibility."

Major Bowen leads us into a large hall. An assault course has been set up around the perimeter of the room, with a boxing ring in the middle. Off to the side are various practice targets, along with a variety of guns, knives, and even a crossbow, all of which are being carefully guarded.

The room is nearly full as men in fancy suits consort with one another. There's a thread of excited energy humming in the air, everyone keen to get started with today's show.

"I have ringside seats for you," Major Bowen beams, directing us to four empty seats in the front row right by the fighting ring.

While we take our seats, Bowen disappears off to attend to whatever else he needs to do, and the four of us cast watchful eyes around the room. Everyone here is a criminal in one form or another. Whether they own their own criminal conglomerate, are a dirty politician, or someone from a rival company here to suss out the competition.

Not long later, the last of the audience filters in and Bowen comes to stand in the middle of the ring.

"Ladies and Gentlemen," he begins, his voice booming out through his microphone, ensuring everyone can hear him loud and clear. "We are honored to be able to host you today. We have some excellent talent for you, which we hope you will enjoy. If you have any questions or wish to discuss business further with our esteemed board members, come talk to me after the demonstrations."

With a brisk nod to a guy standing ringside, he makes his exit. Two prominent male fighters, who look to be in their late twenties, enter along with a referee. As the referee starts the fight and the two of them dive in, tearing into one another with their fists, it's clear how much they love the fight, the bloodshed. A gleam enters their eyes every time one of them lands a hit that makes the other bleed. It's the most vicious battle I've ever seen; both opponents are intent on killing the other to claim victory.

Both fighters give it everything they have, spraying the mat, and some of the audience, with blood as they land blow after blow, splitting lips and cutting open eyebrows. Neither of them wears mouthguards, and when the one facing me gives a toothy grin, blood stains his teeth red, only enhancing the maniacal vibe coming off him.

Eventually, the guy facing me manages to get the upper hand, taking his opponent to the ground and beating him repeatedly until I'm sure I hear his jaw snap. Only when the referee blows the whistle, calling the end of the fight, does the guy let up, glancing disinterestedly at his half-dead competitor before looking up at the crowd and grinning madly with his red teeth.

The audience claps and cheers as the guy heads off the mat, his unconscious opponent being dragged behind him.

"What the fuck?" Cam breathes. "That was insane."

A couple more fights take place, and in the last one, I noticed the fighters were more our age, if not younger.

"For this last fight, we have something special," the referee tells the crowd. "Our best fighter fought twenty of our own people and won, so we're going to give you a taste of just how capable she is."

She? I risk a glance at Cam beside me, taking in his tense posture as he leans forward in his seat.

Four people step onto the mat, and as the three large guys move to the edges of the ring, we all get a clear look at our girl. *Hadley.* I'm halfway out of my seat before catching myself and forcing my ass to sit down again. My fists are clenched tightly at my sides as I fight every instinct in me to get to her.

I hear Cam gasp beside me, and there's a small commotion on his other side as Mason most likely stops Hawk from doing something stupid. I can't tear my eyes away from her to look. She looks skinnier than she did before. Her face is sunken, and there's a hardness in her eyes I haven't seen in a long time. She's sporting the same armor she had when she showed up at Pac last September. I hadn't realized until now just how much she had opened up to us, but seeing her all closed off again makes me furious that these fuckers have destroyed all the progress she's made with us.

"What the fuck have they done to her?" Cam growls, likely seeing the same changes I am. She looks nothing like the Hadley we've all come to know and love.

"Are they going to make her fight all three of them at once?" I gasp, watching in horror as the three guys who've spread out around Hadley flex their muscles, stretching before lowering into a crouch.

In the middle of the ring, Hadley does a slow circle, assessing each of her adversaries before settling into her own fighting pose.

My hands firmly grip the sides of my chair as the referee blows his whistle and all three guys move in on her. Blood rushes into my mouth as I bite my tongue, preventing myself from screaming out to her when the guy behind her wraps his thick forearm around her neck.

She's fighting like a madwoman, trying to get out of his grip before he crushes her windpipe. Meanwhile, another asshole is slamming punch after punch into her gut. Somehow, she manages to get her legs up between her and the guy in front of her, kicking him away and using the resistance to push herself backward, knocking the guy choking her off balance.

Once she's free, she delivers several hard kicks to the guy before swiveling back around to deal with the two fuckers approaching her, clearly planning to tag-team her.

It's a tense few minutes that feel like they last a lifetime, all of us sitting on the edges of our seats, watching with a mix of awe and terror as our girl works her way through each of her opponents, systematically taking each of them to the ground and ensuring they won't be getting back up before moving on to tackle the next one.

Finally, she's the only one left standing in the ring, and we all breathe out a sigh of relief. Unlike with the previous matches we've seen today, she doesn't look victorious or satisfied with her win. She seems empty, like the Hadley I love is no longer in there, but she *has* to be. We haven't come this far to lose her now.

As she's swept out of the ring, Major Bowen announces the next demonstration. Still, I barely pay attention to the rest of the events as I stare at the spot Hadley disappeared from, my brain frantically trying to identify a feasible way of getting her out of here.

Time seems to go by in a blur while I'm lost in my thoughts, and it's only when Cam nudges me out of them that I realize everyone is getting to their feet.

"Come on," Cam urges. "We've got that tour now. It's our only shot to get a note to her."

We rise to our feet as a young guard comes over to us. "Hi, I'm Drew. Bowen asked me to take you on a tour of the facilities."

"That would be great," Hawk responds with a tight smile.

"Great. What did you think of today's demonstrations?" he asks as he leads us out the door where Hadley disappeared. This part of the compound is entirely different from where we entered. The halls are narrower and darker, making them appear more ominous, causing a shiver to make its way down my spine as Hawk blathers on with the guard.

"That female fighter was impressive," Hawk tells the guard, inflecting the right amount of interest in his tone.

The guard laughs. "She's something alright. Between you and I, though, she's got a real attitude problem."

"Oh yeah?" Hawk scoffs while I mentally praise Hadley for making these sick fucks' lives as difficult as possible.

"We're quickly bringing her to heel, though."

"How so?" There's a menacing growl in my voice—I'm clearly not as good as Hawk at hiding how disgusting I find this fucker—but the guy doesn't even notice as a dark and twisted grin crosses his face.

He shrugs indifferently, that small act enough to have me fighting back the urge to rip his fucking head off. "The usual methods. It took a few days to get a reaction out of her, but the Major is really good at his job." There's a sick gleam in his eyes. "Sometimes, he lets us watch. There's nothing quite like hearing a girl covered in blood screaming, to get your dick hard, right?" He laughs maliciously. "I just hope the rest of us get a turn soon." *Yup. This fucker's going to die, along with everyone else in this godforsaken hellhole.* I wouldn't consider myself a violent person—I don't relish in it the same way as the others—but right now, for Hadley, I'd happily embrace that darkness.

Glancing at Cam out of the corner of my eye, I can tell I'm not the only one holding myself back from going apeshit on this disgusting cretin. His body is thrumming as he struggles to restrain himself.

"We'd love to meet her," Hawk says casually.

"Ah, sorry, guys. No can do." The guard shakes his head. "She's a bit of a wild one, and we've had to feed her the last few days so she'd have enough energy to fight. She's probably overflowing with adrenaline right now. Wouldn't want her to lash out at any of you."

Fuck. There goes our only idea.

The guard shows us around the compound. With today being open day, most of the recruits are contained within their sleeping quarters. However, a few trustworthy ones are working out, bouting with one another, and generally milling around.

"What's in there?" I ask, pointing to a steel door. Beck was able to give us a brief rundown of the layout and having drawn-up a vague schematic based on what he could recall, I'm pretty sure that's the interrogation rooms.

"Interrogation rooms," the guard confirms. "Nothing exciting. That's where we're keeping D—the fighter from this morning."

"She's not out with the other recruits?" Hawk questions.

"No." The guard looks around before leaning in and whispering, "She actually managed to escape several months ago, and we only just got her back. So she's not allowed to interact with any of the others until we can get her back in line."

Hawk nods his head in understanding while Cam steps up beside the guard, throwing his arm around him. "You mentioned something about a fighting cage, Drew? I'd love to see that."

With a sleight of hand, he slips the guard's pass out of his pocket, holding it out to me behind his back. Quickly taking it, I bend down, pretending to tie my shoe while Mason and Cam distract the guard with various questions as he leads them to the fight cage. Hawk lingers back with me, neither of us daring to move until the three of them disappear out of sight.

When they're gone, I tap the card against the reader and slip into the interrogation block. It's even darker in here, and the stench of piss makes me gag as I look around. Along one wall are steel doors, marking out small cells, with the rest of the room broken up into what looks like several interrogation rooms, with large, darkened windows, showing brief glimpses into each one. In the center of the room is what looks like a small guard station, composed entirely of glass, providing the guards with a three-hundred-and-sixty-degree view of the room. Thankfully, it's empty, with all available guards pulled to accommodate the open day.

"Hadley," Hawk hisses. "Hadley!"

"Hawk?" Her surprised voice carries to us like a soft whisper from several doors down on the left. I'm itching to go to her, but I force myself to stay by the door, keeping an eye out as Hawk scurries toward her.

"Baby Davenport." I can hear the strain in Hawk's voice as he reaches the steel door separating her from us. A broken cry from behind it has my chest cracking open. *Fuck, I never want to hear that sound again.*

Hawk tries the security card on the keypad by the door, despite Beck already informing us only a few guards have access to these rooms, growling in frustration when the light flashes red. Even if we could get into her room, there's no way we'd be able to sneak her out of the compound unnoticed before someone sounded the alarm.

Closing his eyes, Hawk rests his forehead against the door, letting out a long exhale as he attempts to wrangle his emotions.

"Hawk." The relief in her tone crushes me. "What are you doing here?"

I can see Hawk gritting his teeth from here, struggling to contain his anger. "Beck said you were here, but we didn't believe him."

"He told you." I can't tell, through the thick door, how she feels about that.

We don't have time now to get into all that, something Hawk must realize. "We're going to get you out, little sis." His voice is a low growl, filled with dark promises of vengeance. He'll do whatever it takes to get his sister out of here, and we'll be right by his side. "Stay strong, okay? I have to go." His voice breaks and, *fuck*, if the moment doesn't have tears in my eyes. "But we're coming back for you…" He hesitates for a second. "I-I love you. We'll be back. I promise."

Another broken sob, followed by a quiet "I love you too," is the last thing we hear from behind the door as Hawk shoves a folded-up piece of paper through the narrow gap at the bottom of the door. It took a lot of arguing for us to decide who would seek out Hadley and who got to write the note.

Hawk pulled the brother card, and, well, what could we say to that? If it hadn't been for the overwhelming despair of the situation, it would have been a heartfelt moment. I'm so proud of him for opening up and accepting her, and I know this moment will have meant everything to her. As for who wrote the note, Cam won that one, claiming he wanted to be there for her the way she was there to pull him back from the ledge. Regardless of who got to speak to her, or write the letter, Hadley knows we're all with her in spirit and that we're all doing everything we can to free her.

Pausing, Hawk stares at the steel door for another moment, reaching out and pressing his fingers against the cold metal. His shoulders slump on a heavy sigh, and he closes his eyes for a second before standing up.

When he turns to face me, his expression is shuttered, but the fire burning in his eyes is something everyone in this place should be afraid of. He strides toward me, each step filled with purpose and determination. With one final glance at Hadley's door, we step back into the main corridor. It tears me apart to leave her behind, and I can see the same war waging in Hawk as he sears me with a haunted look, his jaw set in steely determination, ready to do anything to get his sister back.

We jog down the corridor in the direction the others disappeared, and thankfully Cam's loud laugh echoes further on up ahead, letting us know where they are. Slipping into a large room with a fighting cage built in the middle of it, I pretend to bend down and pick something up while Hawk strolls to the far side of the room, feigning interest in a collection of knives lining the wall. Actually, he's probably *very* interested in them —in jamming them into the guard's neck.

"Hey man," I call out, gaining the guard's attention. "Is this yours?" I hold up the security pass Cam swiped. "It was on the ground here."

With wide eyes, the guard pats his trousers. "Shit, yeah. Thanks, man."

"Don't sweat it," I assure him, smiling easily, all the while picturing smashing his head into the concrete wall.

We quickly finish up with the tour and get the fuck out of there, and I can feel the impatient atmosphere as the car drives us back toward campus.

I text Beck when we're nearly back at campus, and he steps up to greet us as the car makes its way out the school gates, having dropped us off.

"Well?" Cam snaps irritably when we're alone. "Did you find her?"

"Yeah. She was there."

"She got the note." Hawk looks determinedly at each of us. "Now we just need to come up with a way to get her out of there."

Hadley

CHAPTER TWENTY-NINE

I'm abruptly woken to yet more numbingly cold water being hosed over me. What day is it now? I'm losing count. My head constantly swims from lack of food, making it impossible to grasp onto a single thought long enough to figure anything out.

I've been so close to giving up, so close to losing myself. Every time I feel my will to fight slipping away, I pull out the note Hawk pushed under my door. It's the only reminder that it wasn't all a dream. That my guys were really here. They came to find me.

I'd forgotten it was that time of year—the yearly open day. After the challenge night, they left me alone. My world was nothing but deafening silence. The only noise was the sound of the hatch opening when food was delivered. It might seem better, but all that endless time left alone with my thoughts is just as damaging as what they were doing before.

Things went back to the way they were after the open day. The food stopped coming, my clothes were taken away, and I've spent most of the time living in a quiet corner of my mind where I pretend none of this is real.

The hose passes over me again, the cold water seeping into my already numb bones. I swear, if I survive this, I'm never having a cold shower again, only steaming hot water for me. I want my skin to turn red from scorching hot water.

"Ah, good, you're awake. It's no fun if you're passed out." Bowen's deep, demonic voice pierces through the fog in my brain seconds before a blade digs into my thigh, making me grunt as it tears a path up to my hip. I can feel the blood dripping down my leg, pain flaring when I tense the muscle.

I'm yet again shackled to the fucking wall, wearing nothing and wondering what the fuck he did to me when I was passed out. The only difference this time is that my cheek is pressed against the cold stone, my backside exposed to the elements. Clenching, nothing feels overly painful, but that doesn't necessarily mean anything.

He trails his fingers through the blood dripping down my thigh before pressing down on the wound, the flare of pain making me hiss. I tense when his blood-coated fingers slip between my ass cheeks, the sick fuck chuckling in my ear.

"Not long now, D," he promises. "Lawrence will be back in a few days, and when he sees you're still fighting, he'll more than happily hand you over for me to break." Leaning in, his breath tickles my ear. "And trust me, when I'm done with you, you'll be shattered into so many pieces there won't be a hope of piecing you back together."

All I know for the next however long is the feel of his blade digging into my skin, tearing apart my flesh, and branding it. Although I'm acutely aware of what he's doing, I hardly feel the pain anymore. I don't know if I've just become so desensitized to it all or if it's because I am starting to break apart.

The only thing keeping me going is the note from Hawk and my guys. Every time I'm dumped back in my cell, I dig it out from where I hid it between my mattress and the bedframe. When I read it, that spark of fire I'm so used to holding close for warmth, sparks within me, reminding me I'm not ready to give up the fight.

My body may be weakening, but my mind is still strong. It screams at me to keep fighting, to not let *them* win. Smoothing out the crinkled piece of paper, I read the words scrawled in Cam's messy handwriting. I soak them up like they're a lifeline. They *are* my lifeline. They're the only thing keeping me going.

You're so brave, Baby Davenport. We're coming for you. We love you.

My boys are coming for me. I have to make sure I'm strong enough to fight when that day arrives.

Baby Davenport

EPILOGUE

I tore the dorm apart when we got home, but it still wasn't enough to squelch the insurmountable rage I'm feeling. The things I saw today, what I heard, the way she looked. It took everything in me not to go fucking apeshit right there and then in that vile compound, but that would have been a surefire way to have our parents getting suspicious and watching us more closely—the last thing we need right now.

"What's the game plan?" Cam asks, all business for once. We're all perched on stools around the kitchen island, and there's a fire in his eyes like nothing I've seen before. Cam is one of those people. When he sets his mind to something, he gives it a hundred and ten percent. He doesn't quit until he's the best. That's why he's done so well with swimming, and if he put his mind to it, he'd be challenging West for the top position in the year. Right now, though, all of his energy is focused on getting Hadley back and, looking at the others, they're just as determined.

"I'm just throwing this out there," Beck says, already raising his hands in a placating gesture as he looks at me, "but I take it there's no point in going to your parents?"

I shake my head. "I've thought about it, and I don't think so. I don't trust them to get her back. If they realize how instrumental she is, they may decide to keep her there indefinitely, and if they know that we knew she was there, they will make sure we never saw her again."

Beck grits his teeth, giving a tight nod in agreement, before he reaches out to grab a beer from the table. As his fingers wrap around the bottle, Mason's hand snaps out, holding onto his forearm.

He stares in confusion at one of the tattoos on Beck's forearm. "What's that?" The tattoo he points to is one of his more basic ones. It looks like it was inked on him by a child or a drunk person.

Beck's lips press tightly together as he pulls his arm out of Mason's grip, looking reluctant to share whatever the story is behind the tattoo.

"Seriously?" Cam snaps. "Now hardly seems like the time to reminisce and get to know each other better."

Scowling at Cam, Mason focuses his attention back on Beck. "There's a gang in Black Creek called the Reaper Rejects. Do you know them?"

Beck's brows furrow as he looks at Mason in confusion. "No. This"—he waves his hand at his forearm—"was just some stupid name a bunch of kids with nothing better to do came up with."

"Yeah, a bunch of kids that lived in Black Creek," Mason muses. "What happened to your friends?"

"I have no idea. We lost touch after I moved away."

Mason's fingers tap absently against the counter surface as he thinks. "What if they grew up and started a gang—one that's quickly taking over Feral Beast territory."

Beck's brows climb up his forehead at that revelation.

"So what?" Cam sighs, frustrated.

I see when Beck catches on to whatever Mason is getting at. They better start sharing with the class real fucking soon.

Mason turns his head to look at each of us.

"So, that could mean we might be able to level the playing field."

"I need to go to Black Creek to see for myself," Beck states, his mind running a million miles an hour as he thinks. "There would be no guarantee that they'd help. This isn't their war."

"But it is," Mason argues. "Our parents are lifting kids off *their* streets."

"If you're right, and it's my old friends running this gang, there's no way they'd be okay with that."

"Exactly." Mason nods his head. "What do you think they'd do if your friends got in their way?"

"He's right," I add, throwing in my two cents. "Our parents will soon become their problem. If you can convince them to help, we might actually have a chance of defeating our parents, for good."

We discuss it over some more, and Beck tells us more about the guys he used to run around with back in the day—Cain and Oliver—before he agrees to leave for Black Creek the next day.

That night, as I rest my head against the pillow and stare up at the ceiling, I think about Hadley and what she's had to endure; sick in the stomach at the fact we had to leave her behind today.

We've got a plan, little sis. We're going to get you out of there, and we're going to make every single one of them suffer.

Sweetheart

WHEN HADLEY GOES MISSING

Swiping a hand over my face, I shove aside my exhaustion as I push open the door into the guys' dorm. "Anything?" I ask, already reading the answer from their strained faces and the fact it looks like I interrupted them mid-fight.

Great, all of us at each other's throats. That's just what we need.

"We're trying to figure out where Lawrence could be hiding her," Mason explains.

"What about the compound?" Given the fact we haven't found her yet, I feel like that's where he must be hiding her.

West shakes his head. "Nope. Not since I hacked into her GPS, anyway."

"Still, he could be keeping her there," Mason argues.

"I just think it's too obvious, right under our parents' noses," Hawk dismisses.

"It might not be completely implausible," I say, all four of them turning to look at me. If they knew what I know, they'd agree. But they don't know, because Hadley never fucking told them.

"What the fuck does that mean?" Hawk snarls viciously.

I hold his gaze for a moment before looking away, running my hand through my hair. *Fuck. I have to tell them.* My eyes close and I sigh. "She should really be the one to tell you this, but you need to know." Meeting Hawk's stare, I state, "Hadley grew up in the compound."

"Yeah, right," Hawk scoffs. "Like Lawrence could hide a kid in the compound all those years without any of our parents hearing about it."

"Actually," Mason interjects, "that might be more plausible than you realize. When I was up in Black Creek, I, uh, uncovered something about Nocturnal Mercenaries." Mason spills everything he uncovered over spring break. It's nothing I didn't already know, but hearing that they're taking kids from my hometown doesn't sit well with me.

"Kids?" Cam questions after a moment, sounding confused. "What? Like eighteen-year-olds?"

Mason shakes his head, his next words only sickening me further. "The kid I saw on the video looked more like eight or nine."

"So they're taking kids from Black Creek?" I question, stuck on that fact.

"Amongst other places, but Black Creek seems to be their main feeding ground. They have some sort of deal with the leading gangs there."

"Fucking kids?" Hawk snarls. "What the fuck is wrong with them? Is it not enough that they're already performing a black market service for God knows what sort of underground criminals?!"

I can feel Mason's eyes on me throughout Hawk's tirade. "Why are you not surprised?" he demands of me.

Meeting his steel gaze, I confess, "I knew."

"You *knew?*" West argues.

"And you never told us?" Hawk snaps.

"I couldn't."

West frowns, putting the puzzle pieces together. "That's the secret job they were getting you to do by threatening me."

"Yeah," I admit, crumbling beneath the weight of everything I've done, all in the name of protecting my little brother. When each of them looks at me expectantly, I fill them in on everything my father has had me doing. Every sick part of it.

By the time I'm done, I feel drained. Lighter than I did before, but giving a voice to what I've done somehow makes it all so much more real.

"You could have told us, man," Mason says, but I shake my head.

"Nah. This shit eats away at your soul." My gaze locked on West, I state, "I didn't want that for you," before glancing at the others. "For any of you."

My admission is met with wide eyes filled with surprise and what looks like respect. Perhaps a silver lining to all of this. Everything I did was to protect West and the others. It never mattered to me if he found out or not. He can hate me for the rest of our days, and I still wouldn't regret the choices I made, but if us fixing our relationship can come out of this, then at least it won't all have been in vain.

"So, it's actually possible that Lawrence could have taken her there," Cam muses, breaking the silence.

"I have to go back in a couple of days," I tell them. "I was planning on doing some snooping—try to find out if he was keeping her there."

"I still can't believe you've been doing all of this for me," my brother murmurs, his face all bunched up as though he doesn't know what to do with the information. "How have you coped, carrying that burden all by yourself?"

"Hadley figured it out," I confess.

What I don't admit is that she's the reason all of this hasn't swallowed me whole. The only reason I'm able to get out of bed in the morning. Why I'm able to pick myself off the floor when I get back from that godforsaken place and fall into a pit of despair.

"Jesus Christ," Hawk swears, throwing his arms in the air as he stalks back and forth across the apartment. Apparently *this* is his breaking point. And he still doesn't know everything. As if he can read my thoughts, he bites out, "It's like we don't even fucking know her. What other secrets is she keeping?" Seeing the look on my face, he snarls, his expression deadly. "What?"

I try to figure out the best way to phrase what I have to tell him, before saying, "It wasn't luck that she was able to kill that mercenary. She had all of the skills to do much worse to him."

"There's no way," Cam scoffs, although the furrow of his brows says he doesn't quite believe that. "If that's the case, why didn't she kill my dad and run off years ago?"

My shoulders droop and I sigh. If only it were that easy. I'm sure Hadley has wished she could do exactly that every time Lawrence gets close to her. "Lawrence is her Achilles' heel," I explain. "He's terrorized her since she was a little girl. All the attitude and combat skills in the world won't help her if she can't stand up to him psychologically."

Baby Davenport

HAWK'S DECLARATION

I smack my hand against the marble counter, gritting my teeth as I close my eyes and try to gain control of myself. It's impossible. Anger itches under my skin like a fucking infection, heating my blood and making it difficult for me to think straight, never mind sit still.

I can't take this sitting around anymore. Fucking talking and planning. I need to move. To do something. Something other than sit here and think about her—wondering what that sick fuck is doing to her, what she's having to endure being back in that hellhole. I still can't wrap my fucking head around that. She grew up there? I've played Beck's words on repeat since he told us Hadley's deep, dark secret, but no matter how many times I tell my subconscious he's got it wrong, a gut feeling within me knows I'm only fooling myself. Everything makes so much sense now: how she was able to sneak in and out of our apartment without any of us noticing, her ability to fight, the scars.

The fucking scars.

My stomach twists violently as I think about how small things like not saying, "Yes, sir," or being five minutes late for dinner would earn Mason a similar mark. What did the psychos that run the compound deem punishable by such extreme methods? I can only imagine—and I'd really rather not.

My fist bangs against the countertop again, my short fingernails digging painfully into my palm. Hearing Hadley's broken voice at the compound haunts my every waking moment. It would probably be the soundtrack to my nightmares too, if I slept. It took everything in me to walk away from her that day. And the guilt of leaving her there eats me alive, only exacerbated by the guilt of my broken promise to her. I made her a promise that Lawrence would never lay a hand on her again. A promise I failed to keep. I'm consumed by so much guilt I can feel it gnawing away at my insides, slowly devouring me and making it difficult to breathe. And so it should. I failed her.

Worst brother in the world award, right here!

With a fierce determination, I push down the guilt and anger and straighten my spine. Leveling my shoulders, I harden my features into the impenetrable mask I need them to be. Wallowing in self-pity isn't going to do her any good. Beck's gone to Black Creek. He'll get Cain and his gang of thugs to help us. I've no doubts about it; he has to.

Then we'll make a plan and we *will* get her back. Mason, Cam, West, and I have always had each other's backs. We'd go through fucking hell, endure any storm, to help one another. Hadley's one of us now. She might not know it, but she can count on us. I only hope the note I slipped her is enough to keep her going while she waits for us to get to her.

The words I whispered to her through the door come to mind. *"We're going to get you out, little sis."*

Those words were a promise—one I intend on keeping this time. They're a vow, a warning to anyone who stands in our way. I'll do whatever I have to get her back, to keep her safe. We're going to get her out of there, and I'll gladly annihilate any fucker who stands in my way. I'll be damned if I'm going to let *anyone* destroy my baby sister.

BREAK FREE
Book Four

R.A. SMYTH

Dove

PROLOGUE

Fifteen Years Ago

The party is in full swing when we arrive, precisely as planned. It took a while for everything to come together, but by the end of tonight, the Davenport name will be synonymous with grief and heartache.

"Ow, you're hurting me," the woman beside me hisses as she tries to tug her arm free from where it's linked with mine. I relax my shoulders enough so I'm not squeezing her arm, and scope out the room. Now that I've come this far, I just want it over with, but I have to play my part if I want tonight to go off without a hitch.

"Let's get a drink and mingle," I mutter, grabbing a couple of champagne glasses from a passing waiter. Handing one to my date for the evening, we make our way through the crowd, stopping every now and then to chit-chat with incessant suck-ups.

Just when I'm about ready to blow my brains out, Wilbert Warren shuffles his way through the crowd, the fat fuck already rosy-cheeked from too much alcohol.

"Lawrence, lovely party, isn't it?"

"It is." I return his too-wide grin with a tight smile and zero enthusiasm.

His glassy eyes move to the woman I brought with me this evening, carefully selected so she will blend in and get the job done.

"Who's your ravishing date?"

"Elise," she greets politely, introducing herself. "Pleasure to meet you."

"The pleasure is all mine." He reaches out to take her hand, kissing the back of it, and I have to bite my tongue to hold back my sarcastic comment. The idiot thinks he's so smooth, flirting with anything that's attached to a pair of tits, but it's beyond me how he managed to knock up not one, but *two* women. Money obviously speaks louder than good looks.

Elise emits a girly giggle that I know is all for show, but Wilbert eats it up like it's chocolate frosting, and the two flirt back and forth until Barton steps up to the front of the room, Maria dutifully at his side. Tapping the rim of his champagne flute, he speaks up, gaining everyone's attention.

"Ladies and gentlemen, we are honored to have you here to celebrate with us this evening. I still can't believe it has been five years since this wonderful woman agreed to marry me."

"If you'll excuse me, I need to use the ladies' room." Elise smiles softly, flitting her gaze my way before taking off through the crowd, just like we planned.

The second she's out of sight, Wilbert digs his elbow into my side to gain my attention, waggling his eyebrows like a pussy-deprived teenager. Sighing, I ignore him and pretend to focus back on Barton's pathetic speech. In reality, I'm with Elise, picturing her sneaking upstairs. All of our houses are built the same, so it wasn't difficult to give her directions to the nursery.

With everyone focused on Barton and distracted by the party, she should be able to sneak in unnoticed and take the girl, and we'll all be long gone by the time anyone realizes she's missing.

Elise returns by the end of Barton's boring speech, and I catch her eye. Knowing my unasked question, she gives a small, barely perceptible nod of her head, silently letting me know the job is done. She got the girl and has handed her off to one of my men, masquerading as our driver for the evening.

We mingle for a while longer, and I make a point of congratulating Barton and Maria, even though the words taste like poison on my tongue. The only reason I get through it with a straight face is knowing everything will change after tonight. While they are down here, showing off for their guests, their daughter will be on her way to the compound, where she will never see the light of day again.

As the night wears on, Elise and I get more explicit with our PDA, making it more than apparent that when we duck out early, and I can't be reached, it's because I'm too busy fucking her brains out. As anticipation thrums through my veins, that's *exactly* how I plan to fucking celebrate.

When we do finally stumble out into the cool evening air, we hurry to the limousine I hired. The driver tilts his head when he opens the door, and as I slide into the back seat, my eyes fall on the sleeping toddler lying across the leather seats.

Elise slips in beside me, and the driver closes the door, moving to the front of the car and starting the engine.

"What are you going to do with her?"

I don't know if she's second-guessing her decision, just curious, or simply trying to make conversation, but I don't care. She had no qualms about accepting my money in exchange for her role in tonight's plan, so even if she is rethinking her decision, it's too fucking late.

"That's none of your concern."

She shrugs it off, and we lapse into silence again until we pull up at the hotel I booked us into for the evening. The driver pulls open the door and helps Elise out. Sliding out behind her, I pause as I redo the button on my jacket and say in a low voice, so it doesn't travel, "Take her to the compound and come back in the morning."

"Will do, boss."

I stand and watch as the car leaves the parking lot, and only when the red lights have faded into the distance do I turn around, a victorious grin on my face. For the first time all night, I take in the slutty dress on Elise, noticing how her nipples are visible through the thin fabric and her long, toned calves in the heels she's wearing. My dick hardens. *Oh yeah, I'm more than fucking ready to celebrate.*

By morning, I'm sated and happier than I have been in a very long time. My phone has been going off for the last hour, but it's still early, so I don't answer it—after all, I'm meant to be in a sex-hazed cocoon.

The same limousine as last night pulls up at the steps, and the driver gets out as I open the door for Elise.

"My driver will take you wherever you want to go," I tell her. "I never want to see you again."

She doesn't say anything, all business, as she gives a sharp nod of her head and climbs into the back seat. I close the door behind her and turn to the driver.

"Any issues last night?"

"None. I have someone looking after her for now. When she's old enough, she can join the other recruits."

I nod in agreement, not giving a damn what the guards at the compound choose to do with the girl now. I don't give a shit about some useless child. I've achieved what I wanted, and now I get to revel in the fallout.

He moves to step away, and I stop him, gesturing with my head toward where Elise is hidden behind the blacked-out window. "Bowen, deal with this problem too."

I can't have any witnesses or risk her gaining a conscience and coming back one day. She needs to be dealt with, permanently.

Bowen grins maliciously. "Already done, boss."

As he walks round the limousine and climbs in behind the wheel, I walk toward my own car. Pulling my phone out of the inner pocket of my suit jacket, I dial the number I need and hold it to my ear. The phone rings twice before it's answered.

"You're going to get a call today from Barton Davenport. Whatever he offers, I'll double it."

"What do you want?"

"I want you to send him on a wild goose chase."

Hanging up, I slide into the plush leather seats of my Maserati. I fire off one final text, saying *'the job is done'*, and before I can put the phone away again, it starts to ring, Barton's name coming up on the screen.

Huffing out a sigh, I answer. He doesn't give me a chance to even spit out a greeting before his angry tone comes down the line. "Where the hell have you been? I've been trying to reach you all morning."

"Sorry, it was a late one. That girl I was with gave me quite the workout after we left the party."

I hear him huff on the other end. "Just get to the house. We need everyone from the board for a meeting."

"Why, what's going on?"

There's a second of silence before the angry snarl of his words hits me, warming me up like a glass of dark whiskey, and I mentally pat my back for a job well done. "Someone took my daughter."

Hadley

CHAPTER ONE

The blasting of death metal music—loud enough to deafen me—jolts me out of my semi-dream state, and I groan. My eyelids are too heavy, refusing to do anything more than twitch, and I quickly give up on attempting to open them. The strobe lights I can see flashing through the closed lids are enough to make me not want to open my eyes, even if I could. My exhaustion is bone deep, and I'm too tired even to try and lift my arms to block out the screaming as it threatens to crack my skull open.

A pounding headache starts up behind my eyes, nausea churning in my stomach as I flop over onto my side. I manage to gather enough energy to blindly stretch an arm out and lift a piece of bread from my food tray on the floor.

They keep switching up their torture tactics. They'll starve me for a few days, and just when I think I'm about to die from dehydration, they bring me food and water and deprive me of sleep instead.

I can't do anything but merely exist. I force the bit of stale bread into my mouth, chewing and swallowing it, even as my stomach revolts. I know I'll need the energy, though. Hawk and the guys are coming, I *know* they are, and I need to be ready to do whatever I can to help them when they arrive. I refuse to be a dead weight for them to carry out of here. That thought ignites a fire in my stomach, and I manage to chew the last few mouthfuls of bread with more vigor.

Despite the amplified vibrations of the electric guitar and some dude screaming about how his heart was ripped out, I pass out. But when I next jerk awake, the room is oddly quiet. Deafeningly so. Or maybe my eardrums burst and I can no longer hear anything. I'd honestly accept that reality at this point—anything to not have to listen to that god-awful racket again.

Unfortunately, the sound of a shoe scuffing the floor confirms not only that I have *not* lost my hearing, but that I'm not alone in here. And in spite of my weakened state, my fight-or-flight response kicks in, and I jump upright, ready to defend myself as my ingrained instincts flare to life.

"Hey, hey," a guard hushes in a slow, soothing voice intended to put me at ease, yet does anything but. He raises his hands to indicate he means me no harm, except there's no way I'm buying that bullshit.

My eyes narrow, and I track his every move, ignoring the lightheadedness at my abrupt shift upright and the thrumming of the pulse in my neck as my heart rate skyrockets. Without lowering his hands, he points to a tray of food he left on the floor. *What the fuck? The guards never come in here to leave food.*

His weird behavior only makes my eyes narrow further as I try to suss out his motives. As far as I know, Lawrence hasn't given the *okay* yet for Bowen, or any of the guards, to touch me—beyond beating me. Even if he had, Bowen has already insisted on first dibs, and none of the guards would ever dare go against him. Lawrence might think he runs the compound, but really, it's Bowen. The only reason he hasn't done as he pleases with me is because this is what he truly gets off on—the infliction of pain. He's a sadist through and through. I also get the impression that Lawrence has told everyone I'm still a goddamn virgin—probably to ensure they don't disobey him. I don't even fucking care, so long as it keeps them away from me.

"Eat," the guard grunts, jerking his head toward the tray.

I scoff. Does he seriously think I'm that stupid?

"Why, so you can drug me and do whatever the fuck you want with me while I'm passed out? Yeah, no thanks."

The corner of his lip lifts in a small, barely-there smirk. *Who the fuck is this guy?*

"Not my thing. I prefer my girls to be conscious when giving them the time of their life."

I scoff again, sneering in disgust.

"Eat," he continues to persist, this time using the toe of his boot to shove the tray closer to where I'm sitting on the narrow strip of thin foam posing as a mattress. "You'll need your strength."

"For what? Whatever new torture method you've devised? I'd rather not be conscious for it."

He shakes his head and huffs out a sigh like I'm deliberately being difficult, but seriously, what the fuck did he expect?

"Don't be so morbid," he snarks. "The sun will rise on another day, and may it be better than the last."

His words freeze me in place, and I can't do anything except sit and stare at him. My eyes roam over his face, searching for something familiar, but the room is too dark. Maybe his nose looks like hers did? It's been too long. I try to bring her face to the forefront of my mind, but it's blurry, and I can't recall the finer details.

"What did you just say?" My voice is low, threatening yet unsure, and I notice he's watching me just as closely. A strange intensity replaces his nonchalant demeanor.

"You know that saying?" he questions, his tone sharp.

I hesitate before responding. "A friend of mine used to say it all the time."

He nods his head slowly, before lowering into a crouch. He's careful to stay on the opposite side of the small space in the cell so he's not crowding me.

"My mother used to say it to my sister and me when we were kids." My eyes dart between his, trying to piece together what he's saying. I feel like there's something significant in his words, but what? My brain's too dulled from lack of sleep and food to figure it out.

He continues to scrutinize me, and I can tell he can see my brain trying its best to think straight. "That was before she died. My sister and I ended up in foster care, and we were separated. I haven't seen her since she was five."

My stomach roils precariously as the penny drops, my breaths coming in uneven rasps.

"You're Marcus." My voice is nothing more than a whisper, and the second I say his name, his face collapses in pain, aging him in a split second. The heartache shines through his eyes, making me wonder how I hadn't seen it before.

"Meena was my sister."

I can't do anything but sit and stare at him, unsure whether I'm hallucinating or this is actually real. *Her brother.* I remember her telling me about him. He was the one who essentially cared for her—ensured she was fed and had clean clothes. Their mom was a druggie, too obsessed with getting her next fix to give a shit about her kids. When she died from a heroin overdose, the two of them were put into foster care, where they were separated. The day she was sent to a different home than him, was the last day they saw each other.

When Meena first showed up at the compound, she used to cry herself to sleep every night. Back then, all the recruits slept in the same large room, and some of the other kids would give her a hard time over it. I didn't really understand her sadness. I'd never cared about anyone enough to miss them that much, but I could practically feel the pain pouring off her, and could only imagine how difficult it would be to lose the one constant in your life. Never mind ending up trapped in this godforsaken place.

My eyes roam over his face. "I don't..." I shake my head, words failing me as I struggle to wrap my head around the fact that Meena's brother is here right now. "How?" The word is barely a croak, and even though my head is swimming with questions, I'm incapable of saying anything more.

He's still crouched in front of me, with his arms leaning on his thick, muscular thighs. At my question, his head drops to his chest, and he releases a heavy sigh, fraught with so much heartache it sucks the oxygen out of the room.

"When I aged out of the system, I went looking for her. I got the address of the last foster home she was at, but the people there told me she'd run away three months earlier." A pained expression crosses his features, and in frustration, he runs his hand over his short, buzz-cut hairstyle.

"I searched everywhere for her. I spent months trawling the streets, trying to find her or anyone who had seen her. No one knew who she was, or at least, they weren't willing to tell me anything if they did. I'd gone years without viable leads, and I'd all but given up, until I heard the whispers about kids being taken from the street. I knew it was a long shot, but I had nothing to lose. It took fucking forever to get any sort of proof, and even longer to find a way in."

"How long have you been here for?"

"Just under a year."

So he must have arrived shortly after I left.

"So you know..." I trail off, unable to say the actual words. Only I don't need to. He gives a quick jerk of his head, lowering his gaze so I can't see the grief that I have no doubt is swimming in them.

"I do." His words are choked, and it takes him a second to compose himself before he says anything further. "They told me you were friends."

I swallow around the lump clogging my throat, licking my already dry lips. "We were. She..." I pause, struggling to find the right words, before blurting out the blunt and honest truth. "She saved me."

"How..." He looks away, emotion again rendering him speechless as nausea churns in my stomach, and the memories of that day rush to the surface.

"No," Meena cries vehemently as tears stream down her face. She's on her knees in the middle of the ring, perched beside the unconscious form of a new recruit.

"Kill her, or I'll kill you," the guard snarls, growing impatient with Meena's stalling.

Every day, we have to get in the ring with each other and fight until someone can't get up again, but we've never been asked to kill our opponent before.

Meena sobs over the girl's unconscious form, shaking her head as the rest of us watch on with bated breath.

"Meena," I cry out, my own cheeks wet. Her head lifts to look at me through watery eyes, and the look on her face breaks some essential part inside me. "Please," I plead, ignoring the fact I'm begging her to kill someone.

Her lower lip trembles, a fresh wave of tears streaming down her face, however, she doesn't give in. If anything, the longer she looks at me, the more her resolve reinforces itself.

Her face hardens into a determined mask that only destroys me further because I know what it means. I'm shaking my head, silently imploring her not to do this, but the second the guard told her to kill the innocent kid in front of her, I knew she would never do it. No amount of pleading with her will ever change her mind because, unlike everyone else in this cesspit, myself included, Meena is pure. She's got the heart of an angel. She's been here for about five years, but she's never once let the scumbags in this place destroy the goodness in her. She's got something none of the rest of us have—integrity.

It's because of her that I'm still here, that I'm still human enough to know right from wrong, even though at this moment, I'm begging her with everything I have to do the wrong thing...just this once.

Please, Meena. I can't live without you. It's selfish of me because you're far too good for this place. If this is the life you're meant to live, then death is your only way out. You can spend eternity with the angels in heaven, where you belong. But, *please,* If you're not here to pull me back from the darkness, I'm scared of what I'll become.

"I don't have all day, girlie," the guard snaps. His harsh words break Meena's attention from mine and she lifts her chin when she looks at him.

"No." This time the word comes out strong, defiant, and even though I'm dying inside, I'm so fucking proud of her.

The guard doesn't appreciate her defiance though, and he takes a menacing step toward her, followed by another. Every time his heavy boot hits the floor, my stomach twists dangerously, and my pulse skyrockets. I'm not sure if I'm about to be sick or pass out.

Instead of watching him draw closer, Meena returns her gaze to mine, and I hold it, refusing to look away from her. "I love you," she mouths, even as tears flow steadily and fear shines in her eyes.

"I love you too."

It feels like it takes forever, yet no time at all, for the guard to traverse the distance to where Meena is kneeling, and his hand snaps out, slapping her across the face with enough force that she falls onto the mat, a gasp escaping from her.

He doesn't stop there, kicking out with his steel-toed boot next. The air rushes out of her as his foot connects with her stomach, and she curls in on herself. I don't even realize I'm screaming and trying to get to her, until I receive my own slap. Only then do I notice I'm being restrained by another guard. I barely register the sting in my cheek as I watch the scene unfold, Meena's cries of pain drilling into my mind. It's a sound I'll never forget. It'll haunt my nightmares for the rest of my days.

"Meena," I scream, still fighting off the guard. It's a futile attempt, but it doesn't stop me from clawing at his skin, even as he threatens and curses me.

I don't know how long it goes on for, but eventually Meena's cries fall to whimpers before they just stop, and all that's left is the heavy panting of the guard still attacking her. The solid thud of his boot hitting her small body. Blood covers her face, making it impossible to tell if she's alive or not.

When the guard finally steps away from her, giving me an unobstructed view of her limp form lying lifeless on the mat, I stare pointedly at her chest, waiting on pins and needles to see if it rises or not. When there's no sign of movement, the last of my energy drains out of me, and I collapse in the guard's arms, sobbing and crying.

"Let me go," I cry, pushing against him again, but he still doesn't release his hold. The sick, fucking piece of shit guard who killed my best friend lifts his head, searing me with his ice-cold gaze that lacks any ounce of empathy. For every speck of emotion he's missing, I throw all the pain and devastation threatening to drown me right back at him. I glower at him as fiercely as he's scowling at me, and in the clashing of our gazes, I promise him the most excruciating of deaths.

One day, Major Bowen will be at my mercy, the way Meena was at his. He's going to beg me for amnesty; he's going to pray for it to end. Throughout it all, I'm going to soak up every pained scream and desperate whimper, and when the light dims in his eyes, he will look up at me and know his death was of his own making.

I CAN'T TELL her brother any of that, though. "She died because she refused to be turned into a monster like the rest of us." A single tear slips down my face. "She was the best person I have ever known, and she held on to that until the very end."

He ducks his head, and I glance away, giving him a moment while he sniffs and wipes at his eyes. Tears still shine in them when he looks back at me, but there's a determined set to his jaw that reminds me so much of Meena. It has a fresh wave of tears threatening to break past my defenses.

"We've gotta get you out of here. I wasn't there for Meena when she needed me, but I can at least help you."

I have no idea what he can do to help, not without putting himself at risk, and I won't let him do that for me, but he can at least be on alert for when my guys come, which should be any day now, hopefully.

"I have people coming for me," I tell him, watching as his eyebrows lift in surprise. "I don't know when, but you might be able to help them when they get here."

He nods. "Anything I can do, I will."

Sweetheart

CHAPTER TWO

Despite being on the road before the first rays of light graced the horizon, it takes all day to drive to Black Creek, and I'm exhausted and disheveled by the time the urban wasteland makes its mark on the surrounding landscape.

Too much coffee and unappealing gas station food have me feeling both buzzed and groggy. The combination leaves me short-tempered and impatient as I park the car, throwing up a faint hope to whatever God above that likes to pull on our puppet strings, it will still be there when I return in a few hours.

Walking the streets of Black Creek feels both familiar and also like I'm seeing the place for the first time. It's been ten years since I was last here. Ten long years. And while the streets look the same, they also appear much more bleak and dreary than I ever remember. Walking past an alley, the stench of piss hits me like a freight train, and I can hear the telltale signs of homeless people farther down it, most likely scrounging for scraps and huddling together for warmth.

Staying alert, I make my way quickly down the street until I come to the first bar I've seen. It's the last unit at the end of a row, and the wild roar of a drunk crowd escapes the bar before I even open the door, which looks like it's barely hanging on its rusted hinges. The whole thing squeaks dangerously as I yank it open and step into the crowded, sweat-staunched room. As I push my way through the horde of perspiring bodies toward the bar, I scan my eyes around the room. After all these years, I thought I'd feel a sense of coming home when I stepped foot back in this rundown town, but taking in the scruffy riff-raff surrounding me, I have never felt more out of place. If I don't belong here, and I don't belong in the overprivileged world of Pacific Prep, where do I belong? A voice at the back of my head whispers *with Hadley*, and the rightness of those two words pacifies me. With that reminder of my girl, I push through the throng of people lining the bar with renewed energy.

"What can I getcha?" the bartender asks. He's an older man, in his fifties, with long gray hair pulled back in a bun. There's a cigarette sticking out of the corner of his mouth, and as he inhales, the tip glows, the ash growing along the end until it falls off, dropping into a glass in his hand.

I keep my features neutral as he exhales and smoke curls out from between his parted lips. The stink of cigarettes permeates the air between us and clings to my clothes.

"Beer. Eh, Bud will do," I grunt out, figuring something in a bottle is the only safe choice.

Grabbing a bottle, he uncaps and hands it to me. As he slides it across the bar, I lean in toward him. "And I need some information."

Lifting an eyebrow, he doesn't say anything, waiting for me to continue.

"I need to know where I can find the Reaper Rejects."

His eyes widen slightly, and I don't miss the way his gaze drops, taking in my clean, form-fitting t-shirt and jeans that aren't hanging off my ass like half the idiots in here. I deliberately dug out an old top and jeans from the back of my dresser, wanting to do my best to fit in here. But regardless of my casual attire, my scruffy beard that's grown out since Hadley disappeared, and my tattoos on display, it's obvious I'm not from around here. I look too put-together. I don't have that mix of vicious hunger and hopelessness in my eyes or the same haggard appearance as most of the people who have lived here their whole lives.

"They operate out of a house on River Street," he responds, his gaze lifting to meet mine.

River Street? *Fuck*. I've been skeptical about Mason's theory that Cain and Oliver are behind the quickly growing Reaper Rejects, but it's hard to deny the mounting evidence. Knowing their base of operations is River Street—the street all three of us grew up on, only makes it that much more likely that it's them. Why else would a gang set up there? There's nothing particularly appealing or strategic about that street. It's nothing more than rundown, dilapidated houses, half of which lay empty and had been claimed by the druggies and vagrants that roam this town in abundance.

Nodding my head, I lift the beer bottle, taking a long swig of the cool, frothy liquid. It's cheap and bitter, but it helps to calm my nerves. With one last once-over, the bartender moves to the opposite end of the bar to serve a newcomer, and I sweep my gaze over the rest of the room, not really taking any of it in as my thoughts drift to the friends I once knew. There's so much that could go wrong tonight. There's no guarantee the men that lead the Reaper Rejects are still the same friends I knew growing up. Time changes us all, and living here hardens you in this dog-eat-dog town. It makes you cynical and untrusting. Ten years is a long time, and for all I know, they saw my leaving—and the fact I never reached out to them—as an act of betrayal. By turning up unannounced, I could be walking into a fight, if not a bullet to the head.

Yet, as I finish the bottle, slap a few dollars down on the sticky counter, and push my way through the writhing mass of drunken bodies out into the dark street, there's no doubt in my mind. There's no second-guessing, or hesitation. It doesn't matter what greeting I receive from them, or how high the risk is, I still have to try. For Hadley.

I make it back to my car and drive over to River Street on the opposite side of town. Familiarity crashes through me as I pull onto what used to be my childhood street. The place where the guys and I played chicken with passing cars, where my mother would stand on the front porch and yell for me to get my ass inside and ready for bed. The place where our childhoods came collapsing down and everything changed.

As I gradually make my way down the street, I slow the car to a crawl, probably looking like I'm preparing for a drive-by shooting. I pull over to the curb, stopping opposite what was once my house. Staring out the window, I take in the narrow, two-story terrace house. The place is shrouded in darkness, not a single light on at this late hour. Everything about it looks the same as it did the day I left. White paint is peeling off the front door and window sills, and the front steps still look like a hefty weight will have them snapping in two. Patches of dead grass and weeds have pushed their way up through the concrete slabs lining the house, only adding to the derelict appearance.

With a heavy sigh and a nostalgic ache in my chest, I tear my gaze away from my old front porch, instead focusing on the place two doors down from where I'm parked. Cain's childhood home. Unlike the darkened houses on either side, light streams out from the front windows, lighting up the road in front of the house, and I can just about make out two men standing in the shadows on the porch.

Well, I didn't come all this way just to sit here. May as well get out and see if this guy really is Cain. I push open the car door and step out, striding confidently along the sidewalk with my head up, looking like I belong. As I reach the metal gate, I notice the guys by the door stiffen and stand upright, eyeing me warily.

"The fuck do you want?" one of them calls out.

"I'm looking for Cain," I shout back. "Does he still live here?"

The guy at the door hesitates for a second. "Who's askin'?"

"Beck Jacobs."

He silently assesses me for a long moment before jerking his head in indication for his buddy to go inside, hopefully to get Cain—assuming it is actually Cain in there and not some high-out-of-his-mind drug dealer that I'm about to piss off.

The two of us stand, facing off in silence for a long moment, until the screen door creaks open. With the light from the hallway behind him, it's impossible to make out the details of the man standing in the doorway, and I squint through the glare, trying to work out if the tall, broad, muscular man in front of me is the lanky kid I used to know.

"Fuck me. Talk about a blast from the past."

His voice is a deep rumble, nothing like the hoarse rasp I remember when it was breaking as a pre-teen boy. Regardless, there's a familiar ring to it, and for the first time tonight, a sense of rightness settles in me.

"What's it been? Ten years?" Despite not being able to see his features all that well in the dark, I can feel his eyes roam over me. "What brings you back to my run-down neck of the woods?"

"I heard about some thugs going by the name of Reaper Rejects. Had to come see if I needed to beat up some shithead kids."

He barks out a cold laugh, making it impossible for me to figure out if this is all friendly banter or if my being here has pissed him off.

"Guess you better come in then."

Nerves coat my palm as I push open the squeaking metal gate and walk up the short walkway of cracked and broken flagstones, climbing the rickety steps that protest under my weight to the front porch.

In the dark, with the interior light behind him, it's impossible to get a read on him, even this close. Not that he gives me much time to analyze him anyway, turning on his heel as my boot hits the porch, and pulling the screen door open so he can step inside.

I follow him into the once-familiar house. Growing up, the four of us spent a lot of time here. Eating in Mama B's kitchen and hanging out in the living room. While the interior looks the same, right down to the markings etched into the living room door frame, marking each of our heights, it's completely different. A haze of smoke floats in the air, and following the noise coming from the room on my right, I find a bunch of thugs lounging on sofas, their feet up on the worn coffee table, with beers and cigarettes in their hands as they watch me closely.

Cain gives them a brief nod as we pass, which they all return, still keeping their wary gazes on the intruder and potential threat—me.

"Where's Mama B?" I question as we move past the living room.

"Dead," he gruffs out sharply, and I can't tell if it's from emotion or a silent warning to drop the topic. I swallow my questions and ignore the pang of sadness at hearing of her passing, following him down the hall to the kitchen.

"Out," he barks as we enter the small kitchen at the back of the house. The few guys in the room quickly grab their stuff and scurry out, sparing me a glance as they move past me.

I hardly notice them though, as Cain turns to face me. In the harsh light of the kitchen, I can see everything that I couldn't make out in the darkness. I take in the tight set of his jaw and the hardness in his eyes that never used to be there. Combined with his unruly black hair, brushed up and stylishly tapered along the sides, and his dark stubble, he looks menacing and unapproachable. Tattoos cover his neck, running from his stubble-covered jawline to dip beneath the neckline of his top, and, dropping my gaze, I can see swirls of colored ink running down his arms and decorating his fingers. I can only guess that every inch of skin in between has been branded too. I can feel his eyes assessing me, the same way I'm scrutinizing him. He's got the same Reaper Rejects tattoo scratched into his skin that I do, except his is on his left bicep. Looking at his right one, there's a newer, more professional-looking tattoo that I'm guessing is his gang's insignia. It also says Reaper Rejects, only with a reaper's scythe cut across it.

Pulling my gaze away from the myriad of tattoos adorning every inch of visible skin, I instead notice how much he's filled out since we were kids. He's no longer the scrawny boy he used to be. Rather ropes of muscle make his biceps bulge against the tight fabric of his black t-shirt as he crosses his tattooed arms over his chest and leans back against the kitchen cabinets. He criss-crosses his feet at the ankle, drawing my attention to the dark denim jeans hugging his thick thighs and the black, steel-toed combat boots he's wearing.

My gaze returns to his face, taking in his hardened expression, and *fuck*, if that steely look in his eye doesn't kill a little something in me. What has he had to survive in the last ten years? Or is this all a consequence of that day?

After another tense moment of silence where he continues to take me in, his eyes lift to mine. Just when I'm beginning to think I might have made a huge mistake coming here, a wide grin splits his face and he shakes his head, releasing a chuckle.

"Fuck, man. It's so good to see you."

He closes the distance between us, clapping me on the back, and I sag in relief as I embrace him back, a nervous chuckle escaping me.

"You too, man. It's been far too long."

He steps back, his hands still on my shoulders as he studies me. "You look fucking good, man. Finally outgrew that beanpole body you had."

He laughs again, and I swear, every time he does, it sounds more like the old Cain I remember.

"Shut up, asshole. Look at you! You on fucking steroids or something?!"

He just laughs and shakes his head, pulling open the fridge door and grabbing a couple of beers. He hands one over to me, and I twist the cap off.

"Is O around?" I'm suddenly dying to see him and get the three of us back together again. It wouldn't be like old times—too much has happened for that—but it would be fucking great to catch up.

"Nah." Cain takes a long sip of his beer before answering me. "Dude got himself caught up with The Feral Beasts after, you know…" He trails off, a darkness clouding his eyes, but he quickly shakes it off. "Ended up in prison last year. He's got about a year left of his sentence, and I'm hoping he'll join me here when he's released"—he shrugs—"but we'll see."

I nod my head, not altogether surprised by that news. Honestly, I'm just glad he's still alive. In this world, you never know. I'm sure plenty of the kids we went to school with are long dead and buried.

"So this is all really yours?" I gesture around the room, but we both know I don't mean the house.

"Yup." He beams proudly. "We're a small outfit, but we're growing. With the Beasts gone, we've seized a lot of their territory and started making a name for ourselves."

I nod. I've got a thousand other questions, but I don't feel I can pry into his operation here and, honestly, I might be better off not knowing the ins and outs of it.

"What about you? I bet you made something of yourself." A cocky smirk curls the corner of his lips. He's so damn sure I made it in life. "Bet you've got the whole shebang—white picket fence, two-point-five kids, and the perfect housewife."

I bark out a humorless laugh. He couldn't be further from the truth.

Rubbing the back of my neck, I grimace, glancing away before focusing my gaze back on him, fixing him with a determined look. "That's actually why I'm here. I need your help."

He doesn't say anything, watching me closely before nodding for me to continue. I move to the old, wobbly wooden table that I remember the four of us carving our initials into the underside of when we were seven years old and collapse into the chair, taking a deep breath before I catch him up on the last ten years—more specifically, all the shit that's come to light in the last twelve months.

The whole time, he leans against the kitchen counter, listening intently with an impassive expression that gives nothing away. When I finish, a weighted silence lingers in the air as I wait impatiently to see if he'll help—if he's even able to help. I didn't miss the tight lines around his eyes when I mentioned kids being lifted off his streets, and if nothing else, I'm hoping that threat to his town will be enough to incentivize him.

The kitchen door opens, and a young-looking guy pops his head in. "Sorry to interrupt, boss. We need you for a minute."

Cain gives a sharp nod, and the guy ducks out, closing the door behind him.

With a sigh, Cain runs his hand through his unruly black hair and fixes me with a look. "It's late, and I dunno how long this will take. You can have my old room for the night, and we can discuss what to do in the morning."

"You'll help us?" I question, half in surprise and half in relief.

He huffs out a breath. "'Course I will, brother. Not only are they taking kids from *my* streets, but they've got your girl." He comes closer to me on his way to the kitchen door, clapping me on the shoulder. "You love her, right?"

"I do."

He nods, having already known the answer before I confirm as much. "Then we're going to get her back."

Without another word, he leaves the room, and the extent of my relief almost has me keeling over. Suddenly, getting Hadley back doesn't feel like an insurmountable task. I have no idea what the fuck we're going to do, or how Cain and his guys can help, but the fact he's on our side and willing to try lights a fire within me, sparking hope and a newfound determination.

Exiting the kitchen, I grab a duffel bag from my car that I'd packed just in case and saunter up the stairs to Cain's room. I hear him and some of his men talking in a side room at the front of the house when I amble past, but whatever his gang is involved in is none of my business. I'm not about to shit all over his hospitality by getting caught eavesdropping, so I quickly walk past the closed door.

As I crest the top of the stairs, I pause, my eyes finding the closed door at the end of the hall. Swallowing around the lump of emotion clogging my throat, I head in the opposite direction, knowing my way to Cain's old room like I do the back of my hand.

Pushing open the door, I huff out a dry chuckle. It's not much different than when we were kids. He's upgraded the bedding, from Ferrari sheets to plain navy ones, but other than that, everything's exactly the same. All his childhood shit is cluttering the top of the dresser, and I move toward it when I notice a photo of the four of us. We were only five or six at the time. Oliver's got a black eye, and Cain's sporting a split lip. My head is thrown back while I laugh, and Evie is scowling at all of us. I run my thumb over her face, sighing heavily before setting it back on the dresser and moving to the bed. Dumping my bag on the mattress, I sit beside it, rubbing my hand down my face before pulling my phone out of my back pocket and firing off a text to the guys, letting them know I'm here and all is going well so far.

A second later, the phone rings and West's name pops up on the screen.

"Hey," I greet wearily, lying back on the duvet to stare up at the ceiling.

"How's it going?"

I know he and the others are impatient for good news. All of our hopes reside in getting Cain and his men on board.

"Good, I think. Cain's agreed to help us. We'll put together a plan in the morning."

"Good." Silence falls between us, and all I can hear down the line is the faint sound of his breath. Now that he's got reassurance that I haven't fucked everything up and that we're working on a plan to get Hadley back, I expect him to hang up, but to my surprise, he speaks again. "What's it like being back there?"

His voice is a smooth, deep rumble, and all of a sudden, I just want to be back in their dorm room with them all. *When the fuck did that happen?*

"It's weird. I have spent so much time thinking about coming back, and now that I'm here, I just wanna come home."

He doesn't respond at first, but the silence is comfortable, contemplative, unlike the usual tension that threads between us.

"Well, sort out everything in the morning and come home tomorrow. It'll, uh, be good to have you back."

He rushes out the last few words like they burn his tongue, but regardless, they still bring a smile to my face. We speak for another few minutes before hanging up, and I quickly strip and climb into bed. I drift off to sleep to the thought of killing every fucker keeping me from my girl.

~

When I emerge from my room the next morning, I pause as my gaze zones in on the door opposite the hall. It's inauspicious, and you wouldn't give it a second glance if you didn't know what was behind it. But I do know what's behind it—at least, what used to be.

I don't even realize I've moved, but the next second, I'm standing in front of it. My hand trembles as I reach out, wrapping my palm around the cool door handle. My stomach churns, but wild horses can't drag me away right now as I turn the handle with a clammy hand and slowly push the door open.

I'm not sure what I expected, but storage boxes and old furniture in a white-walled, nondescript room were not it, and some sort of weird half-whine, half-laugh chokes its way out of me as I peer around the bland room.

"I had it converted into a storage room," comes Cain's emotionless voice from behind me. "Couldn't stand looking at it, knowing she'd never step foot in there again."

I nod, unable to utter a single word, as I tear my gaze from the room to look back at him. I can see the pain in his eyes; grief and vengeful anger pour off him.

He blinks and it's gone, an impassive slate replacing the emotion on his face. "No point in dwelling over shit we can't change. Your girl's still alive. Why don't we focus on saving her?"

I give him a tight nod, *still* unable to speak past the lump in my throat and, closing the door behind me, I follow him down the stairs. The house is quiet, and there isn't a soul in sight as he directs me to a small office.

He sits in the overstuffed chair behind a desk with disorganized piles of papers wedged into the small space, and I drop into one of the two chairs taking up the last remaining bit of space.

"Right, so to recap last night. Your dad and his cronies own Nocturnal Mercenaries, and they've been taking kids from Black Creek and forcing them to work for them." He waits for me to nod in agreement before continuing, "And one of them has kidnapped your girl and is holding her there against her will?" I nod again, my teeth gritting as anger flares within me over the whole fucked-up situation.

"Alright. I've told my men to be here in an hour so we can talk about what to do." He leans back in his seat, getting comfortable. "So tell me about this girl. You met her at that fancy school?"

I ease back in my chair. I'm keen to get on with the meeting and get a plan I can take back to the guys. But I guess, for now, there's nothing I can do but wait for Cain's men to arrive.

"Yup, she's a student there." I know he won't judge me, but I do suppress a smirk when his eyebrow quirks in surprise.

"Didn't picture you falling for some rich princess."

I snort, knowing Hadley would be furious if she heard him right now. I ignore the pang in my chest when I think of her. "She's far from that. She's more like someone from here." His other brow climbs up his forehead, and I decide to tell him the truth about her. It's best that he knows she's not some helpless girl who needs rescuing. Yeah, sure, that's what we're going to do, but I know once we get to her, she'll be more than able to hold her own.

"She grew up there. They molded her into a trained killer. She had the guts to escape, to try and make a life for herself. But this sick fuck is obsessed with her, and he dragged her back there. She's strong, *incredibly* strong, but I don't know if she will survive that place a second time."

I watch his expression change from surprise to shock to something much darker. Shadows roll in behind his eyes, and I know exactly where his thoughts have gone. *Evie.* Girls being taken against their will is a hard line for Cain. One he won't tolerate.

There's a hardness in his eyes that I only ever remember seeing once before, on the day Antonelli's men came and stole Evie from her own front yard, shooting up the street while they were at it. That day changed our entire lives. It ripped apart the safe bubble we lived in. Where, as children, we thought we were invincible, and it exposed us to the true horrors that exist in this world. That was the day we stopped being children and became adults, hardened to the world around us. It was a day I'll never forget.

He leans forward in his chair, resting his elbows on the wooden desk. His features are tight, and his nostrils flare as he says, "We're going to get her back, brother. Then we're going to make sure they can't steal another kid ever again."

An hour later, Cain leads me into the front room of his house where, at first glance, about twenty men are waiting for us. They're relaxed, lounging on the sofa, until we enter. Then they all straighten, their full attention on their leader. It's interesting to watch, to see the respect and power Cain has over these men. Long gone is his easy expression, instead he's wearing the impenetrable mask of a leader, ready to direct his men.

Cain slowly looks around the room, meeting each of their eyes and giving a few of them nods of acknowledgment before he addresses everyone.

"My brother, Beck, has brought a serious matter to my attention. He has informed me that kids are being stolen from our streets." He pierces each man in the room with a steely gaze. "Turned into soldiers; forced into being killers. All so some rich fuckers can line their pockets."

I'm watching his men closely, assessing them. While I trust Cain, I don't know any of the men in front of me. So I notice when their jaws clench and their eyes narrow in anger.

No one speaks, though, and Cain continues, "You all know I don't stand for children being taken against their will and used as pawns." A few men nod or murmur their agreements. "As if that isn't insult enough, they've taken Beck's girl."

All eyes fall on me, and I subtly straighten my spine and lift my chin, letting them see the parts of myself that are still very much Black Creek. I allow the darkness in me to rise to the surface and shine through my eyes. Let each and every one of them see that I will destroy *anyone* who gets in the way of me saving my girl.

After an assessing moment, one of the men focuses his attention back on Cain and speaks up, "We can't let them get away with that. Tell us what you want us to do."

The rest of the gathered men give sharp nods of agreement, and the room fills with determination and a willingness to fight as shoulders are pushed back, and everyone leans forward to hear Cain's plan.

Cain lets a small, prideful smile lift the corner of his mouth before he barks orders at his men. "The organization is Nocturnal Mercenaries. Beck here can give us a schematic of the compound where they are keeping the children and his girl. Still, we need to know as much as possible about their setup before we wreak havoc—guard changes, security systems, and any potential weaknesses. Reach out to your contacts, and see if you can find anyone who knows anything about them. We need to move quickly, so get it done, boys."

With renewed energy and the promise of impending violence, the men quickly get to their feet, pulling out their phones and talking to one another as they leave the room.

"What now?" I ask Cain, unable to sit still and do nothing, but not knowing what I should be doing.

"Now you go back to that stuffy school, and I'll call you when we know more."

"The guys and I are going with you when you go," I tell him in a fierce tone that brokers no argument.

He quirks an eyebrow. "The guys?"

I might have conveniently left that detail out earlier. "Her brother…and the other guys Hadley is…dating."

His eyebrows climb to his hairline, and I can see he's smothering a laugh. Questions dance in his eyes, but now isn't the time to get into any of it, something he realizes as he lets the topic go.

"They can handle themselves?" he asks, and I nod. "Fine. We could do with all the manpower we can get. You should get back though, before anyone notices you're missing. The last thing we need is them realizing you've been up here."

I agree. We have no idea how close of a watch any of our parents are keeping on us. Before I leave, I draw up a schematic of the compound, and Cain gives me a burner phone which he'll use to contact us when he's got more information, so we can all work on a plan. He promises it will take no more than a day or two, and I'm holding him to his word. I don't know how I know, but I can feel it in my very bones. My girl doesn't have much longer. It's like I can feel her giving up with each passing day. I *need* to get her back before she's irreparably damaged.

Firefly

CHAPTER THREE

"Fucking hell," I snarl, banging my fist against the table as I glower at the computer screen in front of me, ignoring the tired itch behind my eyes and the jittery adrenaline from too much caffeine. Ever since we got back from the open day, I have spent every moment trying to hack into the compound's security system. To have any hope of getting Hadley back, we need access to the compound's cameras and security, yet I can't find a backdoor into either.

Huffing out a breath, I grind my teeth, and for what feels like the millionth time, change part of the code before grabbing my mug and going to top it up with a fresh cup of coffee. *God knows I'm going to need it.* We can't go after Hadley until we have a way into the compound, and we can't get a way in until I crack this fucking code. Until that happens, I won't be sleeping or doing anything else that takes time away from helping Hadley.

The kitchen is empty, and checking the time with the clock on the oven, I realize it's only four a.m.—no wonder no one else is about. My sleeping pattern is entirely out of sync. Rubbing at my tired eyes, I brew a fresh pot of coffee.

Once it's done, I fill the mug to the brim, taking a long, much-needed gulp of its life-sustaining properties.

"What are you doing up?" Hawk's voice is thick with sleep as he pads barefoot into the kitchen. In his half-awake state, his eyes roam over my face, likely seeing the exhaustion from too many days of no sleep. "Ah, haven't been to sleep yet."

I rub my lids with my fingers and shake my head.

"Not having any luck with the compound's security?" The strain of being away from Hadley for so long is getting to him, evidenced by the fact he's awake at the ass-crack of dawn, but regardless, his tone is soft.

"I can't decode their encryption." My voice breaks, exhaustion and defeat making me feel utterly worthless. This is what I'm good at. It's the *only* thing I can do to help. "If I can't get in, then we—"

Hawk claps his hand on my shoulder, cutting me off. "You'll get it."

I lift my head and look into his eyes, seeing the swirling storm of emotions in his gray depths. We're all a complete fucking mess without Hadley—even Hawk. He might have been the last to come around to having her here, but now he's as invested as the rest of us, if not more so.

"I know you will." He takes the mug from my hands. "Now go get some sleep. You're no good to anyone when you can't think straight."

I open my mouth to protest, before sighing and closing it. Maybe he's right. A power nap wouldn't hurt. It's not like I can do anything while the program runs the new code.

"Yeah, maybe you're right," I reluctantly agree, moving past him back to my room. Glancing at the computer, I don't see any updates, so I take Hawk's advice and grab a quick nap. I don't even bother to get undressed, collapsing onto the bed. I'm out before my head even hits the pillow.

A loud beeping noise interrupts my dead sleep, making me groan. My eyes are so heavy, I don't think I could open them if I tried. The noise infiltrates my foggy brain again, making me jolt upright.

I squint at the computer screen, unable to make out the blurry text as I fumble around on the mattress for my glasses. Finding them, I hurriedly slide them up my nose and fix my gaze once again on the screen as I rush across the room.

Taking a seat, I get to work, my eyes bouncing across the screen, unable to believe what I'm seeing. I did it. *I motherfucking did it.* A disbelieving laugh escapes me as my fingers fly across the keys.

"Guys!" I call out, unable to rip my eyes away from the lines of code in front of me long enough to share my good news with everyone else.

I hear footsteps as the guys come running.

"You're in?" Excitement threads Hawk's voice as he rushes into the room, and I hear the others close behind him.

"I am." I've managed to find a backdoor access into the compound's central system, meaning I can access their door codes and control the gates.

I feel everyone crowd around me as I remain focused on the screen, working my way through the system. My brows furrow the more I search. "We might have a problem, though." I huff out a breath, becoming frustrated when I can't find what I'm looking for.

"What is it?" Cam asks, leaning in for a closer look, as if that will help him understand what he's seeing on the screen. Based on the way his face wrinkles in confusion, it doesn't.

I groan in frustration, having gone through every nook and cranny I've gained access to. "I can change the door codes and lock down the facility, and I'll be able to open the gates to get us in and out."

"That all sounds like good news," Mason says warily.

"Yeah, but I don't have access to the cameras."

"Why not?" Hawk's voice is all business, ready to deal with this new setback.

I shake my head. "They're not on here. They must not be connected to the internal system." I run my hand through my hair in exasperation. "They must have the cameras hooked up to a remote network."

"And you can't just hack into that too?" Hawk asks.

"No." I sigh. "Not without knowing what network it's connected to."

"The compound's not connected to the same network as our parents' houses?"

"I don't think so. I'm still trying to work through some highly encrypted pathways, but I haven't found anything yet."

"You'll get there." Hawk squeezes my shoulder. "This is great, West. Now we'll be able to get into the compound and move around unobstructed."

I give him a small smile, but I'm frustrated about the cameras. I'm desperate to get eyes on Hadley and reassure myself that she's okay. Plus, seeing inside the compound would enable us to pinpoint exactly where they're holding her and allow us to keep tabs on each other once we're inside. I have a bit more time to work on it, in any case. Beck won't be back from Black Creek until later tonight, and it will take us a day or two to put a plan in place.

∽

It's been two days since Beck came back from Black Creek. Fourteen days since Firefly disappeared and nearly three weeks since I laid eyes on her. But tonight, all of that changes.

We've been chatting to Cain ever since, formulating a plan, and tonight's the night we finally make our move. I've been through the company's mainframe, and I know how to change the access codes and lockdown the whole compound. The entire place is set up similarly to a prison so that if there are any issues in one part of it, that area can be locked down until an override code is entered. Once we're outside the gates, I'll change the override code and lock down the entire compound so we can get to Hadley without interference—assuming they are still holding her in the interrogation block. When we got back from the open day and told Beck where she was, he was surprised, claiming he'd only ever seen new recruits being held there, so she may have been moved somewhere else since the open day, but we won't know for sure until we get in there.

Unfortunately, I haven't managed to gain access to the security cameras, so we're going in blind. I'll need to find the control room as soon as possible to deactivate the cameras so no one can track us or sound the alarm.

Pulling up the map I drew of the compound—based on what we saw on the open day and Beck's limited knowledge—on my tablet, I trail the route to the control room and from there to the interrogation block.

"You've got the security side of things sorted?" Hawk asks. All four of us are in the living room, anxiously waiting for Beck so we can head out. He's not questioning my ability; he just needs the reassurance that everything is ready.

"Yup, we're all good." Despite the nerves taking over me, my voice is confident. I won't be much good if we run into any guards or, god forbid, an actual mercenary—although, at least, I've got my contacts in this time—but *this* I can do. I have the same confidence in my computer skills as Mason or Hawk do when they take on an opponent in the ring, or Cam when he obliterates his competitor in the pool.

With a sharp nod of his head, not needing to hear anymore for him to be convinced that the job is handled, he focuses back on his stretches, limbering himself up for the inevitable fight to come.

There's a knock at the door, which must be Beck, and Cam goes to answer.

"What the—"

Wilder shoves his way past him into the apartment.

"What are you doing here?" Hawk growls angrily as he glares at Wilder, pissed-off with his intrusion, now of all times, when we're all on edge.

"You didn't think I was going to let you go without me." He scoffs, uncaring that he's angering an already temperamental Hawk.

The idiot is wearing all black, but in white, across the front of his top, is written #darkknighttotherescue. I can see Mason staring daggers at it, as I ask, "How did you even know we were going tonight?"

He just shrugs, and before any of us can argue with him any further, there's another knock at the door. Fuck, that better not be Emilia trying to tag along too. We don't need even more people to worry about tonight.

"Shall I get that?" Wilder doesn't wait for a response before pulling the door open, a completely out-of-place grin on his face.

"What the fuck is he doing here?" Beck retorts, storming past him with a small bag slung over his shoulder. Just like the rest of us, he's dressed in all black, the long sleeves covering up his tattoos. There's a determined set to his jaw, and his shoulders are pushed back, his chin held high.

"He says he's coming," I answer him, as he drops his bag on the island in the kitchen. Turning, he gives Wilder a cursory once-over before dismissing him, pulling open the zipper on his duffle.

"Fine, but it's at your own risk. We're not going to carry your damn ass if you end up with a bullet in you."

Beck's too busy rifling through his backpack, so he misses Wilder's crazy grin. It's as if the thought of getting shot excites the fucking psycho. I don't know what the fuck happened to him to make him think taking a bullet is something he wants to experience, and I'm relatively sure I don't want to know.

"What?" Hawk snaps, turning his glare on Beck and gesturing to Wilder. "He can't come with us."

"Why not? He's another body. We have no idea what we're going to be up against. If he wants to come, let him." Beck lifts a handgun—a fucking handgun—out of his bag, and suddenly any argument about Wilder is forgotten as all eyes fall on the sleek, black, metal contraption in his hands.

"What the fuck is that?" I exclaim.

He quirks an eyebrow. "A gun." *Asshole.*

I narrow my eyes on him, and he explains before I have to ask him more asinine questions.

"Cain gave me one for each of us, in case we need it."

Cam moves closer, looking at the gun with wary interest, and Beck holds it out for him to take.

"I've never shot one before," Cam murmurs, reaching out to take the gun and weighing it in his hand.

"None of us have." Hawk's glaring at the gun, looking equally unsure as he debates what to do.

"It's easy." Beck takes the gun back from Cam. Pointing to a small lever on the grip, he flips it down. "Safety off"—he flicks the switch back up—"safety on." He tightens his hold on the grip and lifts it until his arm is stretched straight out in front of him. "Point, aim, and shoot." He drops the gun back to his side, looking at each of us. "Easy as that."

I scoff, not buying that bullshit for a second while squashing the questions I have about how he knows how to do that shit. Wasn't he like thirteen when he left Black Creek?

Lifting another gun out of his bag, he hands it to Mason. Well, he tries to. Mason sneers at the thing and waves it away. "No thanks. I prefer to rely on my fists."

Beck shrugs, moving to hand Mason's gun to Hawk. Still scowling at the metal contraption, he takes it, glancing at the safety before shoving it down the back of his pants. Cam follows his lead while Beck hands yet another one to me. Without giving it much thought, knowing I can't rely on my fists or athletic ability like the others can, I take it from him, placing it in the small bag along with my tablet. Despite the fact I haven't a clue how to shoot the damn thing, I know I might need it. I'd be a fool not to at least have it on me. If worse comes to worst, I can at least bash someone over the head with it.

He hands the last gun to Wilder, but he waves him off. "Nah, I'm good too." He pulls a savage-looking knife—like nothing I've ever seen before—out of a holster strapped to his waist, which I hadn't initially noticed.

"What the fuck is that?" Cam gapes at the dagger Wilder is wielding with a proud smirk. The blade is about six inches long, with a sharp tip intended to puncture through flesh and muscle easily. One edge is serrated, while the other is a violent-looking sawback designed to tear a person's skin apart as it's yanked out. It's clear the weapon is intended for maximum damage.

"This," Wilder begins, with all the theatrics of a showman, "is a Marine Recon Bowie Knife, or as I've decided to call her, Marie." He flips the handle in his hand while Hawk scoffs.

"You're going to end up stabbing yourself with that thing."

Wilder narrows his eyes on him. "I'll have you know I'm professionally trained by Sunshine herself."

"Good to hear she's encouraging this insanity," Hawk retorts. "I'll be having words with her when we get her back."

"Well, what are we waiting for then?" An unusual seriousness takes over Wilder's features, and a maliciousness I've never seen before darkens his eyes.

I grab my bag with my tablet and newly acquired gun in it, and the six of us hastily leave the apartment. I glance at the others as we walk in silence to the car, taking in their tense postures and the determined glint in their eyes. All of us are more than fucking ready for tonight. Beck catches my eye, his brows lifting in a silent question. I give him a sharp nod, letting him know I'm good, and focus my gaze straight ahead, mentally running over the plan again.

When we reach the parking lot, we split up, taking two cars. I go with Hawk and Cam in Hawk's SUV, while Mason, Beck, and Wilder take Mason's four-wheel drive.

The drive passes mostly in silence, and when we're half an hour away, Hawk dials Mason's number, the sound of the call ringing over the car's Bluetooth before he answers.

"Let's go over the plan one more time," Hawk says tersely, before Mason can say anything.

"When we arrive," I respond immediately, diving into the plan. I have gone over it in my head multiple times today, as I'm sure Hawk has. However, ensuring everyone knows exactly what we're doing, especially with Wilder's last-minute addition, makes me feel better about our chances of success tonight. "I'll change all access codes remotely and lock the guards out of the system. I'll put the compound on lockdown so no one will be able to freely move around, unless they know the new code. I've sent the code to your phones. Beck, can you send it on to Cain?"

There's a pause where everyone checks their phones before murmurs of confirmation are heard.

"Will do," Beck responds before filling us in on Cain's role. "We're meeting Cain at the back entrance. West, you'll be able to get us in okay?"

"Won't be a problem. Once I lock them out of their system, I'll be able to activate the gate. They'll see that it has been opened. Still, they won't be able to do anything about it, and with the signal jammer Cain recommended, none of the guards will be able to communicate with one another or send for help to anyone outside the compound."

"Good." Beck's voice comes across gruff over the Bluetooth. "Cain and his men will get the kids out and any willing recruits, so we just need to focus on finding Hadley."

Even though he can't see me, I nod and direct everyone on how we'll achieve our part of the plan. I don't know how Cain plans on rescuing the kids, and honestly, I don't care. All of my energy is on Hadley.

Not long later, we turn off the main road onto an overgrown track leading to the compound's back entrance, and Hawk switches off the headlights. Following behind us, Mason does the same, and we drive in darkness for another few minutes, the car bumping over the uneven ground until we come to a stop. Squinting through the dark of night, there's no sign of anyone else around. We must be the first to arrive.

Grabbing my backpack, we get out of the car, and the others meet us at the hood. Unzipping the bag, I pull out the tablet and open the necessary program, getting ready to send the compound into lockdown once Cain and his men arrive. Once I'm sure everything's in order, I pull up the map for the building, and the others huddle around me so they can look as well. With the exception of Wilder, we've all been inside and spent all week constructing the layout as best we can. There are plenty of blank areas on the map—areas that weren't pointed out to us on our tour or that Beck hasn't been privy to, but it's the best we've got. We know enough to get to where they're hopefully holding Hadley, and that's all that matters.

"Currently, we're here." I point my finger to the back entrance to the compound, mainly for Wilder's benefit, but it can't hurt for all of us to go over the route one last time. "The last time we saw Hadley, she was here." I move my finger to the interrogation sector where we're hoping Hadley is still being held and quickly walk us through the plan one final time. I've been over it so many times now that I could navigate my way to Hadley's cell blindfolded and drunk. As I'm finishing up, the beam of headlights washes over us and the overgrown field we're parked in, before they're switched off, and several large vehicles pull up behind our own cars.

All of us watch tensely as a tall, broad man, covered in tattoos and looking like the last person you want to meet up with in the dark, climbs out of the nearest vehicle. I'm guessing this must be Cain. Beck moves to greet him and, despite his thuggish appearance and tight set jaw, he embraces Beck in a quick bro hug before coming to join the rest of us.

Casting my eyes behind him, I notice who I'm assuming are Cain's men climbing out of the vehicles and hovering nearby, eyeing us warily as they wait for further instructions.

"Guys, this is Cain," Beck introduces as the two of them move to join us.

Cain gives a sharp nod of his head, running his eyes in an assessing manner over each of us. His gaze lingers on me for a second longer. "This one's your brother?"

My eyebrows lift in surprise, not having expected him to know who I am, let alone be able to figure out in the darkness that I'm *the brother*. His voice is gruff and unfriendly, and combined with his hard, penetrating stare, I'm pretty sure he doesn't like me.

"Yeah," Beck confirms. "This is West."

His eyes sweep over me again, and I swear I see the corner of his lip lift in a small smile, but it's gone in a second, and I'm left wondering if it was just the darkness playing tricks on me. In a surprising gesture, he holds his hand out for me to shake, and I notice every inch of visible skin on his wrist and the back of his palm, right the way to his nail beds, is covered in ink.

Placing my palm in his, he gives it a quick shake before dropping his hand back down to his side. "Well, we can do proper introductions after we get your girl back." With a final look around the group, he asks, "Everyone ready?"

With my muscles tensed and my body coiled tight, ready for action, I nod along with the others.

"Alright then, let's do this."

Now that we're all here, I pull up the program to put the compound on lockdown and change the security codes. Checking that everyone has the new codes, I turn on the signal jammer, and before we all set out, I lift the gun out of my backpack and tuck it into the waistband of my pants, slinging the bag over my shoulders.

As a group, we move toward the back gate. When we're far enough away that we're still hidden amongst the tall grass of the field, out of sight of any guards, but close enough that we will be able to see when the gate is opened, Cain signals for everyone to stop, and I slip the tablet out of the bag and put in the code to open the gate.

The creak of the metal as it rolls back sounds like thunder in the otherwise quiet night, quickly followed by the yells of guards as they realize something is going on.

Once it's open enough for us to squeeze through, Cain and his men slip through the narrow gap, and a second later, we hear gunshots going off. Beck rushes through the narrow opening next, closely followed by Mason, Hawk, Wilder, and Cam, and I bring up the rear as another gunshot echoes in the still night air.

Standing on the other side of the compound wall, I watch as a guard crumples in a heap on the ground. Following his body to the ground, I stare transfixed at the two dead bodies in front of me. I knew there would be bloodshed tonight, but it's one thing to think it and another to see it unfolding before your eyes.

"Go," Cain insists in a whispered order. "Others will have heard the commotion. We'll distract as many of them as we can."

Giving him a sharp nod, Beck jerks his head for the rest of us to follow, and the six of us take off across the compound toward the main building. We stick to the shadows, crouching low and moving as silently as we can. We're about halfway across the open space when a large explosion goes off, and the sky lights up.

"What the hell?!" Cam whisper-yells as we all turn to look toward the source of the blast. All we can see are the tips of flames as they climb toward the night sky.

"Cain's distraction," Beck explains, quickly turning his back on the fire and moving on. The rest of us quickly chase after him, not about to waste the opportunity. Now that we no longer need to worry about avoiding the guards, we take greater risks, running across the open space instead of moving from building to building, relying on them for cover.

When we reach the main building, where the open day was held and where we last saw Hadley, I put in the new cipher, releasing a silent breath of relief when the keypad flashes green, and I tug the door open. Once inside, we keep our eyes peeled as we move stealthily toward the control room. It wasn't pointed out on the tour we received on the open day, but a guard had opened the door as we walked past, and I caught a glimpse of the room, with wall-to-wall computer monitors showing various camera angles, covering what looked to be most of the compound.

As we approach an intersection, with one corridor leading into the center of the building and the other running around the perimeter, a guard appears in the hallway in front of us, and we all slam to a stop. *Fuck.*

"Hey!" he yells. "What are you doing here?"

His hand goes to the holster on his hip, but before he can get his gun out, Beck fires off a shot, hitting the guy in the shoulder and propelling him backward. The sound of the gunshot seems to ricochet off the walls, alerting anyone who might be nearby to our presence. Although, given the distance between the guard and us, there was no way Mason or Hawk would have been able to tackle him before he reached his gun.

Another shot and the guard drops to the floor, lifeless. We all stand and stare at his unmoving form for a second, before I turn to look at Beck. His face is pale, his features drawn tight, but there's no regret there, only acceptance of what had to be done.

We hear them before they round the corner, the sound of boots thumping against the floor as what sounds like two more guards rush our way. Mason, Hawk, Cam, Beck, and Wilder all charge toward the far end of the corridor, wanting to take the newcomers by surprise when they come around the corner.

Hanging back, I let them do their thing, tag-teaming the guards while I move down the corridor to our left toward the steel door that marks the control room. No one has come out to respond to our commotion, but if there's anyone watching the security tapes, they'll know we're here and are likely frantically trying to get in contact with someone to raise the alarm.

I glance back at the guys over my shoulder, finding them still battling the guards. I can't wait around for them. *We can't waste any more time.* Pushing back my shoulders, I lift my gun out of the waistband of my black pants. I flick off the safety and hold it as steadily as possible in my trembling hand as I enter the security override code. Hearing the door unlock, I take a deep breath, whip open the door, and step into the room.

With my gun raised, I stare wide-eyed at the guard in front of me, who is leaning back in his chair, his legs spread wide, with his head tilted back and his mouth open and eyes closed.

A flashing light on the far wall snags my attention, and looking at it, I notice a list of various gates and buildings, with a lamp beside each one. All of them are turned off, except the one beside *the back gate*, which is flashing, mostly likely to indicate that it's open.

"Fuck, yeah, just like that," the guard groans, as I steer my attention back to him. Glancing down, my nose scrunches in disgust as the guard pushes some girl further down his disgusting dick. I hear her gag, and tears stream down her face as she stares wide-eyed at me.

I'm not even sure if she can see me clearly, but I lift my finger to my lips in a *stay-silent* gesture and return my focus to the guard. Confused about how he hasn't heard the commotion outside, I realize he's got wireless earbuds in. Then, as I look at the desk in front of him, I see he's got his laptop set up, covering one of the monitors. On the screen, some woman is trussed up in a way that looks like it can't be anything but painful as three men fuck her.

My scowl deepens, and I focus instead on the monitors that show Cain and his men fighting several guards out in the yard, and Mason taking down another guard right outside the door. This fucking waste of space is too busy getting himself off to notice the compound is being broken into and destroyed right before his eyes.

I almost can't believe our luck, but then I hear the girl gag again, and I remember that our luck is her misfortune. I tear my gaze away from the cameras and focus on the problem in front of me. Pursing my lips, I know what I have to do. I move on silent feet until I'm hovering over him, so close there's no way I can miss the shot. I raise my arm, ensuring the girl on her knees between his legs isn't going to get hit and, with my finger resting on the trigger, I point the gun straight at his head.

He doesn't deserve to live. He's involved in the fucked up shit going on here. Whether or not he actually touched a hair on her head, he hurt my Firefly. On that thought, my finger presses down on the trigger, and the next thing I know, blood is splattered all over me, the monitors, the floor, the girl, and the guard is slumped in his chair, with an undeniable hole in the side of his head.

My ears ring, and I think I lose track of time, or maybe the noise of the gunshot sent the guys rushing in here, as the next thing I know, Beck's face is taking up all of my vision. I can feel his hands on either side of my head and see his lips moving, but I can't hear what he's saying.

I blink a few times, focusing on him, and the noise around me rushes back in.

"West, West! Are you okay?"

I drop my gaze over my body. "Yeah. I'm fine, I think."

I'm faintly aware of the others talking to the girl, and a second later, she rushes out the door, hopefully to Cain and, eventually, safety.

Beck continues to stare at me for a second longer. Lines form around his eyes, and his lips press together, forming a thin line, before I feel his hand on mine, slowly pulling the gun from my grip and, glancing away, he flicks on the safety.

"You should have waited. You shouldn't have had to do that," he mutters under his breath, more to himself than anything else.

Now that the initial shock has passed, the fog in my brain is clearing. "I did what I had to do. If I hadn't killed him, one of you would have had to."

Returning his gaze to mine, his features are still tight. "It didn't have to be you."

He's wrong, though. I'm not about to let everyone else do all the dirty work. All these men deserve to die, but none of us are killers. Every life we claim tonight will haunt us, even Beck, despite the tough act he puts on. If the others are going to carry that burden for the rest of their lives, then I will carry it with them.

"It shouldn't be any of us, but here we are. We'll all do whatever it takes to get Hadley back."

After a moment, he reluctantly nods his head in agreement, knowing I'm right.

"Well, do what you need to do then, and let's go get her."

Turning away from Beck and the dead guard, I notice the others waiting nearby with worried and anxious glances, except for Wilder, who's palming his now bloody knife like he's about to shank someone. I'm not sure if it's terrifying or exactly what we need to survive tonight.

My hands are still trembling as I turn back to the wall of screens. I get to work and do my best to block out the dead guy dripping blood on the floor beside me. I scan my eyes over the various views of the compound, but when I don't immediately see Hadley, I focus on what I came here to do. I rewind back the security tapes to before we broke in and copy a strip of the recording, which I then set to play on a loop, so if anyone else in the compound, or remotely, looks at the cameras, they won't see anything amiss. I double-check that the communication systems are down, then nod my head at the guys so they know I'm done. Time to go get our girl.

As we rush out of the room, I notice a map of the compound on the wall beside the door. Lifting my tablet out of my bag, I snap a picture of it, just in case, and hurry after the others. All six of us run toward the interrogation sector, desperation pushing us faster with every step we take.

Hawk reaches the door first. His focus is single-minded as he hurriedly types in the access code and yanks open the door, rushing through it and over to the room Hadley was being kept in last time.

The rest of us are close on his heels. Like the last time I was here, it reeks of piss and hopelessness. It's a suffocating combination that activates my gag reflex and has me smothering a cough. My heart slams against my chest, worry for what state we're about to find her in, making me jumpy as Hawk once again enters the code at lightning speed. She sounded so broken when Hawk and I found her, and she's had to endure nearly another week here since then. The second the door unlocks, Hawk is tugging it open and storming into the small room, all of us hot on his trail.

My eyes dart around the drab room, and I feel the others pushing against me as we all try to squeeze into the small space.

"What the—" Hawk's words drift off as he turns in a circle, as if expecting to find her huddled in a dark corner. "Where the fuck is she?!"

Hadley

CHAPTER FOUR

I'm staring at the dark ceiling above me, trying to figure out how many days have passed since I heard Hawk's voice through the door, but the days all blend together. Maybe a week? But it could be as little as a few days, or a lot longer.

Hearing the sound of the door being unlocked, I freeze for a second before quickly hiding my surprise, eyeing the unknown guard warily as he steps into my cell.

"Get up," he barks out. "I don't have all day."

Marcus is too new to be one of Bowen's trusted guards in charge of me, but he's been able to sneak in a couple of times. Each time he does, he brings me a pile of food that I've mostly devoured, but I have kept a few non-perishable items that I've hidden in the dark corners of the cell and rely on for sustenance on the days no one brings me anything to eat. None of the guards come in here unless it's to take me to see Bowen. They definitely don't expect me to have gotten anything past them, so they never bother searching the small, dank space I've been calling home for however long now.

He hasn't been able to do anything about the death metal music on the days they decide to sleep-deprive me, so I'm still functioning on next to no sleep, but with food in my belly and hope flaring in my chest, I'm feeling a million times better than I was. I'm not as disorientated or as out of it as I have been, but as I get to my feet, I make my movements seem weak and disjointed as I stumble toward the guard.

I force myself not to pull out of his grip as his meaty palm wraps itself around my bicep, squeezing so hard I can feel his fingers pressing painfully into the bone.

He hauls me out of the cell, and I let him drag me along the hallway. I expect him to take me to Bowen's special torture room, but instead, he leads me toward the showers and shoves me under the cold spray. The sudden drop in body temperature makes me gasp as my body tenses, and I begin to shiver, even as the guard throws a coarse rag and a bar of cheap soap at me.

"Shower," he snaps, crossing his arms over his chest as his eyes roam over my naked body. I have almost gotten used to the leering looks from the guards—almost. I do my best to block him out as I scrub the gritty soap over my skin. Sticking my face under the faucet, I tilt my head back and close my eyes, taking a second to just be; to just enjoy the feeling of being clean.

"Today!" the guard barks impatiently when I take too long. Sighing, I quickly finish up and turn the water off. He throws a threadbare towel at me, and I hastily wrap it around my anorexic-looking frame, thankful for the minimal coverage, even if the rough material scratches my skin.

Next, he tosses me a pair of black pants and a top similar to what I wore on the challenge night and open day. As I pull the clothes on, I try to work out why I'm suddenly being gifted them. There is no way it's time for another challenge night already.

I have barely pulled the top over my head when he again grabs my arm and pulls me out of the room. With his tight grip on my upper arm, he escorts me down several empty hallways. I assume we're heading toward the fight room, but when he directs me down a corridor I'm all too familiar with, one I've been down many times before, my blood turns to ice, and I trip over my feet as sweat trickles down my back.

No, no, no.

That spark of hope I have been feeling the last few days quickly extinguishes. I'm not even in his presence yet, and I can feel myself shutting down already. Fear wracks my body, making it nearly impossible to breathe, and I begin to hyperventilate.

If I end up back in that room with him, it won't matter when Hawk and the guys come for me. They'll be too late.

The guard's grip tightens—if that's even possible—as my steps falter, desperately trying to delay the inevitable while I wrack my brain for a way out of this. Before I can do anything more than internally freak the fuck out, we approach the door. It looks like every other door in this fucking place. It's unassuming, and as the guard types in a code, ensuring he covers the keypad with his large frame so I can't see—not that it matters, they constantly change the code as soon as I'm in there—the room beyond is just as unimposing. The room is furnished like some small, self-contained apartment with a small kitchenette, a sofa, a television, and a bed. I have no idea what its purpose is when Lawrence isn't occupying it. However, when he's here, it's always this room where we have our fucked up 'dates'. Where he dresses me up like I'm his personal Barbie doll and tells me all about the oppressive future I want no part of. Somehow, I doubt it's going to be the same song and dance tonight.

The guard shoves me into the room, and I struggle to remain upright. Steadying myself, I spin around as he closes the door behind him and locks me in the room. My breaths come in rapid pants, and my hands tremble. As far as I'm aware, Lawrence hasn't visited me since he dragged me back here, so if he's here now, it's because he thinks they've had enough time to break me. Whether he's here to claim me as his or discard me once and for all, it doesn't matter. Neither outcome is in my favor.

Turning in a circle, I struggle to think of an idea. I've been in this room enough times to know they never leave anything in it that I can use as a weapon, but desperation has me pulling the kitchen drawers open anyway.

Empty. Empty. Empty.

Growling, I slam the last drawer shut and turn back to face the room. I don't get the chance to do anything else before the telltale sound of the door unlocking momentarily freezes me in place. I must look like a deer caught in headlights as my worst living nightmare strides into the room. His every step is filled with arrogant confidence, and his unfaltering smirk as his gaze roams over me shows just how sure he is that Bowen has broken me.

I swallow around the lump in my throat, watching him while he takes me in. His gaze slowly lifts until he meets my eyes, and the dark smile on his face grows wider.

"I brought you a present." Lifting his arm, there's a small bag dangling from his index finger with the brand name of a designer clothing store; the same store he brings me dresses from every time he visits.

When I don't move to take it, he walks over and sets it on the small kitchen table. He pushes it toward me, quirking a brow. "Aren't you going to have a look inside?"

I hesitate for a second before slowly approaching the table. The hair on the back of my neck stands on end with every step I take closer to him, and I watch him intently, alert for any sudden movement.

Without removing my gaze from his, I lift out the dress and set it on the table.

"You should try it on."

It's not a request, but for the first time, I don't obey him. I think he might be right; I think the last few weeks here have broken me, just not in the way he wanted it to.

Even though sweat coats my palms and makes my top stick to me, I say, "You forgot the heels."

Instead of angering him, my snark makes his sleazy smile deepen. "I've got a matching pair for you...when you're ready to come home."

Goosebumps pebble my skin, and I have to fight back a shiver at the thought of calling anywhere I'd have to live with him *home*.

In the next second, the smile drops off his face, and the way he looks at me—like I'm nothing more than a possession, someone to control and manipulate, is even more terrifying than his sleazy leer.

"Put. It. On." His words are sharper this time, leaving no room for argument. I clench my fist at my side as I try to stop the trembling in my hands. Licking my dry lips, I wrap my sweaty palm around the edge of my shirt, and with one final strengthening breath, I quickly whip it off over my head, ignoring the fact I'm exposing myself to this fucking asshole.

I quickly shrug off the pants, mourning their loss after only getting to wear them for such a short period of time, before I snatch up the dress and hastily pull it on. It falls to just above my knees, with a small slit up the back of the skirt. It hugs my chest, pushing up my tits in a disgustingly inviting way, and I swear, if I ever get out of here, I'm never wearing anything but pants ever again.

Stepping toward me, he reaches out a hand to fix my still-damp hair over my shoulder. I flinch, and a satisfied gleam ignites in his eyes.

Come on, Hadley. You don't need to be afraid of this asshole and his pathetic dick. I take a fortifying breath, telling myself, not for the first time, that I'm stronger than him. The words have never made a difference before, but it doesn't stop me from reciting them over and over in my head.

"Have you had fun the last few weeks?" he asks, knowing damn well what I have had to endure. At least he's confirmed my suspicions that I've been here for some time. I wonder how long it's been since the guys showed up. Surely, no more than a few days. They wouldn't have left me in here any longer than necessary. They have to be coming soon—any day now. But there's not going to be anything left of me if I let Lawrence have his way tonight.

"Wh—why me?" I ask, stuttering out the words as my palms sweat. I'm not even sure I care why he stole me. The why of it doesn't matter; it won't change anything, but I need to stall for time, because I see the ill intent in his eyes, and it terrifies me more than anything else I've had to face within these concrete walls.

His face pinches, and his hand that was playing with my hair freezes. He doesn't say anything, and I brace myself for the slap or sharp tug on my hair that I'm pretty sure is coming. As his brown eyes darken in anger, I regret saying anything at all, and my chest rises and falls rapidly as I wait for whatever punishment he decides to dole out.

He unwraps the curl of hair from around his finger, and I flinch as he raises his hand, but instead of hitting me, he runs his palm down the length of my blonde hair.

"Did you know your mother and I used to date?"

My eyes widen in surprise. Not at the fact I don't know something about my mother—I know next to nothing about her—but at the fact she would ever date someone like him. To me, he looks like a monster. Then again, as I've said before if you didn't know him as I do, didn't *hate* him as vehemently as I do, you'd probably think he was attractive. He's got Cam's good looks but none of his charisma or generous heart. He might look stunning on the outside, but his core is rotten.

"We were going to get married."

And the surprises just keep coming.

"Until your *father*"—he snarls out the word, spittle hitting my cheek as his face turns into the demonic thing I know all too well—"started taking an interest. One measly compliment from him and I was all but forgotten, kicked to the side so they could run off into the sunset together."

His fingers grab hold of my hair as his anger skyrockets, squeezing the strands in his fist and inadvertently tugging on the roots, making me wince—not that he seems to notice or care, too lost in his past to see me standing right in front of him.

"Then you and Hawk came along, and they had the picture-perfect family." His lip curls up as he sneers. "Meanwhile, the pathetic excuse of a woman I was forced to marry gave me an idiot son who only cares about chasing girls and swimming."

My own temper flares at his demeaning words. He's got no idea just how capable his son is. Cam is *the* top swimmer in the region, and he's got his national meet coming up soon, and I *know* he's going to ace that too. Beyond his swimming achievements, Cam is smart—when he applies himself—and more importantly, he's kind and loyal. He's got something his father will never understand—integrity.

As quickly as my anger ignites, it's washed out in fear as his hand wraps around my throat, and I stare into eyes overflowing with fury.

"What was it that made you spread your legs for him? Are you so stupid that you fell for his fake charm, like every other slut in that school?"

My eyes bulge as he squeezes my throat. I can feel my pulse hammering against the skin at the base of my neck, and my breaths come in short, frantic pants.

"You were supposed to be MINE," he roars. Color stains his cheeks red as his lip curls back, baring his teeth. He looks like a wild animal—unpredictable and dangerous.

His eyes are wide and manic as he stares back at me, disgust and revulsion clear to see. "I have no need for a slut," he sneers, "so which is it going to be—are you a whore, or are you mine?"

I must have a death wish, but then, death would be preferable to any sort of life with him. He resembles every one of my nightmares; it makes my limbs shake and my heart race at just the mention of his name. I have always hated how weak he makes me. In his presence, I'm nothing more than a trembling, terrified statue, barely able to speak, but I'm at my lowest point right now, so close to giving up that the thought of angering him doesn't affect me the way it should.

Lawrence was my own personal monster before I learned how to fight, before I was molded into the killer I am today. He makes me feel like the scared kid I used to be. But I'm not that kid anymore. He affects me in ways I don't fully understand, but regardless of the reaction he evokes in me or how his presence turns my body to lead, he will never, *ever* own all of me.

I tilt my chin and stare into the dark, bottomless pits that have become his eyes. "I will *never* be yours."

Violence flashes across his face, darkening his features, and my whole body shakes. I'm frozen in place, petrified, despite my inner bravado.

With his tight hold on my neck, he propels me backward toward the bed that occupies the far corner of the room.

"Maybe I should just start fresh with the next generation," he snarls. His face is inches from mine, but I can hardly focus on it as my vision blurs from lack of oxygen. Whether that's due to him cutting off my air supply, or my hyperventilating state, I'm not sure.

He loosens his grip on my throat as he shoves me onto the bed, and with the little bit of distance he's created, I'm able to gather my wits enough to calm myself somewhat and gulp down several lungfuls of air, relieved when the fog in my brain lifts somewhat, and I can think more clearly.

The meaning of his words finally registers with me, sickening me to the core. "You want to impregnate me and try your luck with my daughter when you're old enough to be her grandfather?" I bark out a caustic laugh that comes out more high-pitched and hysterical than I'd like. "Tough luck, you sick fuck." I've already pissed him off, so I might as well keep going. He's going to do whatever he wants with me anyway. The last couple of weeks here have undoubtedly robbed me of my sanity because I don't even care if I can't get my limbs to cooperate enough to fight him off. I'm so. Fucking. Done. Done with being at his mercy, with letting him dictate my every thought and control my every movement. Alive or dead, what does it matter, so long as I'm free of him.

So, I'm all in as I say my next words, knowing they're going to infuriate him beyond belief. "You think you have the men here under your thumb? You think they were okay with babysitting a pampered princess?" I laugh in his face, even as his fingers tighten around my throat, threatening to cut off my words. "If I wasn't a soldier, in their minds, I served no purpose...you must know what they do to their soldiers."

The blood drains out of his face, and his eyes flare in outrage. Quicker than I can blink, he's yanking up my dress, tearing it in his rush to confirm what I'm saying. With the fabric around my hips, he can plainly see the small white scars just above my pubic hairline or the one right below my belly button. If you didn't know to look for them, you'd hardly notice they were there.

"No," he gasps.

His fingers dig into my hip, and I know they'll leave bruises, but I don't even register the pain.

"Yup." I've never been so gleeful to have something so basic taken away from me. "They sterilized me. Wheeled me into the operating room like a fucking dog getting spayed."

His eyes are wide with shock as he moves his gaze to the other scar, and I notice when he spots the owl tattoo, with its wings spread out and a dagger driven down through its head, sitting just above it, entangled in the tail of the phoenix tattoo I had done as soon as I escaped last summer. It might have seemed like a waste of money, especially when I didn't have much. I had to forgo several nights in a motel just to afford it, but it was worth every penny. It reinforced everything I'd fought for, and everything I still had to achieve in order to claim my freedom. Since then, I've found something so much more meaningful than simply being free. I have found acceptance, love, family.

His eyes bounce between the mercenary symbol tattooed on my hip, and the small white scars, glaring daggers at them as if he can make it all disappear by sheer will. As fury builds within him, his gaze flicks up to mine and his grip on my neck tightens.

"You have been a complete waste of my time," he hisses scathingly. His face is scrunched in anger as he hovers over me, pushing against my neck and using his weight to drive me further into the mattress. The intent is clear. This time, he's not trying to scare me.

"She never gave a shit about you. She discarded you, wrote you off as dead. You were mine to do whatever I wanted with, but as you grew older and you looked so much like her, I thought I was getting a second chance." He laughs humorlessly, the harsh bark sounding unhinged in my ringing ears.

Unable to breathe, panic flares to life, and I claw at his hand, frantically trying to push him off me. Adrenaline courses through my body, clashing with the paralyzing fear I always experience in his presence. I feel like the two parts of myself are at war with one another.

Black spots obscure my vision as he leans in and presses his lips to my ear. "I know you've come to care about that brother of yours. Maybe once I'm done here, I'll send one of my men to torture and kill him. Tell him how you screamed for his help as I drained the life out of you."

Something in me snaps, and everything goes hazy. It's like I go into a rage blackout. Anger surges through my veins, burning away the all-consuming fear. It's one thing for this sick fuck to threaten and terrorize *me*, but not my brother. He's done everything he can to protect me, and I know he's fighting to get to me now. We only just found each other, and I'm sure as fuck not about to let anyone harm him.

I'm not sure what happens, but the next thing I know, Lawrence is lying on the floor on his back. His eyes are wide, his face pale, as I drive a knife into him, over and over again. I feel the warm flecks of blood hitting my face, and my hand slips on the blade as it sinks with sweat and blood. Yet I don't stop, even as the life drains out of his eyes and his body falls still beneath me.

I stab.
And stab.
And stab.

CHAPTER FIVE

My eyes dart frantically around the empty cell. "Where the fuck is she?!" Hawk snarls, echoing my inner thoughts. He spins, pinning West with his intense stare. "Where else would they be holding her?"

West's tablet is already in his hand, and lines furrow his forehead as he pulls up an image on the screen. Leaning in so I can get a better look, I notice he's looking at a much more comprehensive layout of the compound than the half-complete one we drew up several days ago.

"There's a couple of places, but I don't know for sure." Beck leans in over his shoulder to study the blueprints too, and West spares him a glance before focusing back on the screen. "You don't know where they conduct punishments?"

"No," Beck murmurs, staring just as intently at the tablet. He reaches out to touch the screen, zooming in on a particular part of the map. "But if I had to guess, I'd say it's there."

The rest of us move closer to see where he's pointing. "Why?" I ask, trying to work out how he's narrowed it down to that corner of the compound. The area he's pointed out on the blueprint isn't labeled as any particular sector. It could be a storage room or anything.

He grimaces. "Because there's a small morgue beside it and a loading dock out back."

His words make my stomach revolt, and a desperate need to find Hadley claws at my insides. Tension fills the air as the guys shift uncomfortably, and I can feel the molten hot anger pouring off Hawk as he restrains himself from storming out of here until we've got a plan.

Still deep in thought as he stares at the screen, Beck ponders, "Hadley once mentioned being taken to a room when Lawrence visited her."

"You think my father is here?" I snarl, my own anger flaring.

He shakes his head. "I mean, Lawrence would have ensured that whatever room she was taken to for his visits was secure, so they might be holding her there, away from any other guards or recruits.

I grit my teeth in anger, itching to get a move on. "Okay, so she might be there or wherever they take recruits to punish them." My nose wrinkles just saying those words, and I try not to picture young children being dragged kicking and screaming to some hellish corner of this place where they can be tortured. It doesn't work, and vomit blocks my airway as I struggle to swallow it down.

West, whose gaze hasn't once left the tablet while the rest of us talk around him, points to another unlabeled blueprint area. "There are a few blanked-out areas; they could be keeping her in any of them."

"We need to split up." Hawk's words are sharp. He's just as keen as I am—as we all are—to get a move on. We can't afford to waste time just standing around.

West nods his head in agreement. "You guys check out the blank areas on the map. I can go back to the control room and review the security footage to see if I can track her movements."

"You're not going there alone," Mason snaps. "I'll go with you."

"Wilder and I will check out the blank area beside the morgue," Hawk states before West can argue with Mason. "Cam, you and Beck go through the other unlabeled areas. We'll all meet back here in twenty minutes."

We all nod, and snapping a picture of the blueprint on West's tablet, Beck and I take off, heading for the closest area on the map.

Please be there, baby.

Reaching the first unmarked area, I share a glance with Beck, and with guns at the ready, we pull open the steel door. Nothing but an empty space lies beyond, with doors leading off of it. A pit forms in my stomach. *God, please let this just be a storage space.*

Each of us takes a side of the room, and I enter the code and pull open the first door, ready to shoot any fucker who lunges at me. I breathe out a sigh of relief when I find the room empty. My brows pull together in confusion as I glance around the small space. There's nothing but a bed in the room. Maybe it's sleeping quarters for guards on duty?

My gaze catches on chains dangling from the wall above the headboard, following them down to metal cuffs resting on the mattress, and any hopeful thoughts I had quickly dissipate.

"Beck." My voice sounds strained even to my own ears.

"I see it." The heaviness in his tone only makes me feel more ill, and I hurriedly shut the door, spinning around in the small space as I stare at each of the closed doors. One, two...five, six. *Six.* There are six rooms in here, and I'm guessing each one is laid out the same.

As my thoughts spiral, I stare wide-eyed at Beck, taking in the ticking of his jaw and the darkened color of his eyes. I'm too shocked to move, watching him as he clears the rest of the rooms. As soon as he enters the code for the last room, the door flies open, and a guard comes crashing through it, colliding with Beck. The two go tumbling to the ground in a brawl, fists flying as Beck wrestles to gain the upper hand.

Frozen for a second, I stand and watch them, before raising my gun and aiming it, except I can't get a clear shot. Tucking it back in my pants, I'm about to dive in and help when I hear a frightened whimper coming from the darkened room behind me. Forgetting about the fight in front of me, I take a hesitant step, then another, toward the noise.

Stepping into the doorway, my jaw drops when I find a young boy, no older than ten or eleven, wearing only a pair of briefs and chained to the bed. His eyes widen in fear, giving him an owlish appearance as he stares at me. When his lower lip trembles, it releases my feet and I rush toward him.

"Hey, you're okay," I try to reassure him in a low, calm tone. My eyes roam over the chains and the cuffs fastened around his wrists. "I'm going to get these off you. Do you know where the key is?"

The kid looks at me for a long second, before he glances behind me. Turning, I notice the guard's uniform shirt and holster in a pile on the floor. Moving over to them, I find a key sitting on top of the pile. Grabbing it and the shirt, I hurry back to the bed and quickly undo the cuffs.

"Here, put this on." I hand the kid the guard's shirt so he can cover it up, and he doesn't hesitate before taking it from my outstretched hand.

As he's doing up the buttons, a shadow darkens the doorway, and the kid freezes.

"He okay?" Beck's deep voice seems to echo around the small room.

"Yeah, he's fine. You?" I notice he's got blood trickling from a cut to his brow, and his lip is split, but he nods his head.

The kid's eyes bounce between us, filled with wary suspicion.

"What are we going to do with him?" I whisper to Beck. "We can't just leave him here."

Beck nods his head as he thinks, before moving to the bed where the kid is sitting and crouching down in front of him.

"We're here to get D. Do you know who she is?" Biting on his lower lip, the kid slowly nods his head. "Do you know where they're keeping her?" This time, he shakes his head, and although not being any closer to finding Hadley must frustrate Beck as much as it annoys me, he doesn't let it show. "We have a friend who is going to get you out of here, but I need you to do something for me. Do you think you can do that?"

The boy hesitates before nodding his head again, and Beck smiles reassuringly. Who knew he was so good with kids? I wouldn't have a clue what to do if he wasn't here. "Good. I need you to stay here." The boy's eyes widen, but Beck continues, reassuring him, "Nobody will be able to get in here. The code didn't work for the guard who was in here with you, did it?"

When the kid shakes his head, Beck explains, "That's because we changed it. If you stay here, I will tell my friend where you are, and he will come get you. You'll know you can trust him, because only the good people will have the code to open the door, okay?"

The kid's gaze lifts to mine. I give him what I hope is an encouraging nod, and when he looks back at Beck, he silently nods.

"Good man. You're going to be alright, kid. My friend will be here soon to get you."

Beck gets to his feet, and with one final look at the wide-eyed kid, we return to our mission of finding Hadley.

My brain is still trying to process the fucked up shit we just saw as we make our way back to the main corridor.

"Hold up a sec," Beck says, throwing his arm out to stop me. "Let me see the blueprint again."

Pulling up the map on my phone, I hand it over to him, and his lips thin as he presses them together, analyzing the map.

"What is it?"

"I remembered something Hadley once said." He lifts his gaze to look at me. "Those rooms back there were too small. The way she described her visits with Lawrence…she told me he would get her to make drinks for him, and he liked when they ate together."

My lip curls back on a snarl. "Like a fucking date?!" What the hell is wrong with that sick fuck?

Ignoring my angry outburst, Beck continues on with his train of thought, "It sounded like she was in an apartment. Not a small room like the ones we just saw."

Catching on to what he's saying, I lean in to look at the map with him. Zooming in on one of the unlabeled areas hidden at the back of the building, it seems like one relatively large room away from everything else.

"There. That must be where Lawrence took her."

My blood boils with anger, renewing my determination, and I take off toward that part of the compound, ready to take down any fucker that gets in my way.

Blood rushes in my ears, and my thoughts are only on holding Hadley in my arms again as I run to the far end of the building. I can just about hear Beck's footfalls as he races beside me; my focus is so fixed on finding Hadley that I don't even realize we have company until I hear a gunshot, and a second later, a weight slams into me, knocking me off my feet. I go crashing to the floor, the impact forcing the air out of my lungs.

A fist crashes into my face, and the tangy taste of blood floods my mouth. Snarling, I slam my knuckles into the asshole's side. I shove him off me and roll over until I'm straddling him, delivering another blow to his head. My fists connect with his face, over and over, until he's nothing but a bleeding pulp beneath me. Lifting my gun out of the back of my pants, I flick off the safety and point it at his head. With my finger on the trigger, I take a deep breath and pull. The shot rings out, and blood splatters me, but I'm barely aware of it over the whooshing of my pulse in my ears.

Panting heavily and still in shock, I lift my gaze, finding Beck fighting off two more guards. Stumbling to my feet, I go to help him, but he sees me.

"Hadley," he shouts, delivering a round-house kick to one of the guards. I hesitate a second longer, and he spares me a glance. "I got this. Go get our girl."

I give him a curt nod and, swiping a dribble of blood from the corner of my lip, I race away from the fight to the steel door at the end of the corridor that should have our girl locked behind it.

Entering the code, I pull open the door and step into an empty corridor. There's nothing here except a single door at the far end of the hall, and I rush toward it. Holding my gun in my right hand, the keypad flashes green and the door unlocks. I quietly open it and steady the gun in front of me, freezing at the sight before me.

My eyes dart from the dead man to the deranged, blonde-haired, blood-soaked angel straddling him, as she drives a knife into him like someone possessed.

Stepping forward, my gaze falls back to the dead body on the floor, and this time, I see past the blood, taking in the lifeless eyes of my father.

"Baby Davenport." The words are barely more than a whisper, coming out on the end of a shocked gasp. Nevertheless, they break through whatever trance she is in, and with the knife held above her head, ready to plunge into my father again, she freezes.

She lifts her eyes to mine. "Cam?" Her voice breaks, and studying her closely, I notice how thin her face has gotten. Her eyes look dull, her cheeks sunken, and tears track down her face, mixing with the blood spatter. She should probably look nightmarish, like some sort of born-again demon, but hovering over the dead body of her very own monster, knowing she conquered her fear—that she fucking saved herself—she looks like the fucking queen of hell.

The knife slips from her grip, clattering to the floor, and in the next second, I've closed the distance between us as I fall to my knees beside her. Her lips crash against mine, and her thin arms wind around my neck as my father's blood soaks into my pants.

"It's really you," she murmurs in wonder, her warm breath tickling my lips. My hands roam over her, unable to believe she's truly in my arms, relatively safe and sound. "You came for me."

Cupping her face in my palms, I drink her in. "It's really me, baby. It took too long for me to sort out my shit and let you in, I'm not about to lose you now."

She leans in, fusing her lips to mine once again. With every clash of our tongues, my fear and worry abate, replaced with an overwhelming need to hold her close and never let her go again. My arms wrap around her, and I mentally note how much thinner she is as I effortlessly drag her into my arms, not giving one single shit that she's drenched in blood.

"Cam," she moans, grinding against me. Her sultry tone goes straight to my crotch, and I pull back, highly aware of how fucking inappropriate all of this is.

Refusing to put any distance between us, she follows me, her lips chasing mine.

"Hadley—"

"Cam." Her voice is much more insistent this time, and as I look into her eyes, dilated with adrenaline, I notice how dull they look. They've always reminded me of the sky after a thunderstorm—electric and energized—but right now, they're hollow and listless. Like everything that made Hadley, Hadley, has been sucked right out of her.

Running my hands down her arms, I feel numerous lacerations. Tearing my gaze from hers, there are more cuts than I can count, littering her skin. Some are shallow and partially healed, while others look fresh from the last few days. Dropping my gaze to where her thighs straddle mine, I notice the same slashes across her legs. One particularly savage-looking gash running up the side of her thigh has me gritting my teeth as I struggle to contain my anger.

She places her hand under my chin and forces my gaze back to hers. Her small fist wraps around the front of my top, pulling me into her, and she kisses me deeply until I get lost in the feel of her. "Please," she murmurs. "I need to know this is real."

Those words threaten to break me, and her desperate, vacant look is my undoing. Even though I don't understand, I can tell she needs this now.

Beck's going to cut my fucking balls off if he comes in and catches me taking advantage of her in her vulnerable state, but fuck me if I'm going to let her down.

I surge forward, returning her kiss with a fierce passion. I let her taste every part of the panic and desperate longing I have felt since I discovered she was missing; let her see how much she's been missed, how much she's needed, wanted, and loved.

Holding her against me, I get to my feet, noting how light she feels in my arms as I set her on the small table. She never lets our kiss break, clinging to me like she's scared that if she lets go, I'll disappear, but she should know I'm not fucking going anywhere. I'm never letting her out of my sight again. I've been such a fucking idiot, wasting so much time being pissed at her and angry with myself when all along, I should have been doing this—showing her exactly what she means to me. She's had me captivated since I first saw her in the quad in her combat boots, with her hair whipping wildly around her face. In the last two weeks, I have realized that the way she makes me feel is so much stronger than lust, more powerful than like. I love her in an all-consuming, dark, possessive way, that means I'll always fight to get to her. I'll slay whoever I need to and conquer whatever obstacle is in my way. I don't want to control her the way my father did. I don't need to dictate every part of her life. I want to watch her fly free, to see her vanquish her enemies and become the formidable queen she was born to be.

Our teeth clash as my hands run down her sides. My skin tingles under her touch as she slips her hand under my top, and I groan at the contact. Kissing her passionately, I stroke along her inner thighs, hesitant to go further as her words echo in my mind.

My body tenses at the spark of anger. Questions swim in my head as I wonder, not for the first time, what she's had to endure the last two weeks. She must pick up on my distracted train of thought as she pulls me further into her, leaning back on the table until I'm hovering over her. Her legs wrap around my waist, causing the god-awful dress that asshole has dressed her in to slide up. Running my hand along her thigh, I push it higher and slip my hand between her legs, gritting my teeth at the absence of her underwear.

Breaking the kiss, her head falls back, and she moans as I circle her clit. I dip my head, kissing along her neck and uncaring of the blood coating her skin, as her needy moans spur me on. When I sink two fingers into her, her face falls slack, and her eyes become hooded. She tugs me up to kiss her as I push her closer to oblivion.

Gazing into her eyes while I give her what she needs, I murmur, "You deserve to feel nothing but pleasure."

Her eyes bore into mine, and her fingers dig into my skin as she comes apart. A single tear escapes and runs into her hairline before I can wipe it away, and she begins to tremble in my arms. Her hand shakes as she places it on my chest, over my rapidly beating heart.

"I didn't think I'd get to feel this again."

The sound of footsteps coming toward us has me spinning around, ensuring Hadley's hidden behind me. I move to grab my gun, but my fingers wrap around nothing but air, and I curse myself for being so stupid when I notice the gun lying uselessly on the floor beside my very dead dad.

Lowering into a crouch instead, I ready myself to fight my way out of here as the footsteps draw closer.

"Jesus, you scared the shit out of me," I huff out, sagging and dropping my arms as Beck stalks into the room. His shirt is torn, and he's got a nasty gash on his arm, but otherwise he looks relatively unscathed.

His eyes drift behind me, and they flare when he spots Hadley. As he steps forward, I move to the side. His gaze roams over her, most likely noting the same physical changes I did.

Tears stream continuously down her face, and as she pushes herself off the table to get to Beck, her legs give way beneath her.

Beck and I dive for her at the same time, but he gets there first, wrapping her in his arms, and I hear her sob into his chest. Now that the adrenaline is wearing off, she's starting to crash—hard.

Giving them a moment, I move to the sink and wash the blood off my hands and face. Finding a worn-looking dishcloth beneath the sink, I wet it under the tap and turn to move back to Hadley, wanting to clean my father's disgusting blood off her. Only I pause when my gaze lands on his unmoving body. Stepping closer, I take in his blood-soaked shirt, the shocked look frozen on his face, and the numerous stab wounds that speak of all the pent-up aggression Hadley had toward him. The lack of emotion I feel, or rather the absence of the grief I should probably be feeling, is unnerving, yet it seems appropriate. He was my father in name only. We shared DNA, but that was it. I won't mourn his absence or wonder what could have been. Knowing Hadley will no longer have to fear him makes a sadistic grin brighten my face, and looking away from his rotting corpse, I focus on my girl, still held safely in Beck's comforting arms. I step over my father and, without a backward glance, I move to clean her up, wiping the damp cloth over her face, neck, chest, and arms. All the while, she leans against Beck's chest, watching me. The deadened look in her eyes worries me as she stares blankly back at me, and I stroke my hand over her hair.

"You ready to get out of here, baby?"

She sighs, and her eyes drift shut. "You have no idea."

"You need me to carry you?"

She gives a small shake of her head, burying her face in Beck's chest and inhaling a fortifying breath before pulling away. I'm relieved to see she looks stronger as she pulls her shoulders back and straightens her spine. She moves toward my father with a steeliness in her eyes that wasn't there before. I reach forward, intending to stop her from doing whatever she's going to do, but she sidesteps me, bending down to grab the knife she had. She stares at it for a second before running her gaze over my father, pausing when she notices the sheath on his hip.

There's no emotion on her face as she wipes the blade on his gray suit pants and gets to her feet. *Fuck me*, if I don't get a little hard at the sight of her covered in blood and wielding a deadly weapon. If the look of adoration in Beck's eyes and sudden tightness in his pants is anything to go by, he's feeling it too.

We leave the room without another word or a backward glimpse at my shitstain for a father. I make a mental promise to Hadley to destroy every piece-of-shit scumbag associated with this godforsaken place.

We move at a slower pace, making our way back to the interrogation room to meet the others. I'm sure our twenty minutes are well up by now, but despite Hadley's determined face, it quickly becomes apparent that she's struggling. I watch her closely, and it's clear from her stick-thin frame and the bags under her eyes that she's been starved and hasn't had much chance to rest while she's been here. Not to mention the cuts all over her body. The large one on her thigh seems to catch every time she over-extends her leg as she keeps wincing, and it's taking everything in me not to whip her off her feet and carry her the rest of the way.

Thankfully, we don't run into any issues, and it doesn't take long before we round the corner into the corridor with the interrogation room.

I've been walking behind Hadley, watching her obsessively, and I'm immediately on alert when she freezes. Looking past her, I discover the reason she's stopped.

"Hawk." The emotion is thick in her voice, and even though she doesn't say the word all that loudly, her brother, who's standing further down the hall in front of our designated meet-up spot, turns toward her. The permanent scowl falls off his face as his eyes widen, and he takes her in.

Hadley flies off like a bullet, running toward him at a speed I wouldn't have deemed possible in her weakened state, and Hawk rushes to meet her halfway. The two collide like something out of a movie, and *holy fuck*, if it doesn't make my insides go a little gooey. The two of them are a fucking twinmance for the ages. As the two of them embrace each other, clinging to one another like it's the end of times, this moment epitomizes just how far Hawk has come in the last few months. It's good to see the fucking asshole has a heart, after all.

After what feels like forever, the two of them break apart, and Hawk takes a step back, running his gaze over her. His brows pull together as he registers the red tinge to her skin and the very obvious blood stains covering her previously cream dress.

"Why are you covered in blood?" Without giving her a second to respond, he snaps his gaze to Beck and me. His eyes darken, and he barks out sharply, "Why the fuck is she covered in blood?"

"I'm fine," Hadley quickly assures him, reassuringly squeezing his arm. "It's not mine." She hesitates, glancing back at me with a mixture of emotions I can't place. Turning back to face her brother, she can't meet his steely gaze as she mutters, "I'll tell you later." I don't like how she seems almost embarrassed, or afraid to tell him. I don't give a fuck that my dad is dead, and I know Hawk and the others will be as proud as I am that she overcame her fears and did what needed to be done.

Losing his patience, Mason shoves Hawk to the side, wrapping his arms around Hadley, and West, needing his moment with her too, does the same. So our poor girl is squished between them.

As they pull away, Wilder pipes up, "Good to see you, Sunshine. I was worried you wouldn't get to see my incredible knife skills." He holds up his bloodied blade, and I quirk a brow at Hawk, but he just shakes his head. Guess that's a story for another time.

Despite Wilder's nonchalance, there's a softness in his eyes when he smiles at Hadley, and I can't decide if I like the way he looks at her, or fucking hate it.

She lifts her own still partially bloodied blade, and although it doesn't look as deadly as Wilder's, she grins wickedly.

Wilder's eyes light up. "Twinsies."

It's Hawk's turn to raise an eyebrow in question, and I simply murmur, "I'll fill you in later."

"Let's find Cain and get the fuck out of here," Hawk barks, wrapping his hand around Hadley's and tugging her toward the exit.

"Wait," Hadley calls out, digging her feet in and forcing Hawk to stop in his tracks unless he wants to drag her along behind him. "What about Michael? I was with him when..." Her brows scrunch together as she struggles to remember something before shaking off the thought. "He might be here."

"Michael?" I question. "No, he's fine. He's back at school."

"What do you mean you were with him?" Hawk growls angrily. "He said you'd parted ways before you disappeared."

Wrinkles form along Hadley's forehead as she struggles to think, before sighing and shaking her head. "I don't remember. I think I was drugged. It's all a blur. The last thing I remember was walking toward the lake with him."

"We can sort all of this out once we get the fuck out of here," Beck interjects, but his lips are pressed tightly together, and there's a hardness in his eyes that wasn't there a second ago. When he looks my way, I know he's thinking the same thing I am—Michael didn't say anything about going to the lake with our girl.

Sighing, Hawk nods his head in reluctant agreement and starts moving toward the exit again with Hadley by his side. The rest of us fall into formation around them, moving as a single unit toward the back entrance of the building.

Reaching the exit, we pull open the door and step out into the night. Hadley pauses to tilt her head up to the dark sky, sucking down a deep breath of the fresh air, and I once again curse my fucking father for everything she's had to endure.

Scanning our surroundings, the yard seems quiet. I'm hoping that means Cain has managed to take out any guards that were lurking around out here.

We're making our way silently toward the compound's back exit when we hear footsteps—someone running in this direction. Falling still, I raise my gun while positioning myself in front of Hadley, noticing Hawk doing the same on her other side and the others closing in behind her. Regardless of our attempts to block her, Hadley crouches into a fighting position between us, wielding her knife with all the skill of a trained mercenary.

The second the asshole guard comes into view, I fire off a shot, but he's too far away and it's too dark out, so the shot goes wide.

Spotting Hadley, the fucker's eyes widen and he calls out, "D!"

"Wait!" Hadley shouts, surging forward and throwing out her arms in an attempt to stop us from shooting at him. "I know him."

"He's a guard," I growl, refusing to look away from the enemy, even though he's holding his arms in the air in surrender and no longer advancing toward us.

Hadley gives me a stern look. "He helped me." Turning back to the guard, she calls out, "Marcus, what are you doing here?"

"I heard gunshots. As soon as I realized what was happening, I figured it was your guys. I wanted to help but couldn't get into the building."

I tense as the guard approaches, and Hadley looks at me over her shoulder, doing the same with Hawk, pinning us both with a *behave yourselves* look, before her eyes move to Beck. "He's Meena's brother."

I don't know what that means, and neither does Hawk if his furrowed brow means anything. Although Beck obviously does, as his shoulders relax, even though his brows pull together in confusion. His gaze runs assessingly over the guard before he glances at Hadley. She gives a tight nod of her head, and he returns his focus to the guard once again. "If you want to help, there's a boy inside, in the far-right corner of the building."

"I'll get him." There's a promise in his tone that has me giving him another once-over, but I still don't trust him.

Beck must be hesitant too as he studies him for a second before responding, "The code is four-two-three-five-three-nine. Take him to the back entrance. I'll tell Cain to look out for you."

The guy nods, and with a final glance and a small smile directed at Hadley, he takes off into the building behind us.

The rest of us keep moving forward. The previously silent yard is now ripe with life. Sounds of children crying, along with smoke from burning buildings, filters the air. The place is frenzied, and as we approach the back entrance to the compound, children are running or being carried through the open gate.

We're most of the way across the yard when Hadley's leg gives out, and she falls to the ground, hissing in pain. Hawk is beside her in a flash, hauling her into his arms.

"Shit, are you okay?" I brush my fingers over the reddened skin on her knees, swiping away the dust and grit, relieved to find no fresh cuts from where her knees collided with the hard asphalt. Running my eyes over her as I inspect for any other damage, I notice the deep cut on her thigh has opened up. Blood trickles from the wound, and when I look back at her face, she looks paler than before. Honestly, she seems completely fucking wrecked.

"I'm fine." She waves me away, but there's a fine tremor in her hands which she tries to hide. "Just not used to such strenuous exercise." She tries to laugh it off with a small, tired smile, but none of us find it funny. Hawk's arms tighten around her and his face turns thunderous. My own jaw clenches and I have to look away for a second so she doesn't see just how much her words fucking infuriate me.

"Hawk," she grumbles, pushing against his chest, "I can walk."

He glowers, but none of the heat is directed at Hadley. "I don't give a shit if you think you can somersault the rest of the way. You're fucking exhausted." Huffing out a breath, he clenches his teeth and pleads with her with his eyes. "Just let me help you, okay?"

The two of them share a twin moment, where the rest of the world doesn't exist, before Hadley relents and gives a quick nod of her head, relaxing into his embrace.

We set off again, quickly closing the distance to the back gate. Spotting us heading in his direction, Cain strides toward us.

"Go on. I'll catch up in a sec." Beck focuses on Hadley, before sparing the rest of us a glance. As we pass by, Cain nods his head at us, a gesture I return. Tonight wouldn't have been possible without him.

Leaving the chaos of the compound behind, we make it back to the car, and Hawk slides Hadley into the back seat. I climb in beside her, and Mason slips in on her other side as Hawk gets in behind the wheel.

"You go," Wilder insists, watching Hadley as she slumps against Mason, barely able to keep her eyes open. "I'll wait for Beck."

Hawk nods, starting the engine, while West slides into the front passenger seat. Not having to be told twice, he guns it down the lane, onto the main road, and away from the burning buildings behind us.

Hadley

CHAPTER SIX

The world comes back to me slowly as I groggily wake from the land of the dead. Or maybe I'm actually dead. *Did Lawrence and Bowen finally get the better of me?* I'm struggling to think through the thick fog of sleep, to remember what happened or where I am, and I can't for the life of me manage to peel my eyes open. They may as well be glued shut.

I give up on trying to open my eyes and focus instead on what I can feel and hear. The room is silent, and if it wasn't for the smoothness of the soft sheets wrapped around me, I'd believe I was still in my dingy cell back in the compound.

Someone squeezes my hand, and on instinct, I squeeze back.

"Hadley? You awake?"

Hawk's soft murmur and his worried tone give me the energy to crack open an eyelid, and I groan as light floods in. Lifting my hand to block it, something tugs the skin and, looking down, there's a bandage stuck to the back of my hand, with a tube coming out of it that's attached to a bag of fluids.

"The doctors said you were extremely dehydrated when we brought you in," Hawk explains.

"Where am I?" My throat is so parched the words are barely more than a croak, and my lips are dry when I run my tongue along them.

Letting go of my hand, Hawk stands and fills a cup on my bedside table with water, bringing it to my lips. I down it in two gulps, feeling the cold liquid slosh around in my otherwise empty stomach.

"You're at a private hospital. You passed out on the way home, and we didn't know what else to do." He glances away, and I notice the muscle in his jaw tick. "Given the cuts all over you..." Gritting his teeth, anger overwhelms him. Unable to stand still, he paces back and forth across the end of the bed in my small private room.

Resting my head against the pillow, I sit and watch as he stomps to one side of the room, then turns around and strides toward the opposite wall. His eyes are molten fury, his face like thunder. There's nothing I can say or do that would calm the rage consuming him right now. I know, because, despite the sheer exhaustion threatening to pull me under, I feel it too. That boiling ball of rage and fury, of wrath and malice that grows in my stomach, demanding retribution.

Lawrence might be dead, but I need *everyone* connected with that cesspit of a compound to be punished. The guards, Bowen, our parents. I won't be able to move on with my life until they've *all* suffered.

Hawk stops pacing, spinning to face me from where he stands at the end of the bed. His angry eyes fall on mine, but behind them, I see the pain he's masking; the vulnerability that he doesn't know how to process.

"Hawk—"

He shakes his head, unwilling to hear my platitudes. His fists clench tightly around the footboard, turning his knuckles white and threatening to crack the flimsy plastic.

"Just tell me," he hisses between gritted teeth. Unable to look at me, his gaze is laser-focused on a random point on the plain white bedsheet. "I need to know what they did."

Tense silence fills the room, choking me as memories I'd rather not relive assault me. I endured my fair share of grueling workouts and terrifying punishments growing up in the compound. Still, I was never locked away and isolated for so long or subjected to Bowen's cruel form of torture so frequently. And having tasted true freedom, even if it had been for only a few months, made being back there so much harder to handle.

I can barely come to terms with what I've been through, never mind telling Hawk every grotesque detail.

When I don't answer him, he lifts his head, pinning me with his swirling gray eyes. "Did they..." Unable to finish his sentence, his words hang in the air, their meaning more than clear.

"No," I choke out, even as memories of Bowen's threats, and Lawrence's leer while he forced me to change naked in front of him. Of him shoving his unwanted fingers inside of me, battering against my mental walls.

Hawk's penetrating gaze holds me captive for another moment as he searches for the truth. After a moment, his shoulders drop slightly in relief, and he nods. His Adam's apple bobs as he swallows roughly. Despite the tension still pouring off him, he seems somewhat reassured that at least I wasn't violated in such a heinous way.

The door to the room opens, and expecting it to be the guys, I'm entirely fucking shocked when Barton Davenport, my fucking father, walks into the room.

His eyes land on me and widen in shock. Under his scrutinizing gaze, I can only think that this is the first time he's ever really *looked* at me.

"What the hell are you doing here?" Hawk growls dangerously. He moves to block Barton's view of me and, suddenly feeling self-conscious, I rush to tuck the bed sheet tighter around me and flatten my hair with my hand—not that it does any good.

"I needed to check on you. Someone attacked the compound...What happened?" Barton's eyes narrow, and he tries to side-step Hawk, but the brute follows, continuing to block any advance Barton can make in my direction.

Scoffing, Hawk sneers, "Like you give a shit."

For the first time since entering the room, Barton tears his gaze from me to focus on his son. His eyes narrow in annoyance, and damn, if the two of them don't look eerily alike. It's freaky, and I'm not entirely sure what to make of it.

"Watch it, son."

The two of them stand off against each other in some stupid silent duel, until I huff out my own breath of annoyance. I can feel a headache forming behind my eyes, and I'm way too tired to deal with this shit.

"What are you doing here?" I ask wearily, my voice nothing more than a dry rasp as I look at Barton.

His attention snaps from Hawk to me. His eyes are filled with anguish and sorrow, but I can't understand why. Maybe I'm reading him wrong. Only seeing what I want to see. After everything I've been through, any girl would want her dad in her hospital room with her, comforting her...but not me. Not when my father hasn't given a single shit about me my entire life. His presence here only means more problems to deal with. Problems I don't have the energy to face.

Hawk ensures he keeps Barton in his sights as he shifts on his feet, moving so he can also see me. "How did you even know she was here?"

"I tracked your car. Once I explained I was your father, the receptionist told me what room you were in."

His gaze runs over my bare arms, the only visible skin, taking in the numerous scratches and cuts covering them.

"Who did that to you?"

My eyebrows lift in surprise at his threatening tone, but before I can work out what to say, Hawk scoffs. "Like you don't know."

Barton rounds on him so quickly it's nothing but a blur. "What the hell does that mean?" he snarls. "*You* told me she was in bed with a stomach bug, but clearly, that was a lie."

Hawk's eyes darken, and in the next second, he's got his dad shoved up against the wall, his hands fisting his shirt. The two of them are of similar height as they face off. "Yeah, and you pretended not to have a daughter all these years. Clearly, *that* was a lie."

I huff out yet another breath—not that it seems to do any good—and, deciding if shit is going to go down in this too small of a room, then I'd rather have pants on when it does. I unhook the line attached to the back of my hand and push back the covers, sliding out of bed.

Hawk must see the movement out of the corner of his eye because as soon as my bare feet hit the cold tile floor, his head snaps in my direction.

"Hadley," he growls. "Back in bed."

I glare right back, unperturbed by his pissy attitude—I'm practically immune to it by now.

"No, asshole. If you're going to start shit, I want to be dressed. I can't kick anyone's ass in this stupid gown." I wave my hand over the flimsy gown with no back so my bare ass is exposed—who the fuck thought that was a good idea?! Would it really have been so difficult to add an extra tie to the back so I could maintain at least *some* of my dignity?!

His eyes narrow to slits. "You're in no state to be kicking *anyone's* ass. Get. Back. Into. Bed."

Barton's gaze jumps back and forth between us as he silently watches our argument, but we both ignore him. Glowering at Hawk, I make sure to keep out of his arm span as I stomp—okay, so it's more of a crippled shuffle—toward the attached bathroom.

There's a black duffel bag sitting in a vacant chair and, hoping it has spare clothes in it, I snatch it up on my way past and slam the bathroom door shut behind me.

Alone, I lean against the closed door, tilting my head back until I'm staring at the ceiling. Thankful for a moment's peace. My legs shake, and my hands tremble, that little bit of exertion too much for my fatigued body.

Dropping the bag on the counter beside the sink, I unzip it, breathing a sigh of relief when I find a pair of clean sweats and a top. Looking around, the bathroom is small but functional, with a narrow shower stall in the corner. I can't even remember the last time I showered—at least one that wasn't with cold water and some perv watching me. Even though my legs protest at the thought of holding me up for much longer, the clawing need to have a nice warm shower is all I can think about, and I hastily tear off the gown and turn the dial until steam billows out of the stall, fogging up the mirror. Stepping under the spray, my eyes drift shut as I let the warm water wash over me. It feels like fucking heaven against my skin.

I turn the dial until the water practically burns me, scorching my skin and turning it red. I don't know how long I just stand there, soaking in the moment, relishing the small privilege of a warm, private shower, before I finally grab the small hotel-like bottle of shower gel and scrub my skin raw. I do the same with my hair, emptying both bottles. I still don't feel completely clean by the time I turn the water off and step out, but then I'm not entirely sure I ever will.

Exhaustion hits me like a freight train, and I quickly dry and throw on the sweatpants, top, and hoodie, noting that each item belongs to one of my guys. Burying my nose in the neckline of the hoodie, I breathe in Beck's cedarwood and eucalyptus scent, letting it wash over me and soak into my skin, soothing me in a way that only Beck can.

Rifling through the bag, I find my toothbrush, toothpaste, and a hair tie. I smile gratefully, knowing West will have been the one to remember to pack them. Once I've brushed my teeth and scraped my hair back into a messy bun, I straighten my spine, and with a determination I don't feel, I pull open the door.

Barton has since taken one of the empty chairs beside the bed, while Hawk continues to stand over him. They both look my way as I step into the room and shuffle back toward the bed. My muscles feel looser after the warm shower, although my left thigh, where Bowen—that son of a bitch—drove his knife into it, tugs every time I put my weight on it.

Seeing me struggle, Barton jumps to his feet to come to my aid, but Hawk shoves him back in his chair with a growl before stepping toward me, intent on helping. I wave him away, though, needing to achieve this small thing on my own.

Once I'm settled in the bed again, I look between them before my gaze lands on Barton.

"Did you know?" There's no point in pretending anymore. Lawrence is dead, and all I want now are answers. "Did you know where I was all these years?"

Barton's brows draw together in confusion, and I have to give him some credit as he never breaks eye contact. "What? No. I had no idea where you were until Hawk showed up with you that night."

I can feel tears gathering behind my eyes. The last few weeks have worn me down and robbed me of the energy to keep my usual defense mechanisms erected around me.

"Why did you never look for me? I was your daughter." My voice breaks, and I swallow back the emotion in my throat as I shake my head. "How could you just move on like that?"

With a pained expression on his face, Barton leans forward as if to touch me, but I flinch away, shuffling to the far side of the bed as Hawk's arm snaps out, blocking Barton from coming anywhere near me.

"Don't touch her," he snarls, moving to sit beside me on the bed, acting as a barrier between Barton and me.

Barton's eyes widen and his lips thin, but he slowly sits back in his chair. Keeping his focus on me, he says, "I did search for you. I hired a private investigator, and all of his leads were dead ends. Eventually, he told me there was no point in continuing to look for you. I didn't want to believe him, but ultimately, I had to accept that I'd lost you." He seems pained as he adds, "I had to focus on the family I still had."

Unable to stand looking at him, I drop my head so he doesn't see the tears threatening to overflow.

"That was it? You just gave up?" Hawk's words are a harsh snap, and I can feel the anger radiating off him, the heat searing my skin. I lean into the warmth, reassured that my explosive volcano of a brother will always have my back. There's something to be said about knowing someone will always be in your corner, fighting for you. It empowers your own strength and makes you feel capable of pretty much anything.

Even now, when I'm at my weakest, Hawk's fierce need to protect me washes over me like a balm to my wounded soul, piecing me back together. Perhaps, with his help, I'll come back stronger than ever. "And now you're claiming ignorance of it all? I still don't believe you didn't just sell her off to be Lawrence's little plaything."

Barton looks completely confused as his gaze jumps between Hawk and I.

"What are you talking about? What does Lawrence have to do with any of this?"

"Lawrence is the one who's been hiding her all these years. He kept her locked up in that fucking compound you call a business. Had her tortured and threatened. He kept her fucking terrified every day of her life."

The words explode out of Hawk, his voice rising with each syllable until his chest is heaving, and he's glaring murderously at our father, uncaring of how the color has leached from Barton's face or the way his lower lip trembles.

"You're wrong." Barton shakes his head, and I can see the wheels churning frantically behind his eyes. "There's no way Lawrence is capable of something like that. We would have known if she had been there. *I* would have known."

"How?" My voice is monotonous, devoid of all emotion. "You only visited once or twice a year. And every time you did, I was locked away until you were gone. You and the others left the day-to-day running to Lawrence. He was the one in charge, the one who oversaw everything." My own temper starts to flare, and I feel Hawk slide his palm into mine, squeezing my hand in encouragement. "Do you even know what goes on in there? What the guards do to form the inhuman soldiers you utilize for your own gain?"

If Barton looked pale after Hawk's outburst, he seems like a fucking ghost now. His mouth opens and closes wordlessly as he struggles to process everything.

Leaning forward, I hiss, "They beat children, rape them, break them down using whatever means necessary, until they are nothing but a void. A shell that can be molded and rebuilt into something monstrous and destructive.

"I was tortured, beaten. I've had my skin torn open more times than I can count, and I've been starved for days. I've been so close to giving up that I prayed for death." Hawk's hand squeezes mine, and I can feel the telltale wetness of tears coating my cheeks. "My best friend was beaten to death because she refused to kill another child. She was only thirteen. Thirteen years old, and she had her life ripped away from her. *That* is the company that you run. *That* is the hell that you abandoned me to."

Barton looks like he's about to be sick, yet I have fuck all sympathy for him. He swipes his hand over his mouth, and I watch his eyes dart back and forth unseeingly as he tries to come to terms with what we are saying.

"That can't be true," he mumbles disbelievingly, staring at me like I'm a figment of his imagination come to torment him. I lean back and tug down the waistband of my sweats, exposing the tail of my phoenix tattoo and more importantly, the symbol of the mercenary company—*his* company—hidden amongst the tail.

Both he and Hawk look at the exposed skin for a second until they see it, and Barton gasps.

"They branded you?" Hawk snarls venomously.

I shrug. Really, it's the least intrusive thing they've done to me. "They do it to everyone."

Barton seems lost in his own thoughts for a long moment before he speaks up again, "It was you, wasn't it? You attacked the compound?" His gaze flicks over the multitude of injuries I have on display. "Is that how you got hurt?"

"LAWRENCE TOOK HER," Hawk yells, loud enough to make me jump. "*Again.* He's had her for *weeks. He's* the one that's done that to her."

"I don't understand," Barton murmurs in a quiet voice. "Why? Why would Lawrence take you at all? And hide you in the compound? It makes no sense."

"I think it started as some sort of payback for you stealing Maria from him, and grew into an obsession over time."

If it's possible, Barton just looks even more confused as he shakes his head. "What? The two of them had already broken up before we started dating."

I don't know what to tell him, so I just shrug, too tired to give a shit about why. I'm the innocent victim in whatever shit went down between the three of them before I was even fucking born. People do fucked up shit all the time without good reason. If I get caught up in why Lawrence chose me, or why not Hawk, or both of us, I'll drive myself mad. There's never going to be a good enough reason to justify what he did, and I just have to accept that.

Barton gets to his feet, stumbling before he rights himself. "I-I need to go talk to him."

He steps toward the door, looking dazed.

"Yeah, no can do, I'm afraid." I grimace. "He's dead."

Barton's eyes widen comically as he spins to face me. "He's what?" Hawk doesn't react at all though, so I'm guessing Cam or Beck already filled him in.

"He's dead. I killed him. And I'm coming for the rest of you next."

Hadley

CHAPTER SEVEN

After Barton stumbles, wide-eyed and panicked, from my room, Hawk tugs me down beside him on the bed. I melt into his embrace, drained and exhausted. We lie there in silence for a while before he speaks up, "That girl, the one who died…"

"Her name was Meena. The guard last night, he was her brother."

Hawk mulls over my words before speaking again, "If he was her brother, why was he a guard there?"

"He's been searching for her all these years. They were put into separate foster homes when they were kids, before she was abducted and brought to the compound." I can feel the tears again welling up in my eyes, and my chest hurts for their lost relationship. I know how much it would have meant to Meena, knowing her brother never gave up on her; he'd been looking for her all this time. Hawk's arms tighten around me, and I bury my face into him. "It was because of her that I never lost myself in there. If it wasn't for Meena, I would have ended up like all the others."

We lapse into silence, although I can feel the anger emanating from him. Regardless, it's not much longer before exhaustion pulls me under, and I fall into a deep, dreamless sleep in the reassuring comfort of Hawk's arms.

When I next wake, I'm pressed against a strangely comfortable brick. Squinting, I gaze up at a sleeping Mason. *Huh, I wonder when the two of them switched out and how I didn't even notice.* Lifting my head, I gaze around the otherwise empty room before lying back down and snuggling in tighter against him.

"You alright, Little Warrior?" Mason's voice is low with the perfect amount of sleepy sex appeal, and his arms tighten around me even though he hasn't opened his eyes.

"Yeah. Where's Hawk?"

"We finally convinced him to go home and get some rest. You're being discharged in the morning, so he and the others will come pick us up when you're ready to go."

I nod against his hard chest and try to go back to sleep, but my mind whirls with thoughts of returning to school. I feel like a completely different person to when I was last on campus. How can I go back there and act as if nothing ever happened?

"Barton said Hawk told him I had a stomach bug."

Mason sighs, shifting in the bed so he's lying on his back, and I'm sprawled across him.

"Yeah. He phoned, wanting both of you to go over for a family dinner. We couldn't tell him the truth, so Hawk lied. We've told the school the same excuse for why you haven't been in class."

I swallow roughly. "What about Emilia?"

Cupping my cheek in his large palm, he tilts my head up so I have no choice but to look him in the face.

"She has been driving all of us crazy, wanting to know what's going on and demanding we bring you back."

"Does she…"

"No, but she knows something's up. We figured you'd wanna be the one to tell her the truth." I glance away, worrying my bottom lip, but Mason forces my gaze back to his. "You've got a true friend in Emilia. She was ready to take us all on, thinking we'd done something to you." A fond smile tugs at one side of his lip. "Hawk had no idea what to do with her when she wouldn't back off. He was in shock when she actually stood up to him."

I chuckle. "Damn, I bet the look on his face was priceless."

Kissing the top of my head, Mason fixes the covers around us. "Go back to sleep. We'll deal with everything else in the morning."

Sinking into his warm embrace, coaxed by the heady combination of his uniquely Mason scent, I drift back into a dreamless slumber. By the time I wake up again, I'm feeling a million times better, physically, at least. If only sleep and a bag of fluids were enough to fix me mentally too.

~

Mason and I are sitting on a bench outside the hospital with a paper bag containing a bottle of painkillers they gave me upon discharge, waiting for the guys to pick us up. I can't stop looking at the blue sky, breathing in the crisp, fresh air, and relishing the sound of birds chirping and cars driving past. Just soaking in the everyday mundane that people take for granted. It feels like a fucking lifetime since I had the luxury to just sit and drink in the world around me.

We're not sitting there for long before Hawk's SUV pulls up, stopping in front of us. Hawk jumps out from behind the wheel, and rounding the car, his gaze immediately falls on me. He gives me a once-over as if he expected something to have happened in the last few hours we were apart. Seeming satisfied, he nods at Mason and comes over, reaching out to help me up.

"Hawk," I grumble, waving him off. "I can walk. I'm not a fucking invalid."

He scowls but backs off—a little. He's like a fucking shadow, sticking to me like glue as I shuffle toward the front passenger seat. I can hardly be annoyed, though. If anything, it's sweet to see how much he cares. He grabs the door handle before I can reach it and doesn't move away until I'm buckled into the seat, like I'm a goddamn child. I roll my eyes when he's not looking, even while a slight smirk lifts the corner of my lip.

He and Mason exchange a few words before they both climb in, and we head back to campus. With every passing mile, anxiety ratchets up within me. My leg bounces repeatedly, and my palms sweat. I'm not even sure why I'm so on edge. I've done this before—successfully integrated into normal society. Sure, it took a while. The first couple of weeks were the hardest. I kept expecting someone to come after me and drag me back there. I couldn't get used to no one hurting me on a daily basis, and the tiniest touch from a passing stranger would send me into a downward spiral.

So, I've been here and survived it before. I should be able to get through it again, yet my nerves are still frayed. Anxiety claws at my throat, threatening to suffocate me as we drive through the campus gates and up the drive.

"Hey, are you okay? You're looking a little pale," Mason remarks once we've parked and he's opened my door for me. He takes my hand and helps me out of the car as Hawk rounds the hood, eyeing me warily, like he's worried I'll pass out.

"I'm fine." The words come out more sharply than I intended, and I grimace. *God, I'm such a bitch. They're only trying to help.* I give him an apologetic smile. "It's just weird being back here...after everything."

He nods in understanding and steps back, giving me some space to breathe before the three of us start toward the dorms. The anxiety only gets worse with every step I take, however. I swear I feel eyes on me, and as I bury myself deeper in my hoodie, I glance discreetly around me. Every student we pass seems to stare openly at me and whisper with their friends, and I constantly glance down at my arms, wondering if they can see the cuts marring my skin. Everything is covered, though; the only giveaway that I'm not my normal self is my thinner, paler face.

"What the fuck are you staring at, asshole?" I snap when yet another person gapes at me as we walk past. The jerk startles and scurries off.

"Hadley," Hawk chastises. "What the hell? He was barely looking at you."

"*Everyone's* looking at me."

He shares a look with Mason over my head before pulling me to a stop and focusing on me. "No more than usual. What's going on?"

My eyes dart back and forth between his. *But I swear they were looking and whispering.* It was almost like they were surprised to see me. My brows furrow, and I scrub my hand down my face. I'm becoming fucking paranoid.

"I need to go to the lake." Hawk's eyebrows scrunch in confusion, and I can see the protest forming on his lips, but I rush on before he can argue. "I need to know what happened. How Lawrence got to me." I lean in and lower my voice. "Someone must have helped him. I wouldn't have gone there willingly."

"Alright, let's go to the lake," Mason agrees, earning a warning glare from Hawk. "What, man? She's right. We've been thinking the same, and she needs answers before she drives herself crazy trying to psychoanalyze every kid in school."

Pursing his lips, Hawk returns his gaze to mine, staring at me for a long moment before huffing out a sigh. "Fine, but we're leaving the second you start to feel tired."

I smile at him and nod my head. "Deal."

"I'll message the others and tell them to meet us there."

I'm still jittery with nerves, but the thought of finally getting answers and working out what happened the day I was taken settles me somewhat. I've been wracking my brain to figure it out, but it's nothing more than a hazy blur. I'm hoping being back there will spark something.

It takes us longer than usual to slowly make our way through the campus and down to the lake.

"Baby Davenport," Cam calls out, bounding toward me with a massive grin on his face that I can't help but return. He wraps his arms around me, lifting me off my feet as he spins me in the air.

"Watch it, asshole," Hawk barks. "She's hurt."

Cam drops me like I'm on fire, his eyes wide as his gaze darts over me, checking for any injury.

"I'm fine," I assure him in a soft voice, reaching out to touch him.

He analyses me for a second longer, until he's satisfied I'm telling the truth. "Ah, he's in protective big brother mode, isn't he?"

"More like annoying big brother mode." Cam barks out a laugh, and I return it with a grin while Hawk grumbles beside us and stomps off, only making Cam laugh harder.

I can't help but watch him, noting the lightness in his eyes that hasn't been there in months. He seems like his old self, the Cam I fell for when I first arrived, and I have no idea how he can be so at ease. It was only a few days ago that he found his father brutally murdered…at *my* hands. Yet, he seems utterly unaffected by it.

"What are we doing here?" Beck asks. His eyes are glued to me, and I gently squeeze Cam's hand before I move over to join him. He tugs me in against him, turning me so my back is flush against his chest and his warmth seeps into my body, even through the thickness of my hoodie, as he wraps his arms around me.

I glance at West and Cam before looking past them to the forest stretched out behind them. My forehead creases as I try to think through the fog that is my memories. "I wanted to see if I could remember what happened the day I disappeared."

"What's the last thing you remember?" Beck asks.

"I went to meet Michael. We'd had a fight just before Easter break, and he messaged saying he wanted to talk." I pause, trying my best to remember that day. "We grabbed a coffee in the dining hall and brought them down here."

"You're sure?" Something in West's voice has me looking away from our surroundings to focus on him. There's an unusual darkness coating his expression, and his muscles are tense. Pinching my lips, I shrug it off as jealousy. I thought he'd gotten over that shit, but maybe not.

"Yeah." Slipping out of Beck's arms, I move to the edge of the forest where I last remember standing. I turn on my heel, so I'm facing out over the still water of the lake, with the dark cover of the trees behind me. "We were standing right here."

Mason moves to stand beside me, looking at a point deeper in the forest behind me. "That makes sense. We found your phone back there." He lifts his chin, indicating a spot behind me, and I turn to look into the gloomy depths of the forest.

Something bangs against my consciousness and goosebumps rise along my arm as I move toward the treeline. Stepping into the shadows, I shiver as the heat of the sun is blocked out. I reach out, trailing my fingers over a tree to my right, and I'm assaulted by memories coming so quickly I can't initially process them.

"What is it? What happened?" someone asks, a hint of urgency and concern to their voice.

"I knew we shouldn't have fucking done this," Hawk snarls angrily, but I'm barely paying attention to any of them.

. . .

"Wh-where a-are we...goin'?" It takes more effort than it should to force out the words, and even when I do, I'm not sure how intelligible they are. What's wrong with me? My body feels weird, disconnected, and it takes all my energy just to put one foot in front of the other. Where are we going again?

I trip and stumble against a tree. Someone huffs out a frustrated breath beside me, pulling on my arm until I'm standing upright once again. "Just keep going. We're nearly there."

Nearly where? And why does Michael sound so angry?

"Don't...feel...good." My eyes droop, and my head falls against my chest. I lose all track of time; the next thing I know, pain rattles my bones as my body collides with the compacted dirt of the hard forest floor.

"No problems, I assume?"

I recognize that voice, but everything around me is a blur as I squint up at the two dark blobs standing over me.

"None. Eh, what are you planning on doing with her?"

One of the blobs laughs humorlessly. "It's too late to grow a conscience now, boy. Just take the money and get out of here."

There's silence for a second before one of the blobs shifts out of my view, and I hear footsteps getting quieter and quieter as whoever it is walking away. The other blob crouches down in front of me, and I have to blink several times before his face comes into focus. I wish I could say I was hallucinating the devil's face hovering in front of me, but I'm all too familiar with the grotesque features smiling cruelly at me.

"No," I croak out the word, making his grin widen.

"Oh, yes, Dove. You're all mine now."

I GASP, feeling lightheaded as I blink back to reality, finding all my guys crowded around me with various looks of concern on their faces.

"Did you remember something?" Beck asks, and I lift my gaze until I'm staring into his moss-green eyes, finding none of my usual comfort in them.

My mouth is dry, but I manage to croak out, "Michael."

Hawk snarls, "I fucking knew it was that asshole! I'm going to fucking kill him." His lip curls back, and there's a determined set to his jaw. Murderous intent glows in his eyes, making him look more terrifying than I've ever seen him before—which is saying something.

Beck reaches out for my hand, placing it between his warm palms. "You're shaking. You need to rest." I hadn't noticed the tremor in my hands until he mentioned it, but now that I'm aware of it, my whole body is vibrating. He glances around at the others. "We can discuss this back at the dorm."

Everyone quickly agrees, and Beck practically carries me back to the dorm.

"My room," I protest as we bypass the girls' dorm, heading for the guys.

"Fuck that shit," Hawk snaps, but I know his anger isn't aimed at me. "You're staying with us. I've cleared out a room for you."

I raise my eyebrows at him. "When did you do that?"

He shrugs. "Last night."

"You mean, when *you* were meant to be getting some rest."

The asshole acts like I never spoke, ignoring me as we climb the stairwell to their apartment. I get a weird sense of coming home as I walk in, a small smile growing at finding the place the same as how it was the last time I was here.

"Come on, I'll show you the room, and you can sleep for a while." He must see me about to argue as his eyes narrow in a warning and he continues, "Everything else can wait. We'll discuss it all when you get up."

My lips thin, but I can see that arguing with him would be futile, and I am pretty tired after today. "Yeah, okay," I agree on a sigh.

He shows me to a spare room at the back of the apartment, and I'm speechless as I walk in, finding the walls painted a dark blue, with cream covers on a large California king bed. My meager belongings have been moved from my room in the girls' dorm, and a few potted plants have been placed around the space, making it feel more lived-in. I spot the boxing gloves Mason got me sitting on the dresser and my textbooks on a desk.

"You can, uh, decorate it however you want," Hawk mumbles. His eyes dart around the room, as if he's trying to see it through my eyes.

"You did all this for me?" I gasp, turning in a circle and taking it all in.

When he doesn't reply, I tear my gaze away from the room to look at him, and he shrugs a shoulder. Closing the distance between us, I wrap my arms around him as a tear leaks out of the corner of my eye. "Thank you," I murmur. "It's beautiful."

He pats my back, and I can feel the awkwardness in his movements. He coughs, clearing the emotion from his throat. "Um, yeah. It was no big deal."

I smile into his shirt before letting him go and spin around to take in the room again.

"Get some rest, I'll check on you in a bit."

Once he's gone, I take my time walking around the room, opening drawers and rifling through my tatty duffle bag before stripping down and sliding between the clean sheets. *Oh yeah, this is by far the comfiest bed I have ever slept in.* Despite the horrors of the last few weeks and today's revelation, I feel safe and content as I fall asleep.

I'm pretty sure I've got the best grumpy brother in the world.

Hadley

CHAPTER EIGHT

A noise startles me awake, and I jump upright in the bed, alert and on edge.

"It's okay," Cam rushes out in a whisper. "It's just me."

Even though the tension drops out of my shoulders, my heart keeps slamming against my ribs, and my breaths come in rapid pants.

"Hey, shhh," Cam soothes, sliding into the bed beside me and pulling me into his arms. He strokes his hand over my hair and just holds me until the adrenaline rush passes. "I'm sorry, I shouldn't have snuck in like that, I-I didn't think."

Lying back, I pull him down so his head rests on the pillow beside mine, the two of us facing one another.

"I couldn't sleep. Every time I close my eyes, I worry I'm going to wake up and this will all have been a dream." I can see the genuine fear in his eyes. "I thought, maybe if I just came in and saw with my own eyes that you were really here, I'd be able to sleep."

"I'm here." I lift my hand and run it through his short, blond strands, and he closes his eyes, leaning into my touch.

We lie there in silence for a while, until the burning need for answers and reassurance becomes too much.

"Your dad…"

"Don't worry about him," Cam murmurs, slowly opening his eyes.

How can I not worry, though? "Cam, I killed him."

He reaches out, tucking a stray strand of hair behind my ear. "I know, and he deserved every painful second of what you did to him."

My eyes widen and I stare at him in shock. "You're not the slightest bit bothered by what I did? He was your *dad*."

"He was a controlling, manipulative asshole, who dictated everything in my life, and made it perfectly clear I never met his expectations. I can't think of one fond memory with him—not one fatherly moment. He was nothing but the demon on my shoulder my whole life, telling me to try harder and do better. After discovering what he did to you all these years, I would have killed him myself."

He shuffles closer to me on the bed, until our bodies are flush against one another, his head resting on my pillow inches from mine. "You mean more to me than he ever did. I've never been more proud than I was when I walked in and saw you wielding that knife. You didn't just face your greatest fear, you conquered it and made sure he could never come after you again."

Even in the dark room, I can see the honesty shining in his hazel eyes, and for the first time since Cam stormed into that room and found me murdering his father, I feel like everything between us might be okay.

"It might have been completely inappropriate, but seeing you covered in his blood, knowing you hadn't been afraid to do what you had to do, made me so fucking hard." I snort out a laugh as one side of his mouth lifts in a grin, and a sense of accomplishment shines in his eyes. "Now roll over so I can be the big spoon."

Doing as he says, I shift onto my other side, and he drapes his arm over my hip, tucking me in against him. Just as my eyelids droop, he murmurs against my ear, his warm breath tickling the skin, "I'm pretty sure you're the love of my life."

Well, if I don't fall asleep with a smile on my face after that.

∽

"Where is she?!"

Emilia's shout wakes me from the land of the dead the next morning—damn, those pain meds knocked me out—and I can't help but chuckle as I hear Hawk grumble a response, his voice too low for me to make out the words.

The two argue back and forth, and I feel Cam's chest rumble as he laughs. "Sounds like she's giving him hell."

"I should probably go save him."

Cam groans in protest as I disentangle myself from him and climb out of bed. Grabbing a pair of shorts from my duffle bag, I slip them on and snatch Beck's hoodie from yesterday off the floor on my way to the door.

"She's resting," I hear Hawk snap at Emilia as I walk down the hall, following the sound of their voices as they argue.

"I want to see her. I need to know she's okay."

"She's fine."

Emilia scoffs. "Like I'm going to take your word for it."

The two are standing at the front door, facing off against one another as I enter the room. Hawk's back is to me, so Emilia sees me first, her gaze moving to mine as her eyes widen and her mouth drops open in shock.

"Oh my god," she gasps, and Hawk turns to see what's gained her attention.

She shoves her way past him and throws her arms around me. "I have been so worried about you," she cries, squeezing me so tightly it hurts. I momentarily stiffen at the sudden contact, but after a second, I relax and return her hug.

When she eventually pulls back, her eyes roam over me, widening as she spots the cuts on my legs and the large bandage wrapped around my thigh.

"What happened to you? Where have you been?"

I grimace, looking past her to Hawk. He purses his lips but gives me a nod of encouragement before slipping down the hall, giving me some privacy to explain everything to her.

Taking her hand, I pull her with me over to the sofa and sit so I'm facing her. I chew on my bottom lip while debating how to tell her everything. It's all pretty fucked up, and I can only imagine how it's all going to sound to her.

When I take too long to start explaining, she sighs in exasperation. "Just spit it out. How bad can it be?"

Ha, if only she knew.

Taking a steady breath, I blurt out, "I grew up in a mercenary compound that I recently found out is owned by my parents. I was kidnapped as a baby by Cam's dad, in some revenge plan to get back at my parents, but he developed some sort of fucked up attachment to me while holding me captive. I escaped, but Michael lured me into a trap with Cam's dad, and he kidnapped me *again*. But the guys rescued me. Oh, and I killed Cam's dad."

By the time I'm finished, Emilia's mouth is wide open, and I can see the whites of her eyes. She gapes at me, speechless for probably the first time in her life.

"Michael?!" she eventually screeches, making me huff out a laugh. *Of course, that's the part she focuses on.* Color works its way into her cheeks and tight lines form around her eyes as they narrow. Her lip curls back and she jumps to her feet, unable to sit still as she paces back and forth in front of the sofa. "That asshole! Do you know he's been walking around here like he doesn't have a care in the world?" She waves her arms around her in fast movements that match the rapid pace of her words. "Oh my god!" she exclaims. "All those times I told him how worried I was about you." She barks out a caustic laugh, upping her pacing as she wears a path on the hardwood floor. "He pretended to be fucking there for me—telling me not to worry about you. He fucking *hugged* me." She's snarling like a rabid dog by the time she's done, making me dizzy with her back and forth.

"You, uh, don't have anything to say about the other stuff I told you?"

"Huh?" She spins to face me. "Oh, uh…" She pauses, eyeing me critically before she moves back over to reclaim her seat on the sofa. Reaching out, she clasps my hands in hers. "You're going to be okay, right?"

Her eyes show genuine concern, and I swallow roughly before plastering on a watery smile. "Yeah." I smile coyly. "They might have bent me a little, but they'll have to do more than that to break me."

She smiles placatingly, but I can tell she doesn't believe the lies I'm feeding her. Squeezing my hand in reassurance, she says, "Your past doesn't change anything for me. I love you for you." Her eyes soften. "I'm so sorry for whatever you had to go through and for being robbed of a life you should have led, but don't think you're going to scare me off with all your baggage. You're not getting rid of me that easily."

One side of her mouth lifts in a rueful smile, and I can't help but smile back as I lean in to hug her. "Thank you."

"Please tell me you've got a plan to deal with Michael?"

"Oh, we do," Mason practically growls out the words as he comes striding into the room. Despite the anger on his face, his eyes soften when they land on me.

He comes toward us, kissing my temple before dropping onto the couch beside me and pulling me into his lap.

"We do?" I question. It's the first I'm hearing of any plan.

"We'll deal with him, and you just rest."

I scoff. *Yeah, right, like I'm going to miss out on the asshole who betrayed my friendship getting what he deserves.* "Not happening. If you're planning something, I want to be there."

"Me too," Emilia tacks on. Mason sighs, but before he can protest, Emilia speaks up to argue her case. "He betrayed us both. He pretended to be our friend, then stabbed Hadley in the back." I can see her getting worked up again as she clenches her fists and glares daggers into the couch cushion. A pained expression crosses her face. "I blamed you guys for doing something to her. When all along, it was *him*. Fucking duplicitous shitstain."

Mason is silent for a moment. "I don't blame you for thinking that. We were pretty horrible to Hadley when she first showed up, and no doubt we came across as suspicious when she disappeared. Hopefully, you can understand now why we couldn't tell you anything."

"Yeah," Emilia sighs heavily. "I get it."

"We're still not missing out on whatever you have planned for Michael, though." I cock a brow at Mason, silently daring him to stop us from coming. He returns my look with a hard stare of his own, which lasts all of a few seconds before he gives up and rolls his eyes.

"Fine."

~

"I want a go at Michael," I state after dinner that evening. The six of us are gathered around the island, and the second the words leave my mouth, all eyes focus on me.

"No," Hawk snaps, getting up to set his plate in the sink, as if somehow leaving the table ends the conversation.

"I wasn't asking for permission, asshole. I'm telling you. I don't want to just stand and watch you guys deal with him."

Hawk spins around to glare at me. "You're in no state to be beating the shit out of him."

I scoff, highly offended at his weak impression of me. I mean, he *might* be right—but that is totally beside the point.

"Have you forgotten who I really am? You have no idea what I am capable of."

Hawk's deadpan stare holds me in place. "I'm sure you could obliterate him in ten different ways, but just because you can, doesn't mean you should."

"Babe," Mason interjects softly. "That fucker isn't going to be walking away from tonight. Just let us handle him for you, and you can watch." He stares deep into my eyes before uttering the final words that leave me with no room to argue, "Please. All of us need to do this for you."

I sigh, dropping my shoulders in defeat. "Fine," I relent. "But I want to talk to him first."

"Why?" Hawk sounds exasperated as he throws his hands up in the air.

"Because I'm the one he wronged," I snap back, anger making me raise my voice. "I can count the number of friends I have ever had on one fucking hand, and he was supposed to be one of them. I—" My voice breaks as emotion clogs my throat. "I need to know why he did it."

The room falls silent for a second, before Hawk reluctantly relents.

"Well, now that the subject's been brought up, can we talk about the fact you're a real-life fucking assassin?" Excitement colors Cam's voice, and when I turn to look at him, the shock and horror I expected to see are nowhere to be found. In fact, he looks seriously impressed, like it's somehow cool to be a trained killer.

"Cam," Beck chastises.

I glance around at the others, confused. "You're seriously not put off by, uh, what I am?"

"Baby!" Cam exclaims. "Didn't you hear me? You're a fucking badass. I have never been more turned-on in my life than I am at the thought of you going all ninja on some douchebag's ass."

"Fucking hell, Cam. I don't need to hear that shit," Hawk snarls, looking thoroughly disgusted.

Cam ignores him as he leans in to kiss my cheek, whispering in my ear, "Maybe you can get all dressed up in some tight leather pants for me and go all assassin on my ass."

I gape speechlessly at him as he laughs and plants another quick kiss on my lips. *I'm not even sure what the fuck that means.*

Once I've gathered my wits again, I glance at Hawk, Mason, and West and hesitantly ask, "What about you guys?"

"I'm with Cam, I think it's hot." Mason shrugs, not noticing or deliberately ignoring the threatening look Hawk throws his way. He must see my unasked questions, as he explains. "I like knowing you can look out for yourself if one of us isn't around. It made me feel better when I knew you could fight, but this is on a whole other level."

"Same," West agrees. Leaning in, he places his warm palm on top of mine. "It doesn't matter to any of us. This wasn't something you chose for yourself, and we know you're nothing like those guards or the kids they successfully turned into soldiers. Somehow, you were able to hold on to your humanity. You've learned to trust and let people in—"

"Yeah." I scoff. "I let Michael slip right past me."

"That's not your fault," Hawk insists in a tone sharpened with anger. "That's all on him. He *pretended* to be your friend."

"Don't let one misjudgment undo all the hard work you've achieved," West implores. "And don't, for one second, think finding out about your past changes things for any of us."

I smile fondly at him before Cam speaks up again, looking slightly hesitant, "Can we, uh, ask questions about the sorts of jobs you did or what you can do?"

"Umm, yeah, sure," I agree hesitantly, not entirely sure how much of my life at the compound and what I was made to do I'm willing to share with all of them.

"Were they all jobs where you had to kill your mark?"

"For the most part, but sometimes we were sent to get information from people or scare them."

"How would you do that?" Hawk asks, his head slightly tilted to one side, seeming genuinely curious about my answer.

"There are lots of different ways. I'd usually start off with verbal threats and show them various tools I could use to hurt them. If that wasn't enough, I'd move to carving flesh wounds in their bodies or breaking their fingers. You just keep escalating until they eventually give in…or they die."

My words are met with a shocked silence before Cam asks, far too excitedly, "How many ways do you know how to kill a man?"

I begin to count them in my head, before realizing it's way too many. "At least one for every day of the year."

"Fuck, that's hot," he murmurs, shifting in his seat and reaching under the table to adjust himself in his pants.

"Fucking gross," Hawk snarls at him. "If you can't keep it in your pants, then this conversation is over."

I'm both confused and loving the fact that Cam finds the fucked up shit I can do such a turn-on. But I have to say, out of all of them, I'm surprised he's the one who seems so excited by it. Sure, there's a darkness in him, but it takes a lot to set him off and given everything he's been through this year, part of me expected him to be done with me when he discovered the truth. I genuinely thought it would be too much for him to handle. Of course, I should have known better. When Cam decides something is worth his time and energy, he gives it everything he's got, and for some reason, he's decided I'm worthy.

"How did they stop you from just running away when you were out on jobs?" West asks, moving the topic along.

"We weren't allowed out until we were older and had proven our loyalty to them. Even then, a guard was always assigned to watch over me, since I was Lawrence's little pet." I sneer in disgust, the guys' expressions matching my own.

"Fuck, if that asshole wasn't already dead, I'd kill him myself," Hawk bites out, and every single one of my guys murmurs their agreement.

~

"Hello, Michael," I greet with a bright smile, stepping out from behind a bush into his path as he leaves the library for the night, acting like we're still friends and I haven't been to hell and back in the last few weeks.

"H-Hadley?" His eyes dart nervously around us. "Wh-what are you doing here?"

"I just had a quick question for you."

His face is panicked, and his eyes never rest on me for more than a few seconds before they bounce away again. I'm not sure whether that's because he can't bear to look at me, knowing the part he played in Lawrence's plan, or because he's worried he's about to be jumped.

"Oh, uh, o-okay?"

"Why?"

His gaze jumps back to mine, wide-eyed and terrified, before he quickly glances away again. "W-why what?"

I step in closer to him, and he steps back, desperately trying to maintain the distance between us.

The friendly expression drops off my face, quickly replaced with hardened eyes as I channel Hawk, donning his resting bitch face—which is pretty fucking terrifying—and glower at Michael.

"*Why* did you do what you did?"

"I don't—"

I take another threatening step toward him, cutting off his words as he scrambles back a step away from me. "*Why* did you drug me? *Why* would you betray our friendship like that? *Why* would you do what Lawrence fucking Rutherford tells you to?"

He shakes his head frantically, mumbling something I can't make out. Before he can react, I jump forward, closing the distance between us and wrap my hand around his tie, yanking him toward me.

"What the fuck did I do to you that you thought it was okay to hand me over to that psychopath?" Spittle hits his cheeks as he stares petrified into my eyes.

"I-I didn't kn-know what he w-would do," he stutters pathetically. "He...he said he j-just wanted t-to talk."

"Please," I sneer. "You drugged my fucking coffee. If that's not malicious intent..."

His eyes narrow, and I catch a flash of something I've never seen in him before. A jealous darkness that he's managed to hide. His lip curls back in a snarl, and I'm momentarily stunned as his face seems to change before my eyes.

"You waltz in here and get everything handed to you. Then you string me along like I'm a fucking dog—flirting with me one second, then running off to fuck one of the Princes the next."

What the actual fuck is he talking about?

"You were supposed to be one of us, but just like every slut in here, you had to go and fall for the fucking Princes. Sucked in by money, like every other greedy whore."

My palm cracks him across the face. I have heard enough of that crap from Lawrence; I'm sure as fuck not about to take it from this sorry sack of shit.

"Jealousy is not a good look on you, Michael. Nor does it give you the right to have me handed over to a fucking psycho to be tortured and threatened."

Something flashes behind his eyes too quickly for me to register, yet the dark scowl on his face never lessens. I hear footsteps as the others close in around us, and I lean in with a malicious smirk and whisper, "I'm going to enjoy watching them tear you limb from limb."

His eyes widen, and the dark expression melts away as fear takes hold. "W-what?" he screeches, squirming in my grasp until Mason's large hand claps down hard on his shoulder.

"Good to see you again, Michael."

The pathetic shit begins to tremble, his eyes darting from face to face as he takes in the ring of muscle surrounding us.

"N-no. I didn't know," he cries.

No one pays him any attention as Hawk and Mason pin him between them and march him toward the forest. The rest of us form a tight circle around them, Emilia on one side and Wilder on my other.

I feel like a fucking god as Michael's screams for help are ignored by passing students, everyone looking away as we pass them, proceeding on our death march into the night.

Little Warrior

CHAPTER NINE

I crack my knuckles menacingly as the eight of us form a circle around Michael. The worthless fuckhead is already on his knees, crying like a baby and begging for mercy, like the pitiful sap I always knew him to be.

Thanks to the cloudless sky above, there is enough light from the moon to light up the clearing, eliminating the need for flashlights tonight and adding a macabre feel to the whole ordeal. Fitting, considering this piece of human trash is about to wish he was never born. No one—and I mean fucking *no one*—crosses the Princes, and messing with Hadley is something none of us will stand for.

"Please," he blubbers. I roll my eyes, *fucking pathetic*.

"Jesus Christ," Hawk snarls. "Be a fucking man and stand up."

He doesn't even try to get to his feet, too busy looking between each of us, hoping he'll find a sympathetic face—he won't. Hawk, West, Cam, Beck, and I look like the harbingers of death as we tower over him with stone-cold expressions, while Wilder wears his usual psychotic fucking grin. The dude gets way too much enjoyment from watching others suffer. The rest of us do this shit because we have to, because it's necessary, but Wilder fucking revels in it.

Wilder huffs impatiently when Michael shows no signs of getting to his feet on his own. "Dude, you're killing my buzz. Get the fuck up." Not giving Michael a second to obey, he stomps into the circle, grabs Michael by the hair and all but drags him to his feet, screaming and crying. *Well, that's one way to go about it.*

"Please, Hadley," he pleads, turning imploring eyes on my girl. "I didn't mean to. I-I didn't know—"

"Don't fucking talk to her," I snap, my menacing tone making him jump. "Don't even fucking look at her."

My Little Warrior is so fucking strong, standing there with her back ramrod straight and her chin in the air, her signature *fuck off* expression on her face.

Emilia stands at her side, looking equally repulsed as she scowls at Michael.

"Emilia," he pleads, trying to gain her sympathy next. "Don't listen to them. They've got it all wrong. I didn't do anything."

He starts toward her, and as he reaches out a hand to grab her, Hawk intercepts and grabs him by the neck of his shirt and hauls him back into the center of the circle. "Don't fucking touch her, either. Emilia's one of us. She's not going to fall for your pathetic act." Standing over a head taller than Michael, he sneers down at him, "You know what you did, why you're here. Accept your punishment like a fucking man."

Without further delay, he swings his arm back and drives it into Michael's face. I hear the sweet sound of a bone snapping, quickly followed by a howl of pain. Fucking music to my ears.

I let Hawk get in another few blows before I step forward, needing to sate my own anger before the fucker becomes unconscious. Seeing me, Hawk steps aside, and with a shit-eating grin on my face, I take up where he left off. I plow my fist into his nose, snapping the cartilage, and blood rushes over his face. My next hit is aimed at his stomach, following several more to his ribs. By the time Beck moves to take over, I'm sure he's got a few broken ribs to match his broken nose.

Blood is splattered over my top and dusts my knuckles, and as I stare down at my hands, I feel more satisfied than I ever remember feeling after a fight. There's something about fighting for vengeance that makes it all the more gratifying, and correcting any wrongdoing against Hadley makes it sweeter still.

Cam takes his turn after Beck, followed by West. He might not have the same power behind his punches as the rest of us, but he more than makes up for it with the palpable rage pouring off him.

By the time it's Wilder's turn, Michael is a curled-up ball on the ground. Usually, I'm not one to beat on a man when he's down, but in this case, that fuckface deserves every second of pain he's experiencing. He deserves to feel every moment of suffering Hadley endured over the last two weeks. We haven't gotten any details out of her yet, but the new scars marking her body tell enough of what she's had to survive.

Wilder starts kicking Michael, and just as he appears to be getting into the swing of it, Hadley shouts, "That's enough!"

Surprised, I glance over at her. There's a pained expression on her face, and she's squeezing Emilia's hand tightly, yet I don't think her reaction has anything to do with Michael.

"But—"

"Hadley's right," Hawk snaps, talking over the top of Wilder. "He's had enough."

Stomping over to Michael's bleeding, curled-up body, I crouch down in front of him. "Hey!"

He groans but doesn't open his eyes. "Hey! Don't pass out on us yet," I snap more harshly, smacking him on the cheek. The surprise sting spikes his adrenaline, and his eyes jump open. He blinks several times, struggling to focus on me, but I don't need him to see me; I just need him to hear what I have to say. I lean down, getting as close to his ear as possible. "If you tell anyone or show your face back here again, we'll tear your entire fucking life apart."

I take his responding groan as an agreement that he'll heed my warning. "Glad we understand each other." I give his cheek a condescending pat and stand up.

"Uh, what now?" Emilia asks, frowning at Michael's unmoving body.

We all look at one another, expecting someone else to have an answer to her question.

"Ugh, fuck me," Wilder groans, tilting his head back and rolling his eyes like the dramatic weirdo he is. "Put him in my backseat. I'll drop him off at the hospital and say I found him like that in town."

We all share a look, and I shrug my shoulders. "Sounds like as good a plan as any. I'll help him get Michael to the car, and then we can meet you back at the dorm."

Between the two of us, Wilder and I haul Michael off the ground, none too carefully, and drag him back through the forest. Parting ways with the others just before the forest meets the campus pathways, Wilder and I remain hidden in the trees until we're near the parking lot.

Once we reach his Mustang, he fishes his keys out of his pocket and unlocks the back passenger door, so we can maneuver the passed-out shithead into the back seat.

I *accidentally* knock his head against the top of the door as I shove him into the car. "Oops, my bad."

Wilder chortles ridiculously. "Don't get any blood over my seats, asshole."

"Dude, he's unconscious."

Wilder quirks a brow at me. "So? That's no excuse. Do you know how difficult it is to get blood out of that upholstery?"

I gape at him for a second before shaking my head. "I don't want to know."

He laughs and slams the back door shut.

"You good here?"

"Yeah, man. You go back to Sunshine. I'll make sure he doesn't die."

"Thanks, man." I tap my finger against the hood of his car as I pass and make my way back through campus to the dorms.

I feel like a weight has been lifted off my shoulders. I knew I never liked that fucking dweeb. The way he'd look at Hadley always got my hackles up, but Jesus, I never thought Lawrence would get his claws into him. It doesn't matter that he doesn't know what Lawrence is capable of, he had to have known what he was doing wasn't right. There's no excusing what he did. Hopefully, with him and Lawrence gone, this campus should be a safe place for Hadley. Now we just need to sort out the rest of our fucked up families then we might actually have a shot at a free life for all of us.

Walking back into the dorm, I find Hadley, Beck, and Cam on the sofa, with West sitting in a nearby chair. The four of them are chatting away like it's any other night, and a smile brightens my face as I stand and watch them. This is what I want to come home to every night—my best friends and the woman I love. I've never been able to picture a future for myself other than the unwanted one my parents set out for me. Still, everything's changing, and now that we've found Hadley, and Beck has joined our ranks, I'm starting to see a different future, one that I actually want.

"Hey, man," Cam greets, when the door closes behind me. "There's beer in the fridge."

Grabbing a bottle, I join them in the living room. "Where's Hawk?"

"He walked Emilia back to her dorm."

I quirk an eyebrow at West, who just shrugs. *That's strangely thoughtful of him.*

"Well, now that the violence of the evening is over, what are the plans for the rest of the night?" Beck whacks Cam around the back of the head, and the idiot just laughs.

"I think we're long overdue for a chill night on the sofa with popcorn and a movie," Beck responds instead.

"Mmm, that sounds good," Hadley agrees.

Lifting Hadley's legs off him, Cam gets up to sort out the popcorn and West flicks through the films. I take advantage of the open seat beside Hadley and slip into it, draping my arm over the back of the couch cushions.

Hadley watches me. "Can I try some of that?" she asks, pointing at my beer.

"Uh, you sure?"

"Yeah. I'm curious. I had a sip of champagne once with Emilia and—" She pauses, unwilling to say his name before changing direction. "Well, it was nice, so now I'm wondering what beer tastes like. Besides, I think I deserve a drink after the last few weeks." She laughs, but there's no humor behind it, and it quickly falls flat.

"What about the pain meds you got at the hospital?" I question, knowing it's not wise to mix the two.

"I only got a couple of days' worth. They're all gone now."

I hand over the beer, and she sniffs the bottle before bringing it to her lips and downing a large gulp. "Huh, not bad." She takes another long swig before passing it back. I'm barely paying attention as she pushes the bottle into my hands, too busy watching her. I take in the bags under her eyes, the dampened color of her irises, and the hard edge to her that I haven't seen in quite a while.

"You know, you don't have to be so strong all the time. It's okay to not be okay. You've been through more than most people experience in a lifetime. It's alright to take some time and just process it all."

"I'm fine. I'll *be* fine."

There's a determined set to her jaw, that newfound hardness solidifying further. I'm not sure if she's trying to fool herself or me, but I don't push her. If that's what she needs to tell herself, then so be it. I—*we*—will be here when the words are no longer enough to hold her together. For now, I pull her in against me, kiss her forehead, and hope I'm not losing the one thing that makes me feel alive.

∼

Prying my eyes open the next morning, I groan when they land on Cam's sleeping face, lying on my goddamn pillow. So fucking close I can smell his god-awful morning breath. *Fucking gross.*

Sitting up, I'm surrounded by half-naked men. *Jesus, fuck, what has my life become?* Hadley's gone, and when I check my phone, it's not even five a.m. yet.

Climbing out between the sleeping bodies, I pull on a pair of sweats and saunter through the apartment, quickly realizing she's not here. When I check her bedroom, I notice her gym bag is gone. *Damn woman doesn't know the meaning of rest.* Huffing out a sigh, I grab my own bag and head out the door after her.

As I walk into the gym, I pause in the doorway and watch as she beats relentlessly on a bag. Sweat coats her skin, and it's obvious she's been at it for a while. Regardless, she delivers blow after blow like she's not the slightest bit tired. The way she attacks the bag, she's like a woman possessed, and I'm pretty sure I know what demons are chasing her. I just wish I knew how to help her.

"Are you here to work out or watch me?" she pants breathlessly. I don't know how the hell she knows I'm here, with her back to me and all of her concentration on the bag.

"Can't I do both?"

She puffs out a laugh, dropping her arms and taking a step away from the bag to grab her water bottle. She watches me over the lip as I move to the weights bench and get set up. Seeming satisfied that I'm not here to keep a close eye on her, like I imagine Hawk would do if he knew where she was right now, she gets back to work.

Stepping up to the bag, she rolls her shoulders back and swings her arms. She moves into a wide stance, centering her weight before starting another punishing round of punches. I notice she's favoring her right leg, though, and despite the determined look on her face, she's sweating more than usual.

I watch her as I go through my usual morning routine, and when she shows no signs of letting up, I decide I need to interfere before she hurts herself.

Swiping a towel over my face, I move over to the mats.

"Little Warrior," I call out, "come spar with me." She stops and turns to look at me but doesn't move or respond as she debates what to do. "Come on. This is probably the only shot I have of beating you."

She scoffs. "Even with my injuries, you have no chance of beating me."

She still doesn't move, and I soften my features, pleading with her. "Just get over here. Trust me, hitting a bag isn't going to rid you of that anger. You need a human outlet. To hit flesh and bone and feel the damage you inflict beneath your own hands."

My words break through that hard exterior she's erected around herself since she got back, and for a second, I see the real Hadley hiding beneath it all. She's putting on a brave face, acting like everything is okay, but that can only last so long. She has to work through everything she's feeling and struggling to process.

The only thing that worked for me was fighting. I *had* to find a physical outlet for my anger, or it would have eaten me alive. Every time I felt an opponent's skin break beneath my own, their blood coating my hands, it was like I could breathe again. That insurmountable rage abated, at least for a while, and so long as I pretended every blow I delivered was directed at my father, I could find some sort of inner peace. I couldn't attack the source of my problems, so I used surrogates.

Hadley and I are alike in that way. I can see the flames of anger in her eyes, and if she's not careful, all that animosity will burn her alive. It'll consume her, until it becomes all she can think about. Dream of. Live for.

She moves toward me, until she's standing opposite me on the mat. "You better fight back this time, Hayes."

I smirk back at her. "Don't you worry about me, Little Warrior. Just focus on not letting me kick your ass."

She barks out a laugh and lunges toward me. Going straight in for a jab, she jumps back out of my arm span before I can retaliate.

We go round after round, neither one of us going easy on the other—okay, I definitely hold back a little, but I'm not about to tell Hadley that. Every punch she delivers is precise and well-balanced, delivering maximum damage but with the least amount of impact to her hands and wrists. She grits her teeth, and there is a determined set to her jaw. I can feel the fury burning off of her with every hit she lands, and see the flare of triumph every time she one-ups me. I've never been up against such an experienced opponent, and damn, if I'm not seriously turned on right now.

I'm blaming it on the fact that all the blood in my body has rushed south as to why I get distracted and give her the in she's been waiting for. She slips past my defenses, swooping my legs out from beneath me, and before I can comprehend what happened, I'm flat on my back on the mat. She stands over me with a smug smirk on her face, even as she pants heavily.

"What was it you were saying, Hayes? Something about kicking my ass?"

"No need to rub it in," I grumble, holding out my hand for her to help me. When she slaps her hand in mine, instead of letting her pull me to my feet, I tug her down on top of me and roll us over so she's pinned beneath me.

As I look down at her, I'm pleased to see a lightness in her eyes, and she appears more herself than when I first walked in. I don't know how long it will last, but if I've been able to bring her peace for at least a little while, then that's something.

Her hands slide up over my chest before she winds her arms around my neck and pulls me down until my lips brush hers. *Fuck.* It's been way too long since I tasted her lips on mine or felt her soft curves beneath me. I'm wholly lost in her touch. The second her tongue sweeps into my mouth, it's as if nothing else exists. My hands slide into her hair as I return her kiss, my tongue tangling with hers until we're both breathless.

Everything in my body is encouraging me to keep on, but I force myself to slow down—which is seriously fucking difficult, especially when she starts grinding against me.

"Hadley." The word is a half pant, half groan.

Ignoring me, Hadley hitches her leg over mine, using the momentum to turn us until she's hovering over me. She presses her finger against my lips. "Shh, don't talk." Leaning down, she kisses me again while she slips her hands under my muscle shirt and pushes it up my body until she can tug it off over my head.

My hands land on her hips as I look up at her reverently. I still can't believe she's here, that she survived. That I got so lucky as to find this amazing spitfire of a girl in this crazy, fucked-up world. I slide my hand into her hair, holding her still as I pillage her mouth, and roll us again so I'm settled between her spread thighs.

I grab her thigh and hitch it over my hip, opening her more as I grind against her, making her head fall back as her eyelids close and she moans.

"Mason," she pleads in a breathless pant.

I kiss my way down her neck and over the swell of her breasts, pushed up by her sports bra, then along her toned stomach until I reach the high waistband of her lycra shorts. I tug them and her panties down her legs until she's left bare before me, pausing for a moment to just appreciate all of her. My eyes roam over her fresh wounds that will leave new scars, noting how prominent her ribs have gotten, and by the time I lift my head to meet her gaze, I imagine the fire in my eyes matches hers.

Crawling up her until I'm once again situated between her thighs, I slide my hand into her hair and kiss her deeply. "You're fiercely beautiful. I'm in awe of your strength."

She looks up at me with a rawness I've never seen before, and I realize, for the first time, she has stripped herself bare, and what I'm seeing is all the vulnerability she works so hard to hide.

"It's tiring, being strong all the time."

"Then don't be. Fall apart, baby. I'll be here to put you back together." I rest my forehead against hers so all I can see is the turbulent thunderstorm whirling in her eyes. Nothing else exists but her. "It's you and me."

She tilts her head so her lips meet mine. In that kiss, I can taste everything she's not ready to say yet. I can taste how lost she is, the hopeless void she's on the cusp of falling into, and I return her kiss with all the ferocity of someone begging her to hold on, to keep fighting, to stay with me.

"I love you." Her words are a quiet whisper against my lips before she captures them in yet another kiss. She wraps her legs around my waist, crossing them at the ankles and using her heel to push my shorts over my ass. Lifting, I tug them down and check she's ready, then I line my dick up with her entrance and slide into her. My eyes roll back in my head, and I let out a blissful sigh. This, right here, is the best feeling in the world. It's like coming home after being away at war. When we're one like this, everything I've had to endure to get here suddenly feels worth it.

She moans and her legs tighten around me, encouraging me further until I'm so deep inside her I won't ever want to leave. I can't tear my eyes away from her face as I pump lazily into her, and she watches me back with that same open and awed-expression, like she feels the same things I do when we're together. The air seems to crackle around us, filled with sexual tension and something so much more meaningful. Something everlasting.

I drink in the flush that rises on her cheeks, commit every breathless moan to memory, until she's falling apart beneath me, and I follow her over the edge, reiterating my promise to her: *I'll be here to put her back together.*

Hadley

CHAPTER TEN

"What exactly do you think you're doing?" Hawk demands when I step into the kitchen later that morning, dressed in my school uniform.

"Eh, going to class? It is a weekday, after all."

"No, you're not. I've told your teachers you need another week off."

"No need, I'm all good."

"Firefly, you just got back. Why don't you take a couple of days to just relax? Chill on the sofa and watch some daytime television," West suggests, his tone more soft and coaxing than Hawk's sharp bark.

"Honestly, I'm fine. I have missed so much work, and I don't want to fall even further behind."

Hawk scowls at me for another moment before finally relenting. "Fine," he huffs out. "But don't overdo it, and stay with one of us."

"I don't need a babysitter," I seethe.

"Tough shit," he barks, sounding just as annoyed. "That's the only way I'm letting you out of this apartment."

"*Letting* me?"

West steps forward to stand between us, glowering at Hawk before turning to me, his eyes softening around the edges. "Please," he pleads. "We're all going to be stomping about like angry bears all day if we can't keep an eye on you."

My posture relaxes as I smile at him. "Of course. It's not like I'd want to spend the day with anyone else." His smirk grows, and we both ignore Hawk in the background as he throws his hands up in the air in exasperation and grumbles under his breath before stalking off like the grown man-child he is.

West moves to make me a cup of coffee, setting it down in front of me as I slide into a seat at the island.

"So, what have I missed?" I question, looking up at him over the lip of my mug. "I bet this month's girls are brewing up a storm over the fact that none of you have been around much the last couple of weeks."

West chuckles. "I bet they're more upset that we once again put a stop to the whole tradition."

My eyebrows climb up my forehead as my eyes widen. "You, what? When?"

"As soon as we got you back. We couldn't risk saying anything before then, and bringing any more trouble to our door, but we're fucking done with all of it now."

"But, what about our parents?"

West shrugs. "They're going to be too busy scrambling to rebuild the compound while freaking out over Lawrence's death and the company's future, to worry about what we're up to at school."

I gape at him for a moment before finding my words. "So it's done? For real this time?"

He leans across the island toward me, until he's so close I could just lean forward and kiss him. "Yeah, Firefly, it's done. We're sick of hiding our relationship with you. I want the whole school to know you're ours."

I quirk an eyebrow and smirk. "You mean that you're all mine."

He grins and murmurs against my lips, "That too," before stealing my breath with a dirty kiss.

Half an hour later, we're making our way to the dining hall. My palms are slick with sweat, and my body tense as my eyes dart around our surroundings. I'm not even sure why I'm nervous. My uniform covers all my healing cuts and new scars, and other than being the only girl wearing tights in May, I look like everyone else. Yet, my pulse is pounding so hard I can barely hear over the rushing of blood in my ears, and I feel like I can hardly breathe.

We pause outside the door to the dining hall, and I squeeze my eyes shut and take a few deep breaths to try and shake off the clawing anxiety threatening to overcome me.

The guys decided to send out a mass text telling everyone about the end of the tradition, so of course, since today is the first day they've all faced the school since then, it's guaranteed to be an epic shitshow. I can just imagine the carnage waiting to erupt behind these doors.

"Hey, guys, Sunshine," Wilder greets far too enthusiastically as he shoves his way between Mason and me, throwing his arm over my shoulder. "What are we all waiting for?"

"Get off her, asshole," Mason snarks, jamming his elbow into Wilder's ribs and shoving him backward before reclaiming his position beside me.

"Alright, man," Wilder wheezes from where he's hunched over, struggling to take in a breath. "No need to get violent."

He takes a minute to recover before standing upright, an obnoxiously bright smile lighting up his face as he stares at me. "Sunshine, good to see you back in your uniform again. Shame about the fake dating, though. I thought I made an excellent faux boyfriend."

"Dude, what the fuck is your problem?" Mason snaps. "You're just asking to get the shit beat out of you."

Wilder rolls his eyes, unbothered by Mason's growly tone or furious expression. "Calm your tits, big guy."

I fail miserably at holding back my laugh, as Mason's eyes narrow to slits.

"Hadley knows it's all in good fun."

I'm not sure that I do. I have no idea what Wilder really wants, but I find his honesty and the way he just blurts out whatever he's thinking without giving a shit what people have to say, refreshing.

"Come on, let's get on with this. It's been too long since I had pancakes, and I'm going to be a bitch all day if I don't get some before class starts."

"Sure you don't want a grapefruit instead? Much healthier start to your day." Hawk laughs at his own joke as I scowl at him.

"If you ever force a slice of grapefruit on me again, I'm going to ram it down your throat."

My threat only makes him laugh harder as he opens the door, and surrounded by my guys, the five of us walk into the dining hall. The whole room goes silent as everyone's eyes land on us.

Out of the corner of my eye, I notice Wilder slip in behind us and head over to Emilia before I turn to focus on the top table. I nearly stumble over my own feet when I find the most recent girls of the month sitting there, waiting.

"What the fuck?" I hiss under my breath to Mason. He doesn't say anything, and when I look up at him, his face is set in its usual stony expression, but I don't miss the tight set to his jaw or the anger burning in his eyes. He's just as pissed off about this as I am.

"What the fuck are you four doing here?" Hawk barks, not even trying to lower his voice. He doesn't give a shit if the whole school bears witness to him humiliating these pathetic girls.

"What are you talking about?" the one he's been "dating" asks, batting her eyelashes at him. "This is where we always sit for breakfast."

"Didn't you get our text?" Cam snaps irritably.

"Oh, that?" One of the other idiots giggles. "Wasn't that just some silly hoax?"

"No," Mason growls. "It wasn't."

The smile falters on the girls' faces for a second before they fix it back in place, but this time there's a sharp edge to them.

"You're joking, right?" Hawk's girl snaps. "There's no way you're doing this to us —*again*."

Hawk's jaw ticks, the only warning sign before he stomps the last few feet to the table. He grabs the back of the chair the girl closest to us is sitting in and drags it away from the table.

She screeches, but we all ignore her.

"Get. The. Fuck. Off. Our. Table," Hawk shouts, stomping to the next girl and doing the same thing. The last two catch on and scramble out of their seats before Hawk can reach them, the four of them scurrying off to sit elsewhere. His nostrils flare as he looks out over the rest of the hall, his turbulent gray eyes searing each and every person. "At the risk of repeating myself, this stupid, fucking tradition is over. For good. None of us are interested in dating you, fucking you, or doing anything else with you."

All three of my guys move to surround me—West on one side, Cam on the other, and Mason behind me, with his hand resting possessively on my hip. I feel his chest vibrating against my back as he speaks, his voice booming around the room in a declaration for all to hear, "We're dating Hadley. She's ours, and we're hers." Whispers immediately break out around the room. "Anyone who gives her any flack will answer to us."

I grumble under my breath about being able to take care of myself, and Cam nudges me in the ribs, smirking when I catch his eye.

"Ewww, like *all* of yours?" Bianca speaks up, wrinkling her nose in disgust as she glances toward Hawk, making her insinuation crystal fucking clear.

"What the fuck is wrong with you, Bianca?" Hawk snarls.

"Wait, hold on," Deke calls out, getting to his feet. "Her name's Hadley again? I thought it was Elizabeth."

"It's Hadley," I confirm forcefully, running my eyes over everyone else in the hall to ensure they understand me. I won't answer to Elizabeth, or any other name. If we're done with the pretense, I want to be done with it all. Fuck following the rules and doing what our parents want. I'm done hiding; done giving a shit.

Quirking a brow, Deke just looks baffled as he shakes his head, as if that will help him make sense of it all. "Jesus, your drama belongs on a shitty daytime TV show. I can't keep up with it all. One minute you're doing this or called that, and the next, it's something else. Who gives a fuck?"

I think that's the most insightful thing he's said all year.

"We give a fuck," Bianca snaps, the girls around her murmuring their agreements. "You've been messing us around all year. One scholarship girl can't just come in here and upend the whole system."

"Watch it, B," Cam growls in warning. "Hadley's a Davenport."

Hawk pins her with a ferocious look that brokers no argument. "Regardless, it's done. Get over it."

"What about you?" a girl asks. I vaguely recognize her as one of the girls Hawk chose back at the beginning of the school year, but I don't remember her name for the life of me. "If you're not dating *her*, then why are you not continuing the tradition?"

There's an underlying current of hope in her voice, and I can't decide if it's sad or just fucking desperate.

"Can't you all see how fucked up this tradition is? You offer yourselves up for us to fuck and throw away, and for what? We would never pick any of you to be anything more than an easy lay. Your ability to fuck our brains out has no bearing on any business decisions made by our parents. None of us are interested in any sort of relationship with shallow, vapid, social climbing brats."

Oh, wow. Hawk has gone full asshole. Even my eyes are rounded in shock as I stare at him. His nostrils flare as he glowers around the otherwise silent room before storming off.

Cam sighs beside me. "We should probably follow him."

"But pancakes..." I pout as my stomach grumbles in protest.

"Go check on him," Mason encourages. "I'll grab breakfast for us all." He winks at me, and I return it with a bright grin before he moves over to the kiosks to order food to go, and the rest of us make a hasty exit. As the door closes behind us, I hear the hall erupt into chatter.

Glancing around, I spot Hawk storming back toward his dorm. "Why don't you two help Mason with the food, and I'll go talk to Hawk."

"Sure." West gives me a quick kiss, and Cam wishes me good luck before I take off after Hawk.

"Hey!" I call out, but he doesn't turn around. "Asshole, don't make me chase after you."

That gets him to slow his pace, allowing me to catch up.

"Do you need a tampon?"

He stops in his tracks to stare at me in a mixture of confusion and disgust. "What?"

I point over my shoulder toward the dining hall behind me. "I figured that was a PMS bitch-fit you had back there."

"Ha ha," he snarks, rolling his eyes.

I grin. "I've discovered ice cream is the best thing in the world when I feel crabby. My personal favorite at the minute is peanut butter, but it changes like every week."

"I'm not PMSing!" he snaps.

I quirk a brow, unfazed by his outburst, and pull my tablet out of my bag, firing off a quick message while I wait him out. Eventually, he sighs, scraping his hand through his hair in frustration. "I'm just so sick of all this shit." He waves his hand around, indicating the campus. "I'd reluctantly resigned myself to the life our parents wanted for me, but with everything that's happened recently…" He trails off, shaking his head and huffing out another frustrated sigh. "Life's too short for me to be so fucking miserable all the time."

I shrug. "So, what will make you happy?"

At my question, he chuckles humorlessly. "That's the kicker. I have no fucking idea."

I knock my shoulder against his and lift one side of my lip in a soft smile. "I have no idea what makes me happy either. I don't even know where to start to figure it out." I notice the others coming toward us out of the corner of my eye, but I keep my focus on Hawk. "We could work it out together?"

He stares back at me for a long moment, and the guys have nearly reached us by the time he responds. "I'd like that."

"Like what?" Cam asks.

"I'd like to get some breakfast before my stomach eats itself," Hawk retorts, making Cam laugh.

"Why don't we eat on the grass?" Mason suggests, and we move to a grassy area just off the path. It's a gorgeous sunny morning, albeit it's spring, so the mornings are still on the chilly side, but it's nothing a warm breakfast and a cup of coffee can't fix.

Mason passes around the containers with each of our breakfasts in them. "Here's your ice cream," he says, handing me a tub and spoon. I thank him with a smile and pull off the lid, inhaling the nutty goodness before digging my spoon in. It tastes like fucking heaven in my mouth, and I struggle to hold back an obscene moan—pretty sure Hawk won't appreciate that.

Licking my lips, I pass the tub to Hawk beside me. He looks at it for a second, not immediately taking it from me. "I promise it helps." Leaning in, I add, "And where's a better place to start figuring yourself out than deciding your favorite flavor of ice cream?"

He still looks hesitant as he takes the tub and tries a small spoonful, before he smiles. "Mmm, that *is* pretty damn good."

Emilia and Wilder join us, and, even though I can't seem to relax, and my eyes dart anxiously around our surroundings, as if I'm expecting an ambush at any moment, I feast on my pancakes like nothing's wrong and listen to everyone around me laugh and chit-chat. I wasn't lying when I told Hawk I don't know what makes me happy. I have no idea who I am, or what I want to achieve with my life, but I didn't tell him that I don't even know how to be happy or even think about a future when I'm struggling just to get through the day.

West nudges my shoulder. "You okay?"

I plaster on a fake smile. "I'm all good."

By the time math rolls around that afternoon, my head is pounding, and I'm exhausted from being on edge all day. I nearly jump out of my chair when Emilia drops her backpack on the table beside me.

"Jesus, do you have to be so fucking loud," I snap irritably, and immediately regret it when her eyebrows jump up to meet her hairline and her jaw drops open.

I blow out a breath and close my eyes for a second, trying to rein in my anger. "I'm sorry. It's just been a long day."

She casts her eyes over my face before slowly sitting beside me. "Sure. It can't be easy to be back here…after everything." She chews on the inside of her cheek as she internally debates something before she glances warily around and leans in to whisper in my ear. "I can't pretend to understand what you've been through, but you know if you ever need to talk, I'm here."

I smile softly. "I know. I'm good. I-I'd rather not relive any of it, however. It's in the past."

She nods in understanding, and the teacher starts the class, thankfully ending our conversation. I barely take anything in for the next hour. If I'm being honest, I haven't heard a word anyone has said all day. I'm struggling to focus. Every time I let myself relax into a lesson, my palms start to sweat, my heart rate picks up, and the little voice in my head questions whether or not any of this is real. Maybe I'm still locked in that cell or strapped to the wall in Bowen's torture room, and this is all just a hallucination.

I feel along the side of my thigh, identifying the stitches holding the two sides of the wound on my leg together, and press my fingers into them. My face scrunches in pain. *Real. All of this is real. I'm not dreaming.*

Now, if only I didn't have to keep telling myself that just to make it through the day.

Hadley

CHAPTER ELEVEN

Do you miss me, Dove?

I awake with a gasp, quickly sitting upright in the bed as I clasp my chest. With trembling hands, I reach out and flick on the bedside lamp. I can feel the pulse hammering at the base of my neck, as I work to calm my breathing. *You're safe. You're in your room on campus. You're not back there.*

I toss back my covers, noticing how my top sticks to my clammy skin as I get out of bed and throw on my gym gear, not bothering to check the time. I can tell by the lack of light coming through the window that it's not even dawn yet, but there's no way I can get back to sleep now. My mind is racing in tune with my pulse, and the only way I know to stop the thoughts is to exhaust myself at the gym. These few hours each morning have become my only moments of peace all day. I don't know what's wrong with me, but when I'm not beating on a bag, or Mason, or pushing myself on the treadmill, I can't seem to focus. I've been snapping at everyone all week over the stupidest of things, and it's only getting worse, no matter how hard I try to hide it.

I push open the door to the gym and pull on the fingerless gloves Mason bought me. I drop my bag on the floor and quickly go through my warm-up routine, jumping up and down on the balls of my feet and windmilling my arms to loosen them up.

Once I'm ready, I fixate on the bag in front of me until I can clearly picture Lawrence's grotesque face—his too-bushy eyebrows, the way his nose curved slightly, the dimple in his chin—then I beat and beat and beat on that bag. The whole world fades around me. Nothing exists but Lawrence and me. This is the only time I feel in control, when I feel like *I* have all the power. The rest of the day, his ghost chases me around, whispering in my ear and taunting me from afar until I'm a strung-out mess. I can tell the guys are starting to worry. They keep asking if I'm okay, and the words *I'm fine* are beginning to lose all meaning.

I sense when he enters the room, the same way I get an inkling whenever he's nearby. It's like the air around him reacts to his presence, sparking to life. I respond to the change in the air like it's an extension of my own skin, yet I don't stop pummeling the bag. It's been the same all week. He stands and watches me for a while, before moving to the weight bench and going through his usual routine. When he's done with that, we duke it out on the mat, and I don't know what it is about us tackling one another, but when I'm facing off against him, drinking in his ripped abs and broad shoulders, I feel more like my old self. It's not the same feeling of control I get when punching the bag, but it's a different kind of contentedness. I can *almost* forget all the shit that happened to me. It's the same when I'm around any of the guys. The adrenaline that courses through my veins, creating a constant buzz just under the surface of my skin, seems to die down for a while, and I feel like I can breathe again.

But it never lasts long. Eventually, the fear seeps in, and I become consumed by runaway irrational thoughts. It's like an electrical typhoon in my brain that messes with the synapses and prevents them from firing properly.

By the time we're done with our workout, showered and ready for class, Cam is entering the apartment with breakfast for everyone. Since our showdown in the dining hall on Monday, we've avoided going back. Instead, Beck, Emilia, and Wilder join us every morning, and the eight of us enjoy a nice, peaceful breakfast before we have to leave and mingle amongst the prying eyes of the rest of the school.

Since Mason announced I was dating the three of them, the whispering and staring have gotten ridiculous. I can only imagine how bad it would be if they found out I was also dating the school counsellor. I don't miss the whispered 'slut' when girls walk past me or the filthy looks guys throw my way. I don't even want to know what disgustingly dirty things they're picturing. Thankfully, none are brave enough to do anything more than whisper or leer.

A pounding I'm becoming far too familiar with has started up behind my eyes by the time lunch rolls around. I meet the guys at the dining hall to grab our food, and we take it to eat back in the dorm.

As I'm walking out of the hall, the guys behind me, Bianca stomps past and scowls at me. "If it isn't the Slut of Pacific Prep," she sneers.

I spin to face her, my fists clenching at my side.

"What the fuck did you just call me?"

"You heard me. Anyone's vagina that's loose enough to take three dicks at once is obviously a whore."

Cam snorts behind me, and I think I hear him mumble, "That's not how it works," before someone whacks him around the back of the head.

"What the hell is your problem, bitch? What the actual fuck did I ever do to you?"

"You ruined everything when you showed up here!" Bianca cries.

I roll my eyes. "Grow up, Bianca, and take responsibility for your actions. I didn't do shit."

"HE LOVED ME!" she yells, before breaking down in tears. "We were going to get married. Then *you* showed up, and he changed."

I quirk a brow at Cam, who rolls his eyes at her dramatics. "That was *never* going to happen, B."

"Not you!" she sneers. "Lawrence."

We all freeze. "Lawrence?" Cam repeats. "As in my *dad*, Lawrence?"

"Yes," she snaps. "We were in love."

Damn, I kinda feel bad for the girl. He was most definitely *not* in love with her. I'm pretty sure he was incapable of giving a shit about anyone other than himself.

"Then *she* showed up here, and he became as fucking infatuated with her as you idiots." She glares thunderously at me. *And my moment of feeling sorry for her disappears just like that.* "He'd make me style my hair like yours." Her lip curls back in disgust. "And call him Sir." She steps toward me menacingly, unaware of the precarious churning of my stomach. "It was *your* name he'd call out when he was balls deep inside me. You and that fucking magical pussy you have that makes men drool all over you like fools. You're like the Pied Piper of dicks."

Bianca looks like she's about to launch herself at me and claw my eyes out. Hawk must see the unadulterated hatred in her eyes as he pulls me back a step. "Is Lawrence your baby's father?"

Bianca's gaze jumps to Hawk, her menacing expression melting away as a fresh set of tears well up in her eyes. Her lower lip quivers. "He told me to get an abortion, but I couldn't. He was just worried because I was still in school. It wasn't part of the plan, but I knew that he would see it differently once I graduated and we were married, and he'd regret making me get rid of it."

"I have a brother or sister?" Cam gapes.

"Half," Bianca snaps, her hostility making Cam scowl.

"If you've been with my father this whole time, then why have you been chasing my ass all over campus, demanding I pick you every month?"

Bianca's tears quickly dry up and her snooty attitude re-emerges, making me question just how much of this whole act is genuine.

"Lawrence has been weird all year. While I was certain I could bring him back to me, I couldn't put all my eggs in one basket. Not when I have a child to take care of now. I figured if something happened and Lawrence left me, I could convince you to marry me instead." A conniving smirk lifts one side of her lips. "That would teach Lawrence not to mess with me."

Dear god, this psycho bitch is as duplicitous as Lawrence. Perhaps the two of them would have been perfect together.

Cam gawks at her, likely seeing for the first time just how crazy she truly is.

Bianca dismisses him, once again searing me with a look of disgust. "But you just had to dig your claws into him too. You're such a whore."

I shrug my shoulders. "What can I say? I love me some good quality dick."

I bite my lower lip, holding back my laughter when I hear Hawk mumble, "Gross," under his breath.

Bianca snarls, stomping her feet like the entitled brat she is. "Just give me Lawrence. You can keep these idiots, but Lawrence is mine!"

Cam hedges forward, as if he's trying to get closer to a feral cat, but is unsure if it will scratch him. "Bianca," he starts hesitantly, grimacing as he blurts out, "my dad is dead."

Bianca spins toward him with wide eyes. "Wh-what? N-no. That can't be right. He's just been angry with me the last couple of weeks, because I couldn't do what he wanted. But he'll get over it. He always does."

Cam glances at each of us with a pleading look, not knowing what to say or do next. He needn't bother though, as Bianca, who's muttering to herself, pulls out her phone and dials a number that I'm assuming is Lawrence's. When he doesn't answer, she dials again, glowering at each of us with deadly eyes.

"You're lying," she snaps when he doesn't answer for the second time, dialing his number yet again as she shoves past us and away from the dining hall.

On Thursday, I'm on my way to my session with Beck when someone calls out my name. I turn to look over my shoulder, and I swear the world stops spinning for a second.

"L-Lawrence?" I squeak.

No. It can't be. I killed him.

I blink, and instead of Lawrence, I see Barton striding toward me. My breaths come in short pants and I swallow roughly as I glance around me, as if expecting Lawrence to jump out from behind a door or something.

What the fuck is happening to me?

"I've been searching for you everywhere."

I'm still looking nervously around me, but when he speaks, I try to shake off whatever the fuck that was and focus on him.

"I don't...What are you doing here?"

"Hawk hasn't been returning my calls, and I needed to talk to you."

I don't trust him, and his showing up here like this is just weird. It doesn't help that he looks nervous as he shifts awkwardly from foot to foot.

"I, uh...how have you been doing?" he asks.

"Fine."

An awkward silence passes between us for a second, and when he realizes I'm not going to divulge any more of my life to him, he jerks his head in some sort of a nod. "Good. Good. I'm glad. I, eh, wanted to give you this."

He holds out an inconspicuous white envelope, and I hesitate, reluctant to take it—or anything—from him. Seeing that I'm not going to accept whatever it is without more explanation, he says, "It's, uh, a bank card. I've set you up with an account and transferred funds over, so you've got the same as Hawk."

Frowning, and even less sure if I should accept it, I simply continue to stare at the envelope. "I don't want your money."

"It's your money. It's everything you would have had access to if you'd...you know." He looks away, unable to meet my eye as he cringes, leaving the rest of his words unspoken.

If I'd grown up under the Davenport roof, with my brother.

I'm still debating my response when I hear a door open behind me, and Beck's voice as he calls out. "Hadley?"

I turn to find Beck poking his head out of his office, his eyes darting between Barton and me. Straightening, he steps out and closes the door behind him, never taking his eyes off my father as he strides toward us. "What is going on here?"

Still clutching the envelope, Barton's hand falls to his side. "Ah, Beck. I just wanted to have a word with my daughter, in private."

Standing at my side, with his arms crossed over his chest, the edge of his tattoo sleeve creeping out from under his crisp white shirt, Beck stares deadpan at my father. "I'm afraid I can't let you do that."

Most likely shocked that someone has the audacity to say no to him, Barton stares surprised at Beck for a moment, before his brows pull together and his eyes darken somewhat. "I don't believe my family's business is any of your concern."

Beck takes a threatening step forward, and I can see him gearing up to tear Barton's head off. Before he can do any such thing, I place a hand on his arm and stop him, then look at Barton when I say, "Actually, it is his business. He knows everything." I can practically see the questions running rampant in Barton's head. "Besides, I'm not going anywhere alone with you. The last time I ended up alone with Lawrence, I was drugged and dragged back to Hell. God only knows what you'd try to do to me."

Barton's eyes bulge in shock, and the color seems to drain from his face. "What…I… No," he splutters, shaking his head as if the thought of him doing anything to me is outrageous. However, he's more than shown he doesn't give a shit about me.

I notice Beck glancing nervously around us, checking that no one else is around before he murmurs, "Why don't we discuss this in my office?"

I'm not fussed about being stuck in a small room with Barton, but he's here, and he's probably not going to leave until he's said whatever he has to say, so I guess I may as well get it over with. "Sure."

He holds his arm out, gesturing for Barton to go into his office, and we follow closely behind him. I haven't heard anything from him since he showed up in my hospital room. No doubt, he left and went straight to his buddies, to tell them all about what happened in the compound and of my little threat. So, the question is, what is he doing here now?

Hawk and I filled everyone in on Barton's little visit, so Beck is probably just as baffled by him showing up here unannounced as I am.

"What do you think he wants?" I whisper conspiratorially to Beck while keeping my eye on Barton as he moves to sit in one of the chairs in front of Beck's desk.

"No idea." He shrugs. "Guess we should find out."

Stepping into the office, I lean against the wall beside the door, refusing to move any further into the room when a threat lurks nearby.

Beck closes the door after himself and sits behind his desk, resting his arms on the table and pinning Barton with an assessing look. "What is this all about, Mr. Davenport?"

My father shifts in his chair to focus on me. "After, uh, what you said in the hospital, it got me thinking…about the night you disappeared."

The thought of finding out more about what happened to me perks my interest, and I straighten slightly against the wall, darting my gaze to Beck before focusing back on my father.

"Your mother and I were celebrating our wedding anniversary. We had a big party like we do every year." He sighs and shakes his head. "I honestly don't remember anything in particular about that night. It was just like every other party…until the next day, when I went into your room to check on you and Hawk…you were gone." There's a genuine look of sadness in his eyes and a heavy ring to his voice, but I refuse to let his show of grief bother me. "I looked everywhere and interrogated all house staff, but no one had seen you. Then I called a meeting of all four families.

"That morning, I couldn't get a hold of Lawrence, which isn't all that unusual. Nonetheless, he was the one who gave me the number for the private investigator."

"Why didn't you just go to the police?" Beck interrupts, frowning.

My father sighs, and I swear he looks years older than he did when he walked in here. "I wanted to. I argued with the others about it, but ultimately, we couldn't risk bringing the police in and having them dig too far into the company."

"Right, so you chose the company over your daughter. Real nice, *Dad*." He grimaces at my snarky attitude.

"Lawrence promised this PI was the best in the country. He said he'd do a much better job than the police—that this guy was my only hope of finding you." The last sentence is exhaled on a forlorn sigh, and despite my mental chant to not let him sucker me in, my heart clenches in my chest. Not so much for Barton, but for Elizabeth. Perhaps she could have been saved if he hadn't listened to Lawrence or done what the others wanted. I can see the same thoughts in Beck's regretful gaze.

"So I'm guessing Lawrence paid off the PI or something?" I ask the question in the same tone I'd use to ask about the weather, using it to mask my inner turmoil.

"I'm guessing so. At first, he'd update me on leads he had and show me pictures of girls who could be you, but nothing panned out. After a few years, he tried to convince me to stop. I wasn't ready to hear any of it, and I just kept throwing more money at him, but eventually, your mother gave me an ultimatum. She had managed to move on with her life—her own way of coping, I imagine—and I ultimately had to do the same. I still had Hawk, and I needed to focus on him."

"Except you didn't," I bite out angrily. "By the sounds of it, you were never around."

He grimaces, knowing he's been caught out. "It wasn't easy. Every time I looked at him, I saw you. It became easier to keep an eye on him from afar, but just because I wasn't always around doesn't mean he was ever far from my thoughts."

"He deserved better." I sigh, broken-hearted for the lives both Hawk and I lost out on.

Barton lifts his head, looking me in the eye for the first time since he walked in here. "You both did."

The office door bursts open, making me jump as Hawk stomps in, bringing with him a hurricane of emotions. He strides right over to his father, towering above him. "What the hell are you doing here?"

He doesn't wait for an answer, his gaze roaming around the room until he spots me leaning against the wall behind him. His eyes critically run over me before he meets my gaze, asking a silent question—*are you okay?* I nod, letting him know I'm fine, and he returns his intense stare to Barton, cocking a brow as his impatience wears out.

"You weren't answering my calls," Barton barks, "and I wanted to check on Elizabeth."

"Hadley," I interrupt, my sharp tone cutting across whatever Hawk was going to say next. Barton's gaze snaps in my direction, his brows pulling together in confusion. "My name is Hadley."

"No, it's—"

"Elizabeth died," I seethe. "It doesn't matter what happened, or why. The daughter you knew died a long time ago. I'm not her, and I'm never going to be."

Barton looks like someone tore into his chest and ripped his heart out. His face crumples, utterly grief-stricken, and he seems to sag into the chair, boneless.

I hear footsteps racing down the hall, and a second later, the others come running in, breathless as their eyes dart around the room to assess the situation.

Cam's wide eyes land on me, and he comes over, brushing a thumb over my cheek. I'm not sure what I look like to him, but it must be worse than usual, given the concern etched into his features. "He didn't hurt you, did he?"

I give him a soft, reassuring smile. "No," I assure him. "Not in the way you're thinking." He looks at me, bewildered, and I can see the unasked questions in his eyes. Thankfully he knows not to ask them, not here, and instead slips his hand into mine, leaning against the wall beside me as we survey the room.

I notice Barton looking at where our hands are joined, before Hawk's pissed-off growl garners his attention. "Why are you suddenly giving a shit?"

"Watch your tone, son! I have *always* given a shit."

"Right." Hawk scoffs. "Like when you didn't look for her for fifteen years, or when you signed a business contract that involved marrying her off to some guy she doesn't know. Were you giving a shit when you—"

"Alright," Barton snaps, a mixture of regret and anger flashing across his face. "I get it. I've failed as a father, but I have only been trying to do what I thought was right."

I've got no idea how the fuck he thinks that, and apparently neither does anyone else, based on the various *what the fuck* expressions the others are sporting.

"It's fine, Hawk," I mumble, but the words only seem to stoke the fire of his anger.

"It is not fucking *fine*, Hadley!"

I turn to face him, my lips pinched. "No, it's not, but it is what it is. Nothing's going to change what happened."

Hawk and I share a moment, thick with all the memories we should have shared, but underneath all that pain is our newfound solidarity and a strengthening of the promise to always be there for each other from here on out.

When he looks away, Hawk straightens his shoulders and fixes Barton with a hard stare. "Alright, well, while you're here, we need to talk about what you know…and what you've told the others."

Unbothered by the sudden tension that has leaked into the air and the menacing glowers he's receiving from each of us, Barton returns his son's arduous stare. "I haven't told the others anything about your involvement in what happened at the compound, or Lawrence's death." His gaze flicks briefly to mine.

"Why would you do that?" I question. I half expected him to go back to his wife and West's dad and tell them everything.

He looks incredulous, like he can't believe I even have to ask the question.

"You're my children, and as hard as it is to believe that Lawrence would do such a thing, if I'd known where you were, I'd have done *anything* to get to you."

Pretty words, but that's all they are.

"Even at the expense of your precious company?" Hawk sneers.

Barton sighs, sinking deeper into his chair. "I know you'll find this hard to believe, son, but I never wanted any of this. I argued against recruiting children for years, but they outnumbered me in the vote, and after El—uh—Hadley disappeared, I just gave up caring." He shrugs. "I let them do whatever they wanted."

Sounds like a great excuse to me—blaming everyone else and shouldering none of the responsibility yourself.

I share a look with Beck, and I can see he doesn't quite believe Barton either. "What is it you do want, then?" he asks, watching him closely.

Barton glances at Hawk, then at me before he responds, "I just want my family back together."

Yeah, I can't see that happening anytime soon.

Hawk and I share a look, and I can see he's trying to figure out if we can trust him.

When he focuses back on his father, he's got a serious, no-nonsense expression on his face. "As far as we're concerned, Lawrence is dead, and the compound has been destroyed. Do we have anything we have to worry about?"

"I'm not going to tell your mother, or Wilbert, any of this. If they ever found out…" He shakes his head, not finishing his sentence, but he doesn't need to. We might have burned their compound to the ground, but they still have plenty of mercenaries working for them that are away on jobs and live elsewhere. If they had any reason to suspect it was us, we'd be dead.

"Why wouldn't you tell your wife?" I question suspiciously.

"She's as invested in the company's future as much as the others. She's been making the decisions for our family and running things for a long time now. I'm essentially just the figurehead."

Looking at the others, I'm not the only one surprised by that statement.

"She and Wilbert are planning to rebuild. They think a rival company attacked the compound."

"A rival company?"

Barton quirks a brow at me. "The mercenary business is extremely cutthroat. You didn't think we were the only ones out there, did you? The high level of security was intended for more than keeping people in. We've had issues in the past with competitors taking out our people, so the working theory is that this was an escalation in their attempts to wipe us off the map."

"At least that works in our favor." West chews on his bottom lip as he thinks. "They won't have any reason to suspect us."

"As long as no one gives them a reason," Beck sneers, glowering at Barton in warning.

"I've already told you I'm not going to tell them anything," Barton seethes, getting angry.

"I'm sure you'll understand if we can't trust you," Hawk states bluntly, not sounding as though he gives a shit about whether or not his dad understands.

Barton presses his lips together, and I don't miss the hurt look that flashes across his face. "I get that. I never wanted you this involved, not in this side of things. Unfortunately, you'll have to continue to play along for now."

"For how long?" I snap. "They've been playing by *your* rules their whole lives. When do they—any of us—get to start living our lives, *our* way?"

I can't place the look in Barton's eye, but I'm surprised at the strength of the promise in his words. "I know you don't trust me, and I don't blame you. Play along a bit longer, and I *promise* I'll help you shut the whole thing down. Then you can do whatever you want with the rest of your lives."

Sweetheart

CHAPTER TWELVE

I don't trust Barton Davenport, and thankfully it doesn't look like anyone else does either, as each of us share distrustful looks after his little *promise*. He's just as likely to toss us under the bus to save his own ass.

Unfortunately, if what he's saying is true, that they're talking about rebuilding the compound, then we might have no choice but to rely on him. We thought that with the building destroyed, and both Lawrence and Frank out of the picture, we'd be fucking done with this bullshit. But of course, you have to chop the head off a snake to kill it. Unfortunately, this snake still has three heads left.

"Fine," Hawk eventually spits out. "But we do things *our* way." Barton doesn't seem pleased, yet he doesn't argue. "Oh, and just so you know, we're done with the tradition."

"But—"

"And I'm not marrying Wilder," Hadley throws in, ignoring Barton's protest.

"She's not marrying *anyone*," I growl out before he can get any ideas about setting her up with someone else. He looks at me in confusion before he tries to argue again.

"I don't—"

"It's non-negotiable," Mason interrupts this time, stepping closer to Hadley so his arm brushes hers. Her other hand is still clasped tightly in Cam's, and I can see Barton getting more confused by the second. It's almost comical.

Seeing that there is no point in disagreeing, he stops trying. "Alright." His gaze keeps bouncing between each of us, questions swirling around in his head, but wisely he doesn't ask any of them. Not long later, after placing an envelope with Hadley's name scrawled across it on my desk, he leaves.

It takes longer for me to kick the rest of the guys out, so Hadley and I can salvage what remains of her session—ah, who am I kidding, our hour is long since over. I just wanted time alone with my girl. I've hardly gotten any since we got her back, and I've heard from the others that she's not sleeping well, and she's been jumpy and on edge. All perfectly normal considering everything she has been through, but it just makes it harder for me to keep my distance from her and maintain this pretense. Especially now that the guys are being open about their relationship with her. I'm mature enough to admit I'm jealous. A few times I have spotted her with them on campus, with their arms wrapped around her, kissing her, and *goddammit*, if I don't want to claim her as mine too.

The second the door clicks closed behind the others, I drag her into my arms and kiss her like she's the oxygen I need to breathe. "I think we need to look at upping the number of weekly sessions you're getting."

She laughs, her warm breath brushing over my lips before she kisses me again. "I won't say no to that."

Before I can let my dick start calling the shots, I drag her over to the sofa and bundle her into my arms. For a long moment, the two of us just lie there. It feels surreal to have her back in my arms again. I tried not to think about the worst possible outcome while Lawrence had her, but it was impossible to stop the dark thoughts from creeping in. The possibility of never seeing her again, of never having another quiet moment together, or watching her face light up when she tries a new flavor of ice cream. There are so many firsts she has yet to experience, and I want to capture every single one of them. This spitfire of a girl hasn't had the chance to live yet, and I can't imagine what sort of person I would have devolved into if Lawrence had robbed her of the opportunity to find out.

"What's in the envelope?" I ask, pointing at where it's still sitting, untouched, on the desk.

Hadley sighs and turns her head toward the desk, a frown tugging down the corners of her lips. "Barton set me up with a bank account."

"Is that a bad thing?"

"I don't know. I don't want his money or to be tied to him in any way, and I definitely don't want to feel indebted to him."

"I wouldn't necessarily consider it *indebted* to him, but more as acknowledging what is rightfully yours."

She turns to look at me. "That's what Hawk says too."

"Well, you don't have to decide what to do about the money right now. Let's just focus on getting to the end of the school year."

We lapse into silence for a bit before I dare to ask, "How have you been coping?"

She lets out a long exhale at my question and focuses on her finger as it trails a pattern across my shirt for several minutes before responding.

"It's weird being back here. Everything feels so…normal. I'm not sure how to go back to the way things were before."

"No one is expecting you to just dive back in like nothing happened. You went through a trauma, it's natural for you to have trouble adjusting."

She just sighs and snuggles deeper into me. She's got such solid protection barriers erected around herself that if you didn't know her as well as I do—as we all do—or be on the lookout for small tells, you'd think she had assimilated back into her regular routine without any issues. She's more standoffish than she used to be, and the defenses she had in place when she first showed up here have been reconstructed and reinforced with steel. It's like she's here, with us, but she isn't. A part of her is still trapped back in the compound, and I have no idea how to bring her back to us. I'm a school counselor, not a goddamn psychiatrist. I'm not equipped to deal with post-traumatic stress. I know enough to know that's what this is, and that I don't have the necessary training in cognitive therapy to help her. I'm afraid of pushing her too hard and making things worse, but equally, letting her struggle alone isn't going to help her either. So instead, I'm settling for some middle ground where *hopefully* she knows we are here for her, except I'm not pushing her to talk about anything before she's ready.

I roll us over so we're lying side by side on the narrow sofa and I can look into her eyes. "Whatever you're feeling right now is perfectly okay. It doesn't make you weak or less of a person. Taking another person's life can take a huge toll on you, mentally."

Hadley scoffs softly. "I've killed people before, Beck."

"This is different, and you know it. Lawrence wasn't just some nameless, faceless hit." I tuck a strand of hair behind her ear. "It's okay if you're happy he's dead or if you have mixed feelings. It's even okay to not know how you're feeling about it."

She lowers her eyes, but I see the sheen of tears before she blocks them from my view, and I pull her in against my chest, stroking her hair reverently.

"It feels so surreal," she murmurs. "I see him sometimes or hear his voice…it's like—I feel like I'm going crazy." Her words are a barely heard whisper, but they break my heart all the same, and I wrap my arms more tightly around her, kissing the top of her head.

∼

"We need to talk about Hadley," I tell the guys on Sunday night. Hadley is at her movie evening with Wilder and Emilia, and it's the first time since she's been back that I've had a chance to sit down with the guys and actually talk. I hate talking about her behind her back like this, but I don't see that there is anything else for it.

"We do," Mason agrees. "I'm worried about her. She's running herself ragged. She's at the gym for hours every morning, and last night I caught her sneaking out for a run after we all went to bed. I don't think she's sleeping, not that she will let any of us in to sleep with her."

"I snuck into her room the first night we got her back, but she's started locking the door." I can see the hurt in Cam's face and the worry in his eyes.

"She seemed okay the first couple of nights, but since then, she's been distant," Mason explains.

I mull over his words for a second before saying, "I think she's having nightmares, and she doesn't want us to know about them. The painkillers she was on when she first came home probably knocked her out at night, and now that she's no longer taking them, she's not able to sleep as well."

"It's not just nightmares, though," West mentions. "She's not herself. Someone's phone went off in computer class the other day, and she nearly jumped out of her skin. I could see it in her eyes, she wasn't there anymore. It was as if the noise triggered something, and she disappeared somewhere else for a few minutes. She shrugged it off but was distant for the rest of the day after that."

I chew on my bottom lip before deciding to tell the others what she confessed to me the other day. "She's seeing and hearing Lawrence." I feel like I'm betraying Hadley's trust by telling them, but honestly, I don't know what to do. I know they're just as worried about her as I am. If we have any hope of helping her, we need to work together, and to do that, we all need to know what's going on with her.

"What?" Cam looks paler than he did a moment ago. "But he's—"

"Dead," I finish for him. "Yeah, you and I both saw him. There was no surviving that."

"That bad?" West's nose scrunches.

"I'm pretty sure I could see his intestines."

"She was in some sort of trance when I arrived. It was as if she couldn't stop herself, and she just kept stabbing him."

I sigh. "I think she has PTSD from it all."

Cam nods thoughtfully. "Who could blame her? Anyone else would be a curled-up ball, rocking back and forth on the floor, muttering nonsense to themselves."

"What can we do to help her?" Hawk asks. There's a serious set to his jaw, and it would be impossible to miss the underlying anger. "I have tried getting her to talk to me, but all she ever says is that she's *fine*." He spits out the word like it's acid on his tongue.

"Same," Mason agrees, and West and Cam nod their heads as well.

I wipe my hand down my face, feeling exhausted and unsure. "I don't know. I'm afraid of us pushing her too far, and she snaps or has a mental break or something, but it's becoming pretty fucking clear that she's not coping."

Our conversation halts when the door opens and Hadley walks in. She pauses, seeing us all gathered in the living room, probably looking suspicious as fuck.

Her eyes narrow, and she tilts her head slightly. "What are you guys up to?"

"We're just trying to decide what to do about our parents, if they're going to rebuild the compound," Hawk explains, his lie coming out flawless.

"Oh." She walks over to us, and West moves over to allow her to squish in between us on the sofa. "What are you thinking?"

"I say we tell them to go fuck themselves," Cam states, crossing his arms over his chest and leaning back in his seat, like that solves the problem.

"Yeah, that will go over really well." I roll my eyes.

"Any chance they'll just leave us all out of it?" Hadley asks optimistically, but the look on her face says she already knows the answer.

"No chance. We know too much, and it's only our parents and Wilbert left."

West scoffs. "Yeah, and my dad's going to be fuck all help. All he gives a shit about is drinking and fucking."

"We need to stand up to them and tell them we're not taking their shit anymore," Hawk snarls angrily. "Without the compound, what can they really do?"

"They still have the adult mercenaries," Hadley wisely states. "They don't live in the compound."

"Lawrence was the one who dealt with them, though, right?" Hawk asks her.

"I think so."

"And you said the rest of our parents never really bothered with the compound or getting to know the mercenaries. So they are unlikely to have any of them in their pockets. It's not going to be as easy to just phone them up and ask for their help."

"True." Hadley chews on her lower lip as she thinks through what Hawk is saying. "It's still a risk, though."

"I don't care. I'm fucking sick of them ruling over me." Hawk shifts so he can lean forward in his seat, placing his arms on his knees and looking intently at Hadley. "The compound is gone. Lawrence is dead. I'm not going to let them be the next ones to dictate your life for you." He looks at each of us. "I say it's about time we *all* claim our lives back."

Glancing at the others, everyone has an equally determined look in their eyes as they nod in agreement. When my gaze fixes on West, he catches my eye, and with a steely resolve, he silently tells me he's ready to get out from underneath our father and start his own life.

"Alright," I agree. "I guess we're telling them all to go fuck themselves."

Cam whoops-whoops. "Told you that was an excellent plan."

∽

TWO DAYS LATER, we pull up outside the high-rise our parents' legitimate business operates out of. It's my first time here, and I optimistically hope it will be my last. I have no issues with the legitimate side of their business, but I want no part in any of it—legal or otherwise. This corporate world is not for me, and I'm more than ready to wash my hands of it.

We climb out of the car, and I follow the others through the glass door and across the lobby, into an elevator, and up to the thirty-seventh floor.

"Boys," a young receptionist purrs, her eyes bouncing over us like she can't choose which one of us she wants to focus on. The only one who doesn't get a mental undressing is Hadley. "I didn't know all of you would be stopping by today."

"We're here to talk to our parents," Hawk says sharply, barely paying the girl any attention.

"Oh, well, they're busy right now."

"We don't mind waiting."

The girl pauses for a moment before she gathers herself. "Of course, follow me." This time her smile is tighter and less flirtatious, as she leads the way down a hall.

We follow her into a large board room with an impressive view over the city.

"Can I get you anything to drink?"

We all murmur, "No thanks," but rather than leaving us to it, she walks over to Cam, placing her hand on his forearm. "I'm so sorry to hear about your father. If you need *anything*, just let me know." She trails her long fingernails down his arm, making it clear precisely what she means by that, before giving him one last lascivious look and leaving the room.

Cam's lip curls up in a sneer, and my gaze darts to Hadley, who is glaring daggers into the door where the girl disappeared. "Bitch," she mumbles under her breath, making me chuckle.

The others move to take their seats along one side of the large boardroom table, but Hadley and I hesitate a second before taking a seat each on either end of the row. Despite being told they were busy, we aren't left waiting long before the door is pushed open and all three parents stride in, wearing various expressions ranging from confusion, to anger, to curiosity.

"What's this all about?" Maria snaps. The three of them move to sit opposite us, and I don't miss how Maria nudges her husband out of the way so she can sit in the middle of the table. *Interesting.*

Her eyes assess each of us, lingering longer on Hadley before focusing on her son. Hawk takes the lead. Leaning forward, he rests his arms on the table and steeples his fingers as he eyes each of our parents.

"We understand you're planning on rebuilding the compound—"

"That's right," Maria cuts across, sounding more enthusiastic than she did a second ago as she misunderstands where Hawk was going with his little speech. "We'll be soon calling on all of you to help us get back on our feet. We will need to rebuild as quickly as possible. It's great to see you all so ready to prove—"

Hawk smiles tightly. "I'm afraid you've misunderstood why we're here, *Mom*." Maria's eyebrows lift and her lips thin. "We're done with all of this. We don't want a part in any of it. Taking over this company was never something any of us wanted, and we certainly never wanted to run some fucked up organization that snatches children off the street and forces them to become trained killers."

Maria's gaze roams over Hawk's face. She never once looks away from him. Instead, she leans in, matching his pose. "Is that so, son? And what makes you think you can just walk away from your legacy? You have no money, prospects, and apparently no common sense." Now she turns her steel-cold gaze on each of us. "Have you all forgotten what we said would happen to West if any of you stepped out of line? Maybe you need another demonstration?"

My hands form tight fists beneath the table, and *god*, do I want to dive across it and slap that fucking smirk off her face.

I notice the annoyed tick in Hawk's jaw, but it's the only tell of how angry he is. "It appears you've forgotten you have no mercenaries, no compound, and"—he glances at the two empty seats on their side of the table—"you're missing two board members. Would be a shame if that number became three."

"Are you threatening us, boy?" my father snarls, his double chin wobbling. Hawk barely spares him a glance, dismissing him as the non-threat he is.

Maria throws her head back and laughs, this high-pitched tinkling sound that lacks any humor. When she fixes her steely gaze on Hawk again, the corner of her lip curls up in a cruel smirk. "You think you can threaten us?" Her smirk morphs into a sneer, and the look she spears each of us with is one of pure disgust. "You're nothing but spoiled little children. You have *no* idea what it takes to thrive in this world. All of you should go back to school, and we'll pretend this little…visit never happened. We'll call you when we need you."

She goes to stand, but Barton speaks up, surprising me, "If they don't want to be involved, we should just let them be. We don't need them anyway."

Maria freezes in place, and the look she gives her husband is pure malevolence. It's like nothing I have ever seen on her face before, making me reconsider every moment I've seen them together. They always looked so happy—was all of it for show? Surely not.

Her lips pinch and she pins him with a look that would slay weaker men. "I always knew you were fucking pathetic," she spits, and I'm pretty sure I'm not the only one gaping slack-jawed at her hostile tone. "You know as well as I do that's not possible." She glowers at each of us. "I have had enough of this nonsense. You'll return to school and await our call, or there *will* be consequences."

Having said her piece, she gracefully gets to her feet, quickly followed by my father and Barton, and strides out of the room. My dad is right behind her, but Barton hesitates, looking between his son and daughter. He looks like he's about to say something, but after a second, he closes his mouth and follows after his wife.

After they've all gone, all six of us share a look, no one willing to say anything in case we're overheard, before we get to our feet and quickly make our exit.

Hadley

CHAPTER THIRTEEN

I'm still stunned by what went down in our parents' office by the time we make it back to the dorm.

"Dude, did you see the way your mom turned on your dad?" Cam exclaims as we all walk into the apartment.

"Have you ever heard her talk to him like that?" West questions.

"Never. Sure, they've argued over the years, but for the most part, they seem to get along—at least, I thought they did."

Hawk grabs a six-pack of beers while the rest of us spread out across the chairs, getting comfy.

"It's pretty clear your mom only cares about the company but is it possible your dad was telling the truth the other day?" I can see West mulling over all the possibilities.

"That he gives a shit about us?" Hawk scoffs, running his hand through his hair. He drops into an empty chair, tilting his head back to stare at the ceiling. "Fuck if I know."

Silence settles over us as we each process this afternoon's events. My mother couldn't have looked more indifferent when she looked at Hawk and me. She may as well not have been looking at her own children at all. And the casual way she threatened West. Anger flares, and I feel the sting as my nails dig into my palm.

"What are we going to do now?" I snarl angrily. "We can't allow them to keep threatening West."

"We won't," Hawk promises, and the sharp edge to his tone, giving away how furious he is, has me looking his way.

"My dad cares more about his cushy life than the company," West pipes up, and I can see the wheels churning in his head as he thinks.

"We could scare him into disappearing," I say, thinking aloud. "Show Maria that we're making good on our threat." A wicked grin lifts one side of my lips. "I've found a knife to the hand or thigh is an excellent way to get people to listen to you."

"You're going nowhere near him!" Hawk growls aggressively, making me roll my eyes.

"What if Maria then makes good on her threat to send a mercenary after us?" West interjects before I can snark back.

"Once we've scared Dad off, we go back and spell it out for her," Beck says thoughtfully. "Make it clear to her that *we* are the ones who got Frank arrested and killed Lawrence, and tell her if she doesn't let us go, we'll come for her next."

There's a moment of silence as everyone thinks it over.

"That could work," West muses. "We'd have to watch our backs, in any case. I don't trust her not to send someone after us, even if she agrees to let us walk away."

"Let's sleep on it," Hawk suggests. "It's getting late."

Murmured agreements go up from everyone, and we all get up to call it a night. Beck says goodnight to the guys and kisses me before he leaves, and as I'm heading to my room, Cam wraps his arms around me, burying his nose in my hair.

"I could keep you company tonight," he murmurs against my skin. Damn, does that sound good, but I shake my head.

"Not tonight. I still have a bunch of schoolwork to do before I can get some sleep. I don't want to keep you awake."

"I don't mind."

"Raincheck?"

Something I can't decipher flashes across his face before it disappears as quickly as it came, and he plasters on a smile. "Sure." He gives me a quick peck on the lips before slipping away from me and into his room.

Mason and West have already entered their rooms, not even trying their luck. I've been turning them away all week, and I know they're starting to worry.

Sighing heavily, I let myself into my room and lock the door behind me. I strip out of my clothes and begin my new nightly routine. A set of press-ups, followed by sit-ups, finishing with a round of lunges, then I repeat the three moves until I'm drenched in sweat and feel like I might finally be able to sleep.

Wiping the sweat off me, I pull on a pair of sleep shorts and a top and climb between the sheets, but the second my head hits the pillow, sleep evades me as unwanted memories creep in. I can practically smell the dampness in the air, feel the cold breeze as it blows over my bare skin.

My eyes snap open and my breaths come in rapid pants. I throw back the covers and climb out of bed. Stuffing my feet into my trainers, I flick the lock and slowly open the door, peering out into the hall. All the lights are off, but I can see the light shining under Mason's door, letting me know he's still awake.

On silent feet, I stealthily move down the hall and out the front door. The campus is quiet, not a soul in sight as I set a fast pace, running along one of the longer trails that winds through the forest. I don't care that it's pitch-black and I can hardly see a foot in front of me. Nothing matters except exorcising me of these thoughts. I can't think straight when I feel like this.

My senses are on overdrive as I race through the dark forest, preventing me from thinking about anything except my next step, and for a short time, I feel free. Free from the nightmares, free from the fear.

By the time I make it back to the front door of the dorms, I can hardly put one foot in front of the other, and I have a stitch in my side, but for the first time all night, my mind is quiet.

I pause when I spot a dark shadow on the steps.

"Nice run?" Mason asks, and I release a sigh of relief.

I move to sit beside him, practically collapsing onto the step.

"You know you can talk to us, right?"

"I know."

"We aren't going to judge or think any less of you."

I don't respond—what can I really say?—and he sighs in frustration. "All we wanna do is help, but you have to be willing to lean on us. I know you don't know how to do that. I know you're scared, but it doesn't make you weak to ask for help. Knowing your limitations and realizing when you can't go on alone makes you more powerful. Then, when you're unable to fight your battles, you have others who will stand up and fight them with you." I swallow around the lump of emotion in my throat, blinking away the tears I can feel welling. He moves to crouch in front of me, so I have no choice but to look him in the face. Reaching out, he tucks a flyaway strand of hair behind my ear. "You're not alone anymore. You've got five guys, all of whom would wage war for you, but right now, none of us know what to do. Hawk's on the verge of losing his shit if you don't let him in, and the rest of us aren't far behind him."

"You don't need to talk about what happened or tell us anything you don't want to. Just tell us if you're struggling or if you're having a bad day. Tell me when you need a hug, or if you need to go for a run, or if you just want to be left alone. If you want to spend the day in bed with movies and ice cream, or you need to beat the shit out of someone. Just tell me what you need, baby, and I'll get it for you—whatever it is."

The tears spill over and run down my cheek, and Mason quickly swipes them away before holding out his hand and helping me to my feet. He doesn't say anything else. He just walks me back to my room and makes sure I'm settled in bed before saying goodnight.

∽

"Dad's been blowing up my phone all day," Hawk grumbles the next evening at dinner, when his phone goes off for the third time.

Shoveling a fork full of food into my mouth, I mumble, "Why?"

He just shakes his head in frustration. "He wants us to go over for dinner, probably so he can chew us out for showing up at their offices unannounced."

"Maybe you should go see what he has to say," West suggests. "If there really is conflict between him and Maria, and what he said in Beck's office is true, he might be able to help us."

I'm not sure if we can trust Barton, but he knows a lot more about Maria and the inner workings of Nocturnal Mercenaries than we do. For that reason alone, his help could be instrumental in taking down the company.

"Maybe we should give him a chance? At least go and hear what he has to say?" I suggest, looking at Hawk.

"Couldn't do any harm, right?" Cam questions.

"What if he's actually working with Mom," Hawk counters. "He could be trying to lure us into going along with their insane plan."

"Maybe, but there's only one way to find out." I cock a brow at Hawk and wait him out. Eventually, he groans.

"Fine, I'll text him back and set up a dinner."

Barton replies to Hawk's text almost immediately, confirming dinner the next night.

∼

"Where's your mom?" I whisper as Hawk and I ascend the steps.

"You mean *our* mom, and I have no idea. This is why I don't trust him. How can he live under the same roof as her if he never wanted to be a part of all of this? He makes it sound like he just went along with whatever she wanted, yet he's not a prisoner here. He could have left at any time."

I shrug, not knowing what to say. I understand what he's saying, but I also know you don't need to be locked behind bars or steel doors to feel trapped.

He pushes down the handle of the front door, and we step in, the smell of food hitting us immediately and making my stomach grumble. *Damn, if nothing else, I'll have gotten a tasty meal out of tonight.*

"Hawk, uh, Hadley." Barton's smile falters for a second over my name before he rights it, greeting us, and the three of us stand there awkwardly for a second, no one sure what to do. "Eh, come in. Dinner will be ready shortly. Can I get you anything to drink?"

Hawk and I share similar *what the fuck* looks. I feel like I've entered the Twilight zone. Barton is more casually dressed than I have ever seen him, in a pair of jeans and a polo shirt, with brown loafers on. And, contrary to previous visits where he has been standoffish and unapproachable, never able to meet my eye, he appears relaxed and at ease this evening. Something is definitely up.

"Uh, no thanks," I respond, smiling tightly.

"I'm good," Hawk says when Barton looks his way.

"Ok, yeah, no problem. Please, have a seat."

He gestures toward the same sofa set we sat on when Hawk and I spilled the beans on my identity. *Oh, great, now the three of us can sit awkwardly instead of standing. That's so much better.*

"Where's Mom?" Hawk asks, looking around as if he's expecting her to suddenly appear.

"She's been staying at our apartment in the city since, uh, you showed up at the office."

This small tidbit of information gets both of our attention as we look at him in surprise.

"Why?"

Barton sighs and seems to almost collapse into his seat, the ice in his whiskey knocking against the side of his glass. There's an apology in his eyes as he looks at me. "I've already explained that I struggled to focus on work after you, uh, disappeared. Well, your mother's way of coping was to keep herself busy. Which worked well at the time, but she's become so invested in it now."

"You're saying she wasn't a cold-hearted, emotionless bitch before I was kidnapped?" Somehow, I find that hard to believe. What mother treats their children so indifferently? She couldn't have cared less that I was alive.

Barton flinches, confirming my suspicions. "She's not the most maternal of people."

I hear Hawk scoff quietly beside me. "Neither of you has ever acted like parents.

You put in the bare minimum of effort when I was growing up. You did just enough to make me believe you gave somewhat of a shit but nothing more."

The last of Barton's energy seems to drop right out of him, and he hangs his head. "You're right, son. You deserved so much better. I have no excuse for my behavior, and I can't speak for your mother, but she loves you in her own way."

She's got a funny way of showing it, but then what do I know? Just because she's been a complete bitch to me, doesn't mean she's always been that way to Hawk. She's always seemed distant, yet somewhat fond of him. It's possible Barton is right; she may just have difficulty expressing how she feels. She and Hawk have had nearly twenty years together, developing whatever sort of mother-son relationship they can, whereas I have absolutely no relationship with her at all.

I catch Hawk's eye, and I can tell he's not sure what to think. "So why is Mom staying in the city when you're staying here?" he asks, moving the conversation along.

"Your mother and I haven't seen eye to eye in a long time." Barton looks at me with a hopeful expression. "Now that you are back, I want to work on restoring our family…" He trails off, and it's clear he doesn't want to continue.

"But Mom doesn't, right?" Hawk finishes for him.

Barton grimaces. "No. All of her focus is on the company, especially now, after the attack on the compound. We've never agreed on the direction of the company, and I was hoping now that Frank and Lawrence were gone, and with the compound destroyed, I would be able to talk her into abandoning the whole idea. Between the legitimate side and the adult mercenaries we inducted, we were doing more than well enough for ourselves. We never needed to bring children into any of this."

"So why did you? How did all of this even start?" He's piqued my curiosity, although I'm probably better off not knowing. Just picturing these assholes sitting down over cognac and cigars, casually discussing the destruction of children's lives for their own gain, makes my blood boil.

He runs his hand through his hair, unable to meet my eyes. "We'd been losing clients for some time to Onyx, our primary competitor. They claimed they had the most highly trained, ruthless assassins in the business. We were just spitballing ideas when Frank mentioned using kids. At first, I didn't take him seriously, but the others were intrigued by the idea."

A cough interrupts our conversation, and I look over to find a butler standing at the room's entrance. "Mr. Davenport, dinner is ready, if you and your guests would like to make their way to the dining room."

"Ah, yes, thanks, Geoffrey." Barton gets to his feet, gesturing for us to follow. "The chef's pot roast is delicious."

We move the awkward conversation over to the dinner table, and Barton changes the subject as the food is set down in front of us.

"So, uh, how are you liking Pacific Prep?" He's staring right at me, and I have officially decided that having his attention is way more unnerving than having him ignore me.

"Umm, yeah, it's good."

I side-eye Hawk, not entirely sure what to make of this change of conversation. I'd almost prefer we went back to talking about assassins and mercenary companies than have him prying into my life.

"You've made friends okay?"

I slowly nod my head, saying, "I have," which earns a beaming smile from Barton.

"That's great! Hawk and the guys have been doing well there. They have bright futures ahead of them. I'm sure you're the same...Do you have any plans for next year?"

What the actual fuck? He's acting as though everything is normal, like he and his scumbag associates haven't been forcing the guys down a future they don't want, and he didn't try to marry me off like I'm a fucking possession.

"Uh, no. I've been a little busy, what with Lawrence trying to kidnap me again and helping the guys escape the clutches of *your* company. Simply making it to graduation alive is about as far in the future as I've gotten."

My snarky words seem to bowl right through Barton, knocking the wind out of him, and the congenial expression he was wearing crumbles, devastation marring his face.

No one seems to know what to say, as it looks like Barton mentally falls apart in front of us. Eventually, Hawk sets down his cutlery and I notice a flash of regret cross his face before he asks, "Why did you invite us over tonight, Dad?"

Barton blinks a few times, struggling to reorient himself. He clears his throat and reaches out a shaking hand to lift his tumbler of whiskey, taking a large gulp.

"Uh, right. I wanted to ensure you didn't have any other hair-brained ideas like the one you had the other day."

I scoff. *Is he for real?* "At least we're *trying*," I sneer. "Unlike you. You claim you had nothing to do with any of this, that you were just going along with everyone else, but what have *you* done to try and stop any of it from happening? To try and get yourself, or Hawk, or any of the other guys out of it?"

He has the good grace to look thoroughly chastised, even as it means nothing.

"You're right. I haven't done nearly enough. However, threatening Maria and Wilbert isn't the way to go, either."

I share a look with Hawk, but neither of us is willing to share anything with him regarding our plans. If he doesn't approve of our unexpected visit to their office, he undoubtedly won't approve of the next step in our plan.

We don't respond, and with the remnants of the shitstorm that is our current situation sucking all the oxygen out of the room, none of us seem to know what to say and an awkward silence falls over the table. In fairness, Barton appears wholly lost in his thoughts. I'm not even sure if he's aware we're still here.

After what feels like fucking ages, but is probably only five or ten minutes, Hawk jerks his head in a *let's get out of here* gesture. More than happy to comply, I jump to my feet, and the scraping of the chair legs on the wooden floor jolts Barton out of his trance as he looks up at us.

"We've gotta go," Hawk explains.

"Oh, right. Of course." Still looking dazed, Barton gets to his feet, showing much more grace than I did. I make a move to head toward the door, but Barton stops me. "Before you go, I just..." He holds up his index finger, indicating that we give him a second, and he quickly darts out of the room.

I quirk an eyebrow at Hawk, silently asking where the fuck he's going, but Hawk just shrugs. A minute later, Barton returns, holding a wooden box in his hand. The way his palm is placed flat on the bottom, his other one wrapped around it, he carries the box like it's important to him, a priceless possession.

He approaches me, chewing on his bottom lip before holding it out for me to take. Still, I don't immediately move to accept whatever it is, instead eyeing him and the box critically as though he's trying to hand over some sort of explosive device—I mean, he could be.

He licks his lips nervously. "I-I know I've let you down, and you have every reason to not trust me, but hopefully this box will help you understand. Just because you weren't around, didn't mean I didn't think about you every day."

I still hesitate, even as he pushes the unassuming box closer to me, and with unsure hands, I take it from him, seeing the relief in his features when I do. I just stand and stare at the box, not wanting to open it, but my mind whirs with the possibilities of what's inside. Whatever it contains though, isn't enough to offset everything that's happened. Pretty words and a box don't make up for the fact Barton didn't try harder to find me; for the fact that he gave up on me.

I feel the heat of Hawk's palm on my lower back, grounding me and, with a tight smile, I turn my back on Barton and walk out of the house.

My eyes are glued to the box as I settle myself in the car and Hawk climbs into the driver's seat. He doesn't start the engine, and after a while, I glance up at him, finding him looking at the box as well, with a slight frown and lines furrowing his forehead.

I sigh and shake my head, trying to clear it of my jumbled thoughts. "It doesn't matter what's in here," I say aloud, more for my own benefit than anything else. "It doesn't change anything."

Hawk nods his head slowly, but his face still has a thoughtful expression. "I remember seeing that box before..."

"You know what's inside it?"

He shakes his head. "No, he would snap it shut as soon as I entered the room. When I asked him about it, he told me it was a special box where he kept his happiest memories."

My gaze falls back down to the box perched on my knee, and an overwhelming need to know what it contains overtakes me. With sweaty fingers, I flick up the latch and slowly open the lid, peering cautiously inside. I feel Hawk lean over the center console to get a better look, and as the top drops back, we both take in the various items inside.

There's a small pair of pink baby shoes, no bigger than the length of my finger, and I can feel a lump forming in my throat as my eyes burn at staring at them. Blinking away the building tears, I look over the other items, noticing a collection of photos, a small, yellow baby blanket, and two knitted hats—one pink and one blue—that are so small, they must have been made for newborns. Noticing something wedged at the back of the box, I lift out a small book.

My eyes skim over the front cover. *Baby's Firsts.* Opening it up to a random page, I read, *Baby's first steps.* Scrawled underneath, in barely legible handwriting that can only belong to a man, is the date I took my first steps. Flipping to another page, the date I got my first tooth is recorded, and the same is on the page for my first word. I flip through the pages until I get near the end, noticing the last few pages have been left blank. I'm guessing I hadn't achieved those milestones before I was kidnapped.

Unsure what to make of all of this, I glance at Hawk, only his face is expressionless as his eyes roam over the box's contents. He leans in and lifts out the stack of photos, slowly flicking through each of them. There are some of just me and others of the two of us together, but there are also photos of Barton, Hawk, and I, out on day trips to the beach, or at a fair, or even just playing in the back garden.

"What do you make of all of this?" I ask, my voice a soft whisper.

"I don't know." There's an unusual gruffness to Hawk's voice, giving away the maelstrom of emotions affecting him, the same way they're affecting me. Careful to put all of the items back in their rightful places, I close the lid, and we start down the drive, making the journey back to campus in silence.

Hadley

CHAPTER FOURTEEN

My mind whirs all night when we return to campus, and I'm second-guessing our plan to threaten Maria. The problem is, my brain is too sluggish to think straight. I'm just about getting through the day—with the lack of sleep I'm running on—never mind adding all this extra stress with our parents.

With all this talk of Nocturnal Mercenaries and rebuilding of the compound, I'm waking up even more frequently during the night. I don't know what else I can do to try and abate the demons nipping at my heels. I already run myself ragged every night and beat the shit out of the bag in the gym every morning, and *still* Lawrence's voice haunts me from the grave, and nightmares of the compound wake me at night.

The next morning, I'm attempting to kickstart my brain into action with my third cup of coffee when Hawk stomps in, looking barely alive and having just woken up, already pissed off at the world.

He bangs around in the kitchen, making himself a cup of tea with absolutely zero fucking grace.

"What now?" I moan, not ready to deal with any more shit, but evidently something has him in a pissy mood.

He frowns at me over the rim of his now full coffee mug. "We've been called to a meeting with our parents tonight."

Fucking. Great.

That text was the first indicator of what a shitty day it was going to be. I should have realized it then, called it quits, and gone back to bed. Foolishly, I didn't. So, when things go from bad to worse at lunch, I lose absolutely all fucking patience.

I'm spending some quality time with Emilia and Wilder, listening to her talk us through her *very* intense study schedule for the upcoming end-of-year exams that, honestly, has me freaking the fuck out on the inside. Every minute of her day is planned out, with ninety-nine percent dedicated to classes or studying.

On the other hand, I haven't given a single thought to our exams or the importance of passing them.

"I'm hoping that with four hours sleep a night and only fifteen-minute breaks for meals, I'll be able to fit everything in that I need to," she says, sounding panicked as she chews on her bottom lip, frowning at the little laminate cut-out of her study schedule. "Maybe I should—"

Wilder plucks the schedule out of her hand and looks it over. "I don't see any time to have fun," he remarks, looking more and more appalled the longer he looks at it.

Scowling at him, Emilia snatches it back. "Not every minute of the day is about enjoying yourself," she snaps. "Just because you like to flit from minute to minute with no plan or purpose doesn't mean that's how the rest of us like to live."

Wilder's brows climb up his head and he lifts his hands in surrender. "I just think you need to reward yourself every now and again to help keep you motivated."

Emilia stares at him for a second, before frowning and looking at her schedule thoughtfully. "I guess I could—"

"Hey, babe." Deke steps up to our table, his gaze running over Emilia in a disgustingly sleazy way that immediately has my hackles up.

"What the fuck do you want?" I snap, noticing Wilder watching him intently.

The asshole doesn't look at me, keeping his eyes on Emilia as he leans in toward her, planting his hands on the table right beside her plate.

He bites his bottom lip in a pathetically clichéd manner, giving her yet another once-over. *We get it, you're interested. Get to the fucking point already.*

"I don't know how I didn't see it before."

"See what?" Lines form on Emilia's brow as she looks up at him in confusion.

"How fucking hot you are."

Emilia turns beetroot red, and I want to deck the guy just for making her uncomfortable.

"I'm willing to overlook the whole scholarship thing if you'll come to this week's party with me."

"You fu—" I snarl, before Emilia can formulate a response, but Wilder jumps to his feet, looking ready to tear Deke to shreds.

"Get. The. Fuck. Away. From. Her." He bites out the words with more venom than I have ever heard from him, and I don't miss the way Emilia gapes at him in shock.

Deke sneers at him, and I can see the comeback forming on his lips. Wilder isn't a Prince, so he doesn't command the same respect from Deke, but that doesn't mean he should be any less feared. If anything, Deke should be even more afraid. My guys at least have lines they won't cross, things they won't do. I wouldn't have the same confidence that Wilder won't chop your body into tiny pieces and feed them to the pigs if you looked sideways at him.

"You heard him," I snap. "Get the fuck out of here."

He glowers at me, and I return it with a cocked eyebrow and an unfazed expression —does he honestly think he's that intimidating? He looks like a pissed-off kitten.

Returning his gaze to Emilia, he winks at her. "I'll catch you another time...when your guard dogs aren't around."

He saunters off, swaggering like the fucking dipshit he is, completely unaware that I'm mentally picking out what tools I'll use to castrate him.

"Where the fuck does he get off?" Wilder snarls, collapsing back into his seat with a dark expression.

Emilia's eyes bounce from Deke's retreating form to Wilder, finally landing on me. "What the hell just happened?"

That dickwad just signed his own death warrant, that's what.

～

THAT EVENING, all six of us are lined up in our seats in the boardroom, overlooking the city spread out before us. Instead of focusing on schoolwork and our upcoming end-of-year exams like normal teenagers, we've spent all day speculating what this meeting could be about. Still, every possibility was worse than the last and we eventually gave up.

The swoosh of the door opening has me looking over my shoulder as Maria strides into the room, perfectly presented in a professional, yet attractive gray dress and matching sky-high heels that I could never pull off. She doesn't once look at any of us, keeping her head held high and a slight frown on her face as she strides into the room.

Barton is behind her, and his gaze goes straight to mine. I can see the questions in his eyes—Did you open the box? What did you think? Does it change anything? It's too much, so I quickly look away, focusing back on Maria as she takes her seat opposite Hawk. Barton sits on one side of her and Wilbert on the other, clearly placing Maria in the middle and silently portraying her as the one in charge.

"What's this all about?" Hawk snaps, the second their asses all hit the seats.

Maria quirks a brow, looking irritated at Hawk's pissy attitude, but it's Barton who speaks first.

"I have offered Maria my shares in the company." My eyebrows raise in surprise, and I hear Cam's intake of breath beside me. "In exchange, she has agreed not to involve you in any further business with the company."

I glance at Hawk from the corner of my eye, finding him watching his father closely, suspicion and a subtle flash of hope in his eyes. After a long moment, he focuses back on Maria.

"That's true? You'll leave *all* of us alone in exchange for his shares?"

Maria smiles cruelly. "While Barton's gesture is *touching*"—she spits the word out like it tastes disgusting—"unfortunately, his shares aren't enough."

"What, but you agreed," Barton stutters. Color coats his cheeks, and his eyes narrow in anger.

Maria smiles placatingly at him, and for a moment, I can almost see how she managed to manipulate him all these years, and yet, it's not enough for me to believe he just blindly agreed to whatever plans she and the others devised.

"Yes, I know, but I've changed my mind. I want the majority share of the company."

"I'll give you mine, too," Cam pipes up. I don't pretend to understand anything about this corporate world or the importance of company shares, but I trust Cam and the others to know what they're doing. "With Lawrence dead, his quarter of the company goes to me. I don't want it, but in exchange, you *have* to agree not to come after any of us. I don't know about the others, but I don't want to hear anything about Nocturnal Mercenaries ever again. I don't want to see your face or come back to this office."

We all murmur our agreements, and there's another moment of tense silence as Maria thinks it over before her gaze moves to Mason, and he tenses beside me in the chair. She tilts her head, scrutinizing him. "I want Frank's shares too."

"I don't have them. They're still in my father's name."

Mason's words spark a flash of anger in Maria's gaze, and her nostrils flare. "Then get them for me."

Jesus, demanding bitch. I grit my teeth, holding back my retort, and thankfully Hawk speaks up before I say something scathing that will only further piss her off.

"We'll get them for you. Then you'll leave us alone?"

She waves her hand dismissively. "Yes, yes. Get me the shares, and you can go live your pathetic little lives. I won't have any need for pampered children."

It takes everything in me not to snarl at her like a rabid dog, and I feel Mason's hand squeeze my leg gently. He can probably see me practically vibrating with anger and the clenched fists I'm hiding beneath the large boardroom table.

Maria doesn't hang around, having delivered her orders, and like the pathetic sap he is, Wilbert follows her out of the boardroom. On the other hand, Barton hesitates, glancing at Hawk and me with a pained expression on his face.

"I'm sorry. I couldn't let you do something rash that would only escalate the situation. I thought, with both of your dads out of the picture"—he gestures to Cam and Mason on either side of me—"that owning the full Davenport quarter of the company would be enough for her."

"It's not going to be enough until she owns the entire thing," I tell him. What I don't say aloud, because I still don't trust him, despite this 'gesture,' is that her owning the entire company is unacceptable. Handing everything over to her might buy us our freedoms, but it won't solve the problem that is Nocturnal Mercenaries. Without anyone standing in her way, she will simply rebuild and go back to destroying children's futures. I *won't* allow that to happen.

His lips flatten, his only response to what I've said, and he glances at each of the others before his gaze comes back to meet mine. I can tell he wants to say more but won't with everyone else here. Eventually, he gives a sharp jerk of his head and strides out of the boardroom without another word.

∾

"How the hell are we going to get Frank's shares transferred over to Maria?" Cam asks that night, once we're all back at school.

His question is met with thoughtful silence, none of us having a good answer for him.

Eventually, Mason sighs, running his hand through his short strands before he drops his head back to lean against the couch cushion to stare up at the ceiling. "I'm going to have to go see my father."

"What?" I argue. "No. You can't go see that shitstain!"

Lifting his head, he pierces me with a resigned look. "I have to."

"Should we even be handing them over to *her*?" I continue to argue. "What's going to happen when she has the majority? We might be free and clear, but if she rebuilds the compound, she can pick right up where they left off and go back to stealing kids. I" —I shake my head and sigh—"I can't stand back and let that happen."

Beck pulls me into his arms. "We aren't going to let that happen," he promises, but I've got no idea how they plan on preventing it, especially if we hand over control of the company to her.

"Even with majority control, it will take time for her to forge the necessary relationships and rebuild the compound," Hawk states.

"Could we get your dad to sign over his shares instead?" I ask West, desperate to avoid Mason having to go see his father. I saw how he acted when he was forced to be around his father at parties, and I *refuse* to put him in that situation again.

"We probably could, but she'll know they aren't Frank's. She probably thinks she has our father wrapped around her finger, which is why she's demanding Frank's shares instead. Our father will do whatever she wants, giving her full control of the company."

"No." I shake my head adamantly. "We can't allow that to happen!"

I see West thinking something over before he finally speaks, "But we *could* get my father's shares and keep them for ourselves."

"What would the benefit of that be?"

My question garners West's attention as he looks my way. "I've been through the company bylaws enough times while trying to find a loophole to get us out, to know that even if she has the majority shares, she can't make huge decisions like deciding to rebuild the compound without a unanimous vote from the board, i.e., us."

"So, what, we just keep blocking her by voting no?" I question. "That's not a long-term solution. It's a bandage on a gaping wound at best."

"It would be *something* for now," Hawk says, although his expression is tight, so I know he agrees with me. He focuses on West and Beck before speaking again, "You think you could get Wilbert to hand them over?"

The two brothers exchange a look before both of them nod. "Yeah," West confidently states. "I think he could be persuaded."

"Okay, so we just need to sort out how to get Frank's shares." Hawk sighs, looking grimly at Mason.

"Yeah, and to do that, I need to go see my dad," Mason states with a finality that lets me know he's not going to change his mind.

∽

THE REST of the week goes by in a blur. Between the stress from our parents, the pressure of upcoming exams, and how far behind in my schoolwork I am, not to mention the lack of sleep and constantly feeling like I'm barely keeping my head above water, I'm honestly beginning to struggle.

After Mason's chat with me last week, none of the guys have asked how I'm doing, and I appreciate them backing off a bit. I know they're worried, but how the hell can I even begin to explain to them how I'm feeling? I feel eyes on me all the time; I'm hearing a dead man's voice; every morning when I wake up, for those first few seconds, I'm convinced all of this is a dream and I'm still locked in my cell in the compound.

They've shouldered more than any sane boyfriend, or boyfriends, would when it comes to me. Finding out that my brain might finally have snapped and I'm probably losing my mind would push them over the edge.

It took me weeks to assimilate into 'normal' life when I first escaped from the compound and, while this is different, I'm confident it's just going to take some time. All this extra stress isn't helping, either. Once we get shit sorted with our parents, the company, and finals are out of the way, I'm sure I'll start to feel better. At least, that's what I keep telling myself.

"Shall we agree to meet in the library after dinner?" Emilia asks as we exit the main school building. Class has just finished for the day, and while all I want to do is just go back to the dorm, curl up on the sofa and ignore everything for the rest of the day, I know I really, *really* need to study.

"Yeah, sounds like a plan," I agree.

"Super, I'll see you then." Beaming like we're going on a trip into town or doing something fun, she takes off toward the music department for choir practice.

Continuing along the path toward the dorm, I'm not far from the dining hall when my tablet buzzes in my bag. As I go to grab it, a passing student knocks into me. In the blink of an eye, the campus grounds around me fade away, replaced with dark walls, as someone grabs my arm roughly and tugs me down a familiar hallway. The one that leads to Bowen's torture room.

Panic flares to life within me and I tug, trying to get out of the guard's grip. I wriggle and writhe until he loses his hold on my arm, and I spin to face him. Despite my petite stature and weakened state, I tackle him with all the pent-up rage I've been harboring all these years. Catching him by surprise, I quickly take him to the ground, and with him pinned beneath me, I pummel my fists into him over and over until he's bloody and beaten.

"Hadley!" The shout comes to me as though in a dream, and I pause with my fist drawn back, glancing up. The voice comes again. "Hadley!" And I blink. "What the hell are you doing?" Hawk barks.

Everything swarms back into view—the school, the trees, Hawk, and Mason running toward me. I'm aware of the grit from the path digging into my knees, and I look down. *What the fuck?* Some kid I don't even recognize is trapped beneath me, his face bloody and his eyes wide in terror as he scrambles to get free.

I hardly feel Hawk as he grabs my upper arm and pulls me off him. Mason helps the guy to his feet and whispers something to him before he scurries off without a backward glance.

"What the hell were you thinking?" Hawk snaps, stepping in front of me so he's all I can see. Not answering him, I blink down at my bloodied knuckles, trying to work out what happened. "Hadley! Answer me!"

"I-I don't know," I mumble, glancing up at his worried, furious face.

Mason comes to stand beside him, looking equally as worried as he checks me over. "Let's get back to the dorm. We can discuss this there."

I look past him to where the student has long since disappeared. "What about him?"

"He won't say anything." The sharp edge to Mason's voice has me wondering what he said to the kid to get him to keep his mouth shut. I don't have the wherewithal to ask, though.

Hawk tugs on my arm, maintaining his tight grip as he drags me to the dorms. I follow him, dazed, unable to stop looking at the dried, crusting blood on my hands and picturing the guard I could have sworn was trying to take me somewhere.

When we reach the apartment, Hawk throws open the door and storms in, making West, Beck, and Cam jump.

"What the hell's going on?" Beck demands, scowling at where Hawk is still holding my arm in a firm grip.

"Hadley here thought it would be a great idea to beat up another student," Hawk seethes, using his tight hold to turn me to face him. "Wanna fill us in on why you did that?"

My mouth opens and closes several times soundlessly before I snap it shut, refusing to say anything until I've worked out myself what happened back there. I've had moments where I forget myself for a second and forget I'm not in the compound again, but I have never lashed out at anyone like that before.

Hawk's lips flatten as he presses them together and his nostrils flare. I can see the effort it takes him not to snap or say something that he knows will only make this worse. Eventually, he closes his eyes and sighs.

"Hadley," he begins, opening his eyes and capturing me in his churning gray-blue gaze. "What's going on? We know something's wrong. Just talk to us."

"I'm fine, Hawk," I grit irritably.

The asshole scoffs. "Come on, Hadley. Everyone knows when a woman tells you she's fine, she's far from fucking *fine*."

I look at him like he's crazy. "What? Don't talk shit. That is *not* a thing."

"That is absolutely a thing," Cam pipes up, earning a dark glare from me before I focus my glower back on Hawk.

"I'm so fucking sick of hearing that word from you when it's obvious you're not *fine*," Hawk continues to press.

"Why are you pushing me? Just back off and leave me alone."

Hawk shakes his head like he can't believe I'm not getting whatever he's trying to do, and steps forward so he's crowding me. "Because I'm the asshole brother who lives to piss you off, and I'm not going to stop until you're honest with me."

My lip curls as I scowl up at him. "You wanna know what's wrong," I snarl, shoving him hard in the chest. The fucking asshole doesn't back up though, which only infuriates me further. "I can't sleep because every time I close my eyes, I'm back in that room with Lawrence, trapped and terrified. Every time I stop to just breathe, or take a moment, I hear Bowen's voice in my head, telling me all the fucked-up shit he wants to do to me. If someone plays loud music, I have a panic attack 'cause the guards would pump it through the speakers for days, so loud I hoped it would burst my eardrums, so that I could get five minutes of sleep. The slightest noise makes me jump. I can't get my mind to shut off, and today…I have no idea what the fuck happened back there. So you wanna know if I'm okay? No, Hawk, I'm so fucking far from being okay, I don't even know what direction to go in. I feel like I'm fucking drowning, and I don't know how to swim, so I'm treading water, just trying to stay above the surface. But I'm tired, Hawk. I'm so. Fucking. Tired."

A tear spills over and runs down my cheek as the wind goes out of my sails, and I collapse in on myself. In the next second, I'm wrapped up in a crushing hug and as soon as Hawk's arms encase me, something inside me breaks. The dam I've been trapping all my emotions behind cracks and comes tumbling down, and I fall apart in his arms.

I'm faintly aware of the others joining us, of bodies pressing in all around me, Although, instead of feeling suffocated, it's like all of them are holding me together, and Mason's words flitter across my mind—*When you're unable to fight your battles, you've others who will stand up and fight them for you.*

I'm not alone. I never was.

Firefly

CHAPTER FIFTEEN

The moment Hadley fell apart in Hawk's arms, we all felt it—the change in the air—and we moved as one, crowding around them and embracing them in a group hug. I don't know what happened that she ended up beating up some kid, but I think it was the catalyst she needed in order to realize she's not okay. She's not coping, and she's unable to get herself through it alone. I think we've all been waiting for this moment. It was only a matter of time before it all became too much for her.

She cried herself to the point of exhaustion before Hawk carried her to her room.

"Is she okay?" I ask when he enters the room again.

Sighing, he collapses into a seat and shakes his head. "Far from it, but I think she will be." He pins Beck with a look. "This is a good thing, right?"

Beck nods. "Yeah. She's been living in denial, trying to shove everything she's feeling in a box and avoid dealing with it."

"What happens now?"

"I'm not sure. Let her dictate that, and we can go from there."

"I take it we all heard what she said?" Mason states, looking at each of us with an expression I can't quite place.

"About Bowen?" Hawk sneers.

"Do you think he's the one that cut her up?" I question, feeling both furious and devastated for Hadley all at once.

"Probably," Hawk spits out the word, and I can see he's struggling to hold his anger in check.

Beck nods his head in agreement. "He was the one in charge when Lawrence wasn't around."

Tension is thick in the air. "Did anyone see him when we were at the compound that night?" I look around at the others, everyone shaking their heads. *Great, so we've no idea if he's alive or dead.*

I sigh, running my hand through my already messy hair. There's nothing we can do about him right now. But there *is* something we can do. "This extra stress with our parents can't be helping her," I state. "We need to deal with them as soon as possible. She deserves to leave school and start fresh, with none of this shit following her."

Beck nods his head in agreement. "I say we go after our father tonight."

"Tonight?" Hawk questions.

Beck shrugs. "Why not? What's the point in waiting? Graduation is only a few weeks away. Don't you want to be free of all of this by then?"

Hawk thinks on it for a moment. "Alright, what are you thinking for tonight then?"

"Leave it to me. I'll make sure we get his portion of the shares."

"No." I pin Beck with a look. "I need to be the one to do this." He opens his mouth to speak, but I cut him off. "*I'm* the one he's been using to threaten all of you. *I'm* the one that was belittled by him. Told I was never man enough, never tough enough, but I'm not the weak kid he thinks I am."

He must be able to see the adamant look in my eyes as, after a moment, he reluctantly nods his head in agreement. "Alright, fine, but I'm coming with you." He holds his hands up before I can protest. "Just as backup, in case you need it."

"Alright, fine, but only if I need you."

∽

IT'S late by the time the two of us leave to make the journey to our father's house.

"You don't have to do this, you know."

I glance away from the road to look briefly at Beck. "I do. You have no idea what it was like growing up in that house, always hearing you're never enough. He always signed me up for sports teams, then gave me a hard time when I sat on the bench for the whole game. He constantly compared me to the other guys, wanting to know why I wasn't stronger, tougher, more outgoing. In his mind, that's the definition of a man—which is fucking ironic, given what a fat fuck he is."

I can feel Beck's gaze on me, but I don't look away from the road, not needing to see the pity in his eyes. My childhood might have been shitty, but compared to his, Mason's, or Hadley's, it was nothing I couldn't handle.

"What about your mom?"

"She couldn't handle having a cheating manwhore for a husband." I glance at him out of the corner of my eye, hesitating before continuing, "Finding out he had another son was the final straw for her. She fucked off to Europe when I was six, and I haven't seen her since. There's the obligatory *Merry Christmas* email, but that's all I hear from her."

"I'm sorry, you didn't deserve that."

I shrug, not sure what to say to that.

"You have a good family with the guys, though."

"Yeah. We've only ever been able to count on each other. Our parents were too self-centered to provide us with the families we needed, so we made a family for ourselves —one we wanted." I pull my gaze from the road once again to look at him. "They're your family now too…if you want them. I have no idea what your plans are after all of this is over."

"My plans are wherever you, Hadley, and the others are. I already lost one family, I'm not about to lose another."

Our conversation is put on hold as I pull up to the gate of our father's residential estate and type in the code. Once it's opened, I drive through and pull into the driveway, parking the car and turning off the lights.

Moving quietly and carefully, the two of us slip out of the car and silently close the doors before we sneak up to the house. It's the early hours of the morning, and my father should have long since passed out. The dark windows peering out at us confirms that assumption.

Inserting the key in the door, we let ourselves in, and I quickly turn off the alarm and jerk my head toward the stairs, indicating for Beck to follow me.

Keeping our steps soft and light, we climb up the stairs and along the hall to my father's suite. I can hear the snoring coming from his room before I've even opened the door, and Beck snorts softly behind me when I open it, and the snores become deafening. The sound of them is followed by the whirring noise of a machine on his bedside table that has a tube running from it, attached to a mask covering Wilbert's face.

"What the fuck?" Beck whispers.

"Sleep apnea."

"He looks like he's on a ventilator."

The two of us share a look, not entirely sure what to do next. However, true to his word, Beck lets me take the reins and gestures for me to go ahead. I hadn't exactly thought about what I'd do or say once I was here. I just knew I had to be the one to confront him. Taking a moment, I think about Hawk's deadly anger, Mason's stoicism, Cam's flippancy, Beck's steeliness, and Hadley's strength and channel each of them.

Stepping up to the side of his bed, I stare apathetically down at him before reaching out and poking his arm. He doesn't stir, so I poke him harder. When that still doesn't get his attention, I slap my hand down on his large, protruding belly, and the idiot jolts awake, staring up at me with wide eyes.

"Ah, you're awake." I smile spitefully down at him. "Good, we need to have a chat."

It takes him a few minutes to prop himself upright and remove the mask from his face, turning off the machine so we can all hear one another without yelling.

"What is the meaning of this?" he eventually splutters, breathless just from trying to sit upright. His gaze focuses behind me, and I know he's finally spotted Beck.

"I just wanted to stop by and have a quick chat," I tell him, garnering his attention once again.

"A—what? It's the middle of the night, West. Go back to school."

"Yeah, I can't do that. See, you have something we need."

I watch as my father's cheeks redden in anger. "What are you talking about?"

"We want your shares," I state bluntly, getting straight to it—no point in beating around the bush, after all.

My father stares at me incredulously, before huffing out a laugh. "Are you high? I'm not giving you my shares."

I sigh and shake my head as though I'm disappointed in him, although it's not like I expected him just to hand them over anyway. I tilt my head, feigning a thoughtful expression. "Did you ever wonder what happened to Frank?"

His brows tug together in confusion. "The idiot got caught murdering his mistress. What does that have to do with anything?"

"How did he get caught, though? Don't you have private security in your houses? No one should have had access to that…unless someone hacked into your system."

His mouth opens and closes wordlessly before he finds his speech again. "Th-that was you?"

"What about Lawrence?" I question, neither confirming nor denying my involvement in Frank's demise.

My father has the audacity to scoff. "Now I know you had nothing to do with that. Hiding behind your computers and hacking into cameras is one thing, but outright killing someone is something you're not capable of."

He says it like murder is the making of a man. He's got no idea what I'm capable of, though; what I'm willing to do for the people I love. I certainly don't feel like more of a man for killing that guard. I did what was necessary, and that's it.

I don't let him see any of my inner thoughts or feelings. Instead, I fix a sick sort of macabre mask on my face and do my best to mimic Wilder's insane grin. "Is it? Then how come I know he was stabbed—brutally. Attacked with such savagery that only someone who truly despised him could have torn him apart like that?"

My father's eyes widen to saucers, and he splutters incoherently before finally managing to string together enough words to form a sentence.

"What do you want?"

"I told you what we want."

Sweat beads along his forehead. "I can't get you out of the company. Maria is in control now. She's not going to let you just walk away."

"We can deal with Maria. We *want* your shares and for you to report back to us with what Maria is doing. Once we've made this deal, we don't trust her to stick to her agreement. I want *you* to spy on her."

"I—what? I can't do that!"

"You're also going to transfer the deed to the house into West's name and empty half your bank account into his," Beck speaks up for the first time. I quirk a brow at him but quickly return my focus to my father as his shock is replaced with anger, and his nostrils flare.

"I'm not doing that," my father snaps. "And I'm sure as fuck not about to hand over half of my wealth to you ungrateful bastards." He sears Beck with a hateful glare. "I should have known you would be a bad influence. I should never have pulled your sorry ass out of Black Creek. You and your mother—AHHH!"

The knife I stole from Hadley and had concealed under my oversized hoodie is sticking out of the mattress, between his thighs, inches from where I imagine his limp dick is.

"Do you want to end up like Frank or Lawrence?" I question in a dark, sinister voice that sounds nothing like me.

His lower lip trembles, and he frantically shakes his head.

"Then you'll do what we've told you." I wrap my hand around the handle and yank it out of the mattress. Without sparing my father a glance, I turn my back on him and head toward the door, Beck following close behind with a proud little smirk on his face.

"Holy shit." Beck laughs as we climb back into the car. There's a fine tremor in my hands, but ultimately I feel fucking great for having finally stood up to my old man after all these years. "Where the hell did you learn that fancy little trick with the knife?"

I chuckle. "I might have asked Wilder to show me some tricks Firefly taught him."

"Damn, well, he looked totally terrified. I wouldn't be surprised if he pissed himself a little."

I snicker, starting the engine and driving us back to school, feeling lighter than I have in a long time.

The guys are still awake when we let ourselves into the apartment, and I'm surprised to find Hadley wedged between Cam and Mason on the sofa. She jumps to her feet as soon as we step into the room, rushing toward us until she's got one arm wrapped around each of our necks.

"I was so worried about you both." I hug her back, enjoying the feel of her in my arms. When she pulls back, there's a stern look on her face, but I'm too busy noticing she looks so much better than she did earlier. The few hours of rest must have done her good. It's probably more sleep than she's gotten in weeks. "I can't believe you'd go without telling me," she argues, but her words have no heat.

"You needed to rest," I say soothingly. "How are you feeling?"

"A little better," she answers in a shy voice. "I, uh, owe you an apology." She turns to look at everyone else. "I owe you all an apology for how I've been acting recently."

"You don't owe us anything, sweetheart," Beck assures her, sliding his arm around her waist and pulling her in against him.

She smiles softly, looking at Hawk. "Still. You were right earlier. I'll try to be better." She fidgets with her fingers, giving away how nervous she feels. "I can't promise to be very good at it. I have no idea what's going on with me, but I don't want to lose any of you."

"You're not going to lose any of us," Beck promises her. "We'll figure it out together."

We all murmur our agreement, and Hadley ducks her head with a rosy tint to her cheeks and mumbles a thank you.

"Well, it's late. I'm off to bed," Hawk says, waving goodnight before disappearing down the hall.

"You should get some more sleep, too, sweetheart," Beck encourages. Hadley nods, chewing on her bottom lip.

"I don't want to be alone anymore."

I step in front of her, holding her chin in a firm yet soft grip. "You were never alone, Firefly. We've always been here, waiting for you to accept our help. Now, tell us what you need?"

She stares into my eyes, and I swear I lose myself in the swirling depths of her gaze.

"I need you," she murmurs, before her gaze bounces over the others. "All of you." She tilts her head back to look up at Beck. "Will you all stay with me tonight?"

"Of course, we will." He leans down, brushing a kiss over her lips before we all head to her bedroom, everyone going through their nightly routine before climbing into bed. It's a tight fit with all five of us, but no one seems to mind. We're all just relieved to be in the same room as Hadley. Nestled against her back, I bury my nose in her hair and knowing she's safe in my arms, tiredness tows me down into its dark depths.

I jolt awake as Hadley jumps, another nightmare having woken her. It happened several times during the night, and each time one of us soothed her back to sleep. My heart ached for her every time, and I hate that she's been struggling alone with this.

Cam must have woken too, and I hear him murmuring to her, soothing her. I pull her in tighter against me and bury my face in her hair, breathing her in while I listen to Cam whispering to her. I'm nearly asleep again when I realize he's not trying to soothe her back to sleep. *Horny bastard.*

Unperturbed by my arm around her waist, he presses himself against her, and her breathy moan goes straight to my dick and *fuck me*. I try to talk him down, because, unlike Cam, I do not let my dick rule my life.

"Do you remember what I said to you in the compound?" Cam whispers, and I feel Hadley tense against me. I'm about to chew the asshole out, when she relaxes again.

"That I deserve nothing but pleasure."

Another breathless moan follows her words, and I can only imagine what he's doing to her to make her sound so fucking divine. My dick is rock-hard now, and suddenly, all I can think about is watching her fall apart. It's been so long since I have seen anything other than frown lines and tight smiles on her face.

I rock my hips, grinding my erection between her asscheeks, and she groans again, arching so her ass is pressed firmly against my hard length. Cam shifts, forcing Hadley onto her back, and settles between her thighs, kissing his way down her chest and abdomen as he pulls her top up.

He works his way to the waistband of her sleep shorts and pulls them down as I slide my hand up her stomach and cup her tit, squeezing it gently before tweaking the nipple. Her head falls back against the pillow and her eyes drift shut.

"Keep your eyes open," I say softly. It's not one of my usual harsh demands, but she obeys me anyway, snapping them open and looking up at me like I'm her entire world. "I want to capture every minute."

"Of what?" she asks in a breathless voice.

"Every minute you feel alive."

She reaches up and slides her hand around the back of my neck, tugging me down until my lips meet hers. Her lips part beneath me, and as I slide my tongue into her mouth, it's like my whole world rights itself. Everything that's been off-kilter the last few weeks suddenly slots back into place, and for a moment, everything is right again.

Fingers brush over mine as they slide along her body, and I know either Beck or Mason have joined in the fun. Hadley vocalizes her approval of another player with a dirty groan that turns into a gasp when Cam gets busy between her thighs, putting his tongue to good use, and I take advantage, claiming her mouth in another heated kiss that sends us both spiraling.

When we finally pull apart, Hadley is a writhing mess underneath our combined touches, and I find Beck sucking her tit into his mouth. I spot Mason watching the four of us, running his hand over the front of his boxers as he tries to soothe his hard-on.

Catching Hadley looking at him, he smirks and moves to join in. He shifts to the head of the bed, leaning in to kiss her as I shift my attention to her nipple, and under all of our touches, Hadley is crying out her release in no time.

Satisfied, we all collapse onto the bed, snuggling in against her. Her stomach grumbles, and I snicker. Laughing, Cam goes to get up. "I'll make us breakfast."

Hadley pouts. "But we're not done yet."

Cam gives her a dirty wink, leaning down to kiss her. "Far from it, baby. But you'll need your stamina for what I have in mind."

She laughs as he climbs out of bed, and the sound is like music to my ears.

Mason grabs his phone from the bedside table as Cam gets dressed, the rest of us unwilling to leave the bed just yet.

"Hawk's text. Says he's got stuff to do today and that the five of us should take the day to do something."

My brows lower. "What does Hawk need to do?"

Mason shrugs. "No idea."

"A day out sounds fun," Hadley says, looking at each of us.

"Oh, yeah, we could go to the beach," Cam says enthusiastically, jumping onto the bed and forgetting all about his breakfast plans.

Hadley laughs. "I don't have a swimsuit."

The look Cam gives her is positively evil. "Who said anything about needing swimsuits? Our parents own a private cove nearby. We could go there. No one else would be around."

Thrilled by the thought of us all spending the day together, away from school and all the other shit that constantly surrounds us, we all climb out of bed and get ready for the day.

Hadley

CHAPTER SIXTEEN

"Wow," I gasp as we pull up on what is nothing more than a gravel area at the top of a cliff overlooking the ocean. Getting out of the car, the wind whips my hair around my face, and I can smell sea salt in the air and hear the distant noise of waves crashing against the rocks below.

"Over here," Cam calls out, leading the way toward the cliff face. As I approach, I notice steps carved into the side of the rock, and as we start to descend, a small strip of the beach comes into view, stretching out below us. It's well hidden, so no one passing by on the road would think to stop and come down here, although the outlook is absolutely spectacular.

"Who the hell owns their own private cove?" I gape when my feet hit the sand. I look around, completely mesmerized by the shimmering sand and glistening ocean.

"We do." Mason winks as he moves past me, carrying a large cooler filled with drinks and food. I catch Beck's eye, and I can tell he's just as amazed by all of this as I am.

We both let out a disbelieving chuckle and follow the others over to where Cam is laying towels on the sand.

"What do you think you're doing?" Cam asks, reaching out to grab a hold of me just as I go to sit on the towels. "We're going swimming."

I laugh. "Cam, I can't swim."

His eyes widen to saucers. "You, what?! Well, we will have to correct that as soon as we're back at school. For today, I guess you're just going to have to stay real close to me." He winks, and I shake my head, trying to wriggle out of his grip.

"Baby, you have five seconds to get your shorts and shoes off, or I'm carrying you in fully clothed."

"You wouldn't," I gasp.

The asshole just quirks an eyebrow. "Five."

I scowl at him, refusing to believe him.

"Four."

I still don't move.

"Three."

He steps toward me, and I can see the intent in his eyes. He's one hundred percent serious.

"Two."

His arms wrap around my waist, and I shift slightly out of his reach, frantically kicking off my shoes and unbuttoning my shorts. They're not even halfway down my legs when he wraps his toned arms around me and lifts me off the ground.

I scream, kicking my shorts the rest of the way off as he runs with me to the water, the other assholes laughing as they watch us. I give all of them the middle finger and scream again as the first drops of cold water hit my legs.

"Cam! It's freezing!" I yell as he runs deeper into the water, quickly submerging us. I move in his hold to wind my arms tightly around his neck, my legs doing the same around his waist. I'm clinging to him like a goddamn spider monkey, and he seems to find it fucking hilarious, based on the deep boom of laughter he emits.

"Baby, I've got you, but if you strangle me, someone will have to come in here and rescue us both."

"Shut up, asshole," I snarl, but I do loosen my hold around his neck—he is my human life vest, after all. "I can't swim."

"You're not going to drown. We're not far enough out. If you put your feet down, you'll be able to touch the ground."

I stare at him incredulously. "Put my feet down?" The water is already at the level of my nipples. There is absolutely no fucking way I am letting it go any higher.

"Trust me. I've got you, but I promise you're fine."

My nails dig painfully into the muscles on his shoulders as I slowly loosen my hold on his waist and lower my feet until I can feel the sand bed beneath my toes. His hands remain firm on my waist, even when I'm standing on both feet. The water is no higher than it was before, but it's still too close to my face for my liking.

Digging my toes into the sand, I take a bolstering breath.

"See?" He closes the tiny bit of distance between us, his bare chest brushing against mine as he looks into my eyes. "I won't let anything else happen to you."

He dips his head and presses his lips to mine in a passionate kiss until the sound of the others coming toward us has us pulling apart seconds before a splash of water washes over me, and I scream.

Cam grabs me, dragging me against his front and using me as a human shield as the others continue to splash us. His arm is like a steel band around my middle, making me feel safe as I get caught up in the water fight, laughing and splashing them back.

Lifting me, Cam places me on his shoulders. His hands are holding tight to my thighs as the five of us wage a water war against each other, until the need for food to replenish our energy calls a time-out to our antics, and we all traipse back up the beach to where we left our things.

I pull off my tank top, leaving me in just my bra and panties, and wring out the water so it will dry more quickly.

"Damn, forget food," Mason murmurs against my ear. "I wanna eat you out for lunch."

I laugh and lean back against his damp, sun-kissed chest, tilting my head up for a kiss. "I won't say no to that," I say against his lips, earning myself a warning growl and a spank to the ass that only has me wishing he would make good on his promise.

We spend the rest of the day talking and laughing, switching between messing around in the water and just chilling out on the beach, and as the sun starts to set on the horizon, I feel more at peace than I ever remember feeling before. I'm still a long way off from being okay, but today I wasn't haunted by my demons, so I'll take that as a win.

"Let's make a bonfire," Cam exclaims in excitement, not waiting for anyone to agree with him before rushing off to gather twigs. He's like a giant child, and it's hilarious to watch.

West sighs but gets to his feet, taking off to go help him, and Mason grumbles something but does the same.

Left alone, Beck drags me into his lap. "Wanna go for a walk?"

I smile up at him. "Sure."

He helps me to my feet, taking my hand in his, and we walk down the beach, away from where the guys are collecting sticks for the fire. The cove isn't big, but there's a bunch of rocks at the far end, and once we're hidden behind them, Beck tugs me against his hard chest.

My hands land on his warm skin, and I love how his muscles tense beneath my touch.

"I can't stop looking at you today," he murmurs in awe, drawing my attention to his face. "You look so happy."

I smile. "I am happy. I needed this."

He leans in to kiss me, and my hands slide up his chest, winding around his neck until my fingers are buried in his windswept hair. His fingers dig into my hips as he holds me against him, and between the thin fabric of his trunks and my panties, I can feel how turned-on he is.

He breaks our kiss, staring deep into my eyes. "Do you want this?"

How can he even question that.

I grind against him, making him groan. "So badly," I murmur, claiming him in a hungry kiss.

He pushes me back until I feel the cool surface of a rock at my back. His hands tug frantically at my bra strap before pushing my panties down, leaving me bare before him.

He groans, running his dilated gaze over me and heating my skin, before pressing his lips to mine in a desperate kiss.

I push my hand beneath the waistband of his trunks and wrap my fingers around his wide girth, stroking him until we're both panting heavily, and neither one of us can take it anymore.

Pulling his trunks down, he grabs a hold of my thigh, hitching my leg over his hip, and slams into me in one hard, long move. My head falls back against the rock, and he rests his forehead against my shoulder, stilling inside me. He kisses along my collarbone and up my neck, behind my ear. "Nothing could ever beat this feeling," he whispers. He starts to move, and *holy fuck*, the world feels like it's coming apart at the seams.

Nothing exists except the two of us here, in this moment, and as I get lost in his eyes, I can't picture being anywhere else. Beck is it for me. He and the others are all I'll ever need.

I feel him swell within me, and I plant my lips on his, kissing him with everything I have as the two of us fall over the edge, entangled in one another's arms.

By the time we walk back down the beach, the others have a fire lit, the embers blowing into the wind. It's the perfect view, watching the three of them goof around, with the sun setting into the ocean in the background.

I lean my head against Beck's chest. "I could get used to days like this."

He kisses the top of my head. "Me too."

"Hey," Cam calls out as we approach. "Where did you two disappear off to?" He waggles his eyebrows suggestively, and Beck reaches out and slaps him across the back of the head, making the other guys laugh.

It makes me smile seeing how easily they have come to accept him as part of the group. He and West are still getting to know one another, but West's attitude toward him has completely changed now that he's realized Beck isn't here for money or status. I think finding out Beck only ever wanted to get to know him has resonated with him. Sure, the guys have always had each other, but they've never had anyone else really give a shit about them, and I think it just took West some time to believe Beck was genuinely here for him.

I slip away from Beck to join West on a log one of the guys has dragged over in front of the fire. I rest my head on his shoulder and just stare into the flames, feeling so at ease, as his arm wraps around my waist, his heat enveloping me. I wish we could just stay here forever.

"Are you having a good day?" he murmurs softly.

"The best."

"It's not over yet," Mason chimes in, handing out beers to everyone as the others join us around the fire. He holds one out to me, but I shake my head. I tried some a couple of times when they were drinking, and I liked that it helped me forget about my problems for a while, not to mention the deep sleep. They were the only nights I'd wake up without nightmares. Nevertheless, I don't like that feeling of losing control when I drink more than a little bit. "We've still got marshmallows to melt and starlight skinny dipping to do."

I bark out a laugh and cock a brow as he sits down on my other side. "Really? The four of you are going to strip naked and go swimming in the ocean?"

"Hey, I don't care if my sword crosses one of theirs, so long as you're naked and wet and writhing between us."

Well, damn, now I really want to go skinny dipping.

Cam groans and adjusts himself in his trunks.

"So," I start nervously, picking at my fingernails, "now that you won't have to go work for your parents, what are everyone's plans after graduation?"

My question is met by silence which only makes my stomach twist tighter.

"Well, I'll need to find a job," Beck pipes up.

"You're not going to stay at Pac?" Cam questions.

He shakes his head. "Nope. It's not for me. I only agreed to work there for West. I always wanted to help kids that grew up like I did." He shrugs his shoulders. "Maybe I could get a job as a counselor in an underfunded school, somewhere where I could make a real difference."

I smile warmly at him. "You would be great at that."

"I agree, but you don't need the money, man." West tells him. "You're entitled to half of everything I have."

"Nah, that's yours. I told you, I was never here for the money. I've never had money, and I'll never need it."

"It's still yours," West insists. I can see how much that means to Beck. I know he doesn't need or want the money, but West offering it to him, especially after spending months believing that's the main reason Beck was here, is a huge deal. It shows just how far the two of them have come, and it warms my heart.

"Okay, so we're going somewhere with some underfunded rundown school where Beck can go be some child's hero. What else do we need?"

I'm momentarily shocked at Cam's easy-going attitude. Just like that, he's on board to go wherever Beck is, assuming that we will all stay together after school ends. It brings a bright smile to my face, one that he notices and returns as I cuddle deeper into West.

"We obviously need to be near a college with a good swimming program," I state, watching Cam's brows climb up his forehead.

"We don't need that—" he begins.

"I could do college," Mason muses.

"Same. I'd definitely be interested in doing a tech course or something."

Cam gapes open-mouthed at West and Mason. "Guys, you don't need to go to college just for me."

"We're not," Mason assures. "None of us have ever had a chance to think about a future for ourselves that wasn't being chained to our parents' company. You've got swimming, and that's great, but I have no idea what I want to do with my life. Besides, they say college is where you figure out who you are."

Well, if that's the case, I need to go to college.

"What about you, Firefly? What do you want to do?"

"I'm with Mason—I'm all for going to college and spending the next four years working out who I am and what I want to spend my life doing."

The four of us look around at each other with slow grins forming.

"To college," Mason toasts, lifting his beer into the middle of our little group.

"To college," we all cheer.

"And saving disadvantaged children," Cam tacks on, making us all laugh.

The sun has long since set by the time we put out the fire and pack our things to head back to the car. It takes us much longer to climb up the steps in the dark, with only our phone lights guiding the way.

"Shotgun," Cam calls out as we reach the car, and Beck climbs in behind the wheel.

"Fine, idiot, that means West and I can have Hadley all to ourselves in the back." Mason smirks smugly as he pulls open the back passenger door.

Cam's face is comical as he realizes his error, and he curses himself out under his breath as he gets into the front seat, with West and Mason both laughing at him. I'm overcome with sadness as we pull onto the main road and leave our day in the sun behind us.

"Promise me we can do that again soon," I pout to Mason, who chuckles.

"I promise."

He drapes his arm over my shoulder, and I shuffle in closer to him. My eyelids start to droop, tiredness hitting me.

"You're not tired, are you, Little Warrior?" he whispers in my ear, and the seductive ring to his voice has my eyes popping open as my tiredness recedes.

"It depends. What did you have in mind?"

His dirty smirk has my panties all but disintegrating, and my skin flares hot beneath his touch as he achingly slowly glides his hand up my bare thigh. His fingers dip beneath the cut-off edges of my denim shorts, inches from my apex.

"But I mean, if you're too tired…"

He moves to pull his hand back, but I latch onto it, not letting him get too far.

"I'm not."

His smirk only deepens. "Are you sure? You look pretty tired."

"I'm not."

He cocks a brow. "I wouldn't want you to fall asleep on me now."

I return his cocky smirk with one of my own. "Then you better make it good."

His dreamy blue eyes flare at the challenge, and his fingers move to rub me through my shorts. I'm faintly aware of Cam and Beck having some sort of discussion in the front of the car, and without turning to look at him, I can feel West's heated gaze burning into me, serving only to heighten my desire.

My head falls back against the headrest and my legs fall open. Mason deftly undoes the button on my shorts, lowering the zipper so he can reach his hand inside my panties, and the second his fingers connect with my clit, I jump and have to bite down on my lower lip to suppress a moan.

"Shh," West says, leaning in to bite my earlobe. "You don't want to distract Beck."

Right, no, that would probably be bad.

He pulls the strap of my vest top down my arm, low enough to expose my breast. My bra was still damp when it started to get chilly, so I took it off when I put my top on earlier and never bothered to put it back on again, so I have just granted West effortless access to my aching nipples.

He dips his head, flicking his tongue out before sucking my nipple into his mouth just as Mason's fingers slide inside me. The combination of their touch is too much, and a small moan escapes me.

"What the—Ooh."

I pry open an eye to see Cam staring transfixed at my bare chest while licking his lips. "Goddammit," he mumbles to himself, "I'm never claiming 'shotgun' again."

My gaze lifts to the rearview mirror where Beck is watching me with equally heated eyes, before he tears them away to look out the windshield, grumbling something about trying to get all of us killed. I'd laugh, if Mason and West weren't playing my body like it was their favorite instrument.

"Climb onto Mason's lap, baby," West instructs, and he helps maneuver me, so my back is pressed against Mason's chest, enabling West to pull down my shorts and panties while Mason pushes down his boxers. As I settle on his lap, I feel his long dick slide through my folds, my pussy clenching around nothing but air as it screams at me for what it really wants—as if I don't want Mason buried balls-deep inside of me too.

Reaching between my parted thighs, I wrap my hand around his length and give it a pump before lining it up with my pussy and feeding it into my dripping core.

"Oh, fuck," Mason groans, thrusting shallowly and driving himself deeper. "Fucking incredible."

I moan as he slides all the way into me, my head falling back against his shoulder.

"Spread her legs so we can have our fill." The desire dripping from Cam's voice has me clenching around Mason, and he buries his face in the crook of my neck, softly biting the sensitive skin.

West helps me kick off my panties and shorts, and Mason hooks my legs over his, spreading me wide for Cam and West to see. I don't even realize we've stopped moving, but I sense another pair of eyes on me as Mason slowly rocks in and out of me, and I look up into the rearview mirror, spotting Beck watching me intently. It's only then that I realize he must have pulled over to watch.

His eyes are hooded, and glancing down, I can see his arm moving as it tugs on his dick. Looking at Cam, I notice he has undone his seatbelt and turned around in his seat, leaning back against the dash with his hand down his shorts too.

With all of their eyes on me, and Mason's deft fingers rubbing my clit in time to his slow thrusts, it doesn't take long to reach that ultimate high. I cry out as I spasm around Mason, feeling his seed hit my inner walls as he grunts into my neck.

I turn my head to kiss him, even as I feel hands lifting me off his lap, and the next thing I know, I'm straddling West. My knees are pressed into the leather seat on either side of his hips as his dick slides through mine and Mason's combined juices.

Even though I've just come, I can feel the telltale clenching in my lower belly as I rock my hips and stare into his eyes. His thrusts are rough and demanding, but the look in his eyes is full of adoration. I forget about the others watching as I get lost in his touch, until I'm once again diving head-first off that cliff and into oblivion, collapsing against him as he reaches his own release.

I take a second to catch my breath before climbing off him and turning to face Cam in the front seat. He meets me with a hopeful expectation shining in his lust-blown eyes, and I smirk as I squeeze between the front seats and climb into his lap. His back is still resting against the dashboard, and his hips rock against mine as I settle over him.

"You don't have to, if you—"

I press my finger against his lips, cutting him off, and slide my other hand between our bodies until my fingers circle his dick. "I want to." Lifting myself up, I position him at my entrance and slowly slide down until he's fully seated inside me. His hands squeeze my hips and he leans forward, capturing my lips with his as I begin to move.

"Fuck," I hear Beck groan from beside me, drawing my attention.

"Think you can suck him off while I fuck you, baby?" Cam purrs in my ear.

I lick my lips and bite my bottom lip, which is all the consent Beck needs before he pushes his seat back and pulls out his dick. Cam lifts me off his lap, and I sit on my knees on the passenger seat, leaning over the center console toward Beck as Cam shifts so he's standing with one foot on the floorboard, his other perched on the seat cushion to give him some leverage. I can feel his chest against my back as he leans over me, positioning himself at my entrance before pushing inside me once again.

I moan as I grasp the base of Beck's cock in my hand and run my tongue along his length. His hands thread through my hair, pulling it away from my face so he can watch me bob up and down on his dick, while Cam slowly builds the momentum higher and higher with every thrust into my pussy.

I lick and suck on Beck's dick until I feel his hold tighten in my hair, letting me know he's about to come. I hollow out my cheeks, taking him as deep as I can, faintly aware of his spluttered curses as he spurts down my throat.

Using his grip on my hair, he gently pulls me upward, slamming his lips against mine and tasting himself on my tongue. I feel Cam's fingers circling my clit, and it's like a bomb detonates somewhere inside me. I come so hard I see stars, screaming into Beck's kiss as I practically strangle Cam's dick, feeling when he finds his own release.

Sweaty and breathless, I collapse against Beck, and he strokes my hair, murmuring sweet nothings into my ear. I'm still coming down from my high when I'm lifted into the backseat, and Mason and West fix my clothes back in place. They wrap a blanket around me as I pass out in a post-orgasmic haze, surrounded by the four men I love.

Hadley

CHAPTER SEVENTEEN

After our day at the beach yesterday, it is jarring to come back to reality, but sadly the real world is calling; in the form of homework, studying, and Emilia banging on the front door.

"Do you have a death wish?" I hear Hawk snarl, and the threatening tone of his voice has me wriggling out beneath the manmeat I'm sandwiched between and rushing around in search of something decent to throw on.

"Please, Davenport, like you would do anything to me."

I groan at Emilia's comeback, and I hear someone snicker from the bed behind me.

"Why is she taunting him?" I grumble to no one in particular, finally finding a pair of shorts to pull on. Snatching up a random top, I launch myself out the door, barely getting it pulled over my head before I reach the pair of them.

Emilia has her finger shoved in Hawk's chest, and he looks about two seconds away from ripping her head off. *Jesus, help me.*

"Emilia," I exclaim brightly, hoping to diffuse the situation. "What's up?"

I had to cancel our study session at the library the other day, after my little *episode*, and with being at the beach yesterday, I haven't seen her in a couple of days. She looks slightly different than normal, but I can't put my finger on what it is. She seems more annoyed than usual, or maybe she's carrying less tension in her shoulders.

The two of them glare at each other for another moment before she turns her attention to me, and just like that, the pissed-off expression she was wearing morphs into one of excitement as she holds up a flyer.

"Look!" she squeals.

I cast my eyes over the flyer. "A graduation party?" I fail to see why a graduation party has her so excited, but, no doubt, she's about to explain it to me.

She huffs out a sigh like she has no idea what she's going to do with me. "It will be our final hoorah. The last time we get all dressed up and go to a party on campus."

"So?"

She rolls her eyes. "*So*, it's the end of an era! We have to go!"

"Ugh," I groan. "Do we really?"

"Yes! You're going. We need dresses."

"You have the dress you wore last time." I grimace, remembering what happened to mine—such a waste of money.

"You can't wear the same dress to two parties in a row! We need to go shopping. A new thrift store opened up in Liberty Point, we should check it out."

Hawk leans over and whispers in my ear, "Remember that money I mentioned before?" When I just look at him in confusion, he continues, "You deserve to have some fun. Go spoil yourself."

Emilia squeals, having apparently overheard him, and we make plans to go into town the weekend before the dance. It isn't for another couple of weeks. Unfortunately, we have final exams to get through first. Exams I am guaranteed to fail if I don't start logging more hours studying in the library.

The problem is, we have to deal with *my mother* before I can even think about studying and exams and typical school problems. So that evening, instead of heading to the library, where it seems like every other student on campus is going, I head to the guys' dorm room so we can all discuss our next move.

Mason grabs all of us some Thai from the dining hall for dinner, and we sit around the island as we tuck in.

"Any word from your dad?" I ask West.

"Nope, but my bank account is fatter than it was a few days ago, and I spoke to our family lawyer today, who confirmed the house and shares have been transferred into my name."

I absently nod my head, unsure what to say to that. I mean, it's good that he's now financially secure, but I don't like the thought of any of us having shares in our names or being tied to Nocturnal Mercenaries in any way. It's bad enough that our surnames are associated with it, never mind having legal documentation linking them as well.

"You should probably transfer your shares into my name," Hawk says, catching me by surprise. "I don't know what my mom might try to do if she finds out you have Wilbert's quarter of the company."

"And you don't think she will come after you when she finds out you have them?" I snap, scowling.

Hawk shrugs a shoulder. "I'm kinda hoping she draws the line at threatening or trying to kill her own son."

Somehow, I highly doubt that. "Well, why not put them in my name if that's the case?" I counter, calling his bluff.

He's shaking his head adamantly before I have even finished speaking. "Absolutely not. You just got rid of the target on your back, I'm not about to put a new one on it."

"But you're okay putting a target on your own back."

"It's a non-issue," Beck speaks up before Hawk can form some sort of comeback. "Right now, she doesn't know any of us have the shares." He looks at me and frowns, and I know I'm not going to like whatever he says next. "Hawk is right, though. He probably has the strongest relationship with her. If there is anyone she might soften toward, it's him." I go to open my mouth, but he cuts across me. "But for right now, we should focus on getting Frank's shares. We can sort out the rest once Maria is no longer breathing down our necks."

The others murmur their agreement, so I zip my mouth. It's not like I have a better plan anyway; I just don't like the feeling that we're getting dragged further into this mess rather than extricating ourselves from it.

Everyone looks at Mason, who sighs heavily. "I have a meeting with my father at the prison on Saturday. I'll get him to transfer the shares over then."

Not wanting to push him, knowing he hates talking about his father, the others silently agree. I don't miss that he never mentioned *how* he plans on getting his father to hand over his shares. It's not like he can just ask nicely and expect his father to comply. I drop the subject though, letting him enjoy his meal in peace as the conversation moves on to lighter topics.

∽

AFTER SPENDING all day with my ass superglued to my chair in the library, I'm practically vibrating with energy as I make my way through the forest to the clearing for this month's fight night. It's the first one since I got back, and I'm actually a little nervous about it. I usually live for the blood and violence, but with anything and everything triggering me these days, I can't be sure how I'll react, and that lack of control scares me.

The fights are already underway, and I can hear the faint sound of cheering as I get closer to the clearing, soon intertwined with the noise of a scuffle as two boys duke it out in the ring.

Moving to join the guys, Mason drapes his arm over my shoulder, pulling me in against him as one of the boys takes the other to the ground, and he quickly taps out. The two of them move to the side, joining the crowd again, and Mason and the guys scan their eyes over everyone, looking to see who will step forward next.

My eyebrows raise in surprise when Wilder steps forward, the threat of violence clear in his gaze as he grins psychotically at Deke.

"What the fuck did I ever do to you?" Deke snarls angrily before Wilder can call him out.

"You've been harassing Emilia." At Wilder's words, my gaze flits to Deke, and I feel Mason straighten beside me. What the fuck is he talking about? I know he approached Emilia that day in the dining hall, but as far as I'm aware, he hasn't bothered her since.

I open my mouth to demand answers, but Hawk beats me to it. "What the fuck do you mean by that?"

Wilder's scowl deepens. "He's suddenly started showing an interest in her, most likely because of her relationship with Hadley and the fact she's been seen hanging out with the *almighty Princes*. He's been cornering her when she's alone, pushing her to go on a date with him, and not accepting when she says no." He grits his teeth and glares at Deke with a look of death in his eyes, and I just know whatever he has to say next will make me want to kill Deke myself. "Last time, he left bruises on her."

Yup, I'm going to fucking murder this shithead!

I take a step forward, intending to do just that, except Mason's hold on my waist tightens, and Hawk's next words freeze me in place.

"Deke." His voice is as dark and deadly as Wilder's. "You better get in that fucking ring with Wilder, or you'll be facing all five of us, and you sure as fuck won't like that outcome."

Deke's pissed-off expression melts away, quickly replaced with a healthy dose of fear as he steps into the ring, but he still doesn't look fearful enough as he stands opposite Wilder, eyeing him up and assessing his likelihood of winning.

I can see it in his eyes. He thinks he can take on Wilder and walk out of this ring, and sure, Wilder is lean, and he doesn't have any of the muscle mass Mason or Hawk carry, but what he lacks in brawniness, he more than makes up for with his completely savage nature and lack of a moral compass.

Deke strips off his top, and Wilder follows, and I realize this is the first time I've seen Wilder topless. I'm not the only one who gasps as the beams from the flashlights illuminate his skin. Along one side of his torso, from under his arm to the top of his pants, and spreading out along his back, the skin is scarred and discolored in relation to the rest of his skin. The way the skin twists and undulates, it's obvious he's been burned badly in the past, and something he once said comes back to me—*Yeah, but I bet you didn't kill her.* What happened to him, and is that why he is the way he is?

Whatever he suffered in his past, I revel in his brutality as he attacks Deke with a ferocity I have only ever witnessed at the compound. It quickly becomes painfully apparent Deke never stood a chance.

The crowd watches on silently as Wilder batters him, delivering crushing blow after crushing blow until the sweat drips from his forehead and blood runs down his fingers and splatters his chest. He's heaving by the time he's finished, and Deke is unconscious, covered in blood, and definitely in need of a hospital visit—not that I give a shit about him to make sure he gets to one. Wilder loosens his hold, and Deke slumps to the ground. Standing up straight, Wilder's face is drawn tight, his pupils dilated, making him look beastly, as he surveys the crowd before storming off out of the clearing and into the trees.

Fucking hell, I think we just caught a glimpse of Wilder's monster.

∽

"Ugh," I groan, dropping my forehead to rest on the wooden table in the library. "There's no way I can learn all of this in a week. I'm going to fail."

Emilia, the bitch, just cackles beside me.

"For the number of hissy fits you've thrown, you could have finished an entire subject by now."

I lift my head and glower at her but keep my mouth shut. She's probably right. Studying just isn't my thing. Especially with everything else hanging over my head right now, the guys insisted I come and get some work done. Cam had to go to swim practice anyway. The national championship is right around the corner, and even with everything else going on at the minute, he's intent on winning it.

Mason's been subdued the last few days, spending more time alone than usual in the gym. I think he's stressing about going to see his dad, not that I can blame him. He's never really opened up to me about his childhood or his dad, not that he really needs to. The emotional damage is plain to see for anyone who looks closely enough. As someone who's been through what he has, I know it's best not to push these things. He processes his feelings in his own way—at the gym—and clearly, that's been working for him. He had the patience to wait for me to finally come to my senses before confiding in the guys about what was going on in my head. So I can at least have the patience to wait for him.

West has also been flat-out keeping tabs on his dad and my mother. He practically sits glued to his computer screen, watching them every second of the day to make sure one of them doesn't make a move against us. I think it's safe to say we're all on edge, and none of us are making healthy choices right now. We need this fucking shit done with before it ends up killing us. We haven't come this far, fought this hard, to let fucking stress take us out.

Beck is the only one out of all of us who seems capable of looking toward the future at the minute. He keeps shoving college brochures under our noses and telling us to pick one, so he knows where to apply to for jobs, but I have no fucking clue which one to choose. Do I want to live by the beach? In a mountain state? Do I want to see snow in the winter? And that's just the weather and terrain. Then there's the type of colleges—community, regular, or fancy-as-fuck private ones. Not to mention, whatever we choose must have a reputable swim team, probably some sort of wrestling team or something for Mason and me, and it needs a good computer program for West. There are *so* many factors, and that's not including the most important one of all —Hawk. I haven't spoken to him about any of this, and I have no idea what his plans are. We've only just found each other, so I'm sure as shit not going anywhere he's not going to be.

The really fucking annoying voice in my head also keeps whispering Barton's name every time I think about it too, but surely, things are too up in the air when it comes to him to know whether or not he's a factor I need to consider. For all I know, he could be playing us, in which case, I see his death playing out in the near future—along with Maria's.

But yes, all the recent talk of the future and going to college is why I'm here, complaining for the eighteenth hundredth time about how I'm going to fail these exams—in which case, all this talk about college will be futile.

Wilder enters the library with a frown on his face and makes his way toward our table. "I've seen far too fucking much of this place," he grumbles, slumping into his chair. He doesn't make a move to pull out any textbooks or his tablet, however. He just sits there, sulking.

Emilia just frowns and rolls her eyes at the pair of us before returning to her work, and with a heavy sigh and zero enthusiasm, I do the same. I have made it through about half a page of notes before Emilia snaps, "Aren't you going to at least do some work?!"

Wilder looks completely horrified at her suggestion. "God, no, why would I do that?"

"Eh, so you can pass your exams and go to college or whatever it is you want to do once you graduate?"

Wilder waves off her words. "Pfft, I don't need good grades for any of that."

I scowl at him and grumble, "I wish I didn't," which earns me a bark of laughter from Wilder, one which is loud enough to draw annoyed looks from the surrounding tables.

"You don't, Sunshine. You've probably got more money than I do. You can buy your way into any college and future you want."

My mouth pops open. *Daaaamn, I'm that rich?*

"Seriously?" Emilia snarls, looking seriously fucking pissed, and I quickly close my mouth. She waves her hand over herself. "Do you *not* see the scholarship kid here actually *working* her ass off to get into college?!" She slams her textbook shut, and *holy crap*, I don't think I've ever seen her so pissed. She gets to her feet, all the while scowling furiously at Wilder. "Some of us don't have the fucking luxury of getting everything in life handed to us. Grow some fucking respect for the people around you, or keep your goddamn mouth shut next time."

Snatching up her belongings, she storms out of the library. Wilder's gaze follows her, not looking the slightest bit chastised. He doesn't look away from her retreating form until the library door closes behind her. When he does finally turn to look at me, I swear I see goddamn hearts in his eyes.

"I think I'm in love."

I snort. "You seriously pissed her off, you dumbass!"

"And I'll do it again if she throws that fire my way. Nothing hotter than having a girl blow a fucking fuse at you."

I shake my head, not knowing how to respond to that. "You should go apologize to her."

"That's an excellent idea!" He waggles his eyebrows suggestively. "Girl could do with some de-stressing, anyway."

He quickly grabs his still-packed backpack and rushes out of the library after her. *Fucking idiot's got no chance.* Emilia's more likely to tear him a new one than fall for his unique brand of charm.

After telling her off for not confiding in me that Deke was bothering her, I told Emilia all about what went down at the last fight night. She was shocked, but she also seemed furious with Wilder for what he'd done, and ever since, any time he's around, she gets unduly agitated. I can't figure out what that's all about.

I finally got the truth from her about what was going on with Deke, and it turns out that every time she was alone, the fuckface would approach her and demand she spends time with him. Every time she said no, he got more and more aggressive. Wilder noticed the bruises on her wrist one day—it infuriates me that I didn't—and cornered her about it until she told him the truth.

I'm not entirely sure what it means. Wilder cared enough to encourage her to open up to him and he went apeshit on Deke's ass—who is still in hospital, by the way, with a punctured lung and bruised spleen—and then the fact he was able to look out for my friend when I wasn't. He has his name permanently etched beside Emilia's in the *best friend* category for me.

Left alone, I focus back on my work, and with Emilia's words playing in my head, I actually try to focus. While the thought of just paying my way in somewhere sounds so fucking sweet right now, it's not how I want to get by—relying on money and the Davenport name. I want to make my own way in this world, and that starts with not completely failing these exams.

Little Warrior

CHAPTER EIGHTEEN

The day my father got locked up was surreal. It was one of those things I'd always wished for—that, or for him to just drop dead. Or better yet, die a slow, painful death. He deserves a fate far worse than rotting away in a prison cell. Although, honestly, so long as he's out of my life, I don't care where the fuck he is.

He turned my childhood home into a place of nightmares. Made me scared to go home at the end of the day, fearful of leaving my room, and terrified to be in his presence. His temper was so volatile the slightest thing would set him off—stuff like if the server dripped a single drop of red wine on the white linen, if I had the slightest scuff on my shoe, if my mother had a hair out of place. He looked for any excuse to unleash the horrific creature that resided inside of him.

My mother hid behind her specially produced makeup that covered the marks he left on her, and I hid behind excuses—a broken arm from skateboarding, a fractured eye socket from fighting. The only ones who knew the truth of what went on behind closed doors were Hawk, Cam, and West. They were the ones that would help clean me up when I was left bruised, bloody, and broken on the floor. They'd bandage up the lashes from his belt and provide me with the necessary excuse to spend the night elsewhere. They'd listen when I vented, be there when I cried, and spar with me when I needed an outlet. They were my saving grace when everything else around me seemed hopeless.

What was worse than the always present fear and the beatings though, was the blank expression my mother wore as she watched him break me into pieces. I don't know if she was just so immune to the violence that it didn't affect her or if she genuinely didn't care. Or perhaps she was just so broken herself. Whatever the reason, watching her sit there, unresponsive, while I cried out for her help… was what shattered me. It wasn't the physical pain, or the embarrassment, or the fear. It was knowing my mother was sitting *right there*, watching it all, and she did nothing. There was no pleading for my father to stop, no crying, no soothing me after he'd stormed off. Like the dutiful wife or manipulated puppet she was, she'd rush after him, apologizing and begging *him* to let her make it up to him. I understand that she was a victim too, but I just can't wrap my head around that level of detachment.

The clanging of the gate as it slides open jolts me out of my inner turmoil, and I step forward.

"Arms out to your side, legs apart," the guard barks.

I do as he says and wait for him to pat me down. When he's satisfied I'm not smuggling anything illegal into the prison, he waves me on, and I quickly join the back of the line at the reception desk.

My foot taps impatiently against the floor as the line slowly shuffles forward, and eventually it's my turn at the desk.

"Inmate's name," the woman behind the desk asks, not even bothering to look up from the clipboard in front of her.

"Frank Hayes."

"Relationship?"

"He's my father."

She ticks a box and points toward a small waiting area. "Take a seat. You'll be called when they're ready for you."

Doing as I'm told, I take the last empty seat beside a young woman with a crying infant in her arms. She's not paying the baby any attention, too busy on her phone to do anything more than bounce him up and down on her knee.

Mary, Mother of Joseph, please don't let me have to return to this hell hole again. Once is more than enough.

Hadley was incredibly persistent that she come with me today, but she's seen the inside of prison walls more than anyone should, so there was no way I was about to let her accompany me. I managed to talk Cam into distracting her while I slipped out this morning, and I'm sure she's blowing up my phone with all sorts of pissed-off texts, but I left it in the car, wanting to focus purely on what I came here to do.

Getting my dad to hand over his shares will be no small feat. He's a callous man, one who only ever gave a shit about his own wants and needs. He'll want to maintain control of his quarter of the company, but I placed a call to his lawyer before I came here today, and he explained that my dad is looking at a life sentence without parole. He hasn't had his trial yet, but with the extensive evidence against him, it's effectively a slam-dunk case. The lawyer has been pushing him to hand over power of attorney; the stubborn bastard just hasn't done it yet, so I'm hoping it shouldn't be a huge struggle to convince him.

Despite his lack of regard for anyone other than himself, he's a very traditional man. He's always believed in the eldest son taking over the responsibility of the company and stepping into the role as head of the family when the time came—I just don't think he expected that to be any time soon. His reasons for being so 'tough' on me—as he described it—was because he was building me into the man I'd need to be to continue on the family legacy. I have no doubt there was probably some element of truth to his thinking, knowing what I know now about Nocturnal Mercenaries. I'd well believe it's a cutthroat industry, something Barton already confirmed. But the thing is, I am *not* my father. It might be his blood in my veins, his genetic makeup in my DNA. Only that's where the similarities end.

Cam has struggled a lot these last few months, carrying the weight of his father's crimes, and I can understand where he's coming from, but it's not a burden I bear. I had to realize at a young age that the sins my father commits are not mine. The things he does, the person that he is—that's not me. Every time he beat on me and whipped me bloody, I didn't see how alike we were; I saw how *different* we were. Every whoosh of his belt through the air only strengthened my resolve that I would never, ever, end up like my father.

Of course, right now, sitting in this plastic chair with an expensive suit on, my hair slicked back as I appear more like a lawyer than a visitor, I—very fucking disturbingly—look like the spitting image of my father.

Nevertheless, going in there pissed off and demanding he hand over his shares to me isn't going to get me anywhere. I need to play this smart, and that's precisely what I'm doing. Even if every second I sit here, my skin itches, and the need to punch something ratchets higher.

"Mason Hayes," a guard calls, and I get to my feet, my heels tapping on the linoleum floor as I cross the waiting room toward a metal gate that the guard stands on the other side of.

"ID, please."

I lift up my driver's license to show him, and he looks at it for a long moment before lifting his eyes to run them over my face, ensuring I look like my photo. Eventually he nods his head, and I tuck the license away in my wallet as he opens the gate.

"Follow me."

He leads me down a corridor until we stop outside a door. "Visitation time is one hour. A guard will be stationed outside the door and your visit will be recorded. No touching the inmate. No passing anything to him or accepting anything from him. If you are caught breaking these rules, your visitation rights will be revoked, and you could incur a hefty fine. Understood?"

I readily agree, keen to get this over with, and he ushers me into the room. I hear the lock turn in the door behind me, the sound making my heart rate spike. The thought of being alone in the room with this monster makes my collar feel tighter than it did a second ago.

"Son, this is a surprise."

Looking at my father, he's sitting on the far side of a worn table that has been bolted to the floor. I breathe out a sigh of relief when I see he's handcuffed and chained to the table, restricting his movements. It's fucked up that I can't even be alone in the same room as my own dad without fearing what he might do to me. It's been a long time since I've received anything more than a black eye or split lip from him, but it still doesn't stop my long-ingrained reaction to his mere presence.

Puffing out my chest, I push back my shoulders and straighten my spine so I'm standing at my full six and a half feet, effectively towering over him.

Every ounce of hate I have toward him is tucked away in a box, tightly shut, and instead, I fix a nonplussed expression on my face.

"I needed to talk to you."

I stride confidently across the small space, pulling out the chair opposite him and sitting down, acting as though being this close to him doesn't make goosebumps pebble along my skin.

He quirks an eyebrow but doesn't say anything, waiting me out. He's always been good at that. The silent treatment. I guess that's where I've learned it from. Perhaps even why I'm such a reserved person. I've mastered the significance of silence. It unnerves most people, but having had it used on me my whole life, I'm immune to it by now. And I let him see that.

Leaning back in my chair, I watch him back, noting the new lines that have formed around his eyes and mouth. His hair is more disheveled than I have seen before, and his beard is longer than he would ever have worn. Along with the bags under his eyes, he looks years older than before he was arrested, and smug satisfaction warms my blood. I'm careful not to let it show, though.

"I've been stepping into your role at the company."

He mimics my position, leaning casually back in his chair and keeping his fingers linked as his arms rest on the table.

"I figured as much."

"I take it you've heard about the compound and Lawrence."

My father's lips flatten. "I have." He shakes his head before sneering, "I get arrested, and the whole place falls apart. Typical."

Of course, the self-centered asshole thinks he was the only one holding the company together.

Despite my inner scoff, I nod my head as though I agree with him.

"I need your help to get everything back up and running. We've been left in quite a predicament, and *Maria* has taken it upon herself to take charge."

My father's lip curls and his hands form fists on the table. I knew he would object to hearing Maria attempting to take the reins. The misogynistic bastard would have a heart attack at the thought of a woman running a company all by herself. Women are arm-candy, made for producing male heirs and beating your aggression out on—at least in his mind. Regardless of his prehistoric, misogynistic views, it works in my favor for now.

"Of course, that sniveling idiot, Barton, is letting his wife take control. The guy probably can't piss without her telling him how to do it. He's never had the balls it takes to succeed in this business. Lawrence and I were the only ones who had the guts to strive for more, to fight to be at the top of this industry."

The anger pouring off him is palpable, and it takes everything in me not to jump when he slams his fist down on the table. It's interesting to hear him speak so openly about the others, though. I had no idea there was this disputation between the families.

"Wilbert will be useless," he mutters, continuing to shake his head. "We can't let them run everything I have worked so hard to build into the ground."

"I agree." I most definitely do *not* agree. "They're going to destroy the Hayes legacy at the rate they're going. Look at how much we've already lost because of their incompetence."

My father sears me with a critical look, and I know he's trying to ascertain how genuine I am. I can sit here and pretend to be invested all I want, but at the end of the day, we both know there's no love lost between us. I'm not here for him, so he has to believe I'm here because I want to be. After all, *I'm* invested in the welfare of the company's future, in the progression of the Hayes legacy.

I meet his steely gaze with an unflinching one of my own and let him look his fill until he finds whatever it is he wants to see. At the end of the day, he's trapped in a corner. He's never going to see the light of day again. He'll never have the freedom to run the company the way he wants. He *has* to pick a proxy. I just have to give him whatever justification he needs to make that person me.

"What's your plan?"

Despite not wanting to be any closer to him than I currently am, I lean forward in my seat, resting my elbows on the table and interlocking my fingers. "There's no place for women in this industry. And you're right about Barton and Wilbert. They're useless. The guys and I have been talking, and we want to take control. We have big plans for the company now that we've been fully brought in. Not only do we want to rebuild the compound, but we want to expand. We want to build similar camps across the country and further afield."

I can see the hungry greed in his eyes at that idea, even as every word tastes like ash on my tongue.

"Cam already has Lawrence's shares, and West is confident he can get his hands on his father's. Hawk is in talks with his father to get his."

"And you're here for my portion of the shares," he astutely states, to which I nod.

"I am."

There's a long moment where he looks me over, before he asks, "Why should I hand them over to you?"

I take my time mulling over his question before responding—silence is more powerful than words, after all.

"I know as well as you do, you're never getting out of here. You might have the cutthroat personality for this business, but you can't run it from a prison cell. You need someone who can fill your shoes, who can not only carry on the Hayes legacy but can make it more prominent than it has ever been before."

"And you think you're the one to do that?"

The catch is, I'm the *only* one who could fucking do it. The idiot only had one son—me. My sister is too young to deal with any of this shit, not that my father would even consider a woman to continue on the Hayes legacy. So, there's no one else, and he fucking knows it. The sick fuck just wants to make me work for it.

With my expressionless mask in place, I curl my lip in a confident sneer. "I know I am."

~

THE SECOND I'm back in the dorm, I shrug off my suit jacket and pull the tie over my head, needing to divest myself of this fucking suit as soon as possible. I feel too much like my father, dressed like this, with the grimy air of the prison still stuck to my skin. Shucking off my trousers, I head straight for the shower, not wasting a second as I turn on the faucet and stand under the hot spray. Pressing my hand flat against the tile wall, I press my chin to my chest and let the water just wash over me.

Today was a win. My father agreed to sign over the shares, but it took a lot out of me to go toe-to-toe with him in that room, alone. Since I started Pac and moved out from under his roof, I've rarely had to spend time alone with him. And as much as I like to think I'm over what he did to me, when I'm face-to-face with him like I was today, it's challenging not to remember the way he made me feel as a little kid.

I feel a warm hand on my back, and I don't even have to turn around to know who it is. She stands on her tiptoes, wrapping her arms around my upper arms, clinging to my shoulders, and pressing a kiss to my shoulder blade. The two of us stay like that for a long while, and I just let her nearness take the edge off my jitteriness. Now more than ever, I can understand how Lawrence's presence had such a debilitating effect on her. It doesn't matter how much you tell yourself you've come to terms with your past, that you're bigger, stronger, more powerful now. When you come face-to-face with that one thing, that one person who has always gotten under your skin, it tears through every barrier you've ever constructed, breaks apart every positive thought you've repeated to yourself, and strips you bare of the armor you'd carefully placed around you.

It doesn't matter if you're five years old, twenty-five, or fifty. Trauma is trauma, and no matter how much you tell yourself you're over it, that you're tougher than the ghosts that haunt you, you will always be weakened in their presence. They are always going to have a hold over your inner psyche. This is why you need people around you, people you can rely on, lean on, and stand up beside you and remind you that you're not a weak kid anymore.

Hadley is my strength, just as I hope she can now see that I am hers, as are the others. Together, we can face any challenge and come out stronger.

I turn in her arms, pulling her in flush against me, and rest my head on her shoulder. She strokes her fingers through my wet hair, the gesture soothing, and I feel the last of the tension leave my body.

Eventually, she shuts off the shower and grabs towels for us, and quietly leads me to my bedroom for us to settle on the bed. I drag her into my arms, and she slots in perfectly against me.

"Tell me about today," she whispers. It's not a demand, and I know if I told her I didn't want to talk about it, she would let it be, but she deserves better than that, and honestly, now that it's done, I feel like I have gained some closure. Today drained me, but I feel stronger for having faced my father. I feel fucking great for having deceived him. He's going to be absolutely furious when he discovers the truth, but by then, it will be too late—not that he can do anything about it from behind bars.

I bury my nose in her hair, breathing in her vanilla and honey scent. "I got the shares."

She doesn't say anything, waiting me out. She doesn't care about the shares, not really, and that's not what she meant anyway.

I sigh, relishing in the feel of having her pressed up against me. It's not easy for me to talk about my feelings. It's not something I've ever had to do before, and it doesn't come naturally. But slowly, I open up to her, telling her how it felt seeing my dad again today, and once I start, the words flow out of me until I'm telling her all about my past and the dark cloud he shrouded our house with.

The whole time, she just lets me hold her and silently listens to me, and by the time I'm done, I feel lighter than I ever remember feeling. Huh, maybe there is something to be said for this whole *talking your feelings out*.

She's reticent for a bit before she speaks up, her voice husky and clogged with emotion. "You're never going back there."

Abso-fucking-lutely.

"Have you had any more, uh, episodes?" I ask her once I'm all talked out. I have no idea what to call those moments when she's not in the present, but finding her beating up that kid scared me. Not the fact she was attacking him, but the vacant look in her eye. It was obvious she wasn't aware of what she was doing.

"None like the day you and Hawk found me...but sometimes I struggle to remember I'm not back there. It's like, I can be here, in the present, then something small sets me off—a certain smell or noise—and suddenly, I'm trapped in that cell again. Usually, it's only for a second or two, but it's terrifying." Her admission is a quiet whisper, like it's something to be ashamed of. Only I can't begin to imagine how difficult that must be, to feel so out of control. It certainly explains her need to burn herself out in the gym.

I pull her in closer to me, feeling her snuggle into my side, and it's not long before we drift off to sleep.

Hadley

CHAPTER NINETEEN

For the third fucking time in as many weeks, we're all sequestered back in the boardroom at our parents' offices. Honestly, I've seen enough of this fucking building to last me a lifetime.

"Do you have the shares?" Maria asks as soon as she enters, skipping right over any pleasantries. Probably for the best. There's no point in pretending this is a civil meeting; this is a war between people that hate each other.

Barton and Wilbert enter behind her, and interestingly, Barton doesn't sit in his usual seat on her side of the table. Rather he pulls out the chair at the end of our row. Maria barely spares his change of seat a second's glance. Refusing to think about what it means that he's sitting on our side of the invisible war line running down the center of the long board table, I instead focus on Wilbert. The man himself is sitting beside Maria, looking loyal as ever…except he's sweating bullets and looks like he's about to pass out. What the hell? He looks suspicious as fuck right now with the way his gaze bounces around the room, never settling on one place for too long. He shuffles in his seat and coughs to clear his throat, and I'm almost convinced he's about to give away what we've been planning. Still, thankfully, Maria doesn't seem to notice his suspicious behavior, too focused on the paperwork in Hawk's hand to give a shit about Wilbert or anything else going on in the room.

"We do." Hawk slides the documentation for Cam's and Mason's shares across the table, and Barton adds the documentation for his shares to the pile.

Maria looks positively gleeful as she hungrily snatches up the paperwork, meticulously checking through each page and ensuring it's correct.

"It's all there," Hawk assures her. "Just like you asked."

"Yes, it appears so," she finally agrees, setting the paperwork on the table in front of her. Resting her hands on top of it, her talon-like claws begin to tap impatiently against the paper.

"And you'll uphold your end of the bargain?" Barton clarifies. There's no fancy paperwork to sign or legal documentation to ensure she does, in fact, uphold her end.

None of that will actually stop her from doing whatever the fuck she wants. We just have to hope, on a wing and a prayer, that, now she has what she wants, she will just leave us the fuck alone.

Not that that's good enough. I can't just silently sit back and live my life, knowing she will be rebuilding her empire here and, before long, be back to stealing more kids off the street and subjecting them to the harsh realities of the compound.

The problem is, I have no idea how to stop her. Okay, well, I have a few somewhat permanent ideas, but I'm not entirely sure her death is the desired outcome here. While personally, I have no issues with killing her, I don't think it's what Hawk wants. Despite her cold attitude, she's still his mother, and I can't just fucking kill her if he's not okay with it. It's not something we've talked about, but the fact he hasn't just suggested offing her himself is all the conversation we need to have.

"Yes, yes," she snaps, far too dismissively for my liking.

"You are going to let *all* of us lead our own lives without dragging us into the company," I say, spelling it out for her. "You're not going to threaten, bribe, or coerce any of us into doing your bidding, or anything for the company."

For the first time, possibly ever, she actually looks at me. Like, properly takes me in, and sees me as more than just some stranger in her house, some girl her son has brought home, or some pawn she can maneuver around a chessboard at her will. There's still no motherly love in her gaze, merely recognition that I've spoken and an assessment that I'm worthy of a response. She probably doesn't look at me for more than a minute, yet it's enough time for me to determine that I will never care to know this vapid, narcissistic woman in front of me. She's not a mother to me, and she never will be. And surprisingly, I'm okay with that. Sure, I grew up dreaming of the traditional family, but who the fuck wants traditional? The world is full of non-traditional families. I'd take non-traditional and happy, over traditional and miserable as fuck, any day.

"I said yes, didn't I."

Jesus, this woman's attitude is infuriating.

I smile tightly at her. "Just making sure you understand the terms."

"Yes, you all want to give up your legacies, like the entitled children you are, for the freedom you *think* it will gain you." She pins each of us with a serious look. "Just know, I won't be interested in taking any of you back when you come begging me to."

I can tell I'm not the only one holding back my snort. *Yeah, fat fucking chance of that happening.*

"Well, if we're done here," Hawk says tightly, wrapping up the meeting. Before he can get to his feet, Maria lifts a finger, indicating she's not yet done. *Great, now what?*

"Just one more thing." She focuses her gaze on Barton. "You've handed over all of your shares, and as such, I think it's only fitting that you step down from your position."

"I intended to," Barton responds curtly.

Maria nods. "And I also want a divorce."

You could hear a pin drop; the silence is so intense. Surely this is not the appropriate place to have this conversation, in front of all of us? This is a private matter between the two of them. And yet, despite being painfully aware that we're intruding on an otherwise personal conversation, I can't tear my eyes away from Barton's face.

His eyebrows have lifted in surprise, except that's his only reaction. He clears his throat and fixes his suit jacket before responding, "I think that's for the best." With that, he gets to his feet, and we all follow, pushing back our chairs and standing. *Seriously? That's it?* Twenty-one years of marriage, and it ends just like that? I don't know if it's for the best or the saddest thing I've seen all day.

We all follow Barton out of the room and into the elevator, where we stand awkwardly. The others cast glances at Barton, as if waiting for him to have a meltdown. He just stands stoically as the lift descends, looking surprisingly unbothered by the events in the boardroom.

The awkwardness continues as we all shuffle out of the elevator and through the building's reception, onto the street.

"Uh, we'll see you back at campus in a bit," Beck says, looking between Hawk, Barton, and me before leaning in and pressing a kiss to my temple. The others give their own kisses and hugs goodbye and climb into Mason's SUV. Part of me wishes I could go with them and leave this awkwardness behind. I have no idea what to say to Barton. For all intents and purposes, it *appears* he's on our side. He handed over his shares, and he doesn't seem the slightest bit fazed by the end of his marriage, but none of his recent actions add up with his previous ones. Why, all of a sudden, is he putting us first? Above his wife and the company?

And yet, if what Hawk said about the wooden box is correct, my father has perhaps been more affected by my disappearance than his actions dictate. Maybe he was telling the truth, and he thought he was doing what was best. I mean, it definitely wasn't for the best. There's no excusing his past behavior, but is it possible that this is him trying to make up for it? I don't know, and trying to work it out is just giving me a headache.

"Maybe we should go grab lunch and talk?" Hawk suggests, sounding unsure.

"Lunch sounds like a great idea." Barton's voice holds none of the hesitation or heaviness that Hawk's did. "There's a great little Italian place around the corner."

I quirk a brow at Hawk, who just shrugs, uselessly, and we follow Barton as he leads us to the Italian restaurant.

Once we've all ordered and the waiter has taken our menus, I look at Hawk expectantly. Barton doesn't appear to be in any rush to discuss today's meeting, but I, for one, need answers. I need to know if we really can trust him.

"Uh, so..." Hawk begins hesitantly, taking a sip of his water. "About today..."

Barton lifts a hand to cut him off. "Don't worry about it, son. It's been a long time coming. Honestly, I'd been planning on having the same discussion with her, just...in private. We're both after different things in life."

"And, uh, what is it you're after?" I question, confused.

The way Barton looks at me, it's as if he can't believe I even have to ask that question.

"Now that I've got you back, I want to get to know you, to spend time with you..." He looks away from me to focus on Hawk. "...with both of you."

Unsure what to make of his raw honesty, I look at Hawk, and I can see he wants to believe in his father, but he's just as unsure as I am.

"I know I have made bad decision after bad decision, and nothing I say or do can make up for that, but I'd really like it if we could start fresh and get to know one another."

I have so many questions, but I guess the answers don't matter. I probably wouldn't understand his reasoning for many of the things he did—like pushing me into the tradition at school or trying to marry me off to Wilder. At the end of the day, if he's willing to move forward and doesn't try to direct our lives any further, I guess we can see where this goes.

I can feel Hawk looking at me, and when I meet his gaze, he lifts his brows, wordlessly asking what I think. Honestly, I don't know. Does part of me want the chance to get to know my father? Yeah, of course, but I'm also so burned by people that I don't know if I have any more trust left to give.

"You won't have any say in our lives," I state, fixing Barton with a serious look. "You won't dictate what we do or force our hands on anything. If there is to be any hope of a relationship between us"—I hold up my hand, pointing my finger back and forth between us—"it's on *my* terms."

"I understand. I don't want to control you, or run your life for you, I just want to be a part of it—in whatever way you're comfortable with."

Not sure of what else to say, I nod and take a drink of my water, needing to quench my dry throat. I'm not entirely sure if I'm making a massive mistake by inviting him in or opening the door to a relationship I have always craved but never thought I'd have.

∽

THE REST of the week goes by in a blur of studying, spending time with the guys, Emilia and Wilder, studying, and did I mention studying? So. Much. Studying. If I never see the inside of a library or have to open another textbook again, I'll die happy. But exams start in a few days, and to say I've been slacking is an understatement.

Unfortunately, with all this studying, we haven't had a chance to sit down and discuss our next moves regarding Maria. She's off our backs for now, but apparently the next shareholder meeting is only a week away, and West will have to be there, which will ultimately reveal to Maria that the company is not all hers to do whatever the fuck she wants with.

There has been no more talk of putting the shares into Hawk's name; honestly, I don't know that it would make a difference. We're all a target, regardless of who has the shares. The only benefit to whoever owns the shares is that Maria isn't going to kill that person and risk losing them altogether. But that doesn't mean she won't have any qualms about killing the rest of us.

I'm not okay with her hurting any of us, which is why we need a plan in place, because there is no way she isn't going to be gunning for us when she discovers the truth. This is why I bring up the conversation on Thursday night, even though it's late and we're all already exhausted from our busy schedules.

"We need a plan in place before West has to go to this shareholder meeting next week."

My words are met with exhausted sighs and groans from everyone except Beck, who leans forward in his seat in the living room with a serious expression. He's been staying here every night since my little breakdown, and either all five of us crash in my bed or the others start off in their own rooms, but usually, at least one of them ends up in bed with Beck and I at some point during the night.

"I agree," he begins. "I know you've all been busy with studying for exams and everything, but we're running out of time, and there's no way West is going into that meeting without a plan in place."

His words have everyone else sitting up straight and paying attention, no one willing to put West's life at risk.

"Okay, does anyone have any ideas?" Mason asks, looking at each of us.

I have one idea, but I bite my tongue, unwilling to voice it. Killing her is obviously the best way to deal with this, but I'm not going to unless Hawk mentions it. I won't be responsible for putting him in that position; of making the decision whether or not his mom lives or dies.

Thankfully, Beck speaks up, "We need to focus on protecting ourselves. I've been wracking my brain, and honestly, the only plausible solution I can come up with is to"—he looks at Hawk and grimaces—"kill her."

Hawk's lips flatten as he presses them together, and he doesn't immediately respond to Beck's words.

After a long moment, he sighs, running his palm over his face. "I don't know," he groans. "I just—there must be another option."

"Are we really those people that resort to killing off their problems?" Cam pipes up with a shrug. "I mean, no offense, man, but your mom is a bitch. She's as bad as the rest of our parents, but I don't know how I feel about killing her. I know she's going to be furious with us, and maybe it's stupid not to consider it. Nevertheless, I just think if there's another option, we should take it."

I squeeze his hand reassuringly as my heart swells. This is why he could never be like his father. He's too good. Where I—or probably Beck—wouldn't hesitate to behead that bitch. He wants to be able to walk away from all of this with his soul still intact, and goddamn, if that doesn't make me love him even more.

After a second's hesitation, Beck nods and we swiftly move on as he continues. "Alright, then we need to try and cut her off at the knees, prevent her from coming after us."

"How do we do that?"

Beck looks at West. "Do you know how the company gets jobs to the mercenaries working for them—the adults that aren't being forced into this life?"

"Eh, yeah, they have a highly encrypted portal that they advertise jobs through, and whoever wants to take it, accepts and receives the details via an encrypted email."

"Do you think you'd be able to get into that system?"

"Yeah. There should be a backdoor through the company's mainframe, which I have access to."

Beck grins. "Good. Once you're in, crash it. That way, she won't be able to reach out to any of them and get them to do her dirty work for her."

West nods and goes to grab his laptop.

"Okay, so that'll prevent her from sending any mercenaries after us, but there's still plenty more she could do. Even if we take measures to protect ourselves, we can't live on the defense for the rest of our lives."

Beck sighs, running his hand down his face in exhaustion or frustration. "I know, but that's all I've got for now."

Several hours later, West has successfully sent out a message to all the mercenaries for hire who are in our parents' employ, telling them that the company won't be taking on any new jobs for the foreseeable future, and crashed the system, so Maria can't gain access to it.

It won't solve our problem, but it's a start.

∼

APPARENTLY, impending exams do not mean the weekly Friday night Pacific Prep party is canceled. Actually, after spending all week staring at the bland walls of the library, trying to cram so much knowledge into my head that my brain is nothing but mush at this point, I'm kinda looking forward to sitting by the lake and just relaxing for the night.

"Ahh, it's been so long since we've had a night out," Emilia squeals in excitement when I answer the door to her on Friday night. She looks fantastic in booty shorts and a tube top, showing off her tanned skin and flat abdomen.

She pulls me in for a tight hug, and I can already smell the sickly-sweet odor of alcohol on her breath. She giggles as she pulls away, moving further into the apartment, and Wilder comes strolling behind her with a crazy-ass grin on his face.

"Sunshine." He nods his head and moves past me to the kitchen, lifting some beer and wine coolers out of a bag he's carrying and filling up the fridge.

"Can you believe it's the final party of the year?" Emilia exclaims when I join her on the sofa.

"We have the dance next week."

She shakes her head and rolls her eyes, like she doesn't know what to do with me. "That's different. This is the final *Friday night* party."

Yeah, I'm still not understanding the difference. Even if I did, it's all the same to me. A party by the lake in skimpy clothes or a dance in the dining hall with gowns and suits. Either way, people get drunk, sleep with inappropriate people, and regret their decisions in the morning.

Hawk strides in, wearing a dark green shirt and cream chinos, pausing on the threshold before he makes a beeline for the fridge. Lifting out a beer, he joins us in the living room. I notice his gaze linger on Emilia for a second, frown lines wrinkling his forehead before he looks away. I have to suppress my eye roll. The idiot needs to learn to get along with my best friend. She's not going anywhere, and neither is he, so to save all of us the headache, they need to learn to be in the same room without pitching a fit.

Emilia makes a point of ignoring him, talking my ear off about one thing and another, catching me up on the school gossip I couldn't care less about. Not long later, Cam walks in, looking fucking drool-worthy in a tight pale gray shirt and dark denim jeans. The way his eyes drop over me heats my skin, and I have to suppress a shiver of desire. He smirks, knowing just how much he affects me, and squeezes into the space beside me on the sofa, dragging me into his lap.

Leaning in, he bites my earlobe, making me squeeze my thighs together. His dark chuckle does nothing to abate the need coursing through me. "You look absolutely fuckable tonight."

Hoooly shit, someone get me a fan.

Thankfully, before I can self-combust, the others stroll in, and we keep the topic of conversation light as we all down a few pre-drinks.

The party is well underway by the time we make it down to the lake, but regardless of the mass of bodies writhing in time to the music on the pebbly shore, the plastic chairs the Princes always sit in around the fire remain unoccupied.

I'd half expected someone to have claimed the seats. In fact, I'm surprised no one has tried to claim the title of Princes. It's not as though the guys have been all that present recently, but the threat of their wrath seems to be enough to keep people in line. As for the girls, there hasn't been the same uproar to the stopping of the tradition as there was last time. Maybe it's because the guys explained they're in a relationship—

although somehow, I doubt that's the reason—or perhaps they've just gotten sick of all the drama. Now that I could understand. Whatever the reason, I'm not questioning it. We're down to the last couple of weeks of school, and everyone's thoughts seem to be on the summer and college. You can practically taste the excitement in the air as everyone looks toward their futures with the kind of optimism that only comes with youth.

We all take our seats, West pulling me into his lap, freeing up a chair for Emilia.

"What do you want to drink, babe?" Mason asks, flipping open the lid on the cooler, revealing a selection of beers, wine coolers, and water.

"Water, please."

He hands me the bottle, before moving on to dole out drinks for everyone else, and I inspect the lid, ensuring it's properly sealed before unscrewing it. It's become a habit ever since Michael managed to get one over on me. I still don't know how he managed to sneak something into my coffee without me noticing. It's not something I'll ever allow someone to achieve again, though. Now, unless I get the drink myself, I make sure it comes sealed, and I always double-check the seal and bottle for any signs of tampering. Of course, I trust Emilia, Wilder, Hawk, and my guys, but we didn't carry that cooler down here, meaning they got someone to do it for them, and who knows what the fuck some random asshole might have done to our drinks.

We all lapse into easy conversation, watching the party rage around us. It's honestly the best party I have been to all year. No one approaches us or tries to make conversation with the guys. While they still receive *come fuck me* looks from girls dancing nearby, none of them do more than that, and it's fucking bliss not having to watch desperate wannabe housewives grinding all over *my* guys.

As the night wears on, the music gets louder and louder, and I can feel sweat gathering at my temples and along my spine, even though I've done nothing but sit in West's lap. My heart rate starts to spike, and when the music switches to a new song and a loud bass starts up, I flinch.

It's just music. It's a party. You're outside. You're at school. You're safe.

I repeat the mantra over in my head, sucking down huge lungfuls of air as I try to breathe through it.

"Hey," West whispers in my ear. "Let's go for a walk."

Nodding, I climb to my feet, and he slips his hand in mine as we head down the shore, away from the loud music.

"Are you alright?"

"Yeah, I'm fine."

He quirks an eyebrow. *Right, saying I'm fine isn't an acceptable response.*

I huff out a chuckle. "It's like, I can be fine one minute, and the next, I can feel myself getting agitated, and I struggle to keep myself grounded in the present."

He mulls over my words for a second, before asking, "What happened back there?"

I chew on my bottom lip before sighing. I keep my gaze glued to the stony shore beneath my feet, unable to look at him as I say, "Sometimes they'd blast death metal music into my cell, for what felt like days on end. The constant noise and lack of sleep drove me crazy. It would get to the point that I would have done just about anything to get some peace."

He squeezes my hand, and I glance up at him. He smiles softly, pulling me to a stop as he wraps his arms around me. "Any time you start to feel yourself losing control, just tell one of us, and we'll distract you or go somewhere else with you. Whatever you need."

Returning his hug, I bury my nose in the crook of his neck. "I know. Beck showed me these really useful breathing exercises, and I've found if I repeat a mantra in my head, it helps to ground me."

"You're so strong, Firefly. Scarily so. Sometimes, I worry you don't need me," he confesses on a quiet whisper.

Leaning back, I lift my hand, running my fingers through his hair before cupping his cheek. "I'll always need you, West. You're so thoughtful and always thinking of me and my needs. You could see that I was getting stressed, and you fixed it. I could feel myself spiraling, and while I probably could have talked myself down, getting away from the party for a bit was exactly what I needed."

I press up onto my toes and place a soft kiss against his lips before we continue on our walk around the lake. Only when I'm feeling thoroughly relaxed and back in control do we return to the party.

As we approach the fire, Cam lopes over and purrs in my ear, "Dance with me, baby." I might have two left feet, but there's no way I'm about to deny him when he talks to me with that deep, gruff voice that has my lower belly clenching.

Taking my hand, he pulls me toward the writhing mass of bodies, careful to stick to the outskirts of the crowd and staying on the opposite side of the lake to the DJ. How he even knows to do that is beyond me.

His hands rest on my hips as I sway to the tune—some upbeat pop song—and wrap my arms around his neck. As the song continues, our bodies gravitate closer until we're pressed up against each other.

He rests his forehead against mine as his hands slide around to my lower back, somehow managing to pull me in even closer. His eyes never leave mine, and the rest of the party fades away as I get lost in his gaze. The mischievous glint in his eyes holds me captive. It was missing for so long, I worried I'd never get to see this side of him again, and now that he's found his way back to me, I want to capture every second of it.

"My life was nothing before you," he murmurs. We're standing so close that, even with the thudding of the base and the boom of the music being pushed out over the crowd from the large speakers, it would be impossible not to hear him. "I was lost, going through the motions. I didn't even realize how unhappy I was."

Our lips are a hairsbreadth apart, and I couldn't look away from him now, even if a meteorite flew by overhead.

"I thought I had all I needed in life, but you've shown me how much I was missing out on. I never thought I could feel this way." A shy yet awe-inspiring smile brightens his face. "For the first time in my life, I'm excited about the future. I can't wait to spend every day with you—to wake up together, go to sleep together, to argue over stupid things, and just revel in the mundane."

To most people, that might sound like nothing special. It's no grand gesture, but for me, it's the biggest gesture of all. Normal is all I've ever wanted—to live a normal life... with Cam, West, Mason, and Beck. I want Hawk to piss me off, and have Emilia make me laugh. I want to do crazy shit with Wilder, and at the end of the day, curl up with my guys and know that life can never get better than this.

I return his shy smile with one of my own and press up onto my toes, placing a chaste kiss to his lips. "Good, 'cause you're never getting rid of me. You're it for me;

you're all I'll ever need. All four of you. I want everything you just mentioned. I want the mundane. I want to share every boring moment of my life with you."

He chuckles. "Oh, baby, absolutely nothing about our life will be boring."

He slants his lips over mine, stealing my breath with a passionate kiss. Just as I'm getting lost in his touch, he pulls back only enough to whisper against my lips, "I love you."

"I love you too." He swallows my words with another kiss that has me forgetting about everything other than the parts of my body he's touching as my skin lights up like wildfire beneath him.

Hadley

CHAPTER TWENTY

I link my fingers with Cam's and pull him away from the writhing mass of bodies in the direction of the boat house. His body is flush against mine, pushing me faster as we rush away from the party, the loud music quickly fading the farther we go. I glance back at him over my shoulder as I giggle, the hungry look in his eye making my vagina flutter with need.

Out of the corner of my eye, I notice the bonfire, and sparing it a glance, my gaze lands on West watching us run off into the night. His lip lifts in a half smile and he winks at me. There's no jealousy on his face, no anger that I'm spending time with Cam and not with him. He knows, just as I do, that I might be with Cam now, but I'll always have time for West. Just as I'll always have time for Beck and Mason too. I love when we all hang out as a group, but I also love my one-on-one time with each of them.

Once we reach the boat house, I slip around the side so we're hidden from the rest of the party and any nosey onlookers.

He pushes me against the wall, the coarse wood chafing against my peaked nipples as he pins me in place with his hips. His lips trail up the sensitive skin of my neck before he bites down on my earlobe, making me whimper and grind my ass back against his erection.

"I can never get enough of you," he murmurs against my ear. His voice is a seductive husk overflowing with hungry need. "I want to wake you up with my tongue in your pussy and make you come around my dick every night. I want to have lazy Sunday sex on the couch and be that annoying couple who can't keep their hands off each other when we're out in public."

Fuck me. I'm all for dirty talk, and what he's describing has me fucking gagging for him. I can't do anything but moan obscenely as he presses his hard cock between my asscheeks, demonstrating just how fucking much he wants all of that.

His hands slip under my top and skim over my ribs. He squeezes my tits, pinching the nipples and causing me to groan in delight.

"Do you want all of that too?" His husky voice and dirty words have me incapable of producing words.

"Mmmhmmm."

My skin burns everywhere he touches, and my breathing hitches, each breath nothing but a rapid pant. Trailing his fingers down my abdomen, he deftly unbuttons my shorts and pushes his way beneath my panties until his fingers are stroking over my sensitive nub. I jerk in his arms, throwing my head back against his shoulder and groaning.

He kisses the base of my neck. "I love how much I turn you on. Love how wet you get for me." His fingers slide lower, and he pushes his way inside me, teasing me mercilessly. "You feel it just as much as I do, don't you? That deep ache in your chest that only recedes when we're locked together."

His fingers sink deeper into my pussy, and I'm already so close to coming from his words alone. Is orgasm by dirty talk a thing? 'Cause I'm pretty sure I'm about to make it one.

"Yes," I pant. "I feel it. You burn me up inside and make me feel alive, and when you're not around, it's like something inside of me is missing."

He bites along my neck as he slowly pumps his fingers in and out of me, driving me wild. Just when I think I can't take it anymore, he pushes his thumb firmly against my clit, and I go off like a rocket, screaming my release into the night.

He doesn't give me a second to recover, spinning me around to face him. My shorts fall to the ground and he rips my panties clean off me. In the next second, he's hauled me up into his arms, his fingers digging into my asscheeks as my back smacks against the wood of the boathouse, and he slams into me in one swift thrust.

I spasm around him, my fingers clawing into his shoulders, as I lift my head to the sky and cry out. When I lower my gaze to look at him, I find him staring at me, mesmerized. "You're so beautiful," he murmurs. I lean in to kiss him, and it quickly turns wild as he sucks my tongue into his mouth, biting and sucking on my lower lip. He still hasn't moved, and I grind down on him, pushing him impossibly deeper in an attempt to get him going.

He groans into my mouth and pulls back, so only the head of his cock is resting inside me. In one forceful thrust, he slams into me and sets a fast pace that quickly has me climbing closer to the stars above us. Our kiss turns sloppy, and my pussy clenches around him as I cry out his name. He continues to hammer relentlessly into me, dragging out my orgasm and starting me back up that cliff again. It feels like I'm on a rollercoaster, being pushed impossibly higher, but I know once we reach the top, it's going to be a hell of a journey back down again.

My head is spinning, and my breaths are coming so quickly I'm not entirely sure I'm getting any oxygen into my body. My skin feels like it's about to burst apart as, with each thrust, Cam pushes me toward my third orgasm of the night.

"Cam." The word is nothing more than a half-plea, half-pant. I'm not even sure if I can come for a third time, but I know my body needs *something*. This chaotic ball of energy building within me needs some sort of release.

"I know, baby. I feel it too."

I'm delirious, out of my mind with need, but I register the feel of Cam's fingers on my chin as he tilts my head so I'm looking deep into his eyes. Once he's locked me in his gaze, it's impossible to look away, and I watch riveted as he drives himself toward his own release.

He picks up the pace, and his hand moves down between our bodies, until it's circling my clit. He pinches it, and I swear I must black out for a moment, as the next thing I know, I'm lying boneless in his arms, panting like I have just run a marathon and feeling sated like a cat who just had a whole bowl of milk.

"Fuck," I breathe out against his neck, unable to even lift my head. He leans against the wall, steadying us, and I can feel the rapid rise and fall of his chest beneath me.

He chuckles breathlessly, planting a tender kiss on the crown of my head. We stay like that until our breathing has returned to normal, and I'm confident my legs aren't going to give out from under me when I put my weight on them. Then we get cleaned up and re-dressed before heading back to the party.

∽

THE NEXT MORNING, I'm awake before everyone else, including Mason. I still don't sleep well at night, and usually by four a.m., I've given up trying. Mason will be up in an hour to go to the gym, so I typically use that time to get my caffeine fix and binge-watch TV.

There's this show where people buy old, rundown houses and renovate them. It's riveting to watch. I love how they take these buildings that other people have written off and turn them into something beautiful.

Still in my sleep shorts and hair like a rat's nest, I pull open my bedroom door and freeze. I blink rapidly, trying to clear my vision and make sure I'm actually seeing what I think I'm seeing.

"What are you doing?"

Emilia jumps a foot in the air and spins to face me with wide, panic-stricken eyes. I quickly drop my gaze, taking in what she's wearing—her outfit from last night. Returning to her face, I notice last night's makeup smudged around her eyes, and her hair hasn't been brushed yet.

My own eyes widen as understanding dawns, and my gaze bounces back and forth between her and the door behind her—the door to *my brother's* bedroom.

"Did you…Were you…Are you…" Words fail me as I struggle to comprehend what I'm seeing.

"Let me explain," she rushes out, but before she can say anything more, the door behind her opens, and none other than Wilder fucking Clearwater steps out, also wearing last night's clothes.

My jaw drops open as Emilia turns beet red. Wilder, cool as a fucking cucumber, glances between us, smiling. *Smiling.* Like absolutely nothing about this situation is entirely mind-altering.

"Coffee?"

Neither of us responds to him. Instead, I just gape at Emilia, who looks everywhere but at me.

Eventually, he must realize he isn't going to get a response. "Alright, I'll put on a pot."

Yeah, that might be best. God knows my brain needs coffee if I have any hope of wrapping my head around what I just witnessed.

Still not looking at me, Emilia makes a beeline for the bathroom.

Oh, no, she's not getting off the hook that easily.

I push open the bathroom door as it slowly closes behind her, and once I'm inside the bathroom, I flick the lock behind me and stand in front of the door with my arms crossed, waiting her out.

She takes her sweet time, splashing water over her face to remove the last of her makeup before running her fingers through her hair in an attempt to flatten the bedhead look she's sporting.

"Eh, wanna tell me what's going on?" I eventually snark, when it becomes pretty apparent she's not going to bring it up on her own.

"Nope. Not really."

I roll my eyes. The girl who's always asking inappropriate questions about *my* sex life, and can never seem to shut up, suddenly has nothing to say? Ironic.

"Did you have sex with Wilder last night?" Her cheeks turn crimson. *So that's a yes, then.* "In my brother's bedroom?" My brows tug together in confusion. "Where is Hawk?"

If it's possible, her cheeks redden even more so. You could fry an egg on them at this point.

"Oh. My. God." My mouth drops open in shock. "You didn't." She looks at me through the mirror above the sink, and the guilt is written all over her face. "Emilia, please tell me you didn't sleep with my brother last night."

Her lips press together, and her eyes take on a pleading look.

"Oh my god, you did." I run my palm down my face. "You slept with my brother. And Wilder."

"It was an accident," she rushes out, spinning to face me.

"What, you just slipped and fell on their dicks?"

She grimaces. "Well, no, not exactly."

"What does this mean? Do you *like* like them? I thought you hated Hawk?"

"I do...hate him," she's quick to assure me, which only confuses me further, although I guess I don't have a leg to stand on. I was attracted to the guys even though I hated them. Hell, I slept with Cam and made out with Mason, even though they were actively trying to ruin my life.

She groans, running her hand over her face as she sinks to the floor. I sit down opposite her, resting my back against the door.

"It doesn't mean anything. I still hate him. I just had too much to drink last night, and...I don't know." She groans again.

There's a long moment of silence while I try to process everything, and I watch silently as Emilia beats herself up.

"It would be okay, you know...if you did like him, or Wilder...or both of them."

Emilia slowly looks up from the spot on the floor she was staring at, her eyebrows raised in surprise. "It would be? You'd be okay if I wanted to go out with your brother?"

I shrug a shoulder. "I mean, yeah. Why not? He'd be lucky to get a girl like you. God forbid he go out with one of the Pac skanks." I wrinkle my nose in disgust at that notion.

She chuckles weakly. There's a knock at the door before she can say anything more, and Wilder speaks, just as I'm about to tell him to go piss outside, "There's coffee at the door."

Huh, that's actually quite thoughtful of him. Once I have heard his footsteps fade away as he disappears back down the hall, I flick the lock and crack the door, peering out to check that the hall is empty. Snatching up the mugs, I quickly close the door and lock it again, passing a cup to Emilia before reclaiming my spot on the floor.

As soon as I'm comfortable, she shakes her head, picking up the conversation again. "It's not like that anyway. I don't like your brother that way. He *infuriates* me. Even just being around him has my blood pressure spiking."

"And yet, you slept with him."

She scowls. "I told you, it meant nothing. It was a drunken mistake. The scholarship kids don't talk to me, and I don't know whether it's because I'm a scholarship student or because I hang out with you guys now, but no one else in the school will talk to me. Pass it off as being horny and having limited options."

Having unfortunately just taken a sip of my coffee, I snort and quickly swipe at my nose, catching a few dribbles of coffee that went up the wrong pipe. Coughing, I take another few gulps, this time managing to get the coffee into my system.

"And what about Wilder?"

She frowns into her mug. "If it's possible, I'm even more confused about him. I mean, he was *your* fiancé, and I guess we were kinda friends before you, you know...disappeared. I don't know why, but when you were gone, he took it upon himself to check in with me and keep me company. He'd listen to me rant about the guys and freak out over you...he was, sweet, almost." She must see the completely flabbergasted look on my face as she says, "I know, I know. I can't believe I'm using Wilder and sweet in the same sentence."

She's silent for a moment before continuing, "Then he beat up Deke, and I was furious with him. I still am. I didn't ask him to do that or need him to. I can fight my own battles; I don't need him stomping in here like a neanderthal and pissing all over what isn't his."

I snort at her analogy, and we lapse into silence as I watch her glower at a spot in the floor, thinking something over.

"I've, uh, actually, been invited to go on tour with Death on a Matchstick this summer," she says hesitantly.

My mouth drops open. "No way, seriously? I didn't even know you kept in touch with them."

She shrugs casually. "They've sent me a few emails. Well, Axel and Jared have."

"I can't believe you're only telling me this now," I gape, faking outrage.

"I wasn't going to go, but..." she trails off with another shrug. "Now I think I should. I've done nothing but study and live in the small bubble that is Pacific Prep for the last four years, and I'm about to go to college and do the same thing. I think...I think I want to just enjoy life for a bit."

I nod, understanding what she's saying. "You should. It would be good for you, and besides, they're hot as fuck. No sane person would turn down a chance to spend the summer with a rock band."

She chuckles. "Right? I must have been crazy to question it."

Another moment of silence lapses as we both sip on our coffees. "So, you're not angry at me?" I can hear the nervousness in her voice, and without a second's thought, I put my mug on the floor and crawl over to her. I wrap my arms around her in a tight hug.

"Never!"

The two of us sit on the bathroom floor, drinking our coffee and chatting about the fantastic summer Emilia's about to embark on, until there's a hard thud against the door and Hawk's gruff voice interrupts our chit-chat. "Hadley, Jesus Christ, you can't occupy the bathroom all morning. Some of us need to fucking shower."

Emilia and I just burst out laughing, leaving him to huff for another half hour before we finally emerge.

Once we've showered and dressed, we catch the bus into town—much to the agitation of Hawk and the guys, who wanted to drive us—to pick out dresses for the dance.

I have the new bank card Barton left for me, burning a hole in my pocket, even though I'm still reluctant to spend any of it. I haven't even dared to look at how much is in the account. I'm reasonably certain that I will be shell-shocked no matter what the amount is, so I'm better off not knowing.

"Shall we try that new thrift shop?" Emilia suggests.

"Sounds good."

We make our way to the shop, and for the next hour, we try on a multitude of dresses before picking the ones each of us like. It might not be the fancy, designer dresses we had last time, but we have just as much fun laughing at each other and mucking around in the changing rooms, before going to the checkout with our purchases.

Thankfully, I can pay for the dress from my scholarship stipend instead of using the card. I know Hawk told me to treat myself, but it feels weird, especially considering my strained relationship with Barton. However, I use the card to treat us to lunch afterward—somehow, it feels more acceptable if I spend the money on both Emilia and me, as opposed to buying myself something frivolous I don't need. I know it doesn't really make any sense, but that's how I feel.

We go to a sea-front cafe and order more food than the two of us could eat in a week, filling the table with various dishes, and laugh and enjoy ourselves as we gorge on the food until my stomach feels like it's about to tear apart at the seams.

"So the guys and I have decided we're going to go to college," I tell her, once I'm so full, I can hardly breathe.

"That's great. Do you know where?"

I shake my head. "Not yet. Obviously, we're too late to apply for anything this year, so we'll take some time once school is finished, and we've sorted out this crap with Maria and the company, to think over our options."

"I'm so happy for you." The smile drops off her face, and she sighs. "It's going to be so weird being away from you next year."

"I'll come visit you, and you can come to wherever we are anytime you want. Plus, there's the phone and video chat. West showed me how to set that up, so we can do that every week."

She grins and holds her hand out across the table. "I'm holding you to that, Davenport."

I laugh and shake her hand, ignoring the prickle of tears in my eyes. *Damn, I am going to miss this girl.*

∽

It's late afternoon by the time I let myself back into the guys' dorm, finding all five of them huddled together in the living room, talking in low voices.

"What's wrong now?" I sigh, the good mood from my day out quickly evaporating.

Dropping my shopping bags, I plunk myself on the sofa between Beck and West, snuggling in against Beck when he drapes his arm over me.

"I found this on the cameras today," West says, pressing play on his tablet and holding it up for me to see.

Maria is sitting at her desk, when her cell starts ringing. Lifting it, she looks at the screen before answering.

"Everything in place?"

There's a moment of silence while whoever is on the other end responds.

"Good. I need everything to go smoothly. No hiccups."

Whoever she is speaking to says something and then Maria hangs up.

West pauses the video, and I glance from him to everyone else. "What does this mean? Does it mean anything?"

"That's the problem—we don't know. It could be something, or it might be nothing," Beck answers.

"Well, have you talked to your dad?" I ask, looking at West.

"Yeah, I phoned him earlier. He claimed he didn't know anything, but we can't trust him. Just because he transferred the shares and money, doesn't mean he's not in Maria's pocket."

He's right. I know he's been keeping eyes on him, just like he is with Maria, but we can't trust him.

"Maybe we should pay him another visit?" I suggest.

"Yeah, except we all have exams this week, and I'm not even sure it would do any good." I can hear the frustration in West's tone.

I chew on my bottom lip, thinking. "Can you track the call or something?"

"I tried that too, but it mustn't be her normal cell. There were no calls at that time registered to her number."

"So it's a burner phone. That's suspicious."

"Exactly."

"Well, let's see if she does anything else suspicious this week. We don't know enough to make a decision yet."

We all mumble our agreements, but I can tell none of us are happy with this development, and I'm unsettled for the rest of the evening, unable to focus on studying for my first exam on Monday morning.

Hadley

CHAPTER TWENTY-ONE

The next week goes by in a blur of exams and studying, to the point that words lose all meaning, and just looking at math equations gives me a headache. More than once, I contemplate breaking my arm just to get out of doing these exams, but as Emilia wisely reasons, if I don't do them now, I'll have to do them when everyone else is enjoying their summer break. *Girl makes a lot of sense sometimes.*

So, instead, I knuckle down and do my best to not fail every subject.

"How do you think you did?" she asks as we step out of our last exam on Friday.

"Eh, I don't think it was a complete failure." I'm hoping it's at least a C. I'm not expecting top grades in any of my classes. I've barely scraped through the year, what with my lack of a formal education before now. Honestly, if I was still a scholarship student, I'm pretty sure I'd have been kicked out long ago. Anyone looking at my grades can see that my transcript is visibly fake. All A's to barely getting by? Yeah, that, or it's a cry for help, and the headmaster is doing a shit job of ensuring his students are thriving here at Pacific Prep.

"You?"

"Yeah, I think it went okay."

I have to suppress my eye roll. She's said that about every exam so far, but I know for a fact that in all her practice tests, she was scoring in the nineties every time. So it definitely went better than 'okay.'

"You've got that board meeting tomorrow?"

"Yup," I answer on a sigh. We have our first—and hopefully last—ever shareholders' meeting at Nocturnal Enterprises tomorrow to celebrate the end of exams. On the plus side, I get to see the look on Maria's face when we tell her we own the remaining shares, and give her a big, old, fuck you as we watch all of her future plans for the company go up in flames.

"Whatever you and the guys are planning, you're going to be safe, right?" she asks nervously, looking worried for me.

I haven't told her exactly what's happening—it's better if she doesn't know—but she knows shit's going to hit the fan tomorrow.

"We'll be fine," I reassure her. When she still doesn't look mollified, I tack on, "I promise. We've taken all the precautions we can." I sigh heavily. "I'll just be glad when this is all over, and we don't have to worry about insane parents trying to come after us."

She chuckles. "You won't know what to do with all that spare time. Although, I can think of a few things you could get up to." She waggles her eyebrows in a suggestive motion that makes me burst out a laugh.

"Have you worked out what your plans are yet? There's only a week left of school."

"I know," I groan. "But not yet. I need to talk to Hawk and find out what his plans are. I have a pile of college brochures on my desk, but no idea how to narrow it down to one. I can't even decide where I want to live, and besides, this isn't a decision that I can make alone."

"Well, you've still got several months before you need to be picking a college. I think as long as you work out where you're going to live after next week, you can go from there."

"That's true. Hawk says Barton has mentioned more than once that we're welcome to live with him." I give her a look, and she just laughs.

"Has he been making more of an effort recently?"

I nod my head, still unsure what to make of it all. "Yeah. Every day he texts, telling me something about himself. He hasn't pried for any information or asked any questions. I think he's waiting for me to reciprocate."

"And you haven't yet."

"No. I don't know what to say to him."

"Do you want a relationship with him?"

"I don't know...I mean, maybe."

"I never knew my dad, so I don't know what that's like, but I have a great relationship with my mom, and I couldn't imagine not having her in my life. If your dad is genuine about trying to be an actual father, I think you should give him a chance. You might regret it if you don't."

We part ways outside the girls' dorm, and I mull over what Emilia said as I continue on to the guys' dorm. She might have a point. As a kid, I would have jumped at this opportunity, but life has made me cynical, and even though the little girl in me still wants that relationship with her dad, I'm not sure if I can handle the possibility that this is all a scam.

I let myself into the apartment, drop my bag, and collapse into the chair. Pulling out my phone, I open the chat with Barton, looking at his message from today.

> Barton: When I was in college, I had a motorcycle called Shirley. Everyone thought I was referencing a girlfriend whenever I talked about her. In hindsight, it was pretty embarrassing having to explain that I did, in fact, have an unhealthy relationship with an inanimate object.

I bark out a laugh, even as a small voice in my head tells me not to let my guard down. But, dammit, I want to. I really fucking want to. It might be incredibly stupid of me, but I *want* to believe he could one day grow to be a father I could turn to and rely on.

With my heart in my throat, I type out an unsure reply, sticking with his theme of sharing stuff about each other.

> Hadley: I'm slowly working my way through every flavor of ice cream, and this week, my favorite is butterscotch.

The sound of the door opening has me looking up as Hawk strides in.

"Hey, how was your exam?"

I shrug. "Fine, yours?"

"Same."

He moves to join me in the living room, and I chew on my bottom lip before blurting out, "What, uh, are your plans…for, like, the future?"

He gives a casual shrug. "I haven't given much thought to it. If you're asking what my plans are for after next week, when we're kicked out of here, then what are yours?"

I have to fight back the grin threatening to form at his words.

"I'm not sure. The others have talked about going to college, and I'm game to give it a try—assuming I get the grades to get in—but obviously, it would be next fall before we could go."

"Yeah, I think I want to go to college. Hard to say no to four years of keg parties and sleeping 'til midday."

I snort out a laugh.

He moves to sit beside me on the couch, nudging my shoulder. "Wherever you and the guys go, I'm going too. We always talked about going together if we could convince our parents to give us those four years before going to work for them. I'm not about to let you all go off and have the college experience without me now."

My lip lifts in a grin.

"As for right now, maybe we should stay here while we work out our next move. There's still stuff that needs to be sorted, and Cam, West, and Mason all have houses that they need to decide what they're doing with. Plus, it will give us a chance to spend some time together…and with Dad too, if that's something you want."

I nod my head thoughtfully. "Yeah, that works. I guess there's no need to have everything planned out right now."

"There's some excitement in not knowing."

∼

"Can I ask you something?"

When I look up from the book I'm reading, I find West standing beside me, chewing on his bottom lip nervously.

"Uh, sure."

He hesitates for a second longer, and I frown, trying to figure out what could be bothering him so much.

"I was, uh, wondering if you'd be able to help me with something."

"Of course. What is it?" Setting my book on the coffee table, I stand, expecting him to lead me to whatever he needs help with. Only he continues to stand there, looking unsure.

He frowns and huffs out a small breath before blurting out, "I was hoping you'd be able to teach me a few things, self-defense moves or whatever, just in case shit goes down with your mom tomorrow."

A weighted silence fills the space between us before he continues to ramble.

"I'm just sick of being the weak link among us. I couldn't help when the mercenaries attacked us at Christmas, and I wasn't of any use when we went to rescue you at the compound."

I stare at him incredulously. "What are you talking about? I would never have gotten out of there if it wasn't for you."

He frowns, and I don't like how it scrunches up his face or the way he's talking about himself, as though he doesn't have these exceptional qualities that are so wonderfully him.

"West, you have such a unique set of abilities. I'm envious of your skill with computers. Anyone can learn how to fight and defend themselves, but it takes a certain way of thinking to do what you do."

He still doesn't look convinced. "I still feel ridiculous asking you for help."

"Well, you shouldn't. You didn't think less of me when I asked you for help in computer class. Even though I *know* my stupid questions drove you mad." One side of my lip lifts in a smile. "But I am curious, why didn't you ask Mason or Hawk instead?"

"They've tried teaching me before, and, well, let's just say it never ended well. Usually, they'd get frustrated and storm off, or I'd get angry and snap at them."

I give him a rueful smile. "Well, I'd love to teach you. Let me grab a few things, and we can head out to the clearing. That way, no one will interrupt us."

"Sounds good, I'll grab some flashlights for us."

I dart down to my room, grabbing my boxing gloves and some tape, and a couple of other items that might come in handy, and as West and I reconvene in the living room, Cam appears.

"Where are you two off to?"

I glance at West, not wanting to tell Cam anything if he doesn't want him to know, but instead of the uncomfortable look he sported when he asked me for help, he looks absolutely at ease.

"Firefly's going to show me some of her moves."

Cam's face lights up. "Ooh, can I come?"

Again, I hesitate, looking to West for direction. This is his thing, after all.

"Pleeeeeease," Cam pleads, batting his eyelashes like an imbecile and making me snort at his childish antics. I quirk a brow at West. It's his decision. If he doesn't want Cam to come, I know Cam will be okay with it, despite how he's currently acting.

Huffing out a breath, West rolls his eyes. "Fine."

"Ahh, yay! I get to watch my girl be a kickass ninja. Oooh, are you gonna go all Dominatrix on his ass?"

I have no idea what that means, nor do I get the chance to find out as West shoves Cam in the shoulder and ushers us out the door.

Once we reach the clearing, I drop everything I brought on the ground and walk West through a few exercises to limber him up while Cam places the flashlights in a circle around us, similar to the setup on fight nights. It's still early dusk, but it won't be long before it's too dark to clearly see each other. Once he's done, he sits beside my things and silently watches us as I walk West through a few basic self-defense moves.

He watches my movements diligently and quickly puts them into practice when I pretend to attack him. The advantage of what I'm teaching him is that you don't need brute strength to beat your opponent; you just need to keep a cool head and think your way out of the situation. It's about finding your attacker's weak points and using them to your advantage.

I start by showing him a few easy ways to deflect an attacker and how to get out of their grip, whether they're holding onto your wrist or have their hands wrapped around your throat. Once he's got that down, I show him some offense techniques so he can take down an attacker and escape.

"Okay," I start when he's gone through the motions a few times. "This time, we'll go through the whole thing. When I come at you, try to get out of my grip and take me to the ground."

"What? I'm not actually going to fight you back."

I huff out a breath. "Why not?"

He glances incredulously at Cam before returning his gaze to mine. "I don't want to hurt you."

I chuckle softly. "You won't, I promise."

"Still, it's one thing to go through the motions, but to actually fight you off…"

"Ooh me, pick me! I'll do it!" Cam exclaims, throwing his arm in the air like we're in class or some shit.

"Yeah, I'll practice on Cam."

I throw my arms up in the air in exasperation. *Boys! There's no fucking dealing with them.*

"Fine, tackle Cam then."

Cam jumps to his feet, looking far too excited about the prospect of ending up face-first in the dirt, and does some weird thing with his arms as he shakes them out before lowering into a crouch and grinning ruthlessly at West.

I quirk a brow at him. "Just go through what we've talked about, Cam."

"Sure thing, boss."

I roll my eyes and step to the side to see both of them clearly. "Alright, go."

Cam moves on lightning-quick feet, closing the distance between him and West. He grabs West's wrist and tries to pin it behind his back, but West does exactly as I taught him, enabling him to break free and use the momentum to twist Cam's arm. Cam hisses in pain as he's forced to bend over to prevent his arm from being dislocated. With Cam's balance off center, West easily pushes him to the ground, giving him ample time to escape.

"Good! That was really good." I grin proudly at him as he helps Cam to his feet.

"You alright, man?"

"All good," Cam assures him, rotating his shoulder and pumping his hand to get the blood flowing through his fingers again.

"Let's go again. This time, use a few offensive moves, West. Don't be afraid to really go for it. Cam will survive a few bruises."

"Ouch, baby! You really wanna mess up this handsome face?"

I roll my eyes, even while I suppress my laughter. He does have a gorgeous face, but that's not to say he wouldn't look any less handsome with a bit of bruising. It would totally give him that alluring bad-boy look.

They go again, and West holds nothing back, giving Cam a good dig in his ribs when he tries to tackle him and swiping his cheek to get him to back off.

Clapping starts behind me as West again manages to take Cam to the ground, and I spin to find Beck, Hawk, and Mason watching us.

"How did you guys know we were out here?" I ask as they move to join us.

"Cam sent us a video of you and West. We thought we'd come watch the show." Mason smirks.

"We're not here to entertain you, idiots. It's important that he—that all of us—knows this stuff."

"I know, babe." Mason leans in to kiss my temple. "I was only joking. It's good that you're able to show him some things. I must admit, I was never very good at explaining it."

"We'll just sit quietly over here and watch," Hawk assures me, moving to sit in Cam's vacated spot. Mason and Beck silently agree and move to join him, but when I focus back on West, he looks more nervous than before. Great, he's not going to be able to concentrate if he's too busy worrying about what they'll think of him.

Sighing, I spin toward the three intruders. "Hawk, up," I snap.

"What? I don't need any lessons. I'm good to watch."

At his cocky attitude, I place my hands on my hips. "Really? You don't think you could learn a thing or two?"

I see the second he realizes how his words could be misconstrued.

"No...uh, I didn't mean it that way. I just...I can handle myself."

Lifting a brow in challenge, I goad him. "Prove it." It's all I need to say to guarantee he's going to get up and do precisely that. Just as expected, with his perpetual scowl in place, he rises to his feet and stomps toward me.

"Right, I have been teaching West how to break out of an attacker's hold and take them to the ground, so when I come at you, try to do that."

He gives a sharp jerk of his head and focuses all of his attention on me. Quicker than he can blink, I rush him, darting around his side so I can wrap my arms around him from behind. This is a hold I taught West earlier. Although I don't spare him a glance, needing to keep my focus if I'm to make my point—which is basically that Hawk is wrong, as per usual—I'm confident he's already assessed the situation and ascertained the best way to get out of it.

Unfortunately for Hawk, he does not immediately suss out my weak points and instead tries to use his extra strength to shake me off. I simply tighten my hold around him, as if I'm giving him a giant bear hug from behind. He leans forward, and I can already tell what his next move will be. As my legs leave the ground, I don't hesitate to wrap them around his waist, only further securing my hold. Yeah, okay, unless my aim is to squeeze him to death, I'm not going to do any actual damage. It's not like I could drag him off somewhere like this, but the intent of this exercise is to shake off your opponent.

From his bent-over position, he tucks and rolls, and I ignore the shouts from the guys as the air is knocked out of my body and I suddenly find myself flat on my back, with the enormous fucking weight that is Hawk Davenport on my chest. It's a clever tactic, but I'm not about to give up that easily. With the way my arms and legs are wrapped around him, Hawk has no use of his arms, no matter how hard he tries to raise them and knock me off. That leaves him with just his legs, and now that we're both on the ground, he can't do anything more than shuffle around and wait me out until I run out of oxygen. However, now that my legs are pinning his arms, my hands are free to do whatever I need them to, like, place him in a headlock that will have him going unconscious long before I run out of air.

I do precisely that, making it clear exactly who is in control here—i.e., not him—

before I let up, loosening my hold and letting my arms and legs go limp. Coughing, he quickly rolls off me, and the others rush over.

"Dude, you could have hurt her," Mason snaps, helping me to my feet. I give him a soft smile, letting him know I'm okay, as I brush the dust off my backside.

He continues to scowl at Hawk regardless, who promptly ignores him as he climbs unaided to his feet.

"Your turn," I tell Mason, who only stares wide-eyed at me. Before he can fob me off with some ridiculous excuse or say something that will only backfire on him, I jibe, "Show me what you've got."

Instead of backing out, he smirks at my challenge, and I quickly move in to tackle him. Having already watched me with Hawk, he's much harder to pin down, but eventually he gives up, unable to break my hold on him, and I turn to Beck with a smug look on my face.

He just chuckles and shakes his head, stepping up to the plate without protest. Beck's the only one of the three of them that I haven't fought before, so I don't know his fighting style, but he was able to take on Mason, so I know he's more than capable, and given his background, he'll most likely be scrappy.

He lets me get him into a chokehold—yeah, I'm bringing out the big guns—and the second my arm wraps around his neck in a tight hold, he sidesteps me, hitting at my groin and elbowing me in the chin. None of it is done with full force, but enough to let me know he knows exactly what he's doing. Distracted, my hold loosens, and he easily breaks free, but instead of stepping away from me, he spins, surprising me as he kicks my legs out from beneath me. His hand whips out, slowing my descent to the ground as he comes down on top of me, pinning me beneath him.

I gape up at him with wide eyes. "Is it completely inappropriate that I'm turned-on right now?" I mutter, making him laugh darkly. He grinds his pelvis against mine, letting me know I'm not the only one affected by that act of dominance, and I have to bite back my groan. *Now isn't the time, Hadley!*

He presses a quick kiss to my lips before lifting me off and helping pull me to my feet, and we all break into pairs to practice a few more valuable moves. I'm hoping none of them will ever need to know this, but everyone should at least be aware of it.

When it looks like they've got that all down, I move to grab the few other things I brought with me. I still remember Cam's bafflement over me carrying a knife, and I don't like the thought of him walking around unarmed, especially with the threat of Maria coming after us. After everything we've already survived, I know she's just one person, but just because she doesn't have any close connections with the mercenaries in her company doesn't mean she's incapable of finding someone who will do her bidding. We need to be prepared for every eventuality.

Palming my own knife in my hand, I hold the other two I brought in a loose grip at my side and turn to face the guys.

"Knives?" Cam exclaims, and I can't tell if he's excited by the prospect or nervous.

"Yup."

"We already have the guns Cain gave us," Hawk reasons, and I nod, knowing that.

"Guns are great and all, but they have limited use when your opponent is right up on you, whereas a knife can always be useful."

I hand a blade each to Cam and West, who both hesitate before accepting them, and I quickly run through how to handle them and point out the main things to aim for. Large arteries are the best. My personal favorite is the femoral artery. People seem to expect it less. The neck is an overrated, overused artery that any half-decent opponent can see coming a mile away. However people never seem to expect a dagger to the groin.

I also take each of them through the best places to wound an attacker. Injuries that won't kill them but will incapacitate them, and make it much easier to get the advantage, or escape.

Despite appearing unsure, each of them listens intently to what I have to say, and I watch as they each practice a few simple movements with the knife, attempting to jab it into an invisible opponent.

When we're done, I focus on West. "Does all of that make you feel a bit better, or is there anything else you wanted to know, or go over again?"

"No, that was great, Firefly. I'm a little scared of ever pissing you off, but what you've taught us tonight was amazing."

He presses a sweet kiss to my cheek and I blush under his praise. When he goes to hand back his knife, I hold up my hand. "You keep that. I have a bunch more. Besides, you should really keep something on you at all times. It astounds me that you don't."

I bend to tuck my own blade back in my boot, and when I stand up again, I catch Cam's expression. He's biting on his lower lip, his pupils dilated with lust as he stares at where I tucked the knife away. Catching me looking, he gives me a dirty wink before giving himself a once-over, debating where to store his blade only to realize he doesn't wear comfortable yet sensible combat boots like myself, and stuffing it in the pocket of his hoodie instead.

"There should be a couple of blades in my old room I can give you guys, unless you grabbed them when you got my stuff?" I tell them, directing the question at Hawk.

"I didn't even know you had knives in your room."

"Well, I don't want to remove the ones I have stashed around your dorm, and I don't have any others just lying around."

"You have knives placed around our dorm?" Hawk asks, sounding incredulous, yet I can't for the life of me understand why.

"Of course I do. And I have a couple at Beck's place too."

"What—Where? When? Why?" Cam stutters out, looking shocked, although I can't for the life of me work out why.

I shrug my shoulder. "I dunno, I started stashing them when I moved in, but I had one or two already hidden before then. You can never be too careful." I don't tell them that I have hidden a bunch more around the school since what happened with Michael. I've even strapped one to the underside of my chair in the dining hall and buried one in the ground down by the lake. It helped make me feel like I had more control over my surroundings, even if it's not really true. After all, I had my knife on me that day, which didn't do me any good. But just knowing I always have something nearby, should I need it, helps me sleep better at night.

Nobody seems to have anything to say to that, and we gather up the flashlights and head back to the dorm, stopping by my old room so I can retrieve my knives and give one each to Hawk, Mason, and Beck. A calmness settles over me as I hand them over. I hadn't even realized how stressed I was about each of them, but I'm glad West suggested this tonight. I feel so much more at ease knowing they're better prepared to face whatever is coming our way.

BECK, Mason, Cam, and I huddle around the computer screen, watching as West and Hawk walk into Nocturnal Enterprises. Unfortunately, only shareholders are invited to the meeting, so we couldn't all go—something I was most disappointed about. West had to go, but none of us were comfortable sending him alone, so Hawk went with him for backup. We're hoping once Maria finds out that we've fucked her over, she'll be less likely to do something irrational and stupid if Hawk is there. We're relying on the fact she might give a bit of a shit about her son and not act out in her anger. Honestly, I'm not convinced she's capable of caring about anyone other than herself, nonetheless Hawk seems to think he might be able to get through to her if shit goes sideways.

However, we weren't about to sit around with our thumbs up our asses and wait for them to come back, so we attached a small camera and microphone to West's suit jacket so we could all watch. No fucking way was I about to miss the look of shock on Maria's face when she discovers we've screwed her over.

I hate the fact I'm not there in person, though. To say I'm nervous about them facing off against Maria alone is an understatement. Still, the guys have assured me there will be plenty of people in this meeting, so Maria won't be able to do anything to either West or Hawk when she finds out what we've done. Pretty much everyone else who attends these meetings is clueless as to what goes on behind the curtain at Nocturnal Enterprises. They are only involved in the legal side of our parents' operation, and as such, Maria won't be able to do or say anything that could raise suspicion.

The elevator pings as the guys arrive on the thirty-seventh floor and are escorted to the boardroom. I chew on my bottom lip and my leg bounces anxiously with every step they take, until Beck reaches out and squeezes my knee reassuringly.

As West pushes the door open to the boardroom, we're greeted with a nearly full table of businessmen and women, with Maria Davenport seated at the head of the table. Wilbert is sitting dutifully on her left and my eyes narrow on him. He's been suspiciously quiet since handing over his shares and half of his wealth, but West hasn't found anything in the cameras to suggest he's spilled the beans to Maria.

The woman herself looks up at the intrusion, and her lips flatten in disapproval as her brows scrunch together in confusion.

"Hawk, what are you doing here?"

There's a sharpness to her tone, and it's obvious she's all business right now. She's about to inform the board that she's the majority shareholder and that she will be taking over the running of the company, so no doubt she's keen to get on with her one-woman show.

I can hear the smugness in Hawk's voice, and damn, do I wish I could see his arrogant expression, but I know him well enough by now to picture it in my mind's eye. "Why, we're here for the shareholders' meeting, Mother."

He strolls toward one of the spare seats at the top end of the table, next to her, which I imagine were the seats Barton and the others occupied at previous meetings. He's careful to keep a seat between himself and her at the head of the table, and West claims the empty seat on his other side.

"This meeting is for shareholders only, *dear*. Of which, neither of you are." Her gaze darts back and forth between Hawk and West, and I can see the anger radiating in her blue depths.

"Actually, I have recently acquired shares to the amount of 25% of the company," West states, lifting the necessary documentation out of his inner pocket and placing it on the table in front of him. His tone lacks the same smugness as Hawk's, but it's no less victorious.

My gaze is transfixed on Maria's as she glowers at where West's hand rests possessively on top of the paperwork, and I can see her jaw working in agitation. Her lips are pressed so firmly together they're nothing more than a thin pink line.

After a long moment, she tears her gaze away from West's hand, sparing a glance around the rest of the table as she works her face into an impassive mask. Focusing back on West, she manages to sound indifferent as she asks, "Where did you acquire those?"

By now, Wilbert is a bucket of sweat beside her. I can see the pit stains from here, and his hair is sticking to his forehead. On the other hand, West sounds cool as a cucumber as he casually states, "Father here decided it was time to hand them over to the next generation."

With trembling hands, Wilbert lifts a handkerchief out of his jacket pocket and dabs at the sweat lining his temple. He's going to need a lot more than one measly square of cotton to mop up all that perspiration, however.

Like something out of a horror movie, Maria's head slowly swivels to fix Wilbert in place with a Davenport special glower. *So that's where Hawk learned it from.* He shifts uncomfortably in his chair, deliberately avoiding eye contact, and I can tell he's resisting the urge to bolt. I'm actually a little impressed. I have seen kids all but crumble when Hawk has turned that look on them.

He doesn't say anything, and she quickly dismisses him then focuses back on West, before fixing Hawk in her sights. "And what are you doing here, son?"

I notice the sleeve of Hawk's suit shift as he shrugs. "Moral support."

She could easily tell him to get out since he's not a shareholder—it's honestly what we expected—but instead, she dismisses him, huffing out a frustrated breath before calling the meeting to start.

She takes her time, her gaze slowly drifting over every member at the table and making it perfectly fucking clear who is in charge here.

"Who is everyone else?" I whisper to Mason.

"Heads of departments, people on the board of directors. Honestly, I'm not entirely sure. None of them are aware of Nocturnal Mercenaries, though. They all only work for the legitimate side of the business."

"How do you know that?"

"West did background checks on them all—on everyone in the company—when we first found out what our parents were really up to. As far as we can tell, everyone inside that building is clueless as to who they really work for."

"So the only people who know the truth are our parents and the guards at the compound?"

"Seems so. I guess the fewer people who know, the better. Between the four families, they were able to ensure all aspects related to Nocturnal Mercenaries were managed by themselves. Frank laundered any cash, so it looked like it came from legitimate sources, and he was able to justify the purchase of the compound by claiming it was a training facility for the men they recruited to protect their clients. With Barton and Maria in charge of security, they would have been able to keep an eye on things and make sure no employees were snooping anywhere they shouldn't. While Lawrence was in charge of the day-to-day running of the compound, those at Nocturnal Enterprises believed he was responsible for overseeing the running of the training facilities and private security personnel, and I doubt anyone would question Wilbert's client meetings."

Maria's voice interrupts us, and I focus my attention back on the screen. "To start us off, I'd like to update you all on a few changes regarding leadership." She side-eyes Hawk and West. "West has already—rather unprofessionally—informed us of the change of ownership of the Warren quarter of the shares, but given the unfortunate situation Frank has found himself in and Lawrence's untimely death, I have absorbed their responsibilities, along with their control in the company. With the unexpected return of our daughter, my husband has also decided to step down. All of this is to say that from now on, I'll be running things.

"I, of course, will be looking to fill the positions within the company that have been left vacant by the sudden absence of my fellow colleagues…"

For the next hour, they drone on about company-related things, most of which go over my head, but *finally*, everyone gets up to leave. Not waiting to hang around for Maria to catch up to them, Hawk and West are the first two out the door, and the elevator doors slide shut before anyone else can filter into the small space with them.

They descend in silence and make their way onto the street. With the meeting now over and the two of them out of harm's way, Mason leans forward to close the lid of the laptop, when the screen suddenly goes black.

"What the hell just happened?" I question, looking puzzled at the laptop. "Did the camera just cut out?"

"Maybe West turned it off?" Cam suggests.

Maybe.

"Shush, do you hear that?" With his brows tugged together in confusion, Beck leans in closer to the laptop, turning the volume up full. Whatever is covering the camera must be muffling the sound as well, but with the volume turned up, we can hear what sounds like a scuffle and the unmistakable sound of West grunting, followed by what sounds like a car door slamming.

"What the actual fuck is going on?" I snap. "Are they being kidnapped?"

I look desperately to the others, but Beck is the only one who looks away from the screen to meet my gaze.

"I think so."

Baby Davenport

CHAPTER TWENTY-TWO

I groan, and it takes a second for me to recall what happened. I distinctly remember something hard smashing across my temple. The second I remember that, the rest of my memories flood back like a tsunami, not that I remember much of use. I remember exiting Nocturnal Enterprises after the meeting. Of course, we knew we were putting a target on our backs by turning up today, but I didn't expect a retaliation so soon. The second our feet hit the pavement outside the building, someone threw a bag over my head, and two or three people must have surrounded me. When I hit out at one of the fucktards—and I know my hit landed well, causing some damage—someone else closed in behind me, pinning my arms.

I could hear West struggling beside me, but it wasn't long before we were both neutralized and thrown into the back of some sort of van. I was screaming obscenities at the fucking shitheads, vividly painting their deaths with my words, when something hard whipped me across the head. The next thing I knew, the darkness was calling my name.

The hood is still drawn over my head, but I draw on my other senses, noting that I'm tied to some sort of a chair with my arms tied behind my back. I try to move my legs but find them equally restrained. *Fuck.* I'm only left contemplating my options for a moment before I hear a faint groan from my left. I immediately recognize it as West's, and I hiss out his name. I've no idea if anyone is around to hear us, but I have to know he's okay. Fuck, Hadley will have my balls if he isn't.

"West," I hiss again when he doesn't respond.

"Uuuugggghhh." It's the only response I get. *Better than nothing, I guess.*

"Dude, wake the fuck up," I rasp more urgently, trying to keep my tone low in case anyone is nearby.

There's a long pause before he finally responds, and I breathe out a sigh of relief. "Fucking hell, I'm awake, asshole."

"Are you okay?"

"I'll survive, you?"

"Same. Do you know where we are?"

"No. They knocked me out."

Fuck. Neither of us mentions it aloud, but I know he's as perceptive, if not more so than I am, so without having to say it, I know he's hoping the others will have seen through the camera what happened and be able to track us somehow.

"Cough," he tells me, and without questioning him, I start hacking up like I'm having a fucking asthma attack. Over the sound of my own wheezing, I can faintly hear him talking, and I know he's speaking into his mic, likely reassuring the others that we're okay and relaying any information he can. I just hope we have reception and they actually hear what he's saying, but it's not like we have any better options at this point.

When he's finished, we lapse into silence, both of us lost in our own thoughts. The fact we were lifted right outside Nocturnal Enterprises means this has to be my mother's doing. Does that mean she knew about the transfer of shares before we arrived today? There's no way she would have had time to arrange for us to be kidnapped during the meeting. I watched her every move the entire time we were in that room.

That only leaves one option—that we were double-crossed. And there's only one person who would have gone running to Maria. Wilbert Warren. That limp dicked, pathetic sack of shit. I'm going to fucking carve out his insides for this.

Time has no meaning as we sit, both of us restrained to our chairs, and wait for whatever the fuck is to come next. We make a point of not talking much, not wanting to draw any unwanted attention, but we confirm that we're both tied to chairs and that neither of us saw who kidnapped us. The consensus seems clear, though—my mother is behind this act. Who else could it be?

I'm bored out of my fucking mind and dying to piss when the hood is finally pulled off my head in a dramatic flair that is completely lost on me, and I stare into the frosty eyes of my mother. The apathetic look in her eye makes me pause, but regardless of her expression, I carefully rearrange my face and give her a bland, unsurprised response. "Mother, about time."

She doesn't need to know my heart is racing in my chest and that my palms are sweating. Despite my outward appearance, I've never been held fucking captive, and to say I'm a little unsettled would be an understatement.

One side of her lip curls up in a cruel smirk. "You never did have any patience."

Her gaze drifts to my left, and I know she's eyeing up West. If I thought she looked at me with a cool gaze, it's nothing compared to how she is staring at him. My best friend. My brother, for all intents and purposes. To her, he's nothing more than a bargaining chip. Someone she can use to manipulate and threaten her way to achieve what she wants. It only makes me hate her more. She's my mother, and despite her callous attitude, I want to believe she wouldn't hurt me, but I'd be a fool to think that leniency would extend to anyone else.

I'm not even sure she would show Hadley any laxity. I have seen the way she looks at her own daughter. The detachment in her eyes. It's not normal, but then nothing about our situation is normal. Barton has made excuses for her, saying removing herself from the situation and focusing on work is her way of coping with everything that happened, but is that really true? At what point does she stop hiding and just accept that she's not that sort of mother? Does she care? Did she ever?

I made sure I was the one to come with West today, hoping Maria would listen to me, but honestly, I'm not sure she will. I want to believe that deep down inside, she doesn't mean me any harm, except the harsh reality is that I'm not entirely sure that's accurate. Yeah, she and Dad didn't treat me with the same distant callousness as West's dad or inflict the same judgement on me as Cam's. They definitely never beat me like Mason's dad did to him, but does that mean they cared? Barton is making a point of proving himself, but Maria...well, I'm still unsure about her. Regardless of how skeptical I am, the little boy inside me wants to believe his mother isn't capable of hurting him.

She moves to pull West's hood off, and regardless of the fear I can see shining in his eyes, he glowers defiantly back at her. Looking away from him, I focus on the threat in front of us. "What do you want?"

She takes her time, fixing me in her sight and tilting her head. "Why, son, I want what's mine. I want my company. *All* of it."

I shake my head. "We can't let you rebuild."

She laughs, this empty sound that lacks any sort of humor. Any emotion at all, really.

"What you're doing is wrong!" I snap, getting angry. "You're stealing kids!"

Her face transforms before my eyes into this heinous thing, and she snarls, stepping close to me and squeezing my cheeks in her hand. "I'm giving these children a future they wouldn't otherwise have. They should be fucking grateful! Without me, they'd have no prospects. They'd be dead in a gutter, high out of their minds, or shot in a gang war before they were even old enough to vote."

The longer I look into her eyes, I realize she believes the shit she's spouting. She truly believes she's saving these kids. And maybe she would be, if she wasn't subjecting them to a childhood of torture and forcing them into a life they might not want. But as it stands, what she's offering these kids isn't some sort of safe house. The compound isn't a haven. It's one of the levels of hell, and there's no escaping it once you're taken captive. It's not a place fit for children. No one should be subjected to the fucked-up shit that goes on in there.

Hadley has so many strengths, and I envy her tenacity; her ability to keep going in the face of adversity. Even so I can't help but wonder how she would have turned out if she'd led a normal childhood. If she'd grown up with the rest of us. I know she's fighting her own demons, and some days her PTSD wins, but the point is she shouldn't have to deal with any of it. No eighteen-year-old should have to go through what she's experiencing, what she's had to live through. She should have grown up with a mom and dad who loved her; and with a brother who drove her crazy. She should have attended sleepovers, where she gossiped with her friends about her latest crush and experienced the typical awkward teen moments at school that are essentially a rite of passage. She should have sent Valentine's cards and received flirty texts. She should have gone on first dates and gotten all dressed up for school dances.

She should have had it all.

Instead, she wakes up screaming at night, has trust issues, jumps to the worst-case scenario, and can't relax unless she's got her knife nearby. It's not a life I would have ever wished for her, and if I could do it over, I'd trade places with her in a heartbeat. Unfortunately, life doesn't work that way. We don't get a do-over. We must live with the choices we make...but that doesn't mean we can't avenge past mistakes.

"And what about your daughter?" I snarl, that ever-present anger I feel burning beneath the surface, sparking to life and flaring up at the thought of all the injustice. "What was she being saved from when she was kidnapped and hidden away in the compound? From you? From Dad?"

Mom tenses, and a flicker of surprise crosses her features before she masks it. "I didn't know you knew that."

Eh, what? That was *not* the response I was expecting!

I frown, scrutinizing her impassive expression. *"You knew?"*

Her lips purse and she gives a small shake of her head, but she doesn't answer me. A desperate need to know what she knows builds within me, and I glance at West, finding the same confused, questioning look on his face.

"Did you know where she was all this time?" I demand, my voice coming out strained yet insistent.

As if I asked her what's for dinner, she waves away my question like it means nothing, spinning in her high heels and striding away from us.

After several steps, she turns back to face me, and I can see what I didn't before. The malevolence marring her face. "She was *supposed* to be fucking dead," she spits out the words, her lip curling in a sneer. I honestly can't do anything but stare at her. I fucking gape, wondering how I ever thought I knew this woman. Wondering how I ever called her mom, 'cause at this moment, she is more reminiscent of a nightmare than any mother I know. "That fucking asshole screwed me over. He couldn't even keep a *child*" —she sneers out the word—"under control."

She huffs out a humorless laugh. "The fact she was able to escape under his command is laughable. It's a testament to the wayward nonsense he was running in that compound. Under my leadership, such shirking of responsibility will *not* be tolerated."

My mind races as I try to process what she's saying, only West beats me to it as he croaks out, "You knew? All this time, you knew where she was?"

"Don't be ridiculous," she snaps irritably, gesturing to me. "I had no idea she was even alive until you brought her home and told me who she was. She was supposed to be dead or buried so deep in the foster care system no one would ever find her. She was *not* supposed to be right under our noses, on our own goddamn property."

My head is spinning now. "So you did play a hand in her disappearance?"

She stops in front of me, her gaze hardening. "We're not here to talk about *her*. She won't be a problem for much longer." What the fuck does that mean?! It takes everything in me to not struggle against my restraints, but it's hard to fight past that clawing need to get to Hadley. She's been through so much, and I *refuse* to let anything else happen to her. Not under my watch. No fucking way. I don't give a damn what it takes, I will protect my sister with my life. With every fiber of my being, I will ensure she leads a long and happy life.

"What I want is the shares you stole from me." Maria's next words cement me back in the present though and remind me I can't just storm out of here to go to Hadley's aid. I want to be the one to save her, but I'm fully aware of the fact she's capable of looking after herself. We didn't expect my mother to come after us this quickly, but we *are* prepared for this, and I try to take some comfort in that knowledge; in the fact that Hadley can take care of herself, and she has Beck, Mason, and Cam to look out for her. I'd trust them with my life, so I know I can entrust them with hers too.

"I'm not just going to hand them over to you," West sneers, lifting his chin.

The condescending look Maria throws his way stalls the breath in my lungs. "Nor did I expect you to." Lifting her hand, she raises two fingers in a *come here* gesture, and from somewhere behind us, two men dressed in black appear. No further instruction is needed as they lay into West.

"NO! STOP!"

I fight against my restraints, screaming for them to leave West alone, but it's futile. It's only a minute or so, but as I watch, I feel like they beat on my best friend for fucking ages before they eventually relent. They're not even breathless as they move to stand in a soldier-like fashion, their hands clasped behind their backs and their legs hip-width apart. Their expressions are blank as if they weren't just beating on a kid a second ago.

I gape at them in shock, before focusing on West. His head is dropped against his chest, and a string of blood-tinged drool hangs from his lips, but his chest rises and falls in exerted breaths. He lets out a pained groan, reassuring me that he's still with me.

"What the fuck?!" I snarl furiously at my mom. I'm not surprised by her actions, but I am taken aback by the display of violence and the apathetic way she just stood by and watched.

Ignoring me, she approaches West, tugging on his hair until he's looking up at her. She smiles at him, and it almost looks gentle, reassuring, if it wasn't for the cruel gleam in her eyes. The longer I sit and watch her, the more I wonder if I ever really knew her. It's a question I've been asking myself on repeat all year, ever since I found out the truth about my parents. I have been going back through old memories, trying to put together the pieces and see the truth behind their facade, but everything is so murky it's impossible to tell what was real and what was all for show. Nevertheless, observing her now, I can't help but think *this* is the real her. Maria Davenport without her fake socialite mask on.

"Was any of it real?" I ask, drawing her attention my way.

She removes her tight grip from West's hair and his head flops forward as he groans. She doesn't spare him a glance as she stands upright again and turns to face me.

"Any of what real?"

"The time both of you spent with me? When you'd come to my football games and cheer me on, or when you showed up at my middle school graduation with a smile on your face and clapped like you were proud parents...was it all for show? Did you ever care?"

She tilts her head to the side, a pitying look on her face that confirms what I thought. Knowing I'm right doesn't make me feel any better, and I can feel something inside me shrivel up at the knowledge.

She pushes her lips out in a pout. "Aww, sweetie, did you want your mommy to love you?"

My lip curls back in a snarl as I go into my default protection mode. "What the fuck is wrong with you?"

The mocking look on her face drops off, quickly replaced with one of fury, and her hand flies out to smack me across the face. My head whips to the side, and I can feel the sting in my cheeks, but I use that pain to fuel my own rage, glowering at her with so much hatred I can feel it burning through my veins and turning my insides to charcoal.

"What is wrong with *me?*" she snarls furiously. Her lip curls back, making her features appear grotesque. "Just because I never wanted children, that means something must be *wrong* with me? Your father is the one who couldn't accept living a life without sniveling, snot-nosed gremlins running around—although I can't for the life of me work out why. Not once have you disproved me, and now that you've finally started to serve a purpose, you fuck *everything* up."

I can't do anything but gape at her as she rants. The disguise she's been hiding behind all these years is long gone now, and for the first time, I'm getting a glimpse at the despicable human being that lies beneath. Growing up, I spent so much time wishing my parents were present more, that they gave enough of a shit to be around, but now, as I look into the eyes of the monster that birthed me, I'm seriously fucking glad she played a minimal part in my life.

"Everything was fine until *she* came back." I watch as my mother visibly unravels before me, and I cast a quick glance at West out of the corner of my eye, finding the same *what the fuck* expression on his face. "She was meant to be DEAD!"

My eyes snap to her face. That's the second time she's said that, and the thought that she had anything to do with Hadley's disappearance only adds fuel to the burning fire of rage building within me.

"What did you do to her?!" I yell. My harsh words pull her back into the here and now, and her gaze snaps to mine. Fire burns in her eyes, and rage pours off of her.

"I gave her life a purpose. Since I was forced to carry her around for nine months, giving up my size zero figure and dealing with fucking cankles, I was going to make goddamn sure I got something out of it."

"What the fuck does that mean?" I snap furiously, needing to know and simultaneously dreading the answer.

A cruel smirk stretches across her face, and the gleam of pride at what she's done is sickening. "I got rid of her to break your father. He was such a fucking sucker for you two. I knew losing his *little girl* would send him over the edge. The pathetic waste of space all but gave up after her disappearance, leaving me to take control. Between Lawrence, Frank, and I, we pushed the company to new heights. We made Nocturnal Mercenaries number one, the go-to organization."

She sounds so fucking proud of her achievement, and I sneer at her, not even recognizing this conniving bitch standing in front of me. Why was I so hesitant to kill her? It's all I can fucking think about as she glowers at me.

"But, Lawrence…"

"Lawrence was obsessed with me. He would have done anything I wanted for the chance to get me back—he *did* do everything I asked of him." She laughs humorlessly. "And the pathetic sap thought it was all his idea. A dropped hint here, a subtle nudge there. He loved fucking me while we spitballed ideas for how to destroy Barton."

Her insinuation is more than enough for me to gather she and Lawrence were working together back then. However, I'm guessing once Maria got him to do her bidding, she was done with him. Over time, as he became increasingly infatuated with Hadley at the compound, he became less interested in pursuing Maria, instead seeing Hadley as his second chance to start over. It's all incredibly fucked up.

My mother's expression turns sour. "Of course, I didn't expect him to double-cross me. To keep that little whore all for himself and use her against me." I can tell her focus is lost in the past as her eyes cloud over. "It makes so much sense now. How accepting he was when I broke things off with him. I had no other purpose for him. He was useless to me, just like Barton. All I have ever wanted is the company." Her gaze hardens as she snaps her attention back to me. "Now, enough of this nonsense. Give me the goddamn shares!"

She starts to stomp toward West, ready to pick up where she left off, but I call out, "You can't kill him."

She pauses mid-stride, looking at me with a feral look in her eye. "Who said anything about killing him?" My shoulders sag in relief, not realizing the prematurity of my actions. "That's what I have you here for."

Fuck.

A malicious grin curves up her botoxed lips, and without hesitation, she changes direction, striding over to one of the men dressed in black. He doesn't even move as she lifts the gun out of the holster on his belt and, flicking off the safety, she turns to face me. There is no emotion in her eyes as she lifts her arm and points the barrel at my head.

"Now, West," she says in a sickly-sweet voice, "give me the shares, or Hawk here, dies."

Fucking shit. I grit my teeth and glower at her, even as sweat forms along my back and my heart hammers against my chest. Until now, I never thought she was capable of it, but if all the shit she spouted in the last few minutes isn't proof enough, then the unwavering set to her face is definitely all the confirmation I need. My mother won't hesitate to kill me.

My tongue flicks out to run along my bottom lip, and I glance briefly at West, seeing the same *oh shit* look on his face before I return my focus back to the gun pointed in my face.

He opens his mouth to speak, and I know he's about to offer her anything she wants, but he doesn't get the chance. I jump as a blaring alarm goes off, delaying my execution...for now.

Hadley

CHAPTER TWENTY-THREE

The four of us sit in silence, listening to the sound of a vehicle driving away, with my brother and boyfriend inside it.

"We need to go after them," I insist, jumping to my feet. "We need to go *now!*" I push more urgency into my tone when no one else moves. *What the fuck are they waiting for?*

"They'll be long gone by now, babe." Mason sighs, his brows furrowed as he thinks.

"So what, we just sit here and do nothing? We have to do *something!*"

"We can track their phones…assuming they're still on," Cam suggests, and my ears perk up. I knew I loved that gorgeous man for a reason.

He pulls his phone out, and I lean in to watch over his shoulder as he pulls up an app.

"What's that?"

"Fam Finder. You can add people to it, and so long as they have their phone on them, and it's turned on, you can track where they are."

"Handy," I mutter, watching as each of our names come up on a list on the side of the screen.

"Yeah, we added you and Beck to it after you disappeared." He maintains his focus on the screen, clicking on Hawk's name. An image of a map comes up with a flashing green dot in the middle. I lean in to get a closer look.

"It's moving."

"Yeah, they're heading West on Greenwich Street. It looks like they're trying to get out of the city."

"Where do you think they're taking them? The compound?"

I notice Beck shake his head and turn to look at him. "I'd doubt it. That place will be in ruins by now. The company probably owns other property—they could be taking them there."

"It doesn't matter where they're going," Mason says. "If we leave now, we can follow them."

We rush around, gathering bits and pieces. I shove on my combat boots, checking that my trusty knife is there, and with purposeful feet, I stride into the living room. Bending down, I reach under the coffee table and retrieve the knife I'd taped to the underside. Moving to the kitchen, I do the same with the knife taped to the top of the undercounter cabinet.

I'm faintly aware of the others watching me. Cam has made a game out of trying to find all of them. So far, he's found the one I had under the coffee table, but that's it. Idiot didn't even think to check the cistern behind the toilet or under his own damn mattress.

"You've still got your knives?" I ask, and everyone nods.

"Here's a gun, too," Beck says, holding one out to me. I notice each of them has one tucked in the back of their pants as well. Taking it from his outstretched hand, I do the same, and we all share a final look—a fierce determination burns in their eyes, which I imagine is reflected in my own.

With a sharp jerk of my head, I bark out, "Let's do this," and turn on my heel, striding out of the dorm without a backward glance. I don't need to. I know each of them is behind me. I can hear the promise of retribution in every thud of their boots as we make our way down the stairwell and out of the building.

∼

We waste no time getting to Mason's car, and we all pile in. Cam, who's sitting shotgun, pulls up the map on his phone. "It's stopped," he exclaims, zooming in. He rhymes off directions to Mason, who doesn't hesitate to put his foot down on the accelerator and gun it down the road. "Looks like the industrial part of the city on the outskirts on the West side."

"Nocturnal Enterprises probably owns property out that way," Mason muses absently, most of his focus on the road in front of him.

I turn my attention to Beck beside me as he works away on his phone, before a video feed showing some sort of warehouse appears on his screen. Leaning in, I frown at the screen.

"It's West's camera," he explains.

I scan the image for clues as to where they are, but it's just a large, generic-looking room. It could be any warehouse owned by anyone, anywhere in or outside the city.

As I watch, someone moves into view, and I gasp when I recognize my own mother. I mean, I suspected she was behind this—who else could it really be? But I didn't expect her to show up to do the dirty work herself.

Her mouth moves, saying something.

"Turn it up!" I bark, staring wide-eyed at the screen as I desperately try to read her lips.

"What do you want?"

I let out a sigh of relief at hearing the strength in Hawk's voice.

"Why, son, I want what's mine. I want my company. All of it."

I watch, agape, as right before my eyes, Maria turns into something inhuman. Any pretense she had before is discarded as her hatred and rage rise to the surface and overflow. My hand flies to cover my gasp when two brutes come into view and start beating on West. I can feel Beck vibrating with anger beside me, and my heart clenches as all I can hear is his heavy breathing and pained groans.

"Hurry up!" I cry in earnest to Mason. "We have to get there *now!*"

He pushes the car faster, and I know we're going well above the speed limit, but my eyes remain transfixed on the phone in Beck's hand as the horrifying show continues to play out before us. I mentally store away the implication that my own mother was involved in my kidnapping. I don't understand how. Lawrence made it sound like he took me to get back at her and Barton, so it makes no sense how she would have been involved, but I don't have the time now to think about it.

"How long?" I cry, glancing out the front windscreen, and watching as large industrial warehouses fly by at breakneck speed.

"We're nearly there. Five minutes." Cam's voice is tense, and I know everyone is freaking out as much as I am right now.

Focusing back on the screen, I watch in horror as my mother strides toward one of the guards and lifts out a gun.

"Oh god," I gasp. I can feel vomit rise up the back of my throat as she points the handgun at Hawk, and says, "Now, West. Give me the shares, or Hawk here, dies."

"This is it! Up here on the left!" Cam shouts, already unbuckling his seatbelt, ready to dive out as soon as Mason pulls into the lot and slams on the brakes. Not hesitating, the second the car stops, I hurtle myself out of the backseat and run toward the warehouse, desperate to reach Hawk before it's too late, all the while straining to listen over the high-pitched blaring of an alarm for the sound of a gunshot that may as well be aimed at my own heart.

I mentally chastise myself for not considering the possibility of the warehouse having a perimeter alarm. We must have triggered it when we drove into the lot, and no doubt guards will be on the lookout for us now, so we need to move quickly.

My senses are alert to everything around me as we approach the warehouse. Annoyingly, the loud noise from the alarm makes it difficult to communicate with the others, preventing me from hearing if anyone tries to sneak up on us. On the camera, Maria has two guards in the warehouse with her, but she could have more lurking around out here.

How did she even amass people to help her so quickly? She shouldn't have the connections or the necessary pull with any of the guards to get them to do her bidding. Nor does she have access to the server to contact the mercenaries, and yet, she clearly has help. The gut-wrenching feeling in my stomach tells me we've greatly underestimated Maria Davenport.

Keeping low as I approach the warehouse, I wait for the others to catch up and signal for them to keep quiet before I ease the steel door and peer through the crack. I do my best to treat this like any job and go into work mode, but knowing my brother and West are in there make it infinitely more challenging. I've never had an emotional connection with anyone I worked with, so I have never had to deal with this. Suddenly, the way the compound raises us, tearing apart our humanity and teaching us not to care about anyone other than ourselves, makes sense. It's the only way to focus completely on your objective and not let emotions cloud your judgment.

Finding the room beyond empty, I pull the door open fully and enter the room, the guys closely behind me. It appears to be some sort of storage room we're in, consisting of nothing more than a few large crates. I make a move toward the door on the far side of the room, my objective single-minded, when the alarm cuts out, and the space seems to fall deathly silent as we all share a look. As I start toward the door again, a hand latches onto my wrist, and Beck hisses, "Hold on."

Frowning, I look over my shoulder at him. Not put off by the look I'm giving him, he states, "We need a game plan. We can't all just go barging in there."

"I agree," Mason pipes up, and I purse my lips, knowing they're right.

Sighing, I nod. "Alright." I mull it over for a second. "We should split up. Mason and I will continue on this way"—I point to the door behind me—"you two go around the back of the building and see if you can find another entrance."

Cam looks between Beck and me. "Maybe we should call the police?"

I don't even need to think it over, shaking my head. "They won't get here in time. She had a gun pointed at Hawk's head. Even if they did get here before she did something, I'm not satisfied with her just going to prison. After everything she's done, everything she's doing, and everything she wants to do"—I shake my head again—"she's not leaving here alive."

The deadpan tone of my voice leaves no room for argument, and after a tense moment of silence, Beck sighs. "Okay. We'll go around back but be careful."

He and Cam don't hang around, moving back toward the outer door and slipping out of the room. Glancing at Mason, I silently check if he's good to continue. With a grim expression and a determined set to his jaw, he jerks his head, and I continue moving across the room to the door on the far side.

As I approach, I hear muffled voices on the other side, and I bring my finger to my lips before pointing at the door. Indicating that he hears the voices too, we both remain still as we listen. More muffled words that are impossible to make out, nor can I tell who's talking. Mason doesn't seem able to discern the voices either, based on the concentrated frown on his face.

I guess there's nothing else for it. Carefully, I reach out and pull down the handle, slowly inching the door open until I can peer in. The room beyond looks like the central part of the warehouse, consisting of an ample, open space. There's a giant metal shutter on the far wall that looks like it can roll up to allow forklifts to move easily in and out, with another steel door to the side of it.

I hear the voices again, drawing my attention to the middle of the room. *What the fuck?* I ease the door open further so Mason can see, and the two of us stare at Maria, standing in the middle of the room, with her gun aimed at...my father? Why is he here? Two guards are standing behind her, like a wall of muscle, while another two are manhandling Barton. Tied to the chairs in front of them are West and Hawk. Their backs are to us, so I can't see their faces, but other than West slumping a little in his chair, they appear to be unharmed. Hawk doesn't look dead, and the sheer relief I feel at receiving that confirmation has my knees nearly buckling.

I quickly scan the room for any other entrances or exits, noting none. *Okay, so Beck and Cam will have to make their entrance via the steel door beside the roll-up shutters.* Once again searching the room, there is a stack of crates near the back wall.

"Do you think you could get over to them?" I whisper to Mason, pointing out the crates.

He takes a moment to work it out, assessing the distance and cover points and weighing up how likely he is to be caught by Maria or one of her goons.

"Yeah, that should be doable. What are you thinking?"

"I'm not sure yet, but Beck and Cam are going to have to come through that door," —I point out the only other door on the opposite side of the room to us—"so if you come from there, and I approach Maria from here, we would have them pretty well surrounded."

He mulls it over before nodding, and I step back so he can slip out. He shifts toward the door, but before he leaves, he spins around. His hand comes to rest on the back of my neck, pulling me in as his lips find mine in a searing kiss. "Be careful," he murmurs, slipping out of the room and stealthily making his way across to the crates at the far back corner.

I don't breathe again until he's hidden behind the crates, giving me a thumbs-up to let me know he's okay. As my heart rate settles back to a normal rhythm, I focus back on Maria and Barton.

"How did you even know we were here?" Maria asks him suspiciously.

"You forget, dear, I was the head of security. You might have been running the illegitimate side of things, but I still have access to anything associated with Nocturnal Enterprises. I was alerted to unusual activity here, and imagine my surprise when I signed into the system and saw my own son tied to a chair." He loses his cool by the end, snarling furiously at Maria and pulling against the two guards holding him in place.

From what I heard of Maria's speech earlier, it sounds like Barton, out of the two of them, has been the only one to give a damn about our well-being all these years. If what she said is true, she was the one that never wanted kids, but it sounded like Barton did. Is it possible he was the one that dragged her to Hawk's sports games and school events, wanting to have a more active part in his son's life? Regardless of the reason, he wouldn't be here now, trying to help his son, if he didn't care on some level. For that, I have to respect him, but it does complicate the situation somewhat.

I notice a small movement on the far side of the room, and my gaze snaps to the steel door, seeing it's ajar. I can just about make out Beck, who catches my eye, and I signal toward where Hawk and West are being held. He purses his lips, nodding, and I see his mouth move, likely relaying what he sees to Cam.

When he looks back at me, I do my best to tell him where Mason is, but he doesn't speak shorthand, and I end up huffing out a breath in frustration. It takes me a second to wrack my brain before realizing I can just send him a text.

Pulling my phone out of my back pocket, I notice Mason already sent one to a new group chat he set up that doesn't have Hawk or West in it—probably not wanting to accidentally set their phones off in case Maria or one of her gorillas reads the messages. Quickly scanning through the message, he's already described the warehouse layout to Beck and Cam and has informed them where he's hiding.

As I finish reading his message, a new one pops up.

> Beck: What's the plan?

> Hadley: You two reveal yourselves and distract them. I'll sneak up behind Maria and catch her off guard. Mason, you stand by in case things go sideways.

> Beck: Ok. Be careful.

> Mason: *thumbs-up emoji*

Putting my phone away, my palms sweat as I wait for Beck and Cam to reveal themselves. I have done plenty of jobs not dissimilar to this before where me or my teammates have been at risk. However, I've never put anyone I care about in danger like this, and my stomach is threatening to revolt as I second-guess my decision. I can't afford to lose any of them. I have no idea how I'd survive if I was responsible for any harm coming to any of them.

I don't get the chance to spiral any further as the door Beck and Cam were hiding behind is whipped open, daylight flooding the room and casting them in shadow as they step in, guns raised and pointed at Maria.

Maria turns slightly, and the guards shift to stand in front of her, protecting her from the new threat and giving me the advantage while their backs are turned to sneak into the room. On silent feet, I hurry toward a small collection of large wooden barrels and duck down behind them.

Peering my head around the side, no one has spotted me, and everyone is still focused on the new threat Beck and Cam have presented. I'm not paying attention to the conversation going on as I work out my next move and then quickly sprint toward the next item I can hide behind.

I continue to do this until I'm within firing distance of Maria. With the guards standing in front of her, blocking her from Beck and Cam's shot, her back is exposed to the unknown threat lurking behind her—me.

As I lift the gun out and flick off the safety, the voices start to escalate, and for the first time since Beck and Cam stepped into the warehouse, I actually focus on what's being said.

"It doesn't matter where your friends are hiding, you're outnumbered. This is your final warning. Give me the shares!"

The confidence in Maria's tone has me narrowing my eyes on her. She's so fucking sure that she's on the winning side here. That her goons are enough to protect her. Well, she has seriously underestimated us.

She swings the gun, pointing it at Hawk, and I see red. Her face is in profile, but even from here, I can see the intent in her eyes. She has no qualms about killing her son. If I was unsure about it before, the last of my hesitation disappears as I get to my feet.

I'm a trained killer. I know that once you decide and start down that path, you have to see it through to the end. So my decision was made the second I stood up. Which is why, as soon as I have my feet planted firmly beneath me, I pull on the trigger, and the sound of a gunshot rings out around the room.

Time seems to slow as the bullet shoots out of the chamber, and several things happen simultaneously. Maria must see my movement out of the corner of her eye as she turns her head, but keeps her gun focused on Hawk. Her eyes widen in surprise. At the same time, the two guards holding Barton spot me, and they drop their hold on him to reach for their weapons. No longer restrained, Barton dives forward in front of his son just as the sound of a gun goes off.

That one was definitely not mine.

Hadley

CHAPTER TWENTY-FOUR

Chaos erupts around me, but I don't pay attention, swinging to point my gun at the guards going for their weapons. I'm faintly aware of the sound of more gunshots, and the other two men blocking Maria hit the floor.

My ears ring with the aftershock of the shots and the rapid pounding of rushing blood, and as I look away from the dead bodies of the guards and Maria, the world comes to a standstill. It takes me a second to process what I'm seeing, unable to tear my eyes away from the blood spatter on Hawk's face.

"Dad!" he screams, and the tremble of fear in his voice is what breaks through my trance. As I blink back to the present, the reality of what I'm seeing crashes into me. Hawk is thrashing in his chair, trying desperately to get to Barton, who is lying unmoving in front of him, blood seeping out from a gunshot wound to his abdomen.

Beck rushes toward Barton, tugging off his top and pressing it to the wound. Barton's face scrunches, and he groans, the only indication he's still alive as Beck keeps putting pressure on the wound, attempting to stem the blood.

Mason moves to quickly tear through the bonds holding Hawk in place, and he falls to his knees beside his father. "Dad." The word sounds more broken this time, and it fractures something inside me. My heart breaks for Hawk, for what he's about to lose, but it also bleeds for myself, for the relationship I never had the chance to foster. I have been going back and forth for weeks, but suddenly I realize how right Emilia was. I *want* to know the man who's my father. And now I might never get that chance.

My feet are glued to the floor as I watch on in horror. The feel of Cam's warm palm slipping into mine is the only thing grounding me right now.

"We need to get him to a hospital!" Beck yells.

Now free, West drops onto the ground beside Hawk, and Mason moves to Beck's side and asks, "What can I do?" His expression is tight as his gaze darts over Barton's supine form.

"Eliz—Hadley." Barton's weak croak has all of them pausing, and the way his eyes dart unseeingly back and forth, trying to find me, makes my heart hammer in my chest.

My feet feel like they've been laid in cement as I watch helplessly, unable to move closer.

Cam places his hand on my lower back, applying gentle pressure to get me moving. "Go see him," he whispers in my ear, his voice full of heartache.

With his support, I move over to where Barton is lying, and West shuffles out of the way as I collapse to my knees beside Hawk.

"I'm here."

I hadn't even realized tears were coursing down my face until Barton lifts a shaky hand to swipe them away.

"I'm sorry." His words are a weak rasp, followed by a coughing fit that sounds horrendous and leaves him looking paler.

"Shush, it's okay. Just rest." I can't look away from his face as the life seems to drain out of him, and he smiles feebly. I'm faintly aware of the guys' hushed whispers around me, but I can't seem to concentrate on what they're saying. All my focus is on memorizing every crease and line of my father's face, wanting—needing—something to remember him by.

"I wish I had the chance to know you better."

The tears are flowing freely now, and Hawk wraps an arm around my shoulders as I sob. "Don't say that. You will. We'll get you help."

He manages another small smile, though I can see it in his eyes. He knows he's not getting out of here alive, but I refuse to accept that reality. I refuse to believe my luck is so fucking shitty that, just when I'm handed the opportunity to get to know my father, fate—the psychotic bitch that she is—is going to come and take it all away from me.

"Hawk." The urgency in Beck's voice has my gaze snapping up to his. "We need to move him."

"Did you phone an ambulance?" Hawk asks.

Pursing his lips, Beck shakes his head. "They won't be here in time. Mason can drive him to the hospital faster."

Hawk gives a sharp jerk of his head, and between the five of them, they sort out how to lift and maneuver Barton out of the warehouse.

"Hadley, I need you to keep this pressed firmly against the wound. Can you do that?"

My voice wobbles as I respond. "Y-yeah." Beck holds my gaze for another moment before confirming I'm present enough to follow his commands.

"Mason, go bring the car around. Park it as close as you can get it, and be ready to fly out of here as soon as we've got him in the backseat."

Nodding, Mason rushes off to do just that, and between them, the rest of the guys get Barton to his feet with his arms slung over Hawk and Beck's shoulders. The second he's upright, I press the shirt against the bullet wound.

Awkwardly, the three of us move toward the door as Beck and Cam come through. Glancing over my shoulder, Cam is helping West, who is looking worse for wear, with a black eye forming and blood trickling from a cut to his brow. As we approach the outer door, Cam runs ahead, propping it open as we shuffle through it, finding Mason pulling the car up.

Cam yanks open the door to the backseat, and Hawk and Beck carefully ease Barton into the car so he's lying across the seats. His eyes are closed, and his breathing has this god-awful rasp that doesn't sound good.

My hands are shaking like crazy when Beck clamps his hands over mine, taking the blood-soaked shirt from me. "You did good, sweetheart. I'll take it from here." He gently kisses my temple and climbs into the backseat, careful not to jostle Barton as he checks his vitals and continues tamping the wound. "We've gotta go!" he shouts.

"Hadley, get in!" Hawk barks urgently.

"What? No. You get in! We'll get a cab and meet you there," I insist, pushing Hawk toward the front passenger seat.

"No. I'm not leaving you." Without waiting for me to argue with him, he pins West with a look. "West, get in. You need to be checked out anyway."

West's mouth opens in protest, but Beck has had enough of our shit. "West," he snarls. "Get in the fucking car."

Huffing out a breath, West glances at me with what looks like an apology in his eyes, but I'm not sure why, before he climbs into the passenger seat. He hasn't even closed the door before Mason is gunning it out of the lot and down the road, out of sight.

When they've disappeared, I look to Hawk, seeing the despair in his eyes. Despite the lack of hope I see there, I ask, "Do you think he's going to make it?"

He wraps his arms around me, and I bury my head in his top, stealing some of his strength. I don't miss the fact that he doesn't answer my question, and the sick feeling in my stomach solidifies.

When he pulls back, I run my eyes over him. I take him in for the first time since everything went down. He's got a split lip that looks like it's scabbed over. Other than red marks around his wrists, he seems relatively unharmed. He's definitely in better condition than West.

"Are you okay?" I ask quietly, scanning him over for any injuries I may have missed.

"I'll be fine. Let's just get to the hospital."

"I've booked a cab," Cam pipes up helpfully. "It'll be here in fifteen."

I look over my shoulder to the warehouse behind us. "What, uh, are we going to do about the mess in there?"

Hawk grimaces. "I'm not sure. Maybe Beck can see if Cain knows anyone who could sort it out?"

"Maybe."

It's not the best of plans, but I'm too concerned about Barton to try and figure out a better solution.

The three of us make our way toward the main road to wait for the taxi. Hawk all but collapses onto the sidewalk, placing his elbows on his knees and sighing heavily as he goes to bury his face in his hands before realizing they're covered in blood.

Pausing, he stops and stares at the blood on his hands, like he can't recall how it got there, before he frowns and crosses his arms instead while hanging his head.

I move to join him, suddenly feeling exhausted, but as I bend down, I notice the absence of my gun from the back of my pants. I quickly straighten and pat myself down.

"What's wrong?" Cam asks, watching me closely.

"My gun, I don't have it."

"Does it matter? You probably can't take it to the hospital anyway," Hawk mumbles, looking up at me.

"My fingerprints are on it. I don't want to leave it behind."

I start back toward the warehouse, but Cam's arm snaps out, his fingers wrapping around my upper arm. "I'll go get it."

I give him a small smile. "It's okay, I'll get it. I can't just sit here and wait anyway."

His lips flatten, but he lets go of me. I don't waste any time jogging back to the warehouse, not wanting to hold us up if the cab arrives while I'm gone.

Pulling open the side door, I scan the floor, my gaze bouncing over the dead bodies as I search for my gun. Spotting it lying on the ground, I swallow around the sudden lump in my throat as my eyes bounce to the puddle of blood beside it. I can't think about what might happen to Barton right now. One thing at a time. Retrieve the gun. Get in the cab. Go to the hospital. *Then* I can think about him.

My footfalls reverberate around the large space as I move to retrieve my gun, yet as I go to bend down, the sound of stiff boots on the concrete behind me has me spinning around, crouching and raising my fists in preparation for whatever shitstain tried to sneak up on me.

My eyes widen as I come face to face with Bowen, pointing his gun in my motherfucking face, like I haven't already had the day from hell.

"Ah-ah." He waves his gun, indicating for me to step away from mine, which is uselessly lying on the floor at my feet. Keeping my eyes trained on him, I slowly side-step until the gun is out of my reach, holding my hands out to my sides, making it clear I don't have any other weapons within reach.

I watch him closely, on alert for any sudden movements, as I try to work out where the fuck he came from. Was he here this whole time? Hiding out? Why?

"You couldn't have made this easier for me, D," he purrs, his beady eyes eating me up. The way they flare in excitement at having me trapped, sickens me, and I struggle to regulate my breathing as my pulse spikes and my palms begin to sweat. "I thought I'd have to chase you down, but here you are." His lips curl up in a cold smirk that sends a shiver down my spine. "It's almost like you missed me…did you miss me, D?"

I can hardly focus on his words as images flash before my eyes. One second I'm standing opposite him in the warehouse, and the next, I'm chained to the wall in his torture room back at the compound.

In my distraction, he manages to get closer to me, and when I blink back to the present and find him towering over me, I scurry backward on shaky legs, desperate to maintain some distance between us while I talk myself out of my panic attack. *Now is not the fucking time to be having traumatic flashbacks!*

I take a second to give myself a mental reprimand. I have been doing well since I opened up to the guys. Sure, there have been the odd moments when I've struggled or woken up from a nightmare, but talking to the guys and opening up to them has really helped me adjust. Knowing that we have been systematically working on bringing down our parents and the company has been an enormous help too. I can't let this sick fuck destroy all that progress.

Thoughts flitter across my mind of Hawk and how fucking grief-stricken he will be if he loses his dad. Or if I allow this asshole to destroy me, along with what losing me might do to the guys. Would West and Beck's relationship survive if something happened to me? I know it wouldn't take much for Cam to break. He might appear like he's back to his normal self, but his wounds are still healing. One strong pull on the stitches, and he would fall apart. And Mason…he's only started to poke his head out of his shell and feel confident enough to be himself. I don't want him to go back to the cold, impassive person he was when I first met him.

Those thoughts bolster me, and I straighten my spine, glowering at Bowen as I refuse to let him intimidate me. My little act of defiance has one side of his mouth lifting, excitement for the chase flaring in his eyes.

"I always knew there was more fight in you than Lawrence believed. You wouldn't have survived all those years if there wasn't." He chuckles malevolently, like we're sharing some sort of joke. "You had him fooled, in any case. He thought he had you broken and reliant on him, ready to do just about anything he asked of you." He tilts his head to the side ever so slightly. "But that wasn't the case, was it? You've been deceiving him—all of us—all these years, planning your little escape." He shakes his head and sighs as though he's disappointed. "But, D, you should have known you could never have a normal life." His mocking laugh echoes in my head, along with his next words. "Who would want to be with someone who can't bear children, after all? Face it, you can never escape your fate."

Instead of shrinking back from his words, which terrify me more than he could ever know, I match his smirk with one of my own, loving how a little line forms between his eyes as he tries to make sense of my reaction. "Maybe not, but neither can you."

The gun goes off as I dive to the left, sliding along the gritty concrete floor, ignoring the pain that flares along my side as I reach for my gun. Quickly flipping onto my back, I point the barrel at Bowen as he spins, glowering at Hawk in outrage, adrenaline masking the pain he must be feeling from the bullet wound to his shoulder.

"For Meena, and for me," I whisper as I fire off a shot straight into the side of his head before he can raise the gun at my brother. Enough fucking people have shoved a gun in his face today. I won't let one more piece-of-shit scumbag get the chance.

His eyes widen comically before he crumples to the ground in a heap. I stare at him as if expecting him to come back to life and attack us again, as I try to wrap my mind around the fact the man who killed my best friend, who tortured me relentlessly over the years, is dead. It almost feels too easy. I'm waiting for the other shoe to drop…but it never comes.

Instead, I feel the warmth of Hawk's presence at my back as he pulls me into his arms.

"Are you okay? Hadley! You're bleeding."

I have to blink several times, but as the adrenaline wears off, the sting of torn flesh along my arm cements me in my reality—one where Bowen truly is dead.

Looking down at my arm, the long Henley I was wearing has been ripped open, and the underlying skin scraped off from where I slid across the ground, leaving it red and raw looking, with bits of blood forming where the grit has broken the skin.

"I'm fine," I assure him, not that he listens, lifting my arm to inspect it himself. Seeming satisfied, he lets me go, helping me to my feet. My side aches a little, but it's nothing I can't live with.

"Where did you get the gun from?" I ask, brushing the dust off myself.

"When you didn't come right back, I got a weird feeling. Something was just telling me I needed to get in here, so I grabbed it from Cam and came to find you…although it looked like you had everything handled." One corner of his lip lifts, and I can see the proud gleam in his eyes.

I scoff. "I don't know about that. He definitely got the better of me for a second there. I-I kept remembering what it felt like to be back in that compound, chained to his wall."

Hawk's eyes darken, and he places a hand on my shoulder. "You'll never be back there again. And look at how far you've come. You were able to work through the trauma and fight back. I'm so proud of you, Hadley."

Tears prick my eyes. "I couldn't have done it if you hadn't come looking for me."

He smiles placatingly. "I'm pretty sure you'd have found a way. Now let's get out of here. The cab should be here, and Cam will be wondering where we are."

I glance around at the dead bodies strewn over the ground, noticing Hawk's gaze linger on the unmoving form of his mother, and a look I can't place passes over him.

I nudge my shoulder against his. "I'm sorry about your mom. I know you wanted to believe the best in her."

He lets out a long, exhausted-sounding sigh. "Yeah, I did." He shakes his head, as though he's annoyed at himself. "But she was never the mother I wanted." When he looks at me, lines mar his forehead. "Did you hear what she said?"

"About how she got rid of me and that I'm supposed to be dead?" I snort. "Yeah...I just don't understand how she was involved."

He shrugs his shoulders. "I don't know."

"Lawrence told me he and Maria were meant to get married until Barton came along. Do you think they were working together?"

Hawk wraps an arm around my shoulders, pulling me in against him. "It sounded that way, but whatever their plan was, it doesn't matter now. They're both gone, and we're still here."

"Did you hear gunshots?" Cam shouts, rushing into the warehouse. He freezes when he spots Bowen lying on the floor, and his expression darkens. "What the fuck was *he* doing here?" he snarls.

"It doesn't matter," I say, repeating Hawk's words. "Let's just get the fuck out of here."

Cam continues to stare at Bowen's body until Hawk's phone goes off, drawing each of our attention.

Pulling it out of his pocket, he puts it on speaker before he answers, "Yeah?"

"They've just taken your dad into surgery," Beck says, his voice sounding grim. "They weren't able to tell me anything more."

"Thanks, man. We'll be there soon."

"Don't worry about the warehouse. I've spoken to Cain, he knows someone. He'll get it sorted."

Before any more assholes can crawl out of the woodwork and attack us, we leave the warehouse behind and head to the hospital. With every passing mile, I pray to god that Barton makes it through his surgery. I have lost so much, I can't lose him too.

Hadley

CHAPTER TWENTY-FIVE

*H*ours go by as the six of us wait anxiously in the waiting room for news on Barton's progress. All we know is he's still alive, but that's not much comfort considering he's been in surgery for the last four hours and could still die at any moment.

The only positive is that West has no lasting damage, just some bruising that will heal in a few days.

Beck's phone buzzes, and he looks at the screen before showing it to me. There's a picture of a building being ravaged by flames, and it takes me a second to realize it's the warehouse from earlier.

I guess Cain's man came through. At least that's one less thing to worry about. I smile at Beck. "Thanks for taking care of that."

He wraps his arm around my shoulder and kisses my temple. "You know it."

We lapse into silence. Hawk's foot tapping incessantly against the linoleum tiles is slowly driving me insane. He's had a scowl on his face since he sat down, and he's only gotten increasingly more worked up the longer we've been sitting here. I can't tell if he's just worried about Barton or if something else is bothering him.

Eventually, he lets out a long, frustrated sigh and runs his hand through his hair. "What did Bowen mean when he said you can't have children?"

My throat is dry as I stare wide-eyed at him. *Shit.* I didn't know he had heard that.

He stares at me with a look I can't quite place—a half-plead, half-blood-thirsty rage. I'm incapable of forming any sort of response as I swallow around the lump in my throat.

I can feel the others looking between Hawk and I, but I cannot look away from the maelstrom of emotions flittering across his face. His stare holds me captive, practically pulling the dark secret out of me.

I lick my dry lips and chew on my lower lip. "He—" Fuck, how do I even explain this to everyone. Tearing my gaze from Hawk's bewitching ones, I glance at each of my guys, hoping this final secret won't be the one that breaks us. We've already survived so much, but this is…different. While I'm not sure if I want children in the future, that doesn't mean the guys are willing to attach themselves to someone who will *never* bear children and are ready to accept the possibility of never having their own kids.

My face crumples as I sigh, turning my gaze back to Hawk. "Several years ago, I was, uh, sterilized."

My words are met with a deafening silence, which feels like it lasts a lifetime, and I swear I see something break in Hawk's eyes as he stares at me with such a profound sadness it constricts the air in my lungs.

"I don't—" Beck begins, and when I finally look at him, lines form across his forehead as he tries to process what I'm saying. "They performed surgery on you?"

I nod my head. Leaning back in my chair, I push down my pants enough to show them the barely visible scars on my lower hips. They're just tiny white lines, and in comparison to the marks on my back, they're nothing.

They all lean forward to see where I'm pointing, and the second Hawk sees the marks, he storms off, looking ready to punch someone. I watch him go with concern, but Mason's hand on my thigh draws my attention back to the guys and where he is crouched in front of me.

"Let him go," he says, giving my thigh a reassuring squeeze. "Talk to me."

I give a small shrug of my shoulder. "What is there to say? I can never have kids." Unable to look into his blue eyes and see the concern there, I drop my gaze to my lap. "If you stay with me, you won't ever have your own children." I can feel the tears welling in my eyes, the guilt of robbing the guys of that opportunity riding me hard.

"Baby." Mason presses his finger under my chin, forcing me to look at him. "Has a doctor ever told you that? Or is that just what Bowen or someone at the compound told you?"

My brows scrunch together, and I respond in a quiet, unsure voice, "Some guy at the compound told me."

A small smile graces his lips. "Then let's talk to a doctor and get a second opinion before we make any decisions, yeah?"

I give a hesitant nod. "But, what if…"

"If it's true, then we'll deal with it like we have everything else." He strokes his thumb down my cheek, and how he looks at me with such earnest devotion leaves me speechless. "Nothing you say or do will ever scare us off." He must be able to see the doubt in my eyes, as he continues, "If you can't have children, then, if and when we decide we're ready for kids, we can adopt. Or look into surrogacy, or…I don't know, but we will work it out. As a team. The five of us."

A small grin lifts one side of his lips. "You're stuck with us, Little Warrior. It's you and me. Always."

I glance up at Beck, West, and Cam, and the three of them move to surround me. Beck clasps one of my hands in his, and West takes the other. Mason scooches to the side so Cam can kneel beside him in front of me.

"Always," Beck promises as Cam and West nod their agreement, all of them looking at me with impassioned gazes. The amount of love pouring off them has tears overflowing and running down my cheeks.

"I love you, all of you."

Beck presses a kiss to my forehead as each of them murmurs loving sentiments.

Mason and Cam eventually pull up chairs, so we're all huddled together, which is how Hawk finds us when he finally returns. As soon as he steps into the doorframe, my head snaps up, and the anguish in his eyes has me standing up, moving toward him as he steps into the room.

His arms wrap around me as mine wind around his neck, pulling him in for a hug. He whispers apologies into my ear, and I run my hand up and down his back as I soothe him. None of this is his fault, and he shouldn't have to bear any of the pain.

"We'll talk to a doctor and find out for sure. We will do whatever it takes to fix this, if that's what you want." I smile into his hug, loving how this grumpy brother of mine who hates everyone except his family is always ready to fight my battles with me. He always has my back, and I know he always will.

We pull apart as a man dressed in scrubs walks into the waiting room. "Davenport family?"

"That's us," Hawk rushes out, turning to face him.

"I'm Dr. Gallaher, can we, eh, talk in private?" The doctor glances at everyone else crowded around us.

"It's okay, you can tell us in front of them. How's my dad?" Hawk asks, desperate for answers.

I feel Cam slip his hand into mine, and I hold on tightly, terrified to hear the doctor's next words.

Nodding, he looks down at the clipboard in his hands. "Your father was shot in the abdomen. The bullet nicked his aorta, causing massive internal bleeding. He lost a lot of blood, and it was touch-and-go a few times during the surgery, but we managed to stop the bleeding, and he's currently in recovery."

"He's alive?" My voice is a harsh croak as tears overwhelm me.

"He is. He's still under anesthesia, and it will probably be a while before he starts to come around, but he's alive. He's currently getting a blood transfusion and will require careful monitoring for the next twenty-four hours, but after that, he should be out of the woods."

I practically keel over with relief and feel someone's arms around my waist, holding me upright.

"Can we see him?" Hawk asks anxiously.

"Immediate family only for now," the doctor explains, glancing behind us to the others.

"We're his children," I clarify.

"Then the two of you can sit with him, but no other visitors for now."

We both nod in understanding, and I glance over my shoulder at the guys, who all wave me on before I follow after the doctor and Hawk.

He leads us into a room, and I'm taken aback by how frail Barton looks in the bed. Monitors are hooked up all over the place, and he looks as white as the sheets draped over him.

"As I said, it will be a while before he's awake. I'll come back to check on him in a bit."

I murmur a thanks, unable to take my eyes off Barton as Hawk moves to the bedside. His gaze runs over him, stopping on the various tubes and wires attached to him before he glances up at the machines.

We pull up chairs and sit beside him, both of us watching him closely for any signs of movement. We rarely talk, only passing a few remarks back and forth.

I lose all track of time, but at some point, a nurse pops her head in. "Visiting hours are over. Why don't you kids go home and get some rest. We'll let you know if there's any change in his condition overnight."

I can see the reluctance in Hawk's expression, but before he can argue, I speak up, "Thanks. We'll leave in a few and come back tomorrow."

Nodding, the nurse closes the door, once again leaving us alone.

"We need to get some rest ourselves. They'll call if anything happens," I assure Hawk, taking in the bags under his eyes. We all had one hell of a day, and I still haven't updated the others on what happened at the warehouse with Bowen after they left.

Sighing, Hawk nods his head in agreement, and we mutter our goodbyes to a still-unconscious Barton before we leave.

Cam wraps me in a bear hug when we return to the waiting room, and I sink into his embrace.

"You didn't have to wait for us," I say as Mason does some sort of bro-hug thing with Hawk.

"We wanted to wait in case you needed anything. How's your dad?" Beck asks. He looks exhausted, and glancing at the others, I see the same weariness tugging at their features.

"He's stable. We'll know more tomorrow," Hawk answers with a small smile as Cam pulls me in for another hug, not yet ready to let me go.

Extricating myself from his embrace, I link my fingers with his. "It's been a crazy long day. Let's go home."

～

ONCE WE'VE all showered and thrown away our bloodied clothes from today, we all collapse onto the sofas in the living room, and Cam hands out beers to everyone. I can already feel my eyelids drooping, exhaustion from today's drama taking its toll.

"Can we all just take a second to talk about what a complete and utter psychotic bitch your mom is," Cam states with absolutely zero tact as he drops down into the only remaining empty seat. "I never thought she'd have it in her to off her own kids."

I notice Hawk rub his eyes before pressing his face into his hands and sighing wearily, and I turn to look at him. "I didn't think she had it in her to actually kill me...but I saw the resolve in her eyes when she pointed that gun at me." He lifts his head, and there's a sadness in his eyes. "Never mind what she said about you." He shakes his head. "I don't understand how any parent could do that to their child. To a harmless baby."

Neither do I, but I don't see the point in dwelling on it. "Me neither, but it doesn't matter. She's dead, and Barton's going to be okay. We're free and clear."

"Yeah, except for my father," West grumbles from beside me.

I squeeze his thigh in reassurance. "We'll deal with him...tomorrow. You need to get some rest."

"I'm fine, Firefly," he assures me, lifting his arm so I can cuddle into him, being extra careful not to jostle him or press on any of the bruising around his ribs or abdomen. Even sitting here must be painful for him.

Just as I'm getting comfortable pressed up against him, Cam's next words have me groaning. "So, guess who showed up at the warehouse after you left."

Mason, Beck, and West all look at Cam before their gazes bounce to Hawk and me.

"Motherfucking *Bowen*," Cam continues, knowing damn well his words are going to get the other three all riled up.

"What the fuck? What happened?" Mason exclaims, running his gaze over me, inspecting me for any injuries.

Bar a little road rash, I'm fine. I have kept my arms covered all day though, first with Cam's hoodie at the hospital and now with one of West's long-sleeved sweatshirts, wanting to put off any questions that were sure to arise from the others at the state of my arm.

"Nothing. I'm not sure what his angle was—maybe to try and take me." I shrug my shoulders, not sure what Bowen thought was going to happen when he snuck up on me. "Not that I was ever going to let him do that. He's only ever seen me in the compound when I was weak, and even though he knew the training I'd received and what I'm capable of, I think he thought he'd be able to cower me. He's always been the one in charge, the one in control, yet outside the confines of the compound, he doesn't have that same power over me."

"And your PTSD?" Beck questions. "Were you okay?"

"Not at first," I mumble quietly, ashamed of how I panicked when he first approached me. "But I was able to work through it."

"She was amazing," Hawk speaks up, a proud note in his voice and a prideful glint in his eye. "Took him out with one shot."

I blush under his compliment, returning his heart-warming smile with a shy one of my own.

The six of us sit and chat for a while longer before everyone starts to yawn, and we call it a night. Hawk makes his escape down the hall, and I kiss the others goodnight.

"I'm going to stay with West tonight, and make sure he's okay."

"Of course, Little Warrior. I'll see you at breakfast." Mason places a searing kiss to my lips before heading to his room, and Cam takes his turn before following after him.

"You can stay in my room tonight," I tell Beck, who nods and glances at West.

"Look after him." With a kiss, he heads for my room, and I turn to West.

"Come on," I say, taking his hand. "You need painkillers and to go to bed."

He doesn't argue, letting me get him a glass of water and tablets before leading him to his bedroom.

As the door closes behind me, I trail my hand down the front of his t-shirt before tugging it up. He raises his arms so I can pull it off over his head, revealing his chest and abdomen. He watches my every movement with a keen eye, so I'm sure he doesn't miss the way my face scrunches in annoyance as the dark bruises that are beginning to form on his skin are revealed.

I lightly stroke my thumb over one, feeling that familiar spark of anger flare to life. He tucks his finger under my chin, lifting my head until I'm looking him in the eye.

"I'm fine," he assures me. "I'm here. You're here. Forget about today."

Closing the distance between us, his lips brush mine, stealing my breath and setting my skin on fire. I run my hands over his firm pecs, and he tugs on my hoodie. I pull it off as he steps out of his sweatpants. We discard the last of our clothes, and I can feel the sheer need pouring off him as he drinks me in.

He reaches out a hand, grasping my arm and turning it so he can see the abrasion better. "It's nothing," I promise him. His lips pinch, but he thankfully lets the topic go as I step into him. My nipples brush against his chest, hardening at the contact, as my hand moves to cup his balls, giving them a gentle squeeze that has him groaning before I wrap my fingers around his length to work him up just the way he likes.

"Fuck, Firefly," he groans, staring mesmerized at where my hand is wrapped around him. "Lick me." The words are a husky demand, and when I glance up at him through my lashes, his pupils are dilated with lust.

Slowly, I get to my knees before him, flicking out my tongue to run around his head, catching a bead of pre-cum and relishing the salty taste on my tongue before licking along his shaft. I pump him slowly as I suction my lips around him, giving another swipe of my tongue over his tip that has a low growl rumbling in his chest. The noise has me clenching my thighs together with need.

"Touch yourself," he orders, and I don't hesitate to press my fingers against my swollen nub as I suck him deeper into my mouth.

He lets me have control for a moment, but when I sink my fingers knuckle-deep inside my pussy, and moan around his thick shaft, his restraint snaps and his fingers pull my hair out of its hair tie, tangling in my messy strands as he thrusts into my mouth, and hits the back of my throat as he takes control.

I circle my fingers in tandem with his hard thrusts, and just as I feel the telltale tingle of an impending orgasm, West pulls back and I release him with a pop.

"Ah-ah," he chastises when I whimper with need. "All of your pleasure will be at my hands tonight."

All of my guys are different when it comes to sex. Beck fucks me like the process is an exorcism, ridding him of his demons. Mason can be surprisingly sweet and soft but no less dominant. Cam is all about making sure I come as many times as possible—he's definitely a giver in the bedroom. But West…it's not enough for him to make me come. He has to own every second of my pleasure.

In a move that must have his muscles screaming in pain after today, he sweeps me into his arms and carries me to the bed, dropping me onto it with a bounce before he wraps his arms around my thighs and pulls me to the edge of the mattress. Getting on his knees between my spread thighs, he doesn't waste any time before diving in and lapping at me. My back arches as I fist the bedsheets, already breathless and desperate for release.

All I can think about is the spiral of lust unraveling within me when I feel his finger, coated in my juices, press against the tight ring of muscle at my ass before pushing in. I tense for a second before relaxing, letting him slide in further. He begins to thrust shallowly in time to the movement of his tongue, and I quickly fall apart, crying out his name.

He doesn't give me a second to recover as he maneuvers me up the bed and hovers over me. In one swift move, he sinks inside me until his pubic bone grinds against my sensitive clit. My mouth drops on a gasp as I stare into his wild, lust-hazed eyes.

"Arms above your head," he murmurs in a deep husk that has my lower belly clenching with need, already forgetting that I just had an earth-shattering orgasm.

Doing as he asks, he leans over and pulls a satin tie out of his bedside table, tying it around my wrists. The material is soft against my skin as he pulls my arms further up the bed, securing them to the railings on his headboard.

He trails his fingers over the sensitive skin of my inner arm as he slowly works his way back down my body. His shallow thrusts drive me wild, tempting and teasing me.

He pulls back until just the tip of his dick is inside me, and towering above me, he takes his time to look over my blushed, heaving chest and peaked nipples before his gaze rests on my face.

"Now, no moving," he orders in a serious tone that brokers no argument, spearing me with a stern look before he slams inside me in one quick motion that has me crying out.

His eyes never leave mine as he continues his relentless pace, pushing me back up that peak until I swear I can taste my orgasm on my tongue. My hips involuntarily buck, and he draws back as soon as I move, slowing to a stop as his eyes narrow in disapproval.

He holds himself still above me, lifting a hand to press it flat against my sternum. I can see the question in his eyes, feel the hesitation in his movements, but I know I'm safe with him. Despite being tied to the bed, I know he won't ever go too far or do anything I don't want him to do.

If anything, handing over control to him like this has provided me with moments of relief over the last few weeks. I spend so much of my day trying to gain control that there's something ultimately freeing about being with West and handing all of that control over to him.

"It's okay," I assure him. "Do it." I tilt my head back, exposing my neck to him, and he stares into my eyes for a long moment before he slides his hand up my chest, wrapping his fingers around my neck. I'm sure he can feel my pulse as it thuds rapidly beneath his hand. My response isn't one of fear but excitement.

He flexes his fingers, testing his grip before he again sinks inside me. I feel his hold tighten around my throat, limiting my breathing just enough to add to the heady sensation that comes from being slowly driven toward ecstasy.

I'm truly held captive beneath him, my body wound tight as I try not to writhe, my breaths coming in pants the higher he pushes me.

"West," I moan needily, lost to his ministrations. "Please."

"I love it when you beg," he rasps, picking up his pace.

"I can't take any more," I cry, half delirious.

"You'll take what I give you," he growls in a demanding tone that leaves no room for argument. It only ratchets up my need for him.

His fingers tighten further, but it's still not enough to have me panicking. If anything, the entire world seems to fall away until I'm aware of nothing but his tight hold on my throat and the way my pussy clenches around him with every thrust, as I stare up into his deep green eyes that watch me in wonder.

"Come for me, Firefly," he growls in a breathless pant, rutting into me until he finds his release. The feel of him swelling inside me pushes me over the edge into an orgasm that feels like it goes on forever until I'm left lying limp on the bed.

West kisses me gently as he reaches above me to undo the ties and rub soothingly at my wrists before he flops over onto his back, taking me with him.

I curl into his side, careful not to put any pressure on his bruises, and as my eyes drift shut, I feel him press a kiss to the top of my head.

"Go to sleep, baby." His fingers stroke through my hair, and I feel sleep tugging me under as he murmurs, "Everything's going to be okay from here on out. I'm going to give you everything you've always wanted."

Hadley

CHAPTER TWENTY-SIX

I jerk awake at some point later in the night and lift my head, looking around to see what woke me. I'm just about to pass it off as a nightmare when I hear a floorboard creak in the hallway.

Careful to keep quiet, I slip out of bed, grab a pair of West's sweats and a top, and pull them on before stuffing my feet into my boots and cracking the door open to peer out into the darkened hall. I can make out a dim light and hear the sound of movement coming from the kitchen. Slipping the knife out of my boot, I move on silent feet out of the bedroom.

Slowly, placing one foot in front of the other, I close in on the kitchen. As I approach, I tighten my hold on the handle, ready to drive it into whatever asshole broke into our dorm, but as I step into the kitchen, I stutter to a stop when I come face-to-face with Beck.

"What are you doing?" I hiss, dropping the knife to my side.

He glances down at the steel blade in my hand, and instead of seeming surprised—you know, a *normal* reaction—his pupils seem to dilate, and one side of his lips lifts up in a smirk. "Were you about to stab me, sweetheart?"

"You're not supposed to find that a turn-on," I grouse, tucking the knife back in my boot. "What are you doing up?"

He steps back to grab something from the island, and I take in what he's wearing—He's dressed head-to-toe in black. "Or maybe I should be asking *where* you're going."

When he turns back to look at me with a black backpack in his hand, his expression is tight, his lips pressed flat.

"Where are you going?" I repeat more insistently, tilting my head slightly and quirking a brow as I wait him out.

After a moment of silence, he huffs out a breath. "To deal with Wilbert."

"Alone?" I'm already shaking my head. "I don't think so. Give me a couple of minutes to change."

"No, sweetheart." He reaches out to snag my wrist as I turn away, forcing me to turn back to face him. "Go back to West. I'll sort out this last hurdle for us."

"I'm not letting you go alone," I insist. "I'll be your backup in case you need it."

My wrist is still held captive in his as he stares at me for a long moment before relenting. "Fine, but no stabbing people unless it's necessary."

"No promises," I mutter under my breath as I turn away from him and scurry back down the hall to my bedroom, grabbing some appropriate clothes and throwing them on as quickly as possible in case the asshole so much as thinks about trying to sneak out while I'm changing.

I'm relieved to find him still standing where I left him when I return to the kitchen. "Ready?" I ask, and he nods, throwing his backpack over his shoulder and heading toward the front door.

The campus is quiet as we walk through it to where Beck's car is parked in the staff lot. His car is an eyesore, parked amongst various brand-new Audis and Mercedes, but he doesn't seem to give a shit as he strides toward it.

Inserting the key in the door, he unlocks the car, and we climb in. It takes a few tries before the ignition starts, and I side-eye him, wordlessly hoping the car doesn't break down halfway there.

He pats the wheel in some sort of weird, loving gesture before putting it in gear and driving us away from the campus. Neither of us talks, comfortable in the silence as we make our way along the seafront and up the cliff to our parents' residence—although all but Barton's house belongs to the guys now, so I guess it's their residence. *Weird.*

We pull up to the gate and Beck enters the code, waiting for the gates to open before driving through them and parking at the entrance to Wilbert's driveway.

"You have a plan in mind?" I question before we get out of the car.

"Not really. I'm fairly confident we can wing it. He probably doesn't know about Maria yet, and if he was in on her plan, the last thing he would expect tonight is a visit from us."

Nodding my head in response, I push open the car door and get out, careful to close it quietly behind me. With a knife in my boot and another in my hoodie pocket, I'm more than prepared as we stealthily move toward the darkened house. At this late hour, he's probably sound asleep, giving us the element of surprise.

I follow Beck as he enters the house and, without making a sound, begins to climb the stairs. He stops at a bedroom door, glancing over his shoulder at me. I give him a quick nod, letting him know I'm ready when he is, and he slides a gun out of his pocket before easing the door open.

The second he does, I can hear the sound of a machine whirring. Nevertheless. Beck pays it no attention, so he must have heard it before, when he was here with West.

He pushes the door open further, until we can step into the darkened room, and I can just about make out the outline of the bed. Before I can determine whether or not Wilbert is lying in it though, I hear the recognizable click of a gun being cocked from the far side of the room. The loud noise has both Beck and I spinning, raising our weapons in anticipation of an attack.

"Stop right there," Wilbert growls angrily, pointing what looks like a fucking shotgun at us. We both freeze. "Weapons on the ground." Slowly I lower my knife to the floor, and Beck does the same with his gun before we both stand upright and raise our hands in the air.

Wilbert reaches out to turn on the light on the table beside where he's sitting, lighting up the room. Now that I'm not having to squint through the darkness, I can see pillows or clothes or something have been stuffed underneath the duvet to make it appear like there's a body lying in bed and then there is some sort of device sitting on his bedside table making the annoying whirring noise. All of it was set up to make us think he was asleep in the bed. *Sly, Wilbert. Didn't know you had it in you, you fat fuck.*

"I set the gate alarm to alert me whenever it was opened. Didn't want to be caught unaware again."

At his words, I return my focus to him, and the large gun pointed straight at Beck, obviously deeming him to be the greater threat out of the two of us.

Glancing at Beck, he looks utterly unperturbed by the gun pointed in his face.

"Gotta give you some credit, old man. We didn't think you had it in you to deceive us."

Wilbert's face reddens in anger at Beck's words.

"You think I was about to let some *children* take everything I have worked for?"

I quirk an eyebrow. "Doesn't sound like you've really contributed much. You just leave all the decisions up to everyone else and reap the rewards."

His gun stays pointed at Beck, but Wilbert's furious gaze bounces to me, and his lip curls up in a snarl. "Stay out of it, girlie. You have no business sticking your nose where it doesn't belong." His gaze darts back and forth between Beck and me. "Maria's the one you should be chasing anyway. She's got your brothers."

So the piece of shit knew that.

"And you don't even give a shit that she could be doing god knows what to West?" Beck snarls furiously.

"He shouldn't have come after me or tried to win one over on her. We weren't about to let him get away with that."

"So you let Maria do all the heavy lifting," I begin, shifting slightly so I can move closer to him. "You let her organize his kidnapping." Another small shuffle. "Let her have her goons beat him up. Let her threaten him." I let the monster inside me rise to the surface and shine through so he can see exactly who the fuck he's messing with.

I relish as the sneer drops from his face, quickly replaced by fear and astonishment.

"H-how do you know that?"

I grin savagely at him. "Because we killed her." I don't give him any time to process that information, taking a large, deliberate step toward him. My sudden movement has him swinging the gun in my direction, but this is the thing I *hate* about guns, especially huge, long-barreled shotguns—they just don't work in small spaces, and I'm far too close for him to get any sort of a decent shot.

The second the barrel swings in my direction, I reach out and grab a hold of it, fighting him for control. With him distracted, Beck quickly rushes to his other side, and in a move that turns me on *way* more than it should, he pulls a knife out of his fucking boot and holds it to Wilbert's carotid.

The fat shitstain stops struggling, immediately falling still at the press of cold steel against his neck and letting me rip the gun from his hands. Flicking on the safety, I chuck the stupid thing on the bed and turn back to grin manically at the look of utter terror on Wilbert's face.

"Is it inappropriate if I tell you how much I want to fuck you right now?" I ask Beck, ignoring Wilbert's splutters.

Beck laughs darkly, his own monster stirring just below the surface. When he looks up at me from where he's crouched behind Wilbert, I swear, I fucking gush for him.

That titillating combination of darkness and lust brims in his eyes, and I am so fucking here for it. "Not at all, sweetheart. If only you could see the boner I'm sporting for you right now."

My grin turns genuine as Wilbert's wide-eyed gaze darts between us.

"What the—"

"Shut the fuck up," Beck snarls, focusing back on his scumbag father. "I think we've heard just about enough from you."

"Definitely," I mutter in agreement.

Wilbert's breaths come in rapid, panicked pants, and sweat coats his forehead.

"Now," Beck muses, glancing up at me with an excited gleam in his eyes, "what are we to do with you?"

I lift my finger to my lips as I mull over our options. I'm all for gutting him here and now, but given Maria's death earlier, we probably shouldn't be drawing any more unwanted attention our way.

An idea comes to mind, and Beck quirks an eyebrow when I grin at him. "I have an idea." He waits patiently for me to continue. "It involves a cliff and a long, *long* fall to the bottom."

"What? Wait—"

"Sounds perfect," Beck agrees, his fucked up grin matching my own. "Come on, fatty, let's get some fresh air."

"What?! No!" Wilbert insists, pushing himself further into the chair and gripping on tightly to the arms as if that will save him. It's fucking laughable.

Beck seems to think the same as he chuckles, digging his blade deeper into Wilbert's neck, nicking the skin. "It wasn't a suggestion," he barks.

With much pushing, Wilbert eventually gets to his feet. His knees are practically quaking as Beck shoves him in the back, causing him to stumble as he takes a step toward the door.

I retrieve the gun and knife from the floor, handing the weapon back to Beck before I open the bedroom door. Keeping ahead of them, we make our way at a painfully slow speed along the landing and down the stairs. Wilbert blubbers and cries and protests with every fucking step, but Beck and I pay him no attention.

It feels like it takes fucking forever before we finally reach the doors leading out the back of the property. I've never ventured close to the edge of the cliffs, but I remember West telling me about them, and somehow it feels like a fitting end to all of this.

Opening the back door, there's a slight breeze in an otherwise still evening, which swirls the sea air around me. I take a deep breath, and I don't know if it's the sea salt or how close to being finished we are, but damn, the taste of freedom is so fucking sweet.

"Please don't," Wilbert pleads for like the fiftieth time as Beck shoves the end of the gun in Wilbert's back, rolling his eyes at me. I laugh, and Wilbert looks at me like I'm crazy.

"You're both sick," he snarls. "What normal person would do this to someone?"

The laughter drops off my face, and in the next second, I'm standing in front of him, so close I can feel his disgusting breath on my cheek. "What sort of person turns children into monsters for a living? What sort of person makes his son feel like shit and pretends the other doesn't exist until he has a need for him? What sort of person forces his children to do what you've made Beck do?"

Stepping away from him, I shrug, letting my anger at his words bleed out into the night air. "Besides, we never claimed to be normal. We are what you made us. We're a product of our environment. *You* turned us into who we are, and now it's time for your reckoning."

He just looks confused, and I'm pretty sure he's got no fucking idea what I'm on about. Not that I give a shit.

"Now come on, Beck and I have better things to be doing with our night."

Beck shoves Wilbert forward again, and he begins to sob like the pathetic waste of life he is. Slowly, we make our way toward the cliff edge, the sound of the waves crashing far below getting louder with every step, and the smell of sea salt in the air grows stronger.

There's something so peaceful about it all, and this unusual sense of calm settles over me as we approach the cliff. When we're a few feet away, Wilbert collapses to his knees.

Beck and I both huff out a breath of frustration. This is taking so fucking long.

"Jesus Christ, be a fucking man about it," I snarl angrily.

"I can't," he sobs. "Please."

"Please, what? Show you mercy? Spare your life?" I wrap my hand around the hair on the top of his head and wrench his head back, so he's staring up at me, not that he can see me through the tears streaming from his eyes. "Where was your mercy when you were killing kids? When Meena was being beaten to death? When you stripped us of our fucking humanity to line your own pockets?" Letting go of my hold on his hair, his head flops forward until his chin meets his chest.

"I didn't—" he blubbers, and maybe he's right. He didn't pull the trigger. It wasn't his boot that kept driving into Meena. But it *was* done under his purview. Whether or not he was directly involved isn't the fucking point. It was *his* company. He is just as much to blame as Lawrence, Frank, Maria, and even Barton to some extent.

Unfortunately, I wasn't lucky enough to be able to throw Lawrence, Frank, or Maria off the side of a cliff. Regardless of how each of them met their demise, it was more than deserved.

The sound of a gunshot going off makes Wilbert scream before he breaks down in a fresh round of tears.

"On your fucking feet," Beck snaps, having reached the limit of what he's willing to tolerate. Knowing his father isn't going to stand up on his own, he grabs him by the back of his pajama top, and I help yank him to his feet.

With the gun shoved deep into the middle of his spine, he stumbles forward another few feet, until he's hovering at the cliff edge.

I can see his entire body shaking with fear now, and Beck and I make sure to stay a few feet back from the edge to be safe.

"Please," Wilbert continues, his words falling on deaf ears.

"Go on, over you go," I encourage him, but he shakes his head furtively, continuing to plead for mercy.

"Fucking hell," I grouse. "Get it through your thick skull, you're not getting out of this. This is the end of the line for you. The only decision you get to make is whether you go out like a man or the bawling baby you're acting like."

An ominous crack follows my words, and in the next second, the ground beneath Wilbert's feet gives way, and he and the ground he was standing on disappear. My mouth drops open as I lean forward, not daring to step any closer to the edge. Not that I need to since his screams float on the air until there's a crash of waves below, followed by a reverent silence.

We both listen intently for another moment or so, almost expecting to hear him crying for help, but when we hear nothing but the sea hitting the rocks far below us, I turn to Beck, a disbelieving chuckle bursting out of me.

He returns my smile with a dark grin of his own, wrapping his arms around me. "Damn, that felt good." He chuckles.

"I just wish all of them could have met the same gruesome death."

He tucks a stray strand of hair behind my ears, cupping my cheek. "I know, but it's over. That's all that matters."

I nod my head, but then I pause. "Actually, not quite. Do you think Cain would be able to get someone inside Ashfield Prison to take care of Frank?"

Beck's eyebrow lifts in surprise. "He's going to be sentenced to life in prison."

"I know, but I'm not willing to risk him ever getting released. After the things he's done to Mason, he doesn't deserve to live."

Nodding, Beck pulls me in for another hug. "I'll reach out to him and see what he can do."

We stand on top of the cliff behind West's house for a long time, and the faint pink and red of the sunrise is gracing the horizon by the time we head back to campus.

When we return to the dorm, I pull him into West's bedroom with me, and we quickly strip off our clothes before climbing into bed.

As Beck slides in behind me, I can feel his erection pressing between my asscheeks, and I push back against him.

He nibbles on my earlobe. "What is it about killing off the last of your enemies that is such a fucking turn-on?" he whispers in a low growl into my ear.

I turn my head, capturing his lips with mine in a heated, sloppy kiss, full of tongue and teeth. "Fuck me," I half-plead, half-demand.

He smirks into my kiss, shifting us so I'm on all fours. "Climb on top of West," he orders. "See how many times I can make you come before he wakes up."

Doing as he says, I place a knee on either side of West's hips and press my hands into the mattress on either side of his shoulders. Beck lines himself up behind me, and after checking that I'm more than ready for him, he pushes all the way into me until his balls slap against my clit, making me moan.

He sets a slow pace, taking his time building up our climax, and I shift my weight to one arm so that I can stroke my other hand down West's gorgeously naked body. Trailing down the center of his chest, I stroke over his happy trail, holding back my giggle when his dick twitches under my touch.

Wrapping my fingers around his length, I pump him slowly, in time with Beck's thrusts, and my focus is so intent on watching him grow in my hands that I don't initially realize he's woken up, until he lifts his hands to press his fingers against my clit.

"What do you think you're doing, Firefly?" he questions, his voice thick with sleep and lust.

Lifting his head, he kisses me before I can answer, and between his fingers and Beck's dick, my orgasm hits me, and I moan into his mouth. Beck continues with his thrusts, dragging out my climax, and when I finally come down, he pulls out. I don't get a second to miss him though, as West pushes his dick into my pussy instead, and as soon as he's fully seated inside me, I feel Beck pressing against my ass. *Fuck yes, a hot brother sandwich!*

Inch by achingly slow inch, he pushes into me, until I'm so full I can hardly breathe. "Is that good, baby?" he asks, his voice dripping with need.

"Mmmhmmm." It's the only semi-coherent response I can form as the two of them start to move in tandem, one sliding out as the other pushes in, so I constantly feel full. I can feel their hands roaming over my body, setting my skin on fire as I rush toward an even more explosive orgasm.

"Oh fuck," I pant, as my skin begins to feel like it's about to rip apart at the seams. "I'm going to come."

Beck's fingers dig into my hips, and West's hand slides up my chest to wrap lightly around my throat, and the combination of their possessive touches pushes me over the edge as I scream out my release, faintly aware of their grunting as they find their own.

After we clean up, the three of us collapse into the bed, and I quickly drift back into a deep sleep filled with all my happy thoughts for the future that I've never let myself dwell on for too long...until now.

Baby

CHAPTER TWENTY-SEVEN

I shake out my arms, doing a few stretches to loosen the muscles as I step up to the side of the pool. The last few days, since Hadley and Beck snuck out to kill Wilbert, have been strangely quiet. I could get used to the peace, though. To carefree breakfasts and afternoons spent lying on the lawn. To movie nights and climbing into bed with the only girl I'll ever need.

Of course, there has also been a lot of time spent at the hospital over the last few days, but thankfully, Barton has woken up and seems to be recovering well. There have also been many conversations about the future and everyone's plans for after graduation. We're down to the final days of school, and this time next week, we will have packed our bags and said our goodbyes to this place. Today is the last school competition of the year—nationals—and we should receive our exam results this afternoon. Tomorrow is the final dance of the year, then graduation is next week, and after that, we're officially done with all things school related.

Barton should hopefully be discharged next week, and Hadley and Hawk have discussed at length about staying here for the next year so that she can foster a relationship with him. I think it would be good for her, and I'm all for hanging around here for a bit longer. Besides, just because we live here, doesn't mean we can't take the year to go on a few sex-crazed adventures of our own. We have the money and means to go wherever the fuck we want on vacation, and I've been encouraging Hadley to make a list of everything she wants to see and do. I want her to experience everything, and I know the others do too.

I push thoughts of the future to the back of my mind as the whistle goes off, and I dive into the pool, intent on making this my best performance yet. Without the weight of the company and our parents' bullshit hanging over my head, I put everything I have into every stroke, kicking my legs as hard as possible. Reaching the far end, I flip and push off the edge of the pool, gliding through the water. Nothing exists except the sound of my heart racing in my ears and the cool water as it laps at my sides. I don't hear the noise of the crowd, nor do I register the movements of my competitors on either side of me. No, these moments of peace are all about me, and I give every second of it my all.

The whistle blasts as I slam my hand down on the tile, lifting my head to check the time. A new personal best. *Fuck, yes!*

The next hour is a whirlwind of handshakes and congratulations.

"And this year's national swimming champion for the freestyle is Cameron Rutherford," the chairman announces, a round of applause going up from around the pool. I hear a wolf whistle from the stands behind me and turn to grin at Hadley and the guys, all of whom are on their feet, cheering and clapping, before climbing the steps to shake the chairman's hand and accept my trophy.

There's another round of applause and handshaking before I'm free to go shower and change.

Before I can make it that far, though, I'm accosted outside the changing room.

"You were fucking incredible, man!" Mason exclaims as Hawk smacks me on the back and Hadley pulls me in for a hug.

"You were amazing out there," she says, smiling brightly at me.

I give her a quick kiss, unable to get carried away and celebrate the way I want with her brother standing right beside me. *Cockblocker.*

"Hurry up and change, Emilia messaged saying the exam results were up."

I can see the nervousness in her eyes, and I know she's been anxious about the results. Given the lack of formal education she has received until now, I can understand why she would be nervous, but she's worked hard this year—which is saying something, considering all the other shit we've had going on. If anyone deserves passing grades, it's Hadley. She might not be the smartest, but she tries the hardest, and no one else I know deserves a fresh start more than her. Not that she needs good grades to do that. None of us gives a shit what college we go to. In fact, the less prestigious, the better. Sure, all of us could just buy our way into whatever school we wanted, but I know Hadley intends to earn her place wherever we go next. Something that I both respect and admire about her. I don't give a flying fuck if we're at some community college or fucking Crestmore—the most prestigious college in the country—so long as we're all together.

"Cameron." I turn around as a well-dressed middle-aged man approaches us. "My name is Richard, and I'm a scout for Ridgeway College. I appreciate that it is a little late in the year to be asking this, but what are your college plans for next year?"

"Ehh, I don't have any. My friends and I are taking a gap year. I intend to apply in the fall for next year."

Richard beams. "Fantastic. Let me give you my card. When it comes time to fill in your application, give me a call. If you can keep up your swimming training next year, I think you would make an excellent addition to the Ridgeway swim team."

He reaches into his pocket and produces a card, and I take it from him, completely flabbergasted.

"Uhh, thanks."

"No, thank you. It's been a long time since I've seen such talent and determination in a young athlete. You could have a bright future ahead of you, young man."

Tilting his head in goodbye, he walks away, leaving me gaping after him and trying to work out if that was real or if I imagined the whole thing.

"Holy shit, Cam," Hawk gasps. "That was insane! Did you hear him? He said you have a bright future!"

"And that you'd make an excellent addition to their swim team," West tacks on.

"Yeah." I stare at the card in my hand. "I mean, it could all be bullshit. For all I know, he's a sexual predator who likes to hang out at high school swimming meets and try to lure kids into his car with fake cover stories."

Even as I say it though, I run my thumb over the very real business card in my hand.

Richard Steltzer, athletic scout for Ridgeway College.

He didn't seem like a perv.

I hear someone snort, and I tear my gaze away from the card in my hand.

"Go on," Hadley encourages, shoving me toward the changing room. "Get changed so we can get our results and start celebrating." She's got a massive grin on her face, and she looks fucking amazing right now. Brighter than she has in a long time, like she's no longer carrying the weight of the world on her shoulders anymore.

"Yes, boss." I wink at her as the door swings shut behind me, cutting off her tinkling laughter.

∽

"Ahh, oh my god," Hadley squeals, flinging her arms around me. "I only failed one subject."

I laugh, wrapping my arms around her. "What one?"

"History." She chuckles. "But who cares about that?"

After my swim meet, we all returned to the dorm and pulled out our tablets to check our results, although I don't think the rest of us give a shit about our grades, so long as Hadley is happy with hers.

Mason, Beck, West, and Hawk all take their turn congratulating her, and I don't think she could wipe the stupid grin off her face if she tries. It's fucking adorable.

"I'm so proud of you, little sis," Hawk murmurs quietly when he wraps her in a bear hug. A soft blush forms on her cheeks as she faces the rest of us.

"How did everyone else do?" She gnaws on her bottom lip as she looks between each of us.

"All good, Little Warrior," Mason assures her.

"Same," I pipe up. I have a healthy mix of letters, mostly B's, so I'm good. I've never been much of an academic person, and so long as I didn't flunk, I didn't really care about my grades. The only time I put in any effort was when I was paired up with Hadley for our English assignments. I guess I wanted her to see me as more than the guy who gets by on his good looks and parents' money. I wanted her to see when I put my mind to something and how I gave it my all. At that time, all of my focus was on getting Hadley. Of course, there was a fuckton of unexpected road bumps along the way, but now I've got her, and everything is finally looking up. She might not know it, but I'll dedicate the rest of my life to making her happy.

"West?"

He grins at her. "Second in the year. I can probably guess who came first, so I'm happy with that."

Right on cue, there's a peppy knock at the door that can only belong to one person.

"Open up, biatch," Emilia calls through the door, following it up with another round of knocking, which persists until Hadley opens the door, and the little black-haired girl flings herself into Hadley's arms.

"I came first!" she squeals in a high-pitched tone that only dogs should be able to hear. "In the whole year! The. Whole. Year! Can you believe that? I never thought...I just wanted to do well enough to get into Halston."

I hide my snort of laughter behind a cough. She must be the only one out of all of us who didn't think she would be Valedictorian. She and West have vied for the top place for all four years at Pac. If she had been up against Hawk or Mason, she would have come to blows with us years ago, but West never gave a shit about his ranking. He just enjoyed studying—although I can't fathom why. Dude clearly needed to get laid. Although, he's been getting plenty of sex this year, and still beat everyone else's ass.

Anyway, with the amount of hours Emilia has been logging in the library, and dragging our girl along, there was no doubt in anyone's mind she would be top of the year.

I obviously missed part of the conversation, as the next thing I hear is Hadley saying, "Give me a sec, I just need to grab my dress," before she rushes off down to her bedroom. She and Emilia had agreed to get ready in Emilia's room before the dance tonight, and we'll pick her up on our way there. The two have been trying to spend as much time together as possible the last few days before school ends. I've no idea where Emilia is from or where she will be spending her summer, but I can tell Hadley's going to miss her terribly when she leaves. I guess I'll just have to treat my girl to a few weekends in Halston so that she can have herself some girl time...and I can definitely get some mind-blowing thank you sex afterward.

Hadley enters the room with her dress slung over her shoulder and waves a quick goodbye, saying she'll see us later, before rushing out the door with Emilia, a grin plastered on her face. It's been kind of jarring seeing her so happy, but I fucking love it.

"Guess it's just us guys for the rest of the afternoon," I say with a shrug, grabbing beers for all of us.

"Here's to the end of school," Mason says, raising his bottle.

"And to finding lost siblings," West adds, smiling fondly at Beck, who returns it with one of his own.

"Cheers!" We all clink our beers together and drink from them before moving over to comfier seats in the living room.

"Bet you can't wait 'til school's over and you don't have to hide your relationship with Hadley anymore," I say to Beck as I plunk my ass on one of the couch cushions.

"Fuck, I can't wait. It's been driving me mad, especially since you guys announced to the school that you were dating her."

I grimace, not having given any thought to how that might affect him. "Sorry," I mutter, but it's a pointless apology. He waves it away.

"Don't be. It had to be done. I'll just be glad when I no longer have to hide what she means to me."

We all sip on our beers for a bit before Mason speaks up, "So Ridgeway college? That's not too far from here. We should go check out the campus."

I shrug my shoulders. "It's just a card. Doesn't mean anything."

"Don't sell yourself short like that. You were on fire today. They'd be lucky to have you on their team." Beck sounds sincere, and when I look his way, he's wearing his serious 'school counselor' expression.

His confidence bolsters me, and I straighten my shoulders. "Yeah," I say, turning back to Mason. "It would be cool to go look around."

There's a knock at the door, and we all share a knowing look. I roll my eyes as I get up to answer the door, knowing who will be on the other side before I even open it. Since Emilia has just left, only one other person would dare knock on our door.

Wilder comes bouncing into the dorm like a two-year-old on a sugar high. "I just bumped into the girls, and they said something about a guys' afternoon."

I don't think I'm the only one who stifles their groan, but when Wilder lifts his hand and says he brought beers for everyone, I decide I can put up with an afternoon of his craziness.

I know Hadley likes him, and I must admit, despite his unhinged personality, he's really stepped up. He was dumped in this school, not knowing anyone, and expected to marry a girl he'd never met. Most guys would have cowered when they discovered their fiancé came with four pissed-off boyfriends and an overprotective brother, but not Wilder. I have to respect the balls on the guy—so long as he never sticks them anywhere near Hadley!

I think letting something happen to Hadley on his watch messed with him slightly —not that he'd ever let on—but he accepted responsibility and insisted on coming with us to rescue her, even though he didn't have to. And I know he kept a close eye on Emilia when Hadley wasn't around. The rest of us were too concerned with bringing Hadley home to even think about Emilia. Still, Wilder, without having to be asked, immediately thought about what Hadley would want, and was there for Emilia at a time that I'm sure was confusing for her. If nothing else, I know that meant a hell of a lot to Hadley, however her weird friendship with him is more than just that. They seem to get each other in a way we can't understand. Whenever I tried asking Hadley about it before, she just shrugged it off, claiming something about his darkness being similar to hers—whatever the fuck that means.

Regardless of what it is, I guess he's kinda wormed his way into our friendship group, and thankfully has stopped flirting with Hadley—although he still insists on calling her fucking Sunshine—ever since we told the school we were dating her.

When I tried to broach the subject with Hadley about whether or not she was interested in dating him, or adding him to the harem or whatever, she nearly pissed herself laughing, and looked at me as if *I* was the crazy one. It had seemed like a genuine question at the time before the shit hit the fan and my fucking scumbag of a father got his grimy hands on her again, but I can see her friendship with Wilder for what it is now. He's a genuine, albeit slightly psychotic, friend, and Hadley needs more of those in her life. Michael—even thinking his name has me wanting to beat the shit out of him again —battered her already very limited trust in people, so it's good to see her letting Wilder in. He's actually worthy of her friendship.

"Did you hear the good news?" Wilder asks, flopping down on the couch beside Hawk and dropping his arm over his shoulder, which Hawk quickly shoves off. "We've upgraded from bros-in-law to pussy brothers."

"Dude, what the fuck?" Hawk snarls, glaring at him with such fury. Any normal person would be backpedaling at this point, climbing over the back of the sofa to get away from him, but not Wilder. He just grins like a fucking loon.

My nose wrinkles in disgust before what he said registers with me. "Wait, what? You banged the same girl? Who?" I can't think of a single girl on campus Hawk would willingly go near, except, maybe...no. Surely not.

"Fuck me," Mason groans, glowering at Hawk. "Tell me you didn't."

My mouth drops open and I gape at Hawk. "You both fucked Emilia?!"

Hawk buries his head in his hands, mumbling curses under his breath as Wilder bobs his head like a puppy looking for a treat.

"Dude, why the fuck would you do that?" West snorts, trying and failing miserably to keep a straight face when Hawk scowls at him.

"Hadley's going to skin you alive when she finds out." I chuckle. Damn, I need some popcorn and a comfy seat for that show.

"Oh, she already knows," Wilder states casually. "She ran into Emilia and I the next morning."

If it's possible, my mouth drops open even further. *Fuck, I bet that was awkward as fuck.*

Hawk groans into his hands, obviously not having realized that little tidbit.

"Emilia?" I'm still struggling to wrap my head around the whole thing. "But, why? Out of all the girls on campus, you had to fuck Hadley's best friend?"

"I don't know," Hawk groans.

"Does it mean anything?" Beck asks, leaning forward in his seat, his gaze bouncing between Hawk and Wilder.

"God, no." Hawk's quick response and vehement 'no' has my eyebrows rising in surprise. "It was just sex. I can't go near any other girl at Pac without them expecting a fucking ring at the end of the year...and Emilia was just there."

I kinda get what he's saying, but still...Emilia? He's such a fucking idiot for crossing that line. I'm beyond shocked Hadley hasn't handed him his ass for it.

"What about you?" Beck asks, jerking his head at Wilder, who just shrugs.

"Dunno yet."

Jeez, what a response. I can hardly restrain my eye roll.

We drop the subject after that. I'd well believe, to Hawk, it was just a one-night stand, although, with Wilder? Fuck, never thought I'd see the day he'd be down for sharing a girl, let alone with a dude he hardly knows. He must have been drunk off his ass at the time.

"What are your plans after graduation?" I ask Wilder instead.

He gives another one of those infuriating shrugs. "Haven't decided yet. Thought I'd hang around here for a bit."

Well, that's vague, but then, I guess so are our post-graduation plans.

We drink and chat for the rest of the afternoon until we have to get ready for the dance.

"Don't we clean up well," Wilder preens, checking himself out in the mirror as he fixes his canary yellow bow-tie that matches his yellow sneakers. Along with his black suit, he looks like some sort of deformed wasp. "Come on, pussy brother, let's go check out the Pac sluts one last time."

"Don't call me that," Hawk grumbles, but he follows him out of the apartment nonetheless, leaving me alone with West and Mason. Beck had to leave earlier as he offered to supervise the dance tonight—basically, he just wants to torture himself all night by watching us grind all over Hadley.

Checking my outfit in the mirror one final time, I turn to the others. "We ready to go get our girl and give her the best dance of her life?"

Hadley

CHAPTER TWENTY-EIGHT

*E*milia left a couple of minutes ago, and I'm smoothing out the creases on my forest-green dress when there's a knock at the door. Giving myself a final once-over, I move in my kitten heels to answer it, the skirt of my dress flaring out and swishing around my thighs.

Pulling open the door, I couldn't keep the grin off my face even if I tried, as I run my gaze over the three handsome men, all dressed up in suits, standing in the doorway —*my* men. My stomach is a bundle of nerves and excitement. The last dance I attended was a disaster, and I want tonight to go better, so we can all end the year on a high.

My skin heats as each of them roam their eyes over my outfit. "Wow, Firefly, you're stunning," West praises, stepping forward to plant a kiss on my lips.

"Absolutely gorgeous," Mason murmurs, when West steps aside, staking his claim with a heated kiss of his own. I melt under the softness in his sky-blue eyes, and a blush forms on my cheeks as Cam shoves him out of the way so he can stand in front of me, a dirty smirk curling his lips and a wicked glint in his eyes. Before he even opens his mouth, I know whatever he's going to say would be inappropriate, so I shut him up with a dirty kiss that I have to break off before we both get carried away and don't make it to the dance at all. I'm all for stripping each of them out of their suits and spending the night licking every part of them, but Emilia will never let me live it down if I miss out on tonight.

Pulling away from Cam, I look up at each of my guys. "Should we go?" No one misses the breathiness of my tone, but thankfully they overlook it.

"Oh, hold on," Cam says, digging in his suit pocket. "I wanna get a photo of all of us."

Pulling out his phone, he puts it on selfie mode and lifts his arm as we all huddle in for a photo. I'm grinning at the camera like a loon, with a blush still coating my cheeks, and Cam is making some stupid face. West looks stoic as ever, and Mason is staring at me instead of the camera. When I turn to ask him about it, he captures my lips with his, his hand resting possessively on my neck as he kisses all the sense out of me. I'm nothing but a puddle of hormones when he pulls away, whispering against my lips, "I love you, Little Warrior."

I can see the sheer honesty in his eyes, his words warming me from the inside out as I murmur my response, "I love you, Mason Hayes."

Cam ushers all of us out of the room, and we can hear the music and sounds of partying coming from the dining hall as soon as we step out of the dorm and make our way over.

The hall is packed with what looks like every student enrolled at Pac squished into the hall. Unlike last time, with the exception of a drinks table set up along the far one, the rest of the room is basically one giant dance floor, already packed with students dancing with one another and in large groups. I spotted tables and chairs set up under a string of fairy lights on the lawn outside the hall, the fairer weather enabling students to go outside if they wanted to sit or get some fresh air.

I'm looking around for Emilia, when my gaze meets Beck's on the other side of the room, his lips quirking up in a barely-there smile of acknowledgement that he sees me. His gaze drops, taking in what he can see of my outfit—which is basically just the way it pushes my boobs together and makes them look pretty damn good—and I can see the flare of heat in his eyes all the way over here, before a teacher nudges his shoulder, gaining his attention as he breaks eye contact with me.

I continue my search of the room for Emilia, and spotting me, she comes bounding toward me.

"Come dance." Without waiting for a response, she grabs my hand and drags me into the crowd, toward where Wilder is being his usual brand of insane with some weird-ass dance moves. He grins when he spots me.

"Sunshine!"

Returning his grin with a smile of my own, Emilia lifts my arm in the air, tugging my body in rhythm with the beat. Laughing, I move my hips, getting into the swing of it as the three of us dance our hearts out, until we're all panting and breathless.

"Need a drink," Emilia pants.

Wilder nods his head in agreement. "Same."

We start to push our way through the throng of people, but a hand clasping onto my wrist has me spinning around.

Coming face-to-face with Mason, a smile graces my lips as I quickly forget about my need for a drink and get lost in his pearly blue depths. A dirty smirk curls up one side of his lips as he pulls me into his arms, placing his large hands on my hips and grinding against me to encourage me to move.

I wind my arms around his neck, unable to look anywhere but at him as another song starts.

"Are you doing okay?"

I know he's talking about the fact I'm in the middle of a densely crowded room with loud music, and you know what...I'm actually not freaking out. I felt sweat coating my palms when we first walked in here, and the heat hit me, but somewhere along the way, I got lost in having fun with my friends and just living in the moment. Not to mention, there's something about not having obsessed psychos chasing after you, and not having deranged parents controlling your every movement that has me walking taller and breathing easier these days.

A soft, genuine grin spreads across my face. "I'm fantastic."

He matches my expression with one of his own, and the relief in his features has me leaning in, pressing my lips to his, and I drown in the taste of him. He slips his leg between my thighs, and I grind shamelessly against it. His body is perfection and presses against mine in all the right places.

Pulling back, he bites his lower lip before spinning me around. With swollen lips and love-drunk eyes, it takes me a second to compute the gorgeous hunk of man-meat standing in front of me.

"Cam," I purr as he places his hands on my waist, just above where Mason is holding possessively onto my hips.

"Baby, you're a sight for sore eyes." His words come out in a seductive husk that goes straight to my greedy pussy, and I fist the tie hanging loosely around his neck, pulling him into me, so I'm wedged between his lean, athletic body and Mason's huge, muscular one.

The three of us move in tandem, swaying and grinding to the music, and I feel Mason's hands slide down my sides, over my hips, until he reaches the hem of my skirt, and his fingers dance along my bare skin.

Arching my back, I press my ass against his hard erection, loving the deep groan that escapes his lips. Cam's hands slowly work their way to join Mason's, his fingers stroking along my inner thighs and making my breath hitch. As his hands slide under my skirt, Mason slides his up my body until his large palms are spread across my ribs, his thumbs brushing the side of my breasts.

My head falls back to rest against Mason's chest as Cam's fingers get closer to discovering just how fucking soaked my panties are for him—for the two of them. Mason ducks his head, running his nose up the column of my neck and occasionally flicking his tongue to taste me.

My hands cling desperately to Cam's shoulders in a vain attempt to hold me upright, but let's face it, Mason's solid body and firm hold on my waist are really what's holding me up, because my legs are fucking quivering under their ministrations.

Cam's fingers *finally* brush along my damp panties, and the glint in his eyes is positively wicked as his tongue runs along his lower lip. His dilated pupils bore into mine, the carnal need in his eyes holding me captive as Mason sucks and bites along my throat.

My lungs empty of all air when his finger presses firmly against my nub, making my hips buck. Mason chuckles into the crook of my neck, the noise sounding more like a rumble reverberating from his chest. He subtly brushes the pad of his thumbs over my nipples, most likely able to feel their hard peaks, even through the fabric of my dress.

A shiver of desire courses up my spine, and my cheeks are flushed from both heat and the wicked things these boys are doing to my body. I fall apart under their touch, my breaths coming in rapid pants as Cam's fingers slip beneath the thin fabric of my panties and easily push their way into my wet core.

My eyes drift shut as the two of them send me rushing toward a climax. Just as I feel my core tightening, my eyes pop open and looking over Cam's shoulder, my eyes meet Beck's lust-addled gaze.

Knowing he's been watching us get hot and heavy in the middle of the dance floor is my undoing, and Cam slams his lips down on mine as I come on his fingers and moan into his mouth.

"So fucking sexy," he murmurs against my lips when I come back to reality.

"Mmmhmmm," Mason agrees, still nibbling on the sensitive skin along my collarbone. "The sexiest."

I snort out a laugh as West, Hawk, Emilia, and Wilder join us, and the seven of us form one large group, dancing the rest of the night away. At one point, West and I break away from the others to get some fresh air, and when we come back in, I notice Wilder and Emilia arguing at the side of the room. Emilia's brows are drawn in confusion as her arms gesticulate wildly, and Wilder scowls at her before he snaps something out and storms our way, not sparing us a glance as he skirts past us and storms out the door.

Looking back at Emilia, her shoulders drop on a sigh, before she shakes her head and turns to grab a drink from the table. I worry my bottom lip, trying to decide if I should check on her or give her time to cool down, when West drags me back onto the dance floor. I decide I'll wait for her to tell me, in case she doesn't want to talk about whatever that was.

An hour later, Wilder returns, his usual grin plastered on his face, except I can tell it's sharper, more forced, and he watches Emilia with a weird expression. Emilia ignores his presence, but other than that little awkwardness, all of us have a great night. The sun is gracing the horizon by the time we all fall into our beds, and even though my feet hurt and my jaw is sore from laughing so hard, I don't remember ever having so much fun.

∽

DRESSED IN A BLACK GOWN, I fix my hat on my head, flattening my curls beneath it.

"We're gonna be late. Come on!" Hawk gripes, his own graduation gown billowing out behind him as he strides into the kitchen, just as there's a knock on the door, and Emilia shouts through it, "Open up! It's graduation day!"

The sheer excitement in her voice has me laughing as Hawk scowls at the door, refusing to move to open it.

Rolling my eyes, I shove my way past him and open the door. Emilia's eyes glisten with excitement, and she can't keep the grin off her face.

"They have everything set up on the lawn. It looks like they're getting ready to start soon," she says, bouncing up and down on her toes.

"Is your mom here?"

Her face falls. "Someone called into work, sick, last minute, and she had to cover for them."

"I'm sorry," I murmur, pulling her in for a hug. "We'll take loads of photographs to send to her, though."

She nods her head, fixing her smile back in place. I know having her mom here would have meant a lot to her, but I get the impression Emilia has gotten used to her mom not being able to make important events in her life because she has to work. It's sad, but she understands her mom is only trying to provide for both of them, and I know when they do get to spend time together, they both appreciate it much more.

"Let's go graduate!" Wilder calls out. There's still some weird tension between him and Emilia, but for the most part, they seem to both be ignoring whatever happened at the dance. Emilia hasn't mentioned their spat, and I haven't asked her, so I'm assuming it was nothing significant.

We all file out of the dorm and make our way down to the lawn, where they've set up a stage, with rows of chairs lined up in front of it that are quickly filling with students. Surrounding the stage and chairs are stands which are already overflowing with parents here to celebrate their children's achievements—or what is more likely, here to socialize and connect with other entitled, elitist assholes.

There's an excited thrum of energy in the air, along with a constant buzz of conversation and girly squeals as students meet up with each other and find their seats.

The rows seem to be set out in alphabetical order, and grinning at the others, Hawk, Wilder, and I move to find our seats near the stage while the others go in search of theirs further back in the rows. As Valedictorian, Emilia has to make a speech, so she has to sit up on the stage, along with the Heads of Departments and the headmaster.

I'm wedged between Hawk and Wilder when Mr. Phister stands up and moves to the podium. The noise settles down to a quiet hum as he speaks into the microphone.

"Ladies and gentlemen, I am honored to be here with you all today, to celebrate the Class of 2021. A graduation is always such a special occasion…"

He rambles on for a good few minutes about the bright future ahead of us and makes a point to remind us that it was Pacific Prep that set us up with the necessary foundations to achieve success—seriously, dude, is getting donations all you think about?

Glancing at Wilder out of the corner of my eye, I see him frowning at Emilia on the stage, and I lean in to whisper in his ear. "Are you okay?"

Tearing his gaze from her, he meets my eye, still frowning. "She's going on tour with some band." His lip curls in disgust.

Tilting my head, I try to get a read on him, but as usual, it's impossible. "Yeah, I know."

He doesn't elaborate on his thoughts, just shakes his head and returns his focus to the stage. Does Wilder like Emilia? Or does he just not approve of her summer plans? I can't work him out, and after a moment, I give up, returning my attention to the stage as Mr. Phister finishes his speech, and Emilia stands.

As she approaches the podium, I nudge Hawk. "Record this so she can send it to her mom," I whisper in his ear. He huffs but does as I say, lifting his phone out to start recording.

After thanking the headmaster and faculty, Emilia looks out over the sea of assembled students. Her gaze latches on to mine, and she smiles timidly before she glances down at her page of notes.

"Fellow students, today is both the end of everything we have known for the last four years, and the beginning of something new and exciting. After today, our futures are up to us to do with as we please. Whether you're going off to college, starting work, or heading off to find yourself, the future is yours to grab ahold of. Life is an adventure, and every opportunity to do something is a chance to learn more about yourself and push yourself to new limits. So make the most of this opportunity you have been given. Do something that scares you. Take the trip you keep putting off. Talk to the guy you have a crush on." She glances my way, one side of her mouth lifting in a grin, and I can see the tears forming in her eyes. "Take a chance on the new girl. Because you never know, she might just turn out to be the best thing to ever happen to you." I grin back at her, blinking away my own tears. "Live your life with no regrets, because every misstep is a chance to learn. Every mistake enables you to make the necessary changes and do better next time."

The guy in front of me turns to the girl beside him and rolls his eyes. Leaning forward, I smack him around the back of the head. His head whips round to glower at me, but seeing my furious expression, combined with Hawk's looming presence beside me, the pissed-off look on his face drops right off, and he mumbles an apology before turning around and paying attention again.

I glower at him for a second longer, making sure he's going to sit there and shut the fuck up before I focus back on Emilia's speech. "Pacific Prep has given me so much, and I'm not just talking about a high-quality education. It is here that I discovered myself, that I met my best friend and found a group of people who accept me for who I am, where I was pushed to stand up for myself and for what I believe in. No doubt, my time here came with challenges and low points, but even those I look back on with renewed clarity and know they helped to prepare me for what's to come. So, as we all, together, take that step out into the real world, let's remember the lessons we've learned here, appreciate the friendships we formed, and embrace whatever challenges we may face in this next unknown phase of our lives." With a bright grin lighting up her face, she finishes off her speech. "Congratulations, Class of 2021!"

I jump to my feet, clapping and grinning like an idiot, closely followed by Hawk and Wilder. I'm pretty sure I hear Mason whistling from somewhere behind us, and, more slowly, the rest of the year get to their feet, applauding.

With a final look my way, Emilia reclaims her seat, and the headmaster steps up to the podium again and begins calling out student names. Each student walks across the stage, accepting their certificate and shaking his hand before descending the steps, and the next one goes up, until the headmaster calls out, "Hadley Davenport."

Emilia grins at me, and I hear several whoops and whistles from my guys as I laugh and walk across the stage. Accepting my diploma, I glance first at Hawk, standing at the side of the stage, fist-pumping the air and grinning as brightly as I am, before I turn to face the sea of students in front of me to seek out West, Mason, and Cam. I then search the stands for Beck, and my mouth drops open when I find him standing front and center, clapping and smiling harder than anyone else. Standing right beside him, looking worse for wear, is my father—who is supposed to still be in the goddamn hospital. He's got tears in his eyes and an equally blinding grin on his face.

I walk off the stage as Hawk's name is called, and when he returns to his seat beside me, I lean in to whisper in his ear. "Did you know Barton would be here?"

He shakes his head. "No. He's not supposed to be released until later this week."

The headmaster continues through the list of names, and I clap equally as hard for all of my guys, until *finally*, the ceremony is over. Once we're released, I go in search of Beck and Barton.

Spotting him in the mass of students and parents, I push my way through the crowd toward Beck, and when he sees me, his face lights up. As I approach him, I jump into his arms, winding my arms around his neck as I plant a kiss on his lips, no longer giving a shit who sees us. Beck handed in his resignation a couple of weeks ago, and school is officially over. Now is our time, and I'm never going to hide my relationship with Beck, or the others, from anyone ever again.

He returns my kiss with a passionate one of his own, and when we break away, I can see the same happiness in his eyes that he can no doubt see in mine. He slides his fingers through mine, holding my hand, and I turn to look at Barton, taking in the way he's hunched over slightly and leaning on a walking stick for support. He's pale looking, with bags under his eyes, but the fact he's even up and walking about is a vast improvement. Hawk and I have visited him nearly every day, and with each day, he looks healthier and healthier.

"What are you doing here? We thought you didn't get released until the end of the week."

"I managed to talk them into letting me go early. I couldn't miss your graduation." He gets a nostalgic look in his eye. "I have missed so much of both yours and Hawk's life. I wasn't about to add this occasion to the list."

I smile appreciatively. We've been talking a lot recently, all three of us spending time together, getting to know one another, and establishing some sort of family unit. Given how he dove in front of that bullet for Hawk, not giving a damn about his own well-being, more than solidified the fact Barton had turned over a new leaf and wanted to put Hawk and me first. I feel nauseous whenever I think about how things could have ended differently that day.

Given his heroic actions, I have been making a concentrated effort to open up to him, and we've had some in-depth conversations about Maria's involvement in my kidnapping, and I've shared some of my time in the compound with him. Mostly, though, I've just talked to him about Pacific Prep and everything I have experienced this year.

"Dad!" Hawk has a wide grin on his face as he comes toward us and hugs Barton, careful to keep it light and brief so as not to hurt him. "I wasn't expecting to see you here."

"Wild horses couldn't keep me away," Barton jokes.

We spend the next hour or so getting various photographs taken, until Barton holds up his camera. "Okay, one last one of all of you, then dinner is on me."

He herds us all into the shot, Emilia on one side of me and Hawk on my other, with Mason, Beck, West, Cam, and Wilder surrounding us.

"Say Princes," Cam shouts out.

Emilia and I share a wicked look, and as they all say *Princes,* we call out, "Pricks," and cackle our heads off as Barton takes the photo and the guys start up a protest.

Hadley

EPILOGUE

Local prominent businessman, Frank Hayes, who was recently arrested for the homicide of Lauree Hamilton, was found stabbed to death in his cell yesterday morning. There were no witnesses to the crime, and the prison hasn't reported any suspects at this time...

I set down the newspaper, snorting out a laugh. Of course, Mason got a phone call from the prison yesterday, not that it came as a surprise to him. Once Cain confirmed he could get the job done, I told Mason what I had planned. The way his shoulders lifted and he pulled me in for a bear hug, made me kick myself for not thinking of it sooner.

He would never have burdened us with his fears, but he was obviously worried about what his father might do in retaliation for us destroying Nocturnal Mercenaries.

"What are you laughing at?" Beck asks, walking into the kitchen carrying a large box. He sets it on the table and looks over my shoulder at the paper in front of me.

"Ah. It's always nice to see the news reporting happy stories, isn't it?"

He kisses my temple as I nod. "It definitely is."

"What are you up to?" I ask, eyeing up the box.

"Just helping the guys move the last of their stuff in. Who knew the lot of them had so much shit—I thought it was only girls who got sentimental about every belonging they own."

I laugh and shake my head. The five of us agreed to move into West's house, opposite my dad's, for the year. Of course, we've closed the door on the main bedroom suite and won't be setting foot in there until it's been completely gutted and redone. Moving in here seemed like a weird choice at first, and I wasn't sure how I felt about it, but none of the guys seemed bothered about coming back to live on the little cliff they grew up on. Understandably, Mason didn't want to live in his old house, and there was no way we were moving into Cam's, so that just left West's house. It's only for a year anyway, before we head off to college, and this way, we are close by to help Barton if he needs it over the next few weeks—although he's recovering well.

Cain has been struggling to find homes for some of the kids he rescued from the compound, and Barton offered to take some of them in. He's got this huge mansion all to himself, and I think a mixture of guilt and not wanting to be alone encouraged him to offer up his home. So he's got four teenagers living in the house now, and he says there's more life about it than there has been in years. He seems happier too, and I think most of that is down to him having both Hawk and I nearby.

Hawk, after much arguing, agreed to live in Cam's house, and the three of us make time for family dinner once a week, and I'm learning so much about both of them. It's amazing how much I actually enjoy our weekly dinners. My relationship with both of them has come a long way. It's crazy to think that not even a year ago, Hawk would glare daggers at me in the hallway, and Barton couldn't even stand to look at me. Now we hug and laugh, and I know without a doubt that Hawk would jump on a grenade to save me—just like I would for him. We're a family. A large, dysfunctional, perfect family.

Hawk also reluctantly agreed to take on an unexpected roommate. Wilder had no plans after graduation, and he looked so down after Emilia left, I didn't want him to be alone. It just made sense that he lives with Hawk. It's such a big house for one person, although I did question my decision when I told Wilder, and he responded with some fucked up shit about living with his pussy brother? Nope. I do not *ever* need to hear those two words used in a sentence together, especially not in reference to my brother. *Fucking gross!*

We've only been living here for a week, and there have already been more shouting matches than I can count between the two. I've stocked an entire kitchen cupboard with popcorn bags so I can munch on something while I watch the blow-ups between them. It's more entertaining than TV, and since Beck and I only had a fraction of everyone else's belongings, I have had a lot of time to sit and watch The Hawk and Wilder show.

Sitting on the stool beside me, Beck asks, "How are you feeling after yesterday?"

"I'm okay. It was what I expected, although I'm a little overwhelmed with all the options we have. I don't know which one is right for us."

I had an appointment with a gynecologist the other day to find out for sure if I truly was sterilized at the compound. It turns out, I was. It was a nice thought for a moment, that perhaps it was all a ploy to make me think I couldn't have children, but of course, Bowen doesn't like to take risks. There's no way he would just say he sterilized us. It was still a shock—having it confirmed—but the biggest surprise was that this didn't mean I could never have children. I admit, it's not something I have ever given much thought to. Why would I, given the upbringing I've had?

The prospect of having a family of my own one day was never one I allowed myself to dream of...until now. Now that it's an option, I have no idea if it's even something I want. The good news is, we don't have to make any decisions right away. The gynecologist gave me a whole bunch of leaflets on my options. Everything from having surgery to undo the sterilization—but apparently, it has a horrendously low success rate—to IVF, to surrogacy, and to adoption. The five of us need to decide what we think is the best option for us, but there's no rush. For now, we just want to live our lives. We want to go to college, travel, learn to live together as a family, and get to know one another better. We have more than enough to keep us occupied.

Beck kisses the top of my head. "The good thing is, it's not a decision you have to make alone. When the time is right, we'll make it together."

I smile warmly up at him, taking some peace from his words. They've all said similar things to me since the appointment, and I know that, regardless of what happens, nothing will send any of the guys running for the hills. No matter what the future brings, all of them will be there for me, and that unwavering support calms me whenever I get anxious about it.

The others filter into the kitchen, carrying their own boxes of belongings, and I slip out of my chair to put the newspaper in the recycling bin before Mason can see it. He already knows; he doesn't need to see any reminders of his dad. He got what he deserved, and that's that.

We're all starting a new phase of our lives, and no parents will interfere with our plans. This is our time—our time to do what we want, to live the lives we've talked about, and enjoy the newfound freedom none of us thought we would have.

Thick, muscular arms wrap around my waist. "What has that smile on your face?"

I turn in Mason's arms, pressing my hand flat against his chest. "I'm just thinking about our futures."

"Oh, yeah, what about them?"

Tilting my head back, I look up into his eyes. "How amazing they're going to be."

I feel the others close in around me. West on one side, Cam on the other, and Beck at my back. I look up at each of them with the same love in my eyes that I can see shining in theirs. Yup, so long as we have each other, the future can throw anything it wants at us. No obstacle is too hard, no challenge too big. Don't they say love conquers all? Well, our love is a force to be reckoned with.

Baby Davenport

THE WAREHOUSE

Gunshots go off around me, the white noise ringing in my ears while momentarily disorientating me. I hadn't even realized my eyes had closed, and when I snap them open, my whole world tilts on its axis.

"Dad!" My voice sounds strange, choked and distant, and for a second I can't comprehend what I'm seeing, but as the blood seeps into my father's shirt and spreads across his torso, reality crashes down around me and my chest caves in.

I don't even realize I'm fighting against the ties binding me to the chair until Mason gets me loose, and I collapse to my knees beside my dad.

"Dad."

I'm faintly aware of Beck saying something about a hospital, but I can't focus on anything but my father's face. It's already pale and clammy looking, and I swear I can see the life dimming in his eyes.

He croaks out Hadley's name, and a moment later she drops to the floor beside me.

"I'm here."

I can hear the heartbreak in her voice, and I know, even though she's only known him for a short while and most of that hasn't exactly been amicable, that this is destroying her as much as it is me.

"I'm sorry." His words are followed by a coughing fit that takes way more out of him than it should and only intensifies that ache in my chest.

"Shush, it's okay. Just rest," Hadley coos, putting on a brave face for him, even as tears stream down her face.

"I wish I had the chance to know you better."

I wrap an arm around her shoulder as a sob escapes her. As many regrets and *what ifs* that I have, at least I had eighteen years with my father. Hadley hasn't had any of that. She's only just started to open herself up to him, and now this.

"Don't say that," she sobs. "You will. We'll get you help."

He seems to get weaker with every passing second, and I hold Hadley against me, taking as much comfort from her as she is from me.

I have no idea what to do. We probably need to get him help, but I'm terrified of moving him and having him die. Part of me just wants to sit here with him, so he knows he's not alone when the time comes.

"Hawk." Beck's authoritative tone grabs my attention and I tear my gaze away from my father's pale face and dulling eyes to look at him. I can see the panic in his expression, but he's in *take charge* mode—something that I'm ridiculously thankful for as I'm incapable of working out what we should do in this moment. "We need to move him."

I nod absently for a second. "Did you call for an ambulance?"

"They won't be here in time. Mason can drive him to the hospital faster."

Right, okay. I still feel lost and unsure of what to do, but when I look at the determined set of Beck's face, and the others gathered around us, ready to jump into action, I take some strength from that and give a sharp jerk of my head.

Between us, we manage to get Dad to his feet, and Mason rushes off to get the car. It's slow progress, but eventually we get him outside and into the back seat. Beck climbs in, getting my dad settled. "We've gotta go!" he shouts, the urgency clear in his voice.

"Hadley," I bark, "get in!" If only one of us can go, she should be the one with him when he dies.

"What? No. You get in!" she argues. "We'll get a cab and meet you there." She pushes me toward the car, but there's no fucking way I'm going without her.

I'm shaking my head as I shake off her efforts. "No. I'm not leaving you. West," I call out, knowing I can't waste time arguing with her. Besides, I already know it will be pointless. I rarely win an argument against her. "Get in. You need to be checked out anyway."

"West," Beck snarls impatiently, "get in the fucking car."

Thankfully West does as he's told, and Mason's peeling out of the lot before he's even got the door closed. I watch as the car races down the street, turning a corner at a dangerous speed while I pray to God that my father doesn't die before he can get the help he needs.

"Do you think he's going to make it?" Hadley asks, her voice sounding small.

I wrap my arms around her, unable to give her an answer. He's in bad shape, and as much as I don't want him to die, I'm not holding out much hope.

"Are you okay?" she asks, pulling back from our embrace.

Fuck, what a question. Physically, yes. I can feel my lip is split, but I barely register the pain. It's inconsequential to the fear threatening to suffocate me.

"I'll be fine," I assure her, even though we both know it's a lie. "Let's just get to the hospital."

"I've booked a cab. It'll be here in fifteen," Cam states, and I give him a grateful look.

"What, uh, are we going to do about the mess in there?" Hadley asks.

Fuck if I know. How the hell does one go about cleaning up dead bodies? We can't exactly contact the police. "I'm not sure," I admit. "Maybe Beck can see if Cain knows anyone who could sort it out?" I really have no better ideas right now, and with everything else going on, it feels like a minor issue; although I know we can't just leave this mess for someone else to find. Then we will end up with the police at our door, asking questions none of us want to answer.

"Maybe," Hadley mutters, sounding like she gives as little of a shit as I do right now.

The three of us move to the main road to wait for the taxi, and I collapse onto the sidewalk. I go to bury my head in my hands, needing a second to just fucking breathe, when the red stains of blood—my father's blood—stop me, and I end up staring at my hands. Will I ever see my father alive again? There was so much blood. And Jesus, fuck, my mom's dead too. I'm not remotely upset about her demise, but fucking hell, how did my life become so messed up? How did it come to this? With one dead and one nearly dead parent. What the fuck did I do in a past life to end up dumped on in this one?

Hadley drops onto the curb beside me, her presence drawing me out of my dark thoughts. She's the only bright side that's come out of all of this. Finding her has been like a balm to my damaged soul. I never noticed it before, but I think I somehow knew something was missing all these years. I just didn't know what... or who. Since she wormed her way into my life, I haven't felt so lost. My sister is the keeper of my soul, and I'm the guardian of hers.

"What's wrong?" Cam asks, drawing my attention to Hadley, who has stood up again, frowning as she looks back toward the warehouse.

"My gun, I don't have it."

"Does it matter? You probably can't take it to the hospital anyway," I tell her.

"My fingerprints are on it. I don't want to leave it behind."

"I'll go get it," Cam insists, stopping her before I can, as she starts back toward the warehouse.

"It's okay. I'll get it. I can't just sit here and wait anyway."

I can see he's reluctant to let her go, but I get that she needs a moment alone. I'm feeling the same weight in my chest too. It's only growing heavier with every passing second we sit here and wait.

"We'll give her five minutes," Cam tells me when Hadley's out of earshot. "Then I'll go get her."

I nod my head in agreement, suddenly feeling like even talking is too much of an effort. I'm fucking exhausted. Beyond exhausted.

Cam leans against the chain-link fence behind me, giving me my space while we wait for Hadley to come back and the cab to arrive.

As the seconds tick by, a buzzing starts under my skin. I initially pass it off as emotional exhaustion and stress, as I wonder how Dad is doing and if he's made it to the hospital yet, but the sensation grows until I can't sit still, this itching need to move taking over me.

I get to my feet, pacing back and forth along the sidewalk. I can feel Cam watching me, probably thinking I'm on the verge of losing my shit. Fuck, maybe I am. Is that what's happening right now? Has life pushed me too far and I've finally lost the fucking plot?

Something tugs in my chest, and without even meaning to, I take a step toward the warehouse.

"Stay here," I tell Cam. "I'm, uh, going to go check on Hadley." Just before I walk away, I pause, looking back at him and holding out my hand. "Actually, give me your gun." I can't explain what the fuck is going on with me right now, but the buzzing beneath my skin has become an overwhelming urge to return to the warehouse. Even though I'm not sure what, I can just sense that something isn't right.

My heart races with every step closer to the building, this urgency that I can't explain taking over and pushing me to move faster. When I crack open the door at the side of the building, I hear a male voice coming from inside. My brows knit together, and on instinct, I lift the gun out of the waistband of my pants, flicking off the safety as I peer through the door.

I spot Hadley standing near the chairs West and I were tied to, a man with his back to me preventing her from seeing me.

"But that wasn't the case, was it?"

My muscles tense, my finger flexing against the trigger. I recognize that voice, and hearing him talk to Hadley in that smug-ass tone has me seeing red.

"You've been deceiving him—all of us—all these years, planning your little escape."

I move, silently, farther into the warehouse, keeping my gun pointed right at the shit-stain's head. I don't have a clear shot from where I'm standing, and I won't risk accidentally hitting Hadley.

"But, D, you should have known you could never have a normal life. Who would want to be with someone who can't bear children, after all?"

I falter at his words. *What the fuck does that mean?*

"Face it: you can never escape your fate."

Storing away the questions he's raised, I take another step to the side, bringing myself into Hadley's field of vision. I lock eyes with her as I lift the gun, pointing it at the fucker's head.

Despite the fear I can see in her eyes, she smirks at him, knowing I've got her back —that I'll *always* have her back. "Maybe not, but neither can you."

She dives to the side as my finger presses down on the trigger, the gun recoiling in my hand as the bullet shoots out from the chamber. It lodges in the asshole's shoulder, wounding him instead of shooting him dead like I'd intended. Even though he's injured, he raises his gun as he turns to face me, but before I can fire a second shot, the sound of another gun going off echoes around the large, empty space.

Bowen crumples to the ground, blood gushing from his head, before he face-plants into the concrete, dead as a fucking door nail. It takes a second for me to realize Hadley shot him, but once I blink past the stupor and find her lying on the concrete, I rush toward her.

"Are you okay?" I gush out, crouching in front of her. "Hadley! You're bleeding." I grab hold of her arm, inspecting the red scrapes of skin visible through her torn Henley while ignoring her grumbling about being okay. Satisfied that there's nothing more than some superficial cuts and scratches, I let her go and help her to her feet.

"Where did you get the gun from?"

"When you didn't come right back, I got a weird feeling. Something was just telling me I needed to get in here, so I grabbed it from Cam and came to find you." I don't even know how to explain what I was feeling, but now I'm thinking it was some sort of twin intuition, like I could sense she was in danger or some shit. Although, it looks like I wasn't needed. Even though the PTSD had her in its clutches, she was fighting through it. I know without a doubt that if I wasn't here, she would have survived just fine on her own. Like she would with everything else life has to throw at her, except she won't have to struggle through anything alone again. I'm here. I will *always* be here for her. The corner of my lip lifts in a ruly grin. "Although it looked like you had everything handled."

She scoffs, not believing me, but that's okay, because as time goes on and she builds that confidence in herself again, she will realize it on her own. She'll see what the guys and I do… that she's an unstoppable force. She's capable of achieving anything she sets her mind to. Hell, her strength amazes me.

"I don't know about that. He definitely got the better of me for a second there. I-I kept remembering what it felt like to be back in that compound, chained to his wall."

I fight the urge to beat the shit out of the dead motherfucker at my feet and place a reassuring hand on Hadley's shoulder. "You'll never be back there again," I promise her. "And look at how far you've come. You were able to work through the trauma and fight back. I'm so proud of you, Hadley." I mean it. She's come a long way from when I found her beating on that kid on campus. She look so lost and bewildered that day when I dragged her off him, like she had no idea what was happening. But today, she fought through that fear. Instead of letting it overcome her, she conquered it.

"I couldn't have done it if you hadn't come looking for me," she says, her voice a tad squeaky as she blinks away the tears building in her eyes.

"I'm pretty sure you'd have found a way. Now let's get out of here. The cab should be outside, and Cam will be wondering where we are."

I follow her gaze, as she looks around us at the dead bodies littering the floor, pausing when I spot my mother. The absence of guilt or grief over her death should probably be concerning, but all I feel is regret. Regret that she couldn't have been the mother Hadley or I wanted her to be; regret that power and money meant more to her than her own children; regret for how things ended here today.

Hadley nudges my shoulder, drawing me out of my thoughts. "I'm sorry about your mom. I know you wanted to believe the best in her."

Don't we all want to believe the best in our parents? Mine were never cruel to me. They were never mean or unkind. They were just absent. The neglected kid inside me believed—hoped—that they loved him, just in their own, distant way. Man, I was so fucking wrong. Our mother truly never gave a shit about either of us. All those years I spent growing up with her meant absolutely nothing. It twists my stomach, and a quiet voice at the back of my mind wonders what I did to make her hate me so much. But I shake it off, not needing to fall down that rabbit hole today.

"Yeah, I did." I sigh and shake my head. "But she was never the mother I wanted."

She was never the mother either of us deserved, and honestly, I'm glad Hadley didn't have all those years of distant mothering, being left to wonder why she was never enough. My mother's words from earlier come back to me. Other than confirming she played a vital role in Hadley's disappearance, I was too caught up in trying to figure out a way for West and me to escape to give much thought to what she said, but now...

"Did you hear what she said?" I ask Hadley.

"About how she got rid of me and that I'm supposed to be dead?" she drawls. "Yeah... I just don't understand how she was involved."

That's what I'm struggling to piece together. "I don't know," I admit with a shrug of my shoulders.

"Lawrence told me he and Maria were meant to get married, until Barton came along. Do you think they were working together?"

I wrap an arm around her shoulders and pull her against me. "It sounded that way, but whatever their plan was, it doesn't matter now. They're both gone, and we're still here." It's the truth. I'm not exactly sure what part my mother and Lawrence played in Hadley's kidnapping and last fifteen years of captivity, but they're dead now. We might never get answers or know the whole story but we're both here—alive and well with our entire futures ahead of us. And ultimately, that's what matters.

Hadley

FOUR YEARS LATER

"Hadley! Hurry up," Cam calls.

"I'm coming," I yell, hurrying down the stairs. "What's the rush? Where are we even going, anyway?"

"You'll see."

I glare as I step past him and out the front door. The others are already waiting in the car as I climb into the back seat, smiling broadly at West before dropping into the seat beside him. Cam clambers in beside me, the three of us pressed shoulder to shoulder as Beck pulls onto the road.

"So, is anyone going to tell me where we're going?" I ask when we've been driving in silence for several minutes. There's a strange energy in the car that I can't quite pinpoint.

"Patience, sweetheart. You'll find out soon," Beck says, lifting his gaze to look at me through the rearview mirror before focusing on the road again.

Blowing out a breath, I sit back in my seat and watch the scenery go by, until we turn off the main road onto a one-track gravel path that leads up to a familiar cliff. I can feel the guys watching me as a broad grin stretches across my face.

We've made a point of coming here at least once every summer, and it's become one of my favorite places in the world to be. Isolated, deserted, and breathtakingly beautiful—what's not to love?

The second Beck brings the car to a stop, I'm out the door, grinning like a maniac as I tilt my head back, baring my face to the sun and sky above as I inhale the sea-salt air. It's September now, so it's cooler than it usually is when we come here, but it's still warm enough for shorts and t-shirts.

"First one to the beach is a rotten egg!" Cam calls out before rushing past me and hurrying down the steps.

"Slow down!" Beck bellows after him. "You'll break your neck if you trip!" Cam pays him no attention as he continues his race with himself down the steep stairs to the beach far below. "Fucking idiot," Beck grumbles.

The rest of us take our time descending to the beach, Mason carrying a large picnic basket and Beck with a backpack slung over his shoulders. By the time we get there, Cam has already gathered logs, and it's not long before the bonfire is lit, with the flames stretching up to the heavens and the warm heat washing over us.

"So what sparked this?" I ask once we're all settled. "We never come here after school starts up."

The guys all share a look before Mason shrugs a shoulder and says, "We just felt like it. Thought it would be good to have a day away before the insanity of senior year kicks off."

"Besides, do we need an excuse to have a day out?" West teases. "We deserve a day of fun before Cam's crazy competition schedule starts and we get bogged down with assignments, Nocturnal Enterprises, and applying for jobs."

I scrunch up my nose, nowhere near ready to think about what comes *after* Ridgeway. I've spent the last four years *finding myself*, and I'm not done yet. Despite taking all sorts of various classes, I still haven't figured out what I want to do with my future yet. I don't feel ready to put myself in a box for the rest of my life. I still feel like I just got out of the damn box.

"No talk of that today," I order, making the guys laugh. They find the fact that I'm burying my head in the sand about our impending graduation absolutely hilarious. It's all right for them. They all have some idea of what they want to do: Cam has swimming, West has computers, Beck has his counseling job at a local school, and Mason… well, Mason is probably the closest to me. He's still not sure what he wants to do after college.

The conversation changes to lighter topics, and we spend the next few hours laughing and forgetting about the real world beyond our little stretch of sand.

"Come on," Cam encourages later that day. "Let's go for a swim before the sun sets."

I change into a bathing suit and we take off toward the shoreline, leaving the others cackling by the fire. As soon as my feet are submerged, Cam hauls me into his arms, carrying me out until the water swishes around his middle.

With a mischievous grin, he grasps my hips and launches me into the air. I squeal as I go down, down, until the cool liquid engulfs me.

Pushing off the seabed with both feet, as soon as I break the surface, I start splashing Cam, the two of us mucking around until he tackles me, sending us both under water as we're once again submerged in our own cocoon. His lips find mine in a bruising kiss, his arms holding me close as we drift beneath the surface, until the undeniable need for oxygen outweighs my desire to remain wrapped around Cam.

Only when we're both breathing heavily, grinning like buffoons, and the sun is beginning to set, do we drag our asses out of the water.

Beck meets me at the edge, holding up a large beach towel, with my clothes grasped in his hand.

"Where's my towel?" Cam asks as we emerge from the sea.

"Wherever you left it."

I listen to their banter as Beck enfolds me in the soft material.

"Well, I guess I know where I stand then," Cam huffs.

Arching a brow, Beck counters, "You mean, you didn't know before today?"

I bite back a grin at their teasing. I love how easily it comes to each of them now. Beck has become fully integrated in their friendship group over the years, and the time when he was a suspicious outsider and a brother West hated now seem so long ago.

"Let's hope I don't freeze my balls off before I make it up the beach," Cam grumbles, quickly taking off toward the fire.

Smirking, Beck rolls his eyes at Cam's back. "Such a drama queen."

"You wind him up," I point out.

His face breaks into an all-out grin, showing off his white teeth. "I know. He makes it too easy. How can I not? Besides, he deserved it after switching out the whipped cream for shaving foam." His face scrunches, and I can't help but laugh as I remember the night Beck and I got a little adventurous on the kitchen island.

I think Cam was just planning on playing a prank by having us put shaving cream on our pie at dinner the next day. But, well, Beck thought it would be tastier to eat the cream off *me*. Safe to say that experience was ruined as soon as he ate a mouthful of shaving cream.

"Join me for a walk?" Beck asks as I dry myself off and shimmy into my clothes.

I smile up at him. "Definitely." Just like play fighting in the ocean is my and Cam's thing, going for a walk has become my and Beck's thing. Every time we come out here, the two of us sneak off for a walk along the beach, which usually ends up with my back against a rock as I scream at the cliffs, fighting to be heard against the crash of the waves.

"This is my favorite place in the world," I tell him as we walk hand in hand along the shore.

He chuckles. "You say that every time we come here."

"Well, every time we come here, it reaffirms it. No matter where we go or what we do, this beach will always be my happy place. This is where we had our first date, all together, as a family. The place where we can all come and forget about our problems."

Wrapping an arm around my shoulders, he kisses the top of my head. "I know, sweetheart. This beach is special to all of us."

We watch the sun set, various shades of pink, red, and purple blazing across the sky as dusk settles while we meander along the beach. By the time we pivot and begin our return journey, the sun looks like a fireball being slowly lowered into the ocean and the stars are starting to make an appearance.

Against the darker backdrop, the bonfire stands out like a beacon directing us home, appearing larger than it had earlier in the day.

It brings a smile to my face, knowing the rest of the guys are there waiting for us. I bet Mason is grilling food over the fire while West keeps an eye out for our return, and Cam is probably chilling on a log with a beer in hand, talking their ears off.

As we grow closer, I notice flickers of movement beyond the fire. "What is that?" I ask Beck, squinting to get a better look.

He doesn't answer as his hand on my lower back applies pressure, encouraging me forward until the indistinguishable shapes take form.

Flames.

Each flicker is a candle flame.

Dozens of them are spread out along the beach, illuminating a path that leads to the bonfire.

"What..." I lose track of my train of thought as I glance up at Beck with questions in my eyes. He stares back at me with nothing but pure love and adoration, a charismatic smile on his face.

He slips his hand into mine, tugging me forward. I follow him on numb legs, and as my eyes shift over to the fire, I spot my other three men standing front and center, watching us approach. When we are encased in a circle of candles, Beck drops my hand and moves to stand beside West.

"What's going on?" I ask when I finally find my voice, taking a second to stare into each of their faces.

All of them are wearing the same expression as Beck, and beneath their scrutiny, my body begins to hum.

Instead of answering me, Mason steps forward, his eyes firmly glued to mine. Heat blazes in his lustful gaze, and I can't do anything but stare as he begins speaking. "From the very first moment I stepped into that gym and saw you beating the shit out of a bag, I was intrigued, but it wasn't until the night you beat Hawk that I knew I had to have you—in whatever way I could. It's you and me, Little Warrior. For now and always."

Moved, and a little confused, I stare as he steps back, joining the others in their line. At the same time, Cam steps forward. He has a mischievous smirk on his face, but the same fierce love burning in his eyes.

He stares at me for so long that I begin to wonder if he's going to say anything, but then the smile drops from his face, and he grows serious. "Baby, you are my sunlight on a dark day, my rainbow when it pours, my lighthouse in a storm."

Silent tears slide down my cheeks as Cam recites my words from so long ago.

"Every day you give me a reason to get out of bed, to breathe, to laugh, to keep moving forward. I love you, for now and always."

He steps back, and my gaze slides to West as he steps forward. He licks his lips nervously before lifting his chin. "Firefly." He breathes his nickname for me like it's the oxygen he needs to survive. "You upended my world when you crash landed in the vacant chair beside me that day in computer class. You were the chaos I didn't want but desperately needed in my life."

I give a wet chuckle as one side of his lips quirk up. Tearing his gaze away, he glances briefly at his brother before returning his attention to me.

"You have given me more than I could have ever hoped for in this life, and I can only hope I can give you half as much as you have ever given me."

I swallow roughly around the lump in my throat. I may have become more in tune with my emotions over the years, however I am *not* an emotional person. But damn, these men of mine sure know how to get past my defenses.

"I love you, Firefly. Now and forever."

Blinking away a fresh wave of tears, I shift my attention to Beck as he steps forward, a soft smile and that same adoration in his eyes.

"You already know you saved my life, sweetheart." Placing a hand over his heart, he says, "I am beholden only to you. Without you, my life is forfeit. I am yours, forever and always."

With the affectionate declarations over, I stare at each of them, unable to scrape together a single word. My throat is raw, my eyes burning as my heart swells with so much love for these four men.

They all say that I saved them, that I changed them, that I'm the reason for who they are today, but what they don't realize is that they are all of those things to me too. Without each of them, I would not be the person I am today. I'm not even sure I would be alive, and if I was, I would be a shell of the woman standing in front of them now.

Before I can get my voice box to work, the four of them step aside, and I see what was hidden behind them.

A strangled cry escapes my constricted throat as my hand flies up to cover my mouth. More tears gather in my eyes, quickly overflowing, but I barely even notice, too caught up in the magical words written in the sand.

Will you marry us?

I'm speechless, frozen in place as the waves crash against the shore behind me and seagulls cry from overhead. None of it registers, everything fading into the background until all I can see—all that exists—are the four men standing in front of me, promising me forever.

"Well, baby, what's it going to be? Think you can put up with all four of us for the rest of our lives?"

Cam's teasing snaps me out of my stupor, my gaze flicking up to meet his. Despite his playful tone, I spot the flicker of vulnerability in his gaze.

I lower my hand from my lips as I smile at him. I take another second to drink in each of the other three, my grin growing wider. "I think the better question is: can the four of you handle *me* for the rest of our lives."

"Is that a yes?" Beck asks while Cam bounces on the balls of his feet, West scrutinizes me as if trying to read the answer from my body language alone, and Mason silently observes, patiently awaiting my confirmation.

With tears in my eyes and more love than I ever thought possible gushing from my heart, I nod my head. "That's a motherfucking yes!"

ACKNOWLEDGMENTS

There are so many people, without whom, this series wouldn't be half as good. The biggest thanks goes to my PA, Nikki. Not only does she keep me in line, but she alpha'd the series, and made all the gorgeous teasers. She was there every step of the way, helping and supporting me and for putting up with me, she's an absolute superstar!

A MASSIVE thank you has to go to my editor, Angie (Lunar Rose Editing). Not only is she amazing at her job, but a truly fantastic friend! Thank you so much for all of the blood, sweat, and tears you have poured into this series!

Thank you to Dez for the amazing cover and Michelle Lancaster for use of the gorgeous model. And to my beta and street team for all their hard work.

Lastly, thank you to all of you for picking up this book and reading it. Without you none of this would be possible!! If you loved this book, please help me spread the word by leaving a quick review.

Printed in Poland
by Amazon Fulfillment
Poland Sp. z o.o., Wrocław

Pacific Prep: The Complete Series
Copyright © 2022 R.A. Smyth

All rights reserved. No part of this book may be reproduced, or stored in a retrieval system, or transmitted in any form or by any means, electronic, mechanical, photocopying, recording, or otherwise, without express written permission of the publisher.
The characters and events portrayed in this book are fictitious. Any similarity to real persons, living or dead, is coincidental and not intended by the author.
ISBN: 978-1-915456-07-6

Cover by Pretty in Ink Creations
Photographer: Michelle Lancaster
Model: Indi
Editing by Lunar Rose Editing Services.
Formatting and interior design by Rachel Smyth.